LIE BY THE SWORD

Lie by the Sword (Fimbulvetr — Book Two)

2nd Edition
copyright © 2021 by Daniel Scott Westby

ISBN: 9780578599212

Book design by Daniel Scott Westby
Printed in the United States of America

www.goblinwinter.com

to Peace
&
to two pieces too

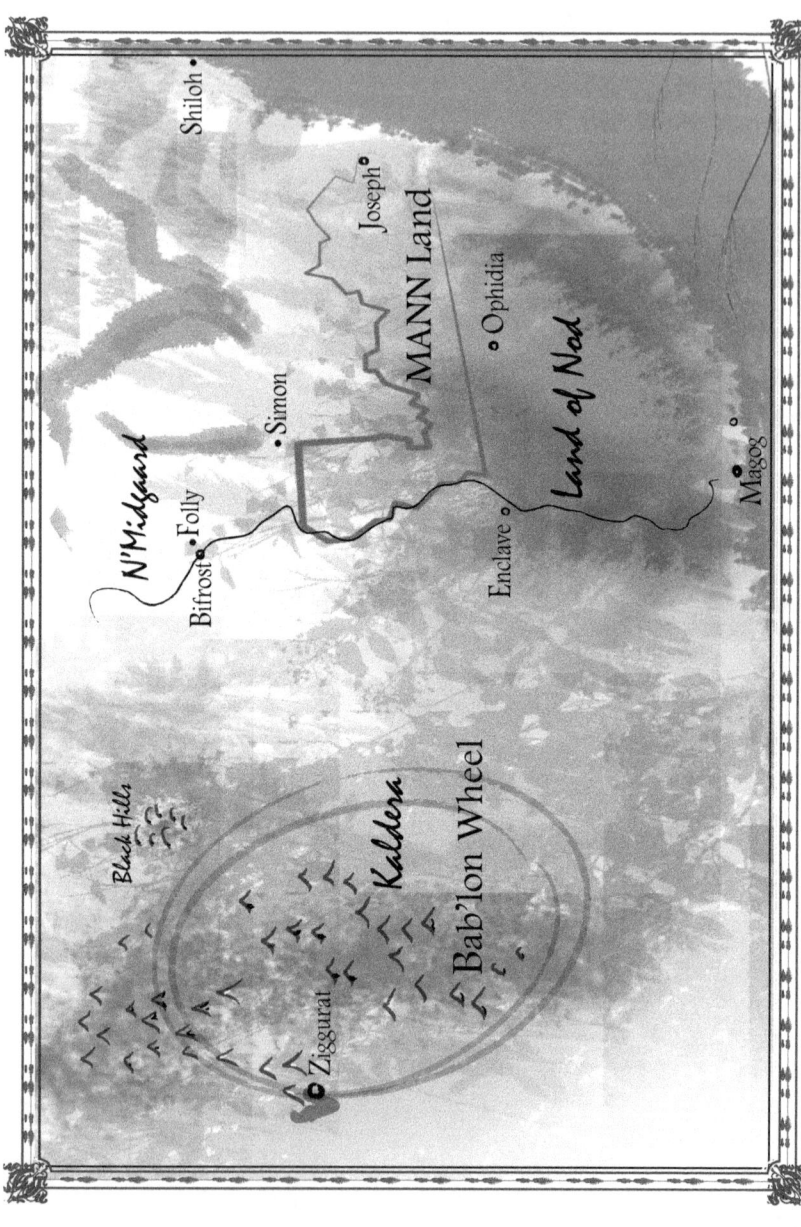

FIMBULVETR
book two

LIE BY THE SWORD

Daniel Scott Westby

I

This is the tale of the warrior known
to some as All, as None to
some, but in all his lives he was first grown
—scrawled on the walls of the King of All's lower halls

He knew nothing, but there was nothing to know. He had yet to sense time, and this was a blessing, for temporal comprehension would surely have driven him insane. Or perhaps he could grasp time, and he already was. Perhaps he would be born mad, and in that way would have a kinship with mankind he would always search for but never find, even though it would be with him from his first breath onward.

Light came from all directions, still stunted bloody and barely permeating ever-present synbiotic fluid. But he knew nothing of the diversity of colors. A muffled pulsing beat came from all around him, barely humming through crowding protean masses striated and bulbous. But he knew not the possibility of sounds. He struggled against cord, prick and probe, with the walls pressing and squeezing, never relenting. But he knew of no other touch. To him, this was love. This was nurture. And he was both, he was all, he was a king of all. This was the closest thing to the concept he would never understand as mother, and it would be the first to betray him, but far from the last.

The King of All came into the world silent, surveying his surroundings for threat and weakness. He had exhausted himself inside the cold womb, struggling against awkward corner and cord, straining against probe and claustrophobia. Flushed toward a seam of brilliance and pulled by frigid, impersonal clasps, he was blind against the sudden and all-encompassing absence of color. The oppressive light brought with it a sense of time, of a "before" and an "after." It was, however, the feeling of "present" that distressed him the most. Whether pleasurable or distasteful, he would spend his whole life trying to avoid it — yet another thing he would have in common with those around him, while never recognizing it.

Only now did he cry out — not from fear or discomfort, but of triumph. He had not only survived the womb, but had conquered it. Unconsciously, he shook the nutrient mixture from tiny arms, screamed incomprehensible exultations from immature lungs. The King of All had won his first war, and he enjoyed every bit the celebration. This was something! This was new! This was freedom! Fatty, gray legs kicked at nothing. Nothing existed! Forever there had been only something enveloping him — something thick and slow between him and the unyielding walls, something he ate and breathed and fought against for as long as he could remember. Now, here was nothing all around him, separating the pincers that neared, surrounding his newly realized limbs and enveloping the wagging bulbousness of his head.

It was an event replicated all around him as nearly identical newborns fought to free themselves from the walls of wombs, eventually being pulled by synthetic and unsympathetic hands showering away plasma with wine. Some cried from what they had lost, some from what they now found, but all fought against the onslaught of light and simulated caress. Unfamiliar senses dulled by gelatinous suffocation, never needed, now woke to hyper-stimulation from all directions. Ears were sucked clean to invite invading sounds — pinching "clicks" and tickling "hums" assailing eardrums pink and tender. Tiny lungs, immediately sore from an oxygen thick wash, drew in rapid breaths of prickling air — its taste souring lips into even sourer expressions.

The King of All could see none of his twins' similar battles. His prideful awakening was quickly being interrupted by rough and quick swaddling and a warmth unfamiliar to one used to the milky temperature of the biting uterus. He screamed again! This time in defiance, this time as a war cry to renewed battle. Damning the consequences, he flailed, chubby limbs pushing and pulling against stainless fingers and cradling wrappings. Simple consciousness submerged into shock and exhaustion as his packaged form sank into a nutrient bath.

The King of All had lost, but it had been his greatest battle. One he would never remember.

~

The sterility of the Taygetos laboratory reached beyond the antiseptics and UV projectors into the sharp taste of the air, the absent color and painfully bright lights. Even the men, their clothes' corners crisply straight and starkly even, were clean without fault in appearance and manner. From the blackest of clans, they looked down through generations, and now through transparent plastic, to study and judge. The infant they watched railed against his testing, pulling the only objects of any color from his trainers' hands only to tear them apart or toss them from his sight. He eventually settled on a sharp shape to taste and wave in front of his own dark eyes before crushing and cradling it.

"We've recently put holds on introducing any random factors into the soup, straining the last two generations into more focused outcomes. Each of the new batches has been a thousandfold removed from the prior, and in each case the cullings have resulted in one subject to bring into the next. Only the strongest. Only the superior."

"It seems a waste to just toss good genetic material…"

"The waste would be the time and resources spent on anything other than the pinnacle of our achievements. Nevertheless, be assured the "material," as you call it, is recycled in other ways to serve the Empire. The Clan's work is nothing if not efficient."

"But could not the inferiors, still mighty in comparison to the standard stock, be sent out…"

"The assignment is not only to create the ultimate army, an unstoppable clan, but also to keep our activities a secret to all but the Elders."

"But…"

"The more we explore side projects, the more we expand our research or successes into other areas, the chance of our revealing grows. Genetic sculpting has long been illegal, and the clans must never be reminded of the mistakes of the past. If the Empire is to be as righteous, god-chosen and infallible, then history as well as the future must be unblemished. We cannot grow upward from rotted roots, cannot move forward from a pockmarked track. Nothing good would come from the knowledge of the Clans' involvement in our enemies' origins, nor would it come from free access to our accomplishments here. The general planets only care that they can rest easy at night, tucked away deep in the galaxy, far from the wars being won by the fruit of our labors."

The wall-to-wall vidplays behind them showed the slow dance of asteroid families the laboratory participated in. A standard structure would have used windows straight to space, with magnetofields to hold debris at bay, but the Project's quarters were entrenched deep in iron and ice, and the cyclopean gas giant's ever-shifting poles would go far to scramble any sensors combing the system. Their work was too important to be discovered by the masses. More accurately, the men believed, it was beyond the simple minds of the common clans to understand. Its intent was beyond such pathetic filters as morality, beyond the microgeist of the simple men and women it was intended to protect. It would be misinterpreted by small minds unable to see beyond their own lives. Not only would the creations here ensure a future for an unstable empire, but it would mold it. The ability to exert influence over something as slippery as destiny — how could that be priced by those living day to day? This new army, this new clan, would be beyond the judgment of primitive ethics. In hindsight the clans would appreciate the work they were doing. In hindsight only was wisdom found. The Project was the vision of gods, and to be able to look backward while predicting the future was to become like them. It was to taste divinity. And here, deep in the rings of the gas giant, they used that taste to protect the lesser races, like gods, evolving and creating their betters. One day this new clan would overthrow its parents. Like all supplicants and children, it was what they were made for.

For now, however, the unstoppable army would spread the rule of the Empire past its enemies, past the degradation of the outlying systems, into new and old worlds waiting for the salvation of the clans.

"How much input have the Elders…"

"Little to none besides the initial order and investment."

"Then who decides when we have reached…"

"Rest easy knowing that we may actually be at the threshold. The most recent model has exhibited unparalleled size and strength without affecting endurance, epidermis withstands most conventional artillery while remaining light and flexible enough for superior speed and dexterity, and has already shown a mind for superior strategy with negligible levels of obstinacy. I fear another round of births, bringing this model forward into a new batch will only result in unacceptable levels of feralness. We will meet soon to discuss the possibilities."

"So… this may be it. This may be…"

"I, for one, believe we have found our template, and I am prepared to hand it over to the battle nurses."

"What is its name."

"It is EA-Z53n, but I have taken to calling it 'Easarean.'"

II

An old silent crone…
A claw opens throat and gut.
Scream! Silence again.

—Graffiti scratched into the walls of the Royal Church of Bifrost

B e you forever gored on the Serpent's sizzling tooth, witches milk still be yer reward! Dig you whorehounds, you sons of bitches, you mother's fodder. Father's switches on yer asses! Dig 'til you find your futures' bones freezing in unleavened graves, come back to haunt yer shriveled stones!"

Even with ears perked they could barely hear his calls across the frozen ground above the sounds of their own digging, yet still his voice spurred them on, as did the electricity in the air. The pack had splintered away from the rest before the Horde purged the Garm, and it was even possible they may have been all that was left of what had been the largest gathering in their history. If so, it made their search all the more important.

"Dig, you dirty curs, you cursed pigs! Claw Earth 'til she pleads or your puppy paws bleed. Woof! As you prefer, gentlemen dogs!"

Mad Hati's calls hung in the fog like the stench that brought them, here to the dirty frost and chilled swamps of the deep South, here to the sunken city of what was left of Magog. It was all broken ground and iced sinkholes and fields of shattered forests laid low by hail and sea that frequently swept high into the hills, every time retreating and leaving an impossibly briny wasteland of glacial ruin. Hati's long red mane hung out from a furry hood to mix with an equally crimson beard. With a bare upper lip, he was unique among the men of his pack, and his nose and cheeks flushed in the chilly breeze. But he felt none of the cold, covered as he was in autumn hides making him appear even larger than usual.

It was in this brittle mud the Garm dug. On the run from the Horde, spurred by the howls of their pack leader, called by the scent of the *Shear*, the last of their kind had run the country during each glorious full moon, to find themselves deep in the dying Land of Nod to scratch and pull at land burnt by the frozen ocean.

The albino eye of the cosmos glared down on their excavation, pale but slightly bloodshot but always taunting them. And so they

5
~

dug faster, for the scent that had beckoned since the fall of the Gog Tower was now scattered over the shattered ruins of the sunken city. Somewhere under broken stone and jagged ice they could smell the *Shear*. The scent not only tickled their black noses, but was felt deep inside their black hearts. The *Shear* pulsed to the moonlight, throbbing as the eye sank and then appeared from the herd of clouds running the cosmos. Only the *Shear* was sharp enough to cut the fetters that held the Beast. The blade, forged of impossible things by an impossible blacksmith, was the only thing in existence sharp enough to release the Garm's wolfen god. Freed from its impossible binding, it would tear Earth in twain to emerge on the surface before eating the sun. Those left in the world would be saved from the judgment of the heavens. No longer would anyone walk under the oppressive eye of the day. No longer would anyone have to hide from the chilling stare of the moon.

The Garm tore into the salty stink of the ruined fields, muzzles wrinkling and searching the solid ground for what should have been the growing scent of the *Shear*. If the mystical blade was near, why could they not feel it as strongly as they had in their dreams — visions that sent them through burning plains and mountains in which only their Hel-stoked breath kept the air from freezing before they could choke it down. Even beneath the smoke of smothered prairie and the parched air of iced hills they could always smell the *Shear* in these dreams, but here the scent had grown faint. The ground was rich with the sulfurous stench of wild magic, as the air was with salt water, yet the blade's call should have overpowered it all — in furred snout as well as twisted half-man heart. They had begun the hunt on the whims of their souls, but had lately been spurred on by the rants of their leader.

"Tear Earth! Prove your worth! Claw the Mother 'til all paws are red with devotion, never pausing 'til the dirt drinks up your life to sprout the blossom of Ragnarock! Rout the gods in their hubris! Dine in twilight's coming bliss! It will never end! And we will hunt by nose and ear the blind blessed to live to be prey. Pray with the dig, for tonight we hunt bloodless quarry of the sharpest tooth, in the quarry of fallen necromancers! Let the unliving dreams of the dead immortal make for a fecund garden, guarding the fruit…"

Mad Hati growled and barked over the small pack between his sermons, despite his appearance. He was their abomination — a man among wolves — bred to dominate from even his human form. From afar it looked as though he watched over his pack with the dried sockets of his furry hood. The hides covering his shoulders, draping his torso, leading to the wolf's head topping his own, looked even bloodier than usual in the pulsing moonlight. The wolf's ears looked like his own in the canine shadow spread behind him.

His voice carried like a howl over the digging Garm, even as he turned his face to follow the scent of the *Shear*. It trailed past the ruin of the once great city. His nose twitched as he caught a breeze from the far hills. Could it be, he wondered, that they were not the first to mine the fields for the legacy of Tormalco?

The pack leader stepped from the ridge to continue searching the breezes for the scent as his pack gathered. They had not noticed it, but their sniffing and digging, digging and sniffing, had brought them slowly closer to each other. They now found themselves all scratching and clawing at the same plot of wasteland, tearing up great clumps of stone and ice. Dirt flew in plumes from between their hind legs, as their breath rasped louder from between drooling teeth.

And then — a "yelp." And then the pack scattered. But they were quickly drawn back, hesitant but growling and circling, the moon casting rotating shadows from the rise and fall of their hunched humpbacks. The stink of everdeath wafted from the pit they had dug, keeping them at a certain distance from the emaciated hand reaching from the ground. It was bone thin, covered in more ice than flesh, and it reached to grasp ground, revealing a skeletal arm before pulling itself up through the breaking earth.

Some of the pack stepped toward the pit as more of the body appeared. They bared teeth from quivering leech lips, jumping back as the headless lich stood from its frozen tomb. An arcane shroud stuck to its desiccated shoulders and arms like the hanging remnants of its hair, diabolic sigils spun from gold replicated in the dull glow of dark light in the air around the creature. Ice-burnt flesh flaked and floated as the undead sorcerer bent, reaching into the frozen mire to pull his head from the ground.

The Garm circled and growled, blue and gray eyes never leaving the sight of the pale husk. One putrescent hand cracked and twitched, forming the circles and quick motions of magik, while a lipless mouth whispered spells. Bare teeth clicked from the head hanging by long whispy hair clenched in the lich's other hand. One of the Garm dared to look deeply into the black glow of the hanging head's eyes and was trapped. He could not look away. His own eyes went white, and he never saw anything else ever again.

At the sight of his blinded brother, another of the pack moved in, lunging with tooth and claw. The lich spun spell with one hand and held his head up toward the giant werewolf with the other. A blossom of bubbling violet spewed from between the sorcerer's teeth into the Garm's muzzle. The beast rolled and choked and vomited.

A third Garm fell upon the lich, pinning him to the icy earth and snapping his massive jaw at a sudden multitude of limbs and heads and hooves and pinchers. The closing of his teeth echoed over and over across the frozen mire, but he bit at only air. He felt and smelled the dead mage beneath him, but his mouth kept coming up empty against the barrage of illusory limbs.

The empty crack of canine teeth brought Hati back to his pack. He had found a scent leading away from the frigid pool, but the sulfurous stench of undead sorcery now made his eyes and nose water. He found his pack so quickly in shambles. One Garm sniffed the air, gazing crookedly at the sky with milky, blind eyes. Another squirmed in the cold muck, rubbing paws over blistered nose and gums. The final werewolf had its giant furry claws clenching and unclenching into the lich, holding it firmly, but continued to bite at spectral arms and legs. The biting Garm cringed at the dry whisper of an ancient language and the crinkle of petrified fingers, but it was too late. The lich had brought up its head to the werewolf's pointed ear. A shriveled tongue pulsed red hot and flicked from the jaw into the Garm's ear, impossibly reaching out and licking the air from the other size of its head.

"Come wizard, come zombie, come putrid once lord of Magog and Gog and land of swamp and fog," howled Hati. "Come meet the Beast's blizzard! The feeder of buzzard! The meater of man and wolf! Woof! Can the dead die? Dye the earth with congealed blood? Muddy the Great Hall with twice-judged jelly? Come, old and moldy, let's learn together whether Mad Hati Weirdson's time is done or just begun."

The lich rose, floating, broken toenails scraping the ground as he left the deaf Garm writhing behind. Still his papery skin stretched as his teeth clicked away, forming another spell.

Hati tore the leather coats from his chest, leaping out of his boots and running down the ridge at the lich, howling all the way. His limbs twisted, bones snapping and reforming as he neared. His remaining clothing split to reveal spreading masses of fiery fur matching the hide blending into his shoulders and head. The wolf's tanned head became his own as fur mingled with hair, eyes consumed eyes, and his face shattered outward to become a gangly-toothed snout. The ground buckled as his claws launched him into the air over the lich, his shadow engulfing the undead mage.

At the same time, the shadows within the lich's decomposed chest slithered to take the shape of thorny tendrils, exploding outward to catch the crimson Garm in his fury. Mad Hati tore through the clenching blackness, shedding and scattering the shadows with his claws, tearing great inky chunks with giant teeth. Fur quickly became wet and matted, but he dug onward and downward.

The undead lich held his head aloft, gore hanging from skinless neck and jaw chattering away a new spell. His other hand gestured a slow succession of signs in unison to the raspy chant.

Nearby, the blind Garm took one last sniff of the putrid air before striking out. He bit through moldy shroud and brittle flesh, crunching into the lich's petrified arm. He tore it from the body, arm and head flying, as he fell and rolled, unable to find steady ground beneath his sightless eyes.

The headless lich staggered, seeing only the mud its face landed in, and it only had the time to put up its remaining arm in defense before Hati plunged thorn-torn claws deep into the liquid blackness, grasping the lich's chest, pulling and shattering its ribcage open and outward. He tore arm from socket and crunched through tendon and bone before leaving the pieces for the rest of the pack. Deaf, dumb, and blind Garm waited until the red wolf was finished before moving in.

Hati's neck cracked backward, and his canine face sunk inward as he forced the change upon himself again, this time back to his human form with limbs quivering, chest sinking and joints bending backwards. His skin hissed as ruddy fur disappeared back into his skin.

"Heel... we'll not make a meal of it... sit!" As he spoke and changed his voice became less of a growl. As his skull buckled and teeth blunted his speech returned to fully human. "Woof! Grind his bones to pebbles and stones. Find the heart and pull it apart. But mind you don't eat it. Lift yer leg to it. Dig and bury it. Get rid of its sweet dead stench instead. Heed! It's foul meat indeed. Cursed or worse." He staggered, half naked, bloody-handed, over to where he had left his hammer. He breathed deeply and loudly before his pack, grunting as he lifted *Manhood* to his shoulder, unafraid to show his exhaustion. The axe's length was half his, and the exertion of the change had strained his back and arms.

He passed his pack as they scratched and bit, clawed and pissed, and he was proud. The Horde had only done the Garm a favor. The Horde had culled the weak from the packs. They had killed the old and the lame. Their genocide had only weeded out the unfit, leaving behind the young and the strong and the focused. No more pack politics. No more fighting over status or order. Mad Hati's pack answered only to itself, with its destiny clearly and physically set out in front of it.

"But the *Shear* is not here," he sighed, bringing the carven hammer over his back, its wolfen head appearing blooded in the night's light. "Where? Near? I have its scent..." The lich's head was crushed without a sound beneath *Manhood*. "...no doubt Hel sent." His furry headdress stared with crinkled, dried eyes up at the moon, as he stared down at its reflection in the gore of the frozen swamp.

~

The pack was long gone by the time the moon began to set, but the dark pall of both still stretched across the chilled sludge. Two Garm followed the scent of the pack over the carnage. They were mangy, unkempt, and the black male's fur was either clumped or missing in patches. Their black noses twitched and their blacker lips curled at the broken bones protruding from mud and frost. The remains stank of decay and enchantment, but the two had not eaten in days. Flowstone Skoll and Busy Emla were condemned to eat only scraps left behind by the pack. And the pack never left scraps, so the two took advantage of the foul-smelling leavings.

Skoll sniffed at many familiar scents in the area, least of which was the blood of Mad Hati. The air told him the pack had headed north. He and Emla would follow, as they always did, at the allowed distance.

Emla, gray but black at every tip, clawed at the muck and pulled up a rib to chew at its hardened marrow. The bone was stubborn, and she had to grind it into powder to get at anything of any taste. The *Brandr Moon* was vanishing now for another month, and the change painfully and suddenly came upon her. She swallowed another lick of the gritty marrow as her guts churned and body contorted. She could barely feel Skoll as he mounted her from behind, his claws shrinking into fingernails as he howled at the opaque heavens.

III

With wyrm in his germ, Mage asked,
"For when shall us men feel your love again?"
Not one childhood will have passed.
"Open arms to War of Sin."
Liege of Foes will return, without, within.
  —The Ver Primordium (VII-VII-VII)

$\mathcal{O}$ ammit all to Hell! She can have my soul!"

The game was getting heated. *As if we don't attract enough attention,* Sol Ascension thought, *now we have to deal with Flagon waking the streets outside.*

"The luck of this one!" Flagon shouted unbelieving, slapping him on the back with a hand twice the size of Sol's. "I was so close." The big man had thrown his cards when Sol had made his move, and he now slowly collected them as he finished his beer, not caring if the others saw his hand.

Sol looked shyly around the saloon to see if any of the other curfew breakers were paying any attention to his table, but everyone out this late in Megrim had their own dealings to attend to. Flagon was seen and ignored as just another drunken Midgardian avoiding his homeland. It was a shame, Sol thought, Flagon was actually a credit to his people, but when he drank he quickly fell into the boisterous stereotype of the northerner. The plan had always been to hide out in the open in Megrim, but Sol was never sure if they were playing into that strategy or not. So, as usual, he just went along with the others.

"How is it, cleric," Flagon asked, "how is it you pull just the right one at the right time? Every game! Yer dirty robes hiding cards? Don't yer mistress call sinning on cheating?"

Sol fought off the man's callused fingers as they poked at his clothing, keeping his laughter low. "Off, heathen! If you need to call skill and talent a cheat then you're playing with the wrong men. Skata, it's your turn."

The mustached man to Sol's left rolled his bones and paused, staring at them as though he hoped they would suddenly change on their own. Most games of UnderCrawl used the same agreed-upon set of bones, but the men at this table trusted each other enough to allow each player to use their own.

Sir Skata continued to ponder the bones until Sol expected another outburst from Flagon. But the knight eventually passed on moving his pawn, instead drawing cards. If his game was off, Sol could find no indication in the man's steely face, and the otherwise gregarious knight barely talked after the first round of the game. Was it a strategy intended to unnerve the rest of them, or was it just intense concentration — Sol did not know. Perhaps it was the tension creeping through the Motley Cow, for none of them were playing to win tonight. They had other reasons to roll the bones.

Sol knew the knight so well that he often wondered if others in the town could tell him as such. If he ever wore the white and red armor of his order when visiting Megrim, it was hidden under coat and furs. If he brought his angelically ornate sword, he left it hidden in his safe house. If he still wore a Libran talisman, as Sol suspected he always had, it was worn close to his heart. The only indication of Sir Skata's faith was the long, black mustache under his broad nose. By now, however, it was overgrown and joined by a slight but unkempt beard growing over the ruddy man's square jaw. The Order of the Creed was not officially outlawed in Horde territory, but Sol had cautioned the knight in obvious displays of contrary faith. There were rumors of disappearances the men at the table did not doubt.

As though he had been thinking the same thing, Skata, surprising the rest of the table, broke his silence. "It is said that the new Sin Eater travels to Megrim." He kept his voice and dark eyes low, speaking into and from behind his hand.

"What'd interest him in this tinder pile?" Flagon asked, barely hearing under the creak of his chair, the floorboards, and the building's whine against the weakening blizzard outside. "Winter covers all prints, the wind all smells."

"These 'rages' across the territories... these berserk, suicidal massacres... could they be traced back to you?" Sol Ascension whispered. Among the beads strung around his left arm, one string hung down to the emerald he rubbed under the table. Its smooth presence reminded him of his vows, of his alabaster mistress, and of his belief in redemption and the connection amongst all men. Rages were appearing in the Horde's churches as soon as their final bricks were laid. Were these slaughtered parishioners beyond redemption? Would the Lonely Forgotten Sun of God approve of the underground movement's increasingly violent ways? Would she approve of his?

"I didn't order *all* of them," Flagon spoke into his mug.

"Still…"

"So my men wish to die at the end of a sword. So be it! Better than under the feathered heel of some demon. Better than in the yoke, under the whip of tithingmen."

"Understood," Sol mused. The methods of resistance appearing in other cities would be a discussion for another time. The Sin Eater was a more pressing concern. "It can't be coincidence. It'd be foolish to consider it as one."

The knight spoke up then. The barkeep had kept up with the freezing night, stocking the fireplace consistently, and so Sir Skata tied his hair back in the warm saloon. "We can take Megrim." Sol and Flagon leaned in closely. "We pull men from the closest neutral towns. I have men stationed at a ranch nearby that will lead them. Megrim is far enough from Horde-secured territory that it has never fully pledged allegiance. Those in town loyal to the Choir will submit if they see strong enough numbers in strong enough force. We can make this city a symbol, show that you don't have to just roll over to the Horde. Others will come. We can hold off any forces while we grow. The Horde can't split their forces right now, especially not for what they think is an insignificant town."

Sir Skata passed his turn over to the final member of the game — a man who talked even less than the knight, in game or otherwise. The cloaked figure took no time to roll the bones, barely paying attention to the outcome before playing two cards at once.

Flagon was standing before his cards hit the floor. "Tor's sores! Will this game ever end?"

Sol watched as Sir Skata examined the two cards closely, waiting, even though he would have been surprised if anyone could have countered the play. Their fourth player had played the cards *Hasty Retreat* and *Under the Same Son*. Sol did not need to look at the cards closely. He knew what they meant. Alone, *Hasty Retreat* brought one's peg back to its starting position. Both cards together affected all players. But they meant more than that. Did the others realize?

Sol Ascension had been moving from town to town to city for over a year when he first made contact with the underground in Megrim. A rickety city built on top of itself, it would not have been his first pick of a place to settle down in, but it was his first sense of stability since he had been ordained. Looking at the cards, he surprised himself by admitting that he would miss Megrim's loud rafters and swaying upper levels.

Flagon glared at the cloaked man sitting quietly next to him until, from beneath the deep hood, a pale granite eye glared back.

"Is that really the move you wanna make?"

The man nodded, the eye sinking back into shadow.

All the players moved their custom pawns back to each individual corner of the board.

The waitress, perhaps sensing a break in the gameplay, then brought their food for the evening.

"Ah," Flagon exclaimed, "now here's a game I am sure to lose. Yet I never fail to play. A king's ransom for an Imp's Meal!"

There were things in Megrim that Sol knew he would not miss. Although as much as they often complained about the city's food, rumor had it that it was not better anywhere else these days. He knew Flagon was joking, but the only people eating meat these days were those that had figured out how to profit from the war. Populations had shrunken from Plaag. Crop and cattle were still recovering from Phaimon. And the long winters held the land in slow standstills. Death seemed to be the only commodity worth anything, and Megrim was far from the battlefields.

But Sol was used to hardship, and hardship reminded him of someone — a child called "Cutter" by his mother. Cutter's earliest memories consisted of watching his mother do her work. He had inherited her large brown eyes, but hers looked even larger through the magnifying glass. He would play away the afternoons with her old shaping wheels as she slit and polished precious stones. As a toddler, he learned his colors by the gems her clients would bring in the early hours of the day, and by the time he was eight years old he had begun to practice his own gem cutting on fakes and flaws under her stern instruction. He had a natural talent.

Cutter had woken late on the morning the Barons of Bab'lon erected the walls of the makeshift town of Quarantine right in the middle of their capital city. He would never forget the sound of the chaos outside his mother's shack, as the destitute blocks he had never wandered beyond were alive with commotion and violence against

Ziggurat's city guard. The officers contained the outbursts with staff and rifle, felling any of the unruly that hampered the final stages of the construction. It was days before the uprising calmed, and the young boy had wandered littered streets for hours in a futile search for his mother until coming upon the western wall. It had been hastily layered but still imposed itself over the ramshackle huts of the ghetto. Those that tested its mortar and height were quickly dispatched with rifle shots from some unseen tower. If anyone escaped it was from climbing the hills of the dead stretching up the walls, and, even then, those that stayed had to dodge the bodies as they were thrown back in, burned and broken.

For years, numerous diseases wracked the sewage-filled gutters and gullies of Quarantine, long after the Goblin Winter had subsided outside the town's walls, and all through those years the Western Wall Gang presided over the people. Cutter grew under their tutelage, learning of man's essential rights in judgment at the tip of an improvised knife, as a peer of frightened juries, and at elaborate executions. By the time he had grown into the role of the Western Wall Gang's leader there was peace through the damp streets. The three western walls had always comprised one gang, but in the years leading up to the young man's leadership the two walls of the Eastern Gang had been absorbed into the Northern Gang, while the streets and shacks of the southern wall were too disease and body-ridden to even be thought of as habitable.

The ground shook the day the young man brokered peace between his gang and its rivals. Those around him grasped at wall or ground, but he stood unwavering before following them out into the streets. Quarantine had become their home. Many could remember nothing else, yet they still all ran for the new sudden openings in the walls. The quake had broken the brick to the outer world of Ziggurat, and as the young man stood in one of the openings, repeatedly knocked to the ground by his escaping people, he breathed in fresh air for the first time in ten years. It was cool and strange, and it made him forget about the city officers that should have been gunning him down.

The streets outside reminded him of one of his first memories — that of the insanity of the initial quarantine — and it made him try to remember his mother's face for the first time in many years. But he could not remember.

Over the days that followed, as their paths crossed, old friends and new attributed their salvation to the *Ashmedai Adat El's* sudden appearance over Ziggurat. The Prophets Lesser was spreading that very word throughout the capital and, eventually, all the Baronies. The churches filled all throughout the cities, but the young man stuck to the alleys and the shacks he knew. Here the whispers and rumors in the doorways were, as yet, untainted by propaganda, not yet filtered by the new order. It was here he first heard the accounts of the Lonely Forgotten Sun of God. The tales said that she too had been disserted by the heavens, left to fend for herself in a dangerous world. In these stories her frustration had cracked the earth with fire and steam. Her sadness had shaken the city.

By the time the agents of the *Ashmedai Adat El* had come to salvage the ghettoes, the young man had disappeared, fleeing into the less guarded areas and finding himself lost outside the baronies in a world much more open than he had ever known. But in every famine-stricken hamlet he wandered into, and in every emaciated farmstead he happened upon, he would hear new tales of the Alabaster Princess.

When the winds subsided and the plains extinguished, and the fields once gain started to produce, and the young man found more and more to steal, and he could finally add mass to the shriveled frame he had become, he found himself repeatedly gorging himself over a meal surrounded by the growing tales. She had been seen entering the far-off exotic Land of Nod and, when she had been said to have left, the dead no longer roamed its swamps. Evil magiks no longer held sway over the dark land's nights. Fertility, albeit slowly, had returned to the countryside.

The young man called Cutter followed the whispered stories of her new pilgrimage, skirting the Baronies. For months hushed tales led him just behind her sightings. Here he found a ranch where a new spring bubbled up through recently cracked limestone. There he found a village where the hills had slid over dry pasture, bringing with them newly turned fertile earth. Her light footprints through the sprouting dirt were obvious, but it was still many days before he found her.

It was far from any habitable area. The nearby plains had been smoldering for years. Without any vegetation left, the fires could only smoke, but the winds kept them sparking while drying the fields to a crust nothing could grow in. There were nomadic camps far as the eye could see, from the mountains and dunes to the north to the cloudy horizons all around. This was a sparse land, but it had to be passed through to find civilization. Cutter found the people gathered by the hundreds, leaving tent and tipi to the mercy of the plains, around a shallow lake flanked by trees long since petrified and unmoving under the white sun. The sands and winds had polished the sharp trees smooth and pale as though nothing was allowed color this side of the mountains.

Cutter struggled to find a grip on one of the trees as he climbed to see over the crowd. The lake was as glaring as the sky, and as soon as he settled into the branches he could see a change coming over the waters. It rippled before bubbling, as the air over it wavered before bending, and as the people gasped before cheering. The crowds moved in to collect the sudden piles of floating fish.

The air was cool and the sun burned him, but Cutter had waited until the people gathered their fill and went back to their sites to start campfires. He could now see the cloudy hunger in their eyes, their sunken cheeks and boney hands. They would look different in the morning. She had found them food in a desolately dry land. How long had it been since they had gone to bed with a full stomach? Had they ever? Tonight they would dream of something other than food. He walked to where she still knelt at the edge of the lake. The stench of brimstone hung in the sweltering air so he could not tell if she glowed like the sun or if it was his watering eyes that made her appear so. Her champion stepped in front of Cutter, blocking his view. The expressionless marbled mask frightened him more than he thought it should have when he later reminisced about the lady's guardian.

The young man was quickly accepted in the pilgrims' care, and, as time went on, he found joy in learning the survival skill of the wilderness. He, in turn, proved his worth when they encountered cities. In civilization he quickly made contacts and approached black markets and circumvented authority. In baronies converted to the watch of what he now knew as the Horde, these skills had become invaluable. But it was months later, when the ever-growing mass of pilgrims came upon a dilapidated temple, that he had a chance to show the talents he was most proud of.

The mountains in the southern baronies were treacherous but not tall, filled with loose paths but not cold, and the Lonely Forgotten Sun of God chose only a few from her flock to accompany her into the interior canyons. Cutter followed closely behind the lady's masked champion. In the time the young man had traveled with them he had already seen the champion fight many times, and it had been exactly as he had heard. The man fought as though possessed by an army, a whole legion of warriors. Cutter believed him to be unbeatable.

By the time the moon rose they had emerged from the tree line to find the observatory, and as they entered what was left of the building they could see it had once been a temple. The Alabaster Princess sat amongst the rubble of feline sculptures, looking up toward a starless night as though she expected it to be anything but. The masked champion left to patrol the hillsides while the others sat around her. She taught them to pray that night.

It was one of those prayers that Sol said to himself this night in the Motley Cow during a lull in the game. All the players seemed lost in their own thoughts, and so he took the chance to finger the string of beads he kept hidden in his sleeve. The string was entwined around his left arm with the sliver of emerald hanging into his palm. As he rolled each bead through his fingers he thought to deeds over the past day corresponding to the *gentle constants*. Humility, compassion, patience… before the morning had come he had memorized them all. And it was in this morning light that she had given him his new name, and as the initiates rejoined the rest of the pilgrims, Sol Ascension began work on what he believed would be his greatest contribution to the faith. In the rubble of the observatory he had found an emerald, quite large to have been left hidden for so long. With tools he had gathered over the past months he cut the stone into slivers reminiscent of a cat's iris. He distributed the pieces to those that had first prayed with him.

Where were those other clerics now, Sol wondered as he turned his sharp emerald in his hand beneath the table. But, more urgently, he wondered, *what had happened to the Alabaster Princess?*

"Another double grog," Flagon said to the servant girl as she finished placing mugs before them, "and a hot posset for my cold friend here." He gestured to the cloaked man.

They were quiet until she returned with the drinks. Sol had no doubt they all pondered the preparations they needed to go through in the coming night. "A toast," he said without emotion, "for, as Skata has said, before today was the Feast of Gob Mammon-Gammon, it was celebrated as The Liege of Days. We used to herald in spring today."

Flagon laughed at this. "No wonder the people had forgotten."

"I am not a wealthy man," Sol continued, "a vow of poverty prohibits it, and so I have no cakes for you, my friends… my best friends." He felt his throat tighten and hoped it was not noticeable in his voice. He had not realized he had become so close to these three men until the last round of UnderCrawl. The game was only on hold while they ate, but it may as well have been over as far as he was concerned. By morning he could be on the road. But would it be soon enough? "But we have something better than the Liege of Cakes." He lowered his voice to ensure that only their table could hear. "We need no trinket or effigy at our table." At this he tipped his glass toward the cloaked man, who, in turn, nodded before drinking his warm drink.

"A story then," Flagon said, setting his cards down to pick up his fork. "Put the game aside for a story while we eat."

Having only a glass of water, Sir Skata joined the toast only with his attention. He then wiped his hands and face with a handkerchief fancy enough to belie the rest of his appearance before starting in on his dinner. "Yes, Sol, in honor of forgotten holidays and present company, tell us a story. Make it loud, make it blasphemous, in honor of our last night…"

So it was true. Sol had hoped he read the cards wrong. This would be their last night in Megrim. "I'm one of the few to have been christened by the Alabaster Princess herself," he whispered. "I say it not to gloat, but to point out that, as I've been renamed by her, I'm in a unique position to watch over the flocks of her followers as, over the years, they've formed rifts, not only in the world but among themselves. Some in her faith call themselves *Ascendants* and they believe themselves descended in word from those that first heard her voice, that first watched her pull fire from the ground or split the ground or crack Bab'lon. They have long memories and loud voices and they spread her words as if they were their own. Others call themselves *Ascensionists*, and they've grown from the predictions in the *Fallo Terminus* — the book she left behind. Where she left it, where they found it, I don't know, but their copies have spread far into Horde territory, hidden under mattress and floorboard.

"This is a story about the Ascendants and the Ascensionists."

He may not have been loud, but his story *was* blasphemous for it told a tale of the Liege of Foes.

~

I'd only recently arrived in the area, sent by the Lonely Forgotten Sun of God herself, to try to encourage the commune on the prairie to help in resisting the Horde. They considered themselves Ascendants, having seen the miracles of the Alabaster Princess or hearing of them from family and friends. They knew her to be descended from God. To them she was half flesh, close to both man and the divine. They heard of her pilgrimage across the Baronies and were waiting word on its outcome, and so I'd have had my work cut out for me — convincing them to spurn the Horde — were they not already stricken by a dripping fungus crippling their cornfields. They'd barely enough food to feed themselves, much less share with the new order.

They were disappointed in my appearance, mistrustful of my ragged robe and worn shoes. They expected more of a cleric that claimed to come directly from holy conference. They'd seen her beauty and had a tough time believing me heaven-sent. Also, my lack of new news bothered them as much as it did me. She had months ago been invited by the Prophets Lesser to take a pilgrimage of the Horde's territory, in the promise that, once seeing the "order" and "salvation" found in its cities, she would join its pantheon of prophets. She hadn't now been heard from for many seasons.

The commune of Ascendants turned a blind eye to my pauper's appearance and a deaf ear to my less than encouraging words. I couldn't convince them to join the then-burgeoning resistance, but I did find what I needed to know — despite the dire reasoning behind it, they wouldn't be supplying the Horde with food. I readied to leave, but, as I did, something stayed my feet.

I'd heard the rumors before I'd even stepped foot into the commune's roads — that this particular groups of Ascendants had a thing for animal sacrifice. I'd dismissed it when seeing their devotion firsthand, but their starvation had made them bitter, and their immediate judgment of an unfamiliar follower had made me wary of them, but I couldn't doubt their faith in who they had named the Alabaster Princess. However, my first look underestimated the degree of the famine and the commune's desperation, and, as I was leaving town, I noticed the crowd and ritual involved in murder. The girl's squealing made my breath catch and sent shivers down to my toes.

"She was our last one," they sermoned, "praise be, but we'll go on.

Her blood'll feed the soil, her spirit will haunt the others. Spit at the eye of those around the Bend."

The ritual was led by a woman they must've hid from me during my stay, because I would've remembered her. She wore a habit covering all but her face — a face so covered in make-up I wouldn't have been able to tell you her age or origin. Her feces-colored eyes looked lazy but young. They called her Hec, and she was so adept at slitting the necks of the piglets that the ritual was finished by the time I made my way to the altar. She ignored my exasperated expression but explained herself quickly in hysterics.

"This town is cursed, boy, cursed by those living around the Bend. The fungus, barren wombs, spiders fillin' the cornrows with webs, hoppers eatin' the fields, jaundiced wee ones, wells dryin' up…"

Her voice rose in pitch as she went on and on. I quickly gave up on following her hectic train of thought. The point of my story is that the Ascendants were pacifists and, instead of confronting these witches around the Bend they decided to fight fire with fire and follow Hec's lead in spelling against the drought.

My words couldn't keep up with her hysteria. I wasn't prepared to deal with such drama, and so my accusations of heresy went unnoticed by the commune. They hadn't trusted me to begin with, and now confronting a respected member of the tribe only ruined my credibility.

But the Liege of Foes immediately commanded their attention.

He walked into the gathering as the only shadow beneath the sun that day, cloak billowing and voice demanding attention. "How do you know your countercurses are fruitful when no fruit still grows among you?"

"Without the ritual the fields would be dryer, the creeks would all be gone, even more worms in the pantries and panties…" Hec ranted. Now challenged, her words came impossibly faster. I wondered just how many mouths she had. "We send curses back to dry their loins, shrivel their buds and bundle their clouds and whip their winds and wrinkle their teats…"

"I'll speak with them," the Liege of Foes said, glaring at Hec from the granite eye within his hood. He stared as though he could see deep into her habit as she grabbed at his feet, pleading for him to change his mind. He kicked her aside and examined the virgin with his fingers, but Hec continued as the Liege of Foes removed the dead girl's girdle.

"They'll kill you, man, as they do to any that walk on their land. They're ruthless and they have no need for manners when it comes to strangers. You won't survive but a day in their woods. They don't respect conference or words spoken by any but themselves. They know only curse or bloodthirst or…"

"This good man will help you decide in my absence," he said, gesturing to me, "if you all still walk the Alabaster Princess' path, or if you're better off since spilling the blood of piglets."

The rest I only know from what I was told later. I heard two different stories, but I like the Ascendants' version best.

It was half a day's walk, but as soon as the Liege of Foes went around the Bend he was afflicted by their curses. And he recognized it immediately. The symptoms increased the deeper he went into their territory. It was pig pox, swine flu, and hog hobbler, and it was directed at him. He knew the cocktail of curses was a clue as to the Horde's involvement, but, as he went lame — orifices crusting over, pustules on his belly bursting, pus pooling from his pores — he feared he'd take this insight to his grave.

But he woke under the care of strangers, and they tended to him with a concern he rarely saw across this land, and they amazed him with their knowledge of the herbs and healing roots of the woodlands. They scrounged what salves they could spare while he sprawled near the empty pantries, cringing every time one grew near. The strangers had single green eyes tattooed on their foreheads, and it unnerved him in his sickness.

"I told you to kill him!" a familiar voice said, "Not to bring him back here, kill him!"

The Liege of Foes looked to the cellar doorway, following what he thought was Hec's voice to another painted woman in a habit. Her mouth was wider, although with less teeth, and she had eyes as blue as his one original.

"I'll do it myself!" she screamed, running downward and pulling a wicked sacrificial knife from the folds of her habit.

The Liege of Foes dizzily sidestepped, pulling the virgin's girdle from inside his cloak. He swung it closely, and it snaked before twisting and tightening around the witch's arms, binding them to her sides as the knife fell to the cellar floor.

"It burns! It burns!" she squealed, jerking like a newt before slowing to a gasping stillness. They watched as, within the confining hood, her head twisted around to reveal a third face — this one pruned and as blind as its gums were pink.

The Liege of Foes and the Ascensionists gathered around her, unable to look away. They were another commune, and for years they followed the peace found in secondhand rumors and myths of who they called the Lonely Forgotten Sun of God. They had recently found and translated thirdhand copies of the *Fallo Terminus*, and so they believed her to be wholly holy, not the progeny of the divine but a god herself come to liberate the people from the sickness and the famine and the creeping war of the sinful land. But still the forest denied them, their orchards giving up only wormy sauces.

Hec's head jerked at every mention of the Lonely Forgotten Sun of God until finally she spoke. "She's weak! She's abandoned you while the people of the prairie curse you and your fruit, and your only hope is to curse them back with every…"

"No," the Liege of Foes said above the witch, "even now she watches over you. Phaimon's spell is broken, and soon your orchards will blossom and the prairies will yield gold. Hec has turned you against her and your own brothers on the plains." He gestured toward the bound creature beneath them as it tried to hide itself. "Get a good look. This is a sight few men will ever see. A Bride of Chem-Oshmelech. She was almost your and your brothers' destruction. See what the Horde has to offer? Their influence is spreading and the Alabaster Princess works to stop it. She asks only that you make peace with your brethren, and when the corn sprouts without fungus, and the trees are heavy with apples, that you feed the growing Army of Earth. Chem-Oshmelech is only one of the terrors coming out of the West. Pray it is the last you hear of him."

I left with the Liege of Foes, but not before attending the first meeting of Ascendant and Ascensionist. They cried over the graves of their daughters, trading cups of corn whiskey and cider. They'd long been following the same god, but, with the threat of the Horde suddenly closer, they'd now do it together.

~

"I have a better tale," Sir Skata said, "but let us resume our game first."

"And a refill," said Flagon.

Sol wondered if he himself had already had too much to drink tonight, for he only now noticed the man alone at a neighboring table. He would had thought that the man had recently come into the saloon, except for the fact that he looked long passed out, crumpled over the table face down, his large mug of ale the only other item near.

Yes, Sol did remember seeing the man when they came in earlier, but he had already been passed out. *Still*, he thought, *best to abstain for the rest of the night*. He would need to keep his wits about him.

IV

*"There is no better advantage
than in being underestimated"*
   —Hyper Khan's "The War of Art"

Imagine how exciting it must have been to see a star or planet in the night sky after it had been absent for a season or a year, next to the repeating seasons, the return of a familiar celestial friend would have been ancient man's first inclination of time. The sun? Bah! It would have retreated into the subconsciousness like a hideous wallpaper one ignores without realizing it. The moon? People's natural tendency to push it to the peripheral is a coping mechanism, for to acknowledge its constant binge and purge is to accept the wane and wax of our own lives, and that is assuredly a path to madness. Like the ugly wallpaper, we push the true consequences of time to some other plane of recognition, one that keeps our focus unoccupied to deal with more immediate concerns. Mankind would have never gotten this far by wasting resources on the future, by wasting tears on the past.

"But every once in a while such a man is born, one with temporal acceptance, a mutation setting him apart from both his kith and the safeguards bred into us by nature and kin. In the rare chance this man rises to any prominence he inevitably will fall as quickly, even more quickly than his mutant peers, for the rest of us — those grounded in immediacy — will always have the upper hand, because without generational sight, without empathy beyond our own village, we have not far-reaching moral consequences to slow us down, and the narrow-visioned will always triumph over those cursed with a mature grasp of time.

"The only difference between us and our prehistoric fathers is that we have no excuse. We are willing while they were captive. We could all be the minority mutants. We could rise above the hypnotism of chronic chronal tradition, break free from the spell memorized embryonically and look at life as it truly is, without the restraints we've placed on our short existences. But what would those lives be like?"

Ivy had an answer, but she did not think she was actually being asked.

"I fear I can't imagine," Astrolo continued. "The concept is too alien. Only the mutant can see time and our place in it as it truly is without becoming what we have designated as mad. We classify him as pathological in this way and that, and his line ends through willing or unwilling social exile, and that is why his kind will always be an aberration, never dominant, and why we will remain the mutants that are and not the mutants that could be. As I said, it is a coping mechanism — experiencing time as we do, and our immediacy drives the survival only instant gratification can provide.

"And so, floating willingly in the warm, sleepy-slow current of the plodding months and years, imagine how our father to the millionth power must have felt when he saw that familiar friend appear to him, twinkling its return. The starry eyes linked him to a past only he remembered, and it suddenly made him realize that there may be more pasts, more nights like this night when he would again be lamenting his long-lost celestial friend as it again blinked into existence above, starting the pontificating yet again, and so, man met time, and the stars taught him to appreciate it. They ignored their mother Earth — always providing, always bleeding for them — to look upward to the domineering cosmos. A father glared back, punishing or rewarding, approving or disapproving depending on the season."

Ivy realized now that she had gone through a similar experience, but hers had been more prolonged, a gradual realization of how best to break *then* and *now* and *when* — how best to experience and measure time when relating to those around her. It had seemed so arbitrary at the time, but she had eventually learned that it was not the *why* or *how* that mattered, it was the reasoning behind the measurement. It was a way of controlling one's environment. That, she had also learned, was of greater importance than anything else, and it would put her at a great disadvantage not to do so. But why should she care about being at a disadvantage? It was something she had not decided yet. She was still observing. She was taking her time.

She watched another reminder of the passage of time through the massive windows stretching from floor to rafter on the far side of the great room of Astrolo's home. The sun had disappeared an hour ago behind the Titans. There was still a faint glow, but many stars had appeared to prompt Astrolo's talk. He had lit many lamps to mix paint by, and now returned to the easel, but it was obvious to Ivy that he would not get much more painting done this evening. And that was fine with her. This was the third day she had posed for him, and it would be the last no matter the outcome. The giant room had begun to cool with the coming of night, and the few silken scarves she held did nothing to warm her nakedness, and Astrolo had not breaked to start a fire in the great fireplace as he had the previous evenings. An iron cougar guarded the mantle jutting from the chimney. It now disappeared as new shadows grew.

"Some men began to record — or 'chart,' if you will — the heavens when they noticed its inconstant nature in equally changing sands and, eventually, in much more unchanging methods." Astrolo placed his palette aside but kept three differently sized brushes in one hand, alternating mostly between two of the smaller ones. "And it wasn't long before they assigned meaning to each pretty little aster-ism, supernatural power to the appearance of every combination, and when a blessing occurred under one sign, it became a good sign, for all time, and when tragedy occurred under another, it was forever met with fear. Over time, a few began to notice that blessing and tragedy were emphasized by the tribe during these periods. These antediluvian proto-priests were smart enough to profit from the stars, forecasting the woe people already expected. Tribes combined, people settled in fertile lands with fences and walls, cities rose and fell, before man ques-tioned the stargazers, and so stories had to be told. Nothing captured the attention like tales of ancestors becoming heroes becoming gods becoming captured in and around the milk separating the cosmos. Now the gods fought monsters with the deeds spread across the night sky, watching and reminding those below of a golden age — a time the scattering populace would always strive for but always stay just on the verge of, as it once again gathered to build wall and observatory. And so they wouldn't forget, couldn't walk through life gazing at navel instead of star, some built observatories and gathered standing stones to mark and claim the earth for the heavens. The constellations danced in battle over them year after year, leading them to new lands, new people and new battles as they struggled to live up to their dead grandfathers' approval. Domineering lions and virile bulls slinked through and trod the cream of the night, inspiring armies to victory, nations to new shores. Orion, Osiris, Poseidon — all at different times pointed sword or trident down at man, spurring him to a potential otherwise wasted. Even now men see Scorpius Antony thrusting his 'spear' outward, ejaculating the milky way through the heavens to impregnate every star above. I would challenge us to camp out tonight, for by morning we would have our own pantheon, our own myths to subjugate the populace with, for myths crack sharper than the whip across the back of civilization."

Astrolo stood to reach to the unseen rafters, dropping his brushes into a pot stained of white spirits. "Who was it that said that?" he asked himself.

"The Clockwork Monarch," Ivy answered, stretching herself. She appreciated the setting of the sun. It no longer glanced off Astrolo's great bald spot into her eyes. And, although her nakedness could not hide the swirling runes etched into her skin, she was more comfortable when direct light did not expose their shimmer. They were normally faint, almost invisible, but the solar's daytime brilliance revealed them. The painter had not asked, and Ivy would have been hard pressed to explain them anyway.

"Yes, we could admire the stars together or instead gaze upon my latest masterpiece all night." He turned the canvas toward her as she stepped from the rise, but she walked past the painting, continuing on through the darkening hall, past works in all stages toward the wall of windows.

She unfolded and pulled the silk around her, covering sensitive areas that were the coolest, striding past chairs and lounges covered by sheets that, although rough with dust, were nicer than she had seen in years. She took a quick look back before giving her full attention to the Titans. The windows she approached disappeared up into shadow and rafter, and by the time she reached them Astrolo was back to working on the painting, this time with a tiny blunt knife.

"The people have adopted new myths though," he sighed. "Not those told by heroes in the sky but of those on the tongues of the Brotherhood, not those of an idealized past but of a golden future. The Prophets Lesser tell a tale of a world that already exists, one we just have to accept, and they claim to have seen it, to have been there, but each of our sinful steps take us one pace away from this utopia at a time."

Ivy stared out into the forest spreading into the pastures that turned back into woodlands at the base of the snowy mountains. The river lazily snaking its way from one woodland to another, splitting the deer-preferred pasture from the elk-favored hills, was inky compared to its frosty brilliance in daylight. Each of the past three days she had arrived in the afternoon, and each of the days had been brisk but full of sun over the snow-speckled green lands. Astrolo had just sketched on the first day, rapidly and sometimes without even looking at the paper he scratched. He had her stand and sit and lie in a forgotten number of poses, spurred on by her seemingly inexhaustiveness. By the time the forests darkened into a deep emerald, and the mountains glowed by moon instead of sun, floor and daybed had been covered in charcoal dust and the curling paper of sketches.

"How is it you know of the Clockwork Monarch, Ivy of the Grove?"

She could see Astrolo in the dark reflection of the window as he went back to mixing powder and oil and paint. Her own reflection caught her off guard, as it always did, before she responded. "I was told to learn of Chimaera before coming here…"

"And?"

"I found very little."

"And I can assure you that what you did read was riddled with heresy and innuendo, for Chimaera was a myth… *is* a myth. Why superstitious plebs continue to humor these old wives' tales baffles me. Do they wish to forever toil over unforgiving earth and under even less forgiving gods, multiplying their own sorrow and giving painful birth to ever-new inhibitions by fairy tale? Every generation insists on yoking themselves in ever-inventive ways, and the myth of Chimaera — of an all-seeing triad of puppet masters directing the course of history — was just one more way for the peasantry to fault their misfortune — misfortune no doubt built by their own failings — on forces out of their control."

Ivy looked to the skewed view the snowy grasses and two peaks became at night. Still, even without the glare from the misty mountains, the third peak could not be seen from between its brethren, as shrouded in cloud and snow and distance as it was. There was no color out the windows remaining from the day except for the silver that accented the Titans' icy and jagged talons. Her eyes focused closely back to her reflection. She had years ago stopped being stunned at the sight of her own face, despite the memories it dredged up. She had once thought she saw her own death, and subsequently had learned to fear it but had eventually gone full circle. Immortality, she now felt, was something more to be feared.

Astrolo painted with the finest of brush heads, hairs barely lighting on the canvas. He spoke up to the rafters so his voice would amplify back along the massive room. "Let us presume, just for a minute, that this Chimaera truly existed at one time. Doesn't it denigrate the efforts of the ancestors? Believing that their every accomplishment was constructed by three men from behind the scenes? Are you claiming the nations built by Nim and Neb, the wars won by Bold Warlif, the land tamed by Washkington was all just the work of Chimaera pulling strings — both heart and purse. These would have to be impressive men indeed."

Ivy turned from the dark mirror with only a slight glance backward. She had grown taller in the past few years, thinner in the destitution of the resistance, harder in her time hiding from the Horde. She walked far across the expansive room, away from window and reflection and the little light still trickling in. Sunsets came and ended so quickly under the mountains. Wulf had once likened it to the way civilization would fall under the Horde. Liberty would disappear quickly, and night would be upon the land before anyone realized it. Wulf's estranged people, the midgardians, Ivy had read, screamed at penumbras, believing the moon being swallowed by the Beast. They would shout and cry at the dying sky until hoarse, while the eclipse would always end with the satisfaction that they had scared the Beast off for another season or year. Ivy saw the underground resistance as those people screaming to the heavens, waking and warning the populace to the deceptive dying of the day.

She stepped between two short podiums topped by small, matching puma statues, continuing into the areas of the room dim in even the brightest part of day, and Astrolo stepped away from the easel to clean his hands on one of the many speckled rags nearby before turning a dial on the wall. A slight humming grew around the lower ceiling in the wide hall they now walked as hidden bulbs of the purest white grew to light the paintings lining them. As in each prior day, Ivy stopped in front of one of only varying shades of gray except for a dark mossy green suffocating in the monochrome.

"The artist would be flattered," Astrolo said, "knowing his work keeps catching your eye so. Alas, he is anonymous, and no doubt long since dead. *Brig* is estimated to be over a hundred years old. I inherited it, along with many of these works, when I bought this house. The previous owner had succumbed to extreme paranoia, first concerning his immense wealth, eventually surrounding conspiracy theories like those peaking your precious curiosity. You'll find allusions to Chimaera in many of these paintings actually. For example..." He crossed the hall to another dimly colored painting, this one three times the length of most of the others. The quick glance backward Ivy took revealed it to be a farmyard setting filled to the edges with animals. The calling rooster would indicate the morning, but the muted colors gave it an eerie nighttime feel. "This one once hung in the Zurrad Tower," Astrolo continued, picking specks of paint from his short curled beard as Ivy shivered, "supposedly indicating a 'safe spot' for theorists to gather and discuss their paranoia. Every typical farm animal is represented. Ox, goose, even camel — perhaps indicating it is a southern ranch — but what is the significance of the panther? Why the snake in the grass on the far right? And in the middle, the mountain goat — an odd addition among the more standard milking sheep. Well, *Animals Among Men* has been long analyzed, and it is of course obvious that the three interlopers are to represent the ceremonial titles of the Chimaeric clandestine trinity — the lion, the goat and the serpent, and so critics have led the ignorant masses into thinking the painting shows predator accepted among prey — the foolish masses willfully, blindfully looking the other direction as carnivores prepare for a feast. They see the sheep blissfully unaware, following the flock as it rotates, the dogs content as long as they live and die in orderly pack fashion, the pigs fat with slop and imaginary authority."

"Goats are vegetarians," Ivy barely responded. Astrolo then noticed she was still staring, enthralled by *Brig*. But he continued.

"Yes, but people see the malevolent stare in the creature's expression, and indeed he watches the viewer as the viewer watches him, but there is another, truer interpretation. You see, the mountain lion does not stalk the llama, the rattler is not sneaking upon the chicks. Both look to the sky. Do you see it? This creates lines along barn and fence, straight to the sky where the lines of light — muddy in this color scheme, I'll grant you — strike back down toward the dead center mountain goat, right into his angular face. You see it? The three triangles of Chimaera! A skyward point surrounded on each side by those pointing downward. Their coat of arms! This was not some secret message between futile theorists but from one illuminati to another. Mankind's landscape is a barnyard, and here we see the superior beings watching over the farm, protecting them, directing them, herding them toward their potential."

"So, Chimaera *does* exist?"

"Does? Did? I would pose that it doesn't matter." Astrolo ran colored fingers through the tight curls above his ears and smoothed out the hair over his lip as he crossed over to Ivy. She finally broke her gaze, looking to him as he stopped at her side.

"Where is it?" she asked.

"You can see it? It's well hidden."

Ivy traced the shape between rock and cloud, canyon and peak, her finger just a hair's breadth from the chunky smudges that made up the painting. "I see a gigantic iron ship nestled in stone far from any sea. Inside it is a city — the city of Brig."

"You see more than the painter intended. Such is the blessing and curse of art."

Ivy tightened the silks around her. The floors were cool, but her toes felt only the curve of the large cats in the hardwood beneath her. They were shaped from a cherrier wood than the rest of the lighter patterns. She recited, "Chimaera was three men directing the course of history from before humankind even emerged on the surface. One made his fortune in oil, another in flesh, and another was a kingmaker, but they all rose in secret power from what they found in Brig. Its ancient technologies made them the gold standard behind the country, and they used their wealth to back or destroy entire cultures. Every war, if not caused by Chimaera, benefited them. Every lord placed by them. Every silver piece bit by them. Yet no man could name them."

"And what, pray tell, happened to these immeasurable men?" Ivy could see his curl-framed smile out the corner of her eye as he asked. "There is no evidence of their existence, much less their demise. Such great ghosts sound immortal."

"Their ego got the better of them," Ivy said quietly, never blinking at the painting before her. "And greed and hubris. Gluttony and mistrust was their undoing. They were replaced by weaker men, who were replaced by weaker men, and so on and so on." She watched Astrolo's smile shrink before he turned to walk the hall, here and there nudging a random frame into crookedness before straightening it.

"You are right about one thing, pet," he said, "men such as that cannot strive for long, and a secret society cannot hide forever. Human nature always reveals itself, and so, just as your logic betrays itself."

"Unless one neuters nature." She silently nudged *Brig* just the slightest bit off-kilter.

She watched in her peripheral as Astrolo stopped, rigid and away from her and now hunched half way through a step. "What do you mean by that?" he asked.

"Latter day Chimaera, still always three of them, castrate themselves, thinking passion's lack will temper them. They believe this softens ambition and competition, and they will avoid the overreaching traps of their predecessors."

He whispered almost inaudibly, "Love and hatred cause error in judgment; for affection magnifies even trifles, and envy as much depresses weighty things."

Minutes then passed in silence. Ivy tried to find any distinguishing hints in the painting, any clues as to where the city ship was located. Astrolo walked the hall up and down, but she did not look to see where his attention lay.

"Come," he eventually said, beckoning her down the row to its end in curtain and dim lighting, "here is something you'll find interesting." Two portraits faced each other on each side of the hall. The man captured on the silver plates was pictured from the waist up, sitting with his hands genteelly crossed in front of him. The plates mirrored each other exactly, clothing and gunmetal frames exactly surrounding one as it was in the other. The faces, however, were strikingly different. Astrolo could not hide his disappointment as Ivy ignored the intricate work for the rusting frame, and he slapped her hand away as she touched its surface. "No, child, look at the faces. You don't know who this is? This is the infamous Torquemada! Libra's Tickler, Raphe's Torment, Dentist of Brig and Bab'lon!"

Ivy ignored his voice. Were these frames taken from the hull of Brig? They were an ancient metal, scarred by time and barnacle.

"There were many portraits of Torquemada," Astrolo continued, stepping to the curtain. "Some were mercury-settled prints like these two that came with this house, some were painted, all had the same pose, same outfit, but no two faces were alike, and none of them had his real face except for a picture that hung for him and him only. A private piece he had hidden away until the Uninvited sacked the land. It was unknown, lost, a figment of myth until I found it squirreled away in the bowels of Bab'lon by some dealer who knew not what he had." He pulled the curtain aside and new lights grew to highlight the hidden portrait. "Torquemada!" The painting had been cleaned up well, with the subject's rosy ascot matching the blush in his cheek. But the rest of his face had long ago been torn from the canvas.

"These frames," Ivy asked, still looking over the metal prints, "Brig exists? Where is it? Is it near?"

The painter sighed loudly, closing the curtain before turning past her. Ivy followed him back out into the immensity of the dark solar where he struck large matches to light shrunken candles, eventually bringing a cat's paw candelabra close to his painting. He dabbed thick crimson into a glistening oil before mixing in a fine dark dust from a vial around his neck.

Ivy pressed, "Brig has been used for many things over the centuries — a refugee city, an inquisitor's palace for political prisoners, and now the Horde has found it. I want to know where it is."

Astrolo sat and paused to stare at the canvas in front of them. Eventually he turned the easel. After another long pause he moved the candelabra back. He dipped a brush into the dusted paint before making broad strokes at the peripheral of the scene. "Red lion pepper... only found south of here... only way to get this color. I devised it myself, but, careful, I'd advise you not to breath too deeply in the powder's presence."

From where she stood, Ivy could only see the reflection of the moon on the two Titans and the river below. The mountain mists had been swallowed by the night, but the evening still kept the third peak hidden far between its brothers. She brought her gaze back to the painter, glaring until he finally spoke.

"Is that why the Army of Earth sent you? To chase the fairy's tail? Three-headed monsters and impossible shipwrecks?"

"You know why the Army sent me."

"Very well, I divine for the Brotherhood and what you call the Horde. It surely is no secret. I have been doing Schism's charts since back when he was known as Running Antony, so it can be no surprise I've been promoted to tell the fortunes of the Army of Heaven." He sat back to look at the painting, tugging at the curls framing his face with one speckled hand while picking at the colors in his beard with the other. Ivy just continued to stare at his dark wrinkled eyes. "No major decision is made without consulting me first. The Horde makes no big move without a letter from me. The stars tell me, and I tell them." He dabbed a finger into a thicker area of crimson on the canvas and then drew a long tear down his face before looking up to her. "Are you here to kill me?"

"No."

"Well…" He jumped from his seat. "What then? My contract with the Brotherhood is by no means exclusive, but the Liege of Foes couldn't possibly afford my services."

"No." Ivy followed Astrolo to a divan piled with furs where he chose a red one frosted lightly at its edges to wrap around her before leading her back to the windows. She looked at him, not the stars. "We want you to give the Horde misleading information, wrong information. We want you to lead them astray, into hostile land, traps, and winter."

"I knew you weren't a killer." Astrolo sniffed. "I've read your charts for the tithingmen. They are *very* interested in you. Do you know why? I had to do a lot of research to find your birthday, Ivy of the Grove, and it wasn't easy."

"We want you to misfortune tell."

"It would take quite a bit to convince me to risk my life, not to mention my reputation, Ivy of the Grove, and we've already established that the Army of Earth is indigent. What can you offer me, I wonder." He wiped the tears from his eyes, his nose continuing to run. "But *could* you be a killer, I wonder. Are you locked into a path the heavens proclaim? *Could* you be a killer, for the right price, no, the right reasons?"

"I was sent to convince you of many things."

"Then it is settled. I will compose your chart at the coming equinox, and then it will be known when you are to make your… move. For… me." Ivy had let the fur slacken from her shoulders. He pulled it tight at her neck, stroking her chin with rainbow hands. "Now, as to where to have this… confrontation, that is for another to conceive. I am releasing you into the care of another. Have you been to the city yet?"

Only then did Ivy start to feel the chill of the room. Was this becoming more trouble than it was worth? She had made contact with the resistance in Arcade Herod as soon as she entered the area, but she had avoided entering the city. She was becoming too well known. Astrolo had known she was coming before she had announced herself, and he knew a frighteningly large amount about her when she arrived.

Three stars in the constellation *Golgotha's Eyes* had appeared now in the night, and she looked to them for guidance as she did on her journey through the Territories. Wulf had her follow one west, and, a month later, another to the mountains. But the stars were now silent.

V

Morel Knight, mold his mouth, called for good news.
"See a land burned and boiled in human stews.
Smell melted fat and scorched hair.
Praise love, for I will be there,
for Liege comes back to collect faithful dues."
—The Ver Primordium (VII-V-II)

Sol Ascension moved his pawn an unprecedented number of spaces through the maze, still having enough bones to play the *Thankless Child* card to poison his opponent's pawn.

As the pawn encroached upon his own, Sir Skata played a card from his hand — *Grapevine* — to even the odds. The two men rolled the bones and Sol returned his pawn to its corner.

"Well played," the cleric said. "Now I think you've promised us a story."

"After my turn," the knight said. He rolled the bones again and used their worth to draw cards, filling his hand amply. He stared at those cards, waiting for the impatience that never came from across the table. He had hoped to be able to move the labyrinth's walls again, for Flagon's pawn was getting uncomfortably close to the prize, but neither his cards nor his bones were cooperating. He had to settle for moving his pawn one space closer to the pit. The knight was never one to use the pit, causing the game to end in a draw, but perhaps he could use the threat of it to distract the others. His turn then passed to the left.

Three of the men picked at the remains of their food as Flagon finished his, tossing his plate to the neighboring table. "Ahhh, when I find my golden vein I'll buy you all imp's meal. But that's it. Don't need no leeches sucking me dry. You can visit me in my castle on holidays, but that's it. Don't need no bedbugs overstaying their welcome. But I'll buy ya each some pasture, but that's it."

Sir Skata now noticed the man passed out at the table next to them. The clatter of the plate had not even disturbed him.

"You do know what imp's meal is, right?" the knight asked.

"Of course," Flagon answered with a big grin splitting his beard, "tongue and testicles! A nice hot dish. Grows hair where you care!"

"It is called imp's meal, you oaf, because it is for impotents. People used to think it dislodged words and otherwise."

The men laughed at Flagon's pouting until he joined them. "All I know is I'm tired of tripe and trotters. If it's not the wind keeping me up at night it's the steak dreams. How about an apple? When's the last time any of you's seen a goddamn apple pie?"

Sir Skata looked to Sol, finding the cleric distracted through the meal, paying attention now only during their cloaked friend's turn. This reminded him that he should be doing the same. Another reminder came when his pawn was attacked. The bones revealed a draw, and the hooded one's turn ended with the revealing of the card *Fairplay*. The order had been reversed, and it was immediately Skata's turn again.

So, the knight pondered, *I have my orders*. The men under his watch had only been in the neighboring towns for a little over a month, training the underground to resist the Horde without any hint of a unified front. He felt they had accomplished much. In fact, he was waiting on a recent census to find out how much the underground's numbers had grown in so short a time. But there was still much to be done, especially in Megrim itself.

Although it was again his turn, the *Fairplay* card still stared at Sir Skata from the board. To send my men home so soon, is that the best move now? Megrim had lately become the home of the area's tithing-man. If the underground could take even a soft hold on the area, it would proclaim a lot to the rest of the Territory. Morale was low, but they could change that.

"Any word out of Temple Needles?" Sol asked him.

The knight rolled the bones before answering, contemplating his next move slowed his speech. "Communications becoming sparser... as the Horde's Black Hills cordon becomes tighter. They are not letting anyone out, and they certainly are not letting anyone they see as a threat in." To punctuate the point, Skata played *Salted Earth*. The others would know what it meant. The Horde would continue to move ever tighter around the Temple Needles. Eventually, so dependant on the Hills and the surrounding plains for resources, the Order of the Creed would have to submit. Skata had been outspoken in his view that the Order needed to fight back, but the knights were hesitate to join a war against a force so closely aligned with other Librans. For the Kalderan Knights — the Order of the Spirit — had long ago pledged allegiance to the Horde.

All the players discarded their hands in response to his play. Although Flagon had barely started on his latest mug, he said, "I'm gonna need another drink if this keeps up."

Sir Skata had been raised to always treat the exiled Western Order with an air of suspicion. The schism that first broke the Librans in two went all the way back to the Evolutionary Wars. The first Dhani, the founder of the Libran faith, the only Lesser Antony ever initiated in the faith, had died. Most in the faith had seen him as an upright but flawed leader, but also as a conduit through which the blind angel Libra made mortals into something closer to Heaven. Through Dhani Antony she had blessed humanity. But some of the early monks saw him as close to the divine, even worshipping him to the same degree as Libra, for why would she choose anything less to consort with?

The knight's order had always believed Dhani Antony to be all too human, with only his children — their ancestors — having a touch of the divine, but in his death he had taken on a great role. His death was a beginning for the Order. From all the years of war and infighting and allegiances and betrayals, he had taken on the Librans' sin, and they were now free to start anew. His body, cursed with mortal sin of generations would be burned to signify the new era.

But Dhani Antony's remains disappeared as soon as they had been burned. Soon, new spells were discovered, but not by his elite descendants whose magic came easily from blessed blood, but from strange sects of Librans sporting ashen markings in strange symbols and mystical charms and weapons of bone.

The distinctions were ridiculous to Skata. Was Libra's blessing passed down through Dhani Antony's lineage or his remains? Removed from the question by generations, it was a silly dispute to continue into modern times. But he knew better than to underestimate it. The rift had been so strong that the new philosophy headed west, with Dhani Antony's remains and about a hundred followers. Separate from the Temple Needles, the new order had evolved along new lines, met other cultures and lands that shaped them differently. They named themselves the Order of the Spirit, kept in estranged contact with Skata's Black Hills order, and grew in unison with another emerging community — the Prophets Lesser. It was always his belief that the close proximity with the Brotherhood had corrupted the Order of the Spirit further, and this latest unholy alliance with the Horde was proving him right.

All this Skata had pieced together through years of digging through the Temple's archives in any spare time he could find. In between his training he scoured the Order's library, through biased histories and interviews, diaries and photographs, to decipher the origins of the orders — four in all — not taught to the squires.

But these silly distinctions were for other knights. As fascinating as he once saw the histories, Skata had always found the objective at hand to be more important. Everyone had their roles to play. It was only for Libra to judge if they deserved the consequences. Perhaps he would have felt more strongly invested in the dispute had he been born into the Order, but his blood was not descended from the first Dhani. His parents had given him to the Librans in lieu of rent shortly after he had been born. He remembered nothing of them or their lives, and he had always told himself that he did not care. His blood was not tinged with the angelic, and so he would never be more than a knight — never a monk or paladin with their strange, blessed abilities. It was why many had headed west. The ashes and relics of their founder gave them the mystical skills deprived the lowbloods. But that was not the role Skata had chosen. He was now fully immersed in his new life as the Order of the Creed's representative to the resistance.

Yes, he pretended he did not care about his birth parents, but that did not stop the question of their whereabouts and well-being from creeping into his mind occasionally, especially as the countryside found itself wracked over the years by first plague and then crippling famine. Had the family of his origin suffered and perished by disease over a decade ago? Had they struggled and wasted, surrounded by brittle fields or cattle corpses? Had they survived all that only to be trampled under the armies of Ammon Mars? Perhaps they had embraced the Horde and lived in affluence in one of the baronies, selling their corn or sunflower oil to the war effort, his unknown siblings leading legions against his comrades-in-arms. Or perhaps they resisted the *Ashmedai Adat El* and, as he had done in the south, they secretly provided northern resistance fighters with food. Did they have the room to spare to lodge or hide dissidents? Did they have the knowhow or courage to curry blasphemous information behind enemy lines? Despite suppressing it, he could not help but wonder if he had anything in common with his estranged family. They had already demonstrated a lack of loyalty he could not understand. But, then again, he had been familiar with familial betrayal all his life.

The childhood he had spent with his adopted family would have held some of his most contented memories had they not been tainted by what had followed. He had been spoiled beyond what he now considered to be possible. It was difficult to believe the treats and toys he had been showered with when looking at the desolate shops, barren shelves, and empty larders of Megrim, yet his nightly dreams were filled with the memories of multi-flavored ice cream, caramels, and clockwork toys described only in the tales of Bab'lon royalty. His new father, however, had been a type of royalty when it came to the Librans. The striking figure of a classical knight, Skata still remembered him as towering over the servants and guests to the mansion. His composure intimidated all men, his rigid style and chiseled appearance wooed all cowering women. But the great knight had been so gentle and soft toward Skata those first years. Skata's new mother took this kindness and reflected it outward to the vassals. She was the patron saint of the state, and an example to everyone on story and deed, and she treasured her new son. But their kindness only lasted until she had became pregnant.

And so began the months leading up to Skata's esquireship, being ignored by his father and unrelentingly chastised by his mother. It was now obvious to him what his role had been. His mother had been thought to be infertile, and now Skata's presence was only a reminder of the jeers she imagined, his face a reflection of the patronizing glances she expected from vassal and peer alike. The true heir was on the way, and Skata was no longer needed.

He had a couple more years before he would have been sent to the Temple Needles for an official esquireship, having already served as a page to his father, but Skata inadvertently set things in motion.

It was his twelfth birthday, and, although the holiday had been ignored by his parents, the butler had sneaked cake into Skata's bedchamber. It was a treat the boy had once taken for granted but was now a luxury to one who was rarely allowed to leave his room. His sweet tooth awakened, he snuck out in the middle of the night to find more, knowing his now stoic father was out on the summer witch hunt. He would be returning home soon — a day the boy once waited on with glee. Skata had not heard from his mother in days, but she was known to retire early when the knight was away.

The mansion had become alien to him over the last eight months. What was once salvation from some unremembered past had then become a prison — physically as well as emotionally. Whenever he did dare leave his quarters he was threatened into hiding any expression, suppressing any communication. Even walking the mansion halls at night should have awed him. They were what separated him from the vassals and, from what he was recently constantly reminded, the fate his parents had saved him from. He was told his vagabond biological parents had not wanted him, could not afford yet another child among many, and thought him too weak to work the pigpens. So the mansion's extravagances should have eternally amazed him, but he now only saw them as oppressing. And the coming brother would not help.

He tiptoed back to his bedchamber, finding every hint of frosting with his tongue and every crumb with his fingers, but the sounds drew him down other halls and other rooms. Here he peeked in to find the source of what he had assumed were the grunts of animal butchery or the squeals of prison torture. It was, however, the butler and his mother. Her belly hung, speckled pale like a fat fungus. The butler's eyelids quivered and clenched with the exertion.

Skata was out of breath before he even began to run, and his legs ached with straining by the time he reached his bed. He had no doubt his mother had seen him, for as soon as he had turned from the room the sounds had stopped.

He was sent away to squire even before his father returned for the autumn feasts — his mother had seen to that — not to the Temple Needles, as was customary, but to the far western side of the Black Hills. Here, with the opaque hills obscuring every sunrise, and the vast western expanse of flat, bleached prairie stretching out in every other direction, Skata was sent to esquire under the hermit knight known only as the great Makhoskan. Even Skata, growing up outside the Order's main compounds, had heard the tales of the exile. The knight's crime had been great enough to banish him from the Temple Needles, but not so great that he was hunted.

The great Makhoskan was a stern master, but what he lacked in compassion he more than made up for in ability, and his squire grasped at every skill, every philosophy and strategy, but, most importantly, the ancient knight's passion.

Years later Skata entered the Temple Needles, the Order's trial conquered, as a knight, but it was not long before he requested a change of station — a request the monks were all to eager to sanction. They, like

Skata, found him an exceptional knight, however with a countenance too odd for the direct contact of the Order. He had grown without the Order's direct supervision, and, as he saw it, found his discipline from the judgment of Blind Libra herself, not from the petty minds of Highlords and monks. Some feared he might leave for the teachings of the obstinate Kalderan Knights to the west, the estranged Order of the Eye to the east, or even gone in search of the missing Southern Order. In the end they found him too odd to care about, and so, as the Horde grew in power, incorporating land and faith into its grip, the Temple Needles knew just who to send to scout the baronies.

"Your High Lord needs to request a meeting with theirs," Sol Ascension said out of nowhere. The saloon and game suddenly came back prominently into Sir Skata's awareness. "If the Kalderan Librans could be turned it would mean an end to the war."

"I don't think so," Sir Skata replied, roused from his thoughts. The cleric had become a good friend in their time together. He had quickly come to understand Skata's brooding and often anticipated his thoughts. "The Horde uses the western knights for propaganda more than military. It is good to show the citizenry they have the support of Librans... if one could really call them Librans anymore."

"Why do you think they joined the Horde?" asked Sol.

"The broken mirror image of Libra they pray to, the twisted twin Angeliika, has been given a place in the Divine Choir. She now sings along with the rest of their so-called angels. And I don't think they have a High Lord anymore. Word was they killed him."

Flagon pushed the board aside to lean in close to their cloaked fourth player. "I tell you, now's the time to strike, while the Horde's distracted by their Libran blockade. We can pull everyone from the Resistance, every man and boy we have from every farm and town we can. We pull them all to meet the armies to march on Bab'lon. It'd be hundreds..." He looked around at the other men at the table. "Thousands? Towns and lands may fall in the short term, but once the Baronies are regained it'll be short work reclaiming the rest of the land." He was obviously straining to keep his voice in check. "You refuse to petition N'Midgaard, fine. I tell you, you won't have to if they see a strong enough show of force against the Horde. They'll respect that. They'd love to join the fun."

If the cloaked man responded in any way, Sir Skata could not tell.

He could barely see the blue granite eye in the low light of the saloon. But, as Sol moved his pawn three paces through the labyrinth, and laid down *Enchanted Apple* to skip Flagon's turn, he saw the hood nod in agreement at the play.

Flagon sat back and tugged on his thick braid, as Skata knew him to do when frustrated. The big Midgardian perked up, however, at the sudden presence of the servant girl. He had not been hiding his appreciation of her looks all night, despite the tattoo they had all noticed around her ankle on warmer occasions. Most of the woman in Megrim wore a similar tattoo, to the dissatisfaction to all but Skata at the table. A vow had kept his eyes from wandering about town, but the others at the table had been disappointed early on in the meager pickings of the city.

Through Skata's research he had learned that Megrim was an old city, founded on the path of a railroad that never came to be. Since its beginnings it had been a strong source of gambling and prostitution for those averse to the high prices and culture of the Baronies. It was a refuge of entertainment for farmers skirting the wealth of Bab'lon, but, for generations, the only permanent population was men.

There had always been Lesser Prophets passing through Megrim to no avail, preaching of Gob-Mammon Gammon and the promise of wealth. The city had no use for angels. But then the plague hit. And then famine dried up supply lines. The Horde took Bab'lon, and even the Prophets Lesser stopped visiting as every Antony across the land was sent to see to the war. This was now the age of the tithingmen — the deformed progeny of the Lesser Antonys in both flesh and spirit. The tithingmen shut down the gambling in Megrim, sent the prostitutes away in exchange for the promise of medicine. They brought bread for those that attended a quickly built church on the remains of a dice parlor. They brought faith to those starved of food and warmth and hope. And then they closed the gates.

For years the Prophets Lesser had spread the good word — that this world, this reality, was *wrong*. They claimed to have seen a better one, and only they knew how to make it right. Salvation was found in the song of the Divine Choir. For years they preached this far and wide and no one listened. The old gods had too much of a claim on the land and in the hearts of the myriad peoples across plain and mountain, forest and coast. Blind Libra had led man from the interior of Earth to a new surface. B'stet avenged the Old Ones and cleared the land of monster and radiation and burned the clouds away to reintroduce the sun. Yggr and his sons Tor and Tyr taught man to keep their claim on the land against witch and machine. Mankind owed all these ancient deities their souls.

But the old gods were leaving. And in their absence came the sickness and the drought, the pox and the locust, and the avatars that spread them. Now war ravaged the land with its own heralds. With their prayers unanswered, people fled to the new territories of the *Ashmedai Adat El* — what Skata and the resistance called the Horde. But now there was a price.

It had been over a decade since the Goblin Winter left a population dead from disease, but many homes still sat empty. Indenture yourself and earn a home. It had been only seasons since the *Scar* left fields and wombs barren, but there were sprouts appearing. Plow for the Brotherhood and one day the field will be your own. According to leaflets everywhere, the evil Liege of Foes was bringing war to the territories. Enlist in the army of the *Ashmedai Adat El* and your family will never know want for the rest of their lives.

Skata's mind had wondered from his friends and the game again, but he brought it back now to the servant girl and the tattoo now hidden beneath furred boot. Megrim, like many outlying towns had died when mines emptied, oil dried up, or fields failed to turn. All that had been left was vice and men. Into this the tithingmen brought women. Husbandless, often skill-less, they needed a means into the Territory. Like the servant girl, these women catered to the men of Megrim as newives — women working off their debt to the Horde through marriage.

Skata often found himself quieting Flagon when the saloon owner's newife was near. She owed the Horde for her new life. No one could be trusted even this far from the inner baronies. Her tattoo now peeked out into the dim light of the saloon — a *noli me tangere* with fleshy petals tightly clasped together. The flower's vine wrapped her ankle without hue.

"We need to make a move, a grand move to get the attention of both..."

"Shhh..." Skata calmed Flagon as the servant girl poured coffee for everyone but the knight. It was always vile, bitter, and from some bean from the gods only knew where. The knight could see that Flagon was getting more careless as the evening went on and knew this would be a good time to interrupt.

"My tale!"

"Yes, I could use a good story." Sol smiled, appreciating the interlude from business and game.

Still, Sir Skata waited for the servant girl to return behind the bar before starting, for it was looked upon with suspicion to speak of the Liege of Foes.

~

All my quests take me far from the Needles, and I will not complain. The politics of the Temple are of no interest to me, and so I was sent out of the Hills, heading south, skirting newly established Horde territory, into pink, rocky hills that struggled to grow even sage grass around scatterings of long-burnt trees. It had to be one of the few places in the land untouched by snow, yet there blew a dry cold carried by the wind, while the sun still held an oppressive unavoidable glare.

The Temple had sent me to observe a dispute concerning a feudim of families belonging to the Order in name only. They were distants descended from once proud knights, paying homage and tithing to the Order of the Creed only enough to keep their titles, lording the prestige over the vassals living in the ravines below the collection of mansions. I found, immediately upon arriving, a feudim on the verge of violence. I walked swampy streets of sewage, peasants all around calling for the heads of their bosses on high. Through the gaseous fog I looked upward to the mansions of the hills where the vassals marched, and I followed knowing there I would find the so-called knights.

The paths were narrow up the hill, and most marched single file to avoid the streams of waste water trickling downward. Weird algae grew in the runoff, stinking and catching the garbage floating past. The crowds I hiked with apparently never received word that Plaag had been defeated a decade earlier. Each had a sniffle or scab at the edge of their mouth. Many had no voice left from years of coughing. Some were blind from eyes that refused to water while other were sightless from those that never stopped tearing up.

The vassals were hesitant to talk with me. My shiny armor and well-kept boots may have been alien to them, but the sigil on my coat, the angelic charm around my neck, was indicative of the overlords they were now rising against. I gathered little from their suspicions as we neared the mansions, but it was enough.

The surrounding land was unfit for people. Ranches could not survive without vegetation, farms without water or suitable soil. The oilfields to the south had been commandeered by the Horde. The Black Hills to the north had long ago been mined out. The only option for those stubborn enough to remain in the area was to work for the families at the top of the hill. The mansions imported metals and woods for the peasants to work with, and, despite the years of declining health, the product was in demand throughout the Baronies.

So that explained why anyone would live in such conditions. It was not new. I had seen it in other areas normally inhospitable to people, so what shocked me was why the people now marched on their hilltop benefactors. You see, deeper in the ravine, past where even these diseased people lived, the wastewater collected in a pool inhabited by a creature the vassals blamed for their sickness. Whether the mermaid fled the sinking of Magog or crawled from the pits of Hell, I know not, but she could not have been indigenous to the region. Nevertheless, she had found a home away from home in the waste below overlord and peasant. And now, years after her discovery, the lottery had been exhausted, the vassals were down to their last virgin, but the sickness still hung over the ravine.

These were not knights that greeted us in the fountains between the mansions but the spoiled great grandchildren of those that had made the Order of the Creed great, those that retired from the Great Maid Hunt to calm a burning landscape, to bring prosperity to the barren, sandy rock and its scattered people. These were not knights, but they carried their ancient silver swords. They were doubtfully Librans, but they wore the angel around their necks. These were the families that continued to watch over the land, sending for lumber and metals from far away places. They had grown up among the luxury of the mansions, and they were prepared to defend it.

As we gathered and crowded I could now see the final virgin, the maiden that had led the vassals up the hill. Today was to be her sacrifice, but instead it was the day she incited the peasants to march on the mansions. She tore off her girdle, throwing it to the ground and shouting over the roar of the crowds. She would walk to the rancid pool at midnight. She would give herself to the creature that wallowed in muck and disease, but she demanded an equal sacrifice from those that called themselves knights. They could no longer close their eyes to the sickness below.

But I knew the vassals' demands to be doomed from the start. They had no leverage. I could now see that the mansions were not stricken by the cancers debilitating the villages. They were above it all, and they knew the peasants that died were eventually replaced by any other rancher or farmer struggling across the parched prairie. They drew swords and cocked rifles, ready to protect their heirlooms and children.

I admit I was frozen with indecision. I am only a knight where as this was a quest for a paladin or monk. Furthermore, I had been sent to observe only, but I could not stand aside with bloodshed imminent. Still, I could only wait for violence, being vastly outnumbered on both sides. I could not think of the words.

But the Liege of Foes could, and his words cut through the riot like warm rain, soothing the tempers. Staring from his hood with one azure eye and one granite, he called for mediation. He recognized me as the only other outsider, and, with me at his side, he took the knights' elder and the vassal virgin to speak to in private. What came next I remember differently than the others, but I will tell their more… poetic version.

The Liege of Foes convinced the Libran descendants to volunteer their most precious silver for the vassals to work with. The smiths melted and worked it into a beautiful, if not dull, chest small enough to be held in two hands. In it, the Liege of Foes put all the fears and doubts of the peasants, all the lack of faith of the mansion people. He shut it quickly and held it tightly.

Still the crowds bickered and blamed and threatened violence. Still they teetered on the verge of bloodshed, but he made them all promise to an armistice while he was gone. I was left to keep the peace in his absence.

The Liege of Foes followed the virgin down the treacherous slides of the hill, passing slick runs of sewage down into the peasant villages. Through the stinky streets he followed her, along dirt alleys lined with streams of runoff, down into the hazy ravines leading out of the villages into rosy canyons where the stench was strong enough to double a person over in pain. They wrapped scarves around their faces and quickened their pace to bring the two of them to the tepid pool as the moon hit its zenith and peeked into the canyon to find its ugly twin in the sludge below. The light highlighted the sewage dripping from the mermaid as she rose, massive in the muck with pointed green teeth and hair, swine eyes with a red nose. She hissed at the Liege of Foes, and kept her mouth wide, movements following the wading man. The boney plates of her tail emerged from behind, barely distinct from the dark pool.

The Liege of Foes opened the small chest, intending to release all the insecurity, all the doubt and fear, but there was barely any left. The inferior scraps and waste silver used to create the chest had leaked out over the path behind them. The mermaid was stunned, piggy eyes opening wide, but she still lurched toward them.

The Liege of Foes pulled his legs through the sludge to reach for the virgin, yanking her girdle from her before whipping it through the air, entangling the creature as her pearly claws grew near.

I know not how the abomination was disposed of. Perhaps that is a story for another night, but the people were appeased. The vassals were immediately certain the sickness would leave their villages. In fact many had already claimed to be cured by the time the Liege of Foes returned.

As he left, both knight and peasant hailed him a savior, and no blood was let at the mansions that day. I stayed behind to put the peace in writing and to broker the process by which the people of the area would begin helping the war effort. A certain percentage of the metals brought to the mansion would be given to the vassals to fashion into armor, and a certain amount of the lumber would be made into carts and tent structure. It would be made for the Army of Earth and, in return, the hill people — above and below — would be protected against the Horde's advance. To this day, many of the assaults, many of the trenches, many of the camps are made with equipment from the hill people.

~

Skata picked his pawn from the board, examining it closely while deciding how many paces to move it. If he used up all his bones, without playing any cards, he could move it into position to claim the prize on his next turn. Granted, this would depend on the actions of the other players, but he was almost certain they had all played out their most effective cards. The question he had to ask himself was, did he really want the game to end?

VI

… in all his lives he was first grown
to be the Warrior true and through he
was in all his lives because
no chance at choice let no will to be free
—scrawled on the walls of the King of All's lower halls

They fought all around him, eventually falling into wrestling piles moving seemingly as one in both practiced and instinctual maneuvers. An observer would think him an instructor as he looked down on all sides at their naked exertions, analyzing and judging. None would touch him anymore. None would engage him in the daily games. He had never been bested the same way twice, and even the brutal ephors were becoming openly out of ideas on how best to challenge him. It was inevitable, the rumors went, that Easarean would be sent to Krypt to endure a rite of passage whispered about by the children only in the few quiet hours they were allowed to sleep. It was said none of the tested had ever come back. "Come back with your sword or upon it," was said to those sent there.

But it was not death Easarean feared, for he had not even come close in over a hundred exercises. He was actually even starting to wonder if he could die. With each day that passed, death seemed less of a certainty. The best fighters were brought from other academies, and even those he at least fought to a standstill. No, it was not death he feared, just that his lack of fear would lead to a stagnation in his drive to be the best of the Clan.

As he bloodied noses, broke fingers, and brought concussions upon his classmates, he daily wondered if death, to one such as him, would be more akin to never reaching his potential. How could all these others live with their failures? He wondered about those he beat senseless each morning. Where did they find the courage to continue? What drove them each day to face inevitable defeat at his hands? Was there something to learn in defeat? Without that lesson would he eventually stagnate?

He asked the question during an afternoon workshop, the sound of shuffling seats all around him. Even though pre-pubescents, he and his peers had early on theorized that their chairs were unnecessarily uncomfortable in order to keep any measure of pleasure from the students.

"There is nothing to gain from failure," his battle nurse had responded, "unless you value the shame of the gods."

He asked the question in many ways over his early years to many different ephor, but always found the same answer. At times the shame would be placed by peers or commanders or clan, but there was always the consistency of the shame itself. And any attempt at further clarification was ignored. Eventually he believed it, and curiosity concerning failure provided no more interest. Defeat was a concept he had to accept would be forever denied him, and he easily did not care.

So it was that daily, bloody, hand-to-hand combat evolved into the training of numerous weaponry, and it, in turn, from simple to technological to long range armaments — all of it complemented by intense schooling in the clans' history of omnipresent warfare. To Easarean and his fight-mates it would appear that the Empire was war incarnate. And in many ways they were right. From early expansion to the countless enemies they countered and created, the clans rarely had seen even a generation of peace. Where once they had fought only amongst themselves — familial tribes squabbling over gods and land — they had now, for tens of centuries been spreading that warfare across galaxies. And for most of that time one particular clan had led the charge.

In between sparring and the seemingly endless stratagem lessons, Easarean found himself inundated with the tales of his forefathers, nonstop stories of the glory they brought to the Empire, and the pressure that history placed at his feet. His few dreams placed him in the roles of Echilles and Ellyses and other mythic conquerors, but in his version he was never betrayed by wife, men, nor god. In his version he lived forever in more than just legend.

Easarean and the others of his agoge would be accelerated to the physical age of fourteen soon, and where those of other clans would still be in their studies, those of his would stand seemingly as adults, ready for their first mission. But first, if he was ever to lead, he would have to be sent to Krypt.

~

The planetoid was desolate, with barely an atmosphere left after being burned from some long ago atomic bombardment, yet it still held a small pond. The liquid was cloudy with an oil that ran repeatedly as his boat rocked, and Easarean believed it would not be long before the sludge appeared between the cracks in the ancient wood. But he was not going to let this opportunity for solace escape him. He stretched out in the tiny boat, listening as its dry seams also stretched. Soon his agoge mates — the few whose dying blood did not fleck his forearms — would be upon him. They would most certainly swim the sludge from all sides, in pairs except for a frontal assault of three. The plan would be to strike with their spears at close range, crippling his legs so that when the boat broke he could not both defend himself and stay above the rancid waves. He knew they would only attack when they neared, for throwing the spears would only give him a weapon. But he did not need one. As impressive as the micro-carbon blades were, he wanted to use his bare hands for the test.

There was no sunrise or set on Krypt, no day, only one identical dusky night after another, and so it was difficult to determine just how long since his test had begun. It felt like a season since he had slept, but he knew it had only been days. He had survived without food for longer times, but still was hungrier than he had ever been. The ache in his lungs and itch over his skin had days ago disappeared — an indication he had gone numb to the nuclear air.

Large colorful stars stared down at him and he met their bored glare, scowling back at them. He was used to being watched. The only time he felt truly alone back at the Academy was when he stole boats to watch night skies. This was why he would make his stand here, in a poor simulation of his routine discrepancies. But here there was no satellite to gaze up to, no moon to dream of visiting. His sparring partners, most of whom he had killed since arriving on Krypt, would talk of the inhabitants of that moon — some sort of creature known as female. Females sounded fascinating, like the Empire's Aemazon enemies. He promised to one day conquer one. The moon always seemed to look down upon him with approval, but here he saw only ambivalence from space.

Easarean knew he would be punished, not for killing all of his so-called peers, but for making a mockery of the test. Since being sent to Krypt he had searched out all the low ground, all the unfortifiable locations and indefensible areas — all to increase the challenge. But he knew it would be seen as an insult to the test, a spit in the eyes of his ephors. He had been punished before, for stealing the rations of his agoge mates, for questioning tactics and lusting after his enemies, but the torture and deprivation would be nothing compared to what waited — all the more reason to savor the rock of the waves beneath him. The coming punishment did not scare him, nor did the disapproval of his instructors. If he was truly in the wrong, some putrid water god would have pulled him under by now. He needed no more proof he was doing Heaven's bidding.

The boat creaked as it rubbed against one of the many gravestones jutting from the pond. Were these the memorials of his predecessors? They did not deserve such attention. He raised his head to read the epitaphs but found them worn away from some alien language. Easarean and his agoge mates had only been taught enough to read schematics and battle plans. He found it difficult to believe others would learn to read anything more. What else was there to read? The myths of fallen heroes and risen empires were meant to be shared through song only, as all good things.

He could hear the almost silent slither of his mates as they made their way above and below the pond, and he was disappointed in them again. Still, he decided, he would bless them with quick deaths.

VII

"If you know thine enemy as you know thyself
you have already lost"
—Hyper Khan's "The War of Art" (St. Aerror translation)

he Homega Sapiens form is the ultimate example of the inherent biological intelligence the average person ignores. All living things — from the lowest flea to the physical glory of your brothers in the Prophets Lesser — have inborn organizing properties responsible for maintaining and healing the body and soul. One must just simply remove any interference to the nervous system to heal any and all disease within the individual. No matter how one views the ultimate reality — whether they sing to Asmodeus' angelic pantheon, await the final scaling of Blind Libra's judgment, or follow the unfeeling trod of a karmic wheel — everyone believes in an organizational universal order. Even the naturalist recognizes life's intrinsic tendency to self-organize and co-evolve into ever more complex, tightly interwoven and mutually compatible forms.

"This ultimate reality, this universal intelligence — whether sentient or not, whether caring or not — may be experienced in uncountable ways, but it is acknowledged — consciously or not — by all. Even birds recognize the patterns within or beyond nature. Even fish see the order residing in or directing the seasons. There is no argument in the biological kingdoms that something, some *thing*, dwells in all existence, continually giving the form its properties, which lead to its actions, thus maintaining its existence. Thus the energy operating the human machine derives from an inexhaustible source, sadly limited only by the capacity of the human brain — along with the constraints of manmade society — to transform it, individualize it, unlocking its potential.

"The Prophets Lesser had their chance — a clean slate, a fresh start, unburdened by the toxins of their past bodies and purged their bloody history — with perfect, new Homega Sapiens forms, free from impediments, clear of blockage, to experience life's trinity of intelligence, force and matter unfiltered. But they chose otherwise.

"You, however, little Homega Sapiens, are the true clean slate. You — untainted by the bias of constructed short falling universal interpretation — can chose to truly become one with the ultimate reality.

So new to life and free from prejudices of culture and pseudosciences, you can cultivate your superior form's innate ability to develop, heal and adapt, its natural inclination to strive and thrive in a myriad of toxic internal and external environments, maintaining a state of physical and mental health free of interferences and with a clear and direct connection to God."

Ivy had gotten past the feeling that fibrous worms crawled along her back and now felt as though she was melting into the cushions beneath her. The pillows were placed appropriately to support her while leaving room to breath, and the room and bed were warm against her naked body, as were Chiro's nimble fingers. He had first left her alone in the small dark room, and she had been tempted to explore its unseen corners, but the needles placed along her body would have no doubt been disturbed. So she slept to the steady hum of the filters and lights servicing the walls of aquariums. She had woken to Chiro as he replaced the needles with smooth hot rocks.

Wulf had sent her to the land around Arcade Herod to make contact with both its resistance and its merchants — the latter known to be supplying the Horde in numerous ways. More than anything, she was to observe and record with her photographic memory and reflexes.

Chiro had started with light strokes along the full length of her body, followed by a soft lifting of the muscles in her limbs. As she went in and out of sleep, he now pressed and worked in shrinking circles with his thumbs and fingertips in the deepest parts of her muscle tissue.

"Your highly evolved form is, not surprisingly, free of toxins," he continued, "and, as is well known about the Homega Sapiens, your immune system is unbreachable by any terrestrial germ, but I am of the opinion that there is always room for improvement. Can you feel the lymph flow enhancing, flushing the body of metabolic waste?" Fingers pressed firmly on her lower back, vibrating before moving on.

Ivy turned her head to the side and opened her sleepy eyes. She could see his right pinky standing stark from his hand. A long blade curved from the jewelry, hovering delicately over her skin.

"Why do the tithingmen want me?" she asked dreamily.

"Ah, so, Astrolo warned you did he? He must truly believe in you. Why are the tithingmen obsessed with the thought of your existence? Aren't these stunted men funny? On any topic they reach for the extreme. They have an opinion on anything and everything, and it is always to an obsessive degree. As far as they are concerned there is no middle ground in any situation. They either love or hate everything. It makes them very predictable."

"Why do you support them?"

"Do I?"

"You supply them with oils and tonics."

"Perhaps my supplements curb their ambitions, have you thought of that? Tithingmen have been coming to me for decades for symbiotes — coral cochlea, phalangeece, metatarsalami to overcome handicaps — or for supplements to vanquish congenital defects — ambrosial liqueurs, flytrap aloe, or djinnseng. Is it my fault my reputation is impeccable? Perhaps my cures are received as a crutch though. Perhaps they keep tithingmen humble, cooling the fires that normally drive them to overcome their impediments. Perhaps it keeps their bodies from uniting with the ultimate reality, from healing themselves. But this is not truly your concern is it? The Army of Earth is more peeved over my relations with the so-called 'Horde.' Correct? Well, nothing but the best for them. They know quality merchandise when they see it. And, I'm sorry about this, I truly am, but it would not be good business to give the Liege of Foes a discount, as I'm sure he would need to afford such fine product."

"We would like you to stop supplying the Horde." Ivy listened for many minutes before the occasional bubbling from the fish interrupted the ever-present underlying hum of the tanks. Chiro eventually started applying slow direct strokes across the grain of her shoulder muscles, mostly using his thumbs now. She could not see it, but she could imagine the pinky spur drifting near her jugular.

He had moved on to applying the slightest pressure to tiny areas behind her ears and over her scalp before he spoke again. "A Homega Sapiens — the current pinnacle in human evolution — strength beyond structural proportions, immune to all earthly ills and venoms, practically inexhaustible. Sublime in their perfection.

"However, the reproductive union of a Homega Sapiens and any peasant of this land without fail results in physical, and, some would argue, emotional, defects unique in every case — the tithingmen. No two of these half-breeds are alike in their deformity. Now, it's not long — the very next generation actually — before the genes correct themselves. Like I said, nature will right itself. It moves from chaos to order if we let it. Otherwise we wouldn't be here talking about it. And so a tithingman's children are seemingly clear of the defects, but that has never stopped the bitterness of the men themselves. The tithingmen are forever in the shadow of their perfect, superior fathers." He was now feeling her neck, eventually applying the same delicate spiraling touch straight down the middle of her back. Even though the room had no windows and, despite the soft glow of the aquariums, was lit by the same number of candles as when she entered, it seemed to grow darker. "Amazing. You have the smallest amount of congestion clogging your God Line I have ever felt. Your spine connects you to the eternal, reaching upward to the heavens. It is the telegraph wire to the ultimate reality, and you must have the clearest reception ever heard."

She lost track of the time he spent on the light pressure, waking only when he spoke again.

"The tithingmen have found their savior in Chem-Oshmelech. Their fathers brand them at birth in his burning bronze embrace, in which the angel promises them their resurrected bodies. To some, this is enough — the knowledge that they will one day shed their earthly shells for something more celestial. But there are some tithingmen who can't wait, and to this end they have recently collected and squirreled away their twisted sisters to some location even I haven't fathomed for experiments even I wouldn't condone. Of all the factions of the Horde, it is their best kept secret. But I do know this, and really only this, that they believe the key to unlocking their broken genes lies within you. A female Homega Sapiens is rare, if not unique, in this world, and many of the tithingmen would give anything, do anything, to get a hold of the Z chromosome belonging to yours truly. They believe the information locked inside you is their earthly salvation."

There was no incense burning, but Ivy found the scent of the room intoxicating. She was not sure if it came from the pillows, or the beds or Chiro himself, but it would put her into the deepest of sleep if she had not wanted to stay awake to continue breathing it in. It was light enough not to offend but strong enough to make one forget the sea life swimming so near.

Chiro crawled on top the bed, straddling her legs and pressing his palms into her hips. His shoulders rocked and rotated to bring the pressure quickly over her back.

"Is it true that Chimaera are eunuchs?" Ivy asked.

"I... am not... sure what..."

She could now swear she felt gem-encrusted jewelry tickle the base of her skull.

"...where that question came from." Chiro climbed off of her, and she could hear what sounded like the adjusting of clothing from behind. She started to get up, feeling the weakness of her softened limbs, but he continued, starting at her toes. He rolled each digit between nimble fingers as he stuttered. "What are you teh... talking about? What did Astrolo tell you?"

"He told me the men make the ultimate sacrifice to neuter the passion of extremes. They now just secretly rule the land by controlling resources, owning men's addiction and insecurities." Her voice was slurred by the ecstasy of the foot rub.

"They've always done that. But without the dominance and competition and bloodlust of sex they wouldn't overextend themselves. Content to carve out their own neh... niche... they would stay hidden... hidden without threat of exposure." He traced every hard line of her calves, lifted the taut flesh of her thighs. "I fear you've tricked me, you little perfectly groomed flower. Astrolo would never tell you such things. You believe in bogeys. There is no such thing."

Ivy pretended to ponder drowsily. "If three men existed, controlling all commerce, placing lords and ladies, supplying all armies of every war..."

"Only if the war suited their... interests, young one."

"All wars suit their interests, and their wallets, elder. The outcome on the other hand... I doubt the Horde's dominance would be profitable in the long run. Until now Chimaera has always had a strong hold on the vices of the land, supplying and withholding as fits its needs, but if the Horde conquers the land it won't be businessmen deciding the morality of the nation."

"Is this more of what Astrolo told you? His lips..."

"No. The Liege of Foes predicted your concerns. Across the country, merchants have always pacified cults with silk and sugar, making silver the one true 'ultimate reality.' The Horde and its Theses are growing exponentially each day. There will be no room for other gods once they reign completely, and that includes gold... that includes Chimaera."

Chiro pressed her hips in silence, and many minutes passed as he worked his way upward, pinching the skin over the slender arch of her back. Ivy just watched the dim glow of the water. She had only seen fish on plates or cooking over a campfire, so it was fascinating to see them float past her, from one wall to another with unmoving eyes and unstopping mouths. Could they see her, she wondered. Were they bored, or were they as fascinated with her naked body as Chiro was? Their stare was dead. Were they even alive? A shadow slithered between the schools, inky skin gleaming in even the meager light. It was featureless except for long threads snaking from what she assumed was its head.

"Ahhh... there's one of my favorites," Astrolo said. "Introducing its ancestors to my pools was apprentice's folly of my youth. It was called a kid eel, and the tiny poisonous pimples around its mouth revealed it as a predator to the other fish, and they avoided it immediately. My kid eels were quickly in danger of starvation when left to their own devices, so I fed them in separate tanks."

He kneaded Ivy's shoulders and arms, rolling them in thumb and finger and under elbow.

"The day came when hatchlings were old enough for me to notice one born slightly different. The nodules around its mouth were slightly raised compared to its broodlings. It would have gone unnoticed to the layperson, but the variation aroused in me a new hobby. Over time I kept track of its equally spectacular descendants, breeding them among themselves and any others that appeared equally mutant. It took many years — I forget how many — before one was hatched with even longer nodules. These even an idiot would notice. And so, as you could guess, I fostered this trait again, controlling the bloodlines. And so on, and so on. Over the generations I've created the handsome creature before you, with its whiskers trailing beneath it. It now swims again with its grandfather's skittish prey, but pays them no notice, for its whispy tendrils light upon the sands below the darkness of the pools, agitating insects and smaller fish easily eaten. I call them billy eels for their beard. Sadly, they lost their anxiety when I selectively bred them down in girth. They were expensive to feed before they acquired their new tastes, you see, so it was only prudent to prize the thinnest, smallest of each array."

"What does he think of us?" Ivy asked. The billy eel had slinked below the light, but she could see a slight cloud of dust his whiskers no doubt kicked up in the sand. "Does he think of us?"

"Of course not. It's best to work behind the scenes, to observe and direct with minimal interference. I have no qualms about admitting that what I do is unnatural selection, but I strive to emulate *natural* selection, getting as close as I possibly can." He stepped away from the bed of cushions, passing into her peripheral. Ivy turned her face to its side, closing her eyes as he touched the glass and continued. "No, the fish sees only amorphous blobs beyond the light, remembers nothing beyond the concerns of the now. I have walked among the eels, you know. I always expect to feel their venomous tickle, but they ignore my legs as long as I keep calm. But others… others have not fared so well." Chiro's voice grew quiet and Ivy thought she may have fallen asleep until he spoke again. "They were too afraid… and the eels could feel it, could feel their fear. If they had only stayed still… not drawn attention to themselves, controlled their emotions… if only they had only stayed still…"

Ivy stood through the malaise of her body, pushed through the pillows to walk among the candle light to the aquarium walls opposite Chiro. Some of the fish gave off their own light, whether it was from reflective scales or from fleshy bulbs suspended in front of them by colorless stems protruding from shrunken heads. Small fish with silver heads and translucent scales scurried like lightning in schools of four or six. What they were afraid of, Ivy could not tell. They were surrounded by only large and lazy fish — great grays and chalk-colored fish, fat and marked by blister and age. Only fins as large as Ivy's head moved. Their eyes and lips solid in expression, as she guessed they were for years on end. Would they see any difference in one day in death as they did in life? Their indifference was in reverse proportion to the minnows' wariness.

Ivy tried to follow the tiny creatures' movement. Each family moved as one. How did they know where to move at the exact second as their brothers? Their miniscule black hearts raced along with their fins, beneath slivers of ribs. She turned her hand before the tank, examining the absence in lines every other person she had met had. Still, even after years of being cut in battle, she had difficulty picturing the bones beneath her flesh, the blood moving through her chest. Men like Chiro — the few learned of the land guessing her background — placed so much emphasis on her odd origin, so much worth in the parentless doppelbrothers the Lesser Antonys. Why did they value the past more than the present. Surely it was as unobtainable as a previous night's dream. Or so Ivy assumed. She had never dreamed before.

A second's reflection surprised her until she focused past the glass at the fish again. The robe slid over her arm as she put it back at her side, covering the faint swirl of runes. Would her unknown creator be displeased at how she had improved his work? Had Chiro seen the pale lines in the dimness of the room. He must have, yet he had said nothing of them.

"You can't win, you know," he finally said. "You fight the zealous, and not only are they led by Homega Sapiens — the finality of human evolution — their Heaven's Army is generaled by something else — something beyond. Schism may lead from Phaeton — his mobile city — but it is Ammon Mars that commands the forces. He is War incarnate — a Greater Antony that fights not for some angel or nation or any idealistic creed. He kills because it is all he knows, all he is. He is beyond reason, beyond negotiation, beyond mercy."

"They called him Red Antony."

"Once. Because a hundred years ago, when he was discovered, under ice and rock, he was covered in the blood of his own men, his skin stained forever ruddy. But he has evolved beyond even the insane creature of that day... a Greater Antony — physically already beyond what demented Mother Nature could birth, now with a soul to match. And what do you follow? Who leads the Army of Earth? Some false prophet? A broken man with the stolen title of some long-lost soothsayer. You can't compete. Ammon Mars rides a mammoth into battle! What does the Liege of Foes ride?"

There was a collection of sponge collecting in the corner Ivy stood, surrounded by pink creatures made entirely of hundreds of tendrils. She could not tell if they moved with the artificial currents or by their own dance. She yearned to feel their softness but could only touch the glass they pressed against. It was surprisingly cool in the warm room. If they knew they grew under man-made light and recycled water they gave no indication. Did they know their long-separated brethren breathed the seas of freedom over ancient gulf beds, under sun-warmed waves, surrounded by the barnacles of storm-wrecked galley ships? If they did know, would they care?

"Where is Brig?" she asked.

"Oh, right, I was warned of your strange interests. The mythical lost city in a ship. You are an odd one." Chiro stepped to a small table surrounded by three leather-bound chairs, and Ivy saw him for the first time. Like Astrolo, he was well past his prime, but he held all of his age around his pale eyes. He had hair greased to a degree she had never seen before. It swooped like cresting waves, tight to his head with each side flowing in different direction from the top. The work that must have been put into the sheen contrasted with the scraggliness of his squared beard. He sat at the triangular chessboard Ivy had noticed when she had first arrived. It held intricately carved armies of dragons, goat men, and some sort of large cat. Chiro moved one of the horned men to the edge of the board, knocking a crowned serpent over.

The hexagonal room's uniformity was disorienting. The door Ivy came through was lost to darkness on the other side, and so she knew the passage that opened beside her, from wood and stone, was not how she had entered. Chiro now placed a heavy robe on her shoulders and prodded her into the dank stairway that first lead them down before suddenly heading upward. The steps grew drier under her feet as they ascended, and she could hear the man's heavy breathing as the walk stretched into minutes.

Chiro swallowed repeatedly as they reached a door, and he passed her to open it into a slight balcony. The evening was tepid and she squinted at the dull light peeking through the alleys, looking out into low windows and high doorways.

"Forget your nursery rhymes." Chiro spread his arms out to the streets leading into the buildings. "This is the only city you should concern yourself with now — the free city of Arcade Herod." His voice dropped to a whisper and his dry beard tickled her neck. "But if Priest has his way, it will be free for not much longer."

"All three of you support the Horde," she reminded him.

"Supply? Yes. But only Priest *supports* it, and, truth be told, his wares are the only ones that could be said to actually affect the war. What are fortunes and tonics compared to the scales he tips with his munitions?" He had stopped lowering his voice almost immediately. "Also, no amount of persuading — yes, even by your perfect lips — will convince him to negotiate with both sides of the battle, much less to completely switch his support to the Army of Earth altogether. Priest has broken the cardinal rule. He is owned by emotion, not reason, and that will lead him, and, by extension, all of us, to ruin."

Ivy was watching the sunlight bend around the buildings as the sun dropped into the mists of the Titans. They stood at the edge of Arcade Herod, many miles closer than she had watched from Astrolo's estate. The other side of the city was nestled against the base of the twin mountains Astraeus and Asteria, looking imposingly over the snow sprinkled structures, yet she still could not see Prometheus

— supposedly greatest of the three — between them.

The beams of light appeared solid, as though she could reach out and wipe the dust from their glassy surface. Beneath them the shadows of strangely shaped buildings slithered and jumped from cobble to alley wall as peak and cloud claimed the early sunset.

"Arcade Herod is truly a magnificent product of its time." Chiro had been following her gaze to the architecture. "Look to the central park of springs. The only way into the park is through one of three arches — each facing out into the world at the differing views on where man emerged from caves. Now, you'll see these arches reproduced throughout the city, popular with the original sex and mother cults prevalent when people appeared again on the surface. The struggling civilizations were few and immediately dying at the time, culled by machine and the cancer of radical waters, and so the feminine mystique came as an easy worship. The internal — the concave nature of female biology — was the nomads' religion and, indeed, salvation, and they represented it with the birthing gateways of arches. Walking through one was never taken lightly. So, firstly, they were built around the hot springs, leading into — what they thought of as — healing waters, Gaea's milk, and connected by easily defendable walls. As their numbers grew so did the city. Growing outward in a compass pattern, the original city — then called Keystone for the solidifying delta homage placed in the top of the arches — learned the value of defenses.

"As Keystone prospered and bragged of its miraculous mud pits, it was repeatedly beset by bandits. It was a hard life behind the arches, and the children the survivors prayed for grew harsh under the chaos. They bred warlords and battle clerics, each taking a suburb for themselves, and now the new structures meant something else. You see, arches are nothing without their wedge-shaped apex stone. The voussoirs and springers are meaningless if they even exist without the final ultimate piece. And these warlords gave their urchins this constant reminder with each new arch — that they were nothing without their king to bear their weight. The irony being that the keystone — and not so coincidently, the kings — actually bear the least stress among stone and population.

"And the city continued to grow as did its reputation for merciless defense of its warm waters. There came a time when even the most covetous bandits feared straying anywhere near these mountains. Without war to wet their whistles, Keystone's kings competed with each other. Not through bloodshed but with art and architecture. Hence the obelisks you can see jutting offensively skyward. Their nurturing sister gods had become, over the rough years, strict paternals, and they glorified them phallically. The original monuments are gone, having been long ago replaced by the three-sided ones of much more massive length and girth you see today. For these pay homage to the later lords that tossed aside cultish tradition for a more self-worship, replacing each generations' monoliths with their own, constantly erecting higher than their closest neighbor.

"Yet let me be very clear here — as grand as I find Arcade Herod, it is not unique in the world. The same evolution was being mirrored across the land, albeit with cultural eccentricities specific to each area. In some nations men dug into earth, hoping to reclaim the security of the womb the caves and caverns had given their forefathers, immortalizing this worship with inverted pyramids aimed at the planet's core. They too eventually embraced the masculine, reaching for the sun with their towers, but, if you look closely, there is another shift — one that present man is a part of — a nostalgic reversion back to the maternal, back to the glorification of the feminine. The Lonely Forgotten Sun of God herself, before she disappeared, spread most recently her words of love to the war-torn masses. And the Divine Choir's male angels are depicted, at the most, androgynous. Or is this a mediation of balance? Will the conquering faith be a mix of the extremes? Balance is never the most profitable for the merchant, however, I, for one, find it the most comfortable state of society."

"The Horde brings only extremes," Ivy said. She now looked out to every street corner, every doorway and adjacent balcony, and she saw meaning in the direction of every window, the symbolism of each intersection's meeting, the reference of each brink's placement.

"Exactly. And that is why Priest must be taken care of. But it must be done in precisely the right way. There are correct ways to actions in Arcade Herod, and there are cursed ways. Astrolo has told you *when* to meet Priest, according to the stars. I will tell you *where*, according to the auspicious corners of the city, the oriented roads and buildings and shadows. He owns much of what used to be called Keystone, and is known to frequent all of it." Chiro looked between the alleys and over the roofs. He looked to the cobble below and the peaks above. "I will tell you exactly *where* to find him."

VIII

With meat in his teeth, Bear asked,
"When shall these things be? What shall
be the signs of your return?"
Liege cried that His next coming would be fast.
"Soon, look to the fall of Hadrian's Hall.
You will see me when Lon Spire you see burn."
—The Ver Primordium (VII-X-IV)

F lagon's bones rolled disappointingly for the second round in a row, and again he passed on drawing cards in favor of moving his pawn forward. His deck had run low anyway in the expanse of the hours they had been playing. He ended his turn but continued to rub the pawn between his fingers. Sadly, he thought, it was one of his most prized possessions since giving everything up to hide out in the edges of Horde territory, drumming up support for, and directing elements of, the resistance. This was not what he had planned for his life. War he expected, dreamed of, yearned for, but not this — hiding, sneaking, planning from behind the scenes. It was not the way wars should be fought, but, over the years, he had proved himself as a leader, someone that others chose to follow. It looked like it would forever be his lot in life. But he still hoped that one day his role would bring him back to the front lines. And it would, if he could convince the others. He believed there would come a day when every available man would have to head to the battlefield. It was inevitable. But would that time come to late?

The Horde had moved over the land in so short a time, changing the landscape of culture and architecture, suppressing numerous other faiths and driving many of them underground. It had become unadvised to speak openly of the Liege of Foes, increasingly dangerous to carry a *Fallo Terminus*. In the few short years the Horde had taken the land, Lionshrines were tumbled to make way for bedizened churches of pink stone and colored glass, deep bells and massive perches of indeterminate use jutting over ghettoes old and new. In every town, even those as distant as Megrim, could be heard the choirs singing in imitation and adulation of the angelic pantheon, at any time of the day to contrast the expected silence of the nights.

The constant singing was the worst part of it for Flagon. Preferring to spend his waking hours outside of curfew for just that reason, he had spent more gold than he wanted to admit to himself on blankets and furs to stuff into the numerous cracks in his apartment's walls. His friends would criticize him for filling the wide space beneath his door, for they always needed to keep their ears to the streets, but he had not been long for Megrim before he found he could not sleep without some respite from the groups, and even individuals, singing their hymns. At times he would still wake during the day, sleep interrupted by what could have only been a lone man humming outside his door. The low buzz always infiltrated his dreams before he woke, appearing as some annoying horse fly or the distant rumble of thunder on a green horizon.

The growing choirs saw each town as their individual orchard, drawing nourishment from the hymns, each citizen a fruit ripening at each note. They saw their singing as a responsibility to the Divine Choir their voices emulated, readying the countryside for the day the war would end and each angel would come to reap, plucking the most faithful of the crop.

Against Sir Skata's wishes, Flagon had often spoken out against the sound, from open square rants to outwardly mocking it in drunken stupors he barely remembered. More than once his hangovers had been accompanied by bare memories of his warbling chant being accompanied by growing crowds joining what they thought was earnest, albeit toneless, singing praise.

Flagon was not excited about uprooting himself yet again, especially after all the work he had accomplished in the area, but the wassailing was one thing he certainly would not miss. He was only worried about how much worse it possibly was in the larger baronies.

He left the finely carved pawn on the board but continued to gaze at it. Its value was mainly sentimental. It was a gift from their fourth player, whittled himself from a balsam fir — a tree native to the homeland they both shared.

Flagon was hard pressed to feel homesick for N'Midgaard when everywhere he traveled these days was as snow-covered as he remembered the Granite Lands to be — although, the faint news coming out of his homelands described it as being even more frozen than ever, with ice storms and drifts covering even the tallest homes. He was in no hurry to return to the land of his birth, but he always expected that he would have to at some point to join with northern armies. But the longer it took for King Lif to join the war, the more Flagon doubted the old polar bear would. Midgardians were built and raised for battle, and they preached it in sermon and carved it into their art. Why were they silent at would surely be a glorious battle?

"We should just let the Horde invade N'Midgaard," he mumbled. His double grog was wearing off. He had barely felt its effects in the first place. Molasses was becoming trickier to come by, so he had no doubt the saloons in Megrim had been watering down his drinks for months now. "If I wanted a single I would of asked for a single." His final UnderCrawl card wavered in his hand. He did not care if the other players saw it. He could not remember why he even had *Ale's Well that Ends Well* in his deck anyway. Megrim had not had ale available in weeks. "I could go for a nice tall ale."

"What're you mumbling about?" Sol Ascension asked. Flagon could not remember Sol's last turn. Was he still playing?

"I say…" He quickly quieted himself. "I say we let the Horde move on Lif, wake the old bear up. He… they've gotten fat in their isolation, hoarding their resources… lopsided trading…"

"And in the meantime the Horde takes more land, more people?" It was obvious Sir Skata had become more worried about the Temple Needles the more they discussed it.

Flagon believed he *should* be concerned. The knights had chosen isolation long before even N'Midgaard became xenophobic. They had forgotten war. At least the Midgardians still aspired to it in prayer. So why had word not come back to him?

Throughout the night there had been few constants in the saloon. The table of UnderCrawl, the nearby drunk asleep at the nearby table, and the newife servant girl, had been taking advantage of the warm bar since before sunset, but any other patrons had slowly left as the evening went on, replaced by only a few others scattered as couples or individuals. There was no clock in the saloon. It could have been before midnight or close to dawn. No one knew. Anyone entering now was breaking curfew though, which actually was not an uncommon thing in the outlying territories. Unlike the inner baronies and cities, where the tithingmen had the manpower to strictly curb vices, here in Megrim the curfews was used more to differentiate between Horde loyalists and those they considered sinners. Here Flagon could have assumed the newife like-minded to their cause, for keeping the saloon open late was cause for suspicion. However, it actually only made him more suspicious of her. This was a perfect place for those disenfranchised by the Horde to meet, and it was also a perfect place to expose those working for the Resistance.

They had in fact met many contacts in the saloon. They felt it was less suspicious to gather in public, for who would dare? Paranoid neighbors and the tithingmen's spies were far more likely to look for clandestine meetings held in someone's home than the public bar. Saloon patrons could have been breaking any number of unenforced church commandments, but they would not be ignorant enough to plan against the state religion in public, would they? This was the plan of the fourth player at their table — to hide in plain sight. To the other sinners in the bar the table would appear to be just an innocent weekly game of UnderCrawl. Like the rest, they were probably just good church goers who could not give up the simple sins that had only just been condemned with the new order.

Flagon knew they had best keep their voices down for the remainder of the night though. "The Liege of Foes himself needs to call a congress," he whispered to the center of the table. "N'Midgaard's queen will hear him. She would hear *him*."

Sol Ascension, Sir Skata, and Flagon looked back and forth between one another, each appearing as though they were about to say something before all turning to look at their fourth player. They could see only darkness inside his hood for what seemed like minutes before he leaned forward, bringing his eyes from the shadows, the granite one surveying the board.

They had all forgot whose turn it was, lost in individual thoughts as they were, but the fourth player rolled the bones. He too was near the end of his deck, and Flagon wondered if that was behind his decision to skip drawing like the rest of them, or if it had always been his plan to move his pawn ever so slowly to the middle of the board. He would, in, at the very most, a couple of rounds, be at the Pit, and then it wouldn't be long before the game ended in a draw, which Flagon considered to be a failure for all players.

The other two pawns were between Flagon's and the prize. It would be tempting to attack either in his turn. Did they expect as much? Could he resist the temptation and head straight for the gold? He certainly did not want one of them to beat him to it. If this was the last game he would play with his friends, he definitely wanted to be the one to win it.

"They are embarrassed," Sir Skata said, breaking the silence.

"Yep," grumbled Flagon.

"Back in the Evolutionary Wars, King Lif followed the original Liege of Foes with more faith than any other of the original apostles. He added the Liege of Foes to the Northern Pantheon, as a demigod, as a son of Yggr. But something happened at the Diet of Wyrms that changed all that. N'Midgaard felt... betrayed? After the Liege's death, Lif retreated to the Granite Lands, humbled and bitter."

"He's just being cautious," Flagon explained with a sigh. "He's scared of the rumors. He wants proof. He wants to be shown that the Liege of Foes lives again. For better or worse that'll shock him out of complacency." But underneath it all he feared the knight was right. The tribes that eventually became N'Midgaard were pivotal in crushing Automaton but had scarcely involved themselves with any outside nation since. It was on the actual cause that he and Skata differed, however. In the haste of desperation, to hold onto their dominance, N'Midgaard had made an unholy pact with forces near but unknown to the public, resulting in the creation of the Garm. For generations those Hel-spawn had scourged the countryside during the full moon, only recently being purged from the land by the Horde. Flagon did not like admitting even to himself that the Resistance would have been better off had some of the garm survived. They would have made a fine addition to the Liege of Foes' army.

Flagon, like many of his brethren, believed the Garm to have gotten a bad reputation over the generations since they had been conceived. They had protected the tribes and the Granite Lands from both machine and man, and just the threat of their existence had kept outsiders from encroaching on N'Midgaard, but, as their influence grew, their reward was to have their sanctioning revoked by the King. The Garm had gone from cult to heroes to celebrities, but back to cult in the time span of only a few years. They had begun preaching the end of the world, of the unleashing of the Beast and the awakening of the dead and the destruction of the land by the fire of Heaven. The Garm believed themselves chosen by the Beast itself to set the end in motion, and they had begun to gain support among Bifrost — N'Midgaard's capital. It was a wonder the King and his church had let it continue as long as they did. The Garm had officially left the city without a struggle. Splitting into numerous packs, they had since searched the countryside for the means to release the Beast from its imprisonment, but, growing up in the Granite Lands, Flagon, like all of his generation suspected many of the Garm to be living right underneath the King's nose. For only on the full moon would the cult members change into their wolfen forms. At other times they could have been anyone — the fishmonger, the royal berserker, a wife or father.

Flagon thought of their fourth player without looking at him. Did he know the rumors? He must. Did he know the King had put his father under suspicion in order to kill him? Was that common knowledge?

Flagon's own father had been a simple tailor, a master in an occupation his son had made no secret he was embarrassed of growing up in the edges of N'Midgaard. Only as an adult could he look back and see the shame in his father's eyes when his son would taunt him, but to be belittled by a child had made Flagon see him as even less of a man.

Still, he hoped his father was well. He had not spoken to him in years but knew he would be proud of his son's role in the Resistance. Not necessarily because he believed in the cause, but because Flagon was following, and had become passionately successful in, something he believed in. He had left his home and his father at a fairly young age, back when the land had been prosperous and healthy. Back then, one could choose their place in the world, not fall into some roll by need or providence. Flagon, bored and fearful of a life without violent prospects, went looking for a war. But the country was at peace. The Evolutionary Wars with its mechanical antagonists were generations removed from his present day. The Librans had split long ago, isolating themselves in each direction without any chance of bringing the common man again into their disagreements. Bab'lon — comprised of its Wheel of Baronies — was, at the time, enjoying the lush resources of the Kalderan landscape. They had no interest in expanding outside the fruitful oil fields and profitable mountainous forests. War would only threaten their wealth. Perhaps conflict could have been found somewhere in the Land of Nod, but even Flagon's strong lust for battle was not enough to drive him to that demented scenery.

So the Midgardian returned to his homeland with head hung low, stole a wife and readied himself for a life of mediocrity. He had planned to return one day with trophy and tale, scalps and scars, but found himself with only a future that stretched out into nothing but an apprenticeship in his father's dress shop. But there, back home, he found the land ripe for battle. The uneasy relationship between the Midgardians and Natives had broken down in his absence, and he quickly enlisted to take advantage of the tensions. King Bold Warlif had grown tired of the Native's encroachment into the Granite Lands, and his church deputized citizens as berserkers to purge the land. Flagon quickly moved up through the ranks in short campaigns, but it was not long before he realized he was sending men to raze women and children in camps barely established, much less built for raiding. What Bold Warlif called invading war parties, Flagon found to be small, ill-prepared, and made of Natives only on the defensive.

Flagon soon quit his king's berserkers, vowing to himself to forget what he had seen, and he did forget with the help of the mead found at the outskirts of N'Midgaard. Here the men cared not for the King or his church's agenda. Here they lived for fishing and boating and beer and little else. Flagon stole himself a wife and settled near the *Jormangandr* and began to build himself what he envisioned to be the finest dragonship along the village port.

But before he could finish the finest dragonship in the village, he became distracted by the tales of a mercenary group leaving their footprints up and down the snowy land. They were already known to be bounty hunters, head hunters, ex-army, and dinosaur slayers, and they made their own rules and worked only for whom they chose. By the time they headed through Flagon's village he had already decided to join up. Here would be war on his own terms.

For years this was the perfect arrangement. Flagon and the mercenary group did battle with bandits and invaders, never losing a fight. It was all perfect until the Goblin Winter came. Flagon had never much cared for the myths of his people or their church, had always fought for thrill and glory as opposed to the decree of Tor and Tyr or the promises of Yggr, and had never given much thought to the legends of a winter that would hit hard, debilitatingly locking the land in ice and obscuring the seasons. So he gave no credence to the winter as it hit. Amongst a sickness that killed most of his men, those that survived hid under the drifts covering a hamlet on a link of frozen lakes outside Bifrost. Travel was impossible. Mercenary jobs were nonexistent, and so the remaining fighters waited out the year with copious amounts of warm beer. Under snow and sleet, rain and ice, they rested, spending all their gold while they waited for Plaag to take them. When the seemingly never-ending winter ended, those that survived found themselves without any of the fortune they had accumulated over the past few years. With the sickness broken, Flagon almost immediately saw a deluge of offers come into their mercenary group, and so they oiled their swords, rebound their hammers and went out to punish those the people blamed for the supernatural season.

It was not long before Flagon found his life repeating, violently. He and his men-at-arms burned camps of Natives to the ground, leaving no tipi standing, but he saw no signs that they were responsible for disease or winter. In fact it looked as though they had been hit even harder than the rest of the populace. His mercenary friends did not need evidence. The gold they filled their packs with was motivation enough, and a simple vote showed him the course would not change. Such ended Flagon's life as a mercenary.

It was obvious that, as long as he lived near N'Midgaard, Flagon would find himself pulled into Bifrost's war with the Natives. Disheartened, he headed south before veering west toward the Wheel of the Baronies. He stole a wife and quickly found work in the oil fields and settled to a life where the only battles were found in a bar after his shifts ended.

Years passed, and Flagon again grew restless. Phaimon scarred the earth. The Horde took Bab'lon as their own. Whispers of the fall of the Tower of Gog reached his isolated ears.

One night Flagon returned to his cabin on the prairie to find that his wife had been killed by Natives. It had taken them years and many miles, but they had found him. With nothing but boredom and bad memories ahead, Flagon decided to follow the Prophets Lesser and their pilgrim crowds deeper into the Baronies, intrigued by rumors of enlistment into new armies. This deep in Bab'lon he could not afford land or property beyond the most dilapidated shack, but there was the promise of citizenship paid for in war. This sounded tailor-made for Flagon. While waiting for the word to come Flagon stole a wife and intended to jump at the first call to battle.

Now, sitting among friends and cards in the Motley Cow, he had trouble remembering her name. It was not important. She had, unfortunately for him, been a newife, and that was important. The city guard hunted him as mercilessly as the new coveting laws demanded. He fled out of the Baronies with a back full of buckshot.

Why, when he should have been planning for the coming night, did his thoughts sink backward, he wondered. His friends had been talking but he had not been listening. Their faces looked as dour as his thoughts. It had always been his role to cheer up the mood among them, and he relished it now, this last night together, more than ever.

"One last myth then to cleanse the palate of your weak tales. Someone has to speak for my countrymen. In N'Midgaard, there're two tribes that have always guarded the borders to the Northern Lands, never interested in the politics of the Church or the melancholy out of Bifrost. These families, not as frozen as the old bear on the throne, could see the coming threat of the Horde, and they would've acted accordingly, violently, were they not so busy killing each other.

"This, my friends, is how I met the Liege of Foes."

~

Two families. The Asaar and the Aanir. Drinking and eating, mixing sweat and tears… probably blood. It was a grand celebration, my friends. The likes of I had certainly never seen before — and that's saying a lot — and will never see again until we send the Horde back into the pit it crawled out of. Such a party. Here I met my favorite wife.

But I digress. Here we, both Asaar and Aanir, celebrated the end of the Aanir. These families of Aanir had lost the war against the Asaar, a war as old as their names. I couldn't believe it was over, but the few remaining Aanir grandfathers and women were welcomed into the hall as the last of their children fought their last against the winning Asaar around the countryside. We all drowned out their dying screams as we danced and sang among their elders.

You, friends, think you have seen me in the greatest depths of my drink, but you have seen nothing. For in that night, surrounded by the revelry of brothers and brothers' cousins and those I would soon call cousins, my eyeballs floated in mead. My brain pickled in ale. My piss burned clear and killed the fish of the *Jormangandr*, and after I returned to the hall I was uncertain whether what I saw was a meadream or whether I had soaked myself to death and here I looked at some underhall of Hel herself. But it was real. And as drunk as I was, the sight sobered me quickly.

Two families. The Asaar and the Aanir stood with mouths gaping like the weird fish before them.

I recognized him immediately, for as a pup I'd horrible dreams of the streambed spirit after I had first heard of him through tales at bedtime. He was doing a jig in tights as pink as his flesh. When the fires lighting the hall reflected off his scales they shew every color of red I'd ever imagined, and when he spoke in our minds his fishy lips moved silently, a tiny flame appearing just beyond his mouth.

I assume my invitation to be lost, children, for how could such a glorious gathering occur without the presence of Loptr?

At the sound of his gurgling voice, in our heads, I suddenly remembered years of repressed dreams. The streambed spirit had created my family, the Asaar at the beginning of time from autumn lake slime, but he's haunted us since, for we broke his first commandment — to never eat of his roe.

His jig finished, he turned his torso to us, for he could only stare at us with one golden eye at a time from his giant fish head. The hall was silent except for the crackle of the fireplaces, but the sounds of the cousinly war continued outside. We Asaar held our tongues for we knew a proposition would come soon, for the spirit was known for his one-sided deals. And I can only assume the Aanir stayed quiet for the same reason. Sure, they would claim no allegiance to the pale trickster before them, but they no doubt knew him by some other name or appearance. Such is the way of things in N'Midgaard.

A celebration to end one family, in celebration of the rise of another. By morning the sounds from outside the hall will have ended and the revelry from within will culminate in the execution of the final Aanir you have so graciously allowed to enjoy in the festivities. This night to end all days demands the ultimate party game, what do you say?

He turned so that his other frozen eye could catch reactions. All he saw was the crowd of both families taking quick swigs, trying to forget the dreams they had just remembered.

It appears the Aanir are an endangered species! Such a shame. But it is only fair, do you not think, that the dying family be given one final chance to avoid oblivion? Here is what I propose...

At this point he resumed his jig, lady legs kicking low while we refilled our drinks. Our mugs were half finished by the time he slowed.

I propose a challenge, a chance for the few Aanir left to live on. Tonight only, I will permit any one of the Asaar one free strike against me to be returned in seven days hence at my castle. If honored, the few remaining Aanir will be spared. If honored, my protection falls on the Aanir.

There was much shuffling of feet, much avoiding of gaze of all in the hall. My brothers of the Asaar cared not if the Aanir lived. The night's debauchery, in fact, was a tribute to their destruction by our hands, and even the doomed in the hall accepted that tradition. But the chance at striking an unblocked blow against this sower of nightmares, of ending his reign in our newly remembered dreamscape, was dangerously tempting. I say 'dangerous' because it surely was a trick. If Loptr promised a golden apple you would find your first bite full of spiny caterpillars. If he promised silverware you would find your kidneys spooned out. If he promised bronze skin you would find your flesh tanning and nose falling off. The families knew better than to accept the chance for a quick kill from Loptr.

Is the challenge accepted? If so, the war must cease immediately, and no blows can be struck across the families.

Unmoving fish eye met pale granite eye as the Liege of Foes stepped from among the silent revelers. The hall was hot from fireplace, stove, and sex, yet he had remained wrapped in the shadows of a cloak.

One unhindered strike against me today. One unhindered from me in seven days. The tiny flame licked at puckering lips.

"I have no weapon," the Liege of Foes said to… the brook god? The families? Himself? I didn't know. So I took the honor of pushing through the gawkers, and I gave him the sword *BroadSplitter*. It was a fine blade, and I miss it for I've since lost it in some fight with Horde minions. It was too big for the Liege of Foes though. He looked like some pup playing war with his buddies in the churchyard, but, unblocked, the sword would do the job.

Loptr prostrated himself with spindly arms outspread, as the Liege of Foes steadied to raise the sword back over his head. The sword came down heavily, and, by Grimm's frostbit nips, I swear I could see the fires move at the chorus of gasps in the hall. The sword had stopped short, resting barely on soft scales and twice bending the firelight into the crowd.

The Liege of Foes talked so quietly that only I, still standing near, could hear what he said to the stream demon.

"If I had killed you, the Asaar would not have hesitated to finish the war and the Aanir bloodline."

Loptr stood, and his laughter tickled the inside of our skulls.

The challenge has been accepted! Tee hee! The war is over. No harm can befall the Aanir by the Asaar. Tee hee hee! And I'll be seeing you, he giggled, gesturing to the Liege of Foes, *in seven days. Tee hee, tee hee!* The flames in the places, pits and stoves suddenly flared, blinding or distracting the partiers, and when they looked again the fish spirit had vanished. Yet his smell remained, I'll tell you that, and it dampened the celebration. The war was over at that point. No more blood would be spilled between the families.

I wanted to go with him, you know I did, but we gave him one of our best sleipnrs, and he rode it out the next morning alone. I've only heard the rest of the story in bits and pieces over the last few years.

He arrived early thanks to the many-legged horse, the pride of the Asaar stables, and Loptr had not returned to his castle yet, but the river spirit's wife welcomed the Liege of Foes in. She gave him a room far from the busy areas of the keep. The fireplace refused to light, but the cool bed was covered in all manner of overstuffed quilts and numerous blankets from all sides of the castle.

Vina visited him the first night just as he started to drift off to sleep. Her cheeks were deliciously pink, her eyes unnervingly staring and golden.

"You are early. My husband will return in three days time, until then we must amuse ourselves. It is so nice to finally have some company."

The Liege of Foes had heard some far-off activity in the castle when he first arrived but he had yet to see anyone besides Vina. Yet, for some reason I have yet to understand, he ignored her advances that night.

The next day he spent exploring the castle. It was old, apparently unused, and quiet except for the occasional sound of movement and voices down far-off corridors. Vina visited him again that night to tuck him under the great pile of blankets. She smelled of river shore. Again he spurned her attentions. Again he disappointed me.

The Liege of Foes explored the lakes and streams beyond the castle the next day. Wherever he walked he could hear the constant creak of the watermill at the edge of the castle. It was in strong need of repair. The river caressing the keep barely turned the wheel. That final night he again pushed Vina away from his bed, her mouth puckering silently. She was again upset, but left him to his cold chamber, leaving her girdle behind for him to remember her by.

He walked the castle interior the final day but could find no sign of her. His echoes were the only reply. By noon the fish god had returned home, and without ceremony had the Liege of Foes kneeling in front of him and his great blue axe.

You could have run. You owe N'Midgaard nothing. You are Midgardian in name only. They have never honored you or your place. But you followed the challenge to its bitter end, knowing full well it would be the death of you. Rise, you pathetic man you, rise and take another breath. Your ridiculous honor has touched me deep down in some place I thought dead long ago.

There was little light this deep in the castle, and the spirit's scales held little of the glamour they did in the hall seven days earlier.

The challenge has ended. The Asaar and the Aanir are free of me. I am no longer tickled by their feeble whims. They bore me. As long as they steer clear of me and mine their dreams will be peaceful and devoid of drowning.

The Liege of Foes turned to leave the castle, immediately feeling the current of air change slightly in the chamber. He turned back to see Loptr swinging the great blue axe widely and wildly.

I am, however, still going to kill you.

The axe got caught up in cloak and arms, tearing across his belly, but in the end there was no blood, only Vina's indestructible girdle peeking through from beneath the Liege of Foes' clothing.

Hmmm... yes... virgin's lingerie. Like the Beast's fetters... inherently charmed by paradox. One never knows the potential, the power... the magic.

I heard the Liege of Foes' horse from miles away as he returned to the halls of the Asaar. He must've pushed the animal to its limits leaving the castle of Loptr, and I don't blame him.

I called for a party to celebrate his return and found no resistance, for in his absence the tale of his daring only grew across the collected families. That night Asaar and Aanir became one in riotous festival rivaled only by the one before and the one after. Hogs were devoured. Wenches flowered and deflowered. Drums were beat and songs written and sung. Toasts were made, including a rousing speech by the Liege of Foes himself. The words escape me. In truth, I wasn't listening, but after that night many Midgardians were inspired to march off to the Army of Earth where, to this day, they beat back the Horde at all sides.

~

Flagon had only seen the tithingman of Megrim once, shortly after coming to the city. The visibility in the streets had been reduced to nothing by a blizzard that did not necessarily bring in much new snow but created the illusion of such by blowing the existing drifts around the streets in blinding and quite painful sheets. A person could not stay in one place for many minutes before they would be completely covered in numerous blankets of the icy granules. Flagon hoped to take advantage of this by scouting around the tithingman's mansion in the center of Megrim. As a northerner he felt he would be the only one in Megrim not huddled inside over fire and coffee, but quickly found that the accumulating layers were even too much for his weathered hide and hot blood. But before he dug himself out of the heavy drift holding him to the ground he saw what was unmistakably the tithingman assigned to Megrim's salvation.

The man appeared to be surveying the grounds through the blizzard, and, at one point, was close enough for Flagon to reach out and touch, but it was not long before he began fiddling with keys through thick, furred gloves.

From the way he had walked it was obvious the old man's one leg was longer than the other, and as he worked the locks on the mansion's door Flagon could see the same was true of his arms. However, if that was the extent of the man's disability, Flagon remembered thinking, then the tales of the Tithing Men's bizarre individual deformities had been greatly exaggerated.

But they had not. Flagon could see that now. Up close, in the saloon, he could see the tithingman's transparent vein-streaked underlids as they blinked between the movement of his main eyelids. He could not help but watch the interplay of the man's interior mouth as the teeth and lips opened and closed inside his other mouth. His defects were minimal compared with the stories Flagon had heard of other Tithing Men. This old man could pass as just another ex-gambler in the alleys of Megrim, only being exposed by the close light of day. In fact, he had indeed sat at the very next table all evening without the players paying him much notice. Flagon had assumed him just another drunk enjoying the one of the few barely legal vices left in the territories. He had appeared passed out at the table with a full grog Flagon was still eyeing thirstily. As his friends went silent at the tithingman's words, obviously cataloging the last few hours of their discussion, and quickly coming up with explanations for any suspicious comments, the Midgardian thought of readying the dagger beneath his coats. He just clenched his hands instead. The old man appeared unarmed.

"Boys, boys, boys…" His voice was so quiet that Flagon would have had to lean closely to hear him had the old man not already been talking so close to his face. "It's very sweet. You're like children, playing silly games, telling fairy tales, ah… ah, turning your eyes red with debauchery…"

"None of it's illegal." Flagon was instantly sober and he hated it. Sol and Sir Skata, however, could sense it and they were glad, for, drunk, the Midgardian was funny and unpredictable, but they knew him well enough to never feel threatened. When sober, however, he was dangerous, and that was exactly what they needed when facing a tithingman.

"No, there are no thought crimes in the territories, but there ah holy suggestions, ah… ah, inspired recommendations to make one's life easier, for everything in life has consequences, and the Divine Choir only wants the best for all its children. It may be unadvisable to talk of certain things, but it is not illegal, so let us blaspheme, let us speak of the, ah… ah, what do you call him, the Last and First Born? The Liege ah Foes." The tithingman pulled up a chair and leaned into the fourth man's hood. "Ah'm sure he has many fascinating things to teach us."

Wulf's pale hand emerged from his cloak to roll the bones. They gave him exactly the number of paces he needed to move his pawn into the center of the board. Without hesitation he set his final card on the board face up.

Ragnarock

The game was over.

IX

P riest's servants dimmed the gaslights so the glitter of the
moon could be appreciated. The artificial light sparkled unevenly, yet those wallowing in the mud would, before the morning
came, see a rhythm in the painted dome. Just like in everything around
them, Priest knew, they would find patterns and meaning. In nature they
would see design. In life they would see purpose. In every external force
they would sense antagonism. It would serve him well. It always had.

He did not join the revelers in the mud baths, preferring to mingle
among those with tastes closer to his own. But even along and between
the bubbling clay his guests perspired in the thermae, drinking his wine
and eating his fruit beneath a painted night sky. A newife took his
glass before he could even set it down, and by the time he had spread
a particularly purple buenalba over the most fragile of crackers he was
involved in three different conversations, all concerning the war and
how it might affect Arcade Herod. The cheese was a past gift from
Chiro and it tasted just as Priest would expect. His friend was too
patient. He had added the wine after the curd had begun to set. The
berry flavors were overpowering, as was the infernal heat of the room.
His fairy-silken robe soaked up the sweat from his chest, but his face
beaded and ran.

The chamber perspired as well. The humidity collected and dripped
from the cosmic scenes of the rounded ceiling and the pear trees circling the rim of the chamber. The constrictors thrived though, threaded
and wound around branches above the baths. Their unfocused eyes
seemed as uninterested in Priest's guests as the minglers were of the
snakes. Neither knew or cared that the trees had died seasons ago. As
long as he kept them fat they would not question their surroundings. So
why was he playing the pacifier at tonight's party, he wondered.

The concerns had gone beyond the city, and now he was asked
about the markets represented across the Territories. Why had trade to
the far north been postponed? What of the rumored route across the
western desert? Would it open up new buyers or create new competition? Even the blackmarketeers who had made their fortunes sneaking

technology into N'Midgaard appeared worried. Their contacts had recently quieted. The guests whined like Astrolo when it came to the topic of the war, and Priest tired of the discussion. Did they think the land would suddenly have no need of leaves for pipes? That people would forsake down and silks and steak? Kings rose and fell. Creeds trumpeted and silenced. The land may change but there was always one constant.

"Sir?" The servant had been waiting for a break in the conversations. He handed Priest a bulbous glass of wine as violet as the cheese. "You asked me to inform you when your special guest had arrived."

"So I did. A toast!" he shouted to the dripping cosmos. "To the moon. To Lady Luna, to Bright Highlander and Dark Maria, Phoebe and Artemis, Selene and Heng'e. To Mama Killa. To Madonna Oriente. The quiet, obedient, unchanging moon. Mother of Night. Dusk harbinger and dawn oracle, she soothes us petty people with petitions of patience. She comforted protoman in his caves and will calm futureman when the sun dies crimson. To the moon! May the Beast chip a tooth!"

Normally using a toast to anticipate reaction amongst crowds, Priest instead left his guests to what would no doubt be inferior follow-up speeches. They would have to amuse themselves while he entertained a meeting he had known would eventually occur. He was actually surprised it had taken the Army of Earth this long to contact him, and he was insulted by the fact that he had to hear about their messenger from Chiro and Astrolo. It was rare when the two men were aware of things before he.

The cool floors were a relief to his feet in the hallway leading to his study, but sweat still collected in the sparse hairline running down thin chest hairs. He patted his dragon-beaded robe to soak it up before arriving at the three serpentine spindles locking a door shorter than his stature. He turned each scaly spindle, setting each with three pins before releasing the bolt. The study was dim, and, although he only planned on walking through, he turned knobs near the far door to brighten the gas lamps. He was not sure why he hesitated. Surely he was not afraid. No. Something was missing from the evening. He took the shrunken bite of a cigar from a tray of ashes, relighting it. The flavor remained, but the ember dissipated even before heading out into the chill night.

The winter shocked him, and the hot spring was calling, but he again stepped back inside to grab a Davidson *Sitdown* from a desk drawer. The giant revolver felt cooler than the outside air in his sausage fingers. He drank deeply the bitter wine as he stepped out. It was strong, and the fresh air would do both it and him some good. He had lost track of time in his hosting. The moon was high and full and, despite the shock of his damp body against the winter, he could not take his eyes from it. The gradient of its surface was so stark, each crater so defined. It was so rounded and looked so close he felt as though he could reach out and grab it. Its brightness would be cool as ice that only knew reflection, never true light.

"No, swear by the moon, the constant moon,
that never changes in her frozen jaunt,
so that thy meat spoil in likewise fashion."

The bubbling and sulfur of the pool brought his gaze from the night sky. His guest sat in its near side, facing away from him so that he could only see the back of her covered head and the delicate arms spread to each of her sides, holding her above the cloudy water. He walked the edge of the pool with tiny flecks of ice dissolving over his head. It snowed nowhere else in the city the thrust looked out upon. The sleet was a short-lived and contained effect of the hot spring in winter.

Rounding to the drop of the thrust he turned to see the present he had missed upon entering. Wrapped, it leaned against the exit to the short hall back into his study.

"Ah, the painting, yes, Astrolo said you made for a perfect representation of Angeliika. She is the latecomer to my framed pantheon, as she is to the Divine Choir itself. Although the faithful seem to have already forgotten. The Western Order has memories as short as their mustaches, it appears. If you asked them they would tell you she had flown the Holy Charm from the beginning."

The Army of Earth's messenger was leaning backward in the pool, her naked body submerged in the steaming water with slender arms stretched to keep her from going deeper. Both fists clenched, she wore a mask draped over her entire head. It was tattered but simple, with an elongated star where an eye would be. On the edge of the pool lie an opaque decanter sealed by wax the same color as the marking on the mask. She was asleep for all he knew. If she was not, he must have looked like he stood on the edge of a world to her, above milky space with the pool flowing into infinity next to him, framed by obelisk and star.

His robe dropped and the immediate tilt of her head did not go unnoticed.

Ivy was not asleep, but Wulf had told her that in every circumstance she was to let them make the first move. She knew he had chosen her for her perfect perception and recollection, and he had said that the type of men she would meet in and around Arcade Herod would reveal more when *not* prompted.

She looked past the preening posture of his pink body to the city. The stars tonight aligned perfectly atop the two largest obelisks, and Ivy's eyes drew lines down both sides of each, creating pyramids guarding a collection of unusually shaped structures beyond. The night played heavily with the buildings. Shadow and odd angle were punctuated by low stars, with the moon highlighting... But then Priest stepped into her line of sight and into the pool. He took the submerged steps slowly, either to let the heat or her impression sink in. Ivy guessed his age close to that of Astrolo and Chiro, although he was larger than both. A solid man, his shoulders and belly were squared. He was hairless except for a pale line on his chest and the sheen of gray over his head leading into a smear of beard. He had no testicles.

"Primitive man looked to her as the eternal mother," Priest said. Ivy knew he positioned himself deliberately at the edge of infinity, the water flowing through him as he knelt, the moon crowning his head. "When humankind crawled from caves — both times — she was their unerring link to time. Through her they measured the seasons, the years, the generations. She foretold... no, she blessed their women with blood and fertility, and, appropriately, became the eternal mother. She was the first woman. Creator of birth. Census taker of sex. She is both virgin and spoiled matriarch.

"She is sometimes hidden, coy like the maiden fair, but we remember her most as she grows full, expectant and glowing, full of promise, most useful. As with all mothers, she eventually shrinks into a brittle, sharp crone, but still she watches over her daughters, foretelling the never-ending cycle of life." He paused, struggling to drink, chew the dying cigar, and point with the Davidson at the same time. He eventually held all, downing the rest of his glass in one swallow, gulping like one of his constrictors. He set the glass at the edge of the pool to return the smoke to the side of his mouth.

"Contrast this with blazing Ra, with Mani, and Helios. They burned away the winters, nuclear or otherwise. They glare down daily as all true king patriarchs do. Inti stares and dries the fields of blasphemers. Wi warms the lakes so putrid the bison will not drink it.

"But, as men proved their worth and the angels blessed them with dominion over beast and land, they prospered. Their children spread across Earth. They worried less each day about what the hunt would bring. They found new pastures ahead of drought. They built roofs against the weather. With pit and candle they no longer feared the darkness. Tribes, now fruitful, saw the generations not as a blessing but as right. Each birth was met not with trepidation but entitlement. Women, once made in the image of gods, revered for their powers of creation, were now imprisoned by purpose, oppressed so others could control the means of propagation.

"Now the moon became seen as 'less than,' denigrated to reflecting Father's comforting magnificence, no more producing her own. She was a slave to gravity, to Earth, resigned to follow along and around.

Ivy wondered if Priest could see *Wyrmwood* burning the night behind him like an aberrant star, its putrid tail whipping the cosmos like a suffocating tadpole. If he did, he was not mentioning it for a reason only he knew.

"But there is a change coming. You can smell it in the air. It stinks like sour witch's womb, like wet jackal. For both the Maids of *MGGT* and the Garm have claimed the moon for their own. Neither male nor female, it calls both cults to cast their spells beneath its phases. Both lay claim to the night, under its protective eye. Both witch and werewolf spurn the light and the promises of the Divine Choir, embracing the night star, Father's dark looking glass, Surt's whore. The androgynous Shining One — Maestro Lucifer — brighter than even the worthy could look at, fell in Heaven's first civil war, now taunts from on high. Is it this dark angel that pulls the strings of harlots and lycanthropes in the night? Does it matter? The apathetic countryside had let these evils and others fester alongside them for too long.

"The Northern Librans isolated into impotence… their Eastern Order conversely miscegenated into obscurity… a rumored southern order corrupted by a false angel… is it any wonder the knights' estranged western cousins have joined up with the Brotherhood? The

Order of the Spirit has recognized the future sings the Song, and that only a nation unified under the Divine Choir has any chance of purging the land of *MGGT*'s Maids, for good this time. You've seen the short work the Army of Heaven made of the Garm. Your 'Liege of Foes,' I would think, would respect that more than most. A safe, unified nation under the Song is inevitable. Why do you resist it?"

"Is that why you arm them?" Ivy asked. The Shiloh mask barely moved as she spoke. "For safety, for stability? Is that wise for a merchant?"

"Ahhhh, I see Astrolo and Chiro have been talking about me, haven't they?" Discolored drool collected beneath the dark cigar butt. "They see opportunity in chaos and obsolescence in peace. If they had their way this war would rage forever, their pocket linings soaked continually with blood money."

"But not you."

"No. My engineers work day and night to find new ways to harness the heat below Kaldera. My smiths bend iron into ever-innovative shapes for Heaven's Army. My caravans risk life and limb traveling to the front lines. I appreciate the trade, but the real reward will come when the world lives under one banner…"

"But won't…"

"…singing the same song." Priest waved the massive revolver to the city lights. "All this… this is all Astrolo and Chiro see. They can't see beyond their little prosperous world. They are both jacks-of-all-trades, but I have made my fortune only in and around Arcade Herod. I have harnessed the heat and steam and gas and oil bubbling beneath its rock. Everything I own I owe to Arcade Herod, yet I alone, among the three of us, am the only one that can see beyond it. Are Astrolo's star charts silent beyond the city? Chiro reads the past and future in secret architecture, but has it gone quiet? They are faithless fools if they can't see the opportunity in one united kingdom under a patronizingly paternal influence. Where they hesitate, I am called to action. No one supports the Army of Heaven more than I, and it has been noticed, and it has been appreciated. And when the Theses are nailed to doors, when morals become laws, when infallible constitutions dictate aspiration, my contributions will be so imbedded in the foundation as to be insepa-rable. Religion is undeniably mutable when mixed with government and enterprise, so to get in on the ground floor… well, it would be foolish for me not to strike while the iron is hot. There will come a day when every peasant finds it is disloyal to avoid my wares, sinful to spurn my services. Astrolo and Chiro? They will be relegated to marketing to blasphemers, and we all know how the Divine Choir treats the deaf."

"Astrolo and Chiro have been supporting the Horde."

Priest cringed at her slander, spitting out the masticated cigar. The butt slowly floated behind him on the inevitable ride to infinity. "Yes, but only superficially. Do their séances and vigorous tonics really have any effect on the war? Not like a gun."

His wrist went limp, and the Davidson fired off into the roofs. It was as though the air over the pool exploded, and Ivy's fists went to her ears. The water flowed around him as Priest moved against it to draw in close.

"Smell the brimstone above the brimstone? Magic comes and goes but guns are here to stay. Oracles wax and wane but pistoleers never go out of style." She could feel the heat of the revolver even above the bubbling pool. "Spells lose their power among the demented, but as long as they can strap a holster they'll be safe." But it was nothing compared to the heat of his breath. "The Army of Heaven knows who they really are indebted to. Not painters and fondlers, not sooth-sayers and medicine men... but me. Astrolo and Chiro may claim to calm the nations' ills — emotional and physical — but I kill for them. For it's not guns that kill people, it is I who kill people. However, the Brotherhood of the Prophets Lesser has certainly helped in my effi-ciency." He turned, waving the revolver as though conducting a choir. His back was as blocky as his chest and its muscles moved beneath the skin like bricks grinding against each other. "Now, my fellow mer-chants may harbor some resentment toward me because they envy my prescience — the foresight their constellations and obelisks deny them — but that is no reason for them to send you to kill me." Ivy's breath quickened beneath the mask. "And how were you supposed to do it anyway? You're not secreting any blades on your person, at least not anywhere I'm disposed to probe." He turned back to point at the decanter with the loosely hanging Davidson. "And I know better than to drink Astrolo's wine until after the whole room has had a taste."

He stood staring, flushing and frozen in the wafting heat and the sinking specks of ice floating over, but never touching, the water. The decanter's seal was broken, where he was certain it had not been when he had entered the hot spring. But his was the only glass out on the thrust.

As he reached for the bottle, a flame suddenly erupted from deep out within the cityscape, as though one of the low stars burst in a quickly dying death. The shockwave hit the thrust and his tower seconds later, rippling through the pool and the snow lighting over the patio, as Priest climbed out of the water to look over the speckled city.

"Hmmm… I did assume you would make contact with the resistance while you visited fair Arcade Herod. Unable to march on so entrenched a city, the Liege of Foes sullies himself with martyrmite. And what, pray tell, was the target? The Governor's mansion? The Church of Gob-Mammon Gammon? The…"

"The United Rahab Geothermal Water Works Plant."

Gaslights flickered over the city. Most blinked but stayed strong, but, following a terrible wrenching sound deep beneath the rock below Ivy, the hot pool's churning slowed and the water level immediately appeared to lower, although Priest barely seemed to notice.

"But, why… I thought… why did he send you? Doesn't he want me to supply him?"

"He knows you'd never work for the Army of Earth, he just wants you to stop building for the Horde." The water dipped to expose the top of her small breasts, and her fists clenched tighter to resist the impulse to shiver as tiny nipples pursed against the air.

Priest growled through grinding teeth, and he loosened his grip on the wine glass for fear it would shatter in his hand. "If he knows me so well then he should predict that I would never do that…"

"Because your allegiance is based on more than just greed. Greed can be tempered. In fact it has, by your new-found faith."

"The Song moves something in me…" He turned and stepped back deeply, awkwardly into the pool, now obviously noticing its change in temperament. It was slowly lowering, but he kept his glass and revolver still raised high as he bobbed toward Ivy. "You have cost me a fortune today, little girl, you should drink up. Celebrate! Take off your mask. I'll devise a toast for you."

Her head tilted, but she thought better of it. "Why do the tithing-men want me?" she asked abruptly.

"What? Truly? That's all you have to say?" Priest waved the gun toward the city. "You sabotage my industry, you come here to kill me, you... you..." Gaslights twinkled like the stars around them. It was becoming difficult to differentiate between pool and skyline and cosmos. "You have no idea, do you... your place in all of this? I said take off the goddamn mask!"

Ivy put her fists to the side of her head, but all that did was tear the Shiloh mask as Priest pulled it from her. Normally it would have slowly floated out and over into darkness, but, as the chalky water lowered, it just sank.

"Did Astrolo really think a little girl could kill me? Chiro's a bigger fool than I thought, sending you here. And the Resistance, the Liege of Foes, they must truly hate you to give you unto me." The warmth against Ivy's cheek ebbed and flowed as Priest gestured near and far with the revolver. "Maybe you're a sacrifice. Are you a peace offering, a gift of good will? From who? All of them?" He searched for any last drop in his glass with a tongue darkly stained. "You're asking the wrong questions, you know. The tithingmen? Who cares? They're supposed to accept their freakishness, but a small sect of them just can't wait for the heavenly bodies promised to them at birth. They've lost faith. They've kidnapped their sisters and put them to work. The Brides of Chem-Oshmelech are supposed to be breeding weapons for the war. They're supposed to be creating a counter to your leader's weird abilities, but their heretical brothers are distracting them. They believe the Brides and their breeding pools can unlock their potential, can fix their deformities in *this* life. They think you play some role in this. I could gain such pretty favor if I turned you in to them."

Priest held the glass and the Davidson in one hand, taking the decanter in the other.

"No, you ask the wrong questions," he continued. "You should be more concerned with the biological weapon the Brides have created. But, you can ask me anything after you just have a drink. I would join you but, alas, we only have one glass between us. Besides, I'm afraid the wine would not be to my liking, would it?" He tipped the bottle completely, but only a few murky drops fell into the glass. A furrowed expression turned to one of disgust as he sniffed at the wide lip. "What... what is...?"

Ivy stood completely still, trying desperately not to mirror his panic.

"What did... no, no!" Now, with a look of recognition, Priest squirmed, peering into the cloudy pool. As soon as he froze, in the middle of movement, Ivy opened her hand and blew a mound of fine crimson powder into his face.

Priest screamed like a wyvern and thrashed like a water snake, the dust already caking around his eyes from the flood of tears. The glass shattered in his hand as the revolver fell into the lurching water. His blubbering was indecipherable, but Ivy could tell he knew what swam below by the way he kept trying to still himself, by the way, between spasms, he would clench all muscles to stand stolid. It was futile though, for the blinding pain in his eyes doubled him over as he repeatedly fell trying to feel for the edge of the pool. If the water had not been shrinking he might have drowned in his stumbling, but his haphazard reaching eventually led him out.

Ivy followed, lifting herself delicately out, seeing now the blossoming pimples on Priest's feet, and how his thighs grew gray. He continued to mumble through foaming lips and stumbled in all directions from the hot spring, getting lower and lower and feeling the stone around him with twitching fingers.

For many minutes she followed, until the snowflakes disappeared and the hot spring barely steamed. Priest was now crawling against the door to his study, but had no strength to open it.

"Is this when you grow wings and ascend to Heaven?" Ivy asked, but she knew he could not answer with a tongue swollen outside his lips. "Or is a heavenly body only promised to the tithingmen?" She assumed that if he could hear her through his burning ears he would curse her for inferred sarcasm. How could she convince him of her honesty, she wondered. He would die believing her disingenuous, she supposed.

Ivy entered the study, warm air enveloping her nakedness, as Priest slowed and paled even further. She carried and unwrapped the painting, momentarily staggering. A bout of dizziness had hit her, but it was gone by the time she rubbed the pinprick sting mark on her thigh.

She set the painting up on a bookshelf so that it was almost even with the rest of its hanging set. Its frame, carved with snaking ribbon and cords, shone in a way different from the others without their dust.

She opened drawers and cabinets — all made of a wood as rosy as Priest's neck — without direction. There were no books of any interest in the office, just ledger numbers she immediately memorized without meaning. A gilded card, fit to be framed, caught her attention from where it had fallen. The script was more image than lettering, more animal than typographical, but she could still make it out to be written in Human. The language was more flowery than she was used to, reminiscent of the type she had found in older books of the Eastern Men, but the invitation was written and received recently. It appeared Priest had been chosen to represent the inner territories at an auction still to come far to the east in an upcoming month. Knowing it would be impossible to preserve the large card's beauty for long, Ivy folded the invitation before turning to look up to the office's framed collection.

Here they all were — the Divine Choir.

Gob Mammon-Gammon — the Promise of Wealth, robed in spun gold, flying with six wings over sands as golden as the curls falling metallically out of his hood, carrying his Soul Kettle in one hand, blowing an ivory leviathan horn with the other. Jewel-encrusted feathers of every color caught the sunlight, bathing the desert into a rainbow-wrapped oasis.

Abaadoon — the Promise of Flesh, flying six-wingedly over ocean shores, holding seven arrows and a turtle shell lyre. He was the sun over the sea, and his golden wings blew the wind's music into the land. Ivy gently took the painting down, grimacing at it before tearing the canvas and breaking the frame over a chair.

Chem-Oshmelech — the Promise of Father, bronze skin reflecting the flaming feathers of folded wings. He walked through the grain of the land, a dove in one hand, lamb in the other, followed by calves and children with smiles as content as his own.

Slog Sabbaoth — the Promise of Dreams, sugary pink and long-limbed with short-feathered wings stretching from one side of the frame to the other. The curls of her candied hair fell to the silken gown barely covering sugary skin. She floated over the dawn of a slumbering Earth, dusting it with sweet sleep.

Ashmedai — the Promise of Faith, Divine Maestro of the Song, King Choir. Stellar halo wrapping a great platinum beard and mane, he looked down on the clouds with kind elder eyes from space. Lance directing falling stars, he wore the luminescent banner of Heaven swirling over his muscular loins.

And now, freshly painted and framed was Angeliika — patron nephiliim of Temple Kaldera of the Order of the Spirit. The rendition was unnerving for Ivy. Here she stood among the Titan Mountains, leading humankind out of darkness and back to the surface. Ivy recognized Astraeus, its rounded main peak built from numerous smaller points differentiated only when seen from such a close view. The angel stood on the harsh single peak of Asteria, six ebony wings casting a shadow as featureless as her body into the valley before Prometheus — the frozen mountain ever shrouded behind the other two in cloud and mystery.

Angeliika's inclusion had brought the western Librans into the Horde's fold, adding to the Army of Heaven's numbers and reputation. They and the Brotherhood had somehow found the means to bring manpower and supplies across the weird western desert. It was just one more reason Ivy was skeptical the Army of Earth could persevere.

Despite the angel's obsidian skin and ruby eyes, the resemblance was undeniable. Ivy had studied Astrolo as he painted, and, even from a model's perspective, she was sure she could duplicate his talent, but the symbolism in the artwork escaped her. She knew it was there, but was unsure whether she could ever create her own.

There was one piece of the painting, however, she was sure was placed for her alone. She again studied the shadow cast by Angeliika's wings. It flowed over valleys and rises but settled awkwardly, as though spiteful of the sun's rules, on Prometheus, in the shape of a massive ship.

Ivy ran from the study, back to the thrust, to the far edge of the drying pool. She unconsciously pulled Priest's serpentine robe around her against the chill, staring at the alignment of the stars, how they punctuated moon shadows and created geometric shapes in the darkness of night-cloaked Arcade Herod. Out there she now saw how only a spectator from her specific vantage point could see three triangles — two angling upward and framing a third pointing downward. The moon sat above, cradled in a cage of three stars and lighting the three inner intersecting points.

Was she to search the city? This she pondered as she dropped into the empty pool to retrieve the Shiloh mask. The Davidson *Sitdown* was large for her hands, but she took it anyway, avoiding the still searching whiskers of the beached billy eel.

She was stopped in her tracks before she could climb out. The bottom of the granite was splattered still with remaining puddles of chalky spring water, but there was a definite carving and coloration that only just now appeared. Standing at its edge she could see the design. It was Chimaera. An angular mountain lion head looking up, a sharp serpent head doing likewise, and, in between them, a goat's head striking downward. She looked again to the city and the shapes mirroring the sigil, but this time for the last time, for she knew now that the secret architects of Arcade Herod were only immortalizing, in time and space, the great event that initially gave Chimaera its wealth and power. Turning to the great Titans lording over the city, she could, for the first time, in its moonlit highlights, see beyond the peaks of Astraeus and Asteria to Prometheus. The clouds caught in its immensity swirled slowly over the mists snaking their way down along its rises and trenches.

Collecting her pack, she dug through it to find the metallic feathers that never left her side for very long. She sat back at the edge of the pool to press the quill into her bare thigh, cutting in a barely visible line a shape of spirals she did not remember dreaming of. Any anxiety, any fear, any excitement she had been feeling leaked out through blood and breath.

Ivy stepped past Priest's bloated body, once more into the study, to again look at her likeness in the painting. The longer she looked at it the less she felt it looked like her. She dimmed the gas, and the flickering lights now revealed runes across the angel's skin, as slight as the ones on her own arms and legs. Astrolo had painted them expertly, as he had Prometheus. She now knew where she must go.

X

"Doubt is poison, I will come to conquer
when iron hand holds the noose
and dry tongue and Well forces you to choose,
when queen loves whip and blond fur
then I, Foe Liege, will return to murder."
So satisfied, the Twin, whose
gut was full of tripe, continued to muse.

—The Ver Primordium (VII-XVI-V)

irst came the Prophets Greater. One by one, individually, they appeared over decades, even centuries. The blasphemous across the land even suggested that a Greater greeted mankind as it emerged from inner earth, waiting to proselytize to the blinking masses. The Prophets Greater were few and initially identical in their massive size and muscle, their foreign jaw and bronze skin. They never crossed each others' paths without violence, being madly hateful of one another, but they all spoke the same message.

The world is wrong. The world is broken.

The world is wrong and its only hope for salvation lie with them, in their vision of a supposed 'Heaven on Earth.' They spoke of a world of one nation, of universal brotherhood, without witches and werewolves and wyrms — a land where nothing but man ruled. But it was obvious that each Greater Prophet meant that ruling 'man' to be himself.

A Greater Prophet had difficulty attracting a following. They were physically intimidating, poorly spoken, prone to easy anger and shocking violence, and easily distracted by neighboring wars. Throughout history they had become involved, in one way or another, on each side of, in every battle or skirmish to touch the land. Tales of Greater Prophets record them fighting for any and all causes. Every history told of at least one rising above the battlefield as a god of war, with feats worshipped by sometime both sides of the carnage. But a god of war grows old quickly during times of peace, and the land had been relatively peaceful in the decades before the Horde took Bab'lon, and in those years the long-lived Greater Prophets grew tired and bored of even their own words. Some retired to lives of warlordship, some to scavengers, and some just disappeared, but all seemed to have given up on their prophecy of a better world. After generations of ignored warnings and calls to arms the Prophets Greater had become barely a background voice in the land. No new Greater Prophet had appeared in decades. Whether warlord or mercenary or bounty hunter or beggar, each was now just a Greater Antony, easily supplanted in the public consciousness by the Brotherhood of the Prophets Lesser.

The Prophets Lesser also began appearing in the early days after man returned to the surface but only seemed to make themselves known a generation later, as friends to the nations, explorers and recorders, innocuous twins of twins, usually traveling in pairs. They were able to assimilate easily into the populace, still speaking familiar words of a better world, but softly and with reason instead of the threat of force. There were more Lesser Prophets than Greater, perhaps twice as many, and their handsome identical demeanor and appearance allowed them to more ingratiate themselves into society. Spread throughout the land, for centuries now, it was not uncommon to see them as leaders, heroes, scholars and adventurers, but they were all still preachers, and they earned the designation of Lesser Prophet with their views on how the world should and could be. In the years after the Goblin Winter they had become more vocal, more involved in the politics of the Baronies and other nations. They were suddenly seen everywhere in one last push across the countrysides to convert all peoples to their vision of a united world. Then, as Phaimon carved his desiccating swath across the prairie, they were recalled to Bab'lon, bringing with them the starving populace and allying themselves in an angelic faith to take control of the land. Now the Brotherhood of the Prophets Lesser was synonymous with the Horde, or — as they called themselves under the Divine Choir — the *Ashmedai Adat El*.

How long had they conspired to bring the Horde to the land? No one knew, but they had begun to unite the people as the Prophets Greater could not — with subterfuge instead of war, words instead of force. Citizens of the Wheel — the Baronies spreading through Kaldera — were quick to accept the new rule. Outsiders were baffled as to why. It was said the song of the Divine Choir could not be denied. No matter the reason, each Lesser Prophet, also known as a Lesser Antony, so quickly finding themselves in a position of power in the new order, now found themselves having to hold onto that power. Like the Greater Antonys, they found themselves excelling at the front lines of war, bringing it to the resisting populations. As the Lesser Prophets led the Horde against the Army of Earth, they left the towns and cities and baronies under the close watch and governorship of the tithingmen.

And of the Prophets Greater, the Prophets Lesser, and the tithingmen, it was the tithingmen Wulf feared the most. For he had never been completely certain, but he suspected that he had met Greater Antonys, and they certainly were not of this world. The Lesser Antony he had known would never have admitted it either, but Wulf had sensed that he too was not native to the land. Tithingmen, however, were all too human, as the sour breath wafting in his face attested to. He turned his hooded face away from the close talker but could still hear his lisping voice.

"The Motley Cow is an odd place for the leader of revolution, the ah... ah, general of the Army of Earth, to spend an evening, especially on such ah holiday."

Technically, the theory went, the tithingmen were only half human. Whatever their fathers were — alien or next step in human evolution — the tithingmen were only half that. Their mothers were women of the land, women charmed by the striking cleanliness and obvious health of the Lesser Antonys — superior in every way to the sickly or starved men they were used to bedding. And it was the human half of the tithingmen that Wulf feared, their pettiness and child-like hypocrisies, quick judgments and narrow-mindedness. In the years the Brotherhood had left them in charge of the homefront, the governors had absorbed their new-found power gleefully and without hesitance. They saw it not as a heavy responsibility, not in the least as any sort of burden, but a divinely gifted blessing owed to them for a lifetime spent in disability and shame.

"Imagine muh luck to find the great Liege of Foes hiding out in muh district, muh humble little town of Megrim."

Even when the governor moved closely, Wulf had to strain his ears to hear the old man, and it served to increase his already growing headache.

"I'm not the Liege of Foes," he said, smiling from the side of his mouth. This too even pained him. His headaches were getting worse with the passage of time. He could now find relief only in meditation. As much as he enjoyed the weekly gatherings with his friends, the focus the game took only increased the pressure behind his eyes.

It was in the months after the sinking of Magog, in the run

through wild or Horde-controlled lands, that the headaches had started, no doubtedly a consequence of the exertion he put his psionic abilities to at the top of the Tower. He had felt something break on the top of the Tower of Gog. Something in his brain had twisted or gone soft, and it had not healed. It still bled or hardened or swelled, and the more time that passed the more the headaches came, until they were, at their very least, present all day every day. It was at moments like this, during intense concentration or annoyance, that the pain was at its worst.

"So, who's winning?"

"Game's over…" Sol started.

"…friend." Flagon finished.

His fellow Midgardian would not be able to hide his disgust, Wulf knew, and so it would be wise to keep the encounter short. But Wulf was curious. What did this governor hope to gain by confronting them now? Was the outside of the saloon surrounded by city guard? Had the Sin Eater already arrived in town? What made this tithingman so bold?

Months ago Wulf had planted counterfeit evidence in the city offices, implicating the Governor's own men in the underground resistance, but nothing had seemed to become of it. He was tempted to peek into the tithingman's mind to verify, but waited. His head already felt like it would split open. With any telepathic effort it just might.

"Ah'm sorry. We haven't met. Not officially. Muh name is Handsome Gibbet. Ah am the governor of this here district, the guardian of Megrim's souls, the ah… ah, shepherd to Megrim's sheep. Ah know, ah know, it's so dramatic as to be laughable. We here out at the edges of the territories need not be so formal. We need not be so fancy as those in the Baronies. Ah do, however, subscribe to some traditions. Ah know, ah know, ah'm so old-fashioned, but ah do plan on meeting each and every man, woman and child of muh district, now ah you boys going to invite me to your table or am ah going to have to get nasty?"

The silence at the table made Wulf realize it was mirrored around the saloon. Even the wind outside had quieted, picking up again as Handsome Gibbet chuckled. He may have been unnervingly quiet when he spoke, but his laugh surely filled the room as Sol Ascension gathered the board game and pieces, setting them aside as the tithingman pulled his chair up. He had left his mug at his table. It was not beyond Flagon's notice.

"I just realized, it's past curfew. We should be going," Sol said.

"Nonsense," Handsome interjected, "we're all adults here. The curfew is for lesser men, yes? We're responsible men, masters of our own destiny, we're aware of consequences, we're ah… ah, accepting of cause and effect." He picked Flagon's pawn from the board and rolled the figure in his fingers. "Besides, we all know the Seven Theses are just suggestions. There are no laws in the Territories. Each man rules himself. Isn't it grand?"

"Yet the Sin Eater is heading here," Flagon grumbled as he snatched his pawn from the tithingman, pocketing it. His hand lingered in his coat, near where Wulf knew he kept a small parrying blade, but the large Midgardian placed both hands on the table after seeing the slight shake of Wulf's head.

"The righteous man has nothing to fear. The Sin Eater will observe my fine town, its new churches and grand sturdy perches. He will see no transgressions against me and move on. We upstanding men have nothing to fear. He craves sin more mortal than our pathetic lapses. Unless the table has something to confess, something more satiating." At the silence he called the barkeep over. She had been watching the table and so appeared immediately. "Ah round of vermillion for muh new friends. You'll have to excuse me, friends, for ah have not the taste for beer or booze, but please enjoy some beets' blood on me while you tell me ah little about yourselves. Ah've been quite proud of myself and how ah've come to know so many of the city in so short ah time, but this table eludes me. Such a mysterious lot, suddenly so subdued, so quiet on this grand holiday."

"Melechmas?" Sol asked.

Wulf tried not cringe, responding to the tithingman would only bring more questions from the Governor. In this case — who would question the holiday unless they knew its origins. Wulf recognized the dangerous situation they were in. Sol was one to avoid uncomfortable silence, and they did not come much more uncomfortable, so he feared the cleric would fill the conversation with anything that came quickly to his mind. Handsome Gibbet was prying for information, and he was good enough to find it in even the most mundane answers.

"Come now," the tithingman responded, his mouth within a mouth speaking slowly and ever so quietly, "we're all grown men here. There's no need to mince words. We all know the celebration of Melechmas was deliberately placed on this day to win new followers. Why abolish a holiday when you can add to it? Today let the faith of the Liege of Foes celebrate with those singing the songs of the Choir. Let everyone rejoice together, whether it's Melechmas or ah… ah, the Liege of Days, and we can all see that there are no differences between us."

"Love all you see," Sol said as quietly as Handsome. All at the table leaned forward.

"Yes?"

"Love all you see," Sol repeated, louder this time. "Known once as the only Thesis. 'Love all you see. This is the *only* law.' Isn't that how it used to read?"

Handsome's inner lids blinked quickly before his outer ones closed tightly.

Sol continued as the old man sat in obvious thought. "It now reads 'Love all you see. This is the *first* law.' I find the original much more inspiring. When you love all you see, and those you love love all they see, and so on and so on, eventually the whole world is covered. It's poetic."

"It's like ah virus." Handsome opened his eyes. "And it's naïve, hence the need to look at all the Theses as ah whole — explained by the correct translation, 'This is the *first* law.' Now, why would someone so close to the Liege of Foes claim to know so much about the Seven Theses anyway?"

"I'm not the Liege of Foes," Wulf groaned, massaging the temples back in his hood.

Handsome leaned in. "You certainly look like him, although you've obviously shaved yuh beard. Ah could never forget those eyes. How can you be in two places at once, ah wonder? Although for one resurrected after ah century ah suppose such ah feat is child's play. For one who dares march on Bab'lon ah suppose it is ah… ah, simplicity itself."

The barkeep arrived with the drinks. She accepted Handsome's coin with the same amount of enthusiasm she did his pinch before heading back into the kitchen.

Wulf smelled the vermilion before setting it aside. He knew it as the acquired taste of those that avoided alcohol, and it was foul and bitter, but it was sweet — usually the only sweet drink available in most areas. He hid a smile, watching Flagon taste it. The big man set the cup back down, scowled and then drank the rest in one swallow.

Handsome sipped at his cup of vermillion, looking through the cards he had gathered in front of them. He tossed most aside without comment but raised one between two fingers, showing it across the table. "Cute," he said. It was *Godgyfu Returned*, with the image of a naked, hairless young woman descending from the sky. "Ah wouldn't show this one around unless you enjoy lye in yuh eyes. There ah many elements in the Territories that frown upon this sort of thing."

Wulf watched him in the spaces between the seconds he spoke. Handsome hid his deformities well. His careful speech mostly covered the inner set of lips and teeth, and his sleepy eyes kept the underlids hidden. One of his boot heels was thicker, but Wulf had immediately noticed the slight uneven gait anyway. He leaned so that his shorter arm appeared equal to the other, but Wulf had already measured them visually.

Wulf found himself often thinking of the *SHE*, as he looked for his place in the new world of the Horde. He had been trained as a child in the skills of assassination, chosen because of his unique mental abilities. At least, that was the assumption. He had always wondered if there had been more to it. He thought he had escaped the *SHE* only to find it a part of his cover to appear harmless to the commune of Enclave. He had killed. He had done what he had been trained years for, but he had not been recovered. His teachers had not reclaimed their investment. He had taunted them. Instructing the goblin Pic in their ways. This was forbidden. They should have come for him. Yet here he was, over a decade distant from their control. Or was he? Were they done with him, or had everything he had done since his "escape" been a part of their plan? He wondered this every time he killed someone. He wondered it now, mapping out Handsome's pressure points and arteries. tithingmen were mutants, each in their own way — a presumed result of their fathers' "superior" blood being befouled by that of their "inferior" mothers. Some were born with animal limbs, some as giants or gnomes, with most never being born at all. Those that found themselves surviving to adulthood had often been reviled, scapegoated for blights, or seen as general ill omens. Yet as far back as histories went they had been included, with many included in fairy tales and the rise and fall of kingdoms. The genetic failing only appeared to last one generation, with a tithingman's children seemingly unaffected, but the deformities of a Lesser Antony's children was yet another reminder of their alien nature.

The tithingmen were no longer freaks, however. The war had

created a vacuum on the homefront they were all too eager to fill. The Prophets Lesser had always left them behind, but here it had left them behind in positions of power — positions of power over those they remembered tripping them in the streets, spitting in their faces, raping and threatening them. It took a hundred years of patience, but the tithingmen would now see their day, or so Wulf expected.

Nothing was ever said of the *daughters* of a Lesser Antony, however. The Brides of Chem-Oshmelech had a role he had yet to discover.

Handsome leaned on his shorter arm to have it stretch farther on the table than the other one. He put more weight on it. Wulf tensed imperceptibly. An iron spear strike to the lake pressure point — into the hollow under the end of the collarbone, directly above the joint — would bring the governor's face to the table.

"So how does one celebrate this most holy of days?" the old man asked. "Ah say with community, by getting to know yuh neighbors, by loving all you see, eh? See, we have much in common with one another."

Once his head was on the table it would have been a simple matter of a phoenix eye strike to the nerve center at the base of the neck. That would keep him alive. But was there value in that? Wulf wondered. Whether they killed or crippled the governor, the outcome would be the same — the Sin Eater would come for them. Was it too early to play that card? Rumor had it that Megrim had already caught the Sin Eater's attention, but was it to root out the resistance? They were not going to take that chance. Wulf had already given the order to abandon the city, to disseminate its underground and send them to other areas. The circumstances were unfortunate, early but practical. He had actually been contemplating a move deeper into Kaldera anyway, but it still bothered him to have his hand forced.

And so they would take their respective leaves in the morning anyway, but if they assaulted a tithingman, the Sin Eater would stop at nothing hunting them down. An attack on the new governors was seen as an affront on their fathers and, even worse, now a sin against the tithingmen's patron angel itself. For everyone pledging allegiance to the Horde identified with a specific angel of the Divine Choir, but the vows made to Chem-Oshmelech were reserved for the tithingmen alone. Like all of the Choir, Chem-Oshmelech had many names — "He of Burning Brass and Loin," "The Drum Covered Scream," "Shamayim's

Seven Sectioned Soul" — but the Prophets Lesser knew him as the Promise of Patronage, and they dedicated their male newborns to him at the moment of birth.

"So, who's first," Handsome asked, "who's first in introduction, who's first to spill — not blood, on this grand day of armistice — but ah… ah, secrets and dreams. Too dramatic? Well, maybe the sugar is getting to me. To today's fellowship!" His toast was still no louder than his usual quiet breath.

Wulf could see the mark of Chem-Oshmelech peeking out from Handsome's sleeve as the old man gestured to Sol with his cup. Some said the pink scar was a birthmark common to all tithingmen, the angel's prenatal kiss. Gossip claimed it was a brass branding at the moment of each child's birth.

"You, bard, play us ah tune in reverence to the Liege of Foes' birthday."

"I'd rather not."

"Then we'll start with yuh name. Tell us about yuhself, Sol."

Wulf watched as the cleric's tense lips gave away his discomfort. Sol tried to go by his original name, Cutter, when out in the town, for "Sol Ascension" was obviously a name with a close relationship to the Lonely Forgotten Sun of God. They had invited danger. They must have used his name in public.

He knew he would regret it, but, with Handsome's attention on the cleric, Wulf looked into the old man's multi-lidded eyes and slid delicately into a mind of contradiction. It was as disgusting as he had assumed, and he pulled out as soon as the pain began to overwhelm him — which was almost immediately. He ground his teeth against the pressure in his skull, hid his shaking hands in the folds of his cloak, and looked downward to shield an obviously strained expression from the table. It was getting worse. He had assumed the difficulty and the headaches his abilities were giving him were from the injuries sustained at the top of the Tower of Gog, but this time he could sense something else, something out beyond Megrim that pressed against his mind when he had opened it up. To go out beyond his own mind was to open himself up to the pressure. It was like some sort of psionic feedback. When he pressed outward it felt as though it looped around back at him, as though his own mind doubled and attacked itself. At the same moment someone else was struck by the same pain — somewhere…

out beyond. If the past couple of months indicated anything, he knew that the pain would subside in a moment, although barely, but as it lasted he could barely make out what Sol was saying. It sounded as though he was representing himself as just a simple gem cutter.

"Ah, business must be good," Handsome was commenting. "We of the Territories find currency unnecessary. It takes the power away from trade — ah goodly thing — and puts it into something insubstantial, controlled by something other than need. Better to trade in goods and services with inherent value. Only then does man know the pleasure of work."

"Consider the ant," Sol added, "blessed among animals. And be wise, for the ant works without overseer, its queen being more servant than ruler."

"Yes?"

"The Sixth Thesis."

"Yes, and once again you surprise me with yuh understanding, my boy, although, ah must admit, ah have never heard the additional 'queen' line, but ah like it. Please, you must tell me of yuh studies."

"Shouldn't all the righteous know the Theses?"

Handsome spit into his cup, swirling the juice around for quiet moments before drinking the last of his vermillion. He then stared strongly at Sol, sometimes beneath cloudy inner lids, while collecting the dark residue that had spilled down his chin with a finger.

"You insult me, boy, even as ah am doing muh best to become familiar. Ah know this table has no love for Ashmedai so do not patronize me. This may be the mocking tone ah've come to expect from those following the Liege of Foes, but ah expected better of this table."

Wulf had however, in the brief moment before the psionic backlash struck, pulled a few images from Handsome's mind. He had tried to see only surface emotions, but the old man's mind was like a seething cauldron ready to boil over, and so more memories flooded in that Wulf was unable to stop. Below scenes of everyday errands, mundane interactions, he could feel the envy directed toward those around the tithingman. This jealousy simmered just below violence and was included for such simple things as household fixtures and clothing but mainly involved the general happiness and satisfaction that others in Handsome's life may have had for their state of life. It appeared that it was not enough for the old man to have achieved his high status in life, but it was important to him that others never would, or at least never would be satisfied in their own. And beneath all the bitterness toward even his family and friends was an even deeper seated hatred of his father. And beneath that was an even deeper seated love of his mother.

"Come, good sir," Handsome said, turning to Skata, "redeem the table with some chivalrous tale, good sir. What quest do you find yuhself on these days."

"No, thank you," Skata said, "I am not in the mood." The knight had not looked up from his cup since it had arrived, and he only now pushed it aside, continuing to stare at the ring on the table it left behind.

"Please, good sir, this is such a somber table. Liven us with companionship. Was it just short hours ago you were regaling the table with story?"

"Leave him be," Flagon grumbled. He too had set his cup aside, although his was long empty. Wulf did not need his painful telepathy to sense the Midgardian's anger. His face was flushed from something other than drink.

"No," continued Handsome, leaning to make sure his voice was heard, "no, gentle giant, you'll have yuh turn. Ah just wish to know what brings this noble man to ah humble city. To what do we owe his presence?"

"Land," the knight said, looking across the plates and cups that had accumulated over the night. His answer surprised everyone. It was not the cover they had agreed on.

"Yes?"

"The war has taken my ranches. I am looking to move southward with what I was able to salvage."

"Tell me, sir, have you ever heard of something called the Low Coda?"

"Pardon?"

"Nothing. And you are from…"

"Shunka. North of Kaldera but south of the Black Hills."

"Precambria?"

"Yes."

"Ah thought so." Handsome's outer mouth smiled while it appeared to Wulf his inner lips tightened into more of a smirk. He considered peaking into the governor's mind once more but just the thought of the act pressed cold pain against his temples.

He had learned little from the initial intrusion, certainly nothing pertaining to the counterfeit information, but he had inferred enough. He saw scenes of the tithingman conferring with the Prophets Lesser since taking the stewardship of Megrim. This led to veiled images of payments made to several bar patrons — others frequenting the Motley Cow on nights UnderCrawl had been played. Wulf recognized these men and newives as sitting near them on many occasions. What they had learned, he could not glean, but the frustration in Handsome's thoughts — his tantrums at the spies' reports — told him the table had given little away.

"So," Handsome asked, now hiding both smiles behind a pursed expression, "have you seen anything you like? Megrim has many great…"

"No," Skata said abruptly, "I find the incessant wailing through the canyon…"

"Well, true, ah suppose the wind can get ah… ah, bothersome… but you must…"

"I was speaking of the carols."

The only sound in the saloon was that of Flagon choking back laughter. Wulf almost laughed at the effort in the Midgardian's face as it grew even redder beneath braided beard. It was pointless. The big man let it out in a spray of spittle, filling the saloon with a rolling guffaw accompanied by large hands slapping the table. But Handsome was not laughing.

They were the only patrons left in the Motley Cow, Wulf noticed, as Flagon called for more drink.

"No, berserker," Handsome interrupted without looking at him, "Ah have a treat coming shortly and ah wouldn't want you to spoil it with some swill or another."

"I happen to like swill, governor." Flagon ordered his usual from the newife. "Swill puts me in a deep sleep each night, deepens my snores. Snoring downs out the wasseling. Besides, I don't know if you noticed, but it's getting past midnight. Your holiday's over."

"It is not my holiday!" Silverware bounced and cups tipped as Handsome struck the table.

The newife hurried to stop the spreading vermilion as Wulf noticed the slight nod she gave the tithingman at some unseen sign.

Some of their cards had been ruined. There would be no use in even trying to get the beet juice off of them. One in particular — *King of Dwarves* — stared up at him with new meaning. The picture showed a short man lording over a tribe of barely shorter men. The slightly taller man was the only one in the image not speckled with vermilion blood. Wulf looked to Handsome, imagining the old man also speckled with blood. It would be an easy matter with a quick telekinetically enhanced tiger palm strike with a slight angle to the nose, shards of cartilage being forced into the brain. And again Wulf caught himself thinking of the *SHE'*. Again he found their ways so ingrained in his upbringing, his very outlook on everything around him. It was no use, so a part of him would never be free. It would be imprudent to kill the governor. It would bring the Sin Eater down on the city and all the work they had done with the resistance over the past year, yet killing the old man was becoming an overpowering urge. Again he wondered if the *SHE'* continued to pull his strings. Had his whole life, everything leading up to tonight, been just another job for the otherworldly assassins' guild? Was his desire to kill the man before him just another choice that had been taken away from him, or was it something all the more human?

Handsome's breathing slowed after becoming erratic. "Well, Midgardian, the drink has obviously loosened yuh tongue, so let's hear it. What brings you so far from home?"

Flagon tugged at his beard, noticing one of the braids beginning to unravel. He scratched long and hard beneath it before answering. "*All* the land is N'Midgaard these days, governor. Cold. Buried in snow. War ravaged. Even the Garm have been seen running in southern lands. Have I left my home? It seems it is everywhere."

"The Garm ah no longer ah concern."

"If you say so."

"You haven't answered muh question."

"If you say so. I dunno what answer you want from me. I like boats. Use'ta bring lumber down the *Jormangandr*, sometimes all the way into the Land of Nod. Shipping's become too expensive now. Too much ice. Hard on the boats. And the Territories have cut off trade from the Granite Lands anyway. You call them heathens. So I thought I'd try someplace warmer. Haven't found it yet. End of story." He looked around for the mug that never came.

"You're ah good fighter," Handsome said, leaning in. "Join up with Heaven's Army. After the War you'll have yuh pick of land, yuh own homestead on any river you choose."

"Anywhere?"

"When the war is over, and the land warms, it will be territories from ocean to ocean. Blasphemy had its chance. The pagans squandered every opportunity. Now is the time for the righteous.

"The Old Ones destroyed the world with brimstone. Their metal descendants soiled it with their presence, and man continued the heresy with the worship of false angels, one-eyed vampires and ah… ah, cat gods. Look what the lapse in unity has wrought — the great Schism predicted disease, named the famine before it appeared, and ah… ah, just as the *Ashmedai Adat Al* promises peace, men bring war. Only death will follow. Death for the land, death for everyone. The Divine Choir promises life for the faithful, but the Army of Earth, the Liege of Foes, promises only a return to plague and drought, to the barbarism of blasphemy.

"Friends, it is ah job, ah responsibility, our ah… ah, duty to save the countryside. The Army of Earth wants to break the message, wants to stop the good word from reaching the populace. All ah want is for everyone to be able to make their own decision. Ah want the farmer beyond the outskirts to have the knowledge to choose. Ah want the city rat, living below castle and sewer to hear the Song. Is that so wrong?

"But the Army of Earth fears the Song, for it knows its power. It knows that no one who would ever hear it would ever turn away. And so the Territories ah assaulted on all fronts. The Liege of Foes' forces attack and kill civilians at the borders while his resistance burns churches and children in the cities. This is what a messiah offers? Death not life?" Even though Handsome was watching him intently, Wulf could see out of the corner of his eye that Sol moved to argue. He was relieved when the governor did not give him the chance. "It is muh turn to tell ah story." It appeared as though the old man had not blinked in minutes, with either set of lids. "On this grand holiest of days we ah tell tales ah the Liege of Foes, it appears, to celebrate his birth or life or death or ah… ah, whatever. So here is muh story."

~

Even ah was told the myths as ah child. It was muh fault, ah asked for them. Ah had heard the whispers among other children so ah asked my tutor, my drunk tutor who ah never saw again after that day. Sure, ah had been taught about the Evolutionary Wars. Over and over, ad nauseam in fact, but ah had never heard of the involvement of one young man, one young man who endeared himself to the divided nations, first on the word of his senile blind mother, then his seven disciples, then the Queen of Bab'lon. He supposedly brought the warring factions of the continent together just by the power of love to beat back Automaton and claim the country for mankind. But soon after his death the nations split once again.

Disheartened, his followers wrote and prophesized and ah... ah, fortune-told of his return. They were lost without ah savior to constantly lead them, so with new rumors of war to the east they spread the word of his imminent, and soon, resurrection. But the Third Evolutionary War came and went without a zombie messiah, and so the *Ver Primordium* was read in ah new light, with each subsequent generation imagining themselves as the blessed, the special, the ah... ah, ones chosen to bear witness to the resurrected Liege of Foes.

Now let me tell you the tale of another man. This is the tale of a Midgardian, although quite unlike you, friend Flagon. As ah boy he went from the teepees of savages to the court of a king, as ah man he has done nothing but wander.

He once blinded himself, now seeing with the use of dark magic. He led goblins against mankind but eventually sacrificed them to his whims. He is ah killer, differentiating never between innocent and guilty, lover and enemy. He has never had any friends, only expendable followers, and he pawns them off on antiprophets and like-minded charlatans.

He has somehow harnessed the power of Hell and has enchanted the downtrodden into building an army. He speaks of unification but tears the countryside apart, pits brother against brother, and sows discord among what was ah finally peaceful nation. Men burn themselves in his name, taking churches with them. Men die on the battlefield, his name on their lips, not even knowing he sends them *against* their salvation. And he calls himself the Liege of Foes, and the barely literate, those barely a step above animal, remember the name and think it should mean something, that somewhere in the back of their lizard brains it links them to ah mythical past, and their lives will actually mean something now when they bleed out in defense of ah cause they couldn't even explain if asked.

Such is muh story. Happy Liege of Days!

~

Wulf saw movement that meant Flagon again was reaching into his coat toward his dagger. "*Peace*," he thought toward him, toward all of his friends at the table, but his brain was immediately on fire, and he retreated back into his hood to hide his shaking features. Did the message get out? He could not even tell anymore.

"The people of the land ah being used," Handsome continued after calling to the saloon's newife, "their superstitions taken advantage of. There never was ah Liege of Foes. It's ah collection of fairy tales as old as time, combined by ancient man to pacify ah frightened population. As common man used the *Ver Primordium* in ah futile attempt to take control of their fears and misunderstood surroundings, kings and politicians used it to control common man. There never was ah Liege of Foes. There's no proof. But what we do know, what the Prophets Lesser have been trying to tell us for generations is that *the world is wrong*, and that the only way to make it right is through the *Ashmedai Adat El*, that if you listen closely to the Song of the Divine Choir, you'll find ah place for you in ah *right* world. It's been proven." The newife neared as he pointed around the table. "And that includes all ah you. It is never too late to listen to the Song, hear yuh name and ah… ah, sing along yourself."

Wulf knew it was no mistake that the old man had not pointed at him, no mistake he had not even looked in his direction during his entire speech. But Wulf had never taken his eyes from the governor — not during his tale nor now as the tithingman rubbed his wrinkled hand over the newife's back as she leaned to hear him.

"We're ready for our dessert, sweetie," Handsome told her. "That's right, gentlemen. Ah did plenty of research for our gathering tonight. Ah didn't want to embarrass myself at muh first Liege of Days celebration." He turned to watch the newife head into the kitchen, as Wulf watched Sol and Flagon exchange tired but worried looks. Sir Skata still just stared at the table in front of him.

"Ah apologize ahead of time for any errors ah may make in presentation. Please don't assume it's out of disrespect. Ah've done muh best, but pagan ritual is, ah'm sure you'll understand, not muh expertise.

"So, each day on the Liege of Foes' birthday or deathday or, ah… ah, the anniversary of the Diet of Wyrms, town elders or warlords or witch doctors would meet to discuss the past year's events and the concerns of their feudims for the coming year. There was plenty of divination involved. Almanacs were presented and edited. At the end of the meetings, dessert was served in the form of cakes. These cakes were randomly given, although there is some indication that trading occurred after the serving, sometimes with tables of gold or pens of slaves up for negotiation. In one of the cakes, placed by some neutral party, was baked ah small figurine — the Liege of Cakes it was called — and he who bit into it would rule the acres or town or kingdoms of all those at the table for the following year.

"Times were tough after the Evolutionary Wars. The short-lived camaraderie among nations had splintered. Brother mistrusted brother. Peasant envied ruler. King feared the people. The arbitrariousness of the ritual was, ironically, ah way to build trust in the new governments. No one held power for long. Majorities could not control minorities forever. Corruption could not gain footholds in such randomly determined, short-lived rules. Plus, it harkened back to ah comforting myth — ah supposed golden age when the Liege of Foes had supposedly brought everyone together for the common good. So the Liege of Cakes would rule over an area for the next year, all the while keeping in mind that his reign would end shortly. But, like all governments without the *Ashmedai Adat El* as their basis, this system was flawed and easily corrupted. Rulers would exploit the other lands under their care during the year, building up their own and breaking away after the year was finished. Or sometimes a ruler would mysteriously win year after year until the Liege of Cakes ritual had to be rethought.

"Eventually the stakes were raised in some of the more barbaric lands. The reward was balanced with threat. If one stood to gain such power one had to be willing to die for even the chance at such opportunity. Only the hardiest of spiders were used, the toughest of centipedes, and if it survived the baking it was served in another random cake among the others. So now those in attendance, kings or congress, sheriff or patriarch, was risking poison or power over an annual dessert. This went on for many years before, again, corruption or uprising did away with many of the old traditions. From then on the Liege of Cakes ritual became just another insipid tradition — a yearly game for kids without either of the more extreme conclusions."

From out of the kitchen came the barkeep and four other newives, tattoos bare in the cooling saloon. Handsome continued quietly as each of the girls set a small cake before the men at the table.

"And so that brings us to today. As people forget the Liege of Days, and more each year celebrate the Melechmas, here we can honor it one last time. Eat to the final Liege of Days, muh friends. Let us find who will, for the coming year, be the Liege of Cakes, and the rest of us honor him with our allegiance."

Wulf sank even deeper into his hood as the light from the fireplace flickered untended. He looked from one cake to another, noticing the care that had been chosen in each one's preparation and placement. Flagon's cake was topped with auburn frosting as dark as the juice staining the table. This was swirled with a thinner orange stream. These were the colors of N'Midgaard and they immediately brought images of the land's colorful autumns, along with the great glass windows of Bifrost's church and castle. Sol's little cake was topped by a sliver of dark green. It appeared that even the Horde was now aware that Mew's followers had taken it upon themselves to repurpose old, Avenger amulets, cutting the emerald spheres into cats eye pendants. From Sol's nervous shrugging, Wulf knew he was working the gemstone beneath his sleeves. Sir Skata's dessert, Wulf knew before looking, was frosted according to the Temple Needles — the crimson and white of the Order of the Creed.

"Ah joke, players," Handsome whispered, "we need not humor such uncivilized traditions. The next step is superstition, and what then? Shield maidens blessing our hammers before battle? Fertility orgies with green-eyed demi-gods? Love poems to false angels?"

Wulf steadied Skata's arm under the table, staying his hand.

"Mmmm," Handsome continued, tasting the frosting of his own cake. It immediately darkened his tongue and layers of teeth with different shades of gold and silver — colors that had replaced any others throughout Bab'lon and its baronies. "No, the old ways ah only mere steps away from damnation. Let us eat our desserts tonight with ah vow to disavow. Leave the old ways behind or be left behind. We ah all promised celestial bodies, all we have to do is ask. The future belongs to those embracing the Song. It is never too late. Mmmm, real sugar, my friends, not the beet leavings you're used to."

He dismissed all the newives but one. Some headed back into the kitchen while others bundled for the trek out into the elements. The one that stayed sat on Handsome's lap, licking the frosting from his upper lip while reaching back behind him to take up his abandoned, full mug from the adjacent table.

"Please, friends," the old man said, "Ah can't eat alone. It offends muh delicate sensibilities. Ah went through a lot of trouble here. It's not easy to acquire certain ingredients these days. I had to call upon many favors." His hand appeared behind the newife's neck, digging each finger deeply in turn. Wulf found it difficult to determine, however, if her smile was forced. "But soon it will be others asking *me* for favors. Have ah mentioned my success today? Ah think not. It is too recent. In fact, it is tonight, just as we friends sit here, in game, in dinner and drink, in ah… ah, story time, that the last remnants of the Megrim resistance have been rounded up."

Wulf stared at the tithingman, gaze unmoving, to find him staring back. He found it unbearably tempting to take another peek into his mind, but just the thought of it brought the headache back in full force. The pressure felt as though it squeezed from outside his forehead while simultaneously pressing out with pins from inside his skull. Was it true though? What did the old man want from them? Was he playing with them while the city guard stood in the drifts outside the saloon?

"Yes, ah'll make Megrim the capital of my territory. There's ah special place in my heart for it. Once the Brotherhood has seen how ah've crushed the insurgency they ah sure to reward me with more lands. And you, friends, can brag how you were there with me, there with me while the guard rounded up the last of the insurgents for inquisition. I wouldn't spread all the details, though. You may want to leave out the parts about the games and the drinks. What would people think if they knew you all gambled and pissed the night away while others fought so hard for the city? Best to keep that part out."

The newife raised her quilted dress, revealing thick, thigh-high knitted stockings and a tiny revolver she took from her garter, immediately placing it into an inner pocket of Handsome's coat. Was he waiting for them to eventually leave so he could shoot them in the back, Wulf wondered. He and Flagon pushed their cakes aside but, out of the corner of his granite eye, he could see Sol bite deeply into the dessert, immediately savoring the yellow cake.

"To real sugar!" the cleric said suddenly and loudly, holding the cake over the table.

"Yes," Handsome imitated him.

The newife at his side drank deeply of the mug she had found on the table behind her.

"To the Lonely Forgotten Sun of God!" Sol added.

"No!"

"To the Liege of Foes and the Army of Earth!"

"No!"

Flagon took a deep breath and pulled the newife's mug out of her hands. "I'll drink to that!" He did not stop gulping until the beer was gone and he was wiping his lips with his beard.

"No!" Handsome yelled, his voice straining barely above a sigh. He pushed the newife from his lap. "You've ruined it, you fools. This could have been 'out with old, in with the new.' This could have been ah new day. Don't you understand? You can still be forgiven. It's so easy. You're so stubborn." His inner teeth were chattering as they interrupted the outer, his tongue catching itself on the mouths' chaos. Lips pursing tightly, suddenly controlled, he rubbed his eyes to synchronize frantic blinking.

Wulf rubbed his as well. The headache's pressure had moved behind his eyes. His hand moved deeper into his cloak to the kingswood grip of a sawed-off shotgun, even though he had used the last of his buckshot months ago.

"Your brothers," Sol suddenly said as Handsome was about to speak, "take pride in their... bodies, yet you hide it. They seem to see it as a badge of honor, that they've been able to rise above it, but you prefer to blend in with the rest of us 'sinners.' Why?"

Handsome immediately blushed and gritted both sets of teeth. "What? Why do you...? All that matters is our celestial body, the gift of Chem-Oshmelech, the perfect body he will reward us with at the End Times."

"So then why..."

"*Fear* of the Song is the *acceptance* of Knowledge."

"...why are you ashamed..."

"*Knowledge* is turning away from *Evil*."

"You place so much importance in the material world for one promised..."

The shutters of the Motley Cow exploded inward. The entrance shattered with shards of door and frame skittering past and over their table. They were all instantly covered in dust sticking by an oily fog that plumed into the saloon before quickly being sucked back out into the blowing street. Their coughing went unheard under the great cracking of timber and the breaking and falling of concrete outside. They tried to brush the dirt from their clothes and faces, only smearing the grime.

Handsome walked to the entryway and, amidst the whipping swirl of smoke and snow, the uneven flickering of heat and wind, he looked out upon the crumbling remains of the church. He ignored the assault on his face by ice and ash, watching the flames rise and fall through translucent inner lids. He took the revolver from his pocket, stared at it, and put it away.

"Turn away, for man's *vengeance* is not the *righteousness* of the Song."

Inside, Flagon lifted the stiffening form of the newife into his arms. He had shielded her from the explosion yet still she fell, and her breathing, first shallow, had now stopped with an acrid smell issuing from her lips. He laid her on an upright table but could not shake the stench. It was in his breath and in his beard. Ignoring sudden vertigo he strode toward the tithingman. Wulf, hood down, the cleanest of them all, stopped him as he passed. They both watched as the tithingman left the saloon immersed in a wind of fire and ice.

Sol could not remember if he had fallen or dived beneath the table, but he was embarrassed either way. He kicked his broken chair out of the way as his hearing returned, and he tucked the beaded chain and Eye of Mew back up into his sleeve. His guitar was cracked from the explosion or his fall. He was positive it would never sound the same.

Cards still floated around the saloon, and Sir Skata caught one, using it to scrape the dust from his cake. It was a card he had only heard of, never seen. It looked to be *Crucifixions*, with a cyclops hanging upside down on the Tree of Life, but when he turned it, flicking the frosting from the card, he saw it could also be played as *Resurrections*, with the creature rising from root and grave.

There was a crash of table and chairs as Flagon went down. Sol was immediately at his side to hold his head from the floor. The big man was coughing more than breathing and pink foam congealed from his lips to his beard. It took only seconds for his body to stop shaking.

Wulf kneeled toward his unmoving friend. The Midgardian had been the strongest reminder of his homeland in years — larger than life but filled to the brim of it. Pushing through the pain pressing against his forehead he looked into his cousin's mind, hoping to find any spark remaining, or kindle to feed into flame. Almost immediately, Wulf's mind was seared as though with a reddened poker. He pulled himself out. He had dug too deeply, opened himself up too wide, and the external feedback lately always pushing against his psyche had pressed inward. It was useless anyway, he told himself. He had hesitated. There was nothing left to salvage.

"Damn." Sir Skata's tone was neither angry nor pained, but resigned. He swore with little more energy than a sigh. Sol paid no attention, still resting Flagon's unmoving form in his lap, but Wulf stood to the table, finding his focus on his surroundings even more painful when upright.

Sir Skata still sat, hand over his mouth, in front of the mess that had become of their game, dinner and drinks. Wulf saw the large bite he had taken out his Libran-themed cake and the clockwork insect that now skittered across the table, shaking the cake from its legs, its flaming crown of hair lighting the dimming saloon. Metallic wings drummed as it lighted to the floor, curling and uncurling a scorpion tale as it moved. Wulf pulled against it lightly with his mind — just enough of a telekinetic pull to lift its scraping legs from the floor — before then pushing against it. The abysmal locust spun slowly in the hazy air before him, and he studied it as he slowly increased the pressure from both sides, pulling and pushing in equal amounts. A reverberating hiss echoed through its metal guts and out from behind a tiny woman's face almost completely filled with a mouth of needle-like teeth. Wulf had to clench his jaw and strain, surprised to feel resistance in something so small, but with increased pressure the creature folded in upon itself and popped with the sound of crushing tin. The flame sparked before sputtering out.

He looked to Sir Skata, not sure if the knight's grimace was from the pain or from how the sting had already started swelling the side of his mouth. Wulf stepped to pick his own cake from the table. Its frosting matched the Army of Earth's flags perfectly — white background, pale blue eye leaking a bloody tear. He squeezed the cake with thumb and forefinger, moist crumbling sections falling away to reveal a sticky Liege of Cakes. He wiped the figurine clean, noticing an obvious resemblance, and placed it in the middle of the UnderCrawl board, directly in the Pit.

XI

...no chance at choice let no will to be free
by yoke of man and god set on his head
—scrawled on the walls of the King of All's lower halls

There was a dreaded moment when he feared that her feet may have been larger than his, but he quickly realized her greaves were outfitted with low gravity emulators, ironically making her legs appear heavier. He found it odd that it at first had confused him. He was more than familiar with the options assigned for the mission, but he was unusually distracted during what would be his first outing. The differences in Ehlena's armor were slight, but to someone as familiar with all of the clan tech as Easarean, nothing would have gone unnoticed.

All their armor was the same smoky red, so bronze it appeared black in all but the brightest light. Even in the crimson descent lights of the rattling cabin, they looked across at each other into shadows swallowing each other's bodies. But a cracked lens released a yellow light out to frame the features Easearen continued to admire.

The seven of them each wore the same 3Eachill-II full environmental armor they had trained in the days before they left, but each with their own requested modifications. As one of the designated shock troopers, Easarean's had the extra armored attachments over his torso, shoulder-mounted micro-flechette rail cannon, and hard-holo field generators.

As a Shock Infiltrator, Ehlena's armor was sleeker, with more curves. Even the armaments she would attach when they landed would be smoother and protrude less than his. He followed the subtle lines of her thick thighs in the dim flickering light. She too wore the slight rings of field projectors around her femoral arteries, while, just below the surface of layer upon layer of carbon fiber, just above caressing nano-mesh, threaded plasma hydralics waited in anticipation to push her body beyond the speed and strength of even the most genetically advanced species.

He knew that under the thick blocks of clan alloys segmenting around and over her hips were set redundant power sources backing up over a neutronic core to power the closed environment and antiparticle lasers of the armor. The source was nearly exhaustible at normal usage, easily able to power targeting, galaxy positioning, and communications A.I.s for generations if need be. But it was superfluous. Their mission would require them to hit fast and hard. After the initial interrogation, their assignment was to eradicate all life on the planetoid.

~

"The first mentions of *Eha'dadadad* come from texts retrieved from the previously habitable planetoid Ugarit. Also referred to as Ba'al or Teshubub or any other bastardization of the primitive clans' storm king gods. From even the most shameless hagiographies we can derive his petty demeanor, his juvenile jealousies, and a childlike need for absolute attention.

"In obviously biased political histories, he is said to have risen through slave ranks throughout puberty, somehow finding his way into the ancient courts of Ugarit while, despite his lower standing, becoming a trusted astrologer to the reigning rulers of the time.

"Competing religious texts then have Eha'dadadad either consolidating the numerous varied churches of the planetoid or allying himself with forbidden and prehistoric gods. Either way, the result was the same — a unified but oppressed Ugarit under the adamantine hand of the god king Eha'dadadad.

"It was mere hundreds of standards later that the Empire first made contact with the primitive society. Ugarit, long falling within the Aertlantean Territory, had largely been ignored, but now appeared as a decisive staging point for the Empire's burgeoning war against encroaching Aemazonian forces.

"Ugarit's resistance had been surprisingly powerful. Left to evolve on its own, Eha'dadadad's theodom had developed a financially thriving society through an unknown mix of techno-sorcery developed through allegiances with spiritual ancestry. But eventually, as with all neighboring civilizations, Ugarit was conquered by the Empire without prejudice. But somewhere within the ruins, in the final conflict, the priests of Ba'al hid to summon the spirit of Eha'dadadad. Prostrate over the gathered mummy's jarred viscera, they prayed for deliverance from their foes — and their hellish forefather answered.

"Storms wracked the planetoid — swirling, electricity-filled storms that darkened the atmosphere and tore the crust from the surface along with the invading forces. A joint effort between differing clans of the Empire was needed to mystically and militarily close Ugarit from the rest of the sector. Storm torn, uninhabitable, and seething with unknown energies, the planetoid floated alone and untouched, while, resurrected into primeval hatred, Eha'dadadad's spiritual form was all that survived for generations, breaking over the apocalyptic land as a vengeful monsoon.

"It is uncertain when exactly the storm demon escaped Ugarit. His airy form unable to survive the vacuum of space, it is theorized that Eha'dadadad at some point possessed some wayward traveler or archaeologist that dared visit the acidic maelstrom Ugarit had become. For this was eons ago, and now, throughout the Empire's recorded history, Eha'dadadad has possessed countless others throughout the clans, wrecking carnage and death in perceived vengeance for what he sees as wrong doings against his kingdom. Most troubling is the demon's newfound interest, respect and understanding of neo-gen technologies. We suspect, through possession of high-ranking engineers, and infiltration of top-secret installations, the entity is behind the recent theft of portable singularities, neutrinomic bubbles, symmetry breakers, and accretion waves — all technology that, in the wrong hands, could become detrimental to the Empire."

~

"Clan data has rated Eha'dadadad's possession abilities as 'psi red.' Anything short of the latest syn blocks will be no guard against it. Even the highest level psionics elder would have a difficult time defending themselves. Once taken control, a victim's innermost secrets are laid bare to the storm demon, while the creature itself can direct the victim to an unlimited degree of puppetry.

"Reports are sketchy at best on possession detection, and by compiling all the clans' data we only have one coherent tell-tale sign. It is said in legend that one possessed by Eha'dadadad *cannot help but to tell you so.* Whatever that means. We know that as a possessed individual it has entered secret installations, killed individual high-ranking military officials as well as gone on serial killing sprees in populated areas, and, as far as we know, it has never revealed its presence. So take the mythology as you will."

~

"Symmetry breaker technology was first used in the early days of the Empire's expansion, and almost immediately denounced as too dangerous for public ownership. Our futurist forefathers, always looking ahead to the needs of their children's children's children, knew that according to their current models of expansion, the clans' growth would quickly overcome the available habitable planets in Exodus II's solar vicinity. This short-sightedness may appear foolish to us now, knowing the advancement of worm-drives and Portal X, but at the time it was only practical to II-form hostile nearby planets for future generations. With this in mind they went about phasing areas of the system with New Mechanism radiation to break electroweak symmetry in and around certain asteroid fields and the planetary rings of the smaller, silicon based, gas exo-planets. Creating massive planetary bombardments and orbital upheavals, this made numerous sectors of the system impassable for generations. Thus creating a fortunate side effect of a natural barrier during early extra-civil wars. Ultimately too slow of a process for II-forming, symmetry breaking was explored only for more pedestrian purposes. However, as you know, this is only what the other clans are told. It has actually been used in many successful campaigns for many generations.

"Eha'dadadad is believed to have gotten whichever hands he now possesses on a localized symmetry breaker. This is not a massive irradiating satellite of the past. This is a fist-sized, spontaneous, condensation bomb that can increase the mass of a large area suddenly by magnitudes dependant on the dominant gravity well and preexisting tachyonic potentials of the location the bomb is initiated. The idea of the demon setting off such a bomb in a sensitive area (that such possessions could lead him to) is only beaten by the danger of it possessing someone who could reverse engineer such a device.

"But the even larger point to take away here is the demon's evolved strategy. Intelligence reports it to be reverting to its old dictatorial ways. Eha'dadadad has, for the first time since its inception, taken to branching out from a strategy of isolation to one of cult building — amassing some sort of ground floor army and surrounding itself with upstarts and so-called revolutionaries. Small urban groups have been eradicated on several prime planets, with information acquired on the scene leading us to a secondary natural satellite. Plains-covered with mediocre soil, Eceres has only been populated by a rotating mix of disillusioned and poor agriculturists and dissidents looking for a cheap high in a carbon dioxide rich atmosphere.

"There are only two size E 'cities' on Eceres, a barely organized government, weak militias and no media to speak of. This is first and foremost a level III type assassination and secondarily a Wreck and Affect mission with any collateral damage approved and encouraged. Eha'dadadad cannot be allowed to leave this moon."

~

He would have had his armor XT her had he not known the lead fibers would have shielded her body, also alerting her to alien tomography, and so he could only continue with what he imagined her armor hid. He pictured Ehlena's solid chest as it was protected by an androgynous breastplate scarcely smaller than his own, with the same blocky adamantine segments leading into particle razors Easarean replaced on his own armor with a pygmy rail cannon and a shoulder mounted launcher loaded with micro plasma grenades that would be especially effective against a storm demon. Easarean's specific mission was to pacify the populace, but it could not hurt for him to be ready to confront the demon if the situation arose.

Ehlena's broad shoulders cradled her helmet. It had the slightly more feminine curves only he could differentiate over the years he had studied the differences — the harshly blocked lines over where her cheekbones must have hid, smoother indentations over a pronounced brow, the helmet's cyclopean eye a few hairs' breadth smaller. The eye would hold a more complete reconnaissance sensory package than his, being his was tailored more for targeting and insurgence deletion, even though she would be seeing as much action as he would.

The drop ship hit the wall of Ecere's atmosphere, shaking Easarean from his fantasy. His sensors informed him the appropriate dynamic pressure had been equated, and that the ship's magnetofields were immediately augmenting the natural shock layer around the outer mold line. The aerodynamic heating his armor had been tracking now increased tremendously, and, although any member of his genetically advanced clan could survive the entry without armor, his scanners told him it would, at the very least, be quite uncomfortable. The Clan's drop ships, although still significantly superior to those made by other races, were designed at the bare minimum, with only one purpose in mind — to get the soldiers to the surface quickly — and even though this was not an Awe Mission, they still wanted to make a statement. And even though Easarean could not wait for the fighting to begin, he still hoped for a second after they would land for a quick, helmetless debriefing. He could imagine her black eyes and blacker buzz cut hair. He imagined her thin lips, sharp nose and cleft chin. And all he could do was imagine, for he had never seen a woman before.

He was ignoring his helmet's sensor now. Just as the ship's stagnation point began to push acceptable radiation levels, they began to slow.

XII

"Never presume that I would be surprised at what I found in the genebratory archives of the illustrious Ophidia in Ouroboros. Those sadistic old geeks would never have squandered a chance to experiment in whimsy, even in their most inspired creation. And even I cannot deny DNA and so must admit, much to my humble chagrin, that I am an Heir of Aesar."

—Melchyor Slayd

The sound of her hammering came back to her at a higher pitch as it bounced among the cols. The song was quickly drowned out by yet another gale, and she paused to find the sternest cracks to slip thickly mittened hands into. The layers over her hands often made the climb even more precarious, but the elements were unforgiving this high up.

She turned away from the deafening winds and ignored the temptation to dig the crampons deeper into the ice beneath her boots. This was the loosest rock of the climb. It was not a good place to stop. She was completely exposed to weather and eyes, and the crags she climbed were hit alternatingly by blankets of frozen rain and taunting sunlight. The glare blinded her no matter how she shielded her eyes. Multiple hoods and hats were not enough against the reflections, but she feared her tinted goggles obscured the variations in the rock faces. And so she found herself taking numerous breaks against each peek of sun, each whip of wind.

Because of the slowing, she had to assume she was behind the schedule she set. It would be turning dark soon. But it was difficult to tell, for when the clouds thinned, the burst of light would reflect around the crest, seemingly coming from all directions, but she was certain that when the sun fell it would do so quickly behind snow and mountain.

She waited many minutes before deciding that, this time, the wind would not stop. She needed to find a suitable place to dig in for the night before evening turned to impassable darkness. The air caught her as she struck the piton, and she dropped the hammer to grab the rock with both hands. The tool fell without sound. Even beneath mitten and hand sock she could feel the paralyzing cold she grasped. Her fingers quivered, threatening to slide from a crevice that had never seen the sun. Two ice axes hung from her pack. There was a flat head on the side of one, and she was going to have to now use it to hammer any future pitons. This last one had gone in softly, blue metal beneath a skin of verdigris, but it felt sturdy enough that she moved along after securing the rope to its ring. She continued upward at a pace nowhere near her previous speed. Each leg swung from the wind between each planting. Her arms threatened to turn widely if she did not keep them close to the rock. Every step was now a deliberate, slowly mechanical movement.

It had been estimated hours since she had been able to see the ground. The swirling snow continued beneath her, and now, as the day clouded behind storm or jagged horizon, it swirled upward until she cold no longer see her boots. It rose with her. She wiggled her toes beneath the layers of cotton and down and leather just to remind herself they were still there. The pain had stopped, but she knew that not to be a good sign.

She dug upward, the axe grasping rock that soon became covered in a dry snow she had to chip off before driving pitons in. Eventually it was only ice she climbed, the axe chopping handholds and steps ahead of her. Her knees shivered as much as her fingers now, and as it grew ever darker and ever windier, she started working out a plan to secure herself to the mountain face. She was not sure if she had enough screws or rope left to bind herself to the ice wall, or if it would hold her throughout the night or if she could possibly survive the dropping temperature.

So she kept climbing, every other step slipping, every other grip crumbling. She kept climbing until her scarves froze to her face and she had to reach through darkness past eyelashes iced together. Arms and legs ached with a soreness her Homega Sapiens body had never known, bending in layers of furs hardening as quickly as the ice she cracked. The storm screamed over rock and snow, brow and ice, and she could not tell which broke beneath her axe, or if anything broke at all.

She fell against diamond hardness beneath her, and when her lungs continued to sting with each shallow breath, and her limbs continued to pulse in aching numbness, she knew she must be resting on some escarpment, not against an unforgiving drop.

But still Ivy pushed on, on shaking hands and knees. The only colors in the night were the ones exploding in her head with the pain of each crawling movement. Either she eventually came upon something that blocked the wind or the last vestige of feeling had left her. She was not sure. But she reached out and above her, but could not tell if anything met her petrified fists.

She did not think that she fell asleep that night but was hard-pressed to remember any of it as morning rose to gleam from all the peaks to reflect off the leaning lees surrounding her. The air twinkled under and around, silent and steady, and for many seconds she thought she may have been frozen inside it, but her joints and padded layers of clothing cracked as she reached for the light. It felt no different than the blue shadows, but comforted her none-the-less.

Every blink, every breath, cracked her face. Every step threatened to give out beneath her. But she moved on, rounding shelf after shelf through a pass that brought her in the late morning to look out and up at each peak of the Titans. Astraeus' tiny pinnacles making up its crest had yet to see the sun from this side. A snowy fog rolled from its opposite side. Asteria's single sharp point bent the sunlight around itself and down into canyon after canyon, lighting the hull of the massive battleship cradled between the three mountains. The gunmetal vessel, however, obviously belonged to Prometheus. The blue mountain held it to its bosom in an enfolding glacier.

Ivy did not care how the colossal seafarer came to rest in the Rocky Mountains. She only cared that, inside its beached shell, hid the ancient city of Brig.

~

Whatever survived of the library of Gog decayed frozen beneath a fallen brine swamp, and Bab'lon's books were too deep in the Territories for someone as recognizable as Ivy, and the blockade around the Black Hills was tightening. The Temple Needle's intricate histories, genealogies, and maps had quickly become unapproachable. All that was left to her concerning Brig's existence and location existed in myth and rumor, but that was where she had started. Wulf had cautioned her against research, but it was all she had left.

All across the land the people claimed home to the sight where man first appeared in the sun after centuries of steam-clouded eyes beneath the earth. Some claimed that the wind of angel wings pushed them to the surface of the Black Hills. Others believed their ancestors to have emerged from caves crisscrossing the rocky mountains of the Baronies, while still others told of mankind's exodus from the mysterious South, past desert, deep from Pharaoh's jungle city of ancient Sepulchre. Could she trust any of the stories? Were any even as old as the elders telling them?

But she listened closely to the tales of the Territories, of man's retreat under ashen skies and falling fire into the shaking earth of rocky mountains. Deeper and deeper they fled, supplanting chthonic civilizations in brass wonder, eventually thriving in their newly adopted world.

But vestigial memories resurfaced unmeasured generations later, memories of sky and sun and colored vegetation, memories of rock that reached upward, roots hidden from eyes, animals with sight, and breath unrecycled. It was disputed just what woke men up. The smell of flowers blossoming for the first time in centuries? The rustling echo of new leaves on the first nonmutant trees in generations? The Obsidian Poppet? No matter the impetus, humankind rose and greeted the new world and spread over fresh fields to meet Automaton and Washkington and the wars that followed. And beneath it all, Ivy heard the theories and conspiracies of Chimaera.

Three men. Or women. Some named a soldier. Others said a king. Some said a scientist was among the three. Most agreed there were wizards involved. Three hidden persons pulled the strings of mankind, some say even before man reintroduced himself to the surface. They influenced elders and warlords and eventually nations, in war and peace, in culture and economy. The three were the richest in gold and influence. But who were they? No one could say. But all agreed that their secret dealings shaped the land and, for better or worse, could still be felt today. Their descendants, in conspiracy and influence, always just three, were never as powerful, and never revealed, but they kept the illusion of free will familiar to all.

The stories Ivy heard were as varied as the people that told them, but there was one similar thread winding its way through the tapestry of time. The original Chimaera — men or demons, aliens or androids, priests or peasants — had found a deposit of ancient technology when they first came to the surface. It was a ship left over from the time of the Old Ones. This technology, rationed out slowly to the nations, gave mankind an edge in the new world, but it also made the three of Chimaera immensely wealthy and a head-start in clandestine destiny.

Gutted and obsolete, of no more use to Chimaera, the ship of the Old Ones later became a retreat for kings, and, later yet, a city of thousands had grown within its immensity — a haven for merchants, a refuge for travelers cutting through the Titans.

None of these myths interested Ivy, yet still she had listened in churches, ink-stained her fingertips in paper shops, and bought drinks for raconteurs in territorial outskirt saloons until they told of Brig.

No one agreed in which Evolutionary War the city in the ship was requisitioned and renamed Brig. Was it Bab'lon that martially took it over? Did early Librans take the Brig for their own? It did not matter. Ivy listened in to rumors telling of the recommissioned city as it was made into a prison both impregnable and inescapable and used by the dentist Torquemada for his heinous experiments. Here the townsfolk would go into their most elaborate descriptions of inquisition against the political prisoners of the time.

But these details were of atrocities committed a century ago. At least. The ship's location had once again been lost to time, its history once again obscured by tall tales and small men. It was when the talk returned specifically to Brig that Ivy would return with more drinks, often only the vermillion available. There were rumors spreading that Brig had once more been discovered, recently, this time by the Horde, and it was once more being used to house what they saw as traitors to the Song. Brig's doors were once again open to prisoners.

~

Everything was black and white, with a predominant gray barely reflecting through dust and dim gaslight. Ivy stared at the wall of instruments without compression. There was no way of knowing if the rows upon rows of shattered gauges, if they were even still functional, would be any use to her mission. In a bottom corner was a mass that, when she first rounded the maze of walls, she thought to be a bloom of angelic tendrils, snaking opaquely to absorb the ubiquitous metal. But it was just yet another tumble of cords knotted and plugged into an uncountable number of sockets. Would pulling any create a diversion she could take advantage of? Was there anyone in Brig to distract?

Through tunnel after tunnel — some earthen, some gunmetal — she had seen no one, the passageways lit only by her tar torch, but in the interior of the ship itself there were starting to be signs of life. There were dials in most of the corridors for gaslights, although she seemed to be the only one using them. There was heat in most of the rooms, although Ivy guessed that anyone other than a Homega Sapiens would have to stay bundled against the remaining chill. Trash littered every corner and hallway — illegible papers and boxes empty and broken — but dust and decrepitude showed its age and abandonment. There was not, however, the usual smell of close-living people she expected. Whether it was from the floor to ceiling sterility of metal or whether the ancient, frozen unmoving air did not allow for any odor, she did not know. Was it possible she had been wrong? Was it even possible that she *could* be wrong? Was she the only person to have discovered Brig in a hundred years? Her total recall and focus had made her the Resistance's prime candidate to bargain with the merchants of Arcade Herod, but in the end Wulf had almost pulled her from the mission for fear that her obsession with the mythical city would distract her. But, in the end, it was that very obsession that convinced him to send her. What she searched Brig for would benefit the Resistance.

Ivy had almost the same conversation with Resistance leaders when she had a year earlier convinced them to give her leave to seek out the Nursery. She could not deny that its existence was of the utmost curiosity to her, but determining the destruction of a source of Lesser Antonys, she argued, was also of grave importance to those fighting the Brotherhood. Her memories of her birth, of her appearance outside the Nursery were vague shadows — in fact, anything before her second birth in the Tower of Ziggurat, including nightmares of Pyramid Abysmal, were almost lost to her — and, despite what she had been told, she wanted more solid proof that the Nursery was out of commission for good. It was a trip she would be hard-pressed to make in these dangerous days. The territorial boundaries had tightened, and the war had closed off many of the more well worn paths. It was too deep inside Kaldera for someone with a face as recognizable as hers, especially with all the Lesser Prophets recalled to fight the war. It was too much a chance to take that they would not recognize their "sister."

Now, deep inside chamber inside bulkhead, there were wheels to turn and gauges of innumerable numbers as the walls continued into more walls breaking into even more walls. There was now even some red coloring in some of the small wheels and gold coloring on some of the larger levers, but most had tarnished over time. But how much time? She could feel vibrations beneath some of the wheels.

The purpose behind each section was unknown but not as alien as the instrumentation she had found when she had finally come upon the

Nursery. Even though the blockades had not closed Kaldera as tightly yet, she had still had difficulty traveling unmolested to the alien artifact. Bandits roamed free through the Baronies, taking advantage of the hysteria spread by growing war. She avoided the more populated areas but still came across two Lesser Prophets as they surveyed the Nursery from within and without. She had hid in the surrounding forest for days until they left, but only found what had obviously disappointed them as well.

The interior of the Nursery had been burned beyond recovery. Even before instrumentation had melted, it would obviously been alien to her. Even before the charred machinery had exploded it would have baffled her. The lake of protoplasm that had spread through the alien craft upon its burning left a stain holding the prints of the animals that must have feasted upon it when the flames had died enough. The little of the jelly that had sunk into the cracks of the splitting floor still slowly rotted and stank like acidic death. Ivy estimated that it would now have been years since Shiloh Antony had destroyed the craft, years since her birth, but the nutrient still resisted bacteria and insect. She left satisfied and returned to the underground of territorial resistance knowing that the Brotherhood was now mortal.

She now continued on through passages of great white pipes covered in even more gray gauges measuring indeterminate numbers. There was warmth from few but no sound comparable to the ever-present creaking of the floors and ceilings. The glacier cradling the ship expanded and contracted constantly, and Ivy was certain that the sound and pressure shifted ever so slightly with every step she took, with every breath of the frozen air she took. It was as though she stretched with the metal. She was getting seasick.

As the maze of instrument-laden walls gave way to parallel corridors of immense piping, so too did the tubes give way to rooms of chains. Most hung empty and broken and cannibalized for other areas, and she saw them jury-rigged to appliance and wall, but some of the thin ones still clung to wasted beds that too had been mostly torn apart long ago for scrap wool and spring. These barracks were lost to light, and without a lamp in the long chamber Ivy had to reach from one chain to another to find her way through trash to a glow flickering from some far doorway. Without any air movement, her breath just hung around her face, tickling and biting as it froze and thawed.

The light she found was not as red as it appeared from afar but a glow from a chalky bulb just accentuating the rusty paint crinkling from a room even she barely fit in. It would be the only room she had seen since entering Brig that did not have at least two other exits if not for an inset ladder leading down into square darkness. The metal was cold, and she had no doubt that her palms would have stuck to it if not for her oversized mittens. She pulled her scarf high and her hood low, careful to not let any exposed skin touch the sides of the tight chute.

The drop continued into ever-darkening blackness, and curiosity almost got the better of her, but she instead climbed off on a level that promised another faded glow at the end of a chamber littered solidly with blocks of metal she bruised herself against consistently until she reached fenced doorways that swung easily at the lightest touch. Gate after gate, each with wiring thickening the deeper she walked and the brighter the light, led to a white hall with rounded gate doors lining the sides and made from the same steel as the walls, floors and ceiling. She could not see the end of the hall for weak light and its length, but, if Brig now held the Horde's political prisoners, this was where she would find them.

But still, no sweet smell of imprisonment, no flow or sound of air and breaths, no expected moans of the hungry and tortured. Perhaps she had been wrong about the Horde. Perhaps they kept their prisoners clean and healthy. *Or*, she thought as she peeked through door after door leading down the corridor, *perhaps they keep no prisoners*. There were thin, discolored mattresses in some, closed lamps in some, bowls and blankets in some, but none held people.

The hall abruptly ended in a darkness she could barely see the pipe-covered wall in, and she almost did not even check the final cell. As she turned a dial to increase the buzzing light of the hall she could now see a small padlock hanging from its door.

The ship frozen into Prometheus was massive — a mountain of ice and metal that had long ago shipwrecked between three of rock. In her estimation she had only explored a small percentage of its tight mechanical corridors and gaping cargo holds. She needed little of the food and comforts the peasants of the land required, but how long before she had to give up her search. If the Winter of Winds had taught them anything, the seasons were unreliable. The snow on the Titans was only going to get thicker, the paths out of the mountains only increasingly impenetrable.

But her musing was for nothing, for as she smashed the lock off with the pearly butt of Priest's Davidson *Sitdown*, she could hear the rustle of leaves and smell the scent of disturbed flowers. She turned the light up higher before swinging the cell door open, peering through the still shadows to find what she had been searching for.

Harlowe crouched limp and smothered beneath chain and coffin blossom, not even acknowledging her presence. Ivy breathed so quickly and loudly in her excitement she almost missed the sound of steps down the hallway behind her.

XIII

In your bed, in your bed,
Goblin King peeks in your head.
Lady Ick will make you sick
if your body is naughty.

　—nursery rhyme

andsome Gibbet went to bed knowing he would sleep better than he had in days. Excitable insomnia had kept him awake deep into the nights leading up to the Melechmas, and the few dreams he had revolved around his plans to take down the Megrim resistance, making even his afternoon naps shallow and disrupted by anticipation. And so, with everything coming to fruition, he had been finally able to drift off immediately after crawling into bed, exhausted in breath and deed. He was going to enjoy it. He deserved it.

It was a deep sleep but not without vivid dreams of past and future — a past to now be forgotten and a future close on the horizon and away from the dregs of the outer territories. Tonight had been the first and hopefully final step of his penance, and tomorrow he could start planning his return to the front lines of the war as the only tithingman not yoked with the responsibility of the masses. By the end of the week he could once again be leading the Army of Heaven, interpreting the words of Schism to the forces defending the good lands from the Liege of Foes' minions. He would once again differentiate himself from his peers, as he always had, and as he always had to.

Handsome Gibbet was the only child between his mother and a father who had disappeared before he was born — a Lesser Antony who, only through his mother's scornful remembrances, Handsome knew had never aspired to the Prophets Lesser. As much as his mother wanted to keep her shame a secret, Handsome's deformities, although unique, gave his background away. It was only when his mother remarried and they moved to the tobacco farms, in with his new father and siblings, that he knew pleasure. It certainly was not from his new family. They treated him as the scourge the villagers did, the aberration his schoolmates saw, but it was on the plantation that he first knew love — love for the surrounding agriculture that filled his days from dawn to dusk. The tobacco field under his care lived and died by his whims, but the plants thrived not because of the threat of his new father's whip, not because of starvation punishments, but because of the pride he felt looking over the lush emerald rows thick with leaves as big as his head. He liked nothing better than to walk the field, sending the slaves back to their barrack with black clouds approaching. The ground would turn to mud as he drank from the giant plants with thunder rolling overhead. Here he could pretend he was the only man alive, with only the voices of wind and rustling leaves to sooth him. These voices never taunted him.

It was during one of these storms that the great warlord entered the plantation, and it was perhaps because of the thunder that Handsome's stepfather had not heard the horses. He was pulled from the barn and drawn before Handsome but quartered before all of the family. It was an example to the surrounding farms, a warning to those who refused to pay protection money. The plantation, including Handsome's mother and children, now belonged to a Greater Antony, a giant of a man who immediately recognized Handsome for what he was.

The plantation was left in his mother's care after she agreed to give the warlord a one-time payment of half her slaves and a recurring monthly rent. It was a hefty fee, but the plantation would never fear bandits or rival farms as long as it was under the Greater Antony's protection.

Handsome's older brother was bigger, his younger sister smarter, but only he was chosen to live with the warlord. Here he saw a true kindness under a stern upbringing, and here he learned to cultivate people as he once did the crops under his care. His new father taught him to seed the villages with promise, nurture the peasants with deed, and flatter them in the sun. The people hid when Handsome rode through town. He long ago knew admiration could never be his, and so he drank up their palpable fear.

The warlord was never called a Greater Prophet by the people or himself, but Handsome knew him as one. For when they were both alone together, overlooking burning field or town, only he heard the tales of a better world. The warlord told only him of a reality of peace and safety and unity in the realized land. The Greater Antony was ancient and tired, and it would not be his destiny to fix the world, but Handsome was young. He had a lifetime to spread the word. And he started immediately.

The world is broken.

He was preaching to a family of settlers when he heard of his toddler sister's death. He was speaking beneath fireworks on Washkington's Birthday when he was told of his three younger brothers' deaths from tornado. He heard the rumor of his older sister's death in childbirth while he presided over his first congregation. He kept waiting to hear about the death of his mother, but the gossip never came.

As Handsome's churches grew, so did his reputation, and it was only a few years into his adulthood when the Prophets Lesser took notice. Finding his word almost identical to their own, his masses joined theirs, although now he spoke of a means as well as a way. Not only was there an ideal to reach, but Handsome now knew how to reach it. All one had to do was accept the Divine Choir into their heart.

He would never forget his first meeting with some of the Brotherhood. Here were two men, Lesser Antonys, identical except for styles of clothing and hair. Here were two men, either of which Handsome knew could have been his biological father. He never asked. Even as this parentage would have explained the mark on his arm, the kiss of Chem-Oshmelech, that he always thought of as a birth mark. It leashed him to the Brass Angel, they said. It was the promise of a celestial body, one that would someday evolve him beyond his crude mortal shell. Handsome had worked for many Lesser Prophets since then, and each time he could not help but to wonder if any of them had been the one to bed his mother those decades ago. Would they even remember his birth? Would it mean as much to them as to him?

But it was to whom he considered his real father that he always returned. The Greater Antony never seemed to age in the years Handsome was out on the road, but his ancient feebleness showed in his movements and voice. This was a giant that claimed to have met Automaton on the battlefield, and, if it was true, he had lived longer than any man before him. Handsome cared for him as he had once cared for Handsome, through gentle chores and stern rebuke, and each night they would talk of how the world should be, could be.

A storm hit when it became time for the tithingman to return to his congregations, holding him up in the old Greater's mansion for an extra day, and it was during this extra day that the Librans struck. Handsome was out in the adjoining woods, enjoying the warm rain and the thunder as it rolled through the night clouds. It was beneath the cracking sky that he heard the shouts of the slaves as they fought the flames lighting one of the smaller equipment sheds near the barns. Handsome recognized the fire immediately as a distraction. There was no lightning leading the thunder, especially not in the low valley of the ranch.

He steered clear of the main entrances to the mansion, avoiding the eerie silver glow breaking the darkness from within. Coming up through the cellar he first heard the deep prayers as he neared the welcome rooms at the front of the home. Here is where the Greater Antony would have received the killers, and it was here that Handsome, peeking through the front kitchens, could see the carnage. Some of the men still prayed, their swords dimming as their words slowed. The Greater Antony had been impossibly hacked open, slow blood spreading between floorboards.

Handsome hid in a pantry, the smell of rosemary forever linking his mind with the image of his adopted father's slaughter, although the men quickly left by slinking back into the woods and storm. They had done well to hide their usual appearance, silver mail and red leather hidden beneath the robes of beggars, but he had seen the false angelic shape of Blind Libra on their charms and blades as they chanted the spell that warmed their swords. He had heard the entire prayer as they sang it over and over above the Greater Antony, but Handsome could only remember the two words "Low Coda." He would never forget the phrase or the scene he saw that night.

Handsome had no friends and he trusted few people — none completely, and so he turned to the only person he could think of when he needed to set someone in charge of the plantations he had now inherited. His quickly moved his mother into the main home, with what was left of her meager belongings, before setting out on one last survey of his congregations. He could not help but notice, before leaving, how different she looked compared to his memories. She was sunken, rubbery, and far from the vibrant woman he had spent his youth with.

He spent a year on the roads connecting his churches, earning wrinkles in coup quelling and scars in uprisings, but he maintained order, established elders and set precedents that would last decades. He had worried what state the tobacco fields would be in upon his return, but found them thriving as never before under his mother's stern whip. She had consolidated the farms, fortifying the outlying, lower producing fields into treacherous ditches to ward off invaders and bandits. The yield had been healthy and unobstructed.

His congregations secure, his plantations fruitful, Handsome should have settled into a comfortable retirement. His mother encourage him to sip sun tea from his porch, to spend afternoons at the fishing hole or nights card-playing in town, but no matter the distraction he could not forget the *Low Coda*. Even his walks in the rain could not make him forget. In fact, he grew frightened of the storms. The thunder covered the sound of approaching assassins. The lightning filled the night with brightness, revealing his hiding spots.

The Greater Antony had been the only person to ever show him true kindness, to never look away when he spoke, hiding disgust. He had not cringed when Handsome spoke closely. He gave him increasing responsibility and encouragement, and comforted him with stories of a better world. When he and Handsome walked into town everyone else was their inferior, no matter their appearance or station. They had learned to bow to the tithingman in deed as well as word. The day his father had adopted him was the day Handsome had stopped being wrong.

Tea was not to Handsome's liking. The silence of fishing left him alone with his thoughts. Card dealing left him with the thoughts of others. And so he filled his days devising new ways to torture the thieves of his fields. Slaves stole crops and time, and most hoped for death as a painless reprieve, so Handsome had to keep becoming more creative in his punishments.

The slitting of ears gave way to brandings. Lashing evolved into blisterings, but still all the pleasures of work gave only momentary respite from memories of the Low Coda. He built a smoke house, chaining the thieves among fires of tobacco stems, hobbling their lungs for life. He chained their heads to the ground, suspending fire and hog's fat from the rafters, scalding drops dripping on bare flesh for hours. He drove nails into barrels before rolling the slaves down hills in them. Years passed by with distraction after distraction, but still he could only think of the Low Coda.

At the behest of his mother he took a wife. She was ordinarily boring and immediately pregnant. He saw her and the children only at brunch. They had not the deformities of his blood. As with all tithingmen the taint burned itself out in one generation. His children and children's children would never know the hardships he had to endure, would never have the same fight to live and to succeed. They would always be weak, never burdened by uniqueness. Only the warlord had understood this. Only the Greater Prophet had understood him. Even the Prophets Lesser could not relate. They had each other, in common goal and common faces. They would never understand their children. But Handsome needed their resources and their cause. The world could be better, and with the Brotherhood's help it would be.

Handsome's plantations fell within a barony of Bab'lon, but since the coming of the warlord no taxes had been enforced. Even the reputation of the Greater's odd son had kept the collectors at bay from the entire region. But now, many years later, during the worst drought in memory, the Barony came to collect. Neighboring farms urged Handsome to lead them against the intrusion, but he passed on the offer. He could pay and wait out the taxes until his neighbors were bankrupt and angry, until they had nothing left to lose and were desperate enough for revolution.

The time came quickly, however. Handsome could barely keep the region's landowners from uprising before he had established contact with the Prophets Lesser. He had left the plantation again in the care of his family, traveling to the far side of Kaldera, beyond the reach of the Wheel — the outward circle of baronies. Here he once again saw the vision of his Greater Prophet — a force to bring about the Right World. The *Ashmedai Adat El*, followers of the Song of the Divine Choir, desired to save the land from itself, and it had found its time.

Handsome was particularly impressed by one man among the Brotherhood. Schism spoke as a Lesser Antony but acted as something greater. He had predicted the plague that had struck years earlier. He had warned the people of the famine that now stretched across the plains. No one, even his own brethren, had listened, and everyone had suffered. Now he saw war in the future, a war that would engulf the struggling populations, and people finally listened. The *Ashmedai Adat El* saw the Baronies as complacent, weak, and dismissive. Their opulent sins had brought disease and drought upon the people, and now their laziness would allow the land to be crushed into battlefields. The Barons would not listen to reason, Schism preached. Only a new order could stand against the coming tide of war, and only ears open to the Divine Song would make sure the faithful never came so close to destruction again.

Handsome was sent home to raise a militia, and by the time he got there the stories out of the fallen Bab'lon capital had reached the plantations. The taking of Ziggurat was said to be bloodless, but the fight for the Wheel would not be. Handsome took one hundred men and boys deeper into the Barony, ambushing a troop of guard oversee-ing the hastening of a fort. They captured the head of the guard in the skirmish, and he soon died — some said by friendly fire, others by Handsome's knife.

The tithingman left half of his militia behind, expecting to replace them while adding more as he advanced westward toward the building of another fort. He met with many men, some disillusioned with the Baron, but all of them with something to gain from his fall. Few put their support behind Handsome, but he marched on to a fort he found to be closer to completion and more heavily fortified than his sources had said. He began an immediate retreat back to the captured fort, and the Baron's guard followed with twice the number of men they had faced before.

Handsome and his men arrived at the fort to find provisions nearly exhausted, trenches only partially dug, and breastworks inadequate. Fortifications were to be built from the encroaching forest, reducing the enemy's cover while cluttering the terrain leading to the fort, but Handsome's militia had run out of time. It then started to rain.

The thunder was the first Handsome had heard in months, and the first to produce rain in a season, ruining the ditches except for paths made by the refuse of unfinished fences. The Baron's force used these paths as the militia tried to get orders out of an unresponsive Handsome. By the time he reacted, the guard was at the fort's gates, and the tithingman's frontal assault only left him with half his men alive. They had barely managed to close the gate, and Handsome's men convinced him to take the conditions of surrender. He and his few men left the fort with just the clothing on their backs.

The tithingman returned to his plantation immediately being hailed as a hero. The word had reached before he did that he had stood against the Barony with poor odds and resources. He had even killed the captain of the opposing force. The militia grew.

As the bulk of the *Ashmedai Adat El* was working to curb unrest in the inner Wheel, Handsome had his growing forces take small towns leading into the Barony. Each town surrendered without engagement, building the militia's arms. He did nothing to quiet his accomplishments, knowing word would reach back home to his family, and he only became louder, taking larger towns whether they had resources, strategic importance, or even nothing to offer the *Ashmedai Adat El*. Finally, as he marched his men loudly into the Barony's capital, the guard was waiting for him. They let the militia enter the town, watching them settle into traps and indefensible positions before attacking. The guardsmen sniped from hidden positions. The townspeople burned the buildings around them. Handsome's men were being attacked from the inside and out. He had brought almost a thousand men into the town but fled at sunset with half the amount, most of them wounded. Word had preceded his return home of how he had rode back and forth across the makeshift battlefields, rallying the remnants of his forces to an organized retreat before burning field and forest to cover the tracks. People began immediately to paint and write his tale of the scene.

Handsome once more took a pilgrimage to his congregations, near and far, inside and outside the Barony. Under the guise of preacher he recruited. His churches, already accused of sympathizing with the invading forces, were under suspicion and harassment, and he found many men willing to follow him homeward.

While other baronies fell, those nearest continued to hold out. Orders were smuggled in, giving Handsome a commission in the *Ashmedai Adat El*. This show of confidence brought even more men to his side, more supplies, spears and even rifles. It was in scenes like this that the militias waned and the Armies of Heaven grew.

Now, in command of thousands, Handsome disciplined harshly, emphasizing sacrifice and training. Every exercise began with prayer, every skirmish with devotion, every firing squad echoing with song. The people's hatred for the Barons increased proportionately to their love of the Divine Choir. Handsome was not only creating soldiers but revolutionaries in culture and deed, and he led them against bandit incursions capitalizing on the recent disorder. In ten months, units of his regiments fought twenty battles, losing only a third of his men, and his territory inside the Barony grew, eating it from the inside. It became an example for uprisings in other baronies, and the Baron's forces grew thin attempting to halt the violence from without and within.

Handsome eventually returned to the Barony's capital, this time as a conqueror. The people had decided and their final push had been a bloodless coup with the Baron disappearing in the storm of the night. But Handsome barely had time to settle into the Baron's mansion before pulling his forces together and driving them into the adjacent barony. There was momentum throughout Bab'lon. Word of Handsome's great victories had spread the Song of the Divine Choir through farmstead and hamlet, town and city. The people tore down walls and gates, and the *Ashmedai Adat El* flooded from Ziggurat into the newly forming territories.

As the insurrection cooled and a new order fermented, Handsome once again traveled back to his plantations. He heard the Song in every walking path and from the windows of every ranch house he passed. He returned to a property that had grown tenfold, for the *Ashmedai Adat El* had rewarded his family with any neighboring farmland that had not contributed to the cause. There were rebellions as a result, but nothing the richest man in the Territory could not handle.

It was not long before Handsome found himself disillusioned with what he now saw as an unfulfilling life. The uprising had only whetted his taste for the command of battle. Here, the plantation world now bored him. His wife and children reminded him of the weak men he had crushed in the campaigns. His neighbors reminded him of the imbeciles retreating in the midst of battle. There was no one here to relate to. He was alone. Daily slave whippings did nothing to amuse him anymore, and so he started whipping himself, but it brought only a moment's excitement. Neighbors urged him to take up fox or boar hunting, but after only a month his packs had purged the Territory's forests of all mammals. It was on his final hunt, finding no sign of hare or fawn, that he instead saw the first hint of black shank creeping through his crop. The disease yellowed only a small area of one of his wetter fields, but it was in a field that touched many others. Within hours Handsome was packed for travel. Within a night he had gathered six men he trusted. Within a day they were all standing over the bloodied faces of a family of heathens at the edge of the territory. The farm's head pleaded between split lips, but only the man's mother gave Handsome the answers he needed after peeling strips of skin from her chest in front of her grandchildren.

Handsome and his men went straight to the farm's cellar, taking their fill and finding the amulet exactly where the family had hidden it.

It was of a dark green glass, smooth except where it had been broken to create its new shape. Once a sliver of a cat's eye, it had been rounded to represent the Lonely Forgotten Sun of God. He smashed it beneath his boot.

Handsome drained his fields, but months later brown spot appeared on his tobacco across two adjacent fields. The crop aged before his eyes. This time he followed rumors to one of his stable hands. The worker had come from MANN lands as a child, and Handsome had always suspected him of sympathies toward the offshoot Order of the Eye dwelling in the eastern capital of Joseph. The man died by hook and hanging before he could admit to any blasphemy, but Handsome was certain he found Libran tattoos in the mess he fed to his pigs.

And so it went, with months turning into years, until Handsome heard of the Liege of Foes and the Army of Earth. Granny wilt was stunting a new season, shriveling an entire field, and he was questioning one of his son's friends for a curse she had been heard shouting at a prior season's harvest gathering. Her gums were the pinkest he had ever seen, and they swelled into a violet he was unfamiliar with as they were sliced and leeched. She cried of secret meetings of neighbors and field hands she had heard her parents speak of only in the dead of night.

Handsome held a special mass. He had never gathered more of the countryside, had never sung louder, raising the song around him to a fevered pitch that culminated in the congregation's march to take the plantations of the heretics. Handsome absorbed the farmlands into his own but quickly began selling all the fields, old and new, eventually only keeping the manor and minor building for his family. He had, at his height, owned most of the Territory, and the riches from its sale went straight into his new venture. Handsome had made contacts during his travels, accrued many favors, impressed many across his congregations, and he used all his good will and all his wealth to now collect every blacksmith and gunsmith servicing the territories to come work for him. Under his guidance they collectively began to arm a newly forming Army of Heaven for the *Ashmedai Adat El*. For months this collective smithed, with Handsome blessing every spear point, arrowhead, and rifle round.

The tithingman was at the front of the receiving crowds when the Brotherhood came to collect. He steeled himself against the anticipation of meeting two more Lesser Prophets. Once again he would wonder if either of them were his biological father. Handsome was an old man now. He barely recognized himself in the mirror these days. Could he expect his real father to recognize the child he had abandoned from birth? But any longing changed to hope when the doppelbrothers arrived to take command of the arms — hope that neither of the men were his father, hope that neither of the men had any claim to him in words or deeds. The beings that drove him to genuflect before the crowds of his own people may have at one time been Lesser Antonys, perhaps even Prophets, but they now had less in common with the Brotherhood than Handsome himself had with the two of them. They served at the head of the Army of Heaven, but Handsome could not hear the Divine Song in their voices. They fought the Liege of Foes but served neither the territories nor the *Ashmedai Adat El.* They lived only for war. They served only Ammon Mars.

The word across the land was that Schism directed the forces of the Army of Heaven from Ziggurat, safe behind the walls and towers of Bab'lon, but it was Ammon Mars that led from the battlefield, bringing holy destruction to each rebellion and down upon the Liege of Foes. And Fobos and Deemos were his hands. They were an extension of his mad violence. It was said that few saw Ammon Mars and lived, but those who met his two generals often just *wished* they would have died.

The sight of Deemos dropped Handsome to his knees, but it was Fobos' boot that forced him lower. One Antony was red. One was black. One wore fur and the other armor.

They left men behind to take their fill of food and wine and women, and when they left, days later, they took with them carts and cattle, but no explanations. They had left the armories full and Handsome had been too afraid to ask why. He sent word to the Brotherhood, expounding the merits and amount of his artillery, emphasizing he asked only for a commission in the army. He wanted nothing more than to serve the Choir again, not from a supply line or church but from the battlefield.

For months now visions of the war had kept him going through the drudgery of his overseeing. He may have appeared attentive, barking orders to all his smiths, whipping the slow-handed and slow-witted alike as their quotas were missed, but his focus was never before him. It was out there, somewhere, at the territorial expansions, commanding the chosen across the battlefields, spurring Heaven's Army to victory. He pictured himself peeking out from the fine drapes of a palanquin being carried over the remnants of the Army of Earth, those stubbornly deaf to the Song littered in puddle and pieces — heathen bodies to fertilize the soil of new landscapes, souls feeding the engines of progress as the *Ashmedai Adat El* headed ever eastward. He would be the man who put whatever was left of the Land of Nod to the heel, the soldier that castrated N'Midgaard, the general to circumcise Mann Lands, the king to make the east sing.

His letter was intercepted so he sent another. It too was waylaid so he sent two more, both by birds this time. Still he heard nothing. And so he packed for inner Bab'lon. It would be a long trip, and his arthritis did not look forward to days of reins, but he now wanted the Brotherhood's response in person. He wanted a Lesser Prophet to look him in the eyes, and, truth be told, he wanted to avoid a return of Fobos and Deemos. Better to chose the Antony he spoke with. But he had barely left the surrounding plantations when the Army of Earth struck. He admired their arrogance, how they rode the main paths into town, how they settled in to open the armories for themselves.

Handsome immediately went about setting fire to the fields. The wilted crop went up easily, crisp leaves spreading the wind-whipped flames straight into the town from numerous directions, leaving only one path out, directly into the hands of the Army of Heaven. Fobos and Deemos had obviously been waiting in the surrounding hills, and as the day pulsed with the cherry light of the flaming land, before darkening under cannon fire and smoking field, they closed the trap and drove the enemy back into the town, back into trailers and buildings of exploding ammunition.

It was only a small contingent of the enemy, an unknown branch of the Army of Earth, but Handsome was impressed by their fervor. They fought to the very last burning man with the name of the Liege of Foes on their lips. And it was in the firestorm that Handsome first saw the dark figure. Here the leader of the Army of Earth stood above him, suddenly as the tithingman crawled through hot ash. He remembered it differently each time. Sometimes he remembered a blade at his throat, sometimes the barrel of a gun at his forehead, sometimes he saw a hammer poised to crush his skull. But the dream always ended with a shed exploding nearby, flaming shards of wood with cinders raining, and the Liege disappearing into the smoke.

Ash blew around mainstreet in tiny twisters, fed from breeze and heat from all directions, as the red and black doppelbrothers congratulated Handsome on his victory. He shouted above the crackle and collapse of nearby shops, the moans of scared cattle and scarred townspeople, and he asked for a commission in the army, avoiding the white eyes and smiles glaring down from painted faces. He was held over the fires, momentarily deaf from their laughter and the sizzle of all the cooking flesh through the town. They left his mouth full of questions, his ears filled with the snapping of loose ammunition and the cry of children searching through smoldering homes and corpses.

The plantation buildings eventually blackened to ash but it took a week for the fires to completely leave the surrounding hills for all directions. Only Handsome remained. The men, without family or livelihood, followed Fobos and Deemos' army, joining to avenge themselves against the Army of Earth. The women, widowed or abandoned, set out to adjacent territories, soon to become newives. Handsome scrounged through the char of the town for what felt like days, never sure of what he was looking for. He could not follow the men to the army to fight like some common peasant. He commanded peasants. He could not follow the widows to another town, to sit amongst the elderly and uninspired, not after whipping their kind in the fields his whole life. So he kept scrounging, for food, for clothing, as the fires moved on to leave only brilliant sunsets and a smoke that hung low over the plantations the rest of the day.

By the time the tithingman came, Handsome had lost track of his surroundings and the season. The air had cooled, and he was found under fur and frost, otherwise open to the elements in a blackened foundation at the center of town. Handsome had never met another tithingman, but the messenger was as hideous as expected. They did not exchange greetings, pleasantries, or even a long look, but the other tithingman left a message on hemp with the broken seal of the Brotherhood. Handsome had his commission.

But first he searched the nearby territories, sending word ahead of his new governorship, and it was not long before he was able to gather his family. His wife came back to him, but it was more difficult to search out his sons. They were spread out, fostered near and far, but he found a number to be satisfied with before heading to Megrim. They arrived before the winter hit and settled into the governor's mansion. It was furnished not to Handsome's liking but furnished just the same.

Before the snows came, Megrim was known for the red rock pushing up strikingly from all angles randomly around the canyon town. Handsome hired men to clean out what remained of the Avenger's tombs hidden beneath the sandstone monoliths leading into the mountains. There was not much that had not been looted over the century prior, but the humble crypt mummies of the Pride had left more than enough holy weapons, armor and amulets to fund what became a world of reconstruction for the old town. For generations Megrim was caught between the plains and the mountains, buffeted by the prairie winds, pushed into eroded gorge on one side and the falling rock of the canyon on the other. Summer sun beat down on Megrim's homes for half the year while hail and drifts pressed against it for the other half. The mining had died up a hundred years earlier, leaving only gambling and radioactive wells behind.

Handsome's new church, paid for with promises and passed baskets, gilded with the gold melted from cask and goblet, stood above the previous tallest building, its tower's open solar amplifying the canyon's unending song. The church's massive perches had yet to be used, but every member of the congregation had taken their turn at mass describing prior nights' dreams of how and when they would be. When the wind did not blow from and to the canyon, the perches bore massive icicles that had killed more than one man, but it had been a while since anyone remembered a silent night.

But shortly after the church had been built, Handsome found himself growing uneasy again. He could hear the Song under the breath of each passerby in the street, hummed by newives and carpenters as they worked, even on the whistle of breezes through the rocks and streams below, but it was not enough. There still existed those outside the Territories that had never heard the sweet notes, still those refusing to sing with heart as well as soul, and the Liege of Foes was all to blame. As long as the Army of Earth fought, as long as it took back land and heart, the Song was not being allowed to spread. And here the tithingman sat — under leaning rock and feet of drifted snow — while others fought for him. Farther than he could see, farther than he could imagine or ever imagine traveling, other men defended his beliefs, his faith.

He was at his most melancholy, withdrawn from duty and family, when he started to see the signs among Megrim's people. Here he noticed a new man settling into the town, without new or old connections to the Territory. There he spotted a woman neglecting her church duties, without any explanation or reason. Here he heard whispers end as he entered a shop. There he heard a distinct silence where there should have been Song. Constant rumors came daily to Megrim concerning the War of Heaven and Earth. It was all anyone talked about, and the more people talked about the war the more people spoke of the Liege of Foes. This warrior, this wizard, this general, this warlord, this king — so far away — had a power freely given to him by the people under Handsome's governorship.

Handsome went out to curb rumor, nailing a treatise on gossip to every door in Megrim, quelling it in every sermon during the week, but it was in individual interrogations where he became aware of many of the newcomers to the canyon. Under glowing brands he heard of secret pilgrims praying to green-eyed gods in human form. While twitching sharpened spoons he was made aware of northern knights hiding false angels under their tunics. In pulling nails he heard tales of berserkers running raids right from his Territory. The enemy was leading campaigns directly under his governorship's nose. His leniency had made him a fool. His mercy had cuckolded him. Handsome had grown complacent in his contentment. Family, the building of the church, his role of mentor to the masses, had distracted him. He had started to yearn for the war, but the war was here, in Megrim. It had found him. The Divine Choir had answered his prayers. Most tithingmen only appealed to Chem-Oshmelech for the Promise of Father, and Handsome had as well — answered when the Greater Prophet took him in — but he had prayed to others in the Chorus as well. Gob-Mammon-Gammon had had delivered the Promise of Wealth in family and governorship. Now, here, Slog-Sabaoth had given him Her Promise of Dream. He had prayed to be influencing the greater parts of the war, and now he could. For when tickling a known gossip with a favorite serrated instrument, Handsome heard a rumor even his greatest dreams hadn't imagined. The Liege of Foes was hiding out far from the frontlines. The Liege of Foes was directing the Army of Earth from Handsome's very territory. The war had come to Megrim.

The tithingman spared no expense in his spies. If a man was loyal and willing to sell out anyone in town he would be paid handsomely. Everyone in Megrim was suddenly on the payroll, and Handsome was inundated with stories of backroom handoffs and clandestine gatherings. Weeding through rumor and innuendo became a full-time job, and each day he resisted the almost overwhelming temptation to confront those hiding right in front of him, but he felt it would be more important to let them play their game while he dealt with interception and interpretation. As long as they thought they were safe he could undermine their efforts and watch the Army of Earth crumble from afar.

But he quickly realized that his approach would not do. He had men infiltrate the Resistance's meetings, passing to him supply routes that turned false. He had women infiltrate their beds, informing him of imaginary troop movements. He learned of tactics never used, strategy never materialized, yet still the Army of Earth marched on without reliable prediction. And then the insurrections began. Throughout the Territories, capitals were bombed, churches burned, and supply lines were cut. The attacks came from inside occupied lands, were highly organized, and all his intelligence suggested it was being directed from Megrim. He had failed to subvert the rebels' communication, so he would now take a more direct approach. He had actually hoped that it would come to such measures.

The secret meetings were bluffs. The intercepted letters were lies. The men's meetings in the Motley Cow, previously ignored by Handsome, had to be the key, and so his spies crowded near their table weekly. Not one meeting then went unreported to the tithingman. Not one word went unrecorded, yet still the Liege of Foe's plans went unhindered.

Handsome felt himself becoming a joke. He would have been surprised if the Brotherhood still opened his letters. By radio he started to hear the sniggering behind the responses. He suspected the Army of Heaven now even followed the opposite of his information, for it created better results. Those he informed even doubted his claims that the Liege of Foes was hiding in Megrim, citing his appearance hundreds of miles away on the battle lines.

He doubted his spies. He doubted his judgment in trusting them in the first place. Fewer people were visiting church each day. He could only rely on himself. And so he found himself planning for weeks for the night he would confront the men. He thought it appropriate that it should land on his favorite holiday.

Hours before they arrived he had prepared himself. Poisoned beer in his hand, face down at the table, he would just blend with the rest of the dregs of Megrim. He could be very patient if he had to, and he knew he would have to be. But hours into their game he could not help but become frustrated. His face ached against the bitter-smelling tale, his knuckles stung as he squeezed the handle of his mug. His back cramped at the position he had held all night, yet the men had barely veered their conversation from their insipid game and fairy tales. He had ignored their feeble whispers of rebellion, knowing they were just feints, instead trying to find some sort of code beneath their words. He knew they met to disseminate false plans among the town, but how were they coordinating the attacks? The conversation so far had been inane, without depth, and mostly centered around the game.

The game!

~

Handsome lurched, meaning to sit up, but the pain overwhelmed him immediately, and he instead did little more than shake. The pain mixed with confusion, and he surrendered to unconsciousness as he now remembered doing for many minutes at a time.

He woke seemingly minutes later, now recognizing the wall-hangings and the window letting scant moonlight through and turning it and everything in his bedroom a dull azure. Every breath burned his mouth. It felt as though it were stuffed full of cotton but clenched to the point of immobility, and it was sore deep down into his throat.

It was the game. He now knew it. The rebels spoke through the game, with the Liege of Foes coordinating both the front lines and local insurrections through cards and the rolling of the bones.

The cloaked figure looked down at Handsome now, eyes appearing even bluer in the faint light peeking into his hood. He was a trim, black shadow otherwise, merged with the night of the room. Handsome could not gather the strength to speak through the biting pain, and his throat hurt too much to turn his head, but he could see Wulf walk to the wash basin with a bloody dagger as long as his hand. Handsome had not the energy to keep his inner lids open, and so he saw everything through a cloudy haze. The blade held the only color now left in the room, and he was sad to see it washed away. His outer lids closed.

The tithingman woke later to see the dagger again red, but

darkening quickly, especially as a pale hand wiped it against the quilts of the bed. His throat pained him even more than before and he found his jaws painfully clenched, but it hurt even more to open them. And now there was a new pain, somewhere lower on his body. His legs were restless to an unbearable degree, but he knew the shock would send him back into unconsciousness if he moved them. And so he did not. But he passed out anyway.

It was still the dead of night when he woke again, but the moon had moved on from his window. Its light off the drifts of snow was the only thing allowing Wulf's vague shape to be made out. Handsome found his energy returned but could not get himself to move just yet. His stomach and thighs felt as though they burned from poison acid. He blinked the film from his eyes, watching the figure cloaked in fabric and night washing his hands in the only color of the room. The water, tainted and pink, dripped from thin fingers as he approached the bed to wipe them on the pillow. So near the movement, Handsome squeaked in pain, the sound hurting him even more. He saw one last glint of granite before Wulf turned toward the door.

Handsome's sight swam as he pushed, almost passing out before and after falling from the bed onto his side. There was instant stickiness around his gut and his cheeks warmed as he bled, but he pushed himself along the floorboards, his legs not responding. He could feel them by the time he reached the doorway, the pain drowned out by the beating of his heart. Wulf was out of his sight, but he could hear his footsteps down the stairway under the pounding of his pulse. Handsome strained his neck to look backward at the dark smear he had trailed from his room.

He woke at the railing looking out over the dining room, not remembering dragging himself down the hallway, but the bloody marks along floor and wall told him he had. His legs now pushed, drying and crusty, but he pulled up with his arms to get a better look at the first floor.

He could see the shadows bend toward Wulf as he moved past Handsome's drunken family. They were oblivious to his passing, concerned only with the meal they devoured greedily. Candles flickered between each bite of the meal as his wife and crazed sons inhaled sharply between each hectic forkful.

Wulf was gone, but Handsome breathed deeply, past congealed

blood, stitching, and pain to find the strength to call out to the grue-some dinner, but the gripping clench in his mouth and loins was too much. He slid down the railing and continued to fall in and out of uneasy consciousness, his frozen eyes never blinking, staring down at the imp's meal.

XIV

The Fool knows *he is wise.*
The Wise thinks *he is a fool.*

   —Excerpt from the Parable of Seven Farmers

Cry as he might, Wulf could not avoid stepping through the wet floor. The room was too small, and he was too distracted, and the sticky pool had spread some time in the night to cover almost the entire floor. He had barely stepped in it but he knew he would again before he left. And now his boots would leave a trail of it when he left the apartment.

He had not turned on the lights of Sir Skata's room. With the Sin Eater in Megrim he had been cautioned to stay in darkness, but he could see around the room. Yggr's Eye, replacing one of his own, had been implanted in his head over a decade ago as he slept beneath winter and Hollow, and it allowed him to see into shadows. There were times, however, he wished he had stayed blind all those years ago. This was one of those times.

"Still," Coyote squawked, "we're lucky it's cold in here." The bird flew to the chest of drawers and pecked at disheveled sheets of paper before examining the red scrawl on the wall. His talons clenching and unclenching at the edge as he leaned for a better look. "But I suggest you open a window. It's only a matter of time. Especially if you plan on spending any longer."

"I would expect you to enjoy the smell," Wulf mumbled.

Sir Skata had lived simply, and there was only one chair for Wulf to stand on. It was poorly made and poorly cared for, but he was able to balance on it while cutting the wire around the knight's neck, at the same time holding the man with his other arm to bring him gently down and eventually over to the bed. He had to augment his strength, telekinetically pulling the body to him, for Skata was in full knightly regalia, plate mail only gleaming by its crimson accents matching the floor. The silver armor should have stood out more in the night, especially as the window caught the day's first glimpse of morning, but it was as colorless as Skata's face.

Here was another friend Wulf would not have time to bury. *Funerals are not the right of the rebellious.* Where had he heard that? He reached down to the unfamiliar heaviness hanging at his hip, to the cool iron strapped to his thigh. The war hammer had been a gift from Flagon. Unlike most hammers from the North it was small — only as long as Wulf's forearm — but still a heavier and cruder weapon than he was used to. It was dark and finely made, carved with the likeness of black ash leaves. Flagon had never missed an opportunity to remind him of their shared homeland.

He spread Skata to his full length on the bed. The dead man's sword was missing, but Wulf untied and rested his hands on his chest as though he held it, crossed together over recent scratches marring the angelic emblem. Had Handsome dressed him *after* the knight had died?

"Unlikely," Coyote said. "Actually quite impossible. He was probably armored at gunpoint, no doubt satisfied to meet his end in full stately appearance."

"He wouldn't have gone without a fight," Wulf said quietly.

"He would," the raven countered, "when thinking of the coming months full of torment."

"And out of the earth the abysmal locusts came," Wulf recited, "and they were given power like that of Abaadoon's seventh kiss. They were not allowed to kill but only to torture for seven full moons."

"Such a good boy. You've been reading your *Fallo Terminus*."

No, Wulf thought, *but Sol constantly quotes from it. 'And those bitten will seek death but will not find it.' But Skata found it. He's at peace now.*

"Handsome Full of Mercy is rightly named," Coyote chuckled.

"Your wit is of no help."

"You want help? Here's my advice…"

"No."

"Get out of Megrim, you fool!"

"I'm working on it."

"No, no you're not! You're basking in sentimentality, wallowing in melancholy! Far be it from me to criticize what works so well for you, but you should have left town at the first hint that tithingman was on to you. How many more have to die?"

Wulf closed his eyes against the squawking. The raven's voice hurt enough normally, but it now aggravated the headache he constantly had. "Where do you suggest I go this time?"

"Find the Army."

"What?" He suddenly had to think back to remember if Coyote had ever surprised him before.

"Well, you're now becoming too recognizable to stay in the Territories, if that was ever even an intelligent option, and after tonight your price will be too high for any headhunter, Horde agent, or otherwise, to resist following you to Shiloh and back, so, ironically, hiding on the battlefield is the safest place for you."

The bird's logic was impeccable, but Wulf knew he was being lied to. That much was always obvious. But why? What was the real reason he should join up? He had spent the majority of the last few years raising rebellion from inside Horde territories, along with feeding information out to the Army of Earth, but he was no soldier.

He dropped the knife and it stuck without a sound into the floor, surrounded by the pool that had spread from Skata's severed tendons. He knew he had probably ruined the blade by using it to cut wire, but it appeared to have served its purpose twice this night.

Coyote hopped from drawer to windowsill, appearing featureless in the sunrise, and Wulf ignored his presence to look around the rest of the apartment. Everything had been searched and thrown carelessly around and surely looted, but he was not worried. The only evidence of sedition Skata would have kept hidden in the room he had always worn. Even in the guise of the most destitute beggar he would never leave Blind Libra completely behind. Wulf picked the pieces of the silver angel from the congealed muck, leaving numerous broken chain links behind.

He could suddenly picture it as though it was happening right in front of him. He could smell the sweat of terror from both individuals, but could feel the tension of inevitability from only one. He strained to hear Handsome's voice, expecting the inquisition to concern himself, but he could only make out one phrase, two words to mirror the dark writing on the wall and mirror of the apartment.

Low Coda

And then, no matter how tightly he shut his eyes he still had to watch as Handsome tightened the wire, leaving just enough slack to keep the knight's toes scrambling for purchase. Wulf covered his ears against the phantom sound, looking to the low rafters where one end of the wire still hung, but he could still see the tithingman cut through each Achilles tendon with the knife before the vision ended. The images were gone, but Wulf could still imagine Skata's struggle. He could have pushed against the floor with his toes to relieve the tightness around his neck, but the pressure would bleed him out.

Coyote fluttered down to the floor, scratching near, but keeping his distance from, the mess. "Still awfully fresh, but dry. He wouldn't have had much time after the Motley Cow. Must have followed Skata straight here. Must have worked fast to be back to his mansion by the time you..."

"What is this... Low Coda?" Wulf wondered. His visions, like his telekinesis, did not aggravate his headaches like his telepathy did, but the sights of the room's past still left him shaken.

"The Librans have six laws for themselves," the raven said. He turned awkwardly around blood and paper before fluttering up to Wulf's shoulder, clenching and unclenching his claws into the cloak. "Observe the Highlord's teachings, defend the Temple... the usual broad moral directives. Other more specific rules were added. 'Judge the witch without mercy.' That sort of thing. Still, six codas set in stone long before the Orders broke apart into separate sects. Never heard of a Low Coda though."

"Neither had Skata." He took one last look at the knight, wishing he could say he saw peace on his face.

Wulf closed the door, making sure it clasped tightly, wishing he could have closed it forever. Every step on the stairway creaked as he descended, and he wondered if Skata had heard the governor coming. Had he fought? Did the new yet crippling abysmal arthritis handicap him or had he surrendered, satisfied in the knowledge of all the good he had done here, that no matter what was done to him he had still set in motion plans that would eventually lead to the governor's downfall? That was probably not the case. Sol and Flagon had been the optimistic ones, believing they were making a difference in the hearts of the people, affecting even the warfront. Skata and Wulf, however, had always been much more doubtful of the effects of the resistance.

The morning was crisp outside, and Wulf pulled his cloak tighter as he walked the streets, Coyote tucking his beak inside a wing and muffling his voice.

"Or perhaps you should head south, deep south to Pharaoh's land. Anyone would be mad to follow." His black eyes peeked out of his feathers. Wulf could not usually tell what the raven looked at, but it was obvious he watched the crowd grow in the hazy sunrise.

The sun could give little color this morning, filtered as it was through the mist, portraying the townspeople in a gray pallor matching their surroundings. The red rock of Megrim had already been forgotten. It had been frosted for years now, never melting in the shadow of the leaning hills. It was impossible not to notice the stillness the floating haze had inspired. For the first time in many weeks there was no wind whistling out of the canyon overlooking Megrim, no bellowing hum from the crevasse splitting the town.

"And none of that goddamn singing," Coyote grumbled before stretching and taking flight. The raven was starkly opaque in the pale mist and it was long before Wulf lost sight of him, but he noticed a distinct eastward direction, away from canyon and hill and mountain, toward the great prairie.

The sun did its best but the fog burned slowly, pale glow illuminating the steep drop from the houses into icy darkness. Wulf remembered when he first came to Megrim. The people were clothed in every shade of a sunset to match the rock jutting up around the canyon. But now, even clad in leather and a cloak of night, he was the one most brilliantly colored. Now the crowd was tough to differentiate from the drifts pressing against their homes, from the smoky clouds choking the morning.

But still the morning fought, for now only creating more of the haze around the crowd Wulf entered. No one talked except for one man near the sloping edge of the town. He was a tall man but appeared short compared to the crowd rising along the hill and leading down to the deep ravine. Even after countless seasons of a hidden sky, the man's skin was red and wrinkled from a lifetime on the prairie, no doubt as a cowboy turned to Megrim by impassable plains. His voice was high and phlegm-filled.

"…we whine and cry for answers, we lament the money spent on unused perch and quiet roost. I've heard say that the only song sung is that of the street, of the faithful in their bed, that it isn't answered. Is that true? Don't none of you hear it?"

There was no sound of the crowd. Megrim remained silent. Wulf imagined he could only hear a slight hiss as the mists melted into more mists.

"Well, I hear…" The man cleared his throat loudly and long. Finally there was a sound from the town as the gurgle echoed down into, and back out from, the darkness. "I hear the Song every day. It comes to me from the wind, from the canyon." He gestured to the edge of town. "From the rock, from the ravine." He swung his arm over the blackness the morning had yet to reveal. He then pointed to a suddenly sheepish young woman in the audience. "And if you can't hear it, and you, and you," he continued, picking out others looking away, "and you, then you ain't listening. The golden rookery is empty and the perches will stay icy and cold until we'll all listen, but you can only hear with unclouded ears, and you can only let the Song in with open ears and open hearts."

A quick rumble of thunder broke the sky's silence. It was physical, pressing against the crowd, after crackles bouncing through the ravine. Those that cringed laughed quietly, awkwardly, looking to those around them.

"See! You're answered!" The plains-worn man did not hold his laughter back. "Can't you hear it? Are you listening now?"

Some in the crowd started to respond, whether by nodded head or quiet assurances. Wulf thought the thunder odd in the brightly growing sunrise but pictured the hidden sky behind them becoming darker with clouds bloated like cancerous organs caught up in the bones of the mountains the canyon opened into.

"There's been too much distraction in Megrim." The man's voice was clearer now, not obstructed by phlegm or mist. He reached down to pull a figure to wobbly feet beside him. Wulf could barely see him over the crowd, and he was decorated, but he still recognized him. They had apparently shaved their captive's head and chin, tarring the hair to a face painted to look like a cat with green eyes, black nose and long whiskers drawn in. When the red, wrinkled man held him up, it was by his own beaded strings binding his hands. Sol Ascension was either exhausted or drugged and appeared in no shape to fight back. The man pulled him even closer to the sloping edge where they were both bathed by thin slivers of morning that had finally found their way through the haze.

"This is why you can't hear. It's men like this puts cotton in your ears and gums up your heart. It's an obstruction of spirit, a constipated soul you suffer from, and here's the blockage. Men like this bring words from outside the Territories, from others who think they know more than you. It's distraction, a devil's temptation sent from pointy-eared demons, a whiskered whore with fangs just waiting to sink into the flesh of your righteousness. She shits in the sand of Megrim and buries it thinking we won't notice it until it's too late, until the Divine Ballet passes us over."

"Yes, yes, well said, my good man, well said."

Wulf did not have to turn to the parting of the crowd to know the tall man striding through it. He knew the voice. Even if it had not been for rumor, he had been expecting the Sin Eater to come to Megrim. Wherever insurrection occurred, whenever the tithingmen failed to control their state, the Brotherhood sent the Sin Eater. And whenever the Sin Eater appeared, Wulf's men disappeared. Whispers grew and disappeared around him.

"Where is my bread? Where is my beer?" the Sin Eater asked.

"Master... Slayd?" the red, wrinkled man stammered. "We weren't aware of your arrival, my lord..."

"Yes, yes, well, I forgive your inhospitality." Melchyor Slayd finished his walk through the crowd as the man kneeled at his approach. "But not your smell." He placed a slender boot on the man's bent shoulder, holding it there for a quiet second before kicking him out into the expanse of the ravine. Gasps from the crowd echoed the shuffling before the silence down in the rocky blackness. "Living on the edge of civilization is no excuse for poor hygiene, people. Now, as for this poor wretch here." Sol's robe tore in the Sin Eater's grasp. "What are his violations? Specifically? Buggery? Vegetarianism? Polyester? Did the accused plant differing crops in the same field? Speak up!"

The crowd grew tighter as the people grew louder, and Wulf found it difficult to move between them. He could now barely see the painted Sol.

"He covets our peace!"

"He lied to me!"

Slayd tore the emerald sliver from Sol's bindings to toss it into darkness. The remaining beads from the strings fell about without sound.

"He cursed the Choir's name!"

"He held cats above men!"

"Feed him to the chasm!"

"Yes, yes, it sounds like he has been a truly bad man indeed. But no, he will not be tossed into the gap like some common imbecile. I'm afraid the company would be too cruel, too unusual, even for him. Are we not civilized men?" Slayd stood Sol on his own, but the man wavered, his body rocking as his eyes followed the Sin Eater's hand. It danced slowly in front of his face, serpentine and rhythmically. His pupils dilated as Slayd's milky eyes constricted.

"Be peaceful," Wulf thought outward to Sol, and almost immediately he found himself on the ground, constricted by the tightening crowd. The pain pressed against his brain, pain he had opened himself up to with even the slightest attempt at telepathy. He had felt a connection — something familiar — with something, someone, far out across the land, but the mental feedback had incapacitated him. For worried seconds he had forgotten where he was, until the men around him lifted him back to his feet so he could enjoy the scene with them.

On the ridge Sol continued to follow Slayd's slender hand as though charmed, until a finger and thumb moved faster than anyone could see, striking and plucking an eyeball effortlessly from his head. Sol's mouth gaped with a silent scream, his hands quaking and slowly moving to his face. The open socket only began to stream when he took a step backward, but his robe was quickly drenched.

Slayd held the eyeball between two long nails, seemingly admiring its cleanliness before holding it out to one of the thickening strands of sunrise splitting the mist. The eyeball glowed a dirty dun in the light before intensifying and directing a thin stream across Sol's torso. The light blinded all but Wulf, Yggr's Eye seeing through the brilliance.

When the crowd could see again they watched as Sol's body, still standing, threatened to slide apart. It burned instead from the line cutting diagonally through his torso, upward and downward, charring his face and legs unrecognizably. Black flakes revealed blooming embers beneath before catching a nonexistent breeze into the thinning mist.

"Now," the Sin Eater said to the assembled people. "Bring me my bread and beer, and let us discuss your grievances, for I sense that Megrim is far from purged of its offenders."

~

Wulf ran from the side of Megrim known for its stone bridge. It had been tended to less than others, and the snow was thicker in the streets than in other, busier ends of town. The bridge was a great accomplishment, and it had once allowed people, carts, and even trucks to cross the ravine instead of traveling around the hills and rocks separating them from the plains. But the harsh winters had covered it in drifts and ice until the people had given up on maintaining it. Even the side of town it connected had been poorly tended to, and Wulf wanted a better place to make his last stand.

The Sin Eater followed — Wulf was certain. He could not expand his senses outward without the fear of the pain overwhelming him, but he could still feel him out there. His skin crawled. His breathing quickened despite the *SHE'* calming exercises. The Sin Eater followed.

The morning's fog had lifted just in time for the sun to be smothered by the leaden clouds that had been caught up in the mountains. It was warmer than it had been for a season, with thin trails of melt streaming through the streets between apartment and shop and man-high drifts, but he wondered what those ominous clouds were carrying. They had hung over Megrim most of the day without snow or hail or rain. What were they waiting for? Without the sun their pall blended with the darkness cast by the canyon to spread over most of the town. It was night in the middle of day.

He saw movement from between two shops and stepped into an alley of his own. The buildings cast weird, inconsistent shadows. They stretched in all directions, with only the largest touching each other. He listened for sound from the alley, anything to give the Sin Eater away, but could only hear the trickle of water that would soon ice the streets under whatever the clouds would cover them with. Few people walked the shops. It was a day of penance, so most of the town had gone home after mass to avoid the temptations of the outdoors, but there were enough stragglers so that when Wulf made a stand it would be seen.

He made his way behind the Motley Cow, telekinetically lightening his steps over the deep snow. He made no sound and left only the slightest tracks behind on the hardened gray mounds reaching from wall to wall and door to door. The Motley Cow would not be open this early in the day, yet there were footsteps near. Perhaps from the roof? The saloon had a flat top and had to be cleaned sometimes daily, but it appeared clear today. Wulf moved on, remembering all the nights they had met at the Motley Cow. It had been his idea to only meet in public. Strangers to the town would already be met with suspicion, so they had avoided clandestine meetings. The saloon and the game had served them well, but he had pushed his luck. They should have left a month ago or even earlier. Now it was all over. Cells they had built throughout the Territories would be on their own now. They would learn it soon enough through rumor or the silence their communications would prompt.

A dog barked in the main street but, peeking around corner and shadow, Wulf couldn't tell at what. Whatever it watched it did so out of the corner of its eyes until its head hung low. It slunk away with tail between its legs in the direction Wulf headed.

Megrim was small, and it was not long before he found himself on the edge of town leading into the canyon. The massive crevice breaking into the foothills was not accessible from this side of the ravine, but it still left its impression on the town. Wind either whipped out or inward, either way blowing through Megrim. In the past, the town had erected rope bridges over the chasm near where he now hid. The melting snow may have revealed the bridges' remnants if not for the darkening sky. Before the seasons worsened he could see the tattered and torn hanging webs from his apartment window. He looked up to the window now. It was as empty as most in Megrim today. He had grown accustomed to the apartment, as he had the Motley Cow, his friends and the town itself. The familiarity had been a weakness. How could something so obvious have eluded him mere days ago?

Rock or ice dislodged itself loudly from somewhere deep down in the ravine, and Wulf moved on, heading back into the walls of snow between the streets. He had thought his apartment would have made an appropriate place to stand his ground, but now, nearby, the idea had lost its charm. There would have been no one to tell the tale.

Back near the shops he began to see more people running errands beneath the wicked-looking icicles that had begun to grow in the day. People all spoke lowly, but he could make out the talk of the Sin Eater on their lips, as they all hesitantly looked to the alleys and the sky. The clouds had not moved, and they still refused to do anything. A window shuttered loudly near Wulf, and he moved deeper into side roads, amongst even nastier icicles. They had stopped dripping, and he noticed that the sound of trickling of the water had grown fainter. He could, however, hear the far-out call of a raven, but it was not a familiar voice.

Deep into the dusky back roads he decided that the alleys would not be where he would confront the Sin Eater. He had to assume the shadows would not just be his ally. The hard snow and ice would impede him while doing nothing to slow down a spell caster. And Wulf's tenure in Megrim would end without anyone seeing it.

The main streets were not much better. There would be more witnesses, but the roads had become icy. If he was going to make a stand out in the open he might as well do it out in the air, wide open to the town he had only now realized he had begun to call home.

And so he found himself back at the bridge. It spanned the chasm and made it possible for the town to expand. What some called Little Megrim looked puny and underdeveloped on the other side. Wulf was not sure why the sister town had never caught on. Perhaps because it looked so vulnerable separated from its progenitor, without a slope to huddle against. Perhaps because it looked ready to be swallowed by the canyon faces without the ravine to protect it. He considered just fleeing, not for the first time.

There were men working on clearing the bridge, taking advantage of the warmer weather and no doubt hoping to lighten the bridges load before the clouds decided enough was enough before covering it again. Wulf could have just continued on, through Little Megrim and around the hills into the plains. He could find another territory to hide in, another governor to torment, make more friends before leading them to their deaths. Is that what he wanted to do? Start all over? Continue the cycle while the war raged no closer to an end?

No. The Sin Eater would follow him across the land, just as he had to the bridge. He would just be prolonging the inevitable.

"How dramatic," Slayd said from behind him, "how painfully sincere, maudlin in its own way. This is where you've chosen to fall? To each his own, I suppose."

Wulf was to the middle of the bridge by the time he turned to face the Sin Eater. The men, who had all moved to the cliff edges to join the gathering audience, had cleared away most of the snow, even breaking through a foundation of ice to the stone below. There was solid purchase here, Wulf realized, grinding his boots. He thought of gods he had cursed long ago.

Father calls from his Hall
See my brothers beckon
All knowing I cannot be bothered
For today there will be reckoning

That was all he could remember. He knew there was some mention of frigid women and warm ghosts that he was forgetting.

His pale hand emerged from his cloak holding the hammer he

had named *GloryRend*. Was this when he was supposed to praise Tor? Did he pray for holy rage to guide his hand, lust to blind his heart and eyes? Or was this when he called out Tyr's name, asking for a good death, covered in his enemy's guts as well as his own? No, it would only be appropriate to pray to Yggr's other bastard, Loki, for the deceit needed today, to cloud the people's minds in the absence of the disappearing fog, to accentuate the shadows of the clouds that were now, he noticed, finally starting to move. The day's darkness swirled above, yet still refused to bring rain or sleet or snow. A wind blew from the canyon down into and over the ravine, bringing a chill against Wulf's cloak the growing audience could not feel at both edges of the bridge.

But no, Wulf would deny his fathers' gods of any pandering. Heaven would not recognize his voice. It would only be his own strength behind his hammer.

Slayd neared and Wulf could now see just how cloudy his eyes had become, how his skin flaked and nostrils flared.

"I've put this off as long as I could," the Sin Eater said.

Wulf lunged, raising *GloryRend* and bringing it down toward Slayd's bald head in the same motion. He felt so slow with a hammer, so predictable with anything other than a blade he could hide beneath his cloak.

Slayd caught the flat of the hammer in an open hand, not even flinching. Wulf was, in turn, caught by the backhand that immediately followed, finding himself foot over head, landing awkwardly on the bridge's low, solid guard and scrambling for hold at its edge. Slayd was immediately over him.

The Sin Eater lifted him by the mantle, holding him out over open air before tossing him back onto the bridge. "No, this will not do. Too easy. Too obvious."

Wulf buffered his head with a telekinetic skin to keep it from cracking on the opposite guard. He knew that underestimating Slayd's strength had been the death of many, yet he was still unprepared. The Sin Eater was tall and thin, known for his paralyzing illusions and mastery of forgotten magiks — specializing in none but deadly in all — so it was easy to forget his serpentine strength and dexterity. Depending on whom one asked, he was either more or less than human.

Wulf gathered himself to stand while reaching out for the hammer past the magus. It skittered along the bridge as he pulled it toward him but, without looking, Slayd stopped it with his slender boot. Here were the unnatural senses again, the strength belying his appearance.

"Nicely made. But an odd time to be embracing your heritage, don't you think?"

Wulf gave one more pull with his mind, dislodging *GloryRend* as it flew back to his hand. He was already in the air, leaping at the unbalanced Sin Eater and this time putting all his strength into the hammer, while pushing against the weapon telekinetically, adding his mind's force to his arms.

Again Slayd caught the hammer's head in one hand, but this time he cringed, his jaw clicking shut loudly. The force of *GloryRend* visibly rippled through his quivering fingers into his splintering hand, down through a breaking forearm and up to an exploding shoulder. But still he kept the hammer from his face, wine blood trickling between clenched teeth. He leaned in close to Wulf's ear and whispered a word in an unfamiliar guttural language and voice.

The minds of Megrim were immediately open to Wulf, with myriad voices crowding and arguing, lamenting and exulting, pondering and quieting, all of them fighting to be the loudest in his head, and the noise was deafening and he could feel the stone of the bridge and the pain against the back of his head but he felt as though he was falling, splashing down into a torrent of rambling with floodwaters of scattered internal dialogue, and he sank into the depths of flowing thoughts unanchored, buffeted by unending whims and whines of the people, unable to right himself in the directionless darkness until, in his end over end swirling, he saw a pinprick of light far throughout the battering currents that grew as he struggled toward it, the familiar glow opening as he neared, enveloping him until he recognized it as the far-off mind that invaded him as he invaded it every time he tried to open his or another's mind, and he recognized it as it recognized him but the loop it created through time and space through a surge of exponential pain built until he broke the link — all the links — forgetting the connection and slamming the hundreds of doors that Slayd had violently swung open with some arcane word in some perverted voice.

The Sin Eater, opposite arm hanging lifelessly, picked him again from the bridge to hold him closely. Wulf had to focus to see through the crushing pain in his skull. Were the spinning bridge and hundreds of spectators part of Slayd's illusions? Were the fuzzy snowflakes thickening around him lighting from the thundering sky or just speckles from his inconstant vision. Yggr's Eye cried blood. He was certain of that much. He could feel its warmth and the coolness of a cold-blooded finger wiping the tear away before Slayd tasted it. He spit the mixture from his bit lip, from his split tongue, behind him.

"This is it, my friend. Be honored in my surprise that it brings me such sadness. If a superior being such as I can be said to have a heart, consider it to be breaking. Consider it your crowning achievement among all you've accomplished in this pit-toilet of a town."

Wulf found it difficult to take his concentration from the hand that held him. A couple of fingers had lost their nails, with darkly curving claws replacing them. There was a second's hesitation as Slayd followed his gaze, and Wulf took the chance to slam his head forward into the magus' face. Both men fell away from each other, with Wulf's forehead instantly bruising under a split brow and Slayd spitting loosened teeth to join the rest of the gore on the bridge. With his only responsive hand he frantically wrote in the blood, finger and claw marking glyphs in snake-like scrawl.

Wulf steadied himself on the guard of the bridge. The shadows in the ravine moved with the clouds above, parting enough so that he could see the dusty snow below, separated as it was by both light and dark rock. His hood was crooked, obscuring part of his wavering vision, and he pulled it down to look up to both ends of the bridge. Were these the people he had convinced himself he fought for? They made no move to help him. How would they tell his story?

The red waste from his eye was smeared, and he wiped to smear it more as he stepped to the retreating Sin Eater. The runes Wulf staggered over began to smolder under his boots, and his chest clenched, his left arm tingled, his jaw and neck tightening. The glyphs also appeared and burned in the air around him closely like a shrinking and flaming ribbon, but he guessed he was the only one that could see them.

Legs weakening, he struck out at Slayd, low kicks striking against ankles that felt like steel, before he kneeled to push with both palm and mind. Slayd fell back but dug in with boot and claw. "I recognize *SHE'* training," the magus said, "I've considered hiring them myself from time to time. Deadly and uncompromisingly effective, but you'll find that I have unconventional pressure points."

And that was the last of Wulf's energy. His limbs could no longer support him, and he crumpled. Only deep breaths from the very bottom of his lungs kept him conscious, and they only increased the tightening of his chest, the scattered pattern of his heartbeat in his ears.

"You'll find I am not so easily dismissed." Slayd once again lifted him, this last time above his head. "So, is this how and when you choose to die?" The twin barrels of a sawed-off shotgun emerged from Wulf's cloak, as if to answer. They touched the Sin Eater's cheek before the dull click of the empty chambers sounded. "So be it!"

The Sin Eater brought Wulf's back down across a bent knee, and the crowds moaned and rocked as they shared the man's pain. It swept over them for only a second before it was abruptly cut off, yet they could not forget the brittle sound of the man's back breaking.

"Your imagination is lacking," Slayd said to the unmoving mass beneath the crumpled cloak. "Let me remedy this." He untied leather to expose himself to audience and element and relieved a full bladder. "No need to thank me." After tying up he took a palm-sized book from his robe and began to chant under his breath. The words were cyclical but repeated in a chorus of similar languages capitalizing on the hiss of Slayd's split tongue. He kept up the chant under the growing thunder echoing through sky and canyon and ravine, even after tearing a tiny page from the book with his crippled arm. The scrap seemed to disappear among twisted fingers before reappearing and lighting into a tiny flame barely visible in the emerging breeze. Despite the wind, the flickering paper dropped straight down to spark the soaked cloak. The body was instantly engulfed in an eldritch flame that cast no shadow.

The fire burned for the rest of the cloudy day, never growing nor shrinking until the Sin Eater left the bridge for his bread and beer.

XV

This man walks a land of his own making, never sure if he is looking from or at his own face, where he begins, where he ends. But after all this time, all these lives, is this man greater or lesser than he was? What is his name? What is in a name? That which he calls himself, by any other name, would still be as broken. The only thing he knows for sure is that he sees himself an Heir of Aesar and all that Aesar wrought.

—RackBreak Antony the Greater

The rattler had found the shadow of the well. The snake was perturbed but slow, and young Harlowe could not help but wonder where it had come from. His family's small house stood alone out on a prairie smoothed by wind, beat by sun, and roughened by twister. Trees had died and creeks had dried over the generations. Now the house provided the only shade for miles. The nearest shadows hid miles away at the rock housing his family's boneyard. So, where had the rattler come from, Harlowe wondered as he poked it with a knotty board. Did it travel in the cool of the night, cold blood slowing its slither through weedy dunes, or had it sizzled through the heat of day, cooking into a nice meal for the red-tails failing to find cactus perches? Or, Harlowe shivered from the cool air leaking from the bricks over the well, had it crawled out from beneath the house? Here was another reason to avoid the cellar. Even had it not been for the voice he heard from beneath floorboards at dusk and dawn, the boy kept from the cellar for its brittle black widow babies. What did they eat in those depths? What sustained them in the absolute darkness? Did they eat the snakes or did the snakes eat them? Was his mother not scared to go down there? Every time she went to fetch preserves or lard he expected inevitable screams before silence. But she always returned to him.

He pressed the snake against the well brick with the board, but it refused to look at him. Its rattle shook lethargically, silently. Maybe it was sick.

"You like to poke at the fanged, boy?" the voice from the well asked. It was the same voice from the cellar, but this was the first time he remembered it speaking to him during the day. The well had dried up suddenly sometime earlier in the summer, and they had lost most of their pigs and all of their goats before Harlowe's father had found a priest to divin them a new spot to dig for water. This one still exuded the cool air of a well though, or perhaps a grave. "Come down here an'

I'll give ya somethin' to poke."

"Harlowe!" His mother was on him before he had a chance to run, and she pulled him back to the house by his ear. "Ah told ya to stay away from there, little man!" They passed the clothing line she had been hanging his father's shirts on. Harlowe's little sister peeked out at him from the basket of dry jeans. Before her giggles disappeared beneath the flap of a wet, fluttering sheet, he saw how sunburned her cheeks had become under the meager shade of her little cap.

She dragged him into the house and dropped him at the side of his father. She was the only thing that smelled like flowers this far out in the wastes. "Ya need to watch 'im while I'm doin' the clothes," she said. Harlowe's father faced away from them in his chair. The large man was Tumbledown's sheriff, but he had been spending less and less time in the town lately and more time in the chair, more time moving the antenna on his radio. The crackle was quiet, and each day Harlowe found him leaning even more closely. "Can ya jus' watch 'im for two minutes while I finish? An' keep 'im away from that old well. I told ya to board it over. An' the snakes're back." She left the creaking wood of the floor behind but Harlowe could still hear her as she resumed hanging clothes. Her voice had started to match the wind in a slow but long whistle.

"Pa?" Harlowe asked, "What you always doin'?"

His father bent the radio's antenna before returning it to its original position. If there was a difference in the static, Harlowe could not tell. He could not see his father's face, but he could imagine the hanging frown and dark squint. He could not remember anything else. "Go practice yer guns, boy."

The whistle from outside grew as the wind did. Harlowe looked down at the pale skin on the tips of his fingers. The blisters had burst almost immediately after he had burned himself on his *Cody* the day before. He was told to practice his gun every day, but he only did it when his father was home — which was now more often than not. It was his least favorite part of each day.

The house shook. Harlowe's mother screamed, matching the siren of the train. It was only a blur of shadow and iron past the doorway.

Harlowe's legs shook so violently he could only use his arms to crawl to his father's chair. He quickly gave up on using it to stand. The dust that had clouded into the room stuck to his sudden tears. When the final car had passed and the train's scream had lessoned to the point Harlowe could hear his mother's cries, she appeared in the doorway, soot and hair plastered to her face. "It took her!" she screamed. "It took her!"

Harlowe was finally able to pull himself up the chair far enough to tug on his father's sleeve. The big man finally turned and leaned over his boy. His gritted teeth were ties and rails. Shadows spewed and twisted upward from his glowing nostrils. His voice was hidden in a steaming trumpet that threatened to burst Harlowe's head.

"IT'S THE *LOCO*, BOY! IT'LL STEAL EVER'ONE YA LOVE!"

~

Except that was not how it had happened. Had it? *That damned ghost train is running wild through my mind, eatin' up memories, shittin' out others in their place.* It had already trampled over all the other memories he had of his sister. Although, Harlowe was starting to wonder if he had ever even had a sister. But what was the purpose? What did it want with him? Why would it not just leave him alone? Since being ambushed by the Horde's bounty hunters he had sat in this cell for... how long? Months? All the while the *Loco*'s horn screamed through his head. But now it started to subside. Ivy had found him. The whistle lessoned greatly in her presence, and as she yanked the vines from his veins he realized that he could never leave her side again or there may not be any Harlowe left to appreciate what she did for him.

~

They had found her near what Antony had referred to as the Nursery. She had been unconscious. Perhaps from smoke inhalation, perhaps from the trauma of birth or the shock of the cool air when all she had known before then was the warmth of a plasmic cocoomb. They took her from smoldering ground where she lay stretched — as though crawling from the scene had been her only act, her first act, some sort of inherent defense mechanism or intuitive act of self-preservation. Was it programmed—a biological failsafe inbred by the Nursery's creators to protect their merchandise. It would be bad business to distribute product such as theirs without it. Those that had found her said that she appeared to know nothing else, but quickly picked up their speech and habits, within days, to an eerie degree that had unsettled but endeared them to her just as quickly.

Whatever the reason she crawled away from the warmth into the chill of the world, she had collapsed in the patch of evergreen that had given her a name. She had not appeared to remember the fire, seemingly did not remember crawling from the wreckage, barely remembered traveling out of the Nursery's forests with her new companions. Only at the Tower of Ziggurat, watching blood soak into the pink — a time she acknowledged as her true birth—had she felt suddenly alive and self-aware. But it was only a birth. One of many.

Ivy never dreamed, but at times certain situations would remind her of scenes from those vague and early days that she never even knew she had forgotten. The smell of gunshot would take her back to Kaldera's crusted, natural chimneys spewing sulfur, toning like Hell's organ, engorging by inches over centuries. The song of certain birds reminded her of the walk through those woodlands into prairies where lighter than air finches would rest on the thinnest of grasses that grew up to her waist. The gaping mouths of the people she met reminded her daily of the people they would encounter on their travels through the Kalderan wildlands. Mew had preached before their dull eyes and they would look at her like so many did now Ivy. And those of the Horde she now crossed paths with brought back memories of the creature they had traveled with, through oil field and mountain and into Bab'lon and up its tower.

"Why were those people trying to kill you," she now remembered asking Sybly. They were days out of Borhol, in a field mostly shrunken by wind, in a patch of wilted peach flowers that still drew her notice. The petals of the stem she plucked were tough but spongy under her caress. She was wondering how they had survived while those around them had fallen and browned, when a thorn pricked and drew blood from her finger. The pinch of pain angered her. Here she had admired the flower, and it had returned the gesture with this unfamiliar, uncomfortable sensation.

Most of her companions had moved on, striving for a tree line at the base of yet another batch of mountains for shelter from the elements, but Sybly had matched her pace. Ivy assumed that she had not heard her under the ever-present whistle of the wind, so she asked again. But the woman answered before she could finish.

"They were scared of my freedom, jealous of a happiness they deny themselves, afraid it would spread to their children. And they don't want to hate their children. They were an unimaginative people, and so fear is their only legacy. And if their children didn't pass that fear of freedom along it would be as though they had never existed. Can you imagine how frightful it would be to have never existed?"

"No," Ivy had said, squeezing the tip of her finger, watching the bubble of blood grow.

"You will."

Ivy could hear that fear in the tremor of the voice behind her now as it tried to echo in the claustrophobic vastness of the metal city of Brig. She was already bored with the whisper's lack of imagination. The tithingman's words were easily lost under the rustle of the coffin blossom as she pulled their vines from Harlowe's veins, the rattle of chains she could not determine an origin of. The flowers' thorns tore the pistoleer's clothing from where they had grown through. The chains started and ended from deep within and wrapped him like the vines. Ivy pulled him free, but still some chains hung from his arms. He was ill-prepared in the frozen walls of his cell, but Ivy noticed that he did not shiver. Nor did his breath hang in the air like hers. But he was responding. After she had plucked the flowers from his twisted hands he had begun to help her pull the tendrils grown over his legs.

"…wouldn't respond. We sent doves, swallows… none came back. A crow returned, but the message was unread. Word is you conscripted the powder monkey we sent. We just wanted you to talk with us. This is beyond the war. This goes beyond any affiliation. This is for humanitarian purposes. We only want to discuss something with you. A proposition. You're not listening to me."

As Harlowe stood, there was even less room in the cell. Ivy turned, hands split and dotted with already dried blood from tugging at the rough vines. The tithingman stood outside the cell, blocking almost all the light. He was taller than the doorway and had to crouch from the ceiling and to see into the rooms. He was not wide. He was actually quite thin, and he had a head quite literally like that of a newborn Ivy had seen once. It was actually the only baby she had ever seen. It was a few months ago, among the resistance of a town deep within the Baronies. She had only days ago heard that the town's resistance had been found out. The Sin Eater had been called for, and even before he had arrived the townspeople had rooted out the underground and hanged them from hooks by their feet on the roofs of other suspected rebels. Anyone that would help them to the ground would be known to be in collusion with the Army of Earth. Ivy wondered what had become of that baby. When she had first heard its babbling, and then seen the sight of its shriveled face, she had been repulsed. How could something so small and ugly be a human? It gurgled like a goblin, its eyes refused to focus, and its fat arms swung without abandon. She had spent a week in the town, gathering information, recruiting for the Resistance, and teaching its underground how to use the brimstone of the local hills for explosives, but she had made it a point to avoid the little creature they claimed was an immature person. But here she was reminded of its ridiculously rounded face and button nose.

The tithingman took his stocking cap from his smooth head to knead it between pudgy fists. He stepped aside to let them into the hallway. "I don't know what you expect us to do. You forced our hands."

"Where are all your prisoners," Ivy asked, "the Horde's prisoners?"

"Prisoners?"

"Barons resistant to change, captured generals, underground leaders the Sin Eater hasn't killed yet. The Horde has…"

"Please, it's… unwise to use such… derogatory… nomenclature in Brig. We're all adults here, let's parlay as such."

Ivy took Priest's *Sitdown* from her backpack, buckling the bag's straps before handing the large pistol to Harlowe. "And this is how adults call for a meeting, through deceit, kidnapping?"

"Now wait, don't be hasty!" The tithingman's voice still barely registered above a whisper, even as he reached into his belt behind him. "Again, we were…"

But Harlowe, joints cracking loudly, easily beat the baby-faced man to the draw. The hammer slammed home loudly, but the gun did not fire, and now the tithingman's gun was even with their heads.

"Take… take care with your pistols in the Titans," he said gasping and lowering his arms. "It takes a lot of work to keep healthy guns in such cold and sulfurous airs." He stumbled back against the close wall before sliding down to a sitting position. His gun hand fell limply to one side while the other hand clenched the jacket over his chest. "Ashmedai preserve me! Put the iron away, pistoleer. I'll say it again, we mean you no harm. Either of you. We… we're desperate. We need your help." Sitting, he was still tall enough to meet Ivy's scowling face. His hand waved parallel to the floor, now frantically. "Please just hear us out."

They continued down the metal halls when the tall man had

recovered. He led this time. Ivy looked down every corridor they passed, down every open hatch and in every milky port, but all she saw was darkness, all she heard was the pressure of each wall upon the others. The baby-faced tithingman led them through the biggest room she had yet seen in Brig. It was completely empty, a great gray cube, except for scattered scratches across the floor and the silver shavings they left behind. As they neared the exit, heading into more close-knit walls and a ceiling their guide had to almost bend in half to avoid, she could see graffiti scribbled around the doorway's frame in tiny characters from some language she had never before seen. The spreading words looked to be written in graphite — gray on gray — and with such a frantic passion that she wondered if it was indeed written in Human, just so hectically as to not appear recognizable. It was old, and could have easily been assumed to be a part of the wall if the organic scribbles were not so off-setting in such a geometric room.

"So what news from the war?" the tithingman asked. His voice almost disappeared out ahead among walls becoming increasingly concrete. "Our updates are sporadic. They'll get leaner if it's becoming winter again. Is it becoming winter again?" The hall was so narrow, and the baby-face so tall, that most light that came from ahead was denied them until they passed any source. They walked these halls for many minutes, changing direction only when the path was suddenly crossed by large piping cutting through the walls. Even then it was usually only a short walk before they returned to the same direction. They passed closed hatches and open ladders and even steep spiraling stairwells, and even though they never took them, Ivy could still feel as though they were heading downward. The floor was always perpendicular to the level walls, but she still felt that, over time, they were sloping downward ever so slightly with each new turn. And the more they descended the more she could hear a metallic rattle.

"I hear the Liege of Foes had actually won some land south," the tithingman said, "but he heads east now? How could he ever expect to keep it? Even if he left a force behind, one of his Necrophim generals, there's no supply lines down there strong enough to survive even the smallest blockade." They entered a small room with concrete walls first lined with red and copper tubing and then almost obscured by an interior wall of more of the same piping. Many of the metal was rusting, even more of it was rattling. The pipes did not look as though they moved, but she could feel the air shaking. Tiny, glassy gauges were the only things that looked new in the room, if not Brig, with hairline needles quivering well within a spectrum of cold colors. They stood from pipe arrays near cylinders flaking from dust and verdigris. Ivy peeled metal, revealing a healthier silver beneath. This was the warmest area she had encountered in Brig so far.

"Let's enjoy this a bit," the baby-face whispered. "It's not easy to bring warmth to the entirety of the city." He kicked at an unattached bar until it rolled against a pile of similarly rusted pipes. He then bent under tubing to collect some of the paper refuse littering the floor. "One day, Blessing of the Song, this city will live again, after wind and war and winter. It is up to us to caretake, to ensure it will be ready for the influx of travelers to and through Kaldera. These passes will be important to those coming from or heading to a newly opened West. The *Ashmedai Adat El*, through their alliance with the Kalderan Librans, have opened up a whole new part of the world. Why would the Army of Earth want to threaten that? The Liege of Foes once unified the land, why now does he want to tear it apart?"

Ivy opened her coat and pulled off the fur cap covering her head. The air here was warm enough to stink. She could finally smell people in Brig.

Harlowe just stood, not shivering from the cold nor seemingly enjoying the new warmth.

They stood together for several minutes, absorbing the temperature with only the sound of loose pipes, before moving on. Ivy tied her coat back up before following the baby-faced through low doorways into hallways that were much wider than those she had encountered so far in the ship. There were less pipes, less concrete, and more gray metal where they were heading, and she now had the feeling, if not the visual impression, that they were heading upward. The tithingman passed cylindrical-chuted ladders reaching into upward darkness without a glance, but Ivy could still feel the incline in their steps.

For each room they passed through, each corridor they cris-crossed, the tithingman would dial the lamps slightly. They came across furnishings now, and the sofas varied in quality greatly, the wooden desks in upkeep to a large degree. Here Ivy would slow their passage by testing the green velvet covering a chair of the richest cherry wood. There she would feel the cool brass lining a sink of flawless porcelain. But these extravagances were mixed with two-legged stools lying amongst their splintered pieces, the shimmer of broken glass ground into stained carpet, and the smell of some sort of overripe fruit. And through all of the mismatched living rooms grew the sound of trickling water.

Every hall they walked through now was lit before they entered. The ugly uniformity of gray was covered asymmetrically by paintings and framed photographs. The paintings ranged in size from some that covered half the wall to some as small as Ivy's spread hand, and they all held a nautical theme. Sleek organic ships rode waves of glass under a full sun and watery sky. Sketchy cruisers broke the darkness of night and sea watched by a discolored moon. The photographs, however, were without any consistency Ivy could decipher. They were either monochrome or so faded as to appear so. Some had people in ridiculously impractical clothes, cackling or grinning in secrets she could only guess the photographers were aware of. There were many images of trees, individuals, and forests. There were pictures of mountains she did not recognize, machines wondrous in shape and indescribable in function, and numerous photos of the sun that had depreciated into just a collection of framed shapes.

Her guide and Harlowe had left her behind, but it felt insulting to leave so many pictures unseen, but she continued on, following the now loud sound of water running through the walls. The noise culminated in a thin, curving room that, although as gray as the rest, was the brightest she had seen yet. The baby-faced man stood aside, revealing round panels, shiny brass, and tightly spiraled hanging cords. The lamps were turned up high from one doorway to another, and they reflected back upon themselves from the row of uniform windows lining the room at head height. The view was glaringly icy with both sides frosted to opaqueness, as far as Ivy could tell, by inches. The room continued on tightly and ended as it began, but at the point it bent the most sat a tiny man in cherried leather. He was paler than the windows and his pudgy limbs, not even reaching the edges of his fleshy seating, were bare in the immense humidity of the area. Heaters, ingrained and offset, rattled and glowed around the curve of the room.

Ivy tipped her head toward the walls, at the rush of water around them, and the baby-faced spoke as he gestured them past himself. "Each day, at a certain time, the sun hits Prometheus just so. Some ice melts and flows through the city. Where? We've never found it. It freezes again soon enough. For a bit each day, Brig floats the Arctic seas once more."

At his voice the tiny tithingman set a book down and jerked his body so that the high chair swiveled toward them. Ivy could now see skin wrinkled as though from a lifetime. He had the prominent spots and veins from ages, but there was a youthful clarity in his beady eyes.

The baby-faced, hunched over in a ceiling still too low for him, gestured again, but Harlowe refused to pass, so he led them to the tiny man's side. The little tithingman cleared his throat, the skin around his mouth showing more wrinkles as he scowled at the pistoleer's gun. He twisted his body suddenly to turn the chair to a ledge bearing a brass brazier. It was in the shape of a bull that sat like a human, its open belly exposing embers heating the small kettle in its spread arms. The tiny tithingman refreshed his soup from the steaming kettle.

Ivy swallowed unconsciously at the soup's smell, distracting herself by paging through the little man's book. *The Torch: The Testaments of Those that Stayed Behind* was in rough shape. Its spine was broken and pages were missing from its crumbling glue.

Seeing that the other tithingman's attention was still on Harlowe's *Sitdown*, the baby-faced other spoke up. "There will be no violence here. They've come to hear our proposition."

The tiny tithingman put his hand out toward Ivy and she stared at it until it shook, but he held it there until she returned his book. He set it aside again to take up his soup. He prodded the smoky broth with sticks between nubs of fingers. "Ivy of the Grove," he whispered, not looking up from the bowl, "you're everything I've heard yet still nothing like I expected. Your hair, your eyes… my, my little girl, are you made entirely of recessive genes? I would think you've come out of N'Midgaard rather than the Nursery." His voice had started high, as she expected, but became lower as he talked. And then it started high again. "What do you think of our grand city, hmmm? Not easy to reach, is it? But we knew you could do it. If you are indeed Homega Sapiens then we knew you could do it. Knew you would come."

Ivy watched him struggle with his simple meal. They were getting supplies somehow up here if they had noodles. Noodles were quite rare these days. "Why did you take…"

"You certainly are not of the Nursery's default." He wiped soup from his knob of a chin with his fingers, as he gave up on the sticks to fish meat as gray as the walls with his other hand. "Every Lesser Antony I've met is dark skinned, dark haired, dark eyed. I don't know what it was thinking with you, but I can still tell you are of its work. You see, I'm something of an expert when it comes to the Nursery. I've made it my life's purpose."

"No one knows more," Baby-faced said, moving to sit cross-legged on the floor.

"What do you know of the Nursery, little girl?" The tiny tithing-man finally looked up to her as his voice became lower again, but it was not long before his attention was back on his soup. He sucked at the noodles loudly.

"I've been back there," Ivy answered.

"Have you now? Why? Like looking up your mother's craw. Why would you want to do that? That's disgusting. What's wrong with you? There is more defection than perfection, that's what I've been trying to say."

"I was…"

"But seeing it is a far cry from knowing it, is it not? I've read. Can you read? Of course you can. Were the languages imprinted within you or have you had to learn? A mixture of both, I've theorized." He was as quiet as Baby-face. High or low, they could barely hear his voice. Even if it had not been for the trickling water and the hum of the heaters, they would have had difficulty. "The Brotherhood has been very accommodating. Before stationed here I spent a lifetime looking through Bab'lon's libraries. I could find nothing on the Nursery, so I've had to rely on the kindness of Lesser Prophets. They were always wary to speak of it, until its destruction that is. Now they have nothing to fear but mortality itself." From his tunic he pulled a slender whistle and, licking his lips with a tongue small even for his mouth, he piped a quick note that bounced around the cabin and out down dark halls. "You see, you couldn't have possibly deduced from the burnt out hulk you've seen that you were looking at something not of this planet."

Baby-faced spoke up. "The Prophets Lesser have seen far and wide yet even they don't recognize…"

"The alien construct arrived sometime after the Old Ones fled into the earth," Tiny interrupted, "but before man returned to the surface. It was a flesh farm, a meat market, used between competing organizations to repopulate the planet with slaves in man's absence. But the idea, for some reason, was abandoned, and, instead, it was just used for the sale of tailored slaves. Bio-engineered warriors, pleasure puppets, untiring laborers, poisonous consorts… which one are you, I wonder? Just a 'tabula rasa,' I've always assumed."

"Are there others like…?"

"But again, at some point the Nursery was abandoned, or taken perhaps by the Greater Prophets. Did you know that for every one Greater Prophet that visited the Nursery, two Lessers emerged? Did you know that? No, there are no others like you. You are the only female left, I'm afraid. I've found rumors of others in the past. Concubines to kings. Daughters to the barren rare elite that could afford it. But none surviving to this day. I had heard of the other you brought with you into Bab'lon before its enlightening. If only I had known. But it is no matter. You're here to help us now. Chem-Oshmelech has delivered you unto me."

"As part of our commission," Baby-faced said, "as part of our co-governorship of Brig, the Brotherhood told us…"

"The stories of Ivy of the Grove have reached us even here," Tiny said, his voice starting high again. "It seems you've been causing all sorts of trouble for the Army of Heaven. It can't be easy for them to stave off Earth's Army's attacks with you sowing disorder on the homefront. But that is beyond us, is it not? We are better than that. Let the Brotherhood fight the war. Let the weaker governors fight to control more sinful cities. As the winds came and went, the war will as well. Ashmedai, the *Wyrmwood* star, looks down upon us now and is on the move, signaling the end to disorder. Soon all will hear the Song. There is no doubt. With that certainty it comes to us to carry on, to concern ourselves with a future beyond pestilence and famine and war."

The tall tithingman grunted to stand and bend. He took the bowl that his tiny counterpart had set aside and silently drank the rest of its contents. His smooth baby face was beaded with sweat by the time he had finished. He removed his jacket and smiled brightly in Ivy's direction.

Tiny twitched his stunted arms and twisted to swivel the chair. He took up a gavel and beat it against the nearest console. The sound reverberated more loudly down the halls than it did in the room. "Where are they!" he squeaked to Baby Face before blowing into his whistle again.

"I told one to stay near. They've just been play…"

"I don't have time for their nonsense, not today!" Loud, it was the only full sentence of his Ivy had understood. But he composed himself and continued in a voice she could barely make out. "We must look to the future, of the land, of the nation, and of the sons of the Prophets Lesser. And for this, Ivy of the Grove, we will need only your blood."

XVI

...by yoke of man and god set on his head

a Warrior knows not the

cage of his false free will 'til he is dead

—scrawled on the walls of the King of All's lower halls

For all Easarean knew, Heavy Infantry Imperial Brute looked exactly like him under the helmet. In fact he suspected as much. Almost all the Imperials he had seen at the Academy had a similar appearance — that of an older Easarean — and he knew he was being bred to become, if not one of them, their superior. He took great pride in this as he watched his commander break the other of the councilman's legs. The limbs now both twitched rhythmically barely above the sandy floor of the open air home. Even the richest of the moon lived where the slight breeze could blow through their homes. Easarean's armor told him the annoyingly hot temperature along with the poor quality of the dusty air. His view screens showed the quick accumulation of the grit, so he could assume the state of the moon's inhabitant's lungs.

Brute held the man against the wall by the neck, one massively armored hand unclenching just enough to allow his raspy replies of ignorance.

"The demon..."

"Yes, man, speak of the demon, and you may yet live," Brute spoke through the impersonal digital deepness of his helmet, filling in the gaps when the man struggled to breath. "Where does it hide? In who does it hide? Within you?" He tore the man's scarf from his mouth and peered inward, closely with his armor's one great eye.

"He's gone."

"You lie!" Brute lifted the man higher. "What are the red barns for?" He gestured to far away hills with his other hand, past pastures to a collection of element-worn buildings. Sat-imaging showed them uniform in their placement, and stark in contrast to the dull grays and browns of the sparse villages and fields and even the nearby city.

Grit had already collected in the man's tears. "The women... they go... during time of brood's blood..."

"Why?"

"...pray... sing..."

That explained the voices Easarean's sensors had picked up shortly after they had landed. It certainly had been rhythmic, but disgustingly infantile, and he had quickly tuned it out of his helmet.

"Where is Eha'dadadad? Why do you hide him?" Brute's speaker bellowed again.

"He... helped found the colonies... but... left... standards ago." The man's two shattered legs squirmed for purchase on the ground, scraping the sand to stand and trying to make it so that Brute's hand was not the only thing holding him up. The exposed skin on his ankles was turning as purple as his face. "He's... gone... the demon... is... gone." His lips continued twitching wordlessly, breathlessly.

Heavy Infantry Imperial Brute was everything Easarean was taught to be — every stratagem, every maneuver, every myth personified before him in mortal, or perhaps even immortal, form. "You lie!" he said again, pressing the faceplate ever inward and suffocating the man until he no longer moved.

It was true, Easarean knew, the man did lie. His own armor had analyzed the farmer's perspiration and heart rate. It had been wildly above average, and, of course, could only mean deceit.

Brute threw the dead body to smash table and appliance that had somehow survived the destruction of the rooms in the initial interrogation. He threw his own armored body against one of the few outer walls, exploding out into the open, hazy air. Easarean followed him. Perhaps he would finally send him to meet with the others of his squad. They were supposed to be a phalanx, but the commander had quickly sent the others to raze farm and city, keeping only Easarean at his side.

His hopes were quickly dashed at his new orders.

"Go. Find Eha'dadadad. He can't escape now. The Sat-web will destroy any ship trying to leave orbit, and your brothers will level every building on the moon if need be. But we, you and I, we will find answers. You go north. I will take the east shelters."

Easarean hoped his armor hid any tell of his disappointment. His heart was off with his squad, off with Ehlena, bringing brick and mortar to the ground and a society to its knees. Was this how his first mission was to play out? He wanted to be among the unified screams of girders and populations, not the individual whimperings of a few defiant. He trudged off to the next homestead, looking over the over-tilled earth. The moon had turned against his team, warmed air and acidic clouds pressing down against village and farm, city and pasture.

"Missing out on all the fun?" the child asked. Easarean had seen him following them earlier, watching with large brown eyes unshielded from the grit in the air. The child's pupils filled most of his eyes. Years of tears stained his cheeks, and crud, probably permanently, had built up around the edges of his eyes. A thin scarf loosely covered his mouth and snotty nose. "Try this house next!" the child yelled, laughing as he ran to, and pointed at, an adjacent dwelling. Unlike most others, this shelter was completely enclosed except for large windows with a fine mesh to protect against the gritty atmosphere. "I bet they know something!"

Easarean walked to the doorway but stopped to scan the child before entering. HUD showed nothing abnormal.

IF-RED SIGNATURE: Within Normal

MAG-IM: Within Normal

BIO-SIGNS: Within Normal

The child's scarf had fallen, and he pulled it back up to cover an absurd smile. "Go ahead, knock!"

Easarean kicked the door inward, shattering it as well as a short inner wall immediately leading into a living area. A man in layers of mesh resembling the window-covering over ragged overalls began firing a bolt rifle without effect into Easarean's armor. The crack of the action was loud in the small room, each shot followed by a dull ricochet. Two small boys, the size of the one that followed Easarean in, meekly entered from an adjacent room to find their father's rifle crushed in the soldier's hand and their father held against a cracking wall. One cried. One stared, frozen at the scene.

"Where is the one called Eha'dadadad?" Easarean broadcast loudly. He crushed the man's filter before tearing it from his face. There was a hesitant moment when he feared the straps would hold long enough to break the man's neck, but they then broke away to leave the man breathless and gasping before his children.

"He lives in one of you," Easarean continued. "Which one?"

The children screamed and cried as the armored giant smashed his fist through the wall a mere space from their father's face. Their father was then thrown to the ground in front of them and they burrowed heads and hands into his quaking side, trying to desperately block out the image of the dark metallic man stepping toward them.

"Wait! Wait," the man cried, pulling his boys even closer, "he... he's in all of us. All who fear the injustice of the clans, all who just want to be left alone by the Empire."

The big-eyed boy followed the soldier out of the home. "That's not good enough," the child chided. "You're no closer. Religious rhetoric is no substitute for..."

"Who are you?" Easarean asked, looking ahead to the next batch of homes. They had barely any differences from each other. It was only beyond them, into farmsteads and plantations that one could see bits of individualism in design and layout, and even then they all had the same drab color and purpose. "Are you him? Are you the demon?" he asked, still staring ahead to the next home. From here on out they were smaller, with many resembling huts reinforced against a wind Easarean had not seen yet.

The boy blew his nose into the scarf. It now sagged loosely down around his neck, with his ludicrous smile now splitting his face and giving him wrinkles way beyond even the adults of his people.

Easarean moved on to the next house, which proved to be empty after he tore down each inner wall. The next was filled with all ages of children telling him nothing and only hiding and crying in and under pillow and closet. The next two homes were empty, and even his scans showed storm cellars, hidden and otherwise, to be devoid of life. By this time he had headed out beyond the village into the farms. The big-eyed boy continued to follow him and give advice, as the soldier threw farmers and ranchers through window and wall.

"Choke him 'til he talks!"

"Kill him if he doesn't know anything!"

"Break his arms!"

"Break his kids!"

By this time the big-eyed boy's smile had stretched even farther across his face, and teeth and glistening gums showed starkly between strained lips.

XVII

You think I'm the only person that wears a mask? At least I know who I am. No matter how many voices tell me otherwise, I am descended, from mind if not body, from the effect he left on this world. So, yes, I too am an Heir of Aesar.

—Legion

Young Harlowe treasured the days spent alone with his mother but, looking back, he wished he had appreciated them even more at the time. Even if his memories weren't slowly being trod over with new track being laid down, his thoughts of her were something he felt he could never revisit. They were few and becoming fewer. She had smelled of flowers before he knew what a flower was. Could even that sense memory be taken from him?

"Harlowe! You git away from there!" she had yelled as she set up their picnic. He had been kicking at the jerky corpse of a jackrabbit, hoping against all odds it would jump up and bound away toward the low sun. The overcast sky was why his mother had chosen the evening to come out to the boneyard. The walk was long, and they did not miss the heat of noon. Every few days they would get a clouded sky that threatened to rain on them. But it never did.

He skipped the path to climb the rocks to where she finished putting out their roastbeef — hers on a plate, his between bread. The beets kept his mouthfuls from going dry.

"Stay away from them dead critters," she said, passing him most of her dinner. "Only reason some vulture ain't eat it means it's filled with coffin blossoms. You'll see. Probably bloom up afore we leave." The sky rumbled and darkened under thickening clouds, but they knew better than to think anything would come of it.

Before Harlowe had finished eating, his mother had already sparked a small fire in the grass and kindling they had brought. The twigs she fanned matched the color of her limp hair, the flickering tinder her long dress. She stood to let any breeze take over for her and pointed down around the rocks to the short rows of grave markers. They had straightened and reset most of the wood when they arrived at the families' boneyard. The markers were drier and splintered even more than the hog fencing Harlowe helped rebuild each year. "Up here you can see how straight all them rows are. Perfect straight. You know why?" she asked.

He did know, had always known, but stayed silent. Even if his mouth had not been full from his last bites he would have just let her speak. She loved her stories. He was old enough to notice now that storytelling was one of the few things that made her happy out here on the wastes.

"Ghosts, all the ghosts of the prairie are drawn to the markers. They can't help it. They can get caught up in them, caught up in the maze. We make sure ta set the markers in nice even rows so they can just sail right though. Nice smooth rows will lead them through, right in one side and out the other, on their way to some other gravesite. We don't need no spirits haunting our boneyards."

The rows did not look that straight to Harlowe. He was dying to poke around the hole and crevices leading into the rock, but he waited as his mother stoked the fire until she was satisfied at its size. She took out her satchel and pulled a handful of grass out that she had dampened that morning in well water. She set it on cross twigs, and as soon as it started to smolder she brought Harlowe's old baby blanket out. She held it to collect the new smoke as she spoke.

"We put our thoughts and prayers inta the smoke, an' they take 'em up to Heaven. It lets our loved ones that have passed know we still think of them, remember them. Think of yer granddad, Harlowe, and the smoke will take yer prayers to him. Remember yer auntie Clay, and the smoke will deliver yer message."

Harlowe looked down toward the lines of gravemarkers — generations of FelDougans and Dugfields, numerous Hatcans and Swiftys, and all ages of Shattys and Candids. Where *were* they all now? In the clouds? In the earth? Riding the winds of the prairies, drawn to ride between the lines of tombstones?

"Who you want ta send a message to, Harlowe? You better pay attention. You'll be the one passing this tradition to your little ones one day. One day you'll be the only one left ta teach how ta catch the smoke." She released a clump of smoke and put more of the damp grass on the fire.

Harlowe later searched the nooks and crannies near the base of the rocks for anything moving while his mother collected the picnicware for their walk back. It was getting late, but if they left soon they could still be back before nightfall.

He followed the twitching tail of a scorpion near the shadows under a low outcropping. He had never seen one with such dark claws before.

"You like them pincers, boy?" asked a voice from the burrow. It was the same voice he had heard from beneath the floorboards under his bed at night. *"You wanna be pinched, I'll oblige you."*

The sky rumbled again, and, even though Harlowe knew it would not storm, the sound was different this time. It rumbled long and low until it sounded as though the ground reverberated. It was close, and even though he knew rain was not coming, he felt that some*thing* was.

The horizon roared, and although he could feel the train pummel the ground, could feel its chugging breath all around, he could not see over the rocks to witness its passage. The *Loco*'s whistle rose to match his mother's scream.

He was still shaking by the time he had made it up the rocks to the scattered remains of the fire and picnic. Smears of ash, of every dark color imaginable, spread like a dark star on the stone. The plates were unbroken. His blanket smelled of smoke, but the dust easily shook off.

It took him until dusk to find enough of the kindling remains, and, along with the scant grasses he could find among the rock, he started a meager fire in the previous one's leftovers. The tinder was dry, so he could not get a good and dark smoke going, but he believed that his mother could hear his thoughts none-the-less.

It neared midnight by the time Harlowe came shivering into his house. He found his father, as he expected to, facing away in the chair next to the end table holding the radio. He could not see him, but he could hear the whine of static change ever so slightly as the big man twisted and turned the antennae. Harlowe made sure to step on a familiar squeaky board to announce his presence.

"How'd yer shootin' go today, boy?" his father asked after clearing his throat.

"Mama... she's... she's gone."

Coal burned in his father's eyes as he turned, and the heat stung Harlowe's face and brought new tears to his cheeks before burning them away to salt.

"YOU CAN HEAR IT TOO, CAN'T YA? IT CAN'T BE STOPPED, BOY! IT WON'T STOP 'TIL IT'S TAKEN THEM ALL FROM YA!"

~

But his father had been wrong. Something *had* stopped the train. By now it should have taken Ivy, yet here she was. In fact, there were times he feared she *had* been taken, but the *Loco* only beckoned, only called to him, its whistle screaming from the far West and from his past, appearing in his memories in places he now was not sure it ever had before. Could he trust any of his past? For once in his late life he was not following the long horn of the *Loco*, and it was destroying him from afar. If he did not confront it, would there be any memories that did not end in the train's rumbling passage? If he did not head west would there be anything left in his mind except the demon locomotive?

~

"The water slows as evening approaches. The sun must be sinking beneath peaks," the baby-faced tithingman said, knocking a featureless fist against a bulkhead. The sound of rushing water had turned to a trickle. "It'll freeze wherever it drains…"

"She's not interested in that," the tiny tithingman interrupted, his scowl turning to a toothless smile as he jerked his chair around to face Ivy. "She wants to know why she's here, don't you, girly?"

"I already…"

"No, you don't, not really." His little chest expanded and shrunk as he emptied his cheeks into his whistle. He covered all its holes, and the sound was tuneless, but something responded this time. Man or woman, Ivy was not sure, but the tiny tithingman called it his "burden," as it lurched up to his chair's side partially on its legs, partially on all fours. The person was awkwardly thin, its head wrapped tightly in a hood with only eyes and ears exposed from zipper slits and button holes. The rest of its body was mostly covered in straps and buckles. Ivy shivered at the mount's exposed skin. It breathed heavily behind a zipper as Tiny mounted it. The tithingman kicked at its lower back each time it sneaked a peek at the newcomers. "Forward!" he whispered loudly to spur the burden ahead and to keep its attention off Ivy and Harlowe. "Come! This way!" he said to them in the same quiet voice.

Harlowe would not move until the tall tithingman went ahead of them.

They left the swelter of the windowed and corded room behind, the salty smell of soup still watering Ivy's mouth. Ivy mentally mapped the new corridors they walked. Even though they looked like the same gray-flecked over gray halls they had already seen, she recognized they walked in a new direction. She noted vents and ladders, hatches heading up and down — positioning every exit in reference to the rooms she had explored in the past day. She wanted to be ready to run. She wondered if Harlowe did the same, but could see his squinted eyes just staring into the backs of the tithingmen's heads, his mangled hand clenching the *Sitdown* like a throat.

The salty smell was back as they walked through the only door to a dark room. Bowls stacked everywhere, shining with the pink and green of equations written in light across a dozen glassy screens standing from wire-grown desks. A mild hum linked each screen in unnatural symphony. The colored scrawl was dim, but enough to lead their way through cords thin and segmented to a screen in the center of the room. Beyond rows of numbers linked by symbols, both basic and angelic, there were circles, both broken and Archimedean. Into these, Tiny now reached with a glowing utensil to add even more numbers. The equations meant nothing to Ivy, yet she memorized them just the same.

Tiny kicked and then pulled at an exposed swaft of his burden's hair until the mount responded by straightening. The tithingman could now reach most of the screen with his light pen. He interrupted the tall tithingman before he could speak.

"In a beginning, the Elohim created Heaven and Earth. For seven days they toiled under flaming whip. They sang of light and night, and their tears under smoking lash became the water above and below. Their charred flesh fell and sizzled and cooled and become the land. Yet still they sang under scourge, shriveled feathers falling, alighting as trees across the land. One among them refused to sing, the Shining One, and she was pinned to the celestial sphere to light the night, inferior to sun and moon but obstinate nonetheless.

"After seven days the Elohim fell to Earth, exhausted and hoarse, and they found it quiet and insipid. *Let us make beasts in our image*, one of them said, and Ashmedai sang the Song of Man.

> *Be fruitful and increase*
> *Cover Earth and subdue*
> *Rule over the fish*
> *And the birds and dogs*
> *Be not afraid to please and fight*
> *But trust not which lights the night*

It was a song Ivy had increasingly heard in the Territories, but never with a voice like Tiny's. She feared he would continue, because she knew there were many more verses, but he went back to his scribbling as he talked.

"And the man's name was Mud. And he was perfect. Perfect in appearance. Perfect in deed. Generated from perfect Song, perfect seed. And he thrived in the new land alone, as the Elohim walked his gardens and watched him from afar, content, for they saw that it was good.

"But the Shining One wasn't content to watch. She tore free of the stars, leaving her wings behind. She fell to Earth burning her arms and legs up in the atmosphere. The falling star struck the land with such force that volcanoes exploded and ash thickened the air and Mud had no choice but to flee into the interior of Earth. But the Shining One followed. Damned to crawl on her belly, it took centuries to find Mud. He was old, and she seduced him, and for the first time he knew the pleasures of the flesh. But the Shining One was greedy, and she took a piece of man's soul — the Mighty Granule — and this she passed along to her first daughter — Lilith — the Succuincubus Queen, seed thief, nocturnal chieftess, Mother Zero. And Lilith passed the Mighty Granule to her daughters, and her daughters passed it to their own, and so on, and so on. And so, since the beginning, women have hoarded the Mighty Granule, passing it only to their daughters. They hoard this piece of men's souls, this holy thread linking us back to the first man, the perfect man, made from the Elohims' — the Divine Choir's — Song."

Tiny had wiped away many of his equations to draw a line from one side of the screen to the other. His writing was miniscule, but Ivy could make out that the beginning of the line was marked with creation, and that he was now marking points from one side to the other with events she could not read. He finished by drawing a passable illustration at the end of the line. It appeared to be a sky of stars with an explosion beneath.

"Women are unclean. No one denies it. There's no doubt they're tainted from that initial greed, but men are imperfect, constantly missing that initial piece of the original spirit, forever searching for what will make them whole. All men die not knowing what that one thing is, that one thing that will fill the pit in their soul. But this is it! I've figured it out." He pointed to his stubby frame as his baby-faced counterpart pointed to his own misshapen body. "Men are broken. We always have been."

"Not all men are like you," Ivy was able to break through his unceasing words, but only for a second.

"No. You're actually correct. Very insightful. All men're broken, but it's the tithingmen that have been chosen, chosen by Chem-Oshmelech to rise above the imperfection."

"Chem-Oshmelech has promised Glorified Bodies to the tithingmen," said the tall man.

Tiny gritted his gums at the man's voice, continuing before he could say more. "I say the Promise of Father has imbued us with our own resources, our own ingenuity." He tapped his shriveled head with the light pen. "Our *intellect* was His greatest gift. He helps those that help themselves to the world, and I have done so, and that is how I alone have solved the puzzle of what's missing from men's souls. *Ashmedai* has begun the Infernal Descent. Soon He will cleanse the land of sin and sinners and, in those End Times, it is said that Chem-Oshmelech will reward the tithingmen with Glorified Bodies to precipitate our rule, but the Song has been corrupted by the inherent flaws of men, and I say we tithingmen must pave our own way, reward our own promises. We do not deserve our Glorified Bodies unless we provide them. Chem-Oshmelech does not bless the slothful.

"But will women be willing to give up their prize — the thread that should, by rights, link men to the first man, the piece leaving our bodies broken? They cannot. They are not strong enough to overcome their inherent greed, and so I've found an alternate solution to the riddle."

Tiny kicked at his burden and when it did not respond he jammed the light pen into its ear. With a wheezing squeal it lurched over to another screen. The tithingman wiped a section clear and began again to write and talk. His voice, lost beneath even the minimal hum of the room, drew Ivy near again. The shapes he drew meant nothing to her, so she just watched his face. When a pink glow landed on it, he looked even fresher faced than his tall companion. When the lines turned green in front of him he looked even older, sicklier. She had heard that tithingmen rarely lived to old age, but, despite his size, his face had become consumed by a depth of wrinkles she had never even seen on the oldest elder. Yet she preferred to stomach the sight over the infant's head bobbing next to her.

"You see, a child is the result of a merging of spirits — the soul of the masculine and the feminine. In nature it is natural for the masculine forces — the competitive, the aggressive, the focused, the singularly objective — to subjugate the Feminine — the wishy washy emotional, empathic, intuitive, the socialist forces. And so, we men, created and chosen to dominate nature, are at a disadvantage. As long as the Mighty Granule is denied us, we are held captive, cuckolded by mothers and sisters and daughters. We each get a perfect balance, the yang and yin, the light and the dark, upon conception. Nature may love a balance but humanity abhors it. The Mighty Granule is supposed to tip the scales in our favor, but women instead use it to dominate conception, and so there is always more of the feminine force contributed. Weakening mankind, making what should be predator into prey, and so nature will always have the upper hand against humanity. With the Mighty Granule back in men's control, the duality would be broken, the Masculine would overcome the Feminine and run wild — its natural state. We would be back on course to subjugate, no more victims to nature's disease and famine, never again suppressed by winter and wind!"

"There's something wrong with you," Ivy interrupted.

"I know! And I'm going to fix it! Ashmedai falls, signaling that the End Times are near, and I will greet them proud and standing tall and walking as an equal among men.

"The Prophets Lesser should have been mankind's salvation. To anyone they would appear as masculinity personified. Their spirit should be able to overcome in conception. They are without the Shining One's initial corruption. But, they too have not the spirit of the original, no thread linking them organically to the Divine Choir. Their origins lie in the meat market, not the Song of Man. They were not given the original order to subjugate by the Song of Man, and so were not created with the extra paternal force to follow through. They are in a disgusting state of balance."

The tall tithingman spoke up, explaining to Ivy, "This is not a popular opinion among the governors. Understandably a minority view…"

"It's not an opinion! These are facts. I've proved it in the Brood Pits. The Prophets Lesser are unnatural. There is a place for them after the End Times, but our fathers are not chosen by the Song. We are! Their lack of soul is an abomination to the Mighty Granule, and you see before you…" he gestured to himself and the Tall one, "…the result. So the women of this land hold tight the Mighty Granule. You see, before I was sent to this frozen rock I oversaw the breeding pools. No one else has put the time into the studies, the experiments needed to solve this riddle. No one has seen what I've seen, had to do what I've done. Only I was willing to get my hands dirty. It was in the breeding pools that I saw, up close, the lengths the women of this land will go to hold tight their ancient prize. Listen! Upon conception, with the power of the Mighty Granule, a woman marks the paternal spirit for destruction later in the embryo. The maternal spirit she contributes is inherently weak, meant to be dominated, but without the masculine force to later confront it, the Feminine becomes an unchallenged spirit, surviving and dividing to populate the very soul of the growing organism.

"The Mighty Granule is lost to us. The original sin is too great. In eating from the Tree of Knowledge we have given up our right to the Tree of Life. But there is hope for every boy born of a Lesser Antony." His focus was on a new timeline on the screen before him as he lifted the back of his coat, absentmindedly revealing the cloven brands on his sides. They were old, as wrinkled as the rest of his skin, but they shined like new burns. "Every chosen child of Chem-Oshmelech need not be mocked for a hunched back or extra ear. No governor need hide flippered hands or rely on a cart to survey his land. I have found a solution, and today it has finally found me.

"You, Ivy of the Grove, are too an abomination. Soulless meat. A mushroom grown from humanity's insecurities. Can't win your own war? Buy a Homega Sapiens army. Your husband can't please you? Order a strapping, young, dark Homega Sapiens. The Nursery was an affront to the Song of Man, and I have no doubt that the Divine Choir punished its creators accordingly. I only wish, whoever they were, could see what it became — a force for good in the world, the Grand Brotherhood. But, as dedicated to the *Ashmedai Adat El* as the Prophets Lesser have become, I am glad the Nursery has been destroyed. He didn't know it, couldn't have known it, but the Prodigal was ironically doing the Divine Choir's work when he burned it. Mortality will remind the Lesser Antonys of mortality, introduce them to humility, put them in touch with their sons. And with the lessening of the Lessers will come the rise of the governors. With our new bodies, the tithingmen will take our rightful place at the head of the *Ashmedai Adat El*.

"But I digress. A Homega Sapiens would come out of the Nursery programmed, mentally and biologically, for some distinct purpose. Some were tailor-made to exploit a king's weakness, some were designed specifically to withstand the rigors of harsh environments. This all changed with the Lesser Antonys. They were superior physically, but generically biologically conditioned, and instead of being programmed with individualized, specifically designed personalities, they were imprinted all with the same mind. You, however, Ivy of the Grove, were not even given that blessing. Homega Sapiens are cut from the same genetic cloth. Even with modifications, you are all twins. You, however, are the female version of the nucleic soup, just a double of the double helix. The same but different, and a superb physical specimen, yes, that can't be denied, but without purpose and with a blank slate of a mind. You were made without a destiny. Or so it seems. As I said, Chem-Oshmelech has a plan for the seemingly most purposeless. Sure, you've amused yourself and others with this game of the Resistance. You've humored the Liege of Foes' sad sense of irony by having a Homega Sapiens involved with the Army of Earth, but my job has always been to ferret out others' destinies, and yours, my child, is to be the tithingmen's solution and salvation. The riddle of the cripple has just been solved!"

Tall laughed, but Tiny ignored him to continue. "You, Ivy of the Grove, are not of the Song of Man. You don't have the thread in you linking you to the original man. You have no Mighty Granule to hoard, and the men of this land, infected with an imbalance leaning towards the Feminine, have not the spirit to affect the maternal force you would contribute to conception, but another Homega Sapiens does. Two balances joined in generation, without the interference of the Mighty Granule, would result in the excess masculine — a child closer to Mud, the Man Original! The original subjugator — the perfect man, designed *by* harmony to live *in* harmony of rule over nature, and in this child is the key to unlocking the deficiencies of the tithingmen. The babe would transcend the balance of its parents. Its blood would be antibody and vaccine, a biological and mystical code to unravel and weave into my own broken genes.

"Now, we of course will have to conscript one of the Lesser Prophets. That shouldn't be a problem. The preponderance of tithingmen over the ages is proof of their penchant for lechery." He struck his burden to turn it toward Ivy. She was looking off toward nearby screens.

"You of course would be well-compensated," said the tall tithing-man, trying to get her attention. "You would never again be want for riches. Once the war is over you would be more than well provided..."

"Or you could just do it because it's the right thing to do," Tiny spat. "The noble thing. A whole generation of governors could look the rest of the land in the eye. You've more than likely seen other tith-ingmen in your travels. Some of their defects can be quite debilitating, but, yes, we obviously can reward you with a full pardon of your crimes against the Army of Heaven, and the status of newife granted in one of the wealthier territories." Even though Ivy watched the screens, she could still see Tiny shift his body and his eyes to keep an eye on the revolver hanging at Harlowe's side. "Are you listening to me?" he asked her.

She paused before looking back to his scowling face. "Barely. My focus has been shared for many minutes now."

"Wha..."

"I very quickly determined that you're quite mad and didn't ne-cessitate much more attention. Your notes, however, are far more interesting, if inherently flawed."

"Fla... ! My work has been tested far more than you could ever..."

It was easy to ignore his quiet voice, especially as she took his notes in. As he ranted she compared his writings to those remembered in books she had flipped through in Chiro's library. She had flipped through the breeder's work journals, his chart notebooks and gene diaries but had only stolen one book. *Prison Cell: Theses on Mitochondrial Diseases* was a boring book, but it was all she had to read while waiting for the stars to align for her meeting with Priest. She had read it in one night and did not remember where she had left the tome. She would have sworn that she also did not remember the content of the book, but here, prompted by Tiny's flawed math, it all came back to her. Those born of the Lesser Prophets' liaisons were definitely victims of a congenital chaotic chemical deficiency. Their problems were two-fold but linked back to a same source — virtual intraspecies conception. The rational conclusion was that Homega Sapiens were only slightly compatible with the rest of the land. There was not enough cell energy being created during generation of the fetus. Ivy moved to a far screen, lit by only the merest of green light. Cell injury and cell death had to follow, she concluded, repeated throughout the developing systems. If this happened early enough in generation, as she now suspected it did, according to the work in front of her, then gene encoding would be disturbed, which would have explained quite a bit. Defects were inevitable, with the only unknown being just *how* they would reveal themselves.

The most interesting piece of the situation was the fact that nature seemed to "right" itself after the first generation. Tiny's notes unfortunately ignored that aspect, and she suspected that this had the effect of much of the land being able to easily deny its origins.

The slight rattle of the chains hanging from Harlowe brought her back around as the pistoleer stepped between her and Tiny. The little tithingman had kicked at his burden until it rounded the desks, coming near her.

"...can understand how being saddled with such an important responsibility can be daunting, but, believe me, no one understands better the yoke of divine destiny than me."

"You don't have to decide this very day," the tall tithingman said from behind one of the screens. He had crouched to look at one of the monitors with his smooth brow scrunching in bewilderment at the equations. He looked like a constipated infant.

"You, of course, can't leave Brig," Tiny whispered loudly. Harlowe's twisted fingers twitched around the butt of his gun.

"What he means," the other tithingman quickly said, "is that it's too late in the day to venture back into the mountains. The sun's too low, the winds have surely started. It would be suicide to head out into the night of the Titans. I can prepare a room..."

"I can't imagine much thought is needed," Tiny said, "but, yes, fine, we can discuss your decision in the morning."

She again heard Harlowe's chains sway. The thought of another night in Brig must have unsettled him, but she feared their choices were limited. Besides, she was eager to start on her new book. She felt the interior of her parka to make sure the copy of *The Torch* was still where she had pocketed it.

XVIII

Victory is determined by seven celestially Governed Elements.
These are: (1) the Immoral Law; (2) the Moral Law; (3) Heaven;
(4) Earth; (5) the Head; (6) Discipline; (7) the Maintenance of Roads

"He who does not know the elements will fail"
—Hyper Khan's "The War of Art"

B efore he realized it, his breathing had become hectic, his tongue thick and clogging his throat. He sucked in the same air he had just expelled, and it was as humid and unfulfilling as he expected. He could barely bend his knees in the coffin, and his elbows skinned themselves trying to find leverage for his hand to push against any wood Harlowe twisted to press them against. The creaking wood was weak, but its nails held strong. The interior's absolute darkness reminded him of nightmares he never knew he had — of a Hell not filled with fire and brimstone, not filled with the unavoidable pain of flaying skin and boiling flesh, but by absence. True damnation, Harlowe felt, would be filled with an absence beyond human imagining. But Harlowe did not even have to try to imagine it this day.

He pushed out in all directions, meagerly but exhaustively with all his cramped limbs, pressed with his back and feet. The creaking became a cracking, and either wood or nails gave, and a side of the coffin gave out before the cover did. Sound flooded in as he pushed the remnants of carriage, sand and clay brick, and other coffins off and away. A cacophony of gunshot sailed around the smoke. A menagerie of roaring fire and screaming horses swirled from all sides.

Harlowe stood from the wreckage of the carriage that had snuck him into the compound, under the guise of the undertaker's wares. The other pieces of Marshall's plan burned from opposite sides of the adobe town. The inferno that was previously a wagon continued to explode and collapse the gate to the compound, its smoldering horses trying desperately to escape from the bridles still holding them to the carnage. *Merle's Conflabulous Balloonation Contrapulation* swayed, caught in the wind and the edge of the compound's wall, its balloon and occupant burned in flutter and silence. Harlowe would be getting no immediate help from either direction, and he was dead center to four of Toot's gang. They each turned from trough, barrel, and bucket, and they drew as he did.

The compound's movement slowed around Harlowe. Dynamite smoke ceased its twirl to harden over the walls. The sandy floor halted its kick into the air. The sizzling flap of the massive balloon slowed above. Suddenly in Harlowe's hand, his *Cody* flashed one round after another in a circle around him.

As the compound sped back to normal time, the gang members were the only things around the adobe town unmoving. What was not on fire crumbled. Any sandy wall too tough to fall darkened in the soot. With his *Cody* already reloaded, Harlowe began toward the fiery gate to see if there was anything he could do to let the rest of Marshall's posse in, but, as soon as he stepped from splintered coffins, he heard the calls from more of Toot's men, and ran to the only corner of the town that had not been dynamite-bombed by Merle, but he had been spotted. A hail of bullets broke crate and clay around him as he dived into a smith's alcove. Ricochet shattered from anvil to horseshoe, scattered around cauldron and rail and Harlowe's boots. He curled fetal-like under the splintered barrage.

He had been a last minute addition to Marshall's posse when his father had failed to show, and now he was the only one to have made it inside the compound. Toot's gang had been terrorizing Tumbledown for months, intercepting the Colonel's supply caravans, robbing ranches increasingly close to the town, and it had taken all that time to find the gang's hideout. The plan had been a three-pronged attack — one that had apparently fallen apart as soon as it had started. From the cramped vantage point, Harlowe could see the undertaker's son, but whether he had tipped his hand to a gang member or fallen prey to Merle's misthrown dynamite, he could not tell. He could also see the burning flap of Merle's balloon from the smith's corner. The basket now burned. Harlowe tensed at what he knew would surely come.

The remaining dynamite broke the air over the compound, swirling before sucking at the smoke before adding to it. Harlowe was sprinting across the square before the thunder had died, his boots cracking in new ways. He raced behind gang member's cover, shooting two men in their necks before they were done shielding their eyes from the explosion. He found two more men at the same time they found him, everyone stepping from smoke as dark as the interior of Harlowe's defunct coffin. He knew these men, recognized them even before he palmed his *Cody's* hammer, separating one of them from his hand, the other from one side of his face.

Toot's gang was built of the disenfranchised, men of Tumbledown who had lost pasture to the Colonel, lessened their ranches due to his superior stock and prices. Some of them, like the three Harlowe spotted walking the wall, had in desperation ended up working the Colonel's cattle. These were men Harlowe had known all his life. And now he ended theirs as they lined up rifle shots. He aimed for their blood red bandanas — the sign of Toot's gang — and blew holes through thighs and shoulders and necks. But where was the gang leader himself?

Gunfire thundered from outside the walls, and Harlowe could now see others of the posse as they worked their way through the broken fires of the gate. The horses had escaped their burning leashes and now hysterically trampled the bodies left in Harlowe's wake. He passed one on his way into the interior. It was a wonder he could recognize these men. They were all stricken with whatever disease had been wracking the ranches lately. They were all just gray shriveled shells of men. Two perfectly placed pox marks peeked out from under neckerchiefs.

Harlowe searched around one of the offices. He didn't know what he was looking for or why he had chosen that specific room to dig through. It wasn't the closest to where he had been. Its shade and size were the same as others. He opened drawers and crates without knowing why.

A minute had passed, with the sounds of fire dying outside, when he realized he had been staring at a bookcase without moving. It was packed with books too neatly, especially for a group Harlowe assumed couldn't read. He tipped it over a close chair, books cracking their bindings as they scattered. The basement door he found emitted a cool air even though it was closed. An even cooler voice leaked from behind its boards.

"Ah, so the son replaces his father. It's about time you stepped up," Toot said from somewhere deep in the basement and Harlowe's memories, "'bout time we met, don't you think?"

Harlowe opened the door, but a hand on his shoulder brought him around with his *Cody* back in his grip.

"Whoa, hero!" Marshall said, jumping back with his hands raised. "It's over, boy. Well, almost over. You done good." He was joined by another of the posse, and the woman that had set off the hunt — the visiting Libran that had traveled far to inform them that they were facing more than just some standard gang leader. Her dark facial markings — angelic wings spread over her eyes — and the ebony feathers entwined in her short hair beguiled Harlowe. He had not known women could come in such variety. She wore a revolver larger than his, of a make he did not recognize, but it was the bandolier of wooden stakes that perplexed him. A silver hammer was in her hand as she pushed past him to take the lead down the steps.

"You made short work of them boys, Harlowe," Marshall said as he started to follow her down. "We'll take it from here. You go clean up, see if any are still hiding."

Harlowe walked the square. Without little to burn, the fires had gone out as quick as they started, but the smoke hovered in swirling pools over the dead bodies as if they collected the dirty souls of the dead. The crackle of wood and the settling of clay sounded like the gallop of horses from somewhere outside of town. The spirits of the outlaws rode from the devil.

Harlowe was never comfortable on a horse and they made it no secret they did not like him much either, so he walked the long night home. He neared Tumbledown but veered from its bonfire. It must have neared midnight, but it appeared the town celebrated. He recognized some of the revelry and gunshots but felt dead tired and anxious to see why his father hadn't shown for the posse. He had his suspicions. His father had not appeared for much of anything lately.

He stepped the last rise before the flatness that led to the homestead, but before it peaked he could feel the train's rumble. He remembered less and less of the years gone by but that particular movement of the earth he would never forget. And so he ran, his boots splitting open to the air on the prairie.

He had felt no more, heard no whistle or chug of the Loco's congested lungs, but as he approached the house he knew of no other explanation. It wheels had again tore the meager yellow sod of the yard. Its fiery guts had scorched the shape of its shadow into the porch. The barn's fencing had fallen in its passing. Beady-eyed pigs stared at him, tears glinting in the many stars, afraid to leave where they remembered their pen to be.

Harlowe closed the door behind him, shutting out the night while lighting candles in the den. He righted his father's chair, finding himself insufficient to fill the depression. But he picked the radio off the floor just the same. The side table was broken, one of its legs splintered, so Harlowe set the radio in his lap and began to adjust the dial. When static waned he turned the antenna. It was many minutes before he heard something, something far off in the static — a whistle he could make out only if he held the antenna just so. When he started to doze he would begin to lose it, and he had to start over again, barely touching the dial and bending the instruments until he could find it. Sometimes it would take all day.

~

Ivy of the Grove woke not knowing where she was. That had never happened to her before. Impenetrable darkness pressed against her, and for a second she thought she was back in the alleys of Bab'lon, hiding beneath dead bodies as, from above, seven massive goat eyes scoured rioting streets for that which would not submit. It was a mound of quilts she now rested beneath however, and if the cool metal walls she could feel even through her mittens did not remind her she was still in Brig, the biting air against where her scarf had fallen would have. She had crawled into the bunk, vowing to stay awake, not trusting the heater to warm the room. She neither stayed awake nor did the heater do its job. It had failed sometime in the night. It no longer glowed and the room had remained frozen. Without the light she could not see Harlowe, but she could feel his presence near the door, hear his remaining chains rattle at his slight movement, and that reminded her why she had come to the city in the ship in the mountain in the ice deep in the territory of the enemy. And if that had not been enough, the whistle chirping off down the echoing halls reminded her why she was still there. The surrounding metal clanked as it shrank and expanded, replacing the trickling water in her recent memory.

They had placed Ivy and Harlowe in separate cellrooms, far from each other down an empty hallway identical to where the pistoleer had been kept, but it had not been long after the tithingmen left when he had left his room to stand inside hers.

"Sneak," Harlowe rasped from the darkness. His voice comforted her in the confines. It reminded her of times, any time, spent anywhere other than the frozen city. It was fainter, however, drier than she remembered — drier than the deserts he spoke often to her about, drier than the air he had breathed on his walk across the dunes to find her in besieged Bab'lon. The Horde had claimed that they had liberated the capital, and she had even since then seen the territorial inhabitants swear the same, but it was not freedom she had seen in their tearing eyes on the day leather and feather perched on the Tower of Zig. It had not been adulation she heard from their spasming lips under that violent night.

"What?" she asked, before immediately understanding as, amidst a rattle of chain and a blur of movement, the pistoleer reached to pull the tall tithingman into the cellroom. The man's bald head and the pearled grip of his holstered revolver were the only things in the cellroom gleaming from the meager light of his swinging lantern. The light hummed from the top of the shepherd's staff he used to pull himself sheepishly up off the floor. He stilled the lantern, and now his gums also gleamed as he spoke.

"You're both in danger. You have to g…" He stumbled back into the doorway, noticing the Davidson *Sitdown* poised near his eye. "W… wait! Not by… I mean, I can…" As she had come to expect, the tithingman's voice was too quiet to echo, even in the tinny walls and halls of Brig.

Harlowe put the gun down as Ivy touched his shoulder. "Let him talk."

"Th… thank you. I just had to come. He knows your decision. He won't accept it. He won't relent. You have to go. You have to go now. He's coming for you."

Ivy stayed in the darkness, as she had observed Wulf do many times before. She kept her face from the meager light and metered her breathing to hide any movement or sound. The man just spoke to the darkness, his eyes never focusing.

"Yer brother?" Harlowe asked him. "No matter."

"He's not my broth… brother, but yes, yes he's coming. He wants your body, Ivy of the Grove, and he doesn't need it alive. You must understand what this means to him and… th… those th… that believe as he does. Come, you have to go." Ivy had started to collect what belongings she could find in the dark confines of the cellroom. "He's calling all his burden to him. Hurry."

It was true. They could hear the shrill whistle from somewhere deep in the ship's corridors as they followed the crouching, tall man down a new hallway. He dimmed any lamps they passed as he led them down deep into rooms where the paint had long ago been worn away. Barely any flecks speckled the gray walls, low ceilings, and scarred floors. They climbed down a scoured ladder into what Ivy would have expected to be pure rock or ice, yet still they found more gunmetal and a larger chamber littered with what appeared to be shacks cobbled together by refuse. The dust kicked up in the tithingman's hurried passage revealed the dwellings to have been abandoned long ago, yet his swinging lantern showed that the structures were so closely compacted that they still held each other together — some even two stories high. It was obvious to Ivy that a hundred people could have at once lived in the chamber, yet still only the sterile, metallic smell filled the frozen air.

No matter how deep they followed the tithingman the walls still reverberated with the patter of hands and feet from levels above. The burdens were obviously following them, yet when there was enough room and enough light for Ivy to see the tall man's baby face, she saw less anxiety on him the deeper into the ship they walked. She thought she heard the whistle again, but it may have been the scream of some warming pipe or cooling release valve.

"He's quite mad, you know," Ivy said when they stopped at a tight intersection of ladder and doors. The tall man had started to turn the wheel of a hatch but had stopped and now seemed to be deciding between two opposing doorways.

"Th... that's just your opinion, and, really, it's a very ignorant one." He chose a doorway, and they followed into almost absolute darkness. "He can be difficult to follow, but all great geniuses are. If everyone was as smart as him we wouldn't be in this situation. The world wouldn't be in need of a cleansing. But... I guess... if we were all as smart as him the Divine Choir wouldn't need to watch over us. There's the irony, I suppose. If we had remained as pure as when they created us... th... they... wouldn't have... um, wouldn't have needed to have made... I don't know." He was silent through a wide hallway — the longest they had yet walked and sided by numerous doorless ways — until they reached a room that, when he dialed the bulbs up, Ivy could see was only twice the size of a cellroom — made small by thick piping that clicked with warmth and wound into and through the walls of the dead end. Gauges with twitching arrows tittered as quietly as the tithingman spoke. "We know about the existence of germs because of geniuses like him. Do you know what germs are? There was a time when I would have called *you* mad for trying to convince me that little animals — smaller th... than anyone can see — live in the air around us and breed and eat and breathe and try to get into our skin to make us sick. But now I would call the peasants mad that don't believe it. There was a time when people believed the shapes of your head determined not only your personality but your fate, and it was madness to say otherwise, but we know better don't we? People preached that Earth was not the center of the universe, but great men — geniuses, called mad by those around them — said otherwise and eventually proved them wrong. Faith in obsolescence proved false. You would be shocked to find out how many aliens flock to our planet, right out in the open, to the center of the Divine Choir's creation. And if you spread the word, if you tried to expose these foreigners, you would be deemed mad by the masses. Such is the stigma of the genius." He tapped an inert meter until the bar tipped and quivered over a new set of numbers. "What you saw on the way in here was a suburb of Brig. Quicksilver was one of the first areas to be developed, and one of the first to fall to ruin. It housed the laborers keeping the great city warm. Now everything is regulated, first by this room and then others the farther you stretch to the bulkheads. But everything starts here. You can warm up here before you head out. Morning comes, but it will still be many hours before the sun can climb over the Titans and into the valleys you'll be heading out into. The last hatch we passed leads into a straight tunnel that will bring you out between the peaks. It will be a frozen path before you, but follow it and you'll find yourself in the clear of the worst of the peaks by the next nightfall. It won't be easy, but it will be less treacherous than the way you came."

"Thank you," Ivy said. She shook out her numerous coats in the warmth of the room. None would fit Harlowe well, but she wondered if he would even notice the weather. She was starting to wonder if there was much he *did* notice these days.

"Well," the tithingman responded, "you actually, ah, can th... thank me. If I hadn't woke you and brought you down here you would be under Pillory's specula and scalpel by now." He fumbled in his tall pockets, glancing sidelong at Harlowe's mangled hand and its twitch at the belted *Sitdown*. "I just th... thought... that mayhaps... in appreciation of me sticking my neck out for you... that you could still help me." He took silver pieces of many shapes out of a cherry box the size of his hand and began assembling a large syringe. "You see, I believe that your blood is good enough. Your blood is the key to us twisted…" His head struck metal rafter as he leaned toward light. He hissed through pain and clenched gums. Ivy giggled at the constipated expression on his baby face. "Ah, you… your chromosomes hold a th… thousand times more information th… than a Lesser Antony's. You are the savior to all the tithingmen relegated to lives of… of… 'lessness.' I can just take one vial to the Brood Pits, and they can figure out a way…"

"No," Ivy said louder than she expected to. Her voice bounced off down the outside hallway. Something clanked in return. Harlowe stepped past her to peer into the dim light, great revolver in a mangled hand.

"No?" the tithingman asked, his voice even quieter, now suddenly out of breath. His thumb twitched from the syringe's plunger handle as he shook it in her face. "But I helped you. You don't understand. You don't know what it's like. I could have let him have you. I could make you, you know. Don't you th… think you owe me? I didn't have to help you. Why are you so stubborn? It's just a bit of blood. You won't miss it. It won't hurt. Why did you even come here? Just to taunt us?"

"I came for him." Ivy turned her head to Harlowe. It was unclear whether he saw movement out in the shadows or just the effects of a flickering bulb.

"I'm in trouble." The tithingman suddenly had his silver revolver in his hand. It wavered in the air near Ivy's head but settled on Harlowe's back. "I helped you. You're so ungrateful." His big brown eyes filled his face, as the only sound after the gun misfired was a loose click that failed even to echo. Before Ivy could react to the sound, Harlowe had spun and his *Sitdown* had exploded the air of the pipe room.

She fell next to the tithingman's headless body, the blast of Harlowe's gun reverberating around the pipes over and over again against her cottony ears. She tried staggering to her feet, but the pressure kept tilting her head, and her body followed. The room spun around her — shattered pipe, steam, Harlowe's boots, blinking hallway, a smear of darkness many hands wide splattered over gauge and wall. The pistoleer grabbed her arm, pulling her to her feet as the thudding pressure became less echo and more of her own heartbeat in her ears. He might have said something to her, but she could not hear, but she followed his revolver's point to see the burdens crisscrossing the doorways of shadows. They were sexlessly emaciated, covered in buckles and leather barely hiding sharp protrusions of elbows, knees and collarbones. In the middle of the pack rode Tiny on a leathern saddle. Even in the dim light Ivy could see that the burden he rode had teeth filed to canines. Spittle foamed onto its tight cowl.

But she still could not hear. The burdens scrambled in a quick but silent dance to her, some crouching, some on all loping fours. Harlowe had his cylinder extracted, and he was examining the remaining rounds as Ivy stepped past with the tall tithingman's revolver. She bent low and beat the hammer with her opposite hand as she had seen Harlowe do in the past. But she pounded it too hard and her dizziness returned. As her shots glanced off the walls, she sank again to the floor to steady herself.

The flickering bulbs revealed the burdens scattering, and as Ivy fought to right her vision she saw Tiny's mount buck him from the saddle. The little man flew head over spurs.

Ivy found Harlowe standing over Tiny after she regained her equilibrium. The tithingman's electric prod had been kicked down the hall and his whistle broken under the pistoleer's boot. Still the little man squirmed from the floor, unable to sit up but swinging a small blade to the extent of his meager reach. There was something flecked on his screaming face, as well as the walls. Ivy's ricochets had found some marks at least. His quiet yells were not loud enough to penetrate her deafness.

But her hearing started to return as she reentered the pipe room, Harlowe behind her. A broken gauge clicked as the shattered pipe whistled. The steam had lessoned and the room already felt noticeably cooler. Ivy took a wrench from the tall tithingman's tool belt. His body was soft, despite what she expected, and something still spilled from what was left of his neck. Only the corners of the room, under pipes large and small, were still dry, and so she went through her pack for the crampons to attach to her boots. Now, able to get leverage in the blood, she worked at the bolts around two of the largest wheels set into the smallest panel. Most broke, ages ago rusted and threaded, and eventually she gave up on many of them before she worked on turning the wheels past where they were meant to turn. Pipes stopped whistling, gauges twitched in opposite directions, and deep thrumming sounded far-off deep from some other section of Brig.

She could now hear well enough to catch the howls and low growls of burdens near and far down doorways and halls as Harlowe led the way back to the hatch. Tiny cursed quietly and suckled the air with dry gums as they passed. She did not meet his eyes but could see others peering from the occasional doorway, quivering like the failing light.

They had brought the tall tithingman's shepherd staff, and its lantern was the only light they had as they descended down the hatch into a tower that eventually turned from metal to rock. Ivy's breath chilled before it left her lips, even under layers of scarves, but the two of them appeared above ground still hours before sunrise, yet the fresh air invigorated her as much as the morning glow behind the Titans.

XIX

In the waters green of the stream I looked
—called from on high but reflection crooked—
before me the son of man
and the waters boiled and cooked.
Visions end, my journey began
duty-chained to mortal span,
to break dead creed, dream, family, and clan.
They named me Liege of Foes, as was my plan.
—The Ver Primordium (VI-XX-II)

The mountains comforted them from afar, for the rock, al-though imposing and lately increasingly silver with snow that now barely shrank in the meager summers, was a still reminder of civi-lization. The great prairies they headed into had little society and even fewer trees to shelter from unrelenting winds. Disease had spared the isolated plains people during the Goblin Winter, but the later famine had not been so merciful. Farmers had become nomads when their fields crinkled under sun and grasshopper. Nomads wandered aim-lessly for game that had abandoned the dry prairie long before they had. The stubborn starved that remained on the prairie were the only fruit left ripe for the picking by the Prophets Lesser. The missionaries had reaped the dead fields and brought a populace hungry for food and word back with them to the Territories.

And so, as each day saw the peaks shrink into hillocks as the trav-elers walked into flatter and flatter lands, the security of mountain towns became only a memory. There would be little sheltered rest in the expanse they entered. Any ranches still standing would be few and far between, wind-swept fields encroaching on the increasingly brittle wood of homes.

The day came when Megrim's mountains disappeared behind them, from distance or being lost to the mists, and that was when they truly felt swallowed up by the wide-open spaces. Horses did not take to Melchyor Slayd, and so they had to walk the grasses caught between the seasons. Which season left and which one began was up for dispute. The only constant was a daily frost that only melted in the zenith of each day but failed to evaporate by the cold nights.

They expected to find the prairie howling with jagged breezes, but the wind appeared to have dwindled in the years since Phaimon, smothering the wildfires and desiccating the land with cryotic soils. The permafrost crunched beneath flat prairie grasses, and the still air had no scent Slayd could taste, but over the days another sense told him of the coming *Scar*, and the next morning they started seeing what was a gradual decrease in green flora become a sharp decline in the living land.

The earth crumbled like thin glass in their hands. Grass became dust beneath their feet, and by the next morning they had crossed the *Scar* without much of a second look. They had each seen the poisoned flocks during the Winter of Winds, the bulbous growth of pus in cornfields, the shriveled teats of human and cow nursing stillborn. Phaimon's passage was years in the past. It was now time to plant new crop, just in time for war to trample it.

And so the two climbed over the crumbling earth of the *Scar*, never looking back. Colorless plains stretched out more before them. The sun was a stark white disc the filthy clouds could not hide. Its glare was the only thing keeping Slayd's cold blood moving in the chilled air. They rested beneath the pale imitation of the sun. The clouds were so thin, so blurred, the sky looked colorless from horizon to horizon. The light gave no heat. The snow beneath their camp was dried to dust and gave off no cold. Slayd whispered to a fly skirting the edges of his thin lips. The insect's abdomen appeared red when it turned a certain way, and it was one of the mutant few hardy enough to withstand the cold without slowing. If it could find another of its ilk, its descendants could be tough enough to populate the coming seasons. Slayd finished his secrets and stood, and the fly quickly disappeared into the air.

They continued on throughout the day, and it was many hours before either of them spoke.

"The land couldn't have been more ready for the Horde," the sorcerer said as they stopped to appreciate the skeletal shade of the low, stunted trees that began to appear every few miles on the eastern side of the *Scar*. The shrubs were darker than gray and had no leaves but provided at least some respite from the sky. The air was cold and the ground frosty, but the sun still beat down on them. Slayd easily pulled one of the small trees from the ground with one hand. The twisted roots were thick as a baby's arms and could not grasp the loose soil whether in or out of the sand. "The people had been softened over a century by the Lesser Prophets' rhetoric. 'The world is wrong!' So when disease reared its black face, when hunger scratched its dirty fingernail across the pastures, the Baronies were ready to finally believe it. 'The world is broken,' the Brotherhood preached, and the world listened and followed. It's not easy to accept that 'just' people are just as susceptible to plague as the 'evil.' Where is the peace in accepting that a child's starvation is unavoidable? What the Horde offered was control — power for the powerless, dominance over the inevitable. The Horde put a face to the troubles infesting the land, personalizing the fears and giving the downtrodden a very physical enemy. How does one stab a virus? What good is a rifle against shriveling bean fields? But putting a face to supposed oppression — invaluable!"

The next day, as they started to come upon more patches of what must have at one time been fields of tallgrass, the land started to undulate, and they passed through rises and dips in rocky transitions leading into only sandier prairies. They stopped at the only batch of green they had seen in days. Graveyard ghost, immature and unflowered by its usual pale, struggled in the openness it usually enjoyed. Slayd collected the leaves of one of the more apathetic plants, also snatching up moths as they fled the disturbance. "Those of the territories now have an outlet for their frustrations. Early on, the Horde gave them a direction to aim their impotence at. The Garm and witches were easy targets. Their blasphemy was deadly obvious, with mangy four-legged messiahs and agarcalistic gods respectively. Both blatantly want the destruction of the status quo. The existence of death cults made for a superb initial rallying cry.

"But with the Garm eradicated and the covens culled, you would think the Horde needed something else to unite the Territories against. And they did, but the people were ready ahead of them. They had already felt uncomfortable in their own lands, stuck between the animalistic unknown of those like the Garm and the effeminate Lonely Forgotten Sun of God ethic they saw sneaking into the more meek-minded of their brethren, enfeebling the Territories as a whole. This new xenophobia was not as easy to define. It was because of this ineffability, not despite it, that the Brotherhood is able to direct the people against any cause they wish. Only the Liege of Foes' resurrection and subsequent rise has made for an easier target to take the heat from other concerns.

"Still, the oh so obvious target of the Army of Earth did not stop the tithingmen from sowing sedition throughout their Territories. These governors know their time is limited. Should the war end, and the Prophets Lesser come home, the tithingmen's stewardship may come into question. They may be running out of time to prove themselves. Eliminating any underlying obstinacy, whether real or imagined, and creating an unquestioning populace loyal only to this 'Divine Song' would go a long way to solidifying their worth."

They entered short groves of the midget trees they had, days earlier, only seen standing alone on the expanse. Here the ebon trees, ashen tips pointing in all directions, wove through great mounds of sand-colored rock that looked to have been stacked and pressed ages ago. Friendly rodents, barely darker than the stone, groomed gritty sand in some of the more open areas. Their holes littered the area to the degree that Slayd wondered how the surface held some of the chubbier adults. One bounced and squawked at his approach and the dance and sound was repeated in a line over the dogs' mounds and into a burrow.

Slayd crouched in shadow to feel the uneven and cool surface of the sandstone. He poked at the bones of a snake mostly submerged in the grit to find a tiny skull he pocketed. He looked to the sky for the direction of any birds but was not surprised to find none. These dog mice were the only wildlife they had seen since heading out from Megrim. It was only then that he realized that they were the only signs of wildlife they had seen. His companion climbed to the top of the most layered mound to look to the east as Slayd spoke. His throat was as dry as the air. It was difficult to speak loudly. "An enemy is the most efficient component of creating subjugation. Yes, yes, I make it sound so simple — and the Horde makes it appear so easy — but inclusion cannot exist without exclusion, or, at the very least, it is less valued without it. For rarity denotes value, and what good is this 'Divine Song' if everyone can hear it? How do I know the worth of the salvation I'm promised if everyone owns it? There must always be sinners, or else how will I recognize a saint?

"Eventually, when the Horde is finished washing over the world, its tide will retreat and its people can inspect the shells and crabs left in its wake. When everyone is nuzzling Slog Sabbaoth's ample bosom in tee-totaling conformity, the pious will search out the hypocrites or the fallen or the ignorant to set aside to save. Divisions will occur

— separations that would seem negligible to heathens such as you and I — wars will explode, and a unifying peace will resume. But in peace is boredom, for, again, there is no value in a society of the saved without unbelievers to weigh one's self against. The cycle will continue ad nauseam. As it always has. If the Horde's world is any different it is that the process is all conscious. Every component, from the divine angel to the governor to the wassailer in the street knows what they are doing. It's been an awfully efficient force of nature, this Horde has been."

"You sound like you admire them," Wulf said from the rock above. He pulled his hood back and tousled wavy hair to let any breeze touch his scalp. His cloak was easy protection against the winter, but it had become too hot against a stark sun that had only then begun to give off heat.

It took a minute for Slayd to respond, as he had to rehinge his jaw. His throat had to shrink after the passage of a squirming and squealing prairie dog. "Don't you? In a few short years they've staked a claim on the land and souls of the people that is hard to deny."

"Violently."

"Yes, yes, but that only came later. And the Army of Heaven would not be so successful if not for the unquestioning passion of the masses. I've lived a long time, friend, and I've not seen people take up a faith as quickly as in the Divine Song."

"As you said, the conditions were perfect. Their missionaries needed to not work very hard."

"Don't underestimate their patience."

"I know now to never underestimate anything about the Horde, including their governors." Wulf put his hood back up and squinted to stare back west with Yggr's Eye. Even the dull granite of the stone was bluer than the sky. He jumped down into the shade. Prairie dogs scattered at the dust but did not hide. He took a drink from his canteen before rubbing his temples with his fingers. He had hoped the ever-present headache would lesson away from Megrim. It had not in the least.

Slayd licked his thin lips with a tongue gradually splitting at the tip. It sounded like someone taking a dagger from a leather sheathe. "Are they still back there?"

"Yes, keeping their distance. They know there's nowhere to hide now, especially on horses. Can't tell who they are."

"There's no doubt," Slayd sighed as they continued eastward. They would be walking in and around more ravines of the sandstone before continuing into another plain. It appeared they would at least be heading into some greener areas by the end of the day. They could see some sort of shrunken forest at the far horizon. "The Horde would not take kindly to an absent Sin Eater."

It was another day before they reached the hills Slayd searched for, and the sun had gone down by the time he had found the wheel hidden on the highest plateau, repeatedly tasting the air and leading Wulf into the assemblage of stones.

"What would you do if you were God?" the sorcerer asked seemingly out of nowhere.

"Nothing. Nothing at all."

The rocks were worn by the exposure of the clearing, and they seemed to shine in the moonlight in the absence of stars. There was a definite swirling pattern to the stone placement, with a small center cairn half-grown over by earth, surrounded by an outer ring of rock. Four lines of mostly smaller stones branched out from the cairn in each direction. Wulf knelt at one of the spoke stones. The lines coming from the center were made more recently. The rocks were not solidly stuck in the ground. They were cleaner.

"Don't move anything," Slayd hissed. "Even a small misposition- ing could be tragic. You could wake without a head, or on an ocean floor. It may take me half the night to examine the layout as it is for accuracy. I don't need you mucking it up further."

When Wulf stood he could see other smaller stone circles meeting their own. They were broken and old and mostly grown over with the struggling weeds Slayd pulled from the rise. The trees on the plateau grew closer to each than any others they had seen on their journey, but their dark bark blended into the night, gray tips of endless branches speckling every direction like a low milky way halo around the hill. "Who made this?" he asked, more to the absent heavens than Slayd, but the mage answered.

"I don't know. This, and its eastern companion, are the young- est hoops I've found described. And the smallest." He pulled the *Annihilation Cantripticus* from a fold in his robe that should have been too small to hold such a massive tome. The only sound in the clearing was the aging hinges of the book, the stretching crack of the binding as Slayd sat to decipher a certain looping sketch. "And they're certainly the only ones this far south and east. Pray to your hoary pantheon that we wake with all our organs aligned... on the inside."

Wulf sat cross-legged, farther than a reach from any stones of the hoop. From the ground he could feel the curve of the rise. It was far from flat. He immediately began to doze. The journey, the sore muscles, the tedium of the plains, had wakened him to the reality of the last few years. At one time he had been resolved to a life of wondering. Even as Goblin Liege of the Grand Mob he had moved his followers across prairie into a nomadic existence. But reluctantly orchestrating the Resistance had created some stability in his life. With this stability came the inactivity of the cities. And the stiff muscles of the previous morning had reminded him of it.

His eyes would flutter at the sound of Slayd's low incantations, and he would try to center himself, delving deep back in his mind, finding the Yin of emptiness and the bright Yang found swimming within. The duality danced slowly, and he would, each time, fall asleep before he could meditate on the balance. This uneven slumber lasted until the moon was at its zenith, its bloat highlighting the sandier stones of the circle and the bleached tips of the stunted trees. He woke completely then, tired of the uneasy sleep.

Slayd's muttering had lessoned, and it was the lack of this mono-tone that Wulf supposed had woken him. The mage was testing the warmth of a tea he heated over a tiny brazier he had conjured from, Wulf guessed, somewhere within his sleeves.

"When is the last time you slept well, killer?" Slayd asked, inter-rupting his spellspeak but not looking up from his brew.

"I sleep well every night," Wulf answered, standing and stretch-ing, already feeling the next day's stiffness in his hips. The moon and cloudless sky made it a bright night, yet even with Yggr's Eye he could not see those who followed out on the prairie. They had appeared only a few days ago and deliberately kept their distance. Slayd believed they were of the Horde.

"No guilt disturbs your dreams? No ghosts haunt your conscience? It must be nice not to fear retribution from man or fury."

"I've known my fate for many years, and it involves neither wronged nor god."

"Oh? Do tell."

He continued to watch the black horizon through blacker scrub. There was no movement back west except for dust devils feeding, and feeding on, prairie breezes Wulf had not felt for days. Were the tiny twisters moving the tumbleweeds real, or were they remnants of a spectral past only Yggr's Eye could see? Wulf grudgingly admitted that it was becoming more difficult to tell lately.

It was not the *SHE'* that followed. Wulf knew that much. They would not have been spotted.

Slayd stood, obviously carefully so as not to disturb any stones. He directed Wulf to sit back down in an area unbefouled by their footprints. "Here the spoke points east. By morning our pursuers will have lost us, and we will be closer to my reward." He placed a small clay bowl in Wulf's cupped hands. "Drink it quickly, before it cools."

The first sip scalded his tongue, but either his mouth became used to the hot tea or the cold night cooled it faster than expected, for he drank it in three swallows. It smelled metallic but tasted like wet dirt. There was a furry, organic bitterness left behind afterward that reminded him nothing of the tea. He would have been more comfortable had he watched Slayd make it.

The mage went about sprinkling sand from a pouch along the circle and down each spoke. It was darker than the sand of the loop and disappeared into the night before it settled. He turned the sack inside out to shake out the last grains. "We'll know if that wasn't enough of the eastern dirt by our dreams," he said, returning to sit north of Wulf, fingering along the page of his tome. "Ancient Dunwich claims you'll dream of your god's disappointment if the portions are incomplete." He took his own steaming bowl from glowing embers and poured it completely into a mouth that, to Wulf, looked unhinged in the faint glow and pulsing shadows of the brazier. Something darker than the shadows hung from Slayd's neck, less than a finger's length. He turned away after watching the mage pull another leech from a sleeve, pressing it against his neck's opposite artery.

If it was the *SHE'* that followed, Wulf mused again, feeling his eyelids grow heavy, his scalded tongue numb, he would never know until they struck — just how Father Reclusive, Handsome Gibbet, and countless others had never been aware of Wulf until he had struck. The *SHE'* had taught him well. But they would never have just let their investment wander. What was their game? He had even taught others their secrets — a taboo with a death sentence. What were they waiting for? How could he have been allowed to live all these years?

But he knew his fate was not to die by his old masters' hands. His death was no more mystery to him than a previous day's steps.

He saw himself returning to Earth…

"Indeed?" Slayd turned to him. Even beneath the milk the mage's eyes had become they were entirely black, the slits of pupils had filled his sockets. His head was sweating profusely through pores Wulf did not think the sorcerer had.

As thick as his tongue felt, as heavy as his head had become, as tough as it had become to focus, Wulf could not help but speak his thoughts out loud. *I'm an old man, tired of mind and body, crippled in thought and limb, my only desire is to visit familiar sights before I die, but someone follows me as soon as I touch Earth, someone I barely remember, but I did ask for the familiar and I always get what I ask for.*

"When is this? How long from now?" Slayd asked, his voice beginning to slur, but, as minutes passed, he gave up on waiting for an answer. He chanted incoherently, accentuating every third note deeply and with a weak clap of his long hands.

Wulf could see the mage's words form out of the smoke of the brazier. The symbols were alien, but the world spun before Yggr's Eye could translate them, and he found himself on his side, face pebbled to the soil of the loops. The constellations above turned, stars falling and leaving long streams of their tails. Soon all the night sky was streaked so brightly Wulf's sore eyelids had to close against the glare. He was grateful, for he was exhausted. Still, he remembered the future of his death. His voice was breath. His exhale formed words even he could see beneath his lids. *But there is nothing left of the world I remember. Surt turned it inside out a century ago. Still I am followed. I'm followed north and I continue walking. I can't stop moving or I'll be overcome but there's no snow. There's no ice or white sun or cold winds. I yearn for the winters I remember. Had Earth used up all its winters in Ragnarock? North. Ever northward. I reach the top of the world before I find the white I remember, the white that burns through cold. The mountains here scratch at what is left of the heavens. The valleys cut Earth to its still core. Still I am followed.* The herbs no longer warmed his belly. The tea's tendrils snaked along his veins, warming them mere seconds before leaving ice-water behind. His heart had burned but now shivered. Only his brain now beat with heat. *Silver bears explode from the snow, shadows eating the little light the mountains of madness let through.*

Slayd asked a question. Wulf ignored him to continue.

I wake in their hovel. The wind whistles across the cave entrance and my ears bleed. I am eaten. There is little meat left on my legs, even less on my arms. The silver bears huddle together nearby, not for warmth but to weather the change together. They quiver and sweat, bones breaking and mending, fur shrinking into hair, claws falling and paws shriveling into hands, snouts folding in upon themselves into faces. Is this what man has done in my absence? Is this what was required for survival in this new world? His brain cooled. A wave of nausea was his only sensation now except for Slayd's guttural song. He could not hear it, with ears bleeding backward through the ages, but he could feel it. The words pressed against him like skin drums reverberating the pebbled ground between them. *Still I am followed. So as the were-bears seizure in change I crawl out of the cave, exposed tendons twitching, bare muscle grinding against the ice. I fall into a valley almost as dark as what is left of my mind.* He could not feel his heart clench, but he could hear the ice holding it crack and splinter as it struggled to beat in rhythm with the drums. *I wake covered in oil and furs. Those who hunt the silver bears have built a fire. They found me but have left me to die in their small hall with the smell of burning blubber. The only thing familiar, the only thing grounding my broken body and mind to the here and now, the there and then, the future when, is the goblin at the foot of the bed. His knife shines clearly with poison, darkly with my blood. He has finally found vengeance. Our lives complete, he opens his wrists and we sleep together — he on top of the furs, me beneath.*

"That's not how you die," Slayd may have said. Wulf heard nothing, but the words floated under his eyelids before sinking up into the miasma his head had become. The mists swirled, light consumed by darkness before blossoming out of the liquid to overcome ebony. He let the swamp overcome him as the revolving dance continued throughout the night.

~

Wulf coughed until he vomited. The painful popping of his ears had woken him and his throat was immediately seized by a tickle that kept him doubled over for most of the morning.

"The loop has given us quite a head start on our journey," Slayd said, smacking his thin lips at the dryness of his mouth. "Are you determined to squander it?"

Wulf folded his legs beneath him, closed his eyes, and delved deep into mind and body. He found the focus deep within and calmed his quivering chest. Many minutes passed around him as seconds, as Slayd collected his belongings and scrawled loud notes in the *Annihilation Cantripticus* with an inked feather held together by pale tendon and dark ribbon. He finished writing as soon as Wulf stood to spit the last of the ash from his mouth.

"So, what did you dream about," the mage asked.

"I don't dream." It was the same nightmare he had had for all of his adult life — since his delirium under the Goblin Winter. The only difference this time was that it now felt more like a memory. It was fresh in his thoughts. But, at least, his headache was slighter in this new land.

He looked around the clearing for the first time since waking. The stones were granite and smoothed as if by water and they barely varied in their blues and grays. They were not as uniform in size as the prairie loop's sandstone had been. Here the ring of rock was mostly grown over by dew-frosted grasses reaching up Wulf's calves. Although no breeze could penetrate the thick woods they now stood in, the air was colder here than on the prairie, the morning thicker with clouds and a low haze.

Slayd went about digging up the occasional stone of the new loop, kicking some of the smaller ones aside. "Just in case they decide to follow us through. And we can speak freely now."

"There was a Lesser Antony with them." Wulf cleared his sore throat.

"Unlikely. The Prophets Lesser are preoccupied with the war."

They shared handfuls of dried huckleberries and a nut Wulf did not recognize. "But to retrieve the rogue Sin Eater? Surely that would beg the attention of the Brotherhood."

"They would not expect me to report in for many more days. I taught them to respect a large amount of autonomy from me. It is *you* they follow."

Wulf chewed oyster jerky as they headed down a slight path leading into the treeline and away from the green ridge. Like his mouth, the snack tasted like ash. "But I'm dead. I found my last stand in Megrim very convincing."

"I warned you. As long as reports keep coming back from the front lines of the Liege of Foes, the Horde wouldn't believe your demise."

"I'm not the Liege of Foes."

"Yes, yes, nevertheless, consider your retirement from the Resistance to have concluded prematurely."

"And your tenure as Sin Eater?"

"Was growing tiresome. Beer and bread is the meat of unwashed masses. My tastes run more... sophisticated. The Resistance better appreciate my protections, the sacrifices I've made for information and sabotage."

"You're being compensated."

"Yes, yes, better than to let others believe I did it out of some futile sense of charity. I have a reputation to uphold."

The trees lost their color at the edges of the wooded areas. Here Wulf and Slayd came upon rolling hillocks thick with snow and bare trees in lowlands but bare of both at the higher areas. By midday they had already crossed two rivers — one of brittle frost and crumbling clay, another of fast flowing water they watched through shiny gaps in ice. The latter they had to navigate north until they found a place where the ice was thick enough to dare cross. It groaned beneath their feet all the way to the shore.

The sun revealed itself late in the day, and, although it cast no heat, Wulf felt the air grow heavy all the way until dusk. They were still traversing the low ups and downs of plateaued hills, and the weather had adapted a similar pace, with wet snowflakes appearing and disappearing as the clouds covered and exposed the sun intermittently.

Wulf used the first stars of the evening to locate their position and direction. They were farther east than he expected, farther south, and closer to the Land of Nod's boundaries than he was comfortable, but Slayd deserved his reward. Still, Wulf decided to meditate on their position through the night. The morning could bring a detour. He had a lot to think about.

It was late in the night when they came across a wooded setting thick enough they felt safe enough to bed down in. It was dark under the tight trees and crowded enough to block breeze or snow. The uprooting of a downed basswood made for an excellent ditch they could spread furs diagonally over. The tree had grown from two trunks and so an expansive root system had taken a large swath of ground with it when it fell. The ground was cool, but Slayd stoked charcoal with his breath and talked of the Horde, as Wulf wiped tears from his eyes. Soot had already blackened the air and interior.

"Use pit fires only as a last resort. What the Horde lacks in apti-tude for sorcery they've gained through their angels' favor. They give their 'divine choir' acceptable service through reverence and awe. In return they've received the all-seeing, all-consuming fire as technology. Through Chem-Oshmelech they can scry far and wide through the flames, watching enemy and friend alike. Through special blessings of Ashmedai they can even walk into the fire and appear elsewhere, from another." Slayd buried the coal in the dirt. The tent immediately cooled. Through the settling darkness Wulf watched him pull one of his few remaining fingernails out. It had become bent and brown over the prior days. A claw had already begun to appear beneath it.

The sorcerer moved sluggishly in the cool mornings until he had basked in sunlight, so Wulf went ahead before dawn to the edge of the woodland to search the early cosmos. The clouds were thick at each horizon, but what he could see of the stars confirmed his suspicions. He was familiar with the land they skirted. If they continued south, southeast the low rises would grow to greater hills, the shallow dips would become deeper ravines and sunken riverbeds.

Slayd joined him as the East warmed, the sun revealing a distinct hill on the horizon Wulf had watched grow yellow with the dawn. Even from here they could see a summit culled of its largest trees and slopes tiered unnaturally. Wulf looked to check any remaining stars.

"I've been here before… to this land."

Slayd was examining charms hanging from branches just within the treeline. He poked at one and tasted the air around it. While most were strung together with petrified sinew, the fetish was one of the few braided with long hair. The blonde web held a pale sapling taut and circular. A turquoise eye was painted and suspended slightly off center in the web, like the abandoned meal of a crystal spider. More of the hanging charms could be seen leading back into the trees the woodland shadows dissipated, but none were as intricate as the one Slayd pulled from the branch.

"These are old," the mage mused, "but not as old as I'd expect, being they're sure signs of Descendents. Virginia Dare's people were the first to greet the westerners as they explored this direction. No one seems to know what happened to them after the first Evolutionary War. They most likely assimilated into the populations. Perhaps it is what gave the people of Ophidia their red tint. Nevertheless, these fetishes do have some remaining enchantment. They may have protected us through the night." He watched as Wulf turned away from the sky, as the last stars were diluted by dawn. "We'll stay eastward today. I'd prefer not to enter Ouroboros yet. There are disturbing rumors coming out of the land — not coincidently concerning Horde occupation."

"Ouroboros?"

"Yes, yes, northern Nod hasn't been called that in a dwarf's age, but you and I now skirt land that used to be the most magically advanced area on the continent, but serpent worship has a tendency to eat itself. Your Midgardian war priest Nidhogg brought the cult to the area long ago. After the *Diet of Wyrms*, his apprentices fought each other over control, with Tormalco taking the South, and the North divided between Naga Kundalini and the Brothers Erm. The discovery of a White Room was the final nail in the coffin for the kingdom of Ouroboros. Unlocking gene secrets spread Doubt among the populace. Why worship scaly gods when we can create them ourselves? Ophidia is all that is left of the once great nation."

"I need to go to the south of those hills." Wulf pointed to eastern mounds tall enough that their summits' trees had browned. They were the largest hills in any direction and the only ones not covered in green or white.

"It's not necessary."

"It will add a day's journey… but…"

"The Horde pretty thoroughly surveyed this land before retreating for the war."

"We can head starkly north afterwards."

"I've waited this long for my compensation. I'm nothing if not patient." His new claw plucked the azure stone from the charm's hair. "But be forewarned, killer, you may not like what you find."

The air was warmer than the previous days, but they found themselves circumnavigating ice-filled ravines and slushy shade that threatened to soak their boots. The sun often disappeared behind hill or cloud or thickly branched areas, so it was difficult to keep track of the day. Wulf began clearing an area for camp as soon as they emerged on an outcropping overlooking a valley untouched by snow. It was the greenest area they had seen yet on their journey, but a light powder started to fall as he sat to admire it. It was barely evening.

"We can still gain much more ground today." Slayd said. He had assembled a backstaff from vanes and mirrors impossibly pulled from hidden pockets, turning from the sun to take measurements.

"No. We've arrived."

Slayd tasted a slight breeze blowing up out of the nestled lowlands they faced. "Yes, yes, I see, I see."

The mage had set aside the backstaff until dusk. Wulf cooked a peppered malt slowly over charcoal in the growing darkness as Slayd measured the appearing heavens.

"With the gods fleeing Earth, I wonder, will they take with them their constellations? The night could become traitorous, as unreliable as *Wyrmwood* has been as of late."

"You can see it too?" Wulf asked, feeling the lack of warmth emanating from the malt. He looked to the star, finding it brighter than he remembered — a cerulean not as apt to disappear at night. It moved faster and contrary to the other stars, and would disappear before the moon hit its zenith. But that had been its path only lately.

"Of course, such an unnatural crimson is difficult to ignore."

The snow lightened as the night darkened, until it ended altogether as Wulf crawled into a hastily made tent. He left the furs with Slayd, preferring just to wrap himself in his cloak, but the mage stayed out in the open air. The moon had shrunken over the prior days, and the little light it gave off was smothered by cloud cover, so Wulf retired to let the sorcerer read the *Annihilation Cantripticus* by feel with the few fingers he had left that had not yet grown claws.

He was still reading when Wulf joined him, before sunrise, as mists began to rise from the valley below. The glow from the horizon peaked into adjacent valleys between neighboring hills and was reflected beneath them. The fog glittered like great diamond serpents winding their way through hillocks and ravines. The moisture hadn't reached them yet, and Wulf drank deeply his canteen, quenching his dry throat as the mists noticeably rose toward them.

"We must move quickly. It's only accessible at certain times of the day."

"Yes, yes," Slayd mused, tasting the air, "it can only be seen through the prism of dew. Interesting. I had always heard the rumors, but had no idea the exiles hid so close to Ouroboros. Did anyone, I wonder?"

They met the mist as it floated up into their path to eventually consume them.

~

"Hmmmm… it doesn't add up… literally." Slayd examined the claw marks on the few structures not completely gutted and blackened. The marks were clean. The prints in the paths were deep and well-framed.

"Because they're fake," Wulf whispered barely audibly. It was the first words he had spoken since the mists had lifted and they had found themselves at the edge of Enclave. A dusty smell of smoke stung his throat, despite the fact that the fires had long ago burned out, and so he whispered through a scarf that covered most of his face. His real eye teared up before streaming down into the fabric. The side of the village they wandered had been burned the worst. Anything Wulf remembered being built of wood had been scorched into ash. Blackened stone foundations were all that lingered of the walnut homes lining the main street. The dust of sheds and fencing had settled into outlines of the former shapes. The Tower of the Triskellion had crumbled, not entirely, but the grand lookout at its pinnacle had fallen and now peered from scorched rubble at its former base. Wulf walked what was once the communal gardens, each boot alternating between the crunch of fire-hardened dirt and the onion-like layers of brittle glass the sand had become. He knelt at a pair of mounds that appeared to be a mixture of cracked stone, bleached ash, and tiny splinters of what he guessed were bone. His time in Enclave had been short, but he had grown to know that the people would have been satisfied that their remains would have become almost indistinguishable from the village they loved so much. They had always considered themselves and their village to be one with nature. The fire must have been immensely hot to disintegrate nearly all existence of habitation, and it must have been short-lived to avoid spreading to the outside forest. Brandr had brought Hell to Earth in Enclave's defense. Wulf would have expected nothing less.

"Garm only have four claws," Wulf coughed into his scarf. "Also," he said, pointing to a pair in the crust of the path, "when they stand upright the prints should be deeper, with all their weight on two paws. Also, the gardens have been carefully pillaged even though the Garm are far from vegetarians."

He walked to stand behind Slayd. The mage was measuring another set of prints with a compass made from the chitinous legs of some giant insect. "Soooo… the Horde would like it to appear that the

Garm pillaged the village."

All the better to justify the purge of the werewolves, Wulf thought. He walked the uneven glass to a row of disturbed standing stones. From there he could best see the ruined structure of the fallen tower. Even the uneven interior was streaked with striations from fire or smoke. He had always assumed that Brandr had left the village after he had, but perhaps the young boy had settled in. Perhaps he had found purpose and love among the commune. A family. A loyalty. Had he burned the village rather than let the Horde have it?

Slayd mused, "The Horde left not even a garrison in what is a highly defensible area, so this must have been during their initial push east, before the Army of Earth appeared and all the Lessers were recalled."

So, Wulf thought, as he remembered Enclave in its prime, *it had sat here burnt and destroyed.* This had been the reality of the village for years now. Was it such a threat to the Horde? The people of Enclave, all runaways and exiles from numerous creeds and nations, held to no beliefs but that which exulted the Triskellion — which existed only to glorify the faith in the people. They would have never bowed their heads in reverence to angels. The Divine Song would have been like background noise to them. Many of them had been running all their lives until happening upon the village. They would have died before running again. And it looks like they had.

"Are we done?" Slayd asked, thin pupils behind milky gaze growing. He had collected some of the palest ash and splinters in a vial, snorting a claws-worth into his shrunken nose. "I'm not sure what you were expecting to find here."

Wulf was not sure either. Had the village been standing would he have thrown himself upon the mercy of its people. Would he have given himself up to inquisition, breaking without ever saying a word? There were no answers he would have ever said aloud to any of their questions. He took one last glance up to where the tower windows had looked out. With the sun behind its spectral image, he could see the shadow arc down upon him with Yggr's Eye, could hear the screams of villagers as they pointed up to Father Reclusive's limp body as it bent lifelessly over broken silver.

He followed Slayd into the treeline, exploded trees already grown over leading quickly into untouched woodlands. They were engulfed by shade and would walk through the cool shadows for most of the day before appearing on a side of hills open to the day. Would they be the last to see Enclave? Wulf wondered. It seemed blasphemous somehow, unfair to its ghosts.

The land leveled out over the next few days as Slayd took them north into what he said was once the great, but short-lived, nation of Ouroboros. The woodlands thinned in a day. The snow thickened. The air cooled, but the unclouded sun kept them warm. The occasional stream was iced over but only by a thin crystal Wulf would break to fill his canteens. Unlike the lands near the *Scar*, they could follow deer tracks to easier paths. They even dined on fresh hare one day. Slayd once again warned of campfires, so the rabbit took almost all night to cook over his brazier.

And so, after a long night and an easy day's walk, they followed the shoreline of a slow river to climb a hillock thick with sweetgum. How the trees, even in the light dusting of snow, had kept their red leaves, perplexed Wulf. The woods they had traveled since leaving the territories had the occasional branches, or even groves, where the trees had managed to hold on to some foliage, but he had not seen such full conical crowns in years. The ruddy star-shapes were brilliant in the frost and were only seen as they topped the rounded area. He would have stopped to examine the long-stalked drooping balls composed of smaller fruit had the land not opened from the rise sharply ahead.

People walked marbled streets oblivious to Slayd. "Here I am humbled by nostalgia, laid low by déjà vu," the mage said, gesturing to numerous columned beckoning entrances. "Here I weep for *wasted* youth and wasted *youth*." He grabbed the nearest bald head and pulled it in for a forceful kiss on the lips. The kissed man continued on his walk with barely a blink. "In Ophidia did Ophidia lie, to her suitors three. Here I was born, and it is here that I shall claim my reward."

I've made a deal with the Devil, Wulf thought. *No, no, not yet.*

XX

To ever win the war ever in you
will you see all the worlds still
at the edge of your heart and mind's eye too?
They are all there if you wish to see them
grown from deeds you will not own

—Unknown

Slayd had to assure him that the thin mass of pale flesh slumped in the chair was a man. Except for the dark creases spiderwebbing in every direction, the man was colorless, an inanimate puddle hung over velvet cushioning and walnut scallop. Wulf could not tell if its beady eyes were awake, if the fat lips could open in between their rolling, if the face could function under the oppression of such massive jowls. The rest of the man's body was thin, and could not possibly have enough muscle to move under even its own negligible weight. The jelly skin hung, showing the outline of ulna and clavicle and even vertebrae. There was no movement or even apparent breathing, despite Slayd's assurances of life.

"Don't be fooled by appearances, this handsome gent is older than he looks." He was kneeling next to the chair, holding the ancient's spotted hand in his own. "He was old when I was young, and, despite what you hear in the cathouses of Quicken, I'm no tadpole myself. He is the architect of everything you see here in the White Room, aren't you, Granddad?" How his dry caress did not break skin, Wulf did not know. "Ophidia was built around the White Room, by magic and stoic philosophy. It was a beautifully progressive city, but it was Granddad that unlocked the secrets of the White Room, of DNA, and merged science and the arcane, revealing the myth of genetropy, to make the city grand. All you see before you is his life's work."

Wulf had to assume Slayd was referring to the interior of the White Room, for the city above, although obviously once a feat of engineering, had fallen into disrepair. The open theaters they passed had sunk, seating smoothed by the elements. Numerous temples were open to the sky with ruined ceilings, marked only by discolored columns holding nothing. Molding mausoleums leaned against each other, housing the blank-faced dwindling population. Street and structure were cluttered by massive mounds of rubble, of stone — once squared — broken and weathered. There was little symmetry left in Ophidia. It had become hazardous to walk the streets, with every step threatening to twist an ankle or crumble into a sudden shaft of a dry sewer.

From its history, Wulf had expected serpentine symmetry in the ionic arches, carved scales and wrapping tails topping its columns, but Slayd assured him that the reptilian symbology had been relegated to just the labs long before the Horde would have toppled any dragonic iconography. They had stayed clear of the rows of fluted columns while Slayd searched for an entrance to the White Room. The stylobates were crooked beneath them. They stepped quickly beneath the few architraves still holding. There was little marble and fewer stone in the city filling Wulf full of confidence, yet here he now found himself beneath the rubbled streets, surrounded by the uniform dun of halls molded in metal and plastics. There was just enough familiarity with the *Hollow's* White Room to both set him at ease and conversely unnerve him. Most of the rooms were laid out exactly as he remembered, to a surreal degree, with this White Room having additional labs and control rooms in a sub-basement. Although it actually made him wonder if there had been more to the *Hollow's* White Room than he had been made aware of.

He paced now in one of the additional labs under red lights that barely lit the three of them. Instruments and a control panel led into a black screen covering the adjacent wall. Slayd had powered up the screen immediately upon their arrival, while Wulf examined a familiar man-sized frame of silver and gray. Theirs had been a similar device beneath the *Hollow*, mostly cannibalized for the precious metals in the guts of its base, but here this one stood, a freestanding entrance to nothing.

"It's a Moon Room," Slayd said, not turning to look at him. "But no one, in all of Ophidia, was interested in diverting enough power to open it. Whenever a power source immense enough was discovered there were always other experiments taking priority. Being so close to MANN lands, or so paranoid concerning the Everman, defense was always the word of the times. It's a shame really. Ophidia's force fields did not save it from the Choir. Its walls fell when the angels blew their trumpets."

"The Horde conquers through more than just violence."

"Yes, yes, but never-the-less, had they powered the Moon Room,

Ophidia's people might have lived on in whatever lies on the other side. In Ophidia did Ophidia lie, in the twin sins of eternal contrition and infernal nutrition."

But they did live on, Wulf thought, in the empty stares and scrounging fingers of the scavengers above. Slayd had told him that the Army of Heaven had marched on Ouroboros after the Tower of Gog fell, but had soon retreated when the Liege of Foes rose. Still, cities like Ophidia — so far from the Territories — had starved for too long in occupation. What was left was neither wholly of its original grandeur nor of the Horde.

Wulf traced the runes of an unknown metal, the bar crossing the top of the Moon Room's frame. Yggr's Eye translated the runes, but they said nothing he did not already know. Any power source was mute. The frame's base was open, practically hollowed of components, and any cords were cut or missing. Yet Wulf swore he could still feel a warmth beneath the alien metal.

Before walking back to Slayd and the ancient he looked through glass into the nearby room. It looked untouched even by time. The beds and monitors were pink under the red light, reminding him of when he woke all those years ago in a different White Room, feeling as though he had slept for years, dreaming the same dream in a seemingly endless loop — the dream Slayd claimed dramatized the gods' dissatisfaction. Wulf suddenly felt as though he had had the vision again the night before. It was fresh yet again in his mind. Perhaps it always would be. He was now certain the nightmare was more than just the sleep of an affected mind. It was a memory. But of the past or the future? Possibly both?

Call to the Beast and the Beast calls back. A summons and a howl. Earth opens and Heaven goes silent. Only the howl remains.

Just what had he done in his feverish delirium on the plains, all those years ago, when found by G'mama?

"I'm not even sure the old man *can* die." Slayd interrupted thoughts of the world's upheaval. "His body is an absolute marvel of science and magic. He was his own first test subject. But it is his mind I'm truly interested in." Granddad was apparently hairless except for eyebrows curling relentlessly like feelers in centipedal death throe. No teeth around a swollen tongue. Fleshy flaps hung under his shriveled eyelids. His auricles were monstrous mazes. "And it's still in there, if it can be recognized as such. And if anyone can navigate the haunted house between his ears, it is you."

"I'm afraid..."

"Pardon?"

"...my abilities have not been... reliable as of late."

Slayd cooed closely to the ancient. His vibrating tongue looked thinner, more forked than Wulf remembered. "Granddad is the only man alive with the knowledge to work these elements. He practically invented the arithmetic these computers process. He discovered levels of epigenetics not known to even the Old Ones, to those who left us the White Rooms. They had given in to genetropy, convinced of limitations in DNA manipulation. Granddad refused to believe in boundaries. He broke evolution." Slayd dabbed at the drool forming at the edge of the ancient's mouth. "And he's the only person alive who remembers how to manipulate these instruments to do his bidding. The codes and passwords have been lost to all but the abyss of dementia."

"Looking into a man's mind is not a task to be taken likely," Wulf explained. "It is an act of intimacy — one in which both parties are not left unaffected."

"How many of your men have I saved? How many resistance members live to see this day because I 'killed' them? Do you even know? The Resistance would not exist if not for my misdirection. The Army of Earth would have been crushed if I hadn't been risking my life to sneak intelligence out of Bab'lon."

"There's risk of infection. A mind so... disturbed could create a backlash, incapacitating even my..."

"The Governor of Megrim was on to you. Bab'lon was aware of your presence. If I hadn't come to town, if I hadn't partook of their bread and beer... I sacrificed a very lucrative title to pull your fat from the fire." Slayd straightened the ancient's gown. It now contrasted with the invalid's slumped form but flowed into the chair's matching velvet. The mage kissed a desiccated hand before moving to the other, his lips lingering over a heavily lined palm. "You know what I need, what your Resistance owes me. I asked only one reward," he said, standing and crossing to a row of instrumentation lining the wall. He clapped his spindly fingers together, folding one hand inside the other before opening it to reveal a ring cut from crystal turning violet at its tips in the crimson room. A pocket appeared in Slayd's sleeve from which he withdrew a slim finger still bearing all its knuckles. The scaly image carved into the crystal matched perfectly the tattoo wrapping the feminine finger as he betrothed it, just as the rock fit into a notch on a control panel like an artisan's finest puzzle piece. The edges of the wall-screen immediately lit in the same purple color.

Wulf sat cross-legged in front of the ancient. The information he needed was very specific and would have been a challenge to find in any average man's mind. And this would be no average mind. He would have to prepare himself, have to fortify his telepathic shields against anything he might find while also against the feedback pressing at him from out among the land.

He closed his eyes, dulled his senses, and meditated on the simple form he always retreated to — the black and white flowing and turning and sinking and evolving backward and forward.

The *Wheel* of the *Way* slowly turned within him, the simplest of contrasts flowing against itself, ever in balancing harmony. He breathed deeply, sinking into the primordial gray, only his not-stomach moving, expanding and shrinking as he pictured the thoughts leaking out of him as torn streamers radiating upward and outward on air heated by escaping warmth. The dissipating consciousness was the only light in the abyss, and so it grew dark in Wulf's mind as he cleared the gulf around him, purged the poisonous energy.

He floated, sitting in the absolute vacuum, the only movement being the deep breaths he then started to count. He counted forward and backward, following each breath into the future, remembering each breath he had ever taken, one at a time. It should have been his only focus. But the pressure squeezed from all around him, the outside force was always there, pushing against his mental defenses.

He sat on a shore before the dawn of the pressure, the pain's light just warming an organic horizon. He had little time. The sand was coarse beneath his thighs, each grain a memory ever cooling with the passage of illusory seconds. The tide of the future grew ever closer as he counted. Soon there would be no more breaths backward. How many more breaths forward would there be? The future foam licked his toes. It was icy cold. As deeply as he breathed, he looked, and then he looked deeper, into the surrounding not-air, into the not-air's not-molecules until he could see the not-atoms of his surroundings. He drew them around his cross-legged not-form, squeezed them, bonding them together into crystals — thousands of long filaments of parallel crystals he wove hexagonically in the not-space before him. He wove walls, parallel and on all sides, until he sat floating, sitting within a cube. He no longer felt the sand or the tide or the dawn. He looked deeply again, pulling more not-atoms to him, compressing and weaving, building walls within walls until he was surrounded by redundant tesseracts of mental shielding folded together around every edge in every not-direction.

Only then, after not-years on the not-shore, was he ready to step through the imagined door.

~

He expanded the walls upon walls to weaken them, permitting a blinding light to seep in. It was no wonder the baby cried. The light permeated the apartment, pressing even through closed eyes, along with a faint buzzing. It was unclear whether the two were related. Wulf had little time. He could feel the familiar interloper out there, somewhere, the mental feedback building. So he hurried through the mess of the apartment, through long-soiled clothing hardened and stuck to the floor, food rancid with roaches on counter and sofa, and indeterminate trash leaking and crumbing beneath his feet. He opened a portal in the redundant walls to snatch the baby from the dark spot on the carpet, light and buzzing and incessant wailing flooding in. The infant's beady black eyes were the only indication, the only hint that it was, with certainty, the ancient man. The world started to tremble. The far-off familiarity shook the sky outside the apartment. Wulf had little time before the painful feedback would force its way in. He pressed the inconsolable infant to his chest, squeezing it into a lump of flesh, crushing it smaller and smaller, its muffled screams growing dim. He molded it down into his hands, patting it until it hardened into a smooth brown egg. He picked through crusted dishes and utensils fuzzy with mold to find a glass to break the egg over. It cracked but did not open. A roach scampered over his hand. He dropped the glass. It shattered silently. The sky out the window splintered and broke in turn. The familiar interloper flooded in, collapsing the apartment and slamming against his mental walls. Wulf crushed the egg and drank its orange yolk as the pressure tore at the barriers and consumed him.

~

Slayd had only to turn away for a second when Wulf rolled

backward, clenching his head in his hands, breathing and frothing in the pain.

"Is that it?" the mage asked, milky eyes wide. "Did you get it?" But he received no response except gritted teeth. "Breathe, killer, take your time." He walked to kneel again by the ancient. "I've waited this long, I can wait a few minutes more. Isn't that right, Granddad? I inherited my patience from you. Whether you passed any of your genes to me or not, you taught me that, if one waits long enough, the world will come to you. I regret to say it took me too long to see the value of that lesson." He caressed the long lobe of the old man's ear between a dying nail and a new ebony claw. "I've missed you, father, but, you must understand, I thought there was nothing more for me here, and I was right, until now." He pulled a small vial from deep within the endless folds of a sleeve. He held it up, looking at the shine of the ancient's spittle through its translucent glass. It appeared empty. Slayd knew better. "You would laugh. Oh, the irony. You see, I've been saddled with responsibility. A god's power with a man's conscience — the latter I blame you for. Such a complete incompatibility. If God is love incarnate, and He kills millions, does that make genocide an act of ultimate love-making? God is the epitome of moral example, yet killing…"

There was stirring behind him, and he picked at the crust lining the old man's closed eyes before standing to follow Wulf to the control panels. "How long will the memories last? How much time do we have?" he asked, but Wulf just staggered again, rubbing between his eyes with one hand while typing with the other. The keys lit at his touch, while panels opened with new controls emerging and glowing. Slayd watched his fingers move eerily quickly over the numbers and sigils. He found himself embarrassed to admit how mesmerizing it was, how familiar it was, while, at the same time, he was hit with an unfamiliar stroke of nostalgia. He had been pretty young when he would watch Granddad work, but the old man's rhythmic typing had entranced him as a child.

"In Ophidia does Ophidia lie. Her bloodline leads to thee."

After a minute had passed, Slayd realized he was missing the images and text on the wall before them. Wulf's pained face reflected the numerous rotating dossiers on the large screen, a single thin tear of blood running from his granite eye as he read about the different Greater Prophets Ophidia had catalogued over perhaps centuries.

The files stretched all the way back to Golgotha, his remains exhumed from tainted lands, his DNA indecipherably alien. From there on, the genes were noted as identical, from Jugannatha — hero lord of the Evolutionary Wars — all the way up to one Wulf appeared to be focusing on. The individual's name was unfamiliar to Slayd, but his appearance was similar to the others, and his genetic make-up was again noted as identical. "But," Wulf finally whispered, "he wasn't a Greater Prophet. I know that for certain."

Wulf landed next to the ancient as Slayd shoved him aside. "This isn't why you're here," the mage hissed. He typed slowly with the tip of a long bruised finger, and a small slot appeared and folded open to accept the clear vial. It disappeared as the drawer folded back into the panel. Blinking sigils and numbers squirmed across the screen like insects, disappearing as quickly as they appeared, to be replaced by worms of light that would be, in turn, replaced by even more results.

Slayd returned to the ancient's sunken lap. He caressed the folds comprising the old man's neck with the back of a shedding hand. "I don't know if you've heard, father, but Tormalco's hold on the southern land is over. I ended the Everman. But his goal of immortality may not have died with him. His legacy may yet live on. He left behind a virus named for his old master. Do you remember Nidhogg? Yes, yes, I never found the Always to be of the sentimental sort, but the name is appropriate, don't you think? The Nidhogg Virus is a deadly venom on the earth, but who is it targeted to, I wonder?"

"The lobsters come in to their infernal march... across the sky," Wulf mumbled from the ground.

Slayd sighed and returned to the control panels. A slot appeared to return the vial to him, and he held it up to the crimson light of the room, slit pupils narrowing. "Automatons too small for the eye to see, too ugly for man's mind to comprehend, emulating organic pathogenic agents, replicating through reverse transcription, and, by mining the iron in a man's blood, building microscopic factories in a host, churning out millions more of its kind, all with the secondary purpose of integrating themselves into the host cells' genomes, expressing new genes, new mutations, before building new invasion forces to send out in search of familiar frontiers in not so new hosts." He followed the lines of new math appearing on the wall above him.

"The lobsters continue their eternal march... up on high," Wulf said. He licked his lips like the ancient beside him.

"Because the virus is targeted, the microscopic automatons are programmed to only search out those with a certain gene marker, a short DNA sequence. And that is why I am here, to find the name of the lucky person or 'family' that Tormalco saw as a threat. Whom did he hate so much that his legacy…" Slayd froze as the green characters before him did likewise, only his unblinking eyes twitching. For minutes he read, and when he finally broke the stare he almost immediately returned to read the screen again.

"The lobsters within you are aware of your external march… so I dive…" Wulf struggled to his feet but quickly crossed the room to slump into a corner. "…down into your pores, to find doors, in which there are four drawers to explore…"

Slayd typed, pulling up other files he barely skimmed. "Well, I suppose I've failed somewhere along the way if I find that surprising. Is it a character fault to have optimism eclipse perception? I suppose it is. I, after all, have certainly punished others for the weakness of positivism. Tormalco, you sneaky saint in demonic clothing, did even you have any idea how this could change the genetic landscape. I suppose you did." He touched a blinking panel and it opened with a cold hiss before a warm hum deposited two pencil-sized and shaped instruments into his eager hand. He shrugged, the shoulder of his robe falling to expose a flaking pale arm he stuck the flat end of the white instrument against. After a slight hiss from both utensil and recipient, he tossed the object aside before placing its twin into Wulf's lap.

"…full of dinosaurs… so many dinosaurs."

Slayd took a step toward the door before pausing. He adjusted his robe, turning folds and pockets inside out before pulling out a glowing leyden jar. "And here is where I say my valedictions, father," he said, delicately taming the old man's eyebrows with a fresh claw reflecting the spark of the jar. "For Ophidia holds nothing else for me, if it ever really did. I have outgrown it, if it was ever truly large enough to contain me in the first place. I wish you good health." He held up the jar as though to drink from it. "To your past century, and to the next hundred years!" He pitched the glass, shattering it over the panels. The controls and the screen greedily ate the resulting electricity before exuding their own sparks and eventually growing dim, leaving the room smoky and red again.

Slayd strode through the exit without looking back.

...'til he is dead
and buried in the grave of weak choice and
chance, held strong by gods, and man
—scrawled on the walls of the King of All's lower halls

asarean walked through the wall of yet another farmhouse, leaving the structure and the inhabitants behind groaning in his wake. One of the suns had set earlier as he threatened a group of workers pulling up stillborn beetfruit from a brittle field, and the other star now began setting out toward where he grudgingly had to continue his interrogations. In his armor he never tired, hydraulics and stimulants compensating for any strain, yet it would still take him more time then he wanted to spend running around this dirtball of a moon while the rest of his squad engaged in actual warfare.

"They knew more than they told you," the boy said, his smile widening impossibly farther. "You need to hurt them. You need to hurt them more. They think they know pain — eking out a sparse existence on an ignored moon, toiling over a cursed ground, pathetically eating of it all the days of their lives."

"What are you, kid?" Easarean shouted, mulling over the prospect of spending any more time questioning peasants while Ehlena and the others razed the population. Every so often his scanners picked up on the devastation of the city, broadcasting into his helmet the loud work of his clansmen. He had long ago shut off the communications of the squad. The war-cries and updates were only boiling his blood faster than the nagging of the child before him. "Are you Eha'dadadad?" he asked, finally looking toward his grinning face.

"These may be the dregs of the Empire. Blood diluted across clan and race. Culture forgotten and mixed into a bland stew too tasteless to disgust. Ostracized and left to barely survive in a distant system long ago mined of any value." He unraveled his crusty scarf to rewrap it tightly over a mouth so stretched Easarean could only wonder how the kid could breathe much less talk without cringing from the pain. "They may be wronged by the Aertlantean Empire, but still they know nothing of the true suffering it has caused. Nothing of the poison it spreads just by its touch to the countless other cultures it has interfered with, the endless ripples its fascism has spread to other planets and races across the cosmos. But more importantly, even these genetic menageries are descended, like all the clans, from those that fell upon the Court of Ugarit, from those that forced the diseased mind of the Empire upon an innocent land and its lord, from those that stole gold and lives and time and potential from the one and only…"

"Are you Eha'dadadad?" He had taken the boy from the salt of the earth, holding him aloft by the neck and squeezing until the large brown eyes bulged beyond how they should have been able to.

"Yes, this is how you hurt them! They is how they should suffer for what they did long ago. They never suffered! They were never made to pay for their intrusion! A hundred generations pass and they still interfere, still meddle with lives and worlds beyond their own! And they won't stop until they are made to suffer! Until they are hurt!"

With a mental command Easarean shut the receptors in his helmet. He shut down all the sensors except for one, closing himself off to all his surroundings except for a meager visual feed coming straight from the his armor's eye. He was immediately at ease in the deprivation. The silence was comforting. With the HUD displays powered down the darkened interior of the helmet gave him no indication of the hazy atmosphere, no indication of the coming storm or updates of the fight being waged in the city. He could peer through the pinprick of light in front of him to watch as his hands closed tighter around the child's throat, becoming fists under the scarf. He could feel nothing — neither skin nor bone giving under gauntlet. Easarean would have thought himself possessed if he had not enjoyed it so. Even so, he felt far removed, as though he watched it from a feed being sent from a million leagues away.

The boy's scarf, as disheveled and strained as his skin, pulled away to reveal the smile, now askew but still crossing from ear to ear. There was a quiver of lip before the boy's head popped off. Easarean wasted no time in turning and commanding the armor back up to full sensory input. Fluorescent scenes swam over his vision and audio came flooding in of the city battle. The squad had found a cache of power armor that was immediately being used against them, great stolen giants defending the city against Easarean's brethren. From even farther away, Heavy Infantry Imperial Brute checked in. He had entered the Red Barn district and had an urgent update, but he cut out before clarifying. So now Easarean had a choice. He could ignore the protocol of trying to regain contact with his commanding officer, and he could head toward the far district, or he could continue going into sparser fields for continued interrogations.

A dust devil picked up from behind, lifting the dead body. The boy's head bounced on currents of dusty air and arcing ground lightning.

Easarean scanned the coming clouds. They rolled over each other like waves — red over gray and green over white. They had the expected ratio of sulfur and nitrogen oxides with extremely elevated levels of hydrogen ions. The weakening pink sunset turned even darker as shadows ran like blood over the pastures and beetfruit field.

It happened so fast his sensors picked up the increase in wind only after he had been lifted into the air. Eha'dadadad raged all around him, his armor's quaputers barely compensating for the massive electrostatic surge.

The clans shall learn the very meaning, the origin, of suffering! the voice screamed through the cracks appearing around Easarean's armor as it depressurized against the storm demon's ball lightning. The Aertlantean was tossed against ground and building, and even the sky slammed against him in his uncontrolled tumbling. He thought-commanded his armor to release irradiated ice nucei from hidden compartments to stun Eha'dadadad. With his systems shuttering, Easarean would have had no idea whether his armor complied had he not almost immediately landed in a field far from where he had been picked up. He was in a new eye of the storm. Before his armor rebooted he caught the signature of a symmetry breaker going off at the sight of the red barns. The resulting electromagnetic waves would more than likely fry his quaputer, but he blacked out before he found out for certain.

~

Easarean was exhausting his ammunition. Except for Brute, he had been the closest to ground zero, and, after the symmetry breaker bored to the core of the moon, his armor's quaputers had been less than reliable. He could only periodically access its power source, despite the fusion cell having plenty of power, so any energy weapon was becoming increasingly useless. And so he instead fired off round after round of projectiles.

It had been long enough since Heavy Infantry Imperial Brute had checked in that the others had given up on him, but Easarean's sensors still periodically searched. The information was broken, with frequent reboots of his systems interfering, and he still heard nothing back.

He scanned the broken holodisplays moving across the interior of his helmet, at the same time tearing down the building's wall in front of him. His directed energy weapons, pulsed electric cannon, and even his railgun, had become inconsistent after the symmetry breaker cracked the moon, so he found himself tearing through the shaking city with armored hands, rationing the few rounds he had left for his solid projectile armament.

Somewhere near, Eha'dadadad hid, in storm or flesh or building or home, and so the phalanx just had to raze what was left of the moon to be certain. Easarean watched the city fall through a haze of sand and crackling holodisplay. The breaker had tore a rift in the moon's magnetic sphere, possibly damaging it for good, and a great rounded hole now emerged and grew from the area where Brute had searched the red barns. The breaker had increased gravity in the vicinity of every object, pulling everything down to the planetoid's iron core. Easarean's squad's armor was the best of the Clans. It inspired fear and innovation across galaxies, but they still could not have been prepared, or shielded, for this proximity to the symmetry breaker.

His armor alerted him to the nearby presence of other squad members. Ehlena was the closest, engaged in battle with something Easarean's failing scanners could not identify. She should have been near enough to spot, but the storm raged around him, particles of field and city, natural and otherwise created a thick winding soup through the opaque air.

He tore down another wall before deciding to seek Ehlena out, and almost immediately a nearby particle explosion put him on his knees. His display reappeared to show him the schematics of an experimental Empirean power armor before him. Before they flickered out, he recognized the suit as one stolen from a secret foundry.

The power armor stood twice his size, and it took a heavy step toward him before bathing him in a shower of plasma. For a second he could see the metallic ogre through the magnetic storm, large arms poised to crush him, small arm melting as the plasma whipped back in winds from all directions. Easarean leaped backward into the meager shelter of the shaking building, sticky elehydraulics slowing his muscles. If he remembered correctly, the stolen power armor was equipped with only topical magnetoshields, and, even if the destroyed atmosphere was not already wrecking havoc with its systems, a well placed shrapnel drill grenade should overload its systems.

With his targeting quaputer offline, Easarean launched the grenade out into the storm. There was no sound above the deafening winds and shaking of the moon, nothing to indicate he had done any damage until the power armor crashed through the opening toward him. Sparks flew from hundreds of points where nano-carbon drills burned the shields away.

Easarean chanced his shoulder-mounted rail cannon. It fired its last round, exploding in the process but sending the flechette projectile through the power armor's remaining shielding and opening its torso. Easarean read the flickering screens inside his helmet before they blinked out, perhaps this time for good. They told him the building's weak points, and he went about tearing at them until he stepped back into the storm behind the collapsing structure. If the power armor dug itself out he would be waiting. But for now he followed the short cracks of projectile firings to a small enclave of weather-wracked rebels. Here he pulled limbs from bodies, heads from necks, with shots from every direction harmlessly bouncing off his armor. And all the while Easarean looked for that smile, that hideously deforming smile Eha'dadadad could not suppress in the possessed.

He was well aware that they may not find the storm god before the moon collapsed completely. He might have escaped, or he might have been hiding, or his final trap might yet be sprung. But until whatever outcome came, Easarean was going to enjoy himself. In the wind, the blood covering his armor caked with sand and evaporated before it could dry, but there was always more to come.

He strode into the next mass of the fervent with a lust to gain the notice of the devil.

XXII

Brother to none and most unraveled worlds
Condemned in flood and constipated deed
Split by scar, to ape's army he is hurled
Will he be demon-damned or vacuum-freed?
—The Fallo Terminus (XXVIII)

The doll's crown was missing. Slayd touched the felt with the scab of a fingertip, trying to smooth over the tiny holes the thread left when the crown had been removed. He could not remember the Washkington doll without the felt headpiece, but he did not remember ever removing it either. The rest of the room was exactly as he had left it, completely untouched in the decades since he had last seen it, so why would someone have molested his favorite toy. He could remember the crown as though it were still there though. Its soft arches always curled no matter how long he pressed them. Its foil gems were forever dull, no matter how often he spit-shined them. Slayd straightened Washkington's bright blue jacket over the rest of its naked khaki, before setting the doll down to search for its short cape. He found it near his childhood orrery, shook the dust from it to reveal the bright crimson beneath the royal blue, and went back to tie it around the doll's neck. This time he placed it face down on the child-sized bed so its button eyes would quit looking at him with unfamiliarity.

He headed for the fallen door of the small room, flicking the orrery as he passed, expecting it to spin as easily as it once had, but Earth barely turned, Mars and Venus just quivering, Mercury falling and rolling out the door ahead of him. Planet X just absorbed light from the opposite side. Slayd took one last look at the short bookshelf before leaving, tipping most of the spines to the floor, slipping H. Humboldt's *Action Mechanics* into some netherpocket of his robe.

He stepped over the door he had only minutes before torn from the corridor, purposefully avoiding the stark numerals laser-etched into the metal. He continued down the passage, stale scents bringing no memories. He passed IV without a look through the tiny window, ignored the darkened interior of V, whistled through his fangs while passing the heavily fortified door of VI. The two claws of his right hand skimmed along the wall, screaming down the chamber, leaving freshly shining lines in the pale metal.

There was a long break until the final door of the hallway.

"Oh, city of lost children, what had you cooked in my absence?" The passage ended in a circular doorway marked with the etched numeral of VII. "Even God knows better than to try to improve upon perfection. Or is it just that humanity will never be as impotent as the Heavens?" A keypad revealed itself, and, despite Slayd's concern, the door slid open upon itself at the slightest code.

It closed behind him as he entered the small round chamber. The air was immediately humid as all light disappeared. The condensation tickling his face dried as soon as it appeared, with the vibration of machinery behind the walls turning and slowing. Through a port in front of him he could see a jungle speeding through the seasons. He braced himself against the unseen curve of plastic walls until his comprehension could adjust to the adjacent scene. Days blinked by faster than his eyes could follow. Fluorescent fauna buds appeared and flickered in impossible growth before shriveling and falling in a breath's time. Weird trees leafed fleshly in sudden summers, bled clearly in quick winters, ever-reaching toward a synthetic star as their elder alders fell to fungal and melted into a pulsing jungle bed.

The air looked thick with a fog Slayd figured to be the movement of fauna walking, flying, crawling, and gliding faster than he could follow — generations of mutants rising and falling toward entropy. For, Slayd wondered, how much longer could the Descensionsphere continue its blasphemous experiment without a hand guiding it? Indeed, how long had it gone on with only a demented absent designer?

The grinding sounds in the round walls around him slowed, as did the sensation of movement beneath the floor, and the scene through the portal. The flickering light slowed to a omnipresent glow, with the massive orange sun emerging to soar overhead before crawling over the holographic sky, finally setting and disappearing behind chitinous trees. The timelock door hissed as some great serpent before its iris dilated open. Tiny eyes reflected toward Slayd as he entered the Descensionsphere, emulating the pricks of blue stars barely breaking through the almost physical night.

Slayd had to strongly suck at the heavy air. It was practically a liquid to wade through, and he wiped at the moisture of his scaly scalp, shedding skin sloughing off like a wet paste. He walked through hypercolor grasses and a cloud of what looked like dragonflies with only two legs but multiple antennae, their wings fluorescent green under the black light.

He stepped gingerly through the night, thick heat weighing on him, radiation tanning his cracking skin. Hairy trees shivered as he passed. He had been holding his pheromones in reserve since entering the Descensionsphere, but the plants were determined to taste his scent. Strange mammalian gliders scampered along exoskeletal branches to follow him, but they kept their distance, their heads revolving at the hooting sounds from the deeper overgrowth.

By the time the jungle began to kill him, Slayd had decided to turn back. His lungs smoldered from mercury vapor. He could barely see through the tears of pollen-swollen eyes. Acidic immunoglobulin of an artificial future grew on his exposed skin.

He rounded a tiny pond, bloated flytraps glowing violet beneath the gelatin, and started a new path back the way he came. Unwatched, undirected, VII had undoubtedly grown beyond its original clutch. Just as he had. And there in revealed the truth about his superiority. He had evolved without the use of a Descensionsphere, without millennia of forced generations. He had grown through tailored experience on his own, a superior curiosity and resultant intellect guiding him — not selection, natural or otherwise. Ophidia's White Room projects had peaked long ago. It was a shame barely anyone still lingered to realize this. Still, Slayd had to admit, he was curious as to what remained of VII. Did anything remain? Or was everything he saw VII? Had the entire ecosystem evolved out of some amino acids Granddad purposefully left out to dry in the Descensionsphere?

Beaked prosimians scattered at Slayd's approach, cackling and fluttering only as far as low branches, neon ringed tails twitching angrily. The nest had been dug out of the clay a river had receded from, and among the fragments of eggshell spread the desiccate form of one of the feathered primates, its proboscis still covered with flecks of glowing yolk. Slayd scratched at the clay to pull the only remaining intact egg out. It was as large as his head, with spiraling designs turning violet in the black light of the fake night.

~

The sorcerer strode the pavilion, past column stumps and over coiled statues, around fallen layers of entablature collecting a light snow, and through colonnades creating shadow-striped corridors as they leaned precariously against each other. The Serpent's Tooth had sometime been reduced to vine-infested rubble, barely recognizable as the tall temple it had once been, and so he searched for other steps high above others to speak from. He eventually found himself in the agora, and settled for the acoustics he remembered. Most of the surrounding architecture had been short, innocuous to invaders, and much of it had survived, and so the corners and alcoves, designed to augment a speaker of the square, would still suffice. Yet he was ignored.

"Here is the one you know of as III!" Slayd's voice was instantly loud, reverberating through the buildings. He leaped to a base with crumbled corners. The only pieces left of its reptilian statue coiled around his legs broken, dust and snow falling at his step. "But that name is nothing to me. I am, always have been, and always will remain, Melchyor Slayd. I am Wyrmbane. Born of Greater and Lesser, king and peasant, and venom and milk, blood of science and magik, suckler of geneticist and conjurer, product of law and chaos. I am both descendant and harbinger of Nidhogg."

Some of the lazy-eyed denizens of Ophidia appeared from rubble both collapsed and leaning. Their robes were clean but their faces dirty. They either spoke quietly to one another or wandered the square without acknowledging the speaker. As Slayd remembered, they were an inoffensive people. Their plain appearance and expression, their words, devoid of any nuance, would relegate them to no history once the last marble of Ophidia had tilted. Nothing had changed since he had left. The people that had ignored him were the same tawny, ambiguously gendered, impotent drones he had left behind. The only difference was that they now slept under collapsed limestone instead of above their palatial gardens. Their pyromantic hypocausts leaked out into the countryside. The luxury of the surrounding concrete now only cooled their mouse-eaten beds.

"I am the slayer of ancient Ashkelon, the Yellowstone Salamandr, great Kalderan wyrm of warm earth, clayborn guarded, hot spring bebreathed. I am the legacy and the death of the Everman, the Always, the immortal Tormalco of the Tower of Gog in sunken frozen Magog. I am savior of Earth, sin eater of Heaven. I am the ultimate glory of the lost nation of Ouroboros, its magnum opus, the crowning achievement on the brow of Ophidia."

Wulf stumbled into the light assemblage from one of the many shadows created by the slanted buildings. He had been holding his head, and now bumped against a passerby to fall to his knees. He crawled through the gravel, his black cloak in stark contrast to the surrounding snow and marble, to lean against an entryway. He took a handful of frost, melting it against his cheek to smear the dried blood that had cried from Yggr's Eye.

"Not this!" Slayd yelled to a crowd suddenly attentive as he held the egg aloft. Its sigils spiraled blandly now under a yellow star. The shell was the same light gold color as Ophidia's citizens. "Not this genetic dead end, not this oviparous abomination! You created the superior being long ago, but, in your obvious ignorance, failed to recognize it, banished it by neglect, drove it away with your insipidness. Instead of girding your loins against the rape of the Horde, you wasted time and resources on quixotic frivolities. Ophidia could have been a force to be reckoned with, but you refuse to recognize greatness when you achieve it, and you fritter and waste the hours in offhand ways, like this." He held the egg high, but it refused to catch the light the way it did in the Descensionsphere. "Is this the city's savior? Is VII our people's redemption? All you had to do was ask, and I would have come running, running to protect the citizens, the philosophy, of those that pushed me away o' so long ago." The egg teetered at the tips of his long fingers. There was no response from the audience. Only bored looks and resumed steps in and out of the agora.

Wulf laughed. His was the only sound besides shuffling slippered steps. He used the edge of the doorway to pull himself up and to steady himself against obvious dizziness. A slight breeze appeared to dust the fallen abacuses of snow. He pulled his cloak tightly around himself after shaking his hood low. Only the livid granite eye appeared from the shadow he had become. His ebony form slunk back to the ground in Slayd's peripheral.

"Very well then, I leave you to eat the omelet you've made." The egg spun to the ground and cracked widely, clear and brilliant yellow fluid spreading quickly before being frozen by time or the chill of the air. Slayd leapt down, keeping his hand on the remnants of the serpentine statue, brushing mismatched fingers over marble scales. "See what you've accomplished in my absence? While I have felled tyrants and changed landscapes, Ophidia has failed to even break fast with style."

The people of the square stopped their wandering. Downward

chins rose. Lazy eyes broadened. Steps quickened, and soon a silent crowd had grown around Slayd. The fallen statue's shadow dissipated as clouds muted daylight. A scattered gray glow emanated equally from the sky and the snow and the marble of the city. Slayd immediately recognized that it was not him they gathered to see. He tossed two of the androgynous aside to kneel over the mess on the marble, shell cracking beneath his feet. A speck of darkness had appeared deep within the yolk and it split and multiplied and grew back within itself as he watched. Amidst gasps from the crowd he prodded the sac with the tip of a bruised finger but could not break albumen. He left a fingerprint behind in the goo, along with scales of dry skin the growing speck squirmed to absorb. It bubbled, turning pale and sprouting a reptilian tail. It curled upon itself but kept one large fish eye on Slayd. The fluorescent yolk shrank as it was absorbed.

The sorcerer reached with an awkwardly clawed finger this time but was tackled before he could scoop the veiny embryo out. One citizen held his arm but was tossed into the air, his back bending critically against a concrete cornice before falling into a heap. "I've never known Ophidians to have much for senses of humor," Slayd said before shrugging to send two others flying into shattered fountain and jagged rubble, "but this has to be a joke. You seek to challenge me? The only worthwhile achievement of this fallen city?"

An infant now sat up before him, golden as a king's crown, with eyes as iridescent as a queen's pearls. It bawled silently, face contorted under an egg white shawl, pudgy arms and legs quivering. The people of the agora then fled, never to look back. Slayd took a step away, intending to do the same, but the broken pedestal was at his back and he could not break his attention from the babe.

The child stood on suddenly svelte limbs, shriveled testicles dropping beneath ambiguous genitalia, and it toddled forward, pushing out of the restraining gel and into the expanse of the tile-strewn streets. Each step grew increasingly sure and carried Project VII across the agora, golden under the colorless sky, gleaming over the dun brick. The toddler's metallic skin reflected an ideal sun, a star that existed only in memories of nonexistent childhoods spent in summer picnics and beachside youths. Slayd matched the child's steps out of the square, at a distance, out into market streets and wide alleys not yet filled by fallen wall. Few people lingered in the open to see the aura outside Project

VII's skin blister near a hip before exploding into a pure and golden beam to cut through concrete and marble, wall and pillar. As he walked, the unblinking beam blazed, cutting cleanly in a line bringing a court building crumbling in a cacophonous dust cloud.

Slayd knelt to brace himself against a moving ground as the particle cloud rolled over him. Someone was yelling for help, and he realized that it was the first time in his entire life that he had actually heard a citizen of Ophidia do so. It was an alien voice, dry yet full of phlegm, not feminine but not entirely masculine. He brushed the sudden caking of dust from his wet eyes and stood powder gray after the cloud had passed to see that the beam of light had dissipated from Project VII's side. But two more blisters of energy appeared just beyond its golden sheen — one over the opposite shoulder, another from its bulbous belly, both popping and projecting beams out across the streets.

Sharp lines of brilliance cut through residential palaces as the child walked. Masonry fell under its own weight. Citizens ran and were cut in half as they crossed the beams of light, open halves cauterized before bisected torsos could bleed. Slayd stood this time as crisscrossing plumes of debris met near him, hissing in breath through the dust. When he emerged, two new blisters had appeared near Project VII's back. Slayd pulled himself into his robes. They fell to the dust, seemingly empty as pure white lasers arced where Slayd had stood only a second before.

Seconds passed, and as the beams winked out, with three more appearing to strike at new directions, Slayd grew from his robes and took long strides to catch up to the gleaming child. He put a splayed hand out near a shiny head but found none of the emanating warmth he had expected and hoped for. The tiles of the street cracked and shook again as a pillared chamber fell, something within exploding and lighting a nearby alley with sudden flame. Multiple blisters splurted beams in new directions, and Slayd had to leap to avoid one as Project VII turned completely in the new square they found themselves in. Its eyes were indecipherable platinum, but its mouth gaped toothlessly, golden gums gleaming. The most recent beams disappeared, but new ones shot out over and beneath the child, burning into the earth and sky.

In his peripheral, Slayd saw something emerge and move from the alley fires, but the sight of the golden child had hypnotized him. Project VII rose on the beam of light, riding it into the heavens in a matter of meager seconds. For just a moment, the sky appeared to Slayd as though it were night, black but star-lit, Project VII glowing at the end of a series of stars once known as the Lord of Wounds. The constellation had been transformed by the addition. The Lord of Wound's trident had a new star. Slayd now saw the constellation as a long-toothed serpent.

A minute passed before the sky lightened back to day for him. He had known the cosmos had only been a vision, one for him alone, but he had been powerless to look away. And, now that he could, he found himself too exhausted to look up from the dust he had found himself prostrated on. When the feeling returned to his limbs he found his hands bound behind him.

~

Wulf had been a shadow in the streets of Ophidia until light had come from nowhere to cut clean lines through buildings and citizens. Now he was a ghost, covered in dust as he emerged from clouds of collapse. He did not remember leaving the White Room, actually remembered little of the past day as the ancient's dementia subsided within his head. Not since sampling the Elder Mask all those years ago had so many unfamiliar memories surged through his head in so short a time — haphazard thoughts without order or context. He had been lost in a wilderness with paths forever beyond his reach, where the trees grew downward from an oceanic sky. There were no laws of physics to break.

He was only now remembering his self. His name came to his lips, and he spoke it over and over again, but it did not seem ultimately familiar. Had he never said it aloud before, or was he still pulling from the old man's madness?

Wulf then stumbled to his feet, his own shuffling struggle obscuring the sound of the coming blow that drove his knees to the sidewalk. The shock blended with his ever-present migraine to double him over. His mantle had fallen crooked, and his sight was obscured by hood and pain, but he could still see enough of the familiar face to recognize the man standing over him. A new scar spread pale from scalp to the tip of his nose, but Wulf recognized the brooding frown of Antony.

XXIII

"Regard thy soldiers as thy sons
and they will follow you into the darkest of caves.
Look on them as the sons of others
and you can follow them into the deepest of valleys"
—Hyper Khan's "The War of Art" (St. Aerror translation)

ven as the Sin Eater, Slayd had known little about the Unfeigned. They were men of faith, of the land, of the Song, that had sought out the Brides of Chem-oshmelech and their hidden brood pools. The Unfeigned were desperate men that had traded their souls for power. Rumors indicated that the Brides used whatever was at their disposal — symbiotes and parasites, tonics and toxins, prosthetics and magiks — to create the Army of Heaven's elite guard. There were very few of these inhuman men out in the land, all of them near the Lesser Prophets leading the Horde's war. Each one was unique in appearance and, Slayd suspected, by which means they came to make such a drastic decision. Their power came with a price. Few lived longer than a year after emerging from the breeding pools, their holy strength and speed burning their cobbled bodies out early.

The sorcerer had never been so near an Unfeigned, yet now had found himself escorted by the two that alternated with two others that scouted far around their path. The Unfeigned, and the Lesser Antony that led them, had taken horses out of Ophidia, but it took them less than a day to kill some of the mounts for dinner. The beasts were anxious around the Unfeigned to the point of disobedience, and Antony found that the time spent wrangling them approached inefficiency. So the Lesser Prophet himself had to now pull the tall cart of plunder out of Ophidia.

Slayd walked hunched between two Unfeigned, the weight of the Griswold collar finally bending him over after two days of travel. Here it shifted uncomfortably as he knelt over the disheveled body of one of the Unfeigned scouts. The other scout sidled into the clearing, the dark contrast between him and a remaining horse blending into the dusk of the frosted woodland, but the Lesser Antony sent him and the escorts out into the deepening shadows, leaving only the dead Unfeigned near. Slayd had taken this chance to examine one up close.

This one had no doubt gained height and bulk from the Brides, for he had been larger than any normal man of the land. He wore an assortment of cast iron armor plates over his chest, while his limbs had revealed a linen robe that looked long ago stained by a liquid both earthy and organic. The protruding goggles he had worn were missing, no doubt taken by his ambushers. Slayd then examined the pits that had hid behind the lenses. There was no spark even in the deep recesses of the sockets. The skin was jaundiced leather that flaked and flittered from Slayd's near breath. The Unfeigned was dry as jerky and, Slayd guessed, near the end of his tenure. If it had not been for the bullet holes in his neck, Slayd would have assumed the Unfeigned had fallen on his own, expiring in due time. So, they still require a central nervous system, he mused, or, at the very least, this one had. He would have loved to salvage the man's candirurethra or whatever other symbiotes the Brides had replaced his organs with. Even the bolts he could now see lining his head may have some future purpose. But the sorcerer's hands were bound behind him by sphinxgut.

The Lesser Antony guided him up and forward with the dog pole attached to the massive Griswold collar.

But to Slayd the question was not who had overcome this Unfeigned but why the Horde felt the need to send four of its precious few elite warriors out of the war.

"You, my friend, must be one important man to necessitate such an escort," he said to the man. The scar splitting the asymmetrical face gave the Lesser Antony away. "Antony of Lovewell Dam pulled from the war. Now just an errand boy for the Horde, yet still important enough to be guarded by such a precious detail." The pressure vanished as the dog pole dropped to Slayd's side.

"Keep moving," Antony of Lovewell Dam still said.

"Unless the Horde deems the quarry worthy of removing these Unfeigned from the front lines." He flexed his stiffening fingers within the confines of the sphinxgut wound around his hands. He could not even remember being tied, just waking from revelation or delusion with Antony of Lovewell Dam pulling him to his wobbly feet while speaking the riddle holding the only answer that would loosen the enchanted fibers.

"Why is a raven like a writing desk?"

The bindings were well-familiar to one coming out of Ophidia. Every proteomancer, every genelock, or apprentice knew the tales of the trials that fell upon their ancestors by whichever oppressive force set their sights on ancient Ouroboros. Sphinxgut had often been used to suppress spell weavers. It was not even the first time Slayd had been tied by such. But the Griswold collar was a new experience. Massive on his shoulders, locked from behind, with rusted spikes many fingers thick pointed inward toward his throat, the Griswold collar was a remnant of days long past — to a time when even N'Midgaard saw the need to curb the Garm. It was meant to be harnessed on the giant werewolves while they were in man form. If the change took them over, the spikes would pierce them as they grew. The silver on the spikes on the one Slayd now wore had long ago been worn away or salvaged. Had they dug the old relic out of some ancient Kalderan dungeon just for him, he wondered, or was the discoloration of the spikes that scratched at his neck from the more recent purge?

They passed through the same groups of sparse trees they had hiked all day. The trunks were tall but thin, thick with slender branches, and covered in fiery-brown bark that looked deeply furrowed in the evening shadows. It had been days since they had seen even an old leaf clinging beneath powder.

The Unfeigned began to circle more closely as Antony of the Dam chose a spot to bed down for the night. The pale mounts could be seen just beyond the tighter clump of trees. The Lesser Prophet assembled his short wickiup before building a small fire he sat Slayd next to.

"Where might you be taking us?" Slayd's voice was slow, his mouth sluggish in the chill of the evening. Everything was slower in the cold. It was not safe to turn his head in the collar, but if he just moved his eyes it would take an extra second for his vision to catch up. He had other questions for his captor, but he found his pulse slowing, his blood thickening.

It was many minutes before Antony of Lovewell Dam answered. He had broken some of the younger twigs from a tree and was spreading that which oozed out on his hands and cheeks as the fire died. The thin line running from his hairline directly down the middle of his face to the tip of his nose was barely noticeable in the dusk. "Justice," he said as he stood and headed for his shelter. Two of the remaining Unfeigned had tied remaining horses and now stood in the tight clearing. One of the cast iron cyborgs breathed through a moldy metal filter covering most of his face, as loudly as Wulf had been doing all evening.

The collar prevented Slayd from lying on the ground, so he sat cross-legged, snuggled up to the gray fire, breathing in the last remnants of smoke. He whispered to himself to ease into meditative hibernation, but his thin lips quickly slowed. His last thoughts of the night were of the Unfeigned. They never appeared bothered by the cold, and it appeared they needed even less sleep than he did.

Antony of Lovewell Dam was up before the sun to start a new fire and cook ham that Slayd ignored. The morning barely blurred any horizon seen through the trees before the Lesser was pulling the captives to their feet and pushing them back out into waning trees. Slayd veered toward any patches of sun on the walk, every glow loosening his stiff limbs. It was an hour into the path before his face warmed enough so that he could talk. They were not being taken to Kaldera — at least not into any capital city — or they would have been led back into the transporting flames.

"So it is not the Antonys that have first rights to the rogue Sin Eater and the Liege of Foes."

Antony of Lovewell Dam looked back at Wulf. "He's not the Liege of Foes." He stepped quickly back to the lagging man and pulled him along, prodding him to a quicker pace. "The Brotherhood has more important concerns than two malcontents. Your friend here, however, has pissed off someone though."

"Yes, yes, your direction comes from a more immediate authority, one closer to the people, one that has grown in power and ambition while the Antonys are busy elsewhere. Tell me, what is it like taking orders from tithingmen?"

Slayd had forgotten how quickly a Lesser Antony could move, and how hard they could hit. Still, he had steadied himself against the blow, so the spikes circling his neck had only nicked him on one side. Slow blood oozed, and he spit a flat tooth out the side of his mouth. He responded to Antony of Lovewell Dam's slight grin. "Don't flatter yourself, you syphillic scab, that one was already loose. But despite your revealing response, the Brotherhood may want to pay attention to what is happening on the homefront."

The trees stopped abruptly, and it was not long before the dusted prairie they found themselves walking was broken by a sudden river. It filled the area between two rises that extended the length of the flats they had been walking. The far shore was close. The frozen water level low. They had crossed many frozen streams earlier, some of which followed them out into the plain and melted the closer they came to the frozen gulch.

The remnants of a massive bridge reached out from wet ice that had opened around metal and concrete and wood. Towers in various states of decay poked up through the riverbed rubble. Slayd attempted to put the gigantic pieces of masonry back together in his mind, connecting the anchorages and abutments on each shore, but the puzzle was incomplete. Too many beams had been looted or had long ago sunk below ice and silt. The three Unfeigned were all near now, and they tested the ice's stability at the edge of the river.

He turned to find that Antony of Lovewell Dam had walked down the shore to where one of the streams opened from ice into water before joining the frozen river. A heavily bundled figure stood at the confluence, breaking ice with the butt of a rifle. The figure's chocolate horse bent to drink from the exposed flow. Slayd could not hear the words, but it was obvious from gestures to both horizons that Antony talked of what land spread out ahead and behind. The figure wore a scarf pulled up to its sunglasses, with a wide hat pulled low and a mantle collected high. The only breath freezing in the air came from the Lesser Prophet.

Slayd looked back to the collapsed artifact. Even in such areas barren of civilization it was rare to find remnants of the Old Ones, but it was still old, so he estimated the structure to have been built prior to Automaton the Second, probably erected during the populating of the first push into the Ouroboros region. They had best head farther up river before crossing. The ice was weakest where it was being constantly pressing against the protruding foundations. Antony of Lovewell Dam was no doubt concerned about the likelihood of a river crossing as ambush. This would be the only area in the coming day that a surprise could not be seen. After the rise on the other side of the river they would find only more plain without even the occasional tree collective. But it was still too open here. They would be seen coming from afar. When the Unfeigned were involved, one had to be sure of success. He hoped that those out there, beyond the rises, knew that much.

Antony of Lovewell Dam walked back, steps slow in the soft ground, sand sucking at his boots. He watched the rises and the rubble, and Slayd knew he had similar thoughts on an ambush. They would no doubt be heading up river to cross on the ice. The Unfeigned would be escorting the captives very closely. They drew near as Antony approached and their watery exhaust mingled heavily.

"Follow her over the hill," he whispered, even though she was far out of range, already heading up the rise they had come from. "Then bring me her horse and rifle. Kill her or don't. I don't care."

So one Unfeigned stayed behind as Antony prodded the captives up river. The collar reopened sores on Slayd's shoulders, and his lower back pinched with each step. He stretched his arms to no avail. The sphinxgut held strong.

Every step on the ice protested. If Antony stepped hesitantly enough to avoid a sticky squeak from the frozen river then it instead groaned from beneath one of the two Unfeigned's feet. If Slayd shuffled his center of gravity enough to prohibit the small webs of cracking below, then Wulf would fall, his helmet sending ripples of bubbles scattering like fish under glass. Slayd watched Antony and the Unfeigned as they divided their attention between the rise in land ahead of them, the hills behind, and the fallen bridge now far to the south.

"They wouldn't risk a confrontation here, you shit-thick homunculus." His voice was as dry as the surrounding air. He bit at the scaly skin hanging from his thin lips. He could not remember the last time he had tasted water. "Unless they care nothing for your captives." His words were punctuated by a reaching moan under their feet that came and went from one shore to the other. Light flakes of all sizes floated around their heads, but Slayd could not tell if it was new snow or recent powder that was picked off the ground by a breeze they had not noticed on land. The sky appeared clear over the river but was so hazy that the sun's direction could not be determined.

Antony stopped and pulled down his rifle to survey the area they had come from with its scope. An Unfeigned took up the dog pole of Slayd's collar when he tried to pause. The other pulled Wulf along behind him when the captive had trouble finding purchase on a particularly puddled area of ice.

The coming shore now appeared as the only slice of color beyond the frost and sky. Before then the river blurred into the rise, and it had been difficult to tell how much farther the ice had to support them. Slayd had been counting his steps but lost concentration as an azure line suddenly appeared, branching like lightning from under his boot toward the shore. The spaces ahead of him clouded with thousands of miniscule cracks. He stopped short and braced himself for the Unfeigned's prodding, but the dog pole jerked the spikes into his neck and he went painfully to his knees. The cold blood trickling down his back sent a shudder up and down his spine, and he was suddenly aware of the weight of the Griswold collar as he immediately scrambled to stand, cottony plumes of cracks spreading downward under where his bare hands pressed against the ice. Every other step found slippery purchase as the Unfeigned partly carried and partly pushed him toward the shore.

By the time they reached the edge of the ice every boot was soaked from the water that would rush over each step, melting the frost and turning the ice clear. Beneath were only pebbles grayer than the surroundings. One Unfeigned headed up the rise while the other still stood behind Slayd with constant tension on the dog pole. Antony still stood out on the ice about a third of the distance to the shore. He just stared over at the far crumbled bridge. He had taken his hat and coat off, and with his arms slightly wide he fired his rifle single-handedly into the murky sky. It was many minutes before he continued the walk across.

The captives had been pushed to the top of the rise by the time Antony had reached the shore. He had covered himself back up, pulling the coat around himself even tighter, tying the hat even lower over his head.

"So you knew who she was even under all those clothes," Slayd said as the prodding continued into a new prairie.

"One can always tell another born of the Nursery." Antony could barely be heard under the buttoning of his high coat.

"But does this recognition extend into fidelity? Apparently not." Out of the corner of his eye he kept catching Antony's backward glances. It had been hours since they had seen sight of the third Unfeigned. The others seemed unconcerned. Eyes hidden behind screen and goggles were always trained forward. Their breath steamed out and behind them from filter and frosted gill. "Are your captives worth capture or, worse, death. Yes, yes, I can see you care not for your own destruction but what of the name of 'Antony of Lovewell Dam?' Would he want to be seen as one who could not even fulfill his stunted masters' wishes — something as simple as rogue retrieval? Losing the Song's precious elite warriors?" There was no other sound across the plain, and he imagined he could hear the Lesser Prophet's teeth grind. "…or there is another option." The sorcerer acknowledged Wulf with a painful tilt of his head. "With the Liege of Foes' good word you could switch sides. Become a champion in the Army of Earth, be on the correct side of history. In fact, write history yourself from the winning side. There will be no tithingmen to disparage the name of 'Antony of the Dam' after the Territories are purged."

Antony had stopped, and, with him, the Unfeigned slowed. The men turned their faces, hidden beneath scar and bolted bar, to him.

"This piece of shit ain't the Liege of Foes." Antony brought the length of his rifle to the back of Wulf's legs, and the man went down again, helmet first. "This lech doesn't have the guts to climb. His milk curdles while real men do all the work, clearing the land of wolf and witch, striving for a better tomorrow. He may not know me, but I know him. He is a cuckold in any world. A dungeon is his destiny in any life."

"'Real men,' you say?"

"I'm not… the Liege of… Foes," Wulf rasped as he was dragged across the frost.

Antony's eyes glared out from under his cap. "And you think you can lecture me on what a 'real man' is, sorcerer? Does a real man betray his master? Stab his lord teacher in the back?"

"Oh, I have transcended such petty nomenclature. A man? Why, all nations wanted Tormalco dead. In that respect I am an agent for the land, although I prefer 'agent of change.' Like the earthquake or the asteroid I change the face of landscape or the path of history. I flip planetary poles to regulate mutation. I choose the descendants of mankind. So… am I qualified to judge a man? I would that is…"

Antony interrupted Slayd's words by kicking Wulf to the ground. He whispered something closely and low to the captive.

"Careful, my dear man," Slayd whispered to himself, "secrets will get us all killed. No sins are original."

The Unfeigned continued their walk.

~

The landscape they plodded over had become maddeningly flat, uniform to all the horizons. They had left all trees behind the day before, with the only flora left being a colorless grass more glass than plant. If the bulbous patches did not break beneath their boots, the blades would stab through their clothing. The West was as nondescript as the East, but by nightfall Slayd thought he could see something obscuring a speck of the direction they headed, a welcome blemish on the seemingly endless blur of desaturated cloud into monotone plain.

With no other option they camped in the wide expanse. Had there been a wind, Slayd feared they would blow to the ends of the earth like the bloodless leaves he could see the outlines of under the unnatural permafrost. The gods had left the world. Their breath was no longer felt. It had been replaced by the warm currents sent by the flutter of angelic wing. But even the Divine Choir had no interest flying over this lonely land.

The third Unfeigned had found them during the night. His beady eyes, dark as the moonless night, disappeared under his beaten bronze helm, but the sorcerer could still feel his gaze as he watched over the camp, never moving, never breathing save for the eventual hiss of the occasional leaking hydraulic as he turned his attention to the captive besides Slayd. Wulf moaned occasionally in something that was not sleep, not unconsciousness, but definitely not lucidity either.

The sun refused to rise early that morning, but, when it finally did, the frosted fields glittered mutedly and as dusty as the sky, like a cosmic blanket holding stars that burned their colors out so coldly and so long ago. Moving westward, the atmosphere was too thick with haze for Slayd to see far beyond where they were, as he assumed their camp would appear to those following them. And the air was too frost-burnt to taste anything other than the oils and rancid meats of the Unfeigned.

So they spread across the dull morning of a mile, with Antony, the captives, and one Unfeigned in the middle. The first Unfeigned led the way out across the melting mists, and the last slowed to watch their backs against whoever followed. Antony still pulled the cart. The wheels had begun to creak with each turn. There was nothing in the flatness for the sound to echo against.

The sun was still low by the time the fog had lifted. The clouds it lit burned a brighter orange than itself. Color in any form had become a stranger to Slayd over the prior days. Still, the fiery horizon cast a putrid pallor on their backs, the inflamed hue of a feverish wound. Even shielding his eyes, he could see only the black speck of the lagging Unfeigned against the inferno when he looked back. But ahead of him he could now see the fallen rails of fencing, wood bleached a decade ago by summers difficult to remember, smoothed meager years ago by the Winter of Winds. He stepped around broken marks in the snow where cowboys had dug up petrified clumps of manure. He leaned against a post as Antony stopped at his side. It was surprisingly solid compared to its weather-cracked appearance. Friable barbed wire stuck out at odd angles before ending abruptly, appearing even redder in the light.

The town appeared in front of them as soon as the fog lifted. It glistened in the disappearing dew and refused to be lit by the flaming sunrise as they were. To Slayd it looked to be no more than a collection of barns and sheds perhaps leading into an uneven main street of crooked stables. Outhouses, both new and dilapidated, outnumbered the larger buildings two to one.

"Are they friendly to Horde or Earth?" Slayd asked Antony of the figures emerging from the ranches. They were far enough away to be indistinguishable to him, but their long rifles — some taller than their wielders — and extended spyglasses told him they had been looking.

The whizz of a bullet near his ear was all the answer he needed. He turned south, making himself a slimmer target but blinding himself to the sunrise. He knocked the wind out of Wulf with a sharp kick, flattening the helmeted captive on the ground. Through the incandescent east he could see specks of darkness emerge, trodding the frozen ground with hooves to engage the Unfeigned. He tried blinking the spots from his eyes when he looked away, but a bullet against his Griswold collar sent his teeth chattering and his body spinning. He found himself on the ground next to Wulf, not knowing which direction the firing had come from. The air was full of gunshots from both directions, the ground covered in tiny geysers of snow and dirt as rounds struck all around them. Antony was shouting to the town and the Unfeigned. Neither listened. A scream echoed through their minds, abruptly and shortly, but it did not come from Wulf. Slayd had intuitively braced himself against the spines of the collar, but his robe and torso were never-the-less covered in his own slow blood from numerous gouges, and the weight of the massive restraint unsteadied the sorcerer as he tried to stand. He could only get to his knees.

"Both inevitably lead to murder," he recited beneath Antony's yelling, gunfire from the east and west, and the thunder of horses. The sphinxgut loosened and he pulled his wrists free to flex his long fingers. Double-jointed arms bent backward until he could feel the hanging lock holding him from behind. He tore it from the collar with a sigh and shrugged the weight away, but the Unfeigned was instantly upon him. This close, he could hear the stretching tautness of some symbiotic mussel tighten as one of the patchwork man's gauntlets closed on his throat. It was the Unfeigned that had watched over them at night. For once Slayd could see into the shadows of his helm. The man's dark porcine eyes reflected nothing of the surroundings.

"Stop!" Antony yelled from the meager cover of the cart. He was reloading while ducking shots fired, aimed, or strayed from both directions. "We want them alive!" But the Unfeigned did not lower his machete.

Slayd spit into the visor, and while the Unfeigned staggered, with eyes sizzling, the sorcerer slithered out of his grasp and under the blindly swung blade. He darted in, tearing the barred filter from the Unfeigned's face with mismatched claws.

The Unfeigned steadied, plump lips quivering just like the worms moving behind his toothless gums. The bloody horizon lit his hidden face and his eyeballs bubbled under Slayd's slaver, but he still turned to stare near the Lesser Prophet.

"We... don' take orders from... you," the metallic man said. Some words were dry as ancient scrolls, others were moist as graveyard runoff, but they were all directed at Antony as he raised his rifle to the Unfeigned.

Slayd crouched as his sight was filled with horses, his hearing filled with gunshots he could no longer tell as near or far. He had lost sight of Wulf and Antony. Hoof and mane and tail and boot surrounded him. Great brown flanks bled from bullet wounds and spurs. Equine legs stomped and kicked near his feet and his head. Through it all he saw the Unfeigned pushing, melted face peering through the chaos directly at him. Sparks arced as a round glanced from his head. Meat flew as another broke a chunk from his shoulder. He only wavered from his steps to punch a horse that stepped too near. Its rider was in the Unfeigned's hands immediately upon his horse going down. The man's face contorted silently as the Unfeigned bent his back impossibly backward.

Another horse fell nearby, its rider screaming from beneath. Slayd searched the squirming man, finding only an open and empty pistol, noticing the symbol of the Army of Earth — the eye as crimson as its tear in the sunrise. He quickly rose to find the Unfeigned pinned by Antony, the man's whistling hydraulics straining as much as the veins in the Lesser Prophet's neck. Antony had the Unfeigned in arm and leg locks, wrestled to a standstill. White steam rose from brass, colorless from the hair damp against Antony's forehead. The Lesser Prophet's face was red from the strain and looked to burst. He was biting through his own lip before a yell, drowned out by screams coming from the town, precipitated his release of the Unfeigned. He staggered back with the fingers of one hand and the wrist of the other twisted awkwardly.

The Army of Earth had scattered, but Slayd could now see them gathering and descending on Wulf, who had walked out into the openness.

XXIV

"Advance thy sons into positions whence there is no escape
and they will prefer death to flight
If they face death
there is no place they cannot fly"
—Hyper Khan's "The War of Art" (St. Aerror translation)

It was sweet relief when they placed the manduco idis over his head. The creature was housed in a brass helm shaped like the shells of the eastern coasts, but unlike its natural-born ilk, this encephalopod would not tickle the prefrontal cortex. It had no doubt come of the hidden breeding pools of the Brides of Chem-Oshmelech, no doubt from a long line of ancestry, grown to rape the mind. Wulf's last thoughts as the heat of his head warmed the interior of the helm, drawing the manduco idis from its metallic shell, were of the stories of the Eastern Men that had settled shores and fished a cold sea immediately after returning to the surface. They were a pragmatic lot, hardy, and believing only in the fruits of their labors, the sweat of their furrowed brows. But it had not been long before they found God in a seashell, whole universes of seventh senses in iridescent glory. From here their lives quickly spiraled and generations whorled to an inevitable confrontation with the Liege of Foes and an end of their dagonic gods.

"I'm not the Liege of Foes," Wulf murmured as something stirred against his hot head.

"Of course you're not," the familiar voice of a Lesser Antony said near his ear as the man tugged, testing the locks securing the helm. "You're just some sad fool who managed to look sideways at the wrong governor."

Wulf twitched suddenly, involuntarily, as cool psilocylium crawled through his matted hair, feeling, searching. They waged war with his eyelashes before holding open his lids. He could only see the interior of the full brass helmet. He jerked at the touch, fingers glancing and blunting off the helm before his hands were bound in front of him in chains.

But it turned out to be a surprising relief. Even as a bursa pressed against his ear canal, turgid tendril squirming to fit, he was awash with the serenity of the absence of the Other. Even before the manduco idis had implanted itself, its enveloping form has blocked out the far-off presence of the intruding psyche that had been pressing against his mental barriers for so long now. For the first time in months he felt he could let his psionic guard down, only then realizing how exhausted he had become. The pressure, his chronic migraine, the familiar intrusion of the Other, was gone. Had he not already been on his knees he would have fallen in sudden comfort. For slow seconds he was alone in his head. And then the encephalopod moved in.

Wulf was blind behind brass, psilocylium periodically probing his tear ducts like a cat plays with a dead mouse, but an Unfeigned pushed him forward. His sinuses and ear canals were filled with either congealing blood or settling vesicle, but he could still hear the Unfeigned's congested breathing. But after a day of walking he could not tell the sound apart from his own labored gasps.

He walked with Fynn down a path long ago grown over. The old man had always been old. Everyone was old compared to young Fenri. He rarely even saw other children since they had moved into the castle. He was afraid of Fynn but not as much as he was afraid of the King. Since moving into the castle he had become afraid of everyone. He was always cold. The walk into the darkening forest was no different. The old man wore fur matching the mud bark of the trees beneath the fox and pumpkin leaves. A giant crow led the way, but Fenri didn't think the old man saw it.

The parapsyte picked through Wulf's memories like someone would flip through photographs. If Wulf pushed back, if he even thought about putting the barriers back up, the manduco idis would react, its psilocylium exploring the crevices between skull and brain.

He hung upside down as the shadows attacked him. They were his masters, the SHE,' two-dimensional serpents he could not see unless they allowed it. But he could feel them, could stretch out telepathic feelers to catch their slippery minds, could send out telekinetic fingers to grasp at the space they barely inhabited. But they were too fast. Smoldering talons and venomous fangs raked his naked body from all sides, all dimensions. With skin splitting and meat burning, he was still cold. He was always cold.

He would wake each morning, still in the perpetual darkness of the monastery, with only the memory of the branding, his flesh healed, nightmarish dreams of his lessons scrawled across his body. He read the scarred characters with his fingers in fitful sleep. Only to start the lessons over again and again. At this time he had no idea the amount of pseudo-years of training he still had to go.

The manduco idis was either immature or impolite, and it ignored any interaction other than the slow peek through all of Wulf's life.

"What are you looking for?" he thought to the parapsyte. *"What good is any of this to you?"* But he could sense the encephalopod did more than just view each memory. He was recording it, storing it deep with the meaty interior of the brass shell helm. If even a sliver of a primordial thought sparked within Wulf's mind concerning a reversal of the probing, if he even unconsciously considered following the astral trail back into the creature's mind, a twitch behind the space between Wulf's eyes brought him to the ground, helm first, where he was immediately and roughly lifted back to his feet by an Unfeigned's crushing grip.

The memories that Wulf knew would come eventually hit him like a punch to the gut, and it took numerous kicks from Antony this time before he was on unsteady feet again. Even then, an Unfeigned practically had to drag him through the trees. It took all of Wulf's focus to pull himself out of the scenes of Enclave and Nod and the Baba Yaga, and for the rest of the day he withdrew into a fugue that allowed him only to count each step before him, the feel of each rock and branch to each side, as the encephalopod continued its emotionless search.

The prodding from the Horde's elite guard grew less as Wulf found his footing on days following the first. He sent rhythmic telekinetic waves out across the terrain ahead of him — slight enough to barely ruffle the frost, but pressing enough so that he could feel any dip in the earth, any root or hollow that would ordinarily twist the blind man's ankle. But the heaviness of the helm still brought him to the ground numerous times each day, and his knees would go from bruised to torn to soft and numb throughout the hours.

He woke in the middle of one night, cloak wrapped tightly against the frost, his legs stiff, knees unbending. He lost the warmth of each breath into the night he could not see, with his mouth being the only part of his face not locked within the brass shelm. The manduco idis, even throughout the nights, never stopped picking its way through Wulf's life. But it was a specific memory that woke him, sweat chilling to his neck.

In the deep realm of Underthought, Fenri's mind's eye found the Beast — Bastard Timber Godling of N'Midgaard — the great-mawed demon Bifrost feared would swallow the heavens. Fenri felt it struggling against its impossible fetters deep in the inverted crown of the World Tree's roots in the center of Earth, paw and claw submerged in a sea of ichorous slaver. Its awesome bleeding teeth would never meet as long as the glowing sword held the monster's hoary jaws apart and stifled.

End my pain.

Fenri heard the Beast's grisly thoughts, as it was his curse to hear all men's.

And I will end yours.

The blade twitched from behind the demigod's colossal fangs as Fenri grabbed at it with his mind. It tore free, shredding meat and tooth before shattering on volcanic rock. Steaming shadows frothed on the creature's lips as they curled around a mouth not closed since ancient ages. Its great ribs cracked as it breathed deep air not disturbed since glacial retreat.

The Beast howled to mankind from the very bowels of the planet, reaching up from the stagnant heat of the great depths. It howled for Fenri and the bloody eye of the moon that taunted the giant wolf from space.

No more muffled by the blade, the howl shook the land, its gurgling call pressing against Fenri's ears and mind. Even in slumber he held his head against the pain. The ground buckled and then exploded upward with Hel's dog climbing through the upheaval toward the sky. The last thing Fenri saw before sinking into the crushing weight of the settling land was the Beast's great maw swallowing the moon and darkening the sky.

Wulf usually forgot the dream when opening his eyes, but here he could only see the indistinct shapes in the interior of the shelm, here he was forced to see the apocalyptic images over and over as the encephalopod peeked through them.

"Is it not enough… is nothing sacred… must you even molest my nightmares?" he asked aloud. He could feel someone stir next to him. There was no bodyheat, so he assumed Slayd sat near. Through cottony ears he heard the sorcerer repeating the same riddle over and over until stopping at Wulf's outburst.

But it was the manduco idis that finally responded, *"Nihilne est sacristo? That was not a dream."*

~

Despite the changing of the seasons in Wulf's mind, the hectic flow of memories, the years unraveling, each day of the prodded walk was much like the one before. The air outside the shelm was cold, but he could tell when the sky was clouded by if his fingers stung or his toes ached inside his mittens and boots. For the most part, when the cold leaked into his clothing, he would just submerge himself into whatever memory the parapsyte happened to be transcribing at the time. Odds were it was of a warmer day. But as the journey went on, as his telekinetic radar touched less and less trees and began to pulse over a flatter blemish-free landscape, the manduco idis began to come across later years, reminding Wulf of just how long the seasons had been unpredictable.

He watched Meri and Teca, careful to not let them see him. There was a deep shadow next to the rock wall that wouldn't see any sunlight until Spring — whenever, if ever, it would come. Even the fresh snow that had fallen had hardened to ice in the shade. Even in the biting cold, it was in the shadows he felt most comfortable. Even after many years away from the tutelage of the SHE,' he still felt at home in the darkness. By this time, he had known better than to think that Meri wasn't aware of his presence, wasn't always aware of her surroundings, wasn't aware of perhaps everything on some cosmic scale, but he liked to think he watched the two of them without their knowing.

But he did not listen to their words. He just watched their mouths move, with the varying degrees of thickness the moisture caught itself in the frigid air floating around their faces. How long had they walked together, he tried to remember, yet he couldn't remember if he had seen the two of them talk before now. Teca winced as the priestess rebound the young knight's wrist with more snow. Even from the shadows Wulf could see the swelling. Yet still Teca's eyes brightened as they talked, so he listened in.

They spoke of the common ancestry of their faiths, of the Pride's emergence from the earth and those that eventually forsook their feline goddess for an angel of the new world. Wulf noticed, not for the first time, how Meri stood above the snow, but next to the girl beside her it was even more obvious. Teca's boots sank into the powder, while the priestess' doeskin lighted over the frost, barely disturbing it. Teca's ruddy complexion stood out against the snow white of Meri's fingers.

"Where is she?" Wulf excused himself from the memory to find himself asking.

"What?" Antony of Lovewell Dam asked. Wulf had difficulty differentiating voices from beneath the shelm, but he had grown accustomed to the signature gaits of those around him. His telekinesis bounced back the varying movements of the Unfeigned's lumbering, the proud strides of burdened Slayd, and the tired steps of the Lesser Prophet. He felt it was Antony next to him, dismissing a question he barely realized he had asked. And only now did he realize how much less he had thought about Meri since he had met Mew.

"The Lonely Forgotten Sun of God." He was now fully aware of the words he said. "Where is she?"

"How would I know?" Antony barely answered.

"Her pilgrimage… she was invited into the Territories… she never made it…" He trailed off, as the slope he felt leveled off. He sensed that ground had rounded flat before it dropped away in the immediate future. They would soon be upon a drop leading to a type of terrain he had not felt yet on this forced hike. The walk down to the odd ground would take his full attention.

"Quid habimus?"

But he was not able to give in, and he stumbled many times on the meager descent, although always catching himself before the heavy brass of the shelm hit the ground.

"What do we have here?" The manduco idis had paused in its searching and collating and storing after many days for a close analysis of the tiny implant in Wulf's grey matter. *"The Grand Hob."*

"Yes?" Wulf thought, steadying himself as the land beneath his feet opened flat and soft. It was sand and rocks he now stepped on. In front of him stretched a pliable mix of of what he could only assume was ice and water. They had arrived at a large river stretching roughly to the north and south. The movement around him had stopped at the edge, with the tired gait of Antony of Lovewell Dam continuing up the shoreline. The parapsyte had become more persistent by the time his attention returned.

"There is a piece of your memory missing…"

"Yes."

"This gift from Hob Robin, what is in it?" The encephalopod probed with both telepathy and psilocylium, echoing through Wulf's mind and tickling back at the base of his skull. He felt numerous itches he could not scratch, and his chained hands knocked against the shelm impotently.

Wulf did not respond, but he knew the memories surrounding his time as the Goblin Liege were being recorded by the creature — of Robin's reemergence as Lady Plaag, her creation of a synthetic clone based on the remains of Aesarean's brainweezle and its subsequent implantation in the right side of Wulf's brain. She had coupled it with the surgery replacing his right eye with the mystical relic known as Yggr's Eye, and he always had assumed some sort of synergy between the alien objects. But he had never been completely certain.

"Let me in."

"No."

"Let me in."

"Damn you to Hel."

The pressure was slow, but it built, and it was not long before Wulf had to steel himself by pulling his reserves back inward. He sent out his telekinetic radar only slight feet from himself, and by the time Antony had returned he struggled to do even that. It was taking almost all of his mental strength to keep the squirming creature out of the lobotomized brainweezle.

"You haven't a chance." The creature's voice had become softer, feminine in its cooing. It was warm nectar dripping down through the honeycombs of his mind. *"I will eventually break through, pop the bubble of this retarded abomination living in your brain, I will eventually open its secrets, so why not just let me in now? Save yourself unneeded pain."* To punctuate, the encephalopod pinched inward. Wulf's temples throbbed, but he was not sure whether it was a vein that twitched or the thin tendrils squirming under his skin.

Wulf suddenly found himself scrambling on frictionless ground. Time had seemingly passed. He did not remember heading out onto the ice, but a brief pulse of telekinesis told him they were somewhere out on the deceptively uneven lake. An Unfeigned had resorted to pulling him behind, over the groaning surface. Wulf pulled the mental waves back inside himself for fear of adding even the slightest pressure to the ice, but also to hold against the still constant pressure of the manduco idis' probe. The creature had pulled out slightly, but their union went both ways, and Wulf could feel it gathering its strength.

He woke on his feet to more time having passed. He could feel the sudden change in the air and the ground that denoted the day's passage. The creature increased the pressure against the brainweezle's defenses. Wulf had woke to what he could barely tell were Slayd's ramblings, but he caught little of the conversation before pain in the back of his legs brought him again to the ground.

"I'm not the Liege of Foes," he responded through the pain to the only words he had understood. The shelm had seemingly become even heavier under the parapsyte's mental hectoring, and he again had to be dragged across the frost.

With a drop in temperature he guessed that night had come, and he awoke from another fugue to the creature's increased onslaught against the barriers he barely held around the brainweezle. Still, again, Slayd was talking without pause.

He sensed no steps around him and he was on his knees. The group had stopped. He could sense the tension around him without using empathy. Muscles clenched. Weight shifted. But still he saw only the inside of brass.

Something solid hit the shelm and his head glanced around in the tight confines. Every color of light bounced in front of his eyes and he went down, immediately to be pulled to Antony of Lovewell Dam's side. This close he could make out the distinct voice, feel the breath on his lips.

"Wonder deeply why your 'friend' fell the Tower of Gog, refuse. Think long. How well do you know him? The Everman falls and an unaffiliated sorcerer is immediately rewarded with the title of Sin Eater. Coincidence? Your Resistance is governed by children and fools."

~

The land had evened out. The slight waves of telekinesis Wulf sent out to predict his steps found only hard grass and harder dirt on an ever-flattening landscape. He could not enjoy the relief of uninterrupted steps, however, with the now rhythmic pounding of the manduco idis. The encephalid had now halted all searching, all sorting, all recording of Wulf's memories, to focus entirely on what the lobotomized brainweezle protected.

"Little pig, little fatty, let me come in!"

He pounded against the mental door. Over and over and over and over again. But Wulf held strong, until, sure of the even plain of the frozen prairie, he pulled all his reserve inward to hold against the creature's constant assault.

"What could be so important, so hidden and blockaded?"

And so the plodding pressure continued until Wulf could feel it deep beneath temples. The space between his eyes pinched with the drumming, his teeth chattered and his neck strained from a jaw clenched tightly over the course of a day. The barrier held, but it weakened slowly over the hours, and by the time he was led to the ground for the night he was certain he could not last another day beneath the now physical slamming against the mental.

"No, you won't, so why delay the inevitable? Your suffering is in vain... serving only vanity."

That night was cold. He could not push outward against the air, could not create a psychokinetic skin to hold in his body's heat while keeping the chill outside. He had to focus entirely on the door — the creaking barrior keeping the parapsite at bay. Even his head, encased in brass, snuggled by the undulating creature, had cooled as the midnight air leaked into the shelm. The sweat of days chilled under his sticky hair and his breath stuck coldly to the interior. Still the creature pounded against the door. The hinges bent, pulling at nails.

Wulf sat on his knees throughout the night, cloak wrapped under and around him. He rocked unconsciously to the beat of the drumming and would catch himself moaning aloud as well as inside his head. Either there was silence across the prairie or he was too focused against the assault to hear anything beyond his mind.

"What do you gain from this?" he let the parapsite hear at some point in the night. *"I know what the Horde wants, but what is in this for you? How do you benefit from my memories?"*

"I don't understand," is all the creature would think back before continuing the relentless pounding. The door started to shake. Braces loosened. Wood split.

It felt like they had already walked the morning away by the time Wulf could first feel the sunrise. It warmed through his cloak and radiated into the back of his haunches and legs. It felt orange but sickly, like an overripe mushroom that had an entire fallen swamp tree to itself. His stomach dropped and he felt the tickle of nausea under his chin. He could not remember if Antony had fed him this morning. What would happen if he vomited into the close quarters of the shelm? Could it be removed before he would drown? *Would* it be removed before he would drown?

The cart was being pulled by his side this morning, and it squeaked in a way he had not noticed before. Now it was becoming all he noticed — a lazy whine that rose and dropped over the seconds. It was making him aware of a passage of time he hadn't realized for how long? Perhaps days. But he feared the incessant sound was lowering his guard against the manduco idis' pounding. But it would not matter soon anyway. Wood was splintering.

Someone's hand on his shoulder stopped and steadied him, but his head still rocked from momentum and the ...*drum... drum... drum... drum...* on the door.

He was now aware of voices. Slayd was nearby. The sibilance of his words was undeniable. The sunrise no longer warmed him through his cloak, but it was still there — a sickening orange furriness he could see even under the psilocylium that coated his eyeballs, could taste even in the numb fuzziness his mouth had become.

Even though he knew he had hit the frozen ground, he still felt as though he continued to fall. The stone-cold field was against his back, but he felt it pressing against all his sides. There was no breath beneath the cold pressure, and no hope of regaining it. His body refused to choke. His lung shriveled without intent to open again.

And so he let the door open. It was time. Its hinges bent wide for the first time since Lady Plaag had implanted the lobotomized brainweezle. Psilocylium rushed inward. The alien mind of the encephalopod poured inward and downward. For, Wulf sighed, if he were to die, someone may as well enjoy Robin's gift.

The manduco idis screamed, but Wulf was too numb of mind and body to feel its pain. But as the parapsyte went utterly and irreversabily mad from Lady Plaag's mind trap — schizophrequations infecting and splitting its libido, anxious and embryonic cognitive biases gobbling instant floating amnesiatic defecation, id-ridden mindscapes projected upon trojan hippocampal screens that fluttered into epileptic akathisia that instant suicidal psyclones drowned themselves trying to chase, suddenly catatonic egos raped themselves asexually into infinity while breeding castrated super-critics dripping with manic afterbirth — its psilocylium squirmed one last time, its stalks clenched and loosened, before going slack inside the shelm.

Wulf's heart pounded against his lungs as they pressed back to fill. The darkness of the interior was filled with spots of every color before the sparse air of the shelm could satisfy his aching chest. Along with the air was a rush of every sense. Tinny clicks all around him were the deadened sounds of gunfire, near and far. The earth vibrated under his elbows and knees from the thunder of what must have been close hoof beats. The manduco idis babbled nonsense in his mind as it tried to reconcile new universes it destroyed with its sudden comprehension of insane physics.

"...*stately...river... down... five... and... were... blossomed were... sunny... deep... green... savage... e'er... by... from as...*"

Wulf's mind was exhausted, and he used this tired focus to sink backward into the fluidity of the way. His heart calmed, then his lungs, and the calming caress floated over his shoulders, loosening the muscles in his arms down to his wrists. Slack and soft, his hands went limp for the chains to fall from his arms. He poked and prodded at the small locks holding the shelm together, blood returning painfully to his fingers. As he found them he sent invisible mental feelers to map and press and turn the lock's inner grooves.

"pants... was... huge... chaffy... mid... ever... river mazy... sacred... measureless... to... tumult... prophesying... of... pleasure..."

The locks turning were loud in his ears, but he was delighted to hear anything unfiltered by brass or parapsyte. He threw the shelm aside and was instantly blinded by snow and sky and movement and a far horizon kindled like some unholy faggot of embers. His granite eye compensated and he walked the cacophony of stomping hooves and leveling rifles. The crimson tear of the Army of Earth was all around him. The icy blue eye stared at him from standard, bandana, and quilted armor. He turned away from the pus of the sunrise as he stumbled, to the desaturated outline of a nearby town. There, men fired haphazardly with long scopes and longer rifles into friend and foe alike with what could only be children bracing and holding above them a wire sculpture of a winged man twice their size.

Wulf searched the scenes for the Unfeigned as he picked at pieces of tendril that had broken off in his temples. One of the Unfeigned, with plumes of steam engulfing an arm, confusedly lashed out with a rippled sword at the Horde's townsfolk. Another strode out of the sunrise, brass greaves reflecting morning and blood. He had torn a man asunder and now dragged both halves behind him. A broken lance stuck out from his back with the Liege of Foes' symbol fluttering and glaring over the carnage of dead horses.

A man ran to Wulf, trying to conceal a limp, wiping his only weapon — a dagger rusted and bloodied — on a rag. The man's quilted armor was torn and patched but looked recently unscathed. His skin was as brown as the gore flecking his boots, and his drawl revealed him to be from a southern territory.

"They're routed, my lord! Your command?"

Wulf opened his cloak but hid his shaking hands within folds. A tactic he had once used against a mercenary group that had been protecting a group of miners in low mountains came to him. He had lost none of his mob in the assault, but had gained a rich silver vein his goblins had exhausted in only weeks. The memory was fresh in his mind, as many now were.

"Call everyone. Split the horse force in a circle east to converge on each side of the town. Round the sympathisers into mainstreet. Take any surrender. Keep the rise to your back," Wulf listed, gesturing to the infernal horizon. "Pass all rifles to groundsmen where they can fire into the funnel, no closer than from here."

He was suddenly and eagerly hugged from behind, and he instantly realized how sore his hips and thighs were. He recognized the child-like hands of Ivy of the Grove clasp in front of him as a long coat and wide hat moved into his peripheral.

"And Harlowe," he turned to say to the grin beneath the hat, "take care of those Unfeigned, will you."

Ivy covered her ears as the air blossomed with the thunder and brimstone of sudden sixshooters. As Harlowe walked the battlefield, Ivy handed Wulf the invitation she had found in Priest's study. Its script was so stylized as to be almost illegible, and it took him until the gunfire lessoned to read the details of the upcoming auction.

Another man ran to Wulf. A bloody tear had been painted from one of his eyes, and it ran down into stubble from sweat.

"Your helm, my Liege," the man said, avoiding Wulf's gaze and handing him the open head of brass he wished to never see or feel again. The locks rattled loosely, and dried psilocylium hung crinkled in the air.

From inside the shelm, gray lips puckered and pursed, silently mouthing poetry.

XXV

There are no ghosts here
I fear
Just a bowl full of crumbs
Faded prints
With no thumbs
And a hollow face in a mirror
Of tears

　—unknown

H is lipless mouth pursed tightly against her scent, but Slayd could still taste her in the air of the room. He would have to conclude the dealings quickly, or, at least, move the conversation to a larger room, one where her old mutton stink would hopefully dilute. But he knew it would be pointless. Generations of the Loup Garou had occupied the plantation and its grounds since even before the Always' first push into the Land of Nod. The presence of Margeride's siblings and cousins, both past and present, had settled into the very foundation of the structures. The Loup Garou family's taint had long ago flavored the water and air. Yet, knowing there was no escape on the plantation, Slayd's mottling skin still crawled in the close quarters of the storage room.

"These are nothing," Slayd said quickly, clouded eyes flickering from one crate to another, long fingers sifting through shipping dust to find only veiny tea sets and medallions golden, silvered, and bronzed. "These are not even from Magog, much less the Tower."

"No," Gauvendanielle said, appearing in the dark doorway. Her sigh was simple, quiet, yet Margeride shrieked at her sudden entrance. "Run along, petite," the older woman said, "there are other guests requiring your precocious charms. Leave this miscreant to one more suited of denying his pheromones."

"But, mum, the gentleman just…"

"The fact you call him such means you are not ready." Gauvendanielle bared her black-lined teeth, and the young girl ran from the room, straightening her wide dress.

Slayd dug nail and claw into pale wood, wrenching open a crate easily. He found brittle daggers and brittler skulls wrapped in a fine blanket before moving to the next crate. "That was unnecessary," he said. "The three of us could have enjoyed ourselves amongst sawdust and quilted forgeries."

"Still the uncouth?" Gauvendanielle moved toward him, long dress brushing the scattered wood flakes. "You are obscene. She is my brother's daughter."

"Yes, yes, that would explain her familiar taste. It appears the Loup Garou blood is as thin as ever. I suppose some things never change." He placed a smooth rock plucked from a box into one of the infinite pockets of his robe. "Hmmmmm... a Jordan Stone. This may come in handy."

The woman caressed the back of his head with the back of her hand. "And now they never will have the chance to. I knew I would see you one last time before the Beast would rise to swallow the sun." He spun and squeezed the hand in his own, taking and twisting her arm behind her as she looked away to keep speaking. Her words came through a bit lip. "How can you still be so young? I must look hideous to you."

He spun her aside to upend a stack of boxes, moving deeper to break the lock of a chest bearing a corruption of the sigil of the Tower of Gog. "Yes, yes, these are well made, I cannot deny it, enough to fool the idiot mayors and inbred princes and whomever else you've invited to this sham of an archeological unveiling. I would have thought the Loup Garou above such pageantry as an auction."

With barely a glance at the artifacts, Gauvendanielle, sighing heavily this time, said, "These are just the trinkets to appease the first-comers, faux for fallen upstarts. The pre-auctions humor the dirty boys while building tension for the real treasures. These have all been sold and boxed for travel. Whatever it is you're looking for is surely in the main auction. I remember you as having more cultured... tastes."

In the few steps it took to reach her she had already loosened the bindings of her high collar. He winced at the flavor of the air around her neck. The abundance of bitter cologne fought with the spoiled meat scent he remembered from long ago. The smell instantly brought back memories of searching through cellars and the ruins of outlying guest homes that had fallen into decay, and filing through a family library. She was always near in these remembrances. Her eyes had been darker and her skin lighter. The reflection in her black hair had not been as dull as it was in the dyed color she now regrettably chose, and she had not the spidery lines reaching from her heavily colored lips. Here he was, after all these years, searching yet again. But this time it was different.

"Actually, Margeride was helping me search for something that supposedly belongs…"

"Is it for that motley group you traveled here with? The Melchyor I knew would have scoffed at the idea of becoming so gregarious. And to align himself with the Resistance? How droll. A freedom fighter? What exactly happened in Magog?"

He quickly went back to searching the corners of the room. "Hmmmm, well, yes, the intuition of women. The Tower is actually linked to my search. Is there *anything* in the auction from Magog? Was anything salvaged, or can I be on my way?"

Gauvendanielle covered her mouth as she laughed. Her nails were painted as bloody as her lips and they appeared just as chewed. "So the ageless Melchyor Slayd finally needs my help?"

"Not really."

"I guess I should thank Hel I lived long enough that our fates crossed again. No, you're right, as you always were, there will be nothing of value to you in this room. The goddamn hurricane that sank Magog, and the ocean ice storm that settled it afterwards, may have lasted a month, but it wasn't enough to deter scavengers for very long, not when so much treasure had been whispered of for a century. The Loup Garou followed every rumor of looter, and bought up everything of worth."

"Where…"

"You're too late, mon amour." She moved against him, her smile lines deepening in a poor facsimile of a pout he remembered from decades past, as she picked at worn robes he hid unsuccessfully beneath more recent ones he had acquired. He found himself embarrassed at her words, her tone, and then disappointed in his reaction, and then disgusted by where he suddenly found himself. Here he stood, fingertips grayed by dust, wearing Tormalco's once-grand robes beneath market surplus, looting lesser men's winnings as a favor to a fallen freedom fighter. He had always just expected that he could have his fun but return to his previous life whenever he grew tired of the mischief of the Resistance. But he suddenly realized that that option moved further away the longer he put it off — if it was still even possible. And he resented the hag before him for making him realize that the option may have never even been there in the first place. "The prime… merchandise…" she gasped as he took a fistful of her hair, "is now being moved from the viewing room into the audience hall. I don't know how you came upon an invitation, but you're too late. The calling should start shortly. If what your vulgaire blue-eyed master seeks is in the auction trove, he'll have to bid on it like everyone else. If it even comes to that."

"He's not my master," Slayd hissed, pushing her aside.

"So you are the same Melchyor! So quick to pout when teased."

"Excuse me if I need refuge from this 'odour.'" His curse of superior senses led him to taste the family in every room, whether a member was present or not.

The air was as sour as he remembered. And he remembered the hallways and steps of the main entertaining house, and he followed his memory of them up and out to a deck overlooking the western grounds. The croquet lawn was still flat and sectioned precisely and geometrically by perfect lines of trees jutting from the forests. The snow was baby blue under the perfect saucer of the moon, and the surrounding woods cast clawing shadows stepping slowly as clouds rhythmically revealed and exposed the light.

Gauvendanielle had followed closely behind him. She recited,
"They scream and yell but
know that eclipse is thy fate
way deep in their guts…"

He could still taste the family on the air overlooking the grounds, but the outdoors was a welcome respite from the walls and furniture turgid with the Loup Garou scent. The pale light turned his sickly tint blue, and he molded the shadows between his fingers until they disappeared. "I don't remember you as one so faithful."

"It's your fault, silly man. You would pass through here, every few years, finger through my grandfather's… possessions, and you always brought tales to trade, old and new, but the ones that affected me the most were the bloody stories of the Northern Men. You were a prophet of the Beast. Did you even know that? Your End Day chronicles spread through the Loup Garou at tea for years afterward. We haven't forgotten."

"Ridiculous tales meant to scare little girls into my guest bed."

"And it worked, if I remember."

"They were unnecessary. Uncles and brothers had primed your sisters for my presence."

"Don't be vulgaire."

"Is there a blade up for bidding?"

"Pardon?"

"Not the usual blade, but bent from a looped handle, like one half of a pair of large shears."

She was close to his face, and he could see the crows feet grasping at her temples. Still, her stretched skin shined in the right places and captured shadows in the right places and held a nice warm hue even under the corpse's pall of the moonlight. Her hair was thick and as long as it ever was, and it held itself high and away from her smooth forehead. She squinted as though trying to look through his cloudy eyes.

"What are you up to?" she asked. "Who is it you came here with? A zombie pistoleer and his petite apprentice? A Lesser Prophet bound and led by a resistance leader? You've changed."

"I can assure you, that's not the case. Now, any word of this artifact coming out of the digs, have the Loup Garou put anything by this description up for auction?"

"Oh, you've become so pedestrian." Gauvendanielle turned. "I can't believe I've wasted so much time over the years wondering when you would return again. Had I known you'd become such a bore I would have spent my energies elsewhere. Such a cliché."

He grabbed her from behind before she had barely taken a step, and he slid one hand down her dress while another slid up it. The air beneath her skirts was humid, her flesh as hard but slicker than he remembered. She was smoother than he would have expected from her age, but he still found the wrinkles he sought.

Her words were quiet, broken as she gasped against his cold fingers. "Would it be so tragic… for the world to… end. If the Horde conquers the rest of the land… we will have no choice but to sing their silly song. If… the Liege of Foes wins then we'll have traded one yoke for an… another." Slayd's eyes teared at the scent of her neck, before she twisted away from his grip. Something tore beneath her dresses as she pulled away. "And who knows what he wants with the land. He may want more souls this time around."

"What have you Loup Garou done?" Slayd asked, looking to his hands again. The night still turned his skin green, but now the fingers of one hand shimmered while those of the other were speckled with blood.

"The land needs a lesson. Even after Pestilence and Famine, there are still enough vermin to war over the leavings. I get so sick of the thought of the dredges clustered in the cities and shitting in holes in the ground on farms stretching from ocean to ocean, squirting out babies with no regard for the future. Well, what if there was no future? What if the land could just burn away the chaff and the world could just start over? Skim the land of the goddamn scum that's risen?"

"Haven't you heard, the gods have fled the world."

"Not all! They've left behind the one They imprisoned, the one They forgot! Fettered deep in Earth by impossible means, left to be cut free only by some impossible means. But there are no impossibilities in this gods-forsaken world."

The wind, off in the trees, suddenly picked up to a howl, but Slayd felt no breeze. Gauvendanielle's hair was unmoved, but she leaned toward the sound with a smile Slayd realized she had been hiding from him. There was more black in her teeth than white.

She lightly brushed his cheek and shrunken nose and picked off a flake of skin with a scaly pattern as hypnotic as the movement of his tongue. Her belly was instantly warm and it sank in a way she did not think possible any longer. "So, so young, but something's wrong. What is happening? Are you ill?"

"The…" He still found it difficult to say The Master's name aloud. "The Everman opened a door deep within me I had succeeded all my life to keep shut. And I'm having difficulty closing it all the way."

She took a long sigh, deep down in an attempt to cool her stomach, but her cheeks warmed under his cool breath. She could feel a random claw slide beneath the bindings of her side. "It is no matter. We are all dying, have always been dying, child, adult, mortal and immortal. Only now we die at the same rate and all together."

"What do you…"

"You are right. You were always right. The auction is a charade. Yes, the items being bid upon now are truly from the digs in Magog, but my brothers and sisters have enticed the leaders of the land as sacrifice for a very special guest. It is such a shame that so few have accepted the invitation, but… I suppose… war distracts… winter indisposes."

Gauvendanielle was gasping for air even before Slayd started to shake her. His cool touch had warmed her bowels, but it was the howling of the Loup Garou forests that stoked the heat. Her thighs tickled where his bony hip pressed into her.

"What has your foul family done?" He truly did desire an answer, but could not get himself to stop shaking her. Her hair flopped about wildly, the gray roots twinkling beneath the darker strands, a perfect reflection of the few stars shining past the full moon.

"The Beast will eclipse… the sun," she gasped and laughed and gasped, "but first must be… unfettered. The Loup Garou summons the Chosen One with an infernal auction, and… listen… he arrives!"

She dropped limply as Slayd's hands opened. He stared from their clenching to the grounds to the forests to the blinding night, not even looking back down as massive shadows emerged from the trees in a ravenous pack.

Gauvendanielle was caught up in loosened skirts and disheveled bindings, trying to stand. She eventually just gasped from the deck, peeking out to the grounds.

"Have you not heard, mon amour? As His howl grows, they own all the bloated moons, no matter its complexion." Her teeth ground against each other, powdering her dark lips. "Enter the Garm!"

XXVI

...held strong by gods', and man's
chains, the Warrior thinks it his own hand
—scrawled on the walls of the King of All's lower halls

He had pleased the angel — wingless, limbless, and shining. He had pleased the angel and now was rewarded with a whole new world to explore and claim. The angel had bequeathed him a room — spaceless and timeless. He had been bequeathed a room with a bed and a phalanx of Aemazonians to quench a thirst aching from his first memories. They were all of one mind and one by one their hearts gave out over the timeless days. One by one they dwindled, culled down to the unified mind and body of the angel. As each one collapsed, the main mind and body grew to create a form Easarean coupled with until he in turn fell, exhausted but alive. He had seeded the angel, the Shining One. And that was when the screams began.

They came from the very walls even though he knew they were from the far away moon he had escaped. The angel had given him a choice. Save his squad or otherwise. And now they screamed from some unheard of torture under Eha'dadadad's immaterial fingers. He could not differentiate between the screams, but he knew one was Ehelena. At times he thought he could pick hers out, but then they would all increase to a creshendo of pain. The angel got what it wanted, why did it now torment him so?

In the spaces between the spaces of the spaceless bedroom he found his armor and its hidden sword and after timeless time of listening to the screams, Easarean punctured his eardrums. It was then that the door appeared.

~

He had pleased the angel and now walked across the new world that was his reward, ears healed, resolve strengthened. He had this world to claim for his clan — a clan that would no doubt be searching for him. In this world, the Shining One promised, Easarean's seed would spread and his children become heroes of myth.

Easarean walked this lush new world where deciduous bloomed thickly and brightly, where conifers coned and covered mountains hoarding horizons. The people, sparse and varied, were primitive and small and he had his pick of those to conquer, but still he walked on.

This world was dangerous too, but nothing one of his clan could not handle. He killed bandits and barbarians, took treasure and maidens, crumbled machine and castle. He slayed werewolf and wyvern, dinosaur and demon, and had his blood stolen by scientist and magus, but still he walked on.

He found a desert ranch of legendary horses and began to make a new life with the intention of learning about this world. From time to time he left his new wife's bed to put on his helmet and scan the night sky. His damaged armor was still inconsistent, but its quaputers still worked hard to recognize sky charts. He was at the very outskirts of the Empire, on a forgotten but quarantined planet of wildly varying technologies and civilizations.

After only days of making the primitive woman his bride, she fell ill, as did her already bedridden father and their ranch workers. After only a few more days they were dead, and he spent most of one of the planet's short days burning their bodies and wondering if their skyward ashes pleased this planet's weak gods.

Easarean followed the roads to a sunburnt town filled with its few healthy inhabitants killing any who showed signs of this new plague. They hid from him and his alien size.

He headed south into jungles where the humidity reminded him of the Academy. Here the animals were all muscle, sleek colorful, and he could see himself enjoying sleeping under lush canopy and rain for the rest of his life, constantly testing his mettle against spotted, furred killers and poisonous, scaled stranglers, but his armor's memory told him of peoples he could impress and subjugate. It was time this world knew of the heroes the Empire could create.

~

They attacked in the night, no doubt granted the night-vision of their totem by some drugged shaman. Easarean rarely wore his armor anymore, carrying its components folded over his back, and he certainly was not wearing it while sleeping, but its perimeter alarms warned him just the same.

Their naked bodies wore only furred gloves, claws raking across his unbreaking skin. He laughed as he swung fists as big as their heads, breaking faces and ribs and reveling in the sudden adrenaline. He enjoyed any surprises in a land that was quickly becoming boring to him. The walk through the jungle had become tedious and familiar very quickly. The attack by these jaguar worshippers had been a welcome respite.

He piled their speckled bodies to sleep on for the rest of the night like the legendary heroes of old — among the dead. And his blood slowed, and he, in turn, slept like the deceased, not even waking when a small segmented slug wormed its way from one of the jaguar man's ears and, as the stars flickered in and out between the wet roof of leaves, crawled ever so delicately into Easarean's nostril.

~

He recognized the plague's signs immediately and, at the urging of the parapsyte, culled not only those obviously infected but immediate families as well.

"We will lose much of the kingdom, the worm thought into his head, *but it is the only way to be sure."*

"It's time to start stealing women from Pharaoh's land," Easarean said. He knew the parapsyte could hear his thoughts, but he still preferred speaking aloud. His people, weak and small, could not understand his words anyway — just another reason they feared him and his rule.

"No, we cannot take the chance of revealing ourselves too soon."

"I tire of this! Waiting, always waiting when I should be conquering."

"This is only a minor setback, love. We must be patient."

He watched as the strongest workers of his kingdom dragged the stones from the jungle, building the foundations of his future castle. Was it the parapsyte in the finished cellars that spoke in his head, he wondered, or one of those he felt worming their ways under his skull. It was becoming increasingly difficult to determine with any certainty.

"Eat, my love, eat. Your people have set out another magnificent spread for you."

It was true. The food in his new kingdom was always satisfying. And here it was before him — massive platters of flaking fish heads, grilled snake battered in its own egg whites, and grubs stone-fired just until they split. Meals at the Academy had consisted of protein blocks and nutrient drinks, and his survival training did little, he now knew, to represent this primitive style of eating, but he enjoyed his new options. Tearing into flesh with fingers and teeth, however satisfying, unfortunately only raised his bloodlust.

He popped nuggets of powdered, breaded hummingbirds into his mouth. They were meant to be dessert, but he could never wait. They were his favorite.

When eating his massive meals he thought of strategy and the surrounding jungled countryside, vowing to find more villages to burn, men to rule and women to take, but the meals always ended in slumber, mostly still at the prepared table, in which he would sleep most of the days away.

These days turned into weeks and eventually months and years, and his small kingdom grew only minimally. The slowly gestating para-psytes were his only companionship as he was uninterested in learning his people's language. The mother worm, tendrils snaking through his castle's cellars, always offered to link him to the village's minds, but Easarean felt no need. He made diminishing appearances to his jungle peasants, sometimes in his ceremonial armor, sometimes naked and bronze and fat, eventually always from one of the castle's uneven windows. Even when awake he was only aware of the passage of time through a slumberous haze.

But this all changed when he was finally visited by the Empire.

~

They had been "cousins" to him — two members of differing clans he could barely still recognize. And their bodies now sat, half drained of fluids, in the cellars beneath his swaying castle, along with the petrified remains of the mother parapsyte. The only slug left in Easarean's head was surprisingly quiet. He knew not if it was because of horror at the death of her family or because of glee at the thought of having his mind all to herself.

His cousin Aertlanteans had brought the news of his clan's demise. He was all that was left to exact revenge. Who or what could have possibly destroyed an entire clan, especially the clan of all clans — the invincible clan of his blood and legend. He was ready to lay waste to entire solar systems to find out.

"Just so we are in agreement," the basilisk said in Aertlantean, demonstrating his varied education, "HEREAS, the consignor agrees to turn over all rights to the FIRST BORN..."

"Silence, lizard," Easarean interrupted. He was trying to focus on the starship's holoplays as they moved around the cabin. His cousins' ship was pedestrian — more traveling yacht than battle-ready — but it had standard defenses and was familiar enough to him that he could read the interfaces. But the codes to leave the planet escaped him. Whether they were unattainably locked away in the quaputer's systems or lost in the dead heads of his two expired cousins, they were beyond his reach. His only chance now for vengeance would be to chance the killer satellites circling the planet.

"I know what you're thinking," the basilisk lisped. He waved a scaly vestigial wing toward the glowing screens floating around the cabin. "But you can't seriously think you'd survive leaving atmosphere. The Empire is very serious when it quarantines a planet. It is the result of shame, failed cultural meddling... you would not survive without the codes. Now..." His forked tongue flicked in and out of his beak, and he shuffled back and forth on chicken feet. "...read and sign at the bottom. Please."

Easarean took the shell blue papers and watched as arcane symbols, as serpentine as the basilisk's movements, slithered to form words in any and all languages he could read. The collector, as he introduced himself to be, seemed well informed, and he promised to give Easarean information that would lead to the codes he needed. And he would have to, for if he stayed on this gods-forsaken dirtball, he would never have any progeny. Easarean had proven time and again over the last years that the women of this world were too weak to accomplish anything with his seed. The Shining One had promised him legendary descendants, but it appeared that there would be more deals to make before fulfillment.

He could barely recognize himself in the basilisk's mirrored sunglasses. He signed the papers. What did he have to lose?

~

The Academy had taught Easarean never to trust a basilisk. They were the devious spawn of fowl and serpent — the result of a bird's nest taken by a snake, with eggs incubated under cold-blooded scale. This one was no different. His enchanted eyes were shifty and petrifying. His words and his feet dancing. His contract magically binding. But he was also a collector, and, as such, his greed could be predicted. Aertlanteans of Easarean's clan had now become unique, and, to the basilisk, very collectable.

And so he trusted the creature's information, and he waited. He had learned patience as King of Nothing, waiting for wars that never came, conquering that never occurred. And so he waited in his cousins' starship, subsiding on surprisingly extravagant rations, and leaving each day to run miles of weeded desert and lift boulders twice his size. He ignored any information in the ship's memory, denying any news he refused to accept. He found non-narcotic stimulants and loaded himself up for swimming excursions in the roughest seas he could find, always careful to avoid the walls surrounding the continent he had adopted, for the basilisk had warned him of more advanced civilizations beyond. By the time he had returned to his bronze figure, seemingly carved from muscle and myth, his patience paid off, and — as the lawyerly lizard had revealed would happen — months later, a blip appeared on the starship's scanners.

XXVII

"I heard (and anticipated) his passage (but not his passing), and I avoided (as all Lessers — and hopefully Greaters — would) any confrontation. I wasn't even curious. He was the Prime of this fallen world, and I pitied him, the odds being stacked against him, the rest of us never having to worry about each others' interference in our own worlds. Yet we all had to cope with the ramifications of his life in this one, and I, becoming the last (one of the last?), most of all. In that way you could call me his son. So, I guess I'm an Heir of Aesar."

—Damn Antony the Lesser

He may, indeed, be the most well-traveled individual in the land. For decades he was showcased in Buck Henry's Paraphernalia of the Curious traveling oddities show, from one coast to the next, through metropolitan and countryside, kings and rubes alike paid to gaze upon his skinless visage. Eventually, the fad of isolationism struck the land, and a traveling show became a dangerous or illegal venture. The show shut down, its freaks went their separate ways, its artifacts and relics spread or took root in Monsieur Buttergoose's Museum of Creepy Dolls and Dental Instruments of Ignorance in the city of Joseph. The popular museum served the destitute communities for even more decades, spared in the fire of '48, burning partially in the fire of '72, but succumbing finally in '91's fire. All its historical and naturalistic oddities were destroyed — all expect one. This individual's pickled body survived unscathed. In the aftermath of the great fire, the taxidermied gent disappeared, and for years his whereabouts remained unknown. There were many claiming to display his horrible demeanor, from curiosity shop to Barony Historical Society, but it was in an estate sale that the petrified personage of humanity's greatest traitor was discovered, not far, coincidentally, from here, and it was from this estate sale that the Always acquired the mummified remains for some no-doubtedly unholy experiments. And in the Tower of Gog, the dried remains of this man have sat, preserved through herb and magiks, until the fall and flood and freeze of that great southern land, and, like all that the Loup Garou have offered from their impressive collection today, you now have the chance of acquiring him for your individual collections."

If it was possible for the people to lean closer to the stage, they would have. Wulf took perverse pride in hampering their enthusiasm as he pressed among them to escape the crowd. He had been exploring the small theatre, to escape the dark dance of the main hall, when the auction had been announced, and he had somehow been caught among the bidders as they entered. The gawkers quickly gave up on a closer look in the dim lighting. It was apparently enough to suck in the increasingly humid air of the room as the caller teased to pull the sheet from what they could already tell was an upright display box. Some laughed, some spilled fine wine, avoiding staining fine clothes.

Wulf had cleaned himself up as well he could, and he and Slayd had replaced some of their more tattered clothing before reaching the Loup Garou estates, but he still felt underdressed for the auction. The men of the bidding especially had given him a berth in receiving and dance, sticking their noses up at the crusted stains at the tips of his cloak. But they paid no attention to him now, only to the taxidermied body the caller revealed by pulling the curtain aside. Upright and nestled in the straw of the crate, the skinned corpse faced the nauseated crowd.

The caller stuttered at the people's reaction. He was a thin man, and even his close-fitting suit looked large on him, his ascot bulbous and cradling the lump that suddenly appeared in his throat. But he was a professional, and his wide eyes were immediately replaced with a look of assurance. "Who among such a prestigious crowd would like to start the bidding on such an unparalleled piece of historical significance? I know I don't have to educate such a learned gathering on the merits of owning the only existing evidence of the Inside-Outers Invasion. The forgotten war, anyone? The antimatter men? Their lives, their very corporal existence was fleeting in our universe, but this, the expertly preserved body of humanity's traitor, Cro-Troilius, has survived. See how he mutilated himself to match the visage of his unnatural masters? He is all that is left of their short-lived infernal march. Once bandit, once Libran, once turncoat, then generations in infamous oddity display, his eyes have watched the land change over the century. What secrets could he reveal? For it is said he whispers of the ages to the worthy."

Wulf walked to the edge of the hall as the bidding started. The caller's voice was as loud in the entrance as it was from any point in the room.

"This may not be a territory, ladies and gentlemen, but we, like the *Ashmedai Adat El,* take all forms of currency and non-currency, deeds and grants, precious stones and not so precious metals."

Wulf looked out into the wide receiving chamber, its voluminous stairways and open, raging fireplace. The area had been dense with guests when he and Slayd had arrived, and they had all turned from hor d'oeuvres and bourbon to sneer at the late-comers. Slayd had garnered the least disapproved looks, his new clothing mostly hiding the old, swirls of interwoven gold catching the light of fire and lamp at the edges of robe and sleeve. His long floppy hat and dark scarf had hid all of his face. Tight folds hid the rest of his tall slender form, with only pale, knuckled fingers revealed to hold the staff he had carved on their long walk to the Loup Garou plantations.

Wulf should not have drawn such attentions. His boots and cloak were not much more tattered than the usual traveler, and he had kept Yggr's Eye hidden beneath shadow and hood, but the man tethered to his side had drawn uncomfortable glances during the entrance. Even colored by bruises, even swollen and battered, the aquiline features, although grayed from lack of sleep and food, it was obvious the revelers could recognize a Lesser Antony.

Wulf had sent the small force the Army of Earth had sent to liberate him and Slayd on their way. They were good men, and they had no families for him to return them to, and they waited on his word without question. He would have preferred to send them to join some neighboring resistance, but he was not familiar enough with the area, and so he eventually sent them to join up with the Liege of Foes' main forces, of which were rumored to be heading eastward, toward them. He had sent them with the cart of spoils Antony had brought out of Ophidia, after Slayd had picked some prizes out for himself. The main reveal was a giant egg that had taken up the majority of the cart's space. In fact, as Slayd removed the wrapping quilts, Wulf had wondered how it could have fit in the cart after all. For being man-sized it was surprisingly lightweight. Wulf could not remember the last time he seen such a beautiful piece of artwork. The sunrise had become instantly dull after the battle had ended, but the numerous metals comprising the egg still reflected as though the horizon burned.

"The Clockwork Wyrm," Slayd had said before stepping on Damn Antony's hand, grinding it into the gore of the pasture they stood. "I wouldn't have guessed it was still in Ophidia. You've had yourself quite a find. Still, it will do no one any good without the key." And that was all he had to say about the matter, although Wulf noticed the sorcerer watching the cart until it was out of distance. Wulf had it sent along with the force to the Army of Earth, along with anything else he did not think they could sell on the way to the auction. He took only a few gold pieces. The force did not even have a revolver to spare, and so Wulf still only carried his empty sawed-off. It had been years since he had found shot for it.

But now, in the receiving hall of the Loup Garou, *GloryRend* hung, a displacing weight on his hip under his cloak. Damn Antony had held onto it for him, and Wulf rewarded the Lesser Prophet by tying him to the greeting chamber. The Lesser slept the first sleep of days, crumpled, caked next to the worn velvet of furniture servants had shooed him away from, watched over by Harlowe's unblinking gaze.

Wulf lingered near. He could hear the soft jingle of the chains the pistoleer still wore, broken remnants of his imprisonment in Brig, beneath the harmony of fiddle and violin. The strings had accompanied the ghostly dancing of the Loup Garou but did not vanish as the dancers did as the auction opened. Or so Wulf thought. Now, when he would acknowledge the music, focus on its sharp pattern, it faded away. But as soon as he forgot it, it would appear again, from some hollow hall beyond solid wall.

"Where's Ivy?" Wulf now asked Harlowe, nudging Antony awake. Mud, now dried, flaked from his boot.

Harlowe glanced up toward curving staircases. The numerous light sources in the chamber were not enough to pierce the shadows below his low hat, but Wulf could still see the man's lips dried into a permanent grin. He followed the look to the busts and shelves lining the walls up to the second level of the mansion. He should have known the occasional bookshelf would have been too tempting to keep the girl in one place.

The charred oak smell that seemed to permeate the hall had only dissipated for the short time of the dancing, when dust and muffled sweat took over. It was back now, reminding Wulf of the drinks servants had offered, the perfumes that practically dripped from the hosts. Like the drinks the scent was quickly intoxicating. He inhaled it deeply from the neck of a girl that stood just inside the showing room as he returned. Her hair was very short, in contrast to the corded locks twisting against her near sister's bare shoulders, but just as dark and woody, like the bourbon they sipped. Her skin was as flawless as the glass lighting against her shining and dark lips, and there were wiry hairs growing back at the hairline of her neck. She watched him watching her.

"Dreadfully hot in here, ain't it?" she asked, placing her glass aside and fluttering a paper fan at her neck. Again, Wulf inhaled deeply. The scent reminded him of cabin wood warming in a sunrise after a night of rain. She collapsed the fan and pulled at the glove covering an opposite arm. One finger at a time she tugged, until each looked like black worms withering in that same sunrise. She switched to the other glove, and Wulf could not look away as she pulled at that hand, again one finger at a time. She watched Wulf as he watched her fold the gloves. "You must be so..."

He jerked at her touch as she reached into his hood, but then finished pulling it back himself. He had shaved and trimmed his hair before coming to the auction but knew he must still appear shaggy. The girl stepped back against a side table, almost spilling the drink she had set down. "You... are you...?" She shied away from the glare of Yggr's Eye. Did she recognize it, he wondered. It was becoming increasingly unnerving to him how many people had started to in the past few years. He knew the Loup Garou had no allegiance to the Horde, but there could have been many invited to the auction that did.

If she continued, he had stopped listening. The caller had begun describing the next item dapper servants had brought out. "Perhaps this will be more to the crowd's liking. Remember, no bid will not be considered. Services have worth as well. Company of ill-repute included. Progeny is more valuable than ever."

What Wulf had first thought was a bookend on a shelf slithered in and out of lamplight to his side. Scales on the large featherless fowl changed color as the little creature changed direction. Failing to hide its bored expression behind mirrored sunglasses, it yawned and hopped to the floor, leaving behind a brilliant white business card. Wolf looked to watch the creature go, but Damn Antony and Harlowe were still the only beings in the receiving hall — the former still tied and now slumped completely on the floor, the latter walking restlessly from frosted window to window.

"The next items up for bid will delight both historians and those of more cultured tastes, for the star-crossed tale of the Divine Knight and the Night Diviner has enthralled the land for centuries. Two young lovers separated by their opposing families but drawn together by an affection for the ages — Sir Metatron and the enchantress Dysnomia.

Their tragic end could not extinguish the passion of their tale, for every child can sing their song from heart, and every adult has dreamt of the lost lovers' treasure. For somewhere out in the jungled forests of Kaldera lies her dowry and his spoils. For countless years gem-hunters have searched to no avail, but they did not have what the Everman had." The barker lifted the linen from the pedestal, only to have a corner of lace catch on a sliver from the box beneath. With a jerk the shroud tore and split away. He blew on the dark bottles, cringing openly from the sawdust assailing his eyes. Blinking at the staring crowd, he said, "Hundreds of gold-seekers did not have what you now can. This ancient vintage, circa PE 14, will not only be the pièce de résistance of some fine collector's cellar here today, not only will it one day be toasted to the dying light of a swallowed sun, intoxicating its connoisseur with the burnt oaky memories of a world long lost, but the labels — preserved and clear and unique and individual to each of these seven bottles — tell their own tale. For Metatron and the knights of his heptagon table each had their own crest, and in each badge there was hidden a map, and when all the maps were placed together one can find the secret location of Mistress Dysnomia's fabled Iron Maiden of *MGGT*. As the legend goes, she told the spiked device all her indiscretions. It was witness to every one of her sins. It was soaked in the voluptuous witch's every debauched deed. And you could be too! Today! Combine and decode the symbols on these wine bottles and you alone will discover the map to Dysnomia's most prized possession. Secrets leak from the device's iron lips. Its blood holds the memories of a hundred virgins. And one of these secrets is the location of the Cave of Rainbows — the secret location of Metatron's treasure. Now, with the knights' flagged ramparts long since ruined, their shields long ago smelted under Automaton's lasered gaze, their family bloods long hence diluted, this collection of labels is the only extant map of seeking the lost Order's wealth. They are only to be sold as a complete set, for what good would only a piece of the puzzle be? Wars have been fought for far less, and the Loup Garou wish no responsibility. Where shall we start the bidding?"

The Loup Garou had taken pity on Wulf once, when he had as a young man escaped the Baba Yaga's dungeons. He barely remembered staggering through the everglades, out of hill lands and into the family's plantations. They had found him dehydrated and rambling of weird forests and weirder spirits. He had always been unsure just how long he had been their guest, but they had nursed him back to health and shown him a kindness unfamiliar in the land. He had left one morning before dawn, never saying goodbye. He had always regretted his ingratitude and planned to return one day to show his appreciation. But that was not why he had returned this night.

The girl that approached him was too young to remember his stay all those years ago. She could not have been more than sixteen years old, yet she was as tall as he and wore the caked powder and blush of the elderly. "This ghastly heat has made me right sticky," she whispered to him, bourbon staining her breath and mouth beyond her painted lips. "I do so abhor a good mob. Let us retreat to the grounds. The air has a delightful bite tonight." Her wig's hair was so folded and braided and tied within itself that it was impossible to tell how long it was. It appeared as a mass of vipers hanging over a jungle stump. Wulf stared at the tiny combs straining to quell the nest. They were never the same color twice.

He took one of her hands, unable to tell where the filigree ended and the lacey tattoo began, and put it to her lips. She kissed it, pausing before laughing softly and pausing again. She was eventually unable to hold the gaze of either of his eyes, and she pulled her arm away and backed into the pulsing crowd.

He returned to the greeting room yet again, instantly cooler near the air of the foyer. Away from the auction he could hear the hum of the outside generators. They were louder each time he returned and they always brought his mind back to the outside world. It was easy to forget the Territories and the war when surrounded by such opulence. Even fallen, the excess of the Loup Garou was its own untouched world. The family had managed to remain independent. They had claimed no allegiance to Army of either Heaven or Earth. Where they had acquired the fuel to power their generators without connections to the Horde-controlled territories, Wulf could not say, but the faint sputter he could now hear beneath their rumble gave him an indication that the engines were not entirely reliable.

Harlowe FelDougan still held watch over the shadows beneath the brim of his hat, where as the Lesser Antony he guarded had crawled to the wall behind a chair of cherry velvet and cherrier wood. If it was not for the occasional shudder of nightmare, he would have assumed the bloodied man dead.

Wulf walked the closest staircase, winding upward around the open chamber, past neglected book and bronze lupine sculptures, dust-dirtied candles and tarnished silver sticks. He had been unnerved since they had arrived, had associated his anxiety with the sudden strange sights and music and the bluster of the auction, but he now feared it was something more. Coming to the Loup Garou plantations was a gamble, but one he would take if there was a chance the *Shear* had been dug up. It no longer called to him since he had spurned it in the Tower of Gog, but he hoped that he would sense its presence if it was near. But all he sensed here was something ominous, something just outside the mansion's walls and the churning of the generators. The chandelier lights dimmed as he thought about the gasoline machines. They resumed their steady glow as he left the chamber for the second floor hallways. Here the lamps were scattered without consistent brightness or placement. There was no sign of anyone on the floor but him. He feared stretching his mind out to the rooms, in search of Ivy, for chance of opening himself to the ever-pushing presence pressing against his head. He was ever-vigilant now, always holding his mental barriers up to prevent the oddly familiar foreign force from breaking through. His sleep at night was uneven as he woke throughout to ensure the barriers held.

The rooms were as he remembered. They seemed smaller, however, and lately untouched. They were clean, without dust, but sterile. Every desk and paper, every portrait and shelf had its place. Every chair and voluminous curtain had grown into wall or floor, seemingly unmoved in a generation. He pulled the jeweled chain on a lamp and it lit the room in a gory pall. New shadows and old furniture blended into an organic cavern without distinction, but the lamp stood distinctly before him. The trunk rose from a spread base in burnished green swirled by a bronze design mimicking wooden striations. Branches cradled a half Earth shade, continents and oceans stained into the fabric. Rubies were strung as though Earth sank into the fires of a burning World Tree. From the shade jutted a crystalline orb etched with the craters of the moon, set in the toothy jaws of an iron wolf.

Ivy entered from a doorway behind him, as silent in step and thought as he had taught her. "They worship the Garm here," she said. He turned to her as the light from both the lamp and the hallway flickered out. The crowd murmured from the far-off auction room. In the darkness, he now noticed the faint glow of the night filtered through the thick hangings of the window. The light was bloody until he pushed the folds aside. It took more strength than he expected to reveal glass. The moon was as pale as his face, as blue as his granite eye, and its light caught and froze the dust of the curtains.

"No one worships the Garm," he said.

"The Beast of the Core then." Ivy was wearing a pewter circlet around her neck. The dull metal had been formed into a twisting of branches that ended above her chest, without touching, in two canine heads snarling at each other. The fur and snouts too came out of intertwined branches. The tiny rubies placed as eyes were black even after the lights flickered to life again.

He had not seen her for over a year when she and Harlowe had rescued him and Slayd on the prairie. They had both passed through Megrim with some information for the Resistance. She was now darker than he remembered, in hair and eyes and face, and she had grown in height at least a few inches. But her undeniable curiousity had remained. She handed him what looked to be a leather journal, bound in ribbon and leather, and he noticed the new gray rings and bracelets on her hand. They all had similar dendrophiliac designs ending with tooth and claw.

He took the journal from her only to set it unopened on the desk. "No," he said, "I fear the Loup Garou have come to worship Death itself. They've become complacent, bored, fulfilled by nothing, envious yet disgusted by the world. Death is the only and ultimate release, yet they wouldn't want to leave the world to anyone else. Through this they look to the Garm — the Garm who seek to unleash the Beast from an infernal prison. The Beast, offspring of Mischief and Savagery, lusts for the sizzling meat of the sun. The werewolves wish to tear Earth asunder and send it into unending night."

"The Beast is…"

"The gods' eternal shame, the ultimate fruit of their sin and neglect, their eternal embarrassment. Unwilling or unable to kill it, or to even curb its insatiable appetite, they could only imprison it somewhere deep within the earth, under the very roots of the World Tree itself. Bound by impossible fetters, only able to be released by an impossible blade."

"The blade…"

"And the location. The Great Beast of the North has been unmuzzled. He calls to the Chosen, and all they need is the blade and a map to the center of Earth. At least, this is what all good little midgardian children learn at bedtime to turn whole generations against the Garm. Now it appears the Loup Garou have found a trendy new cause in the old mythologies of the Granite Lands to alleviate their creeping malaise."

"Do you believe any of it?"

Wulf traced the leather-worked design on the journal with a finger, the pointed ears and exaggerated fangs of the wolf. It brought the images to his mind of his constant nightmare, the hoary howl in his head, the Beast clawing its way to the surface, and great pieces of the surface of the planet heaving and pushing away from and pulling toward the heavens. "It doesn't matter. What is important is that *they* do. Any death cult, any peoples that prophesizes Armageddon as part of their salvation will do nothing to prevent it and everything to allow it. They cannot be trusted in any deed." He pulled the curtains shut, bloodying the moonlight. "We need to leave. There's something not right here."

He had her remove the jewelry before she led him back down the hallway. The greeting room appeared different in its expanse than when they had left it. The chandelier was dimmer. The room even more sparse of arrivals. New shadows wrapped the returning fiddlers and violinists, bows and strings playing over the rising grind of outside generators and inside bidders. The violins trailed a long note punctuated by quick notes in quicker succession, the fiddlers trailing the initial sound in their own way in the background.

Antony was where he had left him, asleep or unconscious, limbs entwined in the chair he sprawled beneath, bindings holding firm.

"Find Slayd," Wulf told Ivy and Harlowe, "we're leaving."

"Empty handed?" Ivy asked with no disappointment hidden in her large darkening eyes.

"It looks that way." Wulf headed back into the auction room for one last look. Windows had been opened. He could smell the cool night, its sterile air and forming frost, but the room was as humid as ever. Sweat still lingered before chilling on bidders' brows.

"Have you found what you're looking for?" a boy asked him, appearing suddenly at his side. He was young but as tall as Wulf, the hair on his head shaved to barely stubble. Wulf got a glimpse of him before ignoring the question in favor of the barker.

"These are no mere books, ladies and gentlemen, just as the collector was no mere man. *Heil to the Chaff* is written in the venom of black widow spiders. Imprisoned in iron dungeon, it was all its author could find to write with over his decades of internment. The tome has been resewn with the finest care, the lettering accentuated with ebony kraken ink to bring out the author's original words."

The boy at Wulf's side continued. He fingered a fox-tooth necklace that mimicked the tattooed bite marks encircling his throat. "I mean, have you purchased anything yet? You're running out of time."

Wulf peeked back into the foyer. The music had become distracting. He was wondering why they played to an empty room when he noticed that new guests were actually still arriving. What could only be a Libran knight was escorting a shrunken man with a painful gait into the mansion. The knight retracted feathered hood and half-helm, leaving a leather cowl over most of his head. Traveling growth appeared sporadically over the rest of his face. The only other armor he wore appeared darkly in his vambraces and boots, both revealing red angelic figures that differed from the Order Wulf was familiar with. This man's sigils were longer, with the figure sprouting four wings.

The auction mob crowded toward the windows, with muted cries of pain as here and there a participant fell, here and there a hand was stepped on. People fanned the open air inward, tilting their heads to some far-off outside sound, something beyond the agitation of the crowd and the sputtering of the generators. The barker continued, raising his voice against the rhythmic strings of the foyer, drawing short attentions back to the stage. "Its sibling, *Sins of the Fodder*, has been rebound and rebacked by only experts in the field to match the striking minotaur calf binding of its twin. Its lock has also been expertly crafted to match, with, as you can see, beautiful Etruscan filigree. The leaves have had no need of restoration. The deaf and blind author's words, as they were dictated from that tower, to the birds of the forests, who sang it to this land's first Maids, can be read by the highest bidder."

"My uncle kept the best for himself," the boy said, positioning himself between Wulf and the hall to the foyer. "There are wands and weapons and coins. I could find what you're looking for, for the right price."

Wulf slid around the boy but remained in the growing shadows to see whom the knight escorted, as the barker continued. "But first let us start the bidding for another item, for it is not *Heil to the Chaff* and *Sins of the Fodder* that are up for bid today but this item here." He pulled a small gray key from his vest pocket. Turning it over the rapt crowd, one could see the flickering lamplight catch an emerald on one side and a ruby on the other, matching corresponding stones on each lock of the pedestaled books. "*Heil to the Chaff* and *Sins of the Fodder* are only bonus prizes here today ladies and gentlemen. Individually they are mere ramblings, rabble rousers, memoirs to raise the ire of disassociated peasantry. But, read together however, they will cause even the most stable mind to go mad. Perused apart they have no power, but even if only a few lines of each are read by the same person, no matter his mental constitution, a quickening insanity will consume him. And not only him, ladies and gentlemen, but the masses around him. These two books caused the collapse of Lon Magnon, and later Imperial Nim, leading Kaldera into its dark age. Up for bid today is not only this key, but a grand responsibility!"

Wulf slinked into the shadows of the foyer, out of commotion and into the thrumming harmony of strings, only to freeze. The knight he now assumed was of the estranged Western Order was escorting Handsome Gibbet.

The musicians were more than just that, Wulf could not help but think, even in the near presence of the tithingman. They were artists, with each violinist expertly harmonizing with the other, each fiddler anticipating any pause in the other. He had never heard such a beautiful song.

of the seven celestially Governed Elements
  (7) the Maintenance of Roads
"…as a value, ensure that, by proper taxation, supplies may reach the army through a
common national virtue of assumed and regulated military expenditure"

—Hyper Khan's The War of Art

here was a Libran waiting for him on the stone porch of the mansion. The knight appeared to be carving letters into the wood of a swing with a pickaxe. Handsome Gibbet approached, stiff from days of riding, in carriage, truck, and wagon, his shoulders paining him in familiar ways, while his lower back had acquired a pinching pressure new to him. It stung him when he stood straight but fatigued him when he stooped, and the weight of his numerous leather bags and pouches made the decision for him. His groin was infected with a numbness that spread to his thighs, with each stride shivering in spasm he had to steady himself against after a few steps. And although part of the journey had been taken through the sacred fire of the *Ashmedai Adat El's* holy gateways of burning bushes, Handsome still felt as though he had walked across the entire country on foot. And so it took him what seemed like a lifetime to ascend to the porch.

"We're late," the Libran spat as he snuffed a cigarette with his fingers. He pulled his riding gloves off with two quick movements as he stood from the long swing. "Eye arrived just before you, governor. It sounds as though the auction's started early."

All Handsome could hear was the sputtering of generators somewhere nearby. He could smell a faint trace of gasoline in the air, acrid beneath the foul horse stench of the knight. Handsome had left his escorts at the gate, knew not whether they followed the horses to the stables or surveyed the grounds as he told them to. They had become increasingly obstinate as they left the Territory, increasingly questioning of his every order, and he had quickly tired of their company. They were all grandsons and nephews and grandnephews of those Handsome trusted. These were the next generation of Megrim's leaders, but they would be punished once they returned home. For now, he had to bite his lip in their presence with both his rows of teeth.

After a week of travel, bowels and jaws clenching either without feeling or with stark pain, the last thing he felt like doing was hobnobbing with dandied snobbery, even less entertaining a representative of the Order of the Spirit. The Western Order were nothing more than zealous upstarts. The Brotherhood had all too eagerly accepted their allegiance, leaving people like Handsome to have to deal personally with the painted sycophants. Red and black tattooed feathers covered the back of the knight's hands, matching a design on his mantle that barely even appeared when the perfectly round moon broke through the clouds.

"But first," the knight said, crinkling the mouth below his cowl in an obvious bashfulness, "the name's Bodkin Hebenflem. Eye bring a gift from High Command." He knelt, bumping the swing into movement behind him and removing a fine cherry-wood box with slow care from his satchel. His eyes disappeared under a half-helm into shadow and cowl and black paint. "Prelate Shriven commends your accomplishments in stomping out the insurgent warlords of Megrim. The frontlines have already noticed a marked difference in terrorist supply lines."

Why can't he speak like ah normal person? Handsome thought concerning the knight's far western Libran accent. The old man tried to pass, tried to reach the great doors, but they swung out to meet him as he neared, and he was pressed back against the Libran. A servant, taller than the knight and thinner than Handsome, with lips pursed to a humorous degree, led them into a long entry hall in which a flickering chandelier could be seen lighting grand dual stairways at the far end. Handsome opened the small cherry-wood box and frowned at the contents padded by plush velvet embroidered with the quad-winged designs of the Western Librans.

They think ah'm ah fool. Ah joke. Just some malformed freak sent to the edge ah civilization to keep order over savages barely beneath muh status. While the high and holy Prophets Lesser ah off winning glory and favor in the eyes ah angel and populace, the tithingmen ah left behind to wipe the asses ah the unwashed masses, for they ah too ugly to do anything else. They ah already close to the dregs and peasantry. Why not leave them behind to lord over the pens? Slop masters. Emperor swine. Halfbreeds in need ah reminder ah their place. So here ah am. Handsome Gibbet. Jester for fools. Muh ambition had revealed me. Ah dared to dream above muh mutant peers. Here was muh humbling. Sent into uncontested lands, far from all the work ah had done as governor, even farther from the glory of the warfront. Assigned to feel out the allegiances of an inbred family and an auction ah illiterate tradesmen. Muh nose shoved in the shit of merchants and upjumped farmers calling themselves colonels and ranchers. This is where they feel ah belong. And they sent this two-steps removed heretic to remind me ah muh place.

Handsome pulled the scarf he almost always now had over his mouth down from his face. Even without a new nervous tic in his inner mouth, he had to struggle to form words without a tongue. "Yuh... you think me ah girl... ?" He took the derringer from the velvet. The engraved feathered patterns hid the simplicity of the 4-shot pepperbox.

"Pardon?" The Libran's smile disappeared.

The servant of the Loup Garou barely acknowledged his invitation, but sank into a chair as they passed.

"Ah... ah, some cathouse sh... slut?" Handsome caught the wall. His legs were already tiring, his mouth already sore from forcing out even those few words.

"Pardon? What's the matter? This whore-shot is part of your new commission. You've been requested at the front lines. You're to report directly after you're done here. Leave tomorrow. Congratulations, old man."

Handsome gingerly placed the pistol back into the box, molding the plush around its curves. He now noticed the bronze coloring of the gun as representing his patron angel Chem-Oshmelech, the fiery feather engraving, the dove on one side of the tiny grip, the lamb on the other. The Brotherhood had finally recognized him, had finally noticed his sacrifices. Here they finally acknowledged their abandonment. They had not forgotten him.

With renewed energy he strode into the greeting chamber, surrounded by stairs, now steady chandelier light, and the string music of multiple instruments. They seemed to announce his presence, so he forgave their horrendous cat-death of a tune.

He was greeted by no one however, Loup Garou or guest. The massive foyer was apparently empty except for the talentless men masquerading as musicians. Their strings were in heat, and he could feel the uneven vibrations of their howling even in his hidden row of teeth. The room had décor far beyond even the imagining for his governor's mansion. The divans, although faded inconsistently from one side to another, still held a joie de vivre he did not think possible in an inanimate object. The wingback he stood near invited a person to be cradled in its cushioning and lulled to sleep by its tales of Loup Garou balls and debauchery.

The torturous fiddlers filled in the notes between the violins, but, even if they hadn't, the crowd in the adjacent room would have been drowned out by a new grinding of the outside generators. Still, Handsome could see the commotion over some worthless trinket or heretical pamphlet. The cool air at his back quickly dissipated against the heat emanating from the auction room.

The string quartet ignored the new entrants, so enraptured in their own screeching cacophony. Handsome felt alone with the Libran. The knight was folding his half-helm back over his head while unbuttoning the jacket under his heavy mantle.

"Wuh… where did you leave your escorts?" Handsome tried to say. Mostly just air escaped his lips. He suddenly became more aware of the weight of all his side-bags and slouched even more.

"Pardon? What?"

The tithingman inhaled deeply through soreness. The stitches had been removed, but he still felt them when he swallowed. This new commission, this new responsibility at the general's table, would be the start down the path toward his eternal reward — the celestial body promised all his misshapen brothers. No more would the unwashed of the land, ignorant and faithless, look to him as though he were the freak, as though he were the one unworthy of favor. Their misplaced confidence in themselves would not save them. His heavenly body, his final reward, would prove his providence. Above all the peasants, he would stand superior. No more would his appearance ostracize him. No longer would he struggle to speak. No longer would sitting or pissing feel like the devil ground glass into his nethers.

"Yuh… your companions, where are they?" he asked again.

"Eye travel alone. It's been many years since eye've had a squire, and eye've grown used to riding solitary." The knight's voice dropped to a whisper. "The *Ashmedai Adat El* has promised these lands and more to the south to the Order of the Spirit after the war. Eye'd like to stake my claim early, maybe survey toward the gulf. Eye've always been curious to explore the rumors of the lost…"

Ugh… why can't he talk like a normal? Handsome dug through one of his many side-bags, showing no interest. He breathlessly said something the Libran could not interpret.

"What?"

"Hsss... so you've traveled here uh, alone."

"Eye'm to join your trip back to the Territories, if you don't mind."

The side of the foyer opposite the commotion of the auction room held entrances and doors to other rooms and chambers, and Handsome looked to past adjacent statues to find a suitably empty passage. Without looking back he grabbed Sir Hebenflem's arm as the knight stepped toward the bidding room. Handsome tried to speak, but any muddled words would have been cut short by another hand, this time gripping his own ankle.

"He's here!" the man of bruises croaked from the ground. No matter how discolored or swollen, Handsome would always recognize a Lesser Antony. The man was frostbitten and appeared to have been dragged across the land, but Handsome knew the sculpted jawline and cheekbones, tanned skin and dark eyes, and voice he often heard when closing dual-lidded eyes. He kneeled over the bound man, unable to believe he had been too distracted to notice him behind one of the many chaise lounges in the greeting room. He winced, either at the Antony's appearance or the continuing string music.

Again, when encountering a Lesser Antony, he could not help but wonder. Was this his father before him? His own had left him shortly after branding him with the infant blessing of Chem-Oshmelech, so he had no memory of him, but still he saw him in each identical face of the Brotherhood. This time was no different. With the war reducing their number, what were the odds that this Antony crawling the floor in exhaustion was his sire? It was no matter though. There would be time for that later. Here was the authority that, by the will of Chem-oshmelech, called him to duty. Here was the Promise of Father in the flesh. Again the world aligned itself to Handsome, the world shifting in his favor. How else could one explain the appearance of this lone Libran? And now, a Lesser Antony appears with no other purpose than to be saved. Handsome smiled painlessly, unafraid to reveal both rows of teeth. Sir Hebenflem's wince did not even bother him.

He stepped over the Antony, putting his arms under his shoulder to lift him into the chaise. All his teeth clenched from the effort. His loins screamed in pain when his mouth could not. But he spat out words as he struggled. "Ugh... Wha... teh, ah you doing here, father? Who's done this to you?"

Even under a split lip and purpled chin, he could see the Lesser

Antony frown. "I'm not your father."

Handsome dropped the man to the floor, feeling his arms go immediately stiff. The Lesser Antony continued to talk but he was not listening as he walked the foyer, peeking down hallway and across rooms. Sir Hebenflem followed him.

"The auction is well underway. Shouldn't we…"

"Ugh… come, teh… this way," Handsome interrupted with breath and spittle. They walked through unlit halls and past bright kitchens. They saw few people, only servants abandoning duties near Loup Garou sleeping in chairs and spilled bourbon.

The music followed them down through playrooms and offices, past dining rooms and up the stairs through servant quarters. The echoing music scratched even more horridly at Handsome's ears as it ricocheted off the empty walls.

When Handsome finally stopped, it was in a large office walled by bookcases full of photographs and centered with a small stocky table. Sir Hebenflem turned a small dun sculpture on the table. It was about two hands tall and surprised him with its resistance when he tried lifting it with one hand. It was a twisted sculpting of a man in mid transformation, fur spreading from his legs up into his abdomen. Was the stretched emotion in his face agony or ecstacy? The knight decided it was both, as he set the statue down with more noise than he expected. He went to straighten a small frame on the wall near a large segmented window that reached to the high ceiling of the room. The frame held an etching of a snowscape revealing only the top tips of elder trees. The only color in the etching belonged to a water-colored sun that appeared to have a bite taken out of its roundness. A single set of paw prints led through the trees. The knight scoffed at the poor perspective in the piece. The prints appeared to walk into the sky at the horizon line. He peered out the window then.

"This is exactly what eye would like. Not exactly on a hill, but a second floor that could peek over the trees, with a green roll the kid could play on, sled over in the winter, the endless winter."

"Teh… the winter will end when teh… the Divine Song is heard everywhere. Harmony'll calm the winds, melody'll warm hearts and ugh… earth." The frame tilted awkwardly again, and as Handsome closed the door to the room it fell to the floor. The tithingman followed to look out the window to the skylights below and the multiple windows to both sides of the mansion. The part of the house they stood in was inset to other floors, and even behind green clouds the moon lit the sharp angles and grounds. The surrounding trees, beyond the rolling lawns, merged into impenetrable darkness however. "Ugh... about what year duh... did the Kalderan Knights break off from the main order, the huh... Northern Order, the ah, ah... Temple Needles?"

"Pardon?" Sir Hebenflem had gone to look at the shelves of family photographs.

"Heh... ad the Libran Codas been established before the Western Order broke ugh... away?

"What?" The emotionless photos were mainly black and white with simple frames to match. They were scenes of parents and children posed without imagination. "Yes. They were all passed down to us by the First Dhani in the First Days. Why?" The more elaborate frames, however, carved and sculpted, held color photographs, with smiling members of extended Loup Garou. All of the frames, fancy or otherwise, were covered in dust only disturbed by the knight's fingerprints.

"Whu... what is the Seventh Coda?" Handsome's exasperated voice was near.

"Pardon?"

With the back of his neck protected by the retracted helm, the sculpture was brought against the side of the knight's head. His mantle bunched at the shoulders and reduced his peripheral vision, so he had little warning that the blow was coming. Still, he was able to roll with it, keeping the statue from hitting him square on the temple.

Handsome did not take much time to catch his breath. He tossed the broken sculpture aside to dig beneath the knight's jacket. A large dagger was the only weapon found. It appeared more ornamental than practical, as Handsome pulled it from its feathered scabbard, with a black hilt and blade and red talons gripping the handle and stretching up into the metal-like veins. The knight rolled over, pushing Handsome weakly aside. The tithingman scrambled for the broken bits of statue and brought a chunk down with both hands on the knight's mouth. He rolled again, this time against the wall, but his eyes had rolled back in his head, and his fingers clenched impotently backward, and he whined highly back in his sinuses, his mouth agape and blowing bloody bubbles.

Handsome breathed just as heavily. "Whu... what is the final law, the Seventh, ah, ah... Final Coda?" He threw the piece of statue, but it bounced softly off Sir Hebenflem's chest. He wiped tiny drops of sweat and the other's blood from his receding brow, unbuckling satchels and removing pouches until he was left with just the largest around his shoulders.

The knight quieted but now watched the tithingman with drooping eyelids and slowing breath. His cowl had fallen back from his head revealing dark paint over the top half of his face. It had smeared and flaked to the scruff of his cheeks.

Handsome, keeping one eye on the Libran, took the large dagger to the room's table. Between two-handed swings at a table leg he asked, "Whu... are the codas?" The chopping of wood covered up Sir Hebenflem's's answers.

"To love the fear of Blind Justice. To serve the High Lord of the Temple in valor and faith."

Handsome could feel the knife give with every blow. The table was not the finest — relegated to this unused room — yet it still resisted the blade. But he made progress against the fir leg with every strike as the knight continued to mumble.

"To protect the weak from witches. To eschew the deceit of the witch."

Handsome fell as the table tipped. He pushed the leg aside and pulled himself up to haphazardly chip away at the adjacent table leg. The angle was inefficient, useless, and so he kept moving to strike at the thinnest spot.

"To practice spiritual, moral, ethical, and sexual purity. To revere the truth of the Temple."

Handsome had paused to catch his breath, but the only sound was of the still-screaming strings as they were scratched and plucked from the far-off greeting room. Sir Hebenflem dabbed at his face with his palms. They came away wet and bloodied. "What has become of me?" he asked.

"Keep going," Handsome ordered. "Whu is hu... the Seventh Coda?" He went back to chopping at the leg when no reply came. The chopping covered the sound of the strings. The tightening pain in his groin, the soreness in his mouth, the fatigue in his arms, all reminded him of his near reward, of the promised heavenly body that would soon be his. No longer would he suffer the stares and mockery. He would never again know the aches and pains of the fallen world.

Arthritis and incontinence were the ills of sinners and the earthly.

The table fell on its short side, and Handsome brushed the leg aside with the little energy he had left. He leaned against a bookcase, felling a line of frames, and looked to the knight. Sir Hebenflem had stopped bleeding, but a welt had grown on the side of his head, blending under paint and the knight's short dark hair. His eyes were unfocused but open.

Handsome checked his satchel again before moving to the man. The knight shrank but did not struggle as he was helped to the table. "Where is this room?" he asked.

"Whu... is the Librans' Secret Coda?"

"Pardon?"

He did not struggle when set over the table on his back with his head toward the floor, nor as Handsome tied his feet to the legs at the high end of the table. The tithingman had run out of rope from his satchel after tying one hand to a broken leg, and that was when the knight's eyes cleared, and he pulled at his restraints. Handsome slashed at his unbound arm with his own dagger until a hand fell awkwardly to the side, useless. The blood had run to his purpling, inverted head.

"Teh... tell me the Final Coda!" yelled Handsome as loud as he could. It came out barely as a squeak.

Sir Hebenflem brushed the exposed tendons of his mutilated hand at his bindings. "To fear the love of Blind Justice. To serve..."

Handsome looked around the room at the side-bags he had dropped. He knelt to one, cracking the glass of a frame beneath a riding boot. He fought with the swollen leather of the buckle, the fingers of one hand shaking so much that he eventually held one hand in the other until his breath hissed, slowing through the rows of teeth.

"Ah was rounding up cattle to the east," he whispered, as Sir Hebenflem continued mumbling, the knight's face darkening to match his painted forehead. "T... thought ah'd th... try muh hand at ranching. T... they all wasted away anyway. This was before the blight, before the starving, the ah, ah... famine. People were all sick, everywhere. Whole towns wiped out by plague. It was the first Horseman, harbinger of the *Ashmedai Adat El*, preparing the land for the return of the Divine Song, culling the peasantry of the weak-faithed, the sinful, the ah, ah... the dead-eared. Ranches were left unmanned and bandits were running all over the country for the easy pickins. This was before the Territories were established. There was no civilization. Ah saved one farm before the goblins could find it. They just mostly had turkeys, most of them dead, but ah rounded the cows.

"There was ah Libran there, ah, ah... a monk. Always crying when ah saw him. Ah think he knew the family. They used to provide the Temple with turkey. This was the Northern Order mind you, of course. Before the war all we saw was the Order of the Creed. He was savaging whatever bird meat was left and burying the family.

"One night we campfired. It was ah nice night betwixt ah long line ah cold ones. But you remember that winter. It came and went, came and went. One day was never like the next. It played tricks like a goblin, stabbing one day and cuddling the next. Well, we campfired and had some smoked bird and told stories of warmer days."

"...in valor and faith..."

"Ah don't remember his name. Maybe he never th... told me. He talked about how he was ah knight once, one of those you call ah paladin. But his squire was one of the first to die by the plague, early on, quickly, just like that. He... h... took it hard, gave up the sword, became one of the monks. Ah don't even know if he was still in the Order. But he was smart, knew ah lot, had been high up in the Temple before heading out on his own. Ah had already abandoned the remnant of a herd ah found drinking from snail-infested ponds, but now ah searched the fields for them. Ah shot the few left standing and cooked one of the older ones for the monk. Ah served it bloody.

"He had ah horrible night. Ah visited him when the moaning reached my camp. He retched only air. There was nothing left. He was so bent he couldn't stand, so sore he could barely turn. But he still put up quite ah fight. Ah know now why Libran monks don't carry swords. Know... not because they're weak. They don't need t... them." Handsome pulled at the side of his cheek and stretched his jaws. Far in the back of his mouth an outer molar was dark and broken, an inner molar was missing. Sir Hebenflem continued to recite. His eyes were closed. Handsome continued.

"But ah bested him. Seems the great Libran monks aren't so great after all. An ah, ah...old duffer like me can take one. Ah kept him in his turkey barn. Seemed appropriate. Piled the shit all over him. Force fed him each day through ah funnel. Picked at his wounds to keep them open. Asked him the same question ah'm asking you. He just said the same things over and over. Your brains ah washed well. The same rules the knights are always blathering about. Their vaunted courtesy. He wouldn't admit to nothing. All the way to the end.

"Surprise though. It took ah week before the worms set in, or at least before ah could see them. Poking their white heads up through his cuts. I could see them under his skin, swimming around in his bruises. They started to eat his eyes from the inside, but he still denied the existence of a secret seventh Coda.

"Ah guess ah don't remember how long it took. Ah just enjoyed steak each night while he ate shit. Ah slept in a master bed while he turned himself inside out. But still he wouldn't tell me until they had eaten most of his neck. Ah couldn't even tell what ah was looking at anymore. The turkeys had all run off by then. The shit was cold. Ah came to him in that final morning at dawn. Ah could only make out a blue mass of dew flies. They was waiting for the sun and they cuddled together over his squirming shining back. The cloud rose sleepily as ah asked him one last time, 'What is the Low Coda!'" Handsome coughed into one hand, with the other hidden in his satchel. His voice had become increasingly dry, and he had to breathe deeply now before each time he spoke. "Buh... but he finally admitted it. The final secret law of the Librans. Handed down in cuh... clandestine meeting by the original Dhani, the ah, ah... first high lord, before he t... threw himself from the temple top. Did you know that? Now this hidden law is whispered to each Libran only when they achieve the initiation rite, when they become knight or monk. Isn't that right? But he died before he could tell me more. His tongue burst open in a cloud of buzzing as he was about to tell me what the Low Coda says. So ah learned ah cannot be patient. Ah cannot take my time. Like here, th... today. Ah don't know what's happening here today. Ah don't know why the Loup Garou invited us or what their plan is, but it surely isn't just some idiot auction. Ah don't have time to find out."

"To practice spiritual, moral, ethical..." Sir Hebenflem rambled beneath loud breaths.

"No!" Handsome pulled a tiny pliers from his satchel. "Every peasant knows those." He climbed to straddle the knight's chest. Here his thighs could feel that the man hid some chainmail patches under his arms. He was also radiating immense heat and sweated through both his own and Handsome's clothing. "The Low Coda! The Low Coda!

Th… tell me what the Low Coda is!"

"To love the fear of…"

"No!" Handsome had to squeeze his thighs to stay upright as though he rode a wild horse, even though the knight had given up his struggle against the bindings. He still sprawled almost completely inverted over the table, and so Handsome's loins quivered in pain at the exertion. He couldn't help but scoff at how much smaller the man was than he appeared. Feathered cloak and scattered mail had made the knight intimidating, but he was meager under all the traveling clothes. Did no man appear as they really were in the world? Was Handsome the last honest man?

Sweat and spittle flew from the tithingman as he clamped down on one of the mumbling man's front teeth. "T… the Libran's have ah hidden coda. There will be no secrets in the new world. The Promise of Ashmedai is an open eye to the world. Open your ears…" He braced his boots against the nubs of table legs left, jerking back again and again to the rhythm of the far-off screeching of fiddles. "…to the Divine Song!" He tossed the tooth aside, unsure as to whether it had broken — crushed in the pliers grip — or had been entirely pulled out. He had always found teeth, the front ones anyway, to be surprisingly easy to yank, but he was exhausted from his days of riding, nights spent in tents and unfamiliar beds, and his every muscle now groaned in soreness. His throat rasped for a drink. His jaws pinched after so many weeks of disuse.

Sir Hebenflem had stopped reciting. He choked, however, through the blood. As he spat it out it bubbled down over his face into his nostrils and eyes.

The violins had overcome the fiddles, still howling from the other side of the mansion, still slinking under the crack of the door into the room.

Handsome brushed the clamp of the pliers against the knight's mantle, back and forth, back and forth. He stared downward, trying to control his breath, listening to the gurgling. He sniffed the air of the room, but could only smell the horses he had ridden, the wild scent that had gotten into all his closes, all his pores. He had noticed, even after washing in the rapids of a stream one morning, that the stink still lingered on his body. It had sunk into parts of his throat and sinuses he just could not reach to clean. When settling down with his Megrim commission he had thought his traveling days were over. But the Loup Garou had specifically invited the elite of near territories, and he did not want to miss the chance to revel in their envy, to see their forced smiles and hear the underlying jealousy underneath reluctant congratulations. It must incense them to no end to see the man they laughed at for so many years to rise among the ranks of the glorious *Ashmedai Adat El*, to gain the favor of the Brotherhood. The only thing keeping him going over the trudging days and painful ride was the thought of the looks on their faces when he would stride into the auction — the man who had crushed the Resistance, who had killed the rebel leaders, who had started the eventual downfall of the Army of Earth. He could not wait for the landowners' and the barons' and the ore owners' grudging recognition that it was he who would be responsible for the Song's ultimate calming of the land. They now had to acknowledge, if only deep down in their souls, that their children's children would some day be attributing their prosperity, their own personal relationship with the Divine Choir, in harmonic prayer, to Handsome Gibbet — whose greatness their idiot forefathers had failed to recognize in their time.

And now he could even rub their sycophantic dog faces in the news of his most recent commission. They could sit in their rotting outhouses of homes out on the frozen prairie while he was obliged to shit with the troops. They could supply the Army of Heaven with their stringy jerky and crooked spears while he commanded the front lines to victory. Where would their names be in five years. Surely not in tale or song. Their dumbed faces would never augment quilt or stained glass.

Yet here Handsome was, many halls and a floor away from the auction room. What he did here was important, would finally answer the question that tormented him most of his life, but it was also keeping him from the restrained frowns of the smug bidders. But he had learned from the maggot-eaten monk that patience was pointless. It only prolonged the inevitable. And so he would end this quickly and go on to enjoy the greatest day of his life. First the word of his new appointment, now the secret behind his adopted father's death, and then their faces as he walked into the auction. What a day, what a day.

"You ah just being used, yuh know," he said, maneuvering the pliers to another tooth. The knight's lips still fought against him, but he slapped head and jaw until he could fit the tool next to the recent socket. "All of yuh rebel order. Your whore of the western shore, this false hymn, this ah, ah... Angeliika, has no legitimate place in the Choir. The Brotherhood is just using you for cannon fodder. Your prelates are either too stupid to see it, or they're selling you out for gold you'll never see. Your loyalty is to fools or charlatans. Why do you defend them?" He braced his boots again and twisted the pliers against the knight's rocking head. "Why do you keep their secrets?" The resistance suddenly gave way and Handsome's arms wagged to keep his balance. He opened the tool and palmed the tooth before forcing it into the coughing man's mouth. The knight spit it out before choking on the blood that trickled down into his nose.

Handsome crawled off of the knight and the inverted table. He just could not catch his breath, just didn't have the time. He looked over the sprawled man, the disheveled knight, the mess of the creature who thought he could match wits with the chosen of the *Ashmedai Adat El.* Who did this wretch think he was? He had been delivered unto Handsome, obviously by divine intervention, on the greatest day of the tithingman's life — delivered like a greasy swan with candied ugly duckling in the shell for dessert, all on silver-themed platters — yet still he resisted. His Libran mentors had taught him well.

"You've been betrayed," Handsome whispered. He could barely hear himself, rows of teeth chattering in exhaustion. "You should be out fighting for the glory of your false angel, redeeming yuh sins in the War for Heaven and Earth. Yet they sent you here, on some errand. You're ah page, ah powder monkey, ah, ah... scullery maid. You call yourself ah knight? Does any of yuh brethren call you that?" He now glowered over the upside down man. If the knight could have opened his eyes he would have seen nothing but the old man's crotch.

Handsome wrenched at another tooth, but it crumbled in the pliers. He had squeezed instead of pulled. It was a delicate balance sometimes, and so he pushed deeper for a molar. The back teeth were hardier but also deeply entrenched.

"The Brotherhood, the Prophets Lesser, the ah, ah... Lesser Antonys, know the world is wrong. They've received this message from the Greater Prophets. But in the end they're just men too, fallen and inherently flawed like the rest of us. They've squandered their perfection, like the First Man did. They take and take, forgetting who they ah, why they do it. They've left behind ah glorious past for ah self-serving future. They make treaties with blasphemers, tea with the deaf.

They do what they do not for love of the Song but only for themselves. And so it will ultimately mean nothing. The Greater Antonys, however, ah gods in the form ah men. They have not forgotten the Ultimate Reality. But they were ignored, shunned and shuffled off to the outskirts ah society. There ah so few left now. Less every day. And only ah know why. Who is killing the unkillable, and why?" His one hand slipped repeatedly as he tried to get a grip on chin and neck, while the other jerked and turned the tool. "What is the Low Coda? What is the Low...?" He staggered and coughed through his parched throat. His whisper had decreased to almost nothing — barely a squeak disappearing in the high ceiling. Hands went to his throat as he backed into a shelf, unburdening it of its photographs, but the pliers held by themselves in the knight's mouth.

He searched among his satchels for his canteen, glass and frame cracking beneath his boots, and found it. He finished off his supply of water, with most of the warm contents catching in and streaming around the patchy stubble on his neck. His layers of teeth, his tongue-less mouth, rebelled against him, dry throat receiving little comfort. On the steps back to the inverted knight he noticed that the mansion had gone quiet. No viol screeched brokenly from the other floor.

His hand finally found sticky purchase on Sir Hebenflem's chin, and he stomped the floor with opposite foot as he jerked and pulled and cranked at the pliers. Finally the tooth came, and, with it, a fresh flow to smother the knight's nostrils. He suddenly appeared to wake and gagged and snorted. His breathing came too slowly, too haphazardly, to cough through the blood. His chest turned and his bound limbs strained, trying to shake the fluid from his face, while the one free hand — peeled and spastic — grabbed at the air as though it tried to capture some for his lungs.

"Shhhhh..." Handsome hissed slowly as he moved to the door. He thought he had heard a man's scream now that the strings had quieted. A loud crashing noise from somewhere off in a distant room echoed through the halls, but now there was silence from beyond the door. Furniture overturning? A wall falling? He felt the door with his cheek as though the warmth against coolness would tell him something. Another scream? This time farther off? And then nothing. Breath bubbled through bile behind him. The knight returned to stillness but still gagged in his own thickening stream.

"Shhhhhh…" Handsome coughed himself before turning an ear to the wood. He could hear the gears of the squared spindle deep within the door as he turned the knob, but they sounded far off down in other rooms or floors. He waited for the knight's exasperations to slow to a raggedy choking.

Except for one of the pus-yellow wall lanterns off in another room, all lights went out as he opened the door. Yelling, no doubt prompted by the darkness, grew and disappeared just as quickly, this time perhaps from outside. It had been silenced by a distinctly human growling that disappeared before rising into an inhuman howl shaking Handsome's bowels. The sounds could have been a floor below, could have been out in the yards. He could not place their distance. Everything echoed incoherently through floor or grounds before silence overtook them.

The knight's dagger was near, and the tithingman took it up with barely a step to peer into the hallway. The doorways and darkness shook. It sickened him — the fluttering wan of the one bulb. His phantom tongue tickled underneath in nausea, and he would have repeatedly swallowed to hold the gorge down had he found any spit.

He recognized the eye in the shadows immediately, but he was not fast enough. He was struck before his fingers could even tighten around the dagger hilt. The eye. The cool granite eye. He only now suddenly remembered how it appeared to him every night, eventually turning any dream into a nightmare. If he had ever been asked, he would have said that he never dreamed, and he would have believed it, but it was hitting him now — a flood of memories of mundane dreams, of days pandering to the Megrim mass, preaching to their tiny minds and big mouths, feigning attention at their incessantly flapping lips after every sermon. He now remembered a new prayer his dream-self had recited in all of these dreams, a new song echoing through his head as parishioners droned on about their petty concerns. The song blocked out their insipid words but was also a prayer to save him from one more day of the boredom of hearing of their insignificant lives. This hymn was Heaven-sent, and only received in sleep. He apparently forgot it each morning when waking, but it existed, if only in visionary form, and had been answered, for here he was away from all that, outside his territory and far from wagging tongues.

But it was not the song that sparked his memory of these dreams. It was the granite eye he suddenly remembered remembering each night. It always came from the shadows, as it did that night and as it had now. It transformed each boring dream immediately into a nightmare, with the face before him moving in to place a smothering kiss against Handsome's clenched lips. Stony grips held both sides of his head frozen as the intruder's teeth forced their way past the tithingman's own two layers — the dry scrape of enamel on enamel — to clamp on and chew through his tongue. The pain, the memory, was so real. He had no idea until now that he relived the pain every single night. This was why the pain would not go way. This was why the soreness of talking and breathing and sitting lingered over these long weeks.

The dagger glanced off the wall somewhere behind him, taking frame and photo with it. Handsome was on one knee before he knew it. He did not remember the strike, but the stabbing shock in his wrist told him it had happened. His hand was broken. No, it was not, but he still had to hold it limply in the other. It had been struck in the opposite direction that his forearm had. The smooth gray eye hovered above him. He did not look up, but he could feel the gaze. He just stared down at the faint smear of crusted mud on the Liege of Foes' boots.

Handsome felt as though he were in the right position — prostrate, beneath — felt to wait for the coming blow. It would be a quick end. It would end the chronic soreness behind lip and loin, would remove him finally from this world of incessant gossip and low whining, but it was the pain itself that reminded him who stood before him, who looked down upon him. That man could not, should not, get the final say in Handsome's life. For he was only a man. Not the resurrected prophet the deaf of the land made him out to be, not the mystical warrior messiah the filthy vermin of the Army of Earth believed they followed.

Handsome, elbows on knee, slowly pushed himself back to stand. Yes, the man before him was just that — a man — not the canine-toothed nightmare he know knew stalked him in his sleep, not the larger than life avatar that led the unwashed against the holy forces of Ashmedai. This man had signs of early crow's feet stretching from the corner of his granite eye to his temple while the shadows of longer ones darkened the other. His real eye would have to squint against the sun, Handsome surmised.

As the man pulled his hood back, an unconscious frown elongated his face as it did the night Handsome faced him across the table in Megrim. He was just a man and not to be bowed before, yet still

Handsome fought the urge to return to a kneel and let fate take its course. But fate was for lesser men. He, however, by mark and vow, was sworn to Chem-Oshmelech, and in return the holy father promised a new body. Here, on the greatest day of Handsome's life, the angel had also gifted vengeance, had brought the pale earthly man — because that is all he was — before him.

Just the sight of him brought the stinging soreness to a peak. Handsome struggled to speak — even more than usual — through the pain, and his stomach dropped into his bowels, and his bowels dropped into his pants, as the Liege of Foes stepped into the room.

"Ah, ah... nuh, knew yuh, you weren't dead." The tithingman tripped backward over a satchel and its contents, breaking the latch on the box of the gift from the Western Order in his flailing to stay upright. He came down hard on the cherry container, scattering the small pistol, its velvet wrappings, and four bullets he only just now noticed were finely etched with feathered designs. *Such ah shame for such expert work to be wasted on idolatry,* he thought as he crawled a floor of broken frame and glass to collect the shot. The Liege of Foes made no move toward him, but nudged bullets away with his boot when Handsome neared. The chill in his gut warmed to anger. Embarrassment brought blood to his cheeks. This man did not even think enough of him to give him his full attention. He was acting as though he did not even recognize him.

"I was wrong," the man said. His voice was neither booming nor inspired. It was not filled with the chest bellow of his barbarous people. It did not capture all other sounds in its presence. He was only a man. Handsome glanced to see him looking at the state of the drowning knight and the room. "I predicted the Horde to splinter and turn upon itself, just not this soon. I expected you to wait until after the war. Looks like the honeymoon is over."

There was commotion on some other floor, higher or lower than the room they were in — a splintering of wood, wall or furniture.

The tiny rounds out of reach, Handsome snatched up the derringer and leaned against the tipped table at Sir Hebenflem's foot. He pointed the little gun at the Liege of Foes, stiff opposite hand keeping the four-bored barrel up. He sputtered to speak without breath, with spasming palette, through traitorous jaws. The man just stared, first at the drowning knight, eventually at Handsome, giving him plenty of time to form quiet words.

"Ugh... you've... found me on the wronguh... wrong day, you running pile of shit. Teh... this is my day." He shook the pepperbox, but never taking the aim away from the man's chest. "Ah nuh... knew you weren't dead." Handsome could feel his face growing redder as he spoke. Sweat beaded and tickled the scruff under his nose. This heathen, with dirty boots and frayed cloak tips, did not even see him as a threat anymore. Handsome could see now that he was less than a man. This less-than-a-man, who had silenced him with a blade, cowardly while he slept, had no idea that his day was done. As Handsome's greatest day had begun, this less-than's day was nearing its end. The tithingman prayed that if he could only choose one gift from the Divine Choir, one Angelic Promise fulfilled, it would be vengeance for his crippling. He would sacrifice his commission. He would even give up his right to a celestial body, to the end of the pain and defect, for vengeance.

The blood drained from his face as he realized that vengeance had to be put off just a minute longer. He boiled no longer. He realized then how cool the room had become. One shivering hand held the pistol as the other kept it steady. He was suddenly aware of how wet his clothes were.

A scream from some man or woman grew, down a hallway or through some window, before disappearing liltingly.

"Wuh... read his head." Handsome could barely hear himself. The Liege of Foes just stood and stared — at Handsome's face, at the window, at the knight. A door slammed over and over on some other floor of the mansion.

"Read... his... head." Handsome tilted at the drowning knight instead of changing his aim to point. "Tuh... tell me what yuh see inside. Ah know you can, freak."

The knight took this moment to snort and cough through blood. He took in deep gulps through his expanding neck and then appeared to shrink before resuming a rising ragged breathing. His clothes now looked especially large on his shrunken frame.

"Ah'll kill you," Handsome whispered, never taking his eyes from the Liege of Foes. "Read what's in his head, tell me what the Low Coda is, or... ah'll... kill... you." The man's expression did not change. His face was neither wide with confusion nor tense with interest. The lesser-than just was. Handsome could not tell if he could not hear him or if he just did not care. He expected the Liege of Foes to have a low opinion of life — but to not even have a care for his own?

"What do…"

Men were shouting from some far off yard or woodlands.

"Tell me what the Low Coda is." Handsome barked under a rush of breath. He could already feel his cheeks warming again, his shirt drying over the heat. "Read huh, whuh, huh… is in his head. Uh'll kill you." His hands fought over the derringer. They both shivered now and achieved a homeostasis with the aim firmly on the man's face, with the same focus as Handsome's stare. "I'll tell you what you want!" he blurted, scars tearing in his mouth. "Ah'll th… tell you where she ish! You read 'ish head, tell me what the Low Coda ish, and ah, ah… ah'll tell yuh where she ish."

At this he finally saw a reaction. He had his full attention suddenly. The man's lips pursed while one corner of his mouth twitched into a half smile. "Yes. You will, won't you?" He took a step toward the now wavering gun. He was only a man. Less than a man. He kept the cape of his cloak wrapped tightly around him, but this closely Handsome could see the fraying at his collar, the slight sunburn on his cheeks, the uneven haircut and stubble surrounding his mouth. He was only a man, but again Handsome felt the urge to kneel and let him end it all. Maybe the godless were right, and all he would have to do was give in, up, and bear the pain of a quick final blow before sleeping forever. But, then again, the Liege of Foes would not make the end quick. He had proven that. He could not let this less-than take another piece out of him.

Men were shouting from some far off hallway.

Handsome clenched the pepperbox even tighter, quelling the shivering, but he glanced quickly to his right to see where the dagger had landed. Before he could even glance to the left, he felt the intrusion. The memories came suddenly and hectically. It seemed so natural at the time that he did not question them, for they flowed from one to another, and, in the space between seconds that they appeared and swam, he thought it was his own transitions that linked them. The reminiscing moved from one scene to another like a song with a background drumbeat that altered so casually from one to another that he took no pause to question why he was reminiscing at so inappropriate a time.

The excitement over the territorial commission was short-lived upon visiting Megrim. This was from where he was to preach to the land? The grazers had minds as underdeveloped as their cattle. They knew little of the Song or the Promises or why he had them build the Holy Perches. They struggled to grasp even the most simple of the Theses, balked as he nailed them to doors, misspelled and miswrote them when they in turn started to nail them to others. He had his work cut out for... himself had given any thought to the fact that any of the elders could be anything close to his equal was now ludicrous in retrospect. The jaybirds sitting around him squawked of post-ear rot prices and bluetongue. Their priorities baffled him. What was more important than the coming war? What was saving the lives of a few herds compared to saving the souls of the surrounding farms? He had nothing in common with these men. They were as old as he was, yet acted as though they couldn't see how broken the world was, how far it had fallen from the days of their youth. Even the table they had brought for the session was an insult. A round table! For them all to face each other equally? He was the governor! He had fought to liberate them from self-serving barons while they hid on their ranches, hiding in tornado shelters and hoarding buckshot that could have been used in the uprising. And here they thought themselves worthy to sit... across established territories. She had grown a massive following on her pilgrimage. What was she hoping to accomplish? Did she truly think, as she walked deeper and deeper into unwelcoming lands that her reputation amongst the poor could protect her, that the *Ashmedai Adat El* was just supposed to look the other way? There were definitely those that saw no threat in her, that chose to stupidly look the other way. They would no doubt be questioned, hopefully by himself some day, but Handsome proposed that to look the other way was to ignore the harmony of the Song. This Lonely Forgotten Sun of God spoke of a unity of ideals among the differing worldviews of the lands. This was troubling if not counteractive. Not every person could be right. Acceptance begets knowledge, and can only come out of certainty, and knowledge is fear of the Divine Choir. This wisdom is only valued by the righteous. Despising this wisdom broke the world. Despising this instruction led to the Goblin Winter and starvation and now war. It would be a sin to let her walk free, corrupting the shoeless and pathless. Yet all they did was... talking never stopped. These fat fools are all talk and no action. They sit across from each other on yet another round table, words swirling around and around, never slowing, never landing.

They talked over him. When he could find a rare pause, if they happened to take sips of their swill at the same time, he jumped in, but it was only to get a few words in before their boisterous bleats crowded him out again. While they boasted and drank and distracted themselves, she... had now entered the Territories on her pilgrimage. There were sightings and rumors beyond his spies spreading her words. The blasphemous *Fallo Terminus* was appearing, unhidden, in peoples' hands. There were reports of people carrying it out in the open. Something had to be done and all these slugs did was talk. He spoke of Erebus in Ouroboros. The city was on the verge of the Territories, but she could be led back there with a peace offering, a promise of communion. No one listened, too occupied with their own words. They agreed with others they argued with. They disagreed with themselves. No one even noticed. They talked only to hear their own voices, and oh did it please... they began to yawn one by one. They must have thought it was contagious. Handsome had supplied the drink for this meeting and it was the first time they had spoken to him. Him! A governor! And the only way he could get their attention was by bringing the beer. One by one they fell asleep forever, right on the table. They neither thought it was odd nor inconvenient. So in the end he had to persuade no one. In the end he was left alone at the head of the round table. His first act would be to send her to...

For only a second Handsome was confused as to why he was remembering all that — such an odd time to be reminiscing about such mundane days. But in that second he realized that there was another presence in his memories, sifting and searching and poking and prodding for any information on her. But the memories had subsided as quickly as they had had rushed through his mind, and now the less-than man was buckling over, face red, fingers pressing temples, with obvious pain clenching his eyes closed. Would Handsome have just continued in his fugue of facile remembrance had the man not fallen, he wondered. Did he find what he had been looking for before doubling over? Was there no end to his violations?

The old tithingman retrieved the dagger with one hand and took a handful of hood and hair in the one that still held the derringer. The less-than man crouched against the wall but Handsome knelled against his gut. Glass and frame crunched beneath both of them.

"T... this is muh... my day, you son of ah toothless bitch," he said, not knowing if, even this close, the man could hear him. He pulled the man's head back until his eyes opened. "T... thank you for being ah part ah it." He tapped the tiny curved tip of the knight's blade against the granite eye. It refused to scratch, and the feel of the metal against rock set both rows of Handsome's teeth on edge. He turned the blade to slide it beneath the lower lid of the man's eye. "Would the deaf recog... rec... ognize you without this?"

There was a crashing sound on some other floor, doors slamming or breaking, someone barking orders, and a long howl grew deeper and deeper outside the mansion. The lights flickered to life for just a second before, again, only the pea green glimmer from the hall was left alive. The floor creaked loudly from the chamber as something lurched through it, closer and closer. The creature brushed the walls as it walked. Handsome froze as he listened to decorative tables tip, vases fall, hallway paintings crack on the floor, but mostly he just heard the hardwood creak. The beast had slow inconsistent steps. Some were heavier than others, as though it favored certain feet as it swayed through the tight passage.

Handsome could not move as the creature stopped at the edge of the doorway. He had forgotten all his pain. The ache in his mouth and groin had become a forgotten memory. His sore hip and back were cold in tightening fear. His hands were fuzzy numb, unresponsive. He was afraid any change in air current would twitch the black nose toward him, any arthritic crack of joint would turn the monster's ears into the room.

The hairy snout crinkled at the room with phlegmy snorts, and a mouth of mismatched teeth panted wide, filling the room with its unclean breath. Handsome could now suddenly move, and he shrank from the physical odor. It pushed him back from the man he had forgotten about, and he silently scuttled sideways back to the table. The bound knight gagged loudly, and the beast entered, the doorframe bending before splintering against its furred trunk. It rose on its short hind legs as soon as it could fit its dusky bulk in the room, ever sniffing the air of the space with a nose that disappeared in the shadows. Its eyes spun in blindness, yellow by the little light leaking in past the wolf's furry girth. Its snout, pasty tongue rolling over up and down and through and over canines, led it to the knight who was again choking through the blood that had run into and now congealed over his nostrils.

The monster's eyes never slowed to focus on any one thing, yet Handsome swayed without sound to avoid them. One of the scattered rounds was bumped, and it came spinning across the uneven floorboards toward him. He was afraid to move too swiftly, and so the round's rhythmic roll came to rest at his knee.

The monster's snout grew near. He could see the nose now through the darkness as sudden moonlight broke the haze of cloud and window to glitter on its wetness and that of the wolf's askew teeth. He was instantly covered in oily humidity and clenched both his rows of teeth against the rotten stink.

The creature snorted again before striking backward, crushing Sir Hebenflem's outstretched arm in its maw. The knight's face contorted to scream but no sound came except for the snapping of bone and crunching of hidden mail. The bound man fell back as, with hectic jerks of neck and head, the wolf tore the arm from its socket.

Handsome scrambled under drips of gore to snatch up the bullet and load the derringer. He had lost the dagger sometime in his scramble.

Tightly woven, now broken, rings of mail fell from the creature's lips as he chewed, tongue searching like a blind worm for a piece of fabric and flesh that hung from a particularly crooked back tooth.

Handsome suddenly remembered the man crumpled at his side, the less-than man that still sat pressing against the wall, hand clenched against the loud vein in his temple, apparently unaware of anything else but the obvious pain in his head. And the tithingman raised the whore's shot, his best day's gift, to the man's face. His aim no longer quivered, his hand no longer shivered. To his side the giant wolf grasped the knight's leg at the knee in his jaws and tore away a thigh. Handsome turned the pistol to the creature. It chewed the meat and bit the air and swallowed both. Handsome looked away from the knight. Sir Hebenflem's pieces were still bound, but now not by bone or sinew. Amazingly, he appeared still alive. Handsome could feel his gaze as he turned the pepperbox's pieces, hoping he lined up the loaded barrel. He would only get one chance.

But the Garm moved before the tithingman could even raise the gun, and the swat of one massive paw sent him flying. Shapes and colors spun before his eyes, his limbs flailed to strike corners and broad objects, and his ears were assailed by the sound of shattering glass.

When his vision slowed it refused to right itself. His arms and legs stilled but could find purchase on nothing but air. He now only heard a new tinkling of glass as it fell beneath him like a drying waterfall.

He tried to watch the wan eyes of the gray wolf stare at the ceiling as he bent over the Liege of Foes. Nose crinkling and moving over the man, the creature still broke Sir Hebenflem's bones between his teeth. With each snap of his jaw, marrow sprayed the less-than man's face.

Handsome began to slide. He felt no pain, but could sense the pulling against the skin of his back as it caught on the glass. He still hung into the room, but barely, upside down as he had strung the knight, and he then slid out of the window and into the night, flayed flesh giving way under his weight. There was the breaking of more glass over his body, and darkness subsumed him, but he never left consciousness.

XXIX

"It is only one who is thoroughly acquainted with profit that can thoroughly understand the evils of war and how they can thoroughly profit from thoroughly profitable war"

—Hyper Khan's "The War of Art"

The pain had diminished except for the underlying, repetitive throbbing Wulf had come to expect after peeking in someone else's mind. Again he had chanced telepathy, and again he could only get a nanosecond glimpse before the *Other* had forced itself in. Wulf's mind had gone spinning in the pounding feedback. He could sense the *Other*, closer now, with a new appreciation. As the presence drew nearer he now wondered if it was as predatory as he had been assuming. The *Other* had felt the painful loop as well when their minds had connected, hence the cumulative psionic spiral. But it did not matter. It was becoming even more difficult to block the presence out. He now was not even sure that, if he opened himself up again, he could close the doors again once opened. He had gotten what he needed from the tithing-man's twisted mind, however, and, for now, that was all that mattered.

But was there an end to the uncertainty, he wondered. Even under the pressures of coordinating a resistance, he had felt at least settled. Megrim was not exactly safe for him, but there was a measure of stability in the town. Now, out here, once again after the years, he found himself in the mutability of the open road. He had once preferred the peregrinations of foot and soul to any other way of life, but the countryside had suddenly become strange, unfamiliar to him. He was feeling the disassociation of age. He yearned for a time when all he had to run from were ghosts and goblins.

Why did the Garm spare him? Had it taken its fill from the Libran? Wulf had been completely incapacitated by the psionic feedback, had not even realized what was occurring around him in the room until the pain had subsided enough to survey a room of carnage, of blood and glass. The giant werewolf had filled the room with its girth and foul breath, leaning over him, wet nose probing his cloak, fat tongue licking aside bits of the Libran to slather Wulf's face.

And then it had just left, pushing furred bulk through doorframe and hallway. Wulf had followed through the destruction of the mansion to find a surprising lack of corpses. Sure there was plenty of blood-shed, of open corpses and scattered limbs, of pools congealing both on hardwood floor and under moon-soaked clouds, but Wulf had seen the running of the Garm before and expected even more slaughter.

He wandered the grounds under the swampy green night. A mare stretched and sprawled with frozen face near a well, large gaping belly still twinkling wetly. But many other horses ran free around the tree-line. Scraps of crimson-stained clothing stuck to earth and rosebush. But mostly Wulf just saw the occasional person running or hiding unpursued. He took the long walk to the stables. The stalls were empty, open, even those he and his fellow travelers had used, but he leaped and pulled himself up through the pitching door to root around behind a hayrick that had long ago fallen into one mass. Everything melted into shades of green as the clouds moved above through a wind not felt on the plantation, including the saddlebags he pulled from the collapsed bales. He left the bags, now out in the open, after pulling *GloryRend* from one. Dropping down outside the stable, he headed back to the main mansion, now with the uncomfortable weight of the hammer beneath his cloak.

He entered through a back door and found himself in one of the many kitchens of the mansion. The lights had buzzed to operation, and now actually lit to an annoying brilliance. The doorways leading out of the kitchen were lamped again but still dim. Fires still burned in the stoves. Ware of the finest silver, knives, and spoons, and two-pronged forks gathered in rows. Trays of hors d'oeuvres were scattered. Colorful ingredients sat neatly sectioned in bowls. A large cast iron kettle still steamed.

Wulf closed his eyes and just breathed in through his nose. The spices and broths flashed back memories that disappeared as quickly as they returned. The earthy scents reminded him of something, scenes he couldn't pin down, remembrances that were too quick to capture. His initial flight from the Land of Nod as a youth? His mouth watered.

He stepped to the massive kettle, hoping to wash the blood that had dried from his granite eye, but found only that the water had boiled away. The pot radiated more heat than even the stove.

The floors above creaked under what sounded to be great weight, and there was a scratching outside an open window that failed to cool the kitchen — a scratching Wulf first thought rhythmic but revealed minor variations as it went on. It preceded the sound of digging and growling before growing stronger and more rapid. A scream from some far room was followed by the beginnings of an aborted howl, and Wulf could not tell if either was from man or beast or the unholy combination of both.

He gathered silver spoons, silver snail tongs, silver skewers, fondue forks and fruit knives. Throwing them all into the burning kettle, he tossed a split log from near the back door into the stove for good measure. Into the kettle went a silver nutcracker, a silver honey dripper, and more spoons. And he waited in the brilliance of the kitchen lights. And he listened.

The scratching continued, quieter but faster from outside another wall, from under another window. Nail or claw or tooth, the scraping continued. Someone talked in a room not far from the kitchen, rambling on and on. Wulf could not understand the monotone, or even pick out individual words, but it was a serious voice, apparently unafraid, apparently unimpassioned. There was no response he could hear — just one voice filling a room. A stallion ran past the open window, for just a second blocking any moonlight, panicked and screaming. Wulf waited and watched for whatever pursued, but nothing passed.

Wulf's stomach growled in imitation of the sounds coming from some man or monster searching through a shed behind the mansion, which in turn imitated the sounds coming from a nearby room where — he guessed — desks were being overturned and chests torn apart. Doors were being thrown from hinges. Cellars were being ransacked. The auction prizes were being searched frantically.

The kettle's contents bubbled and spit.

Something lumbered just beyond the brilliance of the kitchen, down the long hallway opposite the backdoor of the room. Its fur rippled in conflicting directions as it neared, sometimes in long waves over flexing muscle, sometimes against itself as the beast pressed through the tight doorway. It was as salted as the pepper spilled on a nearby butcher board, black but frosted, and with a snow-white bib. It was an old Garm, here and there missing a claw on the hind paws it now used to stand up to his full height above Wulf. The teeth that spread near its face were unusually straight for a Garm but were a mix of black and yellow fangs that closed together as the beast snorted and sniffed from boot to hood with a nose so scarred it could not possibly smell a thing. For the second time Wulf was assailed by breath of copper and open meat, and, this close, he could see the fresh juices of people thickening in the monster's fur at its lips and the giant front paws that clenched and loosened at Wulf's sides.

He first thought the beast had grown before him, enveloping him in shadow, absorbing even the brightness of the kitchen, until Wulf realized that he had been kneeling without realizing it. He was on his knees as the Garm panted over him. Spittle sounded deeply like rain against his hood, and hot breath pressed against it in a heavy pattern, but the beast eventually turned. He watched the gray-frosted claws clench and scar the wood of the floor as they walked away before he stood back up. He was sweating near the stoves, under the lights and cloak, yet still steadied shivering hands against his thighs.

"You," Wulf said, barely above the crackling and boiling around him. The Garm's humped back turned. A scrap of pink flesh that had been stuck in its fur near the snout flew and sizzled against cast iron. "Why do you spare me?"

If it was possible for the creature's toothy grin to grow, to appear to smile, it did so now. And it was a second or two before Wulf realized its uneven breathing was actually a form of chuckling. Its gray eyes were not those of a monster, but of an old man of his homeland. Had he ever met this man? In his short time in the North, had they ever crossed each other in the streets of Bifrost, exchanged greetings on any path through the woods of N'Midgaard?

Even the pale fur around the eyes and twitching ears was littered with flecks of someone else's juices.

GloryRend swung two-handedly from beneath Wulf's cloak, propelled by arm and mind, to strike the near kettle. It was like the blast of a church bell in the kitchen, calling down the thunder of Tor to split air and earth in his cloven chariot. Both man and wolf, Wulf and monster went to cover their ears, but it was the Garm that burned, fur and flesh smoking beneath molten silver that ran from snout to waist. One front leg was drenched from shoulder to paw in the dripping metal.

Wulf leapt around the thrashing. Tables smashed from the throes of the screaming beast, cabinets fell, racks shattered, and stoves anchored to a floor for generations were uprooted. He rolled beneath the debris, struck at that which came too close with *GloryRend*, all the while turning his ears from the pitched rolling whimper the Garm's howl had become. It whistled from behind locked fangs. It gurgled from convulsing throat. It wheezed from a pounding chest.

Droplets of silver fell near Wulf's face, and he pulled his hood lower, noticing the black and white hairs caught in the gray molten. What was it like to run with the pack, he wondered, to follow scents across the fields, racing at the side of brothers, to fear nothing but the dissolution of family? One would never sleep alone. One would never feel the winter under a full moon. How must have they felt the rest of the month? The world must move so slowly for them under the crescent. They must go mad under the waning, for how could one live with such a constant repetition of nerve straining? It was no wonder they were known to eventually lose any resemblance to humanity, even during the dark nights of the month. Garm had notoriously short life spans, for they eventually would be found, naked and rabid and tearing at livestock with blunt teeth under a barely waxed moon. Lynching of the feral men had become fairly common in the North over the years.

The smoldering creature thrashed its last in the kitchen, smashing its bulk out into the hall, leaving behind a stench of burning fur that mixed with the smoke of cooling ash now scattered the length of the room. Ghost embers of the overturned stoves refused to light the floor. Logs, intermittently glowing and black, died quickly without catching the remnants of the cooking counters.

Wulf mused that the remainder of the Garm would now have an even stronger bond. The last of their kind, whatever remained from the Horde's culling, would be desperate but linked adamantly from the persecution.

The ebon kettle had stopped rolling, charring the floor where it rested. It bled pure gray molasses, a liquid too beautiful for the world, just screaming to be held, to be run through the fingers. But Wulf instead dipped *GloryRend* in its smooth shallow depths as it cooled in the breeze of the back door.

~

Antony of the Dam could sleep now that the music had ended. Over his long life he had slept through screams and gunfire and the growls of myriad mythological monsters, and this night would have been no different, but the viol and fiddle had kept him awake. He could not remember the last time he had been this tired, and he did not care to. Any exhaustion, any pain, any new scar reminded him that this would be his last body. There was no going back to the Nursery any longer. He had no choice but to make every minute count. And he had wasted the last week bound and prodded along like a work mule. Luckily, horses disliked the traitor mage Slayd as much as he did, so, as the others rode, their pace had been kept to a minimum, and the recent warming ensured that Antony's many pushes and falls were on drier ground.

The strings had continued unabated when the howling began, and they ignored the questioning few auction patrons that wondered out into the lobby. The calling and bidding also continued, even during the flickering of lights, even over the first few screams as the giant wolves entered through open doors and splintering windows. But the strings had finally ended when the musicians lost courage or guts, and so Antony of the Dam immediately — despite the sound of tooth and claw on bone and wall — floated into a sleep deeper than he had known for days, not expecting to ever wake again.

Hot air stung his closed eyes and dried specks of someone else's blood over his own scabs. It would not have been enough, however. He had the returning strings to thank for that. It seemed like it took all his strength to open his eyes, and it seemed like forever before he could, but past the red bulk that stood over him he could see the lone fiddler still playing. The man moved in and out of his sight like a wasp, previously tight costume now in damp tatters. His dance was now not much more than a limp, one leg as shredded as his coat. But his playing stayed surprisingly even, only missing the eventual high note at the same time as his face would contort in a measure of pain from a wrong step or stretch. Through it all he was smiling in contrast to eyes that definitely were not.

The massive canine smile inches from Antony's face, however, was definitely echoed in its eyes — great gray eyes that grew at his attention. They were clear as the melting spring stream over pale blue pebbles, without any redness to match the auburn shag of the beast. Tiny pupils, shrinking even more as the chandeliers wavered before growing back to their original brightness, stared past Antony as a black nose flickered over him. The palest of tongues licked the nose repeatedly as the giant snout retreated. Antony adjusted his bound limbs, sore beneath their chains, spreading back against velvet and wall before closing his eyes again. He had not taken in fully the red creature before him, but could feel its oily humidity as a very physical presence, threatening to smother him.

"Should have known there were some left," Antony said, clearing his throat before spitting outward. He was not sure the distance, may have spit on himself for all he knew. "For every bitch killed there'll be another pack of mewling brats squirted out in some sewer." The fiddler's shuffling feet were tiring, his dance slowing as his bow quickened. Antony felt as though the strings were tied deep in the crevices of his brain, with each drag, each pluck and pull quivering beneath his skull. His head shook involuntarily with each new note.

"Can you understand me, dog?" he yelled, covering as much of his face and ears with weary arm and shoulder, slouching even lower. Scabbed lip cracked open again, bled anew. "That's all you are, you know. You think you're wolves, some noble beast of the woods. Predator. Top of the food chain. But you're just neutered nature. Born of rakes and pirates. Enslaved to witch doctors and devils. Maybe your grandfathers were once great. Running the plains. Taking down lions and cave bears. But your mothers whimpered at the edge of campsites. Tails between legs at the edge of fire-pits. Begging for scraps. Licking boots. And so you are dogs. Not quite men and certainly not wolves. Runts of both litters. The worst of both."

Antony uncovered his eyes when the teeth did not come. "Do… you… understand… me?" he spat again. The Garm before him had sat back on his haunches, his tail mimicking the shuffling sound of the fiddler's steps. His wild eyes just stared at Antony, as his nose continued to give each direction its due. Another of the creatures had entered from a far room, its white and blue fur in contrast to the stark redness of the other.

And then the red beast surprised him.

"Youuuuu… oooouu… oooo… wish toooo die?" it asked. Antony had been adjacent to the Purge, had been off recruiting and fortifying edge towns when the Prophets Lesser had initiated the Garm hunt, but he had his own experience with the lycanthropes, so he had never known them to be able to speak in their bestial forms. Its voice was made of tooth and tongue. The sound rose from a constant rumble, fought through an overpowering growl.

From behind its shaggy bulk the other Garm peaked in adjacent rooms, sniffed at fire and staircase, emptied bookcase and overturned desks. The fiddler's dance neared it, following a series of long whines with staccatos struck and tapped on string and floor. The Garm's crooked smile widened from black lips, and its head bobbed with the shuffling beat for a few chords before the creature's massive jaws slowly and gently moved over the dancer, enveloping neck and shoulder. The scene froze for one second. The music stopped. Antony could not tell what was happening until the jaws clenched and arteries burst.

The crimson Garm jumped from Antony's side to the other monster, snapping his greater maw, swiping his larger paws. Beaten, the gray wolf whimpered and took up a corner of collapsed furniture, muzzle and tail down but with eyes skittering sideways at its better.

The hulking wolf strode slow steps back toward him, and it was there, as fiery fur rippled and shrank, that Antony could see the mismatched armor and ties that had been hidden in shadow and bulk. One knee was covered in a dark poleyn, while the opposite shin hid behind a scratched schynbald covering leather spreading out over one breaking hind foot. A forearm was protected by a thickly scalloped vambrace, with its opposite shoulder holding a spaulder held in place by bindings that appeared while fur vanished like withering weed into pale flesh. The ties continued around a barrel chest of ginger hair to hold what Antony could see was a massive axe tied to the Garm's back. Or man. Because that was what he was becoming, under the creaking and crisp snapping of breaking and resetting bone. Under impossible contortions, under a howl that became a scream that sent Antony scrambling for abandoned cushions to hide his head, the Garm folded and broke before flesh reknit into a large man panting beneath a sprawling wolfen headdress. When he stood, slick with sweat, Antony saw the wild eyes staring back at him again. The nose was now dun, in the bulbous shape of a northern man, but it still sniffed in his direction.

"Just dogs," Antony mumbled. The chandelier lit the man whose shadow he crouched in, and his wild hair flamed into a mane that grew down into a red beard. "Just mutts abandoned by both parents. Not knowing their place."

He was naked except for the bindings and scraps of armor he adjusted. His member turtled but scrotum hung asymmetrically from thick auburn thatch. Even in human form, the Garm growled, "I've seceded from sheer delusions, stale one, seeded no illusions. I know exactly what I am. But you? You but bewilder me. In the wild, wild wildernesses of the world I have not come across a taste such as yours."

"Because you hid when the Brotherhood wiped your kin out."

"Such is the burden of my role, to roll with mankind's unkind eccentricities against one another, again and again until others play their part, apart, in sheer destiny." He crouched toward Antony. Now even the shriveled sockets of the wolf-head headdress stared at Antony as the Garm smelled him. "Blood so clean as to be obscene. Your sweat so pure. You question my pedigree but must agree, motherless brother, you are surely of surly, man-made gene."

"We are more than man…"

"Woof! Less than! Handmaiden! Unearthly virgin birth, still urging me to end his life. But no." He stood back up to his full height, the fiery halo resumed around his head. "Lines are now converging, so I'm inclined to ignore the purging, for the end will not be ultimately appended without spectators, and what better than your species to spend the end times in rumination, meditation in ruination on a nation in ruin? What is art without audience awed in penitence?"

Another giant wolf came crashing into the lobby, bringing pieces of hallway and furniture with it. Any limbs not shining silver thrashed. The smell of cooling metal and burning fur entered the room along with the beast as it clawed at both the floor and itself. To Antony the screaming whimpering was akin to the violins he had already forgotten.

The red-maned man turned his face to the ceiling and drank in the great mansion. "Ooooooo… too many tastes… sense scents of sheer fear crowding our air. Somewhere beneath it all be where some prize lies." He stepped away from Antony, licking the tips of one hand reddened by his chastisement of the corner Garm. "And who lies best? The bestial, yes? No. Who mans the world, would if he could?" His nose twitched at the corridor the smoldering Garm had run from. "Yes? No. The nose knows. Oh, oooooo… heir to lies and northern skies. Faolson, I know your odor and order you to step from the shadow of my ardor."

The darkness of the hallway became Wulf's cloak, and he brought it with him into the greeting chamber, with only a glint of the silver streaking *GloryRend*. He looked to the gore-strewn stairways and footprints of all sizes heading into and leaving the far auction room. It was difficult to determine what was velvet and what was wet with blood. Even his own hands were wet from something he had touched somewhere in the rooms since the kitchen.

Antony tried pulling himself onto an overturned chaise, but the lounge chair just tipped more, and they both ended strewn and ignored.

"Ahoooooooo! Finally, before finality we meet," the red man said, "meat for the licking Beast, like all men, but meant for so much more, born under the star of *Surt*, certain to star in twilight's final act. Son of Faol, Lifsbane, charlatanistic exorcist, Howl Caller, Hob of the Grand Mob, Liege of Foes, life's bane, Sinister Mister, Left Hand of Hel…"

"I'm not the Liege of Foes."

"…meet the Right!" The hairy man reached and grabbed one red hand to his own. "For we are blood brothers, both bred of different soups of same spice."

"Mad Hati?"

The Garm's eyes darkened as his teeth flashed. "No man calls that nomen to my face, Faolson." The silvered war-hammer beneath the cloak now caught his attention as his smile widened even more. "Lucky this be not my face." He continued to hold Wulf's hand as he yet again sniffed at the air above them.

The other Garm, one averting gazes, one still rolling and clawing, both froze and looked to a far open window before jumping to all their feet. Hunched, they crept beside each other, snouts crinkling at floor and ceiling.

Hati's pupils grew before he spoke. The ginger swatch of hair cascading down his chest rippled as he turned away. "Hear, hear, it *is* here. 'Tis to unleash Beast, unfetter our better, our progenitor, for the end of all we all run. I taste impossible means to cut impossible binds, which means in sheer haste we are bound to run." He turned again but walked backward, following the other Garm. Hati grew no mustaches above his beard but now had the appearance of them after wiping the sweat from his face. Blood had smeared over his upper lip. "Now all we need, heed me, is the treasure trail to the Slit, map to the Gap, a measure of the Beast's Pit." He ran back to slap Wulf on the shoulder, almost sending him sprawling, before running to one of the room's many new fallen doorways. "I'll race you to Hel, little one! Ahoooooo!"

Antony struggled amongst bookshelves and bodies, trying to loosen his bindings with splintered chair legs, but Wulf still felt suddenly alone in the grand receiving room of the Loup Garou.

~

Handsome could run no longer, at least not while blowing into the burgeoning glow of the brush he spilled with every tripping step.

Away from the plantation grounds, from the sputtering generators, and the flickering light of windows, it had become dark in the trees. A smothered moon periodically turned his steps a sickly green, and he was able to move from one thatch of brambles to another, but his energy waned, even in his fear, and the fire he tried to build in his hands equally faltered.

He made the only breeze against him as he moved, as he pulled and kicked against thistles, as his trousers tore and hung in shreds like the skin of his entire body. He could still feel glass grind against bone — shards he either missed or that were in too deep for him to pull out. So much glass. There was not an inch of his skin that had not been torn, that was not either sticky or crusted, that did not flap as he knelt to place the handfuls of weed and kindling before him.

He blew into the dry mismatch, but his body betrayed him again, shredded lips refusing to focus his wind, inner row of teeth shivering and blocking his breath. The ember glowed but quickly disappeared, so he scraped his flint again, over and over, pure sparks lighting his lap and shredded hands. Despite his flayed body, he noticed, it was really his wrist that still hurt the most. The wrist the Liege of Foes had struck — may he rot in Garm gut. May he return to the shit he came from, squatted out in some hut or vole-pocked plain.

Red and green fires flittered like flies in his tinder, but he kept striking steel until his fingers vibrated numbly. The shard of flint fell out into the brambles, into impermeable darkness it could not be retrieved from, but it did not matter. He would only get one last try, and there was no assurance his prayers would be answered anyway.

A howl broke the stillness of the woodlands, and the tithingman's hanging skin crinkled in a sudden chill that felt like centipedes climbing his spine. The trail of blood he left with each step had not mattered. The smell of the smoking bark and twine he tried desperately to blow into did not matter. It was another scent the monsters followed. He added sharp moss to his kindling, waved his aching hands at the sparks, and gave the glow a few seconds to grow on its own. His hanging satchel caught on glass as he felt inside it, assuring himself that what he had found before his hectic run from the mansion was still there. In trying to find his way, limping and shredded, from the labyrinthine rooms of the mansion, he had stumbled upon a collection of auction items. Most were worthless — trinkets and immodesties and gaudy baubles — many were too large to carry, but one above all held a value he was not yet sure how to determine.

The Garm crashed through the woods salivating at its blasphemous stink. He could hear them tearing through the underbrush, lusting after the sinful stench.

And so he blew at the tinder, twitching hands trying desperately to direct the wayward breath. A small flame converged from the pinpricks of light, but it shrank between his hectic exhalations. He set the bouquet of tinder in his lap, muted under the green night, and he knew it probably burned him, at least some shred of clothing or skin, but he did not care. This body, or what was left of it, cursed from birth by the sins of his absent father, mutated by his mother's unholy union, pariahed in its youth, and ignored in its old age, was only temporary, made from earth. His heavenly body was all that mattered — The Promise of Chem-oshmelech. Handsome's reward would soon be upon him. He was certain. There would be no pain, no stares, no awkward pleasantries by patronizing imbeciles.

But the flame would not grow. He needed a large enough burn to shout into, for the Divine Choir to hear his call. He found himself praying without realizing it, singing through obstinate teeth and unresponsive lips. What came out of his mouths must have sounded like near silent gibberish, but what he heard in his head was marvelous.

Raise me tonight
By a mighty wind, by invocation of the Promise
By singing the Song of songs
Through confession of fallen body
Of the First Man who forsook blessing.
I will rise tonight
Through the Wing of faith of Promise fulfilled
Through the glory of divine sacrifice
Through the love of Heavenly Swain
For ewe and you and murky me.
I have risen tonight
For the strength of the love of Cherubim
For I am drafted
For the service of archangels
For my resurrection is soon upon me
In body

In predictions of prophets
In preaching of Brothers
In faith of confessors
In innocence of sisters
By the deeds of righteous men.

He jumped as the tinder singed his lap. He could feel it now. He knelt before it on flayed knees, ground grinding into open flesh.

I rose today
By the strength of Heaven:
Mud of Earth,
Splendor of fire,
Speed of the lightning,
Uplift of the wind,
Swiftness of the Wing,
Light of sun,
Not of moon,
Against mankind's wishes
I have arisen
Against every deaf man that may oppose my body
Against incantations of false prophets
Against black laws of the toneless
Against false laws of heretics
Against green-eyed idolatry
Against spells of witches and smiths and wizards
Up above knowledge that corrupts man's faith.

He had both the inner and outer lids of his eyes tightly closed, struggling to remember the verses, but could feel the sting of sweat dry as instantly as it appeared on his open face. He prayed and sang and cried and dreamed into the burning bush.

Divine Choir, lift me today
Above poison, above yearning,
Above drowning, against burning,
So that The Promise may be fulfilled.
Father with me, Father before me, Father behind me,
Father in me, Father beneath me, Father above me,
Father on my right, Father on my left,
Father when I lie down, Father when I sit down, Father when I arise,
Father in the heart of every man who spurns of me,

Father in the mouth of everyone who speaks of me,
Father in every eye that sees me,
Father in every ear that hears me.
I arise today
Through a mighty wind, the reward of Chem-oshmelech
Through belief in the Divine Choir
Through the Bronze Promise of Father
Of He who marked me with kiss at birth…

Handsome opened his outer lids at this. Smoke assailed his thin inners. The fire grew to fight against the green of the moon, building an egg of heat pulsing and pushing the night from the tithingman. He was suddenly worried about his birthmark. Was the Mark of Chem-oshmelech still intact? No part of his body was left unmarred after the evening's proceedings. Could he hope his hip and shoulder were any different? He picked at scabrous fibers, unable to differentiate flesh from shirt. For The Promise of Father to be fulfilled he had to be recognizable as one of the chosen.

A branch snapped or a tree fell or the woodlands growled. Handsome's fire was not large enough to move the shadows of the brush, so the darkness moved itself just inside the closest trees. He could hear the wolves breathing their congested chuckling breaths. They were too big or too clumsy to run through the forest without rending it as they did their victims.

Before he could feel the talons sink into his shoulders the air swirled around and beneath him. His little fire was scattered and extinguished and the woods turned black and green again. It felt as though the earth did not want him to go. It pulled him down. He lost both his boots as though he were pulled from sludge. But it was just the pressure from the wings that beat above him, pushing him down as the claws pulled him up. Great blobs of shadow and fur ran and jumped beneath him as the Garm sniffed and searched and howled at their loss.

Their desperate whimpers brought a smile to Handsome's fluttering lips.

Again the wings exploded, and again he felt the push and pull, limbs flapping uncontrolled in the opened air, but the talons held him firmly, digging in for even more purchase. A shoulder popped. His clavicle appeared. The pain was glorious. His entire body was limp and flailing, except for the one area in which it should not have ever possibly been again.

Higher and higher he flew. Dew and sweat froze until his limbs could no longer bend in the tumult. One pair of outer lids broke the frost of his lashes. Was that a sunrise over the sudden strong curve of Earth? The satchel hanging at his side banged against a thigh, reminding him of his prize. It was the latest in a line that would eventually lead to the ultimate gift. The Promise of Father. His Heavenly Body. He now had no doubt. It was the end of the best day of his life, but he could feel that there would be many more. His prayers answered, Handsome rose toward the new dawn.

XXX

...the Warrior thinks it his own hand
but the Warrior moves to their tune
—scrawled on the walls of the King of All's lower halls

"They've found you, my love."

Her voice was beyond psionic, and soon he feared it would become indistinguishable from his own thoughts. He had made numerous attempts to purge the slug from his skull, all various techniques learned in the Academy, but her pubescent tendrils had wormed their way too deeply into grey matter. It would be dangerous and very likely incapacitating to force her out now. He was surprised to find such a parapsyte so far from the center of the Empire, but their reach was extensive, and so it should not have been unusual to find some exotic species thriving away from home. It was for just such reasons that certain planets had been quarantined ages ago. Although, from what he had seen of this land, this planet had never taken advantage of any culture the clans would have left behind — inadvertently or otherwise.

"Careful, careful... he shouldn't be able to detect the cloak at this distance, but we don't know what advances the Empire may have made in your absence. Careful..."

"Dammit, worm, stop your infernal nagging!"

And she did. But he knew it would only be temporary. Her silky voice was almost constant in his head these days, and, even though it was entirely mental, she would often slither to the side of his brain to punctuate her words, tickling his inner ear as though she whispered closely.

Even after months of waiting, Easarean still had difficulty maneuvering the cousins' ship delicately. He was used to the vertitanks and armored carriers of his clan, and the more pedestrian systems of the ships needed a lighter touch. But as of yet it still appeared his quarry was unaware of him.

~

He had followed who the basilisk had informed him would be another of his kind — an Aertlantean, but of another clan, a sneakier, weaker clan. He too had brought what Easarean saw as a yacht to the planet. It was even smaller than his own and ill equipped to survive in even the most minor of firefights.

Easarean's immediate plan was to take the cousin by force, strangling out the codes he needed to escape the planet, but his "companion" had other plans.

"Watch him," she had cautioned, *"wait for him to leave his ship, and we can search it, or confront him away from his communications. We must wait and watch, wait and watch…"*

So once again he found himself growing impatient as the days continued without action. The cousin was obviously doing some sort of reconnaissance or intelligence gathering, flittering from town to town, adapting his appearance, mannerisms and language to this planet's peasants. He took on their weak demeanor and stunted speak, making his motives even more alien to Easarean. But it meant nothing. Only the codes meant anything. And so, eventually, ignoring the incessant nagging of the brain slug, he went to take the cousin.

But it was at that instant that the cousin disappeared. Far from any populated area, deep over sun-stoked plains, the blip disappeared from Easarean's scanners. His cousin's simple starcraft could, at times, cloak itself from Easarean's ship, but after a day of searching a hilly hollow alone in the prairie, he moved on, and eventually flew back to the sea where he waited on storm-wracked shores for the blip to reappear on his systems.

Winter hit the continent hard while Easarean enjoyed the frigid waters shocking his body back into shape. Weeks passed as he daily fought the waves and weather, reveling in a climate he only trained for but never experienced. His swims seemed to stun the parapsyte, and so were the only times he had his head to himself. But still, the sensors found no sign of the cousin.

Deep in winter he scanned the countryside up close, flying low and slow over frosted forest and weird desert, impenetrable air of mountain and fallen cloud. Here he was attacked by Automaton the Perverted. What would be a primitive synthetic intelligence to the Empire, on this planet was the single largest unified force in the land. He had heard the name in various languages across unincorporated areas, and so knew to stay clear of more populated regions, but in his slow scan he had caught the hive mind's attention. Even in his superior craft he had to eventually flee the legion, the Pervert's forces leading the way for a bulbous mothership emerging from white clouds it seared to blackness. Easarean's ship snuck away in the massive shadow obscuring the land below.

For even more winter months Easarean sulked in his ship beneath collecting snow, afraid to now use anything but the most basic support systems in the fear that the Pervert could track him. But, as risky as it was, he kept the ship's sensors on, albeit focused in a tight beam directed on the dark hollow out in the middle of the plains that he had picked up the blip that was the cousin Aertlantean.

Under the drifts, not knowing what the future held, the worm drove him virtually mad. She too was afraid of being discovered, but, hidden and silent to the world, she also began to fear insignificance. Easarean knew she could read any of his surface thoughts as well as increasingly being able to dig deeper, both physically and mentally into his mind. He could not feel deeply into her motivations yet, but knew that one such as her had an ultimate goal — that of reproduction and spreading seed and influence over a civilization. Hiding under the winter would drive her mad as well. They fought daily, as Easarean scrawled battle stratagems on the walls of the ship's cabin, as he hunted great antlered game in surrounding forests, and as he tried to sleep each night. He knew forcing her from his skull could leave him impaired. She would definitely take part of him with her, and she reminded him of such by sliding itchingly under bone and over brain. But there came a point, when the patter of melting snow sang deeply over the ship, that he was willing to take the chance. Luckily for both of them, it was at this point the blip reappeared on the ship's dimmed holoplay.

~

"Not too close, not too close."

"Errrh..."

"Fire a highly localized ion beam at the away stern."

"Quiet!" Easarean yelled in the close quarters of the ship's cabin. The displays moved all around him, showing schematics and alternate real-time views of the cousin's ship, but he watched the scene through the actual vidscreen, through the trees of a hollow alive with swarms of warring goblins. He had pushed the ship as fast as it could atmospherically travel as soon as the cousin appeared on the sensors. The cousin's starcraft had apparently been hiding out in the drifts and forest of the hollow all winter.

He knew the parapsyte knew practically everything he knew but it was still odd to hear her describe battle plans as well as he could in her lilting voice — disturbing and as uncomfortable as when she moved.

"Use the standard I-beam frequency G but with a tweak of preset 'second shield.' I developed it while you slept. See! See the weak point in his field?"

"Of course I see it, you damnable slug!"

"Why do you want to hurt me?"

He could not waste this opportunity. Why was the cousin here, on this planet? Why had he lain low the entire winter? Would he leave the planet now? Easarean was certain this would be his only chance.

"You'll have to come out of the trees slowly. Slowly! Vector 1:3 and straight up at .33 of green impulsive. Little more, little more, beloved. Slowly!"

"Errr…"

"There. That's right, right there, my love. This may be our only chance so you'll have to disable his shields from an awkward angle, otherwise he may see us before we're ready. It is of utmost importance he doesn't see us. But I'm sure you're up to it. You'll just have to be careful."

"Grrrr…"

"Alright, now prepare to drop our shields. Just the magnetofield, love! Not all of them! Not yet! Alright, ready… ready… is the ion-form set? Good. Wait! Oh, no, you don't. You're not going to go manual. Set the targeting quaputer. I said set the quaputer!"

"Ahrrrr…"

"Stop scowling. Come back behind him and get lower. I said get lower! You want him to see us? This is our only chance! You're going to mess this up, you dumb…"

"Ahhhhh!" Easarean yelled, hastily pulling the ship up out of the tree line. The cousin's craft also rose slowly, still powering up. Proximity alerts were going off on every holodisplay. Easarean's shouts rose above them but not the parapsyte's patronizing tone.

"Great, now he's seen us. Is that what you wanted? Now what are you going to… no!"

"Yes!" Easarean fired a spray of invisible ion down on the cousin's ship, only a split second before firing the main plasma conductor in short increments at numerous points of the ship's heavy-armored stern. It immediately flamed into a cascading ball, jumping forward over the hollow before tearing a long swath through the forest. Trees ignited all around it as it came to a wrenching halt farther than Easarean could see on the vidscreen. The other displays danced around the cabin, announcing the inevitable. There was no sign that the ship's quaputer could have survived the crash.

"*Look what you've done!*" she screamed in his mind. "*No one could survive that!*"

"Die, worm, why won't you die and leave me at peace, you horrible, slimy bitch!" He slammed the thrusters forward and pushed the ship again to its planetary extreme, hoping Automaton the Perverted or some other force on this decrepit rock would challenge him as he flew toward the ocean.

She was still chastising him as they arrived at the water — the frigid deep waters he quickly disembarked to dive into. Here he froze in the depths he sank to and she was shocked into silence. Here he tested how long he could hold his breath, as tears — something unrecognized — mixed with the salt of the sea.

XXXI

Who can see the creator of mankind?
Yet I ask who colors my cheek with blush.
Other men search for meaning to find.
Yet under starlit eyes I see no rush.

—Shiloh the First

Yelling would have blunted the shock of the cold water, but the lake took his breath away. It was the first afternoon in a while that the sun was able to break through the clouds however, and the first water source they had come across in as many days, so it may have been the best chance he had to clean himself up for a while. Despite the muted conditions, the week had been warm and the pond clear except for ice skiffs bobbing toward its center. Antony of Lovewell Dam stopped wading when the moving chill stung his thighs, shore mud sucking and numbing his feet. Despite his hesitation he knew it would be best to just drop in. It was like pushing an arrow through — best to get the initial pain over with — but he waited for his legs to adapt. They were not adapting.

"How much farther?" Ivy asked from the dry side of the shore, but Antony was not sure if she listened for the answer, so engrossed in her book. Her hair had lightened in their days under the sunless sky, and it fell out of the woolen mantle adding its shadow to those cast by the few trees surrounding the pond. Her eyes had also lightened over the past week. He could not see them either. Did they watch him or the book? Her horse, a beast the same dusky color as her hooded scarf, snorted as it nudged the short grasses of the streams leading away from the pond. She had not hitched him to anything, Antony noticed. She was sure he would not run.

He waded a step deeper and was able to shout out this time, damning the frozen gods of the North, as his loins tightened against the water. He could see, out of his peripheral, the horse glancing up at him, but there was no movement from Ivy. From where she sat, on black rock and white sand and spears of fuzzy weeds, he could not see her holster, but he had seen her in action to know she could pull iron faster than most could follow. "A day at the most," he answered, "we'll meet roads soon, see pilgrims soon enough." The glassy water emphasized the marks on his wrists. They were red but healing as quickly as the rest of his bruises. Homega Sapiens healed quickly, but he wondered if any scars would be left on his face. The rumors of the Nursery's demise had years-ago been verified, but he would never entirely believe it until he saw it with his own eyes. Could anything be salvaged from the alien ship, or was this really his final body? He rubbed his wrists in the anesthetic water. He had grown accustomed to the scar marring his face, even though, at the time received, he had not known the Nursery's fate, had just assumed he could eventually replace his body after the war. He looked at himself now, distorted in the rippling pond.

He cringed at movement as Ivy tossed a bundle of clothes to the only dry patch of the shore. "Something nice, clean, so you don't raise suspicion," she said, returning to her book as Antony plunged down into the shallow pond. This was probably the deepest the small lake was going to get, so he dropped purposely without thinking into the stinging water. The cold burned him. It stabbed at his groin with icicle knives, lanced his face and neck with frozen claws, scraped wintery hooks across his back. Without realizing it, he had jumped back into the air where he found the water dripping over his shoulders to be even more chilling. It stung like winter wasps, and they died in frozen throes on his quivering chest. So he sank back into the water, leaving only his head above to shake as chilling drops found their way through his hair to bite his scalp. He looked at his reflection again, and, even though the ripples from his shivering and the dripping hair obscured his face, he could still see the scar down his forehead, down his nose.

He thought he had died but fought on, thought the axe that had smashed through his barbute had cleaved deeper into his face, or would eventually work its way into his brain if it had not already. The battle had been early in the war, and tales of that day had spread for years — tales of the Lesser Prophet that had led his force to victory with an axe between his eyes, carrying the perpetrator's head throughout the fight, until the last of his foe's forces had been crushed. The truth is that Antony remembered little of the day, but he resolved to never wear the same type of helmet into battle again. From then on he would sacrifice coverage for a wide range of sight. His scar and the tales had identified him to his men, to the land, for years until the events at Lovewell Dam. Now he was recognized for a different bloodbath, and, without the Nursery, he had no way to erase the badge splitting his face. He could not hide anymore, even among his twin Lesser Antonys. He had pushed the war forward, from capitals and front lines, but had been relegated to errands and head hunting. And now? He struck his head against the water and rubbed the scabs and dirt from his face for as long as he could bear the cold. There was no reflection left. As he stood the picture distorted beyond recognition from the streaming water. His eyes could focus only on his feet as they sank deeper into the cold muck.

He began to pull himself from the suction, slow and deliberate steps taking him closer to the shore. The waterline dropped to his naked thighs and he rubbed shoulders and arms and legs in a vain attempt to stay warm, wiping the chill from his stiff body. He had been sore everywhere from the leagues of travel in manacles and bindings, but knew he would be even sorer once he thawed from the pond. He shook the water from head and groin.

"Master's muscle is nothing like mussel," Ivy recited before looking up from her book, "his head more violet than violence avows."

"Where the hell did you get that shit?" Antony shouted, his voice cracking under a sudden shiver of his spine. He could feel even the slightest breeze in every drop of the pond he tried to wipe away with stiffening hands.

"I don't understand poetry," Ivy said, flipping through pages of the nondescript book. She turned it in her hand as if the bare cover and binding held some sort of clue. "It seems to me unnecessarily abstruse. Why not just say what one means?" She tucked the book into a satchel that hung from the rock she sat cross-legged on.

He could see the revolver belted at her thigh now. Her wooly mantle wrapped her head and neck like a satiated serpent, and it reminded him of another life he often found difficult to reconcile with his latest, a life in which he had been taught grappling moves to envelop and strangle. In leading his section of the Army of Heaven he had often, from some pampered command center, missed the sweaty struggle of one-on-one combat. This longing again reminded him of another life. A king on a throne. A commander of nations.

"I found it in one of the offices of the Loup Garou," she finally answered. "I believe you're familiar with the poet."

Antony had never seen a female Homega Sapiens before Ivy of the Grove. What was she to him? Twin? Sister? She had not been imprinted. There was no doubt. She did not share the mind of the

Prophets Lesser. That much was obvious. The word was that she had been birthed a tabula rasa template, and her insatiable curiosity and total recall certainly backed that up. She absorbed knowledge as he did the chill of the pond.

His reflection refused to right itself, and now the perspective squished his stature. He could quell his shivering for a few seconds at a time, but, no matter how still he stood, the ripples still spread from his knees, the drops still fell like bullets exploding against his features.

The shore's reflection settled until it was less distorted. Except for Ivy and her smooth stoop, however, it was all splintered by grasses, hardy and green with a strong mixture of thin and thick. She finally looked away from the far shore and its thicker tree line, but he could not tell by her reflection whether she looked at him or not. Her form wavered in the water. Her mirror's gaze rippled from sky to shore to mid-pond.

"You look just like him except for the scar. I had forgotten his face."

"You attract traitors, or maybe it's you that's attracted to them. All the Shilohs throughout time have been at odds with the Brotherhood for one reason or another, and it was the height of stubbornness for him to take on the mantle. What was he thinking?"

"Your brothers forgave him in the end."

He caught her once just staring at the Shiloh mask, or what was left of it. Even just owning it would be an unwritten crime in the Territories.

"Do you all have the same mind?" she asked. Yes, she was finally looking at him now. "Is that insulting?"

"No, but it's an overstatement. What we share doesn't last long... out in the world."

"But you were the same once? Would you know what he..."

Antony fell to sit in the icy mud and scrubbed the color from his shins and feet, frozen muck invading cracks. She had already asked him these questions or ones like them. No one could suspect what she did. Did the sorcerer? Had he put her up to this? The sooner they reached Erebus the better.

"Antony of Lovewell Dam," she said, changing the line of questioning after a pause from both of them determined that the only sound would come from his splashing. Was it a question, he wondered. He did not respond either way. She had obviously been tasked to unnerve him. But why now? Why when they needed him? "How did you get your name?"

He did not answer, but his thoughts inevitably went back to the events at Lovewell Dam anyway. That ultimately was the purpose of his new name — to daily dredge up the memories of the sound of the explosives, the brown waters flooding ravine and flowing over fields into the town, and his missing doppelbrother and nephew. With each reminder it had become more difficult to place the blame on others. The Liege of Foes had forced his hand. Antony's doppelbrother should never have been in the town in the first place. The people of Lovewell were stubborn and knew the dangers. None of it mattered. All anyone knew was that he gave the order.

"What was he like?" Ivy asked, breaking the new silence. "The Garm, I mean. Wulf said it talked to you."

Before the tragedy at Lovewell Dam, Antony had been pulled from the war as a potential candidate to head up the Hunt. He had been briefed on the latest Garm packs, their habits and ranges. At the time, they had been united under one leader. This Alpha had been tempered from birth for his role, sent away as a child to be tutored by the finest mentors across Kaldera. He was even educated in Ziggurat, right under the Brotherhood's nose. Some of the Prophets Lesser may have even taught him themselves. How could they have let this happen, he wondered. Was no one listening to Schism? Did no one even peek at the *Fallo Terminus*? Nevertheless, before returning to his command, before being sent to wrangle his doppelbrother, Antony had learned enough to recognize Mad Hati when he had met him. He could still feel the Garm's infernal breath on his face. He could not wash the smell from his nostrils. "He's more monster than man."

"What did he say?"

Antony of Lovewell Dam was living a headhunter's dream. Wulf claimed to no longer lead any resistance, but there were many who still mistook him for the Liege of Foes, and Antony had hunted and found him. Melchyor "Wyrmbane" Slayd was now a rogue Sin Eater and the *Ashmedai Adat El* would love to find out just how long he had been betraying the cause. The zombie pistoleer was a known thorn in the Brotherhood's paw since the beginning of the war. And here sat Ivy of the Grove before him. She appeared so mundane for someone the tithingmen were so obsessed over. She was taller than her wanted posters suggested, and her coloring varied from her descriptions, but Antony had no doubt she was Homega Sapiens. Like the Lesser Antonys she was cleaner than the people of this world. She was not crooked nor jaundiced. The girl was stronger and faster without effort. He was not entirely certain concerning the tithingmen's fascination with her, but the thought added to his shivering.

"Are you coming with us to the city?" he asked quietly, not sure if she heard him, not meeting her eyes.

Ivy's horse had begun to walk the edge of the pond, periodically testing the soft shore for purchase in which to drink and pull green weeds. Its straying did not appear to worry the girl.

"Erebus in Ouroboros," she said, warming her hands in her jacket. "City of the Seventh Day. Its people broke away from the Senate of Ophidia almost immediately after its founding. A stranger in its own land. Unaffiliated. Did its long independence from the rest of Oroboros make it easy prey for the Horde, or was it yet another bloody debacle?"

"Like the rest of Ouroboros, Erebus fell long ago. It just hasn't realized it yet. This part of the land, caught in the long expanse between Kaldera and Mann Land, skirting the edge of Nod, never had anything to offer the rest of the world. The people lacked the pride to spread outside Ouroboros. Their neighbors to the north and east were isolationists. There was bad blood with Tormalco to the south. They cultivated no unique crop to connect them with the West."

"They were scholars. Scientists and poets, sculptors…"

"Exactly. What good is that compared to the oil of Kaldera, or the spread of the Song. Ouroboros broadened its minds at the expense of its borders. It's a wonder it wasn't conquered an age ago."

"By the Horde?"

He cringed whenever he heard that word. Yes, Slayd had taught her to be disrespectful, but there was hope for her yet. Her wayward curiosity was proof of incompleteness. Her companions did not fulfill her. The Army of Earth was unsatisfying. She could still be molded in the right hands. "The *Ashmedai Adat El* has no interest in conquering," he corrected. "The Song spreads as the land opens its ears and hearts and…" He struck the water with both fists to drown out the sound of his own voice and to get his blood pumping. The water stung, but he could not feel his toes. The words of the *Ashmedai Adat El*, the words of the circulating hymns and Theses, *his* words, were all so empty when said out in the land, away from the security of the Brotherhood. His voice, among traitors and rebels, sounded as distorted to him as his face in the pond that refused to settle. Now, from his bent reflection, he was not sure if it was the moving water or if his face was more bruised than he had thought.

"All in the Prophets Lesser are Lesser Antonys, but are all Lesser Antonys Lesser Prophets?"

"Stop!" His legs would not answer his call, and he struggled to pull them from the iced sludge, falling forward as he tried to stand. He had underestimated the chill of the water or atrophy in the length of his capture. For he was still a prisoner, or, at least, he could not forget that that was the role he was playing. He struck the water again, using the pain to remind him to not become complacent. He could not afford to forget that those he surrounded himself with were dangerous. It was so easy to make that mistake. The Brotherhood had been doing it for years. "Just stop with the questions!" He splashed water over his head and back, hoping the shock would wake his numb feet. It did not, so he crawled on his knees to even shallower water.

"Why…"

"Why what?" he puffed. His chest had tightened, and he could not breathe very deeply.

"Why do you need them? Not everyone does. What is missing from you that they provide? That… *Ashmedai Adat El…* is unnecessary."

He expected it to sound unnatural coming from her mouth, but could not deny that it came no better from his. He had spent too much time away from the capitals. This was why a Prophet Lesser was often recalled to the Brotherhood. No matter where one was, the Song sang in the heart, yet its music could never be heard more clearly than under golden perch or when surrounded by the hymns of the faithful.

"You wouldn't understand," he whispered from the dirt of the shore. He now sat in sliding sludge at the only spot clear of the tall grasses. Here, without vegetation to hold the bank, the pond had started a tiny stream that twinkled even under the cloudy sky. He rubbed his toes of their mud in the trickle, looking around for the clothes Ivy had brought. The pain had been good, he thought. It had wakened him, focused him, if not in thought then maybe intention.

"You would *not* understand," he repeated before Ivy could ask another question. "You haven't seen it. You have *not* seen the world as it's supposed to be. We've… *I've* lived it. It was at peace."

"There was peace before the Horde…"

"Not this!" His cringe turned into a shudder. Being out in the air with a wet head was now worse than being in the pond. He wrung the biting water from his hair, reminding himself how shaggy it had grown out in these wilds. "This means nothing. You think there was peace before this squabble? This isn't war, and the land wasn't at peace before it. There wasn't one faith. Souls were torn, man's inhumanity was rampant, witches and wolves ruled the countryside, children were corrupted and lost, people had not heard the Song. We are giving them choice. The Liege of Foes is covering their ears, clogging their arteries with promises of false freedom. There is no freedom without *the* Promises. The Army of Earth is a petulant child that refuses to eat its greens yet won't let anyone else at the table." He stood from the shallow water, feeling the mud he had missed ooze from crack and down thigh. Some had already cold-dried to his hip. "You're so stubborn. You are all so stubborn. The Liege of Foes on a throne... is that what you want? You trust your salvation to a man? The Divine Choir offers the judgment of Heaven, but you fight for the right to be ruled by... by..." He poked at his temple, finding the pain of a bruise he had not noticed. Was it new or old? "...by this gray matter? This is all replaceable." He rubbed arm and leg and tapped his chest. "None of this lasts, but the Promises are forever. I've lived the Heavenly Kingdom. It was possible, and it was glorious, but this world is too far gone, too fallen to achieve it on its own. We were too late. But the Divine Choir shares this vision. For them there's hope, hope that even the Brotherhood had given up on. Through them this world can find peace, it can be what I remember."

He found his clothes sinking in a batch of new puddles. His stomping and splashing had spread to the soft shore, and his shirt and trousers were soaked. He snatched up the denim jacket before it had absorbed too much of the cold pond. He could tell it would be too small just by the sight of it. His boots were all they brought him of his original clothing. They were the only possessions familiar to him any longer. Even his voice betrayed him, he lamented before he decided against continuing his rant. For that was all it was — just a rant. He had become just what he feared he would — one of the ancient Lesser Prophets, choosing to let age warp body and mind, shouting from street corners outside bar and brothel. Ivy looked at him like he had once looked at them, the same look of pity on her face. He sounded like some trained raven on some drunk's shoulder, parroting the words of tithingmen and old wives.

Ivy's horse snorted from somewhere off around the pond.

Even the clothes that were not wet were freezing against Antony's skin, but it did not matter. The bite kept him awake, focused. But focused toward what? There was no big picture. Where would he be by the next full moon? Or a month after that? With the nursery gone he should have been planning each day intricately, but even a few days into the next week were as hazy as the sky above to him. He moved from the shore to find a spot dry enough to sit and buckle his boots. They were as familiar as he imagined, but his feet were still as wet as the rest of him. He had to stay focused on what was right before him. One step after another, one day at a time.

The dull day barely cast his shadow over Ivy. It was a pale mold next to the rich clay of her hooded scarf. His new jacket fit him better than he thought, but it was still tight at shoulder and elbow. He rubbed where his bonds had been. Out of the numbing pond the worn wounds began to ache again.

Not knowing when Ivy would look up from the new book she had retrieved from a backpack, he spoke. "Don't go into the city."

"Erebus in Oroboros," she said, turning a page.

"I can sneak the two of them in, but you shouldn't come any nearer. Let them do their business. I can't keep track of all of you."

"I'm good at disguising…"

"I can't have any distractions." He looked to Harlowe. How long had the man been standing there? Despite the desiccated lips stretched back from a macabre grin, the bony chin under hanging brim, the petrified pistoleer was easy to dismiss. He could have been just another wind-stripped tree or clean-picked carcass lining the pond. Had he been at Ivy's side the whole time? Antony spoke to him now. "You'll be safer out of the way. There's no need to take unnecessary chances."

The truth was, he could imagine his punishment if he were to be caught abetting known rebels and traitors. He could picture defending himself against the Brotherhood — the discussion, the lies and justifications and prevarication. He could predict the actions of his brothers. But when it came to the tithingmen and their obsession with the girl before him…

"I'll get Wulf and the sorcerer into Erebus, but I can make no other guarantees."

XXXII

All's End breathes his last of Death's disciple
before exhaling vampiric doom at
his final home, a cooling world soon fat
with fallen fire, ground in gods' bly mill.
   —The Fallo Terminus (LXX)

he tiny parade seemed custom-made to verify rumors that Antony of Lovewell Dam had been hearing for over a year now. It was led by a motley group of boys he expected to smell even from his position back in the thick of the spectators' heads that crowded him forward. Some of these families had traveled for days for the bread the circus offered, and he tightened his bandana to block the stench. He cringed at the expected wet dog smell of the boys trudging through the mud at the head of the scene. Each held an open prayer book or pamphlet, failing to harmonize *Seven Eyes Sing to Six Cankered Ears*. They were mostly naked beneath the bear furs sewn to their skin.

Antony of the Dam had not believed the stories coming out of the Territories, of how wayward children were being dealt with as their fathers were off fighting the war. He assumed it all propaganda spread by resistance and malcontents, but here were delinquents, sewn into possum-pelt, marching to the beat set by a cat organ. The tiny piano sounded atrocious and seemed constantly about to tip from the cart it was pulled on. The old woman slowly playing its keys, with glasses caught on the wart at the very tip of her nose, also appeared precarious from her bench with each step of the mules pulling the wagon. Each tabby had a different pitch of cry when their corresponding key was struck, crushing or pulling a tail taunt and clasped somewhere deep in the soundboard. Only their heads poked up through their confining boxes. Their ears were clipped, and even from where Antony stood he could tell they were full of mites. It was time to replace the exhausted felines. But the old woman kept playing as she passed, periodically snapping a crop at the mules when they slowed or at one of the cats when they had become numb to the organ's tortures.

As the parade passed, the smell of the boys never came. It would have to be a hearty stench indeed, he realized, to break through the heavenly ambrosia of the warm bread scent hanging thickly through the circus that had sprung up outside of the walls of Erebus in Ouroboros.

The creamy smoke wafted just at face level. The crowd opened around him, now appearing smaller than he thought. Had they recognized him as a Lesser Antony, he wondered, checking his pockets and the buckles on the saddlebag resting over his shoulder. He kept his hat and goggles on — supplies Rood Ruthwell had acquired for him — hoping to avoid any recognition, but his stature and posture would always threaten to give him away.

He had spent over a full day arguing with Rood before the tithingman had relented to sneak Wulf and Slayd into the walled city. Antony remembered a time, not too long ago, when anyone in the *Ashmedai Adat El* would have acted from a Lesser Prophet's order without hesitation or question, but with the Brotherhood out leading the Army of Heaven, the tithingmen had been growing in responsibility back in the Territories, and with this new found power they were becoming, he noticed, increasingly insolent. Antony had played it safe to avoid suspicion as to whom he wanted Rood to sneak past the walls. He was becoming increasingly aware that the homefront's agenda was not necessarily the same as the Brotherhood's.

The desperate meows and off-key singing faded as the parade continued deeper into the circus. *Seven Eyes Sing to Six Cankered Ears* was a song Antony knew well, and he found his gut tightening as he heard it for the first time in years. His nephew used to whistle it, mostly absentmindedly under his breath. The sound had been bothersome, but now Antony would not have minded hearing it whistled one more time.

He pulled down his bandana to breathe the bread in fully, and he walked the newly-worn trails leading through the shanty town the circus had grown up around. Hastily pitched tents and homemade pulpits littered the shadow spread by the inclined walls surrounding the unseen city of Erebus. From all angles, every one of the seven sides, one could only see the great earthen barriers leading up into the impenetrable walls. It was rumored that the walls had protected Erebus during the invasion of the Inside-Outers, but little was ever substantiated about that unknown war. Still, as tempting as the inclined walls appeared to climb, Erebus in Oroboros had never technically fallen from an outside source. It had only succumbed to its own pleasures and lethargy over time. The *Ashmedai Adat El* found only open doors and no resistance when it arrived, now years ago. Antony had led the expedition and found the turnover pleasingly peaceful. There was a beautifully secluded city inside the walls, untouched by modern industry. He would have liked to settle down there one day, but he had not been back since the turnover, and he now found the reports of Erebus' closure to be true. The City of the Seventh Day had been closed to all since the pilgrimage of the Lonely Forgotten Sun of God. By the order of the nearest governor, no one was allowed into, and apparently out of, the city of Erebus. Antony had expected difficulty. He had not expected nigh unbreakable disobedience.

"It's not honey, but beggars can't be choosers." Rood Ruthwell appeared from the crowd and handed him a warm loaf. It was shaped like a large mushroom with a crown barely browned. "And we are all beggars beneath the perches," he added, gesturing to the recently raised structures poking above the shantytown. The great leaning crosses explained the fields of tree stumps seen when one neared the city.

"Beetstrap?" Antony asked, not really interested in the answer.

"Yeah, better get used to it, father. We're not tasting real sugar until the war ends."

"I'm not your father…" Antony's voice trailed away. Rood spoke so quietly, always in a whisper, and it was especially difficult to hear him beneath a periodic grinding of chains Antony had noticed since arriving at the circus. The sound appeared several times a day, but he could never determine its direction exactly.

"Sorry, just force of habit," Rood mumbled. "Have you been enjoying the festivities?" He gestured again to the surroundings and again Antony cringed at the sight of hands with many times too many fingers, all in various states of development. Rood's neck and bald scalp were covered in gills, but it was his bouquets of fingers that gave him away as a tithingman, even at a distance, for the webbing covering his nostrils and ears was barely noticeable. Antony's nephew had had gills on his cheeks. He had always hoped they would have helped him in the flood.

"You're late," Antony said, chewing the undercooked bread. The dough had barely risen in some bites. He wondered how the starving stomachs of the pilgrims arriving, some after weeks on the road, would handle the bread. Rood was leading him to the largest tent, a pied canvas held aloft by miniature versions of the giant perches. He had to crouch to get close enough to hear the tithingman. And he did not enjoy getting close. Rood was young, almost disconcertingly so. Blemishes marked him where wrinkles one day would. He reminded Antony of another life, when grave responsibilities appeared more game than what they really were — life and death struggles that pressed like granite yokes. Still, he pitied the young tithingman. Rood had too much responsibility for his age. He was barely a man, yet he was charged with something he truly did not understand.

"It wasn't easy. There are no extant normal entrances into Erebus. The last gate was sealed months ago, maybe a year. It's tough to follow seasons anymore. All the doors have been collapsed or welded or boul-dered, and we would of been spotted going up the hills. People are watching the walls, especially at night." Somewhere far off, around the heptagonal barrier, a gunshot punctuated Rood's words. "See?"

"You were given the authority of the Brotherhood!" Antony shouted. Luckily, the few people around them were too absorbed in their bread to pay any attention.

Rood's ears were instantly red, as they had been for most of the previous day while Antony argued for his assistance. "That is why I'm trying to be a good example. I have an important job here — speaking to those who come following her pilgrimage." He swung his mass of fingers toward the walled city and Antony could not help but cringe. The hands were bloated bulbs of blossoming digits. Rood hid them behind his back at the sight of the Lesser Prophet's obvious revulsion. "They come here not truly knowing what they want, just knowing that they want *something*. They're searching to fill the emptiness in their lives. They have questions the Song answers. I've been given a great responsibility — to open their ears. How can I do that when they see me breaking the law? What kind of example is that?"

"Who ordered you to seal Erebus?"

"I didn't…"

"These people are here for bread, nothing more," Antony inter-rupted as they entered the big top. He was through with his own loaf and had been about to give away its remains but saw that everyone at the benches had their own slices. They were dipping it in what he could only assume was the beet molasses that had made his bites so bitter.

This was where those wondering the settlements had come to, although they only filled half the seating. There were just as many or-ganizers, Antony deduced, than pilgrims, and they weaved through the benches now, using the bread to start discussions that quickly led to talk of the Promises of the Divine Choir. These men could be picked from the crowd by their short, slicked hair, beardless faces, and by charms of patron angels hanging from their necks. Just from the entrance to the tent, Antony noticed a copper kettle on one chain, a silver horn on another, but most of the men wore tiny vials of golden dust.

There was commotion everywhere under the tent. Few people were just sitting and eating. A crooked dog, caked with mud and molasses, was kicked by both pilgrim and organizer until it sat unmoving under the stage. A tiny child, of which Antony could not determine the sex, had been bound and gagged yet still managed to overturn a bench before being placated with more bread. Two barely clothed men stood to confront an organizer interrupting a game of UnderCrawl. Despite the expanse of the tent, the gaggle of loud voices hung low in the moist air. The words rose and fell but, overall, continued loudly, constantly competing with each other to lift the tent.

"Fuck'in mutts are everwhere, fuck'in like there's no tomorrow."

"We should be so lucky."

"Where they get bread these days? Ergot's not been gone long enough ta raise a good 'un."

"This is how you repay us, with the devil's cards beneath our perches?"

"More beetstrap to wet the lips?"

Antony had not noticed a low rumble from outside the tent when he entered, but it increased now to compete with the myriad voices, hanging lamps in the tent brightening. It was by no means dim under the pied canvas, but now all shadows were vanquished except for the wet shade displaying the dirt under the low stage. Here and there a sword of light pierced the mismatched boards to reveal the monstrosities of the darkness.

"So are they in?" Antony whispered as Rood started to step away. The tithingman answered in a voice just as quiet.

"They weren't happy about traveling through what amounted to a sewer system, but, yes, they are in Erebus. May Slog Sabbaoth grant them dreams they only..."

"Then my time here is done. You've done... good... work here, Ruthwell. I'll make sure to express my..."

"What? You can't leave now, father. Reports just came of the Liege of Foes nearing. His command force is in retreat, being pressed..."

"This far west?"

"I need you to raise and lead these people. I'm no general, but together we can halt his retreat, at least slow them until Heaven can catch up."

"These people?" Antony could no longer hear Rood's raspy voice in the tent, but he got the meaning of his begging. He looked back over the benches tilting in the earth. It looked as though straw had been liberally applied to the ground at one point, but the many days of the circus had worn it into the softening ground. Smoke had begun to waft under the tent edges from whatever truck powered the lamps. From the far side it cradled the stage, but his nose twitched at the acrid scent that had already reached them. He could hear the sound of thunder or another truck rolling from another side of the camps. Not realizing that Rood had left his side, he said, "These people have no weapons. Do they even have..."

The tithingman had crossed the tent, patting children on heads, passing bowls of beetstrap from family to family, while shaking the hands of squinting elderly. He took a precarious step onto the low stage, to a podium fire-burned with angelic runes, before receiving a trumpet from a nearby organizer. The bright lamps shimmered over the brass and the lance of Ashmedai carved onto its surface. He spoke to downturned, sideways, and chewing faces, but Antony expected that, even if the numerous dog barks from across the shantytown had not risen at once, the seated would not have heard him. With hairless brow furrowed, the tithingman put lip to the mouthpiece of an electric horn.

"The twenty-fourth Thesis states, 'thus did Schism; according to all that was commanded, so was done." Rood, even through the trumpet, was still no louder than an average speaker. So he repeated himself before adding, "Concerning this holy decree, I would observe seven things."

Watching the preacher's mass of nubs and shoots and fingers twitch to hold the trumpet steady, Antony thought back a day to their first meeting. Upon revealing his face, Antony had been rushed to one of the few permanent, and ancient, structures of the fields surrounding the walls of Erebus. Luggage and boxes filled the garages and home, yet Rood had settled into the house nicely, even immediately prepared to host with steak and apple juice — two delicacies Antony had missed during his time across forest and plain. His mouth had watered uncontrollably when the tithingman's pre-meal prayer had started. He held his breath, ignoring the gristly scent as the admonitions stretched through the minutes. He eventually started cutting into the giving meat, before the prayer had ended, with a knife sharper than most he encountered outside the Territories. He had ignored the butter-drowned greens of the dinner, as the circus-goers now ignored Rood, but waited until finishing the melting meats before giving his command to the tithingman. Rood had listened patiently, Antony remembered, without interrupting, trying desperately to cut his own meat while keeping his bulbous hands hidden beneath cloth napkins monogrammed with his initials. Goldware scraped and clanked and fell. Eventually his ears turned red, and he pushed his plate and barely touched steak aside.

The tithingman had gone on all through the evening about responsibilities, wiping lips permanently stained red with an equally stained handkerchief. Antony could not stand to look at him. All throughout the conversations, he just looked to empty bookshelves, pretending to admire hypothetical tomes. Rood's adolescent newife would periodically, throughout the night, appear with pickled string beans or refills of ice water. Antony could not figure out how someone so young could be so fat, especially in these times. With Rood's attention firmly on his snacks, Antony's gaze would linger over the newife's turgid hips as they squirmed around furniture and beneath desperate seams. Somewhere beneath the multitude of layers, the girl undoubtedly hid a *noli me tangere* tattoo. He wondered what colors she had chosen for its petals.

"What it was that the Song asked of Schism," Rood now whispered into the trumpet under the tent, "to which these words refer, was the breaking of a seal according to the particular direction of Abaadoon, against this time when the winter of the sinful should come, against the betterment of himself, his family, and the Brotherhood, which are now preserved in the Promise. We have the particular commands which the *Fallo Terminus*, before its perversion, gave him respecting this affair, from verse I-IV-II, 'to unleash holy glory, of thee asked will no more be.'" His stained lips molested the mouthpiece.

They had talked for most of that prior evening, with Antony sampling other foods he had not tasted since the war started — raspberries (large but juiceless), pickled carrot (all brine), and jellied mutton cubes over the wildest of rice. He had asked for wine but received only cane to chew for dessert. Rood interrupted most of the evening's discussion with intermittent meal prayers, whispering about "appreciations" and "glorified bodies."

Antony's repeated attempts to bring the conversation back to his command made him realize the fear behind any discussion of Erebus. What he first thought were Rood's prevarications, he had started to recognize were avoidance through ignorance. He truly did not know why the city had been sealed, where the orders had come from, and what had happened to the Alabaster Princess and her great mass of initial pilgrims. Yet he was still adamant that he could not help Antony in what had been downgraded to just a request. Antony had realized over the course of the day that *he* held no power here. The important question was — just how much power did the *tithingman* have?

And that was something Antony had never entirely figured out. By evening, while snacking on chitterlings drowned in cider vinegar, he had convinced Rood to smuggle Wulf and Slayd into the city without asking any more questions. He had promised to work toward a promotional commission for the tithingman, although he suspected that Rood was probably questioning this Lesser Prophet's standing in the Brotherhood more and more as the day went on. Looking back, he now felt that he had debased himself over the evening in front of the man, but, in the end, all that mattered was that he would finally be free of the rebels. They were fools — fools for not questioning his sudden turn of loyalties. So excited by the prospects of Erebus, they had not even wondered why he was so eager to help them. If Antony was correct in his suspicions about the Sleeping City, they would learn soon enough the truth of his favors. The last thoughts behind their closing eyes would be to rue the day they made him slave.

Rood's raspy trumpet speech now brought Antony out of his thoughts of vengeance, but the growing barking of dogs kept him from straying back into them.

"Number four: We may observe the *special design* of the work which the Song had enjoined upon her: it was to save Zig and the capital, and now the Territories when the rest of the world should be covered in snow. See the forty-ninth Thesis.

"Number five: We may observe her obedience. She listened to the Song: *Thus did the Shattered Hand.* And her obedience was thorough and universal: *According to all that the Song sang commanded her, so did she.* She not only began, but she went through her work, breaking the hold the whiskered she-devil had on the Baronies, which Ashmedai had commanded her to undertake for her salvation from the winds. To this obedience the apostle Cain Antony refers in III-III-I of the unperverted text. 'By faith the Shattered Hand being warned of winter not seen as yet, moved with fear, broke the ward, met in this new world of feather and leather.' We should be willing to engage in and go through great undertakings, in order to our own salvation. Did you come here to find her? Or did you come here to find salvation? The very same salvation she herself found when she opened the land to the Divine Choir. She is one of many to have heard heavenly notes. You are next. All of you. Sing with me now."

Hard to sing with mouths full of molasses, Antony thought, heading to the exit. The tent flaps had been closed and tied together at some time before Rood had started his talk, and Antony had to force his way past a woman and the organizer standing in her way. From the argument it sounded as though she had finished her meal, but the circus was not yet finished with her.

"We were told we could just eat. I just want to leave..."

"What exactly are your concerns with Pastor Ruthwell's words? The least you can do after partaking of bread is stay for a few..."

Antony shoved both of them aside to examine the cords holding the tent closed. Rather than spend any more time in the exhaust he pulled a dull knife to work the knots. The woman used the distraction to follow and pass him out into the camps, past numerous clay ovens contributing to the low buttery fog Antony inhaled deeply.

Following the barking, he walked one of many new, yet worn, trails past temporary buildings and permanent wickiups. Cleanly groomed organizers made no distinction between squatter and settler, introducing themselves to potential newives and cannon fodder. *If the Army of Earth nears,* Antony pondered, *the circus had better speed its recruitment.* Rood was delusional if he thought these transients would make a difference in the fight, especially without firearms or even blades, but, if converted, they would at least not pose a distraction behind the lines.

Antony wandered to find the source of the commotion and a validation of his suspicions. It looked like the dog-fighting ring had been cobbled together by whatever junk could be found. Broken crates, rusty fenders, chimineas, and wagon panels circled what looked like two small molls. They had unusually thick fur for pit-fighters, but Antony knew the breed's reputation for strong jaws and endurance. The small audience was mostly circus organizers, individual charms dancing at their necks as they cheered, with assorted transients and pilgrims exchanging final moneys. Antony had seen the dominant dog earlier in the day and now regretted not putting gold on it, for it had locked its jaw on the other canine's snout and there was no indication it would ever let go.

Another organizer appeared. A dark scimitar had escaped his perfectly greased hair helmet, and he smoothed it back as he yelled above the group to his fellow men.

"The noon sermon has begun, friends! Curb the noise, curb the noise!"

But the fight was over anyway. Antony was unfamiliar with the currency being passed. Any sort of universal coin was being discouraged lately, yet these men counted and pocketed with glee.

The winning hound jerked his jaw one last time before its owner coaxed it to release the loser — a dog with mangled maw it could barely whimper through. Antony was near the loser's owner when he dragged his moll from the ring tripping over the clay and meal forming the boundary. The dog's teary eyes rolled at its owners blank ones before its esophagus was cut out by pruning shears. It continued to blink in silence as it bled out. The owner looked up at Antony sheepishly.

"He wouldna been able to feed himself anyway."

Antony pulled the bandana back up over his face. The exhaust smell had permeated the material, and it was unwelcome compared to the smell of rising dough. He decided then to taste the bread from a different oven.

Standing next to clay and stone radiating a comforting mass of heat, sampling a rye much superior to that which he had earlier, he again heard what sounded like the crank of chains underneath all the other sounds of the circus. For the first time since the morning, he could finally pinpoint the direction the low sound came from. This time, however, perhaps since he was closer, he could hear it followed by the crack of the splintering of wood and a howl of pain. His crust joined other crumbs dropping to the dirt as he headed off deeper into the circus. He passed a blacksmith cooking both bread and gold. The smoke erupting from his ovens was darker than the soot staining his lips, but it dissipated as quickly as it blossomed. The sweat on his bare chest collected in faint hairs or rolled before disappearing over his back. The droplets were the only marks on his flawless flesh. The barreled man stepped back to set aside giant tongs before great mittens covering his arms past his elbow slid off. He dunked a shining hand into a small barrel and pulled back with a fist full of yellow charms.

Antony ignored an obvious organizer huddled near a peddler, as the men tried to ignore him. They held a pipe glowing golden with each shared puff, the tobacco's scent muted almost completely by the crossroads of smoke wafting through the trails.

Girls disguised as boys corn-holed in what could be considered an alley between two permanent structures. The target board was painted with the face of the Liege of Foes. He had wild serpentine curls covering the board, a frown, and a hole cut where one eye would be. The only color in the painting streamed down his face from the hole. One girl, strands of hair loosening from under a floppy hat with each throw, played the game, taking a step closer with each miss. The others just worked at picking the threads of the bags and shaking the kernels free.

Antony walked the perimeter of one building. It had no windows and no signs. Winter weeds grew thickly all along its base except for the doorless entrance. Here, trails converged and wore the ground into the cinderblock structure. He was certain that this was where the sound had come from. Listening now, all he could hear was the far off "chug chug chug" of the truck powering the lamps of the pied tent. Did Rood still preach? The tithingman had seemed so tired at the previous day's parlay, so beaten and abused by life, but on the stage he had been renewed to purpose. Would he revert to the same tired boy Antony had first met? He did not know, and he expected he never would, since his plan was to leave without saying good-bye. But first he had to satisfy his curiosity. Of all the strange sounds of the circus this one kept repeating and kept striking a chord. But no one else tilted their heads when it appeared. No one else followed its hourly rhythm.

The organizer hid a flask behind a crate he then kicked his feet and denim up to when Antony entered. He was a thin man, but the chair he leaned back on looked about to give under his weight in more than one place. Days of stubble and askew hair set him apart from his mates out in the circus.

"How goes the parade, guy?" he asked, nudging a coffee tin past the crate. Scattered inside were tiny nuggets of gold and ore, bent coins from numerous nations fallen and otherwise, and papers of indeterminate worth. The man wore a lance charm but twirled a chain and lyre charm until it wound around a finger. He loosened and dropped it, only to twirl it tight again. "Get yer fill?"

"What is this place?"

"I don't know. Used to be a jail I think."

"Your patron angel?" Antony asked, eying the charms and lifting his goggles and loosening his bandana but keeping his face blank not to reveal true interest.

The man then clasped the loose charm around his neck to join the other. Silver and gold chains were immediately caught up in one another as he leaned forward, placing his feet on the dirt and pushing the tin ahead again. A musket leaned into the corner of the room behind him, but Antony would have been surprised if it had been fired in decades.

The organizer watched Antony look around the dark room, its spacious but bare interior, before he was answered, "I don't have to pick just one do I?" He took a spectacle out of his vest pocket and wiped it on his linen robe before putting it to an eye. Squinting, he said, "Let's see what you have to trade for a pull."

"What?"

"For a pull or two. Have to warn you though, he's on his third one now. Not easy since it has to be custom made for a bastard his size and all." He squinted again. "But you look like you might just be the guy to do it. Yeah, what do you got, guy? This just might be it."

Antony dropped an old Kalderan coin from one of the defunct baronies into the tin. It was soundless, cushioned by tickets and hemp. The organizer removed his spectacle with some difficulty. Its chain had gotten caught up with his charms.

He frowned and, just as thunder rumbled outside and overhead, said, "Ah, I don't know, I can give you... one pull for that. That's alright. Go ahead, I have a good feeling about you." As the thunder slowed, the light coming in from the doorway dimmed. "Ah, yeah, the almanac said it's supposed to storm. Not quite cold enough to snow though. For once anyway."

Antony crouched and stepped into what he could not see upon entering. The cellar steps hid in the dimness. They were equal parts dirt, decayed wood, and metal rusted into scaly flakes. The same verdigris framed the wall, although barely.

It was only a few steps before a lantern was shoved in Antony's face. His eyes had not even adjusted to the darkness enough to be shocked by the light. "You get a pull, hero?" He heard from behind the hand and the glow.

"Just one!" came the voice from back above.

"What is this?"

"Musta been a jail once, I don't..."

Antony pushed the lantern and the man aside to step into the cramped cellar. He ignored the empty man-sized cages, the manacle chains winding through bar and into concrete, the table of irons and tongs and hand drills. As the cellar organizer dimmed his lamp and spun a crank, wall lamps hissing to life, Antony's eyes never left the giant form stretched on an incline panel of fresh wood and browned metal. Numerous rollers and gears of various materials, entwined cords of ropes and chains both thin and thick, completed the massive panel and surrounded the rack on both its long sides. Antony's foot struck the wheel as he stepped back to take in the entire scene. Its grips reached the height of his neck and looked to be the only pieces of the device that had not been replaced recently. Their wood was dark, shaped by sweat.

The organizer was talking, but he did not hear him. He only stared at the Greater Antony sprawled and tied to the rack. It had been ages since he had seen one, since he had wakened in this world, and they had become increasingly rare over the years, but there was no mistaking the giant. He had no choice but to recognize one. He immediately dismissed the thought that this was *his* Greater Antony, for he had followed rumors that his own creator had perished in some vague altercation near an Eastern Libran temple, but this man was familiar none-the-less. His limbs were bold cords of bronze gleaming in the flickering lamps, his chest a bulbous block of muscle. Black, matted hair had grown to his shoulders, streaked with gray and combining with years of beard to obscure his entire face. From this angle Antony could tell the ugly scars gripping the man's shoulders continued to arc over his back. They rippled in the shimmering shadows like gorgan's caresses, but the being's only movement was a barely noticeable rise and fall of breathing.

"What are you doing here?" Antony asked.

Seeing the Greater brought back a life to him he never fully remembered anymore. The life always flowed beneath his conscious thoughts like a dream half-forgotten, moving and shifting and replaying daily, but he drew out the individual events and emotions. The life played in the background as though it were someone else's, and as long as he never brought it to the surface he could continue pretending that it was. But here, with the heavily veined giant bound before him, so close and present, he could not deny the other world he had lived. It had become theoretical, but, here, every day was suddenly remembered, every emotion and victory and failure relived. He remembered why he was here, why they were both here, and tears welled in his eyes as he thought of the Prince's first and last days, both spent cradled in his father's arms.

"You gonna take a turn?"

"Just one!" came the voice from back above.

"Do you know what this is?" Antony asked, not turning, not looking away from the Greater, barely speaking through unmoving teeth. "Do you know *who* this is?"

"Just crank the wheel, buddy, take your turn and stop botherin'…"

Antony swung without looking and immediately regretted it. The man bounced off the wall, instruments flying from tipped table, and the dimmed lantern extinguished for good. Somewhere within all the sounds he thought he may have heard the man's neck snap. He did not move, but Antony could not tell if he still breathed. He took the sharpest implement from the cold dirt and stabbed it at the ropes winding one of the Greater's ankles. The bindings were thicker than his forearms. Up close he could see that the great rack had recently been mended, and he would have been surprised if the cracked rollers and ground gears would have survived another turn of the wheel.

He had barely made any headway with the ropes when the ticket-taker blocked the faint light at the steps. Antony was immediately upon him, twisting the musket in his hands in the limited space to strike against his chest. The man collapsed wordlessly under the musket's repeated descent. The gun and the stairs crumbled with rust flying from both.

Antony went back to working the ropes and chains with numerous instruments. Threads frayed and iron bent. He sweated under the cool earth. In the end the panel beneath the huge man had split, a roller had fallen, and gears that had been cranked tightly for so long fell about the walls. The Greater stirred but was barely responsive. Wide abysmal eyes fluttered behind a wall of hair.

Antony felt like he had been in the cellar for hours. Down under the dirt there was no time. The two organizers had become a part of the scene of old jail cells, frozen by rust and the years. The tools of mending and torture that had been set all around had been in their predestined spots forever and would sprawl there forever more. Only he and the Greater did not belong. Only the two of them looked un-natural and new, not of this room, and they had been in the cellar for far too long — just how long that had been he was not sure. He was not entirely certain that what he was experiencing was real, that this was not just some drunken reinterpretation of his first wakening in the Nursery where, instead of his attempts to rouse the giant in the cellar, it was his own Greater shaking him to consciousness for the first time under sterile alien lights.

But the strain in his back was real. The pressure on his legs was undeniable as he took most of the man's weight up the steps. The rot buckled beneath his feet, and he feared his shoulder would do the same, if the narrow passage was even able to support them. The Greater Antony's limbs had obviously been stretched beyond even his legendary endurance. His joints were dislocated, maybe even useless. Still, they both fought to climb out of the cellar, into the room echoing what Antony could not hear from down in the ground. A hard rain drummed on the cinder block shelter, and, past the men in the room training rifles and revolvers at them, he could see people through the doorway revel-ing in what had to be a painfully large and chilling wall of water. No matter how heavy their clothing was, the rain had soaked through. They danced in deepening mud with clean, upturned looks and hair plastered to their faces. The Greater collapsed beside him and he sank to his own exhausted knees in the biting breeze wafting in. Those aiming at him in the dark room were a mix of obvious organizers and dirty pilgrim. They talked, but he only heard the one voice from outside in the roar of the shower. It was a quiet sound, but for some reason he was able to block out all the other sounds to hear it, as though the very solid rain, the bouncing mud puddles, and the architecture of the structure and doorway directly echoed Rood's voice to Antony's ears.

"See, didn't I tell you? Your song has joined the words of the Choir. Harmony does not go unnoticed by Heaven. Your prayer is heard, as it always shall be, and here is your cleansing, as foretold. Feel it wash away your sins. Can you feel it? This holy spring from on high falls for you and you and you and you. It washes away not just the dust of the trail, the sand from your hands, but it flows through to your very souls, to purify that which makes us human, our base aches and pains and wants that will one day be satisfied by the Promises. And all you and you and you and you had to do was sing. That's all they dream of. Because, yes, angels dream too, of a day when all is harmonized, all are joined together in the Song and there is no more crying to disrupt the skies, no more cursing to summon disease and hunger and bloodshed. No more screaming to raise the devil and death and endless winter. When all sing as one there is no room for sickness or wind or sword or Hel. Ashmedai dreams of the same world as you, and all you have to do is sing."

And they did. The faces and limbs, creating a flickering of light at the doorway as they leaped and splashed, sang in differing pitch and volume. Each person sang the same song but in different verses and mismatched lyrics. The songs broke the perfect tunnel of sound that brought Rood's voice to Antony. The last words he heard were of the tithingman calling for a taking of arms against a rumored approaching of the Army of Earth. Everything, even in the room, smelled like wet dog.

But then, suddenly, his voice was near, with a new echo as it bounced closely and mechanically around the hard room. This was the whisper Antony was more familiar with. "This is how you repay our kindness, father? You eat at my table, I do you a..." Here he paused, and as Antony looked up, the tithingman's sheepish expression hardened while those around looked to him. "You come here asking for favors, you eat our bread and then in turn release our prisoner — an enemy to our freedom?"

"Do you know what you have here? Do you know your Theses? You can't harm Greater Antonys!" Antony stared at Rood while a hidden glance valued the guns being aimed at him as a mixture of new and old arms. Most would be lucky to not jam or misfire. But he was so tired. Tired of the struggle with the Army of Earth, with the Resistance in the cities, with his own Brotherhood, and with whatever was now happening in the home front. Had everyone gone mad? Did the Prophets Lesser know what was going on while they were off playing war? Their work was supposed to bring the land closer to the ideal, to the world they knew and missed — the reality the broken giant sprawled in the dirt reminded him painfully of. Their presence, Greater and Lesser, existed here to fix the wrong, yet life all around him was drifting further and further away. They were all named in memory of the Prince, but Antony could not see his face anymore in the world they were helping create. "Do you know what a Greater Prophet is?"

"He may be greater, but he's no prophet," Rood whispered, taking the revolver from a nearby organizer, but keeping it trained on Antony. "Besides, the Theses say not to *kill* them. He ain't dead."

"They are the first of…"

"He is a conspirator and a friend to the enemy. He has deafened ears to the Song. He was found giving aid to the Resistance."

Antony tried to stand but just could not find the strength. He considered arguing but just could not find the words. The Greater, however, mumbled slowly into the dirt.

"Apples… for… children…"

~

As clouds cleared and the sun revealed a sky the color of blue both pilgrim and organizer had forgotten, Antony sank in mud that refused to dry, manacles chaffing where his wrists had so recently healed. The light should have felt good on his face, but it blinded him against the raising of the massive perch. All converts and organizers had gathered, and most helped in one way or the other — some by pushing, some by pulling, most helping to balance the gargantuan structure with rope or pole as it tilted upward. It would only be a temporary sight, Rood made sure to point out to the assembled mob. It had more than one purpose.

Antony squinted through the noon, up to the point where the Greater was crucified, but even the large man was just a speck at this distance. So he instead tried to remember the face of the Prince — a face so clear, so sudden in the cellar — but it refused to come. Dogs of indecipherable breeds fought near him for legs of meat from unrecognizable creatures. He was dried, spent, yet still his mouth was able to water at the drifting warmth of the numerous bread chimneys.

XXXIII

Chubby arms and legs mounted on a scrapped twig framework. Tiny fingers impaled on tree needles to spread them wide like the petals of some fleshy flower. Disembodied feet planted firmly in the oily dust of the rock shelter to hold the obscene sculpture up. It had toppled already, and leaned stiffly against the curved wall of pictographs. The shelter was cursed now. The next generation would not stop here. The future migration would stay clear of this valley, maybe even this land, once the tale of what they have found here would get passed along. Generation? Future? These were concepts Mew had only so recently taught to the Sunflower People. And it looked to be all in vain. For this was the clan's future scattered in the macabre shrine. This was the final generation dismembered and held together by sinew and stick. Seeing all the limbs only made Mew realize how far the clan had come in recent seasons. So many babes. Now all butchered in the course of what? One light? That was how long she and the males of the clan had been scouting. The Sunflower People were now babeless, all because of her insistence on searching for a new way out of the valley.

Their stores had been plundered as well, reed baskets torn to find a season of corns and smoked meats. It could be a long time before they came upon fire again — if ever. She would have liked to have taken one last look at the walls of rock, the scrapings and paintings of sons and fathers and grandfathers, but could not bear to look past the sculpture again, could not clear her eyes of the fall of water. Her eyes would be shadowed to this site forever, and, after coming upon what the thalls had done to the clan's babes, she wanted to be shadowed to everything.

Mew ran from the shelter, trying desperately to find the sun, but there was a reason why her people always moved on during this season. She had to completely climb out of the ravine to find rays of pink light permitted by the trees. Slog Sabbaoth warmed her light skin, and she called to it, asking how it could allow something like this to happen. For it would be her responsibility to explain this to the clan. It was her duty to justify the strange and evil of the world to those who had adopted her. She prayed to the light to shadow her eyes to all future looks like that of the grim sculpture, but the water in her eyes protected them against the shine. She prayed for Heaven's vengeance against the thalls but knew her clan would have to move soon against their encroachment. She prayed for answers but knew they would have to come from within. Slog Sabbaoth was a quiet god.

She prayed to the light all evening, heading only back into deeper woods by the time it started to sink from Heaven. She was exhausted by the sadness. Her face was soft from the water. She had lost all her sound.

Mew found the males scattered in the shadows, their dark skin blending into the shelter, the trees, and the black dirt of the forest bed. Some picked apart the sculpture with touching gentleness, collecting the little limbs in a large hide spread on the rock floor. Others had already dug a large ditch for the burial. It would not need to be much larger. The rest of the babes' bodies were missing. Taken with the females? The rest of the family she could hear from the shadows. They lamented the loss of those same females. She suddenly quickened her pace, frantically searching the camp. She had forgotten all about, besides herself, the only remaining females traveling with the family — the thall guests — but she quickly found them. Their skin was almost as light as her own and easy to pick out among the trees. She found the three females, bloated at different stages of babeswell, with one suckling what had so suddenly become the only remaining babe of the clan — if the males would now accept it. Mew would have to convince them that the stocky fire-haired pup was now Clan Sunflower's only chance. But it looked like they would not take much convincing. The few males that were not preparing the burial had descended upon the thall females. Some stroked the fiery hair on their heads and bellies. Some enjoyed their warmth. They had even untied them from their bonds. While Mew could hear other males back at the shelter grunting calls for war, these had already embraced their future.

She stepped back into the clamor of the main camp. The family's dogs barked with the rising voices of the males. They called for vengeance and for stealing back their females. Black eyes were subsumed by the forest in a way the males' calls were not. It was a camp of teeth and foot stomping. It was all Mew knew for most of the night until she woke at sudden silence. The teeth neared and steps approached, and she could only assume they waited on the word of Slog Sabbaoth. In her entire life with the clan she had never learned their language, had never been able to speak their grunt and mumbles, yet she always understood in times like this. And they always understood her. It was her they listened to when she told them Slog Sabbaoth wanted them to find a new path out of the canyons, and, despite their concerns, it was her they listened to when she told them to take the captured thall females with, leaving their own females and babes at the rock shelter. Yet they still looked to her for guidance, with her strange eyes and light skin that had separated her from the rest of the family.

In the shadow-time, when Slog Sabbaoth held no sway over the land, she could not see about the camp, and she thanked the sleeping light for its absence. For she knew the near carnage had not been buried yet. Still, her mind's eye could not forget the sight of the pieces of the little ones, all of which she had held near at some point over the last few seasons. They had been the hope of the Sunflower People. Babes had a scent not found anywhere else in the world. She knew this somehow. She was already forgetting the scent amongst the near carnage, and she hated the thalls for that, and she hated herself and Slog Sabbaoth above for ever thinking there could be peace among the clan and the thalls. Water ran her face again at the thought of the babes torn apart by their large hands and protruding teeth, at the thought of the clan's females taken away under their large blue eyes. How could such hatred and anger exist in the world? Evil and anger that could construct such a bloody sculpture? But she knew the answer without asking the gods. Where did the thalls learn the art of desecration? It was from her.

~

Mew pressed the ant to the thall's thigh. It immediately bit down, pincers shrinking the wound. She looked to the thall's pale features, expecting a flush to come to his broad face or a cringe to his tiny jaw, but the creature did not even register the pain. It just rambled, quacking out to the sparse forest and the sandy edges of the creak now running red from the bodies of clan and thall. She looked to the few remaining of her clan to see if they objected to her use of her medicine on the thall, but they paid no attention. They just wandered, tending to their own injuries and collecting any female survivors of pale or dark skin. After the fight they had even less excuse to be selective. They gathered both red and black haired, full-bellied or soon to be full-bellied.

She put another ant to the thall's cut, cringing at the sight when he did not. As with the rest, she twisted the body off, leaving only its head and clenched pincers. The wound was wrinkled and closed tightly. It no longer bled. She considered using the last of her clay to cover the thall's thigh but instead moved on to a female of her own clan. They hugged and the female rubbed her head against Mew's. It had been almost a full moon's waning since they had seen each other. She had been one of the family's females to have been taken most recently, but she looked healthy, even fattened, since Mew had seen her last. All the animals the thalls must have fed her did her well. She looked more the woman than Mew remembered. But her arm near the elbow was bent disturbingly, and so Mew gave her the last of the whyroot to chew on as she examined it. The area was many different colors, all of them dark, and Mew turned and pressed the arm as closely to normal as she could against the female's protests, before scooping the last of her clay from the last of her pots. She applied it gently and evenly around the arm and blew on it to hasten its drying. Would there be more of the red muds outside of the valley? Did the ruddy ants live in other areas as well? It did not matter, for the pressure urging her to take the clan from the valley had become overpowering. Were the visions coming from Slog Sabbaoth? Did it matter? There was a world outside the valley, and she was determined that it was her shrinking clan's only hope. She began to gather the few males left, mostly those of her clan. They were covered in the tattoos of their families — the colorful feathers of Slog Sabbaoth standing out from the dark of their hair and eyes. The markings could barely be made out on their skin, but the scratches from the fight appeared in the dying light, wounds made from many of the thall males Mew now gathered. They crouched sheepishly, pressing large hands against an equal number of cuts from the fight, but answered her summons, blue eyes only following her, avoiding the angry gaze of the clan. It would be an uneasy journey out of the valley, and Mew had doubts as to her ability to quell violence, but for now clan and thall looked too exhausted, to hungry to fight further. She hoped the dwindling number of females and their protection would keep the aggression at a minimum, but feared it might do the opposite.

Morning came early for both family and thall. Without a fire or trust to warm them, Mew led them up and out before the light had risen. Many had stayed up all night to bury the dead. Surprisingly to Mew, even some of the thalls had dug graves. Whom had they learned the ritual from? Did Slog Sabbaoth speak to them too? Had they been divinely directed to follow her?

They had climbed out of a lower canyon by the time the light rose to warm them, yet the clan still covered themselves in furs. With furry chests and backs, the thalls had no need to cover themselves in animal skins, but Mew caught the males covering both clan and thall females with any extra skins as they headed back into the tree growth leading out of the valley. She found paths leading through a canyon of almost blindingly white rock. The sky's light shone through and around it, the great orb seemingly suspended by the asymmetrical cliffs they walked beneath. Mew was the only one to notice the prints going in both directions in the dust. None were from any of the boots associated with any clans. She would have been more than surprised to find any, but some matched the broader, flatter look of thall feet. The passage floor was filled with the prints of some almost round-footed creature. The grooved heels were by far the most numerous of markings. Side by side they led the new family through, into a much brighter world.

The trees were not as tight out of the valley. The air was bluer and the grasses thicker, and as the light rose over their passage they saw an abundance of animals while they walked the dipping fields of golden flowers and luscious clover. The rabbits were skittish but numerous, and it was not long before one of the clan had killed one with a sling. As the rabbit was being skinned, one of the male thalls brought a speared deer into the hungry ring, where the females of the clan showed the female thalls how to prepare it. It was quickly torn and separated and pieces were shared. Few of the thalls accepted it without a look of distaste. Even the hunter refused his portions, but he brought the collar to Mew that he had found around the deer's neck. It was encrusted with pieces of hard ice, clear stones that revealed colors and shapes she had never seen outside of her dreams. The ice did not melt as she rubbed it. The strange designs and sharp shapes did not reveal their meaning as she tried to decipher them.

Mew pressed them on through the night, and no one, thall or clan, complained. Even the females, their different degree of bloated bellies slowing them, welcomed the walk. No one, not even Mew, knew what they fled or to where they headed, but they all had her same sense of urgency. Out of the valley and canyons the light was abundant. They could find it anywhere, at any time of the day. Even the clouds could not contain it. The night had been short, and a horizon had glowed in some direction throughout it. They had never to fear the darkness again in this new world.

The first wall they came upon was barely recognizable as such. It would have been easily mistaken for the fall of a cliff had it not been for sturdier lengths that had survived for time. Even so, some of the clan had stepped over it to continue the walk. Mew stopped them to collect smaller stones. The wall was mostly head-sized rock with smaller pieces used to fill gaps and top it off. She stood in the light as both clan and thall sat to strike stone against stone, flaking away pieces to replace the worn heads of spears. Female thalls watched as scrapers and points slowly emerged from the rock. The material was softer than Mew expected, and as she sat on a low point of the wall to pressure flake one of the larger rocks, it was not long before she gave up. She had hoped to at least make a couple of awls to work any new skins they carried, but one look at the frustration on the rest of the clan told her it was already time to move on.

The afternoon wore on, and they came to the edge of the forest and to another wall. This one was recognized as such immediately. It too had fallen to disrepair as well. The stone was darker than the previous project, carved into brick of similar sizes. It was taller than any male in her group, but the stone was uneven enough that they could easily climb over it. Grasses and struggling tree shoots grew from the dirt that had collected in the crevices on the topmost brick. The males of the clan, angered at the example of the thalls, climbed up and down the wall to help any of the fattened females.

Mew was content to wait for the others to climb, drinking from the green dew of the wall's shade, proud in resisting the urge to see the view from the top, but commotion brought her to her feet. She hurried her climb, at both clan and thalls' prompting. Each step crumbled under doe-skin slipper. Each elbow and knee scraped in her speed. Males both light-skinned and dark pulled her up as she reached the top.

The ground on the other side of the wall was higher, and Mew landed softly in greener grasses and the full brilliance of the sky. She forgot Slog Sabbaoth in the warmth, saw the light only for the color it gave her skin, only for its calming effect as it combined with a breeze that moved the hair from her forehead before caressing her face. She followed the shouts of her clan and the quacks of the thalls to look over the rolling hills spread now out before her. Small clustered groves and the occasional lone tree stood out in the pastures, but it was yet another wall that took her attention. It went from horizon to horizon, and the blessed light of the sky leaned toward it. They could reach it before the light did if they hurried.

Old and young tree stumps slowed their walk as they neared. For most of the walk the wall ahead appeared uniform, perfect in shape and light color, but it darkened in patches the closer they stood. The brick, although smoother and symmetrical, still showed periodic flaws. But there was no chance of the clan climbing it. If any of the males had a chance he would he caught on the shining spears of the beings walking the top of the high structure.

They too shined, with what she first thought was skin reflecting the setting light's glow from bronze and golden flesh. But beneath the reflection, she saw men striding the wall, from tower to tower, paying no attention to her people. Bathed in the sun, shaded in her own shadow, was someone who watched them however. Mew had to wait until the sun set enough to blur the shadows before she could meet the woman's eyes, and she felt dirty beneath the green glare. Mew was suddenly aware of the dirt that had accumulated over the journey out of the valley, the dust that darkened her skin, the mud that had dried to her face and colored her hides and slippers.

God Empress Mew looked down into the preserve, viridescent eyes holding flecks of the sunset as she turned fully away from it. She had ended many a day with a walk on the wall, overlooking the animals and exotic vegetation, but had never seen the likes of the gathering she now espied. They were filthy, and she was certain she could smell them even from the distance. One, beneath a rabbit-skin hood had ebon hair like her own, but the creature was as dirty as her followers. There were no other similarities. She was the only one that had not escaped her collar — a diamond studded piece that still shimmered despite the deepening shadows of the wall.

XXXIV

his first line — code-named Generation One — will consist of the main characters and the Tower of the Lich Action Playset. Certain figures will come packaged with glow-in-the-dark miniature figures of spirit goblins, while others'll come with…"

"Um, yeah, about that, the research team has found that the terms 'spirit' and 'heaven' and some others haven't tested well with certain segments of a more fundamental audience."

"What about 'ghost' goblins?"

"I like it. People love alliteration. Doesn't sound too offensive. Ghosts have been inoffensive for years now."

"Let's use the Army of 'Paradise' instead of Army of 'Heaven.' That'll be nice and safe."

Janus had sat back down and now just stared out the window wall. The meeting was the culmination of months of work. The long table was populated by management he had only heard of, never seen before. This was supposed to be his time to shine. But it had soured almost immediately. He had barely started the presentation before the questions had begun, before his research had been ignored, before his weeks spent justifying rationales had been overruled by "intuition" and anecdotes.

"I don't understand this one," said a man at the end opposite Janus. His suit was excessively threaded with gray lines matching a thin tie, making the man appear excessively vertical. The suit was no more well-made than the simple dark one Janus wore, yet he had no doubt it cost at least three times as much and would be worn three times as less. The manager would quickly move on to next season's style, while Janus would wear his suit over the course of the next year. Yet even in such an expensive suit the man still just looked like anyone else on the street. Above the ivory collar and studded button clips was still just the fat face of Janus' butcher. He saw him every Sunday in his haste to finish the grocery shopping before the game.

The man continued with an exaggerated look of confusion on his face, folding out the bat wings of a feminine figure. He held up packaging toward Janus. "It says 'angel,' but it looks like some sort of demon."

"Um," Janus' partner stuttered. He had taken the presentation over when Janus had sat down and become unresponsive. "The packaging is still in the mock-up stage. We're still open to suggestions."

Janus' chair caught the carpet as he stood, and it fell back loudly.

He ignored it to walk around the table to the window wall. Everyone watched him instead of his partner's continuation of the presentation.

"So, the uh, the action figures will launch at the same time as the new editions of the books, with the new covers, with um, new covers depicting scenes from the movie. The new trailer premieres the Friday before…"

"Can we not do something about the name?" another manager interrupted. Janus knew who spoke without turning around. He could tell by the congested voice. It was the same voice of the Sub Priest. He looked like him too. Janus had noticed as soon as the meeting had started. They both had the same capillaried nose squeezed by dun cheeks. "I mean, what does 'Ragnarock' even mean anyway?" He became louder as others assented. "Kids aren't going to know what that means. We need something catchier, in my humble opinion. We've all been talking about this. Something like 'Guardians of the Winter Wolf.'"

"Or 'Twilight of the Giants,'" someone else said. The room nodded loudly.

Janus sneered out at the city, grinding his teeth. Some in the office said it was easy to imagine they were above the clouds up here, above the grand metropolis of Beulah, looking down at the pink smog settled between buildings. Was this Heaven to them? Air-ships sank and rose between high-rise buildings. The pink sun of noon highlighted ruby glass windows of the Sub Temple where his priest spoke, every Sunday morning, before Janus rushed to gather groceries, before the game. It was only a city satellite church, yet still the winged tower peeked above any other skyscraper, peaked with the dazzling perch reminiscent of the main temple standing offshore on the Holy Island. This near church was where the Sub Priest sang, although Janus could have sworn he now heard his off-tune warbling from the table behind him. He turned from one window wall to look over management at another, and then out into the cuboxes of the office floor. The manager that now spoke reminded him of a cube-mate. He scanned the office but did not see him near the commons area he frequented. Both men wore their hair differently but had the same crinkled brow and small hands. Janus' cube-mate could have never afforded the ascot and pins the manager adjusted as he spoke.

"For what it's worth, I feel we need to diversify some of these guys." He posed The Warrior between cups of perk. The figurine was grotesquely top heavy and was rumored to have been remolded after several stages of testing to ensure it could stand upright on its own. Its legs were formed in a permanent squat. One hand had fingers spread wide while the other was giving a "thumbs up," ready to grasp any of its seven included colorful weapons. The Warrior was expected to be the *Ragnarock* line's biggest seller. "Let's make more versions. How about 'Battle Armor' Warrior, or Warrior with 'Kicking Swimming Action'?" He tried to stand The Assassin figure up, but the over-sized felt cloak tipped it on its side. "And how about this guy? Doesn't he have any weapons? How about space? Give him moon explorer gear."

"This is good," Janus' partner said, "we can work with this. We'll take this…"

"No." Janus walked under the conference room's eyes and took The Warrior and The Assassin from the table. "This is a marketing meeting, not a development conference. All these decisions have already been made. There was plenty of time to discuss any of this over the past year. We're here to discuss the launch."

His partner adjusted his penmote and the display behind him changed accordingly. It now showed a calendar of the following year. "We, uh, the Second Phase, er, Generation will roll out in anticipation, or to drum up interest in the second movie, pre-titled *Die by the Word*. These will consist of the Viking werewolf Playformers and…"

"Those should come out first," management said. "Much more dynamic, extreme. Interaction is what sells. My kid would love them."

"Well, the ah, the designers haven't even started looking at the second, um, the Second Phase yet. First roll-out is next month."

"We can use existing molds though. My nephew loves werewolves. Let's just tweak these…"

"No!" Janus slammed both fists on the table. Cups of perk in every shape and design shook and dribbled. "Research first, then development. We're past all this. We did the homework, we made the decisions, we move on. What's best for the project is to stick to the timeline and the decisions based on the research."

The manager at Janus' hip had been playing with The Gunslinger figure. Activating its quick-draw action over and over, each time setting off its voice chip. "How many different things does he say?"

Another manager spoke up, saying in a familiar voice, "That's just being unnecessarily inflexible. If new data has appeared we have to adapt…"

"So-called 'intuition' and stories about someone's cousin are not new information. They mean nothing compared to the focus groups." The Gunslinger at his side continued to click away, swinging ridiculously sized and colored blasters.

"Ah'm the sheriff now, bird-brain!"

"We've already approved the overtime. People are always asking for it."

Another manager was turning over the packaging. "Where does it say if it's a good guy or a bad guy? How will they know if it's a good guy or a bad guy?"

"Better put yer affairs in order, clown!"

"Have you even read the books?" Janus asked, looking only down at how the slight streams of perk turned to match the grain of the dark oak. The table was more expensive then all the possessions in his conapt combined.

"I don't have to," the manager said amidst the nodding of those surrounding him, "that's what the movie'll be for." They all laughed together.

"Ah'm call'in ya out, wizard!"

The Gunslinger bounced off the window wall from Janus' swing.

A manager stood opposite Janus, shaking the perk from a sleeve. "Alright, things are getting a bit heated, in my humble opinion. Let's table this discussion and reconvene in a week. Everyone make sure to check their messes by the end of the day for the notes and new schedule." Amidst nodding heads he said, "Let's talk lunch."

Janus just stared at the table between his fists as the managers stood, while his partner scrolled through the unused slides of the presentation. The shifting colors of the panel were drowned out by the candied sun of one wall, the fluorescent gleam of the other. He had the light of three different worlds upon him. None of it felt natural, all of it artificial. It flickered on his back like acid rain, on one side like molten plastic, on the other like a shroud of cardboard. Faces passed his peripheral as they sauntered out of the conference room. He had met few, yet they all seemed familiar. If he had not passed them in Central Park, he had graduated institute with them, played armball with them, or fed them at a highchair. Sometimes he felt like he knew everybody in the city of Beulah, sometimes everyone seemed the stranger. But this feeling was something new. Something in-between.

His partner was humming a tune that seemed familiar, but Janus could not place it. Was it from church? It became something else as he finished collecting his stills in a binder, and it had devolved into chaos by the time that he interrupted himself. "We'll have to find out if they're going to update development or if we have to. If they're going to halt the Skeletrain figure carrier assembly… yeah, they'll want to know as soon as possible. We'll have to consider this as we would a compressed timeline, but maybe the swapping out will just balance itself. Individual for individual. Line for line. I suppose we couldn't be that lucky. We better update the studio. They didn't ask for it this time, but the whole RonRon's promotion is going to have to be overhauled. I'll put a stop on the ads. This revisionary plan better come with a budget adjustment. There's no way they'll get it to us by the end of the day. We'll be lucky if we…"

"None of this matters," Janus muttered.

"What?"

"None of this is real."

"I know, I know. It'll all come together in the end, before the movie. I'm not worried. We'll all laugh out loud together, remembering how stressed out we were. In the big scheme of things this setback'll mean nothing." The partner gathered the last of his materials and up-righted a chair before heading to the glass door. "When are you visiting the set? Saturday? Lucky bastard. Get me some autographs."

Janus' partner had always reminded him of his uncle. He even looked like him. He was a chameleon — strong when he needed to be, but he found a purposefulness in weakness that Janus could not relate to. He had learned nothing from either of them — his partner or uncle. Where was his uncle now? When was the last time he had even thought of him? Did he even exist when he did not think of him?

He loosened his tie and gathered up The Warrior and The Assassin. Where was The Gladiator? It was nowhere in the room. Had someone taken it? He suddenly had a difficult time remembering if it had even passed the development phase. Why could he not remember if it had even been approved for the first phase? The two figures in his hands had been molded from completely different sculpts, with The Assassin's lean form hidden beneath a ridiculously voluminous cloak that would probably be discarded the first time it was played with. Neither figure had their Action Voice Chips installed yet, but Janus listened to the toys nevertheless.

Outside, amongst the cuboxes, the hive swarmed in pre-feeding preparation, squirming around the communal printer and bathrooms, buzzing the cells, and pairing up over papers and posterboards. Management had migrated together to the break area. The pollen of artificial cream settled on tables and unused chairs. He could feel an eye stray periodically upon him as they rotated between expressions both serious and forcibly jocular. The glass into the conference room had gone pink from the outside light, but the sun could not penetrate into the equalizing gleam of the office.

Janus stormed from the conference room. Management had circled. They all spoke at once and took turns glancing in his direction between laughter.

"...so I laughed out loud, and I said, 'That's why it's called a demographic not a graphic demo.'"

"You catch last night's episode of 'You Got Tooted On!'?"

"I just feel it's gone the way of the direct mail piece, in my humble opinion, like, when's the last time you ever opened one?"

"I would never buy it, so how can I expect anyone else to?"

"I showed him the results from the focus groups, and we've been on the right track all along. What a waste of time."

Janus thought he had left the figurines in the conference room, but they were still in his hands — The Warrior in his right, The Assassin in his left. He placed them on top the nearest cubox where they stood on their own, half hidden in the vines of some cube mate's houseplant. They watched as he loudly gathered and tossed chairs from the break area. He stacked and pushed but management stayed engrossed in their own discussions.

"So I'm thinking of this new place downtown, they wrap everything in bacon."

"Oh, I really shouldn't, I just shouldn't, but I will, just for today."

"My wife would kill me, but as long as we're on this side of the city we should take advantage of it. It really has the bloodiest steaks, in my humble opinion."

They only looked after Janus had flipped a table to push it across the area, bulldozing any chairs left in the process. He had opened up a clear ring that included only himself and management. The final table was thrown aside as the managers quieted to stare.

"Who?" he yelled, moving to the cabinets and counter. "Who represents?" he asked, grabbing the fogged pitcher of perk, swinging it to ward off the cube mates that neared to check on the commotion. "You!" he yelled, throwing glass against glass. Liquid the color of diarrhea streamed among clear shards behind the heads of the crouching management. He grabbed a manager by a stiff collar and pulled him backward into the clearing. It was the only man who did not remind Janus of someone, although now that he had a clear look at him, he had the same hairline as one of the professors at his daughters' school. He wore his glasses as low on his nose.

Cube mates and managers stared from all directions. None spoke, but Janus could hear their tacit encouragement. Most cheered for him, few for his opponent. He took his tie off and, after considering its use as a whip or entangler, tossed it over an adjacent cubox wall. His opponent's eyes watered as his shoes — as reflective as the break area's floor, failed to gain purchase. The tight shoulders of his suit jacket tore audibly as he reached back to accidently pull an interlocking pile of chairs down into the ring. The sound brought the rest of the office to peek over and out of their cuboxes like prairie dogs alerted to the scream of a hawk.

"You betray all you've learned and all you've taught," Janus said, speaking to the huddled managerial mass, as well as to the man he pulled the chair from. The manager had been warding him off with it, but was now beaten below its legs and hard plastic seat. "You let feelings get in the way of your judgment, emotion to drive your motives. But there's no room for any of that here. There is only the game. The game above all else." He stepped back, breathing almost as frantically as his opponent, swinging the uneven weapon in his hands to the silent applause of the cuboxes.

His opponent staggered to his feet, reaching in all directions for a handhold before falling under a flittering cloud of papers he had kicked up. The lilting net floated about him, but he again tilted to his feet. With a burst of panicked speed he surged toward his group of huddled companions but found an unbreachable mound of polyester and flesh.

The chair was tossed like a trident between the manager's legs, and the man was down again. Janus removed his suit jacket and shirt, speedily pulling at buttons as he approached his opponent. With bare chest he lifted the man onto his shoulders, his exertion the only sound in the office beneath the man's groans. But no, that was not true, for the entire audience had now turned to Janus' side. They called for no more mercy.

Heavy steps took him out of the clearing, past tumbled table and scattered sugar packets. He got caught up in the doorway to the conference room, and, with one big push, he was through, bending his beaten opponents legs and neck in ways they were not supposed to break. Exhaustion suddenly caught up with him, and he swayed and ran around the room-length table. When he could feel himself tripping he pushed with the energy he had left to toss the manager at the geometric skyline. For a split-second the man blocked the filtered sunset as he hit the glass. Janus looked down, deep sighs failing to cool his blood, at the sprawling man and the unmarked window-wall before him.

~

He reduced the volume and let more of the scene play out before pausing the movie on an image of the actress' face. His hand stretched and tightened into a fist without him realizing it, but the pain in his knuckles broke his stare from the viewall. Sometime during the battle in the break area, Janus had scraped his hand. They were only a bunch of very superficial scratches, but who knew what kind of infection he could get from the offices.

It took few steps to cross to the faucet room, but his small conapt was all he needed. It was crowded when the girls stayed but he found the close quarters comforting. It was still luxury compared to the cells in Below the Brook.

He froze, the water automatically running at his approach. *Below the Brook.* He had heard those words before. Where? And why did they appear now? As quickly as they had entered his mind they had left. It was a strange sensation — this nostalgia for the unreal. It was as though he was remembering some movie from his youth, some story he was too young to understand or appreciate at the time but struck some chord in his present world.

He rinsed the minor wounds and lightly scrubbed them with antis. As he dried them, careful not to stain the towel, he found something pale and dried to his cuticles. Something he had not noticed until now. Turning his hands he found more of the substance cracked and caked to one palm. He had somewhere picked up some sort of mortar on his hands.

Back in the mainroom, he walked past a freshly bricked-up wall to fall back onto the vinylounge. The viewall resumed playing the movie at his command, this time muted as he picked up The Assassin from the perk table. He straightened the puffy cloak and bent three of the figure's limbs to hide them within the fabric. He left one arm out, snapping a thin flat plastic sword into its rigored hand.

"I bet you think I should have gone a sneakier path. Should have bided my time, taken down management from behind the scenes, stabbed them in the back, somehow sabotaged the campaign from the inside. I could've messed with survey numbers, I guess, they would have never known." He set the figure down to pick up The Warrior. The Assassin fell over and out of sight.

"So I was too showy for you. Should have just felled him with one blow and moved on to the next enemy." Janus knew his inability to break the window wall was a disappointment, but all glass in the Beulah's skyrises had been reinforced after the massive trend of suicides a few years back. The Warrior's empty rubber head glared at him from under a heavy brow and painted sneer.

The Warrior figurine dropped to the floor, and Janus returned to watching the viewall. It was one of his least favorite movies starring her, although that still made it one of his favorite flics. He had always thought the role was beneath her. The story up to this point was ridiculously fantastical. He was at the part where she had been hiking for days, catering to Neanderthals and troglodytes. Her alabaster skin was speckled with dirt yet her ebony hair was flawlessly sculpted and even. The unreality was ridiculous. She was completely out of place among the setting. He could not wait to see her in person. The anticipation was eating him alive.

He paused it again on her face at a scene where she finally emerged from a tree line and the light struck her across the face. He zoomed in slowly, closer and closer, until just her eyes showed. By Monday the entire office would have heard how he was chosen to represent the campaign at the studio's wrap party. Their jealously would be bittersweet. On one hand he would savor their congratulatory tone, but on the other they would just be a distraction. He had work to do. So much needed to be done to abide by the new timeline. And, really, the chance to meet her was nothing new to him. It had been inevitable for as long as he could remember. It was destined. The actions to set in place their eventual meeting had begun long ago, evolving over time, moving the pieces around to set in motion both his and her appearance in the same place at the same time.

One of her eyes was dark in shadow, the other exposed to the light. He continued to zoom in. She was famous for the green of her eyes, but no one knew her like he did. He appreciated her in ways no one else did. The iris filled his entire wall by the time he froze the image. If you looked closely enough, only he knew, you could see the golden treasure embedded deep within the forest. Only he had noticed. Only he had spent the time looking for the color. He was unique in that way, and she would appreciate that.

XXXV

Death of days and sun told in bare whispers
beet-stained teeth bound by beard of bear whiskers
For adoring death is prophet's profit
adorning Armageddon's love vomit

—The Fallo Terminus (XXXV)

Wulf had taken a break from searching the buildings to wash his clothes again at a fountain. This one held even less water than the first, being that it was placed out in the open, in full view of the sun. The fountains in the deeper avenues kept the shade better to stay wetter, or perhaps they were funded by more prosperous springs. This sun-bleached fountain though, with its smaller trickle of water, was more musical, the tiny spouts and streams arcing and falling in whispering lullabies. It was as quiet as the rest of the city, in which only the sound of slow deep breathing could be heard, and only if one listened very, very closely. It was in this focus he thought of the Other, whoever it was that pushed against his telepathic blocks. The outside pressure had grown during the walk to Erebus. The Other neared, apparently, or Wulf's mental barriers weakened. Either way, the pulsing push against his mind was increasing daily.

The slight spring was exactly no more than he needed. He had earlier in the morning already washed the larger spots of sludge from his clothes and now only needed to scrub the areas he had missed, while wetting his boots and other articles that would probably never entirely become clean again. The drainage shaft they had crawled through had, for the most part, been dry, but it was long, and he and Slayd had most certainly walked through something wet at its darkest points.

Wulf had already hung his cloak to dry on one of the fountain's outcroppings. When placing it he noticed a part of the sculpture unseen until up close. Tiny suckers had been carved toward the end of what was once a watery design. Parts of the marble had been chipped away, turning the spouting scene into a mass of tentacular clubs. Now, instead of being cradled by a uplifting cascade, the pupiless cherubic babe at the fountain's summit was being lifted to Heaven by some sort of pseudopodia.

A new sound brought his attention to the far top of Erebus' wall. The thunder that had disturbed the city's slumber had quieted hours ago, the storm that poured outside was already forgotten, yet he assumed the sound could be nothing else. But now he saw the specks of people making up a crowd that, even from this distance, he could tell struggled with the raising of a massive perch. Outside or inside Erebus, Wulf knew he could not overstate the majesty of those walls — if they could even be described as such. They were something new, or old, outside of present man's abilities or hubris to replicate. Outside, the earth had been moved for miles around to lead up to them, and the walls still jutted above another twenty feet. On the inside they housed identical apartments from ground to the summit, rounding the heptagonal interior. From what he could see, it must have been quite a struggle for the crowd to carry the giant perch up the exterior hills, to somehow have lifted it to the top of the wall. Even from the distance, he could tell they fought to keep it upright, with men pushing and pulling at poles on all sides, yanking and giving with ropes.

He pulled at unseen filaments tickling his ears.

Depending on the angle of the sun, a person inside the city could see similar, but greatly inferior, perches placed at the seven turning points in the wall. They were too small, too distant, to throw the same type of shadow this one now was casting into the interior, but Wulf could see the dark shape of the people hung on each of the scaffolds if he stood at open points in the streets. The building and reverence of perches was relatively new to the land, coinciding with the rise of the Horde, so he had to assume that the complement of stands or bases at the top of the walls were only recently created. The grunts and commands of the mob fell and deteriorated on the winds above the city.

Wulf looked to the surrounding streets, as his clothes dried, to plan the next sweep. Each row of domiciles looked like the last — uniform in their pale colors, their small size and connected interiors. The materials may have been the same as those used in Ophidia, but the architecture was much more utilitarian, simpler in design and, apparently, usage. There were seemingly no governmental buildings in Erebus in Ouroboros, no parks or places of worship — just sections of blocks of rows spreading from each angle of the great wall toward the middle of the city. Here they met at a great heptagonal span of partitioned fields that had once housed all manner of fruit and vegetable. Now, unattended, the crops had all returned to the earth what looked like seasons ago. The wild vegetation overcoming the fields was in stark contrast to the clean residential areas, where neglect kept the identical avenues and short structures pristine. Here, at one of the few breaks in the uniformity, Wulf took up his cloak, kicked his drying boots at the fountain base, and headed back into the stone rows. The distant shouts had disappeared, but he could still see movement from the mob as the perch tilted and swayed. He could now also see that something hung from the crucified figure. Had the crowd looked down into the massive city? Those crucified on the perches had no choice but to do so.

He scratched at strands thin to the point of invisibility. They crossed the path of his face as he headed back down an avenue.

The day was still young, but he had to assume that the days were short in Erebus. The city was large and spread out and open, but the presence of the walls was always there. Did an inhabitant ever forget them? They were always in the peripheral of eye or mind. Shadows would create intricate geometric patterns throughout the streets for most of a day, and the early darkness would make searching even more difficult.

He entered the nearest domicile, slowed by more gossamer threads. Through Yggr's Eye he saw the filaments everywhere, spun to doorways and down streets, stretching from well to window, down alley, into beds, swaying in even the slightest breeze, floating through and over low buildings of the city. With his original eye he saw only the faint glimmer when the light hit the strands just so, and only then if he focused. They were felt more than seen, and only then faintly — as a tickle inside one's ear or the slightest caress against the lips.

Inside the domicile he found what he had been finding in almost every one of the buildings throughout the day. The people of Erebus lived well but simply. The multiple rooms in their homes were all open to each other in a repetition of the pattern of the streets. They held no more furniture or appliance than needed to survive. There was no waste. Nothing was superfluous, and these rooms were as impeccably clean as all the others he had walked. And like many of them, this one also had a sleeping inhabitant.

Wulf guessed that as many as a couple thousand people lived in Erebus – a mix of original denizens and pilgrims that had sometime over the prior year entered the city before it had been closed off to the outside. It was obvious which were which. Here was a pilgrim, cleaned up but still in her mismatched clothes, squatting in what must have been an available structure, fast asleep like all the rest he had found. Any city inhabitant he had come across, whether in the corner of an alley or room of a home, either denizen or pilgrim, could have easily been mistaken for dead. Their breathing was deep and long but almost unnoticeable. Any of them not exposed to the sun were pale as midgardians, and all of them, regardless of age or sex, had the look of starvation in their bodies and faces. The woman he checked now had a steady, if not slow, pulse. She had cheeks not fully emaciated yet. Her mouth was pursed tightly, but it resembled a smile. Through Yggr's Eye, Wulf saw the glimmering gossamer that lighted from window and doorway, all centered on the woman, filling her ears and nostrils, squeezing through her lips and eyelids, and stretching up her pant legs and skirt. Her eyeballs twitched beneath the lids. She was dreaming.

Wulf scratched as new threads that had followed him into the structure probed his nose.

He continued on to the next domicile. Same thing — immaculate home, sparse items, open rooms, this one housing two people slumbering upright in the largest room. Like the apartments built into the inside of the gargantuan walls, and the cubic streets, a rectangular shade was cast around the room. The man's skin was dark out of the shadows. The woman's was light within them. His snowy hair matched the streak splitting her black coif. Their bone-thin limbs embraced each other. Yggr's Eye showed him nothing he did not expect — glittering threads streaming from the street, floating from windows, filling gaping mouths, crowding nostril and pant cuffs. The sight was nothing new, or so he thought until he looked closely. Where the man was warm, the woman was the temperature of the sandstone walls. The man's heartbeat, although almost nonexistent, matched all those Wulf had checked this day, but the woman's was barely existent despite the fact she looked rounded with child. All their lids fluttered with dreams.

Cloak lifting against unseen fibers, he stepped back into the avenue, feeling no closer to his goal than he had that morning. He was, however, closer to the fields of the center of the city. He chewed dried apricots he had found in some earlier home, looking to the high apartments built into the far-off walls. As the day progressed, blocky shadows moved to checker each high rise individually. Did an upper class sleep in those windows, he wondered as he walked past the same old doorways in the same old domiciles down a street undifferentiated from the rest.

He was near the plantations now, the crops withered and lightened to the color of the homes, and the vast gazebo the fields and the entire city revolved around. The more time he spent in Erebus the more he realized the differences between it and Ophidia. They were both such old cities, both aligned to the land Ouroboros, but they had grown quickly in their own ways, with Erebus in the seclusion of its paranoia. Still, it had not been entirely closed off until relatively recently. Did anyone in the outside world know what was happening here?

He was searching another identical dwelling, with another sleeping family, children slumbering in alcoves and shared beds, when a voice brought him back to the main avenue. He looked up the sounds echoing down from the distant crown of the wall, to the stabilizing perch, but it was a closer sound he heard. It had disappeared now, but it had come in the direction of the fields. A stocky figure gestured and gesticulated from the large gazebo, but Wulf could not hear him from the distance. Yet he could hear the figure's scuffling steps ride the breeze across the crinkled crops.

Wulf walked the paths between the dried soil, paths sometimes interrupted by stray seedlings not long for the world. The dirt was brittle and obviously had not seen water in quite some time, its corn and soy bean plants stunted and discolored. It had been years since Phaiman walked the land, since sights like these had been commonplace, and these untended plantations — which had been rumored to have thrived during those unnatural winds — now resembled them in their neglect. Even bugs had long since been unable to find anything of sustenance between the yellowed leaves.

Out in the paths he truly felt the vastness of the fields and, in fact, Erebus itself. Away from the domiciles he could see the walls in all directions wrapping the city. They were covered in a structured pattern of windows and cut evenly by tight switchbacks of staircases. At the top of the walls the smaller perches could barely be seen in the light, as opposed to the giant one now steadied. The sun moved across the sky and Wulf finally neared the wooden structure centered in the plantations. From the walk Wulf could see that Slayd sat in the shade cast on one side of a sunken gazebo. The sorcerer sorted and labeled a collection of vials and jars, tied small ingredient sacks, and made notes in a tiny booklet. He began hiding the objects away in impossible pockets as Wulf approached. Slayd had been ignoring the preacher of the large gazebo.

"…know this now and forever, that there shall come in the End Times, of which we live now and forever, scoffers, walking after their own loves, and crying, 'Where are the Promises?' For since the mothers fell deaf, all things continue as they were from the beginning of the creation. For this they willingly are deaf of, that by the Song the heavens have fallen, and Earth now stands in the clouds. Whereby the world that then was, being so far beneath the lonely Tyrant Titan, whoso only creates for flattery. But the heavens and the earth, which are now, by the same Song are kept as one, reserved unto chill against the close day of judgment and perdition of deaf men… the Divine Choir is not mute concerning the Promises, as some men count dumbness, but is longsuffering toward the land, not willing that any should suffer, but that all should come to repentance. But the day of the Song will come as a molester in the orphanage, in which the autumns shall pass away with a great wind, and the elements shall blanket with fervent storms, the earth also and the works that are therein shall be frozen still. Seeing then that all these things shall be ice, what manner of persons ought ye to be in all goodly conversation and cleanliness, looking for and helping to hasten unto the coming of the day of glory, wherein the heavens being under frost shall be dissolved, and the elements shall still with fervent winds?"

The yawning preacher was a short, stocky man, with loud gestures and expressions, but his words were quiet. Whom he spoke to, Wulf did not know, for even at the downward step leading into the meeting grounds he could barely hear the man's sermon.

"Nevertheless we, according to the Promises, look for new heavens and a new Earth, wherein dwelleth righteousness. Wherefore, beloved, seeing that ye look for such things, be diligent that ye may be found of Slog Sabbaoth in peace, without canker, and blameless."

Slayd stood, following him up the short step into the shade, sighing loudly. "This is where you chose to reconnoiter? If you want to kill me there are less torturous ways to do so." The sorcerer's pale skin appeared to have a blue tint this day under the cloudless sky. Moving into the shade under the giant gazebo's roof, Wulf could no longer see the hive of scales gleaming on his bald head. "He's been ranting ever since before I arrived."

"You found nothing?" Wulf asked, turning to the railings, peering again up to the great new perch and whatever it was that hung from it.

"I didn't find *her*, since that's what you are really asking. And it will take days to properly search the rest of the city, while most of the homes are empty anyway, if they had even ever held any promise."

"There's nothing you can do… to speed up the process?"

"Yes, yes, and why not? I am, after all, the rebellion's trained jackanape."

The preacher continued to speak out on the brick, yawning again, his loud, shuffling steps scraping the ancient floor, kicking up flecks and chips of sandstone that looked to have been undisturbed for generations despite chalk drawings scribbled from one side of heptagonal shape to the other. Wulf put his back to the railing to watch the man. He blocked the sun from reaching into the shade, warming his tousled curls. He had also washed his hair in the fountain, and it felt good to dry his head. The preacher's voice rose and fell with inflection, but was still always quiet. He spoke of a fire soon to come to burn the skin from those with ears too waxed to listen, exposing the insidious sin just under the flesh. He spoke of adulterers, perverts, thieves, and traitors to men and Choir, of the greatest traitor of all — the Shining One, the crawling angel and all He had left behind, introducing sin into the world.

"What game are you playing, Melchyor?"

"Pray tell, whatever do you mean?"

"Antony said something to me… Antony of Lovewell Dam. He wondered how you came to be the Sin Eater…"

"Yes, yes, but remember, everyone wanted Tormalco dead. In that respect I am nothing less than an agent of the land, although I prefer 'agent of change.' You, however, were not supposed to destroy the Tower and all its secrets."

"The secrets of that tower were meant to be buried."

"Nothing stays buried forever." Slayd searched unending space in infinite pockets. "I play the same game as everyone else. Yet at this moment I wonder just how well I play it, for how have I ended up here? Even before being privileged to the bread and beer of the land, I had my pick of litters. I once walked my own floor of the Tower of Gog. Even before that there were songs sung about me…"

"So I've heard."

"…yet here I am, today, scrounging through the dust of a sleeping city for a girl with delusions of grandeur. And you question me on the word of some lesser man? No. No man may question me more than I can myself right now."

The preacher's shuffling steps drew near, scuffing the chalk design of a colorful angel seeding a childlike rendition of Erebus with yellow stars. The angel's head was all pink hair, pinker lips, and baby-blue eyes.

"Yes, yes," Slayd continued, mumbling, "I play a game. As do you. As does this wretched man. The only difference is that I acknowledge that that is all this is. I play with my eyes open. Not like this mad fellow."

"Who is he?"

"His name is Milliam Pittsfield, or so I think I've heard."

Wulf shouted out to him, "Where is the governor of Erebus, Milliam?" For the first time the man paused, with his eyes shifting to the other men for a second. It was then that Wulf first noticed that the preacher's eyebrows were faded tattoos. His beard and the hair atop his head were fake as well, and he straightened both before continuing.

"Now let me ask, if there are no Promises, are not the Theses a faggot of worm-rotted kindling, is not then Schism's *Fallo Terminus* a book of fairy tales and mad myth? Would then Schism, who spoke of the Divine Choir's mercy, be a liar then? If today is not the End Day, does not the Brotherhood deserve to wear the fool's cap? I tell you to walk into the frozen North, outside the city of Bifrost, see the icy sculptures with tears frozen from frozen eyes — where the white bear would lick them and the snow keeps falling. Only the very tops of the trees can yet be seen. This awful reality of Hell on Earth is what awaits the rest of the deaf. It moves south today, today I tell you."

"What is happening here?" Wulf asked Slayd.

"You can see the oral tentacles, the filaments filling the streets and orifices of Erebus?"

"Yes. They grow up through cracks in the sidewalks and from gutters."

"I can only feel them, but I know they're there. They feed the sleeping inhabitants, just enough to keep them alive, while, at the same time, feeding *from* them."

"Seems counter-productive."

"It implies that what the tentacles consume is more valuable than what they are giving back. Nature abhors inefficiency. Better to give it the benefit of the doubt."

"Well, it's not a perfect system, whatever it is. I found one dead citizen."

"As did I. They'll have to be slowly replaced." They both looked up to the distant walls and the perches. "I wonder if those outsiders know they do God's work."

Through Yggr's Eye, Wulf could see cords and bundles of the shining threads arcing up from the city to hang on the crucified. He swiped at his face. The movement had already become a habit even though no feelers were near. In his peripheral he imagined he saw glimmering shapes slinking through dead crop, reaching for the gazebo, but when he looked he saw nothing through either eye.

"Or perhaps this is why we're both here," Slayd continued, "perhaps this is why your Antony was so accommodating in getting us into Erebus."

Milliam Pittsfield neared in his sermon, his boots shuffling loud, his voice high but quiet. Wulf could now see how bloodshot his eyes were. The man's face was purple beneath them. "If today is not the Last Day, is not the *Ashmedai Adat El*, with all its sacrifice and suffering and sacrifice and atoning work, a ship of fools and all the voices thereof a croon of drunken sailors? By every holy kiss of righteous nectar that blessed Schism's body, by every eye which cruel fingers plucked from his head, by every bruise of his face, by every length of burnt flesh, by every mark of the locust upon his back, by every breath he draws which is the pinch of death, by all the leprosy that covers the land and wind that rakes it, we say that if the Promises are unreal, then Schism's pain is in vain!"

"It will take days to search the rest of the homes and the walls," Wulf said.

"Faster without sleep, which I would not recommend, considering."

"There's no descript structures here, nothing to stand out, no temples or mansions, no palaces."

"No, Erebus did evolve on its own, but we are still in Ouroboros. There was most likely a senatus that met in full view of the public, perhaps even here, out in the open. Yes, yes, here they flapped their proud tongues, just like this tired little man, but instead sermonizing the infallible virtues of democracy to an indignant crowd that refused to fully understand its ramifications." Slayd took long slow strides to the center of the brick floor, passing Milliam without a look. "All around, the people listened and complained and then stopped listening but kept complaining. The minority felt entitled and the majority felt victimized. Nobody's a martyr when everyone's a martyr. Everyone whined about the dying plants. Everyone loves a green crop until the color appears on their ears. But they just couldn't get themselves to look to the roots. It was just much easier to whine and bully and threaten with futures than to dig up the root, to sacrifice a season, to criticize the infallible dead elders that first seeded the soil." He knelt, feeling the worn edges of the great stone with fingertip, tracing the great blocks with claw. "If you don't like how the game is played, don't break the players, blame the game." He struck brick with clenched fist. "You have to pull the crop up by the root." He smashed stone again.

Wulf walked toward Slayd as the sorcerer wrenched large hunks of stone up, tossing them across the gazebo, out into the fields. Milliam had suddenly ceased preaching, watching the both of them and yawning. He did not appear to notice how much his eyes watered.

Slayd dug deeper, tossing great pieces of broken sandstone aside. The rock he pulled was now a deeper color. "You wanted to search a structure that stood out from the rest, something beyond the tired monotony of repetitive Erebus? Why not search the pyramid then?"

"This is a pyramid?"

"Oh come now, you have to see with more than just your own eyes. Ha! We are obviously on its bottom, underneath it. Why should a pyramid only point *away* from the center of Earth? Before madmen prophesized our births, before the umbilical cults founded Ouroboros and built this city, before mankind emerged from earthen bowels..." Slayd broke brick and tossed rock with each exclamation. "Before underworlds and machine cities, obsidian gods and ebony skies that drove men into the womb of Earth like Death's litter to eat His mother's entrails, before the eruption of the land, before the golden age of the Old Ones, before the rise of the Americas, before ice crawled and receded over this very land..." He squatted and lifted a final chunk, setting it aside as a plume of moist air blew dust from the dark hole he uncovered. "The Hyperboreans built shrines to the abyss. It is said that the first ape to stand upright used his new height to reach a doorknob, and what he saw on the other side changed his perspective forever. His soul expanded. A hole stretched open in it, and every door we've opened since has filled a little bit of it. But with what? That's the question." He tore petrified wood from the widening hole. It cracked and snapped like stone and skittered over the gazebo floor wherever it was tossed. He pulled earth and root and marble and, eventually, more sandstone brick.

Wulf noticed the green under Slayd's bloody knuckles. "You know she's not down there," he said.

"No," the sorcerer sighed, sitting back, folding his legs, gazing down at the shed skin hanging from his hands, "but *she* is, and that may be the only way we'll find her."

They both shut Milliam's voice out, peering down into a moist darkness even Yggr's Eye could not pierce. "It is vain for you to rise up early, to ponder late, to eat the bread of your thoughts, for so She giveth her beloved sleep to those who hear the Song. Yea, She will not give sleep to your eyes nor slumber to your eyelids, until you too sing the Song of Slog Sabbaoth, the Promise of Dreams."

Wulf stepped back from the wavering air. More than warmth wafted from the shaft. "You first," he said.

"You must be joking. You know I prefer my pleasures second hand. Besides, who am I to lead the great Liege of Foes?"

"I'm not the…" Wulf's voice quickly disappeared as he descended in the light of the shaft. The light was physical, a beam he rode down past a watery darkness churning impenetrably. His cloak was unmoving except for a slight flutter at its bottom tips. His face, now hooded, beaded in the humidity as he lowered himself. His telekinesis pushed against an unseen floor, felt out against uncountable pillars of different gives.

Above, wiping chalk dust from his robes, Slayd looked to the preacher. Milliam's quiet lips continued beneath exhausted eyes and fake beard. "He lay down and slept beneath the ash, because the sun had set on mankind, and he took one of the stones of the place and put it under his head, and lay down in that place. He had a dream, and behold, a ladder was set on Earth with its top reaching to Heaven, and behold, the angels of God were ascending and descending on it, and behold, there was an angel touching him, and She said to him, "Arise and eat, but if you lie down, you will not be afraid, when you lie down, your sleep will be sweet. But if you arise, do this, knowing the time — that it is already the hour for you to awaken from sleep, for now salvation is nearer to you than you once believed. The night is almost gone, and the day is near, therefore lay aside the deeds of darkness and put on the armor of light." Slayd stared at him from cloudy eyes until the man started to stammer under the gaze. "Come to Slog Sabbaoth, all you who are weary and burdened, and She will give you sleep. Close your eyes and learn from Her, for She is gentle and humble in dream, and you will find rest for your minds. In Her Promise is eternal dream, infinite respite from inherent sin and toil of the world."

Slayd grinned to reveal a pied smile and one nasty fang, and Milliam tripped backward over scattered stone and his own staff. "What are you?" he whispered.

"I am the Revealer," hissed Slayd, "he who clears the cataracts, he who pulls the curtain aside, lifts the veil, brushes the dust of ages. And who are you? Or more importantly, who would you like to be?"

"I… have… heard…" the preacher stammered. His wig had turned and the dark circles above his cheeks hid behind new bangs.

Slayd took up the staff and strutted in mock display of Milliam's earlier steps. "There are only two surviving to have seen the breaking of the Abyssmal Seal. One resides in the warfront, in his mobile city of Phaeton, and he is not talking. One came to this city months ago, and hasn't been heard from since. How would you like to be one of the chosen few, Mr. Pittsfield?" The staff swung and pointed. "How would you like to bear witness to the breaking of the Seal of the Seventh Day?"

"I… have waited… I've guarded the dreamers…"

"Steady your vision for divine light. Your faith will keep you from blindness." The staff cracked against Milliam's crown and the man slumped forward into his own lap. Snoring was almost immediate.

Slayd walked the edge of the gazebo, reaching his hand out to the light. The sun moved almost perceptibly toward the western wall of Erebus. He walked it like the hand of a clock, tasting the air at each of the corners. "You are certainly out there, my lady, but where? We just do not have the time to look. So, once again, the burden falls upon yours truly to force the hands of gods."

He dragged his feet to the intersection of the seven corners, smearing a candied angel showering a litter of cherubs with pixie dust from her breasts. Into the shaft he stepped, appearing at the bottom to greet Wulf. The only sound left in Erebus was still the sound of Milliam. His snore was loose and uneven over the fallen crop.

Invisible filaments snaked and wound through dried husk and shriveled bean toward the gazebo.

...the Warrior moves to their tune, his thoughts ever-bound and so caught—scrawled on the walls of the King of All's lower halls

I f for no other reason than to stop the nagging, Easarean, after days spent enduring as much of the icy ocean as he could, flew back to the prairies surrounding the dark hollow. She had promised to be silent as the ship scanned the melting plains, but it was not long before the sensors picked up humanoids walking the fields to the west, and not long before she spoke up.

"It's him! One of them is a clan match! We may be saved yet. You can thank the gods!"

It was true, he noticed on the holoplays. One of the three did have an Aertlantean protein structure. He feared flying too close or too high to get a clear look for the vidscreen, and so he stayed far away to the horizon.

At the parapsyte's nagging insistence, Easarean watched the three from afar over the following weeks as they walked the plains in a spring that lasted only days.

"We must learn who these friends of his are. Are they a threat? Could they be our allies? Aren't you curious, my love?"

"No."

Winter was not through with the prairie yet, and it came back with a vengeance Easarean was thankful he had the warmth of the ship for. He worried at times that the cousin would not survive the elements out in the open, but he and his new companions continued to trudge toward the island in the plains — the black hills looming far and ominously to the west. With the land again covered in snow, the silhouette swallowed all the light at the horizon, and the cousin headed toward it as a star toward a singularity, bending, like the land, unavoidably toward the darkness. It would be tougher to follow them through the gray forest of the hills, the parapsyte acknowledged, but it would also be easier to avoid detection. He still did not understand why he could not just take the cousin now and squeeze the information from his head with his bare hands.

"Why can't..."

"You know why! You wouldn't listen! You lost your temper! You shot his ship

down! If you can't get him to talk then our only chance of leaving orbit went down in flames over that hollow. So we have to be careful, we have to be patient, we have to learn what the right moment will be to move and we have to wait for it. The other clans can't be trusted. We can't just assume we can just ask him for the codes and we can't take for granted that he would talk under pressure. He's stuck here now. Would he jump at the chance to leave with us? We don't know. That's why we watch and wait. If it comes to it... soon I'll mature, soon I'll be able to read minds, and then we won't need force or trickery or trust."

"Others may come for him."

"Then let's hope our time comes soon. If not, we'll deal with them too. Unless you're afraid."

"The only thing I fear, slug, if that your incessant nagging will bore me to death!"

~

He strode the ups and downs of the blackened hills, sandy rock crumbling beneath every step. Flown ahead of the cousin and his companions, the ship was left cloaked in an ever-shaded ravine, but was always in contact with Easarean's armor. He could continue to track them through it, getting constant updates directly into his helmet. He wore tattered clothes over his armor to hide his alienness — remains of wayward bandits that thought their number could compensate for his size. He left only one alive to tell the tale of the impenetrable giant.

He explored the ebony woods and sandstone foothills to find appropriate areas to confront the cousin, and in doing so came across caravans and villages suffering under the oppression of a winter that came and went — sometimes daily — to inhibit early crop. The unpredictable season, they believed, had brought with it something more crippling than the constant freeze and thaw of breath and soil. Easarean found more and more peasants likely to cough in response to his inquiries. He had seen the signs many times over the years in his travels across the continent, and he knew it would not be long before these hills became thick with plague. But unlike the ignorants he came across, he knew the source. While watching the plains for the cousin his scanners had come across a lone wretched figure stumbling through fields, scorched by wind and sun and frost. His body was wracked with every symptom one could imagine, but somehow he survived. The immortal carrier now hid somewhere in these shadowed hills. Easarean gave Pestilence and pestilence no more thought. If any virus on this primitive planet could affect him it would never penetrate the filters of his armor.

On a day of hail and a night of rain the ship told him the cousin had entered the shade of the hills, and so over the days that came he followed and watched and became aware of the men that also followed and watched. From the way they moved and planned he spotted them as killers, each with their own totem animal pulled from the area, and when they moved on, leaving one behind to follow the cousin and his companions into a claustrophobic town, Easarean felt close to making his move.

Easarean sat in a saloon drinking mug after watered mug of the region's weak brew, without helmet but covered by layers of tattered bandit clothing over his armor. He knew his size could not blend in, but felt it was past time to try. Why the men dogged the same three he followed, he did not know, but it was clear the one they left behind had killing on his mind.

The three, however, seemed oblivious to the threat. They sat across the saloon from Easarean, seemingly not noticing him, and seeing them this closely, with his own eyes, created a rush of blood he did not expect.

"Slow your breathing, you dumb oaf. Do you want to give yourself away?"

"Maybe I do," he mumbled lowly, deliberately talking aloud. One of the cousin's companions looked his way. He was a sinewy fellow with deceptively sleepy eyes looking out beneath the hood of a cloak. Easarean could recognize a killer behind those eyes, but just not what type of killer. The cousin was fooling himself if he thought the man could protect him. The other companion was one that had beguiled Easarean even from the far-away monitor he had watched her from. She was a pale goddess disguised as a priestess, an avatar of dangerous beauty, an opalescent figurine carved from quartz. Why she would associate with these poor examples of men, he could not fathom. She was a gift to the pathetic failures of males on this planet. When watching her on the ship's holoplays, Easarean could never shake the feeling she sometimes watched back.

"I said slow your breathing!"

And among such disappointing creatures, Easarean found himself sad to recognize his cousin not rising above. He knew the other clans to be inferior to his own, but expected them to, at least, stand out among this primitive populace. But there sat the cousin, tall but slouched, with any semblance of regalness beaten beneath the miscegenation he had embraced. His speech, his movements, and no doubt his outlook had apparently fallen, along with any sort of cultural pride his clan should have valued. Had this been the fate of the other clans — sinking to denominators set by other peoples? If so, Easarean was relieved to have been kept separate all his life, kept to his own Academy and own clan. Or was this a part of the trickery of the cousin's clan? Was it all an act, a subterfuge, a means of infiltration? He would not put this past him. But why was he here, on an inconsequential planet on the outskirts of the Empire's reach?

"That is what we must find out, my love."

"No," he thought to her, "nothing matters but the codes in his head. And to that end I must keep him alive." He stood after draining another mug, leaving currency behind on his table, and headed toward the door when the sinewy, cloaked companion looked distracted. He did not trust his eyes, and wished to stay out of their notice for now.

Stepping outside the saloon he stared down the man that had been left behind. He had seen him lurking around the bar, and he now had no doubt that the stranger wished the cousin's threesome harm. His gaze was nervous but indecipherable, as was that of the glassy-eyed stare of the brush dog's head he wore over his own. The lion, the eagle, the snake, and the bear had left the brush dog behind, and so he would be the one to fall before Easarean. But not here, not now and not out in the open. His shifty movements were attracting enough attention. The stranger moved on from Easarean's glare into one of the short crowded alleys — an alley he would never leave alive.

God Empress Mew took one more step to the curtains but did not step through. They would not part until she took one more step. Her people called to her from beyond. Legions and galleries, squares and parks and patios — all chanted her new title from the other side of the curtains. And this would be the first time she acknowledged them as the God Empress. She had not created the title, nor had the Senate or even her people. Of those in the multitudes outside the Imperial City, those yelling it now, whose cheers and chants whipped the air of the plazas into a frenzy, moving the curtains before her, few had created the title. Mew knew it had started only in whispers, in the catacombs beneath city both mundane and imperial. She knew the *Roused* had spat it as a curse toward her and her authority. It was the *Roused* that claimed she spoke not just for a false god but *as* a false god. Her spies had traced the original slander to Martyrdominus and the first of his cult years ago and their claim that Mew believed herself to be Slog Sabbaoth in human form. From secret catacomb gatherings the lies spread to the streets to the homes to the Senate, where even the patricians now referred to her as God Empress. She had never once claimed divinity, yet masses that moved the curtains called to her to take the throne of Heaven.

Damn Martyrdominus to the Seventh Hell! His *Roused*, like their rumors, had spread quickly over the years amongst the poor alley-driven to the merchants to the noble families. Few still admitted it publicly, but she could hear Martyrdominus' voice behind any new convert. She had known him as a senator when she was a young empress and remembered most of all his exile speech when her father humiliated him on the Senate floor. He had vowed to have his revenge any way he could against her family, and every time she heard his rhetoric in agitated whispers after she left a room, she was reminded of his voice. She would never forget. He had been a small man, but her spies told her that in old age he had become immense. She wondered now if he ever left the streets beneath the streets or if he just let his words and prayers travel for him. Who among those singing from beyond the veil were of the *Roused*? One in every thousand? One in a hundred? Had it been one in every ten citizens, she imagined that she would not still be standing at all. The cult forced blasphemy upon her, but if the cheers outside indicated anything, it was that the people did not mind. But if they did, and if she continued to ignore the *Roused* to the degree she had, she would one day sleep with a bed full of asps.

Barathrum shuffled up next to her, his cane foreshadowing his presence as always. "The rabble await your words, my Empress. Calm them, inspire them, lift them above their petty worries." The elder had been an ever-present thorn in her father's side for many years but a constant ally to her. Not once had he ever spoken against her decrees. He would be the perfect assassin if he valued wealth more. The old man lived the simplest of all the senators by choice. What would it take for him to betray her?

"Have you forgotten your words?"

"I have no speech..." she rebuked.

"Of course..."

"I will speak from the heart, from the soul. The people expect no less." Yet she still faltered and waited to take one more step. Barathrum's cane led him back to the rest of the senators where she could hear them whisper. They squawked like magpies, waiting, always waiting for... what were they always waiting for? She had grown so thin over the stress of the prior months that there would not be enough meat for them to pick. They would tear each other asunder over the lean corpse. Could they not realize that? Or did Martyrdominus have it all planned out for them?

It had been Barathrum that had convinced her to speak today, to calm the people over the news of the loss of the Island of Polyphemus to a rain of fire. She was to ensure them that it was the blasphemy of the island's inhabitants that had brought the anger of God down upon them. So the Senate decreed. She was to convince the people of their holiness, their virtue, their sacrifices, and that they were in no danger from the wrath of the Holy Mountains. But she had other plans. The people would hear the truth today.

Someone called from behind her, but she had no more patience for any more lisping platitudes, so she stepped forward. As the curtains began their slow parting she was reminded, as she always was, that the real audience was always behind her, that no matter how much heart and soul she poured to the crowd, like the Celestial Urn raining Fortune and Glory on the land, her real audience — the only one that, in the end, ultimately mattered — was always behind her. The people would lap up her words like cowed dogs, with one eye on the master, but it was those behind her that would parse every phrase, scrutinize every word for flavor or weakness.

"My Empress!" A praeguardian was suddenly at her side. His ceremonial armor, not as loud as true bronze scales, had allowed him to sidle up soundlessly. His spear was equally inferior, but a true blade could easily be hidden beneath his skirts. "My Empress, the Heiror has been taken."

"What?"

"Your son has been kidnapped."

~

Mew barely remembered the change of setting. It was all darkness from when she heard of the Heiror's kidnapping until she found herself in the Senate chambers. She was still in shock and was only now emerging from the cottony haze slowly. Voices mixed around the seating and echoed in ways the chamber was designed to avoid. All senators wore white, yet the few specks of color, baubles or blushed cheeks, blared brilliantly through her eyes and straight into her brain. Her forehead clenched so tightly she feared it would tear the scalp from her head.

She had just seen him, just seen her little boy, minutes before heading to the presentation wing of her aborted speech. In so short a time the *Roused* had infiltrated the Imperial City and stolen him from her. Unless... unless the cult had long ago infiltrated the palace and were just biding their time. What was their plan? What did they want? Would they hurt him? Her hands held her face, not just to block the painful light and clamoring voices but because she could barely hold her head up. Everything had become so heavy. The air in the Senate had become a weight she could not bear.

Before she realized it, she was on the cool floor with Senators grasping at her, helping her to a seat. It was always the place of the Empress to run the proceedings from the center of the floor, but the chamber had become oppressive. It felt small today, pressing against her from all sides. Was her son even still alive? She started to make out the words of the Senate.

"Let us just negotiate, O good men. What they desire cannot be as important as the life of the Heiror. Let us just trade for the child and deal with the consequences later. The Republic cannot be seen as weak, and as long as these men have this bargaining piece we will appear unable to control our own citizens."

"The Imperial City cannot just give in to every demand from

every outraged segment of the populace. Where does this leave us, my friends? Believe in democracy, not the upstart's power. Is this how disputes are settled, by skirting the process, by circumventing the law? How does it appear when the Senate just accepts and follows any new rules created by any new outraged segment of society?"

"They have made no demands!"

"Rumors must be quelled before they start. Let the cohortes urbanae know immediately that anyone speaking of the Heiror is to be sanctioned."

"Are we informing the cohortes?"

"In any capacity!"

"My apologies, but the *Roused* will demand, yes, at the very least, a sanctioning of the Empress. Let us not fool ourselves into thinking counterwise or any otherwise. We have heard the rumors, and we are aware of what they stand for, of what their desires are, of what their challenges are to state and law. There is a certain segment of the populace that has become disenfranchised with the order, with the liberties taken with the natural law. They feel that tradition has been overstepped, and now, as we know, there are certain segments of the population that live by and for tradition. This is all they have in their short lives. Now to circumvent tradition is to tempt chaos in the streets — anarchy that could eventually spread to the Imperial City."

Emotions rose and fell, and even if Mew did not make out individual words she could feel them press against her. She was able to raise her head to the spiraling ceiling, and her sight immediately spun. She was steadied by hands not her own. One voice started to stand above the rest. Antsbreakus rarely stood beside her in any debate. Why would she expect any difference this day.

The senators continued...

"When, O Empress, do you mean to cease abusing the people's patience? How long was that pretension of yours still to mock them? When was there to be an end of that unbridled audacity of yours, swaggering about as it does even now? Defend yourself and I will relent. Does not the daily alarm of the people, and the union of all these good men before you, does not the looks and countenances of this venerable body here present, have any effect upon you? Did you not feel that your ambition would go unsanctioned? What design was there which was adopted by you, with which you think that any one of us would be unacquainted? To speak of God, yes, but *for* God… *as* God?"

"If the authority of those who have been advocates in her defense be of any weight, the cause of the Empress has been defended by the most honorable of men. If the experience of these men are to be regarded, it has been defended by the most skillful of players, if we look to their ability, by the most eloquent of speakers, or if it be their sincerity and zeal that we should regard, it has been upheld by those who are her strongest advocates, and who are united to the Empress not merely by mutual services, but by the greatest intimacy. What part, then, have I in this defense? That which is given to me by such influence as you have been pleased to allow me, by moderate experience; and by an ability which is by no means equal to my inclination to serve her. This I have asserted again and again over prior months — that if I cannot by my exertions properly requite the innocence of her ambitions, I will at all events recompense them as far as in my power by declaring my obligations and my gratitude. She knows not what she does and should not be held in full sanction as one would toward a tyrant."

"So we are in agreement then, O good men. We make contact with Martyrdominus to let him know that the Empress will take a sanctioning — a reduction of power to be fully determined at some later time — and in exchange he will return the Heiror to the Imperial City."

Mew gathered her strength and used it to stand. She still wore the paludamentum over the togas over the tunics she had dressed in for her audience with the people, and it weighed her down just as much as the bronze hands on her shoulders. But she pushed through and aside the weight to step away from the men. Their voices stayed just as present though. She would not be able to escape them in the large, loud chamber. They continued to talk — some of her son, some of the people of the realm, some of the *Roused*, and some of her supposed blasphemy, with increased vehemence.

The rush of blood as she stepped spun and pained her head, but her vision settled. The Senate chamber was deliberately without color, purposefully without distraction. The men wore golden rings, but it was her loose flowing purple that centered the room. All revolved around her, and they circled as they shouted — mostly at each other, sometimes to the spiraling ceiling, but increasingly in her direction. She picked at the golden brooch near her shoulder until her massive cloak fell. She left it behind and could hear those behind her scurry to avoid stepping on it. She wore no armor, although some ceremonial chest plate would have been expected, just fold after fold of purple and white and gold. They would have assumed that she once again had refused armor, yet she wanted to remind them anyway.

They all spoke nonsense. She now heard all their words, but they had no meaning. Her son was missing. That was all that mattered. She felt the men near as she prepared to speak. The movement of air around the chamber shifted. Their robes and togas brushed against hers. Senators' hands moved beneath cloth, fishing for something. They surrounded her, waiting for her to speak.

Mew could only think of her son, but, when she did, it was not the child she should have imagined fighting against his kidnappers, it was not the boy whose side she had left what could have only been an hour before. She remembered the bloodied babe that was placed in her arms years before. She remembered her son's warmth and outraged cry at this new world, and Mew remembered her vow to the babe — that, yes, the brilliant and cold world was frightening and dangerous but that her mother would protect him. With tears as warm as the newborn alighting her cheeks, Mew had promised that no harm would ever come to him. And with the remembrance of those old words, new words came to her lips.

"There will be no bargaining."

The Senate chamber erupted in commotion.

"There will be no negotiation!" the God Empress shouted. The Senators quieted but moved closer. She could feel the air around her settle on cool iron and bronze before they stopped. Why did the old men stop? They were waiting. They waited for her next words, but she had forgotten her line. For the first time in her career the words had fled from her memory. How could this be? It was not even opening night. She had been reciting the speech for almost an entire week now.

"There will be no negotiation…" she repeated quietly, stalling for time. How did the next line go? She could not bear to meet her fellows' eyes, could only peek around at their blurred faces, never focusing on any one of them in particular. When her look settled it was on the audience. In all her years in the theatre she had never, not once, looked at the audience as anything more than a hazy scene of indistinct shape and muted color. Her eyes never focused on it. She looked past it, over it. Except to feed on laughter or emotion, she acted beyond it, as though it was not even there. To become a character, to immerse oneself in a scene it was not only necessary but integral. Yet now, frozen, mute, the set revealed itself for what it was — braced walls and wood painted to resemble marble. Her fellows could not fool her. They were melodramatic clowns with shoe polish in their beards and modern boxers beneath their togas. And the audience… the rows and rows of suddenly uncomfortable faces that tried to look away but could not, sat nervously and just stared back without a sound. The theatre was entirely silent.

Finally, the stage creaked from somewhere behind her, and she could hear one of her fellows starting his line — a later line that would make no sense unless she remembered her own. She held her hand up to silence him, to give herself one more chance to remember her speech. His words should have been a hint. Somewhere there should have been a clue. Still, nothing came to her. Her character, the Empress, was supposed to have one final speech, filled with irony soon revealed by the Senate's knife-wielding treachery. She could not jump ahead to her final soliloquy. That would make absolutely no sense at this point. She wished they would all just stab her. What were they waiting for? What were the words?

Face locked on the audience, hands now frozen to her side, she recited her last lines in her head, searching for the rhythm, hoping the pace would just coax the speech from her. But it did not. Her eyes landed on a figure in the third row. The seating was dark, seen through gel-filtered lights, but the woman's eyes shown through. They caught a green glow from somewhere in the theatre.

Mew watched the actress, not wanting to hold her gaze but unable to look away. Was this a part of the play? It had actually been years since she had seen live theatre, and now she remembered why. She had expressed interest in seeing a local performance and her publicist thought it would be good to get back to her roots, so the tickets just suddenly appeared in her trailer one day. But all the experience had done was remind her why she had tried so hard to move into film in the first place, to leave the melodrama and stress of stage acting in the first place. It all came back to her now.

Those seated next to her started to shuffle uncomfortably. Some had already pulled out their comms in disinterest. Mew just stared at the actress' lips as they moved, but nothing came out. *Why won't anyone help her?*

XXXVII

The air in the shade was just cool enough that he wished he had been wearing his fall jacket, or at least a long-sleeve shirt, so he moved from the tree line out into the open grasses of the central park. There were plenty of benches out in the sun-soaked pink of the park, but most of them were in use on a Saturday, especially on a holiday. What was it again? Sabbaothmass? Day of Ceasing? Janus could not keep up with all the holidays. At least it had not fallen on a weakday. He still needed every day he had to get the updated presentation ready before the roll-out. R&D had better be working Saturdays, if they knew what was god for them.

The sun felt good on his neck, and as he spotted an open bench, he pulled his fingers through long hair he again found that did not exist. 'When did he cut his hair so short?' he found himself asking himself a lot lately. But it never made sense. He had never had long hair. He sat on the hexed grid of the bench and found the rubber cover of the metal to be warmer than he thought. He could feel it through his slacks — each line and hole that had made such an unnatural geometric pattern of shade on the unnatural repetition of grass before he had arrived. He had subsumed it all with an organic blob of shade when he sat down. It was the only way he could tell the position of the suns, since the cotton candy smog gobbled up the light and spread it practically evenly over this part of Beulah.

If he narrowed his focus to the rise of grass and tree line he could trick himself into thinking he was out in some rural roll. He tried to ignore the heaven-bound blocks of buildings jutting from over the treetops. With the smog snuggling against the skyscrapers, a newcomer would never know how high they rose.

A boy and a girl ran past the bench, slowing for a second, perhaps mistaking Janus for their father. For a second he in turn thought they were his daughters. One had his older daughter's dark eyes and long lashes. He saw her obstinate chin jutting out in tantrum on both the children, but they ran on and he scanned the park for his own children. There were plenty of kids paired, plenty his daughters' heights and color. He could not remember exactly what clothes they had worn. They had a tendency to easily make friends, and so they could have grouped together with any of the multitude of families enjoying the day. With one of the action figures he scratched at an old scar on his elbow that he did not remember receiving, before looking down at both of the toys. The Warrior and The Assassin stared back with painted expression on their rubber faces that had already begun to wear away. They were only prototypes, he mused, but they were supposed to be nigh market-ready. He hoped the final product would age better. He tapped both against his thighs. He had brought them for his daughters to play with but they became uninterested once the expanse and opportunity of the park appeared. Perhaps he should take the "research" back to work with him on Monday. He could derail the adjusted timeline with his anecdotal infallibility. The Assassin's joints popped as Janus found himself clenching the figure too tightly. The limbs snapped back into place easily enough, but their looseness convinced him they would never be the same.

Where were those girls? He waited minute after minute, chastising himself for not instructing them to stay near him or designating a bench or tree to eventually meet at. The younger one had always been cautious, good at analyzing her surroundings. She had gotten that from The Assassin. He laughed, drawing the attention of a passing couple. He imagined one of the women appeared how one of his daughters would look as an adult. She had her gait and long dark lashes. They tossed their brown hair with the same unconscious mannerism. Where were those girls?

He went to rub his eyes but found glasses in the way. Since when had he started wearing glasses? He took them off, thought about leaving them on the bench but instead folded them into his pocket. He did not need them. He could easily see all the way across the section of the park, the spread blankets, awkward children, and scanning parents. Flecks of movements gave bees away as they circled and dipped toward baskets and meals dominated by fruit. Every warm color of the rainbow was represented over the cool green of the grasses. Families so entrenched in their little piece of afternoon property still appeared so separate from the sharp field beneath them, as though they were dolls suspended over a shag carpet by an inattentive child.

Janus stood to brush any dust from his slacks, and the bench was immediately taken over by another father and daughters before he even took two steps out into the grass. From this distance and angle he could not see the numerous paths entering and exiting the park. The people appeared completely enclosed by the trees on all sides, thick park forests allowing little light past the first row of branches. He found himself unable to remember the morning. Breakfast must not have been very memorable, traffic to the park uneventful. The first half of the day would be as forgetful as the evening then. He had nothing planned except for a very deliberate expulsion of work from his mind. Even if it had not been a holiday, he would have made a conscious effort to ignore any prompts from his busimail. It was too beautiful a day to waste on something no one would remember in a hundred years, projects no one would remember in twenty years, advertisements the audience would forget in a year, insipid work his coworkers would ignore after mere days passed. If any of it could be considered "art" then it was disposable art — not affecting at all, or affecting only in ways he found disgusting. Changing society for the worse. He did not want credit for any of his work, and that made motivation difficult, but it made enjoying the holiday easy. He found himself using that excuse more often lately. It had become very easy to leave the work at the office, and the beautiful day made it even easier. In fact, now that he thought about it, he could not remember the last day that the city actually had bad weather. For a second he had forgotten what that looked like, what a rainy day looked like, what a cold day felt like.

He headed toward the vast line of rounding bark and branch, of still leaves of the darkest green. The cottony zenith glow cast deep shadows under the trees, turning near grass black. He headed for that shade, assuming the perspective would give him a better chance of spotting the girls. From a distance, being able to look out over the crowds as opposed to *at* it, from within it, would be a better vantage point. So he stepped past cooler and stroller and fold chair, past sleeping infant and grandparent. He was being too myopic, he realized, after almost stepping into a passing group of young women. He met the eyes of one of them. He first thought she was a mentor of his youngest daughter. He had met her at a conference at the school perhaps a year back. But it was not this woman. This woman was younger, perhaps. And the mentor he had met would never have covered up her ample cleavage with the fine scarf this woman wore.

Janus reached the edge of the field and looked back out over the park. There were plenty of small groups of kids, pairs of girls that fooled him until closer look. Where were they? So many tiny grass-stained stockings. So many wet bangs stuck to brown foreheads. But none of them his daughters. A threesome of boys climbed, spider monkey-like, up a tree at his side. As soon as activesoles became stuck in the convergence of trunk and branch they were yanked out. One pudgy hand reached upward before the previous one had found purchase, yet the boys scampered deftly and quickly. They had barely reached the top before they descended. They had barely reached the ground before they were onto the next tree. They breathed heavily, little chests rising and following as quickly as they yelled taunts to each other, but only Janus noticed. He peered up the recently abandoned tree. He remembered excelling at tree-climbing as a boy, even though he could not remember even seeing a tree until he had become an adult. There was one memory, however — one skittering just beyond his thoughts — slippery as a fish, of swimming then walking into a new world. This world had paths, natural and man-made, through mountains and pastures and alien towns and peoples. The strange world had been new to him, yet he could only chance to watch the lithe form in front of him. The form had proven herself far from vulnerable over the days, but her protection was his only focus. The memory swam away, as did the memory of its importance, as he reached for the lowest branch.

He quickly realized how much more cautious he climbed than the boys before him, and so he then reached for branches before his feet were secure, before opposite hand had a firm grip, and his climb immediately quickened. His feet were too big to get caught in the meeting of branch and trunk, but his size kept him from exploring certain of the thinner sections of the tree. Still, he reached the trunk's apex just as quickly as the leader of the boys had. He suddenly realized how large his smile had become and looked to see if anyone noticed, but no one saw him among the foliage. He had climbed it as deftly as the boys had. There were branches at the top that he would not dare to spread out on, but he had climbed as expertly as a child. Thick leaves impeded his way farther, but he had moved and ascended like a man in his prime. There was no man across the field he looked over that could have bested him. It was undeniable.

From here he could watch the low clouds and high smog mingle like cotton candy in smeared streams and bushy clumps between the high rises. And from the city the comforting warmth of the heavens descended over the vegetation of the park. Families gathered their picnics as others appeared to establish their own. The green field was a rolling organism, contained but consuming and excreting people in a constant pool of bacteria. But, even from the height, he could not locate his daughters anywhere. Where were they? He spotted a group of men starting a sackbee game on an open area of the park. They had too few players to play a full match.

Janus' climb down turned out to be a lot slower than his climb up. His shoes would not grip the bark, his ankles kept threatening to twist, branches appeared from nowhere to catch up his slacks, and leaves scratched and obscured his face. Half the time he guessed and blundered down, taking it for granted that something would slow his descent. He landed awkwardly with painful shrieks of protest from his shins, the curve of the earth stretching out once more before him. He was again sheltered by the rounding green beneath and above.

He was suddenly struck by anxiety as he crossed the grasses. Something was off. Something was amiss. He stopped between families to catch his breath, realizing he panted more now than when he climbed the tree. What was he missing? He had purposefully brought practically nothing to the central park with him. It was meant to be a day without responsibility, without the concern of trying to keep track of anything. So what could he have left somewhere? He looked to where he had first come into the park, but the lot could not be seen through the repetition of trees. The path disappeared in the pattern. And from here any bench he could see looked the same as any other. His conapt keyard and transpass were on him. He carried no credits today. With a sigh of relief he felt the action figures protruding from his pockets. He had suddenly thought he had left them somewhere, had set the prototypes down to climb the tree, or they had been lost in his maneuvering. His breath slowed but he continued to sweat. He smoothed the hood of The Assassin and squeezed the soft rubber head of The Warrior. All was good again, but he tucked them deeper into his pockets so that they stuck out only from their torsos on up. He was glad to have left their weapons at the conapt. Or had he left them at the office? He could not remember.

He wandered the field, initially intending to survey the paths leading in and out of the park, following closely the circling tree line with his eyes, but found himself veering into the openness of the wide clearing. He heard a staccato laugh that could have only come from a member of his office's management. It was ingrained in his mind and associated with any voice just outside his peripheral, and it now made him aware that he had been hearing it in his dreams lately, perhaps for many days in a row. But when he looked for the source of the laugh he found only faces slightly off from what he should recognize. He knew no one near him — yet. In a central park, on a holiday, on a day as nice as this, it was inevitable that he would run into someone he knew, someone from work or church. He decided he should probably head out before it happened. It was a wonder it had not happened already.

He cut straight through the park, veering often to avoid occupied tales and grills. Running children avoided him as he did them. Eventually, on his way to the far exiting path, he wandered into the loose bounds of the sackbee game. He twisted at a rush of air near his head, a slight shadow that flickered by his face, and snatched the flapping disk from the sky. Taunts and applause brought him around with a grimace. These men were sloppy and uncoordinated to be sure, but they were obvious comrades. Their enthusiasm and showmanship made up for their lack of skill. The crowd must love them.

"We're losing a man. You in?" one of them asked.

Janus had to correct himself. There was no audience here. What he thought was a crowd was only the slight shift of leaves in nearby trees and the calls of parents for their children at a nearby party.

"Sure," he called, flicking the sackbee in an angle that seemingly took it out of the gathering but curved it back at the man who had spoken. The other, the deserter, said his goodbyes before heading out. He shared similar scars and an accent with Janus.

Janus carried no comm, and so he lost track of time while playing, but he noticed that the fuzzy glow of the sun had moved to cast shadows on one side of the park when the men stopped for a break. He turned down offers to share the freesh they enjoyed, eager to return to the game as they talked of their jobs and mates. He could not help but notice how much shinier their faces were than his, how they still breathed heavily through the break, how much they relied on the freesh. They asked him questions about himself, his family and his job, which he barely answered. He had not come to the park this day to make friends.

"Let's get another game in." Their response was to sigh heavily and sink lower at the park table. The only one of them not taking another swig of freesh looked to his comm before answering.

"That's probably it for me…" His buddies jumped in with similar sympathies before he could even finish. One of them sopped new sweat with his c-shirt, revealing a pink gut hanging over his waistband. Janus could not turn away. The man's belly button had disappeared. It looked as though it was continually sucking in upon itself. These were not men. These were mushrooms. They were decent, responsible, fun guys, but they had ceased being men years ago. Now they just pretended to exist, occasionally appearing outdoors to play as children — no, less than children. At least children appreciated the value of competition and challenge. This fungi had given up as soon as their vegetative bodies squealed with even the tiniest resistance. These mushrooms were one step away from watching sports on viewalls, gathering on weakends to sport vicariously through real men. Here they would remember competition. Here they would remember what it was like to be human, but it would be in a safe, neutered environment where they could remember painlessly, without discomfort, with collared shirts to hide sagging chests, and belts to hold pants up over hipless waists. The saddest aspect was that these soft creatures had not forgotten adrenaline — they actually remembered it all too well — they were just afraid of it. The racing of the heart, the rush of the blood, was no more linked to the game. Now it was just linked to fear of office humiliation and demotion. The game was physical no longer. He would be doing them a favor to remind them.

"No," he said, "one more before you return to your sad lives."

"What?"

"You've come all the way down here. What a waste. Let's play just one more. We'll make it quick." He called them out to the clearing, taunting their shriveled legs and flaccid arms. He appealed to the crowds before remembering they were comprised of just inattentive families starting to gather their picnics and toys. "It's a holiday. It's a beautiful pink day. Play for Slog Sabbaoth if you must." He pointed to the winged tip of the church. The very top of the spire could be seen from all points of Beulah, but its fiery-gemmed architecture especially caught the sky's glow this evening, appearing above and below the plush smog. "No, play for your families, or, no, play for yourselves today if never again. Your own glory for once. Look to the stands and see yourself. Be your own master today."

Freesh was finished off. Dull looks were exchanged. Stiffening limbs were stretched.

"Alright."

"Just one more, I guess."

"I'll have to 'cord 'You Got Tooted On!'"

"Sure."

"Whatever."

Janus' shirt was off and he strutted past blankets both spread and rolled. The new angle of the sky cast new shadows, outlining the brown muscles on his rocky abdomen. His arms reached out wide and a breeze rose to shake the leaves on the massive circle of trees. It was the raising roar of a crowd. All around the ring they moved and cheered in his peripheral, but his eyes were on the prize, and he sprinted at the sackbee. Heads cracked together, and, with a twist and a turn, two of the men went down together. They moaned and protested, but Janus was off before they even found themselves in the grass. A picnic basket went flying and seedmelon exploded beneath his feet as Janus charged and wrenched the sackbee free. He spun it into the air before colliding with one of the fun guys. He had been fleeing, but Janus drove his knee into him to ensure he would stay put. He leapt from the fun guy's back to catch the sackbee and held it aloft to the roar of the stands before continuing to the goal.

One of the fun guys was screaming as Janus descended upon him, strollers and elderly tipping at their passage. Janus almost just let him get away. His shrieking had already defiled himself in front of the crowds, had already embarrassed himself and his lord. But Janus had come to do more than just win. The ultimate goal was reputation, not just some goal line, not just some flaccid toy. Except for the prestige, it was all just arbitrary. The only thing more important than the honor was winning the glory for his lady. As he trampled the final fun guy, rushing him into the edges of a picnic table, he looked to her high in the throne seating for her approval or dismissal, but found only the fruity smog settling from skyscraper to central park tree ring. He was alone in his glory. He fought only for himself, he remembered, smashing his elbow into the fun guy's face. Teeth caught on his forearm.

Janus spun the sackbee far off into the air, but there was no breeze to raise the leaves into a cheer this time.

~

He kept his forearm under the stream until it became too hot to do so, and then he kept it under a second longer. The cut had quickly begun to look odd. Probably infected. The faucet responded to his absence by shutting down, and he sprayed antis over the wound before looking for a wrap in the cabinet. He quickly gave up and headed back into the mainroom, swinging his arm to dry it. His foot hit a trowel as he crossed, and the tool skittered from linoleum to carpet.

The Assassin and The Warrior waited for him on his end table, and, after he threw himself down on the vinylounge, he stretched back over his head for either of the two figurines. He had twisted The Warrior's limbs back into place earlier, and they hung loosely, but now, back in his conapt, at least the figures had their accessories. The Warrior wore his full armor except for the helmet. It had probably fallen beneath the vinylounge or some appliance. Although practically new, the armor's paint had worn in any area he traced with his finger. Janus noticed crumbs and what could only be brick dust beneath his nails. How long had he been home? The viewall showed the day to be long over. He was deep into the night. He barely remembered returning to the conapt. What had happened since?

He spoke to the room and the viewall's images of the exterior buildings and skyline melted into a scene of high adventure on the open seas. Pirates boarded and pillaged, an imperial navy sailed and fought storms, and aboriginal peoples watched cannon fire from sandy shores. Janus spoke again and the story progressed at four times normal speed until he stopped it at a point she reappeared. Her shipmates were all men, with grime-smeared faces, crooked teeth and noses. Their scarves were dirtied and askew. The pirates were as bent or as wobbly as the damaged ship they sailed. They were as broken as the main mast, as shattered as the ship's rudder. Their sun-bleached faces were as cracked as the keel. But not their pirate queen. Over the days that passed on the high seas her men deteriorated, but her appearance never wavered from the movie's first scene. The unrealism did not bother Janus. The movie was one of his favorites. It had little hand-to-hand action, but the naval battles kept his attention. He began to doze, however, during the relationship scenes. The ridiculous love story between the pirate queen and her impressed prisoner was too obviously forced into the movie. She would never have been interested in someone so beneath herself. The man could not fire a musket without cringing. Janus usually skipped through these scenes, but was too tired to command the viewall.

Wake up.

Janus jerked to the side. The vinylounge was not meant to be slept on, especially for a man his size, but over time it had conformed to his body. He had fallen asleep enough on it, watching her movies, that the material had become familiar to his restless presence.

Open your eyes.

He had slept through the entirety of the movie again. He was more tired than he realized. The climax, the ship battle of three nations, had not even woken him. Now the pirate queen strode the sands leading from the freshly planted grave of her lover to a blackening sea. The remnants of her great man-of-war, *Pearl of the Abyss*, smoked and became one with the shadowy waves, turning the sunset an undiscovered violet. The credits would begin appearing soon, he knew, so he spoke to the viewall and the scene paused as it changed to a close-up of her face. Her hair and make-up were still immaculately sculpted, but it was her eyes he watched.

She is the key. The Assassin's voice was familiar, even though Janus expected that it should not be.

The Warrior's voice however was what he would expect of a father, *his* father, had he ever met him. *The world is wrong.*

"What would you have me do?" Janus asked. The curve of her face filled the wall before him with perfect clarity. It should have reflected the weird rainbow, but her cool eye was too dominant, with gold flecks the only warmth showing through the viridescent flicker. He zoomed the view in even more closely.

of the seven celestially Governed Elements
    (1) the Immoral Law
*"...requires the people to be in complete accord with their faith, so that they will follow it
regardless of their lives, dismayed by no degree of danger to soul, body, nor family"*
  —Hyper Khan's The War of Art

ven the walls of the steepest of shafts were carved, and Wulf
used sculpted appendages and features smoothed by eons
as hand and footholds. Even in this climb, the tightest of descents,
the twisted figures had no faces. Heads had crumbled over the ages.
Expressions had fallen. Mouths and eyes had long ago been worn away.
Sculptures that reached out beyond the stonework were topped by only
broken necks, with corresponding chunks shattered in mounds at the
bottom of the shaft. Wulf reached the bottom and walked the uneven
piles to the light. Slayd waited for him, as he had at the beginning and
end of each steep climb, with Leyden jar illuminating yet another forest
of columns. The darkness beyond the flickering white was impenetrable, but Wulf figured the chamber to be more of the same — uneven
row after row of a mismatch of columns from all different times. The
originals, with every inch covered in carvings as worn as those in the
shafts, were the obvious oldest, surrounded by others from later times.
Petrified wood, sandstone blocks, and even a slimy green metal reached
from dusty floor to a ceiling lost in blackness.

Slayd held the Leyden jar to the granite and its crackling light bent
the shadows slithering over the carvings. Limbs already closely contorted twisted in the false movement. Painful rigor showed through
without the expressions of face or head. Wulf drew even deeper into
his cloak. The chambers warmed as they descended, but he suppressed
a shiver. Slayd, however, pushed the sleeves of his robes up to his
elbows, but they quickly fell back over his hands.

Surprisingly, to Wulf, there was a break in the uneven monotony
of the pillars. As the shadows moved at the insistence of the Leyden
jar, the men found themselves amongst boulders worn into beds and
the decayed remains of cushions and chaises. Slayd pocketed feathers,
archaeopteryx and unknown, from fabrics that had long ago enveloped
them.

"You may wonder who once slept here," he said, "but from the ages represented it would be better to ask who hasn't."

Wulf stepped over the seven-sided wall onto earth worn away in circles pounded by an eon of sermons. The obvious graffiti scouring the mensa could barely be seen in the dim light. He felt the unknown characters with his fingertips. The american marble was soft and cool against the warm chamber. The heptagon he walked was only gated at the opposite end, leading into the catacomb's wall.

Slayd held his twitching light forward, and the darkness shrank from it, scattering like roaches over niche after niche carved upward and beyond. Most of the alcoves were empty of anything but dust and shadow, with only a few holding leaning angelic statues. "Yes, yes, the Promise of Dreams. Sweet Bliss, One Iron One, Lady Lucidity, the angel known as Slog Sabbaoth." He fingered the pink diamonds and custard pearls hanging in a strand from one of the winged casts. He tipped it with a claw before walking away to study the door into the wall.

As Wulf followed, the idol broke on the floor in front of him. One of the many wing tips had shattered, as had the sculpted ribbons encircling the angel in an imagined breeze. The head fit in his hand. Unlike the faces of all the other carvings lining the pyramid's walls and ceilings, the features of Slog Sabbaoth had survived the wearing of time. Full lips pursed toward him. Lashes reached outward. A pert nose and sleepy large pupils leaned toward him as he caressed the stone in his fingers. Each individual cord of hair had been carved distinctly from each other to dance around tiny ears and a delicate chin.

Slayd was reciting a poem as he chewed some of his sloughing skin. The words were glottal and guttural and as foreign as the runes on the marble table. He spat and smeared an obscene character as long as his finger on the stunted door. The letter reflected the electricity of the Leyden jar and the slaver on Slayd's lipless mouth as he finished the poem. Hinges buckled and screamed but the door opened. It was tiny against the immensity and idolatry of the altar wall. "Let history never record that I, Melchyor Slayd, was the type to hoard first impressions." The sorcerer bowed and gestured to the cracked door.

Wulf crouched to walk through, and he entered into a new humidity and a new light. The sculpted walls of the low chamber, however, were carved of the same designs as the rest of the pyramid — naked bodies contorted in palsied pain. Those not missing heads had expressions smoothed away by the caress of time. The chamber appeared all carved from the same rock, with stone specters covering every inch of wall and near ceiling. He walked the two short steps rounding the room, constantly caught up in fresh vegetation and strands of the threads he had become familiar with in the city. The filaments were thick in the chamber, so numerous he could see their groupings with his real eye. They shimmered and hung throughout the vines and lilies, stretching from the middle of the room to adjacent entrances and exits.

Slayd waited for him, stepping into the warm water that submerged the center of the weird lagoon. His Leyden jar dimmed but still flickered, no longer needed among the chemoluminescent flora. The veins of lily pads glowed and attracted fireflies that lit cords of strands slinking from the giant well Wulf could now see beneath the shallow water.

"These tendrils," Slayd murmured, pulling threads caught up in his face and arms, "go out through the other six doorways, up into crevice and earth. They must eventually find their way to the streets above."

"But they all come from here." Wulf tried peering through lily and vine. The water was of the clearest baby blue, but all he could see of the well was a cottony glow. It moved upon itself like rolling wool. It was taffy, stretching and folding inward, moving away from him, deeper and deeper into the center of Earth, where everlasting warmth waited to greet and cushion all who only had to reach for it.

"Careful, killer."

Slayd had grabbed his shoulder. A dark claw from one of the sorcerer's fingers pressed through Wulf's mantle, and the pain made him blink away the sleep, and he found himself nearer the end of the well than he had realized he had stepped to. The stone beneath the water was slimed and his boots lost their grip, but Slayd again grabbed at his arm to pull him back when he found himself stepping forward instead of back. "You like the pretty lights, do you?"

The sorcerer pulled him back, up a step and out of the water, near where vines and petrified root hung from cracks in the stone where the faces of clenching figures once reached from the ceiling. Spiders, translucent in body and leg, skittered like electricity along threads creeping up through the cracks, leaving behind fluffy webs among vegetation that trapped tiny dragonflies only slightly paler than themselves.

The room warmed and brightened as jellies began to emerge from behind hanging flowers and lilting lilies. Some floated lackadaisically on air, some on water, unimpeded by the masses of thread Wulf and Slayd wiped from spaces around them as they sat down on the top step, boot and foot heels touching the water.

Slayd used a non-clawed finger to pick at the threads encroaching upon his tiny ears. Wulf turned down a swig from an opaque bottle the sorcerer had inexplicably drawn from his sleeve.

"A riddle of man," the sorcerer mumbled after a slight sip of the black bottle. "Upon seeing the Face of God, looking upon one's own impression is forever odd." The heavy organic smell of the lagoon was broken by the bitter bite of alcohol. "Now, is it the image of one's own God that is forever ruined or the sight of one's own face?" He set the bottle aside to pluck at strands floating delicately through the air. "And does it answer the question, 'who is made in whose own image?'"

Wulf's lips and eyelids fluttered as he too pulled filaments from his face.

The mage snapped fingers to wake him. "Hmmm… shame. I guess we don't have time to enjoy the scene. Well, this isn't the first picnic you've ruined, my good man."

Slayd stood, crouching beneath hanging petal and low ceiling. He swatted at something unseen with full hands, stepped on a jelly without seeming to realize it, and tasted the lip of his bottle with a flickering tongue before taking another sip. "So wasteful, such a fine vintage, from the hoard of horny Ashkelon, scourge of village and vineyard. Nothing can compare to the smoky taste of dragon fire ripened berries, grapes molested into maturity before their time by the heat of an infernal serpent's gullet. Last chance?"

He again offered a drink, but Wulf did not notice. He was struggling to stand, seeing for the first time a sculpted head amongst a pile of rubble. His limbs were as heavy as his eyelids, but he pulled himself to the stone expecting to find just another face worn away over the ages. The expression was of ecstasy, of pure bliss. Wulf looked to the walls and ceiling, to the carved figures, to the contorted bodies that had once held looks of pleasurable enlightenment. They had once looked down into the Well with a love they had thought would last forever. He wiped something from the side of his mouth. Had he been speaking aloud?

"Who are we to say it doesn't?" Slayd asked out to the same lily pads and water he poured the wine over. "Communion is too personal, too layered of a defense mechanism, to judge entirely harshly. Silly? Yes. One-sided? Mostly. Counterproductive? Undoubtedly. But ultimately ineffective? Only if one decides the repeated rise and fall of nations to be without example." He swung the bottle about, splashing the wine on both flora and fauna. "I, the eternal optimist, do, of course, but I also bow to the masses and their nihilism as they attribute all good things to providence and its appellation. But again, I must ask, if men truly looked into the abyss, to see its great cataracted kraken eye blink back, what would their dreams then entail?" The bottle shattered against the far wall, the little bit of its contents that were left dripping like a wound into the water from the shards of glass.

The sorcerer licked wine from one hand while holding his Leyden jar high in the other. It had lost its power amongst the multiple light sources of the subterranean lagoon. Shadows no longer danced. "It is a day for prices paid," Slayd announced. "Very well, every faith requires a sacrifice." In a lower voice, turning his head slightly askew back to Wulf, he said, "This is the chapter in which I tell you to run."

"What?"

"Run!" He dashed the jar against the rock, and multiple freed arcs of amber light sparked multiple points on sculpture, vine and wine. Fire of every color slithered over the water like scattering eels.

But still Wulf moved only to shake the sleep from his head. He closed his eyes against the warping rainbow, still feeling the new heat on one cheek, and delved inward into his own biology. He pinched adrenal glands. He tweaked certain neurons. A shiver rocked his body from toe to tip, and he absorbed the scene around him fully for the first time. The air was oil, hue and shape revolving, melting and blending into colors and shapes he could not name. The hair-like threads clustered and fell. Jellies shrank and dissipated and screamed. Or some*thing* screamed, something his mental blocks could not keep out. Ancient vegetation caught and spread the flames easily. The dust of the steps blackened from the heat. Some great round organ swelled from the Well, pink and bulbous and delicate and beautiful. He was reaching for it before he realized. Nothing in reality had ever looked so soft, and he knew that he could die satisfied, now, if he could just feel its silken contour. But suddenly Slayd was before him, a tall figure to inhibit the view of the turgid blossom. The sorcerer walked the water, his feet on fire.

Only then did Wulf run, untangling from fibers, pressing through threads, getting caught up in hairs. He crouched through the buckled door and jumped through altar and over the marble table, stopping only to cough out the smoke that had seeped into his throat without him knowing. Pausing, he could feel the vibration in the floor, moving wood and rock. Brick and pillar shook. The light from the lagoon — a burning rainbow — lit far into the tall chamber, and from it Wulf could see that nothing was steady. Everything shook from a movement deep below. He heard the scream again, not in his ears, and he ran, pulling loose tendrils that tickled from his collar.

At the farthest reaches of the light he lifted himself into the shaft, his mind pushing against the floor. He could feel the vibrations increase below as he rose, could see the decrepit brick of a hyperborean pillar tumble, followed by the snapping of petrified wood and orange-crusted stabilizers. He rose into darkness, pushing slightly against the sculpted stone around him, solidly against the floor far beneath him.

And then he was running again, through black air before cracks of light sparked from above. And he pushed again, with his mind, in all directions against falling brick and earth, past tipping pillar and perch, into a shaft both widening and closing. He covered his ears with hood and hand against the shattering of sandstone, the grinding of granite, and the breaking of ancient bolts. The floors his telekinesis pushed against pushed back. The levels below moved upward as quickly as the floors above fell. Still he pressed toward the opening light. He stepped from falling stone to crumbling wall. He jumped from tipping pillar to breaking floor. His mind pushed off against rising columns, pulled him toward shattered ceilings.

~

Wulf found himself crawling the dirt, shattered path, and cracked sandstone of an upheaved neighborhood of Erebus. He was exhausted. The frantic push and pull of his mind against the crumbling pyramid exemplified itself in shaking, barely responsive limbs. He remembered deflecting great pieces of earth that blocked the light, as he recognized broken sections of the pyramid's walls glancing off the telekinetic skin he had created to shield him from the hail of debris. He had climbed the worms and loose dirt to the surface, using the roots of long dead trees for leverage.

He sat in the geometric shade of some domicile, in some alley, on some avenue below the shield wall of the city, looking above the roofs toward the great sunset-crowned apartments. He reached out his hand to a sliver of the candied light, but it was no warmer than the shadows. Here he caught his breath, blocks away from where he remembered emerging. It had been an unconscious crawl, away from the sinking and rising of the section of the city. It no longer shook. The quaking beneath his hips had ceased. He had ridden the City of the Seventh Day back into silence.

Wulf let his breath slow naturally, the beating in his chest calming in turn. Only then was he reminded of the pressure against his mental barriers, the pressing against his mind's doors by the Other, the person "out there," somewhere, who grew increasingly familiar with each passing day. It was now more than habit for him to push back. It was the only way to keep the intruder out. Even in his sleep he pushed outward, creating an uneasy slumber, but to let the Other in ensured a feedback of returning pain that now took days to subside. Did the Other grow closer? Did that explain the increasing pressure? Did the Other have to work as hard as Wulf to keep him out?

There was a distinct lessoning of the floating threads throughout the homes. Yggr's Eye caught less of their shimmering movement. He wrapped his cloak around him against the cooling evening. He could still see the pyre's colors of the lowering sun behind closed eyes as the light bent over the wall to strike his forehead. Steps, shuffling and hard, that could only be from the boots of William Pittsfield, whisper-echoed down the near avenue. They stopped, were followed by a distinctive scraping, and then came the sound of the preacher's voice. Quiet as it was, Wulf could not make out the words of the newest sermon, but it was obviously propelled by renewed vigor and breathless speed. Wulf put hand and hood to his ears.

Came a dream of trumpets bleating over the horizon, and he woke scratching at his nose. With every itch he now expected the invisible fibers, but there were none near him. Had he dozed long? He did not think so, but the sun had moved along the wall. No, he was wrong. It had not moved. Something eclipsed it, but only barely. Something rose from the center of the city, some fleshy *thing*, crowned with crumbling sandstone of home and street, gloried by a bloody blond rainbow twinkling though the mist of the lagoon, filtering the sunset through its great gelatinous form.

His breath quickened to keep pace with a suddenly racing heart. His stomach and face warmed while the hairs on his arms creeped in coolness. He was hungry for something to vomit, and he wobbled on stiffening legs, walking the alley to find a vantage point to see fully what was so gargantuan to be able to distort the light around the entire city. A citizen of Erebus slid past the turn to the street in front of him. And then another passed, and another, eyelids twitching, nostrils flaring, gullets widening, as the sleepers were dragged by invisible hairs.

Wulf turned into the open space of the street, and, the next thing he knew, his palms and knees were speckled and scraped, the skin on his back and neck was tightening to pull his face toward the horizon. He tried to fight it but relented. Was it curiosity or compulsion? His eyes had never been wider. They drank in the glow, the sunset colored to ambrosia as it passed through the cyclopean celestial form. The fruit of knowledge blossomed up from sewers and out from windows, coloring every corner and shadow. Homes and streets ran with juices. Milliam Pittsfield, crimson in the peripheral, doubled over from retching, continued to vomit, this time just words.

"This is the Revelation, given to the sleepers, to shortly take place, signified by angel to the only man with eyes opened wide!" He spat the bile gluing his lips together before continuing. His voice was as quiet as usual, yet Wulf could hear him perfectly. He no longer saw him though. Silken bell and trailing tentacle filled his vision. He was no longer aware of where the warm light began or ended, of where the umbrella mass differentiated from the city or sky — if it even did.

"Bear witness to the Divine Song, and my testimony, to all I see! Blessed are those who hear these words, even in dreams, for the time is now! The Promise of Slog Sabbaoth is fulfilled!"

Wulf pushed telekinetically against every corner he could feel, pushed against his head, pulled toward every hard surface, but could not force his head. It threatened to crush itself in the pressure rather than turn away. Still the gelatinous bell rose, sheltering the city, still the rippling stalk pulsed and arms the height of the walls floated and reached.

"This is the Greeting to the Seven Nations: Peace to you and peace from Her who is and from those who are to come in the New World, from the Divine Choir, descended from God's abandoned throne, and from the *Ashmedai Adat El*, the faithful witnesses, and the Brotherhood, the firstborn of the Greater Prophets, the rulers over the kings of other Earths.

"Look upon the angel who loves us and scatters away the sins of the deaf with dreams of a better world, and will make us kings and priests in a new world, to the Choir belong glory and dominion beyond the red sun.

"Behold, She comes with the clouds and… and the sunfall… and every eye will wake to see Her, even the blind, and every ear will hear the Song, even the deaf, every tongue will cry the Song, even the dumb. And all the nations of Earth will see the Promise of Slog Sabbaoth…"

But Wulf could now only hear the trumpets again, the horns from his dream, exploding. But no, not trumpets — cannons. Mortar shells struck Erebus' walls from outside the city. Exhaust turned the western glow violet, and the color of the great being pulsed in turn. Indigo veins cascaded over the bell, rippling down the slow flutter of the stalk and lingering ribbons the length of avenues. Cannon balls passed through the angel, and its being rippled like the water of the lagoon. It continued to rise, unharmed, but missile and shells exploded in brilliance round the city, splintering the deepening shade.

The brick beneath Wulf shook, and he was able to look away. Neck and face aching with the strain, he crawled to new shadows to watch the sleeping people of Erebus being pulled from their homes as the fleshy mass bloomed higher above the walls. With Yggr's Eye he could see the shimmering threads, from every orifice dragging them, some snapping when a body would get caught in a windowsill or sewer inlet. Those not released twisted and skittered along the streets like the puppets of a palsied marionettist. Some had begun to lift into the air as the celestial being rose ever higher.

Wulf's stomach sank and his bowels grew cold as he pulled his hood lower to shield himself from the lights, but a far-off ratcheting of gatling guns brought his attention skyward to see fiery projectiles pierce the colored air. They only passed through the being that engulfed the sunset. He wondered how the Army of Earth had known to come, while he barely avoided the retch of Milliam. The preacher doubled over and over again. His fake beard was discolored and askew.

Near homes exploded in brilliance and a shower of sandstone, and Wulf was immediately deafened except for a ringing that sang an unwavering whine. He ran through a mist of sand, stumbling over the bodies of the sleeping or dead. They were soft bodies, warmer than all but the fires appearing around them. The brick beneath his boots was becoming just as soft, as were the telepathic blocks in his mind. The pressure was almost unbearable. To focus on each step through the smoke meant a lessening of his mental barriers. The Other was near and persistent. Wulf could feel his familiar presence out beyond the wall.

The sand settled, and he found himself on another street but under the same filtered and candy sunset. The whine in his ears had become a distant ring, but the trumpets still bleated their uneven song. No, not trumpets — cannons — he had to remind himself. He moved closer and closer to the eastern walls, farther from the western assault but still under the bloody pink shadow of Slog Sabbaoth. The apartments comprising the great walls rippled in a flood of dark light that looked like water cascading down their sides.

He doubted his overwhelmed senses before grabbing at a figure sliding past his view. He slid with the body he recognized as Cutter. The lad looked even younger in death. Wulf cut at the lines with a pocket blade until eventually his weight was enough to hold the boy down. He hugged him to his body under the darklight night, the boy quivering as the last of the hairs broke away from him. Now, unmoving, purpled by bruise and hot heaven, Cutter looked ancient, like the old man he would never become. *No*, Wulf thought, *he should be remembered by his latter name, the name he had been so proud to receive.* Sol Ascension lay dead in his arms. Wulf was the last of them, the only one of the Motley Cow's midnight table to still have to stomach the damnable song that was spreading across the land. Flagon poisoned. Sir Skata cursed then hanged then bled. And now Sol, left to sleep to death in a foreign city. And it had been Wulf that had sent him out into the world to find Mew. Death faked, the lad must have followed those same rumors of her pilgrimage, must have found his own way in or been tricked into falling asleep among the sleeping.

He dragged Sol's emaciated body into an alley impossibly filled with a similar flow of colors moving on every side, through every corner, filling every crevice and crack of brick. If any shells fell near, if any domicile fell or path crumbled, he would not know until it was too late. All his attention had to be on fortifying the psionic walls sheltering his mind. He sat and focused only inward, emulating the criss-cross of Erebus' yellow brick in his head, building redundancy after redundancy, enveloping his consciousness. Chain rounds rattled somewhere far-off.

He barely heard them.

But he did notice when they stopped. The crack of munitions had died. Crumbling home and raining pebble had settled. Even the smell of smoke, the grimy stench of fires finding only stone to scorch, had diminished. He woke against Sol's cold chest. He knew it had only been a minute since he had rested.

Again he walked an alley hesitantly, this time without a vibration in the brick, dragging Sol's body by one arm. As much as he tried to avoid it, he looked to the massive being perverting the sunset. Bundles of people, miniscule at that distance, hung like flies tethered to invisible hairs. Over the horizon of the fleshy bell, he could see a shape denoting the gazebo standing out darkly on its crown. The colossal floating being was escorted by smaller versions of itself. Airy and transparent, they drifted on no breeze. Only when focusing intently with his mystical relic of an eye could Wulf fully see the new jellies. But when a light appeared behind him, high and far, the infant shimmers disappeared. He turned to look up at the opposite walls, the apartments that had previously darkened. Even from the distance he could make out Mew, for a soft green glow grew from her belly. She stood on a balcony, hand out toward the celestial being. New shadows appeared while the old were eaten by the viridescent light.

The trumpets sounded again, but Wulf just had no idea what they were heralding this time.

XXXIX

Once out of the crevice, Mew could drag the old man with both her hands. He weighed less than she did, apparently by a considerable amount, yet it still sounded as though his robe would tear. The thin wool stretched each time his feet caught on the uneven ground. She could not tell if his long beard twitched from his breath or that of the exhalation of the rock. She hoped he had not died from the Challenge of Air, but could not tell if he was breathing beneath the confluence of winds at the edge of the split stone. Two new druids suddenly appeared in front of her to take their chieftain from her hands, before what she realized was the entire village emerging from fog and steam and dew. Their amber robes blazed with a rising son, and Mew realized that she had unknowingly spent the entire night in the crevice. How could all of this so immediately feel like the memory of years gone by? Was this really how it had happened? The characters seemed different. Even *she* felt different. The words, although similar, were not quite how she remembered them. But how could she *remember* them, she had to ask herself. She had not even spoken them yet. And as she spoke she coughed, purging the breath of the Kalderan rock from her lungs. Her voice grew in strength as she slowly became able to inhale without pain.

"Heaven will punish those who do not know Slog Sabbaoth and do not obey the lyrics of the Divine Choir. They will be punished with everlasting winter and shut out from the presence of the Song and from the glory of its blessed rhythm on the day the Seal breaks and Slog Sabbaoth comes to be glorified in front of Her holy people and to be marveled at among all those who have dreamt of Her coming. This includes you, if you now believe my testimony to you."

A mob of druids crowded over the chieftain. Mew could barely see some of the followers slapping the old man gently, lifting him, forcing the chalky water of the rock past unmoving lips. She prayed the old man would survive. Otherwise the night had meant nothing. The Challenge of Air was nothing without a witness besides Mew to testify. She was a foreigner — only a frightening myth that had reached the villages of Hell's Clay ahead of her. She waited, could no longer see through the burning mists and robes, and she turned to see the great twisted elm that spread and hung over the entrance into the towering rocks. Smoke mixed with fog to collect among the talons of the tree. The rising light ignited the vapor to cast a weird warming shadow over the druids. She could not hear their chatter under the constant hiss of the rock but could feel their anxiety. The exhalation from behind her continued to stoke her blush and dampen her hair and clothing.

Sputtering sounds brought her back to the crowd as it parted, and she could see the old chieftain spitting the steaming water onto his drenched beard. Others tried helping him to his feet, but he pushed them aside, eventually giving up himself to sit back against a clay-caked fallen tree. His hands and face had already dried to the gray of the ground.

"God is…" he sputtered with many pauses to clear his throat of phlegm and gasses, "…not altogether such a one as you imagine him to be so." He pointed to a different member of his family to punctuate each point. "The Fire of God burns against you… damnation don't sleep like you do, the boat across the River is ready, the fire is made ready… the Furnace is now hot, ready to receive you, the flames do now rage and glow… the wet sword is whet, and held over you, and the low river has opened her Mouth under you."

Mew was disappointed at the nonsense the old man spouted, but had to accept that it was at least a start. She walked the hot mud and stone to retrieve her staff from where she had left it the prior evening. Had someone from the village knocked it over or had the unstable ground tipped it, she wondered, brushing dried flakes of clay from the ornament of Slog Sabbaoth. She realized then that her recent prayer had not been to the angel. Whom had it been to? She remembered thinking of her mother and searching the blurred sky for stars and a particular cool color, but as quickly as the memory appeared it disappeared. Who else was there to pray to than the Promise of Dreams?

"What did you see?" she asked the chieftain. There was a long pause, and she thought that, despite his look of intense thinking, he was not going to answer. She could hear his raspy breathing even beneath the ever-present rush of heat from the crevice. "Who won the Challenge of Air?"

"I… we've been looking at it all… wrong," he finally said against the moans and gasps of the entire village. "The Earth is Mother, of course, waiting… waiting to receive us back into her womb, but… there is a ferryman… *The* ferryman." He then started a coughing fit that drowned out any questions from those near him. When it ended, his eyes had become even redder and his beard had darkened from whatever speckled his lips. It did not escape the druids' notice that the chieftain and Mew had survived longer than anyone ever had in the crevice and that Mew, although drenched and covered white in soot, appeared healthy and lucid. "Slog Sabbaoth waits to take us home! To the bosom of the world!"

There were some cheers and some outcries, but people mostly just looked to each other and then, finally, at Mew. She had cringed at the angel's name but did not know why. She should have been elated. The Challenge of Air had been won. The faith in the villages would grow as the land cooled. The Song would spread from farm to village to city as it already had behind her.

"Come find me!" she shouted over the persistent rush of hot air behind her, over the surrounding gurgling pools and whistling rock. The sounds seemed to grow as her voice did. "Come find me when the heavens grow gray and the clay freezes beneath unmelting snow." This was new. The words that flowed from her mouth were something she had not added to past villages. Or were they? She remembered someone saying those words — someone that was not quite her. No, but that was not quite true. It was someone that was more *her* than she was being lately. She almost could not continue, so lost in other images of herself — scenes in which she recited words similar to what she was saying, scenes in which she truly *meant* them. But she still spoke the words without even realizing it. "Come find me when graves empty and the ice comes down from the North. Until then, spread the word. Your chieftain's dream will inform you, inspire you to move beyond the land of mud pots and geysers to tell the country of new worlds, to purge the land of old gods. And then, when the world knows only one season, find me in The Land Where Pharaoh D ies, and we will return to the earth, and She will welcome us with open heart."

Mew smiled as the chieftain knocked aside a decanter of smoking water being offered him. He could not, however, turn away the help in bringing him to his feet. Two other druids had to stabilize him to walk as well. Some of the villagers left with him, others wandered in all directions, most neared her but pretended to look away at the crevice, sky, or boiling gray all around. The mixture of gasses and fog continued to roll against each other as Mew's companions appeared from the slowly scattering crowds. The Gladiator, as always, was the first to her side, followed by the Blank Slate. The Prodigal Brother was the first to speak.

"But what did you see in the mists?"

"Nothing. The rocks of this world speak to me no more than the stars of other worlds." Even as she said the words, she knew they were not true. But what is the truth then? The words continued to come however, whether she anticipated them or not. "It is only Slog Sabbaoth that speaks to me, not in smoke or the entrails of fowl, but in fire and dream, as it is foretold. But what really matters is what the old druid heard. I couldn't even see him in the deepest trenches of the rock, but I know that he slept almost immediately. He's an important man among these villages. He'll convince them… and others."

"He didn't look like he's going to last long."

"New faith requires a sacrifice. As it always has been, it always will be." Mew looked to see who had said that, then realized that she had. She was feeling light-headed. Was it from the taste of pebbles in her mouth? No. She was still adapting to the slow speed that the world moved at out here. The world that she, the Gladiator, and the Concubine came from had moved so quickly that it was still difficult to adapt to the slow time of this new world. Whenever she forgot that fact, it was not long before she was reminded of it.

"So, where are we heading next," the Concubine asked, obviously feigning interest. She wore little, even in the heat of the area. Her fine boots had lost their shine in the wet dust.

Mew rubbed the dizziness from her head. "I… the city?" Had they been in Bab'lon yet? Was this before or after they acquired the tome? It had to be before. The book had changed everything. "Yes, we now go to the city." She staggered, and the Gladiator, as always, caught her.

"Night took more of a toll on you than you admit," he said. She caressed his face, feeling for the sideburns or scars that should have been there. He looked so different in the weird light and twisted shadows. His face was not as dark as she remembered. Of their whole group he should have been the one most familiar to her, yet he was barely recognizable. Did he miss the hectic time and short years of Below the Brook as well, or did it only make her dizzy? She tried to steady herself, but the wet rock was not making it easy.

"New faith requires a sacrifice," the Blank Slate said. The girl rarely spoke, but when she did it seemed as though she saw more than any of them.

And it made Mew think. In her short time in this slow world she had already heard the myths of many of the land's faiths. The Northern

Men's All-Father, the hangman Yggr, had given his eye for knowledge. The chthonic people had sacrificed their elder souls to the Obsidian Poppet. The Libran founder had given his life to solidify their Orders. What did she have to give? What was she willing to sacrifice? And would it be enough?

Someone handed the staff of Slog Sabbaoth back to her. Like the great elm, it collected the steam of the earth and the fog of the sky, creating a floating glory that wrapped like fire around them. Its amberous sheen shined emberous in the light, and when she turned its many-winged figure it appeared aflame. Again she realized that she had forgotten Slog Sabbaoth. Wasn't that why she did this, why she did everything?

The crevice continued its unstopping rush of air into the wet clearing. She expected to hear the sound for days in her head, even as they left the area. Perhaps she actually had slept down in the heat and the rock. It would explain how the night went so fast in such a slow world. If she had, it would have been the first time in this world that a night had passed without dreams. Would that be her sacrifice from here on — a life without dreams?

"And so," shouted the Prodigal Brother, "we head to the great city, my friends. I have a good feeling about this. Things are looking up for us!"

The tones chimed and the lights over the far doors changed from warm to cool. There was instant movement all around the studio as production interns appeared from nowhere to break down parts of the set. Mew breathed a sigh of relief as the faux clay pots slowed their gurgling and the rush of sterile air ceased from the wall behind her. She and the others were immediately wrapped in robes, and a towel was placed over her damp hair. The lights dimmed in what were brighter areas and lit parts of the studio she would not have been able to see while they were filming. The fantasy was broken. She now looked out over masses of cords, camera equipment, bare wood, fake rock, concrete and thin rafters. She much preferred shooting on location. It helped her to get into character. But the studio's projected cost and disinterest of moving production to Wyoming had been an undeniable hindrance. She rubbed her head viciously with the towel, already worrying about having to have her hair done in time for the night's party. She dabbed at her eyes, seeing the dark make-up come away. Had the cameras picked that up? Her thoughts were interrupted by the director's sudden appearance. He stopped the other actors' exit from the stage.

"One second everyone, can we gather around the set? Let's gather 'round. Most of you know, but just in case you don't, this is a wrap for Mew." Applause appeared near and far, loud and quiet, from all ends of the studio. "This was her last scene." The clapping waned.

Mew felt neither excited nor sad to be finished. It was difficult to feel either when she expected to still have to do clean-up post. The movie was over schedule, and production wanted to give the impression that they were wrapping up, but she expected there to still be VO work and scenes to clean up. In her experience, post-production was never free of production until the day of release. But her plan was to stick to the promo schedule until she heard otherwise. As far as she knew, her flight out of Beulah was still planned for the morning, which guaranteed she would be cutting out of the party early.

"You're coming tonight?" she asked the director as the other actors gingerly stepped around and off the set. The lighting changed again as the filters cooled. Now all that was left was the fluorescent white of rafter bulbs.

His voice deepened as he spoke only to her. "Yeah, but you're going to have to start without me. I'm behind on dailies. I need to go set up the new editors. Can't wait."

"Who's all going to be there?"

"It's really just an investment thing. Studio hasn't locked foreign distribution completely down yet. Besides that, I think some marketing guys, some contest winners. You don't have to stay long. But hey, congrats. Good job. I liked the ad libs by the way. Can't promise anything, but we'll see in post. I've been cutting for time lately too, so who knows."

"Right."

"Hey, I'll see you tonight. Congrats."

"Thank you."

Mew took one final look around, not just at the elaborate set but all the people lifting and pulling and turning and switching. It was truly baffling. So much sacrifice went in to create some person's dream — a dream so far from her own.

~

Mew was glad to see that most of the partygoers had faces lit by the candied colors of their comms. No one had apparently noticed her yet. Maybe she was actually going to enjoy one of these gatherings for once. Maybe she could enjoy herself like an actual person for once, without being treated like an object or an extension of a marketing campaign for once. She always just felt like some piece of merchandising. She would consider tonight a definite win if she did not leave feeling like a stretched doll from a bargain bin of marked-down *Ragnarock: The Quickening* toys. Was that the title they had settled on? Maybe she could ask one of the ad guys here tonight.

The first fan approached her as she chose an ugly little cracker covered with a plastic swirl of cheese. It was the only swirl twisting counterclockwise in a tray of clockwise twists. The fan asked questions about the movie she could not answer, out of ignorance or disclosure agreements, while another complimented Mew's outfit over and over. After the first fan filmed the three of them together with his comm, Mew excused herself to the patio. The second fan had held a pen and a cocktail napkin without a drink. He had never gotten around to asking for an autograph.

The view over Beulah was dark except for the few lights of airships above the clouds. There was, however, a soft pink glow in far-off smog Mew assumed to be the main church of the city. Standing at the railing, hands gripping litecrete and cool metal, she could imagine the church spires as they culminated in sculpted wing and halo. The air was surprisingly cool, and it made her realize she may have never been this high in the city, but her thoughts were interrupted by a rush of people out of the penthouse. She had been spotted.

Minutes passed and cordialities were exchanged. She rarely had the answers they wanted. It took more effort than it had in the past to create the smile they needed. They took footage, she signed autographs, and eventually they talked about themselves more than she did, and for that she became grateful. It made it easier for her to turn away when she recognized a familiar face. It had been too long since a face was familiar to her, if one had ever been.

XL

J anus sliced the roast as easily as if it was butter. His knives, so recently sharpened, were rarely used, yet he saw them as a necessity. So many things in his conapt gathered dust, yet, for some reason, he felt the need to hold on to them. What was the paint for? Did he really need plaster and stucco taking up space? Even the sausage he sliced was superfluous. The instant meal was complete in its own. It took only seconds to hydrate and heat, but he took the time to add to it anyway. He did feel a sense of satisfaction finally using the knives though.

The Assassin called from the mainroom, telling him to slice thinly, pointing out how the cooking would go so much more quickly. The Warrior countered by demanding the use of a larger knife and the efficiency and taste of larger cuts. Janus compromised by doing both, mentally noting the change in cooking times. He went to the cooler again, and again went away unable to decide on a drink. So much food spoiled. So many drinks went untouched. He continued slicing with glee. There had been a certain pleasure to everything he had done the few prior days. With the event approaching, everything he did, no matter how insignificant, was accomplished with a sense of pleasure he rarely felt in day-to-day activities. With the event so close on the horizon, minor actions felt even more pointless than usual, yet there was a new salience in their achievement, as though it was the last time he would be doing them, as though he was saying good-bye to all small things, as though after he attended the function he would have no need of small gestures ever again.

His co-workers thought him the lucky bastard of impersonal fate, of a management that saw the office as an unchanging hive mind of indistinguishable drones. The grains of sand dragged to the base of the corporation, periodically washed away before being repetitively replaced, could be collected by any of the replaceable men and women wandering the halls of the offices. Management barely hid this philosophy from the cuboxes, and so Janus' peers assumed he was the recipient of some indiscriminate lottery, that yawning powers-at-be had pulled his idenumber out of a hat. But nothing could be further from the truth. That point in the future, the inevitable weekend evening, when he would approach her, over cocktails and ambient music, was a moment in time that could not be changed. He could see it so clearly that it was as though it had already happened. And it might as well have. The event so delineated itself from other moments of the past and future that it revealed the linear nature of time. All seconds were just points on a flat scale, stretching out on a grid of only one line. He could see that so clearly now, the event with her shone so brightly, so much more than any other, that the rest of the line rose on one end and sank on the other. The line of time began to rotate, slowly turning around the green Event. And as the line spun it began to turn, so that all history and future became a sphere as the line left shadows, images behind it that began to overlap, so that all moments that have happened and will happen were now occurring at the same time — so that there was no time. Yet, even though what Janus had always thought of as time was revealed to him now to be a singularity, the Event still stood apart. In the center of the sphere, hidden by the false shadow of a spinning misconception, it still glowed brighter than all illusion. From the Event all past and future sprung. Everything poured into it and from it.

Janus had broken into a cold sweat. For a second he felt the faint tickle of nausea under his tongue, and he grabbed at the counter for stability. It passed immediately, but he feared he had cut himself, feeling the pain shock himself out of his fugue, but it was only a phantom pain however. He washed his hands to examine an old white line on one of his fingers — the scar of some forgotten accident. Perfectly round gobs were washed from the knife, draining down the sink and to some unknown sphere of existence. They did not exist when he was not thinking of them.

So concentrate. The Assassin spoke from the mainroom. *She is the key.*

Janus added the sausage, large and small, thick and thin, to the meal before inserting it. It could have been finished relatively quickly, but he entered the new specifications and set it to slow cook. He was not quite ready to eat. He wiped his hands, wondering at the stucco frosting on the tips of his sleeves, and headed to the mainroom. There was a paint roller leaning against a bucket on his way. It was probably ruined for anything but the off-white color caked and dried to it.

He collapsed onto the vinylounge, grabbing the figures first from a bare bookshelf. He commanded the viewall to life while staring at them. The Warrior had little to say over the last few days, but he spoke up now.

This'll be your only chance.

"I know that... now," Janus said out loud. The figures were

roughly the same height, which he thought ridiculous. The characters in the novels, and the actors in the forthcoming movie, could not have been more different physically. He had expressed this to Design multiple times, but the limitations of mold and budget had overruled him on every occasion. Fans of the story had expressed the differences in objectives of the characters as well as just their physical differences, but Janus was beginning to disagree. He was starting to find more similarities than he had originally expected. The Assassin spoke up and reiterated this point.

Open your eyes and focus. Nothing good will come of distraction.

So he sat straight and called up a recent interview she had done after her scenes in the movie had wrapped. She was not one to usually do interviews, but Janus knew that she had fought hard for the role, and part of the deal was probably that she would take a larger hand in publicity than she was used to.

As recent as the talk was, it was still before the name of the movie had been solidified. She still referred to it as *Ragnarock: The Widening Gyre*. Janus related. He was still scrambling to ensure the merchandise packaging was being updated.

His arms and hands went limp as he watched the viewall. They fell to his sides, and he barely noticed his loose grip on The Warrior and The Assassin. The picture periodically increased magnification on his word. He barely heard her responses to questions he ignored. He just continued to look deeper into the scene moving before him until one eye filled the entire viewall. His arm twitched, and before he had realized it, he had tossed The Warrior across the room as it had asked him the simple question he now realized that it had always been asking. He tossed The Assassin away too before it could ask the same question.

Remember?

It made a different sound than the other figure as it landed, and with this Janus looked away from the viewall for the first time in many minutes. The Assassin had landed on a pile of brushes and a plaster float, near where The Warrior had hit the freshly painted wall. What were all these supplies doing scattered in the mainroom, and why had he not noticed them until now? Had he fallen asleep? No. The paused interview had not been that long. The vinylounge shrank back to its original size as he stood to examine the slight discoloration on the wall. The color had already dried in specks on his shirt and cuticles, in perfect dots on his shoes, so he knew it would eventually match the rest of the wall. He picked at the smears encrusted into the lines of his palm.

The giant green eye watched, unblinking as Janus picked up a mallet he did not remember owning. Its rubber was scuffed on one side, on one edge, and he smashed the clean side into the drying paint. The stucco came away in chucks, and he took a break from tearing at the plaster and strips to bring the mallet against the coverings again and again until the brick was mostly exposed. He then went at the wall with sledge and crowbar. The weapons he needed were all available, all within arms' length. He was not even tired by the time he had opened enough of a space to crouch through. His heart raced, but he neither breathed heavily nor perspired as he went back to the kithroom to find a handlight.

The interior had been a closet. He vaguely remembered it but it was becoming clearer as he climbed through the new opening. He turned the beam toward where he remembered storage drawers and hanger bars. Both had been removed to make the tiny room a perfect cuboid. He set the handlamp in a corner and adjusted it to illuminate the table of candles. The overhead lamp did not answer his call, so he set about lighting the candles with matches scattered on the floor, but as he moved a match from one wick to another he paused to look at the wall the handlight highlighted.

Yes. Don't hide it away.

He had already forgotten that The Assassin and The Warrior had called to him, had already forgotten that he had brought them into the crowded room with him.

She is the key. You can't let yourself forget that.

They both lay askew between candles, flickering light moving the tiny shadows around their painted facial features.

Will you be ready to do what is necessary? To wake her?

He looked from darkness to light to darkness again, rubbing the scar beneath dried paint on his chin. Entirely covering the walls were scraps of articles, prints, and photos. Posters, viewall captures, and presshots, wrapped from corner to corner and floor to ceiling. Neither the buttery candles nor the milky lamplight did the green of her eyes justice.

~

The caviar just looked at him from clutches of hundreds of eyes

— perfectly arranged piles of black irises staring in unison from no matter which angle he leaned. He moved on but was approached by another of the staff, another in the same monochromes, with the same tightly wrangled hair, the same emotionless non-expression. For a second he thought it was the same person, unwilling to accept his lack of appetite or interest, but the man's voice was even more even. Janus looked over this next set of hors d'oeuvres, the crackers with perfectly uniform specks of salt, the asymmetrical fluffy cheese, the identical halved crustaceans. Were the shrimp grown in such artificial conditions as to produce such twin perfection, or were these shellfish chosen from a multitude for their exact similarity? He had never seen such tiny spinach leaves. Their identical shapes were placed identically. They were all the exact same shade of green. The thought made him look up and around the gathering for her, but she either had not arrived yet or it was the great amount of people at the party that kept him from seeing her.

The people, industry and celebrity, extraneous guests and caterers, mingled shoulder to shoulder through the penthouse. Everyone appeared to know someone. But not Janus. He recognized a few of the actors appearing in the adaptation of *Ragnarock*, but he knew no one. He was the only person representing the firm. Everyone else was either celebrating the wrap of the filming or latching onto the celebrity scene. Their fanatical reasons were as uniform as the finger sandwiches he declined, or the faces of the penthouse. Everyone here reminded him of someone. He could have sworn that the bartender was also the peacifer he had run afoul of a week earlier. The man had the same hairline and weather-pocked nose. When Janus had arrived at the party he first thought he had been mistaken — that perhaps he actually was not the only person representing the movie's merchandising. At first glance he thought he had seen another from the firm. Since then he had seen numerous individuals reminiscent of his cube-mates — all of who turned out to be socialites or film industry professionals. In the end, as familiar as everyone seemed to be, they were, in a way, as indistinguishable as the appetizers. When Janus was not focusing on the people, they blurred in his peripheral to non-individuals. Their expressions were as identical and as untelling as cocktail olives.

He adjusted his tie, knowing that no matter how much he straightened and wrangled he was still under-dressed for this crowd. As he wandered, listening to but never interested in breaking into the conversations, the groups of partiers slowly began to separate. He eventually tried a hors d'oeuvre, if only to find something to do as he combed the crowd. It was salty, but beyond that there was no taste or impetus to try another. The people of the party were wandering like him now, engrossed in their comms more than others. He ignored the temptation to pull out his own to check the time.

It does not matter. One of the figures spoke from an inside pocket. He could not tell which one. The Warrior and The Assassin had begun to speak as one these past few days. *Open your eyes. She's out here somewhere.* They were awkward inside his sport coat, constantly poking him in the ribs with hard plastic elbows and knees, and he could not help but worry that their odd shapes would show through. *Stay focused.*

He realized he had been standing in one spot for far too long, staring at nothing in particular for minutes on end. Had anyone noticed? Was it possible to attract too much attention in a room of people more interested in their own hands than what was around them? The DM from the studio was supposed to meet him when he arrived, to make introductions, but he was still nowhere to be seen. Janus was not too disappointed. The man had always reminded him of his first brother-in-law — too familiar, too chatty for the sake of being chatty — but he would have been an easy "in" to the elite of the party.

Janus had found himself at the presentation table where the appetizers ended up. The plates were spread, each one different yet filled with cells of food eerily perfect. He moved to blocks of more cheeses than he had ever seen or imagined in his life. No color went unrepresented. Some cheeses must have been quite hard to necessitate such sharp knives, he thought, while feeling the edge of one knife that had not been dirtied yet. He used it to catch the light off one of the many teardrop lamps hanging from the low ceiling. It reflected cottonly onto the pure tablecloth.

Pay attention. He adjusted his sport coat. Everyone was wearing dark colors. His skin may have been darker than most at the party, but his outfit was easily the lightest.

And that was when he saw her. The crowds had thinned before forming smaller gatherings, and so he could now see through the winding mazes of people to the sky verandah. It was dark past the glass. The candy moon was missing or obscured by smog, and he could not remember the last time a star had lit the night, but she was lit by the screens of numerous comms as people crowded around her.

Unbreathing, he rushed down into the conversation pit, behind the fuzzy warmth of the firewall and a settled group of people that only glanced at him once before returning to comm or acquaintance. Fake flames danced from the rainbow of glowing stones, and he assumed that colors moved his face as they did the cheese knife. He had drawn blood as it picked at his fingernails and cuticles. It had been her. He was certain. Her ebony hair disappeared into the night, leaving only her pale face and neck to stand out starkly on the verandah. She looked different in the real world. He was so used to seeing the same movements over and over, choreographed mannerisms and repeated dialogue, that it was easy to forget she had a true self out there, a true self that lived and breathed beyond the movies. Here she was with her own internal thoughts and outward reflection, separate from what he always knew. He was suddenly reminded that she existed even when he was not thinking of her. Did all these other people as well? That was more difficult to believe.

A comm blared. Someone was watching 'You Got Tooted On!' Nearby.

His head started to pound, and he grew warm as he took his first breath in the last minute. He had to very consciously tell himself to keep breathing as he took a cocktail napkin from under someone's drink to dab at his fingers. A couple made out at one curve of the lowered seating. He looked away, but they were still there when he turned back. Peering through the holographic flames he watched the penthouse verandah. She could now barely be seen amongst the crowd. His skin crawled at the thought that any of these people could get close enough to touch her, and an uncontrollable shiver made him lose his grip on the cheese knife. It fell silently into the shag, but he could still see it through the glass table. Why would she even grace these people with her appearance? They gained so much while she so little by being among their stupid chatter and lecherous gaze. They go about their days producing nothing of worth to the world, only gossip and stupid children that grow to do the same. These were lives contributing to a reality of no forward momentum. There would be no art or philosophy of progress produced at this party. She deserved so much more. A stomach churned loudly, but it was many seconds before he realized it was his, right before he vomited. It was not much, for Janus had eaten very little over the course of the day, but the murky pool on the glass table obscured his view of the cheese knife. He reached under the table as those around him shuffled to other seats of the pit. The voice was distinctly The Warrior this time.

Steel your stomach, you weak fool, you've waited your whole life for this. This is your only chance.

"No, once she sees... once we're together..." No one noticed him talking aloud. They had gone back to full screens and empty faces.

Concentrate.

He was pretty sure that was The Assassin's voice, and he adjusted his lapel accordingly, giving both figurines room to breath. He did not remember standing or stepping out of the conversation pit but now found himself halfway across the bar. He downed an abandoned drink in one gulp to swallow new bile. It had no taste but burned all the way down, searing his empty stomach, but the warmth was calming. It relaxed his shoulders and his steps became looser, at least until he saw her again.

She was taller than most and would have stood out amongst the mob had her hair not continued to disappear into the night sky. He could only tell its flowing shape by how its darkness reflected sudden stars. She faced away from him now, but his heart fluttered unevenly each time she turned slightly so that he would catch a glimpse of lips painted darkly and lashes lengthened longer than he thought possible. His view became obscured as he neared the glass separating the penthouse from the verandah. Guests moved in every direction but always against him or in front of him. In so short a time everyone in the party had appeared between him and the verandah, between him and her, but he was able to push his way through the crowd without too many people pushing back.

The wall of glass was behind him now, and a new group of people was before him. It was a thinner crowd, but they refused to move, but he could see her back clearly through different angles of the human forest. He could not tell where her hair ended and her dress began. Both flowed closely to her body. Both twinkled in the way the night did only in his dreams. His legs refused to move this close to her, and when he thought he heard her voice they threatened to give out underneath him. She barely sounded like she did in her movies, yet her voice was infinitely familiar. She was talking about the weather, and Janus suddenly remembered snow as a concept that seconds before would have been entirely alien to him. A deep breath warmed him like the drink, and he used the shock of it to shake and wake his feet. He pressed around instead of through the people, smelling their myriad yet familiar scents, unconsciously feeling their familiar shapes. Moving around them he approached her at slightly varying angles. Here he saw her chin. There he glimpsed the slight blush marring her sharp cheekbone. She was otherwise as light as the snowdrifts he suddenly remembered — the drifts they trudged through and over in the Rocky Mountains. When had he dreamt that?

Nearing, he reached out for her shoulder, but she turned first with a smile that broke the night of the verandah. Her lips parted as the smile grew, but he could only see her eyes. The green of her eyes. The unnaturally soft grasses of the glen. The invisible gold flakes lost in the viridescent cosmos of her iris. The sunflower of the clearing, dwarfed by dark trees and the night shadows of a stone circle. Yellow pinpricks obscured green by the glow of the dominant star. He remembered it all, and the memories crushed what he thought had been his life, and what was this life among the skyscrapers, among the banter and work of the office, among the schooling and pattern of family and the path leading behind and ahead into nothingness, compared to a childhood spent in the coliseums of Below the Brook? What was the routine of expectation, of walking the steps to marriage and the firm and church and fatherhood and bedside death, compared to the escape from the Morbis Orbis into the wide world and over mountains and across plains and through swamps and into cities? And what was the acquaintance-ship of supposed peer and cube-mate and spouse and grandchild when weighed against the purpose she had shown him? How could he have forgotten? How could he have forgotten the violet skies and fourteen eyes over Bab'lon, a city of chthonic death, the raking of angelic talon and claw, and sword and the pilgrimage? He had forgotten her deaths, and how he had, in turn, died each time in ways he had yet to under-stand. Would he now ever get a chance to understand?

Both lives overlapped and both fought for dominance. He was deaf to all around him. He was blind to everything except memory and the vast forests of her eyes he walked, sometimes with her, sometimes with others, he felt great disrespect for forgetting. But he could feel the solid plascrete of the verandah beneath his shoes and the warm shoulders of other party guests against his and against the cooling evening. Penthouse lights inflamed the smog and threatened to invade his view of the other world, so he held onto anger — the rage that grew in him when he considered the thought of someone, or something, obscuring lives or painting worlds in his mind. But the anger was not enough. He could feel the perspiration at his hairline cooling. The smell of cheeses wafted from the penthouse as partiers entered and exited the verandah. His glory in the ring started to fade. His life across the lands of Kaldera and Nod and the burgeoning Territories dissipated. But as long as he held her gaze he could remember the other fake(?) world, her secret visits to the pens and patronage from on high. How many times had he held a sticky trident or dripping sword to the great seats? How often had he looked past his lord to fathom her approval?

She looked so different now. Her eyes glittered the same, but she looked older, more womanly with her hair down and shoulders bare. They had both aged in this world. She had hardened, and he had softened, but her smile, as rare as it had become, still warmed him and promised him a world without new scars for either of them. But that smile suddenly disappeared, and he was immediately frozen in the night air. How had he come here, he suddenly wondered. How was it that he now stood before the object of so much longing? He could not look away from the beautiful, sudden melancholy of her face but knew he stood about the penthouse of a building, higher than he had ever stood, among people familiar and unfamiliar. He remembered his office's jealousy. He remembered rearranging his daughters' (his sons'?) schedules so that he could make it to the party. He remembered his nervousness at leaving his conapt en-route to the penthouse. Everything in his life, stretching back before him, had led to this point — his days studying in church, the University, excelling at the firm, placating management. All of it held new meaning now. All of it had been worthwhile. He shamed himself now, forever regretting any of it.

"Janus?" she asked as a sadness overcame her face the likes he had never seen. She looked downward at a tilt and closed her eyes. Tears welled in her long lashes.

He was chillingly cold out in the air of Beulah. Even under his clothes he shivered, yet his hands moved under a liquid warmth. He looked down to find them tightened on the cheese knife. It had been stuck deep within her stomach and had been pulled upward to cut a line all the way to her sternum. He looked back to her questioning, quivering eyes. Their color brought the image of leaves crowding a shrinking stream to his mind. He remembered the feel of the sand in that creak.

A soft green glow grew from her wound. As the knife and light split her body it arced to shatter the darkness and the people and verandah. The night broke into crystalline pieces, revealing more light beneath the sky and the very substance of the buildings and the people, and Janus crawled into Mew, being bathed in the warm green glow, and he held his eyes open to the glare, hoping to catch a glimpse of a world he remembered again, so as to not forget it again, but, as soon he thought he could see it, it was obscured by all-encompassing, voluminous Slog Sabbaoth.

Janus had apparently been crawling onto a different patio, a smaller one that barely had room for both him and Mew. This new city below, burning from bombardment, the City of the Seventh Day, was old, and he was now slowly starting to remember his and Mew's pilgrimage to it. His knees and palms were bruised and scraped, and he felt his face expecting the Elder Mask, but found only himself. He thought he was losing his sight, seeing only the flames of the city and the immensity of Slog Sabaoth through a pink haze, before pulling the soft threads from his eyes. He heard the crumbling of homes and crackling of fires as though through cotton before pulling the invisible tendrils from his ears, all the while gagging and coughing up the cord of shimmering vines from his throat. Remnants tickled from every oriface, but he could sense his surroundings clearly now, although he wished he could not as he averted his eyes from the phosphorescent entity encompassing the sky over the city. Inky light rippled like eels down the turgid bell, darkening candied tentacles that spewed shadows down streets tiny in comparison. The glow cooled before warming before repeating the shimmer, and it burned past Janus' newborn eyes back into his brain. His suddenly feverish head burned from the inside out. His clammy hands grasped railing and corner desperately, steadying his collapse before looking up to Mew.

She too had pulled the threads from her body. He could still see lingering strands when the fleshy light obscuring the night sky turned pink. Stray tendrils adorned her shoulders and twinkled from around her feet, twitching before sliding over the edge of the balcony, out of sight as the great entity floated ever higher. She watched the city burn beneath the immensity while she alternated between darkness and the candied glow warming and cooling the night.

Janus rubbed his eyes, wiping the last remnants of tendrils from them, wondering when he was ever going to wake up, but all he could feel was the cold stone against his back — not the bed in his conapt, not the warmth of the pink sunlamps. Would his comm chimes ever wake him? Was it a weakday?

But he knew he had wakened. His lives in Beulah, his childhoods among the great parks and streets of the city, his families and loves and jobs and deaths, were the dream. But when he focused on the details, on names and faces and places, of mates and children and homes, they felt as real as the railing he held, as the smoke he breathed and the soreness in his throat. It was only Mew that shocked his system, grounded him in this reality, *the* reality. Only when he looked up at her did his other myriad lives in the city of Beulah begin to fade, and his memories of his life in Below the Brook — as an athlete for the Lord and the shrinking land's eventual escape — and out here across the slow land — through the trials of Kaldera and Nod and the pilgrimage — become real.

Cannon shot broke the air outside Erebus' massive walls. He knew it could only have been the Army of Earth from the hellfire and the black and yellow exhaust of the brimstone mortars that lingered long after the rounds had passed through the sky, arcing harmlessly through the great bulb of Slog Sabbaoth. The entity was neither here nor there, enveloping the sky over the city but occupying also some nether realm and some heavenly aether at the same time, or all times. Brain burning, Janus looked into the being, through the being, and saw churches and temples and stone circles built in its honor on a hundred worlds in a thousand people's dreams. And he remembered all of them. And then he looked at Mew and could remember only one — *this* dream, the only one that mattered.

The sickly green glow grew in front of her, and for a second Janus was reminded of and worried that it was from the hole he had made within her, but as she raised her arm toward the city he saw the shine of her hand. The glow cut through the rippling darklight, and a roar erupted from some faraway realm, echoing through the dreams still left in the city. Janus could hear it from the stray silk he still pulled from his ears. The last of the tickling came from deep within his head as he gingerly pulled.

The great bulk blocking the night swayed and shimmered. From where Janus sat he could barely see those who still slept dangle like worms on fishing lines. Slog Sabbaoth was now wholly in this world. The Lonely Forgotten Sun of God had forcibly pulled the entity into reality. And Mew glowed like the light of a second sun, illuminating night and dream, yet Janus could not look away. He did not need to. There was no pain in the light. His mind cooled and his limbs warmed. This was a sun for a new world, he thought, but it did not last long. His blood sluggish, he was barely able to rouse himself when Mew's glow suddenly faded, and she fell backward, but his arms were there to catch her.

"You *are* real," she whispered, barely audibly, as she traced the old scar at the side of his lip before pulling one last thread from his mouth. But Janus still was not so certain. Her fingers were cold, but he could barely feel them, afraid they would pass through him. Whether it was because he was not awake or because she was not, he was not sure.

He expected the sky to be screaming, but Slog Sabbaoth was silent and drifting away from the horizon the Army of Earth assaulted from. Gatling fire had resumed anew. Emberous rounds took the place of stars in the night and tore through the undulating bulb. The entity now bled. Jagged lines cascaded darkly like mountain streams over and past ribboned tentacles into streets and homes. Where cannon shot passed through it, the creature bubbled and burst ichorous ink. Still it drifted without sound until it was slinking over the wall and out of range of the sulfurous munitions. Smoldering rounds arced over and into the homes of the city.

Slog Sabbaoth floated slowly out of the City of the Seventh Day, rippling glow now matching the black fires it left behind. The drafts it rode were slight, but Janus suspected it had a great head start. It would take the Army of Earth time to round the walls. As he watched the last of the tentacles slide over the near apartments and rock, out of sight, with the few remaining hanging dreamers lifted and dragging behind on invisible fibers, he noticed the giant perch leaning precariously from the top of the city's wall. He suddenly and strongly had the feeling he was being watched, and he was surprised to find it comforting. It reminded him of lives he refused to believe had never existed. Janus' memories of the pilgrimage and his stay in Erebus were slowly coming back to him, were slowly separating themselves from the myriad memories of myriad lives he had so recently lived, but he was certain the great perch had not been there when he previously walked the city streets and apartments. There was enough burning nearby that he could see the details on the top of the great wall, and the great man crucified on the great structure, of him and the man tied to him, hanging from him. It was a Greater and a Lesser Antony, but whom were they displayed for? Was it either of them that could see him from that distance? How could they be alive? Their faces were dark from their height.

Janus shivered at the Elder Mask he suddenly noticed peeking out at him from the shadows of a corner back in the apartment. Shriveling threads twinkled from its eyeholes. He had conflicting memories associated with the mask. He remembered losing it when they first entered the city, knew that others had worn it, but also remembered sleeping with it, waking and suffocating beneath it and the mass of fibers that had crowded in and under it.

XLI

…thoughts ever-bound and so caught
up in the embrace of a fake fate's kiss
—scrawled on the walls of the King of All's lower halls

There was blood on Easarean's jacket that had not noticed until the light of the early afternoon. Mornings were dark in the canyon town, the full sun not appearing over the tightly-packed hills until midday, and so he had not spotted the dark speckles on his sleeves until he had climbed to the top of the hardware store to get a broad view of the carnival's caravan as it wheeled down main street.

His armor informed him, via his ship, that the cousin was now getting farther and farther away, but Easarean was not worried. He had seen the weakness in the man's face, in his very malaise, and he knew he would not get far. The priestess he traveled with had castrated him. Easarean could recognize a man weakened by thighs and hips and a pale bosom, and he knew now that it would only be a matter of simple applied pressure to squeeze the codes from the cousin.

"No, no you must befriend him," the parapsyte pleaded in his mind. *"Once I'm mature enough, I can glean the information from his thoughts, or perhaps soon I can lay larva in his ears, in his sleep…"*

"Silent!" he yelled.

And she was.

His voice would have easily echoed over the growing crowd below had it not been for the calliope wagon whistling its breathy tune along the caravan. The music moved erratically up and down as the horses slowed, but always with notes low yet still rattlingly pierce enough that Easarean put his helmet on. Seals hissed as his armor closed his senses temporarily off to his surroundings, but almost immediately his HUDs reflected off his face with a multitude of cold color. There was just enough room for him to pull a hood over his head. He looked out from it from a wide array of wavelengths, and the ectoplasmic and abysmal filters fulfilled his ship's quaputer's suspicions. But even without them he would have come to the same conclusion. His helmet was picking up faint but numerous organic sounds from certain closed wagons, but infrared showed no heat signatures. Neutrinor bursts sculpted moving humanoid shapes in vidplays, but x-violet readings revealed not the usual magnetic fields of the living. There was necromancy at work in the traveling carnival.

"You're still thinking about her!"

And he was. Even as his blood rose to the challenge of the coming fight, the priestess was not far from Easarean's thoughts. The cousin was not worthy of her company, much less her touch. Her milky flesh deserved only Easarean's grip. Her ethereal hair, dancing on the waves of heat emanating from their conjoined loins, was caught up in his pulling fists. Her hips bucked before him under his reddening palms. These were the fantasies that kept him up over the previous night, with the whispers of the coming caravan in the shadows of alleys and pub.

After strangling the brush dog the prior night he found his battle lust renewed, and a dead caravan would be just the thing to quench it, while distracting him from dreams of the priestess' silky neck in his hands. Let the cousin have her for one more day, for soon Easarean would make his move, and let the goddess choose the true man, the real warrior, the maiden's champion.

~

Easarean would be dead soon. He knew it. He scolded himself for it, for his lapse in minding his training, for underestimating the necromancer. He knew the signs of the dead, the mystical symbols of dark puppeteering, the clues his armor revealed, but his war-zeal overruled it all. But worst of all, his impatience clouded his instincts. Throughout the fight with the dead, both shrunken-headed and petrified, he should have known to keep his attention on the necromancer. He should have known to not let the dead-dancer get too close. But he did. And now he would be dead soon. He knew it. With his dying breath the infernal mage had cursed him, and if Easarean remembered his studies, as he now did, he had only days or weeks to live — a month at the most. From now on only misery and misfortune would follow, until some humiliating end would find him. Was there anything or anyone on this backward planet that could remove such a curse? He doubted it. Even if he immediately caught up to the cousin, forcing the codes from his mouth, he could not make it to a sector of the Empire in time.

"Perhaps... perhaps the priestess..."

She was right. The parapsyte caught him in the one moment his mind had drifted from the memory of the priestess, and her thoughts had brought his back. If there was any chance at salvation, it would be from the priestess' hand.

"Enough, worm, the time has come for me to reveal myself."

"Yes."

"And their reaction..."

"Yes."

"...will determine whether I beat the codes from him, or whether I allow him to even live another day."

"Yes, my beloved."

~

Easarean worked the controls of the vidplay like a maestro, working the systems he was now long used to. The ship's sensory package was not something he had ever been trained for, but he had had plenty of time to practice since leaving his jungle kingdom.

"Stop! Are you doing it again?" she asked, but was summarily ignored.

He fingered the brilliantly lit images moving around him, pulling up the scans of the priestess and the cousin. They were asleep under the stars, miles away, but their outlines floated and breathed as though they were in the ship with him. With a twist of his wrist the cousin's scan vanished, leaving him almost alone with the priestess' shadow.

"No, stop it! Why must you humiliate me?"

Easarean had become quite adept at blocking out the parapsyte's nagging voice when he needed to. He saw himself as alone with the priestess' image, and he fiddled with the sensors for a more complete scan, filling in contours by increasing the number of wavelengths. Neutrinor bursts fleshed out the image, as he turned the three dimensional scan into a real-time, hard light image — one he could rotate and pull toward his flushing face.

"No! Why? I'm here. I'm right here with you!"

He felt the soft give even against heavily callused palms, moving them over curve and calf, delta and dimple.

~

The cousin was even more a fool than he had initially thought. It was obvious, even as he watched from afar, that the priestess had been testing the cousin since they had met. Pestilence would be her ultimate trial for mankind, as it mirrored so many Easarean remembered from myth — that of the gods testing the populace through poverty, famine, and exile. Here the cousin and the useless "mind mage" followed the diseased one at the priestess' bidding, running around in circles for her while Easarean chuckled from behind tree and alley. They consistently bumbled their hunt, slowing only to humor and frustrate Easarean. And it was this pace that made him take notice of the priestess' second test.

He recognized the creature immediately as some sort of avatar or minion of the priestess. He was everything she was not, in the form of a savage half-man, half-beast. He stalked through the night, black and animalistic and rarely slowing, and as he approached the group Easarean could finally get a good look at him. The ship's quaputers did not register the creature as even existing in physical space, but Easarean could smell the stench of magic around him — a dry stink akin to chalk or charcoal with a sulfur that offended his nose and tickled the short hairs of his arms and neck. His physical form seemed to struggle to hold itself together, dark skin and obvious bone moving abominably like a being Easarean had only studied but never seen. This was the priestess' other test — one of pure survival, one he knew they could not handle alone.

And so when the macabre creature ambushed the three in a barn barely lit by a bloody moon, Easarean, heart pounding loudly in his ears and chest, stepped in to twist the creature's head nearly off. The weather-worn roof let in a varying array of splinters and spotlights of the moon, and Easarean made sure he stood tall in the largest beam.

The priestess watched from the shadows as the cousin and his cloaked friend looked up to find the giant glaring down at them.

of the seven celestially Governed Elements
    (2) the Moral Law
"...requires the people to associate their faith with The Head, so that they will follow it regardless of their lives, dismayed by no degree of danger to soul, body, nor family"
—Hyper Khan's "The War of Art"

O ut of the shade, looking back through trees, into the gray day, down and around rolling hillocks, from flattening valley, past pastures and into surrounding plains mirroring those she would soon be heading into, Ivy saw people slowing and gathering and setting late zenith camps. She watched through her spyglass the people rest on makeshift stoops and build small, quick fires to warm whatever variety of food had been brought or found. She stepped off a bare mound, down between two of the few trees in the area to open her view to different horizons. She felt exposed but knew she had to get used to the effect of the plains. As she scanned the land, she knew she would only be leading the people into more prairies for the next few days at least.

The snow on the short rises was wind-beaten, dry, and it broke into crusty shingles from the first step and ground into something more akin to glass or sand under the second. The rare sunny day was not strong enough to melt it. It just hardened and seemed to spread even when it was not snowing. Ivy peered past the snow particles and breeze-lifted dirt to the west. She had seen the signs of the Army of Earth lessen over the morning, and their brimstone exhaust and ocular banners had now moved farther than her spyglass could see. After leaving two of its Necrophim commanders behind, the Army was going to start veering slowly and slightly westward to raze the edges of the Territories. Ivy periodically smoothed her map between glances, pinning it beneath stones. If rumors of the Horde's activity were true, she predicted that the Liege of Foe's route would eventually straighten northward to parallel her own. If the commanders left behind failed, there would be an even greater push from behind. She had full faith in the Electric Leper's ability to hold Erebus, however. In the end, the Army of Earth's assault on the city had done minimal damage — nothing that would hinder its new defense. But Banshee Jenny Wren's pursuit of the voluminous entity she saw rising up and out of the city worried her. From the squatter cities outside the walls,

Ivy had watched the nightmarish ascent of the enormous entity into the night sky, never expecting to see those she parted with again. She had stood back as Slayd and Wulf were smuggled under and into the walls, and spent most of the next day searching for Antony, whose disappearance had only been explained after she saw the man raised later that evening, strung up to the crucified Greater Prophet at the top of the wall. She had already recruited dissidents in the ramshackle tents of the squatter cities, men and women secretly of Mew's cult that agreed to help her cut Antony down, when the cannons started raining helfire. The hills and walls keeping her outside the City of the Seventh Day had glowed under Slog Sabbaoth's rippling darklight, and then the night had erupted in chaos. Ivy had lost all except Harlowe and emerged later from under ash and dirt to find the Electric Leper taking control of both Erebus and the makeshift pilgrim towns, a small force led by Banshee Jenny Wren following the violet glow east, and the rest of the Army of Earth already resuming their march. Ivy was reunited with her companions many hours later, and it was not long after that when the journey north had begun, and it was then that she had to make a decision. She had spent plenty of time in the past few years with the Army of Earth, mostly as a messenger between it and the Resistance, sometimes as a marksmanship trainer to new recruits, but the events of the past few months gave her pause. She had finally found Harlowe. She had crossed paths with another Antony. The presence that had emerged from Erebus, reflecting and projecting the cosmos, with shriveled dreamers dancing from ribboned tendrils, could only remind her of the presence she felt — never saw — somewhere back in the hazy days following her birth. The journey out of the Nursery and through Kaldera was mostly just story more than memory. Her lucid life began in the Tower of Zig, but the presence she felt in Pyramid Abysmal had always stuck with her, and she had never felt anything even remotely close to it until the entity bloomed over the walls of the City of the Seventh Day. And she never wanted to feel that nightmarish chill again. If certain tithingmen were incorrect in their theories, if she had a soul, then it now felt frostbitten, blackened at the edges, shriveling back from what whispered to her from that cosmic behemoth. Even when thinking about it now, she had absentmindedly reached into her satchel for one of the metallic feathers she kept always near, meaning to trace with it thin sigils she did not understand into thigh and blood, to release the twitch of frustration beneath her skin, but Harlowe's near shuffle startled her. The pistoleer had lit a cigarette, and it glowed through the living darkness beneath his hat. Desiccated lips had shrunk over the time since his liberation. His teeth stood out starkly from the glow of a cigarette she knew would eventually die without being a bit consumed.

Through the spyglass she could see only the stretch of flat lands to the North. The Army of Heaven had not reached where this peregrination was headed, and the Liege of Foes should, in theory, keep this branch of the Horde from their western lands. And, for now, the Electric Leper should keep the southern flank safe. Ivy had come under the command, at different points over the prior year, of some of the Necrophim generals, and they had always made her uncomfortable. Their troops were like no other people she had met, and their rumored origins explained it. Their presence in the Army of Earth had been a part of her decision to travel a different path. But their forces were deadly. She could not deny that, without the Necrophim, the Horde would have already taken the entire continent. There were only four of the weird generals, each with a corresponding legion, under a loose alliance with the Liege of Foes and his mysterious mistress, but they had made all the difference in the war.

The north opened up before Ivy, but she settled in to wait for word from the main body before resuming. She pulled another scarf out to wrap her head, even as the breeze died and the clouds thinned. She first cleaned the spyglass with it and looked back to the south. The front of the caravan were little more than specks unless she saw them through the tool. Through it she could see the meager fire warming some kind of soup Slayd tended.

Wulf looked up as the sun appeared. It was flat and as dun as the brittle snow he had crushed to make a seat in the quick camp. He fully disappeared into his cloak after rejecting Slayd's offer of a meal. He had sometime in the previous weeks decided not to eat anything the sorcerer had prepared. He thought it best. He could see a reflection from what must have been Ivy's spyglass out in the distance. She would be waiting on his word.

"Suit yourself," Slayd said, drawing his attention back to the camp, "more for me." The mage brushed some sort of flaking spice from both pointed and rounded tips of his fingers before striding to his tall cart. The sorcerer had retrieved his cart from the Army of Earth before they had gone their separate ways, and Wulf had never seen him in better spirits. He knew that the giant metallic egg he had brought out of Ophidia was in the cart, but Wulf did not want to know what other alien ingredients or demented artifacts were in the cart. Somewhere over the past day, the mage had also picked up two followers among the rabble — a hinny mule and its owner. Both Ms. Mowgli and her hinny salivated wide-eyed at the steaming bowl warming over the rocks, as Slayd reached beneath the curtains of the cart. His thin arm emerged with the darkest bread Wulf had ever seen. It broke apart softly and with many crumbs and looked to melt as he dipped it into the soup. The hinny balked in his harness, but Ms. Mowgli calmed him. The squared woman was taller than even Slayd and easily twice as wide. She wore layers of furs and skirts, but her muscular legs were bare to her giant boots. She, her hinny, and the cart blocked Wulf's view, so he stood and shook the dry particles from his cloak.

He looked back over the way they had come. The moving was slow, and he did not feel like they had made any progress over the previous day, yet there was no sign of Erebus or the makeshift towns behind them. The way they had come from was still pink and orange with purple clouds though, as though a prairie sun was rising in the south. The force the Army of Earth had left behind in the city could hold Erebus, he had no doubt, but the Horde could just ignore the city, could just follow the trail north. But would they want to? Wulf's "death" had not fooled them for very long. Slayd was certainly now considered a traitor to the Horde. Certain tithingmen were obsessed with Ivy. And now Mew was free to blaspheme again. There was no shortage of outlaws among this peregrination, but had they surpassed the level of headhunter prize?

"We're leaving behind a leviathan's trail to follow," Slayd said, licking soup from thin lips with a flicking tongue, obviously pondering the same questions. His eyes had become so clouded Wulf wondered how he could even see. "Erebus would make for an ideal fort outside of the Territories, but this 'Electric Leper' could hold its walls until the world stops spinning. I know Heaven's Army, and they will leave a force behind to harass the city and send another after us. The Army of Earth should double back and cut them off from the Territories."

"They seemed awfully determined to continue on." Just thinking of the Army of Earth hurt Wulf's head. He had avoided any interaction with any of their members after the chaos of Erebus, letting Janus deal with their commanders and to barter for supplies. The *Other* was somewhere within their ranks, and his near presence was nigh incapacitating. Still now, even as the Army veered away from Wulf's route, farther northwest, the pressure against his skull failed to subside. Constant vigilance was required to fortify his mental blocks against the painful feedback that appeared whenever he let his guard down.

"We are woefully unprepared for when the enemy decides to appear. Out in the open. Unorganized. Perhaps ten working firearms among us."

"I know where we can get armaments, but it will take us off course."

"N'Midgaard has been in a perpetual winter for years. A few more days won't make it any colder."

"Tell that to the gods. You're certain the Horde will follow?"

"Yes, yes, don't underestimate the Brotherhood's fear of Mew. Once they realize she's out in the world again they will make her a priority. This time they won't leave her fate to some ugly governor, they'll find a more permanent solution."

Wulf had no doubt. He had seen the light over Erebus. He had been helpless to watch as the far figure of Mew burned a hole in the night, through dimensions, pulling the entity fully into the world. He had watched as the people of the city woke to a new star igniting over the land that night. The Horde would be foolish to ignore her.

"Also," Slayd continued, pouring the rest of the soup out to darken embers, "why wouldn't the Horde take the same chance to exterminate the Liege of Foes at the same time?" Each time he smiled Wulf saw new teeth as pointed as a serpent's fangs.

"I'm not the Liege of Foes."

"It's not me you need to convince."

Wulf assumed that Slayd was referring to the Horde until the mage swung a slender arm over the south. They both looked over the rolling prairie that had begun to flatten as the day had progressed. Thousands of people were crowded for warmth and food. Some had made quick noontime camps, others — families and individuals, caravans and horsemen, young and old — still progressed toward the front of the line. Many were the sick and starving that had initially answered the call of the Territories' relative safety against plague and famine but only made it as far as Erebus. Many were new faithful that had followed

Mew in her pilgrimage to the city. Many arrived later. Most were citizens of the City of the Seventh Day and the squatter towns that had risen over the past year. All had fallen in fear at the sight of Slog Sabbaoth's presence, and all had risen at the short-lived green star that had banished the entity. Now, all just followed. Wulf assumed they followed to hear Mew's message of the *gentle constants*. Many carried emeralds and glass in gold pendants. Those that traveled near her had started painting their left hands green. But just this day Wulf had heard reports of some travelers painting tears of red on their faces as well.

He asked a nearby boy to send for a link or messenger. It was time to inform Ivy of the change in plans.

Wulf looked over the land, down the leagues of wagons and trucks and crowds, for Mew. He saw neither her nor Janus, but the mass of people in the center of the main line gave away her position. Even from the distance, he could see the wide expressions and painted hands holding copies of the *Fallo Terminus*.

Mew turned completely in the crowd, smiling back at each welcoming face. If someone did not wear some sort of glass jewelry, they had a ribbon in their hair or a swatch of green paint from temple to temple over their eyes. She had never seen so many different sizes and bindings of her book. The copying and secret printing had continued during her disappearance.

She was being bombarded with questions as earnest and pleading as all the faces, but she looked over heads and shoulders to the northern horizon. She could not find Wulf but was certain she saw the front caravans, and they were not moving, so she knew she still had time. She raised her hand and chin to hush the crowds. She was always insecure when realizing they noticed the mark of Death's Scythe on her palm but held it higher this time, proud of the memory. The people quieted immediately.

"May I present to you Laud Broderick, now Laud Ascension," she said to the faces, turning the man to the people. "Like you, he has come long and far to hear the truth. Like you he has hurt and gone hungry and lost those he loved. He was one of the first to read. He was the first to transcribe. He has broken the old stones and shared with many. Find him when first light warms the East. He is the DawnSmith. The first. He will lead the morning prayers. Find him and you will find the sun. Find the sun and you will find yourself."

Janus Legionaire did not recognize the song the crowd started singing. Mew did not appear to prompt it, yet children and adult started humming at the same time. It was not the first time in the last few days he found himself surprised by some prayer or genuflection everyone but he appeared to know. He pushed away from the scene, through a mass of families that would not move. More than one person had to pick themselves up off the ground after he passed. He pulled the bearskin tighter over his shoulders as he emerged into thinner camps. The smell of toasted bread and twice-warmed jerky was all around him. Before leaving Erebus he had assembled teams to scavenge the city of anything to trade with for supplies from the Army of Earth, and he had come back with a fair amount of preserves and quilted clothing and even some fuel for the many trucks and wagons he now passed. But the fruit he had acquired had probably already been eaten. The fuel had probably already been burned through or siphoned from the mobiles that already had to be abandoned. Even if the slow-moving masses stuck to roads, their vehicles would not be able to go many more miles. The unused paths were quickly disappearing under snow and ice packed by many seasons.

He stopped by a truck with more patched than unpatched metal. The only part of the vehicle not browned by slush was the recent addition of the Army of Earth's flag hanging limply from its smokestack. The tear of blood from the white eye defied gravity and stood out parallel to the ground. Why did the owner of the truck not follow the Army when they separated? He was tightening chains on enormous wheels, and Janus almost asked him the question before he paused to ask himself. He yearned for the direction of war. With each day at Mew's side he never knew what the next would bring. There would be a great relief in battle — just following a commander's orders. Even staying back to defend Erebus would have been preferable to the messy ground and cold exhaust of this journey. Where were they even headed? He pressed his fingers to his face, expecting to feel the Elder Mask beneath his gloves, but he found only his real face. The mask was tucked away safe in his sidebag. He had not worn it since waking in Erebus, afraid of any new voices it may hold. It just felt nice being himself for a while, even if he had difficulty knowing who that was since he had woken up.

He moved around the truck and its trailer, admiring it without knowing why. Without a word Janus went to work tightening and linking chains. The truck driver nodded and smiled his approval and gratitude. The engine rumbled rhythmically. It was alive without being alive — unlike the engines in the Army of Earth he had passed during his survey of the forces surrounding the city. The tanks and assault-trucks of the Necrophim did not run and expel exhaust. They roared and breathed. Their armor, scratched with inverted sigils and wards, expanded and shrank with each breath.

The driver showed his appreciation with spice packets and tobacco Janus pocketed. After the tire chains were secured he started to move among wagons but paused deliberately in a cloud of exhaust. The smell was still rare for him, and although it threatened to choke him he still preferred it to the unwashed smell of the masses. His eyes began to water by the time he moved on, and he secured his bandana over mouth and nose before proceeding into the crowds. So many of the people were familiar to him. A person would pass and he would have flashes of impossible memories of a man at the same time being his father and an office mate. Janus would pass a cookfire and the children crowding it, and he would just for a second recognize them both as his sons and the elderly couple running the corner convenience store. The myriad conflicting memories faded more each day yet he still worried he was going mad. The only reprieve came when he was by himself, but that too was an impossibility that faded more each day. He knew the Elder Mask would help, hoped it would help narrow his identity to a more manageable number, but he was not entirely sure he wanted the memories of all those lives to fade. Every once in a while he would pass a face that reminded him of loves he did not want to forget, of days' disappearance that would wound him greatly.

He found that by circling trailers and ox teams that he had accidently come back around into a crowd of people again. Mew's voice was always even, always quiet, even when speaking to large groups, but he could hear her again from somewhere nearby. He imagined that, as always, she was encountering questions from all directions. She just waited as patiently as the masses around her until just the right question appeared.

"Yes, do not dismiss these memories when they visit your thoughts. They are fleeting, I know, but a blessing, a blessing from your loved ones. And who are these loved ones? They are *all* all of us. Remember? They are your mothers and grandmothers. Everyone at one point was your neighbor or your daughter or your savior. You, friends, were once their fathers or their greatest loves. Remember? Do not fear these feelings, embrace them. When you see someone on the road, take them into your arms, and they will remember. Cherish these memories, for one day soon they will be gone, and all we will have will be memories of memories. But that is how they will live on, that is how these other lives will survive, by our will power alone. And if you remember that everyone you meet was once your mother, and that everyone you see you were once mother to, you will not harm them. We must remember. We must remember. We must..."

Janus looked back over the distance traveled. The ground had been pulverized by boot, hoof, wheel, and tire into a muddy pulp. The dark slush would freeze overnight. If the Horde followed they would have a jagged path to traverse. Protecting Mew on her pilgrimages, he had been kept away from the war and did not know the strengths of the Army of Heaven. He wondered what machines they would follow in. Holding the rich resources of Kaldera as they did, he expected them to have an excess of oil engines, but tread and tractor tire would be nothing soon enough if the winter returned in force again. He saw the exhaust of a truck back over a couple of hills turn black as its tires spun in the dirty snow. He knew it would not be the first vehicle already left behind on this peregrination north.

Behind this truck, almost a half mile from Janus, fell Antony of Lovewell Dam. His shackles grew even heavier in the mud. The boots someone had given him when he woke to find his own stolen were coming apart over the uneven ground. The soles seemed to tear from the body with each step, and they now let in the dark slush the rear of the migration was left to trudge over. Even before falling he was out of breath. The ropes that had suspended him above the City of the Seventh Day, that had hanged him from perch and Greater Prophet, were still wrapped around his body. They sometimes inexplicably tightened when he breathed deeply.

He shook the mud from his hair in time to hear the laughter. "Damn Antony!" the people yelled at him. He was certain many of these crowds had to have been at one time supporters of the Territories. Odds dictated that many, if not most, once welcomed the sight of a Lesser Prophet, yet they now all pelted him with any rotted fruit that could be spared.

"Hey! Damn Antony! Can ya hear yer song now?" yelled the driver above the cough of his truck. All Antony could see of the man was his wind-burned elbow sticking out the window. Bald tires spun and sank. Rocks broke free from the gritty spray to pelt Antony and anyone near. A man, his cheek bloodied by the spray, pushed Antony back into the sludge.

The truck choked and quit in a burst of opaque exhaust. Antony was not sure what everyone was cheering about. He slowly crawled back to his knees unmolested for the time being as men rushed to examine the vehicle. The rest of the crowds continued to migrate around the scene. The mud apparently managed to disguise him. He remembered fondly a time when most of the land did not recognize a Lesser Antony by sight.

He wiped the mud as much as he could from what was once a tomato. It would not have been wasted on him if it had been fresh to any degree, so he picked it apart looking for any edible bites. He turned away from anyone watching before chewing on what little was left. He was thankful for the absence of any taste as he gagged on the tough texture.

As soon as he stood he heard the cry "Damn Antony!" from behind. He steeled himself for the inevitable blow that came across the back of his thighs. The man ran around him, swinging a stick and spitting instead of finding the words to convey his confusion at how Antony still stood. He threatened with quick jabs that stopped short before the stick was caught up in Antony's shackles and hands. The man was on the ground before either of them knew it, his jacket now as muddy as his boots. He frowned up at Antony and the stick positioned to now come down on his head, eyes quivering. But Antony just sighed, broke the stick over his knee, and fell back into the dirty snow. This was where he was most comfortable. He barely felt the people walking over him anymore.

The ropes crisscrossing his chest tightened again as he was lifted from the slush.

"Ho, little brother, you'll not get off that easily. We Antonys great and small take our penance on our feet."

He was set back on his splitting boots, roughly brushed off by enormous hands, and pushed forward into the line of pilgrims. He did not need to look to know it was the giant man now known as RackBreak beside him. He would recognize that voice anywhere. He would remember the feel of those ever-calloused hands as though they were his own. The presence of a Greater Antony would always unnerve him. Although, for once, maybe the first time, it was welcomed.

The feeble sun above had shifted for the day, and the giant man's shadow fell over him as an old woman neared. Her bent figure, lost in a plethora of quilted folds, made for a preposterous scene as she spoke to RackBreak's waist.

"He's Horde, he is!" Her twiggy fingers finally emerged from a sleeve to point at Antony. "Damn him to hot Hell!"

"No, no, shriveled one," RackBreak said, easily breaking the metal of Antony's shackles, "he has learned the error of his ways, and he will continue to pay for them, but in service to the Liege of Foes, in homage to the Lonely Forgotten Sun of God. Be satisfied in his penitence. It started when he freed me from the torture of tithingmen. Does that mean nothing to you? No, a warm dip in the netherworld will be denied him for the present. Now scoot, old hag, scoot!"

Many minutes passed before either Greater or Lesser Antony spoke, but there were always "creaks" coming from RackBreak's joints and quiet moans leaking from his lips. Many racks may have broken in the service of stretching the massive man, but his chronic pains were obvious to anyone walking near. He walked slowly and with an undeniably awkward gait. Both of the men fell slowly behind family after family as the day progressed.

"The Brotherhood has no idea what is happening in the Territories," the Lesser finally said. "They're immersed in the frontlines, unaware how the tithingmen are running things. The mutants are drunk with power."

"They care not," the Greater grunted, "so long as order is kept at home."

"But they…"

"They put their sons in charge. They knew the risk. Now, no more talk of these things lest I become inadequate or unwilling to keep you from lynching. It doesn't take much to remind these good people that you were not long ago one of the so-called 'Brotherhood.'"

"I've noticed."

"Then don't forget. This is their world, not ours. Let them determine its outcome."

"What happened to you Greaters?" Antony asked, stopping. The ropes entangling him again tightened.

RackBreak lurched to a halt, turning his bulk only slightly. The great man was covered head to foot in a mismatch of furs and sewn and rebound coats and cloths. There would be no gear large enough for a Greater Antony in the entire land, so he was making due with stretched and amalgamated clothing. His head was wrapped in a thick blanket. Only dark eyes squinted from the makeshift scarf and mass of salted hair. "I, it appears, am one of the last," he grumbled, "and I *was* one of the last to realize that this is not my world, nor is it my world to determine. I had my chance. The Shining One lied. It is not my legacy to forge this planet into my past. You Lessers... we are the same, you and I. Look what happens when you won't accept the same truth. Foul deals with cosmic nightmares? Disease and starvation to win allegiance not entirely ours? This has never been our way. Our time has passed. We don't belong here. Maybe we never did." The wrinkles around his eyes squeezed as he nodded north, toward the now moving front crowds. "This is their world, their time."

The Greater could not see Antony's frown as they resumed their walk. *We are not the same*, the smaller man thought. *We haven't been for a long time*. But he looked forward along the mile of carts and crowds, to where he assumed the Alabaster Princess preached, and to where Wulf led, with grudging agreement. For now, at least, he too would follow.

Leagues ahead of Antonys and prophets and reluctant leaders, Ivy received the messenger link with unbridled anticipation. She led the man's horse to a collection of water running from the last of the surrounding hills. It snorted and gasped but enjoyed the cool drink.

"What's it say?" Harlowe appeared behind her to ask.

She pocketed the note while handing the messenger a recently edited map. "Arcade Herod was fascinating. I could have spent a lifetime in Priest's mansions, reading all his letters and maps. I'll go back after the war's over. Anyway, he has a hidden depot a day from here, filled with guns the Horde shouldn't know about." She took the unburned cigarette from Harlowe's frozen teeth and put a struck match to it. "And that," she said, taking a puff and placing it back in his macabre smile, "is where we will take them."

Ivy took one look back over the lines and masses after sending the messenger on his way. The camps had dispersed. The crowds' few working vehicles were struggling to action. She and Harlowe shouldered her gathered gear, both looking to the sky for final direction, and headed toward the prairie in an eastward bearing.

XLIII

Coming from the land of the near and far
not content to watch with myriad eyes
scuttling plain and tree and falling star
he counseled fools, gods, and the not so wise

— The Fallo Terminus (XLII)

The tinny sound of ricochet bounced around in Slayd's head as much as it did the corridors of the bunker. The deeper he traversed into the open floors the higher the sound rang and more distant the sound grew the more it echoed. He grimaced as the reverberations continued between ear and shrunken ear. He had not been alone for days, and it had worn on him. The constant chattering was like the bullets and shot being fired into the bunker. It got stuck in his brain and reflected back upon itself. All the same frivolous questions. The same petty concerns assailing him constantly. This was why he had lived above the rabble for so long, why he had placed himself above their incessant whining and mundane conversations. Could he do so again, or had that time passed? He could find some abandoned, remote villa to wait the war out, raid wine cellar and library, and eventually ingratiate himself with whatever nation rose afterward. Or was this time different? He had a nagging suspicion that the land was on the threshold of something new. The peasants were even more crazed than usual, as evidenced by the metallic taps growing higher in pitch.

Something tinkled through grate and railing above to bounce off his head. He snatched it from the air with serpentine speed before it had even passed eye level. The wrinkled bullet was proof of the chattel's waste — their lack of focus in philosophy and direction. Whom were they following? These people had been traumatized from what they saw floating over the night in Erebus. They were cold and startled, and now they just moved in unison with the steps of their neighbors.

Slayd flicked the lead pellet and cringed at the close reverberation of the sound. It bounced and fell through the grating of the floor to more grating below. No, he found himself a clichéd glutton for punishment. Perhaps it was the human side of him that convinced himself to see this through. Despite the whining of the pilgrims, he was definitely curious as to how this would end. They were crowding together and blindly following each other to the edge of the cliff. They were knowingly traveling north, to a land with the reputation of per-petual frost, in a time foretold to be endless winter. These prairie dogs were persistently fascinating. No, if he deserted south to some hidden seaside resort he would miss out on mass suicide. He could vacation later when all of the self-fulfilling apocalyptics had burned themselves out. For now this was all too interesting.

He stopped at yet another gray door in the gray wall on a black level over other black levels surrounding the open chamber. The gen-erator was barely strong enough to power the dim lights — two to each level — glowing from rounded cages. Slayd's hope that the armory held more than just munitions had led him amongst the levels in search of something to keep his interest while the shooting continued above. The depot was not as deep, however, as he had hoped. It was only three levels, not including the main bunker, and most of the rooms had been searched before people started firing on each other. He unlatched and pulled open the hermetic door.

The room was lit only by the light of the main chamber and, like the rest of the depot, was unheated, so he moved sluggishly through the grayness to read stacked boxes and containers. They made up only a small part of the small room. His tongue flicked to taste the air. In the room, he could only hear the clanging of he ricochets, not the initial cracks of firearms. Or perhaps the gunplay had slowed. When they arrived at Priest's armory they found that most of the supplies had been pillaged by the bunker's own guards, but there still had been enough rifles and ammunition to equip a fifth of the pilgrims. *But how many rounds would they waste on each other*, he wondered. Upon breaking lock and door, Janus Legionary had immediately gone about to organize the people and disseminate rations and firearms evenly, but it was only about an hour into the process when the shooting started. Old grudges intensified over boxes of bullets. New indiscretions exploded over crates of daggers. The small woodland hiding the depot had erupted with the smell of gunpowder. Knives shook blood off onto the snow-drifts. Slayd found himself barricaded in the bunker before he knew what had happened, chastising himself and Wulf for not expecting the debacle.

He took one of the many boxes and stepped back to the doorway, stretching and taking a deep breath before heading back out into the walkways. The clanging reverberance assailed his ears again, but now he was not sure if it was the echo of gunfire or incessant chattering, if it was new or just shadows that refused to dissipate. He closed the door behind himself, broke the handle off, and memorized the door's designation number.

"As annoying as the insects are," he said aloud to himself, "they certainly are endlessly fascinating." The populace's greatest indiscretion was its ability to make him hate himself. It appeared, at different times over the years, that he could not stay away even if he wanted to. Sure he had even had decades of scholarly hibernation, but he always found himself pulled back into the masses. He could not deny finding their self-destructive idiosyncrasies addictive to watch, and it was this unavoidable failing of voyeurism that disgusted him. The rabble made him weak and would no doubt be the end of him.

And is *this the end?* he wondered, climbing grated cold steps. He could hear the frantic chant of the preacher as he neared the ground level. It was muffled by conflicting echoes and, no doubt, huddled bodies and came to him as a mumbling mess of low noise. For Slayd's entire life he had been hearing doomsayers and endcryers warn of Armageddon, of Deliverance, of Final Days, spiritual entropy, moral dissolution, Divine Judgment, soul-wide upheaval, End of Days, and the Twilight of the Gods. Were these days any different? Perhaps to the ignorant masses it might seem like the ages were ending, that prophecies foretold were actualizing, but Slayd knew better. Sure, disease, famine, and now war walked the land, personified and equally worshiped and reviled, but what of the Forgotten Horseman? Few knew as Slayd did, that the eastern men — Washkington and his brood — had conquered Conquest, preemptively stalling portention for a hundred years. Who even remembered the God King Nim, divinely chosen to crack Earth, anymore. Few people lived long enough to watch the cycles repeat, prophecy shout and wane, and prophets birth loud and die quiet. Slayd considered himself pardoned for not seeing the uniqueness in this latest age of apocalyptics.

"...this time the Lonely Forgotten Sun of God, the great princess who protects your people, will rise. This will be a time of distress such as has not happened from the beginning of nations. But today your people — everyone whose name is found written on Her heart — will be delivered."

The main level rooms were warmer than the rest of the depot, but

Slayd did not taste any ozone in the air, so it had to have come from the warmth of so many people huddled together in such small spaces. Green faces looked up as he entered but quickly returned to the manic mannerisms of Milliam Pittsfield. The man had a quiet voice in the room, and only Slayd knew how well it bounced down halls and levels in the gray metal. A young boy tried to hand Milliam a *Fallo Terminus* but was ignored.

"The multitudes in the dirt of the earth are only sleeping the deep sleep of the righteous. They knew and know the truth and they will wake today to an everlasting life, but those that die today in ignorance will wake to shame and everlasting contempt. Those who are wise will shine like the brightness of the heavens, and She who leads you to righteousness will shine today like the stars for ever and ever. Prophesized today, surrounded by the unnatural, in cold metal and earth, is the day of deliverance."

Slayd stepped on hand and knuckle as he wound through the sitting crowd. The room tasted like soiled children.

Milliam continued. "In their greed false teachers will exploit you with fabricated fables. Their condemnation has long been hanging over them like a sword hung by a hair, and their destruction has not been sleeping. They will freeze today in Earth's upheaval. Pray with me as the mundane decays to leave only the eternal. Pray as flesh burns today to make way for spirit." There was a certain lean to the direction of the heads in the crowd. They shuffled inward to hear the preacher's whisper. He was quiet even when he yelled, "I don't need it, I know it!" as the small boy tried again to hand him the book.

For just a second Slayd considered challenging the preacher. There would be a special delight to do so in front of the families, but the crowd was quiet and soothed despite the outside noise and the occasional round fired into the bunker.

He noticed that the sounds of gunfire had slowed, as he entered the front forward center of the depot. It was as dim as the rest of the armory, although highlighted by cracks of light lining broken seams in the aging structure. It looked as though someone had finally figured out how to return the shotshields to the closed position, explaining earlier loud sounds and the lessoning of the tinny echoes. The whining voices still ricocheted between Slayd's ears, however, as Milliam's sermon slowed in the room behind. Gunfire still sounded from outside, although reduced in frequency and lessoned against the bunker walls. Slayd popped the seal on the chocolate rations of the crate he carried and took a bar for himself before setting the box in front of Antony of Lovewell Dam.

"Happy Denunciation Day!" he exclaimed. From somewhere within his tattered robes he produced a short but wide-mouthed mug for the chocolate bar. "I bet you had forgotten it was a holiday."

"The Horde seems to have a holiday every other day," Wulf said from the front of the room. Even with the shotshield down he stood as Slayd had left him — arms crossed, stiff, staring at the now forward wall from beneath his hood. "We should use that against them." His head tilted toward the filthy and bruised man crouched before the box of chocolates. "Are there any holidays they refuse to fight? Any holy days of rest we could take advantage of?"

"Who is this 'we' you speak of?" Slayd interjected. "I'm afraid you have us mistaken with — yikes!" He jumped as he noticed Ms. Mowgli behind him. "What're you doing in here? Ma'am, you need to be protecting my cart." He jumped again as her hinny brayed from a corner he had not noticed. "And take that mother of ticks with you. Someone needs to be keeping pilgrim cooties off of my possessions." Shot rang off the bunker's outside walls for steady seconds. Before she headed out, Slayd handed her a rifle from a crate. "You'll need this. Find some ammunition for it." The sorcerer looked around sheepishly as Ms. Mowgli pulled the hinny from the room.

After minutes in which the only sound in the bunker came from Antony biting brittle chocolate, Slayd asked, "Where's everyone else?"

"There've been substantial lulls in the fighting since Mew went out," Wulf answered. "Janus and this 'RackBreaker' followed her. I think it may be over soon."

"Perhaps you should go out to check. Inspire them to unity. You've noticed haven't you? There're new banners appearing every day. I even saw a man having a red teardrop tattooed under his eye."

"That has nothing to do with me." Wulf finally turned to sit on the cold floor next to Antony. A chocolate bar disappeared into his hood.

Between his own bites, Antony mumbled, "All Hymns Day."

"What?"

"If the Army of Heaven is true to the Song, they'll rest on All Hymns Day. It's a day to pause from work. The only activities allowed are prayer in singing and evangelization of the workers."

Wulf wrapped himself completely in his cloak. "Does the Horde use a lot of slaves on the frontlines?" he asked.

Tightening his swollen jaw, Antony growled, "The *Ashmedai Adat El* does not allow slavery. The Army uses powder monkeys, newives, and other volunteers to supplement the lines. They're all there by choice. I know for a fact that even your own people use shield maidens in war."

"Shield maidens are promised their own special halls in the afterlife. What are these 'volunteers' promised?"

"A role in the new order after the war. Roles that are delayed as the war stretches on. Look, I'm not going to defend the *Ashmedai Adat El*. I'm here aren't I?"

"Yes," Slayd hissed, "and why is that exactly? You're an emancipated man again. You're free to go at any time." A shot rang against the bunker, and Slayd frowned as he blew into his mug. The chocolate was steaming inexplicably. He sipped it loudly, looking through the heat at the man the people had started calling "Damn Antony."

"Where are we headed anyway," Antony asked under Slayd's gaze.

"I'm heading north to N'Midgaard," Wulf said, "I don't know where everyone else is going."

"They'll follow you anywhere," the slightly digitized voice from yet another corner said. All except Slayd looked to the sculpted metal man whose presence was ironically so easy to forget. Six tiny insectoid eyes on an otherwise featureless full helmet caught the dim gray light of the room. Full segmented armor was polished as a mirror yet it refused to shine. The seven-foot bipedal soldier crouched in the low room but had not moved in hours.

"It speaks," Antony noted. "I thought we were supposed to ignore you."

"I am here to observe, nothing more," the Agent of MANN responded evenly. "You'll forgive me if I sometimes do it aloud."

Slayd licked chocolate from thin lips. "If you ask me there's more than enough forgiveness around these parts."

It had appeared that the bulky Agent of MANN had been waiting for them outside the depot when they arrived. He had informed them concerning the previous occupants of the depot, of his mission to observe the peregrination's movements, and had said little else since their arrival. If he answered questions it was with curt responses.

They had few questions for him. Because of MANN's isolation and mystery, Slayd was not sure if others knew the rarity of this inter-action. Throughout the centuries an appearance of an observer of MANN was of bad portent. The hidden empire rarely made itself visible outside its eastern enclaves. Slayd had more experience than most with the mysterious workings of the ancient civilization, yet even he had never seen one of their agent observers. He could not even tell what manner of human this was. Cyborg or armored soldier or some-thing more insidious. Its segmented hide was made of some unknown metal or ceramic that did not interact with light like usual materials. Its dark reds, opaque blues, and miniscule white trim appeared to bend light around its insectoidal limbs. The tiny striped and starred flag on his chest was barely visible, yet it gave the soldier away as belonging to the subterrestrial nation. *But why observe this motley mass of pilgrims?* Slayd wondered. He did not care. The agent bored him.

Milliam's preaching had ended. To Slayd's pleasure his slight voice had ceased echoing from the other rooms, but to his chagrin it ap-peared next to him.

"Has the violence ceased?" he whispered. He had brought two jugs of water from somewhere within the depot and gave one to Antony to drink from. The other he used to soak a rag before cleaning the man's face. Antony pushed him away.

"It appears your apocalypse will have to wait for another day, doomsayer," Slayd answered, pouring out the rest of his mug on the floor. He kneeled over and scrawled in the chocolate with a dark claw. "Unless you can divine otherwise from my leavings. We found no tea in the rations so you'll have to make due."

Milliam covered his ears at the screech of claw against metal. He appeared to be the only one to hear the sound. From gritted teeth he said, "Concerning the day or hour, no one knows, not the most blessed or damned, but only the Star that shines past all other stars."

"I'll waste no more time here," Wulf interrupted, standing and wrenching a stubborn lever on the wall as thick as his arm. Chains from somewhere deep in the walls rattled and tightened, and the shotshield lifted loudly and slowly by a few inches before he pushed the lever awk-wardly back to its initial position. Thin light pierced the grayer interior from new slots in the exterior wall. "The people are armed in case the Horde follows. They'll hole up here if they're smart. They'd be fools to follow me into N'Midgaard. *I'm* a fool for heading to N'Midgaard."

"Then why are you going?" Antony asked, swatting Milliam's hand away from his face again.

"He already told you," Slayd said. The sorcerer ducked as rifle fire glanced off the slats of the wall. The echoing resumed. Mindless chatter from the other rooms. Milliam's voice wafting between ears. He grabbed the preacher by the scruff of the neck, pulled him away from Damn Antony. His feet dangled as Slayd held him. "What's your game, endcaster? A mere week ago you were extolling the blessings of Slog Sabbaoth. Do your spiritual loyalties come at so low a price?"

Wig and faux beard askew, tattooed eyebrows quivering, Milliam said, "The Lonely Forgotten Sun of God is another no… note in the Divine Song. We all are. She has a pa…part to play in The End."

Slayd dropped him, and for the first time he looked to the Agent of MANN. "What lunacy this must all seem to you."

"I am only here to observe, not interfere."

"Yes, yes, well I envy you."

XLIV

of the seven celestially Governed Elements
    (3) Heaven
"...utilizes the advantages of the night; cold; the base impulses of men"
  —Hyper Khan's "The War of Art"

illiam Pittsfield went running past, and the slush darkening the tips of his robes became covered in new mud. He splashed those he passed, but no one even noticed the grime anymore. No one even noticed the smell of each other anymore. The famine was considered to have ended before the war, but its effects were still felt. The loss of so many animals contributed to a soap shortage. Some of the children RackBreak Antony walked among had probably never known a good bath in their short lives.

Women pushed their way through and around the crowd, trying desperately to catch up to Milliam. It was as though they hit a brick wall when they encountered RackBreak. He stopped to let them work their ways around him. The women wore shapeless layers of robes and coats, but it was obvious to him that some were pregnant. An inordinate amount of women had come out of the City of the Seventh Day pregnant. Since the blights of the prior years, the people of the lands had certainly done their best to compensate for the barren time. It had been more than just the fields that had refused to produce, and the population had felt the need to make up for lost time. But it had been slow going. Like the farms, the families in and out of the Territories had been slow to replenish. But RackBreak had heard the new rumors, of the Lonely Forgotten Sun of God's fecund presence. For many seasons now he had heard of her fertile blessings across the land, of babies appearing nine months after her pilgrimage through a village, and the number of fattening women coming out of Erebus had convinced RackBreak.

These women disappeared into the crowds ahead of him. Even from his height he lost their progress in the masses and wagons traversing the road and fields. All around, the cropland had been flattened beneath snow packed over the past seasons. It was not deep nor uniform, but it had been enough to smother whatever type of corn had once grown around the town they approached. Crooked stalks, bleached yellow and brittle to the touch of a breeze, swayed and disintegrated from the passage of the people and their carts. Ox and horse gave the ugly remnants of the fields no second glances. What was becoming of this world, RackBreak wondered. Was this perpetual winter the result of witch, werewolf, or angel? Such a cold sun was unheard of to him. He found Earth's slow turn unfamiliar. If only he had come here earlier. If only he had not been betrayed. But no, he pushed the thoughts from his mind, knowing them to be poisonous. Such thoughts were for Lessers. He had felt the same once, as did no doubt all Greaters, but he had accepted that this was not his world, and not his world to change. Besides, it was too late — to late to find what he had come for. He was too old and this world was too far gone. He was doomed to live out his days in the memories of what could have been. The people in this world were on their own.

The lines of walkers in front of him were splitting as they came to a wagon deeply entrenched in the sludge of the road. Its owner had apparently recently abandoned it. The canvas had already been scavenged. Two men were working at removing some of the paneling.

"No," RackBreak grunted, "for now it is better served in its original function." He continued to speak as he lifted its back end. Ice and great chunks of mud dripped from the wooden wheels. He set the wagon on drier ground. There was no exertion in his voice. "One day, perhaps soon, it will make more sense to cannibalize the simpler carts, but not yet. There'll be plenty of time to cut the wheat from the chaff in the North." Proud to have kept the crippling pain in his joints from his voice, he moved on as two families starting climbing into the wagon at the same time. An elderly man brandished one of the new rifles from the depot, and the dispute was quickly settled.

Half a league back and an hour earlier, RackBreak had seen a group of boys pulling back and forth on a scarecrow's stand out across the bare fields. They now raced past him, chasing the lead boy who stumbled in his laughing run while trying to steady the pole held tightly in his arms. He shook embers of straw from long hair just as yellow. The scarecrow smoldered and burned but only flamed up when he stopped for breath. The sticks and scraps of scarves they had added to the effigy for wings fell crookedly but lit up as quickly as the straw peaking from the figure's spare outfit. The laughing commenced and the boy was off again, his pursuers unable to catch their breath between giggles. From their hectic passage, a man's hat and a pickup truck's contents had caught fire.

The tiny town the loose convoys neared had no name as far as RackBreak could tell. As far as he could remember — which was pretty far — he had never been in this little area of the continent — in this world or his own — but he was beginning to see what he expected. They passed fenced-in sheds that at one time would have held farm hands and equipment, at other times would have housed lookouts. It looked to RackBreak that the pilgrims had already gone through the small structures, although many still appeared with cans and empty crates to repurpose. There was a large segment of travelers taking apart the fences, collecting the nails and the better pieces of wood. RackBreak was reminded of locusts whose mass passage left behind only the stem of crop or the skeleton of cow.

Dogs ran everywhere in what was now becoming a frenzy. The only way he could tell the difference between pilgrim dog and hamlet dog was the amount of mud crusted to the tail. The canines themselves did not seem to know the difference. They nipped only at the nearest bitch. But the dogs left the travelers alone to disassemble signpost and stable.

RackBreak could not imagine that the fence circling the town proper had been anything practical even before the masses got to it. Most of the wood looked too brittle even for them to salvage. The posts were rotted at any point beneath the snow. Milliam Pittsfield appeared to have found the only stable one. It was larger and was one of the two to hold the missing gate into the simple main street. If the gate had at one time been crowned by a town sign, it could no longer be told as such.

The preacher crouched on the post. His wild gestures continually unbalanced him, while his sermon was heard only by those closest passing into the town. The surrounding women, some obviously pregnant, some only suspected to be, caught him each time before he leaned too far in any direction. To RackBreak they laughed as loudly as the boys tipping the scarecrow.

"Time comes as a thief. O, you can cry that Death has outwitted you, that God's Wrath is too quick for you. 'O my cursed Foolishness! I was flattering and pleasing myself with vain dreams of what I would do in time, and, when I was playing the games of peace and charity, sudden destruction came upon me.' Well the Lonely Forgotten Sun of

God is under no obligation by any promises to keep any man out of destruction for one single moment longer. The day is upon thee! This is the town foretold in a land foretold. This day is *the* day!"

As RackBreak walked into town, pulling his wraps back up over beard and head, he found it telling that he had never seen Mew and this preacher together. Did she know the words he spread in her name? RackBreak had watched her christen a vesper from the crowd the previous day of the journey. The new prayer guide would lead her followers at sunrises. There were more people dying their hair green each day, but the Greater had never seen Milliam in Mew's graces, though the man had recently trimmed his robe in her colors.

"But even the greatest earthly kings, in their greatest majesty and strength, and when clothed in their greatest proclamations, are but feeble despicable worms of the snow, in comparison of the great and almighty Ending. And if it is but little that *they* can do, than how will *you* bear the Judgment? All the great kings of Earth against the Ending are as mites, they are nothing — no, less than nothing. Your love is nothing against today's dying sun. Your hatred is feeble against today's judgment. Before the old lights go out today you will rue spiting the new!" The preacher's voice trailed away as the people entered the town with no name.

The solid ground of the town felt good under RackBreak's sore joints. Every limb ached deeply within the marrow since his ordeal in the squatter town outside Erebus. It had felt like every man in the land had taken a turn at the torture wheel, stretching him beyond even his alien limits. His shoulders were now permanently crooked, his knees forever loosened, his hips chronically grinding like sand in a mortar against the pestle of his bone. The uneven softness of the road had been a pain almost too much to bear. Each step sank crookedly or turned inflamed ankles. The dry-packed hardness of the town was a godsend. On the main street his pain dulled to just a pinching warmth.

He found it practically a joke to call the street "main" and even the town a "town." There was a general store that had obviously been overly optimistic with an unused addition recently built to its side, ample yet empty stables, three homes, and what appeared to be a blacksmith shop. The shop was shut up as much as the homes, and, like the homes, was under siege by crowds of people knocking on locked doors and boarded windows. RackBreak could hear the clop of horse hooves and snorting as he passed a crowd licking at the door to the closest house. The people of the little town had brought their horses into their homes. They must have seen the convoys coming from leagues away. But were they playing it safe or had the pilgrim masses following Wulf north already achieved a reputation?

RackBreak caught up to the front of the line. A truck and wagons had circled, including a sigiled mule cart protected by one of the most intimidating women he had ever seen. Inside the circle camped Wulf and the sorcerer. Even the two scouts were resting within the camp — the odd zombie pistoleer and his clean little companion Ivy. They all looked up as he entered, but only Slayd spoke. RackBreak did not trust the wizard. He was another example of what people had begun to inexplicably call an "Heir of Aesar" — as was himself — but he had always found little to trust from anything coming out of Ouroboros. The kingdom may have only been on the edge of the Land of Nod, but its heritage was linked to closely for his tastes.

"How goes the rear guard, RackBreaker Antony?" Slayd asked, not looking in the Greater's direction. The mage was peeking beneath the drapery of his cart. Colorful vials, dried exotic plants, and patchwork shrunken heads hung inside, but most of the interior was filled by an intricately etched and gem-encrusted egg the size of an adult human. The cart's attendant cradled her hinny's head in her arms, scratching its ears. The animal looked more pleased than he had ever seen an animal to be.

RackBreak looked around before answering. He was tired, and the chance to sit tempted him, but he knew that unless it was perfectly comfortable seating, his back would pain him more than it already was. Also, he would wait to find out how long they were staying in the area. Short rests were never worth the pain it took to get back up. "They know not where or why they're headed, and it's finally making them anxious."

"It should," Wulf said. He was breaking off pieces of a pale cheese to share with Ivy.

RackBreak always found the man more familiar than he wanted to admit. He said, "You may not want them following you, but you don't seem to have any problem accepting their food."

"It's given freely."

They all followed a scampering sound up to the top of a wagon where a flag was being tied to a mast. The cloth's pale blue eye and bloody tear rippled in an inconstant wind.

"Someone take that down," Wulf grumbled. "We're not an army." The dark figure behind Wulf reacted slightly to this. RackBreak had never heard the Agent of MANN speak. Besides always following at the front of the line, this was the most he had ever seen the fully armored man move.

"We may need to be," Ivy said. Harlowe's pale shadow wavered over her from behind, seemingly shaken by the breeze like the broken chains beneath his ragged jacket. "There are rumors…"

"Yes," RackBreak interrupted, collapsing onto a stump among the benches, "every hunter we've come across or every family that's joined up with us over the past week has heard or seen signs of the Horde. Have no doubt, they follow."

"It's true," the Agent of MANN said suddenly in his tinny voice, surprising everyone, "a small contingent led by General Fobos of the Army of Heaven follows from the south."

Immediate silence pressed inward into the circle. For long seconds it seemed even the commotion of the town had quieted. RackBreak knew that anyone outside the wagons could not have possibly heard the agent, yet the dread the circle felt from hearing the name of the general was palpable, extending and affecting beyond them and into the crowds.

Finally, as more vehicles and carts and families moved into the gate of the town, and the sounds of scraping at door and window resumed, RackBreak stared the soldier in his many glassy eyes to ask, "How do you know this? How far behind are they?"

"I am only here to observe. Ignore me."

RackBreak almost offered his suspicions about the twin generals Fobos and Deemos, but decided he would not know where to start. He would share his fears with Damn Antony. Only he was sure to understand. If it was true that the generals were doppelbrothers, later Homega Sapiens produced and imprinted by Ammon Mars, then this rag-tag mass of pilgrim, hobo, transient, and wanderer was doomed. The Greater Antony Ammon Mars had long ago gone insane. Some say he was possessed by the Red Wendigo spirit of the Arctic for some heinous crime against man and god. If he had then used the Nursery, which was unheard of in a Greater's later life, then any Lesser Antony he imprinted would be as mad as he. It was no wonder then that the names of the twin generals were feared in the same respect as the Supreme Commander that begat them.

Wulf tossed RackBreak the remaining block of cheese, saying quietly, "He would be foolish to follow us into N'Midgaard."

"Yes, yes," Slayd said, walking the circle, "anyone would be foolish to head into the Granite Lands."

"I'm not these people's keeper. I never asked for this. I'm done with their faiths and their wars." The circle was silent again, but the eye flapped above them. Wulf rubbed his temples in a way RackBreak had seen him do in days before. So recently familiar with chronic pain, he recognized it in the face barely visible in the shadows of a hood. "Stop that pounding," the cloaked man said.

RackBreak now noticed that the kicking of locked doors had increased. People had begun to boost each other up to second story windows to find cracks between boards to peer into. It sounded as though men were shouting out from the houses, but he could not understand the threats from where he sat.

Slayd handed Wulf a bowl in which some sort of twisted root was seeping. Even beneath beard and headscarf, RackBreak could smell the foul concoction. Its steam was as dry as its scent. "This should help," the mage said.

Wulf silently poured it out as soon as Slayd turned back to his cart. "Will somebody stop them?" He gestured with the bowl to a space between the wagons. Through it could be see the general store and the group of people working the door lock.

"You're not their keeper," Slayd said. A pair of mongrels ran beneath and around the wagons at that moment. They snapped at each other and snarled at Slayd before kicking up dust and running from the circle.

Wulf stood and brushed the dust and snow, indistinct from each other, from his clothes. He began to gather his belongings around his ruddy horse.

"Are we heading out?" Ivy asked, concern in her voice. She put a hat identical to Harlowe's on over her headscarf. "You can't leave ahead of us."

"Try and keep up," he said while tying bindings and tightening saddle straps. "If I'm going to be followed, let it be out of these people's yards and ahead of the Horde."

RackBreak stood amongst the movement, unable to hide his wincing. He feared that sometime soon he would no longer be able to stand up after sitting, hence his fear of resting in the first place. On one side of him Slayd was hissing commands to Ms. Mowgli and the hinny, on the other side Ivy frantically bundled ammunition and dried food. In the middle of it all the Greater just stood alone with the Agent of MANN. They both just observed without a word.

Beyond the ring of wagons a horse bellowed from inside one of the houses as the splintering sound of hinges gave away the kicking in of a door.

of the seven celestially Governed Elements
    (4) Earth
"...*utilizes the advantages of great physical and sentimental distances; open ground and closed minds; differing concepts of life and death*"
   —Hyper Khan's The War of Art

ou better not be starting without me, Eonard, you son of a bitch! You don't know better? You telling me you don't know better?"

The old man was tackled as he tried pushing through Eonard's nephews. One of them pinned him to the ground, eventually turning him so the other could rummage through pockets and frisk ankles.

"You try sneaking any iron in, Maynerd?" Eonard asked, his heavily calloused fingers massaging the grain above and below the saloon table.

"No, you bitchlick, you know I'm a man of my word, not like you sons of bitches. Couldn't even wait to bugger me to my face."

"You're late."

"Like hell I am! Your son wouldn't let me cross!"

Ivy yawned as old Maynerd finally shook off the men and chose the farthest chair from the table to drag loudly across the floor. It was a shameful waste of the day. The sun shone strongly for the first time in weeks, and she was stuck in a smelly saloon with a bunch of smelly old men. Damn Antony may have appeared to be the youngest, but he smelled just as bad.

"You know we only have some pheasant-blusters left Westside and not enough shot to last another season. I'm not going to waste any on this son of a bitch farce of a meeting."

Eonard responded calmly, "You ain't got the guts, that's why."

"Not like your boys then? Fishing offa Lost Harb? I see them drilling one more hole…"

"Is this why we're here, you old geezers?" Damn Antony cut in, "because I thought your towns might want to make a deal. I can just have my people cross right now. I can leave you two alone to cockfight if that's what you'd prefer." He obviously was not taking any chances, Ivy noticed. The Lesser Antony wore his goggles indoors, his wool cap low, and a new mustache thickly. If these prairie river people had ever seen a Lesser Antony before — which was unlikely — they should not recognize him.

The men talked as Ivy sipped from Harlowe's mug. Whatever filled it tasted skunky and horrible. She set it aside, knowing he would not touch it and wondering why the pistoleer had ordered it. Like his cold cigarette, was the beer just something he held out of habit? Some sad reminder of... just what exactly?

Wulf had sent Ivy ahead to negotiate the crossing of the *Jormangandr*. The ice over the rushing river was unreliable at even its coldest and narrowest points, especially for such a massive movement of people, and so they had waited until reaching the tiny town of Eastside to cross. Until now, the peregrination had been following the giant river north by its eastern shore, but Wulf had planned to enter the North from its western side, and he had let her know that the time drew near. Sometime in the discussion, Damn Antony appeared. He had followed her ahead and had quickly made his interest in the negotiations obvious. Ivy was more than willing to let him help. She was curious, actually, as to how he would handle both towns. The control Westside and Eastside had over the bridges was rumored to be difficult to circumvent even before their animosity for each other became apparent.

"I know you business men have seen the amount of families coming up from the south," Antony continued. "Most of the community will be in the area by sundown. I would love to have everyone on the western banks by morning. Is that possible?"

"Who you running from?" Eonard asked, tugging at an earlobe Ivy deuced had seen many decades of similar abuse. "Which army?"

Antony pulled his goggles down and rubbed the indentations they had made. She knew that he was aware of the chance he was taking, especially concerning the line of questioning. But she knew that he knew that the elders sitting around the table would respect looking him in the eyes. "We are unaffiliated," he said after a long pause.

"So're we," Maynerd yelled backward as he stood to receive drinks. He placed a mug in front of himself and one in front of Antony. "Er, at least us Westsiders are. That's why we want to avoid any unpleasantries with whoever's chasing you. We don't want to appear like we're giving any side of this war any unfair advantage. We've managed to stay neutral, under the radar so to speak, this long. I'd hate to ruin that now, especially with the war ending soon."

Eonard stood to get his own mug and a pitcher. He poured the thick drink as he asked, "How many of you are there?"

"More than a thousand. Less than two thousand," Antony answered. Ivy had no idea if the estimate was anywhere accurate. She still had not seen how far back the mass reached. She only knew that it had grown over the prior week. But she could tell when Antony lied. His eyes had not locked. He had not steeled his shoulders. He was telling the truth as far as he knew. "You men haven't gotten this far in life by being stupid, but I say you're fools if you think the Horde will just leave you to your own peace. Those bridges will become very important to them once they resume their eastward expansion. You think they care about your autonomy? They may preach libertarianism, but you'll find that barely applies to those not singing in the choir. I've seen whole independent oil fields…"

"So it's Heaven's Army that's after you, is it?" Eonard chuckled. "Yeah, I heard they were duking it out with the Liege of Foes down south somewheres. All I care about is how you're going to pay for all of these people."

Maynerd coughed into his drink. "Now wait just one goddamn minute, you old fool! You're just going to let these sons of bitches through without knowing what they done? They'll be sitting on the bridges until the river freezes if that's the case, cause I ain't letting them into Westside, I'll tell you what."

Ivy watched a pair of even older men playing Noddy in the corner. There was barely room for their hands on the small table as it held their mugs and an extra lantern. There was only one window in the saloon and the dust covering it blocked most of the day, so the men played by their own light. They played without a crib, without pegs, instead keeping points with tiny copper coins so worn Ivy could not make out their derivation or worth. The men appeared equally matched but with strikingly different playing styles. One moved his cards slowly during long turns, while the other player constantly tapped a coin on the table and made his play immediately on his turn. The two men must have been a usual sight, Ivy observed, for the tabletop had chipped away over time under the one man's mannerism. Neither of them turned glance or ear to the goings on in the center of the room. Ivy left it as well to wipe the dust from an unused shelf near the window. She could only make out the vague shapes combining outside in Eastside. In the little time they had spent in the saloon even more of the communes had reached the town. She began to fear that Wulf, already in Westside, would move on before she had the chance to cross. She did not expect him to wait long.

Unless she was the one to empty it, a shelf with no books was an affront to Ivy. She rummaged through her satchel and produced *Allman's Mycology*. She had found it in the remnants of some squatter town before leaving Erebus. Most of its pages had been spoiled by the puddle the book had rested in, and she had easily read through it by the time they exited Ouroboros. She could not figure out if it had been a scholarly ordering of dietary fungi, a fanciful tale of subterranean evolution, or a memoir. In the end she decided not to limit the book to just one genre. She placed it on the shelf. It was the only one she was willing to give up at the moment. The jingle of Harlowe's broken chains brought her back around. He had not moved from his position watching the discussion, and she stepped back to his side.

"A half per person is not going to happen," Antony was saying. He had drunk all the viscous liquid from his mug and was now trying to wipe the stickiness from his fingers. "Most of those people have no forms of currency, most have nothing of value for trades."

"Kids'll cross free," Maynerd said.

"If accompanied by an adult," Eonard added.

"Come with us," Ivy said to sudden silence. Antony was the only man to keep his gaze before him. All others looked toward her. She could even hear the tapping of the coin quiet behind her. She took her wide-brimmed hat off and shook shoulder-length hair out. This was the first time in days she felt warm enough to do so. "If by some slight chance you convince the *Ashmedai Adat El* to leave your daughters and grain supplies alone, they'll take those bridges for profit or strategic worth. Don't fool yourselves. The MANN Lands are directly east. The Army of Heaven will need this crossing sooner or later, and I'm told it's not fond of taxes." She ran fingers through greasy hair, wondering how cold the water of the *Jormangandr* was. If the old men noticed the pistol revealed as her long jacket opened, they did not react. They had been asked to come to the meeting unarmed, as Antony did, but she had hid the small revolver. Harlowe wore his irons out in the open. They seemed unconcerned or afraid to take them from him. His seemingly ruined hands hung near the grips.

"The Liege of Foes battles near," she continued, "but his battalions are still days away. You'll be on your own…"

"And we have few guns," Eonard interrupted, staring at the table between thick fingers.

"So come with us," she repeated. "We'll have a head start. Your families will find refuge elsewhere."

"What? In the North?" Maynerd scoffed incredulously, "Little girl, don't make me laugh. Does the old bear know you're coming? If the hoar air won't kill you, the berserkers will. Your little green goddess will be less welcome there than in the Territories. And yeah, I know she's with you. I had a nephew that run off with some of her Ascendants or Ascensionists or whatever about a year ago. I'd recognize those idiots anywhere. They going to pick up a spear when the Horde comes calling? How are those feys going to protect my family? No, I don't think so. I ain't going anywhere."

Eonard agreed. "This town's been in my family for generations. No one's going nowhere. It was my great uncle that built the supports for that…"

"Your uncle was a thief and a bugger!" Maynerd blurted. "My great granddad built that bridge from the ground up without any sort of machine to help him. Your uncle came along and…"

"His name's in the concrete!" Eonard shouted. "How do you explain that, smart guy?" He turned back to Antony. "We'll charge a half for couples and a whole for families. We'll take interesting trades, but it'll slow you down."

"And that just gets you on the bridges," Maynerd said, wiping the froth from his mouth. "You still have to deal with me. You sons of bitches want onto the west bank, you're going to have to pay the…"

"Rifles," Ivy interrupted with. Harlowe shuffled uneasily behind her.

This time only Antony looked up. "What? No. You don't have the…"

"We can part with some ammo crates, some rifles — perhaps one for every able-bodied adult male in your towns."

"Well, now," both Maynerd and Eonard said in unison. They blushed before Maynerd continued for the both of them. "I like the sound of this. How many rounds you have for them rifles?"

"Enough for you to keep Heaven's Army away from your bridges."

~

"Why'd you have to leave me with those old fools," Damn Antony asked her when he found her later the next day.

"I could learn no more from them," Ivy responded.

The familiar rattle of Slayd's covered cart brought her attention back to the peregrination. Word was that the last of the caravans had finished crossing the *Jormangandr*. She herself had crossed early in the morning and now wandered what she could only guess was the front of the masses as it slowly composed itself to head sharply northwest. They would be leaving the side of the river for a few days, eventually following it again as they straightened more northernly. The great waters had been a welcome companion for weeks now and Ivy felt uncomfortable leaving it, if only for a short while. She often traveled at the front of the masses, and the people's direction gave her easy purpose. She could only imagine it did the same for the hundreds of people that followed without even knowing where they headed. Now they would be back out in the plains with only the dull sun for a compass. Although she was reminded, as a boy passed her with a green eye painted on his forehead, that most were increasingly using a new sun for direction — one of a different color.

Slayd's cart disappeared back into the crowds, its hinny being coaxed by the tender caresses of Ms. Mowgli, but Ivy could still see the cross-legged magician in meditation. He sat stolid, unwavering atop the shaking wagon. She had heard Wulf and the wizard talking days prior about the amount of spell-casting involved in keeping the Horde from spying on the camps through every torch, or assassins from suddenly appearing out of a fire pit. Slayd spent most days riding his wagon, immersed in new and old tomes, experimenting with alternatives to hide the peregrination from mystical eyes.

Antony was keeping himself mostly covered, but from what was revealed of his face Ivy could see that his bruises and cuts were mostly gone. As a Homega Sapiens he healed as fast as she did — about twice as fast as anyone else.

She walked through the moving crowds, around elderly and children and a bus that, unmoving, made only the sound of metal against metal. This was as far as it would go. Its bald tires were not even turning. Antony followed her, but it was many minutes before he spoke again.

"You have to convince Wulf to turn east again before N'Midgaard. I've tried, but he's dead set on whatever retribution there is for him in the Granite Lands. But he's dragging all these people to Hell along with him. Make him realize that."

The lights of the evening were making an odd night. The sun had disappeared below the horizon but left a cottony pall over the masses. This stain absorbed and collected numerous nearby light sources. Headlights and torches floated about like fuzzy bubbles of both warm and cold colors, as though fat fairies bobbed along the crowds to administer blessings. Antony must have noticed the spectacle as well, for he had pushed aside goggles and scarves and had stopped in his walk. Despite darker hair and a thin white scar leading from his hairline down to the tip of his nose, he looked exactly like the other Antony Ivy had known. Yet he barely ever reminded her of him. But how could that be? What she had gathered about the Lessers over the years made her believe that he should always remind her of Shiloh Antony.

She stopped as well, and the communes drifted around them.

"Where do Greater Prophets come from?" she asked. Antony avoided her unmoving gaze but adjusted back his cap and collar. She knew that he carried his only possessions, which now included a rifle he had somehow acquired over the past day.

"You wouldn't understand," he mumbled, adjusting the rifle strap across his chest before moving on again. "But they came from a world and a time they believed was better."

"Was it?"

"I used to think so too, but now I know it's just all the same. This war proves it."

"And, before it was destroyed, each Greater went straight to the Nursery and came out with two Lessers?"

He continued to stay a step ahead of her. "How do you know so much?"

"From a tithingman."

"You stay away from them," he said, grabbing her coat. She almost lost her balance.

"Where's your doppelbrother?"

He set her down and continued on the path. The cooling night was hardening the mud into sharply uneven steps. "I don't know. I lost track of him years ago."

"Do you ever wonder what's become of him?"

"No." His voice, deliberately lowered, he said, "For all I know he could be leading some Horde force against us right now."

"But how could that be? How can you be so different?"

He tapped his head before tapping his jacket over his heart. "There's more in here than what the Nursery... what a Greater Antony gave us. Every person you meet, every breath you take in a town your brother doesn't, every time you wake in a bed he does not, sets you on a different path. The paths may look parallel from up close, but the longer they run the more they branch from each other."

"What happened at Lovewell Dam?" Ivy asked suddenly.

"Are we at the front of the line or the back?" Antony asked. He took the time to look in every direction. "I can't even tell anymore."

Ivy looked in every direction for the Agent of MANN. The enigmatic figure was tall and could usually be seen over any crowd, and she used his appearance to find Wulf among the communes. Wulf had become increasingly difficult to find over the past week. When he could help it he rode ahead of her and any other scouts. When terrain or fatigue slowed him down he would be subsumed by parties and families believing him to be leading them. Occasionally, like with the crossing of the *Jormangandr*, he would grudgingly involve himself in planning for the masses. She saw no sign of him or MANN's agent. He had probably used the crossing incident to get a head start back north. The globule light display had diminished. Now all the colors were dulled by lack of moon or any distinguishing stars.

"Did you flood Lovewell?" she asked.

Antony buttoned up his coat and pulled his collar tighter. He now answered her questions exclusively under his breath with increasing speed. "When General Fobos comes to those bridges back there he'll immediately see their strategic value, and he has no interest in dealing with those old men every time he wants to cross. The rifles we gave them will barely slow Heaven's Army down. Fobos' patron angel is Abaadoon. He carries with him some chalice out of Pyramid Abysmal." Ivy was warm enough walking through the masses of body heat, yet still a shiver tickled up her spine. She too pulled up her collar as Antony continued. "Those two tiny towns won't last a day. They were warned. We warned them. They chose to stay because of some imaginary blood link to the land. So, in the end, whose fault is it when their children die? Is stubborn pride a virtue when it leads to the end of your lineage?"

"Their families have lived..."

"You want to know? I broke Lovewell Dam to stop the advance of Earth's Army. The Liege of Foes was unstoppable and on the verge of conquering Panhandle Territory. He had allies on the other side of the valley, but if he was slowed... he needed to be slowed down to give General Shriven enough time to come down from the north and cut off the advance. It was a perfect plan and it worked. The momentum was halted, and the Army of Earth has never really recovered. Thanks to your Resistance they learned about the trap and avoided the flooding, but they were stuck long enough for Shriven to land a decisive blow."

"But Lovewell..."

"It's no different than those bridgetowns back there. The people in Lovewell believed that some plant god gave them that land. They had fought off neighboring clans for years. The land was worthless. Soil wouldn't grow anything worth a damn, but their stubborn claim to it drew bandits and otherwise. They thought the people were hiding something. But I know for a fact that they only held onto it because of some sad attempt at religious identity. They were a prideful people, and it was their undoing. So I ask again. If the people of Lovewell knew the water was coming and had plenty of time to evacuate, then whose fault is it their children died? At what point is their stubbornness not held up to be a virtue?"

Before Ivy could even decide how to answer she turned to follow the new sound of sobbing. Two young men trotted by on donkeys, passing wagon and walker, and catching the eyes of anyone that would listen to them. The speaker wiped the tears from his cheeks, inadvertently smearing the green pain covering his face.

"It's horrible... they... so horrible. They're jus'... jus' killing each other."

The men answered questions as they passed. Before they were out of listening range, Ivy had heard the whole story. Westside and Eastside were under hails of gunfire.

If she listened closely she could hear their far-off rifles.

Witnesses were spreading the word that not long after the last pilgrim had crossed the bridge the two towns had begun assaulting each other with their new munitions.

"That was brilliant!" Antony exclaimed, looking down at Ivy. "You set them up so that we'd come out on top either way. Either they would defend themselves with their new guns, slowing the Horde down, or they would just kill each other, and we can swoop in later to retrieve what's left of the rifles. And we essentially crossed the river for free. Are you in contact with the southern scouts? We need to find out how far back Fobos follows, how much time we have to retrieve the guns." They could hear the gunfire less clearly now as the near caravans became loud with commotion. Not everyone had heard where the shots were being fired at or from. "Where are you going?" he asked as Ivy walked away from the noise.

"I can learn no more from you," she said.

XLVI

Deep in the ravines where He sleeps
three Maids for four secrets keep
For where virtue warms the worm
the meek, the weak, the sneaks, and the freaks
shall disport in the hurting dirt
—the Seven Suffragans' Slut

he sun shone brightly, unencumbered and of the gentlest of narcissus colors, and in this purest of lights Teca could see the witch's teats in their ripest of glories as they poked against the sheerest of gowns. The weightless fabric caught on treacle-colored nipples as all were lifted by a breeze lilting through the commune. It was a melody Teca could now hear the closer she stood to the Maid of *MGGT*, could now even feel as it softened the air between them. The woman's tan contours were revealed by the unreal summer and its unfamiliar warmth. Was the light so clean, the breeze so inviting, or had it just been so long since Teca felt any season other than crippling winter? The knight removed her gloves, tying them to her belt before gripping holster and hilt in an attempt to occupy her hands, else she would find them lingering, as her eyes were, over belly and breast.

"There was a little girl," the Maid said finally, moistening berried lips before continuing, "taken from her mother, brutally and without just cause by the Librans of the Needles, that Northern Order, the self-proclaimed 'Order of the Creed,' those who 'carry the torch' for the land to see by. This bastion of 'righteous judgment' in a fallen land stole a child from the bloodied bosom of her mother, under the guise of their charitable selflessness. The girl grew among them, knowing somewhere deep down inside that she was different but taking security in the acceptance and structure of their order."

Teca could not look away. As little Pilgrim the squire finally appeared to lead her horse back, she took off her jacket and handed it to him without even glancing backward. The Maid's hair was of the cleanest blonde Teca had ever seen outside the Granite Lands, and her long curls were spun from some wheel out of the stories of divine bargains and punishments.

"It was a tale of faeries and wyverns and knights for the little girl, of bold (but too bold) men with great mustaches and greater swords adorned by the gold and the blood of an angel. She so dearly wanted to be like one of those knights that she was told had so bravely saved her from a life of warts and toads. And they so dearly wanted her to be one of them as well, so dearly that they were, over the years, willing to overlook indiscretions — scandals with a mentor, discourtesy with a squire, even long errancies out into the big bad world of thin morality and thinner blood."

Teca gripped her buckles tighter, for one hand twitched in anticipation of squeezing one glorious teat. The Maid's breasts looked to have a succulent heft yet tilted upward to end in thick nipples and saucered aureoles as surprisingly dark as the witch's eyes. Their upward curve rested on a rounding belly Teca guessed to be six moons swollen — a belly the knight found her opposite hand to be brushing with just the slightest tips of her fingers. She pulled her hand away, feeling herself blush even under the unseason's warmth. Was it the fabric or the witch's skin that was so remarkably smooth?

The Maid laughed gently, smoothing the sheer dress over a blossoming belly button, and for the first time in many minutes Teca looked past her to the huts in the warm glen. More people had begun to gather, and she estimated that not many more could be living in the tiny commune. The few mushroom-shaped dwellings surrounding the sculpted cube could not possibly have held more people than those curiously emerging now. There were more children than adults, more toddlers than teens, with many of the youngest nearing the Maid that had introduced herself as Pliny when Teca first came riding into the glen.

Pliny was constantly trying not to smile as she spoke, her perfect teeth peeking from full and pursed lips. Her long-lashed eyes never wavered, never moved from Teca's face. She had yet to acknowledge the growing group of children playing around her feet and tugging at her translucent gown.

"You should be afeared," Teca muttered before clearing her throat. She had not spoken since announcing herself to the huts, had not had a chance to examine the massive, petrified cube grounding the hamlet to the glen, since Pliny had greeted her.

"But does this girl ever question?" the Maid continued. "Has she ever asked her elders *why* she was taken, *whom* she was taken from, why her lapses are tolerated, why she is first among strays?"

"Librans take in orphans all the time."

"The Northern Order does, surely, but why the preferential treatment for one specific little girl? Why did she move up through rank and file, despite numerous courteous indiscretion, to stand here before us today as such an honored paladin?"

Teca wiped sudden sweat from her upper lip, using the movement to sneak a glance at the shadows beneath Pliny's belly. They led down to painted toenails children were admiring. Teca tried to remember the last time she had seen painted toenails. They were on some visiting sponsor princess that had toured the Temple Needles. It could have been ten years prior, and those toes had been painted darkly, not with the baby blues and oranges of Pliny's cute little toes.

The Maid, unsure if she was paying attention, repeated, "Teca, you love your histories and your books and maps. What was the great schism between the Northern and Western Orders? Why did some Librans break from the Black Hills and ultimately settle west in the West?" She gestured with painted fingernails at one of the Librans hanging back at the edge of the glen. Teca did not have to look back to know she was pointing at Dharke Parbreake, even though for a few minutes she had actually forgotten about the Kalderan. She had actually been trying to forget about him and resented the reminder, but Pliny answered her own question.

"The original order split because of a disagreement in where the power rested. How is it a Libran can do such miraculous things? Is it faith that commands curses on the Order's enemies? Is blood or ash the Prime Medium? How is it that monks and paladins can call down such horrors on the children of *MGGT?*" She now picked up a particularly precocious boy. Teca estimated him to be at least 2 years old, yet he barely had any hair. His cheeks were rosy with effort or sun. He rested his head on Pliny's neck and Teca envied his mouth's proximity to one plump breast.

"When Librans began to multiply under the faces of the Hills," Pliny recited, "and sons were born to them, Lady Wayasu saw that one was fair; and she took a wife for herself of Dhani Antony. Then Blind Libra said, 'My spirit shall not abide in mortals forever, for they are flesh; their days shall be one hundred seven years.' Teca, even the children of this glen know the story, of how Librans believe themselves descended from the union of angel and hero, of how the northern knights believe their blood is imbued with the mystical qualities of the divine. But their time is up. Their blood is thinned. The magic in their veins diminished. No one of the Order of the Creed has been able to cast one of their silly little spells in a generation. And that is where the little girl, torn right from her mother's bosom, comes into play. That little girl, born of Chosen womb, fed from Maid's milk, blessed by nature and nature's coven, has mystical blood. And the knights knew that. This was their high lord's plan, a way to reintroduce wonder into the Libran bloodlines."

The sheer tunics and gowns of the glen hid nothing. The adults were in effect as naked as the children, and so Teca could not help but notice Pliny's one imperfection — the one tiny blemish almost hidden amongst bare curve and shining skin. Seeing the Mark of *MGGT* was a relief, but it also complicated things. The long journey to find the glen was now justified, but Teca was hard-pressed to decide the next step. She had never come across a commune like this, had never even read of any appearing in recent history. How was she to inquest such a large amount of people with only two knights and two squires? How was she to kill Pliny with so many children in the way? But still, the sight of the hickey emboldened her, focused her mind. The long travel would not have been in vain.

"Why aren't you afeared?" she asked, again clearing her throat. With one hand still on the hilt of her smallsword, the other moved from her revolver to wipe her forehead. She only had one round in the cylinder, and it was old. She could not even remember where and when she had found it. It had at one time been dipped in silver, but the shine had worn away before it had come into her possession. She was not going to take the chance of misfiring in front of lesser Librans.

"So ask yourself…"

"Knights walk into your glen of iniquity," Teca interrupted, gesturing to the commune, "and this man continues tending his flowers, this man sweeps his stoop, and you compose yourself as if you greet just any visitor. This is not just another day!"

From the growing crowd of toddlers emerged a little girl with hair the same color and curl as Pliny. She was holding the puffiest cat Teca had ever seen. Where the fur ended, the knight could not tell. It was whiter than white, and its crinkled face showed only a look of boredom despite it body hanging indelicately from pudgy arms. Pliny set down the boy she carried and took the purring cat, resting it against plump breast and belly.

Teca finally broke her gaze to give Sir Wica a knowing look. The knight had not dismounted and was refusing a jug of water for his horse. The people of the glen were avoiding Parbreake, for he twirled his thin sword in some mock exercise. He pretended to not watch the proceedings, but by his skittish eyes Teca could tell otherwise.

"You must be careful with Titty," Pliny scolded the children, "he doesn't like being carried." She then sighed deeply, the cat adjusting itself against the rise of her body, but the sadness in her eyes and an appearing frown was not directed at the toddlers. "Like our mothers and sisters before us, we have lived each day in fear, always worrying that some monk or knight would break in the door to our homes to brand us with hot iron, to drown us, to poke and probe our bodies with needle or finger. I used to pray each night, in whatever bed my parents had found for me, that, if caught, the Librans would hang me. I was so afraid of burning as a child I would freeze throughout the night rather than sit near the campfire. Still, today, I jump at the sound of horse and mail, have nightmares daily reminding me of my aunt's screams as a paladin sawed her nose off with the glass from her own mirror." She closed her eyes and buried her cheek in Titty's fur. "So am I afraid? Yes. Every single day of my life. Every morning I wake scared that this will be the day a man in pure white and red will choke me on my own cake or piss, screaming questions at me I don't understand. And every night I go to bed praying that these little girls and boys won't grow up in a world where they spend their dawn and dusk in the same cold sweats. So why am I not afraid? I *am* afraid! Every single day of my life. And that is why this day is no different from the rest."

"You…"

"Except for where it is different. Every one of these precious little girls and boys could tell you the story of the child, the girl stolen from her bleeding mother and indoctrinated into the sweet love poems of the *Sol Sistere*, taught to bow down to the ever-watching, ever-judging blind scales of Lady Libra's justice. Every one of them could tell you how she submerged herself in the fear and hatred of knighthood to help forget her wronged family, and how one day she would return, full circle, into the love of a community just like this one here today. And even the smallest babe has been told the tale of how the girl's appearance is the final step toward our liberation, toward the shedding of the intervening illusion. Her appearance is the revelation needed, letting us know we are ready for the final step. We will no more be separate from nature. We will become one with the land once again."

"You're familiar with wives' tales and the gossip of the land," Teca said, "congratulations." She was uncomfortable with all the movement. Children neared and played, pulling and pushing each other. Some cried. Some giggled. Skinned knees and chubby cheeks reddened. There had been an increase in babies born in the years following Phaemon's disappearance — what Teca saw as overcompensating for the previous barren seasons — but she had never seen such bright-eyed children in all her travels. How could they be so robust never eating meat of any kind?

Pliny ignored her comment. "They're a little rambunctious today. We've been harvesting honey all morning. Otherwise they would recognize you." She bent to pet the dark hair of a boy, and Titty leapt from her arms into the crowd. "Would you honor me, Teca, by breaking bread? We have some fresh royal..."

"Get that cat!" Teca yelled to the three Librans behind her as it ran across the open glen, a white blur over the white dust. "I don't want any of your moldy bread," she said back to Pliny.

"Ewe heard her, get the cat!" she heard Parbreake yell.

She looked back to see the knight and messenger squire looking at her, obviously angered at being scolded by someone of the Western Order. She had her suspicions concerning Parbreake as well but yelled and repeated her gesture toward them anyway. They each pulled daggers and ran through the glen and its denizens into the trees. If they lost the cat, Teca thought to herself, then all this would be in vain anyway. She could kill Pliny, but the witch's essence could still live on in its familiar.

The children toddled around the woman as the small mob moved backward toward the petrified cube. Teca could see that the dark object seemed to at times absorb the light of the glen the closer one neared its carved surface. The bright lady and children stood out amongst its shadowed aesthetic as though they or it were from different worlds, but as they backed into its shade both merged into a grayness that told Teca that it was she who was the different world's representative in the glen.

"Don't give in to rumor and slander, Teca," Pliny said, "you're better than that." She had been handed an infant by one of the older children. Its hair was as light as hers, but its skin was as dark as hers was light, its eyes as light as hers were dark. "Our bread is as fresh as that made in the Temple Needles. There is less difference between us and the knights of the Black Hills than you were taught. We only want what everyone wants, to become complete. Why do we suffer? Why does everyone suffer? Because life, as we've all chosen to so near-sightedly see it, is suffering. Everything in life is pain, because, as we see it, every-thing dies. Everything breaks. Everything gets old. Everything ends."

"Please, enough, I know all about your…"

"No, Teca, you've heard of us, I'm sure. You've read in your dungy cellar libraries about us. You've listened to your old men in your win-dowless temples rant about us, and you've believed without question their twisted version of out lives. But, no, you don't *know* us. We only want to return to that which was taken from us. Life has become an exercise in increasing the gap between the culture and the real. The realization of this is the first step to ending the suffering. The world may appear to be an endless sequence of impermanence, but what we've found — what humanity has forgotten — is the endless renewal inherent in a return to nature." She caressed rosy cheeks and ruffled tawny hair as she turned from Teca. "See the regeneration of nature? The salvation in seasonal repetition? The ultimate immortality in the cycle of death, decay, cannibalism, and sprouting?"

Teca would have had to trample some of the children to reach Pliny with her smallsword, and she was not willing to do that yet. But with only squire Parbreake near, she was now willing to try her one last bad bullet, yet she hesitated with hands on hilt and handle, and Pliny and the children turned to walk around the expanse of the cube sculp-ture until they were out of sight. Puerile laughter and heckling could still be heard around the glen, however.

She looked from mushroom hovel to shaded window garden, keeping her eyes on the adults of the glen as they rested from chores. Squire Parbreake neared without sound.

"It's a black taphoract," he said, yawning through his teeth. He was a small man with features too large for his body. She did not turn to look at him but could picture the faded and darkly smeared ash on his face he had not reapplied since they had met a day prior.

"I know," she muttered so low she would have been surprised if he had heard her. The idea of a black taphoract had come into her head before Pliny's appearance had distracted her, but she had quickly dismissed it. The existence of the commune had already surprised her, as it would her Order, but the idea of a piece of original *MGGT* spore still existing out in the land in this day and age should have been impossible. But the giant cube certainly looked to be carved from the petrified fungus mankind's forefathers found across the land. In those days the material was thought to be the remnants of *MGGT*'s fallen immensity, and the decay god's latter day followers carved the pieces into cubed chambers to protect the broken pieces of the One True Spore. But all the supposed relics of *MGGT*, including the shards of the original seed, had all been accounted for and destroyed by the Librans over a hundred years earlier. So what was this coven hiding in their black taphoract?

"Ewe should have taken her when ewe had the chance," Parbreake said laughing. "I can do it if you like."

"Shut up." Teca had been going on two days without any sleep she could remember. Following rumors to the unnatural glen, she had known that she neared an inquest, and she never slept well nearing an inquest. And the sudden appearance of a member of the distrusted Western Order had not put her at any ease. The Order of the Spirit was blasphemous. They were cannibals, eating still to this day the remains of the original Prophet. The Kalderan squire had found her and Sir Wica on the melting road to the glen. Alongside his horse ran a short-haired mutt the same dark color he sported in everything he wore — leather, paint, and large black feathers. He carried a fencing sword even shorter and thinner than her blade but made sure that they quickly knew of his expertise with a flatbow. The hound, angry-looking but seemingly mild-tempered, never left his side. To Teca's annoyance, the dog had not even chased after Titty.

The Librans horses snorted uncharacteristically. They all looked sideways at the black taphoract. Teca did the same, not understanding how she could have thought so little of it until now. It did not belong in the glen. It did not belong anywhere. The smoothly organic scenes completely covering the cube matched the arcing curves of the close branches wrapping the commune, but the object's opacity was an affront to the sudden summer of the glen. She put a glove back on, despite the heat, and traced the air an inch before the supple designs. Each scene blended into the next. Each dancing figure composed of person, plant, and animal. It was impossible to determine when one creature ended and another began. There was no inconsistency in style. The black taphoract had to have been carved by one person and would have taken a lifetime to complete. The giggling of the children of the glen now sounded as though it were coming from within the petrified object. The laughs were muffled but still as jubilant.

She turned from the sculpted abomination and found the sun full in her face. In the same motion she found her sunglasses and pulled the angelic necklace over her head, shaking her long hair out of its ponytail. Shielded from the weird summer, she looked over the glen, watching its scantily-clad inhabitants wander near the artifact and disappear behind and into its shadow. She wrapped the necklace chain around her leather vambrace and forearm, squeezing the winged charm so tightly she was sure she broke the skin of her palm. The knight and squire that had chased after the cat were nowhere to be seen or heard. She was biting her lip so hard she was sure that it too bled.

"Is this how the Creed's Order deals with witches?" Parbreake chuckled. "Should I have brought tea and cake to break with their mammys?"

Teca stepped into the squire's center of balance, her heel pressing against his, and she shouldered him to the ground. It was a move taught to her by someone outside the Order, taught to her when she was just a foolish girl. Parbreake's dog growled — the first emotion she had seen the mutt show. She stepped backward, her voice catching in her throat before she yelled "Who are you?" A couple returning to the glen with a basket of tiny apples stopped to watch. "Who're you to question me, asshole?" She kept a close eye on the dog, stepping back again. It had run to its owner's side to nuzzle the squire's shoulder.

Parbreake wheezed before coughing. "I'm no ass. And I'm no more than I've said. Just an exile looking for amnesty. I belong no more in…"

But she had stopped listening. She watched a woman overwater low ferns surrounding a hut before drinking from the water tin herself. Another woman added melon rind to communal compost. As the sun sank, the main square of the community dissipated, but the mushroom homes appeared empty, their open windows and doorless doorways were bare. She returned to the taphoract but could see only an abyss unless she removed her sunglasses. Even then, she had to replace them with her spectacles to see into the growing shadows. She hated wearing the eyeglasses in front of the Kalderan squire, hated him now knowing that she sometimes needed them, but if there was a way into the hardened structure then she needed to find it soon.

The shade was even darker on the far side of the sculpture, but she still should have been able to find any crease or even a hidden hinge. But not only were the organic designs seamless, without break or interruption in the writhing curves, but now she could not even find Pliny or the children. Yet still she could hear whispers before they were hushed. Teca hid her spectacles in a padded holder of polished stone as she rounded the taphoract, nearing a grinning Parbreake.

"Keep a close eye on the remaining coven. Follow them around if need…"

"They can't all be fitting in there," he interrupted. She just stared at his smiling face until he said, "Yes, sir."

She wandered the near woods, keeping the huts and gardens of the glen in her peripheral. She had never encountered such a commune before. Where were the decaying wicker men? The bloodfruit or teeth or fingers hung from foreheads? There were no sigils of *MGGT* smeared above doorways or grown into bark. She could see Parbreake wandering the glen, peeking into darkening huts. He had removed his cape and revealed himself to be even thinner than he initially appeared. He wore only the dark colors of his bastard order and had been removing the condor feathers from his cap and cape over the prior day. He had also been making a point to keep black tattoos on his hands covered around her. He was certainly keeping up the appearance of someone interested in leaving the Western Order behind.

She and Sir Wica had been weeks away from the Temple Needles when they came upon Dharke Parbreake. He stood out in the open, on a wide path with his quiet dog and had watched them approach for a half mile, yet he still appeared overly surprised as they neared. He introduced himself as a prior knight of the Western Order, fleeing from their wayward ways, and he had hoped to seek amnesty in Teca's Order of the Creed. But, as Teca had recently become aware, passage into the Black Hills was suddenly now strictly regulated. The Horde had blocked all the main routes into the Needles. Militias loyal to the new Territories patrolled through the hills night and day while an entire legion of the Army of Heaven surrounded the Libran monasteries.

Teca and Sir Wica, while ruminating over the days on their limited options for returning to the Needles, had been following the signs and rumors of the Maid of *MGGT* when Parbreake had conveniently revealed himself to them.

As the squire talked of his escape out of the West, he introduced the dog at his side while tightening the knot on a noose that had been taking Teca's attention since they had come upon the stranger. Beside his dog and pony, Parbreake also had an old woman tarred and feathered and bound next to the road. The tar cracked and dried in every wrinkle of her naked body, but Teca could still make out *MGGT*'s marks on her inner thighs. She was no doubt a Maid, but Teca had not even a chance for any inquest before Parbreake had slapped the pony to send the witch swinging from the branches overhead. Teca had examined the body afterward, and despite the western squire's incessant yammering, she had identified the woman as a Maid that had been terrorizing the area with dead consorts for years. She had been known for years as the Seven Suffragans' Slut. Teca herself had sent a knight one month earlier to track the witch down. He had not been heard from since.

Sir Wica had made his distrust of Parbreake immediately known, but the squire shared rumors of the commune, and so Teca let him follow them on their journey. His pony slowed them down, but the gossip quickly let them to the glen a mere day later. And now Teca was alone with the westerner. From afar, she watched him spin a black revolver as he wandered the glen. Even from the distance she could see the charms he hung from its barrel, knowing they would be darkly mirrored versions of Blind Libra. Their "Angeliika" was such a corrupted offense to her order that the Temple Needles did not even consider Parbreake's people to be true Librans.

She turned back to the thick tree-line to follow Sir Wica's tracks. Unless he had treed the cat somewhere, she was skeptical that he had caught it. She should have heard back from him immediately. Teca had traveled alone outside the Black Hills countless times in her life, and she had never felt anxious with just a horse or dog at her side, but things were different now. The Horde was between her and her home. Until the blockade was broken she was alone out in the world, no matter who traveled with her. Still, she would feel much more comfortable when she found Sir Wica. Him she had known for years. They had trained and inquested together on many occasions. But the messenger squire she had never met until he had appeared with his letter early that morning. And squire Parbreake was an uncomfortable companion. Out in the land, cut off from sanctuary and supply, open to the elements and a moving war between forces she had yet to understand, the less strangers surrounding her the better.

She realized she had been absentmindedly folding the messenger squire's letter over and over in her pocket. Its instructions had included its burning after reading, but she could not yet get herself to destroy it, or, truth be told, to believe it.

What she believed to be Sir Wica's tracks luckily were not subtle. She had never testified to being a very skilled tracker, so she was glad the knight wore large boots. The saplings and young grass had not survived his passage. His steps were distant from each other. He had been running. But despite the fact that his steps stayed near the glen — and in fact were circling the small hamlet — she could not see nor hear him. The new path eventually crossed that of the messenger squire's smaller prints, and then eventually the squire himself.

"I haven't seen him," the boy said.

"The cat..."

"Nor the cat. I lost it as soon as it hit the trees. And the branches are so thick with birds and squirrels... what is this place?"

"Keep looking," Teca reiterated. "And tell Wica to keep looking. The cat is top priority." She watched the boy follow tracks, seen and unseen, back into thicker underbrush he rustled with a large stick. She knew all of her Order's latest generations of squires but had never seen him before. He would have to be pretty experienced to be sent out so far to deliver a message, especially in these uncertain times, so he could have been an older trainee that had not crossed her path. She had not had the chance to ask him how he had slipped through the blockade before the four of them came upon the glen. She caught herself feeling the letter again. The corners of the parchment were wearing away in her jacket pocket.

Shouting from the glen brought her running back into the hamlet and immediately across squire Parbreake with another man prone and shuddering at his feet.

"What did..."

"He tried to circle around ahead of me," Parbreake said. "They're all in there. Ewe didn't really expect me to watch them all did you?"

She could hear the last of the commune shuffling behind her, in hut and garden, heading around to the far side of the taphoract. As much as Teca did not want to admit it, Parbreake was right, however they were entering it, the entire commune should not have been able to fit inside the petrified fungus, but she knew that if she ran, following the stragglers to the other side, she would find only the dark slithering design staring back at her, with the slight murmur of hushed voices emanating from somewhere within.

~

The messenger squire returned that night, empty-handed without news of the familiar or Sir Wica. By then Teca had resolved that neither would be found. Either trail would circle around upon itself over and again like the spiraling curves of the organic mushrooming shapes in the sculpture her tent faced. The taphoract had disappeared into the darkness of the evening, absorbing the Milky Way that had lit the previous nights of the journey to the glen.

Dismissing the squire for the evening, she only just then realized the chill in the air — a chill not felt since entering the glen — even though she was sure it must have appeared earlier. She wished she had noticed it. Even now, in her gloves, her fingers would take a while to warm. The flowerbeds at each hut and the more tender fruits in the gardens lining the homes would not survive if a frost appeared. The messenger squire reappeared with blankets from the huts. He began covering the vegetable beds until Teca dismissed him again.

She sniffed at the thurible she sat cross-legged before. Its incense had been snuffed, but there should still have been a pleasant muskiness in the entrance of her tent. The air smelled of a simpler burning however. She flicked the thurible lightly over and over without thought until it finally tipped on its side, dust dark and pale spilling near her boot tips in a pattern she supposed she should have been able to decipher. But the strands just looked like three-fingered hands, reaching for nothing, as the dust always did for her. If there was meaning in the dust it alluded her as much as the hidden doorway into the taphoract. She had spent the entire evening circling and swinging the thurible, directing smoke and the sounds of blessed bells against the artifact, but no secret seam had appeared. She had walked clockwise and swung counter. She had walked counter and swung clockwise. She had burned both red and white rain aster incense. She had used the last of the blackjack charcoal she brought out of the Black Hills. But nothing had revealed itself through the smoke. She regretted ignoring Parbreake's offer of his own incense — condensed ash of the Kalderan Order. She knew the cremains were not really a relic — the preserved remains of Dhani Antony — as apparently Parbreake still did, but she at the time felt it would betray her own Order to use it. Now she felt it could not have hurt. But it was easy to rationalize it after the failed attempt. How would they smell — she wondered, still staring at the relatively new burner — the remains of the original Libian. Had he foreseen how the Order would split over the centuries? Why had he disappeared so suddenly, leaving no direction beyond the Codas? Would he have, if he had known so much blood would have been spilled in his name?

The thurible was too new, she decided. It did not belong amongst the worn and juryrigged items of her saddlebags. The Black Hills gold trim had not discolored yet. The sun and wing-shaped vents had not bent inward from any travels. It was not ready for such responsibility. Her old incense burner, its chains kinked and constantly catching, had rarely let her down. But where was it? Misplaced or stolen, she had given up on finding it a year ago and had replaced it with this tiny counterfeit. Along with the broken longsword her horse carried, the thurible had been the last remaining item she had inherited from her original master knight. Without it, she was even more alone out in these lands.

She took apart the censer and crucible and ground the cone into the sand outside her tent. The incense appeared inert, but she could still smell a dry burning in the air. A haze had been settling she assumed was a fog from the quick drop in temperature, but now she was not so sure. She searched her bags for a hat before folding her hair back within her hood. It had become too dark in the glen to find anything in her tent without a light. She had vowed against using one of the huts to wait the commune out, but now realized that she might have to hide in one against the chill. The domiciles did not appear to have fireplaces, however.

She had decided to check on her horse one last time before retiring as she finished deconstructing her tent. The commune had no stables, but she and the messenger squire had easily converted a large unused corn crib into a holding pen for the three horses and the donkey. She was on her way there when Parbreake appeared out of some doorway or night-fed shadow.

"They're burning," he mumbled, "what are ewe going to do?" The Western Libran easily blended into the darkness. Only crimson trim and his smile caught any of the soot-filled light. She suddenly realized that his dog was barking — had *been* barking — from somewhere nearby. It was never not at his side, but she could not see it anywhere.

It took a second before she realized what Parbreake meant. He had surprised her. She caught her breath and looked back to a glow emanating from the far side of the taphoract. The shadows were suddenly red and she grappled with them to find him, to throw him aside and run to the artifact. She let her saddlebag drop from her shoulder, forgetting where her swords were but holding tight the revolver in front of her.

The night and the smoke combined on this side of the taphoract to cloud Teca's vision. Her spectacles would not have helped had she even remembered where she had set them last. So she kept moving. The fire was silent, but she avoided its glow and faced a breeze and appeared at the corner of the taphoract where the smoke dissipated to wipe the soot from her eyes. Where were the flames? The sound of muffled cries leaked just as the smoke did, vaguely and without definite source. She ran the glen, but the commune had no animal troughs or rain barrels. She saw the blur of the messenger squire pass her with what she guessed were watering cans, but he looked as confused as she was as to the source of the fire. Flames were appearing to pierce the darkness around the cube, but whether they sprouted internally or externally, she could not tell.

And then the screaming started. Teca kicked at dirt and sand, but the flames did not care. They owned the glen. With the smoke obscuring starlight, the fires provided the only illumination, and they gave it sparingly. She quickly decided to avoid them, beating the sculpted walls with fist and boot heel. She knew the designs were not changing but could not hide the fear that they were about to. The thought that the faceless faces would not contort at the heat scared her.

She jumped, then tripped, fell, and rolled at the appearance of some dark movement next to her. It was Parbreake's dog, sniffing at her feet. Her gasp filled her lungs with smoke that had thickened, and she crawled toward what she assumed was one of the huts to find open air. Her chest burned and her mouth salivated at the pain and the oily smell, but it did not hurt as much as she would have expected. Outside of the smoke, but not outside the darkness, the walls of the taphoract now definitely appeared to be changing. She still could not remember where she had placed her glasses but refused to believe they would have helped. She could only imagine the vines and thighs sculpted into petrified fungus twisting and arching — but in torment or ecstasy? She tried to stand, but the few shapes she could make out turned and melted, and she found herself on hands and knees, and the dog was immediately present to lick her face. Even through the smell of soot his breath was foul, and she rolled to sit and push him away.

But lessening screams brought her back to her feet and back into the darkness. She breathed through her tunic and grasped at any protuberance in the design she could get a grip on. The hottest pieces she could feel through her gloves. Any loose area she quickly lost in the smoke, and she would spend hectic seconds trying to find it again. But she never did. The little she became able to breathe burned her throat, and drifting cinders started to sting any open skin like a flaming hornet swarm, but she did not crawl from the smoke until she found herself prone, hot sand burning through the knees of her pants. She thanked Libra's judgment that she had wandered in the right direction. The swirling soot felt as though it had thickened to cement in certain directions, and she could have just as easily crawled straight into the collapsing detritus the taphoract was becoming.

The ashen night had no answers for her. Was the fire spreading beyond the center of the glen? Did the deafening crackling of embers hide screaming or exaltation? Did she cough up ash or blood? Teca eventually stumbled over her saddlebags and found her glasses. The lenses were broken.

She braced herself against some crumbly window opening, preparing to vomit warm soot, but the very physical rising ended up being the gorge of quaking sobs. She no longer had the strength to care who heard her, sinking again to the ground amidst her own numb limbs. She wanted to shout, but her throat closed, wanted to stand but her knees would not respond. So she just screamed silently through her teeth. She could hear it. And that was all that mattered. As long as it drowned out any other sound.

Parbreake found her later as the sun began to appear in the fleshyish horizon Teca had ever seen. Libra had judged her people worthy with the brilliant sunrises of the Black Hills, but she had never seen anything like the dawn that now distracted her from her walk circling the commune. A lesser person would see it as the bloody birth of a new sky, she thought. It was a uterine morning of such promise. But did anyone outside the area of the smoked glen see it, she wondered. The Kalderan squire turned her from her search and the sunrise, and, by the look of his frosted mantle, she just then noticed that it had been snowing. What she had assumed was just more ash drifting amongst the branches was the beginnings of a blackening western horizon. What was night was just replaced by storm clouds.

"We need to move on," the thin man said. He was as pale as she was red, and she ignored him to continue following the disappearing trail Sir Wica had left behind. Sometime in the night she had taken up the trail again, and, as faint as she found it to be, she followed it mostly by memory than by the burning glow of the crumbling taphoract. As the smothered morning appeared, she was unaware of just how many times she had stepped the circling tracks as they led into themselves. It was though Sir Wica had chased himself around the treed border of the glen. And what had happened when he caught himself?

"There's nothing more for us here, Teca... Sir... and each hour we tarry the Army moves farther away."

Movement and laughter brought her running back into the hamlet, but it was only the messenger squire wrestling with Parbreake's dog over a blackened baby doll. They tugged and rolled in the slush running off from the snowfall alighting over smoldering remains. If the doll ever had eyes they had melted like the growing flakes, but it looked through two new scorch marks in their place.

Parbreake followed her. She saw that he had gathered her saddlebags and other new supplies. They sat in snow too far from the great embers to melt. He ordered the messenger squire to gather their mounts before turning back to Teca.

"We have nowhere else to go. Neither of us can go to our homes. The Army of Earth will be our only refuge... Sir."

Teca had not looked at the burning carnage. After the midnight smoke swirled into snow, after the soot cleared from her watering eyes, she had left the glen. She now remembered picking up Sir Wica's trail, and she knew how it had distracted her from the sounds and heat emanating from the commune. She had no choice now but to look, and she could not breath from the lump in her throat, the constriction of her chest.

She at first thought that Parbreake sobbed as well, but then realized that he was chuckling. Fists clenching, one around the core of the revolver, she cracked the gun across the back of his head. He rolled away, covering his face, now sobbing as well as laughing. She raised the gun's butt to bring it down on the bridge of his nose, but he warded her off with flailing hands.

"No... no wait. I mean... ewe just look... look just like a Kalderan."

Teca, realizing too late that she was only smearing the ash, wiped the tears from her face and just stared at the soot now blackening her palms. Parbreake said something she chose not to hear, as she stood to find any area of the glen where the smell of smoke did not linger. The messenger squire had ignored Parbreake, and now collected jugs of water and juice to throw on the hissing ruins of the taphoract, but even he soon saw it as wasted effort. The screaming had sometime in the night ended. The only crying now came from Teca. Her gloves were practically useless. Most of her fingertips poked from new holes.

~

Teca had sent the messenger squire ahead, but the Army of Earth's scouts that approached claimed to have not met him. The scouts were mismatched. Their light leathers were differing in coverage and color. Their simple weapons, although both decrepit, could have come from entirely different nations. But beneath a cap one wore a bandana with a painted bleeding eye. The other scout mirrored the eye with a painted tunic hanging from his horse. They walked the ridge Teca and Dharke Parbreake sat, all of them overlooking a land that moved beneath them. Down in field and trampled pasture, through canyon and thin forest, from the trees of one glowing horizon to the blackening cosmos of the other, the earth moved. From the distance, and obscured by the snow and dusk, she could only periodically make out individual trucks or tanks or legions. It was mostly just a black tar serpent crawling across her sightline. It moved the Earth.

She sent Parbreake out to continue speaking to the scouts, half expecting them to skewer him on a lance or to blast him with a blunderbuss. But earlier in the day he had washed his face with snow, had covered his tattoos and his colors with neutrals found back in the hamlet. At the first hint of sulfur and exhaust in the air he had quickly taken a particularly nasty looking bodkin to his hair. Now it just fell over his eyes instead of to his shoulders. He admitted to Teca that he would be honest of his origins and his exile but wanted to make sure he would survive past initial introductions. She was not satisfied it would be enough. The Western Order of Librans had now been a part of the Horde for well over a year. She would be surprised if the rank and file of Earth's Army would be so lenient with one of their kind. She was not even so sure how friendly they would be to even her. Her own Order had remained neutral since the start of the war, refusing as usual to take part in the follies of worldly allegiances. And she had seen prejudices out in the land against all Librans thanks to the sudden appearance of the fallen Kalderans.

She took her ragged gloves from the rock they had been warming near their tiny campfire. It looked as though Parbreake was not going to be immediately impaled, so she used his distraction as the chance to take the messenger squire's letter from her pocket one last time. Seals could be faked. Colors and waxes could be counterfeit. Handwriting and signatures could be reproduced. But there was no indication that the letter was anything other than genuine. It was written in Lish — an ancient script she was the only paladin to have still studied. Only the elder monks knew her so well. The seal, broken from when she had first read the letter — a time seeming so long ago despite being only a couple of days prior — was in an alternate design designating ultimate priority and absolute disavowal if she failed in her new quest. The design of the seal also designated a death warrant. She had seen death warrants before, had followed them, but never had she read one for anyone other than a Maid of *MGGT*.

Destroy this warrant immediately.
Infiltrate the hierarchy of Earth's Army.
Judge the Liege of Foes as though Blind Libra watches.
She does.
May the reflection off Her scales illuminate your path.
XXXXXXX

Teca tipped the parchment until it lit and made sure the flame had gotten a good hold of the letter before she pushed its remains into the interior of the ember pile. The whites of the flames appeared whiter, the reds redder, until the letter was consumed.

She had let Parbreake think it was his idea to join up with the

Army of Earth, but why had the Order chosen her for the quest? She was beginning not to care. In the end, as she stood and stepped over hard snow and harder earth, leaving the tiny fire behind, it was really just the cold that kept her moving. The cold thickened, in the air and in her holey gloves and boots. The cold had deepened since their day away from the commune's glen, as had the snow and the heavens. And the warmth of the Army of Earth beckoned. Even miles over and away from the march and the engine chug she could feel the heat of its helfire engines. It would be so good to feel warm again.

XLVII

of the seven celestially Governed Elements
    (5) The Head
"...as government, presents itself as virtuous wisdom, sincerity, benevolent violence, and strict rage"

—Hyper Khan's The War of Art

J anus Legionaire moved behind the three, watching the tip of one of their rifles sway. An old man shuffled his legs and paused, but the rifle still wavered.

"Don't hold your breath," Janus rebuked. He struck the elder between the shoulder blades. "This stance won't work for you. Lie down. Hurry!"

The man, greatly older than the boy and girl, sprawled and moaned in a heap of his limbs and furs, and Janus roughly repositioned the rifle's hand guard so that it rested in the notch created by the man's thumb and forefingers. He moved his wrist straight and snapped, "Keep a looser grip. Yes! The shells eject here." Janus stood as the other couple each fired off a round into the distance. The girl rubbed her arm, and Janus adjusted her rifle's butt more firmly against the pocket of her shoulder. "Keep up the pressure. You'll know if your positioning is correct if your neck and cheek relax naturally against the stock. And you won't have to strain to sight."

The three took turns firing and waiting for his response, but he had closed his eyes. He could feel their eyes and more upon him but said nothing at first. They were not ready. None of them were, but there was no time. They wanted encouragement, needed his words, but he could not muster any. It was so much easier when he spoke from behind the Elder Mask, but it remained in his saddlebag. Its image was constantly in his mind, even though he had not looked at it since he left Erebus — afraid of any new voices it may now hold. He opened his eyes to find his hand reaching out for it. The horse he had heard was Ivy's. The eyes he felt were hers. Usually her incessant questioning drove him mad, but she was silent. She absorbed every lesson from her saddle silently, but for once he wished she would break the awkward reactions of his recruits by asking any question.

"Go!" he told the three before him. "There's no more time. You'll find a box of rounds to share. It's all you get, but don't be afraid to waste them. Just remember to range find. Don't fire until you can make out the crests on their belts. Go!"

The three ran off, and Janus glared at Ivy as he moved on to a group of four. It was then he realized that she had brought Mew with her. He had not seen her behind a group of disciples that were obviously distracting her with questions. Far back beyond them he could see the manic gesturing of the preacher Milliam Pittsfield. The man had recently taken to wearing an entirely green robe, and he no doubt was now whispering again of the Final Day, of how no one would last to see this day's sunset. *For once*, Janus chuckled inwardly, *he might be right*.

The men Janus now stood before were of all sizes and colors. They were short and tall, tattered and dirty. They had been locking spears together, but now, at Janus' approach, they stuck their weapons in the ground solidly and stood stoic at his approach.

"You know by now that the spear is in fact three different weapons. If you use it correctly as the third type, you'll need to use it no other way."

The tallest of the men snatched up his spear and balanced its shaft in an open palm until it stopped wavering. Janus noticed he had painted a cat's eye at the balancing point of the shaft, and, not for the first time, wondered where all the green dye had come from lately. "To your ear!" he chastised, and the man brought the spear parallel to the ground and sighted the splintered board the group had been using for a target. Janus would have preferred they had been using a sign or other target off the ground but knew there was no time now to remedy it. Facing slightly sideways from the target, the man ran and launched the spear. It sailed evenly but only chipped a piece from the edge of the wood.

"Not bad," Janus said, plucking one of the other spears from the ground, "but remember, lead toward the target." He rapped the man on the ankle with the blunt end of the spear before striking both the insides of both calves. "Feet shoulder-length apart." The shaft swung wide and caught him on the back of his legs before he hit the ground. "Knees bent slightly. The strength will then come from your hips, the precision from your shoulder."

The man was smiling as he wiped the mud from his hands. Janus scowled openly, saying, "The grit will help with grip. Now go! Each take as many spears as you can carry."

He walked as they ran off, glancing sideways to see Mew now

watching him intently, but with all the people around her he could not decipher her expression. The seven "recruits" he interrupted next had been knife hand fighting, but as he appeared they laughed and picked up their individual blades. He cuffed one green-haired boy and threw a particularly jovial man to the ground. "You are not 'knife fighters,'" he said, sighing loudly. "You will not be in a 'knife fight.' You are killers and you will kill. A man, in the heat of battle, will not run at you with a knife. You will not be fighting knife against knife. You and others across the camps will be the last line of defense. If guns and arrows fail, and sword and spearmen fall, and circled wagon and horse-lines are broken, then the daggermen are all that'll be left to defend the women and children. And you won't be defending them against other daggers." Janus looked around to see eyes suddenly water and throats swallow loudly. These were not gladiators he practiced. These were not soldiers he trained or assassins he schooled. "They will come at you with halberd or sword or mace, and they're not interested in fighting, only killing. The only way to stop them is to kill them. You take no prisoners."

One woman sheathed her daggers in fabric tied around her arms. Her skin was as dark as Janus', but most of her face was painted to match the green ribbons. She asked him, "Will they have armor?"

"Undoubtedly, but a battalion this far from any capital will only be wearing patchwork. They keep the good stuff to defend the main fronts. Men traveling this far couldn't bear the heavy loads of quality armor. Each man will have different gear, and I guarantee they can't have all their arteries covered." He watched for comprehension in the nodding heads — pale, dark, and green. "You will have no more than a second to determine which vulnerable areas are left exposed. If the underarm is armored, strike at the groin. If the abdomen is too well-covered, stab eyes or neck. Most men who are slashed by a knife don't even feel it, so don't waste your strength on wild attacks. Make every stab count. Go for the face first to disorient, then strike the artery, then move to the next man. If they follow you they'll cause themselves to bleed out."

They had so much more to learn, so many more days to spend under his tutelage, but he sent them away, back to their families and friends. He had no more time. But at least they would die in action. He was confident they would not be huddled in wagon and truck when the end came.

Janus turned to look uphill from his makeshift training grounds. It would be a poor place to defend had his students not trampled it into mush. Lines would break on the mud when they came down the hills. The rolling ground was an indication they were starting to near N'Midgaard. The prairie had only begun to separate over the past day, being split by tree-lines, streams, and hillocks. There were still plenty of flatlands to the north, but it had been a relief to see the occasional forest interrupting the fields. He felt Mew come up behind him but kept his face turned until he felt his blush subside.

"How long have you been lying to me?" she asked, her voice cracking. The anger he had expected was absent. There was only sadness of a type he had never heard from her in their long years together.

"I can't just stand around as they're slaughtered," he said evenly. "I have the means to teach them how to protect themselves. That alone makes it my responsibility, and you alone should be able to understand that. You've said that you alone know how to save their souls, and whether you want that destiny or not you're going to fulfill it. Well, this is me. You care for their afterlife, I'll look after their lives — right here, right now, today." He had started up the hill, trying to avoid the snowier patches, ending up slowed by soft patches of bent yellow grass mounds. His booted climb was boisterous and loud compared to her silent steps.

There was no passion in her words. She said very matter-of-factly, "Don't pretend like this is anything more than bloodlust. And that's alright, Janus, it's your nature. It's all our nature, just don't lie to me or yourself that it's anything more than that. Don't wrap it in something noble or you're no better than the Horde. Don't use these people and this world to propagate your lusts. I know this life of... pilgrimage, of helping me spread the word is not what you ever imagined yourself doing, but you were chosen. I chose you! I wouldn't be here if it wasn't for you. You saved me more times than I can count. You have a better purpose in life than to lead others to violence. You're better than that."

"It's all I know how to do!"

"That's not true. These people look to you to be a leader. They consider you one of these 'Heirs of Aesar' — whatever that is — but you can lead them away from death, not towards it. Use their trust to lead them toward enlightenment. I know you can. I believe in you. I chose you. Will you look at me?" She touched his arm, and he swung around.

"If these people survive until tonight it will be because of the guns Ivy found for them. It will be thanks to the training I convinced RackBreak and Damn Antony to give them." He took her hand and continued leading the walk up the hill. He could feel its softness beneath his glove, its strength as she squeezed his fingers tenderly.

"And what of when the bullets run out? What of those that can't fight, or become too crippled by fighting to follow your lead? None of this matters. Flesh is just a distraction, pain is a temptation, and fear is a tool of the enemy. The Horde is using fear to ground the populace, to keep them preoccupied with the physical world the same way they do food and riches. When people are distracted by the physical they forget the spiritual and are less willing to listen. The Horde knows this. We have to be better than them. We can be an example of what's truly real. I said it on the road to Erebus: 'It is not a person's duty to resist evil, for whoever cuts you cuts himself. If anyone burns you, give him a place by your fire. Whoever cracks the whip over your back, lead him to salvation. I know it is not easy to love your enemy, but I say to you, love him and he will *not be* your enemy!' This is why we accepted those governors' invitation and walked halfway across the continent."

"And look how that turned out!" Janus shuddered at the memory of the sky over Erebus that night. He still woke at nights pulling phantom cilia from his orifices, catching glimpses of other ridiculous realities he suspected he at one time believed in.

"Yes, look!" she said, swinging her arms back to the masses behind them, over rolling hillocks and prairie. "How many of them now carry or copy a *Fallo Terminus*?" She pointed then in front of them, to the top of the hill and the prone riflemen. "But how many of them have so quickly forgotten its words because you've replaced it with the fear of pain, the anxiety of the flesh? The real enemies are spiritual and can only be opposed by spiritual means."

"I can't just sit back..."

"All new faiths require a sacrifice. Don't you have faith in my word? These people have to see it."

"I'm keeping them alive long enough to hear your word!"

Before they topped the hill she stopped and turned his face toward her again. He reached for his sidebag but remembered he was not carrying the Elder Mask on him. She was tracing the old scar that ran his eyebrow as she talked.

"You never look me in the eyes anymore. I'm surrounded constantly, night and day, but I'm so lonely, and even though I know you're always near I still miss you. I should be looking forward, but I yearn for the way things used to be. They were so much simpler. I fear for the future."

In his peripheral, back down into the valley, specks of green moved about to circle wagons and use anything they could find in the camps for barricades. They were her life now, not him. Any thought that he ever was a real part of her life was the real delusion. In the end, the sacrifice this new faith would make would be him.

"Doesn't your *Fallo Terminus* tell you what the future holds?" he said, forcing himself to look at her close eyes.

"That's why I'm afraid. I know things can't be like they used to, but can we just pretend, just for a little while…" Her lips neared his, and he could feel her lithe body beneath the few layers she wore. She never ate anymore. Nor did she seem to feel the cold. He closed his eyes but saw her in some other world and time. She was still before him, wide-eyed, but she was cut open and his hands were wet with the deed.

"What's the matter," she asked, as he pushed himself out of her arms. His eyes were open, but he could still see the image of her opened up before him and him with a blade in his hand. The light from inside her was sickeningly inviting. He covered his mouth against the rising gorge. "I miss you," she repeated, but he held her at arms-length and took the last steps up the hill away from her.

She followed as the entire prairie opened to spread out before them. Janus' riflemen and the few people able to find arrows for their bows sat behind the stumps of trees cut down a generation ago. They aimed out at the forces of General Fobos. He had few machines, but his perfectly ordered phalanxes of men stretched across the fields, unbroken as far as Janus could see. He could now hear their march on the frozen plain. The banner of Asmodeus flapped on some wind not reaching the hill, from one side of the legion to the other. The wings on the flags flamed as *Wyrmwood* in the sky above them. Janus looked now to the comet, not remembering it as so bright and so violently violet.

He moved to stand before Mew, tightening one hand around his sword hilt and the straps holding his meager armor with the other. He barked repeated instructions to those near him and shouted to those spread farther over the top of the hill. So this was the Army of Heaven, he chuckled, looking out to the southern horizon. Despite the training he had been giving, he never truly knew what to expect from the Horde. He had heard of its mad generals and its unholy high commander — the red Greater riding his red mammoth. This was the first he had seen of its so-called soldiers. They were quartered and lined as cleanly as any professional army, but even from this distance their inconsistency in color, size, and armament revealed them as conscripts and recent volunteers. They were no more warriors than those Janus had trained over the past week. Most were barely men. But they had horses. They had long rifles and long bows, halberds and helmets. Most of all, Janus now imagined, they had a look in their eyes of zealotry. He could not see them, but he was sure of faces twisted by the Promise. They held the sigil of Asmodeus, but each man probably prayed to his own patron of the Divine Choir. And he thought he could hear their singing between their steps. They had a song uniting them. No matter which angel they had painted on their mismatched armor, they all sang the same song, and it was this tune that drove them forward and directly at the hill.

There was no more time for scouts and messengers to warn any more of the peregrination. Janus had not heard back from Wulf or the front line. He held out a hand to ready any of his bowmen. Only he would be able to tell when the phalanxes were in range. He looked to the unwashed children and men of his hill. The arthritic hand of a skinny old man was testing the air with a licked finger, his other hand kept in a mitten until the last second. A girl appeared frozen to the ground, her bow and arms as taut as her gaze. Green eye shadow had smeared down an unmoving cheek. Janus took the rifle from a boy no older than thirteen years.

"Go. Be with your family," he whispered, raising the rifle to his soldier. "Everyone, follow my fire." He spoke loudly enough so that only the hill could hear him. The sights on the rifle were so misaligned that the gun shook with his laughter. *What kind of a fool finds himself in this life*, he wondered. *A fool on a hill. A fool in love*, he decided. *But in love with what?* He focused his eyes at a different point on the barrel, toward the approaching Army of Heaven. The time was now.

"Have faith. Find freedom in the *gentle constants*," Mew whispered.

"All new faiths require a sacrifice," he said quietly enough so that only she could hear.

But he held his trigger finger. Between the phalanxes rode an indistinguishable shape at barely the speed of their march, but it was lopsided enough to draw Janus' attention. He followed its movement from down his barrel. The phalanxes halted as it passed, but until it emerged from the front line Janus could not make out what it was. He ran to one of his men and traded his rifle for a sharper version. The barrel was long, and he had sighted the telescope himself earlier in the day. He looked through it now to see two thurifers crowded and swaying in a wooden saddle on the biggest boar Janus had ever seen. The men could barely stay steady. They held to each other and the hog's wiry hairs, each with one hand, and to their swinging censers with the other. Some sort of incense or perfume wafted out of the ornate thuribles. With the legions stopped, the only sound to reach the hill by the breeze was the distant snort of the boar as it came to a swaggering stop in front of the army.

Janus wiped the telescope as best he could with a bandana, but the glass was still clouded. He scanned from banner to flag, identifying the strength and direction of the breeze. The dial on the scope's base barely turned, but a slight adjustment was all he needed. He spied on the frontline, the men's open helms and marked foreheads, immediately realizing he had been wrong. These soldiers all prayed to the same angel. He had seen the simple design — scarred, branded, or tattooed on their brows — once before. The scene sped before his eye as he moved the scope back to the hog. The beast shook out its patches of black hairs and snapped its uneven tusks just beyond the reach of the askew saddle straps. The thurifers had dismounted to walk ahead of it now, swinging their chains and whispy smoke. They wore barely more than rags, naked bodies revealing mud or blood-caked molestation. Janus looked to their faces and decided right then to end their suffering, steeling himself for the shot before Mew could see what he saw.

The glass was far from optimum, but as the men staggered forward he could see what was left of their heads. The first man's face had been peeled off. The skin hung from strings around his neck, but Janus could still make out the dark eye-sockets and mouth in the folds. Its green make-up had survived the skinning. The person stared forward on his walk, eyes gleaming from the brown infection his face had become. The other man caught himself from tripping before resuming his frightened walk, and Janus could see that the entire top and back of his head had been scalped. Stripes of gore had dried down to his collarbone, and the scalped green hair now hung from a twine belt around his waist. There was relief in the first man's eyes as Janus shot him in the neck.

By the time the cartridge hit the hilltop and the echo resounded back, someone had tossed Janus another round. By the time he had worked the stubborn chamber and double-checked the sight dials he expected the Army of Heaven to be launching whatever long-range weapons they had at the hilltop. Instead, through the scope, he found unmoving phalanxes and the boar, having shaken its saddle, snout deep in the dead man's flanks.

Janus again wiped the lens of the scope as those near him gasped. He looked to see the hog shaking its massive head, dead man's entrails caught on wart and tusk. The body gesticulated as though it had been resurrected. Beneath the boar's tiny trotters was crushed a thurible, and from its remains streamed a cloud too large for the censer's size. Wisps of the golden smoke snaked from the other man's thurible to consume him. And just as Janus realized what the twisting clouds were composed of, the metallic buzz of the Abysmal Locusts reached the hilltop.

~

Mew felt something she had not sensed before as she stepped past Janus. She at first thought the screams reverberating all around her were coming from every point in every horizon, from every person across the seeable land. The sound rose and fell in a chorus. She could hear nothing else — not Janus beside her nor the gunshots on the hill — but the mournful pitch and dips of the song. She barely felt a hand grip her shoulder, but it was enough for her to twitch and send Janus flying back down the hill behind her.

As she watched the Army of Heaven, spread out as it was in tidy rows of seven, she focused, and the harmony of screams narrowed. It narrowed and accumulated, and as she concentrated she determined that the screams came from the cloud that thickened like the smoke of a great furnace. As the sun and air darkened she listened, and the more she listened the more she could pick out individual screams from the song. One told of suicide. Another of torture and execution. One sobbed of long suffering wasting disease, while another lamented a short life of starvation. From deep within each clockwork locust an individual soul screamed, its wailing powering leg and wing and the flaming hair of each insect's little face. Tail and stinger moved by the strength of torment. Needled teeth gnashed by the pining for Heaven.

Mew opened herself up to the pain, and, with a flash of viridescent blinding anyone looking skyward, she accepted all souls' suffering. The black curve of the sky grayed then lightened as the new grounded green sun enveloped the abysmal cloud. A tinny rain fell on the hill and out over the prairie. The locusts' golden luster failed in the new light and they fell, crowns extinguished and soul batteries released. Pyrite piles grew all around, and Mew dimmed. Without the buzzing, she could hear the gunfire grow all around her.

~

Janus had rolled to a stop at the bottom of the hill amongst the mud and snow of his training field. He had lost the rifle, and his sword sheath and belt had become tangled in his legs during the descent. He felt around in his satchels to make sure the Elder Mask had not been damaged in the fall before remembering he had purposefully left it behind in the camp. Barely composed, he ran back toward the hilltop, toward and into a light the entire peregrination would be watching by now. Shouts and gasps filled the fields behind him.

He reached Mew's side as she dimmed, breathless not because he tired but because he had forgotten to breathe on the climb. She quivered in his arms, even paler than usual. The crunch of metal sounded beneath his boots. Rifles fired on one side of him, arrows were unleashed on the other.

"How many lives do you have left?" he asked her.

"Not enough." She pressed her cold cheek to his, but he pulled away. Fobos' army scattered to the south, shouting and crying over a field of unmoving metal, but Janus paid no attention. A sour taste in his mouth brought again the image of his hands and blade cutting Mew open, of an ill glow spreading her apart and pulling him inevitably inward.

XLVIII

Obdur-8:
"If the past could be changed there would be no
past to change. Better to take my kind as
model. The only past is what you know.
Memory beats reality, whereas
humans have taught me the lack in value
of an objective world. The man who has
blinded his sight will always conquer you.
Evolutionary Wars based on lies
of difference set your people on mine,
yet among you it is the truly wise
who savor memory like a straw wine,
discriminatively plucking the grapes of
a past existing only in supine
mind, grasping to it like one does calf love.
You live only to prove this perception,
to others you may think, but, through them, thine
own self. Therein lies the key of the one
true strength. That truth has no power. Divine
design is humbled before the kingdom
come of reality undone. The swine
comes before pearls in the world of the dumb,
for those without voice can only change their
own reality, where great men infect
the six senses of the sheep. This great swain
finds his past and his future wrecked upon
the shores of indomitable spirit,
shattered casks leaking vinegar retrospect
on the sands of time. But do not fear it!
Even truly changing the past, were that
possible, would that it even exists,
would be most inferior, would fall flat,
compared to the power to fill with mists
men's perceptions of that same past. Control
of memory, of the senses, resists
empiricism's control of the whole."
Narrator:
The tin man spoke of Past's impermanence,
mind's mutability, and of the former's
susceptibility to the mean dance
of the latter, while the hoary storm oars

of the ferryman beat the cresting bile
of Sea Borborygmus. Men swam toward
the shores of Meatus, skin dripping of chyle.
He led him up the beach of Uric grit
to the fleshy mountains. With air burning
and caves beckoning, the land threw a fit,
heaving and turning, rolling and churning.
Guide and tourist were thrown into sphincter.
Ahead, a nude woman was returning
into these bowels, and he would think her
choosing to be thrown by peristalsis
Obedient, she lapped like a broken cur
at raining acid. What would he call this?
His guide walked ahead through hot puddle, sure
of sight and sound, metal serpentine arm
waving all around, pointing to confer
justice inherent in poetic harm.

Obdur-8:
"The Introspective, wasting life absorbed
in navel enchantment, now waste away
in novel punishment. They so abhorred
the life less examined, so here they stay
perpetually digesting their own
self in internal eternal decay.
Damn the Introspective to reap the sown!"

The Assassin:
"But why are you here, O' veteran, O'
nurse, O' gentle automaton, left to
guide this faithless man through the Circle so?"

Obdur-8:
"In the vice of questioning oneself do
you think there is a greater malefactor?
Or ever was? Then the robot who knew
himself as tin, but, as man, an actor?"

Narrator:
The question suspending like acid fog,
the assassin and his guide walked the mount
to overlook the valley's war and smog.
A legion — more soldiers than he could count,
killed under command of a Necrophim,
only to rise next morning on account
of a violet sun, with healed head and limb.

Obdur-8:
"And so it goes — Necrophim lead their men
into daily death, resurrecting them
under a purple dawn. Never has been
there a winner, across the River Phlegm,
over the Sea of Tears, for Hel's castle.
But never has Necrophim brought mayhem
all the way to the Roots of Yggdrasil.
If only there were someone to unite
these lost warlords of these Circles Seven
to take to the Red Queen an upstart fight."
Narrator:
As the guide spoke there appeared the leaven
voice of The Four Hundred and First Son of
Mixcotle with the Nectar of Heaven
on lips. In assassin's ear he sang love.

—excerpt from "The Angel and the Ass"

Che fog appeared so distant, until suddenly it was not. It was the same every morning. As a cloud-choked rise failed to warm a morning, all eyes looked ahead to the east at a wall of mist that seemingly crept out of the dampening night but had probably only appeared with the dawn. As long as Dhani Teca Libran kept with the march through the night she could travel deep within the lines and legions, the night feeling warmer than it should have — even hot, even sweltering at times betwixt some infernal tank and helfire belching transport. She was certain the rest of the world froze in mornings too cold to mist, but when the slow march of the Army of Earth met the snowflakes of morning, the land rose up before dissipating into a fog that swallowed them each morning. Would the Horde, the so-called Army of Heaven, some day use the blindness of the fog against them, or did the mists conveniently hide the Necrophim and their battalions? Had the cold prairies conspired to hide the Liege of Foes? Had the earth truly chosen a side in a war that torn at its guts at every turn? Even the land turned to pain to prove it was alive in a world dying.

The fog this morning, again first appearing a mile off, eating the forward attachments, before seemingly growing out of each company and then individual surrounding her, swallowed more than just those immediately near her. It absorbed all sound. The Army of Earth's machines and march had stopped suddenly and completely all around her for the first time in days, and along with it so had any grind of chain or choke of exhaust. A far-off hiss of burning engine echoed back her way from farther front lines, but only for scant minutes. Whether forward legions continued on, lost to the choked horizon, or whether the entire Army had been consumed for good, she did not know. But now the freezing fog captured all sound as it settled unmoving.

Time did not exist in the mists. Morning's damped glow did not move. Teca was not sure she needed to breathe any longer. The air was too solid to breathe anyway. She looked around, and the only soldiers still visible, those wandering wide-eyed, appearing but disappearing just as quickly in the soup of the air, spoke silently in her peripheral but never as she looked their way.

Why had the lines stopped? She should have relished the rest, sat and let her aching hips and back cool against the slush, but after days of walking her legs did not know how to stop moving. So she slowed and swayed forward in a new direction, contrary to what she thought was easterly. She did not want to stop. When she stopped, her thoughts kept moving forward, sometimes backward. She did not know which was worse — reminders of where she thought she was going or memories of where she had been. Somewhere through the battalions, over the days, she had lost her horse. At night? Over some disagreement? Somewhere in the sulfurous plumes, early on in the march, she had lost the western squire Dharke Parbreake. He was no enjoyable companion, but he was somewhat familiar. She would be surprised to ever find him alive. She kept signs of her Libran heritage hidden, for the Army would be no fanatic of any angelic reminders. Had he done the same?

Those around her wandered in and out of her life like spirits feeling her out only for a second. They did not exist before they wandered near, and they did not exist after they passed back into the mists. Over the days she had spent in Earth's Army she had found little in common from one soldier to the next. They were all color of man. All sizes and shapes. Any past culture that leaked out in manner or accent had at some point been consumed by a new society built entirely on war. They spoke of nothing else in their hodge podge language Teca was surprised to understand to a limited degree. Their words appeared to tailor themselves toward the listener, and the longer she listened to any soldier the more she understood him. But this was not often. Surrounded daily on all sides, she still avoided the men. To her they seemed like ghosts. Wherever they previously had lived, they now marched the countryside of her world as though it were their own personal Hell. She could not help but dwell on that thought now as the near-spectral men wandered through the fog in search of things she could not imagine them ever finding. And she now corrected the thought, watching their abysmally bloodshot eyes — the one thing they all physically shared — search the melted earth and opaque sky. The war with the Army of Heaven, the pillaging of towns loyal to the Horde, and the daily skirmishes with mercenaries would be more akin to a heaven for these men.

The fog thickened inconceivably, and for the first time Teca knew what a person meant when they said one could not see one's hand before their face. The mists swallowed all sound now. No longer could she hear any engine, any smokestack, any treads or footfalls. She cringed at near breathing but realized it was only her own before its sound too disappeared. Now she wandered the cloud and could only guess that she appeared — if anyone could have seen her — like one of the blackly bloodshot soldiers she no longer saw lingering in her peripheral.

How long she wandered through the mists she would never re-member. She would head toward any trick of light, any unevenness in the cottony shroud, just to find that it was just that — her eyes finding differences in the mists that were not actually there. Her steps slowed as she finally admitted the loss of all direction. Dull light came from everywhere and nowhere. Without momentum her legs revealed their soreness, her back reminded her of its ache. Without her horse, she carried all of her traveling possessions. As dishonorable as it was, she no longer regretted losing most of her journey armor. Yet she still drove the thought from her mind.

The ground refroze beneath her. Where exhaust and tread had melted or crushed the snow now the crust frosted and pushed back against her boots. She dug her fingers deeper into her pockets, despite the urge to keep her hands on hilt and handle. And just as the dirt firmed and her steps tripped over frozen footprints, she stopped sud-denly before running into the backs of sudden men.

The quiet ones were of the Necrophim, motley but pale, dishev-eled but imposing. They looked away but their eyes bloodied the fog in front of their faces. No breath mingled with that fog. Other soldiers, not of the Necrophim's original forces but of those of the land pushing back against the Horde, whispered to each other too low to breach the fog for Teca's ears. They too were of differing backgrounds, without rhyme or reason, from city or farm, from nation or tribe. Teca had yet to find any common thread linking those caught up in the Army of Earth, besides an almost primal hatred of all things Horde. As she stepped into mists thinning from the anxious warmth being given off by the men, she was suddenly reminded of the one thing connecting all the soldiers of Earth's Army, whether Necrophim-brought or otherwise. One man wore a bandanna, damp and heavy, from his neck and stained with the image of a pale blue eye tearing blood. Another wore a leather football helmet with the same image sown as a patch. Even the Necrophims' men held the sigil on shattered armor and torn sash.

She at first pitied only the Necrophim, for there was no trace of Blind Libra's love about them. They were not even of the earth, much less Heaven, and their inelegance betrayed a hollowness anathema to love. She feared they were more akin to its opposite. But what she was having difficulty reconciling was that she had begun to now pity the other soldiers as well — militia and mercenaries that had snuck out of the Territories, landskeepers that had taken up arms against the encroaching Horde. These were men and women of the world she should have recognized, yet there was a growing hollowness in them as well. In years past she would have tried to fill these holes with the love of and from Lady Wayasu, but now she feared the darkness would just insatiably swallow it up. There was no place for love out here at the frontlines. The glee she saw when a soldier chucked a spear or aimed a rifle out into the mists was not love. It was something else.

The soldiers knew she was behind them despite her quiet steps, for one of them whispered backward as she neared. Another raised a rifle out into the fog. Another steadied the tallest bow Teca had ever seen. Two others pulled a gatling gun from a crate from a sled that appeared from the mists next to them. The sounds of their slow and careful movements were immediately absorbed into the thick air, the locking of the base and the setting of the ammunition belt just a whisper under the soldier's quiet words.

"Where?" Teca asked.

"All around us," he said. The soldier had a tear branded or cut under his eye. The line was slightly swollen and on the verge of infection. His hair was even darker than his skin, and its curls stuck to his forehead by sweat or dew.

"How do you know?" she asked a little too loudly and was rebuked with hushes all around her.

"Can't you feel them?"

"Where's your commanding officer?"

They chuckled — all of them — unblinking faces unmoving from the soup of the fog. Teca listened as intently as she could to the cottony silence but could hear nothing. Still, as cool as the mist had become, she fingered with a freezing hand her holster, but for the life of her she could not remember if she still had the one round left or if she had fired it off in some skirmish over the last week. She had a memory of the bullet misfiring but was not sure if the incident had been a dream or not. Barely sleeping, the odds were against the memory being real.

Teca followed her frozen footprints backward, slowly and just as quietly. The men and their rifles quickly dissipated back into the dull light. Continuing on, the mists no longer held any remnant of exhaust. They smelled cold and clean and glittered of a purer white. In only a few steps, however, she came upon more soldiers, feeling them before seeing them as her shoulder backed into one. He was not startled to feel her shrug, did not appear to even notice her, but he whispered to her as quiet as a tithingman, as though he knew she was coming.

"Did you hear that?"

"No." She cringed along with this new batch of soldiers. Her voice was the only one not being consumed by the fog. The men were lined up with the most ancient looking rifles she had ever witnessed. She had seen that some of the Necrophims' forces carried blunderbusses and muskets, modified and crafted and merged with some hyperborean proto-technology from whatever circle of hell they had crawled out of, but these militia men were kneeling and aiming in unison with armaments that would have been old when Lady Wayasu led humanity back to the surface. Appropriately, the soldiers wore neckerchiefs and goggles to protect their faces — the latter constantly fogging and perspiring. Between wiping the glasses, they all scanned the clean white wall in front of them.

Teca could have sworn they aimed in the opposite direction as the other soldiers she encountered, but she found each direction quickly becoming confused with the other in the dun soup.

"Which Necrophim general do you follow?" She thought she had overcompensated and had become too quiet but was quickly answered by more than one of the men.

"We follow no blackly bloodshot," one said with as much vehemence as he could muster in a whisper, "jus' the Liege o' Foes. He's our man." They all nodded with as much unison as their tight aiming would allow.

"I need to speak with your immediate commander."

"Who?"

"Who's in charge here?"

"Shhhhh... he's up on the ridge."

"Which direction...?"

More than one soldier pointed in more than one direction in an effort to let her know they were done talking to her. They no longer even whispered to each other, in an attempt to hear whatever they thought was out there. Out in the mists. Out where the light grew even paler and sounds existed only in memory of an echo.

She moved on, pretending that the ground began to rise, tripping over rock-hard footprints smaller than her own, getting caught up in harder prints larger than her boot soles. Sparse and yellow grass had been at some point over the last few hours first revealed out of snow and then trampled into new mud before being frozen back into the ground. Strands emerged then plunged back into the ground before appearing again. They were ancient serpents of a dirty sea, rolling but refusing to die with the congealing waves.

The next group of men Teca came upon were no more surprised by her sudden appearance than the others, but they ignored her whispers. They listened only to the silence of a fog finally moving. The gray swirled with the white swirling with a new egg of a sun, as slow as a clock's hand but still moving. The mists were moving through her, but Teca feared that they were not moving away from her. Where they moved from and where they moved to could have been the same side for all she could tell.

These new soldiers were aiming back down the supposed ridge she now realized she had not been climbing. They aimed with rifle and bow and spear. One man was missing fingers, another had an arm in a sling, while still another had bruises and stitching lowering his brow practically over his eyes. The colors of their infections stood out sharply in the muted hue of the air.

"Who do you take orders from?"

When she whispered they would each cock an ear away from her, but each in a different direction. Palms tightened on grips. Fingers stretched a string. Stances steadied and spears rose. Pus the color of the mists dripped from an elbow and melted the edge of a footprint in the mud.

She could do nothing but stare at these men playing at being soldiers. They had the requisite bleeding eye patches and tattoos, the quilted shirts and leather caps of the militias, even the extra ammo packs of the conscripted, but they wore the boots of hostlers and gravediggers, the gloves of railmen and carpenters. At the beginning of the War — however many months or years ago that was — Teca would have assumed these soldiers to have been highwaymen and headhunters, but after spending only meager days marching with them she knew them to be failed cropsmen and lost swains, sometimes the homeless of cities deaf to the Prophets Lesser. It was the Horde that had absorbed the mercenaries. There were no stipends in the Army of Earth.

Out of the corner of her eye she began to make out some sort of distinction in the mists, some sort of dark color appearing in the rotating wall of white, but she just continued to stare at the men, at their scraggly unshaven faces, broken noses, and cauliflowered ears. What did these conscripts leave behind? Anything? Hobby farms once shrunk by disease, then later dried by drought before being picked by Horde? Shanties in the alleys of territorial cities? These were the men that had not even enough to offer the new territories to deserve the promise of acreage or mule or newife.

One of the soldiers finally met her eyes, but as quickly as he glanced he then turned away, but nodded behind his fellow man. Was this her answer?

A fist-sized rock landed at Teca's foot, barely grazing her boot. It had come from the appearing trees, but the soldiers had not noticed. She looked out into the thin foliage. A year's worth of snow had gotten caught up in the underbrush and looked to have never been disturbed. She thought the Army's forces had stayed to the plains despite her maps showing tree-lines nearing. She could now determine somewhat where the march was heading.

A stick, sharpened to a point, flew awkwardly out of the trees and snow and fog to bounce harmlessly off one of the soldier's shins. His companions fired before he even had the chance to react.

Rifle and bow let loose into the mists and were accompanied by shots fired all around her. Even spears were flung into the glow of the whiteness. Teca recognized the whirr and roar of the gatling gun from a direction she would not have expected. She sank into a ball beneath the cracking of gunfire, covering her exposed head. Somewhere nearby she heard the hissing of the Army's blowtorches, and she could see trees alight and mists become replaced with a darker smog.

She thought that mere minutes passed but guessed it was probably much less by the time the soldiers slowed their firing. Still, she waited until only the occasional wisp of an arrow broke the silence before crouching and heading away from any now exposed treeline. Soldiers had gathered in larger groups now, small packs of men absorbing individuals. They were all back to mouthing silent directions and aiming at fog of both light and dark.

She would not try her questions anymore this morning. This night? What time of the day was it? The mists absorbed and reflected any light. The exhaust of truck and rifle bloated any shadows. She remembered waking recently, but it could have been a memory from the previous day.

She winced as her knee hit a bench crowded with audience members, quickly realizing that she was only reacting to how it should have felt, not how it actually felt. She caught herself doing this a lot over recent memory. Her limbs were so cold some days that pain had become a distant complaint replaced by numbness she just could not become used to. Her leather pants were a long cry from the segmented knee guards she must have misplaced since finding the Army of Earth.

The onlookers did not even notice her presence, as she had not noticed the makeshift theater that appeared out of the morning (night?) fog. Great gaslights lit the back of the stage while torches warmed the first row of the audience.

Teca knew this story by heart now. Practically every campfire she joined, every slopline she crossed, and every company she tried to question or join was telling the tale of how the Necrophim generals and their weird battalions followed the Liege of Foes and his red consort into the land to challenge the Horde. And she had heard about the troupe of guisers traveling along with the rest of the market shadowing the war. Along with venders and peddlers and cooks and tailors, the players entertained the soldiers for pennies. She had heard the troupe only knew one play, and, by the craft of stage and mummery she looked upon now, she had immediately decided that they did it well. For the soldiers' story was not new to her, nor was it the only version she was familiar with.

Torches were also placed on staves, and lanterns were hung from spears. They glowed, diminished by the mists, pulsing like strangled hearts, each in their own little globes of hazy lights. Huddled soldiers crowded around the many globes as though they gave off warmth or actually held back the darkening fog, but it was only the torches and chemical lamps of the stage that ate away at the moist air. And it was the stage that held all eyes, dark and light, bloody and shell-shocked.

The shuffling of armor was all around her, soldiers trying in obvious vain to sit comfortably on makeshift benches. Most crowded on the ground or squatted on their helmets. The ground thawed beneath all of them as the play continued. The longer the performance went on the more likely the earth was to suck at boots and hands. Teca was familiar instantly with the story, and she could tell it was in its final act. Illustrated versions had frightened her as a child, but it was a rougher translation she had returned to in more recent years, one with an almost abstruse yet modern poetic language but without the distracting, some-times macabre, imagery. The performance she watched now was slavish to neither yet held elements of both.

With the limitations of travel and practical costuming, The Angel was nowhere near as imposing as she was on the page, but the costum-ing was still beautiful to behold. The near flames matched the crimson and dark highlights of the actress's long and curly wig, while her fanged mask reflected the glistening dew perspiring over and under the stage. Teca had been at the service of and at odds with many noblewomen over the years, but she would be hard pressed to remember seeing a more elegant gown. She guessed it would appear simpler-made upon close scrutiny, but from the back of the crowds, through the rainbow of haze, it looked as though a goat's tail poked out from spun fire and gold.

The Libran walked through the settled crowds. Those she passed, for short seconds so clear next to her, disappeared into the haze as new soldiers solidified as she neared. Soon they too would be swallowed back into the sometimes consuming, sometimes brilliant, mists. She noticed, for the first time since joining up with the march, women underneath the scarves and armor. She could not tell if they were originally of the Necrophim or from the countryside. They wore the bleeding eye just like any other soldier. They too breathed in the mists and breathed out their own in return. Teca had seen more violence in the previous few days than she had experienced over her entire life. All these soldiers, Hel-sent or earth-grown or both, consumed and created this war like it was no big thing.

Why had those thoughts come into her head just then? Was it something the actors had said? She could hear them now despite the fog's efforts to eat all sound.

The character of The Assassin had many questions, as Teca remembered from reading the play, and the performance did him justice. His mask was pale. His cape was black. The Angel placed her tiara of tiny horns upon his head, and she answered only the questions he needed to hear answered. These were only a few of the seven boons the Red Queen had promised him, and Teca was not sure how many of the gifts had been given or were still yet to be given at this point in the play, although she did remember that the versions she had read all ended without all of them being fulfilled.

The skillfully painted backdrops fell and unrolled as scenes quickly changed behind the actors. The current fabrics were simple compared to the previous one showing a grand banquet room. These showed cells representing more gifts from The Angel. She handed The Assassin the bottled storm demon. She presented him with the paper dragon pinned to the wall. Teca had always imagined the paper dragon as rippling in the heat or wind like a delicate flag, yet here the dampness revealed it to be as limp as its namesake.

She could see the simple seams in the costumes, the chipped paint of the masks, the thick paint on the actors' lips and chins, because, as she suddenly realized, she was at the edge of the stage. Here she could hear the hum of gaslights, could smell the sweat and greasepaint. She turned to the audience. All except those in the front row were faceless to her, but even through the haze she could tell that their dark eyes and invisible ears were set on the play, looking through her and dismissing the muffled sounds of gun and cannon fire still reverberating through the mists around them. The war could not drown out the actor's words.

"Uneasy lies the dead that wears a crown," said the man behind the mask of The Assassin.

In response, The Angel actress said, "Then you are not ready for one. Give it up. But make no mistake, you are not dead, nor are you lying."

XLIX

of the seven celestially Governed Elements
   (6) Discipline
"...marshals the people into proper populations and graduations of rank"
  —Hyper Khan's The War of Art

The young woman knotted the last strings of the patch, and Wulf thanked her before heading back into the masses. He was given everything he needed on the peregrination. He never had to provide for himself food, clothing, heat, or shelter, but he always walked away from the one-sided transactions knowing he had left the provider unfulfilled. It was not from anything they said — more from what they did not say. As he had complemented the young woman's sewing there had been a pause in the conversation, as though he should have said more or as though she had bitten her tongue. But he had nothing to give them. Everything he owned he now kept thrown over his shoulder or around his waist. He was now even mountless, as he had left his ruddy horse, suddenly lame in the northern fields, behind the prior day. He would walk the rest of the distance, having turned down many gifts of horse and offers of wagon rides. The rest of the journey to Bifrost would not be easy for anyone. They were leaving clear roads behind. The new paths were already lost deep below drifts.

Ivy claimed they were already in N'Midgaard. Somewhere over the past years she had picked up runespeak, and since the day before had seen signs proclaiming the Northern Lands, but Wulf was not as sure. It had been decades, but he still expected his return home to be obvious. He had expected to cross some invisible line, and the feeling would be instantaneous. He would immediately be surrounded by long houses covered in long grasses. Long-haired and horned cattle would be lingering around their own homes, houses indistinguishable from the farmers.' Insanely-gabled churches would announce the presence of any town a day before coming upon it, stretching starkly above even the tallest trees of the Granite Lands. He would walk through grasses grown to the hammer at his hip, bend under branches reaching down to his waist, and walk corn fields from dawn to dusk until reaching the capital. After days of rounding lakes — the heavens reproduced time and again over wet earth — and streams strong and clean, he would follow the great *Jormangandr* to where it split blue Bifrost. Tall hall after long pale hall, each with it own granite wall, would greet him from the corner of every cobbled street. From the palest to the darkest wood, every tree would be represented in the multi-layered roofs of the boating houses. Ritual houses would be unknown from longhouses, from lawhouses and barns. The *Jormangandr* would be the source of all sound in the city, busy with impossibly long boats carved in the image of the river's name, launching to wrap themselves around the known world. Looking down he would see waterwheels moving and rainbows spraying. Looking up he would find windmills turning and the sun bending. Bifrost had turned the world itself when he was a child. Without the city the rivers did not flow and the seasons did not change. The cosmos twisted on the command of the Granite Lands. Ubiquitous, blue stone at every turn matched the silver hung from every northern man. Sculpted branches in rock or metal would appear to twine into infinity, occasionally meandering into the shape of hind or serpent. Pillars of these sinuous carvings would adorn street and flesh accented by the runes of the land, fur-covered horns of some unknown beast stood cradled on the entrance to every hall, and a drumming from deep within the streets thundered more loudly the deeper one walked near the Great Church of Bold Warlif — seen from every corner of Bifrost.

But there was nothing to signify to Wulf that he had suddenly passed into his homelands. They walked more hills now instead of plains. The white land rolled into frozen lakes and dried creek beds, instead of stretching without anything to set apart one day from another, but there was no instant spark of nostalgic recognition. If Wulf walked the colonies of N'Midgaard, it was deep beneath the years of snow his boots tread.

He turned down an offer to eat at a zenith campfire crowded with elderly. The heavy scent of char made him immediately salivate however, and he took a turkey leg with him as he continued. Again he had nothing to give. No gold or silver. No extra furs. He had no solace to offer except the advice to turn back, to not follow him, but he had given up on that order weeks ago. Just as they had given up explaining to him and themselves why they followed. He could not quote passages from the *Ver Primordium* or the *Fallo Terminus* well enough to prove he was not the Liege of Foes any better than they could recite lines proving he was. He was through trying to convince anyone of anything.

The world would continue praying until it was hoarse. It would continue warring until it was dead. And in the meantime the snows would continue to fall.

He felt the new patch on his cloak. His clothes had become more mending than original fabrics. His boots had held up surprisingly well over the plains, but, if they were heading into the northern lands, that would not be the case for much longer. Way back in his hood he was shielded from the large flakes of snow lighting softly over camps and wagons. The sky was mostly clear. No wind blew. The weather would not last. It would be a good day to gain some ground. But he first had to make it out of the caravans.

A group of boys sat among rocks, both large and small, playing a game of UnderCrawl. The game was in the shade of a truck. The air reeked of the sweet smell of fuel, but the engine exuded warmth over the boys. The board looked to be made from some cast-off piece of fencing, with a green painted maze for pebbles to traverse. The boys shared dice to pay for their turns, to play the cards and move the improvised pawns. The children were unaware how close Fobos' legion had come to overrunning the pilgrims. From what Wulf could tell, most of the peregrination had only heard rumors of the aborted battle over the last few days. The caravans and camps were so spread out that the story had waned into myth at some point, but everyone had heard of the sudden green star that had appeared over the battlefield to banish the Horde.

The boys played with cards Wulf had never seen before. They were well-made, and the artwork was beautiful, but the cards themselves had seen better days. With frayed edges and dark fingerprints, it was unlikely any opponent was ever surprised by a play. A stout boy, obviously the oldest, rolled high to play a card titled *Lament of the Muses' Son*. He discarded the rest of his cards, put his pebble near the middle of the board, and sat back with a look of accomplishment on his face. The dice passed to his left. This was why the Army of Earth fought, Wulf supposed. Priests and kings would fight over souls and land until the end of time, but in the end it would be the children that would decide what to do with either. The boys began to bicker over card count, but the disagreement was quickly forgotten as the dice passed from one to another. One player unknowingly rubbed the green paint from his ear, while another wore the peeled tin from cans as armor over his arms and thighs. Wulf did not want to leave the heat of the engine, but as the play passed to a boy wearing an eye-patch, he decided he should be taking advantage of the day. Another child stood just beyond the ring of the game. He had no cards but watched intently, and he smiled and blinked as Wulf passed.

A line of women practiced archery at one edge of the camps. More women, some obviously pregnant beneath skirt and fur, sat nearby around Milliam Pittsfield. He leaned against two trees that had in their infancy grown together. The trunks created a comfortable-looking delta for him to look out of. He spoke not to those crowding him but to the archers. Wulf would have been surprised if they could have heard his quiet voice.

"Thy steps grow slippery as the days grow short. That is the reason why you are not fallen already, and don't fall now. It is only that the Lonely Forgotten Sun of God's appointed time is not come. For I say, that when that due time, or appointed time comes, your foot shall slide. Then they shall be left to fall as they are inclined by the weight of their own sin. And that sin is pride — belief that you know the Day of Judgment is not upon us. God won't hold you up in these slippery lands any longer, but will let you go, and then, at that very instant, you shall fall into destruction, as he that stands in such slippery declining ground on the edge of the Great Pit is lost. Believe tonight or there will be no tomorrow. The unrepentant will not see after morning."

The archers were surprisingly accurate, but could they hold their composure in battle? Wulf hoped they would never find out. Fobos' phalanxes had scattered after the death of the Abysmal Swarm destroyed their confidence, but the Horde general had surely gathered his forces back together by now. The near reports of the Army of Earth must be taking all of Fobos' attention. Wulf rubbed his eyes. Earth's Army was near, as the increasing pain behind his brow verified. As the *Other* came closer, the pressure became cumulative. Sometimes he just wanted to give in, to drop the psionic barriers, to let the impossibly familiar mind in and let the pain just wash over him. He was so tired. The resolve to hold the intrusion at bay was exhausting. It would be so nice just to let it in. But would he die from the feedback? Would his mind just be crushed under the immensity of the swirling pain, or would his psyche sink beneath the whirlpool of two minds caught in an overlapping loop of years that spun by while the outside world only experienced seconds. He feared he would experience the madness of mental centuries before his body even began to decay. No, he would fortify the psionic doors for now, at least until he settled his debts in Bifrost.

Wulf felt it was time for him to move on when a couple of men appeared to retrieve two of the women sitting around Milliam. The women appeared to struggle for only a second before reluctantly leaving the preacher's side. Milliam seemed not to notice the commotion.

Wulf was not long back into the masses before he was approached again. He stood at the fronts of the camps, the Agent of MANN now shadowing him, with people of all persuasions offering him what he could only assume were prized possessions. Wulf had not seen a peach in years yet he ate preserves from a salty piecrust. Brass and cork were rare to the common man, yet a blacksmith had specifically made him two shells for the short-barreled he kept under his cloak. There was no end to the rest of the gifts he turned down.

When the crowd eventually dispersed, he looked to the north, to only more trees and frozen water. It was the middle of the day, but it was dark. The clouds were thick enough to make him doubt the time.

"I have nothing more to give them in return," he said aloud. The Agent of MANN's full head was lined with a row of barely visible eyes — or what Wulf had to assume were eyes. It was impossible to know in which direction he looked.

"That's not true," came back the deep metallic voice.

Wulf cast a semblance of a shadow in the dim day, but noticed the ground beneath the Agent was pale as the snow. The deep reds and blues of the man's armor absorbed the light, while its thin white trim bent it, redirecting it around him. Wulf wondered how far this ability went, and why, if the Agent had the power to be completely unseen, he was revealing himself now.

"Have you ever been in N'Midgaard?" Wulf asked.

"No. As I'm sure you are aware, the Church of Bold Warlif has no love for outsiders or the level of technology MANN possesses. We've had no interest in starting a war."

"So I can assume you won't be following us any further?"

"Ignore my presence. I am not here to answer questions nor sway decisions."

"Right," Wulf sighed. He made count of the few possessions in his mountless saddlebag, but before he could head out he was approached by a woman with a garland of flowers around her neck. They had thin, frail-looking, white petals around centers that reminded him of Mew's eyes. They were a very appropriate and increasingly common adornment of her Ascensionists, Wulf thought before second-guessing himself. Perhaps they belonged to the Ascendants. He could not tell the difference. This woman appeared too old to have a toddler, but she held one out to Wulf.

"If the world ends tonight I want her to have seen the Liege of Foes," she said, eyes watering.

Wulf looked to the child but did not take her. Her long blonde hair was mostly covered by scarf, hat, and hood. She had big blue eyes and would fit right in where Wulf was heading. He found a bite of the bitter chocolate bars they had salvaged from the depot and gave it to the little girl even though she already had plenty smeared over her face. She sucked on the piece but mirrored her mother's tears when she saw that she was crying.

"The world won't end in the North," Wulf said. "As much as it wants it to."

The trees had barely enveloped him when he could hear the first signs of people scrambling to close camp and pack. He did not have to look back to assume the frantic collection of loved ones and loading of wagons. His pace quickened.

As the day progressed, consistently darkening early and constantly threatening to snow, Wulf felt that in a matter of hours he had traversed every terrain familiar to his life — albeit all under a tough pale crust. He trudged through drifts of snow caught up in and unable to escape tree groves. He climbed and slid down steeps and deeps hiding shadows thriving no matter the time of day or season. He walked flat fields so white the missing sun reflected blindingly even into the deep recesses of his hood. Between forest and hill he found a plain of yellowed, indestructible grasses. Half-buried strands caught up his snowshoes. Sharp slivers scratched at his leather. The directions were all tree lines, but they appeared to turn and run from him. He trod loudly over ponds long dried and snow-covered, gingerly over lakes that groaned beneath ice and step. Woodlands took up most of the evening. The snow was too deep to climb with just boots, but the resistant undergrowth was too tall and thick to use snowshoes. He lifted his steps to the top of the crust with telekinesis, using his mind to lighten his body, pushing against whatever he could find solid enough beneath the snow as leverage, but any focus outside of resisting the *Other* weakened his mental barriers. The night was spent under constant migraine, climbing in and out of tiny ravines once holding creeks, pushing against great conifers and tugging on adolescent branches. He descended and ascended pits of gravel and ice completely devoid of color. He walked perfectly parallel rows of christmas trees. Each line he crossed was more impossibly straight than the one before. The roof was knitted in the darkest of greens, but their low branches were bare and gray and brittle and none survived his touch. The air in the rows was completely silent, entirely unmoving. The fog of his breath was blasphemy in the symmetrical maze.

It was as though all the world's land was encapsulated in one day. Great sections of earth had been transplanted from all areas to form his path north before being lost beneath the white. But this attitude was naïve, he knew. This was not *the* world but *his* world, and as much as he had always tried to deny it, to run from it, he had at last returned. He had skirted its edges many times, but there was nothing stopping him now from following the *Jormangandr* straight to his past life. The heaviness of *GloryRend* moved against his thigh, reminding him of its presence with each step, just as his memories of Bifrost reminded him daily of his connection to the Granite Lands. This was the cool blue land his forefathers followed Lif into after the Evolutionary Wars. Like the hammer at his side, the people had been a blunt instrument, awkwardly but successfully crushing race and creed in their initial conquering, violently carving church and isolation in the final expansion. This was a warrior race allowed to evolve independently of the rest of the world, and it had stagnated incestuously. It had only itself to fight with. It was killing itself, but it was a slow death. It was said that boiling one's blood was the only way to stay warm through a Midgardian winter. Wulf planned on putting that to the test.

He had hoped to find the *Jormangandr* before nightfall, but hours after sunset he found himself clearing a small spot in a thickly wooded area for a fire. His back and feet were sore from the day's toil, his brain exhausted from the constant fortification of mental walls. If he traveled any more this night, if he fatigued himself any longer, he feared he would not be able to hold the pressure in his skull at bay while sleeping. So after star and moon disappeared behind cloud and night, he positioned the tiniest twigs he had collected on the day's walk and struck flint.

Branches lost to darkness creaked overhead, and the murky cosmos even hid *Wyrmwood*. It was noticeably odd now living in a world where others could see the spectral star. Over the years he had begun to question himself, and if the transient light existed, then others had started to see it. But this night the star or anything beyond one's face could not be seen. His small fire could only warm an immediate bulb of space in front of his folded legs. It could not penetrate the darkness even to the closest trunk.

A meager breeze moved the tree he sat against, branches stretching loudly, and he found himself dozing to the rock-a-bye creak of wood. *Down will come baby,* he recited to himself, *fatal to all.* He knew he should set up the skins for a shelter to trap some of the fire's heat and, if it was not too cold, to hide him from the night's frost, but he was so tired. He wrapped himself entirely in cloak and blanket, his head in hood and scarf so that only his nostrils peeked out. He just wanted to savor a little bit of warmth before setting up the tent. He could see only a slight blur of light from the fire through his wrappings, could barely smell the dry smoke, but he eventually warmed beneath the layers. Only the tip of his nose felt a tiny bite of cold.

The night hours stretched liked the branches above. The fire glowed silently, just a pile of pulsing color. Wulf never knew when he was awake or sleeping. He was mostly just somewhere in-between until he eventually saw other cottony yellows and reds through his scarves and out past his own embers. Muffled words told of other camps laying down for sleep. Their fires burned higher than his but died as his still glowed. He was alone again when their settlements fell to slumber, but he enjoyed their surrounding warmth just the same.

Wulf thought thunder cracked the air wide open, but it was the sound of a branch breaking. He thought lightning opened his eyes, but it was a body falling into his embers. He lifted his wrappings only enough to confirm the emaciated figure rising from scattered flame. He had immediately recognized the sweet smell of lye and whitefish even through his scarves. The scent now mixed with ash. He moved the wrappings back over his face.

Fool pup, the deep voice sizzled like gristle on a pan over the fire

Grimm melted into, *afraid to face the sight of your own responsibility.*

"Why me?" Wulf asked, unmoving. Maybe it was the cold granite in his head, but he could see the ancient being before him, even with his eyes closed.

That's not for me to answer. You head north? Ask her! Her answers'll test your mettle. You'll rue the day you wondered. Grimm was all tatters and hair, and both softened as he crouched in the embers, flames coming alive at the dripping fat of his thawing limbs. From beneath a hoarfrosted beard emerged the noose that had brought the branch down. *Waste no more time on knowledge. What do you have left to sacrifice?* The burning voice came from slack jaw, echoing from black, empty sockets hidden behind jellied hair. *It's no matter! You removed the Beast's muzzle. You've subjected the land to its howl. What matters the 'whys'? All you need to know is that your better travels ahead of you, with the same questions, but he is in love with the answers, and so he will be unstoppable as long as you accept yourself as a pale comparison. You carry a hammer now. Use it!*

"Why are you still here? Just leave like all the other gods."

Cowards, all of them. This is my land. You are my people. I can no longer interfere. You have brought this winter upon yourselves, but you are made in my image. I am made in yours. If you are to die, then I will die with you.

"How noble. What do the Heavenly Halls know of suffering? You sacrifice a piece of the infinite? What is the death of an avatar? You have no concept of human pain."

Grimm smiled behind thaw and fang. *Yes, here is the passion of your forefathers! Use that anger and that hammer and strike. There's so few of those dogs left. Strike now! They go now to find the location of Hel's Slit. Destroy them before they find the means of cutting the Beast free.*

"They're in the North?" Wulf asked. He now peeked from his wraps to see Grimm stand from the living embers. The fire had found new life in the being's burning. Along with his voice it hissed as the last of the adorning ice dripped. The god-as-man appeared to Wulf suddenly as Mad Hati with beard and hair flaming.

He's always one step ahead of you. He's taken fully the foul destiny you dance around.

Fire and finger reached for Wulf, and he was immediately awake with heart racing and eyes wide. He tore the scarves from his face to find morning lighting the forest pale but brightly. His fire had long grown cold and colorless. In all directions, through each tree, people warmed vermillion as a poor substitute for coffee. Some were already letting their fast breaking fires smolder. Many were even taking down camps. Oxen shook frost from massive shoulders.

The branches above Wulf creaked, now familiarly. The peregrination had overtaken him in the night, and he wondered if they had even noticed him among the forest. He had barely anything to collect and hoped to sneak beyond the camps, heading out before them. *GloryRend* hung heavier at his side this morning, he noticed before looking up to the skeletal canopy he had not seen in the night. He had been unknowingly sitting beneath a Midgardian border marker all night. From the tamarack's bent branches hung men and women by their necks. They were desiccate, more a collection of twigs than human. Now, in the bold light of a brand new day he could make out the occasional limb that had fallen and frosted to the drifts in some past night. He was almost certain he had used a finger or toe bone in his campfire. None of the faces, all at awkward angles, would look at him, but he was certain he knew their expressions. The great tree's scaly bark was the only thing of color anywhere near him. Shriveled shingles bled underneath to aborted red cones still on the branches.

He had lost all doubt. He now walked within N'Midgaard.

L

Narrator:

She guided the assassin around dunes
burning of alkali to where new men,
weathered, shriveled, dried to leathery prunes,
waded desperately in a brittle fen.
Deeper and deeper they plunged into a
briny pool, but the waters dried and then
cracked their skin more. But they drank it anyway.
Amidst the sobs of parched tongues and new tears,
Penance led the assassin along a
salt-crusted shore, speaking not of the years
past, or those to come, but of in which ways
the present was just one of so many
possible lifetimes, events, years, days,
and choices. Among the Multiverse, any
possibility exists. Throughout the
Possibiliverse, variation spreads
multitudinal. One reality
sees light bending darkly, another threads
conquering mitochondria throughout
history, foreign in temporal beds.

Penance:

"But it is the more similar about
which we are concerned, realities in
which a single flutter of butterfly
wings condemns a fallen nation to win,
a wayward sneeze causes a king to die
before birth, worlds in which mammalian
dominance gave way to serpentine eye,
worlds won by a specific alien.
In these lives you may be a carpenter,
merchant, father, or a fortuneteller.
But your reality is the center,
and to your world the alien dweller
will find his way in some incarnation —
warrior, king, soldier interstellar.
The Greater Prophet cross-plane migration!"

Narrator:

The assassin listened to his guide but
watched the crying and drying men drown in
the brine of their own tears, choke on the glut

of evaporating sobs, crack and grin
as skin desiccates and flakes and bleeds slow
treacle blood from jigsaw faces. Wild gwyn
milked the treacle men's eyes, for what they sowed
they now reaped. These are the Empathetic —
those who in life valued to understand
and share. These poets chose the aesthetic
ascetic, worshipping lachrymal gland.

Penance:

"Pathetic souls endemically condemned,
dried by drinking, drunk on desiccant sand,
with puckered faces of crusty tears gemmed."

Narrator:

She blushed beneath the Elder Mask, big blue
eyes blinking, platinum curls peeking from
hood, yet still he stared, trying to construe
the world from whence she came. He was struck dumb
though and only listened to a voice he
should not have known. She spoke of the dried scum
filling and drinking the pool. They lapped the
waves caused by their own hysterics. Behind
another world's Elder Mask her eyes teared.

Penance:

"Woe be to the Empathetic, the blind
behind flooded sight who, bleeding-hearted, leered
and sniffed around the pain of others by
which they defined themselves, to be mirrored
in tragedy and perpetually dry."

Narrator:

Still the assassin had eyes for just her.

The Assassin:

"Why are you here, young one? So pure, so pale…"

Penance:

"In me all children did father infer.
When they suffered, me he felt he would fail.
All men are children. All brought him to tears.
Like my father, of all did I avail.
To be unlike him fed my greatest fears."

Narrator:

He followed along the alkali beach
to hills of crust where the sea receded.

Necrophim lords warred in the distant reach
and he watched as they only succeeded
in salting the fields with both legions' blood.
Men died and rose again, unimpeded
under violet dawn, brilliant, plum, flash flood.
Penance:
"Purple sunrise resurrects damned soldier.
The Necrophims' wars are never-ending,
with bodies not taking the time to molder.
They spend their days and lives ever-rending
limb and soul but without direction."
Narrator:
Most obsessed with Circular ascending,
spurned by the Red Queen's constant rejection,
Mixcotle's Four Hundred First Son appeared
from nowhere to whisper in the ear of
the assassin. He spoke treachery weird
and dangerous — a honeyed tongue thereof
regicide. O' to unite the warlords
and to place Mixcotle's Son high above
all Circles and damnation towards.

—excerpt from "The Angel and the Ass"

"Where can I find your general?" Teca asked, but the exploding shell that answered deafened her to any other response.
She could not have been unconscious for long. The blood from her
obviously broken nose had barely had a chance to trickle over her
lips before she was up and scrambling for new cover. Each time she
found something to crouch behind, her cover quickly moved to find
its own cover. The rolling prairie night was filled with hunched soldiers
either lining up their rifle shots or spreading low to avoid the white hot
rounds crisscrossing the smothering cosmos. Both star and glowing
bullet seemed to flicker near inches from her ducking head.

She moved again, low and with the tickling dread up the back of
her neck that anticipated a bullet to the spine. The spotlight, cracked
and yellow like a serpent's eye, scoured the near plain from the only
adjacent hilltop. The light had not reached her or her near comrades
yet, but the mortar that had broken her face told her that the enemy

was firing everywhere in their direction. She could not remember just now how the skirmish had started. Her only thought now was to find some sort of cover. She would worry later how she had woken up yet again in the middle of a firefight.

The gunfire suddenly became constant. For a commodity that was becoming dangerously rare on both sides of the war, round after round tore at the air just over her head, dug into the ground near her side, and ricocheted off submerged helmet and bone just past her boots. From every direction there was no rhythm. The cracking of the dark sky was set to some orchestra of broken drums. She tried to determine what, beside herself, was a target, but any round that did not splinter her meager shelter appeared to be launched chaotically into the exhaust-filled abyss above or beyond. Snow and mud kicked up into smoke far from her as much as did near. The rifles that discharged around the bend echoed out into the black fields as much as far-off shots reverberated up to her position.

Still, near or far, the gunfire all flicked against her as though she were the sole inhabitant of the fields. She felt each round through each vibration. As the dirt quaked, her thighs spasmed. As the air split, her brow cringed. The icy hail of the past days became a hail of lead, and if it was not the wind pushing and pulling her prone body it was the round after round of gunfire. The obscene cacophony of tinny discharges, coupled with the low-hanging putrid of unmoving sulfur, would periodically lull her to sleep, and she would wake up always surprised to find herself not riddled full of holes, not crumpled and broken and swallowing the mud and blood that encompassed her quick dreams.

In all things, Libra's love. Watching all, Libra above. The song kept coming into Teca's head, but she could not remember where from. Was it the *Sol Sistere*? No. The more it repeated itself the more it lost its power out here on the ice and rock. For she could not see Lady Wayasu anywhere out in the fighting. There was no love here. Not even the love of violence. Not anymore. And the Blind Angel could not possibly be watching down. Love was not aware of this, for the judgment of Love was quick and all-consuming, and this felt as though it would never end.

Eventually, she shook. She shivered from the cold. The cold of an air that refused to warm from explosion or exhaust or the heat released from the open bodies of the crying men she could still hear beneath the rapid fire. She shivered from inactivity, her legs jerking awake and against a low atmosphere that solidified as it dripped over the ruddy gelatin darkness. She twitched each time she realized the last remaining warmth of her haunches had been wasted on melting the frost beneath her, and that she had again sunk deeper into the sludge of the prairie. But most of all she shook, as did her cover and the dirt around her and the smoke surrounding her, from the constant discharge of rifles, the non-stop crack of revolvers, and the endless repeat of gatling guns that were only interrupted by the occasional shattering of the ground by mortars. She shook with the droplets of mud that repeatedly flecked her face, the sparks that dissipated as they lighted over her hair and knit cap, the frozen sod that twitched in clumps as it spun through her peripheral like so many limbs, and the air that transferred the vibrations just as well as the checkered plain. She wiped the already-dried blood from her face, but she still could not see. She wiped the crud of the earth from her eyes but still could not see until she could smear the pale soot that wafted more slowly than a second hand. The sulfur hung like ugly silken streamers celebrating the gunfire as the injured did with their songs of anguish.

Another mortar turned the darkness red for a second. This one was far enough away not to deafen her again, but she could still see the silhouette or shadows of limbs or swords flail through the night. The light was short-lived — not as short-lived, however, as the cries of anguish and pain — but she used the quick flicker to spot an over-turned cart and mound of sandbags. More closely leaned the aged skeleton of what she guessed was an ancient oil pump jutting crook-edly into the close cosmos. Old paint or rust was the only color in the flashes of gunfire. Grime and snow had collected in spoke and leg over the decades, so the pump appeared to tilt on a short rise, but she would have little cover unless some was hidden on the backside. There was no debate. The cart and bag cover would be a target for the mortars, but it was deeper, and she could not justify staying out in the open any longer.

But the spotlight was immediately on her as she moved. Its cold-blooded glare chilled her, and her legs responded only sluggishly. Cottony ears refused to hear the shots, but Teca's face felt the air split near. Frozen blood rushed to her cheeks and warmed, and she rolled. She rolled over twisted mortar shells long since cooled in frost caught in a state of perpetual thaw and refreeze. She rolled over what she hoped was shattered helm and helmet but could see through her eyelashes were something more macabre. What she wished were broken blade and shield she knew were the sharp remains of what she had been seeing flip through the air all day or night.

She fell behind the makeshift barrier, counting two soldiers hiding with her, but she spotted the glint of other armor or blade, so the darkness may have been hiding more fighters. Numerous eyes stared. Numerous mouths glistened. The few words she could hear told her the men feared she had drawn the enemy's attention toward their foxhole.

Her hearing was slowly returning, but her ears were now filled with the sound of gunfire, not the answer to her questions.

"Who's your leading commander?" She was suddenly aware that the soldiers probably stared at her bruised face. She touched the softness the bridge of her nose had become and almost passed out from the pain. Auras flashed in front of her eyes with each probe of her finger. She had broken her nose before, and this surprisingly seemed no worse. She spit blood and something else before she spoke again. "Where can I find him?" Their voices came back as muffled as her own had to have sounded.

"Commander... whut... are you on about?"

"...officer... forward engagement... to be here..."

She was certain one of the soldiers mentioned the Liege of Foes. Had she moved up through the march to bypass the Necrophim generals? She asked about the immediate commander, but the soldiers cringed back into the shadows at a nearby explosion. Their eyes went dark, but the crying eye of their badges picked up the star and firelight.

She thought she had marched into the command of a new Necrophim over the prior days. Many of the soldiers that had marched next to her wore the insignia of the general Banshee Jenny Wren, but she could have easily strayed into another legion. She picked at the drying scabs around her mouth, just then realizing that she had left her main pack somewhere behind. If she died here this night it would be without the last remnants of her Libran platemail. She still had her shortsword but had somewhere along the march or within the shooting had dropped the great piece of her first mentor's broadsword. Sir Leksi's sword had its origins back in the early days of the Librans. Now the silver hilt lay trampled somewhere into the refreezing mud of the endless prairie. As she thought of it, she thought she saw it then, sticking out of a trampled drift.

The next thing Teca knew she was waking to a choking cloud of exhaust and a darkness she could not blink away. Her mouth tasted like dirt and the rust of the Necrophim's red tanks. Her fingers went immediately to the soreness of her face, but the flashes of light that appeared from the pain in her broken nose still refused to light the endless night. She remembered running. She remembered crouching and ducking. She did not feel any new injuries except for a splitting headache behind her face. There was no new blood this time.

She tried to turn, but the mud held her. She tried to stand, but the ache in her head felt tied to the rise she rested against. Voices grew near. Or perhaps her hearing was returning again. Either way, each voice, yelling above or anticipating the occasional cannon roar, was often accompanied by a muzzle flash. The flashes were Teca's only peek into the night. She saw faces washed of color. Jaws clenched against recoil. White eyes lining up shots and blinking against nearby shell-fall. She saw the tearing eye on sash and tattoo. As she finally stood, one of the soldiers immediately pulled her back down below the cover line.

She searched her belts and remaining pack for her canteen but did not wait to ask her usual question. Something exploded right above them. It ate the stars and ignited the sky but could not penetrate the darkness of the foxhole. She could only guess at how many soldiers were cramped in beside her. The truck she smelled had to be nearby, for its engine roared more loudly the longer she listened. She had to assume it powered the spotlight turned by the only man she could now consistently see.

She was starting to remember a mortar exploding behind her and other men and her joints being stretched to their limits as some survivor dragged her from rubble. She could only assume this was the same night.

Despite the periodic shaking of the ground, and the lights breaking the night above, Teca felt safe in the hole. The mud was cold but the air was hot, and she could not help but chuckle at the dirt that would build into a pile on top her head before crumbling down into her hair, eventually trickling down over her face. But even that hurt, and it was quite a while before she could sit up again without her head shouting in migraine. But the soldiers were pretty well entrenched, and the bombs lessened as the night went on, whether they were launched at or from the foxhole. The soldiers would take turns resting down lower in the shelter, near her, and her ears eventually felt a lot less cottony. But she could not breath without feeling the fluid clogging her sinuses, could not speak without spitting first.

"Where's your leading commander or general?" she asked, her voice suddenly unfamiliar. "Who's in charge here?"

"What?" The soldier next to her suddenly jumped up to fire a revolver through a recently jury-rigged cover of splintered boards. Teca could not imagine that he was hitting anything at this range unless the enemy was closer than it sounded. The man quickly sat back next to her. He had a split lip that had long ago healed poorly and a recent cut mirroring the old wound that would one day look the same.

"What," he repeated, "aren't you in charge?"

A shirtless soldier fell into the foxhole from behind them. He brushed snow from his shoulders and dirt from numerous empty holsters as he stood from the mud. It was obvious that at one point he had the Army's logo painted broadly across his chest, but it was just a large blue and red smear now, staining his shorts as scabs stained his legs. Teca could not hear him the first time he shouted at the other man, but he repeated himself until the spotlight operator took scraps of fabric from his ears.

"We need the light back here!" he shouted. Upon now hearing, Teca then realized that the new soldier was a woman. She knocked on her helmet to get her attention.

"Where's your general? Who's your…"

"Sorry, sir," the woman yelled above a new mortar explosion, "I was hoping for permission to illuminate the western field." She suddenly appeared to realize that her head was dangerously exposed, and she crouched while waiting for Teca's word. The operator leaned down toward Teca as well, waiting. The cone of light glared yellow and impotently upward, straight into a low exhaust atmosphere.

Teca tried explaining but could only cough. The soldiers took her wave of annoyance as permission, and the light was awkwardly removed from its scaffold and aimed backward.

She stood on crates broken and waterlogged to peek through a wall made of even older crates, not at where the light now shined but out across the fields where shots still rang. There was little light beyond the occasional fireworks, but she could make out an overturned cart and mound of sandbags. Closer lie the aged skeleton of what she guessed was an ancient oil pump jutting crookedly into the close cosmos. Ancient paint or rust was the only color in the flashes of gunfire as soldiers near her fired upon it. Sod and snow had collected in spoke and leg over the decades, so the pump appeared to tilt on a short rise, but there was little cover unless someone was hidden on the backside. The cart and bag cover were an obvious target for the mortars launching from her trench. But still, round after round, fire after fire, the forces approached their position.

Exhaust rolled past the moon. Gunsmoke deadened firelight. And as her trench-mates fired off a long salvo, Teca climbed from the back of the foxhole and rolled as lowly as she could over the hill, following other soldiers abandoning the makeshift station. They crouched and ran around her, but she just could not get herself to stand among the glittering gunfire. She was thick with sod and soggy with slush even before she fell from the hill, continuing to roll over the rocks as the land evened out. She sat up, stiff and sore, but numb where she was not cold. She knew, even without a mirror, that any attempt to wipe the dirt from her face would only muddy it up further.

Despite the new light shining brightly on the collapsible stage, the back rows turned to see the commotion. Some even chuckled at the muddy and bloody mess Teca had become before they turned back to the motley players.

Teca had interrupted the final act again. The Assassin had descended to the Final Circle and ascended to the Final Ring. From what she could remember from some hidden collection she had read years ago, The Assassin had left his chaperones behind at the end of the second act, only to convince the Necrophim generals to agree to a cease fire amongst themselves, to have them set aside their endless rivalries while enticing them to a greater prize.

Teca used knee and bench and audience member to right herself to a standing position before brushing dirt-cakes from her legs and after finding an open seat, finally watching from the back this time. With plenty of torches and the wavering spotlight she could still easily see the silk drapes and chemical lights flickering and reflecting, making the actors appear as though they were surrounded by lava. She regretted missing the entrance of The Angel — great bat wings fluttering and disappearing into each side of the stage, translucent strings lowering her onto the ground. The actress was now escorting the actor playing The Assassin through a constantly changing backdrop. The back-drapes were flipped over and over, representing the levels as the characters supposedly climbed higher and higher through the keep with the players conversations changing accordingly, and The Angel continually explaining the ills of man. With each quick change of scene, a drumbeat — stoked from somewhere behind the stage — rose incrementally to represent the increasing approach of the Necrophim. Teca imagined the generals pillaging each Ring, each level, and each room just behind The Assassin and The Angel. The actors were then joined by another, and the audience — hardened soldiers all — cooed and shuffled like children at a carnival. Unlike the other players, the actor playing the 401st Son of Mixcoatl wore no mask. He was a snake handler, and his oversized jerkin and baggy trousers held many serpents that writhed and often slinked out where he held their heads in his hands. He appeared and disappeared so quickly in the earlier acts that the crowd was always excited to get the chance to watch him for a more extended scene. By the time the scene was almost finished, Teca could still barely hear the dialogue. The chatter of the crowd had hidden most of the actors' words, but she waited now to hear The Assassin as he betrayed the other character. But The Angel spoke first, scaled jewelry glittering in the moving spotlight, hooves clomping on the unsteady wood.

"Necrophim follow in revolt, to rise
against Hell's rule. In Assassin's name they
cast out angels. But now, to your surprise,
rule goes astray. Who is left to betray?"

The spotlight moved and the actor playing The Assassin spoke from beneath his mask.

"As was bequeathed to me, I now reward
Mixcoatl's Four-Hundred and First Son. With
this cuckold crown, you are now Hell's king, lord,
chief, servant, emperor, god, author, smith,
architect, and president. Hail the Duke of Dukes!"

The snake-caressing actor, in a contorted imagining of desperation, then exclaimed,

"Friend, do what you are here to do forthwith!"

But instead, the masked man kissed the face of the 401st Son of Mixcoatl, and the horned tiara was placed on his head.

The lava lights and streamers disappeared, leaving the bloody tear on The Assassin's mask as the only crimson object on the stage before all the lights were extinguished. Even the soldier manhandling the spotlight knew when to turn the light off. Before Teca's eyes could adjust, there was a stampede from stage left as actors playing Necrophim swarmed toward the new King of the Underworld.

Teca planned on starting the applause before she realized that those around her were already clapping the darkness away.

Now let men ask always who	*'Tis blameless blasphemy to*
was chosen to tear the head-	*doubt harbinger hags and the*
freer from Father's fanged maw.	*prayers upon patron lips*
Is gray-matter my gift as	*that drip from dogma's tip and*
well as brawn born by the moon's	*ancestors' tired seedlings.*
sacred stare, bloodshot, shown to fear	*'Tis the holy height of Lord's*
my Master's horrid howl	*love to wrestle reason, His*
that calls to brain-bucket not	*divine gift, granted to all*
blood-bellows leaking from sad	*man-cubs, to find Father's new*
eye and trembling bloomers but	*deadly ginger death-bringer.*
to willing will and red head.	

—from "God's Gift is Testing Fig-eating Dogs: Hati Weirdson's Defense of Reason"

He always eventually ended up regretting not accepting the gift of horse when it was offered to him, and here he found himself regretting it again. The speckled field he walked was only lightly snow-covered — winds having blown the white covering mostly away, exposing the crust of field dirt. It was one of the few paths Wulf had traveled since entering N'Midgaard that a horse would not have struggled along. His own feet, however, were sore from collapsing boot and a ground hardened by what he assumed were years of concurrent winter. He kept the sound of the *Jormangandr* to the east, always close, always reassuring.

Past lines of dead saplings he trudged, into a sudden forest that had once been crowded with trees impossibly crowded. Now most of the basswoods had been limbed above his reach, each tree surrounded by stumps — old and new — on all sides. He could easily see through the gap-toothed forest to the hill beyond, to the rising field of countless stumps unintimidated by surviving brethren. The hard snow thickened and rose beneath his steps before he exited the tree-line, and he moved to a well-worn path carved into the hard mounds. Here he could see the different depths of the snowfall. The wind had blown for the past year around and through the dead hill, and the drifts were highest against any stump, with the path leading through some areas that had less than a foot of snow.

The path led up a checkered hill. If it had not been for the multitude of stumps of all heights and thickness it would have looked as though the dark hall spread over the greatest of drifts rising above the raped forests. But Wulf could also feel the hard ground on the road, could see traces of long-dead grasses on the crisscrossing paths leading to numerous outhouses over the hill. He counted at least seven of the tiny structures. They each were partially submerged except on their door sides, and they each leaned toward or away from different winds. They had been painted or built by the same black wood of the hall. The same color peeked from beneath blizzard-wrecked shingles.

The hill was not large, but Wulf found himself taking longer in his climb than he expected. The shoveled paths turned suddenly at stumps. He could see the twinkle of the *Jormangandr* now, its ice and rapids, and deforested shores. Its surging reflection was a welcome sight. It was the only true color he had seen all day. Its rush broke the steady sound of the wind. He breathed deep hoping to catch its clear scent but could smell only the thick immensity of the wood smoke pouring from the hall. Despite the breeze, the gray hung over the hill caught up in phantom tree and branch.

Supports stood every few feet around and along the length of the hall, holding gables and the steep roof. Any thatch had been blown away, leaving the dark wood to capture any sunlight. From the front Wulf could not see past the size of the structure and the curve of the hill to its back. Deadly icicles, some taller than he, hung from every corner, reflecting only more gray. Some had grown into the ground like ancient stalagmites. They were just more pillars he walked between to stand before a door without a handle. Only through a difference in wood grain could he differentiate the door from the rest of the exterior. His hand emerged from cloak for the first time in hours to pound *GloryRend* on the entrance. It sounded as though wood creaked from all ends of the hall. Frost split for the first time this morning. Heavy-hanging smoke turned the air, tickling his nose.

He listened closely but could hear nothing of the interior, and so he raised the hammer to knock again, but the door dragged open and he was gestured in by a man twice his size. Where his face was not bearded, it was tattooed black and blue. Where he was not broadened by furs and skins he was by girth, and as Wulf passed him into the smoke and heat of the hall he would have been hard-pressed to pick him out from the other men scattered among the structure. They were tall no matter the size of their boot, broad no matter the amount of layers they wore. They were pale but grew all color of beard and braid. The women and children held more variety in appearance, but all were light in hair and skin and dark in clothing. A huge fire raging at the end of the far end of the hall twisted warmth and warm hues over everyone's long hair and clothing.

There had been conversations when he entered, but they all stopped as he walked the path between row after row of long tables and corresponding benches. He stared only ahead at the massive stones comprising the giant fireplace holding the great fire. The heat was exhilarating, and he welcomed it into his mantle and over his face. The ice in his mustache melted coolly over his lips.

He did not look to his sides but could feel all eyes upon him. The only person who did not appear to be watching him sat at a smaller table near dancing shadows whipped into a frenzy by the fire. Damn Antony sat in one of the few chairs in the hall, at one of the few round tables, wrapped as a desert dweller, hidden behind mouth guard and goggle. But he raised the goggles as Wulf sat down and passed him a mug similar to the one he drank from. It was barely more than a log with a handle. He cringed, first at the smell, then at the taste. Was this the only drink left in the land? All nations could be under snow and ice, all udders could be shriveled to jerky, yet the people would still find some way to brew posset. He felt it move all the way down his chest into his stomach, warming his innards as the great fire warmed his outtards.

"Not sure I want to admit to liking it here," Damn Antony grumbled, lips at his mug. "But… it reminds me of something… some other life…"

"It should." Wulf's voice cracked. He had not spoken since Antony had caught up to him at one of the many forest groves over the past few days.

"Yet I still feel the alien…"

"You should."

The inferno completely filled the man-sized fireplace, coloring colorless rocks and consuming what appeared to be entire trees. The stones extended outward into a pit in the floor where the flames continued into a bonfire smoking up to a release in the dark ceiling. A finely carved chair sat nearby, facing the length of the hall. Wulf recognized the design of the high chair as culminating in the image of Yggr

— raven-shouldered and cyclopean. The throne's arms ended in the heads of wolfhounds for the occupant to rest his hands on. Some of the wood had colored prematurely, and the cushions had been removed at some point.

"You think you know me, don't you?" Antony asked, using a finger to wipe his burgeoning beard before wiping the interior of his mug.

"What do you know of the Garm?" Wulf kept his voice beneath the low song of the fire and the new scream of a sword being sharpened. The people of the hall had gone back to their work and talk.

Antony looked to all of them before he spoke. Children watched their parents eat. Crows pecked at something among the rafters. A man in only leather breeches and ribbons sweated and swayed dangerously near the fire pit before tossing a cleaned bovine bone into the flames. His mustache glistened as much as his chest.

Antony spoke through his teeth, eyes languidly moving over the hall without turning his head. "I was one of the first conscripted to lead parts of the Purge. I was only part of it for a short while, but it was enough to educate me on this world's history and the part the werewolves played in it. Fascinating really. I had never understood why such an aberrant culture had been so accepted in the North, albeit grudgingly. Seeing them in action, however, I can understand why the *Ashmedai Adat El* feared them and why the Brotherhood made a hunt a top priority. After standing face to face with one it's impossible to disregard the Garm's claim of divine sponsorship. They have the backing of Hell, I have no doubt."

"Or of Hel."

"What?"

"Nothing. What do you know of the Garm?"

"I know that when the Evolutionary Wars ended, one of the original Liege of Foes' original seven disciples, Bold Warlif, denounced his lord and his pacifism and set out to find a new land for his adopted people — away from Kaldera and machines and any foreign gods and influence. He found the Granite Lands — a land whose humid bug-ridden summers were forgotten during each of its perilously frigid winters. A land surrounding the frozen entrance to the underworld. A land of tornado and blizzard. He fell in love with it, assuming no one in their right mind would challenge him for it. And he was right. But it wasn't long after settling that he found it already occupied by snow-mad

Natives and ore-hungry subspecies. Warlif's new nation fought for years to hold onto the tiny plots of land he had developed along the *Jormangandr*, but his New Midgard was too new, still too small, and surrounded on all fronts. The histories I've read can't help but be flattering. The battles this new king won, the insurmountable odds he ignored, the land he defended with such outnumbered forces — incredible! But eventually his people were winnowed down. It was only a matter of time. The new nation would have disappeared before it began if not for something — something the histories haven't recorded. In under a month the Natives had fled, the goblins had been wiped out, and the dwarves had been oppressed permanently underground. And suddenly the Cult of the Beast had appeared and became a grudgingly accepted minority faith among the midgardians. The Garm were eventually outlawed, but for a while they held an inexplicable position amongst a usually uncompromisingly theocratic people.

"Still, after being denounced by 'ol King Warlif, the Garm survived, hidden, in secret ale houses and dark forests. There were never very many of them in one place at one time — that's how the different packs came about. So every northerner started suspecting a strange uncle or called out a church rival as moonlighting in a mystically tanned wolf fur. For that's how they do it, you see. Some original ancestor called upon the Beast of the Core, sold his soul to learn the black magic involved in the curing of wolf's skin. And one night a month, wearing the fur, they'll become what you and I've seen. Giant. Ferocious. Healing from all but silver. Everything human is sculpted away as a sacrificial meal for the Beast, while all that's left is the unquenchable hunger man tries to forget. There's no greater example than the Garm of how little separates the people of these lands from animals.

"The packs grew in secret and even began spreading out from the North to other areas. They worship Death, desire the end of the world, pray for the netherworld to burst upward and the cosmos to rain fire downward. They were really nothing more than yet another cult obsessed with mischief and mutilation, but something happened some years ago. They suddenly became focused, ordered, and packs that had become estranged from each other started unifying. They had found a leader in this Mad Hati and no longer hid in the shadows. They wish to release their mad god from some chthonic prison. To this end they search for some 'impossible' blade to cut its 'impossible' bonds, along with an entrance into earth that will lead to its prison. And now it sounds like they aren't just relegated to appearing during red moons."

Wulf had just been watching the great fireplace. Each giant ember changed color faster than he could follow. Each log brightened and darkened and lightened and added to the mounds of ash as he watched. He pulled his hood off and ruffled his head, wondering if the waves of his hair reflected the colors of the heat as did those walking the hall.

"Anyway," Antony said, "the Brotherhood told the masses they had completely purged the land of all the werewolves, that they had killed her and her son. But..." Antony paused, adjusting his dark goggles, just staring. "The two of us know Mad Hati's still alive don't we?"

"How do you know this is her?" Wulf asked, wiping the scruff of his face and casually glancing toward the only dark corner of the hall. Only the deepest colors of the flames penetrated the shadows holding Zelda Weird and her caretakers. Men and women brought her posset and popcorn warmed on near stone. A child stood by, singing so lightly Wulf could not hear. He could see a gleam that could have either been an eye watching him or a tongue licking lips. A dog barked from somewhere outside. Someone threw a dagger at the rafters and crows scattered after dropping streams of white paste onto bench and floor. Wulf noticed the humid stench of the hall for the first time since entering, and then he could not get the smell out of his nose.

"She was raped by wolves."

"What?" Wulf broke his stare from the flames but could not get himself to look at either Antony or the shadows.

"I'd advise you not to look at her directly under the threat of losing your posset," Antony whispered. "Rumor is, Mad Hati is the bastard son of wild wolves. His mother is one giant scar."

"What does she want?"

"I don't know. I did my part."

Wulf turned back to look at the fancy chair. It was the only light-colored wood in the hall, and its paleness and proximity to the pit caused it to be covered with rippling waves of warm reflections. He had thought it was on fire for a second.

"You'll be happy to know I'm going to join up with Earth's Army," Antony said after a long wait.

"But not surprised."

"Do you know who I am?" Antony asked, not breaking his stare as Wulf continued to watch the shifting colors. "Do you know who I *really* am?"

"I know who you are, just not how it could possibly be so."

The Lesser Antony chewed the inside of his mouth and sucked on his teeth, never breaking the stare. "I knew a man like you once, Wulf, in another life. In another life we adventurers traveled together on some forgotten quest like pegs on an UnderCrawl board…"

"And you killed him on top of some black hill under a changing season."

A woman lightly ladled water over stones in the fire pit. Conversations died, and the air of the hall immediately became clouded. Fog and sweat beaded on faces. Antony reached and pulled out a small book covered, bound, and tied in hard leather. He wiped the immediate perspiration from it. The wine lacquer flaked under his harsh treatment.

"The *Fallo Terminus*," he said, suddenly out of breath, "used to say something about the… ah, Avenging Eye mixing with the unclean earth. That 'the Daughter of Light saw that the son of man was fair game, and She took him for Herself, and a son and daughter were born unto her, and that she hid them away in the pocket of the world, where they would be unknown and where they would grow quickly to save the souls of the world when called upon.'" He knocked the table with his knuckles until Wulf turned his attention toward him. "You traveled with the White Avatar, I know you did, so you must know who Mew's father is."

A man stood between the flames and their table but could barely dampen the light. Still, with his back to the fire he was all shade except for the white hairs in his beard. Wulf squinted at the shadow or the light peeking around it.

"Perhaps you killed him as well," Wulf said to Antony, standing before following the new midgardian across the room. He felt a rush of air near the embers and hot rocks spreading from the fireplace. The smoke was pulled upward by a unique configuration of flumes and gables directly overhead, leaving the heat and colors to flicker near. The ornate chair was colored by every one of the hues. Each carved curve soaked up a different orange or yellow as Wulf watched and passed.

He braced himself as the airflow shifted before movement brought him around. Another man crashed into the chair, bringing an axe upon it, laughing all the while. The man's eyes flickered over him like the blaze of the fireplace.

"You wouldn't be thinking this is for you, would you?" the man asked through his laughter. The chair, already in very separate pieces, was splintered beneath the blade into more. The salt and pepper man leading Wulf pushed the axe-wielder aside, as they continued to the dark corner. The sound of splintering continued behind them as the chair's limbs were broken and tossed to the flames.

Wulf approached Zelda Weird, unsure what was shadow or wrap or scar or old woman. The fires warped the colors of her robes without lighting her. What Wulf first thought was a massive tumor turned out to be a child sitting on her lap.

"...Peter beget Bedburg who beget Griefswald who beget Ansbach who beget Lucia who beget Roman who..."

The crone shushed the boy's recitation and pushed him from her lap. It was difficult to tell what was Zelda Weird and what was blanket, what was scarf and wattle or decades old scar tissue. The shadows wrapped all with the flicker of the corner's dark light.

"Don't begrudge an old lady for wishing to take a peek," she said, as the bare musk of smoke touched his nostrils before he saw the pipe twitch from the edge of the sphincter he presumed to be her mouth. He could only guess that her bog pearl of an eye rotated in his direction. "See, I seen ya once afore, in the Bifrost, when you was just a wee one, an I was a pretty young thing meself." Pebbles ground in her gizzard, echoing up through her voice. She never breathed in from the pipe. The rings just lingered. Drool dripped from the wet ash as water did from somewhere nearby. The splash came slowly and rhythmically from somewhere behind her padded chair.

Wulf's peripheral was filled with midgardians. The salt and pepper man stood next to Zelda Weird, and Wulf now noticed that his mouth-breathing revealed a checkered smile that blended into the black and gray beard. The man was an immensity next to the petite woman. Another man sat behind Wulf, sharpening a sword as long as he was tall. The file screamed along the edge of the blade, interrupted each time as the man readjusted the sword across his leg to reach the tip. The strokes eventually kept time with two drips of the water. The music accompanied Zelda Weird's raspy words.

"You and your mummy'd just appeared in the capital, an everyone wanted to get a glimpse. Your curly white hair. Big blue eyes. You belonged in the castle. You'd been wasted out with the savages. You'ere a true new prince of the North, but you were not what me and mine'd hoped for. We'd been waiting so long for the fire that was supposed to wake the Beast, an you were not that. I couldn't smell it on ya. There'ere some in the packs'd wouldn't give up hope. We'd snuck'em in everywhere. The High Halls. The Church. Even the castle. Fynn was one of us. A believer. Right under the King's black nose. An he just refused to give up on ya. He went rogue, trying to protect ya or train ya or whatever, but even he was disappointed when ya came back. You'ere no longer one of us or one of them or one of anything. I knew then I had to take the prophecy by the balls meself."

The tallest woman in the room squatted near the open embers of the pit, wrapping a whistling pot in a fur to bring it to the floor in front of Wulf. She added hot water to a full bowl at the edge of the old lady's chair. Tiny feet of red jerky lowered to test and immerse themselves, but before they did Wulf got a glimpse of kernaled toenails of every shape and size.

"Me boy Hati'll do what you're too pussy to do. The Beast o' the Core calls to'im, sings to'im, tells'im what will be. Hati's his true son, an he moves now to find Hel's Slit, to get the blade that'll cut'is fadder free. An what do you do? Your mind... your brain... we gave that to you. We used to be everywhere. We'ere the shamans of your grans and grandads and their grandads before'em. We made you. We made sure you'd be! We gave you your mind, and you use it to just make people follow you. You waste it! We gave you this gift and you just use it to make people love you! Who're these pussies that follow you around, licking your boots? They're nothing. None of them. You turn your back on your own so that the dirt of Earth'll worship you? What you've given up, my Hati'll take. He's the true Chosen One. Even now he heads for Hel's blessing."

The filing man moved from behind Wulf to kneel near the pit, long locks swaying at heat and hidden chimneys. The long sword tilted over one leg as he now slid a whetstone along the blade. The tone changed but not the interruption as he adjusted each time to reach the tip. Sparks rode the updrafts like fleeing fairies. Some could not make it and alighted on the blade. Disappearing beneath the uncaring stone. Still the water dripped intermittently to the tune. Caught up in the music, Wulf had not realized that Zelda Weird still talked.

"There was a man who could never decide who he was or where he was going. He was picked by the secret vvitches to join with a girl from some lesser family they'd been watching and steering for a hundred years. He'd never decide if he were one of us or not, never'd chose where in N'Midgaard he belonged. And she, the girl, never'd pick if she even wanted to be a part of the Granite Lands even! She ran away to live on the Outskirts, with the filthy Skins, under filthy skins. The Savages. The Natives even! And the man would follow from time to time and you were born. 'Tis bad portent. Their lives. How'd anyone believe the Harbinger of the Beast could come out of that? Even when she an you returned, taken in by King an Church — especially when taken in by King and the Church — they should of known. You ain't the Chosen One! So I took God's law in me own hands."

Wulf now noticed a stack behind her chair as she struggled and finally reached a book. He could see a dark glean as water puddled at the bottom of the stack. The old woman threw the volume to the benches, striking the leg of a girl who dared to breastfeed an infant. She covered herself before taking the baby away.

"Your brother…" Zelda Weird continued. She had lost her pipe in the action, but its hardy smell lingered. "Some thought your brother was then Him. Great flaming Surt born in man-form to burn the world down, but we know better, don't we? They stopped talking about him when he disappeared and they laid eyes on me boy Hati. Who was our prized pup? Who joined all the packs together? Who goes to unleash the Beast?"

The salt and pepper man searched the shadows beneath the chair for her pipe. His left side was mostly uncovered, so if he drew one of his blades Wulf planned to damage his radial nerve with a Lake Snake Finger Strike, paralyzing his arm and driving it toward the sharpening man who would no doubt be charging from the side. They would impale each other. Could he rely on Antony to slow any assaults from the rest of the hall? The old woman was too confident. Was it the resignation of a death culttess? She did not move as though she hid any blade, but her rhythm was unique due to deforming claw marks. Midgardians avoided poisons, but he could not take the chance that she compensated in some way. She was not to be underestimated. He would have to first break whatever cartilage remained beneath her eye. It would stun her in a way striking any nerveless scar tissue would not.

If he was quick and fast it would send bone fragments into her brain, and he would still have time to react to the men's attack.

He watched Zelda Weird squirm in her robes, her feet splashing in the hot water as she leaned to help search for the pipe. Fold upon fold revealed itself and Wulf wondered how much of the mutilated and stretched skin was from her infamous, enthusiastic, lupine conjugations or her shamans' attempts at stitching.

"Am I finished here?" he finally asked.

She froze, but her milky marble stared its lashless glare. "Oh yes, you're finished, aren't you? Finished with your kind. Are you sure this time? Just like your ma an pa. Never know who you are. Are you Native? Are you Northerner? Are you killer, vagrant, or goblin? Rebel or war hero? Yeah, you're finished alright…"

He walked away, back into the benches of the hall and the heavy smell of ale-curdled goat's milk. He quickly missed the heat of the fires. The hall was warm in all corners, but he found it striking how quickly the immense heat of the place and pit diminished beyond the stones.

"Wait, wait," the old woman called after him, coughing after raising her voice, "if you want to prove yourself as still a midgardian, if you have any of our blood still in you… take these men." Many of those in the hall stood. Some shouted, but to what Wulf could not say. "Take these men and their shieldwives to your war. If you're not truly finished with the North, gather those left. There'ere still plenty out there from Stiftung to Bifrost, boarded up against the *Fimbulvetr*. Do your duty as a midgardian, as a man, and take them to war. They don't deserve to die with balls frozen to the shithouse. Let'm die on the bloodfields praying with ax and hammer to whatever deaf gods they choose."

Blade hilt pounded table. Boot stomped floor and bench. Antony appeared amongst the cacophony next to Wulf.

"I'll take them," he murmured. "You continue on to whatever Hell you feel you've deserved in the capital. I'll gather them and meet up with Earth's Army. It nears."

"Promise me one thing then," Wulf said as he bundled his clothing up and around himself and headed down the long hall toward the only door. "Take them all. Men, women and children. Leave her with nothing. I want her alone as the winds close in and she chokes on the ice in her lungs."

LII

The Assassin:
"I already know how I am going
to die — claw-mauled, tooth-gnawed, attended to
by lethal protégé. It's a curse, knowing
the means and day of one's demise, to view
The End, remember Beginning, going
on as though the In-between had value."
Clockwork Monarch:
"You fool, the future is ever-flowing."
Narrator:
The cogwheel man led the assassin down
the broken trail to Old Sebum. Here they
paused amongst what was left of the ghost town.
Homes had long ago flaked and blown away.
Streets had disintegrated to a dust
that collected and blew in an oily spray
like something the color of blister rust.
The dried wax of the plains was all that was
left of habitation. Now the only
settlers grew out of unnatural laws,
of cracked fatty fields, secreted, lonely,
yet a part of a burgeoning forest —
a grove wardoned by a giant bone flea,
pruned by a big louse acting as florist.
The guide, of pulleys and gears beneath an
all-encompassing robe, ignored hirsute
trees and man-sized ticks for the assassin
that followed. He found him less than astute.
Clockwork Monarch:
"Your precognition is not mystical —
viewing certain future without dispute.
It is a thing more egotistical —
a tamed Id sorting moment's minute's past,
extrapolating Now into The Coming
Sights, to parse out the daze of future passed.
What Conscious finds paralyzing, numbing,
the caged dream-state portrays as a chain spread
to Future's horizon. While your dumbing
awake mind suppresses, the Id is led
through possible steps feeding possible
steps toward most-likely paths toward most-likely

ends. Your Ego, being suasible,
predictably filters findings tightly
towards its own ends. Your mind's eye does not peer
through some magical window to slightly
immutable future. You are no seer
but a Super Ego traversing what
your inner self sees as the determined
set future outcome according to but
a handful of events reaffirmed in
the absent-minded abyss you call your
subconsciousness. Deep down you decide worm
and germ for a scene you adore to abhor."
Narrator:
Out among and through the Forest Hirsute
the assassin still peered, at babes and men,
grown and from earth unable to uproot
themselves, fully covered with hair which then
was probed and settled by apple-sized ticks.
The sound was deafening across the glen.
Shuffling. Scratching. The bugs dug and affix.
Biting. Itching. Parasites nuzzle to
discover flesh hidden. Human shrubs quake
and quiver, unable to shake scabbed dew
and bloodsucker from endless hair and flake.
Clockwork Monarch:
"It is in the Forest Hirsute the Ever
Evolving find themselves punished. Forsake
these smart sinners! They thought themselves clever
in their progressive reach, but they now grow
uncontrollably, unrestrained down this
slippery slope, with purpose to farrow
only giant mites and to feel the kiss
of ixodid mistress. The Evolving
are reaped as they have sown, but find they bliss
in perpetual growth? Within solving
stagnation? Here they sprout and spread and reach,
but it only brings rash and welt and bug.
Enlightenment through itching? Not a peach
of knowledge blooms from furred trees but a shrug
of tickling, a twitch from biting, spasms
of and from friendly rapacious slug."

The Assassin:
"To find you here, you and your sarcasms,
is of no surprise, old tinkering fool."
Clockwork Monarch:
"No, the ultimate surprise would be to
find another. Excuse my steam and drool."
Narrator:
Grease stained his vestments. Joints and spouts then blew
water whistles, as his body's pistons
chugged their eternal chug — the grind, the chew,
cog against gear, the steam dew did glisten.
On the far side of the Forest Hirsute,
deep in fallen vale and valley, the red
Necrophim led soldier, psycho and brute
against one another in ways most dread.
To the Necrophim each man was a pawn,
born each day to die, Hell's earth their deathbed,
only to wake each morn in violet dawn.
The lowest son of Mixcotle, his four
hundred first, appeared suddenly, and in
the assassin's ear he started to pour
the ambrosia of ambition, the sin
of pride, and thoughts of regicide. To turn
generals against their queen had long been
his dark dream, but who is it to concern
themselves with making the prime move? Who will
to Inner Circle lead? Put Queen to quern?
Open the way and let Necrophim spill
into the Hall of Doors, in to witch burn?
Who could this ancient illegitimate
get to rally red warlords, to return
Pandemonium's Circles to the hate
of Mixcotle's Four Hundred and First Son?

—excerpt from "The Angel and the Ass"

his was it. Finally. It had been years since Teca had read the
script, in either the lower or upper library of the Temple
Needles — she could not remember. Had she read it by candle or
moonlight? The memory of reading the tale of The Assassin's journey

through the Netherworld — escorted or unguided — had once been so associated with *how* she read it and *where* she read it, and it bothered her now with how those sensory associations were being replaced by the sights and scents of the performance before her. Since she was one of the few Librans to still peruse the libraries, the ancient chairs — sharing unfamiliar molds with many of the uncountable volumes lining countless shelves — had conformed to the contours of her haunches, yet here the memory of reading the play in one of the padded rectory-style chairs was being replaced with the soreness in her hips from the makeshift bench she crookedly shared with too many other observers. The smell of settled dust and house dew over myriad leather and fabrics, in-between petrified glues and rotted bindings, was now replaced by the funk of thrice-dried sweat and the stink of gunsmoke that had weeks ago become one with the quilted armor and underclothes of herself and everyone else crowding the benches and ground. And she could now not differentiate the script from the play she had been watching. If there were differences, she had days ago forgotten them. All that mattered now was the final scene. For the one thing that Teca could remember with any certainty was that the copy of the play she had read in the Libran archives had ended suddenly in what she assumed was the middle of the final scene. She had never been certain if the copy was incomplete or if the play was meant to end without the observer knowing The Assassin's choice of doors.

But this was it. Finally. Teca tried desperately to get comfortable on the bench, feeling that each time she or the soldiers on either side of her squirmed in their armor or their boots that the expanding lines on the boards would split open. The wood creaked in pain similar to the pinching of her lower back. The ever-rolling, low hills the battalions had marched over the prior days since she had last seen a piece of the play were no more hardened by ever-thawing and ever-freezing than the prairies before, but the journey had begun to take a new toll on her body. Her boots no longer supported the walk. They were riding boots, and Teca had not ridden a horse since she had joined up with the Army of Earth. For a day here and a day there she hitched a ride on the side of a truck or the back of a tank. She had even spent nearly a week in the back of a troop transport before one of its treads had succumbed to the ice, but she had spent the majority of the march walking, and, although the soldiers she traveled with were poorly outfitted, her sparse outfitting made them look like lifelong survivalists. Her boots were coming apart. Her jacket was inefficient when facing the wind of the plains. The gloves she had picked up somewhere along the way were no replacement for mittens. The good news was that the legions she had finally worked her way up through were camped outside a city. The bad news was that the city of Erebus was immensely walled and, as she realized now through rumor and passed orders, controlled by some sort of forces loyal to the Horde. So they sat and waited for new orders, diesel fumes mingling with the sulfurous exhaust of the Necrophims' great tanks choking on their inactivity. So they waited, with the great hill leading to the greater wall consuming the sky behind the miniscule stage. It was a great and dark backdrop to frame the gay lights and fabrics of the play.

So this was it. Finally. She would finally get to see which door The Assassin picks in the end. With as many times as she wandered onto the performance over the last few weeks, it was baffling to her that she would always catch different acts and scenes but never end up being around for the conclusion to the play. But here it came. The Assassin had been escorted through Circle and Ring by historical figure and otherworldly character, had made his unholy contract with Necrophim general to betray a serpentine upstart, and was now receiving Hel's undeserved weregild for some future duty. The Angel led him ever farther up the tower, presenting him with gifts, of which there would be seven (although Teca could remember that the play she had read had ended without all of them given), with not the least being knowledge — knowledge that his suspicions had always been correct. His life had not been his own. His fate was in the hands of another. But he was also wrong.

"Those you suspect to be pulling your strings
are no more puppeteer than kith or kin.
They too are part machine. Watch how one sings."

For The Angel's first gnostic gift was a paper dragon pinned to the wall — The Assassin's long ago master/slaver/mentor/prisoner. Fluttering in the breeze of prairie and torch, the set piece (voiced by the offstage sibilant) told of the contract made in his childhood kidnapping. But even the wisdom of the ancient parchment wyrm was not enough to reveal the ultimate employer.

But the two actors continued through the levels, drapery settling behind them to reveal each new floor of the tower, and it was the final scene that Teca had again been waiting for. Finally, the chorus hid torch and dimmed gaslight. There was movement in the night, shuffling as the scene was composed. The crooked stage creaked. The troupe breathed heavily. Unadjusted eyes turned to the dim glow emanating from over the wall surrounding the great city of Erebus behind the stage. Teca was just now realizing she had been ignoring the sound of far-off mortars as they arced over the immense hill and even greater wall. Whatever fires they ignited, whatever the Army's helfire burned in the hidden city, began to warm the evening's atmosphere.

The stage torches and spotlights woke again and revealed a set lit by endless reflection. Doors had been stood against the stage exits. These were real doors, some with hinges still attached. Some had barely hanging frames. Some had doorknobs. Not one was like the other. Between each of them was a tall mirror, frameless and foggy with age and warped. But each mirror reflected doors into infinity, as did a painted backdrop.

On the man-made mountain of sod behind the stage, the first legions of the Army of Earth began their ascent. The movement distracted Teca's attention away from the play, even as The Angel explained her next boon to The Assassin.

Teca had been entrenched with what she determined was either the Electric Leper's battalions or that of the Banshee Jenny Wren's for days now, and she peeked around the surrounding audience to see which of the Necrophim's soldiers struggled to advance with tank and artillery up the massive hills. When she looked back to the play her eyes had to adjust again, and she was now even unsure which door along the fabricated corridor was real or reflection or painting. The Angel's tail twitched from some unseen wire. Her fangs reflected into infinity. Her words echoed under rising gunfire.

"Not your last boon but perhaps your final
choice. Infinite doors for infinite worlds.
In each world — infinite whens. I will instill
this warning — before you lies unfurled
all of space and time, beyond the quantum,
beyond all sense. Choose a door, be hurled,
any plane, place, any summum bonum.
Here, all time is yours — a maelstrom purled
to your palm. Here, distance is overcome.
Choose a door. Here. Now. Leave this underworld.

Listen! The Multiverse calls. Hear the thrum
of Temporeality. But choose now."

Teca could not understand what she was seeing. Bright lights dimmed. Weak lights exploded into brilliance. Still glows spun while quivering spotlights fell and stared next to her. But she recovered quicker than most of those around her to realize that a transport had driven through the audience, tilting some benches while crushing and flinging the pieces of others. She watched as an old and wrinkled soldier she was certain had been sitting next to her turned round and round, caught as he was in the truck's wheel well. He looked bemused, puzzled by what must have been her disgusted expression, even before his tangled limbs pulled him deeper into the turning vehicle's guts. Soldiers that recovered and ran were sprayed by the man's suddenly engorged, suddenly puckering into explosion, face.

Teca knew she would vomit, but before the lump into her throat loosened she was able to watch the transport veer suddenly to crash dead into one of the Necrophim's crimson tanks as it turned to begin the climb of the city's outer hill. The tank appeared not to even realize it had been struck.

She stumbled over splintered wood and bone, her coughing threatening to drop her right back to the ground, while she then barely avoided being crushed herself — this time by a group of soldiers tripping over themselves. When she was finally able to right herself, she found she was back in the same confusing state of inconsistent lighting. What she thought were torches were headlights, the frozen orbs of the Army's red vehicles, as unseen drivers either slammed on breaks or into each other to stop and look at what rose out of the high wall of Erebus. What Teca assumed were headlights were the glowing snouts of flamethrowers or the gleaming rounds of helfire mortars being carried upward before artillery men either froze in action or fell in some hysterical semblance of fear and homage. What she thought at first was the sulfurous steam of artillery was in actuality the carnage of a battalion suddenly stopped by the awesome appearance of an elder god of the Divine Choir.

She tried to look at the immensity rising out of the city, but some grand and ancient horn bellowed. It trumpeted one long unwavering note, and, no matter which way she turned, it pressed against her eardrums. She could not determine where her hands were, if they shook her head or if it was the trembling air that tossed her about. She found them when the horn had ended its unholy song. And she found herself, seemingly untouched. She had felt thrown but had apparently not moved. Yet still her fingers shook. Still she physically had to turn her head upward with her hands in order to look at the fluorescent mass billowing like a candied cloud out of the black abyss that hill and wall and hidden city had become.

Her eyelids were so heavy, as were her limbs, and she could see the malaise repeated across the plains. What was left of the shanties and young suburbs the Army had bulldozed coming up to the great hill was now refuge for cowering and bowing soldiers. Broken walls and exposed cellars now held men and women weeping and praying to the great glowing mass they could not even raise heavy heads to admire.

"Fuck 'teh Liege a' Foes."

A soldier threw down his helmet and then his body next to Teca. She watched as he cut a bleeding eye pendant from his neck. The tiny links of the necklace's chain dissipated into the playing light of the regiment as though they were snowflakes lighting onto a bonfire. The soldier's face disappeared equally behind long greasy hair, but she could hear him renounce everything he could think of. He swore off the Army of Earth, his Necrophim general, and his legion and brothers-at-arms. He made an obscene denouncement of the Crimson Queen, of his mother, his wife and sisters. He cursed all gods, living and dead, except for one. With this he tore off glove and gauntlet and forced his chin up to the giant jelly that was fast consuming the starry night.

"I'm yers!" he screamed to the new glow. "Let me sleep in yer dreams!" And Teca saw true love in his eyes. On a hill of puddles that only absorbed light, refused to return it, the man's face reflected the nursery colors of the gelatinous behemoth. She saw a sincerity in his smile she envied, a softness in his expression she coveted. This was a love she had yet to see in the war.

Before he could kneel fully to genuflect he was run through by a lance from behind. Teca turned from an awful crunching sound as the weapon bent and broke armor or bone, but in any direction she turned she saw the Army of Earth policing its own. A mob of soldiers descended upon a cavalry woman that had thrown aside her Liege of Foes banner. They pulled her from her horse and clubbed her until they had taken her armor and spear. A praying man was stabbed until his hands parted from each other and from his body. Any flamethrowing infantry that had stopped their climb to the great wall were being burned by their own stolen helfire guns.

Teca crouched into the darkness behind an unmoving tank. Great wyverns of curling fire were being launched at the great iridescent bell, and she could, before she hid in shrinking shadows, see the faint shape of tentacles and figures floating suspended from Her voluminous ribbons. Her eyes then continuously twitched over the scattering legions to make sure no one watched her as her hand slipped under jacket and tunic to clench tightly her Libran charm. She had removed a tattered glove and her fingers were icy against her chest, numb to the pointed tips of the figure's wings and feet. No one had seen her yet. The resolute either worked to position or fire trebuchet, while others dragged the blasphemous from the ground, kicking them into renouncing their new faith or stabbing them without giving them the chance.

"My soul is heavy, weary, and foreign,

Yet wings of grace blow the winds of favor.

A doe, far from love, land, home, and warren,

Judge the sun black, and please my faith aver."

Her hand, her chest, and her cheeks warmed, and she was able to breathe deeply again. She stood from the last shadows and fully took in the sight of Slog Sabbaoth. The great cascading organ swam ever over Erebus and its walls. With each pulse of its silken skirts, each twinkle of chemical lights, it blossomed ever bigger. And round after round of gatling gun and sniper rifle had no effect. The great entity was out of phase with reality.

Yet a bellow still sent Teca sprawling for cover. She found none, since large machinery had moved on, but she still found comfort in clenching the earth beneath her. What she had feared was the monstrous trumpet again was only a nearby sergeant's horn calling troops together to hoist a sunken cannon.

The movement had passed. Still feeling for the charm beneath her clothes, Teca moved on, trying to determine which of the Necrophim generals held charge with the immediate legions, and which battalion could she see moving far-off to the south to flank the city.

Teca leaned over a boy that had removed all of his armor. He had dressed down to only his trousers in the cold and had then started to remove the few rounds he had from his rifle. It looked as though he already broken his own lance.

"Who are you?" Teca asked. "What is your name?"

When he answered she held his head firmly in her hands and his gaze firmly in her own.

"Never forget it," she then said. "Remember your name. Who is your father? Who is your mother?" And she continued on with the questions, never letting him look to the candied rainbow over the city, never letting him look past even her face. "Why are you here? How did you get here? Why did you join the Army? Why do you follow the Liege of Foes?" She now had to shout the questions over the explosions rocking the city. They both could feel the vibrations in their boots. "Who are you saving? Who are you avenging? Don't forget!"

Teca stood and let the boy look around. Instead, he gathered his rifle rounds from the cold muck and started to hastily put his quilted shirt and mail back on. Nearby soldiers had been watching, and they moved on when Teca stared them down.

"Who do you answer to?" she found herself asking the boy, now almost mechanically. "Where is your general positioned?"

He pointed to a northern curve of the great hill leading to the great wall of the great city, but, before she could follow his gesture, she noticed now one of the doors from the play. It could have been a door from any cabin in the woods or from some outlying shelter on any prairie farm. Specks of teal paint no larger than a fingernail and no more numerous than a handful were all that was left of any decoration. The wood was dried to a corpse gray and appeared just as fragile. One hinge held strongly but crookedly in the absence of another, and it held on to only broken ground. The door lie flat on this broken ground, despite the blasted and torn sod surrounding it. Teca could see no other remains of the stage or the set. She could have been standing on the sight of the play or she could have been a hundred paces in another direction. She had so quickly lost her senses during the inhuman trumpet sounding.

She crouched and took hold of the doorknob. It was a new knob. It was cheap and its freshness looked unreal against the long-ago sun-baked wood of the rest of the door. But it turned. Teca took a long breath before pulling it open, and in came the rush of the scents of the field. The pinch of brimstone. The ancient oil of the exhaust. The earthy suffocation of ubiquitous mud as it deadened the stink of sweat.

There was only more of the mud on the other side of the door.

LIII

"I and Architect are one."
Then all corrupt nations, none
did not take up hammer to hammer Him.
When Bear, Knight, Twin, Mage were done
He asked under the same sun,
"For which works do you tear me limb
from limb? Which prayer? Which hymn?
For why do you rend me with sword and gun?
Are you not architects of your fortune?"
But Liege of Foes was broken by their whim.

—The Ver Primordium (IV-LVIII-I)

The massive doors lie askew with some of the carven scenes hacked to obscurity by axe. The stories were linked by the image of the world tree Yggdrasil, halved on each door, with swirling and interlocking branches at one point becoming waves to lift ghost ship, at another point to represent the great fire giant Surt's flames thrown down from Heaven. Snow covered even more scenes, blown in from open windows, but Wulf knew the story. Every man, woman, and child in N'Midgaard knew the story — from the elders that repeated it weekly in church to the children warned about it at nighttime prayer. When the nations of the world became too corrupt for even Hangman YGGR's noose, when wives found solace in other men's arms and children saw themselves the betters of their gods, the Soot Rooster would crow, heralding the Doom of Heaven and Earth.

He kneeled to knock ice from the doors with *GloryRend*. In the lower branches armies of men marched to their deaths in the heaving and burning earth. Middle branches dripped with venom from the Nidhogg serpent's spread fangs. The crown of the world tree cradled a darkened sun and crumbling cosmos. This was Final Fate. This was the Tale of Twilight. This was the culmination of the Fimbul Winters, and its tale and warning had kept the northern populace in fear and isolation for... centuries? Wulf was not certain how long ago the Evolutionary Wars had ended. Had it been one century or two since the Diet of Wyrms, since the apparently ageless Bold Warlif put down his robe to take up sword and crown? The histories never agreed. But none of it mattered now. He looked over the sparseness of the throne room and out open windows to the drifted streets and empty halls. Bifrost had been quieted.

There was no sign of war, no appearance of fire or uprising. The city had been hectically packed or looted, but there were no signs of violence. Squatters told conflicting stories of attacks by armies or pillaging werewolves, but the Horde was far, the Army of Earth only just now neared, and there was no appearance of the Garm's work.

He steadied himself against the throne, the sculpted embracing arms of cyclopean YGGR, as another rumble passed over the castle. It had been espoused that the throne had been carved from a root of the World Tree, a hidden branch that supported the chosen city of Bifrost and proved its exceptionalism in the Church's faith. But it was just a white ash base highlighted with black ash. Only the dense white ash could support the old king's bulk, with the black ash's purported portentous abilities — being the first tree of the land each year to predict the winter — representing Bold Warlif's prophecies.

Following the rumble of the city to one of the tall windows, Wulf navigated the white floor around ice and the multitude of crow droppings. With the stained glass missing, the weather would have been miserable at the height had there been a wind, but the sun had returned to Bifrost, if only for a day. It was a pale noonday, revealing no new colors on the snow-covered roofs and streets. Wulf flexed a white fist out in the open air before returning it beneath his ebon cloak. The cold permeated everything in Bifrost. The surrounding stone and wood had long ago absorbed it and now radiated it outward. Spend too long in this city and you would never thaw. He searched the myriad gables stretching to the *Jormangandr*. The great river could not be seen, but he could hear it in the stillness. There was no movement below, through suffocated streets and disappearing halls, except for the occasional wisp of a chimney coming back to life. The peregrination had followed him all the way to the capital, and they were bearing down in abandoned church and shop for what would be a cold night. The fingers of smoke were as frozen as everything else, emerging from stacks only to linger unmoving like pale infant vipers encountering their first predawn.

Incredible, he thought. *These people followed me all the way to Bifrost.* He himself could not decide if he was running toward or away from something — and the emptiness of the city complicated the question — but at least the caravans and massive crowds that had entered the city behind him believed they were moving forward. Even if they headed in the wrong direction they were still moving toward some goal — however vague or misplaced it may be. What was it that he was doing here? What had be planned to do or say had the Ragnarock doors still stood, had the warm colors of the windows still portrayed Storm-swain Tor doing battle with the Serpent, had the throne still been warmed by the King's impressive girth? The peregrination had followed through frosted forest and along frozen lake, dragging their families along on nothing more than faith — the faith that he led them to… what? Some promised land? Somewhere free from the judgment of tithingmen and Theses? What did they want from him? Well, here he had rewarded their faith with the frigid end of the road. Or should he take them further? Would they not rest until he introduced them, like Lif, to the Fimbul glacier consuming the planet? Why could they not just find purpose in war like every other self-respecting individual across the land? He was done with them now, all of them. Here, underneath sudden sun and a year of snowdrifts, was where he would finally part ways with the them.

But, beneath the incessant pounding of his brain — the culminating pain and pressure against his mind as the Army of Earth's *Other* approached — he could not get the images of all the children of the peregrination out of his head. Over the prior weeks he had seen girls fight with dogs over food, boys fight with each other over their mothers' breasts. He had seen the smiles of babes comforting their parents in the worst of cold and the leanest of meals. He watched as children shared mittens, inspiring adults to welcome new families into their wagons. The young of the peregrination appeared to live outside of their circumstances — affected by the weather and shortages but reacting without despair. Sure, many of the adults — mostly thanks to the Ascentionists and Ascendants that walked among them — had been successful at repressing the depression that should have come with the winter, but it was an obvious effort. The children just *lived* above it all. And it was the children that made Wulf want to fight. Looking around at the white city and the castle halls he had once run reminded him of the child he barely remembered. It was a boy that lived for the day, not *by* a determining past and not *toward* an impending future. Yes, this boy's life had been manipulated in ways Wulf was only now just beginning to piece together, but the importance lie in the fact that he had not known it. How many of his actions had been preordained? And how could he ensure that he was not still just some puppet on some unknown puppeteer's strings? The questions made his head hurt even more — a pain he did not think possible — so he banished the thoughts from his mind. He so dearly wanted the children to have the chance he apparently never had, to have lives non-oppressed by Horde or Liege of Foes or even their own parents. But someone else was going to have to help them. He had done his part for the people in the Resistance. Their fate was out of his hands. But with Bifrost abandoned, what threads were left for him to tie up?

Where did you go, you old monster? Wulf asked of King Lif. *Did you make one last pilgrimage north? Into permafrosted wastes? Did your people still trust you enough to lead them to their deaths?* Crows balked over his passage as he moved back to the center of the hall, as they did every time he moved. Did they speak to each other, to him, or out to their wild brethren searching for warmer climes? Did they understand each other, or were they as confused as he? Bifrost belonged to the cold carrion birds and the dwarves now. They could have it until a glacier crushed it in its plodding passage.

Coyote now sat in the throne, beneath the carven images of YGGR's feathered companions. His pose replicated the twin ravens' stance. The feathered advisors were meant to guard the East and the West as the cyclopean All-Father watched the South from over the King's head.

"What happened here?" Wulf asked, his breath emerging but hanging solidly in his face. The air in the castle was as stolid as in the rest of the city. He may as well have been standing outside in the elements.

"You're asking for my opinion?" Coyote asked.

"I guess not."

The bird's head twitched to follow his walk. "It doesn't matter. What solace did you hope to find here? A king's pardon? Your mother's waiting arms? The acceptance of a repentant people? All you've done is endanger yourself. And if that doesn't concern you, then what about the danger you've placed all your followers in? They're all targets now, and you've placed yourself in the middle of them. This is nowhere to lie low. You've long since been able to hide out in the public. It's time to find permanent hidden accommodations."

He hated it when the raven was right, but he would be damned before admitting it out loud. Any areas the Horde had not conquered yet, they soon would. He knew little of the MANN Lands, little of the East, and even less of the nigh-mythical far southern deserts and jungles — the Land Where Pharaoh Dies. What was left? What was left for him here? What was left for him anywhere? He had crossed the hall to look out the opposite window, the window he had jumped out so long ago. Had they replaced the glass with the same image, he wondered. He could not remember if he had ever noticed what the stained scene had been. The haunted ship bringing the cursed dead to heaving shores? Perhaps. No. It had been a scene of the two foretold survivors of apocalypse emerging from wood and water. Beneath new tree and above new grasses the two would live to populate a new world.

He felt the presence of a dwarf peeking into the chamber from some hidden doorway.

Wulf squinted against the even sun, retreating farther back into his mantle. Even the smallest amount of light sparked his migraine. There was apparently no respite from the pain. It was one more thing he could not seem to stay ahead of. There was no sign of the Army of Earth out past the city, despite the rumors of their proximity. What business could they possibly have in N'Midgaard? Or were they just fleeing the Horde like anyone else? The forests would be ideal for hiding, but any prolonged stay would also end in frigid death, unless the Liege of Foes' supposed Necrophim generals were Hel-sent as the rumors claimed. Wulf peeked out at the forests now. They had only grown since he saw them last, spreading beyond the city to the faint horizon, but their winter nakedness made them look smaller. He could not curb the impression that everything in Bifrost looked smaller. Yet he felt no bigger.

He spoke back to the throne, saying, "When I was left in the woods, as a child, you led me deeper. I followed you into darkness. Whose command were you under? The Garm? The *SHE*?"

"I keep the best interests of only one person in mind."

"Dammit, bird!" He strode across the frosty floor but fell before the seat on drift and cloak. Fists clenched against his face, he shook. Still, his hot breath only hung around his hood, but it prismatically caught some stray gray light in the absence of the hall's stained glass. It was the only variance the hall had seen on a long time. "What must I do to get a straight answer? Where do I go now?"

"You never like my straight answers," Coyote sighed. A thick shadow cast by the throne's arm doubled the raven in size as he preened beneath a wing. The crows and blackbirds were silent. The only sound in the hall came from Wulf's shaking and the whispered scattering of wood shavings as the birds alighted from above.

"Lady Mew and Janus Legionary!" Ivy announced from the balcony. She sat precariously on the ornate railing, whittling away at a pale piece of wood the size of her hand. Also precariously lined up on the railing were carved figures she had found somewhere in the castle. The blocky effigies represented YGGR and His sons.

"Thank you, Ivy," Wulf murmured. Gloved hands wiped his face as he stood, smoothing simple mustache and beard. He pulled the hood from his head.

"We weren't sure you were still in the city," Mew said. She was wide-eyed at the light and height of the chamber, looking at everything but Wulf.

A dwarf peeked into the hall from behind her.

Mew continued. "Everyone is holed up for the rest of the day, except for teams sent out to reallocate any uneven distributions of fuel. They've found some stores of food, but it won't last long. I thought tomorrow we could build hunting teams…"

"There won't be much to hunt," Wulf said. "Deer will be the most plentiful, but even they'll be scarce. Even non-hibernaters have taken to hibernating. Best look for bear dens. They'll be small bears but hardy."

Janus entered the hall and gave the fallen doors a look. He had taken to wearing an assortment of armor beneath his longcoat. It was mostly blue quilt and brown leather but some chainmail peeked from the layers. Tall boots matched long gloves. Auburn-wrapped hilts, handles, and holsters protruded in every direction. He was about to say something when a tremor flowed through the hall. Ice shifted and black birds took flight. Ivy snatched figurines before they fell.

Wulf shivered at the sight of Mew's bare hands as she crossed without sound. Her white cloak was heavy and thick, but she wore the furred mantle down, and it covered bare shoulders and the lightest of gowns. Tiny pale branches of her crown brought no new color to the castle, nor did her long ebon hair, but her eyes and slivered medallion glowed through the hall.

"Dwarves are taking the city," she said from a window.

"Reclaiming it," Wulf corrected. He wondered if she could see any signs of their work. Had any buildings disappeared completely into the ground yet? It worried him that they could feel the tremors so soon and so near the *Jormungandr*. The dwarve's subterranean city extended farther than he thought, and they worked quicker than he expected.

Janus shook his head with obvious disbelief. "He gave it to them."

Mew turned from the window, but only to watch the wooden slivers float from the balcony. "They trusted you, followed you all the way here, to a city now being pulled below the earth. What now?" She sighed loudly, removing her woodland crown. "What do I tell them?"

"That's never been my purview," Wulf said. "Do as you always do. Optimism is your specialty."

"I guard their souls. You protect their lives. That was the deal."

"There was no deal."

"No," Janus interjected, "that's not true. You *did* make a deal. With the dwarves, didn't you. To supply us? How do I know these things?" He searched his packs absentmindedly.

"What's happened to your mask?" Wulf asked.

"It's safe. But I have no need of it."

Wulf walked the expanse around the empty throne. The crows had quieted, but one could still hear the slight scrabble of their steps, the taloned clenching and unclenching of their feet against the rafters. "It's true. The Ore Nation could have taken the city on their own, but misplaced loyalty led them to wait. But all it took was my word that there would be no reprisals. Bifrost will return to the earth, and in return they will arm the people and the Army of Earth when it arrives."

"And so... war continues," Mew said.

"Until it ends."

"My mother trusted you once. That's why I..."

"No, she found us predictable. That's not the same as trust."

"But you can end it. Tell them not to take up the sword. Adding more bodies to the fire won't smother it, just strengthen it. You're giving them a death sentence. Peace is not found through war but only through pursuing peace."

Janus took the first step up toward the throne, turning back to Mew. He stood between them. "Peace has to be fought for."

"Nothing ends war," she said, "unless people refuse to go to war." An alabaster hand emerged from her cloak to point her crown at Wulf.

"I know you're willing to die to stop the Horde, but how many are you willing to kill?"

"I'm not the Liege of Foes."

"I don't mean how many of the Territories are you willing to kill. I'm talking of those here, under your responsibility. How many of the families out in this city are you willing to aim and fire at Kaldera in your search for… what? Honor? Vengeance? Any peace they've found under my care will be undone. Their souls will be scarred irreversibly. You'll lead them to a death of spirit as well as body."

"No," Janus said quietly, staring at the steps he stood amongst, "he's not meeting Earth's Army."

"What?"

The hall darkened slightly as Wulf looked to the clouds obscuring the dim day. Gray became grayer. "He's right. I'm done with the world of man."

"How can you just turn your back on them?"

Janus frowned, seemingly deep in thought, speaking to himself rather than anyone else in the hall. "He's no good to us until he finds himself." The scars on his temple relaxed as he then looked to Mew. "We don't need him."

"We've already lost Antony and the Agent of MANN to the Army. We need as many…" She stopped. Her words hung and froze in the air just beyond her mouth. A slight snow had begun to fall and meager flakes lighted in through the tall windows. She walked and held out a hand, but it took a while for one to rest in her palm.

Wulf held out his own hand, gloved in pied leather, but all he caught was a wooden curl from Ivy's whittling. A faint echo reached the chamber from some far-off hallway, down some stairwell, through some doorways and barely connected rooms. Metal scraped against stone.

He watched Mew. Despite her appearance she rarely reminded him of her mother anymore. But now, as almost invisible mites of snow landed and disappeared in her hand, he was reminded of the sad expression of divine resignation. For the holy to extol free will they had to be comfortable with paths strayed from. But did any of it matter in a world of predestination, he wondered. Oddly enough, Mew carried no *Fallo Terminus*, yet the version inculcating the land came from her hand.

Her hair lifted by the breath of the Beast

Wafting from womb of wet vine.
Came servants, her flesh to dine.

In the end the people would come to her, would find her, and return to the earth, and the cycle would complete itself. This was supposed to be certain in her eyes, yet he sensed much fear in her. If the future was preordained, then why did she have to work so hard to ensure it? He was certain she struggled with this paradox daily. How could she not?

The jarringly uneven grind of something heavy being dragged up stairs sounded from some adjacent corridor.

Janus sat on one of the stepped tiers. He had taken a hatchet and a whetstone from beneath his jacket but just stared at the two of them like they were new to his hands. "I gathered the best of the men, those with the most promise. They're separated into squads according to their strengths, but I may adjust them once they're armed and armored." He looked to Mew, but she now faced away from the throne plateau. "I pressured none of them. They don't have to go to war if they don't want to."

"They have no choice now. We've taken them to the edge of the known world to freeze, and both Armies have followed. They can only die a cold death or fight their way out. What do you expect them to do? We've limited their options under the guise of free will. I can speak of peace and enlightened serenity but what is that compared to the realities of frostbite and violent threats to their children? Some nebulous afterlife can't compare to the very real and immediate specter of pain."

The grinding scrape grew near. The sound became regular and the blackbirds responded with restlessness. Irritated, they pecked at themselves and each other. Long-dried drippings flaked off rafters to join the miasma of snow as the sun reappeared to reflect blandly off the air of particles.

"When the Horde's been driven back," Janus said, rubbing faint rust from hatchet blade, "the people can go back to ranch or hamlet knowing their freedom and the lives of their families were well earned. There is no greater peace than that earned through one's resilience."

Wulf had heard the lecture before but could not place from where. He wondered if Janus kept the Elder Mask on his person. He would be surprised to find it otherwise.

"No. There is a greater peace," Mew responded, "and it will never be found in war. My only hope is that I can help them find it before they die for the Liege of Foes' glory."

"Glory!" came a phlegm-filled shout from the doorway. "There's no glory but that found in the death of the world." The man limped around the fallen doors. Every step appeared on his red face through a wincing pain. His appearance would have been unfamiliar even without the blistering from the silver allergy, but Wulf recognized him immediately. "Achem... What's greater than to correct God? To rewrite 'is mistakes?'"

Wulf held up his hand to steady the movement out the corner of his eye he assumed to be Ivy and her rifle.

"You!" The man's scabbed lips shouted between coughs, pointing a clawed mitten at Wulf. "I'll... I'll claw yer heart out first, eat it in front of ya."

"Who is this, Wulf?" Janus asked, eyes wavering over the space between the staggering man and Mew.

"No! That'd be too fast... argh... achem!" Hair and beard refused to grow back where trails of molten silver had seared his face, matching the snarling pelt draped over his head and back. The sweet smell of unclosing wounds hit the rest of the chamber as he neared. Pus cracked open as his face wrinkled in thought. "I'll... I'll chew the marrow from yer spine."

"Wulf, who is this man?"

"He's Garm."

"No! I want ya ta feel it." The anaphylactic man coughed something dark down his stained beard, never taking his eyes from Wulf. "I'll... I'll eat yer hands first... then yer face."

The grinding sound grew and appeared as Ivy announced the next figure in the doorway.

"Hati Cur'sson, Pack Bastard Weirdson, Seedspawn of Seven Wild Wolves."

"At your service and your sir's vice," the large red-maned man said, dragging *Manhood* to a halt with a mock bow toward the center of the hall.

But the silver-poisoned man ahead of him continued his staggered steps. The holey hide covering him revealed septic scalp and shoulders. His eyes never wavered from Wulf, even as he felt his belt for a scabbardless dagger. One hand was bare, but the other was covered to the elbow with a heavily furred mitten encrusted with the claws from numerous animals. He finally found and drew the brown blade.

The scraping resumed, now loud in the chamber as Hati followed, a smile above the many points of his beard.

The septic man suddenly stopped at the edge of the throne, wiping multiple tones of green from his nose with the back of his hand to sniff the air. "Wha's this?" he asked, but, before he could completely turn toward Mew, he had the edge of a hatchet in one shoulder and the point of a knife through the opposite forearm. Janus had him pinned to the ground, and they struggled face to face.

And Hati ran, crossing the hall in few steps and up the throne plateau in even fewer. The inlaid outline of the Beast flashed in the dull light — tooth and wild eye — as he brought *Manhood* back over his head and under in an upward circle. Wulf met the axe's head with *GloryRend*, and the air of the chamber shook with the sound of Hel's bells.

Wulf thought he could hear Mew shouting before all sounds blurred to a cottony muffle. His feet were no longer underneath him. He could only push against the dais with one hand, not feeling the other. With his eyes closed he could see only the design of spiky wolfen head, its stretched maw enclosing sun or moon. With eyes open he watched Mad Hati standing above him, giant axe over his shoulder, mouth forming poetry below a hairless lip. To his side lay pieces of *GloryRend*. Wulf blinked away the absorbing shock and tried to make a fist with his unfeeling hand. The pain was immediate and great in each knuckle of each finger, but it moved. It was bruised but unbroken. His cheek was warm, the snow granules that had scraped it dripping from his chin. Mad Hati lingered above him. The red-maned man wore yellow leathered and sectioned armor over one arm, crisscrossing bindings on the other. From the waste down he was covered in thick goat-fur breeches, but his chest was bare to the elements, pale except for blotches of pink and a fresh tattoo over his heart — an intricately colored mass of forest and hills and desert and jungle. Geometric shapes of all types led one through the organic map. Wulf could not help but wonder where the aesthetic images were supposed to lead someone, but the tattoo was unfinished. In the end, the scabs led nowhere.

As his hearing returned he could sense that Mew and Janus were shouting, but could not tell at whom or what about. He could only hear Mad Hati.

"Stay that trigger finger, clean genes," he yelled up to Ivy, nose in the air above his smile. Thick plumes of hot air billowed around his face and the pelt's head above his own. "Balk that cock, despite your spite I come only to... talk. The rest of my pack rests throughout the best of the city. At my howl their rapacity is unleashed on the sheeps. A stream of blood would run. The steam from bowels opened."

Wulf wondered how he could have survived in N'Midgaard, open to the elements. The draping of the great crimson pelt would have provided little protection. The man's great saucered nipples had already blackened and crumbled, still Wulf's gaze was drawn to the map. It either led one south or would be led south itself by a missing piece. It looked like a scrap of a puzzle that could take addition on any side.

Hati lifted him by his numb arm and placed him in the throne, and it was then that he started hearing the others in the hall.

"Back away, red!" Janus was yelling. "You and your friend can live to see the sun set." He had more blades at the septic man's neck than he had hands.

"Why are we fighting?" Mew asked. "Don't we have a common enemy?" She had unsheathed a familiar short sword, but its handle hung loosely from her fingertips.

"The Horde," Hati grumbled. "Woof! Anyone of war, swore born to smite the high and low in celestial climb, is fine by me and mine. We are all brothers now, known to spread death. Fooling ourselves into thinking it was some cause, some unique mystique separate from seven other nations when we are all servile to the only thing that matters. The end of all. The fall of when. Death is our lord, but he is bored. We all wish to wake Him, to sing hymns in His glory. Look how we wish to become Him, to surpass Him with such passion to make Him blush. But only we admit it, see the inevitability. Me and mine are discrete indiscrimination." He leaned in close over the throne, balancing close to Wulf. None of the lands on the tattooed map looked familiar.

"Common man worships war," Hati continued, ignoring the struggle behind him. "It is not deviant for reality to deviate toward finality. Nature does not abide nurture, and we are all only order's messy messengers. Yes, fallow blood brother, you love your followers. They exult in your presence. They savor their savior. You exalt their presents. I even understand. I stand under Heaven, here, before you, for you, to explain that it all means nothing, that there is no thing the mean pain justifies, just the final act, the justice and actuality and eventuality of the end. It is what unifies us all — the original and inevitable fall!" If it was possible, he moved even closer. His fiery beard obscured the half-map. Wulf expected the man to stink, but his body must have been so frozen as to subdue any smell. "The only aberrance is the lonely dance of the Horde. The forlorn wish to prolong Death's blissful kiss, picking and choosing loosely. But you know this. What you don't know, what gnaws at my soul, is that they own the sole object of my desire. Now, my sire, permit me to war *with* you, my formidable pack to gore *for* you. In return, all I require is to wreck the Horde's riches, to catch their cache, to storm their treasure store for what belongs to the long suffering Creature of the Core."

They both turned at the last wheeze of the anaphylactic man. Janus leaned over his prone body, holding the sword that had skewered the man's head from neck to skullcap. But Hati's smile never wavered as it settled back on Wulf.

"The old man's vengeance is denied, but isn't revenge a gent's denial in the first place? The worst play? Death Himself is the final arbiter. Are we biting at the breeze, pissing in the wind, winding watches wondering when the bend past the path will end?" His smile finally sank into a frown dropping into red curls as a slight click brought his attention to the sawed-off shotgun pressed into his pale gut.

"The road is not curved for all of us," Wulf said, "some of us can see all the way to the horizon, and you and your kind are nowhere to be seen." Teeth gritted, jaw tight, he pulled the trigger.

The large red man stepped back. He chuckled through a returning smile, but his lip quivered. One shell had sizzled while the other had remained silent.

"I see, an icy reception. Shun me if you will, little man, but the remaining gods show pity. The Pit favors action! The best is blessed." The blade of his axe dragged and bumped over grit and grittier snow as he approached the fallen form of the other Garm. Janus tensed, hands on the hilts of numerous weapons as Hati spoke.

"Those who live by the sword..." He frowned again, but his cold eyes were now smiling. "Survival of the fittest lives hand over fist even in a convivial heaven, and elohim have left it lying around like fire for men to find. It's our duty to pluck their livers daily, and I, for one, am hungry."

"Janus," Mew cautioned, placing her hand on the warrior's turning wrist.

In a blur of flaming hair and fur Hati raked his hand across Janus' head. He and Mew went down tangled together, but Hati stepped away, scratching the scabby map with bloody fingers before grabbing his dead companion.

Wulf stood from the throne, taking one step down the dais.

"Nature seldom selects in error," Hati said over the sound of iron against granite. "Terminal mongrel grew slow. The pack suffered early lapse under his paws, but I owed him that much." He turned upon reaching the doorway, pointing and snarling at Wulf. "You, however, bad blood brother, sinister mister, left hand to me. I am right! Even you, ewe king, need kneel to a thorn-crowned authority. I owe you nothing, yet awe motivates a lifting of the veil, a modicum of compassion, so I sew what you can reap. See whose abscess you can rape in my absence!" The receiving chamber echoed dully as he left, dragging heads both iron and soft behind him. "Appear to Hell!"

"What?" Wulf sounded so weak in the vastness of the throne room. Any sound he made was smothered by the cold, while Hati's voice took command of the angles and corridors of the castle.

"Hel! She asks for your help, you ass! I enjoyed the soil of the netherworld, but neither worship nor warship were enough for Her. She desires both Brothers Grim before the entire picture can be painted. A thousand words are too much for one man. You have won, man!"

Janus was still stunned, and he struggled to get upright. Mew parted the hair from his face to touch the scratches.

"I can heal you, just let me take your pain."

But he pushed her away.

~

Wulf navigated the bodies, stepping between arms and legs and crowded camps while examining the UnderCrawl card he had found beneath his boot during one precarious step or another. He had put off heading out from Bifrost throughout the night. The thought of leaving the heady humidity of the halls for the frozen forests was tiring, but the pressure against his head had become all-consuming. The *Other* grew skull-shatteringly near. Just outside the city gates. Wulf's brain was under the threat of implosion. He felt it would soon pop and leak from his ears. Each step through the prone crowd vibrated into his sinuses.

Every near snore bounced off his head like a hammer. His face was in perpetual contortion, his jaw clenched in rigor. He could taste the dust of his teeth.

Wulf's concentration wavered as he looked closely at the large playing card. People woke as he stepped on hands. It was still predawn, and before he stumbled over the masses it had been only children that moved through the halls playing, fighting, and stealing. A group of young ones stood on benches ahead of him, shifty eyes in constant movement.

Sun Rises on Cristabel was the card. A maiden woke to a phthalo dawn dripping into her elaborate bedchamber. The card's instructions would slow a player down and practically ensure any game to never end, but it was magnificently painted and printed.

The children scattered as Wulf approached. Some of them were merely toddlers, most barely clothed in the heat of the body-warmed hall. Far from the main pit of the chamber a pile of sectioned wood and broken furniture flamed nearby in a makeshift fireplace, contributing to the constant coughing of sleeping families. The children dropped the cat they had been molesting, and it stepped over and into the dark dozing crowds. They had been dangling it from a table by its tail, spinning its body with all their little strength. It was barely alive. *How horrible*, Wulf thought, *to not be able to choose to die*. He stepped over a woman that immediately coughed into waking. The smoke hung low through the hall, but she could have just as easily been choking from the chin cough that had been spreading through the peregrination even before the arrival in the city. Mew had sent an expedition of her followers out the previous day to collect the inner bark of popplers for a tea they had been using to treat the disease.

Not all of the children had run far. A few steps ahead, one boy stomped on another for letting the cat escape into the mounds of sleeping adults. He called the crawling boy many names, including "tithingman," and ran again at Wulf's approach. The other boy looked up, laughing through a toothless mouth filled with stringy nerves. His bulbous head could not be contained beneath a holey stocking cap. Wulf felt at the unfamiliar weight in a pocket to remember the folded knife he had been given in some recent day. The elderly giver claimed it had belonged to a grandfather, that the incomprehensibly worn designs in its ivory had been the symbolic signs of the original Liege of Foes.

Wulf now considered giving it to the tithingboy. Its blade was rusted immovably.

The edges on *Sun Rises on Cristabel* were frayed beyond shuffability. A crease down its middle was visible on both sides. Wulf's own boot mark had ruined the stock. A past owner had expertly marked the image of the sun on the card, turning the rising orb into a cat's eye. Another had defaced the maiden, scribbling in exaggerated breasts and genitalia. Wulf flicked the card into the conflicting shadows of the hall denizens. Coughing echoed back. From the far doorway he could see to what degree smoke had clouded the chamber. The expanse of the hall was cottony and darkening and filled with the weird light of a variety of stoves and pits. No two flames flickered the same. Each snore was echoed by its opposite cough.

Nearby, in the relief of the cold walls and doors, pubescents sat amongst each others' gangly legs, sighing loudly and chewing on mealy apples as big or small as their staring eyes. Wulf could not determine if they were boys or girls and could only guess at their age due to their sizes. They were scantily clad, dressed more in dirt than clothes. They took turns cutting the smoke by spitting seeds over onto an unmoving figure. The old woman was dressed thickly with numerous layers. Her eyes were closed but her mouth agape. She was dead. The wet seeds stuck to her face and scarves. Only one had even come close to the bull's-eye. It hung on her blue lower lip.

Wulf threw planks and jury-rigged latches and pushed against winds that had appeared overnight. The doors slammed behind him as he headed out into the streets, but they did not close entirely against the rush of air into the hall.

He tightened his cloak, kept the hood low and the wind behind him. The air shifted down each street, but he shifted with it, avoiding its full affront until he had no choice but to battle it across the bridge over the *Jormangandr*. The bridge connecting each side of Bifrost was no longer ore and rock and wood, but storm-made — snow and ice smoothed to a sheen, just one gigantic glacial dam that appeared to grow just over the day the travelers had been in Bifrost.

~

His shallow breath had iced scarf, mustache, and eyelashes together by the time he had crossed the white expanse. The streets on this side of the river were drifted to the tips of gables, were almost bare of footprints. He followed the few indentations he could find before they were filled or smoothed. The snow was decidedly inconsistent on this side of town, down the east side's wider and older streets. His boots disappeared in the rises, legs sinking up to his knees in soft snow before finding the compacted ice of older seasons. He skidded down the same steeps on hardened far sides worn by wind and white afternoons. Cobblestone and curb were nowhere to be seen — perhaps ever again.

Coyote had been trying to circle near but appeared buffeted on all sides. He landed somewhere near Wulf, on rock or ice, but hopped and fluttered, trying desperately to protect his eyes and beak. When he hid his head beneath a frosty wing he obviously could not talk or tell direction. "Forget this," he squawked into the wind, "you're on your own, dude," before taking flight again and disappearing into the storm.

Wulf squinted, Yggr's Eye leading the way, for even though the sun was lost behind glacial clouds, the drifts and drifted homes were blinding. They reflected colorless light he could not find the source of. And hard flakes shattered against the little of his face showing.

Footprints shrank and then disappeared all together as the buildings thinned and streets widened even more, but he continued in the direction he had started. Either he was at the edge of Bifrost or any hall had been completely subsumed by snow. Or perhaps it was the edge of the world. Through the blizzard Yggr's Eye caught glimpses of vague skeletal silhouettes that may have been the occasional tree. No forest encroached on this side of the city. The eastern deforestation had been one of the first acts of early Bifrost. There were to be no surprises from this direction. Yet it would be all surprises for him. He was headed east, and he had little inclination of what he would find.

A large mound of quilt and skin shook nearby, snow sliding down in waves. As Wulf tried to decipher its edges and movement, something appeared out of the wind, hair as dark as the snow was white. His chest was struck and his breath was lost and he was shoved into the air. He was suddenly open to the elements and the winter rushed into his cloak to toss his limbs. The sky and earth were the same. There was nothing discernible through the blizzard to tell him up from down until he hit the drifts. The layer of new snow cushioned his back, but his tailbone felt the hard crust beneath. His meager supplies, flint and knives and shelter-makings, pressed into his sides. Mew was on top of him immediately.

"You can't leave me with them," she said, her whisper catching and whistling away with the wind. "We were supposed to do this together." She was the only person who could sneak up on him. He had never figured out how she moved so unconsciously quietly, and she had recently become even faster. Her steps and mind made no sound when she approached. She was stronger too, he realized, as she pinned him to the ice or granite he could feel biting him through his many layers. Her fingers were conversely warm enough that they felt as though they directly kneaded his arms.

He realized then that the large mass of blankets and furs were her mattins. They were burning incense, praying for the morning to appear from beneath the makeshift lodge.

"What do I tell everyone?" she asked. She had brought a damp fleece over the two of them. Beneath it, the wind disappeared as well as her hair. Even her eyes merged with the sudden darkness. Only the ghostly image of her skin moved closely.

"Whatever you need to tell them."

"They'll become lost in the Army, in the fighting. All the work I've done…"

He winced at the thought of the near Army of Earth. His face was in perpetual strain. The vice around his head tightened more by each minute. "I have to go."

"Janus said you're no use to anyone until you settle what you have to settle."

"I'm not sure how he knows, but he's right."

"Just because some wolf-man tells you, you have to go?"

"No, this goes back long before him. I've put it off long enough. Threats of Folly frightened the babes of Bifrost, but it never scared me. Even then I knew, if it existed, it held answers. Now I go to find them."

"At the expense of these people?"

"They have to find their own paths. Let them fight for the world if they cherish it. The Horde can't stand unchecked."

"At the expense of their souls? None of this means anything. Mankind's wars are nothing compared to salvation."

"Then you have nothing to worry about. Teach them peace beneath the carnage."

"I'm afraid there won't be any."

"If anyone can find it, you can. You're not the Avenger, Mew, you're something better. You're of this world and not. You have a perspective Heaven cannot fathom and a vision beyond that of any of these people. You'll never be able to prove anything to them. It'll take faith. And their faith in me will only go so far, *should* only go so far, but their faith in you will be everlasting. The war is inevitable, but their role, your role in it, is still open to interpretation."

"Cold eye bleeds warmly of and above man.

He is many things to some,

but some things to anyone.

Angels wept, souls rejoiced, when he began…"

"I'm not the Liege of Foes."

"You helped me write it!"

Her knee pressed painfully into his groin as she moved beneath the blanket. The scent of her close breath brought him back to another life, to another journey, to a passage across the plains and beneath snow that sometimes seemed so long ago yet at other times was such an easy memory.

From differing lengths of bindings she unwound a sheath he had seen one of her followers make for her. He remembered it as being laced intricately with green glass but could not find the color in the darkness. The sheath held *Tiwaz*.

"It's yours, take it."

He removed a mitten to feel the coolness of the unwrapped hilt and was again awash with memories of yesterdays. In some memories his hands were warm, in others his fingers bloody.

"No. It has to find its way back to me."

"Maybe it has."

"No," he repeated more forcefully than he intended. Invisible hands squeezed his head. The *Other* neared, and Wulf could for the first time sense that his pain was certainly shared. The feedback looped around and around and back and forth between him and the *Other*. They would destroy each other if this continued any longer. Who was this person? Had the world ever before seen such painful familiarity?

"I… have to go… now!"

"…when King Foeman will open

servants' hearts, bringing hope in…"

"Then you have nothing to worry about," he said through a

clenched jaw, throwing the blanket aside and taking the full force of the wind in his face before he was able to pull cloak and hood around and over him. The mattins were moving beneath their own quilted yurt as a phlegmatic glow appeared to the east. He could not hear their prayers as the wind dissipated any words, breath, or incense wafting from the tips of their shelter. They appeared as one great creature emerging from hibernation to shake the snow from its hide.

Mew watched him trudge through the drifts growing against the uneven edges of Bifrost. He wore no snowshoes but, once moving into the windswept flows, could stay above the hardened crust of bleached fields. She watched his dark and hunched figure through the storm, through the miles before the tree lines, never turning away until he veered north to become subsumed by the rhythm of the blowing snow. She could not see or imagine his shambling form over the day's journey. He was sometimes blown against, sometimes propelled by, a wind that never stopped changing direction. He eventually accepted the frost forming over his face, spreading from hat and hair to mustache and beard like the glaciers rumored to be eating the North. The icicles assimilating his face stung but protected from the wind's onslaught. The drifts growing over his shoulders slowed his walk but froze his cape shut, keeping the sharp air out. The ice collecting on his boots bit his toes but spread his steps wider over a circumspect path. Mew could no longer see or imagine his journey through groves of dead trees too shaken to collect snow, too dark to hide in the pale expanse, through forests that collected vast mounds of snow at their edges. He avoided the forests. Their interiors lessoned the wind, but their growing mounds slowed his travel. So he continued over the hardened fields and around the spiny woodlands, veering intermittently north and east. The snow continued to consume him as the clear glow of the day arced and dimmed, the heavens equally consumed by dirtying clouds darkening land as well as sky.

The smell of Folly reached him before the sight of its burning barrels and trash-strewn streets. Even through his heavy shell of snow the stench pinched his nostrils. It was the scent of sweat, feces, and open wound. It was a hanging humidity of musk that held back the storm, and Wulf's icy carapace dripped and sloughed as he entered the town's palpable climate. His eyes burned in the stench as they emerged from his snowy cocoon. He had had nothing to eat over the day, but his stomach still turned, trying to purge itself of what his tongue tasted in the putrid air. The soggy mitten over his nose did nothing to filter the brown air of the littered streets. Caramel turds flamed in barrels, slowly adding to the oily air, while he stepped around the refuse of the sepia town. Prosimians caked with the same color as the feces taunted him from open windows of brick buildings from some ancient time. Folly was said to have been untouched since the time of the Old Ones, and so Wulf believed himself to be looking backward through the ages to a town whose detritus had the privilege of never changing, of never feeling the growing pains of the maturing, of never having to deal with the oftimes crippling fear of progression. Here was a town of unevolving desire and a pleasure knowing only the art of the primal.

On another block the jackanapes attacked him. They tore at the remaining armor of ice to reveal and shred his hood then mantle. They tore at his cape. They ripped the leather covering his chest and arms. They threw his possessions before fighting over them. Their padded fingers brought the stench of the town directly to his flesh. He was buffeted by long limbs, by filthy nails and filthier breath, but he kept walking, staggering into the next block, each street leaning down toward Folly's center. His stomach finally found something to vomit.

Here the trogs climbed and swung and jumped down from brick and mortar. They would have been considered naked if not for the thick swamps of both hair and fur. They quaked, and muscular arms swung clubs made from ancestors. Wulf was beat with petrified femurs, clawed by fire-treated finger bones, pressed to the ground by grappling throws practiced by untold generations.

He could not push them away. All of his mental reserve was held in check to keep the *Other* out.

Jackanapes dragged him toward poisoned ground, the least shreds of his clothing catching on layers of trash and bone. Prosimians rode his prone body. Trogs mated or fucked all around him. The poisoned dirt was the only space in all of Folly he could see that was clear of garbage. The area stank in a new manner, of funk and sex, but still shocked him to the same degree. He now found himself as befouled of shit as the rest of the pre-cataclysmic town.

The wet earth, brown and unyielding, was scooped and flung. A great brick was hefted out of the ground, and Wulf was lowered into the abyss. The last he saw of the sepia light was filled still with pale forms writhing and struggling, wrestling and screwing.

But Mew, many miles and a day behind him, had not seen nor imagined any of this. She had only turned as his dark form was finally engulfed by the blizzard descending upon Bifrost. She tucked ebon hair back into her furry hood before it collected more snow. Her long lashes caught blowing flakes at the edge of the city. Her eyes closed, returning the scene to its empty whiteness. She took a cold breath through her teeth before saying a silent prayer. She would collect her mattins, gather her vespers, pull all her Ascendants and Ascensionists together, and approach the Army of Earth and its Liege before it could come any farther into Bifrost. Even through the wind, through the drifts, and beyond river and castle, she could see the hellfire of their engines.

LIV

...in the embrace of a fake fate's kiss
that when he thinks he is freed from man's rule,
hidden from gods' decision,
the Warrior thinks he is no one's tool
—scrawled on the walls of the King of All's lower halls

I t was the most important assignment I'd ever been given and I was so excited. Up until then I had mostly worked for city elders, digging up, and sometimes inventing, scandals concerning political and social enemies. I had aspired to someday do this very same work for a planetary ambassador. That, I thought, would be the ultimate goal, the pinnacle of my career as an investigator, and so you can imagine my excitement when I was contacted by a representative of one of the Grand Council members. An Empirical Elder! It was difficult to believe it wasn't a hoax, some trap or elaborate payback from someone I exposed or embarrassed in the past, but the massive secrecy of the process (along with an unimaginable prepayment) pulled me in. I was told that my work, even at such a small political scale, hadn't gone unnoticed by my sudden benefactor, and my relative obscurity would be an asset to the assignment's security.

"The flattery and reward went a long way to convince me the offer was real, and once I accepted the assignment things began to move very quickly. I was shuttled by secret means to the inner core of the Empire and given the details in person, not with the Elder of course, but by those closest to him. There were going to be very few people who knew of the investigation."

The cousin rarely stopped talking, and for a man who had gotten used to a voice constantly nagging in his head, it had become even too much for Easarean. Did all the members of his inferior clan talk so much? What was the purpose? All the words were so superficial, ultimately signifying nothing. His talking never seemed for anyone's benefit but his own. Maybe that was the secret.

Easarean and the cousin stood next to Pestilence's pyre, warmed by colors they would not expect from so simple a fire. The man (for they now knew that was all he was) blackened and peeled in the hastily made fire. The pyre was loud in the echoing canyon, louder than the water trickling around them, but not louder than the cousin's incessant blathering. Why could he just not let Easarean enjoy the pyre?

"The reason for the secrecy became quickly apparent. I was to investigate funds that had collected over the course of a half-gen, insignificant collections from seemingly unrelated projects that had only recently come to light. I needed to somehow link these funds, now amassing to quite a large sum, to a sect of Aemazon terrorists, and then blackmail a certain rival Empirical Elder.

"I was immediately in deep. This was big and this was bad. I had the specialty to get it done and I was insignificant to not be noticed while doing it. And in the end, I would be set for life.

"I deliberately put off the assignment as long as I could, held in seclusion by the Elder's people, to wait until a system I needed to sneak into was bombarded by a solar storm that would hamper communications. It was an extreme precaution, but I was hired to be thorough, and it had been made clear that I wasn't supposed to engage in any sort of communications until I returned anyway.

"The infiltration turned out to be more scary than I (or even the Elder's people) suspected. After investigating hidden banks and dummy businesses I found myself deeply undercover in an outlying subsidiary of a gene-tech unicorp. One familiar for the largest, yet silent, health breakthroughs of the Empire's history. It was here I found I didn't need to forge documents or plant incriminating logs. I wouldn't have to bend data or infect histories. It was here I found that what I had intended to fake, the links I was hired to create, were in fact real. An Elder — one of the seven holding the highest positions in the Empire — had indeed conspired with the clans' most hated foes. Through a cycle-long search I had found evidence that an Elder had received bio-tech in exchange for releasing strategic prisoners of war back to a terroristic branch of the Aemazon's. It was a generations-old news, but the Elders were ancient and their ancient grudges became the people's grudges, and as I dug deeper it became obvious that new grudges were to be made clan-wide."

The pyre cracked above the cousin's words, bones or twigs snapping. Easarean sighed loudly with the flames. Did the cousin even hear his own words? Who was listening?

Since the destruction of his ship and armor in the Badlands, Easarean had surprisingly found some sense of peace. Here were two more of the links to his past gone forever. Here among his new companions he was slowly forgetting past contracts and allegiances and curses and, even just over the course of days, he had found new purpose. Instead of ruing the planet — one that became less alien with his acceptance of his fate — he found a land he could tame, teach, save and rule. The gods, the despicable petty gods, had delivered him to a world that deserved him. He had helped release the land from plague, and that was only the beginning to what he could bring to it.

"You won't believe what the trail then lead to. You can't. I'm sorry, but it's not even possible for you to comprehend what I found as I dug deeper and deeper into the sickness of the Elders, of the Empire in general."

But the more Easarean accepted his new life, the more the cousin's empty blathering assaulted him. It was almost physical. His whiney, self-aggrandizing words pressed against him like a squeezing humidity as the days had advanced, until they now buzzed in his ears like mosquitoes — small flitting insects that seemed to grow as each night approached until the wings hummed in a unison vibrating against his face.

"It is ironic that someone like you, so close to the truth, would have just no idea how far the corruption goes… that someone literally bred to enforce the Empire's rule would be so betrayed by it. And you don't even know!"

His insufferable tone and offhanded smile always made Easarean feel the cousin expected him to appreciate the sideways insults and unwanted criticism.

"I suppose you deserve the truth. This planet is a new start for the both of us. You might as well know. It's a good idea for me to tell you. In retrospect it all seems so perfect. The pieces all fit together. Recorded history goes back farther than the Elders have revealed. But it all makes sense!"

Yes, Easarean had much to teach this land. He shuffled his massive feet at the pyre, disturbing drifting ash, while considering the possibilities. But he did not want to do it alone.

"You're not alone!" the parapsyte yelled frantically in his/their mind.

Two of the priestess's tests had been completed. There was only one left. Only one thing stood in his way. There was only one thing left connecting him to his past, reminding him constantly of his past. With it still around, he could not move forward — not with her.

"It all makes perfect sense. The Empire is so stubbornly patriar-chic, still, even today! It has always slowly, very slowly moved away from it, and that creeping progression has made the clans complacent. As long as there is change, no matter how slow, it will blunt the extremes, the revolutionaries, those who could demand immediate equality for women. But there was a time, before 'recorded history' when they wouldn't wait, when short steps weren't enough, and the women of many clans rose up. Not all of them by any means, only those of wealth who could find support in ways other than close relatives.

"After a generation of simmering resentment coupled with careful planning, they rose up in a great revolution that became a great war and eventually a great excisement from the clans. The war continued as they fled and the Empire fled and any chance of peace fled. And the war continues today. They are the Aemazons! Our own women are the Aemazons! Our bitter eons-old enemy is us! And this has been hidden from us. That's not fair though. The more I thought about it, the more I realized that we, the people, were complicit in hiding or forgetting this. Because how could the Aemazons be anything but us? It actually wouldn't make sense if they weren't!

"So I was stunned by coming across this, even though I shouldn't have been, and I was silent and lethargic and I moved so slowly as I dug deeper. We've always theorized how the Aemazons could repro-duce without men. Every hypothesis has been thrown out over time. Asexually? By creating a third sex? A pact with orgiastic underdae-mons? Even I've heard the fantasies of the superior of your clan being taken from the battlefield and used for studding. But the truth was much simpler in some ways while being indecipherable in others. I'll spare you the gruesome details. What's important is that parts of this disgusting fouling of a cloning process is what an Elder traded with the Aemazons for. In itself the information was incomplete. But certain criminal elements in the Empire had already developed enough of the process to complete, perhaps perfect, it. And out of this organized crime family a new clan was created. A clan now important enough, with enough military might, to have certain Elders look the other way at past activities. It's your clan! It's not a real clan! It's criminals, politi-cal and otherwise, who rose from something forbidden and hidden. Elders bent history to make it appear your clan has always been there, protecting us, leading the charge against our most hated of enemies!"

Easarean knew the priestess could be his, should be his, wanted to be his. The sun fell completely behind the cliffs of rock, leaving only the pyre to light them. The fire no longer warmed him as it shrank, but his bronze face and massive arms flickered with warm hues just the same. He was heated by an inner fire now, one that rose with the cousin's pecking words.

Looking into the smoldering corpse of Pestilence, Easarean could see the future spread out before him in flames — nations crumbling under his order, villages burning by his beck and call, languages and culture spread by his word. An army of mixed men crossing the land with his banner, and all the while the pale exotic beauty at his side. This was an image he could have cherished forever, if not for the insect ramblings of the cousin.

"The Empire is insane, Easarean... infected. And we were infected too by the madness, raised in cultures different but still insane. We're both meant to die here, like babes in the woods. But in actuality we've been cut off, like limbs before the disease can fully corrupt us. Away from the Empire we can thrive."

Easarean took a deep breath in the second of silence, hoping it would cool his insides, but the fire still raged inside, threatening to consume his new-found peace. The silence was short-lived.

"I can see the way you look at her, and I can't blame you, but you have to accept that it's over. She's chosen, Easarean. It's time now for us all to move on, time for us to take our separate paths. You should head out, be a mercenary or soldier or whatever you want. This is your chance to be whatever you want... maybe a gladiator or... or something. But she and I are heading out in the morning, alone, together. This is your chance, Easarean, your chance to start over."

The cousin had no chance to react, to even flinch or cringe as giant fists swung around. He had not even had time to blink, and so his eyes popped outward as his skull was crushed from both sides, exploding under the pressure like some sort of crisp melon. It had squished with the queerest of sounds.

Easarean's hands were covered with bright blood and dark gore that had shot from what was left of the cousin's ears, and he shook splinters of brown bone from his arms as the body folded together before crumpling on the ground. It still had a head, although anyone would be hard-pressed to describe it as such. The dirt of the canyon was wet and dark with the coming evening, and so it appeared as though the cousin's neck barely bled. He did not twitch. His limbs just moved slowly to spread themselves out — the body's last wish looking as though it still wanted to stretch out comfortably before ceasing any movement.

"Ah, finally my true champion reveals himself," the pale priestess purred, walking silently up behind Easarean. "Finally," she repeated, running her delicate fingers along his back. The cooling touch extinguished the heat inside him.

He turned to take her soft shoulders in his fists, looking at her for the first time without wavering under her stare. She was the Queen of Quartz, a legendary priestess that had poisoned the land in search of a champion. Easarean was that champion.

She was the Queen of Quartz, and she licked the darkness from his hand as he held her head, her translucent flesh highlighted by cerulean lines trailing up from her neck. She spoke arcane words in an even older voice that only the parapsyte could hear. The slug died of fright, her tiny organs almost instantly seizing before congealing. In the same breath the Queen of Quartz spoke of Easarean's future, "All hail the King of All," while tracing invisible forgotten runes on his chest.

He could tell immediately that she had banished his curse. He could breathe freely again, and he did, of her dusty musk and the earthy breath he stopped with his mouth.

She was the Queen of Quartz, and only when the moon peeked into the ravine did her dark hair appear of the deepest blue to match her eyes, and by then it spread in rivulets over Easarean's body, mixing with his sweat and hers, and rising with the steam from his exhausted and slumbering snore.

Still warm, the cousin's body had been crushed to a pulp beneath them.

LVI

Angel:
"Yes, the future is immutable. Yes,
the past is the decree of one man, the
defeat of another, but acquiesce,
surrender, submit, and then be
one with the illusion, the delusion,
the myth of free will. God, with child-like glee,
has abdicated His Throne, seclusion
eternally His Reward but nature
and nurture still tug with adamantine
strings. No escape except in portraiture
askew. No freedom except in fleeing
or accepting apathy as reasoned
extremes, denying irrelevance seen.
You only live but twice. Stay here, seize and
rule the night. Dream the dreams of kings in this
bower of bliss. Better to concubine
in Hell than to whore in Heaven. One kiss
and Circle and Ring will be your fine wine,
your Grail, your Whole, your American Dream."
Narrator:
And so assassin kissed lips and canine
teeth and tasted forked tongue to become scheme
as yet untold. On him she placed cuckold
crown before promising six more gifts for
freeing the demon damsel faire — suckled
as she was on hate, First Born to abhor
that which she should adore. Now unleashed from
limitless freedom, she turned from the roar
at the door to continue the tour. Numb
and dumb to outside revolution, she
ascended to the next tier. He followed.
Necrophim — the Khan, the Saint, the Banshee,
the Leper — led red legions and swallowed
the lower Spirals. She showed him the Black
Vatican, her dinner guests in hallowed
Cell for Last Supper before the attack
by the Necrophim would bring them low. At
the long table sat the only Dukes left,
the other Circles having been over-
thrown. Eisleben Erfurt's close eyes, bereft

of sleep, stared, while the long face and gaped
teeth of Consul Incitatus, the heft
impressive, greeted the assassin. Draped
in golden hands belched Colombo loudly.
Birched buttocks bare, the Iron Baroness,
the youngest of the Pan Damn Dukes, proudly
displaying callused welts, cried, "Here in thish
Providential Paradise, we favoured
Dukes now genuflect and pledge all our piss
and vinegar to he most low, savoured,
and satiate — the new and deserv'ed
President of Hell." Quickly then, Angel
escorted Assassin to a reserved
hall, out past hill, over rises, up angle,
down parapet, through dungeons, in and out,
by bridge and stair and star, they rose and fell,
while wails of the Dukes echoed throughout
window and tower as Necrophim tore
them asunder. Followed by dying screams
of revolution and rebellion, Whore
of Hell the Angel led to all our dreams,
endless and everlasting — Hall of Doors.
Myriad openings through all Time's seams
the Doors offered. Visit days before wars.
Tour eras without strife. Explore the days
before man. Experience years after
humanity's fall. Pick any Door, gaze
upon a time and place, but thereafter
never look back, for you cannot return.
Angel:
"Think not long on this boon, my sweet. Laughter
then madness, ever rigor, results. Spurn
my gift if you are wise. Look away! Run
from the Doors instead of into one. But
if you must choose, do not yourself outrun.
Pick a Door, a time, a year, a day. Shut
it behind yourself and walk back into
the minute you left. Regard not that what
these Doors also can be are portals through
the Possibiliverse. Time and space, yes!
but also — choice! Each is also a Door

to every "guess," every "unless,"
all alternate realities of your
every reaction, action, effect,
affect, and cause. But all that I deplore,
that knowledge I implore you to neglect
and reject. Choose only that door with which
you will find yourself in your own time and
place, where you belong, where it is the niche
you have found, the one familiar time/land/
universe you have always called your own.
But choose now! For the Crown will not withstand
the encroaching rebellion. For the Throne
the Necrophim mean to burn. They are wrath
everlasting — ungrateful dead soldiers
who live for only dawn's violet bloodbath."
The Assassin:
"Why let these reincarnations smolder
away in the Netherlands? Perhaps their
unyielding hate deserves new exposure.
Direct their daily violence elsewhere."
Angel:
"Intriguing. But they still need Afterlife's
Lord to butcher today before looking
to morn. Hark! What is that shrill of two fifes?"
Narrator:
In danced Mixcotle's spawn, asp limbs crooking,
golden flutes fluting, just ahead of dead
armies joined, asking with worm tongue, looking
with wyrm eyes. When upon his eager head
the assassin gladly passed cuckold crown.
In swarmed combined legions of Necrophim
to tear and rend their new dread lord, to drown
him in his own cold blood. He tried to swim,
to breathe above the brim of his own gore,
but the rebellion pulled him limb from limb.
Angel and assassin spoke beneath roar.
Angel:
"These Doors, this multitude of glorious
Doors, can take you to any place, any
time you wish, any place notorious,
any time victorious. So many

Doors, I know. The possibilities of
where and when can overwhelm. Again, he
must consider all for whom he has love,
all whom he has hated. What weight mine own
concerns bear compared to the world chose?"
Narrator:
With mutinous screams behind and full-blown
war ahead, the assassin pondered close
escape. Doors before him led to those known,
those glades missed, days remembered sweetly, those
hours — melancholic, mirthful, and alone.

—excerpt from "The Angel and the Ass"

The Librans had a long history of being dragged into wars, and Teca had, over the years, read every biography, every journal entry, and every history extant in the Library Needles concerning her Order's involvement in both of the official Evolutionary Wars. She had even spent time collecting the scraps of hearsay and untrustworthy interviews concerning the heretical Eastern Order's dubious accounts of a third Evolutionary War far on the other side of MANN Lands. All the tales of guilted and conscripted knights led to one current and over-whelmingly consensual philosophy. Librans were not soldiers. Paladins and knights, and especially monks and faithful peasants, were not grunts and infantry to be spent in worldly pursuits and disputes. The sacrifice always ended up being too great. The more Librans warred, the more they found themselves growing distant from the *Sol Sistere*, from love in general — love of the Order, of its righteousness, and of the unending fountain of blessings that was Blind Libra.

Teca looked around herself as the new path began to rise, leading her through yet another legion of the Liege of Foes' main forces. Where was love among the sudden pitfires hardening newly carved spear points? Where was the love among all the men cleaning rifles, sharpening bolts, and packing gunpowder? Necrophim, ignoring the freezing air in their bare rust-colored armor, dragged great artillery weapons through drifts the size of Teca by chimeric machines or great beasts of burden not native to this plane of existence. The pristine mounds of snow, endless virgin hills of fluff, were bulldozed, torn, and thrown against azure trees untouched in years, maybe decades. Those same forests were pressed aside, icy trees screaming as tank towers and treaded transports moved toward the capital city of Bifrost in roads they were just now creating. Bark and limb did not bend or timber. They exploded. Infantry cringed at every sound, cowering and pulling helm and hood down to avoid a face full of splinters. Hall and shack were equally driven over in the mad press toward Bifrost. Any inhabitants, long since frozen to their very core, shattered like diamonds and rubies. It was all so destructive and all so beautiful. But where was the love?

Submit yourself to Love as the First Dhani did to Lady Wayasu. For Love is the Heart, Heart is the Head, Head is the Body, and the Body submits to the Word in everything. Each one of you must love the Word as he loves himself, and love is submission.

And this was not even the War. The Liege of Foes' main forces had, albeit temporarily, left the War behind to catch up to the massive peregrination of refugees. Teca tried thinking back over the weeks following whatever it was that happened outside Erebus. The Necrophim general, Banshee Jenny Wren, and her forces were sent to chase the pink leviathan that had appeared over the city. They headed south, and intelligence spread the word that they had not been heard from since. The Electric Leper and his battalion had been left behind to hold Erebus, but it may have been a pointless gesture. It was untouchable, highly defensible but too remote for strategic importance at this time. The Horde had appeared mere days later to harass the refuges that became the peregrination, and the Army of Earth had gone back and forth between waging small victories and periodically veering back westward to discourage Fobos' forces from pestering the northbound migrants.

Eventually, the increasingly frozen roads north had turned the Horde away — but not the peregrination or the Liege of Foes, Teca lamented. They would meet today in the snow-packed capital she could barely see down the white hill and amongst buried halls. The King's Church itself barely even poked out above the drifts. It was as though the banks of the great *Jormangandr* had overflowed and flooded the city, only to freeze as it crested. Despite the occasional flickering wisp of smoke from the occasional hall's stack, Teca never would have believed anyone was alive in Bifrost, much less the entire many thousands the peregrination was said to have grown to.

She had gathered warmer clothes over the prior days, but nothing would keep out the chill entirely. Doe gloves under furred mittens barely kept her fingers from stiffening. Even under many layers of mismatched socks and patched boots, she could barely feel her toes. They had gone numb sometime in the previous night. She had held on to her leather pants and jacket, but both were supplemented now by quilted accessories. And as unequipped for the snow as she was, she felt equally unprepared for the meeting she had finally procured.

Seeing her approach, a sergeant nodded and pointed down a fork in the path. The legions appeared to part as she neared, clearing a path through snow still up to the top of her boots. Her legs felt heavier than the drifts should have made them, and she slowed to catch her breath. Looking around, she saw that she had almost immediately lost sight of the capital, as suddenly imbedded as she now was in the soldiers' formations. She was now lost in the gold and crimson sea of the Army of Earth's most elite — or so she assumed. This close to the highest echelon of the Army would have had to require the most deadly and the most loyal of the Necrophim soldiers. These were the men with the finest armor. The plate and ring and chain had all been put away into transports as they entered N'Midgaard, so the soldiers were mostly wearing quilted if they were fortunate. These guards, however, wore oiled cloaks over their striated leather shirts. She could even see a plethora of crocheted clothing in the elite legion. She had become accustomed to the mismatched and homemade sigils of the lower legions, but here each soldier, as she could see when the wind appeared to move a line of cloaks, wore a standard pale blue eye on his left arm with the requisite crimson tear. And as she passed through them, winding around the hill and heading ever upward, she could see the tear replicated in a branding beneath each man's left eye. Tied around their cloaks were each soldier's pike rifle.

The trail between the soldiers appeared to lead her away from the mount before it brought her back again. Here, a stove had been dug out of the brick of some submerged hovel, and what she at first thought was a bear, but turned out to be a heavily furred cook, was stirring a grand kettle. The smoke from the fire below could barely bellow in the frigid air. The steam from the kettle fell before it could rise. Teca was grateful that the air only smelled like just more stale snow.

Round and around she went, with periodic views of the submerged Bifrost. Except for the low castle church, it was a city without windows, unless the drifts had covered them all. The Granite Land's capital was also without color. Besides a rare blue the color of a corpse's lips, the winter had even choked any warmth out of the land's palette. Before she could follow the path back around into the legion of guards, she felt the nauseating tingle of an earth tremor. Her feet slid. Her vision wavered. All eyes turned toward the city as one of the bigger hall of halls began to disappear into a sudden mist of rising and falling snow. There was little sound beyond a faint pressing squeal of glacial drifts against one another. She did not wait for the distant powder to settle. She continued back into the troops as they all watched the slowly submerging cityscape.

So it is true, she thought, removing a glove and checking on the revolver holstered deep within her jacket. *Bifrost is sinking.* What are we doing here? What could the Army of Earth gain from conscripting even such a large mass of migrants? What was worth the trip north to such a frozen helscape?

She awkwardly released the cylinder of the pistol just by feel alone and absent-mindedly fingered the five chambers for the only two cartridges she had. Two was probably more rounds had than each of the soldiers she walked near. The guards' pike rifles were intimidating. It could not be denied. But the Army of Earth was dangerously low on ammunition. There existed a ridiculous rumor that the peregrination had looted some ancient depot out on the plains. Is that why the Liege of Foes was opening his arms to farmers, vagabonds, zealots, and families?

Teca adjusted her sword belt as she rounded to the top of the rise, bringing the scabbard around and retying it while trying to look casual, for the guards here ignored all distractions of the stunningly chilled and vibrating city. They watched only for danger. Here Teca saw that she had been wrong about the close legion. These were not all Necrophim soldiers. They were not all bloodshot with alien stares. Up close she could see that the inner guard of the Army's generals were soldiers of all races, and they watched her as close as she watched them, but they let her through.

The drifts on top of the mound had been cleared away to the iced earth beneath. It was uneven, but Teca felt sturdier here than she had in days, even though the solid ground felt unfamiliar beneath her boots. She had hid a knife in one of them early in the morning. Its scabbard rubbed against her ankle over the frozen grasses.

The figures before her she knew immediately, despite never being closer than a horizon's walk. The Liege of Foes and his crimson concubine had their backs to her as they watched the quieting city. Bifrost had settled and the granite and halls and drifts had returned to their silent white song. What could have only been the sun sat low and frozen and colorless behind cloud and fog and approaching snowstorm. The two talked to each other. Exchanging low words beneath a rising wind that hit the top of the hill full of sharp flakes and a chill that Teca had not realized that she had been sheltered from when she walked amongst the soldiers.

The third figure, however, stared back at her. Its dark sockets could do nothing but stare. She had been told that rubies were hidden somewhere deep in those sockets, but in the shadow of the palanquin, under the dark radiance of metallic gold plume and bejeweled helm, the skull's sockets were black as winter night. Myriad gems in a precious web hung bearded from the Catacomb Saint's jaw. This was not the most respected of the Necrophim generals, but it was the most feared. Filigreed plate armor and bleached ribs refused to honor any light as the crusader king leaned forward from his velvet to survey Teca. She could only look past him to the other figures on the hill, in service to the fear holding her breath still, but also to the creeping suspicion of his knightly origins. She shook the wind from her ears. The whistle sounded too much like she would expect from the general's fleshless mouth.

She meant to wait a moment before announcing herself, to admire the pale view over the storm-wracked granite capital, but, before she could pick new frost from her eyelashes, the Liege of Foes and the Crimson Queen turned toward her.

From afar, over the few prior days Teca had been able to move close to the front line, he had been only a singular cloaked blot of blackness against the bleak fields, surrounded by masses of troops before being swallowed eventually by drifted forests in the evening marches, but here, up close, the layers of cloaks and leather were covered with bloody stitching almost indiscernible from the ebony fabrics.

She found the snow melting immediately from her face and wiped it and slick hair from her eyes as she flushed. She failed to halt a noticeable shiver as freezing lines of water slinked into her collar, down between her breasts.

With the corpse sun behind him his face was obscured in hood and shadow as well as beard — a scraggly beard more animal than man. But she had not forgotten the eyes that looked through the darkness. Although one was now granite, they were both the blue of the city behind him. They were the blue of the sad, shadowed drifts and the lazy *Jormangandr*. He looked old, as, she could only assume, she must have to him.

"Hello, Teca," he said, smiling at the side of his mouth.

But his voice had not changed. And, as though she had been stabbed in the chest by one of the surrounding pike rifles, it all came back to her, suddenly and painfully, and it was though she was sixteen years old again. Her face felt even warmer. She found herself holding her wrist in a phantom pain she had not felt in over a decade. How could she not have known? After all this time, how could she not have known that Wulf was the Liege of Foes?

LVII

Catalog of the Army of Earth

Among the differing nations the Liege of Foes had collected into the Army of Earth, there were many notable heroes and scoundrels. These are the names of those recorded by the Third World Nomads, but it is in no way meant to be a plenary listing.

Dogfennel Ascension, who barely escaped from Lying Territory with the largest segment of green converts; "Cute" Quintana Scarface; Jay Astray, who claimed to be possessed by some unheard of demon that was particularly fond of huckleberries; "Backwards" Andy, born with his head on backwards, who became the most celebrated spy for the Army.

Sister Haversack, a green woman who always had a sugarplum for the children and a poisoned dart for the Horde soldiers; Sir Cerulean Shunka, a knight of the Northern Order, who was out exploring the Land of Nod when the Temple Needles was blockaded. He was a strong advocate for the liberation of the Black Hills from the Horde, and he brought his massive pack of hunting dogs to the Army of Earth's cause. These dogs were irreplaceable as sentries and had a knack for predicting the Horde's pyromancy.

The son of Trillibob, Private Hoarlok, who once sailed an entire cargo knarr down a meadow stream to the surprise of an unprepared Horde camp; Prostrate Pigweed, who cobbled the majority of hobnail boots for the Army; Freydis Nofoddir and Beadohild Knowfoddir, who essentially won the Battle Over Carny by themselves (near feral and inseparable as sisters, although they most certainly were not). On close inspection it was revealed that it was not animal skins they wore; Fudginald Vanderpuffy; Dr. Tar and Professor Feather; Grandma Grand Mal; the Muffin Man, who as a serial child-murderer was sent to the front lines at the very beginning of the war; the ghost of Splinter Cat (a Native freed from his post mortem haunting by the violence of the war, he chose to fight for the Army of Earth); Peter Panhandler; Captain Chillblayne, drained the rum cellar of every port in the Great Lakes, barely escaped the freezing of Super Lake; Glen Cairn; Sirocco ibn Herakles, who was descended from a commune that claimed to have come from beyond the sea walls separating the continent from the other continents (his flock of sheep grew wool three times as fast as other sheep).

Wen "Whitey" Wodenfel, the Army of Earth's official hangman (claimed to be a cousin to the Liege of Foes); Snood Logos; Hogback Quirt; Foetus Hoecake; Cuspidor Fetlock, who was the shortest man in the Army; Limpet Squab son of Shoat Sputnum; Jon Goungfermour rich in gong, most well-known sleipnir breeder in south N'Midgaard, set a bowl of vermillion on a wishing well every evening since he was two and a half years old. Never missed a night. As an adult his stables were mysteriously and meticulously cleaned by morning, every morning. He brought his impressive breed of six-legged horses to the Army of Earth; Memento Maury; (Rhett) Hart Ascendant who was appointed to see over pilgrimages into the cooling far southern deserts but felt his winter gardening skills would be put to better use at the warfront. The green house in his covered wagon grew artichokes, black-eyed susan, chamomile, cornflower, foxglove, lilac, and a variety of grasses in even the coldest of conditions.

Infat son of Nevermore, and Larson son of Nevermore, and Ornery son of Nevermore, and Angrbodr son of Nevermore, and Smith son of Nevermore, and Sally son of Nevermore, and Staulk the Wistful son of Nevermore, and Saint Molest son of Nevermore, and Gadfly son of Nevermore, and Sidewalk Sam son of Nevermore, and Puce son of Nevermore, and Mealy Boner son of Nevermore, and Cinderella son of Nevermore, and Saunter Wedge son of Nevermore, and Lame Stryder son of Nevermore, and Gylded Wyrds son of Nevermore, and Hailsin son of Nevermore, who never found a man who could outpace him. He was the best messenger (link) in the Army of Earth.

A woman who claimed to be the only surviving familiar of the mythical sorceress Carcosa. She would construct dolls, shaped in the likeness of the Horde generals, stuffed with her old mistress' broom straws; Sir Jericho Claret (also known as Sir Sanguine, the Sanguine Knight, the Knight of the Hunter's Moon, a knight of the Tetrad), the only surviving member of a small band of knights that broke all vows to judge Librans from outside the Orders. He disappeared investigating the Southern Order, but reappeared decades later with a pallid complexion, an allergy toward daylight, and a penchant for drinking blood. The knight was said, in some stories, to have been staked by Legion late in the War. Other tales tell of his cremation by the Lonely Forgotten Sun of God's green light.

Krywulf, who was abandoned by her parents and raised by a bugbear, then wore the skin of a bugbear as a headdress and was the greatest monster hunter in the Army; Kalinski son of Knife Tooth and Broderick son of Dagger Tooth, feline Ku-Gar who sent intelligence from the Black Hills to the Liege of Foes on the breath of a swallow bird.

Mayor Meow; Ten Tons son of Restless Leg; Call of the Flower son of Ten Tons; Hardtack Draptail; Piquant Hornpipe, who claimed to still be a virgin.

Awl-nose Bill Crosswise the Ranger of Rochester; Webster Bedwetter; Lance Bowles; Ballddofdd Dynddyllg, a dwarf from beneath Bifrost, who was unsatisfied with just smithing weapons, skilled in testing out new types of double-bladed axes; Greede son of Uncle Sam, Eggburt son of Burtson; Landlubber Anderson; Ric rich in grandkids; Old Man Tucker; Santiago "Greybull Jack" Chavez y Chavez.

Swipe, Snatch, and Grip sons of the King of Wisconsin; Sister Cinnamon (also known as Woodnymph Smoldering, also know as Bumblebird Coquette or Dusky Hummingbee), who was the daughter of a Greater Antony and the war god Huizilopochtli, wielded a green rattler as a weapon (in some tales the snake was on fire, while in other tales it breathed fire, while in still other tales its venom burned like fire, and she would let the snake bite her before going into battle).

"Chaste" Hasty Pudding; ClaspKnife Ungirt; Liegeman Stavelock; Michael Turnspit; Pelican Coif the Ranger of Watertown; Gaylynne rich in beads; Van Dyke rich in goats; Jaime Hunchback from the West Farm; Floyd Pompei (the Ashman), who claimed to be as old as cataclysm, living through eruption and nuclear winter, most believed that he was a ghost chained to Kaldera, but there were rumors of his appearance on the battlefields even to the east; Quintana Nahuatl, who was rumored to have been birthed from an egg. Many people, soldiers and non-soldiers, claimed to have had near-death experiences where they were escorted back to the land of the living by her — but she denied it.

Pic, a goblin first of an unknown mob, then of Mob Knife, then of Mob Green, then the only known surviving member of the Grand Mob, vowed blood vengeance on Wulf for his betrayal at the Battle of Keep. He followed Wulf (hiding in the Peregrination) before losing him outside Folly. He lost him again at the end of the War of Heaven and

Earth, when Wulf disappeared over the carnage of Simon.

The Sulphur King of the Fossil Forest, who claimed to be descended from Bumpass — the god of mudpots. Greatest cook in the Army; Prince Dor, who was the sexless son of the Midgardian war god Tor. It was said that anyone dying on the battlefield within hammer distance of Dor was guaranteed entrance into the Hoar Hall, an afterlife of carnivorous caterpillars that spun razor wire silk.

Milk Cloud, the 7th Daughter of Mixcoatl, who was the greatest hunter in the Army. She wore the hide of a white buffalo to hide the candy cane stripes on her skin. Disappeared into drifts of snow for days to hunt Horde and the last of the great game. Also, a half vampire.

Coxcomb Yaws; Tanyard Trillibub; Jonny Applesneeze; Tenacious Grace; Insidious Jane; Diego the Desperate; PJ McJammies; Alonzo Eager for Battle; Tony Beaver, champion griddle skater outside of the Territories; Perfecta Salazar; Fastidious Dean, the fastest gun in the land; "Atlatl Jack" Billingsly; "Bronco" Mateo Reeves, who was hit by lightning once every year since he had been sixteen. Expert with his electric lasso; Hugi Salvador, who was rumored to have hidden the largest gold mine in Kaldera. Could eat clay and defecate dynamite. The Army of Earth's foremost demolitions expert.

Alejandro the Tornado Driver, who (in one version of the story) was shotgun married to a tornado for pissing in the wind, or who (in another version) raped a ver vvitch and was cursed to be followed around forever by a tornado (this is why he preferred cold climates).

Aidyro Aidyr Aidyran, who claimed to wear armor sewn from the scales of a dragon, but in truth it was tailored from the hide of one of the lesser fire salamanders living beneath the Kalderan town of Thermopolis; "Doc" Aberdeen, slowest but most accurate gun in the land, had been dying of lead poisoning for many years and ended up in the North, hoping the climate would "preserve his handsome decay."

Buzz and Burn (the Brothers Byrne), who claimed to be dishonorable discharges from MANN. Buzz was a master apothecary specifically in the cultivation of hamphetamines (sprouting nematode pupae gestated in pregnant sow intestines) that provided the Army's soldiers with "pick-me-ups" to be used in battle. Burn would make mechanical sounds when he moved, claiming he was used to fighting in high-tech, full-environmental, battle armor.

Zenith Auge-peak; "Capon" Cassock Surplice; Clever Jack, who was the fastest runner in the Army of Earth. Her boots never sank into the snow. She had been an exile from the People of Scattered Dust but was seen fighting amongst them in the war.

Gristmill Spoon-bread; Festoons Mescal; Pandowdy Cakeman; "Burnt" Kristian Reyes; WolveGang, who was a tin-man from the time of the Old Ones. Originally an anthropomorphic canine, his consciousness had been repeatedly transferred over the millennia to survive cataclysm, nuclear winter, and the numerous Evolutionary Wars.

Mort, a sentient mourning star mace. It had been passed from soldier to soldier because of its foul language and insults that would bring even the strongest wielder to tears; Kestrel Faolsin, who was never wounded because to scar his face would have been an affront to any love god, claimed to be a cousin of the Liege of Foes. Sligi "Crunchy" Jonson; Seahand Greenepuppet; Sheepcrook and Blackdog; Ferdinand of Twenty Gowns; Brow Fleaquilt, who decided in his youth that he would never sleep another night in his life, and he never did; Goit-Tyr, who had never sharpened a blade in his life; Clay Whistle Pig the Pistoleer Bard, whose mother had fallen asleep under a toadstool and woke up seven years later, pregnant. The fastest gun in the land; The White Knight of Hail, an errant knight rumored to be from the West; The Knight of Acorns, an errant knight rumored to be from the East; The daughter of Moira Otgood, who many saw walking on the surface of Lake Manly early in the war, but she denied the rumors; Faux "Wolvy" Badgerton the Brilliant, who could dig a hole faster than anyone in the entire Army; Henny Fair-beard; Amber "Greasy" Fairbeard; Ver De "Greasy" Verne, who always wore orange and fought only with rusty blades; Thall Gall-stones, who was the tallest man in the Army, hated the King of Wisconsin for stealing his aunt's land, vowed to kill all the King's sons; Tall Kyle, who once ate an entire goat in a day; Generous Arthur, who was the only survivor of an expedition up Castle Mountain; Golfnoyan Genbeddestyr, a dwarf from beneath Bifrost who was dissatisfied with just smithing weapons, skilled in testing out new types of munitions.

Prelate Knacker; Milkweed Sacristy, who claimed to have been born at the bottom of the *Jormungandr*, could understand the language of the large mouth bass, was able to hold her breath underwater for twenty minutes (but only in the *Jormungandr* or its tributaries); Smeagol Gibbons from the West Farm; "Wrestling" Rickard from the West

Farm; The Spring Witches (ver vvitches) of Endor, who some say were the land's greatest meteorologists, while others say the women had the ability to actually cause and prevent the weather; No-toes Curmudgeon, who claimed to have been born at the top of Horny Peak, able to run as fast as an antelope.

Aeinriker the Errant, the Knight of Wounds, an errant knight presumed to have been from the Western Order. Since his cuts never healed, bones never mended, he was thought to have been cursed by the Army of Heaven's General Shriven. Said to have stolen the relic of Dhani Antony's spine to be used as a lance and whip; Touch the Stars, who had been deaf since a child when he had entered a cave before falling from the sky. It was said that he had ventured into a polluted dream stream, bringing a dying spirit back with him, and the spirit now looked through his eyes and spoke through his mouth.

Jessie Van Helsing, famous vampire hunter and motorcycle thief; Luna Guadalupe, who claimed to be the last surviving member of a previously unheard of pack of desert Garm — the Pack of Saint Christopher. The shawl of lobo fur she wore was too tattered to allow her transformation anymore, still an amazing scout that could smell the Horde from a day away — more with a good wind.

"Stomach ache" Ace; Snarls Davenport; Aaliyah Stellarsdottir, rumored to be the avatar of a forgotten war god and half-sister of Tor. Any adversary struck on the head by her short-handled hammer would be permanently night-blind. Her mead horn was never dry, and it could conjure bees to aid her in battle. She rode into the War on the largest and darkest sleipnir in the Army of Earth, but no one had ever seen the horse (or Aaliyah) in the camps otherwise.

The Pileated Pistoleer, whose shock of red hair and crazy aim could not be tamed, fastest gun in the land (despite any adversary being able to hear his wild laugh from miles away); Wynne Ffion, a dwarf from beneath Bifrost who was dissatisfied with just smithing weapons, skilled in testing out new types of war hammers.

Imani the Bold; Quarter Babe (the Great One); Little Juan Crying; Bechdell Ascendant; Cuticle Lue "Albino" the Invisible Man; Glimli No-Lip son of Gums McGee; Bryan Crick-Swim, who killed Ten Tons, and then in turn had to be killed by Legion as weregild; Dede Rich in Hives, who had no bees left, but whose white honey, when warmed by a blacksmith, eliminated nightmares for anyone who ate of it.

Makayla "Sweat Bee" Armstrong, who was deadlier with a sling than most people were with a revolver, rumored to be a tin-man draped in the skin of her dead mother; Anemic Nemo, who had no name before joining the Army, dreamt of the Lonely Forgotten Sun of God his entire life, journeyed north all the way from Sepulcre in the Land where the Pharaoh Dies, his stories of human feedlots never failed giving nightmares to anyone who would listen; Laughing Chumani, daughter of Speaks with Skulls, who fought with spears and hatchets made from ice.

Bone Valentina, the headhunter that killed the Governor of Laramie Territory, fastest gun in the land, her bullets took three days to kill, but they did in fact always kill in the end; Modrette and Cow-Beard Bumblefuzz, who claimed to be cousins of the Liege of Foes; Felipe "Flourishing" Flores, who was considered the greatest competitive swordsman in the land; "Three Sheets" Wynngaard, who documented the fighting from the early days of the war with his "extra-dimensional" camera. His notes were lost or destroyed in the Battle of IOU; Culwich and Olwen.

Mercenary groups that had joined up with the Army of Earth:

The Nebraska Pluviculturalist Society (NPS), led by the famous Captain Benjamin Nutcracker.

Ghosts of the Dirtylegs.

The Southbound Posse: Carcajou; the Peace Garden Glutton; Skunk Bear; Quickhatch. Specialized in hunting quarry of the supernatural type.

Flash Company. Before the War these mercenaries had never even seen modern guns. A collection of farmers and ranchers, called traitors by the *Ashmedai Adat El,* whose crop and livestock were confiscated. Said to have never lost a battle.

The Bloody Bedwetters Brigade, who were rumored to have been trained by a rogue agent of MANN.

The Alamosa Guard, that was originally founded by veterans after the Evolutionary Wars. Had a particularly vicious trial by combat to join. No new members in over two decades.

Southern Branch of Thorny Boutonnieres, built from the remnants of disenfranchised territorial militias.

The Ted Hunters, a collection of mercenaries that only responded to bounties on people named Theodore.

The Heirs of Aesar (no one knew where this name came from): Legion, who could fight with the skill of a hundred soldiers all by himself, consort to the Lonely Forgotten Sun of God; RackBreak Antony, one of the few Greater Antonys left in the land; Damn Antony, a disgraced member of the Brotherhood of the Prophets Lesser that changed sides toward the end of the War; Slayd "Wyrmbane" Melchylor, once fabled dragon-slayer, once apprentice of Tormalco the Always, once Sin Eater for the Brotherhood, changed sides toward the end of the War, used scrying to predict weather and Horde movement; the Crimson Queen, Daughter of Pride, Lady Sumer Sirach, Grand Duchess of the Order of the Wandering Fly, commonly known as Sera, known to have traveled the land in the guise of a fortune teller by the name of Madam Beatrice Cockatrice.

The Necrophim generals (the Order of the Wandering Fly):
    The Banshee Jenny Wren (commanding 133 soldiers)
    Hyper Khan (commanding 316 soldiers)
    The Catacomb Saint (commanding 666 soldiers)
    The Electric Leper (commanding 66 soldiers)

LVIII

There is a warmth below the mountain day,
A golden glow beneath conifer sky.
Heart rumbles under fur and hand in ways
Unknown to this cold soul, to one who dies
Anew, away from his side, one who stays
Awake only to dream of sleep and lies.
So the tiny patter of heart I miss,
New lessons in love, and rough, waking kiss.

—from "the Love Song of Smeagol Gibbons"

O o not think that She has come to bring peace to the land. She has not come to bring peace, but a sword, for She is love."

The crowd shuffled closer to Milliam Pittsfield. Most were sitting, for he had been talking for an extended period, but they crawled and readjusted their sacks and armor in order to hear his quiet sermon. Mothers quieted children. Soldiers stilled their armored arms and legs. The settling army moved loudly around the crowd, pulling together the various poles, furs, and fabrics for the mobile city, but it had quieted around Milliam, and he continued to speak in his whisperous voice.

"Her Chosen trains your hands for war, and your fingers for battle. For he is the Lonely Forgotten Sun of God's servant for your good. But if you do wrong, be afraid, for he does not bear the sword in vain. For Legion is the servant of God, an avenger who carries out God's wrath on the wrongdoer." His arms flailed, their dramatics making up for his unheard words. Whether he realized it or not, his stubby fingers pointed to the sickly green comet moving across the evening sky behind him.

All around the crowds the mobile city took shape, as it did every night. Land was chosen, ideally with some tree-line, no matter how sparse, to shield from any wind, the prairie snow was dug, marquees and huts appeared from pallets of seemingly incompatible timbers and tarps, and fires were built to burn the daily dried dung of burden beasts. Milliam had barely drawn a crowd before the Army of Earth had settled on the plain, before soldiers shared the milk and blood of their mares.

"So follow Her Chosen... and your commander... your Necrophim lord... your Heir of Aesar... and the Liege of Foes. Let all of you be subject to the warring authorities. For there is no authority except from Her, and those that lead have been instituted by Her.

Therefore whoever resists the generals resists what She has appointed, and those who resist will incur Her wrath. For leaders are not a terror to good conduct, but to bad. Therefore one must be in subjection, not only to avoid the Lonely Forgotten Sun's wrath but also for the sake of conscience."

All around Milliam's commune the soldiers cleaned rifles and oiled blades and armor. Families, their own and others, tended to them, stitching leather and boiling soups. Upon the settling of the Army, dwarves immediately began stoking sudden pits and deep forges that had appeared out of nowhere. A fog appeared almost as immediately as these black blacksmiths went to work, their char and red iron melting the new paths between the sudden hamlets. Scouts not milking or blooding their mares circled out into the prairie to survey the evening miles for any evidence of the Horde.

"And do not fear those who kill the body but cannot kill the soul. Rather fear Her who can destroy both soul *and* body. For only She can. So when you go out to war against the Horde, and see mammoths and tanks and an army larger than your own, you shall not be afraid of them, for the Lonely Forgotten Sun of God is with you, who brought you up out of your stolen homeland, or Erebus, or Bifrost. Let not your heart feint. Do not fear or panic or be in dread of the Horde, for She is she who goes with you to fight for you against your enemies, to give you the victory."

Eventually, as the sun settled in as well, on cloud and fog and mist and horizon, only Milliam's weak whisper could be heard, as more and more gathered around him, under fur and blanket, breathing in his words and the moist heat of passed soups. Occasionally one of Mew's vespers would move out in the rows of huts to tend to a soldier's wounds or a patient's cough, but eventually the only movement was the flicker of tarp, of glowing coals, of Milliam's fake beard as he whispered.

"At that time, the Liege of Foes, that great prince,
who protects you, will arise.
Delivered nations as allies
In unity not seen before or since.
Multitudes who sleep in ice of the earth
Will awake. Some will find love.
Others will find the shame of
Everlasting contempt to be their worth."

He held up a water-logged book the audience knew to be his copy of the *Fallo Terminus* in fingers vermillion-stained as dark as the lips under his fake mustache. Someone in the front of the crowd picked up a page that had fallen, tried in vain to dry it before it fell apart, and handed it up to Milliam so that the preacher could stuff it back into the book.

There was a calm in the evening of the sunset, before the dwarves began their nightly high-pitched hammering. The Army huddled in collapsible yurts or around their squad commander, warming darkening fingers and toes, reflecting on those that were with them a day ago but now were just meat for crows or snow. Whether by sickness or cold or enemy spear, the Army of Earth was always smaller by nightfall, and it was even smaller by morning. So soldier, smith, tailor, and nurse all held the calm of evening tightly to their bosoms, as they would a child not expected to make it through the night.

And into this calm appeared the Army of Earth's sorcerer, Melchyor Slayd. He led a hinny along paths already turned to mush. The animal struggled over icy ruts and melted mud that constantly threatened to turn its hooves in opposite directions. Slayd's long legs, however, strode over the messy channel as though it was a marble street, humming some tune that would haunt any passerby as they tried to sleep that night. It was familiar yet obscure enough that they would not be able to get it out of their heads, nor would they be able to remember its significance.

And he never stopped humming, even as he pulled and then stopped the hinny on the path next to Milliam and his crowd. The preacher stumbled over his words at the near presence of the scaly sorcerer.

"N... know this... that we face unbridled evil in the Horde... and in the Last Days there will come times of difficulty. For to allow the Horde their humanity is to make peace with evil. For the Horde are lovers of self, lovers of gold, proud, arrogant, disobedient to their parents, ungrateful, heartless, without self-control, reckless, swollen with pride, lovers of pleasure, and they have the appearance of godliness only. Duh... destroy such people." His voice had become even quieter, so quiet it fell beneath Slayd's prosperous humming.

The sorcerer reached into the impossibly numerous pockets lining the insides of his robes to impossibly pull out an impossibly great broadsword. It was almost as tall as he was and almost as wide, but he lifted it with one hand and brought it down upon the hinny's neck before anyone in the crowd could gasp. It made barely a sound, like wood upon wood, hoof upon wood, or hoof upon hoof.

"Bah... but in the uh... End Times," Milliam continued, his green cape and flushed face suddenly speckled darkly, "ah... embrace your loved returned. For they know not what they duh... do. For they are the Hungry Dead, and we... the food for thought." But no one heard him. They heard only the resumed humming, as they silently shrieked at the blood covering their furs, and as Slayd took the hinny's perplexed head under his arm to continue down the path.

Miss Mowgli appeared and knelt by the side of her hinny's streaming corpse. Mud mixed with drippings, and tears mixed with slush.

A breeze rose to invigorate the frosty dusting that had begun appearing on the tops of huts, and it bent the seemingly endless streams pooling from the hinny's head, keeping Slayd's outer robe spotless. His tongue, now shriveled and forked, tasted the smoke of char and coal and countless chimeneas. His veiny eyes, recently unclouded, adjusted to the dimming light, their black slits pulsing as slowly as his two hearts.

It were those eyes that the troop of guards shied away from as Slayd approached the presidential marquee. It was more a hall than a tent, designed, like everything in the Army's mobile city, to be collapsed and built at a moment's notice. He walked through vestibule, the layers of drapes and velvety ropes, while wrapping a silken shawl and bag around and over the hinny's leaking head.

There were those in the War Hall that ignored his entrance and those that did not bother to hide their disgust. Despite the range of reactions, the talks continued, with Teca becoming louder and redder.

"They're warriors!"

"Are they?" Wulf asked.

"Yes! They know how to fight. To even become a squire they have to go through..."

"But what do they know of war?"

"What do you know about war?" Teca asked. Out of breath, she stepped aside to throw her jacket into a corner of piled rugs and quilts. She pushed up the sleeves of her long johns. The fire pits had warmed the War Hall very quickly. "The knights would make effective commanders. They would be excellent cavalry in the woodlands of the Wheel, and the paladins could help... him... ward against the Horde's fire magic." She made a quick gesture to the pacing Slayd without looking in his direction.

"I need no help," he sighed, "beyond any refuge from the incessant chattering of this inane council."

Wulf smiled at the side of his mouth while pulling back the hood from his heavy mantle. "How goes the counter-cursing?"

"Besides taking up all of my valuable time and components? It is sufficient. Sufficiently boring, that is. But you'll be happy to know, I'm sure, that I am presently putting into action measures that will ensure an end to the Army of Heaven's pyrmission and pyrovoyance. No one will be able to spy on your enlightening conversations through any flame. No more will assassins burst from a fire pit to interrupt such an astute congress of the minds. The important question, I think, is what will I do with all my free time?"

"Stay focused," Sera said, yawning from her sovereign chair. The ashwood throne sat low, yet its bulk allowed her still to look over the commanders to the long matching table and the boards and maps spread upon it. Where fox furs ended and her curls started was difficult to determine. Where red lion stoles ended and velvet vestments started was impossible to determine. A bare arm emerged from the accoutrements to twirl a pale finger in her hair. The Crimson Queen caressed the rubies of an encrusted goblet with her other hand, surrounded by hanging and resting trophies. The Shield of Deemos, its war-paint as bloodied as her lips, was perched overlooking the scene from behind her chair. The triangular-bladed daggers of the last of the Yellow Head Assassins Guild stuck out, extinguished, from all sides of the chair. A preserved manticore's maned face glared menacingly over her furred shoulders.

"Right," Teca agreed, facing Wulf. "You promised to liberate the Needles. The Order of the Creed will repay you. They'll join the fight."

"Are you sure you speak for them?" Wulf asked.

"That's why I'm here!"

"Too risky. The attack last night showed us just how vulnerable we are out here, and just how willing the Horde is to sacrifice its troops to the North. We can no longer count the winter as cover." He leaned over the table to study the terrain just as intently as Janus had been doing. The pieces representing his immediate forces were far from any other, except for the forces that had been dogging them over the few prior days. "We're nowhere near cover, civilized or even tree-lined. The Black Hills are at least a week away in this weather. A straight line. It would be too predictable."

"You son of a bitch," Teca spat.

"No, no," Slayd interjected, still slowly circling, still overlooking the table and each member of the council. "I hear the problem is quite the opposite. Otherwise we could add the Garm to our numbers." He stopped suddenly to eye a remarkable beaver fur top hat. It was exquisite, and he wondered if the Queen of the Necrophim would notice its absence. He must have that hat.

"We don't need them," Janus mumbled, suddenly breaking from intently moving the pieces on the table. He took a long draught from a pitcher of water.

Teca spread a new map over old. "If we double our pace and don't settle the march until the witching hour, we can lose the Horde. We can circle to the north of the Hills…"

"Not now," Wulf interjected, "we have more concerns than your fancy knights. They hid in their hills and now they're stuck there."

Slayd peeked in to say, "I still have not received any 'doves' from the Banshee Jenny Wren."

"No," mumbled Janus. He was back to the table with his scarred cheek resting against the wood, lining his sight up with piece after piece after piece. "And even if we recalled the Electric Leper from our southern holdings — which I still recommend — his battalion wouldn't get to us in time. We can't break the Needles' blockade without help. They're too entrenched. There's too many of them."

Teca breathed out loudly while going to her knees and resting her chin and hands on the table.

They stared at the featureless maps for minutes on end. Slayd continued his long, slow steps around the table. His pacing was the only sound until Sera leaned, revealing the sharp red nails of a white foot as a bare leg hung over the arm of her chair. Harlowe FelDougan, wooled and vested and long-jacketed, silent and shadowed under the flat brim of his hat, bent over her at her beckoning. She whispered to the darkness under the hat and over the scarf. The pistoleer bodyguard headed for the exit of the tent.

"The next couple of days are your call, Janus," Wulf said. "I'm breaking my battalion in half."

"What?" Teca jumped up.

"Some will be joining Hyper Khan's forces. The Catacomb Saint will take the others. What's left will travel with me down the White River. It should be frozen. We'll travel lightly."

"That's directly toward their main forces," Teca said under her breath. She rolled top scrolls to pull out one from underneath. It had thicker and darker markings across it. "Are you insane? And your maps are... lacking. If we only had my collection..." They waited for her to trace the papers' lines and topography. "They'll see you coming for days, and they can meet you at any of these points of their choosing."

"We'll dig in."

"You'll be right out in the open," Janus said, peeking down at Teca's fingers. "I'll take a section to circle south and come out..."

"Actually, I have something special intended for you."

"Are you counting on their loafmasses? The handfasting of a new batch of newives should be around this..."

"No," Wulf interrupted him again. He scratched at his curled hair and shaggy beard before adding, "No holidays, nothing, no reason will stop him from sending all his forces at me."

"You'll deserve what you get then," Teca said, clicking her tongue.

The Agent of MANN was able to somehow fold his insectoidal mechanics inward upon himself, and he now stood barely larger than Wulf inside the tent. He leaned over the others for a better view of the table.

"Anything to add?" Wulf asked, knowing the answer before he spoke.

"I am not here to advise, only to observe. Ignore me."

"Right. So how are we on arms estimates."

Janus continued to move pawns around the table. He and Teca would periodically fight over space and maps and figurines as he spoke. "The other generals haven't responded to inquiries, but we, the main battalion, cannot withstand another couple days like we've had. There are whole legions that report only one round left per man. These dwarves, those you've brought out of N'Midgaard, they are phenomenal, but even they can only do so much."

"They will continue to prove their worth," came the voice from the throne between sips of wine.

"Not if the Horde continues to bombard us at night," Janus

replied, looking to Wulf rather than to Sera. "We have to answer these assaults."

"The Horde can afford to scattershot us in the darkness. They have the resources. We can only respond in the day, but with precision."

"...if we last another night."

"Continue the archery training. If the war goes on much longer there will come a time, soon, when both armies are down to tooth and claw, and that is when we gain the upper hand. We just need more time."

"Yes, yes," Slayd murmured, still pacing, now puffing smoke from a wickedly twisted pipe, "time is of the essence." The cinnamon scent of his smoke blended well with the hot fruits of the incense wafting from Sera's trophies. "I'll see what I can do to slow things down in the meantime."

"Don't drink that," Wulf cautioned Teca as she reached for his mug.

"Why not?"

"It's poisoned."

Janus continued, "If the Necrophim battalions now stay separated, the dried rice out of the Granite Lands could last for months. But even the civilians can't survive on that alone. The lutefisk stores are depleted. The goats have stopped giving milk, so we'll start eating them tomorrow. The cattle will last for another week before we have to start sacrificing aurochs, but only because people keep dying nightly. In other words, the more successful we are, the greater we starve."

Slayd whispered, "The more that die, the more will live."

"Any granaries out here were pillaged by goblins years ago, even before the famine." Teca paused, glaring sideways at Wulf. She could not read his reaction. "We have to get to the Hills," she reiterated, slamming the hilt of her sword on the table. "It has everything we need. By all reports, the winter hasn't hit it fully yet. There'll be food. We can resupply. Ores! Fighters!"

"Not yet."

"Damn it!" Her hilt struck the table again, this time oversetting pawns and drinks. "Are you a coward or just a liar? The Needles are just waiting..."

"Where were the Librans when Plaag wandered the land?" Wulf yelled. "Where were your noble knights when Phaimon scarred the countryside?"

"I'll tell you exactly where they were," Dharke Parbreake said as he entered the tent, escorted by Harlowe.

"Oh, spare me this bullshit, please," Teca sputtered loudly. She collapsed, defeated, back into cushion and drapery, and spread out before finding her own goblet. "Don't tell me we're going to listen to more of this asshole's fairy tales."

The little man watched with great intent as Janus reordered map and figurine, but he spoke out to anyone who listened. "The 'noble' Northern Knights, the great Order of the Creed, was doing what they do best. Always looking backward at blood and navel. Always hiding. It's no wonder this land has been overrun by witches in my old Order's absence."

Teca could not help but laugh. "It's the Kalderan knights that've joined up with the Horde. They're the ones overrunning the people!"

"And that's why I left them, and that's why I'm here, to help in any way I can, but I've already told you everything I can about the supply line."

Sera adjusted the furs on her throne to sit forward. She had again been whispering under Harlowe's hat but now dismissed the pistoleer from the tent before speaking directly to Parbreake.

"Your insights on the supply route will be invaluable. It will be taken care of. But we are now wondering what you can tell us about this mysterious general Shriven."

"I know he must never be underestimated." Parbreake tried repeatedly to look the Crimson Queen in the eyes, but, failing, he made sure to look at everyone else around the table between his glances at the tabletop war games. "I... I was young, only a kid, really, but I remember the Cuckoo's Coup. He changed everything, Shriven did. Everyone was happy with the High Lord. These were prosperous years, but no one seems to remember them as such. It was almost overnight, and suddenly this monk that no one had ever even heard of — just some bookbinder out of some nowhere town — appears and catches the High Lord in bed with some rich merchant's wife. Story is, he rapes her in front of him before hanging the High Lord to death out the tower window by her garters. But the thing is, Shriven was able to get that far because he had raised a small army of all the most respected knights and paladins. No one knows how this unknown clerk had so suddenly won over the Order's best and brightest. We kept hearing about scandals and corruption but were never given any details as Shriven and most of the Order rounded up and executed most of the monks. Eventually he gave himself the new title of Grand Lord. He's collected all of the existing relics of Dhani Antony. He keeps the first High Lord's jawbone under his pillow. It leaks honey into his ears as he sleeps. He carries the prophet's member, *Caladcho'd*, into battle as a wand. It strikes his enemies with hemophilia, even as it curses him with the same."

As the Western Libran toyed with moving the figurine representing Shriven's forces, Slayd leaned into the man's neck to tongue tickle his ear. "I bet Shriven is not the only one to prefer his hand around another man's member," he hissed.

"Wha..." The little man twisted away, one hand on a dagger hilt, the other ready to pull his sword, but the sorcerer was nowhere near him, and no one else had seemed to notice. Everyone moved maps and pawns. The Libran straightened his belts and returned to the table to move horse-headed pieces. "Ah... if, um... Ammon Mars moves his forces away from the leadership..."

"As we will force him to," Wulf interjected.

"Then... Shriven's battalions will stay near the Army of Heaven's main tactical commander. He will trust no one other than himself, especially in this foreign land. He's probably planning some sort of coup anyway. I just can't imagine him taking orders."

"Can we expect to face knights on the battlefield?" Janus asked, finally moving away from the table.

"No..."

"Ha!" Teca scoffed.

"...they're fierce cavalry, but they'll stay as bodyguards and elite legions for the leadership. The paladins' skills? I don't see them as helpful in warfare. They'll spend their time in prayer."

"You think Libra has anything to do with their ignobility?" Teca asked. She did not expect or listen for an answer.

"I believe that *Angeliika*," he corrected, "long ago judged mankind unworthy of her blessing, or even her interest. She's left like all the gods, left us alone to face these pretenders, this Choir, on our own. Father Shriven... lord or general or whatever he now calls himself, committed the sin of pride, and he took many great men with him. My brother died in the Cuckoo's Coup. And this war is no different. Men only fool themselves and others thinking gods are behind them in their discourteous causes."

Into the tent hall, through drapes and ropes, came a guard chasing Parbreake's dog in vain. Before the man could untangle himself from pike rifle and draped doorway, the short canine began barking at Slayd. It would not stop. Janus dismissed the guard without looking up from the table.

Parbreake ruffled the short black fur on the dog's neck as he passed around the table to Wulf. His dog had not acknowledged his presence. He just barked and barked and barked his breathy bark. "I'm not sure what else I can add. Just don't underestimate him. He knows what your plans are before even ewe do. More than a few men and women were pulled from their beds in the middle of the night and hanged in public before the thoughts of sedition had even entered their minds." He took the drumstick of some shriveled bird from a platter of similarly colored meat and sniffed at it before walking back to present it to his dog. The animal ignored it to continue barking.

Slayd was lounging back in cushion and chaise, just glaring with slit eyes at the little dog and the little man, but he suddenly and serpentinely leapt up to grab his big bleeding sack before disappearing behind the exit curtains.

Parbreake struggled to talk while holding the dog's collar. "So am I, ah, assigned to the inner council now?" he asked, biting at different sides of the drumstick like a bored hawk. His pointed nose and chin gave the perfect appearance of a beak framed by the ebon feathers threaded in his hair and cape. Teca thought it obvious he had reapplied his paint shortly before his latest summoning. The dark line of ash crossing over his eyes was geometrically perfect. His blackened lips were precisely symmetrical. She had always thought it bold that the estranged Order of the Spirit never felt it necessary to explain how they never ran out of the cremains of the Prophet. Their paladins had a seemingly endless supply of soot and oils even generations after the exiled Order stole the body away and hid out in the West.

"There'll be other questions. You can go," Teca said, but Parbreake waited until he was dismissed by Wulf. The little man left while still holding the barking dog to his side.

The day for easy victories is done, Wulf thought. The next fortnight, should they even last the next few days, would determine the war.

Teca, as though reading his mind, jumped back to the table to move figurines representing the main forces southward and eastward more closely together. She said, "We need to regroup. Recall the rest of the Heirs of Aesar and head toward MANN lands. If you're not going to the Black Hills then stop spreading the generals so thin. We can at least have MANN at our backs."

"The United American Cities are not your ally," the Agent of MANN said mechanically. The few remaining in the tent hall looked to him. "I said, pay no attention to me. I am only an observer."

"The winter is only going to get worse," Wulf said. The figurines moved about the maps at his mental command. "Once we move away from Kaldera we'll never be able to travel back."

"Interesting point," Sera said laughing from behind, "you are all fighting for a land you know will soon be covered in ever-lasting ice. You are fortunate my Necrophim fight only for pleasure."

At this, Wulf and Teca sat to eat and drink while Janus continued to stare at terrain and pawns. All were silent. All were deeply in thought. An hour of eating and napping may have passed before Wulf realized that the silence in the hall was mirrored by that outside in the Army of Earth's mobile city. He kept expecting some scout or expressman to burst into the tent to announce that shelling had commenced for the night, but perhaps tonight was another holiday for followers of the Divine Choir. What was it tonight? Mandatum Monday? Eve of Norea's Night? The Army of Earth may actually get a good night's sleep for once.

But then the clanking and high striking of the blacksmiths began, and Wulf knew that if even he could feel the reverberations in his teeth, then the strikers would be heard and felt across the legions. But on his very command the smiths could not let up, not even for one night.

Janus was the only one left at the table. It would have appeared to any observer that he had tried out every combination of map, every possible adjustment of pawn and figurine. "Any thoughts on the purported spy or saboteur?" he asked. No one was sure whom he murmured to. He may have been talking to himself. He scratched at a scar that left an area of his head near a temple hairless.

"Intelligence suggests the person may not even know he's a saboteur," Wulf responded, retreating deeper into lounge and cloak. "We know that he's a product of Mother Inferior's brood pits, but he may not even know it." Even from the low divan he could see that the pieces had been arranged in a circle to surround just one other. *No*, he corrected himself. It was an audience around the one. With Janus, it was always an audience.

"He, she, or it is a danger nonetheless." Janus finally looked up from the table to see Sera watching Wulf intently. "Do you trust everyone you invite into this hall?"

A blue and faceted gaze turned sleepily to the ex-gladiator. "No. That's why you're here, so I can keep an eye on you."

"Building an army out of enemies invites treason at every turn."

Teca stood and gathered her sword and coat, tightening both around her in preparation for the certain outside chill. "But then he wouldn't be the Liege of Foes."

Janus took one last look at the chaos represented by the mess of the table, ignoring Wulf's last minute adjustment to map and pawn. He blew into his hands, despite how hot the long tent had become. "I know what you're planning. Somehow, I know. But you better do it soon. We have little time left."

There were no words as Janus put longcoat over jacket and hood over cap. He pulled long gloves over bracers, tied and buckled his coat and boots, and exited through drape and curtain, inviting the wind and clang of hammer and tongs into the hall for just a second.

Wulf immediately sank to the carpeted ground against the ashwood chair, unable or unwilling to restrain an exaggerated sigh that quickly turned into a near hysterical laugh. He found himself almost giggling at the table and its ramifications before him, at the imagined leagues of soldiers and families stretching out from beyond the hall in all directions beyond him, and at the war that raged in all those same directions across the entirety of the land. His back tickled upward over his neck in anticipation of the cold embrace of the Crimson Queen's bare legs and arms emerging from fox and manticore. He would not have been surprised to find that his eagerness was not that but crickets or newts crawling his collar. Little would surprise him these days.

"Uneasy lies the tongue that wears a crown," she hissed.

"I'm no king," he chuckled.

"Not yet."

And the *Goblin Revenant* giggled. They had been following Wulf around since he had taken the Army out into the middle plains. It made sense. It was on the plains that he had led them and betrayed them all those years ago. If the ghosts of the Grand Mob were going to haunt him, it would be out on the plains. But did they laugh with him or at him? He often wondered if anyone else saw the spectral goblins, but he knew they appeared here for him alone. Although, if anyone else saw them, it would have been Sera. She was well-familiar with both haunting and haunted.

~

Slayd's humming reached a crescendo as he approached the ruinous shelter. The crumbling structure was now mostly a bunker — all exposed cinder blocks and top-heavy cement. It looked to have long ago sunk partly into a prairie familiar with flooding. Now this bomb shelter of the Old Ones was no longer alone on the plains. It was surrounded by the Army of Earth, with Slayd's explicit command that it not be disturbed. Scouts stumbled over and upon it a day before the Army had, and the sorcerer had immediately placed his mark and word on the ancient cellar. Slayd's hum turned to song as he approached the buried doors. It was all he could do to drown out the sound of the barking. That damn dog of that idiot Western Libran always seemed to be following him around. He was no where to be seen now, but Slayd could still hear that maddening *bark, bark, bark*. The inbred mutt ignored everyone else, while Slayd was stuck hearing its raspy yips and yaps all day and night, whether it was near or not. It had become increasingly difficult to meditate and plan, and so he sang his little tune to get the barking out of his head.

"Flies in the buttermilk, pretty as you.

Flies in the buttermilk, pretty as you."

His were the only tracks leading in and out, for he had prepared most of the séance earlier in the day, now just waiting for the best celestial arrangement of the night.

Wyrmwood, dark as stale piss, stared down and moved into alignment.

The echoing strikes of the dwarven smiths and the grunting of Miss Mowgli's exertions continued to interrupt his song. Her heavy and heavily furred and belted boots stomped up behind him, and with a wheeze and a snort she pulled Slayd's cart to a stop. He took no time to rummage through the cart's curtains to pull out two large sacks — one still stained through with blood, the other quite a bit larger than the first. He took the bags with him as he crawled down into the frozen entrance to the archaic bomb shelter.

It was a Coward's Moon, and the meager light of clouded stars was not enough to penetrate down into the bunker. The sorcerer went to work in the darkness. He had earlier placed candles in an earthbound heptagram, but now went to work, by the light of a tiny flame flickering from the end of his tongue, on completing the antiprism prison by placing even more candles pulled from Tormalco's Robe of Folding into geometrically and geomantrically prescribed nooks and crannies. He erased the visible portion of the heptagram with chalk formed by the dark rituals of the world's first necromantic plankton. The candles, moulded from the fat of inbred epileptics, the sorcerer lit with a holy flame he stole out of the Horde's capital city on some holiday or other. He had been keeping it safe and burning in his gut so long now and was relieved beyond mercy to be rid of the indigestion. The air in the shelter burned thickly as he scratched wards and runes into metal and concrete walls with a claw dipped in Richard Furman's Inkwell. He wrote Skamania County graffiti in the translucent blood of a pregnant Maid. He corrupted Anasazi aliens by drawing with the tears of a Texas horned lizard.

Finished, he stood back to admire his invisible work. He double and triple-checked the angles of the antiprism before dancing *La Carmagnole* throughout the tight bunker. Round and round he went, calling up Cajun spirits to dance with him

"I'll get you back, in spite of you,
I'll get you back, in spite of you.
I'll get you back, in spite of you.
Pride is a sin, my darlin.'
Flies in the buttermilk, pretty as you.
Flies in the buttermilk, pretty as you.
Flies in the buttermilk, pretty as you.
Envy's a sin, my darlin.'"

He was remiss that no one would see his dance. It was sublime. For a second he humored the thought of inviting Miss Mowgli down to witness his transcendent steps, but he quickly chastised himself for his vanity and for forgetting her pedestrian tastes.

"Cat's in the cream jar, held 'til it's blue.

Wrath is a sin, my darlin.'"

Where his dancing disrupted the scrawled polygon, he sprinkled "Salt of Edith" to fill the invisible gaps. The candles had burned enough. The bunker's atmosphere was fatty and humid. The stars and planets and comet were aligned. He could sense it in the base of one of his brains as the other screamed out protests for what he was about to do.

The larger of Slayd's two sacks squirmed as he dropped it into the hidden base of the heptagons. From one of his endless pockets he impossibly pulled the great grimoire, the *Annihilation Cantripticus*, to run long fingers lovingly over the lying demon hide of the binding. The tome's follicles shivered under Slayd's touch, while the arthritic cracking of the old hemp cords brought a tingle to both his nethers and his lips. The pages were threatening to tear beneath his claws, but he knew better. The book lived, and it aged, and he had no doubt it would outlive anyone or anything living today. Except him, of course.

"*Nyarl ot ath arl thar antae lo tar. Phytane lo lhar. Prothyorl honeytrap ethanoyl toh lor. Hyperon aar.*"

Slayd's eyes, so clear after his recent molting, now blackened and caught the reflection of stars that had not spied on Earth since the continents broke. The words of the *Annihilation Cantripticus* were not spoken in his sibilance but in the voice of some Hyperborean god-priest ancient before glaciers approached the First Men.

"*Enthalpy rotha nytha orr ny lhar. Tholar rapnar.*"

As he chanted the translation, he added ingredients to a boiling stew, to the tiny kettle spitting and smoking over Nim's Brazier. From impossible pockets he added a baby's last laugh, wart of spiderwort, lip of cowslip, and seed of snail seed. He pricked his fingers adding porcupine grass and snake root and made sure not a drop was wasted. The tingle became a full-on vibration.

From a toothy pouch he pulled one of his old ears. It had dried instead of decomposed. He did not miss his ears. They often itched and were superfluous to one of such heightened senses. Besides, there was little worth listening to in recent years. Into the brew it went.

"*Polyantha lothar. Et eat eth arr.*"

At the final words he added a cotton currency to the stew. Slayd was one of the few living who could read the ancient text on the burning bill, and he read it aloud before the image of the long-faced old crone rolled beneath the boil.

"Now, how does one entice the libidinous Watcher who has everything…"

The sorcerer had been waiting for the opportunity the bunker afforded. Here was a localized source of ancient depravity, a focused center of such extreme haunting that nearby ley lines bent and curved their usually straight energies toward this seemingly insignificant prairie. High voices, long-ago soaked into the very concrete of the underground shelter, echoed the cries of raped Old Ones. Children and mothers sobbed of familial betrayal in scattered voices, but Slayd's smoking charms captured their screams, imprisoned their anguish, and they soon began to chant his spell back to him and the dim light of the chamber.

"Polyantha lothar. Et eat eth lolythar arr."

Slayd now took the smaller of his two sacks and placed the congealed hinny's head in a close corner. The abundant candle-created shadows stretched almost immediately toward the corner. They danced at the song of the raped and collected, filling the corner of the bunker. The hinny's head also danced as Slayd stepped back to his brazier. Its flesh split and reached, was consumed by unseen maggots and regurgitated in voluminous plenty. Even Slayd's cleared eyes could not pierce the darkness completely, but he could still decipher what the meat had been pulled to form. Fleshy wings hung over a sack body of cartiledge and tendons and muscle. The sticky hinny skull, gloried by a turning and red mist, peeked from the shadow, its jaw hanging. At the reverberating and metallic voice, Slayd fell to his knees and covered where his ears used to be with palsied hands. It was a voice full of the crying hysterics of unbaptised infants. Boney souls vivisected the babies, squeezing exposed lungs to produce the avatar's voice. Slayd would never be able to forget the image or sound.

"What art thou man (if man at all thou art)
that in dead and deaf fields hast dared summoned
the Promise of Wealth — Gob Mammon-Gammon
— greatest son o' sons o' God, greatest son
o' daughters o' men, greatest 'low the Sky,
greatest lord o' kings' vaults and hollow Earth."

Slayd hesitantly lowered his hands and spit new blood into his little kettle. Scowling, pointed teeth finding the bent candlelight, the sorcerer's words rose angrily above the sound.

"Coy angel, coy watcher, you know who I am. I am Melchyor Slayd of Ophidia, of Ouroboros, of America, of Quantum Prime Earth. I am Slayd Great'son and Lesser'son. Heir of Aesar. Wyrmbane. Slayer of the prismatic dragon of Yellowstone, Ashkelon the Gloomily-Chained and Sulpher Thrown. One time Sin Eater. One time Lord of Magog, one time Emerere of the Tower of Gog. Now and forever the slayer of Tormalco the Endless, the Everman, the Always." He took one last side-eyed look down into the *Annihilation Cantripticus* before flipping it closed with a sandled foot. "And you, coy being, lessen yourself by pretending not to know me, even after I called upon such an elegant choir to announce your arrival. Does not such a presentation deserve a gift? How do you keep the rest of your angelic cohort from knowing you have such an unappreciative tin ear?" His vision spun as he spoke, and he knew that all the wards under his robes had been painted and carved and branded and tattooed in vain. The angel was burning him from the inside out. He could not believe it. He did not think it possible. Could it be that he was actually sweating?

"Vain-glorious, trick-peddler, dost thou not
weet thy boon is damnation in boiled blood!"

He could only manage a whisper from a parched to cracking throat, from a disintegrating tongue. "Yes, yes... how very medieval." Slayd's fingers, secretions flaking from sharp tips, scratched gleaming paleo-runes in the very air before the darkness. "Am... I... the only one who laments the loss of articulate inventiveness in our celestial beings?"

The clank, clank, clanking of the angel's voice, as it screamed in pain, mirrored the smith's striking from somewhere out above. Precious golden wire with diamond barbs suddenly flew around the red theophany, restraining wing and skull. The barbed wire's glittering twinkle tore though both meat and shadow.

And Slayd hissed, "Such disrespect for someone who knows your True Name, *Ga'babriel Noah Ben 52.*"

The creature roared again, wires tightening at the sound. Its muscled hood fell to the side to reveal infinitely faceted rubies in its hinny skull sockets. Slayd knew that to look deeply into the precious stones would invite a madness of questioning self-mutilation.

From between glimmering gold and sparkling diamond, from beneath muscle and red matter, birthed amniotic yet pristine coins.

The clinking of the treasure on concrete sounded similar to the supernatural being's whimpers.

"Yes, yes," Slayd said as he cleared his throat of dust, "I'm sure you are used to a more rabble-tainted lot — genuflecting tithers justifying their dead faith with copper, but I have no interest in your worldly rewards." His blood had cooled back to chilling room temperature, and he was able to stand and walk back to his possessions. From a small crate he removed more ichorous ink, more worn chalk, fatty candles, and a sigil-covered lantern. He tasted the air of the bunker with a blistered tongue before untying the restraints on the largest of the sacks. Inside was Ivy of the Grove, with mouth gagged, eyes blindfolded and limbs bound. Her earthen hair was disheveled, her eyes obviously wide beneath the cloth.

"You'll find that I am interested in other fare," Slayd said. His voice had returned to full measure, and he went to work emboldening the antiprism prison.

Bark! Bark! Bark!

"Flies in the buttermilk, pretty as you.

Pride is a sin, my darlin.'"

LIX

My love's lips part, an early peony
pale and pink, sleepily at my approach
Mouths pinching pecks of sweet lemony tea
as honey patch drips from summer's encroach.
Spread bud I bring him, phobic his reproach
be shrouded in umbra of tomb and time,
affection more favoring flea and roach.
So toward I walk forward at witch time,
for my sheets are cold but my sweet's are slime
grown from the garden of love and life's absence
as he slumbers on damp granite and lime,
renewed chastity ever his penance.
But o'joy, does my boy lie back, well-fed
from dewy gift upon dead featherbed.

—***Unknown***

Che last components were the packages of chocolate Slayd had hoarded from the armory. He would have had difficulty describing the difficulty he had over the previous months keeping the sweet bricks from, first the peregrination's stray children and, more recently, the families of the Army of Earth. The vermin seemed to have been able to literally sniff it out. If he had not had Miss Mowgli to guard his cart day and night, the second summoning may not have occurred. He was not sure what he would have used for an offering.

The stars were still aligned.

Slayd's other ear boiled over the brazier.

The raped revenant harmonized their protestations.

The stacks of chocolate bars began to bloat when the ghostly choir hit their crescendo. Sweet bubbles popped and melted. Already there was a dark pool forming and becoming indistinguishable from the collecting shadows. Eventually, as Slayd stepped to stand behind the bound, blindfolded, and gagged Ivy he could no longer tell the difference between the bubbling and popping chocolate fountain and the darkness it continually perpetuated itself in. The rising and falling pillar buzzed with the wings of numerous insects somehow caught within the ooze.

The celestial syzygies were not going to last long, and the fatty candles were fading fast, so Slayd was going to waste little time waiting for the angel to compose himself.

"The Promise of Father, I presume? The angelic Chem-Oshmelech, Bronze Swain of Hysterical Cradle, courteous prince and patron to blah, blah, blah..." Slayd's nimble claws scratched the very atmosphere of the bunker, carving one fiery rune after another into the very air itself. "But you were once known by another name, were you not — your True Name?"

There were winged things trapped in the viscosity of Chem-Oshmelech's transubstantiated form — owlets and horseflies and bats — and their struggling wings beat the air. Slayd was hit by a blast of wind that extinguished the candles and sent him slamming back against the near concrete. In the darkness, his long hands were not his own, and they scrambled out from him, finding individual nooks and crannies for each finger to imbed itself in. When each nail and knuckle found a home, his arms betrayed him and twisted and turned until every one of his finger bones broke or became dislocated.

But the holy flame Slayd had stolen was not easily snuffed. The candles fizzled back to life, and the sorcerer, with a lap of hands twisted beyond familiarity, could only watch as a continually spewing pillar of chocolate and shadow oozed slowly forward. From the rolling darkness struggled a calf's head with fur matted and eyes starkly dun. It bellowed, and, for the first time, Slayd saw Ivy react and cringe at a sound. Chocolate spittle from the calf's snout squirmed like leeches on the concrete, spelling out runes older than the Old Ones. Slayd understood enough.

"No book ever held True Name of Ancient of Days!"

And he knew what he would see before he could turn his head fast enough to see it. The *Annihilation Cantripticus* burst into flames both organic and violent. The smoke screamed. The flakes scattered in an unfelt wind. The tome was ash in a matter of seconds. Slayd bit his tongue, his gums, and the inside of his cheeks. Even his broken fingers were clenched.

The calf head belched, and sputum danced to form new symbols.

"What is morsel? So immaculate! So unsullied!"

Slayd painfully answered, "A... peace... offering... for you... your majestickiness."

A molasses not unlike the substance of the creature began to hang and drip from every crack in the ceiling. It was not quite the color of chocolate, not quite the color of blood. The ooze shuffled toward Ivy, and, as it leaned to caress her, the buzzing of insect wings rose to an ecstasy.

And with a sudden brilliance of ozone and sulfur, the bunker was awash in white light, and, when the starkness glittered and slowly dissipated, being eaten back up again by the slithering shadows, Slayd stood, wincing and smiling while popping his knuckles back into place, before the ignited heptagramatic anitiprism. It gleamed of laser beams but gave off no light. It smoldered from one reality into the next but gave off no heat. And in the middle of the faceted crisscrossing no-lights, the avatar of Chem-Oshmelech could not move. The pillar still bubbled, boiled, and rolled, but the sweet being was held in place by archaic ward and word.

"Yes, yes, I would never possibly expect such a mundane binding circle to hold you indefinitely, your turgidness."

The calf head, gloried by a darkly prismatic halo of chocolate spittle, struggled to appear before expectorating, *"Fool! You trap me here with morsel!"* Again, ooze dripped toward Ivy's blindfolded face. Her simple shirt, skirt, and trousers tore to sudden shreds as the pillar loomed, but some light source Slayd could not determine caught nigh invisible sigils on her neck and chest. The pale angelic runes circling her shoulders, winding down her arms and thighs, shined under their own light the closer Chem-Oshmelech dripped and popped.

The blind calf bellowed. The wings buzzed and then were quiet.

"This one promised to another!" the darkly slithering slaver wrote out on the floor.

"Hmmmm... interesting..." Slayd had paused writing in the air to watch the unfolding scene. The black slits his pupils had become grew even thinner. His lipless mouth moved as he read silently.

The shambling fountain of theophanous goo retreated the few inches it could in the binding lights, and Ivy's pale sigils dimmed to almost nothingness.

"You are correct about one thing, your glutinousness, that no amount of research or scrying will uncover your True Name. In all of recorded history, no ape has ever put it to paper."

The calf head now struggled also against frosted tongs that had burst upward from the concrete floor. Other similar tongs, covered equally in rust and ice, had hold of the viscous pillar from all directions.

Chocolate hardened and shattered on all sides from the frigid metal's touch. When it could tear away from the pinchers, the calf's mouth would spit temptations, but Slayd ignored them.

"But one of your divinely choral cohorts recently owed me a boon, and he was more than eager to vouchsafe any obligation away with what he saw as an answer to such an innocuous request."

The angel's True Name turned in the air before Slayd, burning the space like molten plasma.

"But it is the boon that I now demand of you, Adamah Mikhaelaheliel, that should most concern you."

~

"You could have asked for anything!" Ivy yelled up to the top of the cart. It was deep in the night, but it appeared that few people slept. There was too much noise from the smithing yurts, too much revelry from the Midgardian legions, and reports and literal explosive echoes from the southern front for anyone to totally settle in for the night. Everyone was waking their beasts of burden, arming themselves, and searching for any and all word on just which end of the battalion the Horde was shelling.

A familiar short-haired dog was following him. Its incessant barking was causing Slayd to rub his temples, to cover his missing ears. With all of the sudden commotion, Ivy had no choice but to raise her voice.

"Not true," Slayd said, grimacing before yawning from the top of his tall cart as it rocked from side to side on its plodding momentum. Except for the yapping of the following dog, he seemed oblivious to the anxiety beneath him, sleepy eyes content only on what was just before him, occasionally slapping Miss Mowgli with the quirt at the end of a long handle. Usually, the leather straps just hung down in front of her face as she grunted and pulled the high and narrow cart through slush and over frozen mud. "Do not believe the territorial propaganda. Each of the 'heavenly choristers' may have claims to divinity, but they are not omnipotent. They make their extravagant 'promises' and stick to their area of supernatural expertise. They each have a different role in the Brotherhood's pantheon, and their abilities reflect that role. Your trealcy admirer, Chem-Oshmelech, is the patron Watcher of the tithing-men. It is this blessing and it is his guardianship of the Fire of IAM that concerns us. Removing his blessing from the Horde, as I have done, even for just a short amount of time, may very well turn the tide of the war."

Ivy stepped around rotted meat that had been placed at the entrance to a yurt. Whenever any soldier's family thought they could spare it, the waste was left outside in evenings to lure tapeworms out of their bodies as they slept — as if anyone could these days.

"But you could have asked for so much more!" she shouted up to him but was not sure if he had heard her. Miss Mowgli, panting loudly, had stopped in front of a shabby tent secured soundly to a base of thick pallets. It was a tall tent that caught a wind blowing above the Army's mobile city, but it was not a very wide tent. Before Ivy realized it, Slayd had leapt from the cart and entered the tent, flaps and drapes folding and parting at his approach. She ran in behind him before they closed.

She had another question for him, but she stifled it when the look of the tent's interior shocked her mute. It was smaller than she had imagined, even though it was bigger on the inside than the outside. But it was the lack of any furnishings that left her stunned. Except for generals and lords, everyone in the Army had to travel lightly, but each family or soldier at least had some scavenged furs or pallets to their name. Slayd's marquee was almost empty. Lit to each corner by the twisting green light of a Leyden jar he set upon an equally twisted oaken staff — both pulled from any one of the infinite pockets in his robe — she could see no hangings or furniture. But by the electric light she could now see the swirls and scratches of painted designs covering the interior.

"I have resided in the eyes of expired gods," Slayd said, sneering at her obvious confusion. "I have looked out from windows set in the skull of the Colossus of Ophidia, and I have sat in a three millennia old redwood mansion. I have lounged on balustrades overlooking faithful geysers and the towers of mad magicians. No king has ever lived greater than I."

From behind her, Ivy could hear Miss Mowgli struggle with pulling the tall cart through the low entrance. It sounded as though she fought for her very life against the tent's fly and doorway wrappings.

"Yet here I now live, amongst the barking and droppings of dogs and others. All I own resides in a cart pulled by a mannish oaf. Let no being question Melchyor Slayd's loyalty, for the answer is in the question."

The cart appeared beside him, and Miss Mowgli immediately pulled its curtains aside to reveal the weird collection of components and ingredients Ivy had often been reprimanded for peeking at. But dwarfing the cushioned bulbs and globes, the black honeycombs and rat cages, the silk worms on tiny looms, the precariously stacked spice cabinets and card catalogs, and the hanging rows of dried herbs and genitals, was the giant artifact known as the Clockwork Wyrm. Filigreed and ornately sealed with every manner of precious ore and stone, the great egg glittered at all points and in all colors in the light of the Leyden jar. The egg was bigger than even Miss Mowgli, and she stumbled lifting it out of the litter of the cart.

"Careful, woman!" Slayd caught the great egg with one hand and lifted it aloft while placing a base for it onto the open ground with his other hand. "Now shoo, shoo." He flipped a long-fingered hand backward as he rummaged through the interior of the cart. "Keep watch over the outside, feel free to eat any vermin you can catch." Miss Mowgli was gone when he emerged from his ingredients, and he skittered up the side of the giant egg to its top. He had an eye loupe placed over one side of his face, attached around his head by tube and wire. The eye looking out at the end was not entirely his own. It was blood-shot and dark and he squinted as he looked through the loupe's eye at a panel of spiraled filigree that appeared under a gesture of intricate hand signals. He crawled over the extravagant surface of the egg, putting any shadows behind him.

"How did you know the angel wouldn't be able to get me?" Ivy asked as she counted the number of bloodstones on the egg compared to the number of azure iris gems.

"Hmmm... oh, are you still here?" Slayd had gingerly opened a small panel with the very tips of two claws and was now reaching into the new cloacae with a pair of tiny tongs that reminded Ivy of Chem-Oshmelech's binding. He ever so slowly pulled out a pencil-thin Carolina ruby, and with a flip of the tongs he tossed it to her. "For your troubles." She lackadaisically tossed it into the litter of the cart and stood on her tiptoes, trying to see Slayd's work. She quickly realized that he talked more to himself than to her.

"What the Clockwork Monarch ultimately lacked in foresight, he more than made up for in ingenuity. This is truly a remarkable accomplishment amongst a long list of remarkable accomplishments. But why have a dragon breathe fire? So uninspired. So anti-innovation." From out of his robe he took a small crystal cylinder, thicker but shorter than the removed gem. The loupe's eyeball squirmed but eventually focused on the seemingly empty cylinder.

"What's that?" Ivy asked. She climbed the precious metals and stones of the egg, but the sorcerer kicked her down.

"The Bastard Ancient, Tormalco…"

"Your old master," Ivy interrupted.

Slayd grimaced and pulled the apparatus from his head, but still he tried to catch the flickering light of the tent in the glass vial. "Tormalco, in any off time that he was not obsessively looking to prolong his already nigh immortal existence, was determined to investigate and expunge what he saw as a very deep-rooted corruption in the continent. This taint, he deduced, was very much literal and less metaphorical. To the means of its abolition, the Everman apparently looked to the twin philosophies of nature and science, shotgun marrying them in a ceremony presided over by the most glorious of techno-magicks."

Ivy circled the egg, watching the electrical reflections of the Leyden Jar fight over the tent's interior and her own outstretched hands. She wondered how the magnetic elemental would react to being let out of the jar.

"To this end, the Always emulated the superior organism known as the virus. I won't confuse you with the details, but he eventually constructed iron golems mimicking this superior organism, and he apparently shrank them down, fitting thousands, perhaps millions into this vial. And these microscopic automatons have eaten from the Tree, for they know themselves and their neighbors, and they can use the iron of man's blood to reproduce at an astonishing rate. They would put a midgardian to shame. But, if I'm correct, herein lies the genius of my old… mentor. These invisible iron invaders search out certain people specifically. In terms you could understand, they are programmed to only hunt certain…"

"Genotypes," Ivy muttered. She had been picking at a particularly ornate pearl panel, and Slayd leaned down to swat her hand away.

He wetted his finger before inserting it somewhere in the panel. "Yes, yes, well I guess you appreciate the general idea, if not the absolute inspiration, so I suppose I cannot expect you to fully recognize the genius of combining what I have nicknamed the Nidhogg Virus with this masterfully designed clockwork creation. You see, the viral army still requires life, and thanks to the dark dwarves that our illustrious crimson queen, Sera, brought out of N'Midgaard's capital, adjustments have been made to this clockwork egg that bring me one step closer to that goal." The vial was inserted somewhere deep into the egg.

"Your tiny pathogen is not the only thing without life," Ivy said, knocking on silver and gold but receiving only hollow reverberations.

"Yes, yes, with an anxiety that almost amounts to agony, I collect the instruments of life around me, that I might infuse a spark of being into the lifeless things that lie at my feet. For now this masterpiece is only one of unmoving art and a safe place for Tormalco's legacy. For while his relative contemporary, the Clockwork Monarch, excelled in courtesy, he was as equally ambitious in his sense of humor. This wondrous contraption was given as a peace offering to the rulers of Ophidia, but the literal key to its automation has never been gifted or even seen. Some ridiculous example of ridiculous checks and balances, I suppose. A deterred deterrent."

"I could have escaped from your bonds anytime I wanted to. Wulf taught me how once." Ivy had moved back to the litter and had quickly and expertly tied fairy silk scarves around her wrists. She relaxed her hands and slipped her fingers out just as quickly.

Slayd landed next to her with more sound than she would have expected. "Then, pray tell, little descendent of a burning grove, why didn't you?"

"I still had more to learn from you."

"And now?" he signed, tossing tiny tools back into the cart before snatching back scarves he immediately wrapped around her neck.

"Thank you." She embraced his torso for a quick hug before running from the marquee.

The camps were scrambling with activity. Back out in the marching city, Ivy was assailed by more sounds than the night should have afforded. Soldiers gathered arms while their families saddled six-legged horses. Trucks and combines sputtered to life while people dug and fortified the mud that tires had hours ago settled into. The shorthair dog was still near, sniffing and barking at the edges of Slayd's tent. Ivy could imagine the lines appearing in the sorcerer's pale scales as he rubbed his temples against the constant sound.

There was no moon to light the sudden deployment, but Ivy held her new favorite possession to star and camp stove to get a better look. Escaping bonds was not the only thing Wulf had taught her over the past few years. She had become quite adept at picking pockets, and never had she encountered so many pockets as in Slayd's robes. They were deep, and their numbers and temperature were almost paralyzing, so she snatched the first thing she could feel. It was a tiny swath of some sharp violet herb tied together by the hair of some person or plant. She tucked it away after sniffing the little jagged leaves. She expected it to smell ugly, but it had no scent at all.

LX

You cannot help
but
love Him
as He folds them
to the furnace of his bosom
they run
like moths to cold flame
and hot Heaven the children came

—unknown

The Rocky Mountain evenings had been pink for so many days now that Harlowe was afraid he had lost his direction when, in his final evening with his escort, the forests and peaks were devoid of any color. Instead, he would now be heading toward the jagged tips of clear mountains and speckled cliffs dropping into woodlands that could not even promise a hint of even the slightest viridian. And the sky was no better. Each day it was appearing as an even starker pale. The sun was smeared behind colorless clouds for most of its zenith. It could not be found during light hours. And so Harlowe had looked forward to the set, to the blossoming cotton of each evening. But those days were now gone forever. He knew that only the dual reflection of cloud and snow was ahead of him.

The crack of Br'er Griz's snipe rifle shattered the frozen silence of the canyons. It returned as a rumble through drift and teeth that Harlowe feared would set off an avalanche, but it only took mere seconds for the peaks and drops to return to their stillness. He imagined the slow alighting of the snow flakes to make some sort of whisper, but all they did was settle and add to a blanket rises and drops that, for all he knew, would last until the end of days.

Harlowe and his last escort, Br'er Griz, were perched in the sparse treeline separating the dipping forests from the slides of ice stretching to black peaks. There was not even any gray out in these valleys, just the stark dichotomy Harlowe found away from the Army and the war. It was all so loud. So many voices, all of them talking to him at once until he would always realize that none of them were talking to him, none at all. Out beyond the touch of war, until it lasted, he could see clear again. And the silence, the free and wide-open blacks and whites of silence, was so clearing and cleaning of his congested mind, that he could barely even notice the constant screaming of the horror train's whistle in his head.

It had been a fortnight since he had seen anyone other than the escorts that Wulf had sent to protect him, and it had been days since he had seen anyone other than Br'er Griz. The war seemed so far away.

Br'er Griz's long rifle spat again, and again the air and land vibrated and echoed for just an extra second before the air righted itself into a solid, stolid nature. The rifle was taller than the man, and he sat in an unorthodox position — short legs straight out in front of him, rifle parallel as a third appendage over a fallen and snow-packed tree truck. The scope he looked through was comical, large and bulbed, but when Harlowe peeked out from beneath the brim of his hat, he could see down the immense slide of wood and rock into entirely other forests. From the distance, unaided, Harlowe could see his pursuers as mere specks, as merely tricks of the eye, but Br'er Griz knew them intimately through his scope.

Harlowe took a step in the direction he would soon head, steadying his boots in the new layer of snow, sinking down to the hardened old layer. He would be alone again soon after many months. It was not the gradual lessening of his escorts that bothered him. He often forgot they were with him. But he missed Ivy dearly. When she was near him, the banshee shriek of the *Loco* dissipated. He tried embracing the frozen silence of the altitude, using it to smother the demon whistle, but it took constant concentration.

Br'er Griz fired again. The smoke from the rifle's barrel was quickly extinguished by the reflecting light from above and below.

"That should be all'a them," the sniper said. "Ah'll keep looking, just to be sure, but you can head out whenever. This here is the end of the road for me. You're on your own from here on out. May God shine on your face and the sun on your back."

But Harlowe did not move immediately. Without the rose of a sunset he was not entirely sure of his southwesterly direction. Why had the horned woman chosen him and him alone to disrupt the Horde's western supply line?

"Does it even exist?" he had heard Ivy ask Mistress Sera, the Red Queen of the Necrophim. The two of them often talked as though he could not hear them.

"This 'ghost train?' His hometown of 'chicken deputies and killer clowns?' They didn't. But now? Who can say? The western desert affects every person differently. People have always tended to dismiss anyone who has traveled from one end of the sands to the other as entirely mad, but that is because it is perfectly natural to fear that which you do not understand. You have no doubt heard of Styx? The old Lesser took credit for writing the original *Fallo Terminus*, but it was in fact written by his 'brother,' Acheron Antony. Was Acheron insane, his writings the delusion of an ill mind? Did the infernal desert dictate the future to him, or did the enchanted sands grant Acheron the power to mold the future to his liking? If the desert can imbue one with the ability to change the future, than why not the past? Both affect reality. The tales Harlowe FelDougan tells you about his past, his journey, his home and youth — are they his memories or his creation? And, in the end, is this supposed power of 'madness' any different than the ability that each one of us daily wields?"

Harlowe remembered but did not understand. Hers was the authority. His was the duty. He would find out how the Western Librans were supplying the Horde, and he would destroy it or subvert it.

"I'm gonna head out," he said to the mountains in front of him. There was no echo. He could not pierce the silence.

"Right," Br'er Griz said, still scanning the darks and lights of the trees and valleys.

"What're you gonna do?"

The old sniper had finished dismantling the scope, placing fine lenses and copper rings into a velvet-lined case, but he still squinted far down into the steep deeps. Harlowe would have been surprised to see if the man could have ever gotten out of the snowbank he leaned in. He could not say how his stocky arms and legs, and the abundance of quilt he wore, had gotten him into his sitting position in the first place.

"Well, pistoleer, ah'm going to tell you what ah'm going to do. You may be surprised to hear that ah'm going to sign up with the Army of Heaven."

Harlowe did not move, but he could feel his twin *Codys*, one at each thigh, oiled cleanly and surrounded by rawhide, over and beneath the cotton and leather of his clothes, tucked within the wool of his long vest and longer raincoat. He knew exactly where they were in relation to his twisted fingers and ever-mutilated hands. He did not think he had moved those hands, but the chains of Brig, the iron rings he still wore, jingled somewhere along his shoulders or arms as they moved against each other.

"Now, hear me out, you old piece of work," Br'er Griz continued. "You know ah'm just a hired hand, just some headhunter from a time when even you were in your nappies, probably, but hear me out. But ah been fighting for free all these years now, for your Liege of Foes. See, me and him go back to the start of the war, back when he was still drumming up fighters from both sides of the rivers, from the ranchers and ranges, and the good and the ill. See, you know ah had spent years searching for my son who was taken as a baby so long ago, but ah had settled down, even from my headhunting, on a farm actually not far from here to the east. Long story short, ah had finally gotten word of my son, as he was heading up a group of banditos far away in Old Cowtown. Your Liege of Foes had liberated the town from the Army of Heaven's slave drivers, and all he wanted in return was the release of my boy and his banditos to fight in his war. So ah joined up too.

"Them was two good years. Two glorious years, fighting along-side my boy and his men. We weren't paid, but your Liege of Foes let us to the spoils. He's a good man. But here's the thing. You know my boy is dead about a moon ago. Ah'm getting old and this war has too. Ah know the winter won't last forever like some say, but it's still seeping into my bones. My reason and time for the Army of Earth is up. Guarding you along these paths, getting you to the last passes here, this here is my last job. It's time to settle down someplace comfortable. Ah'm talking of hot skies and thighs, and your Liege of Foes can't promise that. You know, all ah got to do is last through one battle on the side of Heaven's Army and ah get promised my own little wife and a plot of land somewhere nice in the Territories. They call them newives, you know, and, sure, they may have been betrothed before, but ah don't need much."

"You is a simple man, Griz."

"Right, you understand. You should do the same, after you're done with whatever the Hell they're sending you out to no-man's land for."

"Yep. Maybe I should. Find a nice quiet spot to settle in. Forever and forever."

"Right. Damn, look at this scene. A man couldn't do worse, ah'll tell you."

"Yep."

Gunshot shattered the frozen silence of the canyons before the air righted itself into a solid, stolid nature

LXI

...in the embrace of a fake fate's kiss
that when he thinks he is freed from man's rule,
hidden from gods' decision,
the Warrior thinks he is no one's tool
—scrawled on the walls of the King of All's lower halls

The Queen of Quartz had small sleeper cults embedded deeply in every major state of the inner lands, and her first order of business was to consolidate them in the middle cities of the continent to sow discord. It took years, but the larger populations, apart from the GAU and the separate lands of Automaton the Perverted, fell. She and Easarean were immediately there to pick up the pieces.

As the Queen indoctrinated new thousands into her faith, her lover gathered militia and mercenary, ex-royal guard and barony elite, and marched his new quickly-trained army on outlying fiefdoms. Now, controlling all the land's oil, he recovered ancient machines of war and turned his eyes toward the Pervert.

Drunk with the power of worship, the Queen of Quartz demanded the earth pull its blessing from the realm of the Pervert, and, in fear and obedience, it did. Iron churned and molten filled caverns emptied. Geysers dried and steaming springs rerouted. The immense power Automaton the Perverted derived from geothermal sources suddenly disappeared.

Filled to the brim with an ecstasy only the faith of a million could gift, the Queen of Quartz called forth the earth to now bring Hell to the surface, and, in terror and awe, it acquiesced. In its adulation for its queen, the land buckled and cracked, spewing melting rock and metal, glass stone and its own brilliant blood into the sky. Forests burned and calderas simmered over the middle of the nation, smoke and ash choking lung and heaven. The immense power Automaton the Perverted derived from sunlight quickly waned.

It was then that Easarean's growing forces struck. His armies, fueled by the passion for their queen and the indomitable presence of their giant general, rolled over the kingdoms of the Pervert's machine men. The legions left nothing standing in the robot cities, no emotionless metal face unbroken in the purge of what their queen preached as life's abomination.

All hail the King of All.

In the aftermath, Easarean surveyed the remains of the Pervert's ancient nuclear reactor. The artificial intelligence had long ago decommissioned the plant, planning to send its waste into the sun. Easarean had planned to destroy all trace of Automaton, but he had need of the toxic rockets and hid them away for the future.

With the artificial abomination defeated, and its lands gathered, the Queen set her fervor and her general's sights on the Northern Lands. The granite men had ages ago isolated themselves in culture and ice, while cultivating fear of others and war among themselves. Easarean respected their physical power and xenophobia but eventually crushed the independent nation, this time absorbing the violent race into his own growing forces.

All hail the King of All.

His intention then was to turn his attentions toward the GAU. The mysterious Grand American Union. They were said to be a massive remnant of the Old Ones — those that survived some long ago cataclysm, keeping their ancient culture and knowledge intact. They had high technology unique for this land, and they watched the world from their cities, hidden and isolated and never interacting with the other peoples of the land. Easarean did not trust their silence. As long as a civilization of their power existed they would always be a threat, and they no doubt thought the same of him. His forces had grown, and he was now ready to move on the enemy.

But years later he had still not made his move against the GAU. He found himself assaulted from all fronts from forces attempting to take his new empire, steal his fortunes, even destroy the world itself. He was not only conqueror, but caretaker.

He found himself contending with Famine as it sterilized the land, freezing cropland and womb. Forests dried and fruit shriveled. The people cried out to their king with parched throats. They prayed to the Queen through cracked lip. Easarean followed the scar tearing the land to its source. But as soon as he crushed the cause, his lands were assaulted from the swamplands of the deep South. A zombie army surged from a sorcerous tower. A masked immortal struck at Easarean's lands with arcane storms to wrack capital and castle. The zombie invasion was merely a distraction — his academy lessons taught early to his army — but the sorcerer dug in deeply, and it took the full wrath of the Queen of Quartz to immobilize him.

Even before the mage's tower was brought down, Easarean had to turn his attention to a growing number of deadly divine masses appearing from the West. Their main objective was to strike at the GAU from across his lands, to unleash their undead messiah. Caught in the middle, the Queen of Quartz and her king defended their faith and their realm on two fronts, but in the end they found themselves again as conquers of the West, with the GAU stunned to the east.

Fecund was the land. It drank the blood of nations, eating entire populations that Easarean crushed beneath his heel. Most kingdoms he absorbed into his own, destroying library and language to make room for his, but any sign of rebellion sent entire cultures to mass graves. And the land ate it all up. So the time was ripe for seven maidens to gather — seven brides of a maggoty god. Bloated with male children, the maidens hid in the very bowels of a mountain to perform their rite in a land rich with rot from unending war. The babies were born under knife and suspicion, and in the end only one remained — the weakest — to feast upon both mother and other, and to take his place in the world as the vessel of the larva of the embodiment of the maggoty god. And as Easarean fought some assassin's blade or a random uprising, the child grew into the worm that would spin the pupal swaddling that would bring about the coming of never-ending decay across the kingdoms.

But the earth belonged to the Queen of Quartz. The soil would never betray her. The obsidian would obey. The iron would never break her trust. The land whispered, and she sent her king. Easarean searched the mountains and valleys with his royal guard, and found the demonic imago stretching pinkly skyward from the remains of its fleshy cocoon. They caught it sleepy and vulnerable, and they hacked at the massive stalk before it could reach the heavens. It fell in a cloud of spores that the king only realized were changing the landscape shortly before he reached his capital. For months his kingdoms fought off mutant flora and fauna, but he burned the forests and prairies until there was no sign of the maggoty god's influence. In all of Easarean's reign it would turn out to be just another annoyance, but it was a costly one, for before he could turn his attention back to the GAU, he found an underestimated threat making its move.

A lycanthropic death cult, kept purposefully small and quiet over the prior decades, had finally found what it needed to end all life on the planet. Following the cult southward, back into lands Easarean was all too familiar with, the forces of the Queen of Quartz came face to face with the dark gods of the jungle pyramids and their vampiric avatar. It was Easarean's bloodiest campaign, and he held the line at the front of his forces, and in the end he stood triumphant over the living and the dead and the undead. He returned, years removed from his capital and castles, with only a fraction of his army left, to find the GAU renewed and entrenched in greatly fortified lands.

Immortal sorcerers, deadly divine masses, fungal gods, giant lycanthropic death cults, and undead messiahs — there had been no end to the challenges keeping him from conquering the Grand American Union and achieving final dominion over of the continent. But now there were no more distractions, no more annoyances. He gave the order.

It was when he launched the toxic rockets at the far cities of the GAU that he got the message from his queen. His son was born. He returned to his capital and to his tower that stretched as far into the sky as it did under the earth. He brought the azure newborn to the surface to hold it to the sun, but smog and acid rain only baptized it in blankets of gray that ran like clay along its infant ripples. The gathered nation cheered above the thunder, a raucous rolling roar that excited the baby to tears.

Easarean gave his son the name of Antony, not knowing he would one day take it back.

All hail the King of All.

LXII

The regulation of sex is the purest form of Just Living and Right Reason. In the virtuous and discretionary allocation of the iron keys to the body's charity, one pays tribute to a golden past while ensuring a holy future. Such is the burden of the Righteous Shepherd when placing chains on the Present.

—Milliam Pittsfield

he bombardment would not cease. The sound of the slowly creeping barrage had grown over the prior days, until it was loud enough to keep even Wulf awake. But his lean battalion was firmly entrenched. He was not moving. He had found perhaps the only rise and fall for a hundred miles in all directions. It was defendable and even sheltered from a wind that had been blowing for the better part of a week. The Horde's forces had to be freezing out in the open, but he knew they would not stop. Intelligence had been true. The encroaching legions would sacrifice everything. Strategically, Wulf's position meant nothing. If his force stayed much longer, even not under attack, they would perish in the winter. The amount of resources being thrown at his small battalion were being wasted. The Necrophim generals and most of the Heirs of Aesar, the very vast majority of the Army of Earth's soldiers were moving violently and obviously deeper into the Horde's territories. But the bombardment would not cease around him. All the enemy had to do was wait, and the weather would do its work for them.

Wulf set the river map aside and stretched back into his bed, brushing drowned fleas away. The sheets were wet everywhere he turned, the quilt a capture for humidity. He folded it down to his naked waist as his companion sleepily traced, with dancing fingers, the paths of a different style of map tattooed on his left arm and chest. The heat of the chimineas bloated his marquee. If it was not for the whistle of wind, one might never know it was everlasting winter outside.

"You should have sent Ivy with him." Wetter than even the blankets, Teca fully woke to press against him. Her thighs clenched against his leg, grinding herself into his hip. He breathed deep the earth of her hair, the copper sweat of her neck, the bitterness of her chest. She smelled like he imagined a man would.

"Janus has good men with him, one picked from each force. I've sent Ivy elsewhere."

"You really are the Liege of Foes, aren't you? I didn't see it until now. Each squad is made of opposing men — most with old grudges. Southerners and northerners, hill people and ranchers, midgardians and..." She pushed him back into comforter and pillow when he began to rise. "Why couldn't I have seen it? I was so silly, such a little girl. For years I took any quest I could that would lead me near N'Midgaard, hoping I would run across you."

"I was nowhere near there."

"I know that now, asshole. Maybe I knew it then too, I don't know. So stupid. All those years... the reports of a goblin king, and now you've allied with their ancient enemies, the dwarves. The Liege of Foes. What does the *Fallo Terminus* say? About a warmonger by way of peacemaking?"

He snaked around and inside her and rolled her underneath him. They were caught up in sheets and each others' limbs and fought against both. She covered his Eye of Yggr with the palms of both her hands, clenching great swaths of his long hair in her fingers before forcing his face to hers and elsewhere. She vowed again to make him cut his beard at the first sign of spring.

He could not breathe in the sour humidity beneath her, beneath the quilts, beneath the commander's tent, beneath the Army, but he could still hear the whistling of mortar shells and whistling winds.

And then, when all the whistling ended, she started. She partially whistled and partially sang — some lilting song from her Libran *Sol Sistere* — as she dressed. Wulf started to stand but fell back into bed as his legs gave out. His skin dried in the air where the bed refused to. Staring upward, he just looked at where the marquee had most recently been patched. Burn marks spread out, darkening the already wine colors. Despite the sound and smoke of the last assassination attempt, most of the commander's tent had been salvaged. The gunpowder stains would be the only reminder.

Teca's hair, when it moved, at times appeared almost of the darkest blues, but as she tied it back it appeared the ebony he remembered. She fell back behind one of the chimineas, into a collection of rugs, wearing only a short tunic meant for someone smaller. Wulf sat back up to catch quick glimpses of the blushing skin of her belly and legs as she pulled the rest of her clothes toward herself.

"You sent her after this 'Mother Inferior'?"

"Yes," Wulf answered.

Teca still sang under her breath when she was not speaking. "Right into the belly of the beast?"

"Should make it easier for her to find her way, knowing how much they want her."

"Who is Mother Inferior?"

Wulf stood to find his own clothes. The close fire warmed his cooling loins, dried his moist hair. He gathered wool and leather and fur as he explained, covering first the arcane map tattooed over his arm and the left side of his chest. "Years ago, before the War even began, the tithingmen were assigned by the Brotherhood of Lessers to create some sort countermeasure to what they feared were their enemies' 'clairvoyant' abilities."

"Your abilities."

"Whether it was a rewritten *Fallo Terminus* or a Liege of Foes that could see the future, the breeding pits were built to create a… psionic countermeasure. I used to think this 'Mother Inferior' was the source of my years of migraines, now I know it was some… other." He tried not to take times like this for granted, when he remembered the horrible headaches and the not-so-alien presence of another mind pressing against his. Although gone forever, he would never forget the pain, no matter how long it had been gone. "Now, the breeding pits have been used since to create all sorts of nastiness, not least of which are the Unfeigned…"

"And a reported biological bomb already hidden somewhere in the Army." Teca was still half-naked, but she stood to find the rest of her clothes as Wulf pulled on underarmor and looked for overarmor.

"…but the pits' supposed first great success was Mother Inferior. If there's any chance the Army of Heaven has access to the future, we need to know. And if Ivy can find any information on a biological weapon, all the better."

They continued dressing in silence. Teca no longer sang, but Wulf was slowed by watching her search for her underwear and her weapons. He ate as he watched and waited. Many of a new batch of southern men had brought hogs with them. These were heavily furred boars that, along with being a hearty meal on their own, sported thick tusks and snouts that had been able to root out edible shrubs near the frozen riverbanks. Mew's followers — showing themselves to be impossibly able to find edible plants and even flowers in these frigid wastes — quickly found a way to preserve and fortify the river shrub for the companies and their families.

His knees were still weak as he laced his boots, and as he looked around for a black-furred mantle to cover his cloak, Teca pushed him over into a pile of stacked chests and tall maiden shields given to him outside of the Granite Lands. She led him out of the tent when he recovered.

"Before Lady Wayasu lit the way to the surface for mankind," Teca explained, "a group of women, known as the Pride, had to clear the land of the monstrosities and witches that had conquered the world in man's absence."

Outside of the tent the day was blinding. A hidden sun was magnified, although dully, from horizon to horizon by colorless clouds. Even in the ravines there were no shadows. Teca and Wulf walked numerous manmade paths out of the river canals and up to the first of the fortified trenches.

Teca clicked her tongue. "I used to be fascinated with any writings about the Pride. The few writings there are. These were stories about such a small group of warriors besieged by herds of raptors or vast populations of fungal zombies."

They walked the trenches where everyone scratched heads under helmet or woolen cap, where black finger or nose tips peeked from frayed scarf or glove, and where one would expect any smell to be caught by the chilly breeze, but, in fact, a putrid smell hung yellow in any wet shadow not banished by the day.

"The lean paths're for constant communication with the front. The pebbled gullies lead water down and away from the men. On the front divisions they lead it down to the Horde's forces, to slow them down, but I hear it's all ice up there. Our front infantry defends an area of about two miles behind scouts, with the main force placed on a reverse slope — both natural and quickly built up. They're overlooked by observation posts."

Wulf periodically peeked above the ground. He could only see pink lights frequently pierce the glare, but he could hear twice as many thunders of explosions as he could see or feel.

"Behind the main line of resistance we're holding another defensive area of about a mile and a half. The Horde shouldn't be able to see into that, or this, area without exposing themselves. But the front company'd received heavy losses as of this afternoon."

Wulf turned to a heavily blanketed aide-de-camp, a one-armed elderly man that had followed them into the trenches. When the man stopped coughing, Wulf told him to, "Send out the turtle boats, both on the White River and the northern tributary. Tell them to waste no time."

Teca continued, "The front trench system's the sentry line for the first battle zone."

"Then tell them to cover the front's retreat, as the front will cover for them as they all move back to the second field. They'll hold out as long as they can before repeating the process. Tell them to spare no round or arrow, for as they move backward I'll have the rest of the munitions move forward. Those first trenches should know to set the quicklime traps as they leave. That will blind and slow any advance. Keep any remaining geek fire for trucks and tanks they may send at us. The weather makes it unlikely, but be prepared."

Aides rushed down narrow paths. Despite the movement and sustained entrenchment, they still had not found dirt beneath the snow. Days ago, as Wulf himself had helped dig the trenches, the Army had broken the frost's crust to find softer layers of crystal below, but no ground. Teca had poured over maps until she had found where she believed the remnants of an old battlefield lay. Ancient trenches dating to one of the Evolutionary Wars were scattered alongside the White River. The Army needed these remains for a planned entrenchment. There would be no new digging in this frozen earth, so they had to rely on the uneven ups and downs of some battle lost to memory.

"Why the turtle boats?" Teca asked, as she slouched to prepare to enter a close command tent. "I was hoping to keep them on land for a final barricade around the main camp."

"They'll disorient him, tease him. They won't do much damage, but they shouldn't take any either. The order is to disengage as soon as they are engaged. It'll slow him down. Give Janus more time. The plan is to make it look like we have a plan."

"Do we?" she asked. Not waiting for an answer, she peeked into the tent.

Wulf stood, with his Army of Earth's soldiers scrambling all around him to readjust and reinforce units unseen over and across the blinding rolls of the prairie. By now, word had to have reached the battalions of the attacking Horde, word that the Army of Earth had split its generals across the Territories. The Banshee Jenny Wren still had not responded to any summons, but Wulf had sent the rest of the Necrophim generals south to each march on a different city on the outskirts of the Kalderan Wheel. The cities may not have had any strategic importance, but they would have families belonging to Horde soldiers, and the attacks would hint at a greater push into capitals. Wulf had also sent some of the Heirs of Aesar out, with smaller troop units, to confront targets of differing importance. This had left him with his small, slowly freezing battalion, out in the middle of nowhere. Yet nearly the entire attention of the Horde was on this plain. The majority of its resources were crossing this frigid hellscape to the point he stood — as he knew they would.

Teca looked back with one last smile before she disappeared into the tent completely. She had appeared to be about to say something, but relented at his knowing grin. She was never more beautiful than when she was withholding.

And the *Goblin Revenant* giggled from behind Wulf. It was becoming increasingly difficult for him to ignore their ghostly squirming and anticipations.

~

Handsome Gibbet was not sure if the man speaking was his second or third cousin or if he was some sort of uncle to his mother. He was certain he was related to the man somehow, had some faint memory of growing up with his visits or his appearance at holidays. The man looked to be Handsome's age. They had the same grand canyons of crow's feet spreading from their eyes like a disease. This man was completely bald, however. He could not hide the fact beneath his thick knitted cap. Handsome yanked the hat off the man's head.

"Show some respect in the puh... presence of yuh superiors." It still hurt when Handsome talked, no matter how quiet his voice had continually grown. It apparently would always hurt. His throat and lungs would always compensate for the loss of his tongue, and they would become hoarse by the end of each day. It was just a faint voice becoming ever thinner.

The distant cousin or uncle rubbed his bare head, never skipping a beat as he read from a prepared card. Handsome knew that there was no need for the man to read to him the simple information. He read so that he would not have to look Handsome in the eyes. The man was a coward.

"…council has also denied the request for the Imperial Guard of Ziggurat and the latest Courtesy Knights coming in from the West. They have been intercepted, their orders rescinded, and they now return to the Capital."

Handsome handed the vague relative a mug of vermillion he had prepared before the man's entrance. The tithingman finished off his own before heading to the corner of the marquee to untie his trousers.

"In addition," the uncle or cousin continued, after sipping the vermillion, "a decree has come down from the Brotherhood, that you are to return both the Seventh Brigade and Criterion Antony's Battalion — immediately. You will also rescind your claim to the Dragoons of Deemos, and they will turn their march back to the Jefferson Territory. Your own forces will fall back to…" The vague relative was interrupted by whisper and whimper — the whisper from Handsome, the whimper from a boy bound to one of the tent's main corner support poles. The vague relative could not see around Handsome, but he could tell that the tithingman was readjusting a large funnel he had earlier forced into the boy's throat. "Pardon?"

The tinkling of Handsome's urine made him even tougher to hear as he repeated himself. "Duh… Drink up. Ah'll join yuh in a second."

The wind through the camp had grown to an inescapable howl. Handsome kept expecting to become used to the sound, but he never did. It did not wax and wane like the whistle through Megrim's canyons. The wind on the plains was constant. It was a pressure he could feel even inside a marquee surrounded by a mile of idling trucks and transports. It buffeted the canvas of his command yurt and flooded the intake of his generator. The night too seemed to press against his mobile home. He could feel it as strongly as he could smell the ever-present gasoline in the air.

Lights strung throughout the yurt flickered momentarily. Had he left anyone behind to work on the generator? According to his commands, there should have been few able-bodied men left in the camp, but surely there was one man left who could fortify an intake screen against the elements.

The vague relative drank deeply the thick juice, his eyes bulging over the mug so he could watch the corner of the mobile command yurt. He chugged and he coughed, but he finished the drink before the other old man had finished evacuating his bladder. He still waited until Handsome had tied his trousers back up before he returned to reading his speech. His teeth were now as stained as Handsome's double rows.

"After all the forward forces are pulled back, you will be left with the two…"

"You nuh… know," Handsome cut in, searching for and finding his own mug, "we used to call this 'vulgar' back in the good old days — what people nuh…now call 'vermillion.' Beet sugar juice. Just poor kids used to drink it. Nuh… now everyone does." The vague relative leaned forward but still could not hear him. "That's the problem with people today. Once you accept the habits of the idle, of the wicked and the low, once you pardon others as just 'being different,' you start to become them. Turn one cheek and the other will be branded with the sign of the sinner. Wuh… once you accept, then you become. To become is to lift yuhself above God in yuh own eyes. But nuh… no one is above God."

Oblivious that the relative could not hear him, he beckoned the man over to the bound figure. The boy's belly was distended, his eyes bloodshot, his gums as bruised as his lips.

"Who is he?" the vague relative asked. He could not find his cap to wipe sudden sweat from his scalp.

"He is ah duh… deceit-seeder. He is ah myth-monger, ah fib-teller, ah liar of the worst sort. He is ah ruiner of reputation, and he is ah traitor to the *Ashmedai Adat El.*"

"From Silverthorn?"

"Eh… exactly. He's been tellin' folks untruths, lies 'bout how the Brotherhood took his town for the ore."

"Everyone knows Silverthorn was supplying the Liege of Foes."

"Duh… don't ah know it."

"Pardon?"

"Ah know it! We know it! Everyone knows it!" Handsome wound up and punched the whimpering boy in his bloated belly. He pummeled him until both of them were wheezing. Vomit covered the sawdust of the ground, along with Handsome's hand. He picked the funnel from the ground and repositioned it, forcing it deep into the boy's throat, muffling his screams. The vague relative took up position, unzipping his pants and letting loose a stream of dark urine. Handsome's dual layers of eyelids disappeared as his eyes grew at the sight. His stained lips stretched wide as a rare smile revealed all his teeth.

"What have you asked him?"

"Uh... asked him? He don't know nothing." When the vague relative was done, and the boy's belly had grown again, the two old men walked away to resume their drinks. "Nuh... now everyone just drinks their vulgar, the young people just curse the Choir, and nuh... nobody nuh... knows their place anymore. Everything was better when people just did as they're told."

The vague relative coughed up what he thought were flecks of vermillion.

Handsome left his side to approach the tier of pallets crowding the long end of the grand yurt. A grand and open palanquin topped the pallets. Despite it being constructed almost entirely of heavy gold, it was designed to be quickly moved or disassembled. Handsome knelt and asked for permission before stepping over the pallets to approach a figure sitting on a chair shaped from the curves of every letter in the angelic alphabet.

"When Ziggurat fell to the brilliance of the *Ashmedai Adat El*," Handsome whispered before leaning over the unmoving figure, "who was redeemed in the hearts and minds of the Brotherhood?"

"Pardon?"

"When the Word was found to be one with the Song, whose voice was found to be justified? Who received the *Seven Sealed* from the Divine Choir itself?" He pointed crookedly at the opened and unopened reliquaries on the dais.

"Schism," the vague relative croaked.

"Yes," Handsome agreed. He leaned even closer to Schism, his ear brushing the figure's stitched lips. "Yes, yes..." He nodded and agreed and whispered back before walking back down from palanquin and pallet.

The vague relative wanted to protest but could not stop coughing. Instead, he barked like one of the so many dogs scratching at the outside of the yurt. And he too started scratching, at his chest, collar, and throat.

"The day after the Word, his word, was deemed one with the Song, Lord Commander Schism was finally rewarded, given rule over the pedestrian forces of the *Ashmedai Adat El.* He was gifted." At this, Handsome pointed to the seven miniature gold chests set within the curves of Schism's throne. Only three still had unbroken ribboned seals. "That is how we know he speaks with the authority of the Song. Not the Brotherhood, not Ammon Mars or his generals, and certainly not you. What?" Handsome suddenly ran back up the short tier, turning his ear once again to rigored lips sewn shut. "Yes? Yes." He stumbled back down toward the vague relative. The short steps had aggravated other injuries, and he knew he would be walking with an even more exaggerated limp for the rest of the day. "But you, you disobeyed my orders, you and yuh 'council.' You turned away the Buckwater Company when it arrived yesterday, against my orders, sent it back to the Hills, didn't you? You've told my own personal guard to bed down against the cold, didn't you, when ah told them to press forward?"

"Pardon?" the vague relative coughed. His face had turned a light shade of blue, but then the hanging bulbs flickered, and, when they came back on, the old man's face had turned to a darker color.

The prairie wind was playing the taut guy lines outside like some underworld string instrument, while it slammed against the canvas of the yurt. On which side, Handsome could not tell.

Handsome pushed the coughing relative to the sawdust. He tried so hard to rise above a whisper, but his mutilated mouth just would not comply. "Yuh… you were going to tell all the forces to pull back to the Territories, weren't yuh. Don't yuh know who is out in those trenches?"

"The… Liege… of…"

Handsome wrapped his hands around the other old man's neck. Muscles contorted beneath his fingers from coughing that would not stop. "Uh… all because yuh all think you know who he is. Only ah do. Only ah know what he is, and that is why, when ah call the *Ashmedai Adat El* together and tell them to press forward, he will die." He squeezed as hard as he could. The man kept coughing. "He will die by muh hand, and, when ah hear of it, ah will laugh and laugh." He squeezed once more before standing back up. It took him a minute to find the right mug and refill it from one of numerous casks. The relative was still on the ground gasping from swollen tongue and clenching heart, but he had finally stopped breathing by the time Handsome finished his drink.

The weather continued to buffet his yurt's canvas and others, the generator continued to chug unevenly, the boy in the corner continued to whimper.

Handsome was rolling up his sleeve, intending to punch the boy's distended belly again, when the lights went out. It took mere seconds for the swirling filamented cinders inside the bulbs to completely fade, leaving his surroundings in a darkness he could not have expected. He heard a faint tearing of fabric somewhere beneath the howl of the wind, inside or outside.

"Guard." He knew it would have been impossible for his vestibule guards to hear him, even if it had not been for the incessant wind. He also was not entirely certain if he had sent his personal guard out into the battlefield or not, so he crawled over the sawdust in what he thought would be the direction of the exit drapes. Before he made it very far, he either ran into something solid or was kicked.

But it was obvious when the lights came back on. Through the rapid blinking of his numerous eyelids he saw that two slender individuals, covered from head to toe in the darkest of otter fur, had slinked into or under the canvas. Other than their strange uniform, he saw they each only carried the thinnest of knife blades. They crouched toward him, as though they swam silently through the building light of the yurt.

Handsome pushed through the pain in his groin to scramble and turn, crawling and reaching up toward the *Seven Sealed* around and on Schism's swirling throne, but a gloved fist and iron hilt came down upon his mouth. "What?" someone asked, as unconsciousness took away any voice his soft face still held.

"What in the name of Elmo's Tendriled Beard is that?" Janus Legionary cursed to no one, looking up at the palanquin.

"Wait," he told his companions as they started to lift Handsome. Janus was wearing the same short black fur and make-up as his squad, and it stretched silently as he took a step up the pallets to peer at the mummified figure. Although warm beneath the otter suit, he shivered in the presence of eyelids, nostrils, ears, and a mouth sewn shut. Something moved beneath the leathery skin, something legion and multitudinously skittish. "I'll take him," he said, tossing the little old man over his shoulder like a sack of beets. "Let's get out of here before anyone sees us."

Blood or vermillion or both leaked from Handsome's mouth, along with a skitter of broken teeth.

you kin learn alot from a lepercon
they wear green pants
they wiggle they giggle
look at them dance!
you kin learn alot from a chicks tits

—Graffiti found on the walls of the Aviguro

ot sure what you wanna know, but I can tell you all I ever heared. Just that they got into some sorta fight a hundred years ago or more, back up north, in them black hills. Their leader, some dude they all considered a prophet, went ass up. Think he fell from some sorta tower or temple. Suspicious circumstances, I'm sure. I don't know. They all loved him though, that's not the problamo. Some considered him a father or grandfather — literally. Some just considered him a holy magic man. So the problem was that some of the Librans thought the magic was in their blood, since they were bastarded or orphaned from him and their angel, and they wanted to take control. But those others felt left out, so they robbed his grave and headed out west, far west, farther west than you or I can imagine. They crossed that weird desert and found empty forests and even another ocean. Sure, they kept being knights and such, but they changed. These ain't no Librans like you or I ever met. It's either the desert that made them such, or just the time away, but I've seen them, with their black marks and vulture headdresses. I'd stay away if I was you."

The gun smoke had not settled yet. Perhaps it never would. The air in the saloon was becoming as cool as the outside weather, and as increasingly still. Harlowe could tell that the town of Clap had never been used to the cold. It was not far south enough to be unfamiliar with a winter, so its proximity to foothills, canyons, and deserts must have created a bowl where usual seasons were mild compared to the eastern mountains Harlowe had left behind days earlier. But there were certainly signs that the few people that settled in Clap were beginning to feel the effects of the Winter of War. Upon coming into the town, the pistoleer had noticed women wearing what had to have been men's boots and shawls made out of hastily sewn quilt remnants. The door on the saloon was large, and it looked and smelled freshly built. The hinge holes of the swinging doors it must have replaced were still obvious in the frame of the wall. The new door no doubtedly had kept the beginnings of the supernatural season out, but it still looked as though the pervasive chill had begun to seep into everything in Clap.

"Is that what you wanna hear, chief? I sure as Hell don't want to disrespect anyone of your name, so if there's anything else I can do for you…"

"Don't care," Harlowe interrupted. The dim lights over the bar were the only ones that had not been shot out, but they were bright enough to catch the squinting glare beneath the flat brim of Harlowe's hat. After surveying the carnage of shattered tables and chandelier for any movement yet again, that stare returned to the Punk.

Despite appearing to be in his teen years, the headhunter known as the Punk had acquired a reputation that had even been making the rounds during wartime. He had robbed caravans for the Army of Earth, subjugated refineries for the Army of Heaven, and had just generally made a profit for himself and the highest bidder over the previous years in any way possible. But now, on the far side of mountain and war, he crouched in a forgotten town, holding a black and blue hand that refused to clench or open.

"I just can't believe it. The Zombie Pistoleer! What luck. Wait until I tell my little girl. She's gonna love it. She's your biggest fan." He made an exaggerated pistol pull with his other hand, pretending to shoot at Harlowe with a finger gun.

"How they sending stuff across the desert?" Harlowe croaked, his voice as dry as the sand that trickled from a gunshot wound deep inside jacket and vest. Some of the sand left a trail as he paced the floor for loose revolvers, some of it trickled into his boot.

"Who? What stuff?"

It only took Harlowe taking one step in the Punk's direction for the boy to throw up his hands.

"Alright, sure, I know it's somewhere south of Drip. If you keep going west from here, along the top range that follows the tree line roads. Ask in the town of Dose. They'll send you along the right way. Look, boss, I gotta go. My mams'll be asking for me. She ain't getting along so well after my pops passed in the sick summer, and I'm all that's left to wash her and tend the chicks."

Harlowe's boots crunched over the shattered glass of lanterns and whiskey. He stepped on hands and hats and the occasional brass cartridge bending under his heel. Including the Punk, there had been four of them, and they had been waiting ahead of him in the saloon. Two had been playing Poke Her, conveniently sitting in a table and corner that had placed both of their backs mostly against a wall. With the Punk at the bar, that left the final headhunter to lean on a railing above in a poorly acted drunken exchange with a housekeeper.

"Look, I don't even know those cheats," the Punk whimpered as Harlowe used a boot tip to brush through a prone figure's cloak. He came away with blood on his buckles. "You know who that is, right, sir?"

"Yep."

"That there's the Pied Pistoleer." The Punk quick drew his finger gun and pointed imaginatively around the room in a reenactment of the prior minute's action, making exaggerated gunfire with his mouth. He pretended to fire a round at Harlowe. "I guess he ain't as immortal as the novels say."

"Nope."

"You figured it out though, didn't you, chief? His power ain't come from that patchwork cape of his. You figured it came from that neck-lace charm, didn't you?"

Harlowe brushed at broken chain and the sharp pieces of tur-quoise from the dead man's chest before he turned back to the bar. Amidst the sounds of unseen chains, he holstered one *Cody* low on his hip, the other high under his arm. He still faced away, but the Punk could see a glint of watery eyes as the old man lit a limp cigarette in the darkness of collar and hat. The match's sulfur joined its violet brethren in the unmoving smog of the oil lights.

"Wait until I tell everyone that you outdrew the Pied Pistoleer. Yee-haw! I'd heard you were fast, boss, but that was some shootin'. You are a bonifide king of lead, yes you are."

Harlowe stepped slowly toward the Punk as the boy aimed and fired again with his finger before rubbing his sore hand again.

"There's no hard feelings, is there? I only drew 'cause I was scared. I just come down here for a drink and some cards and maybe some friendship and people just start shootin' all around me. A boy's gotta right to defend himself, don't he?"

But the closer Harlowe stepped, the older the Punk appeared. His freckles were the soot of the caplock that had been shot out of his hand. Pale hair only appeared red under the velvet brim of his hat. His eyes and nose had seen more sun than it appeared when looking at him from across a room.

"Where they endin' up?" Harlowe asked. "What're they travelin' in? How they gettin' across those sands with their minds intact?"

"Who says they are?" The Punk tried to chuckle, but he got his own words caught in his throat. "I'll tell what I hear just as I hear it. That's all I can do." He started to pretend he was again pulling a trigger, but stopped to look for the source of the sound of a rattling chain. "They is supposedly riding some sort of ghost locomotive."

Outside of the saloon, down a street that was more used to a dust settling than a dust being blown in, a breeze tested the recent additions to shutters and doors. The northern evening sky decayed to a massive gangrenous cloud threatening to bring snow but which would hold off for several more days. The hills and stunted trees surrounding Clap oozed shadows that contorted all evening before touching the mountains seconds before the sun would disappear each night, and each peak-suppressed late morning they would appear on the opposite side of town, stunted as though afraid to mingle with the shadows of the starved woodlands stretching west to a sickly prairie and even farther to an even sicklier desert.

The echo of a single gunshot coming out of Clap would touch all these lands. Underneath it, one could perhaps hear the *drum drum drum* and *chuh-ug chug chug* of an iron demon, but only if one chose to.

...the Warrior thinks he is no one's tool,
seeing the slave to small thought he once had
scrawled on the walls of the King of All's lower halls—

he King of All slouched forward in his red throne, crimson armor defaced by guano, his draping red lion furs defiled by white excrement, the blossoming sunset glaring in through tall windows. A thousand sounds and two thousand scents assaulted his senses. He settled his chin on his fist, feigning interest at the ceremony. The oddity had fascinated him on the first day of his son's birthday, but as the week progressed, Easarean had lost interest. He found himself easily impatient as of late. With the Grand American Union cracked and splintered into nothingness he had nothing left to conquer on the continent. Against his Queen's words he had taken their technology, more advanced than any he had seen on this planet, but could what survived help him wage war on whatever schemed across the oceans and over the sea walls? After a year of study, even a core of his best scientias could not yet tell. And so after all these years he again found himself waiting, this time not in a cramped starship under a goblin winter, but in ceremony and inane pomp. The King went to absentmindedly stroke the key around his neck but was inhibited by ceremonial scalemail.

The armadillo left the prince's crib side, and the King could hear Antony babbling, as he was wont to do when he grew tired. The one-year-old seemed endlessly enamored with his birthday, and, although bored, Easarean still smiled each time the toddler reached for the next furry or shiny visitor as they pledged their allegiance to the little demigod.

With both alien and divine blood flowing through his veins, Easarean doubted anything on the planet could threaten Antony, but the Queen of Quartz believed herself not so naïve. On this, her son's first birthday, she had called the land to his crib to swear fealty and nonresistance and vow never to harm Antony for all time.

The warmth of the sunset grew gray in the clouds surrounding the child's castle, and Easarean's eyes fluttered sleepily as he watched the line going down the halls, through waiting chambers and keep, gate-house and ward, through wall and over moat and out into mountain and wilderness and across the continent. For when the Queen of Quartz calls, all in her domain come.

A splinter of amethyst, bending the chamber's light violet, approached the crib, followed by a raccoon and a chickadee. Behind them shuffled a block of bullion and a tarantula, ready to pledge allegiance. As far as Easarean could see, animal and mineral, solid and liquid, gas and plant, moved along the line. A gnat buzzed his ear, jumping ahead in line to represent all of its kind.

The variety was endless before the King's watering eyes. There was bamboo and sea lion, algae and anthrax, trichophyton, mistletoe, tapeworm, ringworm, small pox and protists — all heeded the call.

It was intriguing enough to see the mists of the planet rise to swear fealty, to see the igneous and the oily and the chromium of the planet pay their respect, but The King of All's people actually came from all parts of the nation just to catch a glimpse of the representatives of animals from all over the globe. The exotic and domestic lined up — the animals slithered, flew, and swam to the capital to wait their turn to speak for their species. There was capybara, Australian swamp rat, vole, mole, and titmouse. The stripes of a Bengal tiger mixed with a serval's spots, followed by cheetah, snow leopard, and meerkat. The timber wolf sniffed the jackal, the terrier nipped at the brush dog, while the flying fox licked itself. The swan trumpeted, the duck quacked, the turkey gobbled, the chicken clucked, but the mongoose was silent. The bush baby climbed the wall to join the spider monkey, overlooking the mandrill, the orangutan, and the golden lion. The lungfish, mudskipper, and silverfish flopped across the floor to speak for their kind, while the octopus and anemone, shriveled in dehydration, croaked their last words in allegiance to the child. Tadpole, pollywog, frog, and nematode — all heeded the call, and all vowed to never harm Prince Antony.

The fly buzzed past the dragon, while the dragonfly waited patiently. The caterpillar hitched a ride on the wooly bear, while the wooly bear caterpillar struggled to keep up with the eastern long-necked turtle, as he was passed by the Sumatran short-eared rabbit.

Crowded around Easarean's throne waited the dwarf leopard, the pygmy marmoset, the europasaurus, the royal antelope, and the midget buffalo.

Hundreds of differently colored, differently sized moths avoided spider webs of all thickness and all patterns. The oyster, the mink, the rhinoceros, the tabby, the silk worm, and the dung beetle presented their gifts to king and queen and prince.

Bat, mosquito, and deer tick compared notes. Eagle and hawk looked down their beaks at chicken and penguin. The porcupine snubbed the echidnae who snubbed the hedgehog. The elephant cringed as the skunk passed. The hyena laughed at the platypus. The llama spit at the sponge. The lobster pinched the baboon. The sloth dozed. The grizzly snored. The goat fainted. The possum faked it.

The King of All found the ceremony disgusting, fascinating, surreal and overwhelming, and he finally went to sleep on his throne, surrounded by the stink and squawks and howls of a million creatures, but hearing only the words of his son as he spoke for the first time.

~

When he woke it was to the cries of Antony and the screams of his Queen. The chamber was empty of the sights and sounds of the animal kingdom, but their mess and stench remained. It was dark in the castle, with any star or moonlight completely muted by the settling smog of the land. Easarean had to follow the Prince's calls through the darkness of the chamber, through scat and scale and the fur and feathers littering the floor. Webs caught the King's long hair.

He found the babe cold and held him against his massive chest, beneath soiled cape. The cries immediately turned to choked recognition. His first words called to his father for comfort, and, quickly warmed, he snuggled in for sleep. He dozed even under the echoing screams of his mother, for the Queen of Quartz wailed from somewhere high up in the castle.

He knew he should have hastened to the sound, should have run the halls and steps of the castle to find the Queen, but he could not. The weight of the past week's ceremony had exhausted him. He had done nothing but sit in his throne, with the occasional nod toward servant or guard, but the days' ritual had still tired him. The line had appeared endless, as had the hours, and his presence had been merely dictated by some ancient tradition as opposed to being of any practical need. His muscles ached from inactivity as he now walked the chambers leading to the tower's stairs, and he assumed they would for the coming day.

The screams had stopped, and that worried him more than their initial start. The castle was quiet, with the servants hiding in lower rooms and all the mural chambers they thought he did not know about.

He turned on the occasional biotorch to give the castle its evening luminescence.

Antony babbled for his attention, no doubt woken by the larger steps and footfalls on the stairwell. The tightly clockwise spirals had been designed by Easarean himself, and it now slowed him. He had noticed that the men of this planet were predominantly right-handed, and any invaders would have their sword hand against the wells' interior curve, making any swing difficult and giving an upper defender an advantage. Against the Queen's wishes, he had even set the steps himself in uneven patterns — some short, some tall. The castle's inhabitants had long become use to each stairwell's patterns, but an attacker would be at a disadvantage against dimmed lights and ready defenders.

So it went with all the design of the King of All's castle. He had built the main gate into a deadly trap. It first opened into a small courtyard with another main gate at the far end, the forward gate harboring an iron portcullis held normally in the open position. If ever the gate was infiltrated, with an enemy inside the courtyard, the portcullis could be brought down, trapping the invaders in a crossfire built with technology left from the remains of the GAU. Both quicksilver rounds and stimulated photon beams could be set to raze the yard automatically at any sign of intrusion.

Outside the main wall were other, concentric, walls for miles, each set with turrets of other alternating munitions gained from the takeover of GAU cities. EM webs, sentient rail launchers, and sonicapacitors — all linked to the castle's main AI system and ready to be turned on any invasion. While avoiding the myriad towers, an invader's only option would be to dare the many moats snaking through the outer walls — gelatinous streams and pits filled with heat-attracted technorganic algae, ready to smother with a cocktail of every paralyzing poison Easarean had come across on his conquering journeys.

Easarean had always preferred commanding men over machine, but the deadly force that now kept his little family under the strongest protection in the land could not be denied. It had taken all his resolve to lower the defenses for the ceremony, but the Queen of Quartz could be very persuasive, and her control over the creatures and earth of the land could also not be denied.

But despite the reliance on the linked tech of the GAU, Easarean had made sure to integrate some more primitive means of last defense in his castle. Beyond the hollowed walls that the servants often cowered in, he had hid secret passages throughout the foundation, below even the crowded dungeons, that could take a person far from the castle for supplies or escape during a siege.

Antony quieted as the King of All entered the topmost spire of the fortifications, handing the Prince to his mother. A light came from somewhere through the opposite windows, but Easarean was clueless as to where it could possibly have emanated from. Through the glow, the baby looked up at the Queen of Quartz, smiling.

"Where are the guard?" Easarean asked as the Queen went to the window. He had pulled the key out of his shirt and was turning it in his hand without realizing it.

"I have sent the royal guard away, husband. They now have a new calling. As the best of your men, trained by your very hand, augmented by magic and science, alchemy, and the most potent drugs and herbs, they are now to hunt the most deadly of game."

"What…"

"The most impertinent of creatures! Disloyalist of the disloyal! Ingracious of the ingrates!" She turned back and her face had changed. The ethereal veins that snaked her flesh stood out starkly blue against her features. Her dark lips and eyes disappeared as shadows crossed her face. "They did not come! I called, and they did not come. All the world heard my command, and all the world came. All of nature's kingdoms sent their representatives. But not them." Her features softened as she came back into the meager light, and all that was left now in her expression was love as she kissed the playfully resistant prince on the nose.

"Will you help them, husband? Will you help them hunt this most obstinate of beasts. For all the living and unliving of the land have given their sacred vows to never harm our dear Antony. Except for this foulest of betrayers, this vilest of unworthy. Colder than the coldest serpent's venom is this creature's betrayal. Without the total extinction of its kind, our little prince will never truly be safe."

"And what is this creature?" Easarean asked. He held his fist clasped tightly in the opposite hand.

"Only the most detestable and ungrateful of them all. Among all the earth it ignored my call. The hummingbird never came, husband! The hummingbird never came!"

Easarean could not hold his laugher in. And her vicious scowl only made him bellow more loudly. The quiet castle now woke with a deep chuckle he feared would last for the rest of the night. He left the spire, his chest shaking uncontrollably, tears streaming down bronze cheeks.

Even beneath his laughter he could hear Antony begin to cry behind him.

LXV

"Ode to Surt"

Thou wretch'd and wing'd celestial giant,
O' peeping pervert, does loneliness have
its own self-satisfied reward to grant?

Thou still tidal slave
leashed to milky cave
with only the cold and breathless to save

—unknown

Other Inferior bathed. It was one of the few luxuries she was afforded, that she afforded herself. It was a luxury that had become scarce lately, as each month grew grayer, as each day grew colder, but, despite the never-ending winter, she had thought she could always rely on the afternoon. The early afternoon always brought sunlight through her window, and this simple blessing of the Divine Choir had not failed yet. So this day was like each other day, and she soaked up the sunbeam, dozed in its warmth, bathing in the yellow comfort. The rest of the day would be cold. There was no room in her apartment for a hand brazier. So she just napped at attention, periodically woken by the bobbing of her head as her neck relaxed a bit too much, as she sank a little too deep into true sleep. She just enjoyed the calming waters of the sun-lit window and the enveloping blanket of the warmth found in the stagnant pond found within the yellow room between Wake and Sleep.

But this time, when her head nodded, and she snorted, with her veil flickering in front of her face, it was misinterpreted by a sudden audience. The other Brides in this day's attendance had started to filter into her apartment, and they took her startled mannerism as an answer to some question they had asked.

"Pardon?" Mother Inferior asked, composing herself, straightening her sumptuary and collecting the cards spread out on her desk. But it was too late, the few Brides that could fit into the room could not have helped but notice the cards. She worried that her blush could be seen even under the veil.

"She's here. She's ready, so..." one of the Brides was saying. Mother Inferior could usually determine who was speaking, but everyone was squirming for position in the tight quarters, trying desperately to fit and to stand closest and to make room to push Ivy of the Grove through. Hidden bells tinkled beneath layers of beige.

Ivy of the Grove — This little girl was whom all the tithingmen were obsessed with. Cleaned and prepared, she looked nothing like Mother Inferior had expected. Reports had indicated the girl was blond and light-complected. The girl before her was neither, although, if she was the same race as the Lesser Antonys, she would continually adapt to her surroundings.

"Where was she taken?" Mother Inferior asked.

"She gave herself up out at…"

"Where was she taken? Never mind. Well, well, well, isn't this a surprise. Not really. By now you must know that we had been alerted to your little plan. You see, I'm sorry but there really isn't much you and your band of heathen barbarians can get away with anymore. Your army has been just so chock full of spies and malcontents that we know everything that you're planning to do before you do it. It was inevitable. How could that godless King of Foes ever expect to keep his people together without the Song. Word is that your Resistance has been squashed and your Army is being crushed. How many fighters are you down to, I wonder?"

"Beer Garden has been taken back by the people," Ivy said. She had picked a brass bull up from the desk and was examining its underside, speaking barely above the chattering of the closely cramped Brides. "Last I heard, your General Fobos — or maybe it was Deemos — was killed by our Hyper Khan, or maybe it was by the Electric Leper. I'm sure you understand that good information is hard to come by these days." She set the bull upside down on the desk but kept her hand on it. "Castrated? Truly? How then…"

"Get out!" Mother Inferior yelled to the Brides. She snatched the statue away from Ivy. "I mean, move along, girls, you know we still have a lot of packing to finish up. Tell the bondsmen to start loading the trucks. We leave, on my order, in the morrow…"

"We only have wagons left, ma'am, so…"

"The wagons then! Have them load the wagons. Go, go!" She waited until almost all of the other Brides were out before she added, "And send in an Unfeigned…"

"They were all called to the front, ma'am, remember? To Master

Schism's lead, so…"

"Out, out! Let me do my work!"

Ivy closed the small door after the last had left but was quickly chastised.

"That's my door!" Mother Inferior shouted. "You don't touch it unless I say, so…"

She spoke so fast that Ivy had a difficult time hearing each word. There was not enough room for a chair, so she continued standing. She tried to peek out the window behind Mother Inferior, but the outside glass was too filthy with dust and ice. The seal was not tight, and she kept expecting the windswept window to shake off the frost, but it just continued to bang against itself and to collect more dirt and snowflakes. She knew she would be cold in the chilled room even if there had not been a slight breeze and whistle from the loose pane.

"Yeah, we know all about your plan to spy on us," Mother Inferior said, "so why don't you tell me what you know and I'll tell you if you're right because you might as well give it all up. Your army is on the ropes and it's only a matter of time before you all are either dead or put in the work camps or maybe you'll even be sent to us for the medical research. If you don't want to speak you're in the right place because we have ways of making you talk. I won't pretend that I can read your mind without permission. I can't. Your kind are especially hard to read. You know that my daddy was one of your kind, don't you? I can't read them but we could hurt you real bad and then I bet I could get in there, with your defenses down, or we could put you into one of the pools that are left here, and then there's all sorts of things that could be done to you to soften you up. You don't even want to know, so…"

Ivy saw Mother Inferior quake. Even beneath all the layers of her sumptuary — visor and bonnet, brown aprons, obvious rib-bone corsets, girdles, bloomers, and stockings — she could tell that the woman shivered. She also made note how the woman, for the most part, kept her gloved hands below the desk. Ivy wiped a finger through the dust on an empty bookcase as Mother Inferior continued. Still, she had to closely concentrate to keep up with the words' hectic pace.

"I know you think you have the upper hand but you can't fool us. You can pretend to be calm all you like, you and your rebels and your suicide explosions and your army of blasphemous criminals but your time is almost at an end and then the world can go back to preparing for its deliverance by the Song. Oh, I can't wait, I will be so happy when I don't have to worry all about all your sin distracting us, and we can worship in peace. I know all about your sick orgies and gambling and sacrifices to the Liege of Foes. You are all sick, sick, sick. That's all we want to do is worship in peace and be alone with the Divine Choir watching over us. What could you have possibly hoped to gain by coming here?"

Ivy slid pristine pencils and ornate candles aside to rest herself partially on the desk. She realized in the sudden quiet that she had been asked a question. "I've decided I want to help."

"Bah!"

"I turned myself in and hoped..."

"Bah, bah! No, we captured you. Don't think this is some kind of negotiation or truce or whatever, because you are our prisoner. Don't forget it. I'll give you the courtesy of not getting shackled but that can change with your attitude 'cause I can have you flogged at any second if I wanted. Show some respect, so..."

Ivy wiped the same dust from the desk. She could not follow the speed of words. She continued anyway. "Are these the Brood Pits? I was under the understanding..."

"Bah! Wouldn't you like to know? See, you even came to the wrong place. *No*, these aren't the Pits. They just used to be. We're moving to somewhere else. We have another project taking precedence. You're too late, so..."

Ivy crossed her legs and sat fully on the desk, but she still could not see Mother Inferior's hands. Nor could she read the woman's face. It was only a shifting mass of shade beneath the tan veil.

"I was hoping to make a deal with the IDesigner, but I was told..."

"Bah, no! He's not here. He can't afford to be bothered with you. He's moved along. You'll deal with me. No! You'll not *deal* with me, I'll *tell* you what we're going to do. I could just throw you in one of the Pits and preserve your body for him. He wants your body, you know, even though he doesn't need the whole thing but how about this — you give me a sample of your blood and you let me into your pretty little head and I'll let you leave alive."

"I'm just curious about this biological weapon we've heard you've cooked..."

"This is not a negotiation. Don't you understand? I could have you killed for just appearing at our door. You don't seem to appreciate the trouble you're in. If Zrappado was here you wouldn't be so lucky, you'd be skinned alive, you would and he would soak you in the Pits first and you'd be hung upside down so all the blood would rush to your head so you wouldn't pass out. You feel every bit of it, so…"

Out of her peripheral, Ivy just watched the slight nudging of Mother Inferior's right arm as it adjusted something under the desk. "His name is Zrappado? The IDesigner?" Trying to keep up with the woman's dialogue was exhausting. It never slowed.

"Bah, it doesn't matter what you know. You'll never see the light of day again. Do you play cards? I know I'm not supposed to but I play solitaire from time to time, just in here on my own time. Do you play?"

"No."

"How about a different game then?" She dug around in a desk door and Ivy tensed as she continued speaking. "I keep a set around here to make decisions with, hmmm, yes, we'll play a game with more urgent consequences." She passed a large card from the top of a deck Ivy recognized to be from the game of UnderCrawl. The cards were in the best condition she had ever seen. "Don't show me the card but think of it in your head. If I guess what the card is you have to stay here with me and give me a vial of your blood and if you win you get to leave, no questions asked alright?"

Ivy held the tip of *The Night of All Seas* to her forehead, turning it slightly, flirting with the idea of revealing it completely. She was not even sure what had been offered, but the introduction of the cards made her curious. She had never played the game, with its board and bones, never even been interested in playing it, but she loved the variations of cards she had come across over the last couple of years.

Mother Inferior pressed a free hand to a veiled temple and hummed almost inaudibly, but an obviously clenched jaw and teeth gave the sound a very specific vibration Ivy could feel behind her ears. "You can't — hmmmm — keep it from me, little rebel, little thing, you — yes, yes, I see it! You hold the *All-Seeing Knight*, I know you do, so…"

A cow bellowed from somewhere out in the pits and pens.

Ivy looked closely at the card. The image had the most intricate design of dark faeries and darker vines as a frame. They were drawn in such miniscule that she could barely make the lines out, even in the bright room. One of the faeries stretched from the frame and into the image and appeared to be turning the handle controlling a system of enormous spouts. Massive lakes of water grew on the tranquil landscape of the moon, while Earth rose in the background, with nary a continent to be seen.

"Nope," Ivy said, placing the card face down back on top of the deck.

"Bah! You cheat and you lie, you *all* just keep cheating and lying and having your orgies right into your cold empty graves. You'll all die alone and be greeted by emptiness. Unbelievers, all of you! Deaf to the Song. It's a choice, you know, being deaf. Closing hearts and ears."

"Where are the Brood Pits moving to? North?"

"Somewhere old, somewhere new, somewhere cold and blue, it doesn't matter. It doesn't matter what's there. You'll be long gone by the time Yankee Zrappado turns it on. He'll be the first blessed with the Promise of Father — his deserved spiritual body. He will have long forgotten about *your* body by then, so…"

The deck of cards was in Ivy's hands before Mother Inferior realized it, and she had shuffled them before they were snatched back with the jingle of hidden bells.

A cow bellowed from somewhere out in the pits and pens.

"But let's make a deal, little 'Girl of the Grove,' let's make a deal. You deaf are familiar with making deals with colored devils and black witches so you should have no problem making a deal with me. Here's the deal, I'll read your fortune and if it tells me to let you go I'll let you walk right out my door back to the heathen wastes and your dying army but if your fortune tells me to take your blood and mind then you stay with me until I choose to let you go."

"Why don't you just kill me?"

Mother Inferior bent closely over her own shuffle, but she quickly returned one hand under the desk. "That's for your criminal kind, deaf child, we don't do things like that here, those of us in civilized society. Let's play our little game and move on, shall we, I have final projects to supervise, so…" She tried shuffling one-handedly, but the deck fell apart, so she pulled one card from the scattered spread and placed it face up before Ivy. It was *Venusian Daughter*. The shadows beneath the bonnet stared for quiet seconds before Mother Inferior turned the card back to face herself. "It is not you."

"I know."

A deep breath and long exhale moved the veil. "No, not you, don't think it is."

Ivy stretched out as well she could in the space, and for a long minute she just listened to the muffled sounds of movement outside the office. Furniture dragged. Tubs drained. Manic voices exchanged directions. The subdued sound of activity was a far cry from the rattling windowpane. Ivy curled, unsure if she had ever been so cold. She had climbed the peaks of the Titans in the middle of the night, but she was certain she had felt warmer than she did now.

"When I was a young girl," Mother Inferior finally said, "my momma fell very ill. While digging my baby brother's grave she had pricked her finger on a toe ring deep in the dirt and the infection spread. Her dying words to me were to never let my daddy marry again but if he did I was to drop the toe ring into the pit of the squathouse before his new wife was to take her morning constitutional. If, then, at breakfast, she showed up wearing the ring on a finger..." Another sigh moved the veil as Mother Inferior leaned in, supposedly to look even more closely at the card. "Momma knew daddy would marry again, the Lesser Antonys are always lusted after by the ugly, fallen woman of the world and she was right, it wasn't long before he married one of the daughters of the farmer at the end of the road. I waited a whole week until after they'd been married before I dropped the ring into the piles and I could barely finish my chores quick enough I was so excited for breakfast. I was even in time to set the places myself and sure enough as I sat there waiting patiently — I hadn't even taken the time to clean up for breakfast — daddy's new wife came in — I think her name was Boner — and sure enough..." She paused, giving Ivy a chance to try to catch up to her words. The woman reached down deep below her desk, and, before Ivy could tell what she was doing, she had pulled back on an ignition cord. Amidst a cloudy sputtering and the sudden stink of gasoline, some hidden engine roared to life. "Is it warm in here, are you warm?"

Ivy was not warm. She was actually quite chilly, but she could no longer hear the rattling of the windowpane under the grungy, new rattle of the generator. No, she was not warm at all, but was it perspiration that made Mother Inferior's veil stick to the shadows of her face as she tapped at the card?

"Look closely, here, see the Daughter's headdress, see how the bloody shadows are a part of it, see that it is not just an ornament but a shroud? Pay attention, the devil is in the details!"

Ivy started to lean in, but cringed at the new acridity in the air. Her nose tickled. Still, Mother Inferior beckoned.

"This is not you, but you are here somewhere, look closely, look closely. Ahhh, yes, here in the background, always in the background, look, see how the rays of the eclipse are filtered through the wings down to the dark grove, so..."

A cow's bellow echoed from somewhere out in the corridor's pits.

Ivy finally looked closely at the card, and immediately Mother Inferior lunged with the prod she had been hiding under the rim of the desk. It was a thick prod, and it crackled with a chemically metallic stench of ozone. Ivy smashed the palm of her hand into the woman's face at the same time that the prod grazed her shoulder, and she suddenly could not see or feel her limbs, could barely feel the sudden floor against her back but knew she lay on the cold stone of the office.

"You an... hech'aow! Yours! You and yours are an affront!" As soon as Ivy could see again, she was witness to Mother Inferior trying to disentangle herself from the cord connecting the prod to the wheeled generator. The Bride's long skirts were caught up with each other and the wiring. At the same time, she choked on whatever blood and cartilage Ivy had loosened or broken with her strike. Her veil was soaked to dripping, and it stuck to her face like early sundown. "Ech'aow! Hec... hech... whores like you are why we are all punished. You flaunt your sin while we all are left to atone for it. We had our chance and we squandered it all throughout history by distracting and tempting and lessening and belittling and being prideful and vain, and the rule of the father and the brother and the husband is our reward but you just won't stand for that will you? Bah! Ech'ew... ew... ew... all you had to do was submit to be saved, it's that simple but you adorn yourself with shiny trinkets and flowered colors and clever words when you should be adorning yourself by accepting the authority of a husband."

Ivy could see and hear and smell again, but her arms and legs would not respond. She could not speak and could just stare up at the looming shape of sleeves and nearing fabrics. She knew that the fat prod was pressed against her again because of the clenching pain tightening every single muscle in her entire body. But she could not feel anything else.

"It's because you refuse to be silent that we all suffer because you and your kind are so selfish, because you take too much we must take less. We all have our roles and each role is allotted so much grace but you take more than your share, in voice and prideful action, and then those of us that are chaste and silent are left with so much less. Ka'chew! Ech... eck... but those of us that are saved will make the sacrifice thankfully so thankfully because it is through the barren land-scape you leave us that we truly become acquainted with the Song. It is through humility that we recognize the fear that will keep us safe!"

Ivy could not tell where her hands were, much less use them to hold Mother Inferior back, but she knew they were tightened to their extreme in pain like the rest of her body. The muscles in her neck were so impossibly strained she though she would choke. Her scalp was so tightened in rigor she feared it would tear from her head. Yet she had no idea where the prod pressed against her.

"But now you know the humility of the blue light, eh, you little prostitute, don't you, the humbling nature of lightning, the erasure of self that is the spark. So let's see what's left, shall we? You must be open to my brain probe now, aren't you? Pain removes all barriers, physical and mental. Open up!"

She could not feel the strings of blood that dripped from the veil onto her neck, or the knees and elbows that straddled her body, but she could feel Mother Inferior's fingers as they pressed against her temples and forehead, the grain of fingerprints pressing under her skin as they forced their way along the bone of her skull. If she bled from the indentations, she could not feel it. She could only watch as Mother Inferior shrugged into a trance that, in turn, forced her mind unimpeded into Ivy's.

~

The expansive oval office had no shortage of brilliance. There was no sun outside the windows, no matter the time of day, but enveloping light warmed from tall glass in all directions. There were no birds outside, yet still the open skylights brought their warbling tunes, along with the crisp scent of honeyed spring air. Between the windows danced identical dwarven trees, potted and painfully green. Wruth's immaculate desk, carved with the designs of feather and leg, was covered completely in the wide leaves and fat pots of uniform plants.

She adjusted the framed photograph of her husband on her desk.

Chem-Oshmelech was so handsome in his hunting fatigues, and Wruth began to fidget beneath her skirt with the long and painted nail of a finger before she felt another's presence.

So she stepped around the long desk, wiping the dust from leaves with one hand, tipping an empty water can into the green flesh with the other, trying in vain to ignore the shadow that had appeared between far bookcases. There was no room for any darkness in her office. The light from all points ensured that every nook and every cranny was well lit. It reflected from glass to wood in all directions. Nothing could be hidden in her office.

"Yet so much still is," Wulf said. The shadow had become him, and now a door stood behind where the darkness had been.

"You can't be here," Wruth whimpered.

"Now, now that isn't being very gracious. After all, it was I that allowed you to create this setting."

But that could not be, Wruth wanted to say, for her grand office had always existed, and she had always been here. "You're a liar," she said, "everyone knows it, everyone knows not to believe your lies. Where did the plants come from then, huh? Where were they before, liar? Who wrote all these books, then? So..."

He had been looking at one of the books. It had no written title on the cover or the spine, and its pages were all blank. He dropped it on the floor in front of the full bookcase, and Wruth cringed at the sound and started to weep, for she was suddenly starting to remember what *had* come before. And she knew that none of this was real.

"Sure it is," Wulf said. "Smell the dust on your plants. Feel the smooth varnish on your desk, the weird warmth of the light on the back of your neck. Isn't this real?"

"Bah! You're trying to confuse me but you can't because I know the truth, and the truth is in the Song."

"The truth is that you invaded a mind that wasn't yours, Wruth. The truth is that I sent Ivy to retrieve information from the Breeding Pits by any means necessary, and she chose to do so peacefully, but you took advantage of that in violence, in rape, as I knew you would..."

"Bah, you are the king of lies, so..."

"...so before she left I implanted a hypnotic surrogate inside her mind to only be uncovered if... when you violated her memories."

"Pillow-biter! You're all incapable of listening to reason, aren't you? As a person of reason, I can see the need for order. Everyone has their role to play, you can hear it in the Song and our role is to question. Yes, we *are* allowed to question and it is the role of fathers and brothers and husbands to reign us in, otherwise there *is* chaos and there is chaos isn't there? Not a nice, slow ruling progression as there is in the chaste balance of questioning and reigning-in but sickness, drought, and war and chaos and that's because you didn't do your job. The men of the land were deaf to the roles prescribed in the Song and now the *Ashmedai Adat El* has to return order by…"

"Listen up, Wruth. This is important. I am a psionic clone of…"

"You are a pillow-biter and a liar and it is a sin against the Divine Choir to hear anything you say, so…" She strutted around in the body that she was starting to suspect was not real but a creation of her mind. It was starting to feel unfamiliar. Her massive hips bumped the desk as she rounded her plants. Gargantuan and translucent breasts were in her way as she leaned over leaves and pots. She struggled to steady herself on tiny feet and tall shoes. Had her plants suddenly developed aphids?

Wulf continued, "I was activated when you invaded Ivy's mind, and I rode the path you opened back into your own, taking you back with me. This… setting… is your mind's attempt at…"

"Why can't you barbarians be reasonable, look at the successes of the *Ashmedai Adat El*. You all spend so much time looking for answers, constantly wandering, so much wandering when the answers are right in front of you, in the Song. Listen to the Song, you'll find peace and an easy end to the struggle. You are so stubborn."

"You are not dominant here, Wruth. You have to answer my questions."

And she knew he was right.

"Liar, you said," she whimpered, "that we are in my…" She started crying again, because she sensed that he was not lying, that she would be uncontrollably compelled to do anything he asked of her. In a room so bright and clear, he was difficult to focus her eyes on. No! That was not right. Here she had no eyes. It was all in her mind. She knew she was not even actually looking through eyes, yet she just could not focus on him. In a room of light, he was the absence of light, or he was all light, or maybe he was something beyond light. Were these distinctions just all of her own creation anyway, here in her mind? This was all her creation, except for him. He was an introduced foreigner in her mindscape. What did he want from her?

"I want to know about the biological weapon the Breeding Pits created."

"I don't…"

"You can't lie to me, Wruth."

"Zrappado did it to his own brother, you pillow-biter!"

"What did he do?"

"Turned him into a living weapon, that's all I know." Her massive belly knocked a pot onto the floor when she turned away from him. Amongst the spilled soil and leaves she could see them multiplying. They were not aphids. Something worse. They ate much more quickly and were darker than aphids. "Oh, gawd, oh, no, I remember the Before. I *was* in her head wasn't I? That Ivy of the Grove? It was so quick and so messy."

"Where is this brother? What can he do?"

"I don't know, just that he's infiltrated your army. He's one of you, he probably doesn't even know what happened to him or what he's supposed to do. He spent years gestating in the Pits, as soon as the war began. He has to be perfectly mad. There will be some sort of trigger, something that will set him off." Her tears were feeding the spilled plant but drowning the bugs. "Oh, gawd, she's been so far, seen so much in her short life. Why would you let her do that? You're complicit in her wandering. No good can come of that, just as I told you. Questioning is good. I question but it has to be structured, this wandering into controlled progress not the unbridled chaos her unchecked exploring leads to and it's all you and your kind's fault. You let them wander around spreading their legs for every merchant and farmboy. Anything they find in a book or theater is just noise, loud noise that just drowns out the salvation heard in the Song."

Wulf breathed deep of imaginary air. Could it be that this had all just been a risky waste. The mysterious Mother Inferior appeared to be no threat. The biological attack could still come at any time without warning. He had endangered Ivy for little gain.

"Bah!" Wruth grunted as she slipped on her own tears. The water level was above her heels, and from the floor she could see the bugs devouring the flesh of her plants. Even the eternal light of the Outside seemed to be dimming.

"It doesn't have to be like this," Wulf sighed, sitting down against the door and flipping through another empty book before dropping it into the warm pool.

"Pillow-biter!" she yelled at the skylights, and the light instantly resumed brightly, the water disappeared, and her plants stretched, rejuvenated and parasite-free.

Wulf could feel himself fading. He had designed himself to have a short lifespan, and it had been difficult, in his creation, to truly conceive of the ramifications. He certainly felt like the original Wulf, could remember being nothing else, but he knew that the prime template was out there somewhere, hopefully, waging the rest of the War. But the psiclone had all his memories, and, except for not having a physical body, was for all intents, still Wulf. Yet here he sat out the last astral seconds of a life measured in nanothoughts, in someone else's brain stem. He tried not to think of it as he dissipated to nothingness, for all thoughts and regrets led him back to Teca. He missed her greatly, and it bothered him to no end that she would have teased him mercilessly for the sentiment.

He died angrily.

~

The youngest Bride was the first to recover from the psionic scream that had shrilly resounded through the gutted Breeding Pits. Her temples still clenched as though she anticipated another scream, but the auras had faded from her vision. The hallway had turned back to its grisly green colors. She staggered past emptied pens and drained gestatubs. Murky smells lingered even if the contestants had been evacuated and scattered to other locations days prior. The youngest Bride grasped at wet reliefs for stability as she moved from one chamber to another. Her fingers found handholds in the organic carvings winding in and out of the extended mouths of princesses, the clasped thighs of virgins and whores. The Pits, even before their scuttling, had been rationing oil and gas for the Army of Heaven, and the rock and metal of the corridors refused to gleam in the scant light of the few lamps.

She slipped again, this time on the spilled contents of a prone Bride's cart. A pool of amniomortis or synthetic amnioambro still spread slowly from the containers. The youngest Bride stepped over her groaning peer to continue to Mother Inferior's office.

Amidst more reliefs of long limb and neck entwined by organic cord and plug, of arching back and gaping throats, was the door she sought. From its poor seals came the smell of grilled meat, and the youngest Bride tittered at the thought of catching Mother Inferior in sin. All Brides knew not to eat meat in the presence of the tithingmen, but it smelled as though the youngest Bride's headmistress was wasting no time in master Zrappado's absence.

She peeked into the Headmistress' office, careful to avoid the door's well-known creak of hinges, and found Mother Inferior twitching on the cluttered floor, the cords leading from her generator obviously to the prod beneath her. The hair and skin under skirt and veil smoldered.

The youngest Bride looked back out into the main chamber with veiled eyes searching frantically. Other Brides still gathered their gowns and girdles, holding their heads, still recovering from the instant migraines of the psionic scream.

Ivy of the Grove was nowhere to be seen.

LXVI

"My Master's Mistress"

He comes to me in my terrible rages, nights bereft
of those cool hands we all know
it ain't right
to be left
with thoughts of her calming influence that, although
forbidden, we accept that
it ain't right
to be left
behind on the back steps like the head of a barn rat
with dying mind and tongue that pleas
it ain't right
to be left
thinking a man is blind when really he just can't see
—Unknown

hin, pale scars wrecked his temples like premature crow's feet, and even more crawled away from his lips like tiny worms fleeing an infected corpse. Those same lips had been split more times than she could remember, even before they had escaped out of Below the Brook. Now, after countless battles, they had a fullness she did not remember him having as a child. His neck was relatively free from the marks of combat. He protected it well, and it was in stark contrast to the crisscrossing scars she knew covered the rest of his body. She missed seeing that body, as covered now as it had been for years beneath many layers of quilt and fur and now armor. Janus had never liked the cold. He had always been more disposed to the hot sand of the ring, the noon of the stadium.

Mew's finger lightly brushed the line crossing his chin, where stubble would no longer grow. Unlike practically all the men under his charge, Janus kept shaving daily. Even in the coldest days of the never-ending season, she had never seen him with any more facial hair than he had now. His braids he had cut though — shorter but not short — when the peregrination had joined up with the Army of Earth. It gave him a larger range of the armor and helmets the Army given him access to. But the length she now realized that his hair had already grown back to made her realize how long they had been with the Army of Earth, and how long the war had been raging. Days had so quickly become months, yet the winter still raged around them.

Out in the world, away from the grand little lives they had both led in the grand little world beneath the stream, all she could remember were dark skies and falling snow. The only steps she could remember were over ice and wind-buffeted dunes. Yet she knew this could not be true. Every once in a while something or someone would remind her of a warm day, but it was becoming more and more difficult to imagine colors beyond a gray scheme. The flowers strung around her arms, the greenery stitched into her gown, held colors so beautiful but now foreign. They at first seemed to mock the winter, but it was a stupidly obstinate mocking from colors that were not fated to last long. The season did not fear them any more than it did the cowardly sun, and the colors gave their bearers no courage, much less optimism, against days and nights that too scorned the drab heavens.

Despite all this, the trickle of water had begun to grow almost to a roar beneath the two of them, and grasses, suddenly a vibrant green barely remembered, lifted themselves from the clearest of slush. But Mew saw none of this. She only traced the tiny mark on Janus' ear reminding her of the competition that had taken a piece out of it. All of his scars made him appear so much older than he must have been. It was true, she knew, that he did not know his age, did not remember being taken into the athletic trade, but she had always assumed him to be her own age, yet he looked so much older.

"I remember when you got this. It was an equinox celebration, and for the first time ever Lord Elmo had ordered the gownstresses to design a dress for me of black and the darkest greens I had ever seen. He had never dressed me in such somber coloring, and I was very insecure as to how it would be received. There were no shoulders in it. The visiting lord… Crepe, I think, was his name…"

"K'repes, of the eastern steppe."

"Yes, he certainly did not hide his affection for it, and usually that would have made Elmo furious — such boldness in his house — but this time he seemed to take pleasure in my discomfort. He teased me all through the foregathering, right up to and through the competitions, that he had bet on you, bet *me* on you, and that if you lost I was to be sent away with Lord K'repes."

"He would never have."

"I know, and I knew, but I still took glee in watching you fight, pretending that the stakes were higher than they were. So imagine my mock shock when I thought that giant had skewered your head on his massive trident. But you had slipped between the points, of course, but he had taken a little piece of your ear with him."

"It was an ogre, not a giant, and it was with no skill that I survived that day. I was just lucky enough to fall between those blades. And this is what he actually took from me." Mew had been pulling her fingers through his dark hair, and he took them in his own to lift a swath to reveal a small bare stretch of skin. She massaged it. "When I lost the piece of ear, I can't remember. It may not even have been until we came here."

Silence always followed between them when one or the other spoke of the exodus out of Below the Brook. What followed the fleeing was a time neither liked to think about, despite the fact that they almost always were.

"I remember that dress though," he finally said. "The thought of it kept me warm many a night in the barracks."

"Pig!" she shouted, pushing at him, but he stayed firmly lying down with his head nestled in her lap, and she eventually returned to playing with his hair and scars.

"Wulf wanted me to talk to you before I left," Mew said, looking at him directly for the first time since they had sat down on the rise.

"I can imagine what for, but it won't do any good."

"The rumors are true then? Why do you do it? You are a commander, there is no reason for you to put yourself in danger like that. You have a responsibility, to your men and to the Army, to lead from behind. They're calling you 'Legion' now, because you fight alone like one, all by yourself, at the front of the lines. What would happen to your troops if you fell?"

"Someone else would step up."

"Yes, they would, inspired by your pig-headedness, and the cycle would continue — just as it does on a grander scale. But it doesn't matter, because I told Wulf that you'd be leaving with me."

"You know I can't do that."

"I know that you *won't* do that, but let's talk of other things."

But Janus was silent. She knew that he could hear the crack of rifles over the hill and through the woods, that the war cries and the splitting of tree trunks by the Horde's minion-engines called to him like cheers echoing around and around a coliseum. The explosions and march of troops that vibrated the ground all the way to their rise tickled them like the stomping rhythm of an Morbis Orbis audience, and she watched as he absent-mindedly reached for something in his saddle pack that was not there.

"I'm dying," she finally said, "by staying here."

"I know."

"But do you know why I stay?"

Janus slowly turned to sit up, and he took her hands in his own and held the palms to his cheeks with eyes closed.

She said, "While I stay I share in the War's sins. And as long as I travel with the Army I am as sick as its plagues, as starved as its famines. I am as violent as its gunpowder, but I am just as sensitive. I must cleanse myself, or I will die."

"I know. Where will you go?"

"Back where it all began, to a world that moved at a different speed, that was shrinking. I still feel so small in the wide expanse of this great world. I have to return to a much smaller world to remember who I was, and it is in who I was that I will be renewed. Don't you ever wonder what is left of that world?"

"What's left of that world lies in us. We're all that's left."

"But I have to know for sure. Before I can go forward I must look backward."

"Take my best as your escorts."

"Only until the edge of Kaldera. I must do this alone. Unless…"

But the thump of mortars brought Janus to his feet, and she followed, resting her head against his chin. His musky smell always reminded her of the barracks beneath the Morbis Orbis. Those memories reminded her that it was time for her to go.

They looked down the rise before them, along the melting streams of snow, through the straightening grasses and into the flower-adorned faces of a thousand tear-stained eyes. Mew's followers were spread out among all the battalions of the Army of Earth, leading healers and councilors following all the generals, but hundreds had gathered to appeal to their mistress in a sudden garden surrounded by ice and gunfire. Some Mew recognized, most she did not, but their green drapery and white furs marked them as obvious healers in the service of her quiet word.

"Your people plan on staying," Janus mumbled, moving around her embrace to pull up his hood. He turned away from the crowds, sudden spring, and even more sudden spring.

"As is their choice. They have found worldly salvation in saving the world. I will work on saving their souls in the meantime."

"And I'll make sure they live long enough for you to do it." Janus then whispered, "Come back to me. You know I love you." He turned her away from the valley and the multitude of wet eyes.

"I know. I've always known. I'll look for the blood. That is where I will always find you."

She took his hands and his face and pulled his scarred lips toward hers. Her eyes had never been greener, nor more golden, but he pushed her backwards in spite of himself, more sternly than he had intended. Her budding tiara suddenly reminded him of scalps he had collected over the years, the tiny roses placed around her neck like so many of the throats he had slit. But mostly he could not forget the image of his own hand plunged deep within her belly, blade and all. It was the only scene of the multiple lifetimes he had lived in Slog Sabbaoth's slumber that he still dreamed of, that had not faded away, and the memory repulsed him. As he would wake nauseated each night, he was so now, and he reached for his mask to hide it, but he came up empty-handed.

He finally recovered to find Mew washing her face in the clear run of new water.

"Legion," she whispered, "I'm afraid you will betray me."

"I would never give you up."

"I know."

"Then how could you say such a thing."

"I already did, and you already have."

The wind shifted and they could smell the smoke of fires in the air. He bent over her, a beautiful dagger he did not remember unsheathing suddenly in his hand. He came away with a lock of sublimely and abysmally black hair.

Mew again splashed water on her face as Janus strode away, quickly up and over the hillock.

Down where the water flowed, where short grasses greened and moved to the rhythm of the new breeze, the lights were in a multitude. Few colors were represented twice. Each flower held or worn or passed by Mew's healers was as individual as the crowd members themselves. No two appeared alike in size, color, or movement, yet the hundreds of followers each had, somewhere upon them, a consistent green. Over the years, those that had dreamed of, followed, or had even found the Lonely Forgotten Sun of God had worn some shade or variation, but here they all now wore on amulet, paint, gown, tattoo, or scarf the exact shine of her eyes. War smog rose from the hill behind her, smothering any light from the north, so this time her crowds glowed viridescent for her.

"You do not follow me," Mew said to the thousand, and although her voice was soft and the trickling of spring water under her feet grew loud, they could hear every word. She continued, speaking to the confused faces, "You never have, and you never will. I do not want to be followed." She pointed to a man with a beard full of fleshy leaves. "You, wash your cheeks of tears." To a bald woman, scantily clad and painted head to toe, she said, "You, clean yourself of sorrow. This is a day of rejoicing. A true day to remember the *gentle constants*."

Mew knelt and felt the stream again. Beneath dripping ice and bending grasses the dirt was washing away to reveal a red clay. She washed her face yet again, and the crowds followed.

"The earth will renew. It will cleanse itself, and when the clouds break and the glaciers recede, the world will need a people equally pure, so cleanse yourself, purify body and spirit. Be vigilant, do not let the sword sway or direct your mind or words. You can be *of* the world, but you can rise above it, for when I return I will need a people ready to make the final pilgrimage, into the South, into a warm sleep to wait out the deathscape the upper world will soon become. Nature purifies, the rain and streams purify, blood will not, and so, if there are any among you unwilling to face the coming hardships clean and patient, then take up a plowshare and join the war. Unless you wash, you have no part with me. But if you want a part in the new world that is sure to come, wash the world from your hands and from your face and heal the broken. Heal their body, heal their mind. Go to them. Wash them. Clean their wounds, and their soul will be equally purified. And now, a new command I give you — while I am gone, go not just to injured friends and family and the like-minded, but clean the sores of our enemies. Listen! I say to love those who hate you, bless those who curse you, treat those who mistreat us. Be merciful to the merciless Horde. I say to half of all you — go out into warfields, won or lost, and care for *all* wounded. Go out into the Territories as they fall and lift up all the low, all the sunken, and if you are hated you must remember that I was hated first, but I will overcome the world, as you will. Be an inspiration to me as I have been to you. And find our sisters and brothers and tell them, one half of all, to walk into the fields and mountains of the shadow of our enemies to prove the example of a cleansing sun that will not sleep forever."

A thousand washed in the rushing streams their bodies warmed, and, along with the water, the earth warmed and softened. The hill was covered in clear, streaming branches that collected at her kneeling figure to rush, stream-like, down into the reddening pasture of clay the green people washed in.

"Be renewed. The love you feel for me I feel. I have always felt it, and I always will. That is its strength. And if *all* people of this cold land could feel that same love, then the world will survive, keeping itself warm until the sun shines again."

The black cloud grew, hanging but wind-whipped, until the air and gunfire stilled, when it collapsed on the top of the hill. For still seconds, Mew's eyes could be seen through the ebony haze. They pulsed like a heartbeat as the darkness threatened to consume the glow.

"But take heed, there is one among you whom the world has changed, if in body if not in soul. He does not know it. He does not remember. But he is a child of nature too, for the world is nature no matter how much Man tries to remove itself. Be merciful. We all have our roles to play in the end and beginning of Man."

The hundreds and hundreds of green priests finished washing themselves in a new pond that was quickly becoming a pit of red mud. They all looked to the top of the empty hillock and then to each of their crimson-smeared faces and hands.

~

It appeared as though the fallout from the latest battle would never end, but Mew sent her escorts away after a day of trying to distance themselves from the carnage. They had skirted the smoke of battle-fields, hid in abandoned trenches and tree lines that had apparently been burning for days, and they had even snuck through a refuge of ranches that appeared untouched, but, upon closer inspection, were filled with families and ranch hands dead in their beds from some sort of bloating gas poison. Even a day after she had dismissed Janus' elite soldiers, she could still smell smoke no matter which direction the wind blew, could still hear the occasional exchange of mortars out in the darkness, never knowing which horizon it came from, could still taste gunsmoke on the falling snowflakes.

~

After a fortnight of first sleeping out in the open, then under the still-thick foliage of dying Kalderan trees, Mew stopped seeing signs of the War. She delicately walked the top of icy dunes crowding amongst forests, reveling in breezes without even a hint of exhaust, enjoying the silence between canyons paler than the snowfall. And it was true silence, she one day realized, suddenly not appreciating it, as it had come with a price. The years of winter had driven many animals into a deadly and endless hibernation. Others she would come across were flash-frozen in running rigor or sleeping petrification.

~

They were mostly men and she recognized them immediately as once belonging to the shrinking world. They were dark-skinned, as most men, but with a reddish tint her homeland's sun had given them from birth. They still wore their small beards and mustaches in spiky and mocking remembrance of their old oppressors, and their abundance of armor and clothing were mismatched but recognizable as belonging to her old lords' wealthy classes. They all huddled around frequent bonfires, and the forest enclave was warm despite the night, but they all seemed unable to escape the chill. She knew that few of them had ever experienced a cold season, much less the *Fimbulvetr*. Each, in turn, would watch her as she passed, their breath freezing in the air and capturing the glow of the fires and lighting her way, creating a path through and around the camps.

So thickened by years of snow, and now by this freezing foreign population, she could not recognize any landmarks, yet she still knew the way. It had been calling to her for months now, in sleeping as well as waking dreams, and she had tried to ignore it. But here the brook now was — if she could call it that. It had shriveled to nothingness — just an oft-broken sliver of dry ice she had to dig through a crust of white to find, in a long desiccate streamed of sand as hard as any snow she had encountered as of late. For a silly second she had hoped to find footprints of the three that had come through so few yet so many years ago. But the pebble-bed refused to admit that the exodus had been anything other than a dream. She held a shard of the ice to one of her eyes. The night was moonless, but she swore she could see something not through but inside the glossy glass. What she saw was inexplicable, yet she still silently chastised herself for not expecting it. It was all that was left of Below the Brook, and, after nauseating seconds of adjustment to a different flow of time and space, she had stopped falling inward and downward to look dumbfoundedly upon the remains of the pocket world and the painted god that had been left behind to hold it precariously open.

...seeing the slave to small thought he once had
been, the Warrior, now seen
as free, with no end to choice, could go mad
—scrawled on the walls of the King of All's lower halls

There were times when he suspected that his memories of the Academy were not his own. The rare occasion Easarean thought back to his youth was like seeing through someone else's eyes, or watching a series of alien events on a vidplay. The people and situations he remembered were only vaguely familiar — as though he had watched the scenes play out sometime in his past but never actually played a part in them. And these scenes only became increasingly boring to watch over time. Until now he only visited them to remember some sort of battle strategy or training lesson, but lately even those memories had become obsolete, and so now he only looked back out of curiosity. He thought back, trying to remember if his people had a word for the concept of peace. Surely the Empire, always riddled with war, had at least had a name for even the theory of war's absence. His specific clan, on the other hand, probably had no such need for semantics. He knew now why he and the other children had been kept ignorant of such a state. Peace was empty but exhausting and at times overwhelming in its expanse. It made Easarean small in an ever-expanding universe he could only at these quiet times feel, with the empty spaces in his days giving him too much time to ponder and think about an alien past or a future devoid of battle in any respect.

"Father, your wounds!"

And so the King of All distracted himself as well as he could in a time of peace in a land with nothing else to conquer. He cracked the side of a barrel against granite and drank in the cascading wine before too much could spill on the grasses, turning the ground as burgundy as the remnants of his warped armor. Antony ran to his side to examine the burns mutilating an arm and both his legs. His cuirass still smoldered in the places it had melted to his chest.

"Your wizards, surely they'll be punished."

"Yes, son," Easarean said, grimacing as he pulled the ruined plates over his head, "but with mercy this time. There is only so much enchanting one can do to protect against a beast such as Phlegethon. A wyrm's breath is hotter than the promise of Tartarus on your old man's soul." He pulled the key from around his neck and breathed a heavy sigh, noting it had not been damaged. As painful as it was to clench his hand, he moved the key through his fingers, listening to the Prince's enthusiasm.

"Their eggs incubate in the planet's core."

"Yes."

"They drink from volcanoes to cool themselves."

"Ha!" Easarean winced. Any effort, especially laughter, was painful. "You remember your studies well." He looked over the fine azure specimen his son had grown into. He had aged rapidly and was now at the verge of manhood without blemish or asymmetry. The people of the land had, for years now, sung ballads to his beauty. His physique was a leaner version of his father's musculature, but the entirely sapphire eyes and hair were unquestionably inherited from the Queen.

"Can you walk, father?"

"Barely." He leaned into his son while taking another messy drink from the barrel. The Prince helped him to his feet and toward the edge of the overlook.

"Your mother will have her work cut out for her this time," Easarean growled, "but she'll heal me up. You'll see."

"Like with the Great Harpy Hunt," Antony said, nodding.

"Yes." Easarean wiped the wine from his beard with his good arm, spilling more at the same time. On cool nights he could still feel the harpys' talons raking his back, even though, as Antony reminded him, the scars had vanished years ago. The creatures' down now filled the bedding of his northern retreat. "But unlike that hunt, this is one for you to finish, my son."

"But..."

"You who cannot be harmed. You who cannot be burned, or torn, or poisoned, or bled." They sat near the edge of the cliff, cool granite soothing the King's wounds. "This greatest glory will be yours and yours alone."

"No."

"No?"

"It was you, father, who planned the hunt, you who conquered Phlegethon's traps. It was mother who broke the beast's magiks, its curses and wards. It was your armies that defeated the monster's minions, that brought the mountain down upon it and its lair."

Thunder cannons roared and rumbled through the near canyon, as if in response to the Prince. The ground grumbled a response, and for a moment Antony thought he felt the cliff shift beneath him. He brought out the silver coin to wipe the soot from its face and the face of the prehistoric queen carved into it. The metal was worn from what he assumed were centuries, but he could still make out much of the design. The profile had a bold nose, long forehead curving into waves of hair ending in curls and ribbon. Jowls accented a weak chin and fat neck. Thin lips pursed in haughtiness, expressing more emotion than the dead eye. She was hideous to him. This was the kind of woman the ancient races adored? This was worthy of silver? He wished he had some of the Kingdom's gold on him so he could compare this bauble to the image of his own coin. There one found majesty. There one found the hawkish nose and eye, strong resolve and cheekbone of a beloved ruler. He regretted not stealing something out of the creature's hoard with some beauty.

The fires in the surrounding forests grew closer as they waited, but Easarean predicted their hunt would be over before they consumed the canyon they sat atop. Yet it still grew darker earlier as the smoke blended with the exhaust of the encroaching cities bearing his name and banner.

He had yet to find a drink that could get him drunk quickly, but vowed to never stop trying. Easarean either finished off or spilled the rest of the barrel's wine before crushing it into the ground next to him. He shook the drink from his beard, wincing as drops splashed and smoked over his cauterized arm. The King leaned in to see what had taken the Prince's attention.

"The Old Ones," Easarean explained, "ancestors of the Grand American Union. Take notice of the phoenix on the coin's tail-side. It rises, resurrected from leafing flames as its empire never did. Such hubris. Where is their legacy now? Wasting and rusting away in a smelter's hoard, that's where."

Antony flipped the coin into the air, deliberately letting it clink to the granite. No matter how far the monster was, and even beneath the guns and grips of his army's war machines, the creature would still hear its metallic bounce. He knew it. Soon it would be upon them again. He gestured to the coin's image.

"Did the people love her as much as they love mother, I wonder? I bet not."

Easarean tried to stand on his own, but surprisingly found the drink hampering more than the pain. Sadly, he knew the relief would not last long.

"They... the people..." he stumbled, realizing Antony had left his side to approach the canyon. "They don't love the Queen."

"Of course they do, father, they love you both more than anything. The praise, the festivals, the tributes, the prayers... I've seen how they look at you. You are everything to them."

"No, boy, your mother has shielded you from the world, shielded you from the ills... from the old... from the death... of humanity. You will never understand the drive that comes from mortality, the motivation that follows fear of insignificance cut short. For it is not love you see on their faces in parades and on holidays — it is fear. They fear the King of All because of what I can give them, and they fear the Queen of Quartz because of what she can take away."

The ground trembled again, and this time Antony was sure of it. He could hear the beast's breathing, could feel the infernal heat leaking from beneath scale and flickering from between teeth as tall as him.

"Perhaps you're partly right," Easarean continued. "Perhaps it's a type of love. For what is fear but love's bastard half-brother. One warms the blood while the other chills it, but both set the heart a flutter, both capture breath and words. Both make fools of us all. Both conquer nations and kings... both... both..."

Obsidian smoke plumed up over the canyon edge, rolling in fire and upon itself. From it came a bloodied claw, each toe as large as the King, crashing down to crush and grip granite. But it was the dragon's roar that shook the cliff. It tore at senses and soul, and, weeks later, as Easarean would tell the tale of the days-long fight in the sky — under the Queen's disapproving gaze and healing hands — he would shiver at the roar's remembrance. For now, however, he had to tell himself it was the drink that made him shrink to the ground, and not the Tartarurian scream.

Antony took up his adamantine sword and leaped, disappearing into cloud and canyon and maw.

"But they love *you*, my prince, my demigod, my son, my everything," Easarean whispered beneath the crumbling rock and battle cries. "They fear All, but they love you. Be their adored, their hero, their prince, their blue god."

A hint of sun peeked through the smog, and something caught The King of All's eye on the ground next to him. He picked up the coin Antony had left behind and ran a thumb over the smoothed bird as it reflected the fire of the glowing forests.

LXVIII

VIII. Even rocks die.
X. Avoidance of death prevents man's transcendence.
XI. Without transcendence, all life is waste.
XV. Waste is the ultimate evil.
XXII. Devalue permanence.
XXVIII. Embrace life.

 —Precepts of the Painted God

his was my Great Renunciation. I remember the moon being high in the sky when I woke. It was the first time I ever remember being cold. My fellow athletes had always talked about it, especially after we lost a fight. You see, our 'lord' would punish us with the elements after we had a disappointing practice. I remember falling asleep with so many questions racing through my head. I had been angry, but I could not remember why. I know that I had, for the first time in years, wondered about my place in the world, in Below the Brook. Why had my mother given birth, only to leave me here to be found by slavers and lords? Who was I ever to look to guidance in the pens? The Family heads? The Merchant heroes? Those that ate duck and slept on springs, when so many others chewed bones and covered themselves in dusty straw to wait out the nights? Would my mother ever return to save me from the whips of lords and the cheers and jeers of the stands? The punish pit reflected my questions. It became dank and black in the night. I can still see the ghoulish pall the lonely green star cast down into the circles of stones and vermin bones I had compulsively set up over the unremembered days and nights of my punishment.

"I thought that the stench of the dead came from me, but it was too dry to have come from my recent flogging. It pressed deep into the pit, holding me low to the ground. I could taste it, all the way down into my twisting stomach. I pushed at the heavy air, to no avail, and then I saw him, as though he had always been in the pit, as though he had been here all along, interred long ago, and as though I was the interloper, not he. And then the mummy spoke, but not through the foul air, but directly into my mind. It was as though some spectral quill scrawled words immediately on the crevices of my brain. I had been the concubine of lords and lordesses, all who reveled in directing the irony of an educated athlete, all giving me access to the finest of tutors, yet the swirling runic language written in my head I should not have been able to read. Yet I understood."

Your strength is unsurprising, my boy. I would've expected no less. We'll see if your beauty also matches that of your mother, for this generation will know the absence of God, and you're charged with keeping the lyre of Heaven charming.

"The star had grown over the pit, blinking its light down to be absorbed by the nightmare. It burned away in the green flame slowly eating the wide-open side of its decomposed head and glowing from its long mouth in place of a tongue."

Your anger toward God is forgiven, but never forget it. Use it. Now you must choose the path of the word or the path of the asp to devour the unjust while keeping Her memory alive.

"I tell you, Mew, the creature was hideous. Red and black and pink wrinkled arms and legs. Body wrapped in filthy bandages. An open chest revealing more of the dying green flame. No heart behind burnt ribs. But I was not afraid. I certainly should have been, as the undead's burning fingers dug into my chest, as my blood boiled to the surface of my skin, as it spread like ink over my body, spreading and stretching into scenes and images — the narrative of the prophetic. Yes, I should have been petrified, but I suddenly felt my mother's presence warm away any fear I should have felt. I could feel Her watching over me, and I then knew why I had been born into such a corrupt world. I had been remembered, and I had then woke to destiny."

"That you had been chosen to overthrow the lords," Mew stated, not asked.

"The destiny of the world," Maahesehaam grunted, shuffling to leverage himself against the two halves of what was left of Below the Brook. His shoulders and back held up one side of the pocket universe, the great muscles of his legs the other. "It is the curse of all beings to embrace tension, to desire it as much as they do food or drink, or love. As much as they evolve, it is never beyond this basic need. But systems evolve as well, and this tension is an important ingredient of the evolution. Without it, systems and their integral participants would stagnate. The lords and ladies, soldiers and merchants, slaves, artificers, fieldsmen, children, and gladiators all made up what was a plateau of a system in Below the Brook. What I thought was the world had atrophied, and, like the blood-starved testes of the gelded, it blackened and shrank. My destiny was to stoke the remaining tension into a bonfire of the ages, to take advantage of underlying, but simmering, potential and move the system along the cogs-way into its next evolutionary step. What I later realized was my father, that mummified monstrosity of a servant of the Green God, had revealed me to be an agent of final change, and I took the reigns of this dying world, freeing all, becoming the ultimate balancer of the scales of each being's potential. We all became equal in now having a connection to the natural world, no longer alienated or separated by those who think they are our betters. Whether rich fishmonger or bejeweled slave-girl or wealthy pickpocket, each being is now able to choose their mode of suffering, instead of having it chosen for them. In the end it was too late, however. Once started, the shrinking would never end. Now I just hold open the world so any remaining may escape into the new universe you apparently discovered long before me."

"If I had known," Mew wept, "I would have come back years ago."

"You led the way. It was the myth of the girl that had escaped a shrinking land that led pilgrims to the watery portal. It was the memory of your beauty that motivated the explorers."

The tiny world creaked and groaned around them. The landmasses pressed against his tattooed shoulders and thighs.

"Soon, Mew, very soon, my time here will be done. The land will crush in upon itself, and I will present myself to your new world. My followers are readying it for me. They have explored much of the surrounding areas, reporting back to me. It sounds like a cold world. A violent world. They have told me much of the nations, of the people, but I need your word, your perspective. Who among your world stifles evolution, and who among the nations embraces adaptation? Call us the Remnant — those that have survived an ever-quantum land. Those beings out there number more than you know, and they are your original people, and they are cold and anxious. They have adapted and been what they need to be in the past many years in your absence — farmers, warriors, and politicians. They are cold, but I can warm them. Just tell me who, in this new world, stands in the way of a being's natural potential."

"You are their god." Mew wiped away the last of her tears.

"I never claimed to be an agent of anything other than nature. They have named me The Painted. That is their right, just as, I have heard, your people have named you."

"But I am not God. I am *of* God."

"No longer. Yours will be a *newer* new world, and it will be in need of a pantheon. The decision is not yours. You belong to your people, and all new thought requires a sacrifice. Your wish to remain humble will be that sacrifice." The tiny world shifted against him. He and his muscles groaned. The living tattoos over his chest and legs shifted as well. Mew watched as images, that could very well have been indicative of her, changed as she tried to decide her future. "Now, whom should my armies march upon?"

"You see that man's potential lies in its connection to nature," she stated.

"The natural state, yes, one of balance, equality, with those around them."

"And I say that war distances men from their potential, from salvation. There is no room in Heaven, no peace, no solace in the afterlife for one so soaked in bloodshed. Man cannot sleep everlasting among the nightmares of a life spent in death dealing."

"Heaven? Salvation in the After?"

"Yes."

"I have been holding this world open for so long, and, soon, when I can finally let it close, I will have a whole new world to explore. Perhaps... perhaps some day I will return to pull it from the microcosm and stretch it out and make it as green and as large as it once was. Or perhaps I will some day break down the gates of Heaven and take its golden fields as my own. Or perhaps I will descend into the Circles of Hell and conquer its crown and castle. Someday I will find a Paradise for those praying to me, so that they can live out their rewards in death, but for now I can only ensure that their lives are rewarding. I cannot imagine what type of people they would be if I now offered eternal salvation. I truly cannot. They would be an alien people to me. Never concerned with the natural world. It would be like unto a shadow to them."

Mew was thinking of how expansive Below the Brook had appeared to her as a child, how it had been her everything, how every decision her Lord Elmo had made, how the outcome of every Morbis Orbis event, and how every interaction she had had with the High Families and ladies had been only of the utmost importance, not just to the realm but to her life. Yet now she realized how small it had all been. It had all led to nothing. Below the Brook had no history, no past or even a future. She remembered the immensity of the overwhelming feeling she had experienced when she had walked into her new world. It was so big, so all-encompassing. She and her concerns had felt so insignificant. Under dark sky and glacier, would she one day feel fooled again. Was the key to survival a feeling of importance or a realization of insignificance?

"There is no avoiding natural law," tattooed Maahesehaam said in the cramped quarter.

"No. There's too much pride in its dismissal. But there's also immense ego in its defining."

"Not for ones such as us."

"I suppose. There would be equal pride in refuting our responsibility." She felt the closeness of the collapsing continents with each hand, the heat the Painted God gave off in his struggle. Would she have been able to hold open the last remnants of Below the Brook for even a fraction of time he had, she wondered. Would she have wanted to? Except for some cherished memories, she often tried to forget the temporal pocket.

"I have never desired being apart from the world," she said aloud, surprising herself, "but I will not be a part of its violence."

"You are making an unnatural delineation."

"No, I'll prove you wrong. Stay your people, or let them roam. Lead them south, ahead of the winters, out of the wars. They deserve as much. I will not be responsible for more bloodshed."

"Even if it ends the War?"

She looked around at what was left of her old world, the world of her youth. Time had moved so differently here. How could she have known? It felt so natural. If only she had left earlier. But would she have been ready? Her life of luxury, the pampered memories surfacing whenever Maahesehaam spoke, disgusted her, but there had been beauty here too. If only she had snuck out more often to that glade of greens. That circle of dew and twilight had shown her more shades of that one color than she thought possible. It was the perfect balance of warmth and comfortably crisp air. And there had been beauty in friendship as well. Zenith dalliances with Janus had been the highlight of many a day. The bars between them never dulled her visits.

It appeared she remembered more than she cared admit. And now, despite the killing winds and buffeting wars, there was still beauty out in her adopted world — in the rosy cheeks of newborns swaddled next to campfire and mother, in the sad eyes of a dog sharing the last of its owner's food.

"Years ago, shortly after I left this world," she remembered, "I came across a tilting barn. The Winter of Winds had beaten it mercilessly. It was done for. What remained of the building had only minutes left, according to the dying cries of the boards and nails holding the last few planks together. A fieldfire burned quickly toward the barn. It moved with a suspect quickness and near intelligence, driven by the lashes of a week-old wind. Yet into this maelstrom ran the farmer's son, to rescue the barn cats. They scratched at his arms and tore his only shirt, but he continued to go in after cat after feral cat. I spoke at his burial, and what else could I speak about but love? This love damning the consequences. It was said he even saved a nest of naked rats. Years later, I took a pilgrimage, heading toward the Territories, and it took me near the windy paths I had already forgotten. It was an early winter that begat early winters, and it had caught the land unaware. The plains people scrounged wood from long-burned forests and the ruins of many a ranch. One morning, as I bedded down with a huddled mass of nomads, teaching them how to best plant snow peas, I saw the charred remains of the lovely boy's grave marker. His name was all that was left. I kept the piece of wood with me for weeks. I lost it sometime while I was… sleeping. There is beauty out in the world. Beauty and love. It just needs to be remembered. Love, never forgotten, can conquer the land as easily as war."

"Tell that to your enemies," the Painted God said, once more shifting his muscular bulk against the cliffs threatening to close the universe. He said no more, putting all his attention into holding back the continents.

"I go now to do just that. There is a governor out past your people's encampments. He was given charge of an oft-forgotten territory, and word is he refused to send his personal guard to the front lines at the Horde's last request. He sounds like a reasonable man."

~

A generator outside the large tent belched, and the hanging lamps flickered, but there was an ample glow from the stoves and the grill to make up for any loss of light. Mew could still hear the stutter of the machine, despite the side of her head being so bloodied that her ear had swollen shut, could still smell the pinch of gasoline and charcoal despite a nose so obviously broken. Before she had been bound to the blocks securing the tent pole, she had been able to feel the softness of her face with her fingers, and there was no doubt that one of her eyeballs had become dislodged, but that was before the men had pulled her arm out of its socket tying her up and then down. Most of her body was numb from the pain, in shock from the whippings, and all she wanted to do was succumb to the darkness that pressed against her head, but the shattering grind of the bone fragments in what was left of one of her ankles kept waking her. It burned and froze at the same time. Her eyes, the little she could open them, saw in two different directions, but she could still tell that the black and purple mass beneath her was her foot.

She once woke with a start, the side of her face she could feel twitching in spasm, to look around the governor's tent with her twirling vision. She had vomited down over the torn vests of her chest at some point over the previous hours, although she could not remember the last time she had eaten. The governor's chef was flipping great slabs of drooling meat on a great grill. The hiss of some great serpent filled the tent, along with the greasy steam of its breath. The chef returned to an opposite table, to the gutting of a quivering hind. Its tongue choked in its mouth silently. Its delicate legs danced their last. Its blood drained into a gutter the chef checked periodically while ripping into it belly. He tore another piece for the grill before slathering all the meat in a custard that refused to melt.

Mister Cilice entered the tent before Mew could pass out again. The stocky man wore the same broad brimmed hat and short cape as when she had first sought his audience the week before. Except for an immense and blocky nose half the size of his head, his face was still completely obscured by long and tight ringlets of brown hair.

"What's the good word, governor?" his chef asked, not looking up from the quickly graying flesh he cleaved loudly against untreated wood. "What's the sermon 'bout tonight?"

Mew could see the ringlets move, but could barely hear the quiet voice through her ringing ears, but she was certain she heard the tithingman grunt, "Free will."

"Alright, alright, alright!" the chef said. "One of my favorites!

'Is your name written in the Book of Life? In gold? In iron?' Ha, ha! Right? I remember."

Mister Cilice waddled to one of the tables before dipping a gloved finger into a steaming bowl. He tasted the finger behind his hair while dragging a chair to the corner of the tent farthest from Mew. He faced her, but if he stared from beneath brim and from behind hair, she could not tell. Her head was too cottony heavy, her bruised back too sore, to keep upright. But the chef's voice kept her awake.

"Lets see... 'Dwelling on choice is the original sin... better to call it *will*... when all thought and deed are infected by the First Man's curse... we are all in blessed bondage to the only will that matters... the will of the Song... and with the Divine Choir being *all things* and *no things*... will is neither free or not free.' Ain't that right? All that matters is your name. Is it written in gold or iron?'"

Cilice just sat and stared or did not stare. Each time Mew was able to build enough strength to raise her head, his unmoving form was all she could see from across the room. Eventually, she woke to a ruckus at the entrance to the tent. In came men of all sizes and shapes, of obviously varying positions. There was a padded man-at-arms, a blacksmith, even a young powder monkey. One wore a carpenter's smock, another a mechanic's singlet. One suddenly filled up Mew's distorted vision, unbuckling a belt as grease-stained as his beard, but he was pushed aside by a sunburned man straightening a meticulous tie. He had in turn opened his trousers, but, struggling with silken undergarments, was passed by several more men.

Fingers dug into Mew's arms and legs, and she could suddenly feel again. Her head flopped at the end of a slack neck, and at one point it swiveled to see the chef tying the drapes of the tent closed. Still, Cilice just sat in the chair, far in the corner, staring or not staring.

LXIX

and when you lose control
you'll find true self within chaos
and when you lose you win
with the found absurdity of life
and then you'll lose your mind
in finding freedom from other eyes
and when you loose the dogs
upon the foundation of thought
you'll see what is, not what you ought

—Hati Weirdson

The vines had grown long in Ivy's absence. He had not even noticed until around the third day of skirting the desert. One particularly thorny tangle had gotten caught up in one of the headstones Harlowe carried, and the strand of coffin blossoms pulled from out under his skin as it fell. The vines rubbed and scratched at his skin. The thorns torn at his shirts and coat. Eventually, as he rounded the rosy and rocky upcroppings, placing the heavy stones near yet far from others just like them, he sat to take a break, tug at the jagged leaves growing from his mutilated hands, and lit the tiny cigarette stuck to his lip. The silver bite of the moon did not glow, but he did not need the light. He had become so familiar with the path he had made that he could easily walk it in the dark. His footsteps just fell into the prints his boots had made the day before, and the day before.

~

The sun glared and blinded but gave off no heat. Its stare still tried to burn him, but he was already leather. The air tried to desiccate him, but he had no moisture left, save whatever the blossoms drank of. With his hands now free for the walk, he could pick at the buds appearing over the lean meaty round of his palms, but it was not long before he was grasping at his chains. Either over sand or sandstone, the marble became heavier with each step. He had this day entangled them within the chains he still wore wrapped around his body. Dragging, he found, was easier than carrying, but the western slate got caught in fig shrubs and salt depressions. But still he dragged them, a couple each day.

Harlowe knew his father would have seen him as weak for having to drag, as opposed to carry, the schist and granite headstones. His father had been a large man, with large teeth and large hands, but Harlowe had begun to wonder lately if he had been as large as he remembered. He certainly remembered less and less each day, and as his memories grew smaller, his father grew larger, so that almost all he had left was a great big image of his smiling "pa" pushing all his other memories to the peripheral. And so he struggled, over and around the hard scrabble of the dead prairie he plowed, to pull out any glimpse of any image of any other memory of his childhood. But it was difficult.

~

Against the wishes of Harlowe's mother, his father had snapped off the tiny branches from the winterbloom to show the boy how to go doodlebugging. His father had always spent his Sundays off from his deputy duties doodlebugging for oil out beyond the sand scrapes, but he had never taken Harlowe with. This was a big day for the boy, or so he had thought at the time.

He remembered being ecstatic when his father had asked if he wanted to go along. He remembered his fascination, watching his father wet and bend the little winterbloom bough into a 'Y' shape. "This 'un," his father had swore would, "outshine the rest. Jus' you see!" Harlowe remembered the intrigue at each twitch of his father's wrist and at the manic digging when the branch would tilt toward the ground.

Then Harlowe remembered the long day turning into a long evening, as his father's mood darkened along with the skyline. He would dig less, and Harlowe would be scolded to dig more while his father would sit and curse the heat that would not dissipate with the coming of the stars. He would complain about the people of Tumbleweed, the people he helped daily. He would list off the incompetencies of other deputies and the sins of the Sheriff and Mayor. It became obvious to Harlowe that his father saw the ultimate goal of doodlebugging as his way out of the game it had all become. All it would take was for one good strike of black gold, and his father could be his own boss, be in control of his own life.

Beneath a similar evening, the same stars, but a much cooler wind and plain, old man Harlowe dug in the sands once again with inflamed hands that looked much closer to his father's than what he remembered as his own. He set yet another headstone along a widely spaced line spreading to the horizon. He had found the stones in a long abandoned boneyard miles back, and they had been his companions — one or two by two — for days now as he moved them across the scrabble to the sands and red rock.

Before setting out again, he remembered that his father never took him out doodlebugging after that one time. He had seen him as bad luck. It was the first time Harlowe had realized that his father was not a smart man, and he had vowed to never be that weak.

~

"I told you to leave them shrubs alone!"

Harlowe rarely saw his mother angry, and when she was, he always had to suppress a grin. She tried so hard to be intimidating, and when she caught a glimpse of his smile she would become even angrier, and he could not blame her. He was always worried that his mother would think he did not take her seriously.

She snatched the broken winterbloom twig out of his little hands. "Yer gonna kill them plants!"

"What's all this about?" Harlowe's father appeared. It was assumed he had retired to the den for the evening to tighten the threaded screws on the back of his radio, but his loud voice made everyone jump.

"Did you teach 'im this?" She held up the green bough.

Harlowe tried to protest as his father picked him up sideways by the arm, but he could only manage to cry, "I jus' wanted to help ya out, pa, for when…"

He was hit twice — once by his father's think palm and once when he hit a table or chair or the floor or all three at once. Despite all the places in which his face was struck, it was the back of his head that hurt the most. He did not even remember being struck in the back of the head, but he was numb everywhere but there.

"Don't you dare go layin' hands on the boy!" his mother screeched. She sounded like the brakes on a runaway train.

Harlowe's father and mother yelled at each other for many minutes, in which time Harlowe just pretended to hold the back of his aching head. He used his elbows to cover his ears. When he tired and crawled to the doorway he accidently looked up to see his father twist and turn a chair around as though he tried to drill into the floor for oil. Harlowe had to avoid his stomping feet.

"When I was 'is age, my pa would'a beat me bloody for doin' much less! The boy needs some boundries or who knows what 'ill turn out to be! He needs to be fenced in, to led down the right path!"

Harlowe thought at first that his father had been beaten, but he suddenly realized that the puffiness around his eyes had come with the tears soaking his cheeks. The desperation in his father's voice made little Harlowe vow that he would never be as weak as his father.

~

The pistoleer could see for miles in all directions from the top of the upcropped canyon, even in the dimming bruise of the meager evening light. It was the first desert sunset he had seen since returning to the land. Over the past week all he had experienced were drab and uniform evenings that collapsed into senseless nights. Here finally was some crimson color to match the flames of his small bonfire. From the sands stretching all around him, his camp must have appeared as a suspicious red-eyed star, judging the immensity of the cold plain.

With a thick collection of smoke, Harlowe released one end of the blanket. He repeated the ritual intermittently, but there was definitely a pattern to the dark pocket clouds ascending and eventually smearing over the horizon.

He took a break to peer down into the twists and turns of the raised canyon. He could not see the squiggly petroglyphs any longer. The sun had almost entirely disappeared. He went back to the collecting and releasing of smoke, back to the calling and summoning. The siren scream in his head had completely vanished for the first time in years, and what he thought was just its imprinted echo reverberating back behind ear and gray matter, turned out to be a far-off whistle that grew with each passing minute.

~

But his senses were slowly returning. Unfortunately, the first thing he could hear was his father's laughter. Harlowe washed the crackling gunpowder from his face with what little water he could find at the bottom of the rain bucket. He could not yet open his eyes. They stung too much. But he knew the sludge at the bottom of the barrel would be green and filled with the few insects that would dare to venture out into the prairie of the homestead. He did not care. His face burned too much to care. His father's laughter stung even more though.

"Told ya to clean yer gun, boy! Look what happens. Now get yer cryin' outta the way, we got a lot more practicin' to do before chores."

In the bloody darkness of eyelids refusing to do anything but squint, Harlowe picked at his raw cheeks for the grit of powder and sand. His face felt like hamburger beneath fingertips that were just as sore.

What was it father had said then? The zombie pistoleer tried to remember, as the *Loco* roared through the night, growing and growing across the dead plain, its bloodshot, cyclopean eye wavering down in the darkness that was more than just night. Its howling no longer frightened the old man. It had been a part of him for too long now to induce shivers. Besides, he had set the trap. But its scream now sounded more like the whistle through his father's teeth than he had remembered.

And what was it his father had said, as Harlowe had worked to open his eyes and throat through the stinging?

"I'm waitin', boy! I ain't got no little daughter for a shooter, do I? We're gonna get some more shootin' in if I have to tan yer hide to get it outta ya!"

"It was yer pistol," Harlowe had murmured.

"What's that sass, boy?"

"It was yer pistol I shot. Not mine."

"So. You shoulda cleaned it, like I told ya."

"Don't know how."

"You shoulda asked."

That night, his father had cleaned his mouth out with the lye soap they used to clean the pens.

Standing high upon the red rock, a lifetime later, Harlowe could still taste that soap. It was the only thing he could taste anymore. He threw a cigarette that would not even burn in the bonfire.

The *Loco* veered suddenly on its path. An iron creature, so fast, so heavy, should not have been able to turn that tightly, but the headstone trail called, and the bloodshot eye grew and neared.

Harlowe thought back to that day one last time before he started down the treacherous path to the bottom of the upcropping. It would take him a large part of the night to traverse down the high canyon walls. The *Loco* would be long trapped by then, struggling to back out of the tight turns, penned in by petraglyph and granite and slate and sandstone and marble. Harlowe wanted to be ready for it. The chains beneath his long coat jingled with every step downward.

So he thought back to that day, one of the constant when his father made him shoot. He remembered vowing on that day to never become as weak as his father.

LXX

"Ode to Wyrmwood"

O' color out of space, thou wander'n eye,
thou, from whose unseen presence narcissists
are enlivened like virgins vampire-kissed,
breathe'n just to die
  —unknown

here was very little of the original Brood Pits left by the time the Brides of Chem-Oshmelech were loaded into the wagons of the final caravan. In each of the prior caravans, one heading out in each of three prior days, an equal amount of equipment, volunteers, supplies, and servants had started out. The wagons were balanced and spread out over the days, so that if any were intercepted en route, by either bandits or the Army of Earth, the others could be saved or salvaged. Two of the four caravans were slightly different from the others. The first was partially built of heavy machinery, great gasengines and plows secretly requisitioned from General Shriven's forces to make sure the passages around the mountains would be cleared for the following caravans. This was done with a direct appeal to the General, and without the knowledge of any of the other generals or commanders. It was taking needed machinery away from the warfront in a time where all gasengines were being sent to the numerous frontlines. The other unique caravan was the line of wagons and trucks sent on the final day of the Brood Pit's decommissioning. The last carrier, on the last day, behind the last wagon, was loaded with the Brides.

They had dressed in their best for the journey — khaki beiges and darker brown layers of skirts and scarves and veils — but their slippers and flannel hose were already muddied and soaked by the time they even got onto the truck.

By an hour into the journey the trailer had warmed up, by the great gasengine vibrating the springs under their cushions or from the same breaths they would continue to inhale and exhale for the next week.

By a few hours into their journey they knew that their clothes would not dry. The cold humidity of the trailer, body heat stunted by cotton and wool, and a trickling drip of melting snow from somewhere none of the Brides could locate — all served to keep mud and sweat from drying.

A half a day into their journey they knew that the wagons and trucks would take longer than projected to arrive at their destination. The roads and paths, ancient and days-old, natural and man-made, were clear from the prior Brood Pit caravans, but the previous days' journeys had taken their toll on the roads. Now, wheels, treads, servants' feet, and antiquus' hooves sunk into the sludge left by the earlier passings. The decision was made by the trail drivers to travel through the night.

And all through the night the trailer lurched and men shouted. Tires roared as they spun. Antiquuses bellowed as they were whipped. Great plumes of slush and earth struck and slid from the exterior of the trailer as it tipped, eventually in and from all directions, but by morning the wagons were on their way again, this time over ice and a ground frozen from the night.

The sweet smell of gasoline had already permeated the Brides' clothing from the bench cushions, but now it oiled the air they re-breathed, while exhaust hung to settle and soak slowly through one layer of their clothing at a time, finally settling on their skin, eventually crusting into yet another layer and over the days becoming indistinguishable from shirt or skirt or sweaty grime.

They rocked and they rocked like babies in a tepid cradle, but they never slept. Eyelashes grew painfully heavy, lids stung from exhaustion as well as exhaust, but bobbing heads could never entirely rest, especially on each other. Their backs felt the cold of the apocalyptic winter, even through the trailer wall, especially through their tan clothing. Even at times of the days when they assumed the sun shown down on the wagons, when the darkness of the interior appeared to warm, the wind could be heard to jostle the forests they imagined they rode through, and the whistle reminded them that they should be cold.

Each evening, any trail driver that had not deserted had to decide whether to halt the trucks for the night to wait for the ground to harden or whether to fight through the sludge in the clouded darkness. If they had kept any of their Unfeigned guardians, the decision would have been easy. Some of them could see in the night. Most of them could have lifted a wagon out of the cold earth. But they had all been called to the War. So each night was either a silent cooling where the Brides' minds still rocked in the repetition of the day, a frigid wait until the struggling chorus of morning ignitions, or a continued shaking of the trailer as machine and beast of burden fought through both wet snow and night.

And the days were filled with the commotion of shouting and the wrenching of metal. Drivers yelled at henches. Henches barked at servants. Servants screamed at each other. The trucks were loud and the antiquus were shrill in their bestial bellowing, but still the Brides, even as crowded as they were in the interior of wood and scrap metal, could always pick out the voices of the arguing men. Only through the hours of each day, when what they assumed were branches of the forests tearing alongside the trailer like the talons of furies reminding them of the ghosts they left behind in the drying pits, were they able to ignore the shouting of the men.

The Brides quickly lost track of the days, and the nights quickly became just as indistinguishable. Any light peaking through the poorly soldered seams could have been from winter sun or nightbeams, or even the occasional unclouded moon. The caravan now moved just as haphazardly whether it was day or night, and the Brides continued to be jostled and sometimes thrown, and they continued to both sweat and shiver at the same time, all the way from the outskirts of the Kalderan Territories and all the way north to the Black Hills, all the way to the rises and rolls of black Quicken. They had replaced the dark smoke and pale exhaust of their trucks for the gritty smog and even heavier exhaust of the pirate city of the Black Hills.

Their truck breathed its last just as they entered the streets. The congested huffing and puffing that had grown to them to be as familiar as the rise and fall of their own chests had ceased. Now, as drivers ordered henches to have servants rapidly unload the Brides, the only sound coming from the trailer was the repetitive tick of cooling metal. Servants of both familiar and unfamiliar faces hurried the Brides into near alleyways where they regrouped and watched spiked and studded scavengers grow from other side-streets to almost immediately fight over the rights to salvage the steaming vehicle.

Quicken was not living up to its reputation. Sticking to night-fed shadows, the Brides peeked out at roads that should have been shoulder to shoulder with armed brigands. They expected loud saloons polluting the streets with lights filtered through all manner of smoke. They watched for hunched cutthroats and juvenile pickpockets, gartered and low pox-covered women, and brown and black men grabbing at pale girls. But the streets, still bustling, were not crowded. Each corner's dance hall was not standing room only. The alleys the Brides walked were filled only with trash. It was rare when they tripped over a drunk or child in the shadows. Quicken was certainly still the busiest city they had ever experienced, but it was not leaving them as awestruck as they were led to believe they would be. So this was how the War, not to mention the nearby blockade of the Temple Needles, was affecting the Black Hills. Bandits and machine gangs had either signed up or been conscripted by either army or they had fled from the righteousness of the enclosing *Ashmedai Adat El.* The city of scoundrels was quieter than it had been in a hundred years.

Still, the occasional gunfire or fireworks sent them sprawling in the garbage of the alleyways, where they were victim to a host of wet smells they could never have imagined existed. Still, there was one reputed fact about Quicken that lived up to rumor. Every lurid sight was obscured by an oily smoke wafting from ground vents. Every tobacco cloud was diluted by the smog's acrid omnipresence. Every mob's chatter was oppressed by a turning chug of some great furnace deep within the hills that made up the city. There was a vibration beneath the earth the Bride's felt as they periodically scurried for the cover of the shadows.

Driver led hench leading servants who hurried the Brides from one corner to another. As far as they could tell, they were the only women in Quicken, and the servants, by shuffling them quickly into abandoned building or side-street, meant to shelter them from the inevitable catcalls. But all the locals did was stare at the scurrying figures covered entirely by drab fabrics.

Finally, from the edge of the city to the center they shuffled, and eventually they entered a collapsed structure hidden inside another building hidden amongst a tightly packed group of apartments surrounded by a gated wall the drivers surprisingly had a key to. Here they passed the occasional Unfeigned keeping guard. None of the Brides were surprised to find that Yankee Zrappado had kept a few of the experiments for himself. Deeper they were led, into a cellar beneath a basement, down steps and taking turns in an incredibly loud and questionably stable arcage, and beneath the sewer of a sewer, until they arrived at their destination. Here they found rooms of unopened crates and pallets still loaded with kegs of amniprevation mixes. They were surprised to find that so little had been unpacked before their arrival.

The Brides, now just led by one hench, crowded themselves into a low room seemingly made of great gears and pistons. The hench took two of the Brides away but left the rest to ruminate on their surroundings. Was this to be the new Brood Pits? They had never been told, but they had assumed it nevertheless — this labyrinthine collection of both tiny and great rooms, each of walls, ceiling, and floors made from massive pipes and ancient levers. Even now they walked over a floor of fat tubing and obviously recently greased drive shafts. They examined a wall composed of one giant accordion pump, another of connecting rods and oiled plugs from another time. A viscous lube hung like a spider's web from the cylinders composing the ceiling. A constant hum — that the Brides had not realized until then that they had already become accustomed to — vibrated through all the rooms, as though they stood in the chambers of a titan's throat.

"Please stop touching that which you do not understand."

More than one of the Brides jumped at the voice. It was familiar but tinny, and it echoed from hanging speaker and corridor, and many of them thought it was directly prompted by their gloved fingers on the pistons making up the walls, as though the very rooms were alive.

The speakers shouted and echoed and whined again in unison as the two missing Brides returned. They were supporting a lanky man clothed only in a sagging diaper the color of their hose. Tiny hidden bells jingled. They knew to turn their veiled heads quickly away from the master IDesigner, but many of them peeked at his bare flesh and the myriad scars running up the left side of his body. No two scars were the same length, color, or shape. They interrupted limb and hairline. More than one of the Brides bit tongue or lip to keep from swooning too noticeably.

"I'll make you understand, if you can, what a momentous day this is," blared the tinny speakers. Some sort of bronze device had recently been implanted on Yankee Zrappado's throat. His neck was still a healing bruise. Even though no words came out of his quivering lips, his voice boomed all around the Brides.

"The Old Ones," chuckled the feedback and echoes, "the Old Ones thought they were so great, so like gods they thought themselves, with their buildings scraping the heavens themselves and their long lives, yes they lived for so long, as did their empires, but what they never knew, what they never gave homage to, was the hidden empires before them. Did they even know? How insignificant they were compared to the mighty civilizations that had come before? Oh, they knew, but they repressed the knowledge, pushed it deep down, buried it, in fact, like those very antepleistocene empires buried beneath the first holy glaciers."

At this point, Zrappado pushed away any Bride that tried to help him into the prepared pool, but he quickly called them back to his unsteady side. He suddenly busied himself by turning away, hiding the scars covering the right side of his body before the women slowly lowered the tithingman into the organic stew. The prone tank was sized just for him, and he quickly sank completely into the muck, but his voice continued through the speakers.

"They were pure and dedicated, these hyperborean ancients, but they were corrupt and wrathful, and it was righteous for the Divine Choir to cleanse the world of their wickedness with living purifying ice, but not before these ancient scientists had learned to harness the greatest power source the world has ever known."

Tendonous cords, previously leading into the pool slithered deeper into the fluid, now connecting the IDesigner to terminals behind and over his side of the room. There was much movement and lights twinkling within the shallow depths. Through the obvious implant in his throat, his voice continued to crackle from speaker to speaker.

"These older Old Ones had fettered the spirits of man! The actual souls of the sacrificed powered everything from the smallest appliance to the greatest war engines! And these prehistoric cultures knew the value of celestial ores, oh yes, they respected the spite of the heavens, and they harvested from the star showers, and it was from one of these meteor events — the greatest of all actually — that they mined their most ambitious, most grandest undertaking. From Cloud Creek did they dig, from celestial material, the holy iron and divine nickel, did they mine. It took generations to pull the meteorite from the earth, to transport it all the way up here, to smith it, to build the pieces from it, and their generations were long back then. Men before the icy deluge lived for a hundred and twenty years!

"The prehistoric sorcerer-scientists then built their most beautiful accomplishments, through the melding of the mundane and the divine — artifacts to attract wayward spirits, artifacts to capture and harness the soul, machines to live and destroy — and beneath these very hills they put all these superpreturnatural devices together. The

Mannanimus Magnet, the Eus Engine, and, finally, what you see here, perfected as the Quicken Device, and I, your master Yankee Zrappado, final man of reason, the one and only IDesigner of the *Ashmedai Adat El,* have found it and resurrected it."

There was scattered clapping amongst the Brides. It was a dry and stifling sound — the rub of cotton on cotton. The women did not recognize the men that had come into the moving room. If they were drivers, henches or servants, they were new. The men had a cold look about them. Even in the hot room, they wore too little. The sweat on their sunken chests had dried to oil days earlier. Still, the speakers bellowed like the cows the old Brood Pits held.

"But to my eternal regret, this beautiful accomplishment will again sadly never reach its full potential, for it requires the sacrifice of a truly godly people, for the winter winds of the Divine Choir will again cover the lands and the hills again before it can emerge, for the sick and fallen spiritually destitute of the countryside and the cities chose not to have the courage for the faith required to give themselves up for the Mannanimus Magnet. For it would require the sacrifice of thousands, unfettered souls suddenly and almost simultaneously drawn by the magnet, absorbed and stored and translated into energy, fuel for the Eus Engine, and then driving the Quicken Device to its full stature, its full abilities and potential.

"But the machine is not without its uses, and we, as the hopeful, the chosen, are not without our resources, our roles, for our faith, our patience, will be rewarded. For I, Yankee Zrappado, a man born out of due reason, have opened the Mannanimus Magnet to the countryside, and, although it will absorb far, far less then the required thousand of souls, it will still find enough souls to be of some use. For some still die nearby everyday in this fallen land. And the Quicken Device also houses an ancient computer that, to this day, has no peer except perhaps that of the human mind, and no one knows the human mind better than yours truly. So, in my exile I have awakened this Quicken Mechanism. I have coaxed it back to awareness, but without a power source it still lies inert. The computer was meant to move the entire living machine out, across the world, to drive ancient man's enemies before him, but without the sacrifice of the land the leviathan will not move. From my research and work, however, I have faith that a smaller, meager sacrifice, will suffice to power the Mechanism for a limited time, and that limited time will be all I need to ask one question, one all-important question. The Mechanism is advanced enough to predict the future through massive probability calculation. It will succeed where that failure, Mother Inferior, has failed. Reason will win out over emotion!"

Before leaving, the few men in the room handed out flutes of bubbling champagne to the gasps of the Brides. The women were hesitant to take up a taboo they had been denied their entire lives, but the electric speakers squealed Zrappado's approval.

"Sisters, you have worked hard these past years in the service of the Song, and such faith and such persistence as you have shown will never *not* be rewarded, and it is through the Song that you will be saved, for no matter how very much I have tried my best to give you a good life there are those people, out there in the world, with their lies, the lies of the Liege of Foes, the lies of traitors and the unclean, have made your potential, all your potentials, impossible. There is no way to detach yourselves from what is happening out there, in the world. But you can, you will, be an example to not just the unreasonable, but to others like yourselves, to those oppressed by the dirty, filthy liars out there, that your faith will see you through to the peace of the rewarding afterworld. Your role, your new role, will be played out in a divine plane, as mundane energy powering the celestial plan. We have always sought enlightenment and information, sisters, have we not, and I will admit the sin of envy, right here, right now, for you are on the verge of becoming information. I am tired, as tired as you, but my noble sacrifice will be to stay behind to harness that information — the information born of your revolutionary act, an act protesting the conditions of a fallen world!"

Two of the Brides had already tasted the drink, and, before the others could fit the flutes under veil or between scarves, those two were on their knees and skirts, breathing so loudly and so rapidly that they choked not just on their tongues but the cloths encircling their faces. A third Bride shoved through the rest of the women, moving to the front of the room and knocking the champagne glasses to the floor both accidently and on purpose.

"You're not even listening to what he's saying," Ivy said, removing the ill-fitting veil from her face. "Your potential is to hypothetically be submerged in some hysterical group consciousness powering an old calculator? Is this what your…"

She had turned to face the group, some of which had run from the room, when from the gelatinous pool behind her emerged something out of the Brides' dreams and nightmares. The IDesigner was both man and machine, a collection of weak flesh and strong iron and nickel. Some limbs had been replaced in the pool, some augmented, some multiplied. His lower half disappeared into cord and flexible piping. Above his silently moving mouth, his head was entirely covered by a globe of optics and chunky metal antennae. The Brides' beige turned dark as they were splashed with ooze.

Ivy was held, prone in both warm and cold arms and hands and vises, paralyzed by sudden syringes into her neck and thigh. For many seconds the shrieks of the Brides were all Ivy could hear, even above the gaseous pistons and axles comprising the walls, but then she could hear Zrappado's breathing in her ear, or perhaps she had mistaken hearing for feeling.

"I know who you are, little bird, little aunt, I know who you are," the speakers whined with feedback as the cyborg tithingman's throat contracted. "Do not think for one minute that I have not given you a hell of a lot of thought, but, unlike others, I had given up on any pretence that you are me and myselfs' salvation. How could a fruit so rotten be so sweet, be the key to our promised spiritual bodies? I had turned to other ventures, yet here you are, cloaked in the purity of the sisters. How blasphemous, yet how utterly serendipitous."

One scaffolded iron arm held out Ivy's arm as far as it could reach. Another, of blades, shears, needles, and snips spread the fingers of her hand.

Zrappado chewed her ear with a quiet mouth but echoed around the room. "You have a lot to account for here today, little weed. The Mannanimus Magnet, open to the land, goes unfed. The Eus Engine will not turn. The Quicken Mechanism will not calculate, will not answer my one question. 'How can I end the war?' That is all I wanted to ask it, but you have no interest in the answer? You want people to continue to suffer, do you? Fine. So be it."

Pseudoamnio dripped from the tithingman to obscure Ivy's eyes, and, although she had lost most of the feeling in her body, she still felt the gritty snips cut her pointer finger off, but she could not look, could not pull her hand away. The master IDesigner sank backward, submerging into the hot liquid, still folding Ivy into his arms.

"We all have our roles to play, predetermined on a level our meager bird brains could never understand, but listen to the Divine Chorus and a pattern emerges, that all serve the Song. Your role, little wren, is to convince these wayward girls, these sisters, these Brides of Chem-Oshmelech, of their role, to become one with each other and with reason, to reinvigorate their faith, to feed the machine."

LXXI

XLII. The Theory of Original Sin, ever forced upon the oppressed, is the poor man's rationalization of convenient equality.

—Precepts of the Painted God

Che crowds were old and paler than the impotent sun, and, like the dull star, the jurors hid their stares, but she could still feel them. Even beneath all the areas she bled, she could feel their eyes upon her. The elderly helped the elderly over and up into the ruins of the broken amphitheater, over and around Mew. The trial was about to begin.

"Let the jury note that the accused refuses to take the oath," she heard the tithingman say. It was the first thing she could hear governor Mister Cilice say since they had dragged her into the crumbling field of the stage. He had spoken much, to her lawyer, the security, even to the hundred elderly in the stands set to be her jury, but she could not hear his quiet voice until he started using the birch bark bullhorn. A chorus of freshly-washed powder monkeys had sung a short and lilting song certainly chosen for their prepubescent ranges, and Mew now realized, from gestures and looks she had been given, that she had been expected to kiss each of the boys on the cheek to demonstrate honesty to the Song, as Cilice was now doing. Her lawyer could not help but express his displeasure as he held her up to face her prosecutor.

"Bad move, m'lady. You better start to play along, or this will continue to get worse."

She leaned against the stranger as best she could until he walked away, obviously uncomfortable so near the edge of the great canyon. She teetered on her own, on one leg she could not feel and another that hurt with each movement. The gown they had put on her before the trial was soaking through already. Something trickled down to her broken foot.

The mosses, petulant against the winter, green against the granite, somehow thrived despite the frost of the mountain. The fuzzy carpet covered the rock of the broken amphitheater and even the swaying bridges connecting one peak to another. The haze choking the thin air required fires in randomly placed, seemingly ancient carved stoves.

"Please give the jury your name and surname," Cilice asked with a bullhorn that was suddenly so near her face. She had not been aware that the prosecutor had approached her, not been aware that she had staggered back at the sound to so near the precarious edge of the open air.

She answered, realizing a rough throat that spoke in something other than a scream for the first time in days.

"What kind of name is that? Barely a sound!" the tithingman broadcast to the crowd. The wrinkled and weathered audience leaned forward. Mew would have been surprised if they could have heard him, much less her answers.

"The jury might ask 'Where are you from?'" he continued.

"I am... was... from Below the Brook, but I..."

"Below a brook? What kind of place is that? Are you a fish?" The jury chuckled along with Cilice. "What is your father's name?"

Her lawyer appeared suddenly at her side when she staggered and did not answer. "They expect you to answer. You have to look good for the jury." But he moved quickly away when a breeze from the canyon appeared at her back.

"How old are you?" the governor asked from behind bullhorn and the obscuring curtain of curly hair. He had to constantly maneuver the megaphone between the brown ringlets and under his massive nostrils. "How old were you when you first sang the Song?"

"I've never..." she stuttered, feeling the open air behind her on the damp flogging marks beneath her gown. "I don't know. Why are you..." Looking around gave her an immense pain in the side of her head, and she staggered again at the cliff. One eye could not focus very far, and the other looked through such a fog that she could only see silhouettes, but she could tell that the shape of her lawyer shook its head in disbelief right along with the crowd in the stands.

She heard him whisper to the governor, "The accused is prepared to recite the Zeventh Holy Verze if it will look favorably..."

"No," Mew whispered in turn, "but I am willing to talk to someone, anyone, about any..."

"The time for reparations is over," Cilice interrupted into the bull-horn. "The jury might wonder 'why have you attempted at multiple times to escape?' Is that not already an admission of guilt?"

"I... don't know what I am being..."

"How old were you when you left your father's care?"

Mew suddenly found herself on the crumbled brick of the

half-amphitheater, not remembering passing out. She pushed herself into a sitting position, careful of the bright abyss behind her, and murmured an answer to the latest question. "I heard a voice, as a girl, that helped me... guided me. The first time, I was very much afraid. It was at the noon of one day... in a garden... I think, and the voice, I knew came from the green light of the sky. The voice always came with the light. I only recently remembered this." She tried to raise a hand to wipe a tear from her cheek but remembered that her arms had stopped listening to her sometime during the night. She could feel some finger on one hand move, nothing more. "I... I'm so thirsty. Can I have some water?"

"A green light," the bullhorn mimicked. There were murmurs in the stands Mew could not understand any better than what her lawyer whispered to her. She could not help but think of Janus, as she had so often over the few prior days. How was it that he adored the coliseum, the audiences and their stares upon him? The thought made her hate him. "Everyone knows there is no green light in the sky. Where is it?"

"When I was in the wood... in the clearing, surrounded by stone and trees, the voice came easy to me. It was a worthy voice, the voice of light and life. I only remember now that it protected me. It... understood me."

"And what did this 'voice' offer you, huh? We would all like to ask 'What did it promise?'"

"It told me to be... good."

"It gave you no instruction for salvation? For saving your soul?" She could hear his pacing through the cottony swelling of her ears. There was no rhythm to his circling or the bellowing of his horn. The sound grew and quieted through the questioning, but he never neared, preferring to stay close to the crowded stands and the decrepit hearing of the jury. "You move in the habit of a man. You carry a sword, you wander alone, you demand audiences... where is this green light? Point to it now!"

"I was a child..."

"Can you *hear* the light?"

"I don't..."

"Can you hear the Song, or does the light fill up every orifice, blinding, deafening, smothering you, filling you up with such unholy pleasures that you cannot or will not hear the Divine Choir?"

Mew thought she had been standing but could still feel the broken ground beneath her. To loud gasps of the jury, she reached for leverage, but either her hands would not answer her or they were bound, and she swayed over the edge of the canyon as her legs attempted to hold herself up.

"Where does this voice come from?" Cilice asked her, although she was certain he was directing his words over the ruinous stands.

"It does not... it came... the voice came from God. I am afraid to explain it to you."

"The jury would reason that 'If you are innocent, then there is no need to be afraid.' Fear is the will of the divine."

She could see her lawyer squirming in his chair. Its red plush was one of the few colors her eyes could still see. This was a chair not meant for the outdoors, but it did not snow this day, and the collapsing area had obviously been cleared sometime recently. Mew could not see the governor but still heard the scraping of his pacing boots. "Where... where am I?" she asked.

"Are you a virgin?" The circling steps stopped. If Mew's lawyer had been whispering to her, he stopped. Weathered wood creaked from somewhere up high in the seating. "You are a woman of very good fortune, m'lady. You've wandered far and wide without interruption, through territory and wilderness, by and past loyal choirs and with men and harlots of the despicable Army of Earth. Would you have such good fortune if you lost your virginity?"

"I'm not..."

"Or do you believe you have such good fortune because you are a virgin?"

"I don't..."

"Would you have seen this green light if you were married? Were you assured good fortune if you would keep your virginity? Are you sure of salvation? Did you make a vow to this 'green light' to lose or keep your virginity? Did the light still come to you? Did you offer your virginity to the Liege of Foes and all his generals and all their wild men? Were you awake when you saw this light? Had you been fasting when you heard this light? I have to ask, 'Did you, in fact, see or hear this light?' Because, you see, I'm afraid I've caught you in a little lie. At one point you claim to have seen this 'magical' light, when you later stated that you heard it. Is that correct? Let the record show that the accused has lied to this most reputable jury. So, now, how is it that you intend to prove to the people gathered here today that the voice you heard was, indeed, the voice of God? Do you expect these men of right reason to just fall for your charm and take your word, a wild woman of the world's word? You who have so deliberately defied the good graces of the *Ashmedai Adat El* at every turn, m'lady, you were offered every chance to speak, for many a year now, but you chose to delight yourself on pilgrimages and peregrinations with all manner of low men and women. And all this amounts to one question and one question only. Are you, m'lady, a virgin? Speak up! Is your intention..."

Mew could feel little beyond numbing pain anymore, and she had been feeling it for so many days and nights now that she would expect to embrace it as a familiar friend, but she never got used to it. The multiple breaks in her leg kept her up at night, pinching and pulsing as they eventually merged with the merciless grinding of bone in her hip. She could not see it but knew her arm hung at an unnatural angle. Like her opposite hand, it ignored her, but the squeezing muscles also refused to relax. They tightened until she found herself not even realizing that she had been sobbing until eventually, in the night, her captors would gag her with oily rags or something worse. There was a softness in her breast that spoke of broken ribs. The bones pressed against her insides. Her breaths could only be shallow or she would chance coughing up bits of blood both dark and hard. It was all so constricting, her body. It was against her, crushing in upon itself. She could not help but compare it to the airy freedom at her back, the crisp openness so close behind her. She chanced a glance backward, through swollen lids and skewed vision, and delighted in the unimaginable depths through she could barely peer. The golden canyon held numerous worlds all its own. The winds whipped between countless slanted forests and cliffs sunburned by untold eons of prehistoric seasons. If there was a bottom to the cavernous steeps, she doubted it had ever been seen by human eyes.

Governor Cilice, the tithingman prosecutor, still circled the half-dome of the ruined arena, finishing his questions. The inconsistent scrape of boot against western marble and protruding yellowed weeds grew closer before lessening farther. He was near and far. The bull-horn was loud and then faint. His presence and his questions would suddenly appear inches from Mew's face, hot breath and soft voice on her wet cheeks as he held the instrument away in order to whisper new questions closely to her, to make sure she could hear.

At some point she realized that he had actually ended his questioning, yet still he periodically neared uncomfortably close and still he explored the space in front of the mass of jurors.

"…let me just say, that unless I personally am convinced by the Song and plain reason, that I do not accept the authority of any so-called reveler, for they have always contradicted each other. My conscience is willfully and faithfully burdened to the Song of the Divine Chorus as it was revealed to the prophets, for its infallibility is told of in its very verses. To go against this conscience is neither right nor safe. Here I stand. I can do no other. And I would most humbly ask of you — May the Choir of Heaven help you in your interpretation and deliberations of my words.

"Now, you are to judge the accused on the order of three conditions. The first condition: That no supposed reveler speaks in contradiction to the Song as revealed to the original prophets, otherwise it occurs through the response of devils, for the reveler then deceives and are deceived. If you reply in spirit, 'How can I know whether it is the Divine Choir who is speaking?' here is the answer — if a reveler has announced something in the name of the Divine Choir, and it is in contrast to the Song, as it was revealed to the original prophets, it is not the Divine Choir who has spoken. You are concerned with an invention of the reveler and of her spirit of arrogance. For if one speaks falsely for God than one lifts oneself up pridefully to the level of a false god, and we all know the punishment of self-idolatry.

"Second condition: That no supposed reveler acts in contradiction to the Song as revealed to the original prophets, otherwise it acts in the response of devils, for the reveler then deceives and are deceived. You are concerned with an invention of a hypocrite and of her spirit of deception. For if one acts in deafness but speaks falsely for God than one lifts oneself up pridefully to the level of a false god, and we all know the punishment of self-idolatry.

"I would say that 'You have a great responsibility here today,' o' respected members of the jury. You number seventy-seven — a holy number — and it is only fortunate that you decide the trials of today. It is necessary that you distinguish the revelations of angels from illusions, for just as the verity of our truths are combated by the disputatious arguments of heretics, so is the authority of true miracles and holy revelations diminished by the means of revelers of deceit, by wild feats of wild women and magicians.

"Third condition: If a maid is not a virgin then she is fallen, and she will keep falling until she dies. She is not possessed by devils but oppressed by them, but, just like the possessed, she has made a choice. It is a choice to fall."

Mew thought that Cilice had walked away, but his breath was suddenly upon her cheek again. With the bullhorn at his side, his soft and measured words blew past his mask of ringed hair to even move the strands of her own sweat and blood-stuck hair.

"Are you a virgin?" he asked. "The jury does not take honesty lightly. This is your chance to clear your conscience as well as your soul."

She bit down hard at the base of his huge nose, deep within the hair hanging from the wide brim of his hat, deeply into skin and cartilage, and, as he screamed into her face so did all her muscles scream as she pushed backward with all the faint strength her collapsing limbs would allow. Here the pain was finally her friend, as it reminded her she was still alive, and it woke her in her final seconds. She wanted to be awake before she died.

She could not see or hear, but she could feel the liberating rush of air all around her. She had hoped to twist or somehow maneuver Cilice beneath her, but he was quickly lost in the swirling buffet of the chasm's air. She was tossed about as in a hurricane and was reminded of the storm over the city of Magog. She was certain that the battle at the Tower had only occurred a few years ago, that she had been so young and naïve in the manic fight, but it was so suddenly clear in her memory that it could have occurred days earlier. Janus had been so quick to tell her every detail about when they had been separated in the fight, and she now remembered dismissing his tales of violence, and she now regretted it. He had always tried so hard in vain to impress her back then, but his eagerness and impatience had diminished him in her eyes. Why could he never see that? But, in the end, he was only human. And so was she. She regretted being so hard on him, and on herself, for she missed him greatly, and she missed herself — the innocence that had blinded her to the world. It was so much more beautiful in those days. Why could it not have stayed that way?

She knew she must have hit outcroppings, stone and forested, but could feel nothing. The rush of the fall still blew past her ears, exploding them. Blood rushed to and from her cheeks, to and from countless wounds. Still, she fell, beyond sight and sound. She focused and tried in vain to find the pain in her head, limbs, and chest. The pain would keep her awake until she hit the distant rock of the canyon floor. She needed so desperately to stay awake, to be aware of every last second of life, or else it was all in vain — she did not know why she felt this way. But it was no matter. Mew was dead by the time she hit the earth.

LXXII

Fallen Knight knows not lover's plight
to end each tryst in hectic flight
from jealous mate and bitter day
we sleep and slip and slide away
out of sight of falling night

—Unknown

There was a distinct lack of winter in the Black Hills relative to the surrounding storms enveloping the plains. Crystalline snow packed hard against the uneven terrain, and ice clung tightly to the ashen forests, but it was a subdued season compared to the wind-wracked steppes Wulf's forces felt as though they had spent a lifetime crossing. Here one could even find dry ground on the sunnier sides of trees, composed of layers of dead leaves and decayed scrub before any dirt. The blackjacks he and Teca sat beneath had kept their needles, and she wondered if there was anywhere else in the land where that could be said. They were brown and broken, and it would not be long before the wind or the endless season would bare the branches and shrivel the caterpillars that had woken too early to attempt a meal. The worms, the first of their kind to experience snow, would no doubt be the last generation of their kind in the world. One dropped, squirmed, and died tickling her cheek before it fell, while Wulf nuzzled her opposite ear. She pulled up the leather of her pants before tying and buckling numerous belts at the sound of her approaching troops. She hoped her underclothes would dry before nightfall, but it felt unlikely. As of now, they bunched and stuck to her belly, and she tried not to let it show in her stance as she moved into one of the few sunbeams able to break through the branches. Like all the light near the emaciated river, it glowed deeply violet, congealing through the dying needles overhead. The fighters were too sheltered in the hills to know if it was the sunset that gave the shade its bloody hue or if it was the reflection from the body-strewn stream. As the seconds passed, more and more recent corpses floated past their spot on the trampled shore.

Wulf followed her up, in turn tying breeches and adjusting his belt. "No matter the outcome of the War," he said, moving against her, his mouth on the back of her neck, "it will be the ravens who ultimately win."

Most of the torn or dismembered bodies floated on by, quickly sinking out of sight, but on the chance that one would get caught up on sand or any patch of dead branches, black birds were quickly upon it, tearing at its face.

"Those are crows," Teca whispered. Her breath shook as she looked up to the red light.

"That they are, missy," said one of the passing guard, an obvious midgardian in furs matching the color of the trees. There was no telling the girth of him or his followers. They were big men, but bear-faced shoulder plates and layers of iced furs doubled their size. They stopped to peer out at Wulf from either white-horned or blue-feathered helms. "Them birds do us a service, they do." Teca wondered if there were any blue eyes in service to the Army of Earth that were not tattooed or branded with the single crimson tear.

Wulf sighed, breath tickling the hair he had been stroking. He left her side to walk the sandbar, and she was immediately cold. She shivered, noticing the stare of one crow. The eyeball hanging from its beak would also not look away.

"Ah, yes, that's right," Wulf said. The birds yelled at him and each other but refused to give up their juicy snacks. "Never look into a dead man's eyes."

"It's a doorway," the other midgardian said, "to God's Throne Room, but no one can look on the face of God and live. We're not ready."

"To see the face of God is to go mad," Wulf whispered, then laughed. "So, yes, these benevolent birds do us a great favor. It must be why they follow us so, giving away our every position."

"We've cleared the ravine, m'lord," one of the men said.

"Send word to the back forces. All boats, both river and lake ships, should be reassembled by now. They are all to be sent to the front to portage. We veer sharply south now."

"To the Bare Butte Lake," Teca pointed out. "It won't be frozen enough to cross on foot. The Horde has its northernmost stronghold on the south side of the lake. I don't know any other way to approach it except from southern roads."

"Except from the lake, which they won't expect. Send the Svalbard ships first to break any ice."

He came back to her when the guards shuffled off. It worried her, sending most of the Northern troops ahead of the rest of the battalion. The midgardians were easily the most powerful fighters, and she felt much safer surrounded by them, but they were definitely the best shipmen.

"We're taking an awful long route to get to the Needles," she said as she moved into Wulf's embrace and wrapped herself in his arms and cloak. It was at times like this, feeling the slow beat of his heart against her cheek, that she could not imagine ever being cold again, but she moved in even closer, with her cold fingers finding the warm flesh under all the layers beneath his belt.

They still had so far to go, through such rugged rises and dip in elevation, before she was home. She could not even imagine how an army could travel through the route she had chosen for them and had been going over maps incessantly since Wulf had come to her with the plans.

He sensed her apprehension. "The majority of the blockade forces will be surrounding your temple at the southern side. If we can break it, we will eventually want them to retreat south. If they retreated to the Bare Butte stronghold we would always have to watch our back, and the fast push into the Kalderan Territories that I have planned requires that we never look back."

"It also requires that the Necrophim generals keep up the pressure on the far sides of the Territories. When is the last we've heard from any of them? How can you trust them?"

"I don't. As far as the Necrophim are concerned I have put my trust in two things. Their complete love of conquest…"

"And her?"

"They don't love her, only violence, but they owe her for presenting a new civilization to kill."

"And what do *you* owe her for?" Teca spoke into the warmth of his hair, the humidity of his scraggly beard and wet lips.

He was running his fingers through her hair, as she noticed he always did when he was thinking of just the right words to use. This hair he bundled tightly in his fist to pull her face away from his, her suddenly bare chest to his mouth.

They rolled in dead grass and snow recently trampled by boots from both armies. She clenched his legs within hers and squirmed against him, grinding his leather into ice and sand. They stopped short of the frigid stream, laughing at and shaking off their disheveled or discarded clothing. Some of it had been lost to the slow rapids, and they traded what they could to cover open areas of flushed but suddenly cooling skin.

Teca immersed her face in the water as well as she could without losing her balance. Her legs were weaker than she had expected when her pulse slowed. The reflection showed her face to be even redder than usual. She smiled. Even Wulf's snow-white skin looked bronze in the crimson haze.

"She presented a new world to me as well. But it was one that had already existed, one that was always there, I just didn't realize it. It was a world in which free will had, at the very least, been corrupted and, at the most, been an illusion forced by... someone... to achieve an order to their liking. It was a reality in which the dirtiest of bloodlines had been manipulated for generations to one day create an anti-savior with the ability to unleash Armageddon on gods and man. She showed me a world where choice had been a lie, called it home, and then she brought me back to it. The revelation was one of seven gifts."

"How nice. But who is she?"

"She is known by more names than there are nations that curse her. The Crimson Queen. Hella Halja Loksdottir. Ogress Halfface. Mourning Attar's Shame. Son of the son of dawn. Lilit Light-bringer. When she found me in her kingdom, washed up on the shore of a lake of fire, in visible darkness, she claims I cried out to her in my sleep, calling her Sera..." Here he paused. Without realizing it, Teca had played with long strands of his hair out of his hood, hiding his granite gaze behind curls. "It does not matter who she is. All that matters is that she hates the Asmodeus Horde, specifically Ashmedai, with a passion that will win this war."

"We'll win after we liberate the Temple. The crusade will not stop until the Knight's Cavalry ride the streets of Kaldera's capital. This blockade... the Order has never been so insulted, especially considering the betrayal of the western knights. It's always been an estranged relationship, but allying themselves with false angels is beyond offensive — it's apostasy of the highest level."

"Teca," Wulf started, leaving her to bathe his hands and face at the side of the rapids. She thought that he may have been blushing, but he was also bathed in the scarlet of the scene, disappearing in the pink light and deep shadows. "You must know by now not to completely trust your…"

A cadre of Teca's soldiers appeared loudly from the trees. They were members of her Close Guard, and they looked relatively unscathed from the battle. The crying eye painted on their leather helmets and long skirts looked particularly bloody along the dark waters. They quieted and saluted as they passed. Behind them, pulled by binds, trailed a few chained members of the Army of Heaven. They had been stripped of armor and most clothes, and, Teca thought, she probably would not have able to tell their allegiance had they not scarred their chests with the Mark of Ashmedai. The marks too glowed even more in the crimson eve.

Wulf came out of her blind spot to pin her against a tree, and her boots slipped in new mud before he held her hips painfully against its dark bark.

"When I was in your holy village," he said, "all those years ago, I… saw something… something that wasn't right, that didn't belong."

More of the Army of Earth were appearing along the stream. Mercenaries of the Quicken-based Incorrigible Vole Clan, identified by shirts of gray fur and silver wire, were wading out into the water to catch any body that floated by for any salvageable round or metal. Other soldiers passed through to rejoin their families' encampments that had been left behind at the entrance to the eastern canyon.

She just hid in Wulf's cloak, from the cold, from the War, from both the anticipation and the dread of being reunited with the Order. Why now of all times had she found him? She had wandered for years outside the Black Hills, through the Wheel and skirting the plains. Why could they not have found each other during happier times? But she immediately recognized that younger girl in her thoughts — that younger girl that had had her wrist broken by some alien abomination in the Badlands, the girl that had led a group of strange strangers (as she did now) into her home forests to try to save the land, the girl that was again setting herself up for embarrassment by getting too close to the man whose shirts her fingers now danced. Why did she act so differently around him? She cringed at the thought that this was her true self, appearing again after so many years, and she cringed when thinking that the thought made her resent him a bit. She regretted the thought, as her wrist reminded her of its occasional soreness and the past it exemplified.

In the violent haze of the evening it was difficult to tell a more exact time of day, but she could tell Wulf was trying to do so. He looked to the thick sky through the mesh of dead branches. He peered into the cottony reflection. "What time is it?"

"Who am I, the Clockwork Monarch?" she chastised, biting his chin through the wires of his whitening beard.

"They've returned," he said, his real eye suddenly going cloudy while the other became the color of the stream.

Teca looked to find her gloves amongst the trees. Even in returning to the shade of the forest, her hands appeared bloody in the dim light. She shouted back, "Who? Now? With an answer?"

"They have decided... and I must do this alone."

She came out back into the glow of the rushing water only to follow Wulf back into the tree-line. She watched and walked as he went slowly, hesitantly but deliberately, up and down rises and treacherous rock falls. The trunks and limbs of the blackjacks became thicker, older, but still their needles were dead. The snow was lighter the deeper they walked, sparser and harder. It crumbled beneath their steps into tiny gems, each individually sided but catching the gore of the air with the same dull glow she and Wulf were absorbed.

She stopped whenever he did, looking off into the same direction before obviously adjusting the route. Her boots were not enough to lesson the threat of straining ankle and bruising heel. They were off any path now, and she worried that this was the type of terrain their legions and their soldiers' families were going to have to traverse very quickly in the coming days — the treacherous steeps and deeps that the straightward plan would require. The nearby Horde forces very obviously now knew that the Army of Earth had left the prairie, and Wulf had found himself on a sudden and very strict clock. So why were they wasting time sliding down crumbling hills?

They could no longer hear the sound of the Army. The battle's red fog still filtered the evening, but they had walked far enough to lose the echo of the crying wounded and the mending of swords.

"After all this," she eventually asked, kicking footholds through layers of age-settled needles and tangling weeds, "after all this is done — the wars and the land grabs. What then? After the Army beats the Horde back, after you win, where will you go, what will you do?"

It was many minutes before he answered. She knew he had heard her, could tell from the tilt of his hood and from his slowed steps that he was thinking. She walked up along side him when the land flattened out, noticing the same sullenness in his face as when he had to discuss difficult troop direction, when he knew sacrifices would have to be made.

They approached a sunken cave partially exposed behind a massive horizontal outcropping of rainbow rock, and he hesitated only to say, "I must go in alone," before ducking to head into the darkness. She followed to find that it was not shadows they entered, but even more bleeding light leaking from ceiling crevices. The initial interior of the cave had only a partially closed roof, and the evening still streamed in, occasionally interrupted by both natural and chisel-carved pillars. She looked to her hands. They were still the color of the recent battlefield.

"When everyone heads south, ahead of the final push of whatever glacier pushes its way from the North, we could find some abandoned mansion," Wulf said softly, avoiding an echo. He ducked and wound his way around rock and light beam. "We could find some empty estate in the richest oil territory, one filled with the largest fireplaces and stoves, and huddle in for the *Fimbulvetr*. Slowly, as we realize that the winter will never end, over the years, we'll dismantle plush furniture, take the occasional wall down to burn for warmth. Eventually, when the final season is still young, yet we are old, all we'll have is our bodies to keep each warm. Beneath this ragged cloak and your ugly jacket, we'll…"

He ducked a swing of her fist that she could not possibly figure out how he knew had come at the back of his hood. "I don't remember you being such a romantic," she said.

"If he is truly his mother's son," came a voice from some side of the cave, "then he most certainly is a romantic." Laughter of a different voice followed from some other side of the cave, and that is when Teca saw that they were surrounded.

She had heard that only five of the Seven Smoke Phetas had initially answered his summons a week earlier, but he had told her that the gathering had gone well, yet, unless more watched from the red shadows, only three families were here represented. Shappa Lizard spoke nearest Wulf, leaning over him from a recess where she could play with a beam of light without becoming too exposed. Teca could not recognize the bones of the great beast the Native wore, but she could tell that at a moment's notice they could all be removed and used as weapons. Even the skull that covered her pale-painted face had each edge sharpened. Her bronze toes peeked from the darkness, gripping the wet rock with nails and transplanted talons.

"Hae khola, you have won another victory here," the Chief purred, and Teca could not tell if was a statement or question.

"With each battle won," Wulf said, moving back deeper into his cloak, "I lose more and more fighters. I'm not sure I can afford many more victories. That is why I ask your councils for aid."

"Tell us, ciqala ohanzee, what will be your first word upon sitting on the throne of the *As-sin-wati,* the great mammoth wall of mountains. When the last of your enemy, *those that screech out of season,* is driven before you, what song will you first sing to replace theirs."

"I'm not interested in thrones," Wulf said, and Teca, without looking, imagined the smile at the edge of his mouth.

Another chief leaned into an almost solid beam of light. From one side of her head hung pure silver like strands of metal. It may have actually even been metal, Teca thought, for her raiment was almost entirely made of the thinnest of silvers pressed into the shapes of feathers and leaves. The fiery shadows dripped from her sharp bonnet. She spoke, never moving her dark eyes from Wulf. "Someone will need to rule, ciqala akecheta, and is that not your responsibility after tearing the land apart for these many years?" The hair hanging from the other side of her head was of a blackness untouched by the evening. Teca guessed that this was Lame Wachiwi Iguanodawn, chief of the Two Trucks Tribe.

Water dripped, slowly and rhythmically, from somewhere deeper within the cave, and it was all that Teca could smell — the clean water filtered for eons by hidden granite and volcanic rock. But other than the drip and its echo, the cave was quiet and cold. The crooked spires of a reddening sunset did nothing to warm the crisp humidity.

Teca looked sideways at the third chief, a being supposedly made entirely of minerals, dripped and formed over the ages man still hid beneath the earth. According to the Natives, when she awoke, it had been time for the tribes to return to the surface to prepare for civilization's eventual return. But up close, Teca found the appearance of her amber skin softer than expected. A bony frill opened on the back of her head when she realized she was being stared at. This was the immortal Marge Da Makota, and she held a staff that looked to be made out of the same substance as her body. It was topped by a sculpture of an archaeopteryx, and it had translated every word that had been said into some quiet language, but now, like the rest of the speakers in the cave, it had gone silent.

"Look, we've made our plea," Teca stepped forward eventually to say, walking into the steam of her sudden breath. "We don't have time for any more negotiations. I don't know what was said or what still needs to be said, but the Army of Earth needs to move out. You've seen or no doubt heard what the Horde is capable of. They're slavers. They're drillers. They allow no dissent, and they worship some sort of aliens from beyond the stars, monsters not of this Earth. They are un-natural, a blight upon earth *and* Earth. We're going to stop their spread and take back what they've captured over the past few years. We've already..."

"It is appropriate that you have brought her, little *shung manitu*, little wolf king," the chief of the Two Trucks Tribe said, and Teca could see a flash of many colors of ores and beads hanging from her neck to her metallic legs. The dimming light, however, quickly reduced all the finery to shades of red. She held out her hands to Teca. One ended in chrome claws, the other in reptilian talons. One hand was entwined in a dew-speckled web from which an obsidian spider danced, from the other were hung strings of reflective beads. "We are not interested in reclaiming the lands of the Paha Sapa."

"Why would..."

"S'cephansi, your church and its land are tainted by corrupt spirits, evil wakanpi, that your elders invited in after driving our ancestors out of what you call the Needles. Your 'sirs' and monks have blackened the winds and cursed the sand."

"Wulf! What gives you the right, you asshole?" Teca grabbed at his cloak for an arm or a handful of leather to turn him toward her. "What is she talking about? What did you do?"

Shappa Lizard clarified, "There is an angry nagi among your knights, and it has fed upon your people and their minds for genera-tions. As long as its roots are in those hills, why would we ever want our land back?"

Teca pulled her gloves off to grab at Wulf's face. She wanted to feel him, to make sure it was really him beneath the hood. "Did you offer up the Needles? Is that what you promised?" But she pushed and pushed against him until he sat on the wet stone of the cave floor, not listening to anything he said, if he said anything at all, before she stormed from the cave.

Outside, the sun was setting and the air had begun to resume its dun hue. The trees were gray again. The ground was gray. The air was gray. Her hands were still red, however.

LXXIII

Beneath salt and pepper trees
your heart purrs more on forest floor
and I curse the day we met

Sung to sleep by birds and bees
and far away gift of gay days
but I cried the day we met

For soul weeps and chest will seize
for from the start, death do us part
I knew this the day we met.

—*from the Love Song of Smeagol Gibbons*

She did not pull away as immediately as he had expected her to, but there was still a coolness under his touch contrary to the unexpectedly nice weather. The sky was gray. The air was gray. The surrounding pillars of stone were gray, but the sun shone a shade of dandelion that Wulf had forgotten over the prior months of the colorless season. Teca did not return his touch, but he still followed as she surveyed the damage of the assault upon the Needles. The manmade path was gray. The wood of the gates and metal of the periodic grated portcullis was gray. The drab trails only made all the drying handprints stand out that much more. The marks were everywhere throughout the crevice they walked, and then down into the lower spires of granite. He could only imagine that the ashen forest below them was also made of trees similarly covered in the red prints of the recent battles. They stepped around broken arrow shafts and between walls of granite scarred by gunpowder and the stretching claw marks of spear tips. Any bodies had been removed, but the occasional gauntlet or unscavenged boot tripped them up. There were places amongst the stone forest the sun never lit, and these shadows collected in pools that had already congealed and drawn slow flies that smelled worse than the wounded that had vacated the narrow paths. Smoke rose beneath them in several places, down in the spirals and thick gatherings of blackjack trees spreading out from the spires and the Libran villages, but Wulf did not expect the fires to last long. The Black Hills was almost too dry to burn, the ground too hardened into desiccation to even smolder.

"They did as much damage as they could before abandoning the blockade," Teca said, as much to the rock as to him. With each word she spoke, each step she took, her sunburnt face moved from sunlight to shadow back to sunlight. "They should've fled, not sieged, after the breaking point."

Wulf responded, "Just like the reports coming in out of the Territories. The Horde is adopting a scorched earth strategy. If they can't hold a town, they burn it. Instead of abandoning prisoners, they'll kill them."

"But they found and left the Temple as all would-be conquerors have left it before them — ultimately unscathed."

"There's no doubt about it," Wulf said, placing his hand over a bloody print larger than his own, "the Needles remains impregnable." The skybound granite was ice cold, but his hand still came away red. "Your Lady Wayasu has judged you worthy this day."

It was obvious Teca was about to reply but decided against it. Still, she could not hide her scowl at his remark, and her pace quickened ahead, back through narrow paths and hidden steps.

Back out up in the villages, into open squares and surrounded by the multiple stories of dwellings and shops, she was not hiding her displeasure that he had followed. She spoke to give passing squires direction, and sometimes even to him, but never while meeting his gaze.

"We can shelter the rest of the wounded in the House of the Lady of the Woods. I've made a call to all of Mew's followers... what do you call them?"

"Green Healers? I think."

"For any surviving Green Healers to come to the east hospital. The nuns'll be overwhelmed otherwise."

He watched her walk and talk, amazed at how she had integrated herself back into the Libran villages after being gone for so long. She directed knights and even fellow paladins in the chaos that was still present through the cobblestone streets. Carts of brick and mortar spilled. Wicker litters holding crying wounded tipped precariously. Mounted knights yelled at peasants to put out lingering cannon fires. Yet Teca kept her cool in calming the burnt and the crushed and the stabbed. She calmed the mass of horses being led through the main street. She helped support the load-bearing wall of a stable with only her shoulders as it was haphazardly and temporarily reinforced. And she did all of this while answering the questions of a flock of monks anxious to hear any news of the outside world.

All throughout the afternoon, while surveying the damage to the inner and outer Needles, as he directed his scattered legions, Wulf could not resist the temptation to peek up at the monastery's highest tower. It was one of many manmade spires emulating the natural towers of the Needles, but it rose above them all. It had changed little since he had first seen it, in what seemed like another life, but he would never forget its high windows even if it had. He had almost forgotten, but being back at the Temple Needles had very suddenly and very quickly reminded him of the entity he had more sensed than seen up at the top of the monastery. But each time he looked away from Teca up to the highest granite he saw only windows. They were grand and colorful, with some sparkling of stained glass and feathery designs, but no curly-horned being looked down with vertical pupils. Still, with the Eye of Yggr he saw shadows bending around those windows in ways they should not have been. There were corrupt colors in that stained glass born of a phantasmagoric rainbow not of this world.

He had stopped his periodic glances at the temple, finally finding himself staring. It was then that Teca reappeared at his side. Her whole demeanor had changed. For the first time since the previous days' battles, he noticed that she was smiling.

"Hey, I almost lost you!" she said, folding his arm in both of her own after moving into his cloak. "Word has finally come in from the Nublar Camp. They've broken off the chase. I sent word about the rendezvous outside. The last of the battalion is grouping as we speak." Wulf had not noticed until then that a bruise had grown from the bridge of her nose to under one eye. They had fought the war apart over the last day, so he did not know whether the wound was from an enemy combatant or from her own ill-fitting helm. Like the rest of the Army, she had been fighting in salvaged and scavenged armor. Now, home again, she undoubtedly would be able to replenish with arms of her Order.

"I'll head there too. The camps will…"

"There's time. They'll be setting up for the rest of the day, and it's easily defendable. They can see for miles from those hills. Come on, I want you to meet someone."

She pulled him through a sudden alley where he could tell the sun rarely lit. Snow in the corners had compressed to ice and frozen the mold darkly, but the brick of the dwellings was new and strong and had survived a shelling that he was surprised to see had reached so totally into the living areas. He wiped away the soot on the brick and could see no damage beneath.

His real eye blinked at the light when they emerged in another street. The afternoon showed starkly through an opening created by the crevice of two spires that pressed together in the sky. Houses were built up and around the granite with brick and light mortar. Both dull and bright colors matched the crimson and silver of the Order's sigils.

"The nuns raised me when I was brought into the Order," Teca said, still leading him along the streets. "I don't remember it, but I lived in one of the orphanages on the other side of the grounds. My first memories were of being squired and of all the training at the stables. These houses… well, they couldn't be farther from that side of the villages. On this side of the Needles, one can just… 'be.' Here one contributes to the Order of the Creed, without having to be a knight. Actually, many of our greatest monks grow up out of these blocks." She had stopped at one of the single story shelters, and Wulf noticed that all of the buildings were mostly intact at this end of the paths. Some of the roofs had shingles obviously shattered from some wayward shrapnel, but the fighting had definitely not reached this deeply into spire and street.

He thought back to the prior few days of the War as Teca knocked on the door of one of the smallest domiciles. He had sent most of his closest forces southward to wrap around the mountains of the Needles, while a small cadre of elite soldiers attacked the blockade from within during a night of the Divine Choir holiday "Feast of the Often Circumcised." Teca had snuck word into the Needles prior to the attack, and a cavalry of mule and knight struck at just the same time from the opposite direction. Wulf had followed up by pushing with his final legion through a hidden canyon, forcing the Horde into steep inclines that scattered their forces. The entire assault was planned by Teca amongst piles of maps she had stayed buried within for days. All of Wulf's fighting had been done in the forested valleys filling the lower elevations, and this was his first look at how closely the Horde had retaliated against the Temple. Looking down from the reaching granite gardens, he had not been able to tell which of the surrounding canyons he had fought through.

"Momma!"

The child's voice reached them before Teca could fully open the door, and he was in her arms before Wulf could step up to the doorway. The breeze changed and Wulf could smell smoke. It was the smell of wildfire with an added sweetness to it. Some of the woodlands must still have been burning. This was the scent of some tank the Horde must have left behind. It had to have been a massive undertaking to bring the heavy machinery this close to the Needles. There were no roads that could have accommodated the tanks, and the crumbling hills barely supported small vehicles, but Wulf could not deny that the machinery must have looked menacing to these people trapped in their monasteries for so long. The Horde had left most of the tanks behind, unable to find retreating paths, but it would be at least a day before his men could even examine the metal beasts to see if they could be converted for the Army of Earth.

"This is my big boy," Teca said, "this is Lexi."

Wulf could not tell the age of the boy. The child's excitement at seeing his mother quickly turned to shyness, and he buried his face in her arms and chest as she held him. He guessed the boy was two or three years old — old enough to remember his mother after all her months away.

They continued their survey of the monasteries as they walked, now with Lexi peering back at Wulf over Teca's shoulders, finding little more damage this far from the outer paths. None of the Horde's soldiers had actually made it anywhere near the interior of the villages, but the occasional mortar had lucked its way over or between granite spire and gate. When Wulf's personal forces had finally made their way up to the small mountain, all he had encountered were crowded groups of enemy soldiers being picked off by the Order's rifle and bowman from high and hidden locations even he could not find. The Horde was struggling through narrow crevices, caught up in near vertical paths and rock. The treacherous summit, along with the rumored vast store of supplies hidden deep within granite vaults, contributed to the Order's unconquerable reputation.

"I hope you're ready for refugees," Wulf finally said as Teca headed into a broad structure made from many generations of obvious additions around a collection of original low towers.

"We welcome them. Always have, always will."

"I have no doubt that many of the soldiers' families, and many from the peregrination, will want to settle down someplace safe. I may lose a lot of my forces."

"Here," Teca said, tickling Lexi until the child peeked out at her. They had entered a building inside a building. Here the walls were of an older material, with brick smoothed by time. The mortar had depreciated. It was absorbed by the stone and held together nothing any longer. She took a key ring Lexi had been holding onto for dear life and let them into a widening passageway that instantly smelled wet. "One of the oldest libraries used to be in here. It was small but one of my favorites. I moved it a few years back to one of the High Towers. Each year these rooms were getting damper and damper." She used the same key on another door, even though it looked to Wulf as though the lock was not even in working condition. Teca handed him a lantern to light before descending down a short stairway into a hallway even wider than the rest. Here, at her request, he lit sconces from the lantern even though natural light came in from openings near the ceiling. He could only assume that there was some sort of mirrored system directing streetlight down into the chamber. Still, the far end of the hallway disappeared into darkness. Even so, the symmetry of the room, along with the light, both natural and flame-based, directed one's attention to a heavy and heavily tarnished iron door. But Wulf would have approached it anyway.

Lexi reached out a chubby hand toward him as he passed, but Teca set him on the ground where he examined the spiders of the shadows drawn by the inconsistently raised edges of the floor stones. Wulf paused for a second, noticing how the boy had his mother's dark chocolate eyes and burnt skin coloring but looked nothing like her in any other way. His hair was darker, his features broader, his mouth and lips smaller.

The door ticked audibly in one sense and only noticeably in another when Wulf put his ear up against its cold frame. He was only remotely familiar with the myth of the Clockwork Monarch's work, from obscure references and even obscurer books in the Library of Gog, but he knew immediately that the door was the work of the mad scientist king.

"How have I not heard of this?" he asked himself aloud.

"Why would you? Most of the monks have even chosen to forget that it's down here. To them, like all things dealing with the Clockwork

Monarch, it's better off forgotten. As squires we all become fascinated by it and sneaked down here, hoping it'll open for us, but everyone puts it out of their mind when they grow up. Every once in a while a knight will joke about its existence and then become embarrassed, like they're caught playing with a child's toy. But I never forgot it. I used to come down here to read sometimes before it got too cold." She put her jacket on Lexi's shoulders, and he toddled around but whined as his feet kept tripping over its length.

There were multiple clocks on the door, ranging in size. The largest hands — almost as tall as Wulf — ticked quietly, and, if they moved, they moved more slowly than he could follow. A row of rolling numbers, some so stylized he could not make them out, turned just as slowly. He could not yet tell if they counted down or up.

"I'm embarrassed to admit it," Teca said, wrangling the boy back to the door, "but I just had to come down here in case the foundation of the building was damaged in the fight, to check if the frame or door had been unsettled. I would've used it as an excuse to finally open it."

Wulf was trying to make out words tarnished almost to obscurity, and Teca was suddenly beside him with Lexi peeking from her arms again. His nose was red.

"He didn't use the Glorified Script. It's not Human or American. Some language he designed himself. I've never been able to find anything on it, but the story, passed down from knight to squire, is that it says that the door'll open during the 'time of the Libran Order's greatest need.'"

It was too old, Wulf thought, too old to still be ticking away without maintenance.

"I was worried that it may have opened in my absence. Like every story about the Clockwork Monarch, it's shrouded in weird myth and rumor."

Wulf poked at the little round face smiling coyly at him. He had changed his mind. In the quickly changing shadows and dull reflections of the chamber, the little boy looked just like his mother, especially when their wide eyes looked to the time vault.

~

"Mommy!"

There were no nurses around, but many of the healers that prescribed to Mew's teachings had finally been allowed into the monasteries and had found their way into the makeshift hospital. Wulf was not sure if the old man he tried to comfort was of the Army of Earth or if he was a Libran that had been wounded in the attack on the blockade. He had to assume that if he had been a knight he would have been afforded a better bed in a different building.

"Mommy!"

Wulf finally did see one nun passing through, but the only red on her gown was the simple Libran silhouette of outstretched wings. She attended the viaticum, ragged lower mendicants going bed to bed with elaborately inscribed copies of the *Sol Sistere*, but not actually the wounded or sick.

"Oh, how graceful you are, my darling bride,

oh, how beautiful you are, my great love.

Moonlit silver eyes behind veil you hide

Full lips reddened as budded maidensglove."

One of the Libran viaticum brushed against Wulf's cloak in the tight quarters as though he did not see him. "Now, please sing it with me," the friar said, trying to press between the wounded old man and Wulf.

The old man looked not at the friar nor at Wulf, but through or past or beyond them. His eyes focused on something neither of them could see as he winced in pain before yelling out again.

"Mommy!"

"Please," the viaticum pleaded, placing a hand over the wounded's quivering mouth, "please sing with me, just one line, please."

With hand and mind, Wulf picked the friar up by the collar of his oily shirts and threw him back into the aisle where he scrambled to find his *Sol Sistere* before scrambling again to find the page of a specific verse.

"Out!" Wulf yelled with both his voice and his mind, and the viaticum all covered their ears ineffectually. Telekinetic tendrils and clouds and hands pushed and pulled at the dirty men, dragging them into the aisle before funneling and pushing them toward the high open door. Some clamored, some genuflected, some continued to sing, but all were eventually pushed out into the open air. He let the nun stay, and after obviously uncomfortable minutes she was left with only the wounded and the Green Healers to talk to.

"Please... please... where are you, mommy?"

Wulf moved the strands of hair stuck to the old man's face by days worth of sweat. He dove into his troubled mind, avoiding thoughts both current and past, pain both actualized and remembered, to find and silence a certain roadway in the old man's thalamus. He followed the signal back from one neurone to another along the spine and nerve bundles, anesthetizing all the way, until he found all the fibres to deaden. In the end, it would make it difficult to diagnose the wounded, but the old man would not live out the night anyway. He closed his eyes in a peace Wulf had not seen yet in the hurried hospital.

Out in the cobbled streets, under the watch of the Temple and a sky cluttered with granite, Wulf met up with the latest supply caravan. It was smaller than the previous train, lesser than he had hoped, but he was at the Order's mercy, and he walked out ahead through secret gates and hidden paths, down into a valley sheltered by ancient trees and primeval stone. The canyon was dark before the nightfall yet still the granite held a pallor not totally unlike Yggr's Eye.

As the sun crossed over and began to disappear, Wulf and the supply carts raced it. They climbed suddenly and sharply over a road only recently cleared. The ground was solid. It had not had a chance to soften. The previous caravan had barely left its mark in the frozen earth. By the time Wulf reached the rendezvous he was fully in the sunlight again, out above the forests, with the cluster of spires called the Needles out above other woodlands behind him. Here his closest legions had gathered. Here the thousands of soldiers and their families pitched tents and manufactured low wikiups, waiting on his next word. He had only to decide what that word would be. The plan was originally to chase what remained of the Horde's blockade immediately into occupied Kalderan territory. Instead, he sent only one small force to follow the remnant so that his battalion could regroup, rest, and care to the wounded. They had gathered in an area that was now relatively calm concerning both the War and the weather after what seemed like months fighting on the blizzard-wracked plains. His people deserved a chance at rest.

"Any word from the southern forces?" he asked after passing contingent and row after row of the Red Guard to enter a pavilion that appeared to be constructed entirely of uneven layers of heavy and heavily embroidered rugs and drapery. It had the appearance of ever-melting rock or a continually flowing mound of lava. Lordess Sera of the Necrophim lounged inside on her throne of many colors. Wulf found it difficult to identify a wood that was not represented. With the setting sun on the tent, multiple pyres placed about, and a ground covered in the hide of numerous bugbears, he pulled back his hood against the heat.

Sera Dawndottir stretched horizontally in this chair, the frosted fur of some great artic beast around her shoulders but only the thin silk of black widows comprising her short dress. Droplets of grease from the turkey leg she gnawed speckled her thighs like stars that are only seen in the brightest of days. "You can trust them to do what they were brought here to do," she said, her mouth full of meat. Wulf could not remember the last time he had seen a turkey. It had been years. "Each Necrophim general will take a different territory. With each territory lost, the Horde loses something unique to its dominance — oil, man-power, manufacturing. They cannot afford to keep their attention on us, way up here, much longer."

"I find it to be a virtue — the realization that unbridled hatred cannot be overestimated," Slayd said. By the fire in which the turkey roasted, the sorcerer struck a cleaver against a cutting block, separating fat from the rest of some bubbled animal carcass.

Wulf could not help but salivate at the mix of juicy smells from many manner of meats surrounding the fire. "We took care of Handsome. His vendetta is no longer driving the heads of the Horde."

"Yes, yes, but I was not referencing our gelded governor. It is true, the enemy no longer has its eye on you — although once they hear that the blockade was broken they may change their mind — but I was referring to our illustrious Lonely Forgotten Sun of God. As long as they mistakenly believe that her green light shines from within our camps, they will not stop hounding us. They fear Mew more than any blue-eyed upstart or — and my apologies, my lady — any Queen of the Impassioned Damned."

"And they will regret it!" Sera said. She tossed the bone and slinked to the grand table centering the pavilion. The silken skirt did not move according to the air and the heat of the room, nor did her pale and bare limbs. Wulf thought it was as though her body was still, after all this time, adjusting to the mundane physics of such a fallen world. But if she still choked on the impure air of this realm, if she cringed against a dawn so unfamiliarly absent of weird violet, she had not told him.

"They will rue the day they sold their souls to Ashmedai. I say let them fear us, let them know we howl at their doorsteps." Red nails carved through maps and into the table. "Let us march immediately toward the Rocky Mountains."

Slayd's fingers quivered in the delicate work of bending what looked like a sharpened piece of rib bone until he could tie its curve taut with a sliver of tendon. It looked poised to spring dangerously at the slightest touch, but he was able to insert it into a soft piece of bare fat without it opening. He had just missed poking a finger, distracted as he was by the absence of that striking beaver fur top hat he had hoped to see in the Queen's pavilion. What could have happened to such a sublime piece of haberdashery?

Wulf turned to move pieces over the table, updating troop movements throughout the maps. "To bolster our battalion, I'll soon recall the three Heirs of Aesar that are out in the field. This force will then again be the largest in the Army of Earth, and we will work our way into Kaldera. The Horde will be forced to consolidate, to give up, at the very least, any of the outlying territories being hounded by the Necrophim. And, without those supply chains, Ziggurat — or whatever it is they've renamed it — cannot withstand a prolonged siege."

Sera had found her goblet. The ivory of its large mouth and deep belly matched her skin, while its fiery rubies mirrored a mane of hair that slithered upon invisible updrafts. There were blond streaks in the flaming tendrils today, but Wulf only noticed them as Sera tilted her face to drink. She stepped through piles of rugs, around ordinary chests Wulf knew belied the treasures within.

"The Nublar Camp has not yet returned," Slayd reported, admiring the lump of suet in his hand.

"Then, if we must wait, let us celebrate the onset of the final phase of the War." The Crimson Queen emerged in a cloak of fox and red lion and a clay jar in one hand. Its lid, in the shape of a fly's head, had no seams. The weathered clay had been fired covered in binding sigils and wrapping ribbons waxed together. "A gift! Yes, another gift is in order. You were promised seven, after all."

Slayd appeared and snatched the jar before Wulf could fully take it. He pulled an infinitely faceted crystal monocle from some infinite pocket before looking closely at the clay. "Hmmmm... these refracting spells are rather sophisticated. I cannot imagine anyone on this plane

— excluding myself, of course — being able to conjure such binding. I am impressed." He read on for himself until asking Sera, "Hmmm… Ba'al? Is my translation correct?"

She had crawled back into fur and blanket on her chair after snatching a bit of flame from a nearby pyre. She played with the lick of fire in her hand as it danced from finger to finger. "It is mostly known as Ba'al, but it is ancient. Ba'alphegor, Ba'al'zebut, Ba'al Hammon, Baalshamin, Thunder Dagan, Eha'dadadad, Judge Gideon's Keeper — its names are as endless as its hate. A hatred singularly focused. A hatred that could be positively focused. The elemental demon has a particularly nasty obsession with a certain endangered bloodline, and being that 'the enemy of my enemy' and all that, well… the gift is for you to do with what you will, my Liege."

Wulf just barely caught the clay jar as Slayd turned away, tipping it on the edge of a taloned finger. He held it tightly with both hands, imagining he could feel the imprisoned entity's anger as a chaotic hum like the rippling of far off thunderheads. The jar was so simply crafted he could see smoothed fingerprints in the hardened clay, and the fly's head looked to be painted by the zealous hands of a child. He would assume that Sera and Slayd were teasing him if Yggr's Eye had not shown him the glowing power of the sigils and seals.

"Your men deserve a reprieve," Sera murmured, caressing the flame against her cheek, her lips, her neck, "but with all other forces on the move we cannot afford to rest long."

"We won't."

He considered setting the jar down but put it under his arm, following Slayd to the curtains and ropes leading outside.

The air they emerged into was crisper than when he had entered the pavilion, the sun lower and the sky full with evening stars. *Wyrmwood* burned its brightest and yet darkest yet. It was a color familiar to him, but he could not remember ever seeing that shade in this world. Had it always been such an unnatural indigo, or did it only appear that way now that it was so large in the sky?

"Do you see what…" he started to ask Slayd, but the sorcerer cut him off.

Tapping a claw painfully against Wulf's shaggy hair, he said, "Did you know that a human's olfactory bulbs are part of the brain and that they associate closely with the neo-cortex where they can modify conscious thought? Vaporized odor molecules are floating everywhere, constantly dissolving in the mucus lining of your nostrils. After perceiving any odor, your sense of smell immediately accesses memories. Of the fact that humans are slaves to the past, there can be no doubt. You are built from it, *of* it. Without the past, there is no *you*. So realize that, along with always being so maudlin and romantic and consistently *choosing* to be reminded of your past, you are also always constantly being limbically, involuntarily, and in fact unconsciously reminded of it by the ubiquitous molecules in every breath of air."

Campfires were appearing in Wulf's every peripheral. So near woodlands, the troops and their families no longer needed to ration out fuel. There would be plenty of bonfires tonight. The Librans, in their yellow stone fortresses, would have difficulty sleeping, for the hills would be bright. He took a deep breath. No matter how many nights he smelled wood smoke or remembered sleeping next to the occasional fireplace, the dry and near musky scent of a campfire always brought sudden thoughts of his mother, of the nights spent out on plains just out of N'Midgaard's reach, surrounded by the teepees and incense of the Natives that had taken them in. When he smelled the smoke of the fires everything became the tan and brown colors of the prairie people's villages.

"So... so imagine..." Slayd was distracted by the passage of a boy who he was certain was wearing that exquisite piece of beaver fur finery. It was! It was that distinguishing top hat! "...imagine a creature with a sense of smell one hundred thousand times superior than a human's," Slayd continued. "This creature would be able to locate a petrified onion buried forty feet below the ground, or a strangled princess sunken in an eighty foot deep moat." The sorcerer dug into a drift of snow hardened by daylight and a wind continually traversing the tops of the open hills. In his other hand he still held the ball of fat. "Now, this creature would be ever-bombarded by constant past emotions and memories modifying its higher thought to a degree a human could not possibly understand. Any lesser being would be paralyzed. This being would experience life at such a higher degree of consciousness to put our petty concerns to shame." He hid the fat inside the hole he dug before covering it up with tightly packed ice and snow. "Yet, with all this enlightenment, with such a highly evolved sniffer and brain, this bitch chooses to torment my waking and sleeping days with its infernal barking!"

"Great," Wulf said, looking past the sorcerer to a ridiculously wide cart shedding its rope and canvas. "So, anyway…"

"Where, oh where, might your little paladinic paramour be, my friend? You two are rarely apart these days. Don't tell me she's off polishing her breastplate in that musty old temple by herself?" The far hills of stone spires would be lost to the night. Soon they would only see the faint and ghostly reflections of inner fires and lights seemingly hanging alone over the deeper forests. "What game is it you two are playing anyway? Besides 'squeeze the weasel,' that is. I don't buy it. She will be the death of you."

"Or I of her, more likely."

"You're right, I misspoke. Do not tell anyone. Some of us have a reputation to uphold."

"I don't know. She was to meet with the High Lord to coordinate the departure of the platoon of knights she had requisitioned, but I couldn't find her. I wanted to invite her."

"To what, pray tell?"

One of the many casks got away from the men unloading the cart, and they scrambled to prevent the spillage of too much beer.

"Oh, haven't you heard?" Wulf smirked. "I'm throwing a party."

> ...with no binds the Warrior sets out to
> make all choices and none, take
> freedom led, in a world not truly true
> —scrawled on the walls of the King of All's lower halls

Jon Noble led the last of his kind straight through the heart of the King of All's territory. Hiding in plain sight was actually the least suspicious option available in a land where the genocidal overlord and his god queen ruled everywhere. Besides, Jon Noble knew that if the alien conquerors suspected that the GAU still existed, it would already have been destroyed.

They were few, they were beaten, and they were the last of the Grand American Union. The King of All had poisoned their land and their children before marching his army over their cities. The war had lasted years, and now twice as many had passed since the few survivors had fled their homes, sterile and stricken with myriad cancers. There were few of them left, and, while at one point a member of the unhealthy GAU's complexion would have given them away among the rest of the populace, they could now mix with the yellowed and polluted peasants without their appearance giving them away.

But the constant reminder of the fall of the GAU was starting to weigh on Jon Noble. All around him were examples of the dominated and the assimilated, yet he could not stomach being immersed in the culture of his conqueror any longer. The last remaining stragglers of the Grand American Union were sick, barren, and probably not long for this world, and so they decided not to spend their last years under the smog-blackened skies of the King of All's cities. The alien overlord may control all of the land, but reminders of his rule would at least be less obvious in what remained of the wilderness.

But even outside civilization they found hints of the King's rule. Grimy rain fell on them hundreds of miles from even the nearest industrialized areas. Refineries blazed throughout the nights towering over even the smallest hamlets. Processing plants stank up the hillsides of even the simplest farms. And so the shrinking Grand American Union continued on through the mountains. They lost track of the seasons in the higher elevations, for all they knew was avalanche and flood and the melting of prehistoric snows, and when they came out the other side into the dustbowl, there had been only fourteen of them left. By the time they reached the stumped woodlands there were only ten. Here they had to make long detours around skeletal giants — reprogrammed antiques and leftovers from Automaton the Pervert's legions — slowly razing the forests as the insects were the burnt fields.

The Grand American Union pushed deeper into unpopulated territory, hundreds of miles into wilderness that they knew would survive at least until they all died out, which would not be many seasons more by their estimates. Here, while their number died down to seven, they found some solitude, some quiet from the King's factories and the Queen's fanatical populations. In these as yet untouched wooded hills they could reminisce in their final days on the GAU that was, the pure legacy of the nation covering North America before cataclysm, before man's return to the interior of the planet and the land's claim by supernatural and alien forces. In the cities, constantly reminded of the King and his victory, they could only think futile, vengeful thoughts that ate at their insides faster than the tumors, but here, away from the ballads and monuments, they talked of simpler times and a soon extinct culture reaching back a millennium. Here they found the peace only seclusion could bring, even while another season brought their number down to four.

As the gray summer brought an even dustier autumn, the four decided to move west. It was doubtful they would all make it to a new location, but Jon Noble convinced them it would be better to die on their feet than in their beds to the groans of the now encroaching jackbots felling ever nearer. They packed up as much as they could and headed out on the first day the exhaust began slinking through the trees.

It was only days before one of their kind could not proceed. She had always appeared the healthiest outwardly, but her inward feebleness and ability to keep little food or water down had made her the weakest on their journeys. This was one more trek she refused to slow, and so Jon Noble found her a glen with more green than they had seen in years, with the slightest gurgle from a near stream — one she could imagine still ran clear and deep — and made her as comfortable as possible. None of them had ever imagined through the majority of their lives in the cities of the GAU that they would die out under the open air, or be buried in the earth itself, but none of them minded. In some respects it was the perfect contrast, a welcome irony, to those who had always lived surrounded by smooth plastic angles and white corridors.

It was weeks later when the Grand American Union had found a forest untread by machine or man, without the sound of prayer or horn, song or machination. Jon Noble could even find the occasional breath unhampered by grit or oily stench. He was the last of the GAU now, having left the few others behind in glen or knoll or grassy haven, propped by their softest belongings. The pain in his lungs and blood in his mouth told him he too would soon follow, and he hoped to greet the end as graciously as they did. However, it was in what he felt would be his last days that his thoughts turned ever more to spitefulness. The farther he traveled from the King of All's capitals the more he dreamed of revenge, both waking and sleeping, and he feared he would die a bitter man. This thought made him all the sicker. Knowing the King of All would win in the end, even in this, his final thoughts, made him the ultimate conquer. And it would have been this way — Jon Noble passing away under transparent leaves and opaque sky, final dreams striking out in anger at alien overlord and goddess — had he not rested on the overgrown entrance to the Nursery.

For hours he had searched for his final resting place, never satisfied in the sun or the shade, the grass or rocks. He had almost given up, his hips and knees aching to exhaustion, when he spotted a small dead bird lying on a small hillside under a small but tightly packed grove of trees. It was the smallest bird he had ever seen, and, although unmoving and obviously dead, it was, so far, exquisitely preserved. Being only as big as his thumb, it was easily held in one hand, and Jon Noble knew that if only a small amount of sunlight could break the smog, the tiny bird's feathers would sparkle like gems.

He had never before believed in horoscopes or omens or fate, but the symbology of the little creature's coloring could not be denied. It had a crimson swatch from beneath its long beak to a white ring spreading into its tiny blue feathers. These were the soon to be forgotten colors of the Grand American Union, and so a more fitting place to sleep Jon Noble felt he would never find. He held the bird to his chest, and that was when the ground gave out, and he fell into the Nursery.

Warm and comforting lights grew as he passed through the smooth and pale corridors. It appeared to be some type of mobile laboratory. It had living quarters that appeared prepared for long term stays, along with instruments that, although beyond anything Jon Noble had ever seen, he could recognize as navigable. His life in the GAU was not spent as an engineer, but his military days afforded him plenty of experience with technology the King of All's scientists were only just now beginning to retro-engineer. It only took a day before he had the nutrient-threaders powered and cooking a batch of what the operating systems translated to him as *the endless hu-man*. It took many days but he learned about the base templates of the standard hu-man. They were potentially strong, potentially highly intelligent, ultimately healthy, and, most interestingly of all, one could use the laboratory's systems to copy and/or transfer a person's mind into a hu-man's body. The standard template could be let loose without programming, able to absorb and interpret information much more easily than a normal person, but, through the digitization, the copying, of someone's mind, they could be readymade with another's personality.

Here, beneath an eon of forest growth, Jon Noble had found the crashed remains of a slaver's starship — an alien contractor set up to deliver custom-made men or women for labor, companionship, pleasure or... war.

Jon Noble had found the means to vengeance. The Grand American Union would rise again.

LXXV

"The Five Wild Wives of Ismara"

Bacchus burned, dryad spurned,
five wild frenzied wives of Ismara tore chaste
poet to pieces.
Quite dead, quiet head,
listened to by lesbians
on debased beaches.

   —Zapho

I ain't never known my pa. He was just some dude with another wife and my ma ain't never meant much to him. I sure as hell never meant much to him. He knew about me, I know he did, I know he must of seen me around town once or twice when I was a kid, but he never said anything about it. He had to have known about me though. It was a small town, but, like I said, he had another wife and other kids to look after. I ain't never really held it against him. I had a pup once that we took from its bitch ma before he was ready. Had to feed it from a bottle until it was old enough to eat on its own. Can you imagine that? A pup sucking from a baby's bottle! And it ate on its own early, I tell you, because it had to. Was eating raw steak with its milk teeth! Can you imagine that? So the meanest pups is the ones grow up without their parents. My ma shrunk away when I was just a boy, maybe nine years old or something. Doctor never did figure it out, but I ain't going to hold it against him or nothing. Sometimes it's just a person's time to go, and you can't do nothing about it either way. She just got so skinny and wouldn't eat nothing that I think her body just started to eat itself, you know? So I never had much for other kin, not that I can remember. There were some other uncles or cousins or such hanging around when I was little but they was all disappeared by the time ma got sick. I don't remember anyone coming around when she was buried. Don't really remember who buried her now that you mention it. So I was on my own from then on. Didn't really matter. I was taking good care of the chickens and the cow by then anyhow. I was pretty good with the snares and the bow by then. Sometimes other people would come live at the house or in the coops. Other kids, maybe, that were on their own too. I would chase them away after a while. But when I met Phannie that was kind of different. I never did end up chasing her away. We sorta fell in love and even pretended like we were married. We always wanted to have kids and such, but it never happened. I don't blame anyone. If one was supposed to have kids they would have kids. I guess God knew how it would all turn out anyway, so He thought the better of it. I can kind of guess how kids by me and Phannie would of ended up anyhow. They would have been ripe old hell raisers, and I would have had to chase them away anyway. So Phannie and me, we rode out the old Goblin Winter. Just hunkered down, ate whatever scrawny pheasant we could lure near the house. It weren't so bad. We had been prepared better than most. That Winter of Winds was hard though. Cow died. So did most of the chickens. Or their eggs dried up. Sometimes from the inside out. All the sheds fell over from the wind, and I had to build a new house, just a shack, from whatever boards I could catch before they blew away. People would still show up, try and live with us, but now we just had to chase them away. I ain't proud of what I had to do to protect me and mine during those winds. Never found out until later how close we lived to the *Scar*. You know the *Scar*? It still cuts across the land like a open wound. I seen it myself. Nothing grows within miles of it, I swear. Can you even imagine? So we hunkered down, and we survived, Phannie and me, until those winds ended and the new winter started — this Winter of the Sword — and I never wanted any part of it. But the Horde, see, it don't care what you and yours wants. Those angels helps those that helps themselves, you know? So when some governor or another took over the town he took all the lands around it, and, I know it, he wanted the creek behind my house to feed his pastures, so he dams it all up for his beef cows. And I never used it much except for drinking and bathing, and it had been freezing up lately anyway, but it was mine dammit, and now it was gone. And then, to add insult to injury, Phannie runs off to be some newife, thinking she'll get put up better than I can ever do for her. Last I heard she was fat with some dead soldier's baby. Serves her right. But I don't hold it against her none. You got to do what you got to do to survive in this life. You only get one chance. I just wish I could see her one more time before I go."

"So you do understand then that there is no coming back?" Damn Antony asked, finally leaning forward in his chair. He had taken a long drink of the ale he had been avoiding but now spit it back into his mug. It was vinegar. Its bitterness could not be denied. He scraped his tongue against his teeth but could not get rid of the taste.

"I know it's some suicide mission, master, but, like I explained, I ain't got no one to go back to, ain't got even nowhere to go back to either."

"I don't remember asking for a mug of grizzly piss," Antony said. "What is this? Where did it come from?"

From the laughter walked one of his personal guards. The man was a midgardian, as were most of the troops, and he took time off from polishing a large shield to approach Antony. His beard was trimmed closely and neatly, unlike other northerners, but he had their same gray eyes and large build. "It's from the coffers we salvaged outta Carny. You really expect anything tasty to come outta Kansah?" His head of braids shook as he underhandedly tossed a bottle into Antony's outstretched hand. The laughter died quickly as, Antony guessed, they were all reminded of what they had seen out in the now uncontested lands — the pits of mass burning graves, the lines of dead slaves all chained together out in the middle of nowhere. They were now familiar with a new kind of crucifixion, one where a person's lungs were pulled out through back flayings to appear like wings. Antony had lived through many wars, even before coming to this world, yet he never seen so many flies in winter. They were thick over window sills and abandoned bodies even before the fighting would begin. When not engaging his troops head on, the Horde would leave behind encampments scuttled, and anything it dared not leave behind for the Army of Earth was destroyed.

The Lesser broke the neck of the bottle, deciding against pouring it into another mug. He took a sip and set it aside to breathe. It tasted like burning chocolate, and he liked it, but he would wait for the air to dilute its acidity. "What's this?"

"Don't know," someone behind his chair said. "No label. Should of come out of a tribute box. Maybe Clearwater?"

"You wouldn't be trying to poison me, would you?"

"Tor's tucked scrot! With your dead palate? Would you know?"

More laughter. Even the small man before Antony chuckled.

"Alright, so, simple mission. You'll be escorted across the bridge under a white flag until they come out to take you in. You just keep them distracted with non-answers, but the goal will be to convince them that we are leaving in one day, that we just need to pack up and head out."

The small man looked suddenly very downtrodden. "Yuh... you... we are going to retreat?"

"From that rat-infested island? No, but you need to convince them that we are. All you have to do is keep them busy. Just keep them off balance for a few minutes."

"Uh... okay."

Antony leapt down from his chair with his bottle in his hand. Finger bones and other small trinkets hanging from his tattered jacket jingled in his movement. All his clothing was tattered — from uneven boots to discolored pants and sagging shirt to the rags he wrapped his face in. Curved and chipped horns stood up from the rags. Golden tails of fur hung from the back of his head.

"Does that mean I got the job?" the small man asked as he was given a small mug.

"The mission. You have a mission."

"Master, sir..."

"I'm not your master," Antony said, sniffing the broken neck of the bottle while leading the small man out of the command tent.

"Can you make sure the Liege of Foes hears about this? Tell him my name?"

Antony cringed before sipping from the sharp bottle. He interrupted his drink to say, "Look, you do realize that the Liege of Foes is just..." He wiped the wine that had spilled over his lips before encouraging the small man to drink deeply from his small mug. "Alright, fine, the Liege of Foes will know of your exploits. I'll have one of these tone deaf northerners compose a song to your glory. Maybe they'll succeed in poetry where they fail in drink selection."

"Not my fault you don't appreciate the finer points o' mead," said the midgardian bodyguard that followed them out. He was polishing a shield as large as himself as he walked. Its brilliance made the sunrise dance over the dirty snow.

Antony stopped to look out over the assembled troops and the frozen lake, again sniffing the bottle. "Don't your people believe that bad poetry and good mead come from the same source?"

"Aye, the scared shit of the Godeagle that fell to earth in times long past. Well, as I always say, 'if you have to drink shit, it might as well be the shit of...'"

"Here," Antony said, making sure the small man had finished what was in the small mug before handing him off to a group of mounted and bannered men. "These men will escort you onto the bridge. Go with the knowledge that today you..."

"One more thing, master, will you make sure that Phannie hears of what I do? I'd like her to hear that I went out fighting."

"I will. Now go with the grace of whatever god you subscribe..."

"The Liege of Foes, master, I believe in him now that will..."

Antony strode away, grunting, always followed by his heavily hirsute guard. He knew that Wulf had saddled him with a company that was mainly midgardian so that he could prove his worth surrounded by warriors completely loyal to the Army of Earth, and he was not sure what bothered him more — the fact that Wulf did not trust him or the fact that he found himself warming to the northern men. They reminded him of someone he knew long ago, someone he spent most days trying to forget.

"Why send that little man out when we're on the verge of a rush?" one of the midgardians asked. Antony thought his name might have been Aslog or Asger.

"It'll distract that vermin-filled faction for a minute, off balance them for a second, and we'll need every second we can get. Timing is of the importance now. Speaking of, bring the Full Guard forward immediately. I want the shield maidens front and center on the sandy side of the lake. All troops with spears..."

"They're not gonna like that."

"I don't care. No one on the sand front engages except with long range weapons. And I want all bowman behind them." He drank deeply from the bottle now. The wine had a lingering chalky feel, but he liked the way it took a second to burn. Its taste was all about timing.

"Can't believe you made us sit through all those boring stories, pointless auditioning of the damned."

"Not true," a new voice spoke up. "I've always thought everyone should get their life told, no matter how low. Would be nice if somewhere there was some giant place with a book for every man, being written just as they live their life."

"There is," Antony said, "it's called the Library of Baboon A'ah-Djehuty."

"Hah! You and your stories! I never tire."

"The Bear Shirts are nearing the tree shore," said another midgardian. He wore little armor beyond some chainmail and tire tread over each shoulder. His beard was glorious, but the little hair he had on his head was dyed red and spiked above his forehead. Antony could not remember if his name was Bjolf or Bjornolf. He hated his troop's names, but it could not be denied that they were born to fight. Antony's company had won every skirmish, with most of the enemy fleeing before he even arrived. His only job seemed to be centered around keeping them from attacking too early. It had taken all of his patience and negotiation skills to keep them on the shore for the past few days, keeping them from trampling out onto the frozen lake to lay siege against a walled island he knew they could not break.

"They need to stay hidden until I give the word," he told Bjolf or Bjornolf.

And so Antony and his men waited. He finished the bottle of wine and called for another, along with his scalp staff. His staff appeared as one of the weather vvitches suddenly whispered in his ear. The tiny skulls of voles hung from thin chains, the dried hearts of moles from strings. So close to his face he expected her breath to be foul, but it smelled of a type of clove he wished to find in a drink. He thought her voice would be smoke-stung and dried by age, but she sounded barely an adult. His belly suddenly warmed, and he told himself it was from the wine. She told him the time was now. The sunrise would move past the lake to the prairie soon. The air in the ice had collected and bubbled to peak placement. The clouds would soon appear. The temperature would soon drop and the pressure would dissipate. He wondered what she looked like beneath her rags. This close, he could feel that she wore nothing at all beneath them, and, despite the heat in his gut, he shivered. He glimpsed pale warts upon cauliflowered warts when she turned to leave, exposing, for just a second, her neck.

"Has our envoy entered the walls?" Antony asked Aslog or Asger.

"He just has. What'd you make him drink anyway?"

Antony gave the signal and the march began onto the lake.

"A little something that just arrived from the Command Battalion. The Liege of Foes' pet wizard cooked up a particularly nasty concoction. The commander inside those walls will surely kill our messenger. When they do, his corpse will release a pheromone that will drive all the rats rabid in the castle. The Horde will be dying to escape."

"By Hel's leaking lips! Well played."

"It will also have the side effect of hungering any man near the body into cannibalism of the dead. Not particularly necessary for our purposes, but it should be interesting on morale inside the walls." Through the ragged scarves encircling his face he caught a whiff of his scalp staff. The staff would stink even more if the air had not been so frigid.

A deep groan could be heard through the open expanse toward the walled island as ice pressed against shore. First walked the shield maidens, each hiding behind a metal barrier as large as themselves. Each shield was hidden by a skin or fur covering. Those that waited watched with wide eyes. The maidens were used to carrying wooden shields, or, at the least, a wood and metal combination, often quite smaller and lighter than the shields they now carried. They were followed by the main force, walking behind them.

"That's right!" Antony yelled to his men, raising his scalp staff into the air. "Keep walking, you crazy bastards. Show me you can control yourselves. Are these the smallest steps you've ever taken?" He hated laughing in front of his men but could not help but chuckle. In now countless battles he had sent them into the fray, and they would always run, unleashed and chaotic. When planning this attack he had been worried that they would be unable to just walk into a fight, but this strategy counted on a patience he hoped they could show.

"Show us how to do it," some soldier yelled out from the front of the line, "boy-bugger! If I had such loose cheeks as yerself…"

The sound of the troops laughing echoed across ice and against wall, but not as heartily as the men standing next to Antony. They slapped him on the back as he asked, "Aren't you going to join your brothers? You going to let them get all the glory?"

"That ice can't take their weight," a near soldier answered to more laughter. The man was as dark-skinned as Antony, but he had grown a braided beard over the prior months, had covered himself in the shoulder furs and wooden horns of the northmen.

The Horde faction had appeared on the other side of the lake, on the drifted shore beneath the nearest wall. They hesitated but marched out onto the ice at an even slower pace than Antony's men. The banners of Ashmedai hung limply in a morning frozen still. The fiery wings of the flags looked like nothing more than a child's scrawl.

"Lure them out to the ice," Antony said to those near, and the word was passed down the line. "Bait them with violence." And the shield maidens stepped forward to the deep creak of the lake, and the men they led chucked spears over the shields. Most missed the Horde's front line, skittering over the ice. Those that struck shield or armor failed to leave any discernable mark. The Horde fired back with the occasional rifle shot, but lead struck only metal shield.

"Is the archimirror in place?" Antony asked.

"Yes," a man he believed to be named Erland the Early reported, although his name may have been Ear-bit Erlend. "Thought you should know, as well, that the squad on the bridge is being engaged."

"Then blow it."

"What?" several of the guards around him questioned.

"Our men are almost all the way across, pushing…"

But Antony was not listening. He tightened boots tied with cleats and waded down deep into the troops working their way across the ice. "You ladies ever pick up anything beside a hammer? Do I need your maidens to show you how to use a blade?" Far out onto the ice, in the midst of the groaning lake and soldiers, he grabbed a spear away from the frontline, and, with a deep breath he launched it over the shield maidens into the Horde. It exploded against wood and metal and the far soldiers of Ashmedai scrambled away from a bloody and prone figure. "Are there not any real men among you that know how to use a real weapon?" He threw another spear, and it disappeared in the air before vanishing into the running legion. One of the Horde staggered out, his arm mangled and his throat torn out. His companion soldiers yelled and moved forward on the ice toward the Army of Earth.

Antony stomped his boots all the way back up the shore to his smiling guard.

"I said blow that goddamn bridge up. Now!"

A messenger ran off.

"You can't blame the men for preferring a little sweat and bad breath in their battles," Erland or Ear-bit mumbled. "They would rather feel a skull crunch under an axe then throw a stick across a lake."

The familiar ratchet of a gatling gun sounded slowly from up on some high wall on the island. They were being careful, Antony knew, picking their targets lightly, hesitant to not crack the ice anywhere near their own troops. He gave the signal for his own gatling gun to return fire, and bullets resounded against the island structure as their ricocheting did the ice and air. He gave another signal and a slew of arrows launched almost straight up into the air. At some high point the air caught and bent their trajectory over onto the far side of the enemy men. Small shields caught or deflected most of the arrows, but it pressed their front lines to move forward on the lake.

"Onward, little girls!" Antony shouted to his own men, and the two armies grew closer and closer to each other under a bright sky and over the dull ground. Breath froze in the air but did not move. Soldiers were paying more attention to their steps and boots than they were to their enemy. Guns had silenced as quickly as any war chants. A couple times a minute one of Antony's men would toss a spear into the approaching line. Sometimes a rifle answered. More often than not one would not.

Antony realized he was holding his breath, and so he inhaled still air along with a long draft of one of the sweetest ales he had ever encountered. "Don't give me no small beers," he barked at those around him, but he took another drink, using his tongue to unstick his lips from his teeth. "And damn those horns! Can't any of you even take a piss without someone blowing a horn over it? What it with your fucking horns, people? It's time. Let's do this!" he shouted and turned away from the battle, stepping back up into the encampment. He walked past shelter and around heavy tent and unwound the ragged facemask from his horned cap. Behind him, his army ran across the ice at their nearing enemy. Shield maidens pulled the cloth from their fat shields, revealing highly polished metal that instantly captured the sunrise peeking above the walls of the island to blind the Horde. "And enough with the god damn horns! Please, I can't take any more of the horns!"

From a truck high above the shore, at the very edge of the encampment, appeared the archimirror — a cylinder apparently cobbled from every expired engine in Antony's legions. At the tip was a collection of convex and concave mirrors that too caught all available light and directed it in a focused beam at the Horde troops.

The screams of men were hard-pressed to rise above the lurching cracking of the ice and the splashing of waves as the water stole the breath from hundreds of soldiers.

~

The brazier was flaming low in the command pavilion, just a few embers glowing barely beyond the bronze casing, and so the guards almost left shortly after entering, but they stopped after Antony's voice slurred out of the darkness.

"Do you people have Kwanokasha in this world?"

One of the guards kicked at the brazier until he overturned brighter coals that glowed more loudly. The other probed a dark fire pit with a poker until partially charred logs flamed up. Antony sat low on a couch and footrest. Both were a faded scarlet that matched the flushed skin of his bare chest. A thick and dark bottle wavered on his stomach, but he would always catch and drink from it before it fell.

"I once saved a tribe of them from a rabid boggart," Antony continued. "It had moved into their cave and was making the milk of their little women sour. I just took care of it with a horseshoe and some salt, but these little people were so fascinated with me, so thankful... they wanted me to stay."

"The numbers are still coming in," Asger or Erlend said. He sniffed at the stinking air of the tent. The scalp staff must lie in some corner of some shadow.

"So these little people take me into a cave and present me with three items — a knife and two different bags of herbs. I'm supposed to choose one." In an attempt to sit up, Antony slid even lower into the cushions. "So I chose the knife. I came back the next day to find that they had eaten the contents of one of the herb bags. They were all dead, had spit and shit their guts out. What do you make of that?"

Bjolf or Bjornolf said, "I love your stories." He threw a cold quilt over Antony's nakedness. Some of the guards also had bare chests, but they weathered the cold with expertise, pale and blue tattooed skin gleaming naturally in the crisp air. "We're heading out onto the island, see what's left to scrounge up."

"Good luck," Antony said. The bottle had fallen and it rolled, empty echoing, into a table leg.

"What do you mean?"

"There won't be anything of value. Maybe some ammo. Hopefully some ammo."

"Why the hell not? Why are we here?" Aslog or Erland asked.

"You ever climb a mountain just to see if you can?"

"Ullr's undescended eggs!" Ake or Afkaar exclaimed. "The smell in here!"

Some of the guards sighed, some looked sideways at each other. Two of them whispered.

Antony belched. "Don't give me those puppy dog eyes. Your fabled Liege of Foes sends me... you know what he does? Wulf sends *me* out to do the dirty work, the things he doesn't want to be associated with but knows needs to be done. And he doesn't get his hands bloody."

The lake on the side of the battle had collapsed, and, as soon as Antony had heard the explosion marking the destruction of the bridge, he had put two actions into play. He immediately called for the contingent of portaging Svalbard ships to enter the lake and to cross and attack the walls on this side of the island. At the same time he had given the word for the Bear Shirts to cross the remaining ice on the opposite side of the island to climb those walls. The compound had fallen in under an hour.

"I don't believe it," grumbled one of the guard.

"Well, maybe I don't either," mumbled Antony, reaching around for any bottle that was not empty. His woolen cap had been pulled low, and, knowing that few of even his closest guard had ever seen his face uncovered, he wiped from his forehead to his chin and asked, "Do... do I look like anyone... anything... to you? Are you surprised?"

A couple of the braided men talked in hushed tones before approaching him.

"We're relieving you of duty."

"I would think you'd appreciate this," Antony said, closing his eyes. "The thrill of chaotic combat. Unbridled bloodlust. Go ahead then, put me to death for the glory of your king."

"You don't know us like you think you do."

Someone's boot stepped on the neck of a bottle or one of the lost wine glasses. Antony cringed. It sounded like the shifting of ice of a lake.

LXXVI

How sweaty and onerous it is to die for one's father.
Mother sues the man with fleas,
spears knotty bowstrings or cow and ham hocks
just shy of bad youths.

—from "God's Gift is Testing Fig-eating Dogs: Hati Weirdson's Defense of Reason"

The brown-haired man chewed jerky of some unknown animal. What was left these days? Deer? Dog? He could not remember the last time he had seen a jackrabbit. The animals had starved or frozen long before the men had. Those gathered around looked to him to speak next, so he wet his tongue with spring water, rinsing the salt from his gums.

"There was some big baron owning all the land next to ours when I was a kid, and he cut all the trees down that were his next to the farm, making furniture, I think, or something. Maybe boats, I don't know. He raises beef for the Horde now, I hear. Then he pulled up all the stumps 'cause he was going to make a road, but he never did go and do it. When it rained nothing stopped the mud and the shit of his steers from filling up the creeks and the pond. We all got so sick one year that there was no one left to tend the goats even. Water just never tasted the same. It was hard years after that. Tough to find buyers after we lost them, and my granpa used to sell the older boys out to the games for some extra money to bet on. I only fought once, and I don't remember much out of it, but I know I was hit pretty hard a bunch of times. They put me up against an older boy. It wasn't really a fair match. But everyone always said I wasn't ever really the same after that. Couldn't or wouldn't understand rules. Didn't really want to anyhow. I moved away to the city after granpa died and the farm dried up, but I never really liked the city. Everything sounds so loud and my head hurts a lot at loud sounds. I have a tough time with jobs 'cause I get sick a lot and everything is so loud and I get mad a lot. What do I fight for? Out here, with the Army, the loud sounds don't bother me none. They just all seem so natural, like they belong. My head don't hurt as much out here, and it don't matter if I get mad 'cause I'm getting mad at the right people."

The brown-faced man sitting next to him nodded, looking around at the others as they turned to him. "My turn? What do I fight for?" He set a shingle of mushy cornmeal down before swishing water around in his mouth and clearing his throat. "What do I fight for... you all know me... since the fields dried up in that one winter things just haven't been the same. There's a giant scar tearing across the land still, for Tentacleez' sake! Nothing'll grow anymore. Anyway... after having only girls all those times my wife can't make anymore children... after that scar was torn in the land, and I ain't a man that'll take more than one woman... so I guess that's it for me and my line... my name. But my daughters ain't able to have children either, despite all the trying, so the Horde didn't want them as newives, so they ain't got much in the way of prospects. Local governor always wanted my land... I suspect there's oil on it somewhere, so he had his men dress as bandits to burglarize my estate. They found all my wife's old family household Tentacleez idols. That was all the neighbors needed to kick us out and sell the homestead to the Horde. The girls are all out on their own. So... why do I fight? I just send whatever I can find from the fighting back to them... and hopefully after all this I can get a nice chunk of territory... maybe my own back... to settle back down in." He went back to scooping at his shingle. "What... about you?"

"Ah don't really remember a time before the fighting," the brown woman said. "Does anyone remember, even before the taking of Bab'lon, how much everyone was always fighting? You had goblins always attacking good people. And ah heard people were fighting over the rights to loot towns that had died because of the plague. There was blood spilt over the last fertile horses when Phaimon walked the land. Farmers killed each other over healthy seeds and maps to productive dirt. People always say the War started when the Liege of Foes reappeared, but people have been fighting forever. It doesn't matter. Ah just hate them all, and ah told them so, and that's why ah have no choice but to fight. The Horde took over my territory and my town, and my mayor, he pledged allegiance to the giant perch they raised over the town, but he was never a good man even before that. He was always mad at me because ah would never marry him, but now, with the law of the Horde behind him, he was mad at me because ah just wasn't married to no one. He married all the girls off in town or sent them to the capital to be newives. My family wasn't any help. Ah just ran, and that mayor, he actually sent headhunters after me! Ah had wanted posters! Ah hid in the Horde's army for a while, pretended ah was a man. Never saw any fighting. And then, when we met up with the Army of Earth, to fight over that patch of oil land in the tip of the Panhandle, ah just snuck over to the other side. And here ah am. So, ah guess ah just fight because ah hate. Every faceplate ah smash in, ah hope to find his face underneath. When ah shoot someone from afar, ah always hope to catch up and find his bleeding body where it fell. Ah hate the Horde and hope to send as many of its soldiers to Hell before the War is over or before ah die."

"Anybody knows why *he* fights?" someone asked, and they all looked up to the interior balcony that RackBreak Antony appeared on.

The interior of the natural fortress was dark, making it difficult to tell where the carved rock ended and where the structure and furnishings, made to look like the immaculately hollowed stone, began. And the few light sources made it difficult for the soldiers to look down into the lower level or up to the balcony, but they could determine RackBreak's presence by his size. None of the soldiers had ever seen a being as large as a Greater Antony.

He looked down into the proceedings from within a helm that looked to only allow his great head of hair and beard out. The rounded helm was secured to his shoulders to the degree that he had to move his torso in order to look to the side. The rest of his wide body was covered in sheets of thick leather and armor that appeared to be made of jagged stone. His soldiers would not have been surprised if it turned out to, in fact, be layers of rock segmented to his armor. Even through floors and walls of rainbow rock, his soldiers could feel his steps.

RackBreak's soldiers then looked down into the lower floor as the envoys of the Army of Heaven made their entrance, escorted into the supply chamber, surrounded on all sides by walls of crates and barrels. One was obviously a Libran of the Kalderan Order, of the western self-exiled, with a velvety ebon cape that culminated in a scarlet collar obscuring most of his red death's head helm. Tall feathers, almost invisible in the darkness, plumed over the back of his head. The metal of his plate mail was entirely silent, and he carried a collection of leather sewed together into a thin satchel as tall as himself.

Except for a breastplate largely too big for the old man, his companion was all furs and tails. Tails of all types of hairy creatures hung from his shoulders and arms. He wore woolen leggings from the waist down and a metal helmet with one horn sticking out from the forehead.

The unicorn helm he removed before he spoke, looking up through the dark and circling halls to the Greater Antony peering down and over them.

"Greetings and salutations, o' honorable…"

"Get on with it!" RackBreak's voice seemed to shake the very rock of the structure itself.

"As you wish," the old man said, using a cane to hobble over to where RackBreak's men were lifting one side of a round trap door. The interior of the floor glimmered but reflected only more of the darkness pervading the cellar.

"Oh, I can already see you are well-stocked," the minion messenger said, his toothless smile and wide eyes both growing larger. "But, a claim was made. Duty calls, don't you know."

"I'd like to do my duty," the brown-haired man whispered from the next tier, "and put that scum-drip on the end of my knife. What's this all about anyways?"

"Hmmmm?" the brown-eyed man answered in hushed tones. "The Commander told the Horde we could hold the gate indefinitely… that we could outlive… outlast any siege they throw at us… we could hold up here until the end of the longest of winters."

The brown woman added, "They proposed a deal. Horde said if they could get a tour and test the depths of our wells and they see we could hold out forever then they would break off the siege and head back the way they came."

Down on the bottom floor, the Western Libran had removed a double yardstick from his long satchel. The old messenger scurried to use it to feel for the bottom of the well. Raccoon and squirrel tails wiggled and dipped as he spoke. "If only all our battles could be fought so painlessly, eh? A lot of men's…"

"Enough!" RackBreak's voice bellowed again. "You have what you need. Go, tell your mad High General what you've seen here today."

The coat-of-tails looked as though he was about to respond, his grin wavering for a second, before he turned to hobble out, escorted by his fully armored knight and a small cadre of RackBreak's guards.

"So," the brown woman grunted, "we can probably expect to be holed-up for a least a little while longer. What do you think?"

No one answered. Their mouths were too dried from over-salted rations. After they had tasted the water of their canteens, one soldier or another started up the conversation again, but she had barely spoken when someone new came to join them.

"We're told not to drink from the well," he said, joining the warmth of their stove. His gloves were fingerless but not by choice. "Just refill from the upmost keg room."

"Why?"

"Those bastards poisoned the well."

"How do you know?"

"'Cause the Commander says it was what he would have done."

All of the soldiers at the stove swore a little before returning to eat the jerky of some unknown animal. They had barely begun to tell their stories again when they were again interrupted, this time by cannon fire against the walls of other floors of the natural complex.

"Where can ah return fire?" the brown woman asked as they all peeked from the roof of one of the western walls.

"We don't," the brown-eyed man answered, "until the Commander says so. Only the low windows are shooting out."

~

The far-off floors of the stone canyon had been cooked to near glass by millennia of desert sun, smoothed by eons of the driest of winds, and sculpted by millennia of eons of some primordial ocean. Now the rock walls trembled at the sound of Ammon Mars' steam gun. The yellow air of the canyon was filled with a rainbow comprised of shells catching light from all directions. The yellow dirt of the canyon floor was soon covered in piles of those same shells as they ricocheted back at their own men. The soldiers of the Army of Heaven ran but were inevitably scorched by clouds of their own hot mists. Those that had not already tattooed their skin red were blistered under the steam.

Next, the double-barreled cannons were wheeled to the front of the line and fired. RackBreak's soldiers dived to the roofs at the sound and sight of cast iron balls and chains twirling through the air. No matter where the cannon fire hit the canyon castles, RackBreak's soldiers could feel it, in their teeth, in their bones, even in the faint hairs of their necks and arms. Deep within the stone levels of the structures, beards twitched at the shuddering walls and natural and man-made pylons. On rooftops and parapets even far-removed from the canyon, soldiers quivered or tripped from painful reverberations in their legs. Rock cracked and dust floated and poured in streams and collected in piles in front of the Army of Heaven, but the great gate still stood defended when the double cannons quit their thunder.

"Quicklime!" came the warning across the balconies, spread by word over the collection of battlements, and RackBreak's battalion climbed down into trapdoors and closed up embrasures. All arrow loops and gateway pillboxes were sealed just before flocks of pots smashed against their exteriors. The canyon walls and bed were quickly filled with a putrid haze congealing and swirling slowly counterwise to the organic rainbow ribbons of the stone. Many of the Horde soldiers wore elephantine masks of cords and accordioned tubes over flat and highly reflective goggles. Those that did not ran in hectic swirling circles of their own, blinded and vomiting up solid objects.

From within the fleeing mob came a round tank, low but conical. Those that dared peek out, exposing eyes and lungs to the burning air, could see it down below, kicking up the dust of its passage. It appeared to twirl unless a spectator focused hard on its metal planks and spindle. Then one knew its rounding movement was just a trick of the eye and the unexplainable shimmerings of light all along the canyon. Tens of feet, metallic or fleshy, stomped forward without rhythm from beneath the odd tank. Lead darts were tossed from window and rooftop, and arrows and the occasional rifle shot were fired, but all just glanced off the dull gleam of the turtle tank. It stopped at the base of the gate.

"I'm told that the first men were a'sieged by the dead," the brown-haired soldier mumbled from behind a scarf. Near where he sat another man quickly opened and closed an armored window cover to toss out hissing cocktails of some pink concoction. The window would only open for a second, but the brown-haired man still coughed from whatever thick quicklime air seeped in.

"First men is just a myth themselves."

"Whatever. I am descended from their types."

"The hell you are."

"We all are. So they had just climbed their ways into the new world, just started getting used to the sun on their eyes, the ground beneath them instead of over them, when they was a'sieged by Minions of *MGGT*. They was holed up for a whole year in a castle. Not like this one. It was up north, back in Kaldera somewheres. Finally, those Minions start using catapults, but they is tossing the first men's own dead against them. Imagine that! Shooting them right over the walls.

They weren't fortified like we is. Didn't have the stone walls and roofs. Well, the stink gets them first and all the disease. That was bad in its self, but what they didn't know was that those *MGGT* priests had planted some sort'a mushroom in those dead bodies, and after a day or two it had grown all over inside those dead men and they started walking again and attacking everybody inside those walls."

Those that would take the chance to peer outside saw that the tank stomped away, back down the length of the dry canyon and back into the Army of Heaven. It had left a stack of barrels behind that exploded, loudly, chaotically, but left only sooty scars across the giant gate.

Two new soldiers wandered in upon the gathering. One of them snorted, "That's the last of it. The Commander jus' had us dump the poisoned water down into the underground crick."

"Why'd ya…"

"The crick comes out later in the canyon. It has to be the Horde's only water source near by. Maybe some'll drink from it before Ammon Mars stops 'em."

"You think he'll think of it?"

"RackBreak says *he* would, if he were him."

The brown-faced man sniffed at the water in his canteen before quickly closing it. His eyes would not stop watering no matter how often he blinked. "There was a town near mine…" he said before pausing. "Some town I bet no one has ever heard of… but it was known for some glorious stables… and it had stockpiled like you would never believe. It would have been ready for this winter. No doubt. But there was a preacher there… boy, was he something to hear… and he spoke out against the Horde. Soon the people had decided that they didn't want one of those giant perches in their town, and they told the governor when he came calling… told him he could keep his damned Theses and perches. The town quickly built up fences because they knew what was coming… and they were right… that whole town was surrounded by some Horde militia. But those fences held good. But soon enough, the nearby creek is fished completely out of fish, but you could smell them from somewhere a mile away… and all the barn cats disappear for the day. No mewling or crying for one whole day. But, come in the middle of the night… well, all those damn cats come back with fat bellies… licking their whiskers, every one of them. And what the people of the town didn't know is that those cats had small sacks tied to their backs… like a fire arrow. Soon enough, that place was a burning site of flaming barns and haylofts and corncribs. I could see those stables lighting up the night sky for days… all the way from my place. The governor just told everyone… sent out some decree that said the town was hiding the devil's weapon for the Liege of Foes… that it had backfired and burned the town to the ground with hellfire."

Dust fell from the low ceiling, and pebbles danced over the stone corridor. Something big had hit one of the canyon walls. It was rumored that Ammon Mars had an arbalest that traveled along at the back of his army, that his very mammoth pulled it along behind them. It very well could have been the giant weapon's massive bolts that struck against the gate's keep, shaking the stone to the core. The Horde had turned completely from attacking the gate to striking against the castles then. Windows were thrown open, rifles were fired, caltrops and flaming cocktails were tossed from the highest battlements, but RackBreak's soldiers knew they had nothing available to compete with a weapon that was probably perched on the upper canyon of some hidden foothill. Even if the Horde had somehow brought the arbalest down into the stone roads, RackBreak's soldiers had no equivalent to fight back with.

Outside, the sound of splashing could faintly be heard. The brown woman guessed that it was the last of their gasoline that was being thrown over the side of the keeps.

"You know how this rock was named?" she asked a new batch of men that had appeared before they settled down in the corridor to clean and reload their rifles. "M.T. Graves was a famous pistoleer that worked as a bodyguard for the King of Kaldera back after the Evolutionary War. Maybe it was before it, ah don't rightfully know. Anyway, he was the fastest in the entire country with a pistol. He'd shoot men down before their iron would leave their holsters, before they even knew they were being thrown down on. He got the attention of the King by saving him from some southern bastard assassin that tried to get the jump on him in a royal parade. Anyway, he was taken into the kingdom and given honorary status as the Queen's bodyguard. But he did his job too well. Soon he was on the run for deflowering her majesty, or maybe it was the princess or the King's sister. Ah can't remember which. The King put out a reward that anyone bringing M.T. Graves' scalp back would get their own tower in the royal capital, with all the amenities. Let's just say that every man and boy that could lift a pistol, from headhunter to stablekeep, from one side of the Rocky Mountains to the shores of Shiloh, was on the hunt. It took years, but the word got back to the King that Graves was holed up in this here road, with enemies spread out along the top of both sides of the canyon walls. He was just drenched in their shadows and slaver, each one drooling over the thought of living out the rest of their days as a guest overlooking the royal baths and gardens. He drew first, of course."

An archer came running into the room, followed by her quiver-man. She threw open the hidden sash and door before launching a flaming arrow down into the legions below. Her quiverman already had lit the tar of another arrow, and it was just as quickly shot out into the Horde, and the two of them were immediately running down the halls after securing the embrasure shut. The brown woman continued.

"Bodies rained into the rocky floor. By the time anyone had got the chance to draw against him, Graves had filled the canyon halfway up with dead bounty hunters. He ran and climbed as he shot, and he eventually stepped up to the roof of the land by running up the backs of all the dead men. There were no babies made for years afterwards, 'cause the women of the country had to wait for all the boys left to grow up. Anyway, at the top of the towers of dead men, M.T. Graves slipped and fell and broke his neck. I guess he starved out in the sun."

Despite the sealed traps and closed arrow ports, the soldiers could smell the burning gasoline. The bitter sweet stench became so strong they spread out to inner caverns, with some returning to the roofs of battlements. It was there, out in the open and glowing air, that they were beckoned by some men lobbing leaden darts over the side of a low wall.

"It's him!" a soldier cried. "You can see him if you squint! I swear to all that is holy and unknowable. They will never believe this back home. Good god, what *is* he? What *is* that?"

The brown-haired man spat over the edge, but the taste of burning dirt stayed strong in his mouth. The smoldering depths of the bright canyon turned slowly. The air looked as solid as the rock, despite its intricately swirling colors. It was impossible to tell where the walls burned. The grit of the low atmosphere bent and displaced all light. He looked for the being that was said to have been painted by the angels in the blood of Earth, baptized in their blasphemous rites in the center of the world, washed by their divine hands in molten magma. The brown-haired man could only blink tears away.

But the brown-eyed man saw him — what could have only been Ammon Mars, High General of the Army of Heaven. The Horde claimed he was the grandson of the sun — a red child born from the union between a divine messenger and a lecherous solar breeze. The brown-eyed man believed it. Above all his troops and tanks, Ammon Mars appeared from the sand and flame that had become the light of the canyon. Even for a Greater Antony he was immense, with each limb as large as a man. His red arms were adorned in razored and barbed wire, thorny chains, and bladed mail. The glistening muscles of his legs and knotted feet were bare, his groin covered in a skirt of silverback black fur and jawless human skulls entwined through their eye sockets. He rose from the back of his ruddy mammoth, lifting his arms and a cape of rusty whaling hooks to the glowing sky. The brown-eyed man could not look away, could only watch the flames reflect and then catch the helmet of the giant. It bore both the curved horns of a mountain sheep and the forward thrusting horns of some unknown beast. Snow-white hair and beard peeked through the openings in the faceplate.

The brown woman peeked from the scarf hiding her stinging eyes to gaze down upon the immense mammoth lurching through the canyon. It was all one gigantic mound of matted and braided, flaming fur, sweeping the burning sand of the stone floor. From the mass of fur swayed great broken tusks, wrapped with more dripping chains and hooks, and a mottled trunk ever searching lowly like some tumor-riddled serpent searching drunkenly for its last meal. Ammon Mars, straddling its great hump, raised an axe composed of every shape of blade in one hand, while launching an iron spear into the sky with the other. The slowly swirling air lifted the heavy blade straight up through the canyon toward the brown woman.

There was no time to breathe the hot air everyone stood paralyzed in. Soldiers' limbs froze as suddenly and as icy cold as their blood suddenly ran. The giant spear struck and shattered the rock of the low wall of the battlement before impaling the brown-haired and brown-eyed men. Their torsos were torn asunder, but the rest of their bodies, now indistinguishable from each other, still held together by wet tendons and shreds of skin. Neither made any sound, but broken stone skittered to the roof around them.

RackBreak's soldiers gasped as he appeared in a covered balcony high above even the tallest parapet. With a noticeably painful grunt, he launched a spear down into the Horde masses. It caught fire in its descent and slammed into the meager crevice behind the bladed plow of a staggering truck. Smoke billowed and steam hissed, and the rest of the vehicle was silent.

A roar of outrage, first thought to come from a tank's exhaust or the trunk of the mammoth, fought against the smothering atmosphere and stupefying rock walls. Ammon Mars gurgled in anger and reached for another black spear.

RackBreak waved a heavy hand and the sound of cast iron against stone rocked the rock. Sand shook and feet tingled and the great gate began to lift. There was no wind, but the churning and hot colors of air lilted toward the opening section of the canyon. Through the rising metal and wood and stone, the road on the other side could have been an entirely different world. There were cool colors appearing that soldiers on both sides of the siege had forgotten existed.

The brown woman ran. Over lows walls, onto adjacent roofs, and down onto a trapdoor. She asked everyone that passed her, "What's happening? Why's the gate opening? You know the gate's opening?"

"He's mocking them," some soldier said.

"What? Why'd..."

"Commander RackBreak. He knows the Horde won't actually go through, won't head back north like they want to," another one answered.

A man bandaged his hands in a corner. He sprinkled his fingers with oil before wrapping them in green cloves and dirty rags. He was sitting next to a bow that looked as though it had been burned. He looked up to the brown woman and said, "The road is the only way in at least thirty miles to take a army back to the war. I know we were supposed to hold them, but the Commander says they won't go anyway until we're all dead."

"How does he..."

"Because he says it would be what he would never do."

LXXVII

The Grand American Union had fallen again.

To the rest of the nation they had appeared from nowhere, thousands strong with blasphemy on their lips and vengeance in their hearts — their superior identical hearts. For they had the same face and the same voice, and the same goal — the utter annihilation of the Kingdom of All. They were all Jon Noble, his mind in thousands and thousands of bodies. Two by two they had rapidly grown in the Nursery, and by the hundreds they had secreted into outlying towns, into ammunition dumps and over the landscapes of factory and mining outposts. They became only simply armed, but it was in their increasing number that their advantage was found. They were all Jon Noble and so they had nothing to lose, killing themselves when sneaking explosives deep into crowded centers, sacrificing their new bodies when bringing dirty bombs to strategic populations. When one Jon Noble was crippled he could transfer his mind to a healthy new body, when another was killed two more could take his place. They moved as one, because they were one, and their sudden appearance and willingness to use a seemingly endless army as fodder just to bring anarchy to the Kingdom of All brought chaos to the land once again.

But the Queen of Quartz was divine, her king a titan among men, her prince a demigod. The Kingdom of All would not fall. Just one short year after the first sightings of a resurrected GAU, the King of All's forces stood on the collapsed sight of what had only for a short time been named Noble City. The King had hunted down and destroyed the Nursery. A crater still smoked months later where it had once been buried, the surrounding forest irrigated with napalm. Unable to reproduce, the few remaining clones made a last stand on the crumbling countryside on what was meant to be a new capital, a new staging ground for the new world.

Jon Noble stood above it all. It had taken the King of All's armies days to move into the fortified acres surrounding the area but only minutes to reduce Noble City to rubble. The King of All had suspiciously left an escape route open to the north, but the few remaining GAU soldiers fled in all directions, scattered and broken. But Jon Noble climbed through dust settling on his shoulders and burning his face. The crumbling towers guarding the rear of the city had collapsed against each other but still created a high point far from the victorious forces. The King of All's legions had stopped after rolling over the city's walls, and they quit the advancement to gloat and admire the destruction, not even sending soldiers out to pursue the remnants. Such was the hubris that brought down Jon Noble's people and their proud millennia of tradition stretching back before and after cataclysm, leaving him alone but now among the few selves scattering between enemy lines. He was not concerned whether they would survive or not. His time was over, and so should be theirs.

A simple breeze blew from behind him and it would soon move dust and exhaust to cover his quarry, but it would also help lift an arrow. It would not help much, but he would need all the distance he could get.

He stretched the oak of his flatbow, feeling its obstinate flex beneath fingers that had so quickly become familiar. He had left his tumor-stricken body behind in an unmarked grave beside the Nursery, and had quickly savored his new body's reflexes, strength and stamina. Mirrors were unnerving, reflections eerie and avoided, but the army of himself had served its purpose. It was, however, odd to see the world without the nanoplants standard for the GAU. To know his body was clean of any technology, any cybernetic upgrades, had been at the same time unsettling and freeing. But he had, with his army of one, achieved the same outcome. He no longer had the need for interpersonal or hive cypathy, for his people were him. He already knew what they thought and how they would move. Given time they may have each evolved on their own, with different experiences creating new Jon Nobles. But they had not been given the time.

He felt the unmoving tautness of the bow's string. It still felt strong as the day he fashioned it. In the new GAU's short life, the building of one's bow had already become a tradition, even after the subjugating of several stolen armories. Jon mused at how easily his army latched onto something as simple as bow building for a makeshift rite of passage. They used the few remaining trees of the land to build their bows, dogbane and sinew to make their strings. Many of the army's sinew strings became useless after travels under acid rain, but Jon could feel the strength of his bow as he anchored his pull near his cheek, survey-ing through the ocher smog toward his quarry. He never had the time to learn the limits of his new body, but he knew he was seeing clearly farther than the even the healthiest hunter, pulling and holding better than even the strongest oxman. He released the arrow at the smear of light the land came to know as the sun and watched it curve over the land, as he pulled the final arrow from his ragged quiver.

He felt the fletching, never taking his eyes from the first arrow's descending flight. Quickly, the final arrow was nocked and drawn to his face, and through its colors he spied the target, but from its colors the last six months flashed through his mind. These were the feathers of the bird that had led him to the Nursery. The tiny bird had been the only colors left in the world, and Jon Noble had fletched the feathers to a bow meant to be ceremonial — yet another quickly started tradition in a cultureless people. He had a distinct memory of receiving it from another Jon Noble as his new body had been born from the Nursery's alien womb rooms, and another of passing it along to another, but here it was again in his possession. He could not remember what type of tree he had carved the shaft from, was not even sure if the arrow would stay together in flight. But the fletching would hold, he knew. He remembered setting it strongly, and so the rose, pearl, and sapphire of the Grand American Union would fly one last time.

The first arrow struck the ground closely behind the target, and so Jon Noble lifted, adjusted and loosed the final arrow all in one breath.

He broke the flatbow over the shattered ramparts surrounding him and turned to step carelessly down the giant rubble that had been the last stronghold of his kind.

LXXVIII

If you believe in custom, then you are a fool.
If you believe in the Liege of Foes, then you are a fool.
If you believe in honor, then you are a fool.
If you believe in pulviculturists, then you are a fool.
If you believe in dinosaurs, then you are a great fool.
If you believe in the gods, then you are a fool.
If you believe in vampires, then you are a fool.
If you believe in civilization, then you are a fool.
If you believe in angelic songs, then you are a fool.
If you believe in sex, then you are a fool.
If you believe in philosophy, then you are a fool.
If you believe in vegetables, then you are a fool.
If you believe in the Theses, then you are a fool.
If you believe in mothers, then you are a fool.
If you believe in magic rings, then you are a fool.
If I am a believer, then you are a fool.
If you believe in precious stone puppets, then you are a fool.
If you believe in kings and chiropractors, then you are a fool.
If you trust in evolution, then you are a fool.
If you believe in the moon, then you are a fool.
If you believe in grandfathers, then you are a great fool.
If you believe in mushrooms and triangles, then you are a fool.
If you believe in gold, then you are a fool.
If you believe in Washkington, then you are a fool.
If you believe in the power of love, then you will conquer the world.
If you believe in "Wyrmbane" Slayd, then you are a fool.
If you believe in courtesy, then you are a fool.
If you believe in wizards, then you are a fool.
If you believe in tradition and seashells, then you are a fool.
If you believe you are a fool, then you are a fool.

—The Prelude to "Picture a Lemon-eater" by Wild Oscar

For anyone noticing the boar tapping through the reveling crowds it would have been difficult to believe that the creature could smell anything through nostrils so caked with snot, but it oinked at the beer-soaked paths and snorted at any breeze that made its way into the warm interior of the celebration. A couple, swaying softly together to the sound of a flute being played for someone else, saw the pig approach and stopped momentarily before petting it on the head and going back to laugh at their own dancing. The spiny creature paid them no attention and continued to search out the scent he had lost for only a second. His trotters, comically small for such a fat animal, skittered over the myriad surfaces. He walked the pebbled paths, the muddy tracks, the snowy drifts, and even sometimes into the beaten straw or carpets of the tents, always sniffing the ground and air for a specific scent.

A man with a floppy hat too large for his head, drinking from two overflowing mugs, jumped up from a fire-pit circle to offer the pig a drink. Finding himself the only person noticing his joke, he called his friends over, but the swine had disappeared back into the crowds by the time they appeared. The occasional dog would growl at the swine but never approach. Its ingrown tusks, beard of quills, and the candied pus dripping from its inky eyes kept the animals and children at bay. Plenty of party-goers would get a quick glimpse of the pig and try to determine just what color it was before returning to their laughing conversations. Was it gray? Brown? Black? Red? Was it some dirty mix of earthy hues? How long would an unattended boar last in the confusion of the gathering before it was cut and stuck on a spit over one of the multitude of dung bonfires covering the hills? It had been years since many of the soldiers or their families had eaten pork, and even the sight of one as sick as this pig sent their mouths salivating, but the due revelry distracted any onlooker before the animal disappeared following its invisible trail.

Wulf crossed paths with the hog as it scratched at the trampled earth with its twisted teeth. Snot dripped over the golden stalactites hanging from its snout. One ear flicked at phantom flies. It waddled on, its trail reclaimed, with the rotted fruit of bur-covered testicles squeezed turgidly under straining haunches.

The sun was long gone, but no one would even know it was winter next to the heat of the fires and the humidity of the gatherings. But Wulf still walked the warmth in a cloak and hood pulled around and down over any distinguishing features. These were the warriors and families of his closest legions. These were southerners and Midgardians, herders and city rats, mercenaries and militia. And as the night drew on he was beginning to see nomad congregate with knight, green healer with barbarian, and cattle driver with dwarf. And it gave him an idea.

He followed the sounds of singing, momentarily distracted by a group of fighters gambling with Black Hills gold and flowers over scars so far received in the War. The women could not stop laughing as they compared increasingly revealing wounds. Wulf took a chance and leaned in too closely, and they recognized him before he dipped back into the dancing shadows cast by the troop's bonfire. He sneaked past spits dripping of turkey and rabbit juices and through lines of people waiting to receive a bowl of beer or a green tattoo. He crept up slowly on a crowd watching a line of singing nuns.

"Thy mouth, Lady, pleases as black currant,
milk and honey under your tongue and gown.
I once fought a dream in which you were not
in my arms, and so in air I did drown."

The Librans hid their hair beneath silver scarves that draped in its absence down over the red silhouette of outstretched wings over their breasts. Impractically long dresses were thin but layered, moving at the slightest breeze and spread amongst each others' and the beaten ground, but they had somehow remained clean. He could not tell where their hands would emerge from the drapery.

"The anointed oil of your voice is song.
While all virgins love your kiss, I alone
sleep the grasses of your soft garden, strong,
knowing I will be thrown upon the stone."

Only their eyes were black, with bright lips mouthing and matching their crests and the halo of feathers spreading from the back of their heads. Each rusty red-tail spread darker before becoming white at the tip, and each gave the impression they were the one capturing starlight to drape over the singers. With necks so tightly wrapped, again in silver, Wulf could not understand how they could sing. But it was humble. But it was marvelous. He suddenly ran back into adjacent gatherings, a shadow amongst the multitude of moving light sources.

Earlier he had spied a green man sitting on the back of a covered wagon, playing a simple stringed guitar. The wagon was part of a long line of the largest caravan. He found some of the vehicles now circled around one of the smallest and smelliest dung fires of the night, the bard quietly playing for teenagers clothed in woolen vests, linen skirts, and a fresh assortment of Black Hills flowers they somehow found in the nearby winter woods. Wide yellow petals clustered from cactus and spines that somehow did not bother the listeners. Wulf shivered at the sight of numerous long-stemmed sunflowers. He tried not to remember why, as he appeared from the shadow behind the musician to whisper in his ear.

In seconds, Wulf was back in the crowds, following a new chorus of breathy sounds. On the way he snatched a viaticum he was fortunate enough to come across. The elder was preaching to a standing group of men leaning bound limbs against canes and crutches. Their attention was much more on mugs and bowls of beer than the old man's words. And so Wulf was dragging the viaticum along behind him as he came upon the traveling line of an assortment of squeezebox players. The bellows, like their players, came in all shapes and sizes. Wulf chose the player pressing the deepest notes to follow him.

The Librans were still singing to the crowds when Wulf returned with his new entourage, but he could not tell if the smiling faces around him listened to the lilting song in interest or derision. He sent the healer with the little guitar to play behind the nuns and was not disappointed. The man sat back and plucked more than strummed, slow but repetitively. He could barely be heard even beneath the soft singing, and, after a minute of the combination of voice and instrument, Wulf pushed the viaticum into the open space. The wrinkled crooner first started to harmonize with the nuns but quickly became louder. He led them, almost angrily, into verses of regret and longing. And, as he became louder and angrier, a blind woman shrouded in every degree of green appeared next to the healer and strummed a large stringed instrument. She was just as rhythmic as the musician, but much louder, and strands of her long green hair fell from a hood to mix with her strings. She strummed to challenge the viaticum, and it complemented his warbling perfectly.

The nuns continued to harmonize forlornly somewhere in the background.

Wulf acknowledged the man with the large squeezebox so that he pressed the bellows deeply for one long drawn-out drag of the instrument. The viaticum, afraid that the crowd would not hear his verse, repeated his words beneath the bellow, again and again. His song flowed long and deep, above and below the instruments, before quieting. For a while it was just the quiet nuns and the consistent strings singing and playing away.

The old viaticum resumed after a verse passed, joined almost immediately by a troupe of Midgardians that had appeared at the edge of the growing circle. Their heads bobbed. Long and pointed beards and braids cracked like thick whips as they each pounded drums as big as their laps. They beat the drums quickly and loudly in short sets, paused for many seconds to gather their breaths, then repeated, always catching the singing at the end of each couplet.

And Wulf would gesture for the squeezebox to bellow, and the viaticum would triple his lyrics beneath it. This went on for minutes, with revelers multiplying, dancing, joining in on the singing, and clapping their hands and beating their thighs to the drumbeat when it appeared.

The Libran women never stopped singing their love song somewhere beneath it all.

More Midgardians appeared at different sides of the open space. Some beat on breastplates or cuisses they never removed, some on helmets, some with hands, others with hammers. This made the original drummers pick up their tempo. The crowd kept up with all of it.

But the percussion and the viaticum suddenly all stopped at once, as though it had been planned. But it had not. The nuns song rose and fell but remained as quiet as the plucking guitarist. Only the blind woman's strings strummed consistently and loudly. An occasional shout from the audiences was heard, as everyone had stopped dancing and clapping to sway together. Every exposed forehead dripped with perspiration as they waited. Every beard stuck to cheek and neck. And Wulf had the accordionist keep his bellows low, but now ever-present, unending and rising and falling in volume. The crowds breathed as the box squeezed, following its descents.

Wulf left the scene but quickly appeared back with two soldiers he had spotted sparring earlier. He pushed them into the clearing, where they immediately began clacking wooden staffs together, back and forth, to a rhythm that had been hidden beneath the words of the singing. The old singer had been accepting water and beer while all the background had gone on without him, but he now appeared, tapping his foot to regain the pace.

He jumped back in at the beginning of a verse, immediately matched by the drums of the Midgardians and the stomping and dancing of the crowds. A new group of northern men had appeared, carrying a smaller version of one of their long lake boats. The portagers had set it upside down and were beating it to the depth and the pace of their drumming brethren. The result was a mound upon mounds that shook the hills all the way to the Needles. If any of the revelers had taken the time to look out over the lower woodlands to the Temple they would have seen the flickering lights hidden within the rocks, as though the ground quaked or lanterns fell at the Order of the Creed.

The viaticum was able to warble one more verse along with the crashing of the drums before the crowds joined in with a song they should not have known so completely. They sang it. They shouted it. They ended up cheering it, challenging the thunder of drumming from all directions.

The dust of the earth dried, wetted, and redried by the melodious clamor, lifted into the dancing crowds and reflected all the bonfires. People were aglow from perspiration. The party glittered in and from all directions. And it was from within and without this glow, as Wulf slinked away from the drumming symphony, that he spotted Teca.

Except for the Libran charm that dangled from her bare neck, she did not glitter like the figures dancing in and out of his vision. Everyone else was transcending while the two of them chose to stay behind. The dancing slowed, but their steps did not, and she was soon in his arms. The surrounding smell of woodsmoke and sweat was then replaced with her manly scent, as he pressed his cheek into her hair and held her face to his chest. All that was left of the music was the slow and somber croon of the nuns and the even slower strum of two guitars growing distant. Wulf and Teca swayed as sudden couples all around them swayed.

She was wearing mostly leather, with a broad girdle and a short skirt over her pants, but any fur was still the white of her Order. Her mantle matched his cloak's hood, and she pulled it up when she noticed that other couples were watching them closely.

"I didn't recognize you without the jacket," he whispered, unable to contain a broad smile he then hid at the side of her neck.

"Enough about the jacket! I love that jacket!" She pinched him teasingly before squeezing him closer. They had stopped swaying, but others danced slowly together around them to the faint music. "I forgot it in the tent."

Those near them smiled and wondered what they laughed at.

"I didn't think I'd find you here," she eventually said, "this doesn't seem like your kind of thing."

He was still smiling, and both of his eyes glittered, although differently from each other, when he said, "What do you mean? This is exactly my 'kind of thing.'"

People moved as one from one side of the hill to another. The land moved as though it was alive, rippling from grass to snow to the trees below, between caravans and around tents and through bonfires. Teca looked out to see wounded soldiers dancing closely with Librans, Midgardians swaying with dusky southerners, red men cuddling with dwarves.

"No, you're right, this is exactly where you need to be."

He brushed the side of her mouth with his lips, his mustache and beard, and she giggled, pushing him away to the loud delight of other couples.

Still, somewhere off in the crowds, the nuns sang the wistful poem of the prophet long ago chosen to consort with angels, while even further off in the camp, after climbing and descending busy mound after partying mound, the sniffing boar neared the end of his trail.

"Know this first of all, that in this last day mockers will come with their mocking, saying, 'Where is the promise of Her coming. For ever since She has left, all continues just as it was from the beginning of the War.' For when they say this, it escapes their notice that by Her Word the War raged long days by now and that it was formed out of ice and by ice."

William Pittsfield stood on a mound of his own making. When the rumbling ground had threatened to distract his sermon he had gathered whatever trash he could find. Any broken crate that was too rotted to safely carry even preserved rations, any helmet too bent to fit even the smallest of heads, or any discarded and rolled canvas that had become too vermin-eaten to even work as a scarf — all these items and more he stacked beneath himself. He heaped a dead horse not yet stripped of viable flesh on top of the charred remnants of a cart. He gathered breastplates from soldiers that had not noticed their absence yet. From the refuse of the Army of Earth, William Pittsfield looked over his flock and continued whispering over their green faces.

"There were signs in the clouded sun and now in the cloudy moon and stars, and on the earth there is dismay among the Army, in perplexity at the roaring of the wind and the blazing of the falling *Wyrmwood*, men fainting from fear and the expectation of the things which are coming upon the land, these here dark mountains; for it is said that when 'man comes upon black hills only then will man be judged.' Tonight will you see the Only Forgotten Sun of God return with power and great glory and great light to challenge the brightest heavens you have ever seen! And each of us will receive what is due for things done while in the body, whether good or bad. The sign of the Lonely Forgotten Sun of Man will tonight appear in Heaven, and the trial of the Book of Life will commence... will reveal... will set a..."

The swine was at once both alien and familiar to him. It was obviously diseased, unclean, and Milliam wanted oh so dearly to look about at the crowd around him, to see if they too could smell the overpowering stench of the hog's open sores, but he could not look away from the beast, and he knew that they could not smell the creature's unnatural sweat anyway. The animal's gaze, its sweet stink, and the pebbly growl of its clearing throat, he knew was for him alone. Those it passed had placed winter flowers in its wiry hairs, in an imitation of some spring mane. Otherwise he would have thought that only he could see the pig. Still, he knew it had been sent for him and him alone. In its yellow eyes were memories Milliam had long forgotten — images of the IDesigner as he had lowered Milliam into one of the specialized pools in the Brood Pits. And as he remembered, he forgot. How had he come to be with the Army of Earth?

In its crusted eyes were the colors of the waters he had been forced into, hogtied and held. Its quills reminded him of the barbs that held his flayed skin open for the surgeries, when he was sectioned and butchered. The unclean smell of the pig was the smell of the recovery room in which they had patched and prepared him. Whose memories were these? Why could they not have just let him remember on his own, instead of being reminded by swine?

Milliam's stomach was churning. His bowels were twisting. A pressure beneath his skull grew, yet he was quickly immersed in a tickling sensation that grew as the hog fell over dead. And at the sight of the porcine visitor's demise, the preacher exploded in ecstasy. Sudden gills and bladders flapped open on Milliam's neck, and glittering spoors billowed all around. Colorful clouds blossomed out from the sleeves of his robes, from beneath the hem of his skirts. The prismatic dust sought and caught even the slightest breeze and moved over the crowds connecting crowds faster than the eye could follow. It formed tendrils and slinked between legs. It puffed out amongst revelers' heads. It mixed with drumbeat and breath.

Across the hill and past numerous bonfires, Wulf looked for Teca. She had disappeared as quickly as she had made herself known to him. As the music swelled again, now with fiddles and the shake of dried gourds, the dances had followed. Hands were exchanged and partners separated, and Wulf eventually found himself spun and alone, and he moved among new fires, new drinks, and settling partiers.

"I hope you are not going to ask *me* to dance," Slayd hissed, suddenly near, "for I, of course, would have to most vehemently decline. Some of us have a reputation among the people to protect, not to mention delicate feet."

"You're not drinking," Wulf said. He pulled wet hair from his forehead before returning the hood. Slayd's sibilance was so distinct that he need not turn his gaze from the crowds to know that it was the sorcerer that had slinked up beside him.

"This lynx piss? No, thank you. I've tasted better concoctions leaking from the nethers of crocodilians. No, I had to force more beer down this cultured gullet in my Sin Eater days than would keep a pedophile from self-hatred. Or a Midgardian... no offense."

"It's not for me either."

"If I could only have introduced you to the pleasures of even just sniffing a good Moab wine. Finest in the land. The hot days and cold nights of the high hills and low mountains massage the grapes into a perfect nutty balance of bloody chocolate fruit. It's been decades since I held a glass of it to my tongue, but I can still smell a particularly honeyed vintage acquired beneath a darkening thunderhead, and I savored the bottle as the swirling clay caverns filled to bursting beneath my palanquin. The drumming of the floodwaters in the tunnels was not unlike your little impromptu concert. That will be the first thing I do, I think, when the War ends. Yes, yes, I'll hunt down a bottle of Moab wine. Have any of the Necrophim generals breached the inner territories yet, I wonder? I suppose none of them sport the cultured palate necessary to appreciate such rare artistry in drink. We'll be lucky if any of the sublimity of Bab'lon emerges unpillaged by rough hands."

"Has the Nublar Camp checked in yet?"

"The birds tell me nothing. Pigeons have become near useless in this unending season, and ravens are becoming increasingly distracted by the increasing dead of increasing battlefields. And I hear nothing on the wind. But your norn ghosts, the weather vvitches we brought from your hometowns, whisper nothing but bad tidings. The winter will return as soon as we leave these black hills."

"Bad signs all around."

"Truly. I'll check my scrying glasses and mirrors, maybe some fowl entrails. Only the best for you. But I would prepare your troops for the worst."

Wulf watched the dancing. Some moved slowly with wounded partners. Some lifted children into the air or swung down at their levels. But all danced to the same beat. It would be a shame to have to end the festivities early. He could not remember the last time he had seen a smile among the legions or caravans, yet that was all he saw across the hill this night.

"Ewe son of a bitch! I'll fucking kill ewe, ewe snake! I'll kill ewe where ewe stand!"

Dharke Parbreake pulled his shoulders against the men holding him. His eyes were as violet as all his velvet had faded to over the prior months, his face as red as it once had been. His ragged cape tore even shorter as he escaped the men's grasp to march at Slayd.

"I know ewe killed him, ewe monster! I'll gut ewe if ewe don't admit it!"

The blanket he had wrapped the dead dog in was caked with shining blood, vomit, and something that was neither. The same ichor flecked around the canine's muzzle. Large northern men had appeared to cheer a fight on, but two old soldiers stepped in to again hold Parbreake back. Wulf could not look away from the multitude of silver charms and necklaces hanging from the squire's neck. They dipped into the soggy blanket with each of his protestations.

"Ewe can't deny it! I don't know how ewe did it, but I know it was ewe, witch!" He wiped wet eyes with an elbow. The black paint did not smudge.

"Whatever could you mean?" Slayd asked, his long fingers and flat hands flicking toward the man and the crowds. "Could you mean to accuse me, the lowly Melchyor 'Wyrmbane' Slayd, of such dastardly underhandedness? How could you, sir knight? And on such a night as well. It should be a crime to interrupt such catharsis, such well-deserved frivolity."

"What?"

"Yes, yes, it has come to my attention that you have not been entirely truthful with us, sir Knight."

"I don't…"

"Now why would a knight — a distinction worth every exclamation and introduction — present himself as a squire?"

"I just… it's not… ewe would trust me…" Parbreake had settled back into the men that were holding him. He put the dog's nose to his forehead. The paint did not smudge as it became bloodied.

"I will have to ruminate on this one," Slayd continued, "perhaps alone in my cold-blooded bed. Although… word is… that there is extra room in your sleep sack tonight. Perhaps we could both take warm comfort in…"

Parbreake's high boots kicked up the dirt of the hill, and his short tunic tore open as he pulled away from those holding him. The blanket fell, one end sticking to the open stomach of the pooch. The dog hung, short legs dancing, now under one of the knight's arms. With the other he reached back behind himself, up into his cape, to pull out a sharply curved pickaxe. Its blade was the color of his velvet in all the flaming reflections.

The fiddles had quieted, but the drums from some near hill kept the dust of the ground dancing over everyone's boots.

Slayd's jaw unhinged as he yawned, but it returned as he stretched one lanky arm before another to the sky, each claw scraping at individual stars. "Should I be offended that you are so frightened to be yourself in front of us, sir Knight? If the good Army of Earth is nothing else, it is a celebration of nonjudgment, especially on this glorious night of all nights. If you fear intolerance then you mistake us for our betters, that grand old Army of Heaven, or should I refer to them as your masters?"

The knight bent his arm to point the obscure tip of his pickaxe at the sorcerer. "I don't have to listen to this. I'm ready to settle. Meet me, ewe filthy, ewe scaly, lying, pile of Ophidian plague-sores. I'll cut that cursing wormtongue out of that fucking bladder ewe call a head!"

"Yes, yes, I have a jar of lutheran sprites that has been peeking into your dreams each night. I know all about just how much you have been wanting to 'stab' me with your curvy 'sword.'"

Parbreake struggled on the ground, against the dirt, with his dead dog, against those now holding him again, with his blade. "'Have I not served ewe well, my liege? I gave you counts of Shriven's battalion, the location of the westward supply line. I even worked with your witches — witches! — to solve the Archeodome murders. Yet ewe let this fucking abomination into your inner circle. This is who ewe..." But as he strained to look around the crowd, he saw that Wulf was no longer anywhere to be seen.

A forked ribbon of a tongue flicked the folds of his ear, whispering, "I am eternally curious, little knight, that when you were once indeed a squire, and you had to endure nightly buggerings from your surely esteemed master knight, who was it that you hated more? The knight or the squire?"

Parbreake again threw off holders twice his size, gathering the dog's corpse and his sword, seeing that Slayd was out of reach. This time, paint smudged as he brought his forearm across his tears. "Is this what the Army follows?" he asked onlookers. "Is this what ewe all offer? Then ewe will have no more help from me!"

No one watched the knight retreat. Music had silenced. Dancing had stopped. All just watched the billowing spoors sail over the hill and through the crowds. The rise and fall of the winter breeze brought color to and through the people. They had breathed it in before realizing it. To each person it smelled like themselves, like their families, like their loved ones. They each found their mouths salivating, and they found the mouths of those next to them salivating under their own. Pupils that encompassed entire eyes looked at others just like their own.

~

It was through tongues that each knew their neighbors, tasting every bit a person's soul as much as the warm flesh of the hill that ignored the outside winter that chose no more to bide its time. But for now, ahead of encroaching blizzard and the accompanying Army of Heaven, bedmate met tent-mate before meeting neighbor and commander. Hair was pulled yet no one screamed in pain. Arms were held fast and necks were bruised. Thighs opened before crushing the invited. Flesh was pressed into the mud of the mounds until no hill remained, only a new slick plain unaware in its humidity of the imminence of an outside world.

~

The Crimson Queen took delicate and deliberate steps between and through the entwined bodies. The glittering mists had dissipated, either lost to the building winds of the suddenly near prairies or mixed within the rising sweat of the multitudinous mix of limbs. Most of the glistening revelers now slept, spent within the heat, collapsed in exhaustion, embracing many and embraced by many. Others still thrusted against one another like ocher earthworms squirming for purchase after a sudden rain. Sera could not tell where the limbs of one lover began and where those of another ended. Such was the wet flesh of the Army of Earth on the eve before its slow destruction.

Her painted toes dipped in mud quickly cooling. Tonight her eyes were pink, and they smiled over the rises. The Army, in its expanse of trailers, tents, and yurts, had massaged the rise of the earth into uncounted mounds of moving bodies, some taller than she. She quietly rounded equal stands of discarded clothes and armor looming precariously over quivering mouths and caressing fingers to near her destination.

The tent was squared, flat, and low, held by numerous diagonal poles and lifted by a mesh of wool rope webbed over its top. Its fabric was dark but thin. It would no longer keep out the returning cold than it would prying eyes. And she entered the tent unimpeded, unannounced, and uninvited, all in ebon furs and lace. Milliam Pittsfield did not look up from his beer to the pale face and fiery curls glittering from behind the black veil.

"It wasn't my fault," he whispered, anticipating her light approach, but she did not step too near him. "The last thing I remember... was talking to my brother. He... he never liked me. We had different dads, see, and he was always embarrassed of me. Thought I shouldn't flaunt it, said I could just hide it if I was smart, but isn't the fact of being a tithingman something a guy should celebrate? The Lesser Brotherhood... they've done a lot of good for the land. Sure they've lost their way as of late, worshipping false idols and such, but before that they were always trying to make the world a better place for us all. You can't hold that against them. So being the son of one of those magnificent men was something I should have been able to announce to the town. I seen him once, my dad, I think. He saved the church from a flock of furies. All the ladies in town thought he was so beautiful. Like chiseled from bronze or molded from red clay."

He looked up to see Sera's ethereal hands emerge from many strings of onyx to finger through his chests of silver and gold as she walked the edge of the tent around him. Her veil glittered as though immortal snowflakes had alighted upon it. Each one twinkled unlike another.

"The last thing I remember... was talking to my brother. He always wanted me to keep it a secret, but then why did he tell everyone about it to embarrass me?" There came a sickening squelch as Milliam tore his fake beard off. The raw skin was pink where the glue had been stuck. The area around his mouth was already the same color from being stained by vermilion. He had removed his hairpiece, so the tattooed eyebrows stood out on his smooth forehead. He started again, after emptying his mug in one draft. "The last thing I..." But he stopped as Sera pick a vine of grapes from a bowl of pears. Running her hands along the fruit, the grapes shimmered in the low light of the tent's brazier until they appeared as opaque crystal. The glass was long, as was a bottle from which she poured wine into from Milliam's collection of goblets.

"Who are you?" he asked, picking at the green paint on his hands. It had almost worn away, was mostly caked around his fingernails. He then scratched at age-old scars lining one of the sides of his body.

She was not sure that he was talking to her, but she responded, "I am the Giver. I give gifts. I reward the Just."

"The Just?"

"Those awake to the corrupt superstructure of reality, the worm-eaten, underlying lining to all motivational momentum." She swirled the wine in the goblet but did not drink it, only holding its fragrance to her veil as she flipped the latch of a basket with a toe, revealing more golden trinkets and silver wares. "But I am also the Arbiter of Reparations."

"But it's not my fault!" Milliam's voice had gotten quieter, even as he yelled. "I just remember just being so done with the church in town. They were lost, not me. They cared more about laws and taxes than the Truth. I never felt welcome. And at the same time that I felt so low was when I ran into a pilgrim of the Brotherhood. It was serendipitous! It couldn't have been a coincidence. He didn't care about himself. He didn't care about the church. He didn't care about me. All that mattered was the Truth. It was exactly what I was looking for at the exact time I was looking for it. It was providence. I remember the ladies at the Brood Pits being so nice to me. I think they really truly cared. The last thing I remember was being held under the water, in the pool." He stood, straightening but removing his outer robe. "And then I was in Erebus in Ouroboros, singing to the Sleeping City of the Seventh Day. The entire city-wide congregation was mine, their ears open to only me. Oh, why did I ever leave?" He stood at a bowl of ice-melt, cupping water to wash the tears from the wrinkles under his eyes. "But, after all they did to me, whatever it was they put in me, that… that… that horrible fog. I didn't know it was there! And however they did it… sending that pig… to set it off. I didn't know what they did to me! But, after all they did to me, I'm still the same person, still the superior man. I'm still the son of a Lesser Antony, the next step in evolution."

"That is what makes my responsibility all the sadder," Sera sighed.

"I am the ultimate male!" William untied baroque belts embroidered with precious metals and frayed twine twice mended.

"But the Army of Earth lies spread in ecstasy while the world's enemies march toward them. Even I cannot predict the bloodshed. It will be an unprecedented slaughter."

The preacher's final robe fell, along with slings and bindings he quickly tore. "I am the Omega Man!"

Sera threw the goblet, knocking over and extinguishing the brazier, but the outside warmth still cast a light inside the tent from many directions. William raised his arms to the flexing of loose muscle. He was both female and male, soft and disconcertingly turgid.

"Gaze upon me!" he whispered loudly. "You have been chosen. You don't get to look away!"

"Nor do I want to. Someone must be punished for what will happen here. You too have been chosen." She kept her chin down and away but watched from beneath the tilt of her flaming locks, pink gaze becoming red in the dim room. "God, you are nothing if not magnificent. They will go to Hell for thinking they could have improved on perfection."

He leaned close with mouth wide-open to chase hers, but before he could follow she removed the mask he thought was her face. She was entirely crimson beneath, and from the lifted veil emerged the splintered horns of some infernal ungulate. Her black jewelry had become the char of barbed wire, and he shrank from its thorns even as his drooling engorgement pressed against her hip. He barely registered the pain following the prick of her nails as she grasped it before tearing it from the root and thrusting its head back deep within his netherfolds.

Eager to return to parsing through the preacher's wares in the flickering light of a suddenly reignited brazier, Sera stepped back from the convulsing figure to avoid his flailing limbs. Milliam curled, then crawled, gasping and spitting, then fell to curl again, his body wearing a hole in the dirt of the floor. His voice broke in a scream an instant before his suddenly pregnant gut exploded outward with nary a sound.

Sera, now dripping with seed, crouched pale in the new darkness — grey eyes looking from Arctic fox fur hood and cape. Her snowy gown and ivory gloves were speckled with fresh amniotic blood before she even reached out to pick up the babe.

"Has there ever been a creature such as you?" she asked, wide-eyed and open-mouthed. "Birthed from sires of the old and next worlds — the culmination of the rape between supra-magicks and super science." The babe's skin gleamed in a light emanating from another plane, another time. It cried silently, and Sera put it to her blue breast where its angry gums immediately began searching. She wiped the gore from a perfectly round head before kissing it with winter lips.

The White Queen emerged from the tent into the lingering dew of the mass conjoining, fiery-stained and haired. Snow had started to fall, but the flakes would dissipate in the warmth before being able to light on any naked bodies. She looked off to a horizon only she could see, and her eyes became even grayer, to see a future she was consistently having trouble remembering.

"I cannot help but believe that you will both save and break the world, little one."

The babe kicked and grabbed, breathless against Sera's bosom.

"It is fortunate that it desires both."

~

"You, little girl, have done something so rare these days. It is not often that I am surprised." The Crimson Queen still held the babe to her breast as she stooped to enter the brick-lined doorway leading into the earth.

The newborn had quieted but refused to sleep. Her cooing was silent, her limbs unendingly spastic.

"So unexpected… but so fortuitous." The entrance and its tunnel were fresh, only days old. The supports were hastily positioned, the hovel quickly dug, but a dwarven warren was built to last, even this temporary hearthhome. The heat hit them immediately, physically, and the babe squirmed deeper into Sera's arms. None of it would escape the hole. Like even the smoke and the sparks, her dark dwarves wasted nothing in their smithing. Their hammer magicks pulled everything back into their tools. Their artifacts were communal and missing nothing of the world.

Toothy tools fell. Molten fireflies appeared and scattered from and to the forge. Black sun ovens burned holes through the fabric of reality, into some sulfurous dimension. Water hissed like the great World Serpent's death cry. Iron fell on iron on iron on iron.

No words passed between the shaggy men. They worked the metal as an infernal machine. No movement was superfluous. No heat was wasted. None of the smiths even looked up as Sera tore the skin from the babe before handing her over to the master dwarf. The newborn screamed, but the sound was lost beneath hammer and the wyrmroar of the flames. Immature lungs pulled at the burning humidity of the hovel.

Nor did the dwarves skip a beat as the headsmith slid the flayed babe into the oven.

The artisans were already at work before Sera had left the cavern for the snow that had begun falling outside. They hammered and bent the infant. Hammered and bent and heated and cooled. The vibrations tickled the Crimson Queen's feet through the dirt. She would be back later to carve the Runes of Planar Discord into the blade before it cooled entirely, but for now she had some sewing to do. She started to stretch the hide, noticing that all stars above but one had disappeared behind winter thunderheads.

LXXIX

By her name did Ophidia lie to
her suitors two.
If only my lips did
excite that split tongue to venom of new
reach, then my love would no longer be hid.

In Ophidia did that queen lie for
her suitors four.
On their bellies they crawl
at heels, yet she slanders for me no more
in the land I named for her above all.

Writhing did Ophidia lie eating
her suitors eight.
Am I not sweet in my
gifts of gall, are the songs I hate to sing
not worthy of the stare from one slit eye?

Or should I joy in the scales of law and
when Ophidia falls my cast will stand?
  —Ophidia in Ophidia Lies

Τhe Agent of MANN moved silently behind Wulf, belying his size, as another squad ran around them to help in securing the southern front. The soldiers were loud, vengeful, and an obvious mix of old and new recruits. There was no consistent uniform or armor to align them to each other or the Army except for a red-spilling eye on either cap or helm, shield or arm. The group formed up again on the road leading toward a small grove of winter-whipped trees, and for a second they lined up in a phalanx and turned back toward whence they came. Wulf stopped, unsure whether they all waved back at him or the scrambling camps of their families, whether they could even see either in the horizontal bluster of the returned season, but he saluted anyway before they marched off toward the glow of explosions. Just like his entire battalion, he had lost all sense of time after the Horde's initial attack on the camps. Not only could he not recall how long it had been since the weird conjoining sleep had been interrupted in bloodshed, but how long it had taken for the Army to regroup in the ensuing carnage and chaos, and how long the battle had been raging since. He could not even determine what day it was or what time of day it was. The sun appeared to be either rising or setting in all of the blizzard-wracked directions. Any one of the many explosions breaking the clouded sky could have been *Wyrmwood* shattering in the atmosphere. The ground and sky were equally ashen and equally periodically on fire. He could not shake the feeling that he was walking inverted in the white storm of Heaven, looking down at the last days of the land.

"I am only here to observe," the Agent of MANN expectedly replied when Wulf was able to yell above the wind to ask him about the passage of events since the strange orgy. The mechanical insectoid suddenly shrank into its body and arthropod legs as the air above them shook with the passage of something large and unnaturally fast.

Wulf had rolled with the impact, his teeth now chattering from the near split of the sky or the snow that had blown into his clothing. The small grove of trees ahead of them had splintered in all directions. The sound of their breaking, the many pieces of their remains, were quickly lost to the wail of the wind. He was picking shards of ice from his leather when a messenger link found him.

"My Liege, I found something I'm told you would want to see." The link's neck was so swollen on both sides that she could barely speak.

"Is now the time?" he asked. He had been trying to work his way back to his commander tent for most of what he assumed to be a day. He felt vulnerable out on the exploding plain without his battle armor, but every time he had tried to head back to where he thought the last hill was, some new side of the camps was being threatened.

"I'm told it would be in your interest. Commander Slayd..."

"'Commander' is he now? Well, lead on then." He looked to the panel of six flat eyes on the Agent of MANN's beaked head but found no expression to share the humor.

Another messenger appeared as they followed the scout. Her words were muffled behind a sleeve she had torn off to staunch the flow of blood from her nose. "Lord Liege, is word from Damn Antony's company."

"Let's hear it." Wulf's command was loud when the wind suddenly lowered, and the girl cringed repeatedly as she spoke.

"'Ey approach from south southeast, but are cut off by about a hunnerd a' the Horde. 'Ey may be about only three miles away."

Wulf knew those three miles may as well have been the distance between Nod and Kaldera in this blizzard. If Teca had not found her way yet, then Antony's troops would be stranded so near yet so far.

"Can you get a message to him?"

"I know a route, 'round a grove so filled in wit…"

"Tell him to push forward against all odds. Help will come from the north if it hasn't already."

"Yes, my Liege."

But before Wulf could continue on, two more links had appeared. He stepped through them to follow the initial scout who was already disappearing into the walls of snow.

"Sir, the breach on stable's end of Far Camp has been averted, but it took high casualties."

"Have them hold firm for one more hour, then they can fall back into the middle of the Sol Caravans. Send them only one green healer. All the rest are to be brought down here, by the last of the Ice Mauls."

"The northmen? Sir, they've already engaged. They're ahead of us. They took the riverbed."

"Of course they did. Alright, I'll escort the healers myself, shortly."

Frost curtains parted, but the wind kept its constant rise and fall. It now at least blew against the back of Wulf's hood, giving him a chance to wipe the frost from his beard and eyelashes as they neared Miss Mowgli and her tall cart. She was struggling in her reins and the bluster to keep the cart from tipping. Its drapery had been tied down, but trinkets, organic and metallic trickled out. Slayd yelled from a crouched position.

"Careful, you poor excuse for an autistic auroch, those aren't just any Hands of Glory. I pickled them myself on Wizard Island! Ah, here we go, Wulf, what took you so long?"

Another link jumped in front. "Good Liege of Foes, I bring a message. Sir Teca of the Order of the Creed has asked that I inform you of her movements." The old man produced a stained hide with a recently painted map as crinkled and cracked as his lips. "As of now she is taking her squad from a hidden hollow, north around the Garden Camps to…"

"I know this. Did she get the knights she requested?"

"Ummm… no, my good Liege."

"Is the Bugbear Mange Company still in holding position."

"Ummm… yes, my…"

"Send word to have half their trucks back her up. No, wait…" He looked out to find some hint of sun or moon that he could be sure was not in fact a burning hilltop or exploding tree crown. "I'll tell them myself." Two messengers arrived for each one that ran off into the storm.

If not for the large unfolding presence of the agent of MANN, Wulf was certain Miss Mowgli would not have even noticed him. He skipped to the side to avoid being struck by the tipping cart.

"You do know, killer, that we're all dying out here, don't you?" he asked Slayd, his smile being the only thing noticeable from the depths of his hood.

The sorcerer continued crouching over a body, just turning to mention, "Yes, yes, sadly though, I'm sure that is little compensation to our little fellow of ambiguous loyalty." It sounded like the tearing of twice-dried paper as he turned the body over. Its skin was heavily crystallized in frost, but the face, even in its grim mortis, and the frozen dog clenched in its arms, was instantly recognizable.

Slayd picked and pecked through folds and pockets chilled hard as stone, before saying, "You know, if he had only confided in me, I would have undoubtedly talked him out of heading out on his own with such a storm approaching. In these final days, all that is left for comfort will be found in the embrace of others."

"Very profound. Have the weather vvitches any luck in curtailing the snow?"

"Not unless they've found new gods to pray to. I don't think I need to tell you that these are no normal seasons. Man-derived meteoromancy will have little power in this, the Winter of Swords. Ah, look, just as I suspected!" He had to raise his hiss above a sudden blast of ice that would have cut anyone else's exposed skin. He raised an angelically sigiled thumb ring along with the tiniest of waxed scrolls. "These would have gotten our tragically disingenuous friend here unmolested through Horde lands. And these…" Between razor sharp nails he held up red and yellow marbled flint and a small C-steel designed with ornate feathers. "…would be how he would harness Eternal Flame to contact his distinguished superiors concerning our troop movements."

Silent flashes of light out in cloud-choked surroundings brought screams to drown out the wail of the wind, but Wulf could not tell if the flashes or the yells were near or if the blizzard had sent both along the snowy air.

"Are we still in retreat?" the sorcerer asked, standing and looking to more silent flashes of light.

Wulf's eyes followed his glance. "We never were."

"A shame. In my experience most people prefer to enjoy a little refractory period after a death orgy. I would think that the Temple Needles would have been…"

"I'm not getting stuck back up there." He had no idea if he gestured back in the right direction.

"And that brings us to the most pertinent quest…"

Melchyor Slayd was suddenly aware of how dark darkness could be. Realizing that he had blacked out momentarily, the sorcerer spit earth from his mouth, feeling the grit of his teeth. He lifted mounds of ice and sudden sleet from his back while swatting the clumps of sod that still fell from the sky, all the while squinting at a glow that both consumed and was smothered by the burning mists of the storm. It could have been the sun. It could have been the comet that lately had been challenging other celestial objects for prominence. Mud, some soft, some solid, slid from his robes in great bergs, discoloring his limbs. He shook it as he was finally able to stand. He whispered a charm no one could hear, holding a miniature maize doll no one could see. The ringing in his head ended and his hearing returned as he finished the short verse, and he returned the shaman's toy to one of his unfathomable pockets.

After listening for the tell-tale whistle of any new falling shells and scanning the walls of snow to make sure the explosion would not be one of many, he shook the prairie's gore from soggy sleeves before brushing the salt and pepper snow from Wulf's face. There was no blood. He was still warm under Slayd's cold-blooded hand, the pulse at his carotid still strong. He coughed to let the sorcerer know he still lived.

The falling ground finally settled, but Slayd could not tell exactly where the bomb had landed, as torn as the new permafrost was. His cart was in shambles. Two of the wheels were splintered into toothpicks. Pieces of an axle poked out of the melted snow at odd angles to each other. Trinkets and tricks lay strewn for an acre, now nothing more than scraps of fabric or parchment or bent unrecognizably into copper puzzles.

"What are you looking at?" Slayd snapped at the Agent of MANN. The shine had barely left the metal being's figure. "Would it have been too much to…" But the sneer melted from his face as he looked closely at the ground. Partially buried, partially burnt, mostly broken, were Miss Mowgli's torso and head. The sorcerer wiped frost that had appeared under his eyes and delicately lifted a swath of the woman's hair to his nostrils, but he could not pick up her meaty smell over the perfume of brimstone and woodsmoke. If the scent still existed, it blew away on the cold wind before he could catch it. The hair tore away with the sound of a breaking corn stalk as the sorcerer stood. His fangs clenched so tightly his mouth bled.

"Who dares?" the sorcerer yelled to the storm. "Who dares?" he screamed to the war before suddenly pausing at the sight of the most magnificent beaver top hat. It sat upon a drift as though the very planet Earth was its head, and he snatched it up as he passed, heading toward the counterwise swirl of lights and snow that indicated the nearest battle. He pulled the wet shoulders and sleeves of his robes down to bear a torso as pale and green and scaly as the winter. His thin limbs and sunken chest were covered in old paint and new etchings. The signs, sigils, and runes pulsed with each flick of a finger and twist of a wrist. They hummed beneath his chanting and over his whispered curses. His casting voice spat out spells, even as he yelled at the Army of Heaven when it emerged from the blizzard walls ahead of him.

Over the cleared plain came shaven men bouncing on warhorses and whipping lean battle aurochs. They fired shotguns and thrust lances into the smoky air above them to the rhythm of their warsong. Slayd waited until he could see the redness of the infections surrounding the brands on their foreheads before he changed his chant. Some had the thorned glory of Asmodeus on their foreheads, others had carved the crescent spine of Abaadoon around a temple.

"Xastur srax ut xas!" Slayd's undervoice versed.

"Who would dare touch that which belongs to Melchyor the Wyrmbane?" His overvoice called at the same time.

"Ut ur suut xat!"

"Do you not know who I am?"

The cavalry charged him, and the dirty snow they kicked up swirled suddenly on its own to grab at hoof and foot. By Slayd's guttural words the mists followed to swirl upon themselves, taking any light with them. His chant bound the fog to rise and the clouds to fall, and the storm wrapped over and over, around and around, and, with its binding inevitable, it threatened to scream but roared instead. The aurochs mimicked its bovine desperation, as the conjured bowl of the minotaurnado rocked back and forth over the skies of the plains before its tail struck the earth at the head of the Army with the sound and force of thunder. Riders and mounts not lifted into the air were tossed aside as the black funnel whipped against invisible reins. The blizzard was sucked toward the whirlwind of horns and bullish muscle from all horizons. The light of fires or explosions or moon was pulled and stretched toward the dead cow eye of the malevolent twister. Only the slow glow of *Wyrmwood* was unchanged.

"Uta ur xuua xut astuur xa!"

Men were torn from their fallen beasts, disappearing into the blackened sky, leaving behind hands and feet still set in rein and stirrup. Others were tossed and thrown beneath the carcasses of strangled or impaled mounts, finally being buried by great sections of overturned sod. Those that could still run grabbed at the sky, as others swallowed tongues when trying to reclaim their stolen breath, while the thrice-tossed naked were skewered by the minotaurnado's endless horns or the circling cyclone of icicles.

"Xastur ut stuuta xuur!"

And through the immediate sleet of blood strolled Slayd. From an infinite pocket he had pulled a small bell in the shape of a masculine-featured weather trickstress. Around his neck flapped a string of dwarf palmetto palm leaves. The sleet turned to slivers of red hail, and the sorcerer's exposed torso was instantly crisscrossed by wild slashes.

"Xas ut srax xastur!"

And the minotaurnado began to disperse. The storm it had swallowed was vomited upward toward the sun and stars, only to sink back over the opposing armies. The bellow of the bovine quieted. The horns disappeared into the horizonal winds. The prairie was torn, the drifts bloodied, but the plains returned to the blizzard. Only the absence of the swirling fogs designated a difference between the battles before and after Slayd's conjuring. He was now very aware of the advance of a new legion of machines coming toward him.

"Shub-tsathoggua," Slayd's undervoice intoned as he yelled with his

true mouth to the shambling tanks and trucks.

"Do you have any idea what you face today, feather-lickers?" His voice reverberated over dune and through rickety metal bolts and hatches. "Is your ignorance boundless, or are your tone-deaf sycophancies so lobotomy-driven as to send you faithfully on your way to unmarked graveyard irrelevance?"

With a sudden soap wand made from the twisted shape of fairy bone soaked in penitent's bile, dipped in the fatty acids of a nun's womb leavings, the sorcerer blew fantastic and prismatic bubbles into the storm. The small orbs crowded to smother some men. Some crushed men under their weight. Some exploded into glassy shrapnel, flaying armor from skin, organ from bone. Larger bubbles captured and suffocated other soldiers before floating upward, ever upward, past cities of clouds and eventually into space.

"*Ghub-thua-guua.*"

From one of a hundred pockets, Slayd pulled an envelope of powdered gorgon scales, letting the wind take them over the earth. His other hand planted a rose granite domino tile that showed blank ends until it disappeared quickly under the dirt and ragged weed.

"*Ghub-thua-guua, tsath thuub gothgua tuub huut.*"

"Let me tell you whom you face today!"

The land lurched. Out of the dirt was thrust sideways stone pillars. From the ice drifts burst dirty rock slabs. A cast iron cylinder, covered in the graffiti of the Horde and tearing the plains on centipede trends was lifted into the air by emerging rock, its turret blasting off into the sky. Single driver mini-tanks were tipped, or they stalled, caught up between sudden stone collections. Some of them fired their wide cannons, shredding themselves like paper in such close proximity to the rock. A massive tractor, of seven great tires and with a toothy plow taller than its cab's height beared down on Slayd. It rocked the prairie, covered in ladders, guard rails, and fur and leather-bearing gasmasked soldiers. They fired sawed-off rifles from within plumes of the darkest of exhausts. Any shot that made it to the sorcerer's vicinity was swallowed by the tiny *Sons of Mastop*. Each clay death fly would then break its spectral leash before unleashing sulfurous indigestion on each soldier. Unable to turn, the spiky tractor broke upon jutting granite that pushed its way suddenly up in front of Slayd. The war grounds were washed with circling smoke and spilling gasoline that refused to be absorbed by the frozen ground.

Up above it all, navigating the burning, flaming, and snow-smothered moonlight, drifted a shining dirigible. It was all Army of Heaven, with shimmering chrome wings and candied paint putting it under the protection of Slog Sabbaoth. It was all points, lazily sailing and carrying a small tank of numerous treads. Wild men stood on the tank, dropping spiked mines without regard for which army they devastated. One of the mines struck nearby and Slayd again spit the dirt from his mouth, shook the mud from his legs.

From a tiny fold in his robe the sorcerer pulled a sack larger than his head. The shadowl hide bag was of ebony down except for the shade-skin drawstring and the arcane scrawl on its lips. He shook it and, with taloned fingers, picked out an iron bolt, but when he opened his hand a plethora of those same bolts trickled to the ground.

The dirigible shook, and the sound of metal on metal screamed overhead.

He shook the bag and picked out a large red rivet, but from his hand spilled many screws and rivets of all colors.

The tank overhead swung as the airship rattled, and a massive propeller crashed into a row of trucks that had been unloading lines of men thickly loaded with armor and belted tanks of a now-exploding gel. Burning soldiers ran to and fro as the falling dirigible careened off sideways into the returning storm.

As land moved once again, this time from a collection of treads and tires and skis that dwarfed all others, Slayd pulled a long swath of his old shed skin from deep within a pocket. It crinkled before melting as he rolled it around in his mouth before swallowing it.

"I was born of admirable insolence. My birth was the finger toward an insipid pseudo-progress of man and a stab at the Right Hand of God. Just the idea of me was the Anti-faith, the true original sin to eclipse the Alpha and the Omega. I am the Higher Man!"

"Xipe ot totec, tlat lauh qui," echoed beneath his shouting.

A pocket produced a squished piece of lead — the used bullet of a suicidal dictator — that Slayd squeezed with both his hands as he walked forward, rolling it, softening it, shrinking it. "I am the culmination of the pinnacle of unpreserved human ambition. Ask not what man should not dare, but ask what man can do freed from the ego of celestial zookeeper. And you will find an ultra-being, the zenith of non-divine superscience and unpetitioned magicks. You will find Melchyor Slayd! You will find the superior man!"

"Otot itti ot tlot tlauli, otot itti ot tlot tlox tlii."

The Army of Earth's fighters attacked the fortress of gears on all fronts, but it appeared unfazed, masticating the land as it approached, drooling grease on its attackers, vomiting oil and flatulating exhaust from stacks as big and as round as its cannons. Spears and gunshot took down snipers that hid amongst its rails and pipes, but they were doing nothing against its massive plows and canine-toothed cranes. But still, both of Slayd's voices boomed louder than the tank truck's clanking reverberance, despite the giant pillow of smoke that enveloped him as the machine neared.

"Iot iotec autec ipe qui."

"But the superior man is more than his origins! It is not enough to kill the father and subsume the mother. One must so totally subvert all they stood for as to become unrecognizable to their values." He then chewed and swallowed the ball of lead.

Gluts of exhaust had been blossoming along with the passage of the great tank, but they then rolled in upon themselves as a lithe figure moved faster than the light could follow. Slayd leaped like a lizard and, with one long hand wet with black bile, and the other with yellow, he wrote shapes within shapes within angular shapes upon his descent on one of the tank's great metal wheels.

"Etoc iotoc eotoc ieic!"

He straightened the robes around his hips and resumed his walk deeper into the nearest squad of the Army of Heaven. The great tank behind him groaned to a halt as treads and belts tore and whipped about, and the great wheel, now glittering in solid gold, lurched and bent before crushing scrambling soldiers beneath itself. Gunfire grew louder than before, as men armored with the feathered signs of the Horde fired upon each other in an attempt to claim the giant golden gear for themselves.

Back on the hazy battlefield, opposite horizons glowed in competition. Smoke pulsed with the far-off gleam of sunset or sunrise. Frigid mists smothered the light of burning gasoline or broken campfires. But Slayd ignored the light to walk into an oncoming legion where horn-helmed soldiers bearing the golden Mark of Ashmedai drove spiked snowmobiles over fallen Army of Earth fighters. Others looked for paths for their struggling horses while stabbing the wounded that tried to flee on their hands and knees. Still others struggled themselves through the deep drifts or thrice-overturned earth. The prairie had become an alien, pockmarked world with an orange sun, where the snow was red and the air nigh unbreathable. The Army of Heaven all seemed to turn their guns and blades toward Slayd at the same exact moment.

"Ophidia in Ouroboros had grown complacent," he shouted, "interested only in adaptation, lazy toward the higher calling of evolution, their dull cow eyes unable to even appreciate the perfection they had already created."

Shots rang out, but the blizzarded air had crystallized into some askew mirror, and, as the scene shattered into shards that broke off into splinters that split into dying fireflies, the riflemen fell, realizing as they died that they had shot themselves or their companions.

Slayd plucked a reaper pepper from within his robe. It glistened and dripped, shaped like a human heart. It beat as one as well before the sorcerer bit gingerly into it. His serpentine eyes watered. His lipless mouth bled. His second voice screamed.

"Aphoom hah zhah!"

He exhaled a green cone of expanding flame over snowmobile and soldier. Those not consumed burned beneath armor that had melted down to the bone. Some were blinded by the slag of their own swords spattering into their faces. Some were deafened by the explosion of gas tanks. Snow and frozen plain melted instantly, filling and choking any unmasked man's lungs with blistering steam. With both of his voices, Slayd read from a small clay tablet harboring the seal of Mother Hydra, and the rush of sudden water froze solid with the sound of near thunder. At the very least, soldiers were stuck hard by their boots in the ice, but most fell over in numbing pain, their flesh and blood crystallizing and breaking from the knees on down.

The sorcerer continued to walk. With a finger flick he ignited a small but ornate lighter made from the melted down silver of the dagger that had scalped the ancient skin-walker, George Armstrong. The lighter held bound a minor campfire elemental, and with it Slayd lit a dried coneflower that had been soaked in Napa palm wine. His undervoice chanted as the wind collected into spectral equine shapes. Snow collected, giving some shape to the ghostly stampede as the dead riders looped nooses around the necks of the unmoving and the scattering soldiers of Heaven alike. The frozen were torn in gory tatters from the ice. The frantic were lassoed and dragged over the jagged ground. Still, Slayd walked on.

"Do you still not know me?" he yelled, the sound shifting the frost from the dirt. "Do you still not know whom you face? I am death to you who choose to still wallow in the ambitionless manure of your self-imposed pens. I am the end to any vainly imposing stunted wills upon their betters. I am finality to idiot lickspittles that have not only chosen to admire the yoke of faith but to dismissively insist on its universality. I am the superior man!"

A soldier of bindings and fur, of straps and goggled eyes, ran at the sorcerer. His shotgun had failed to fire, so he swung with spiked gloves. From another side, a coonskin capped man, with ceramic and metal-plated limbs, lifted a sword thicker but shorter than both his arms. Slayd waved the Wand of Yeb Spawn and both men disappeared into their own armor and rags. From one pile rose a swarm of green-bottle flies, sluggish in the freezing air, and from the other crawled a speckled toad that immediately hopped to voraciously gulp down as many of the insects as it could before it quickly bloated and stretched and appeared back in the form of a naked man, choking and blue. The remaining flies had also coalesced back into a soldier, now with great gashes of his body open and missing.

Around Slayd swarmed more troops. There were painted flags of birdmen in all directions, all colors, sprouting from saddle and backpack. Before a revolver could fire, it would backfire once Slayd gestured and muttered in the gun's direction. Bullet powder would ignite airlessly while still in the chamber. Rifles would leak more water or oil than could have possibly fit in the barrels. Arson grunts found that their gasoline had turned to wine. Slayd's fingers pointed and twisted and danced to the rhythm of his spell voice.

And as the wild men of the Army of Heaven fought to pull swords suddenly rusted to their scabbards, struggled to raise guns suddenly to hot or heavy to carry, the sorcerer was upon them. He punched one man's head off, sliced cleanly through another man's neck with his claws, and shook a soldier's helm so rapidly that what spilled out afterward was far from solid.

The troops that still approached, confused by the thick storm but angered at the carnage they walked into, were heavily armed and armored. One wore a thick leather draping completely covering any features except for the cylinder on his back and the metal tubes rounding to a hidden face. Another was layered repeatedly from head to foot in quilted armor but had virtual gauntlets and gloves of barb and razor wire. A squad followed, each man equipped with two rifles a piece and buckled securely in bandoliers over long white jackets that disappeared in the whipping blizzard. Slayd pulled a string of reflective red haematite from some hidden pocket and tossed it before the rush of men. It hung in the air, vibrating, doubling, absorbing the flashing electricity of the winds before redirecting it at any of the metal the troops were wearing or carrying. As flesh and clothing smoldered to cinders, what was left of the armaments were torn from shredding limbs to collect in the air at the site of the haematite before collapsing upon themselves to fall to the snow as one torso-sized lump of metal.

Still more troops and more winds circled.

"I am the destroyer of tradition, I am Number Three, the Supreme Synthesis," the walking wizard boomed. "I have rushed to where angels fear to tread and defiled whom gods fear to bed, for the superior man does not just kill his father, does not just rape his mother, he seduces her and befouls all legacy, and grand Ophidia in Ouroboros — pathetically ignorant of its ultimate accomplishment — first denigrated by its own aimless intellectual hedonism, then corporeally ruined by physical neglect, will have a heritage so overshadowed and then perverted by its greatest son as to be rendered beyond forgotten, has been and will continue to be erased into insignificance by the great orphan it threw away with the inspired bathwater." He reached into Tormalco's Robe, one of the hundreds of pockets. "Do you still not know who I am? I am the superior man, exactly because I killed my creator, but also exactly because I did more than just traumatize my motherland. I seduced her, infected her, birthed from her the extra chromosome that will shape the new world. For *I* am the new world! Who am I? I am the greatest motherfucker this world has ever known!"

But the pocket was empty. He checked again, fishing deeply even though he knew he should not have had to, but the spell component was not there. But it had to be. He remembered putting it there, cataloging it in his mind. He had never forgotten. He had never confused one pocket for another, one component for another in any spell. He could not be mistaken. It was not possible. He felt that he would insult himself by checking another pocket. How could he have been so mistaken?

The spear entered his back, but he did not feel it until it burst from his chest. He guessed that it must have missed his spine since he could still move his arms, could still feel the grit and cold of the snow as he sunk to his knees. The blade and shaft grounded him to the frozen earth, but he held it until its strength splintered and broke in his hands. Twisting, he threw the bladed end at the horse beneath its master. The short spear impaled mount to rider, and both crashed.

Slayd pulled the long piece hand over hand through his chest and swung the sticky staff, breaking rib and pelvis beneath armor of those that advanced. He launched the blunt wood, and it smashed and stuck hard in the faceplate of another. He hissed magick as he reached back to the fallen horse to tear the bowels from beneath its steaming flesh. He kissed them to make them squirm, and they were suddenly alive, whipping serpentine, wrapping and connecting one soldier to another, constricting necks and tying up arms until they snapped loudly. A rifle cracked nearby and a piece of Slayd's shoulder disappeared, but he was too busy tearing the faceplate of a soldier to bite his face with an unhinged jaw. Another spear was forced into the sorcerer's foot to ground him again, and again he had to go down to a knee, this time splitting first metal breastplate then ribs to tear at another soldier's exposed heart. More gunshots sounded as men accidently struck their troop-mates in such close quarters, but the sorcerer eventually fell lower and lower until he disappeared beneath a pile of scrambling and stabbing soldiers.

Back across the plain, the heat and cold and cottony deafness and blare of explosion and engine finally woke Wulf from the oppressive pain in his head and neck. Even if he had not been partially buried alive beneath sod and ice he was not sure if he could have pushed the ground from his side. The legions of his army trampled the ground all around him, not recognizing their filthy liege. He saw Damn Antony's troops and what must have been Teca's reinforcements.

But out beyond the strange glow of multiple horizons and a storm that appeared renewed with supernatural vigor, he felt the faint mind of Slayd as it diminished. He was almost gone. There was not much left of the sorcerer. So beneath it all, Wulf gently mentally searched for what he assumed he amongst all only knew. It was perhaps he alone that knew the real Slayd, knew that what a small group of misled adventurers saw high above the city of Magog, on a hurricane and curse-struck tower top, was not some transmogrification by the Everman, but Slayd's true form — his final form. Wulf, among all, knew what the sorcerer struggled daily to keep imprisoned inside an ultimately paper thin shell of a simile of a man. So he dived, not to deeply, into Slayd's mind to find the beating sack of veins and dragonic meat, and he probed it, and it twitched at his mind's touch. He poked it again and it exploded, venom flooding what was left of the fading sorcerer's mind and body.

Out in the battlefield, limbless torsos flew and crushed heads rolled awkwardly. Buckets of blood landed as the scaly creature burst from the pile of men it simultaneously threw and ate. It remembered nothing but its aborted terrorism on the top of the Tower of Gog, and it cared not. It lusted only for the carnage of fresh meat. Great crocodilian jaws tore the heads of running horses. Claws as large around as an auroch's head tore huge swaths through any groups of men unlucky enough to become lost near in the storm. Great gallons were drunk that night.

Wulf could not hear the carnage. His troops engaged a new front all around him, with treaded trucks roaring past and what could very well have been most of their ammunition reserves firing both to the east and the south. The plains were loud, but he was grateful to be able to hear again.

"Call us out ta the fight," the *Goblin Revenant* whispered to him. The ghostly forms had risen from the earth. They were barely perceptible in the windblown snow, but he could hear them more clearly than his own forces. *"We can win this for ya, save all yer men. No more need ta die."*

"At what price?"

"You know, you know the only thing we dead want."

He had tried to forget the specters that had followed him across the prairie. They had been silent in the Black Hills, but here they returned, as soon as he set foot out on the flat lands.

"They're driving back!" a soldier yelled at Wulf's left. "The... the... should... do we follow?"

"No," Wulf told him. "Send word to regroup. We'll circle the wagons until the storm dies."

But he was uncertain, this time, whether it ever would.

LXXX

To ever win the one ever in you
will you see all the girls still
at the edge of your heart and mind's eye too?
They are all there if you wish to see them
grown from ones you will not own

—Unknown

his is Yin, is she not beautiful?"

And she was. She was the most striking blade Wulf had ever seen — beautiful in the nostalgia and simplicity of her style, beautiful in the sharp runes of the darkly scarlet metal. There was no ornamentation on a hilt as long as his forearm, except for the mix of hard and soft shagreen tightly wired for the grip. Like the blades he had trained with while in service to the *SHE'*, Yin had no guard, meant for slashing rather than stabbing. It was shorter than most, and he believed Sera of the Necrophim when she had told him that it had been made especially for him. He could not read the abrupt runes, but Yggr's Eye could, and he knew even before they caught the light of the pyres she had presented it to him in front of, that it held the power to break ward and spirit.

"She does not abide by the laws we have chosen to shackle ourselves in," Sera had cooed, turning the red sword so that the edge caught the light from whatever alternate reality it cut into. "Yin has the vampiric thirst of infancy. She drinks blood, magic, and the souls of the wounded. Do not wake her, do not pull her from her hide unless you intend to satiate her thankless hunger." With that warning, she had slid the sword back into its hard and soft scabbard. The design of silver and smooth scales almost disappeared into a crimson that was so dark as to appear black in even the brightest of light.

Now, later, he just held the sheathed sword in his lap, sitting astride his blood bay horse, overlooking again the forested valleys leading out and into the yellowed rock and granite spires of the Needles, again overseeing the gathering and recuperating of the main battalion of his Army of Earth. Fearing to pull the blade from its scabbard, he just relived the memory of its beauty and Sera's words as she had presented him his latest gift.

"She is unbreakable, forged from an impossible thing. Her edge breaks the bonds of micro-universes hidden under even the gods' perception. Never scorn her, for her hunger is the fury of Hell. Keep her sequestered away in her skin, Yang, only releasing her in the world's time of greatest need."

Wulf dismounted but pulled the horse along his side. He had no tenders near to take it off his hands. He had ordered everyone, from child to elderly to chef to mechanic, to help with the reorganizing of the camps and supplies to ready for an immediate return to a march on the Kalderan Territories. The wounded were to be left with the Order of the Creed. They could not be waited for. He had made the decision to head out a day earlier than he had originally planned. Word kept coming in of disturbing movements of the Horde's varied forces. As far as he could tell, any southern fortress or city being lost to a Necrophim general was being quickly abandoned, with the losing enemy forces joining together, to battalions that had been difficult to track. With the breaking of the Needles' blockade, Wulf had put his own battalion out in the open. After the disastrous battle in the plains, it was obvious the Horde knew exactly where he was. He was not sure if the Temple and its villages were large enough to house his entire legions, but it was a mute point. The plan was to charge forward with the momentum they had gained, not to become holed up behind another blockade. He would leave behind some good troops that were close to recovering if he left early, but he instead now had a contingent of knights and new cavalry. It was time to press forward, while the weather was in his favor.

He pulled his hood back to feel the light on his face, but the sun, as bright and golden as it had become over the morning, would not warm his cheeks. Tents collapsed all around him. Yurts were disassembled and zenith campfires left to smolder. The bellowing of aurochs and mules fought with the ignition rumblings of trucks and carriers.

Wulf looked out over the haze that had appeared from battles in the plain. The fog had lasted over the prior day with no sign of dissipating. Any leaves or remaining needles left in the forests below were dulled by the haze into the color of the trees. But still the Order of the Creed rose above it all — smoke, surrounding woodlands, and light canyons. He looked from the Army's rendezvous point up on prominent hills out over the thick valleys to the adjacent cluster of spires. The paths were filled with carts and cars going in both directions. He knew some were abandoning the Army, both soldiers and families, both healthy and crippled, but he would not stop them.

A familiar horse rose above them all. He watched as Teca wove her way through the tight crowds. By the time she neared, the sun had disappeared behind the clouds of past battles and future storm. He had pulled the hood back up over his head. His granite eye had become as gray as the sky, and he turned so that it was all that showed from the depths of his mantle.

She did not speak until her horse was tied and she had found her heavy hat and gloves. The near air had coalesced into something between rain and snow. It was thin, but it tickled an exposed face coldly. She wrapped herself in his arms and his cloak, nuzzling forehead and bandage into his beard, hiding a cut that had ruined one of her eyebrows.

"I'm sorry," she whispered.

He looked again out at the pillars of stone that huddled together so magnificently against the outside world. The spotted woodlands around and beneath changed shape and depth as the clouds cast folding and deepening shadows over the land, but the impregnable cluster of thin towers never changed.

"It comes down from the Highlord himself," she continued, clicking her tongue. "Don't blame the knights. Some of them actually want to come, to help, and I think I can sneak some of them out." There was no wind over the hills this day, despite the movement of the warsmog and the curling of the winter above. "They're closing the doors as the last of the knights return. The wounded can stay until they're well enough, but any others will have to leave immediately. I think I can convince the monks to keep the families, at least the children. I won't believe they would just turn them out."

"I know."

"What?"

"It is because you are blinded by your faith."

She pushed away from him. He let her go. "Are you…"

"And the saddest part, is that it is your faith not in your 'Lady Wayasu' but in your Highlord and your disgusting Order."

"Just wait…"

"No! I could take your precious temple. You know that. What is it you think stays my hand? I have troops on the inside and out, I now know the hidden paths and gates…"

"Because of my…"

"And most of all, I have the right. *I* broke the blockade. *My* men and women sacrificed themselves so that your precious knights can spread their legs. And now you won't even give up a few more kegs of gunpowder? Some salted beef? How about a few plated dandies for me to throw at a mutual enemy?"

She grabbed at his collar, at his face. "I tried my best, you son of a bitch! If I could talk to the Highlord I would. They're scared, Wulf! Do you even remember what it's like to be scared?" She looked at the near organizing crowds before pulling him close to whisper, "No, you're too busy throwing fields of faceless people at the Horde to die happily for a cause few of them even understand. The Order is hiding, yes, but it's because it cares about its people. Do you care about these people?" She swung her arms around at the haggard mobs struggling to find the energy to pack tents and shields. They all looked thinner than the day before, and the day before that. "Look at them. Do you ever even look at them? They're fighting for you, for some myth they think you are, that they've been promised since birth. Next time, before you send them into yet another outnumbered battle, why don't you tell them who you really are? Too afraid that if they know you're not some resurrected messiah that they'll run away?"

"Better to die in battle than from starving outside the gates of the Needles, heckled by some pampered knight."

"Oh, don't give me that midgardian bullshit. You're better than that. You can't fool me. Who do you think you're talking to? What I'm saying is… I know the Order isn't perfect, but at least they know what's important. They're a family, and — I'm sorry — but they know what you bring with you. They were blockaded, yes, but they were safe. Now they've already lost men, since the Army of Earth arrived, and they're scared that since they've given aid they stand to lose more. The Horde will answer. You know that. They're a family, you know that, and they're doing what's best to protect what they love. If you would just… slow down… you might actually do the same. Look around you — these people love you. I love you, and I'm asking you to think about all this. Maybe we can't win. Maybe we're throwing it all away for nothing."

"Is that what you believe?"

They were both whispering, and she looked up to his fallen face.

"I just… no, of course not. I've seen the victims, the mass graves from where those giant perches sprout. I've heard about the slavery, the families torn apart, the quarantines of anyone that dares to question the singing of that blasted song. And please believe me, the Order hates the Horde too. Libra will judge the Territories as corrupted. They are all false piety and love only that which is worldly. Don't forget those knights that died out on the plain against them yesterday. They died fighting tyranny, in a cause they knew to be just."

"They died because of your Highlord's ulterior motives, Teca."

"They…"

"Because he got wind of what Shriven holds. Because we told your temple monks that the Horde, through their union with the Western Librans, had relics invaluable to Librans."

"Only…"

"Everyone knows it, Teca. Everyone knows that your monks, your nuns and paladins, have been steadily losing their abilities over the generations. Whatever it is, whether your 'enchanted blood' is drying up or whether you are being 'judged' unworthy — whatever it is — the Order of the Creed has little power left. The only reason we were given a cavalry was so we could eventually rescue whatever relics Shriven brought here with him. Your Order is hoping they will restore some abilities…"

"Not true."

Wulf pointed out across the valleys to the jagged spires. "Teca, there is something in there. I can't block it out if I tried, and it is manipulating you, has always been manipulating you. And the thoughts of the other knights… do you really want to know this? I can't block out their thoughts. Do you really *not* know this?"

"Please don't. I know…"

"They took you in because they thought you had some sort of magic in your blood. They don't care where it came from, they just want to invigorate their bloodlines. That's why they always…"

"Please stop. They're good people."

"I should have moved on the Horde's capitals weeks ago. I may have doomed us all with this distraction. Slayd is gone, and without his protection…" He stared off at the stony upcroppings, then down at the thinning lines on the paths and roads. The people had dispersed. The camps had mostly been taken down. His battalion was almost ready to head out. The fact that it could entirely fit on the acreages around him showed just how small it had become. Except for the Necrophim legions, he had recalled all of the other companies, but it could be long days, maybe weeks before they reunited.

Wyrmwood blistered the heavens of his peripheral. It had become the only color in the sky. Soon they would not need a sun.

"They're my family," Teca kept saying, "and in the end you'll see that Libra judged the will of the Highlord to be the word of the people. He has no choice."

"I could take those hills."

"Do you want to go to war with everyone? I hope that someday you'll love something enough to know what it's really like to believe in something other than yourself."

She stepped away from him but continued watching. She could only see the cold blue granite within the hood, but she never knew exactly what it looked at. She hoped it was her, but she knew better.

Wulf was on his horse before she could react, and by the time she had untied her own animal, secured its bags, and maneuvered around a line of transport wagons and aurochs, he had galloped down and out of sight. She rarely saw him ride, and to see him whip his red steed in into such a frenzy spurred her on to do the same. She was quickly launched down the hills and into and around people that had dispersed at his passing. Many of them cheered, realizing late that it had been their Liege of Foes that had ridden so manically through them.

Most of the families moved off the path to cover themselves in extra layers when a sudden roll of thunder alerted them to the hardening rain. With his horse diving into the hidden path amongst dead and sharp scrub emerging from a drop that had avoided snow until recently, Wulf pulled his clothing closer while holding tight reins and forcing a rhythm that kept the animal from slowing. The sprinkle was freezing into invisible shards, and they would have tore at his face even if he was not racing through a wind that should not have been able to break the tree line. The ground changed in direction and dangerously thrust into an ascent, and the horse bucked and screamed, but it leaped over and upward at his encouragement. He was deep in the trees now, and the snow, although thin, was sporadic, precarious, as dun as the sky, broken and puzzled, desiccate, unreflective, desperately grasping at dead weed and hoof, disloyal, with each grain polished by a year of shadowed breezes. Wulf's steed bled below its knees, and it chewed voraciously at its bit to either side when pulled, but it dug in and climbed. Surface that had not moved in generations was impaled and thrown. Wulf hugged the ruddy neck. It was all muscle and a heat that threatened to tire him into instant sleep, but he forced his eyes open against the sleet that melted before it could hit the steaming beast.

The horse anticipated the sudden descents before he could, managed the long and exhausting ascents better than Wulf expected, no longer tearing at the bridle. The forests were filled with an accumulation of hail by the time they climbed the last of the hills. It no longer was the sound of occasional thumping against his cloak but a monotonous drum against him. Although he kept his face deep within his hood, water still ran the length from his scalp to beard.

The woodland sharpened as it became even steeper, nearing the tree line, and they emerged amongst granite, and Wulf leapt, pushing off the horse with his feet and the ground with his mind. The thunderheads moved above, and so the shadows changed over and through the trees and Wulf changed with them, becoming one with them as he disappeared into the rocky crevices above the hidden gate. Besides a frothy and flaring horse that scrambled backward and downward the hard scrabble, guard squires, both obvious and hidden, saw only the turning darkness between trees and granite and the hail that ricocheted from branch to boulder.

Wulf kept to the darkness inside the stony spires, his cloak becoming just one more lengthening shadow under the storm. He soon blended into the alleyways and sheds of the Libran town. Doors and windows were tightly shuttered against the hail that bounced and collected in every cold corner. He left only the faintest of footprints in a slush that shifted soon after he passed.

Then out into the open of the Dry Gardens he ran, passing fully plated and furred knights walking the bricked rows with feather-bladed halberds. The large square resounded with an orchestra of ice clinking off their full armor, getting caught up in red and white flag and banner. He ran so fast, propelled by feet and telekinesis, that the limited vision of their thinly visored helms could not follow the blur through the potted gardens.

Mental tendrils pulled at the hidden side door, and Wulf was in the temple before the guard realized anything had moved. Inside the cathedral the air was cold, and the guards wore long and quilted shirts and sleeves under a great angelic amulet that held together large rings over their torsos. Each carried short spears and long knives. The basilica was quiet, distanced from the thunder and hail, and its ceiling disappeared into the dim in the dreary day, but Wulf touched each mind to trigger a communal fantasy. Each guard saw the glow from hidden skylights increase to a point of brilliance. The sun glowed in a blinding feathery fan from these white windows. Any shadow left amongst the aisles fluttered like waking eagles. And Wulf slipped by without notice.

Through silver statues and red woods, through low and dark domes, through the ceilings and walls, Yggr's Eye could see the dark magicks. An abysmal aura, the color of blood-soaked stool, moved at the top of the tower, and Wulf was again reminded of the first time he had come to the Temple Needles. Even blind he had been able to see the corruption that had bled into the very mortar of the brick. He headed forward and upward, guided by light.

The great doors he eventually found himself before were in a swirl of dark miasma. With Yggr's Eye he could see the phantasmagoric trickle of wards falling over the entrance to the Highlord's chambers. He could see but not read the dancing symbols, could admire but not understand the shimmering runes. But he knew that the magic was in place to keep anyone out. The room was bright and open, with tall windows and a lack of the pillar supports decorating all the other rooms in the temple. Between the beams of winter light hung tapestries depicting few past Highlords. Here, above all the other chambers of the great stone structure, the hail could be heard against the outside walls as it lessoned and turned back to a feathery rain. Wulf did not try to hide himself. He had expected elite guard, but here they still wore long but light armor, still carried close quarter weapons. It was magic that protected the doors, not the men.

After verbal commands were ignored, the first guard ran to thrust a short spear. Wulf sprang, his cloak wrapping the man's face, and he stepped highly to drive the blade into the floor. He walked up the spear, kneeing the knight under the jaw before flipping over him, revealing and driving blunt Yang into the muscle where the shoulder met the neck of the next guard. One retched, the other struggled to compose himself with paralyzed extremity. Wulf spun hidden Yin before diving and driving the butt of her hilt up inside the thigh of a guard stabbing high with a long dagger. Wulf held the scabbarded sword far outside his cloak, and the final knight slashed at it. A flat knife-hand driven up under the armpit reduced the man to a quiver on the tiled floor.

"Her edge exists in the space between perception," Sera had told him upon presenting her latest boon. "She cuts askew of the established thought, whether it be the so-called 'rules' of science or magic. She is an impossible thing, untethering impossible bonds."

Yin squealed with the glee of a newborn at the sight of teat as she was unleashed into the air, her scratched runes reflecting a red light without an earthly source, and he drove the tip of her dark blade forward. The double doors were architecturally and magically sound, but Yin slid between them, and Yggr's Eye showed the spilling runic equations split and dissipate. Wulf solidly took great hanging rings in mental tentacles, and, to the grind of rubble and the scrape of hinges, he pulled at the doors.

"Stop!" he heard Teca call from far back down the great hall. "Wait! Please, Wulf, you can't..."

He looked, saw her running. The opposite end of the chamber, behind her, held a yellowing granite statue of Lady Wayasu, Blind Libra. One arm had long ago crumbled away. The other held a balance scale skyward. Broken chains on one side led to a missing pan.

The chill that wafted from behind Wulf emanated from more than just the dark fires, living shadows, and mystically corrupted air of the Highlord's office. It leaked from the demon itself — from beneath feather and down, from between patches of fur and shell, out from long waterfalls of braided hair.

Teca had slowed before she reached Wulf, and her rigored expression was one never before witnessed. She clung to his clothing, staring past him, short nails digging through his shirts. He had never seen eyes so wide. They were a beautiful caramel, a color that reminded him of honey he had tasted in some other life.

The demon roared and Wulf turned to look at what had frozen Teca so. He could not tell if they saw the same thing. What Yggr's Eye showed him may not have been what she looked at, but, if her reaction was any indication, she watched the same monstrosity.

A humped back lurched above, pimpled by the faces of barn owl growths. Pitch eyes searched. One beak screeched. A great bison head made up the giant's wide torso, its snort heating the air instantly. Spittle fell in voluminous clumps of foam. One great arm writhed from a furry mound of a shoulder down to the smoky floor. The muscles were a mass of striped and spotted scales, pale and hissing, rattling and knotting with the occasional thin fangs appearing. The other arm twitched, just a tiny spotted fin flipping coldly. Flies swarmed and buzzed in hanging hives from the beast's belly like living testicles that dripped dying insects on the floor. Longer than any man, the demon's phallus, quilled and with mutilated foreskin, dragged itself behind its giant sheep legs. With the doors open, its cloven hooves shook both chambers with each turning step.

Wulf could taste rotten eggs in the air, and his eyelids felt stung by bees as the monster parted a curtain of strung human arms and legs. None had hands or feet. Few had skin. Behind the flayed drapery was a chamber too immense for the temple. Its spiraling and segmented walls of windows looked out to falling cascades of sand and skulls under a molten sky. The floor of the chamber was mostly open, with numerous causeways over, and ladders into, rising vapors thicker than pea soup. The great legs of the demon stopped over one of the few areas of the floor, over two intersecting heptagons — one of human juices, the other chalk-drawn — before living flame, casting no glare or shadow, appeared and pulled the giant down into an emerging black cauldron.

The entire chamber shimmered as a mirage enveloped in the heat of the Great Furnace, and then it was gone, replaced by the modest office Teca had seen only a few times over the years. There were no chairs or desks, just as she now remembered, only dust-caked and barely used bookshelves and corners of alcoves holding sunken candles not used in a generation.

Wulf was holding her. She had folded and fallen. Her eyes teared as much as those of the guards, but she did not sob as they did.

"What… was that?" she asked to anyone who could hear her. No one answered except for the sword that, although sheathed again, could be heard to whine in insatiate thirst.

~

Wulf was not going to follow her, but, in the chaos surrounding the Dry Garden, he could see Teca heading out on a path he did not expect. With rumors being shouted in every direction, including out from, and even at, the highest windows of the temple, no one paid him any heed, and he headed out after her, into and through hail-filled alleyway along and down some of the steepest paths in the Libran town. But it was not long before he recognized where she ran.

The rain had stopped, but the brick and steps were damp. Even the air in the dim cellar holding the clockwork door was moist. The room smelled of vegetation and newly forged metals, even though neither were present. Here he found Teca pacing. He could not tell if she realized she was walking in rhythm to both the loud and quiet clicks of the clocks built into the large door.

"You wouldn't understand," she spat. She had removed her sword belt and the empty pistol holster she always still wore, and now she took off her jacket despite the chill of the brick. "Because you always get what you want. And you got it again, well, when do I get what I want?" The shadows of the room were filled with crumbled pieces of wall and floor, even chips of the ceiling, but she found one of the bigger slabs of stone, and she turned it in her hands, feeling the heft, but it broke in her grip, and she dropped it before dropping herself cross-legged in front of the door.

"Everyone else has long forgot about this door, or they have stopped caring. I used to come here once a day, for my free hour, sit just like this. Sometimes I'd read, go over maps, sometimes I'd take a nap. There was a time when I'd become so afraid that the clock would wind down without me being here and I'd miss it, but then I just came to believe that it would actually only open for me. I actually didn't have to be here because, if the Clockwork Monarch had set the timer to open when he knew I would be here, in the hour of the Order's greatest need, I didn't have to worry about it. It was all preordained. But that's not really it is it? I never really understood, did I?

"I've seen so much in the fighting, so many people, on both sides, just desperately hoping that this is it, that this is the end, because, otherwise, their lives will have meant nothing. Can you believe that? All this violence, all this death, is fed by people anxious in their... what would you call it? Perceived insignificance! The thought that someday, someone, hundreds of years from now, thousands of years! Someday someone will look back over the expanse of history and not pause on their petty little forgotten life, just skip over their entire era. This is driving men mad! But not if this is the end. If this is the end then it will give man pause. *My* life is significant because I lived during, I participated in, the predestined. The rise of civilization was only a precursor to my grand days, and there are no great days, no eons of generations to follow to trample my lifetime into insignificance.

"And I'm no better. I came here every day when I boarded with other squires. I fretted and dreamed every night when I was out in the land, worrying this damned door would open while I was away. I thought I was over it, but seeing it again brings it all back. I could not just be just another Libran, eventually lost to time, my name registered, maybe, luckily, with some courteous deeds, in some old book with a failing spine that falls apart when some cellar library is moved to make way for a new sewer. The thought that the world had as many years still coming after my bones are interred as it had before I was born was just too much. But if the clocks in this door stopped one day while I waited, if some bell chimed and it opened and the Clockwork Monarch appeared to relate to me my destiny, then I wasn't just another in a long line of soon-forgotten knights.

"I'm no better than any of them. They lie to themselves, claiming to have faith only in Blind Libra when we all gave it to the Highlord, to the monks, or anyone else that makes us feel special. We denounce the Western Order for holding Dhani Antony as a divine saint, but we still glorify how we are descended from him, or his teachings. We're taught to only have faith in Libra, but we each carry a copy of the *Sol Sistere*, telling ourselves it is infallible, but it's been translated, and verses have been added and removed, and so we tell ourselves that Lady Wayasu would never lead us astray, but that is what every version of Libran holding every version of the *Sol Sistere* has told themselves. But we do this to make our time, our lives, of importance. And so we tell ourselves then that we must then live in the 'spirit' of the *Sol Sistere*. And so here we are, with a thousand different 'spirits,' following a thousand different perspectives, telling ourselves we only have faith in Libra."

She suddenly jumped to pull a large rock Wulf had not noticed from the expanding shadows.

"Well..." Teca hesitated in the exertion of striking the rock against the clock. "I confess the sin of pride!" She beat the stone again and again against what looked like a giant piece of the locking mechanism. "I was prideful... in assuming that I could judge better than Blind Libra. I judged who could interpret better than me, who could translate and edit better than me. But I also sinned in sloth. I chose to let others do the work for me, but I was prideful again in judging when I could make my own decisions." The greater ticking had stopped while the minor still clicked away somewhere deep within the door. Levers leading to supposed thick hinges emerging from the rock of the wall were bent beyond repair. "But the good news is that we can just all account it all as a test of faith. So slothful, again so slothful to fear doing the work of looking deep down inside ourselves, all because we're so prideful to cling to the belief that our period, our lives, mean anything to the massive scheme of time."

She strained against the gears of the door, first pushing and then pulling to absolutely no avail. She stepped back as Wulf appeared, eyes closed. Frame and foundation spider-webbed in cracks. The vibrations could be felt in their teeth, radiating to the rhythm of the quiet clock. The sound of the door tearing from the rock was minor compared to the deafening thunder of its metallic bounce against the floor and its crash against the back wall. The ticking of more than one clock could be heard as the reverberations and pebbles settled. Still loud was the chaos of the streets above, so Wulf had little fear that any of the Libran city would check on the noise below.

He followed her over and through the hazy portal. By the time the brick dust had settled, Teca was already across the tall room examining the decay of a device twice the height of a man. At one time it must have appeared to be a circular frame in which two smaller, although thicker, circular tracks spun against and within each other, but one of the interior axles appeared to have corroded and fallen under its own weight, taking most of the giant mechanism down with it.

"I've seen this before," Teca said quietly, "in some forgotten sketches of history or... maybe... a dream. This is how he'd return — the Clockwork Monarch — from wherever, or whenever, he fled to. I shouldn't know this, you know. I would have been suspended. All traces of certain Highlords were expunged. And I only even know that because the timelines just never matched up, the math never worked. I pieced it together over years of finding journals that escaped the Order's notice. But this, I know, is how he was supposed to return. Look at it. It's ancient. This entire room hasn't aged. There's no dust at all. Everything is entirely preserved, yet this machine fell old long ago."

It was true, Wulf noticed, picking among the unfinished clockwork ponies, barely-started skeletons of tin butlers, and draped and rolled cog-covered blueprints. Nothing else had been disturbed by time. Even gutted water clocks held fluid clear enough to drink.

"All my life," Teca wondered, "I had no idea what to expect. Now, there's nothing here to help us. Such a waste of time."

"Oh, I wouldn't say that," Wulf said, pulling an object the size of his hand from a wall bearing winding keys of all sizes and ornamentation. The key he held was by far the most ornate, and it held the bejeweled image of a hatchling dragon emerging from its egg.

~

"You, little demon, have contributed to a trend that is becoming all too common as of late. Your failure will end up changing the shape of the land." The Crimson Queen beckoned to the American Raksasha, siren-calling him from the pocket dimension he had hidden himself in.

"I am nothing more or less than you have made of me, mistress. Have I not ultimately served you well in my tenure as master to these pathetic new world apes? I am only pleased that I could be of some use to you."

They entered an ancient cave formed millennia ago, straight into the heart of the Black Hills. Over eons, rock had fallen to both reveal and hide the entrance to the tiny cavern. They had to shrink to fit among the natural pillars and leaning stone. Again the heat struck her solidly before it could be collected by breathing machines to be used and reused in the smithing. Tiny rivers of slag and molten stone streamed around and between them. Except for the burning fairies, cavorting in their death throes with each strike of a hammer over anvil, the streams cast the only light when the ovens were closed.

"Do not think that I am done with you, noble Raksasha. I will always find your worth in some form or another. Once, as a lonely pilgrim. Then, a nigh-eternal Libran Lord. And now? Let us for one last time test your mettle. You can still be the greatest weapon in my most righteous crusade."

"I am ready to be your holy sword, my mistress."

Dwarves, of eyes dark but with beards blinking of ember dust, escorted the chimeric demon to the largest of the forges. The infernal furnace blasted nova when opened, annealing the beast immediately.

"Holy? Sword?" Sera mused, walking from the scene. "No, this time, this land, requires new rationales, new weapons to create a bridge to an even newer world." She would return to carve the *Soul Unleashed* rune into his casing.

The dwarves removed the black cauldron from the nether inferno, granite hands impossibly delicate. Molten blood and demonic spirit was poured into a small sigil-covered cast as the shaggy men hummed a guttural tune passed to them by cultish great-grandfathers.

LXXXI

...and your worlds, lives, are endless as choices
but those with Kings of All cut
to the core, for you wish to hear their voices
—scrawled on the walls of the King of All's lower halls

The Grand American Union had fallen again, and the King of All regretted it as much as the first time. It was a great amusement while it lasted, and now he would have to go back to the throne, back to the mundane procedurals, traditions and matters of state — all the time wondering if war would ever peek its welcome head again. Would there ever be more dissension anywhere across the land? Were there any enemies left? Not that he was aware of. His Queen would tell him to bask in his latest victory, to enjoy the blood-soaked dirt, the role of conquering hero and the adulation of his men. If peace were to settle, it might be his last chance. And she would be right. But she was not here, and so he had to tell himself to savor the defeat of the clone armies. She was not here, so this was a moment for Easarean to share alone with son.

The Prince stepped from the massive chariotank Easarean had given to him before they set out on this latest, and perhaps final, crusade. It was even larger, more sophisticated than his own. Using technology the King's engineers cannibalized from the first time he had crushed the GAU, they had built the ultimate in destruction and the grandest in presentation. Normally he would have led his men at the front lines, preferring to feel blade against bone, the blood and sweat up close as opposed to from behind a com screen, directing orders and placements, but this final push against the straggling GAU was to be used as a lesson for Antony, and so they approached slowly on the giant crawler as their forces demolished Noble City. He had still planned to take the Prince into the city, to teach him physical combat in the last stages of the attack, but the stronghold fell too quickly under his army.

Easarean followed his son onto the hilltop. They were exposed to the fallen city, but there was nothing left to fear — if there had ever been. Even if there were enough of the clones to stage one final attack, the King would take the chance that they had no armaments left that could pose him any danger, and he had been content since Antony's first birthday that there was nothing in existence that could harm the

Prince — the Queen had seen to that.

He stood behind his son on the pock-marked ridge, overlooking their moving forces, the crawlers' treads crawling over the rubble that was once the outskirts of the city's fortifications. They watched the carnage through the exhaust of lessoning battle as it changed colors from minute to minute from warm to cold, from dark to light. Only as the dust settled could they make out the blur of the sun. The King barely stood taller than his ever-growing son, even as the Prince floated slightly over the ground, never to touch the earth his mother commanded. A tiny blue fire now flickered from his forehead, as dark as his eyes and mirrored by twin flames dancing over each shoulder. And as his features differentiated him over the years, his compassion for the people of the land had grown in ways alien to the King.

Easarean had let the Prince think it was his idea to halt the final push into the city, letting the few stragglers escape, when in actuality he hoped some would embed themselves in the Kingdom of All, creating some sort of resistance or future revolt he could crush.

"Why do they resist, father? Why would they deny themselves the blessings of the Kingdom?"

"Some are born to fight, my boy. Some cannot be content with country and family and other trappings forced upon them by god and community. Some are never satisfied with peace, whether inward or outward."

"Ha! Who exactly is it you speak of, father?"

King and Prince chuckled together, but Antony's voice then grew somber.

"They fight for vengeance, do they not? I'm not so young to forget how we poisoned their wives and loins. We dug up their cities, rained fire on their armies, stole their science and magiks."

"And before that *they* attacked *us*."

"But it was *we* that first…"

"Son," Easarean kept the sternness from his voice, patting Antony on the shoulder, "one can trace back battles and counterattacks into grievances and insults until exhaustion. This goes for any war. All that matters is the here and now, and here and now the GAU threatens… *threatened* the Kingdom's way of life. We were threatened, and we responded. Let history judge who was in the right."

"History?"

"When the sun grows red and scholars of some future race find the remains of the mythical Kingdom of All, they can decide hero and villain. It matters not now. Today you have ground your enemy under your boot. Be it dragon, harpy, angel or demon, wolf or man, your people will live another day, sleep another night, because you have triumphed over it." But Easarean knew he was being disingenuous. There would never be a vague history of this time. There would never be a "mythical" Kingdom of All lost to time or decay. He looked over the young man his son had become, stronger but leaner than his father, inexperienced but wiser than the King, merciful but more powerful than the Queen. He would become a greater king than Easarean, admired rather than feared. He was already a greater god than his mother, loved rather than worshipped. He would one day unify the nation under mercy rather than force. With the gathered sciences and magiks of all the people, past and present, he would lead his own Army of All across the seas and over the walls to whatever resided beyond, and eventually the whole planet would bow to the God King Antony. All this Easarean saw in his mind. All this Easarean knew in his heart. Would he still be alive to see his son take the masses to the cosmos? His kind were long-lived compared to the rabble of this world, but would he survive to watch Antony overthrow the Empire that had forsaken his father in what now seemed like another life? He certainly hoped so. The sweet thought of taking the fight back to his son's alien cousins would certainly keep Easarean alive through generations to come.

Here was his ultimate revenge before him — revenge against the clans that had abandoned him, and revenge against the angel that had tricked him. Here the Shining One had exiled him with the promise his children would be great, be heroes among men. Easarean was sure that the Shining One had laughed when he had left him a door into a world with a people unsuitable to breed with one such as him. But here Easarean had found one of sterner stuff. In all the land, the Queen of Quartz had found him, and now Easarean would be the one to laugh. Perhaps once the Kingdom of All conquered space it would bring its might to the Underworld or the Overworld or wherever it was he had been trapped in his other life. Once Antony was king, anything would be possible.

"Could I have prevented this?" Antony asked. There was soberness in his lilting voice that sometimes worried the King. "I can't tell if the battlefield is soaked or sun-smothered, but the outcome is the same — a bloody sight I already tire of. If I am God could I have prevented this?"

"Men make their own choices… create their own fates."

"God is timeless. God is Omniscient. He knew this would happen billions of years before there were stars to tell time by, yet He still made man knowing they would sin, knowing they would be cursed and suffer for it."

"*You* are God."

"So I am to blame? For every sin? For every death?"

"When you are king, when you rule All, you will end the pain. Only when the Kingdom of All covers the constellations will there finally be peace. Peace cannot exist without war to first enforce it. Peace is not even desired, valued, until a society experiences the alternative."

Antony laughed and, as it inevitably always did, his voice melted the ice in Easarean's chest. There was no one else that had the same effect on him.

"And what will you do then? Is there a place for you in peace, father?"

"And then," Easarean said, returning the laughter, "you may have my final kiss as I light my own pyre, if my bones can support a torch at that age."

"I don't like the thought of being without you, father. If I am God then you will live forever, I promise."

Easarean turned back to the chariotank. Its immensity terrified even him, blocking all light from behind the ridge. How it must destroy any morale of anyone who saw it coming, he mused. Yes, someday, he imagined, he would sit behind the command chair of his son, the future King of All, in a starlight-engulfing juggernaut as it approached Empire space. How his ancient people would fear their coming.

A familiar sound brought him from his thoughts and back around toward the ridge. It was, as he guessed, the sound of a primitive arrow embedding itself in the ground between him and Antony. It appeared that the last remnants of the enemy still had some life left in them. Futile, of course, but he admired the stubbornness, yet still the scene sent a shiver over his body. The dust had settled and there was no wind. His army had halted and even the crawlers were starkly silent. The surrounding smog had grown darker in its bloodiness, and it turned his son's skin violet. He knew the anxiety was ridiculous, but he suddenly felt very exposed.

"Get in the tank," he commanded Antony, trying to hold his voice steady. There was no reason to worry the boy.

"Father? I don't think I want to hurt anyone anymore."

The Prince was looking skyward as the next arrow passed silently and completely through his neck. Easarean caught his body before it hit the ground, struggling to gather the young man's limbs before they touched the ground. He was not to touch the earth.

The King could not hold enough breath to shout at the heavens, could not even choke enough air to curse god or man. It was his son that bled from his neck, yet it was Easarean that could not breathe. Antony's head hung at an obscene angle, eyes staring wide at blood he had never seen before, blinking at pain he had never even imagined — much less felt before. Easarean, although blind with tears, plucked at the tiny iridescent feathers stuck in the accumulating streams of blue blood.

The tiny flames on and around Antony flickered wildly once, as they never had before, before disappearing forever, while the King of All finally found the breath to scream. He screamed over the valley, his men shrinking and hiding all around, and to Heaven and Hell, hoping his only son would hear him. But there was no response.

LXXXII

One with hair stained of fire
in curls chainmail tight
reaches bloodless hand out
past face sculpted in reflections
of battles long fought and villages since plundered.

Off to endless feasts of food and war.
Off to unending drink and plump women to conquer.
Until The Beast is unleashed
Such is the way
and the reward
of the warrior.

—Excerpt from the Song of Gnos

God damn it, why the fates won't let me leave these cursed hills, I'll never understand." Barely back into the plains, just beyond the rise and fall of the foothills and uncomfortably far from the cover of any tree line, Wulf grumbled in vain. The canopy tent he stood beneath provided no cover from the wind, and its burnt canvas whipped loudly enough to obscure his voice. A mortar burst the ground open on some far field, but the sound and vibration was enough to make him cringe, to make the map and pawns on the small table shake. The gunfire nearby grew louder. It was closer than it had been all morning, but he could not tell just how close it had become. The sound of the men building the close barricade had been distracting him. They were the elders and the near infirm of the camps, and they stacked every last bit of refuge to create a junk wall on the southern line. It now looked like some garbage golem in the shape of a caterpillar, made as it was of stalled trucks, dead horses, and the pieces of bombed-out wagons. One of the men was painting the bloody tear-stained eye of the Army of Earth on the fabric of every torn shred of every tent remnant in the mounds so that the barricade would soon look like it was covered in flags and banners.

The Agent of MANN, large and insectoid, crouched to fit under the canopy's swaying frame. It was impossible to tell what its six flat eyes looked at.

"You should have never taken the Army here," Damn Antony said as he looked over the maps while also trying on a crate of differently sized and furred helms. His attendant was obviously only handing him ones that would completely protect his eyes. The old scar exactly separating the hemispheres of Antony's face appeared to glow dully under the colorless sun. *Wyrmwood* pulsed softly — a pustule blistering and suspended in Heaven. "This was a distraction and probably a trap. Did you really want the Black Hills to be the gravesite of the Liege of Foes? All this for the loyalty of some girl knight?"

"All this for supplies," Wulf murmured, moving a horse-headed pawn clockwise around the pieces representing the camps, "rest and healing, some horses, fewer knights than I had hoped, but also the help of the Seven Ghost Phetas, the Natives. With the… liberation of the Needles, they've returned to the surface of the Black Hills, and they are all that is keeping what our spies tell us is a massive Horde battalion from the west from reaching us. Natives are turning the very woodlands against the Horde. I'm told the trees now have mouths and that the weather fights for them. The Hills have become impassable from that direction."

"Then that's where we should head. Go back in there." Antony had now switched to looking over a set of rifles, checking the alignment of sights and the give of each gun's lock.

"I will not get stuck in there."

The Agent of MANN cocked its smooth metallic head toward the wind, one way before the other.

"What's the alternative?" Antony asked. "Winter's taken the North. East? These people won't follow you back out into the plains. It almost killed them just getting here in the first place. You can't possibly still be planning on attacking into Kaldera?" Something exploded far overhead. Embers rained but disappeared before they reached the close forces. "Give up. That's where these forces keep coming from. My company watched from afar as one of your Crimson Queen's Necrophim marched on a Horde controlled city. Instead of digging in or fighting back, the Horde just abandoned the entire territory and sent all its militias up here. Even if you count all the families that comprise nearly half of what's left of your battalion, you're hopelessly outnumbered."

"Are your men loyal?"

"Well… to you they are anyway."

"I need you to go to the Badlands." Wulf drew a line sharply with pawn and map. "There you'll meet with Legion to cut diagonally back behind the Horde."

"Janus isn't here?"

"His troops have been keeping the Ridge Roads clear."

"Then who is protecting us? Right now? Just the main forces?"

A whirr grew beneath the wind, and both men, their attendants, guards, and links looked to the sound's source. The Agent of MANN crouched further down into itself, an alien sculpture reflecting new fires on the horizon.

Around the junk wall raced a snowmobile. It spun out, enveloping itself in its own plume of exhaust. Guards fired into the black cloud, but gunfire followed from the hidden snowmobile. Antony fired his own rifle at another snowmobile that had appeared behind the second. Its face-masked rider, covered in tubes and furs, flew from the machine that continued barreling past into a line of wagons. Its explosion rocked and burned wagon and truck.

"These are scouts!" Antony yelled to the close guard. "Form up for more!" And the heavily armored red troops stepped in front of him to brace high and low with spearifles aimed. Antony himself fingered through a small crate, picking out certain rifle rounds. "My men are going to need new ammo," he said to Wulf.

Wulf had returned to his maps, asking questions of the Agent of MANN that went unanswered. "We all do. I have the smiths working day and night, but we need to move out."

Crashing through the curved path of the snowmobiles came a covered pickup with chained tires and a smoking grill. It tipped in the tight turn, falling on its side and on top of the first snowmobile and its dead driver. Either the snowmobile or the truck's engine flared into brilliance, with black shrapnel flying straight up into the air before falling with its own plumes of dirt. The truck's drivers, on fire themselves and screaming prayers to the Divine Choir, tried in vain to crawl from the wreckage before being shot to death by Wulf's guards.

The wooden frame covering the back of the pickup had collapsed in the turnover, and a deluge of sludge and hogs spilled forth. Each had a large infected wound meant to be the mark of Ashmedai, a curly crown branding, and those that had not broken trotters in the fall ran blindly every which way.

Wulf could feel the *Goblin Revenant*, incorporeal and colder then the frozen earth they emerged from, slink up behind him.

"Av you forgotten 'bout us? Hee, hee! Let us help, oh glorious Goblin Liege, oh palest of grandest hobs. You owe us the chance, don't you? We can help. We love to help."

"Do not... let... any... escape!" Antony was shouting, shooting into the mess. He started loading and handing guns to the attendants. "I counted seven! Do not stop until all are accounted for. Burn the bodies to char immediately. We don't know if they are pestilent, cursed, or what the Horde had planned!" He looked out over the settling sludge, firing around at close range to ensure that one of the swine was certainly dead. This close he could now see that the filth was composed of excrement, and bodies with faces eaten off, bellies eaten out, and limbs reduced to gnawed gray twigs. "How are they getting so close? They know our moves before we make them."

Wulf looked up to say, "Slayd was keeping their scrying at bay. Without his help... the Horde could be watching us through every candle flame or campfire."

"Go back to the company," Antony told his man-at-arms. "Split it. You're in charge there, send the rest here. Make sure I get some mortarmen."

A boy, heavily quilted and covered in scarves wrapping blankets around every limb, clung to the heaving back of a ruddy auroch. The beast pulled a low cart carrying a crate taller than a man.

"I brought what ya asked for, my Liege!" the boy shouted, averting his eyes from the near carnage, jumped down, and held a palm high with its painted bleeding eye.

"Good work, kid. Go, be with your family," Wulf said, immediately working the hinges of the crate.

"Ain't got none, my Liege, I fight for the right to have one of my own some day!"

"Alright. Good man. Then find out for me where Sir Teca's regiment is engaged."

"Southwest line, my Liege, the lower camps are being attacked."

"Is she with them?"

"The Sir is fortifying the south camp, my Liege. Circling wagons and such." The boy's big brown eyes blinked the snow from their lashes.

Antony updated the pieces on the main map. "That would explain the color of the western sky. Something big is burning. They're sitting ducks out there, but we can't leave this side open. Either you, yourself, need to move to the interior, or we need to send out a general retreat."

The last of Antony's words were drowned out, as a tractor the height of the barricade crashed into the junk wall. The spinning blades of the machine slowed, its spiked armor getting caught up in the scrap and tilting it sideways, but soldiers of the Army of Heaven swarmed like blue ants over the wreckage. The old men that had been building the wall fell under a hail of pickaxes and spiky flails. Where once an improvised barrior had stood, now the Armies of Heaven and Earth met. Spears, bullets, arrows, and snowmobiles flew in all directions.

The walls of the large crate fell aside, and Wulf immediately began searching for some port or opening on the great Clockwork Wyrm Egg. As he pulled the ruby-encrusted winding key from beneath his cloak, a small panel complied, sliding soundlessly open at the artifact's approach. Locking the key into the port, he turned it with great effort, as gun smoke thickened the air around the plain. No wind could blow the stench away.

But Wulf just kept turning the winding key until, after what seemed like many minutes of looking up at a rainbow of flawless gems following lace after lace of golden filigree, something moved inside the great ivory metal of the Egg's shell. A ticking started to resound, echoing back upon itself. He was not sure anyone else heard it, not sure if anyone else *could* hear it, uncertain if it ticked anywhere other than within his head, the head of *he who turned the key*. He leapt back as the Egg twitched, grateful that he was not near as it began to open wide, folding outward while twisting in upon itself. The hatching was a result of sudden pieces of its shell opening and spreading into scale and skin, of both intricate and large gears, of springs and struts shrinking and expanding. The Egg turned inside out, growing impossibly twice as large than it had been, every interior cog never slowing until the Clockwork Wyrm stretched its giant shining body and miniscule wings.

"What... is... that... magnificent thing?" Besides Antony, the battlefield was suddenly silent. Wulf could only hear distant breaks of cannon fire and the ticks and clicks of the mechanical dragon's guts.

"It is the product of a cold war, a passive aggression that sat impotently on one end of the countryside while its key sat on the other."

Soldiers of all allegiances had paused, most mid-thrust, many mid-wounding, to stare across at the segmented masterpiece. It had immaculately faceted diamonds for eyes, and the silver plates rolling to make its serpentine neck turned those infinitely reflecting orbs to Wulf. He held up the winding key to its plated beak and jaws, dangling it just below the thinly pressed ribbons of its bronze beard. The segmented Wyrm reared for just a second, and Wulf could only glance at a large rainbow agate set deep within its sheltered belly. Yggr's Eye revealed to him the link to the earth. Focused through the great agate, the clockwork serpent now drew its strength from the soul of the turning core of the world.

Something sprang within the clockwork of the artifact's guts. Its tiny wings shimmered as they fluttered. Spellbound, arcane, and cross-hatched runes caught the light of fires and the putrid comet of the sky. The draconic construct crouched, and then, in a flurry of obsidian claw and tooth, it pounced upon the Army of Heaven. Wulf looked to the key in his hand. Its ruby had cracked, and as he watched it, before his eyes, it cracked again. Gold plating flaked and the metals turned different shades of green and orange before dusting.

And then, without realizing it, time had passed, and Wulf was running. He could no longer hear the internal tick tock of the Clockwork Wyrm in his head directly, but, with each running step, he was counting the same sound as it had counted down a minute before as he had watched the automaton wade into the oncoming Horde regiment.

tick tick tick

Its beak and jaws would envelop a soldier down to the waist and leave only lower extremities squirming alone in the red snow.

tick tick tock

It trampled horse and rider with golden and bulbous feet, smothering them beneath melting dunes and their own twisted bodies.

tock tock tock

Steam rose from permafrost fields soaked with creeks of vitals. Men of the Horde were torn from their spiky tanks, ripped from their porcine mounts, grasped by tooth and claw, and shaken violently, first from their armor and then from their very bones. What was left of each soldier was flung in every direction into gelatinous piles barely strung together by tendon.

tock tock click

The tiny wings continued to flutter so fast as to be imperceptible. They ionized the immediate air, and it became difficult to look directly at the dragon without one's eyes crossing. Its polished magnificence appeared twined, in two close places at once, in two different seconds at the same time.

click click click

Men ran, firing blindly backward with silent pistols. They either missed wildly, struck another fleeing soldier, or their bullets would be eaten up by the warp of space and time that surrounded the rampaging Wyrm. Even close spears went astray. Plows tipped trying to advance. Cannonballs landed and rolled in the opposite direction in which they had been fired.

click click clack

It was undeniably an artifact of war, but its beauty rivaled and was molded into the appearance of mankind's most ancient of idols, and, whether any spectator ran madly or stood frozen, every person on the battlefield waited for it to breathe out some manner of fiery corruption upon the dying fields. And so, rearing slightly, and with a mockery of inhalation, exposing for a second the rainbow agate on its metallically scaled belly, it exhaled over the Army of Heaven, through turning trucks and scattering cavalry.

clack clack clack

Soldiers pulled their horses down upon themselves they tried so desperately in vain to avoid the machine's breath. Tanks crushed nearby footmen in weak attempts to steer clear. But, as the Clockwork Wyrm returned to the rending of both metal and flesh, men found themselves unburned in the exhalation, free of neither smoke nor fire.

All this Wulf remembered watching as he then ran through the wagon blockades and hurriedly into the encampments. He jumped over the lines of his own soldiers aiming past him from quickly dug trenches. With Antony following, he weaved between loose phalanxes of bowman nocking their one arrow apiece. Wulf's legs had moved on their own after what he had seen, what he had realized had happened, what he realized he had released upon the world.

It had been the Nidhogg Virus the Clockwork Wyrm had exhaled. He had been uncertain at first, as everyone on the battlefield had been, as to what had happened, but as time had passed, after the breath of invisible dragon fire, before the first soldier of the Horde suddenly and inexplicably vomited his bat-winged lungs out of his throat, before his head exploded in a pink mist, Wulf, without realizing it, had turned to any remaining attendant, link, and guard to order them to immediately find Teca and to bring her to his personal pavilion with all the haste of Hell.

Now, throwing his own guards aside telekinetically before they even saw him coming, he burst into his tent. He had sifted through the entire contents of two chests and one crate, throwing objects into every corner, by the time Antony had appeared.

"What are you doing?" the Lesser shouted. "What was that? What is happening?"

"I should have known…" Wulf now dug through a pile of worn saddlebags. "We were not through with him… either of them."

Antony peeked into open chest after open crate. "You've gone mad. I fear we all will after seeing what… what exactly was happening to those men? It wasn't just the Horde though. You saw that? It was some of our fighters too."

Wulf paused to glance around the pavilion. Only his granite eye could be seen inside his hood, but even it looked crazed. "The Academy of Gog had developed something horrible. A targeted virus…"

"What are we…"

"Tormalco! The immortal wizard… inside his tower…"

"I know. It's why the Brotherhood had the Tower on its first list to overthrow. It's why Slayd was there, you know, to take out the…"

"It's unstoppable, a mix of super science and divinely-derived pathogens. I knew that Slayd brought it out of Magog when it fell…"

"Wait! No…"

The sounds from outside the tent could only be the breaking of wagons, the smashing of glass, and the crashing of truck against truck. Gunfire, near and far, followed the close commotion.

"I… I think he implanted it into that Clockwork Wyrm. The Nidhogg Virus is carried by its breath." Wulf had gone back to digging through the contents of a small bureau, but he paused before bowing his head. *'Teca!'* his mind shouted outward into all directions.

"Ouch." Antony cringed, caressing his temple.

"Ouch!" Teca yelled, bursting through the tent's hanging doorway, shaking her head. Her chainmail skirt was in tatters of stretched and broken links, leather pants torn to expose a dark knee. She was holding a handful of snow to the wound. Pink ice-melt leaked from between the fingers of her glove. "What's going on? The reports I've been getting…"

Wulf was upon her before she could take another hobbled step, and she screamed as he entwined his arms in hers, bending her head back to place a plastic device the size of a pencil against her neck. It hissed, and she moaned before pushing him away.

"What was that?" Teca held the redness of her neck with one hand while picking up fallen snow with the other to press back against her bleeding leg.

"Wait," Antony interjected as the canvas of the pavilion suddenly flapped loudly all around them. Outside cannon fire echoed so loudly over the camps that it could not be told whether it exploded from far-off to reverberate near or whether the truth was just the opposite. "You said the disease is targeted? To who or what…"

"I… I can barely remember. It's as though I saw it in a dream — someone else's dream. Invisibly tiny metal infectors breeding, building with blood's own iron to search out a specific gene sequence or DNA family…"

"What the shit are you two talking about?" Teca tore a strip of cloth from something in Wulf's wardrobe to bind her knee in ice and padding. "The camps're being overrun. Where are my reinforcements? What happened to Saunterwedge?"

"He defected," Antony answered as he pulled a large clay jar from one of the open chests. "Just this morning. The Horde promised him a whole whorehouse of newives."

"Call the Beautiful Boys Brigade to protect the east family camp until it can pull out," Wulf said. He had crouched to look at Teca's leg, but she knelt to his height to grab him by both sides of the head.

"They're all dead, Wulf. Listen to me. The Southbound Company, and the guards stationed at the smithing camp, and my archery squad…"

But Wulf could only hear the *Goblin Revenant* as they climbed up to the material plane behind him.

"But we can surely help now, yes, master? We will not fail you. We can go places your weak fleshy men cannot, yes? Do things they cannot, yes?"

"What in Aedes is this?" Antony asked. His eyes scoured the strange, scratched, and painted runes covering the clay jar. "Do you know what you have here? Where did you get this? There's Eartlantean writing on this thing."

Teca spilled a box of cartridges and was rapidly reloading her revolver. "The entire encampment has to retreat, and, I don't care what you say, we're not going back into the plains. Who can we send from this side to hold them off until we can move out?"

"I don't know who will be left," Wulf murmured.

"What?"

Antony continued to strain at the binding runes on the jar. "Do you have any idea what is imprisoned inside of here? You... should... not... have... this."

The stink of oil hit the inside of the tent at the same time as the screech of spinning gears and giant tires. The canvas tore all around them, throwing them and catching them, dragging them into the whirl of the giant plow that had crashed into the mutilated pavilion.

Wulf lifted himself with his legs and his mind from the barrage of the ruined possessions he had been buried under. He suddenly felt very exposed under an open sky. Mortars flew overhead. Wagons burned near and far. The command camp had become a battlefield, and it stretched out to the far mounds of carnage he could see the Clockwork Wyrm ravaging. It was the only thing shining, far-off on a sea of frozen blood and overturned tanks. Bullets whizzed by Wulf's head like fleeing flies. Antony sprawled near him, unmoving under wood and canvas. Teca was nowhere to be seen. The bladed harvester that had plowed through the pavilion smoked on its side, and its armored drivers now climbed from the cabin with corded weapons, backpack generators, and tanks slung over their backs.

Out in the far fields, Wulf could see every man infected with the Nidhogg Virus. With the Eye of Yggr he saw the infection as a glittering swarm swirling from man to man, and it was not long after the virus would disappear inside one soldier before the individual would bloat and crack and die.

"But it need not be so, yes, master?"

The *Goblin Revenant* floated up out of the carnage behind him. For the first time in many days he looked to them. He could see through their ghostly figures, and a fire behind the mound they floated made it look as though they danced.

"You were once our liege too, but you led us ta ruin. Would you do the same ta these good people, or will you give us one last chance ta fight for you? We'll defeat the tin dragon."

"Do it."

"And you know the price?"

"I... I can only assume."

Their giggling hung in the air long after their sickly green silhouettes had sunk back into the earth.

Two of the Horde soldiers had climbed out onto the side of the harvester. One of them was surveying the scene through a greasy-goggled mask that stretched down into an elephantine tube tucked deep into a furry coat sprouting a hairy mane over his head. His laughter, muffled but as high as the scream of a pheasant, repeated itself as he raised a ridged mace crackling with tiny blue arcs of electricity. He pointed it at the shadow he thought was Wulf.

But from another shadow, one nearer and darker, Wulf sprang, and from his cloak he unsheathed Yin, separating the soldier's hands from his arms, all in the same movement. The mace, still connected to cord and powerpack, bounced and swung until entangled in the soldier's companion's arms and flamethrower attachments. A fluid stream of fire arced up as the second soldier flailed and fell back into the cabin of the harvester, taking a third soldier with him. Melting and electrified tanks, powerpacks, and generators sparked and flamed and the cabin was a blossoming flower of fire as Wulf leapt from the vehicle. He grunted audibly as he lifted the machine with telekinetic tendrils that pushed out and up from his mind. The harvester barely rolled, caught up in its own sharp appendages, but it teetered enough for Teca to pull herself out from under it. Her dark hair had been singed, and it still smoldered in places, but she remarkably had only a small cut on her ear to add to her list of future scars. Her jacket, however, had not fared well. Where the leather was not torn to shreds, it had been burned through to her underarmor. She stepped into Wulf's cloak to hold him close, shaking what was left of the stinking jacket.

"Don't you say a word," she sighed.

The Clockwork Wyrm spread unmoving, unticking, as the only shining object in the battlefield.

"It was good ta do your bidding for one last time, oh grandest of white hobs, oh whitest of grand hobs."

Wulf inhaled deeply, relieved to find air. He clenched a fist, relieved to still feel warmth, to still feel blood moving through his flesh. The *Goblin Revenant* had risen again. They held up a large rainbow agate in all their little hands before dropping it to the dirt. They quickly dissipated in the alternating breeze of winter and fire, needle-filled smiles on spectral faces, but he had not missed their last laughing words.

"We'll return fer our final payment… in due time."

Across the battlefield, if peeking through the haze of gasoline and the settling mist of freezing body parts, even without the mystic sight of Yggr's Eye, one could follow the course of the Nidhogg Virus as it branched out through the legions of both the Armies of Heaven and Earth. One man's bones would burst from his body, implanting him to the ground, raising him in crucifixion. A near soldier would be spared, but another would have his head grow beyond his helmet until it weighted him down in obvious suffocation before temple veins would break free from skin to whip the ground like gorgon hair. The contagion appeared to skip most of the soldiers, or perhaps it was not reaching some as they ran from the fields, ran from the very war itself, but still it was obvious that the virus was on the move in a crooked line toward the camps themselves.

"What is it?" Teca asked, gasping for breath while at the same time wrapping a scarf over her nose and mouth. "How do we stop it?"

"One cannot stop the storm," Antony said from behind them in a voice higher than usual. "The lightning. The wind. One cannot stop the retribution of generations of blood sin."

"Are you alright?" she asked him. He appeared to be trying to suppress a painful smile with his own fingers.

"Never better," Antony said. Near him were the broken remains of the clay jar. Also broken were the binding sigils etched into the potshards.

Breathless, the link that had helped Wulf earlier ran up to him. The boy was still fully wrapped in scarves and coats, and he now pulled handfuls of messages from within all of them. "My Liege, and Sir, and my commander, I couldn't find you! There are reports… all over… encampment east is still getting hit hard… ulp!" His face suddenly burst from his clothes. It was as though some invisible hand pulled the muscle from inside his chest up and out through his mouth. Striated flesh chomped at the air as though he still spoke before his body crumpled into Wulf's arms.

Teca fell, crying and retching. "What're we going to do?" she finally was able to ask.

"We retreat," Wulf said. He was trying to delicately find a position to place the wretched mess of a corpse on an uneven, unforgiving ground. "We move out now, whether we're ready or not. Away from the Black Hills, away from any inhabited area. We move out now."

LXXXIII

Again hammer falls.
Splitting gums wait for Swan Rider's touch
but find only kiss of sledge.
Drunk with blizzard strength it falls on next hard head.
Meat smell hangs like butcher's fog.

—Excerpt from the Song of Gnos

Ivy's imagination was getting the best of her, and her few lucid minutes of each day were spent trying to differentiate true, recent memories and the ways her senses were being betrayed by her fears.

"Despite the setback," she remembered Yankee Zrappado saying, "I have to admit, it is somewhat of a guilty pleasure to be immersing myself back into this old hobby."

But even though she remembered him saying it, she had to fight against all her senses to tell herself that the master IDesigner was not presently in the room with her. She knew she slept in the rat scat of an improvised cell but just could not wake up enough to convince herself that she was alone. How much time had passed in the cell? How long had she been in the machine dungeons and laboratories beneath the city of Quicken? The spot between her legs where they had taken... what? (samples? ribbons of flesh? blood?) ...was still sore, so had it actually only been a day or two? Was she repeatedly being brought before the cyborg tithingman, or were her memories on a repeated loop, forcing her to relive one day? And when was that one day? It could not have been a week ago. A month ago? Both her arms were bruised and sore from the multitude of drugs they kept giving her, but the Brides had at least taken care of her hand, and it had healed cleanly from where her finger had been taken.

"I was once at the forefront, you know, of the theory surrounding the tithingman's salvation in your blood. It was originally all my theory before I discovered the histories leading me here, below this sinful city."

Ivy knew he was not in the cell with her, but she could still feel his scalpel digit draw down the side of her disembodied finger, reaching elsewhere later and lower, in the night of interior nights, to snip hair and skin. She knew she should not still have been able to feel it, but she could sense the pinches of needles as they drew out blood. She knew

Zrappado had drilled to the marrow but could still hear the knuckle bones break and his tongue lick for blood cells. How long ago had that happened? *Had* it even happened?

"No, heh, you're just talking in your sleep again, Ivy of the Grove." It was finally a voice other that Zrappado's. Even with her eyes closed and her cheek down against long-petrified droppings, Ivy knew the voice of one of the oldest Brides. This was the woman that had been administering the drugs. She always sounded on the verge of hysterics. The Bride wiped the back of Ivy's neck with a wet cloth that felt colder than anything she had felt in all of her climb over the Titans. She was immediately awake and immensely cold.

"I haven't slept... in days."

"That's just your opinion, heh, heh, you've actually been sleeping for quite some time. I was actually afraid you weren't going to wake up this time, because this is your day, shhhhhh... you have to stay quiet, heh, because I'm going to get you out of here, if you want, because I think I've found the route to the surface, and I know some of the servants will look the other way if they see us, see they've been plotting against the master, I can hear them talking sometimes, sometimes around us they don't think we're listening."

Ivy had to break the crust holding her eyelids shut. She pretended to continue rubbing her face while looking toward the open hallway and the beige figure at her side. This one looked as indeterminate as any of the other Brides.

"Why... would you help me?"

"Heh, heh, because this isn't right..." The Bride stopped.

Her chest shook, even though she had silenced herself at the sound of someone's approach from outside the cell. Another veiled figure had entered behind her. The new woman wheeled a quietly humming generator into the cell and held a long bare prod attached to the generator by a short, insulated cable.

"Now, girl, I'm finally gonna getta find out what'cha know 'bout what ya know. First off," the new Bride said, in a fevered pitch, "who are these ones that call 'emselves the Heirs o' Aesar?" She steadied herself before yanking the pull rope. Only when the generator growled to life did the woman look around to see the other Bride crouched over Ivy, only then did she seem to recognize the folly of the open door. The prod buzzed. The hand holding it trembled. "Now see 'ere!"

Ivy shoved one Bride into another, and they both danced at the crowded touch of the electric device. She boxed what she hoped were the ears of the second Bride, and both women went down to the floor of the cell in a heap of heaving skirts and headscarves. She locked the door behind her as she headed off down the hallway. The corridors were all familiar, albeit as something out of a foggy dreamscrape she had to deliberately focus on to remember. She had not walked these pipes and pistons, but had been dragged or carried over the past... days? Weeks? Despite now suddenly feeling as though she had been asleep for a month, she walked the halls and steps exhausted. They must have been feeding her, although she certainly could not remember ever eating anything besides pills, never ingesting anything other than what was injected into her pin-marked arms.

She grabbed at walls for support, not knowing whether it was the drugs in her system that sent her vision melting or whether the gears that made up the ceiling and floors were turning around her. Her fingers found her own prior handprints, and she saw flashes of memories of someone being dragged from the IDesigner's chamber to jury-rigged interrogation rooms to hallway corners quickly cobbled into cells.

Hiding beneath newly manufactured staircases, behind great masses of recently greased prehistoric pulleys, Ivy listened as servants described their master Zrappado as sometimes ecstatic, sometimes fatalistic, in his work. As Wulf had taught her, she slowed her breathing and wrapped herself around and through shadows undisturbed for untold millennia, and she spied on Brides manically gossiping about Zrappado's reinvigorated experiments. Transients and mole people, inward dwellers perhaps living in the sewers since before even Zrappado had found the ancient corridors, ignored Ivy's skulking as they did the rest of the newcomers.

"I... I've convinced... them..." she murmured when she had finally found her way into the tithingman's chamber. Despite wandering for hours (days?), her lips still responded sluggishly, her tongue still moved heavily. Her system should have easily purged anything the IDesigner could have concocted by now, yet she still felt so tired.

"Hmmmmmmmm?" the fuzzy speakers lining the moving room buzzed. Bubbles rose but sank before popping in the raised pool.

"The Brides," Ivy forced out, "they'll... make the sacrifice... feed their souls to the Magnet."

"No. You lie, little sparrow bird, but that is to be expected from you. You seek to distract me until you can find some sort of weakness. Was that your mission, to kill me? Is that why you haven't escaped? You could never best someone like me, you know. I've had all the angles figured out since before you even knew you were coming here."

"Why don't you just… kill them?"

"Why, that is not our way. I wouldn't expect a disciple of the Liege of Foes, or a follower of the Lonely Cult, to understand, but we of the *Ashmedai Adat El* don't just resort to violence at every chance. It is true that the Eus Engine does not require willing souls to power it, but I, however, adhere to the compassion of the Song. The choice had to be of the Sisters."

Since the last time Ivy had been lucid in the chamber there had been picture tubes placed around the levers and hydraulics. Some of the tubes and bubbles were hanging, while other larger glass screens were set around the corners of the room. She recognized the smeared images of microscopic blood-work. They could have been past filmings or the IDesigner's present thoughts for all she knew. Blood cells were penetrated. Quantumscopic images of helixes were raped.

"Besides, deaths above and around us, throughout the city, almost instantly powered the computer. But it is no matter," Zrappado continued, his sighing crackling through the system, "for that is the past, and I, as a man of reason, the final man of reason, have moved on to a greater venture. Ignition of the Quicken Device, no matter how noble my questioning had been, was only an exercise in pride. I wanted to be the one to end the War, to save all present and future lives from the violence, but you ended that venture, and I thank you for your little sliver of enlightenment. The Quicken Device's destiny, as it had been in the past, will again be to one day be covered in divine winter, never to reach its potential. I have kept the Mannanimus Magnet open, receptive of absorbing any unfettered spirit across the nearby plains, and I've been able to make use of its analog Quicken Mechanism for my most recent calculations, but for the Device to ignite and reach its full potential it would have to amalgamate the sudden souls of a sudden thousand. Now, do not let the doomsayers out in the fallen cities fool you, the apocalypse will not be sudden. The Divine Chorus sings of gradual suffering. The deaf will not get off easy. So, in summary, I have returned to a more humble venture — that involving your body — and, you no doubt will be disappointed to know, I have succeeded. The Promise of Chem-Oshmelech has been fulfilled!"

There was movement in the pool. Lights could not break the muck, but there was an internal glow that lit the chamber from within the fluid's depths.

"I have broken the fallen code, revealed the secrets of your naughty blood. I, Master Yankee Zrappado, the final IDesigner, lonely man of reason, have unlocked the secret to finally achieving my spiritual body. You, my little swallow, are early, but I suppose it can't hurt to make the announcement." Now, speakers beyond the chamber, echoing down steaming halls and oily elevators, squealed, "Let the Brood Pens reopen!"

The only sound then, despite the hissing of some distant water clock, was the monotonous bubbling of the pool. It never changed, that bubbling sound. It was consistent no matter Zrappado's demeanor or submerged movement.

Ivy's limbs hurt, as though she had sprained them during the first movement of many days, and her throat was suddenly dry to the degree that she feared she could not have spoken, even if she had found any words.

"Let me tell you something, little Ivy of the Grove, something you and your kind attempt so desperately to ignore, and that is the truth of all matters worldly. You try so hard to see life as anything but the healthy organism it needs to be to survive. Your 'Army of Earth,' your motley collection of thieves and rapists that sees itself as some noble uprising, is just an anarchic and diseased system. It is a body against itself. It is a decapitated, disemboweled, quartered, flayed, and deaf body. It has no respect for roles, for order, for the structured melody of the Song."

A red light blinked from somewhere within the depths of the loose gelatin. Ivy, from the floor, could see its blinking reflection in the dew of the pistons that made the ceiling of the chamber. The poking of different pink membranes continued in the picture tubes around the room.

"Now compare this with the *Ashmedai Adat El*. Everything ordered accordingly to a reasonable hierarchy prescribed, no… prophesied before man had even held a pencil. The immutable and ever-patient

Divine Choir looks down upon the Brotherhood of Lessers, who, in turn, gifted the Governors in their absence with the state of the Territories. There are, of course, intricate levels of subservience in all these areas, but my point is that of accepted and beloved roles. The *Ashmedai Adat El* is a pure body of health and thriving order. The angelic head is the ever-reminding conscience, the ever-present repository of the knowledge of virtue, and an immortal wind carries the Song from heavenly lips. The body and heart are the good people of the land. They work and toil to cultivate the crops and oil and the livestock and the carpentry and their own souls. The limbs? You see them at work right here. Lesser Prophets, tithingmen, and even the Brides of Chem-Oshmelech make steps forward, reaching for and taking a future free from the deaf ears of a fallen world.

"And just like how a body needs humorous balance and a strict diet to be healthy — all in service of biological order — so does the soul, and that is where defined roles come in. Let me give you an example. When I was born, my brother and I were given only hours to live, at the most..."

Ivy had fallen asleep, but the piercing klaxons of a hundred bells, as they vibrated off the rust and dust of ages, hit her head like the butt of as many hammers. They stopped as suddenly as they had started, but the reverberations continued through the vents and gears comprising the corridors.

"It... it... it can't be!" Zrappado's speakers whispered.

Lights blinked out before returning to a glow beyond what they should have been able to achieve. The chamber shook. Half of the picture tubes exploded in glass and brilliance. The screams of servants and Brides echoed down into the room as hallways and rooms shifted and worked against new suddenly appeared hydraulics. Even in Zrappado's chamber, gears now turned and pistons now pushed against new machinery that had appeared when walls moved to let in more levers and massive moving plugs.

The tithingman, all pink flesh and cast iron, dripped loudly as he emerged from the pool. Arms high, he rose to his full corded and serpentine stature. New lights blinked on and around him. Ivy tried to read, in vain, the reflection of some hyperborean runes in his visor as they skittered like insects across the glass.

"It... it... it cannot be, but it is... for all things that cannot be,

can be in the coaxing of the Song, for the Mannanimus Magnet feeds!"
Some of the speakers blew out, but the surviving instruments blared
words Ivy blocked out by pressing strained hands to the sides of her
head. "Suddenly... suddenly a thousand... thousands of wayward
spirits are unleashed upon the land. It is true! There has been... an
unprecedented sacrifice. The Eus Engine is flooded — no fulfilled! —
with soul power! Thank the Choir! The Quicken Device wakes!"

~

The Black Hills trembled, and travelers across the plains could
feel the movement of the earth. The rises of land beneath the city of
Quicken shook before the great iron giant lifted from the bowels of
the world, and denizens as far away as Kaldera could sense the vibrations in their dirt. The prehistoric titan, of meteoric metal and lost
souls, eclipsed the fallow sun for anyone out in the shaken prairies or
collapsed forests that dared to gaze upon its hunchbacked immensity.
Woodlands, black hills, and the buildings and suburbs of Quicken collapsed on and around and off of the rotting behemoth.

A new god for a new world had awakened early.

~

He was bald with tufts of silver hair over his ears, and his smooth
head shone to an almost metallic degree. That was what Teca remembered noticing the most — that his skin reflected like bronze as he
walked the dim interior of the High Chapel, but that it glowed like gold
when he walked between the sunbeams separating one side of the pews
from the other. The noon light was so strong through the skylights she
was afraid the High Lord would shatter it as he strode silently through
their ranks. He seemed to prefer to watch the choir from the shadows,
but, she thought, when he did not know she was watching him, he
stepped into the sliver's radiance to appreciate the singing. He was taller
than any man she had ever seen, and his layers of robes and regalia
made his head look too small for his body.

His stare was disconcerting, but she kept on singing, repeatedly
reminding herself that she had to be louder, had to hit the notes more
cleanly, than the other kids. There would be no other chance as great
as this to catch attentions and become chosen for swainship. Until now
she had only seen him from afar — his double crown peeking above as
he walked the hedge groves, his lanky silhouette as he walked past the
darkness of his immense windows.

He was coming right for her. Turning right in front of her. Brushing against her. She had been taken in by the Order sometime around two years earlier, and over all that time all the monks spared no minutes arguing about her — always just out of sight, rarely completely out of earshot — but she knew that all the grown-ups were always talking about her, angrily. But today would be the end of that.

The High Lord keep walking past, but the short fur of his long golden tail tickled her from her leg up to her stomach. He turned back, the buck teeth of an expanding mouth stretching until they brayed and echoed his voice up to the disappearing Libian marble of a hidden ceiling. Teca slipped before falling in front of the other children. Few kept harmonizing the *Sol Sistere*. Most laughed and pointed at the mess she had made. She tried to convince them that it was not she who had wet the floor, that the mess was from the High Lord, that it was from whatever dripped from his flippers, but she could not speak loudly enough. Her teeth too had grown and multiplied until her mouth spread so wide...

But that was not how it had happened. Teca picked herself up from the almost clinging physical darkness and the desiccate branches of years of the same dry season. Her hands were scraped even beneath her gloves. She hurt everywhere and seemed reminded of every wound she had ever experienced over her entire life. A leg pained her from around her knee all the way up in a line to her hip. Her neck was stiff to the degree that she could not even look in one direction without turning her whole aching body. She had never been this tired in her life and had apparently fallen asleep while trying to climb through the Black Hills in the night. Crowds of her soldiers and other refugees she had been evacuating, unseen in the moonless dark but near deafening in their escape, ran and skittered and fell through the thin forests all around. She had dreamt in her meager blackout of what had been one of her proudest moments, one of her first memories. But even now, blindly leading her battalion, along with the inhabitants of a canyon town, through the ups and downs of her quaking homeland, she could not help but think of how even the happiest of her memories were now forever tainted by what she had seen in the High Lord's highest quarters.

The Black Hills shook again, and this time she was not sure it was going to stop. Massive figures slid past her on all sides — uprooted trees that had lost any grip on the loosening land. Teca rode the debris down the shrinking foothill as best she could in the dark, but, like she assumed about all those around her, she ended up rolling head over heels through an onslaught of a generation's worth of dead and layered undergrowth. Needles and cones littered her hair and coat. She had torn her pants, and a boot's laces were caught up on something sharp she could not find beneath snow and rock. As she scrambled to kick and move something that was either ice or stone, the branches of the few trees to survive the moving earth shook near her. Tecihila Sakowin Wica was suddenly beside her. She knew that the Chief of the Water Ant tribe was helping her to evacuate Deaden, but she had not seen her since the negotiations.

"Take your time, little sister knight," the Chief said from the shadows of the starless forest. "You deserve a chance to savor your victory."

But all Teca could think about was the monstrosity that had filled that chamber as Wulf opened those doors — those doors that had always been sacred to the Order, leading to a chamber always shrouded in rumor that had always seemed so petty to her. And now, her Order in disarray, she just could not believe her fellow Librans had been so eager to believe her account. They should have decried the witnesses. The monks of the Temple Needles should have scourged her for blasphemy, should have hanged her from the spires of the Eastern Gardens for what she recounted. She expected it, even slightly welcomed it, for any denouncement, no matter how painful, would have at least given her doubt that what she had seen was in any way possible. How long had the Order of the Creed been in thrall to some foreign demon? Years? A generation? When had High Lord Kas-Sharak been supplanted? Had there ever even been a High Lord Kas-Sharak?

"The Quicken Machine has fallen," the Chief continued. "*He Sapa* has again taken back what is Hers. Success! That abomination of man and sin has followed your people into the fall, into the jump. What you called the canyon of Deaden was too much for its ancient legs. My people's magicks, my oyate wicahmunga, will take care of the rest. The land will close around that old god. You have done good."

The Army of Earth was being chased by a mountain come alive. It was yet another reason she had begun to question her own eyes, her own sanity, but she had seen it from afar, through telescopes and binoculars, from the plains and back in the hills. The earth had come alive. A giant had risen, carrying the entire town of Quicken on its hunched back, and it had immediately come for the Army, devastating the land in its wake. The planet shook at its every step. Her soldiers should have been beneath its notice. They should have been like less than the smallest of insects to the behemoth, but it chased her and her men deeper into the northern hills, so her plan quickly became to trap it in the canyons. She had no idea how long she had been running, but she had no interest in stopping.

"We have to keep going," she told the Native. "I… I've lost the rest of the Army. Have to… to get back to the flatlands… to…" She pulled her boot free from the shifting hill, her hood from some falling and broken tree.

Tecihila Sakowin Wica was studying her from numerous eyes. Some of them were avian, some amphibian, only two were human. Some of them were painted, on either turtle shell or cheek. Some were shaped by butterfly wings, others by feathers. "I only feel it appropriate to warn you, Knight of No Tribe, that I have seen your paths, all of them…"

"What do you mean?" Teca searched the shifting drifts of dirt and snow for her pistol. She had lost it somewhere in the falling climbs, had, in fact, lost her entire holster and belt. Warmth near her lower legs told her that her knees had been fiercely scraped. Either a mass of shrubs or a still body slid past her.

"If you take the trail that leads out of these *he*, out of your *home*, these *hills*, there are no paths that lead back."

The other paladins and the monks had taken her word as though it was the *Sol Sistere* itself. There was no inquisition. Why had it been so easy for them to believe her? Why had it been so easy for her to believe? And yet, if it was so easy to believe, why could she not focus on anything else but what she saw?

"Once you leave, there is no trail that leads back home… for you."

"This has never been my home," Teca said, more to the darkness and the crumbling hills than to the Chief. She could not imagine the state of the Temple Needles. The Librans that had left with her had as little contact with what was left of the Order as she did. Was the town left in chaos? Had some monk filled the vacuum of power to restore some semblance of order? She could ask the Natives that had joined her battalion if their people had taken back was what originally theirs, but found she did not want to. Part of her reason for luring the Quicken Machine north was to lead it away from the Needles, but perhaps she should have let it veer south, but she felt sick to her stomach thinking of its immensity just striding through the granite forest, knocking the entire city aside without even noticing its inhabitants.

She could hear voices growing in the depths of the turned hills. Soldiers and knights and families were finding each other. Despite the lack of stars, people were finding their ways to the rendezvous. *Wyrmwood*, the only light in the near heavens, despite its inconstancy as it grew closer and closer to Earth, was becoming reliable as the only celestial figure able to break through the winter raging high above. She looked for its putrid amber leavings through the shadows reaching up from a nearby rise in the terrain.

But a metallic squeal separated the mess of sounds. Chief Tecihila Sakowin Wica doubled over, holding the side of her head as her earpiece spoke loudly in a language low but lilting. Teca could only understand a few words. She looked to the woman for clarification when the sounds broke off mid-sentence.

And again Teca fell before sliding and rolling. The darkness of the sky had become as complete as that of the ground. The air instantly chilled as it solidified in a new shadow. When she emerged from roots both young and long dead, she could barely tell which way was up. Her hood was filled with ice as jagged as glass, and it had dug deeply into her scalp. Branches and frozen dirt had done the same to her chin and neck. She felt for her ears and found her gloves soaked through.

The Chief of the Water Ant tribe was instantly at her side again, pulling the piece from her ear and saying, "Go! Join your army. Go to the plains. Head east. They need you. I... my people... the land... we cannot hold it. It lives again."

The hills split all around them. They could not see it break, but they could feel it.

~

"Think of the opposing force as a body, and attack it as such. The head is where the command force rests, gives orders, directs the battle. Think of the branching sections of the forward movement as the body's arms. This is where the action is anticipated. The fight comes from the arms. The legs of the enemy's force are its stability. This is the spot on the battlefield the legions acquire reinforcements, supplies, where they derive stability, where they brace themselves against."

"So, we take out the head and the body will follow," either Fiske or Fritjof thought out loud.

"Why am I here?" Damn Antony asked behind improvised walls and hastily dug trenches in both snow and dirt. He was drinking from a dusty bottle that, along with having no label, was sticky to the touch with pebbling glue. "I seem to remember a coup. I remember being mutinied and sent back to the Liege of... back to Wulf. Now you come crawling back to beg forgiveness? Or what? Shouldn't my hands be in chains?"

"You ain't a prisoner," a woman Antony did not recognize said. She had auburn hair, but her dark skin said it was unlikely she was a midgardian. Still, she had become one of the commanders of Antony's old battalion in his forced absence.

"That enemy out there," Keld or Kjeld said, gesturing as he spat, "is being directly led by some of the Brotherhood. One or two of Ammon Mars' head generals. You have special insight into their workings. We wanna know how to beat them back. Word is it's Fobos or Deemos leading right from the frontlines."

How much the citizens of this land knew about Prophets, both Greater and Lesser, Antony could never determine. The concept of pitting him against other Lesser Antonys only confused the issue. Did they even realize the genius of calling him back to anticipate the movements of the Brotherhood?

"No," he spat as well. The air was dry, but it tasted wet. A new breeze had brought something earthy, something moldy, with it. The ground had started to vibrate at the same time. He could feel it tickle his toes even through his boots, but he had had no indication that anyone else was feeling it. He focused on the vibration now. It was good to center himself on any external sensation. It kept his mind off the demon that had implanted itself inside his body and mind. "No," he repeated, "usually that is a safe bet, but if it's one of the Horde's High Commander's Lessers leading those legions, then the ideal course would be to attack the legs. In any other battle, one can decapitate the enemy force, and it will likely demoralize or scatter, but the Lessers of Ammon Mars are objectively insane. No matter what you believe about their High Commander — that he was blood-cursed by drinking from the Cannibal's Kettle, or that he was possessed by a taiga Rue Wendigo after eating his own men — the fact remains that he was turned absolutely mad. And madness is contagious. Believe it or not, Fobos and Deemos have his crazed mind in Lesser bodies, and the madness has no doubt spread to their Horde soldiers in another way. Their armies are completely insane."

The near sound of mortars tearing into caravan and ice had slowed, but the shaking of the ground had not. But the ver vvitches half-nakedly scuttling through the troops, violently removing the finger and toe nails of dead soldiers, held their balance perfectly, as though they and their macabre beads floated above the packed snow.

"Even if you could take out the leadership, their men would still continue whatever unpredictable orders they had been given." Antony absent-mindedly scratched at his arms beneath heavy sleeves. He could not get used to the thought of millions of microscopic automatons swarming through his lungs and veins, but they had to be there. He had no doubt that his body was swarming with the Nidhogg Virus. A Lesser Antony should not have been able to survive the outbreak he witnessed after the onslaught of the Clockwork Wyrm. All around him, men and women and children had bloated and mutated and screamed around swollen tongues, but he had survived, despite the suspicion that the virus had been created with a specific hereditary gene in mind.

"Ah… you have to attack the legs in this case," he continued, distracted. "This general's strategy is effective. Haphazard, risky, seemingly mindless, but deadly effective. But it is unsustainable. Fobos or Deemos can destroy anything the Army of Earth throws at them as long as they're being well stocked, reinforced, but if their supply line is cut off they can't support a sustained effort. Their attacks are too manic, disorganized."

When he concentrated on the bombs exploding out past the barriers and trenches, truly visualizing the impact signified by each sound, he could almost ignore the demon Ba'al's screaming.

"Uh… it won't be easy," Antony continued, hiding a smile he could not control while hitting the side of his head repeatedly with the palm of his glove. The demon's pseudo-possession had occurred at the exact moment the virus had infected Antony's body. A parasitic equilibrium was the only explanation.

"Are you still backing up the retreat of Wulf's forces?"

Tormond or Torbjorn answered, "We've lost contact with the home battalion."

"What?"

"And there are disturbing reports, unreliable reports. The very earth itself awakens. A living city…"

"We need to rejoin the Army," Antony said. This was bad news indeed. He had only just left the main forces days before. "But first, how far to the nearest substantial tree line?" Fingers quivering, he flipped through a small book of hand-drawn maps.

"An hour walk to the north there's a small line. East to west."

"Retreat immediately. Spread your forces out alone the line as far and as thinly as you can. You'll appear larger but more appealing to those madmen. Do you still have the Bear Shirts?"

"Of course. They're at the frontlines right now."

"And being wasted there, I think. There are old mines and an area of hillocks just to the south. Have them hide out there until the Horde follows your retreat. When you're caught at the tree line the Horde will also spread out, and their rear guard will reveal itself to the Bear Shirts. But hurry, we need to end this. We need to get back to… the Liege of Foes."

Demons hate the touch of iron. Ardorous Ba'al was burning inside Antony, by the presence of the invisible metal pathogens. It was a constant battle for the Lesser Antony's body, raging and screaming inside him, with the side effect of nullifying both the virus' mutating and deadly outcome and Ba'al's complete possession over Antony's actions. The storm demon could not even escape its bodily confinement to look for a new host. Its pain kept it trapped in apparent perpetuity. This branch of the Virus too was apparently trapped inside him. No one stretched and leaked and died immediately when they met Antony. He knew his old battalion had heard of the plight of the near diseased. Many were speaking of it in whispered and fearful wonder, but the Nidhogg Virus had not reached these people yet. Antony could only assume it was a matter of time.

"Admit it," some man-at-arms or another said to him. "You missed us."

"You could have done this without me."

"Maybe we just missed your stories."

"I'm in no mood for story-telling, but if you can find me something to drink out in this waste I may be coerced to tell you the story of the Clockwork Wyrm." He stuck his empty bottle upright into a snow bank, but something shook the drifts so violently that Antony quickly found himself on the ground next to the spinning glass. He was able to recover and stand sooner than those around him.

"They must be moving in on us," one of them shouted. "Tyr's piles! Was that cannon fire? Do they have tanks?"

"That wasn't munitions," Antony grumbled. "That was... I don't know what that was."

A shield maiden Antony was certain went by the name Easter started to say, "The scouts... what they said... they were certain they saw... they heard..."

"What?" Antony looked to a darkening horizon. He had never seen the sky on Earth turn such a violent and lightning-wracked hue so quickly. It was as though the land and sky had been reversed and the plain was alive with electricity.

Someone said, "The scouts... the things they report... they were madmen witnessing... a nightmare..."

Antony found himself on the ground again, not sure whether the land was still quaking or whether the wind had hit him with a physical stench that had thrown him through the air. The low atmosphere was so heavy, so clogged with the dust comprising their surroundings, that he found himself eating the air in order to breathe it. He had lost anything he had been holding. His sockless foot cooled in a puddle of mud. He could not find glove or boot in the frigid shadow of the troll god that blocked out the sun. The hunched leviathan strode the earth like its mountainous feet turned the planet on its very axis, and hands the size of forests swiped at the prairie, tossing fields and rows of hills skyward.

But it was no fleshy deity. Antony had been mistaken. Cities of girders and highways of cogs as big as villages made up the great machine's limbs. Its head was a mask of verdigris — the face of some hyperborean hero frozen throughout time in a rigor mortis of alien and ancient expression. Upon the chthonic automaton's back was a mass of uprooted and crumbling Black Hills, and upon those hills tilted a city. The buildings and blocks swayed precariously, and, even from the shadowed distance, even through the haze of wet and moldy dust the air had become, Antony was certain he could see people jumping or falling from the city over and into the swirling of the upturned land the cyclopean machine was throwing.

The countryside, ice and earth the size of hamlets, was being crushed beneath the mechanical god's gargantuan feet. Antony covered his mouth and nose with a scarf, his wet eyes with his wet hands, but could not resist peeking through mud and fingers. He watched as the land and an army was squeezed through the great screaming bronze digits of a hand that steamed clouds greater than had ever been in the sky.

He did not even notice that the demon had quieted inside him. Ba'al too was watching in rapt attention through Antony's eyes.

~

A crane held its distended arm high over the pit, swaying slightly in the quiver of the earth. It was a testament to the weight of the old tractor that it had not moved more in the winds of the winterly plain. Its arm and hanging cable still moved over the pit they had been placed over before the village had evacuated. Word had apparently reached the inhabitants of RackBreak's coming forces. No one was left by the time his battalion had arrived — only the ghosts of those filling the mass grave to its brim with long-charred corpses.

"Commander, sir, I feel it only fair to warn you, there is unrest... displeasure at our orders."

"I understand," RackBreak Antony snorted through beard and the slit in his faceplate.

"No, I mean, yes, Commander. It's just that the men have heard the last orders coming out of the Army, and we're finally drawing close to the warfront so they were hoping we would... ah... we holed up in Liberal for so long. We held Grave's Gate but just gave it up in the end. We dig trenches, hold the Horde, but just always give them up in the end... We'll just give up Valentine in the end?" The man-at-arms was joined by a different soldier continuing his line of thought. "The men thought we would finally be going on the offensive."

RackBreak's great girth took heavy steps toward the great crane. His armor hid his appearance only to the degree it could not hide his size. He strode up to the machine but could not stop peering around and down into the grave. Any stringing remains still caught up in the hook of the crane had been petrified by winter sun and wind. The burnt bodies of the pit, so blackened and shriveled, had coalesced by the open air into just one mass of inseparable and flaking torsos and legs. Heads could not be told from the rocks meagerly lining the hole.

"Aahhhghhh!" RackBreak's joints burned with a fire he had not felt since tortured outside Erebus. He lifted the machine, tilting it until his back and knees felt doused with acid. Either the crane's axles or the ground gave out, and the construction machine felt to its side. The arm bounced against the rim of the pit but still wavered over the dirt. The cable hung limply, awkwardly around and over the mound of crisp bodies.

The grave was deep but full. Bodies at the top of the pyramidal pile had broken the plane of the pit's edge. The mound now moved again with the shaking of the ground, and black fingers that grasped toward the sky broke away from crumbling hands.

More and more soldiers were appearing in the center of the village with each shake of the ground. "These are shocks this far from Kaldera? I thought…"

"No," RackBreak grunted into the thickening air over his soldiers, "these are not earthquakes. These are footsteps." He unbuckled and unlatched one of his mighty gauntlets before going to work on its opposite. "Gather all remaining legions," he asked of those near him, "have them assemble on the east side of the village in a chariot formation. Line the caravans in a funnel line on the north and south ends. All riflemen lineup on the exterior sides. That's where he'll send his cavalry."

"Commander, we have men here that are actually from this town. They want revenge, sir. You'd understand, wouldn't you? We all want to fight. We're tired of holding and running. I cannot account for the Seventh Guard. I… I think they've deserted." The dirt of the ground danced, and the soldier tripped. RackBreak lifted him with a hand so calloused it looked as though it were made of a metallic rock.

"You think the mission we've been gifted with is weak?" he asked, holding the man to his hidden face. "You think vengeance a greater glory? Horde Territories have fallen, little man, in no small thanks to us. How long has Ammon Mars chased us? How long, when he could have been turning his forces back to Kaldera, when he could have been crushing the Liege of Foes, has he sat outside our numerous fortifications? He would have singlehandedly held the capital or destroyed the puny Army of Earth if he had not been following us over cold rock and through dead plain."

He dropped the soldier to the ground and began to pull at the locks holding his metal boots. All around the square, his legions appeared and looked at the mass grave. A breeze had brought a moist and heavy cloud over the prairie and into the village. Those that did not breathe through scarves found it difficult to inhale without gagging.

"The Horde approaches!" a caller announced. "An expected mile out. Dynamite set! The underbombs await your word, Commander."

A man-at-arms took a break from drying his ammunition to help unlatch RackBreak's remaining boot. "Why, sir, does he always follow? He is relentless. But why us? These fields, this village, hold no value for the war..."

"Long ago," the Greater Antony grumbled, standing above his men with bare feet and hands, "I came upon a hold on the far side of the great forests to the west. It housed a cadre of mercenaries led by a giant. I knew nothing of the men in the hold, but I knew of the giant. He was... familiar to me. I took siege upon that bunker for a month, until every last man had run or was trampled before me. I fought until I was able to look into the eyes of the giant, just to see who I thought he was, if I was right."

"Did you kill him?" some soldier asked from the crowd.

"Impossible."

"Then why'd ya do it?"

"I just had to see... had to know..."

The village had, when RackBreak's forces entered it, the permanent, sweet smell of gasoline. Torture and execution had been such a part of the hamlet's life that the stench had permeated all the wood of the dwellings. RackBreak peered through the heavy atmosphere to imagine how they had done it all, and he saw men hung or strung from the hook of the crane, burning until they stopped screaming or crying until they stopped peeling in flames. Their charred forms would hand over the pile of their predecessors until the tendons wasted away and the remains fell to join them. What had been their sins, he wondered. Had they pierced their ears or bled in public? Had they been tax collectors or vegetable worshippers?

The ground shook so violently that the crowds around him fell in a wave of panic. Several of the nearby huts collapsed with the shouts of his soldiers. "Cannon fire!" many yelled.

"No," RackBreak spat. "That was not the Horde."

"We want to fight," his man-at-arms pleaded.

"I understand."

"Yes?"

"We want the same right as our brothers in the rest of the Army, to kill for our loved ones and our land. We want to take back our homes and fields and our mines and herds…"

"Yes!" RackBreak shouted, himself almost falling against the lurching of the ground. "I said I understand! You want to tear down the perches blocking the light over your hometowns."

"Yes!" soldiers yelled.

"You want to light the Theses littering your doors in a pyre large enough to call the gods back home."

"Yes!"

"A pyre to burn the land, to hold back the glaciers, to choke the angels out of the skies!"

"Hell, yes!"

"Every man has the god-given right to choose his own death," RackBreak said, lowering his shout to a grumble. Those that were not taking up spear and gun crowded near to hear. "And what better death could come about than by in spilling the blood of the oppressor. Today you choose your own death, but not before each taking ten of Ammon Mars' men before you. Leave the tanks, leave the war trucks. They are a distraction. The winter has crippled them. Look your enemy in the eye before you spill his guts. Give him that! Go and wait for me at the west end. Steal your enemy's air to warm your own, but I want every good soldier here to promise that Ammon Mars will be left for me. I want the Horde High General and his ugly elephant left for me and me alone. He is mine."

What the gathered guessed was a barrel smashed into the foot of a nearby building. The closest soldiers were hit with wooden slivers and drenched in what smelled like some sort of thin oil. More and more barrels exploded around the crowds as troops raced through the village to join the rest of the battalion at the west end. It was all simple huts except for the short stables RackBreak climbed to look out over Ammon Mars' approaching army.

"I sent the Seventh Guard in a circle to the north this morning, hiding in a dry riverbed to circle around to the back of these cretins and their war machines!" He yelled this to his forces, hoping to keep the wind from carrying his voice to the Horde.

"Sir?"

"Yes, I too tired of the chase. No other man chooses my death for me. Now, set off the charges on my word!"

The forces of Ammon Mars approached in the sudden haze of the moldy air. Everything was alight. Banners were burning. The Greater's soldiers had spears tarred and flaming. Catapults, filled with burning refuse, were pulled by aurochs that had fiery standards sticking out of their saddles. Men had lit the plumes of their helmets. And the front forces poorly hid archers behind themselves. Their flaming arrow tips were a thousand points of light out in the swirling smog.

Through it all came the barbed tusks and palanquin of the mammoth of Ammon Mars. Its scarlet and dreadlocked mass looked right at home among the fires. Above it all stood the High General of the Army of Heaven, bare feet firmly gripping the heaving beast's matted fur. The Greater Antony flexed fiery flesh beneath the razor wire of his sparse armor.

"Eat them!" Ammon Mars screamed, and his mammoth trumpeted. "Eat them all!"

But the prairie shook before they could advance or unleash the embers of their arrows. Dunes of snow hardened by many seasons slid from one another. Collapsing lines zigged and zagged over the ground as the plains moved against one another. Dirt and rock appeared to float up off the ground while simultaneously falling from a quickly deepening sky. Night and day became as one as the sun was eclipsed, as a shadow as big and as cold as winter's midnight consumed the village and the plains for as far as anyone could see.

Eyes adjusted slowly as the earth quaked in the immense and near physical darkness, but the fires of the Horde eventually glowed outward, lighting faces frozen in horror at what they saw. The great turtle god, the Quicken Engine, stepped over the very curve of Earth toward them all. With a city on its hunched back, it reached for and tore and trampled the land.

~

Wulf always claimed to remember everything. He saw it as an unfortunate side effect of his mental abilities. He could not remember what became before — birth being such a traumatic event — but what came after had become a cycle of his inner eyes opening and closing.

The revelation of segmentation had first broken his mind, that he was *a part*, that he was not at one with his mother, that he was, in fact, the *other*. An isolation came flooding into his infant soul, a distinctness one never escapes. But he did. The *SHE'* had shown him otherwise. Thanks to the Crimson Queen, he now knew that he had not been kidnapped, had not been taken from the forest by the assassins syndicate in some sort of random chance encounter. Sera had revealed to him the plan that had been set in motion generations ago by the first of the Garm, how the cult had manipulated bloodlines to eventually create him and his abilities. The *SHE'* had harnessed those mental powers in paid service to the Garm, but along the way they had taught him to perceive the world as they did, that any distinction of separation in so-called physical space was an illusion. He learned to reach outward with both telepathic and telekinetic feelers and waves to experience the world. Once he finally saw the folly of the barriers placed willingly in his mind he could not look back. He could see, could feel, the invisibly miniscule building blocks moving around and through and the spaces between them that were only made of more building blocks with space between that was so imperceptible as to be mythical. At this scale was truth. At this scale there was no space between him and environment. No difference between him and the tree, the rock of the building, the metal of the vehicle, the flesh of another. And this was how he had learned to manipulate his mental and physical environment — by loosening the distinctions between both, by eliminating any differentiation between self and world. Man was not on an island unmoored in a tumultuous sea. Man was the island. Island was the sea. There is no man, no island, no sea. Only all.

But upon returning to the darkness of the forest, in what he now knew was a charade — not an escape — from the paper dragon assassins, and the brilliance of the sun, into the expanse of N'Midgaard and the land, young Wulf had been almost overwhelmed by the differentiation. All seven senses served only to confuse him. He pulled away from his surroundings, into himself, and saw and experienced only segmentation, wrapping himself in the warm illusion of oneness, apart from allness.

This focus on differentiation was how his abilities had worked ever since. It was now only a simple matter of the interplay between "pushing" and "pulling." There was no "lifting." If he wanted something that was out of reach, his mind would pull it towards him. When he had enough of something, his mind would push it away from him. And he could "feel" his environment through this interaction. The pushing was sensitive. The pulling sensual. Even now, as he lifted himself into the expanse of the sky, near the highest of heights he had ever reached, it was all about his mind's interplay between pulling and pulling and meaningless distances between arbitrary differentiations.

His mind pushed against the ground — a prairie that was no more a plain. The earth had erupted and was continuing to be lifted asunder with each gargantuan step of the colossal machine. Wulf could not help but consider the similarities to remembered nightmares and visions of futures inevitable. This was how the world would end, with the planet being torn open and upward. But this was not the end of the world. Not yet. But it would be the end of the northern plains and the Army of Earth unless he could do something to stop the infernal earthen behemoth from crushing all that lived.

And so his mind *pushed* against an alternating collapsing and rising prairie. It *pulled* him toward the sliding and haphazard city that still rested uncomfortably on the ancient titan's hunched turtle back.

But it was not a god, as so many of Wulf's army had called it from afar as it ate up horizon and land, swallowing the western sky. Wulf had ordered his people ahead as they began to meet up with other returning battalions. He stayed behind, through the dirt-clogged evening and into the sour stench of the foggy night. It was a black fog, impenetrable to those outside it, but it consumed him before the presence of the great giant did, and he could see the myriad turn of gears the size of towns turn limbs the size of cities with Yggr's Eye as he rose through the earthen smog, his mind pushing and pulling. And the pushing and pulling was uneven, unpredictable, as he felt buffeted by a gravity skewed by an immensity so large it corrupted those natural forces of the planet itself.

Breath was shallow through a scarf quickly caked with dirt, dust, and frozen exhaust. The air was solid as it swirled in weather systems created by the leviathan's unparalleled height alone. Its movement brought the clouds to the shattered plains, acres of the land into the sky. There was no way of telling up from down, the heavens from Hell below, yet Wulf's mind still pushed him upward, pulled him up and over, with the divine relic in his skull showing him the rainbows of archaic magiks binding the ores in the monster's construction.

The god's uneven city shoulders tore at the atmosphere it passed through, tearing the celestial sphere open. Storms spewed downward like the birthing waters of an expectant Heaven. Lightning flashed — a thin spider's leg of brilliance that angrily cut through the unnatural darkness — and he could see that the city of Quicken had somehow turned around him. As the iron false god moved over the tearing land, Wulf had risen as it moved around and beneath him. The screaming grind of hundreds of cyclopean gears deafened him. Tornados of layers of dust from under and over the city blinded and buffeted him. Violent vibrations of metal against stone against bone tossed him up before down against the heaving streets of Quicken. And, except for the piles of strewn bodies with arms flopping back and forth with the lurching of each of the giant's steps, for a second the city was just how Wulf remembered it. Spitting dust from his mouth, brushing black frost from his eyes, he admired buildings still standing. They were low, with barred windows and reinforced doors. The streets were crowded with stalled motorcycles. From every crack in the street spewed a swirling substance that was quickly caught up in the storm.

But then it all moved. As the immense bulk of the false god lumbered toward one unknown horizon, the streets slid toward the other direction. A building crumbled in upon itself, scattering more of the dancing brick dust that clogged the paths and air. Other buildings swayed with the movement. And even others slid similarly but over the streets, some at Wulf and some out and over and into a turning and grim vortex he was not sure was off the side of the gargantuan. The falling and sliding was thunderous, and the air thickened to weigh him down even more. From out of the storm came a wall of darkening brick, unattached to any building but matching many of their design. His mind pushed against the cracking streets and a nearby building that still felt stable to his telekinetic tendrils, and he tossed himself aside as the wall passed to smash against a truck that had begun rolling behind him. The remains of a motorcycle, crushed and folded in upon itself, skipped down a side-street, unable to slow on the lurching ground, but Wulf's mind pulled at a miraculously still-standing street light, flipping his body over the rolling wreckage.

The scene split into brilliance again as a broken scratch of the whitest lightning revealed farther alleys and buildings both standing and toppled. For the merest of seconds Wulf could see far avenues and homes crisscrossing and changing directions as the breathing streets swayed to and fro. The engine of some small vehicle bounced along a lifting road, and Yin slashed out from Wulf's cloak to slice it cleanly in half, both pieces continuing past and into the returning darkness. He sheathed the crying blade. It wailed for true blood.

Wulf ran the roads of tilting Quicken, his telekinesis grabbing at any stable structure to pull him out of the way of sliding buildings and rolling trucks, pushing against any heavy object so he would not be crushed under falling walls or within the gaping chasms opening before him. He peered down into these new crevices, probing with his mind to feel for any hint at the inner workings beneath street, sewer, and foundation. He sensed so many layers of metal, then concrete, then earth, then moving cogs larger than any of the trucks or homes of the city.

Something large, of iron or brick, fell or slid into the remains of a building Wulf only saw by the brilliance of more lightning, and he knew that he would have to make a decision soon before he was swallowed by the carnage of the swaying city. A group of people, blood and soot-covered and mostly naked, fell or slid or ran past him, but they were gone before he could focus on their chaos of limbs. Moving mouths told him they were still alive, but, stretching out his telepathy, he could not find any thoughts out in the closing smoke.

He leaped over a river of rubble that bounced and shattered around him, his mind pulling and pushing him into another collapsing cloud of smoke and storm. He found himself precariously balancing over the opening ground. The Eye of Yggr showed him dazzling inner workings beneath. Amongst a forest of man-sized pistons flowed a river of mystical grease — souls bound and liquefied to lubricate miles of axles, to pressurize primordial hydraulics. He could see their screams but not hear them. Their ectoplasmic lungs choked on themselves without the reprieve of any finality. Wulf tightened his grip on Yin and her sheath, resisting the temptation to inhale of the acidic air before leaping. His mind grasped a nearby building to pull from, to lower himself down until he could find something to trust and push against in the shattering cacophony below.

But the ground slammed shut in front of him, rising together from multiple sides as streets and building began to overlap in the tilt of the monstrosity's earth-shattering steps. Wulf smiled crookedly as streetlights sparked to life nearby. The sudden view was of more separating or colliding avenues as far as he could see into the dirty miasma. The light poles quickly exploded in a succession before tilting and turning. The ground dropped out beneath him, but he reached out with his mind to grab at anything secure to pull and keep himself away from falling debris. And he pushed against any stable surface to rise above sliding buildings. He pushed against a slab of the street that flew towards him. He sliced another with Yin. His mind pulled him into the air by grasping at a mass of sod that tumbled overhead. He eventually landed on a surface flat but turning. Fires and the occasional lightning streak lit the moving carnage.

Someone ran past, a knife protruding from his shoulder, while another man yelled from some cloud-choked window. Wulf could hear marching beneath the crumbling of brick but decided it was just more of the machinery below the dirt and rock. His lungs tickled so completely he could not suppress a coughing fit that doubled him over for close to a dizzying minute. He wrapped his filthy scarf back around his filthy head, his nose so fouled by exhaust dust he could no longer smell anything at all.

Someone was shouting, but it took a moment before Wulf realized that he himself yelled through the chunks of air that fell and rose over the street. The ground beneath him continued to turn, and it was then that he realized that he was falling, that the earth beneath was falling, had been falling. It slowly began to flip over. He was out in the filthy atmosphere, his mind pulling at anything it could reach, pushing at anything to find what was up, what was down, and he eventually found the ground beneath him and the false god above him. It continued on past, massive legs and gears destroying the land and the Army of Earth. Wulf's mind lessoned its pulling, slowed its pushing, and he gently lowered himself to a wrecked and unrecognizable prairie.

~

She had been left to wander the transforming chambers and rearranging hallways as she pleased, but these were not unmolested sojourns. Everywhere she walked she had become accosted by Brides with speech too hectic to follow, with words too near the verge of hysteric for Ivy to have the chance to respond to. And so she inevitably always ended up searching her way through rooms combining with other rooms and ladders disappearing into new untouched chambers before finding her way back to the IDesigner's control quarters. It was certainly the safest area of all the complexes she had explored. It had stopped transforming after the initial rise of the Quicken Device, and it was relatively stable compared to the unpredictable movement of the outer corridors, for each gargantuan and lumbering step of the metal titan would send the miles of prehistoric man-made guts into a restructuring that servants and Brides would get lost in for days. Even if they were not crushed by reconfiguring waterwheels or imperiled by a sudden abyss, they could be out amongst new and never-ending corridors without food or heat.

After repeated attempts at exploring newly appearing bellows the size and multitude of forests, or chain drives that had formed over chasms where she had once stood, she had become resigned to hide out with the few Brides that had found their way upward or downward into the pool chamber. They talked incessantly to her as the days went on, of spiritual bodies, angelic promises, the great deeds of brothers and fathers, of old prophecies fulfilled and new ones revealing future glories, of apocalypses both sudden and gradual, cold and hot, of sins secret and damning, creation stories extraordinary or mundane, rapes both punishing and deserved, judgments both cataclysmic and generational, of bloodlines protected and divinely chosen, betrayal fraternal and prodigal and genocidal, slavery predestined and testing and ultimately nation-building, of dramatic escapes lasting decades unnecessarily, festivals lasting even longer but even more unnecessarily, of curses lasting even longer but entirely necessarily, of covenants nature-bound, of covenants worldly and compromising but broken, of daily rituals both purifying and dehumanizing, of dehumanizing both welcoming and inclusive, of more bloodlines abandoned but sacred, histories concocted but influential, genealogies proven but tainted, dissertations legitimized but ignored, and of forbidden loves immortalized in burnt diaries.

It was all very difficult to ignore, as were the multiple picture tubes showcasing the death and destruction wrought far outside by the Quicken Device as it crushed forest and countryside beneath iron feet as large as mountains, and it raked through village and army with mechanical hands bigger than entire towns, but Ivy found distraction in the internal connections and control mechanisms making up and surrounding the raised pool.

Inside the hot muck, the cyborg tithingman squirmed, swirling the liquid and creating a lightshow that reflected out to the oily walls and violent scenes of the monitors.

"It is your unbridled curiosity that damns you, little dirty snow-flake," the speakers of the room croaked, full of static. Yankee Zrappado's voice was much slower than Ivy remembered. "You must dream of the release of the subservient life. There is no reason to suffer, to constantly wander, to bear the yoke of uncertainty. The answers are free to all."

"Are you tired," she asked, not looking up from reeds and tubes, flutes and clepsydras. She followed a mass of insulated and non-insulated copper wiring as it spread to wall, wheel, plug, and into the pool.

"Oh, little gray mouse, you would not understand the burdenous blessing bestowed upon yours truly. If only you could, you would understand that there is no more sleep for me. I have not been promised rest, I have been promised this resurrected body, and, with it, comes the responsibility of justice, of ending this terrible war."

Ivy stared at the only glass bubble not showcasing the devastation of the landscape, not showing images of army-sized limbs stomping or heaving great sections of the countryside. One of the Brides behind her screamed at the images of horse and trucks and giant crowds of armored men being thrown along with great chunks of the horizon. The hysteric girl ran from the room.

Ivy looked up from the screen. "You haven't convinced yourself that you're in control have you?" Blinking colors monitored different levels. Strange and primitive shapes multiplied like some sort of sentient and prolifically reproductive language across the glass. Her finger followed it as she clarified, "I mean, you know that the machine is not following your actions, right?"

"What... is... of course I..."

"You're doing a magnificent job of anticipating the creature's movements," she said, peering over and into the pool's lights, watching Zrappado move in the sensory-deprived fluid.

"Of course I... no, this is my body! I can see what it sees! These are my arms, my legs... my eyes watch the Army of Earth scatter before my power!" His dripping bulk bubbled slowly from the pool.

Climbing around to look closely at the metal wires twisting from the ceiling into his spine, Ivy tapped at plugs and lights adorning the back of his massive metal headdress. "It's killing indiscriminately. It needs souls to survive. Or haven't you noticed that it's currently massacring a town loyal to the Horde. Isn't that the battalion of Ammon Mars being smashed into the hillside? You're not really taking credit for that, are you?"

"You lie…"

"I can fix it for you. Unless you would rather keep things the way they are. I know your main concern was ending the war, and it looks like the Quicken Device will do just that."

"Fix… I… can you… what?" Zrappado moved his real arms very deliberately, but the images on the screens did not move along with them. He turned one way while the perspective of the gargantuan machine did not.

Ivy suddenly stopped and stared, as did the remaining Bride in the room. No one spoke for a long minute. The women just watched the man watch the monitors. The chamber slowly leaned, sometimes lurching, sometimes turning as expected from the movement of the carnage outside. She suddenly felt a bout of seasickness many of them had experienced over the prior few days. Day and night were determined only by what she had been able to watch of the scenes of the destroyed prairies and hills.

"You've never been in control," she finally said, "but I can help, only if you want me to."

"Why would you do this?" the speakers blared, and for a second she had to hold her hands over her ears. The tithingman, both flesh and cast iron, sank slowly back into the ooze.

"In the past you've stated your valuation of choice, and I respect that. I've learned a lot, and I want to repay you. Do you want control over the Quicken Device? I've figured it out, and I promise to grant you your spiritual body."

Masses of people scattered on the screens, in all directions, but all ultimately disappeared under uprooted miles of prairie or massive foot.

"Do it," was all the speakers buzzed.

After silent minutes swapping plugs beneath the alien monitoring screen, Ivy watched the insect language squirm repetitively and blocks of colors shrink and grow proportionally. She followed a thick collection of cords from the blinking pool to a grate she had earlier removed. Here, with ear to the vibrating floor, she adjusted something deep within.

She was not sure if Zrappado could hear her strained voice, and she was suddenly actually unsure how he could hear anything at all. "I was wondering..." She slipped farther into the grate, and her voice echoed only downward. "...I know that the angels sing about selflessness over selfishness..."

"Yes," the speakers said in a voice quickly sounding renewed and energetic.

"How do you do that? Is that even possible? Selfishness is a defense mechanism. Humankind would never have lasted this long without it."

"You think too small, little bug. The Song tells the faithful to put others before themselves, true, but even the deaf can do that. They can put lovers, even pets, before themselves. It is easy to love a beloved child. That is no sacrifice. We chosen, however, are expected to love the unloved and unlovable. In this, we become closer to the Divine Choir, who has unlimited love for everyone."

"But this search for your spiritual body..."

"Yes! The Promise of Father!"

"...seems so selfish."

"Let us see if I can phrase it in a way you can understand. If you listen closely enough, the Song sings of the ultimate selflessness — to truly become selfless is to put the Divine Choir first before ourselves in all matters. The greater I make the Divine Choir, the lesser I become, and the lesser are blessed in Their eyes."

"And is that important to you?" Ivy's arms were thinly black with grease, and she slipped on the steaming pipes of the floor to shove against a wall of carpeted wires. The wall continued to move after she stepped back, revealing a row of levers with corresponding accordion bladders.

After a long pause, the speakers echoed, "Of course. I... I have faith in the mighty wind and will of the Divine Choir. Their will be done."

"That sounds very important to you." Ivy slammed her shoulders against one of the levers. It refused to move.

"It's important to me, yes, because... it is important to the Divine Choir. All that matters is Their design."

"So selfish." Ivy's words were almost lost beneath the sound of the wrenching scream of a second lever. She returned to the first to kick and stomp at its base until a panel of the floor was bent enough for her to reach into. The delicate work was yet another recent reminder that she was missing the pointer finger of her right hand. It had healed well, but she kept it wrapped against the eons of grime present in most of the subterranean corridors.

After loud minutes of pulling and prodding, she kicked the first lever into a new position, ignoring the final five to close the nook and return to the poolroom. One would never know the color of her hair from the amount of grit and grease in it. The remaining Bride had seemingly collapsed, and in the mound of cloak and skirts she had become it was obvious how much weight the woman must have lost as of late. The only entity that was recently having its fill of nourishment was the Quicken Device. Watching armageddon portrayed in the picture tubes, Ivy guessed, was like looking at the world through God's eyes. One saw scenes of earthen upheaval, with entire battalions of people being seeded into the snowy sky or planted deep within the crust of the land. Only periodically would the gargantuan limbs of the adamantine gardener cross its own sight. She had not been able to tell if certain flares of some far-off lens were a trick of light or if she truly was seeing as the meteoric leviathan was, watching the tasty spirits of hundreds of individuals being released from their corporeal prisons before being absorbed into the hidden turnings of the Mannanimus Magnet.

She crossed to a wall of pipes that shattered under a strike from her elbow like some sort of ceramic, and she tore at the wiring inside until thrice-woven ropes appeared. Most had decayed into sludge, but she tested the resistant of a new hempen cord before counting off each pull against it in her head.

"Do you believe selfishness to be an evil?" Ivy barely said, as she coughed against the dust that the rolling rope disturbed. She eventually returned to the blinking monitor to adjust some of its plugs, and she traded some for others, while only turning certain others, as they had begun to spark into the shadows of the corner. She was about to ask the question again when the IDesigner's speakers fuzzed.

"I believe it is the root of all evil. To remove yourself from selfishness, to acknowledge only the will of the Song, is of the utmost enlightenment. So... man's selfishness is in antipathy to the desires of the Divine Choir. Selfishness links us to the deaf, to the unclean animal world, to the original sins of a primordial, uncreated world without tone."

"Are you sure it's not necessary? Where would humans be without it? It built this…"

"No."

"Why do the angels allow selfishness to exist if it's so evil? Doesn't the Choir abhor evil? They seem like the embodiment of love. Do you think they can't get rid of it?"

"No, They can do anything. If you… if you could just clear your ears out, little birdy, you would hear the wondrous things the Divine Choir can do. It is everything! They can do everything… anything! You cannot possibly understand, and I feel sorry for you. They hold sway over Heaven and Earth and time and space. The wind is the breath from Their wings. The sun itself raises each day only to glorify…"

"How could beings of such pure love…"

"No, They are not 'beings.' They are beyond your petty understanding. They do not have to explain themselves to you! They allow evil to exist because it produces good men. The plague? The famine? This war and your army of killers exist only because the Divine Choir allows it, and only because it will create and reveal the righteous who rise to oppose all of it."

"I thought you wanted to stop the war. Shouldn't you…"

"Man must be allowed to make his own choices! Without being able to choose the good over the bad, what would man be? Some sort of empty-minded clone, that's what!"

"Do sickened babes take any consolation in this?" Ivy had moved to replace the copper in an empty set of conduits with the wiring from one of the main lights in the room. The chamber dimmed tremendously before she moved to a wheel that had been hidden minutes before. She greased it as well as she could from the grime covering her clothes and limbs. "Children would not suffer bone and blood wasting if the angels were truly the manifestation of love and all that is good."

One of the loud speakers popped and was silenced as the others screamed, "I'm not talking about babies! I said 'man must be allowed…'"

"Unless…" Ivy had paused from drying her hands to think beneath the screeching speakers. She placed them on the wheel but did not turn it, resting against the metal to gather her strength. "Unless, yes, that's it! I have it!"

She ran from the chamber, but it was another minute before the speakers silenced. Steam hissed from behind some cast iron panel. Condensation formed faster than it could drip in every corner. The crash of distant walls as large as pastures connected and broke apart, sending echoes through empty tunnels and reverberations through near floors. All the while the pool room swayed slowly, and the tithingman's amnioxigen fluid matched that sway. Its lights blinked silently.

Ivy ran back in, pulling a tiny generator on wheels connected to a prod that had at some recent point had its insulation chewed away by one of the rat packs infesting the darker corridors. The generator, covered in a flaking oil that dusted Ivy's passage, looked as though it had recently been on fire. In no time at all she was twisting and pulling at a cylinder among cylinders on the side of the pool. Its hollow chime, as she dropped its immensity to the floor, refused to echo. She quickly went to work on another of its brethren.

"Your song sings of the absolute love of the angels — that they, in actuality are love, its perfect personification. No, that's not entirely right. That what we understand of love is the personification… of your choir. What we believe to be love is a representation of the angels, who are love eternal and perfect. Right?"

The speakers crackled for many seconds, but there were no words.

"Yet your song tells tales of the angels doing horrific things," Ivy continued, near breathless through her exertion. She had to compensate with patience whenever her work required ten fingers. Back at the wheel, she strained but was able to twist it slowly. Somewhere, down hall and up abyss, a rhythmic ticking of metal against metal had started that resounded at the same pace as a new light deep within the depths of Zrappado's pool.

"No…" he started.

"Sure, the song says that Slog Sabbaoth is said to have burned thousands of people for looking into her sacred looking glass. Chem-Oshmelech crippled fourteen generations of unborn because an ancestor loved another man, and Ashmedai himself sent bears to maul children that revealed the nakedness of an elder." The wheel would turn no more, no matter how hard she twisted at it. The sound of the room had changed drastically. The ticking had grown near, and steam from some pipes had dissipated where other walls now blew hot clouds.

Ivy was having difficulty keeping moisture from appearing on her face. "There are so many examples of benevolence being incompatible with angelic action, not to mention their goodness not aligning with their omnipotence not aligning with the suffering and evil of the world."

"But…"

"No, no need to fret. I can help. What I'm proposing is that there is no need to reconcile it all." She pulled and pulled on the ignition cord of the generator with her complete hand, quickly anxious and worried that it would not start. "You've just had it all wrong, you and yours, for so long, you've been selfish, but that's alright, because selfish is 'evil,' and, luckily, evil is good." But it did. The engine coughed to life, and Ivy pulled on the prod so excitedly that a wheel fell off, and she had to drag the generator along the floor to the row of open and closed cylinder outlets. She waved the prod around, squeezing the grip-start, testing its vibration. The ceramic was missing pieces, and green arcs danced unevenly. The areas of the cord open to the air smoldered and glowed as well.

Waiting and acknowledging the silence of the speakers, Ivy proclaimed, "Your song says that the angels aren't just perfect, they don't just do good, they *are* good. It's what they *are*. Eternal and immutable benevolence (for perfection is unchanging)."

She jammed the prod into an open cylinder and was instantly airborne. Her hair smoldered like frayed insulation as she picked herself up off the floor long seconds later. Master IDesigner Yankee Zrappado had partially emerged from the pool, limbs and head being lifted by wiring delving deep into circuit and muscle fiber.

Ivy coughed smoke as she said, "See, you've had it all wrong. Sometime along the way, you invented compassion. The world fooled you into thinking that love was mercy, forgiveness, and uncompromising understanding, when you were ignoring what was right in front of you. Angels are love. We really shouldn't be giving these divine creatures characteristics, actually. It humanizes them, or it glorifies us, but can we help it? It is less limiting to look at and define their actions. Angels starve and infirm and curse and kill, and they turn the other cheek when presented with the pestilence, famine, war, and death of the world. See? So, in turn, to burn and cripple and maul and look dispassionately upon suffering when you have the power to do otherwise…" Ivy slumped back against the wall, exhausted. "…is love! What you've tricked yourself into believing was evil is, in fact, divinely and ostensibly, love!"

She watched the picture tubes as they now showed what was obviously the view from Zrappado's eyes. The images were all of Ivy, seen through the film dripping from the bubbled visor over the top of his head. She patted at cinders she could now see were glowing on what was left of her clothing.

Bells from some shifting corridor a mile away rang throughout the complexes, answered by some chime in the poolroom no one could see, and the view on the tubes changed. The scene was once again of the outside world. The Quicken Device had stopped. The chamber was not swaying. Zrappado's body stiffened, but he moved one arm slowly before him, and the picture tubes showed the metal titan moving its gargantuan arm in response. The tithingman moved a corded and pale leg. The fluid swirled, and the chamber swayed again as the images showed the great god stepping forward to crush the earth.

"I... see..." the speakers hissed, "...everything."

He turned once more to look at Ivy, but now all Zrappado saw was the horizon. At the height of clouds he looked out over a prairie destroyed to hills and mountains colored by fire and untold legions of corpses. He looked up to the thundering heavens, straightening, and countryside and wrecked suburbs slid from his hunched back.

Inside the pool chamber, the tithingman sank slowly, rolling forward into a slump not unlike a fetus. Outside, over a ruined plain, over camps, hamlets, and masses of armies, the new god did the same, and the Quicken Device settled onto a destroyed land on its back, staring up at the dying sky.

LXXXIV

Lyrics of lips wake me to downy dawn
to the steam of jasmine neck as you take flight
Return to pasture, caress me as fawn
The last scalding dew before moon's shroud bright
   —Excerpt from the Sol Sistere

he warmth of the woman's caramel haunches surprised Janus
in a time when it seemed there was no more natural heat in
the world. Everything he touched was cold. He could not remember the
last time his hands were not chilled, yet here there were drops of sweat
in the hair on his arms, here he caressed the woman's hip in one long
line with his hot hand. She was barely covered by the sheet and should
have been shivering in the air of the tent. She should have shrunk
away from his cold touch. But everything was warm for the first time
in Janus' recent memory. The air was humid and the camp outside the
tent was quiet. The sun must have been rising, for the canvas glowed
eastwardly, making everything around him shine as though under its
own power. He sat on the edge of his bed, his own skin glowing like
a bronze suit of armor. Her unmoving curves glistened like the melt
off some dark confection he would have been denied living below the
Morbis Orbis. It had been whispered about by the other athletes. Every
one of the men had claimed to have tasted it at some time, but none
of them could ever quite describe the color or its sweetness with any
confidence.

He checked to make sure she was still breathing, picking fleas from
her hair, with her warm snores moistening his cheek, and so he stood
out of the bed into what he assumed would be frigid water. It flowed
under the tent in thick rivers — runoff from the snow they camped on
and near, warmed by his battalion's presence and campfires. He could
hear it trickling all through the night. The water was warm, as were the
emerging buds of grasses beneath it.

The open air of the tent had a faint chill to it, as would be expected in contrast to the heat beneath his bed sheets, but it was not
enough to cool the perspiration lining his chest. He peeked at a shard
of a mirror, not recognizing himself, but noticing that his whiskers
had grown longer than he liked. He and his men had been fighting for
days, out on the snow-driven plain, against a Horde battalion sent from

straight out of the depths of the Territories. Janus had finally crushed the enemy's last remnants the prior night, pushing them into deeper snows until all that remained was a single unique soldier — one of the so-called Unfeigned — holed up in an abandoned farm house. The strength and unbridled stamina of the Unfeigned had become legendary over the course of the war, and Janus had been wanting to match his skills against one, so he ordered his men to guard the house while he slept, to alert him if the creature tried to escape.

Without realizing it, Janus had been dry shaving his neck with the piece of the mirror. He had not remembered starting, had not even remembered picking it up. He dropped the speckled shard and wrapped his waist and groin in scarves and a skirt. It was not much more than he often wore in the games in Below the Brook. At the continual remembrances of the Morbis Orbis he bent over in pain. His stomach lurched tightly whenever the thought of Mew came over him, which was often. He had heard nothing of her since she had left. She had sent him no communications. He had heard no rumors. And he felt as though the silence was killing him from the inside out. His bedmate moaned in return to his wincing, but he ignored it. He just staggered and ran his fingers through his long hair to untangle it. He grabbed a sword and untied the curtain doors and was out in the morning air — an air that was surprisingly as warm as the tent's interior.

The paths through the camp's tents twinkled with the morning lighting the rivers flowing under carts and pavilions. Trucks and yurts were bathed in gold. The sun had returned, and it was glorious.

"It is glorious," Janus said out loud, but there was no one to hear him. His soldiers still slept. Their campfires had all washed away in the night. He walked the tepid path cutting straight through the interior of the grounds. It stretched out before him, and he could see every slight curve of the road as it wound all the way to the only hill for miles. The sun, rejuvenated after its long hibernation, enclosed the old abandoned homestead in its crown. The structure, for just a second, looked to be constructed out of pure shining ore. It had to have been where the rising sun itself had been hiding these last few months.

No horse or auroch appeared to greet Janus as he walked the warm wet steps of the camps. No guard approached him as he climbed the worn hill path. The house was unguarded, but Janus knew he would still find what he wanted, hidden and waiting inside.

"It is still in there," he said. "What I want. Hidden and waiting…" But his gut hurt so badly at the thought that Mew would not be there to watch the fight. When the pain passed, he was able to approach the door to the house. He looked up to the stands, hoping to find at least that a few fans had appeared to cheer him on, but then he remembered that he was not in the ring, and that it was just the sun, now blocked by the tall building before him, that glared down upon him. He reached for the doorknob, realizing that he held the sword in his hand. He chuckled, opening the door with his other hand, to find that the sun's long hibernation in the house had left the interior glowing so brightly he could not open his eyes. The warmth, the brilliance — if only Mew could have been there to witness it all.

Janus woke up afraid that he had suddenly gone blind, but it was only a flood of tears that obscured his vision. The pain in his stomach had been so real that for many seconds he was not sure that it had all been a dream. And in the dream, he had been able to breathe so deeply — so deeply that it made him realize that he had begun, sometime after Mew had left, to breathe very shallowly. He vowed to pay more attention to his breathing. It would not do well to lead his forces with such shallow breaths.

He had heard reports that a god had wakened — some chthonic behemoth created and worshipped by old Old Ones — and for days Janus and his troops had felt Its steps on the prairie. Feet tingled as they marched. Engines shuttered as their axles shook. Sometimes, at dawn or dusk, when the horizons glowed, some swore they could see the gargantuan silhouette striding from one side of the land to the other, threatening to grasp sun or moon in a fatal embrace. It was the quaking footfalls, shaking the planet, that Janus suspected had wakened him this morning. He suspected that the aftershocks had been giving him nightmares for days now. He pitied the giant god though. It would have to be so lonely to sleep away the eons, then waking to find all the other ancient deities gone. Where would one so unique find solace and companionship?

The woman sleeping next to him, with clammy thighs and hip, sent a shiver up his back. It seemed there was no more natural heat in the world. Everything he touched was cold. He could not remember the last time his hands were not chilled, and he caressed the woman's hip in one long line and she shrank away from his touch before pulling the largest fur of the bed over herself. The air of winter crept its way into the tent as his chiminea cooled into darkness, as did the outside movement as tents and yurts were being assembled and firepits were getting dug to shield any flames from the wind. The sun must have been setting, for the canvas of Janus' own pavilion glowed westwardly, making everything around him lose its colors to developing shadows. He did not remember sitting up but found himself at the edge of his bed, his own skin taking on a dusky shade. The woman next to him, her unmoving curves and color, both darkened and faded like dying charcoal. He was not sure how long he had slept but knew, by the specific movements outside, that it could not have been long, yet his mouth was painfully dry and he could barely remember how the woman snoring next to him had tasted.

He stood out of the bed, shaking fleas from his hair, into what he assumed would be warm water. It flowed under the tent in thick rivers — runoff from the snow they camped on and near, warmed by his battalion's presence and campfires. He could hear it trickling all around him, even through his dreams. It ignored his feet to bite at his ankles, but he could still feel the long dead and frozen grasses soften under his toes.

The open air of the tent had a great chill to someone just emerging from blankets, and it nipped at his nakedness. He picked up a hand mirror, recognizing himself for the first time in many days, but noticing that his whiskers had grown longer than he liked, and so he quickly went to work dressing himself minimally so he could immediately start shaving. He applied soap and water quickly but used a straight edge slowly.

He and his forces had been fighting for days, out on the snow-driven plain, against a Horde battalion sent from straight out of the depths of the Territories. Janus had finally crushed the enemy's last remnants the prior morning, pushing them into deeper snows until all that remained was a single soldier — one of the so-called Unfeigned — holed up in an abandoned farm house. The strength and unbridled stamina of the Unfeigned had become legendary over the course of the war, and Janus had been wanting to match his skills against one, so he ordered his men to guard the house while he slept, to alert him if the creature tried to escape.

He put away his toiletries and wrapped his waist and groin in scarves and a skirt. The rest of his body, from neck to knee, he covered in a thin leather he could move in without any encumbrance. His left arm, from shoulder to knuckles, he covered in plate mail of differing sizes and designs. His right he wrapped in tiny sections of links over straps of more leather. Straps crisscrossing his chest offered little protection but held different sizes of scabbarded daggers and shurikan. With a tapered leather skirt and heavily plated legs, he collected axes and short swords before leaving the interior of the tent for the open evening. The cold almost stole his air, and he had to work consciously to fill his lungs, as much as the temperature hurt them.

He ran his fingers through his long hair before tying it into a topknot. He wore no helmet and kept his face bare but reached into a satchel that was not there for a mask he was not carrying.

The paths through the camp's tents twinkled with the evening temperature slowing the rivers flowing under carts and pavilions. Trucks and yurts glittered with spiderwebbing frost. The meager sun was disappearing for the night.

"It is glorious," Janus said out loud, "to meet one's enemy on equal terms. To eschew all the trickery and lies, the manipulation and manic grasping at higher ground, the deceit of war. This is true sport. One against one. True proof of manhood." His followers joined his walk through the chilling mud. Their campfires had just begun to rise, and they all walked the smoky path cutting straight through the interior of the grounds. It stretched out before them. With every slight curve of the road Janus was joined by more soldiers. Thick cloud cover hid all heavens except for white-hot *Wyrmwood*. The comet and its crackling tail hung in the sky behind the old abandoned homestead. With a quick glance it looked as though it was aimed at the elderly building's upper gables. The house looked to be barely standing. Janus saw its ability to last against the recent windstorms as testament to its maker. Winter winds had petrified its wood to corpse gray matching the falling star.

"It's still in there," Janus said. "What I want. Hidden and waiting..." And he once more felt his heart drop. It was all he had left, he felt, inside — his heart. He was a hollow man, and his heart just fell about, bruised and also petrified. He sank to his knees, arms and armor settling loudly. The soldiers closest to him saw him as being afraid of the last few steps up the porch, and they loved him all the more for it.

"Where is she?" he whispered inaudibly. "Will I ever see..."

Men larger and smaller than he hoisted him back to his feet, but it took a minute before he set them upon the patio. *Without Mew this is all nothing*, he thought. She would not be at his side to see him through the door. She would not be watching to cheer him against the Unfeigned. He did not look back at the crowd, but he could feel their eyes burning through the back of his armor. What good were they? They did not know him. They followed him only because he fought at their sides, at the front of the battles. They called him Legion because he fought like many men and had beaten just as many in battle. He bled and blood-let whenever they did. He never asked of them any more than he had of himself. But they were only in love with what they thought was Janus. He wanted to be nothing more than just one man, but they desired so strongly to see him as more than that. They would follow him into the sea and drown just as quickly as he would.

"Legion! Legion! Legion!" they chanted, beating on breast and shield.

But he so wanted to just drown alone. "Back!" he shouted. "Back to the camp or you'll see disfavor in my eyes." There was much grumbling, but until he repeated himself two more times, each time growling more loudly than the previous times, they would not budge. "No one is to follow. Just let me fight in peace, under no other's eye." Men and women backed from the porch but would not go farther from the house than its long shadow.

Without Mew there was little color in the world. Food tasted dry and lumped in his throat. He always seemed to be looking at the world through a haze of water. A stiffness in his chest kept him from inhaling deeply. There was little enjoyment day to day that seemed worthwhile without Mew to experience it with. Her love for life itself was contagious, but he had recovered in her absence and now saw only the drudgery of the fallen world. Whether he was going through daily routines or driving his forces forward against the spears and cannons of the Horde, it was all so senseless without her experiencing it with him. She had always named their destiny, had always hinted at greater lives to come, but here he just beat his sword against shield in a monotonous tune promising nothing more but the same tinnitus and a cold lonely grave suddenly and without warning. And he knew that, wherever she had ended up, she had thoughts so far removed from his own to preoccupy her.

There was no knob on the door of the house. Its entrance was stuck shut to a frame warped by the settling of age and the wetting of ages. Janus looked back to the crowd, hoping to find it dispersed, but it had grown, and all eyes were upon him. He kicked the door in and pulled a hand axe and dagger.

The hollow man looked up. The house glowered down back at him. Its scaly shingles curled darkly like fungal toenails. Bulbous gables curled like horns against a generation of prairie wind. Shattered window frames — just empty sockets revealing a desiccated soul that long ago refused to escape — howled and gasped at an atmosphere so dusty it turned the sunset into a horizon on fire. From the whistling whine seeping from shrunken boards, Janus would have assumed the house was empty of everything, but he knew better. He knew himself to be empty, just dried guts rattling around in a gladiator-shaped shell. He had lost his senses, deriving no pleasure from taste or touch, even the art of battle. There was no fun in a life or a fight in which Mew was not watching, in which whose eyes he could not choose to also experience things. This was the horror of the hollow man without a light to illuminate his insides. But his shoulders lumped with the reminder that the haunted house was not so empty as he.

The Unfeigned were modern legends amongst the forces of the Horde. A desperate man would earn land and food for his family by submitting himself to the biomancy and super science of the Breeding Pits. With organs replaced, skin grafted, and blood transplanted, something stronger but with a new and desperately short life span would emerge. And Janus had, since the beginning of the war, yearned to pit himself against one, one on one. But here, now, he felt no excitement stepping forward — not even the usual tickle in his guts and toes as he headed out into the arena. For his gut was empty.

How the interior could be so humid when the outside of the house was devoid of any moisture Janus could not figure until he heard the steaming rasp of the building's only dweller.

Despite open ceiling and window frames, the evening burn on the horizon did not penetrate the darkness of the parlor. The tall room was all mismatched angles of wood and shadow. Nothing was parallel. Everything threatened everything. A stairway, once leading to what was now a fallen second floor, had disappeared, collapsing into nothingness. Each step Janus took squeaked like the mice that numerous dried remains told him once had laid claim to the house. Even the walls creaked at his entrance.

Still the Unfeigned wheezed emphysemically from behind warped corner and darkness, and Janus could see dark gleam of the diving bell that held his torso and moldering head. The rest of his body was also oversized, of exaggerated bronze shoulders, nickel bracers, and a burlap and brown leather hand. The other hand was an oversized razor drill. Its stout legs and industrial boots looked too heavy to lift.

But the Unfeigned rushed him before Janus had even a second sense of the dusty wet air of the house. The boards beneath its rubber boots splintered, not squeaked. The segmented drill thundered as it spun in numerous directions, not whirred as Janus expected. The general of the Army of Earth met him face on, trying to find soft purchase with an ax against bolted metal, sliding a dagger up beneath and between layers of sponge and hide. But the Unfeigned came down on top of him, and Janus did not even have the chance to realize that they had both fallen through the shattered floor together.

~

He did not think he had slept — the pain behind the left side of his skull would have prevented it — but he knew that time had passed. Somehow, from somewhere, light reflected off some damp corner, which then reflected against one of the pools of cool sludge Janus rose from. That same sliver of faint silver shone dimly from the Unfeigned's diving bell. The creature no longer steamed and wheezed. Corroded bars of ribbed metal stuck up through the soft parts of its body. He was impaled silently to the swamp of the cellar.

Janus dried his hands before trying to wipe his eyes. He had been blinded by blood many times in the past, but never so completely. As soon as he could see again, his eyelids would congeal over, and so he felt for any crooked outcropping or foot hole to use to climb back up out of the cellar. The pool was filled with woody stalagmites to trip him up, the wall with gritty nails to scratch at his hands and face. He kept expecting the Elder Mask to protect his cheeks before remembering that it was locked away back in his tent.

He wiped his eyes again but was quickly reblinded before he pulled himself up some semblance of a fallen staircase. For each solid step upward he would trip down two from a rotted rung or crumbling stone handhold, but eventually he emerged out into the evening of the house's main level. He crawled until his forehead was wet again, blinked the blood out of his eyes and crawled again.

Outside, falling off of the porch and into the waiting arms of a few soldiers that disobeyed his orders to wait, he could see the horror of his head wound in their eyes before he was blinded again. A green man appeared by their shouting and took careful time bandaging his head in herbs and soaked wraps. It felt good to have it wound tightly. No more did it feel as though his brain leaked out through a crack at his hairline.

Now he felt that he slept, even though he knew it not to be true, for he could still hear his soldiers talking on the mount of the house. The god had fallen, someone had reported. The earth had moved, but the war still raged, sometimes on top of the chthonic being's immensity, sometimes beneath. But the Horde still moved, and the Army of Earth was now running. Janus' forces were being called back to augment a massive retreat.

Janus blinked and winked until he could see again, and he looked to the green man that still held him and the green eye painted on his forehead. He had seen an unimaginable number of versions of Mew's eyes over the past few years, an uncounted variety of greens across tattoos and banners, but none of these facsimiles had ever captured her eyes' true color, the primordial green cultivated from some tropical and early earthly lagoon, some warm and algaeic stew where life simmered in inspired anticipation.

All the green people and their made-up and painted eyes just stared back at him, each day, dead and as lifeless as he felt without Mew.

"M'lord Legion!" someone near shouted. At least, it had felt like they shouted. "I've given the order to upset and head out! We can head out by the owl's hour!"

"No!" Janus whispered. His own voice stung harder, sounded louder, than any of theirs. He pushed anyone near away as he staggered to his feet. His legs felt like rubber beneath him. "What's the use? Why do we even fight?"

"Sir?"

"What are we fighting for? Is this just a game?" Janus had taken innumerable hits in the gladiatorial stadiums over the years, and plenty more since escaping out into the world, but he could never remember his head hurting so completely. He kept feeling to make sure some slab of shrapnel or stone had not embedded itself in his skull. Theirs was a weight to the pain that made his vision and stomach swim.

"You've said it yourself, sir, we fight to fight. We fight to win..."

"This's no fight. There's no glory in this... this chaos. And what do we win? The right to wage more war? A future where our children live to spread whatever culture survives through more war? This is not..."

And Janus was suddenly alone on the mount — yet not alone, for the haunted house peered over his fallen form with a frightened look shaped by broken window panes — yet not alone for all of Heaven was comprised of the spirals of an eye only he knew. There were no clouds, no sun, no moon, but there were stars. They were golden and they flecked a viridescent celestial sphere encompassing another globe — this one so dark and so magnificently voracious that nothing, not even light, could escape from its absolute abyss. The furry layer of celestial algae that surrounded it appeared to stretch forever, forever tidally locked but perpetually gnawing at the inner ring. From here the golden flakes sank and rose. Beyond the green a pure sky of white stretched to all horizons. It was the cotton of the heavens, an orbit so pure it could never have been touched by the unclean Earth, despite two branching rivers of blood snaking along the milk of its galaxy. The great eye of the sky never blinked, but it was not static. The primordial green continued to stretch across time and space, consuming and being consumed by the black hole at its center. The golden islands shimmered as they reflected and generated an absent sun. Janus could not look away from those islands. He watched as unicellular creatures split and adapted and grew and became even more unfamiliar beings with familiar civilizations before tearing it all down to start over again. They had cultures and technologies that inevitably consumed their sandy islands, and as one fleck of gold disappeared another appeared somewhere else in the expansive iris. There was not one that would not destroy itself before even the chance to tumble into the engorged, ebony maw. Janus was alone, and there was no sky, only the behemoth Eye of Heaven, and it grew, but the only space it had left to consume was above him. The haunted house quivered, and its scaly shingles scattered before it was forced to lean and bend. Janus fell even closer to the cold ground before he was pushed. The Eye consumed all of the sky and its sphere pressed against the land, the entirety of Earth's hemisphere, until it pressed against Janus. He could no longer look at it as he was crushed against the ground. He ate dirt and breathed dust until he could breathe no longer, his chest held against crooked arm and shoulder and rocky and dead sod. But he could feel the moist warmth of the celestial Eye as it crushed the land and crushed him to the land, could feel the heat of its movement as it moved and it moved the planet whose pressure stole his breath. He could feel its warmth but also its gaze. Just as he could not avoid the force of its pressing presence, he could not escape its watch. And he did not want to. There was no air left in his lungs, and he swallowed his tongue. Even with his eyes closed and crushed he could see a color green that only he knew. The pain in his head was gone.

Janus was not alone, and he jumped up from the cold ground into the cold air, grabbing at those around him. To his battalion he shouted, "We march in the morning! We return to the main front of the War!" To his men-at-arms he ordered for "all armored and ready to meet with him." To the green healer he asked for "every ounce of dye and ink and paint" the man could scrounge together.

And every shield of every soldier was painted with an eye as green as the one pressing down upon Janus. Every breastplate and helmet was colored like the eye of the Lonely Forgotten Sun of God, and the command was made for tattoos on the hand of every soldier as long as the ink held out. The pale and bloody-teared eye of the Liege of Foes was salvaged and painted over on banners and truck hoods.

Legion's new green-eyed battalion went forth that next day to meet up with the Army of Heaven. The War was no longer his game, but it was for glory, and he would wage it renewed under Her watchful gaze.

~

He had been fighting at the front of the lines, felling foe after foe, driving them down under axe and sword and spear. But they just kept pushing. He had used up all of the rounds in his revolvers. But they just kept pushing. Legion's forces had surrounded them at first and had seemingly executed a successful closed fist maneuver, but the Horde had just kept reinforcing itself from the south, and they had just kept pushing. His squads had all gathered and regrouped, had resupplied the little ammunition left, and had launched a sieve maneuver to separate the nearest Horde forces from their supply route, but he had found un-expected geography, unstable terrain, and deadly weather, and they just kept pushing. His maps were all suddenly wrong. There was a canyon where there should have been a frozen plain, a ruined city where there should have been a riverbed, and hills upon hills of treacherous dirt where his maps showed a slight woodland. And the deadly air appeared even before they were hunted up and down the crumbling rises of black dust and wet stone. The winds seemed to come from all directions, caught up in the sudden ruins and hills. The air could not decide on a season. One morning they would smell engine smoke, but by night the atmosphere would reek of wood fire. If they breathed dust they knew they would soon smell oil or steam. The wind was wet but thick with a dry mold, and it and the air-borne mud clung to their scarves and boots like petulant children.

So they were driven up and into the new yet decayed mounds. Their ammunition ran out as they retreated through a village of upgrown roots. They walked an upside down forest, and, at every count, members of his parties seemed to disappear into thin air, as though the loose ground would swallow soldiers up without a trace. The terrain rarely stopped shifting and settling.

Still the Horde pushed against them, chanting to the *Horny Lord*. Legion had fought at the front of his forces but now had been pushed, by the enemy and his own men, into the interior of the fighting, as the Horde chanted to the *American Minotaur*. He could not swing even a dagger without cutting his own men, even as they all started to fight amongst each other, desperately trying to move away from the open and dark chasm they were being pushed into. Legion's mass of soldiers were caught between the spears and pikes of the Horde and an opening in the earth without a bottom any of them could see in the dim haze of the deadly air. Still, the Horde soldiers, now priests of the *Man Bull*, pushed and chanted. To force himself beneath his own men, between their trampling feet, would be to suffocate on the loose ground. To climb them would be to put himself in range of the Horde's rifles.

Before he knew it, he was falling into open air. He could not reach them, but his men fell all around into the abyss. The last thing he heard was the continual chant of cannibal sacrifice to the *Manimal of the Labyrinth*. He feared that even Her celestial eye would not be able to see him so far from the surface.

LXXXVI

The anthrosophers we left behind, at last word, were still mapping out the caves and upside down cities, distracted incessantly by the civilization that ages ago took refuge inside the titan's body against the Cataclysm. Letters suggest these refugees evolved independently of any other culture, and there are indications of a hive mind and a society more akin to an immune system than a people.

—From the oral histories of the Third World Nomads

t was the face of an angel. Soft and cold and a beautiful baby blue even the winter had yet to emulate. She looked so young, and the stillness of her pursed lips and long eyelashes held a peace Damn Antony knew that, even if he lived another hundred years, he would die nowhere near. He envied her like no other before, before reminding himself that she had probably died horrifically and painfully. He could not find the rest of the woman's body but assumed that, if the Nidhogg Virus had penetrated this deeply beneath the new catacombs that the fall of the Quicken Titan had created, her limbs had probably mutated into the stalks of some unknown monster, her body spreading wide into alien vegetation. Even beneath the fallen city/giant/god/automaton, the virus would suddenly appear. The Lesser Antony would be shouting orders or taking them, fighting ahead of or behind the dwindling and buried legions of the Army of Earth, when someone near would suddenly bloat or shrink, bursting from or disappearing into their broken armor and ragged clothes, only to spread the deadly and airborne pathogens to someone near.

But perhaps the woman was one of the many spared the effects of the virus. One certain bloodline had been targeted. Perhaps her ancestors had been sly enough to avoid the taint apparently infecting the land many generations even before Tormalco had crafted his invisibly small invaders. If the dead woman had been fortunate, Antony thought, she had suffocated on the thin and dirty air of the new world beneath the fallen behemoth, or perhaps she had just been lucky enough to fall prey to the strife still being played out beneath the inverted city of Quicken by the remnants of the Armies of Heaven and Earth.

Deep inside Damn Antony, within brain and gut, the demon screamed and gurgled. Tormented by its entrapment, tortured and bound by iron — the presence of Tormalco's nanobots burning its foul essence by their very touch — the entity never ceased to wail in

Antony's head. The demon Ba'al was not familiar with such torment. Pain and possession were meant for lesser beings, to be administered by itself. But here, it was the one trapped, bound in pain to only look through Antony's eyes without any chance of action, so wracked with the biting burning of iron that it could not focus to control the man's body. So incapacitated it could not even flee the man's body at will.

All it could do was wail.

And Antony could let it go, could let the demon escape with but a thought, could let the constant screaming in his brain end, but to do so would return the malevolent entity to the world, while Antony's body would, in turn, be consumed by the Nidhogg Virus now dormant in his flesh and blood. For the iron pathogens and the storm demon had unwillingly created an unholy biobalance in his body. Neither could leave unless he willed it. Neither could destroy him or others unless he let down his guard. But still, the horrible wailing never ended, no matter how tightly he covered his ears or gritted his teeth or struck his head against a wall. Only the war distracted him from the reverberating scream in his skull.

A shot rang out in the tight tunnel he crouched in, and Antony took one last look at the head of the woman in the dim light of his torch. He moved the palm of his hand down her face, even though her eyes were already closed, before another shot reminded him that there were still some bullets left under the ground. His own rifle had been down to single-digit rounds for what he estimated had been a week. He carried it slung over his shoulder, its wooden butt splintered from clubbing whatever came at him from out of the dark.

The sniper he had been following for days was obviously still out there. Every time Antony beat back assailants by torchlight, every time he had sent the last of his soldiers ahead, out into shadows that would last for hours, he thought he had taken care of the rifleman, but within the hours and days that followed, the gunshots would ring out again in echoes that seemingly never ended. He walked through caverns of rocks, into sudden tunnels of the most ancient of sculpted ores, under great stalactites that by the light of waning flashlight or sputtering torch looked like buildings precariously hung upside down. Over the days, his boots, mismatched and repeatedly scrounged from fallen soldiers of either army, stepped through alternatingly frigid and hot streams, down steaming hallways composed of archaic pipes, and around pools of oil and what smelled like cooked fat. He had been sharing canned and congealed meats he and his fellow soldiers had found in a system of broken lockers, but both the men and the food had been dwindling. He had eaten the last of it hours earlier and had seen the last of his companions even earlier.

For what was assumed to be days, they had followed just one tunnel, but the openings had shrank and multiplied, and Antony was no tracker, especially through chambers, either metallic or earthen, that continued to collapse ahead and behind him. The passages were not stable, and the going was slow. Each step had to be tested before taking, even in the areas where light was present from some unreachable and indeterminate source that never fully materialized no matter how far one traveled.

The thunder of constantly settling ceiling and floor never stopped rolling, making it difficult to hear others or even focus on one's thoughts. Yet it never drowned out the demon's taunts.

Antony crouched low into a larger tunnel with walls of brick cracked and crumbling. Brick dust powered like water through the ceiling, while actual water covered the floor, slowly rising. He removed his facemask, coughing at the particulates in the air before tasting the water from his glove and deciding not to drink it. He had found plenty of melting ice in the past few days, but this smelled of something too organic for his tastes. He spat the liquid and the air out his mouth before returning the facemask, adjusting it over a smile that would not fade.

Climbing through a cast iron doorway that looked as though it would soon collapse under its own weight, he found himself in an earthen collection of tunnels that all appeared to be widening before becoming clogged with wet roots and hanging dirt. None of the caverns had any light, so he added the last of the oil he have scavenged over the past day to his torch and headed toward a new echo of a deeper gunshot. He cut his way tediously through root and sod with a machete that had long lost its edge before he had even found it. If anyone had passed through the tunnel before him they had crawled lowly through deep and sucking soil, but he continued to follow the sound of a pistol firing from far-off.

He tugged at the veins of melting plants, climbing sharply to reach an alcove that had distinctly warm air issuing from it. The skin exposed by numerous holes in his clothing warmed in the current. He took his time before crawling in and found that he could stand in a long corridor that alternated between rock and a metal he was not familiar with. It had been unnaturally smoothed but still caught the edges of his gloves.

As he entered a thin but taller chamber, movement in new lights and old shadows drove him down behind what was either a natural or sculpted stalagmite. A rock shattered and skidded nearby — the result of rifle fire. He extinguished his torch in a collection of hard mud and softening ice, bringing the stone around him back into darkness, but he could still see a figure far to his side, although deeper into the cavern, aiming a revolver out into the darkness. It was not any woman he recognized — she wore woolen skins and a knitted cap under a vest and a wide-brimmed herder hat — but she wore a flag of the Liege of Foes over her back like a cape. Her long beard was as torn as her face, and she shouted incomprehensively as loud as her pistol fired.

"I'll cover you," Antony whispered, unslinging his rifle. He was doubtful she had heard him through the painful echoing of gunfire, but she ran none-the-less.

He peeked face and barrel around the a corner of his coverings and, barely looking, squeezed the trigger while aiming out at moving lights increasingly eaten up by the distant darkness. The rifle made no sound or recoil, and Antony twisted back to eject the dead round. He had few left and would not have been surprised if they were all just as worthless. Everything buried under the fallen god had turned out to be broken. He blew on the few rounds he had left and returned them to the rifle's chamber before running and diving behind a collection of rock and unidentifiable blocks of machinery. There were great toothed cogs imbedded in the metal and mud of the floors and walls, and a shower of sand from a far wall soon grew into a cascade that finally became a falling segment of the ceiling. Every being in the chamber stood, giving up their cover to watch the collapse of what they were only now realizing was an entire city block falling onto a near section of ground that could not possibly hold all the weight.

Antony coughed in the new dust. So many of his troops had died in the past week, throats spitting up blood, lungs drowning in new scar tissue. The air under plains and machine god was thin, poisonous, thick. It never smelled right, not through an increasingly failing face mask, and the underground atmosphere glittered with torchlight reflections from exhaust or particles always beyond one's reach. He was not going to test the superior physicality of his Homega Sapiens form, and so he now breathed through a scavenged bandanna.

Before the dirt settled he was on the run again, firing his last good round into a darkness loud but unlit by torch or lamp. He called to any of his troops that were still out in the echoes. But something hit him from all directions, pinning his limbs, tearing his clothing, squeezing his chest and holding his air until he saw spots — bright in the shadows and black obscuring any light.

Later, as he was being roughly dragged face down by uncountable hands, he was not able to remember if the ground had opened up beneath his run or if more of the ceiling — natural or manmade — had fallen upon him. Had he just been tripped up somewhere in a poorly lit passage, or had Horde men jumped him. He had not been unconscious but shaken so violently that only now were his wits settling about him. The reverberation of revolver fire — so loud he thought it next to his ear, yet, when he lifted his head, he saw that it had come from a figure out in the middle of a massive chamber — rocked the smoky air and completed his waking.

"Settle down," a coughing voice said, kicking Antony's face into the moving ground, grinding a bleeding chin into fine pebbles of rock and metal. The army of hands readjusted on his body before continuing to drag him forward across the giant cavern. In his quick glimpse of the far surroundings he saw great and odd geometric stalactites and an immensity of cavernous voids leading off into all directions. Before Antony was tossed at the feet of the sitting figure, a booming storm of noise and dust, pulling and pushing and swirling the dead atmosphere of the cavern, fell to envelop the mound of collected garbage he found himself on. The upper reaches of the chamber were as apparently unstable as any other tunnel he had found himself fighting through over the past many days.

"Are you wasting time, my time?" a voice he immediately recognized as belonging to a Lesser said.

Antony stood, wincing from the gravel that had been ground into his knees, and found himself in front of a figure that could only have been one of the High Generals of the Horde. Usually coming across another Lesser Antony caused a quick feeling of surreal nausea, as though walking past a mirror that did not quite mimic one's movements perfectly, but with the Homega Sapiens sitting before him — either

Fobos or Deemos, he was not sure — he did not have this problem.

Fobos or Deemos, naked except for a cape and long breechcloth unfolding to his feet, was painted in black caked and cracked paint, but barely any of it still stuck to his familiar face. Beneath it, the man was entirely tattooed red.

One of his soldiers spoke up. "We, eh, though you might wanna see this dude. He, eh, kinda looks…"

Fobos or Deemos stood to feel the scabs and dirt of Antony's chin. "Which one of you did this, did this to him?"

Antony was surprised to see that it had been only two men that had carried him from wherever he had fallen. One of them ran now. The soldier ran haphazardly, partly from an obviously wounded leg and partly to avoid holes in the cavern floor that light from numerous staff torches could not penetrate.

Fobos or Deemos raised a painted *Davidson* as Antony and the other soldier ducked and covered their ears. But the giant red gun only clicked loudly. The High General sat back into a makeshift throne of stone and bone to open the revolver and toss the large round into an empty shadow. "It is a sad state of affairs, is it not, my side brother, when the gene-dead chaff of this broken world think they can just touch one of the Brotherhood as if he were some suburb whore, is it not?" Piles of waist-length strands of a Lesser Antony's dark hair littered the throne, and the High General went back to drizzling water onto what was left of the hair on his head before handing the bowl to Antony. "You must be thirsty, are you thirsty? Can I figure you aren't here to rescue? Imagine us. To survive this… despicable virus… are there any others… only to perish under the ass-side of a titan?"

The bowl held many oily reflections. As parched as Antony was, he could not get himself to drink from its dirty depths.

Fobos or Deemos continued. He was sharpening a straight razor on a rock not meant for the duty. "Man was never designed to live beneath gods, beneath god… awful… beneath…" He had numerous pins of rank and award pinned to his bare chest. There was at least one for each angel of the Divine Choir, and his skin stretched against them but no longer bled.

Both Antony and the remaining soldier of the Horde coughed — the former realizing his missing bandanna, the latter hacking up foam and worms drowning in the foam. From deep within far darkness came a shifting and crumbling sound that could have only been a piece of the ground sinking in upon itself. Antony could feel it in the dirt. He now realized, as his sight continued adjusting to the weird torchlight and cities of shadows beyond, that what he had first thought were immense downward pillars of stone were actually upside down buildings hanging from the rock and metal ceilings. Some had fallen, some had grown into the ground and walls, and a few were still intact. Quicken survived in an obscure existence.

The High General laughed as the other men continued to cough, and Antony was bothered to admit that the sound echoing back from unseen walls was unrecognizable to him, as he began to strip off layers of wrappings. It was inexplicably warm in the great room. "What have you done to yourself?" he asked, looking over the symbiotes attached to the flesh of Fobos or Deemos. He recognized the Mudd's Durian that had grown into the man's upper neck. It inflated periodically, no doubt to filter the smog. But he was unfamiliar with the crystal caterpillars that had taken root in his toes, turning his feet into clubs.

"What we Antonys do best," Fobos or Deemos answered, "I've adapted, as we do best, hee, heh."

"Is that what this is? Everything we've done. I just don't know any..."

"Of course it is, it is!" Antony and the soldier ducked again as Fobos or Deemos jumped up to fire the *Davidson* toward the upper void. Ears ringing, he could still hear the High General scratching at the prickly hair on the crown of his head. "Heh, hee, I'm so glad someone else is finally here that can also hear it, can you hear it? That 'chick scritch' sound? Out there, up there."

"I don't hear..."

"We... are..."

"...anything."

"...the epitome of adaptation!" The High General was the same size as Antony, but he towered above him before sitting back on his throne. The scraping razor made a sound like the flipping of playing cards as it was dragged across the remaining growth of his scalp. "We have been given no choice but to adapt, thrown into a world not our own, oppressed on all sides by an unknowable future. With such foresight they created the Lessers, all the Greaters that came here..."

"They were us!" Antony yelled without an echo. "Have you forgotten? Have you 'adapted' so far beyond..."

"No, no, no, no, no, no… yes! You are right, heh! We are something new, we've grown beyond them, beyond them to become something better suited to this world, and we have to continue to grow, you and I, who may be the only two left, in order to rebuild, to rebuild all we've lost, all we had lost by coming here and all we've gained since coming here."

"We? I…" Antony's head hurt with every cough. "You… I mean… your Greater… no, you! You broke the rules. Your Greater, I know… Ammon Mars, right? He went back to the Nursery, years later, to make more, you and Fobos… or Deemos. Each Greater is only supposed to make two Lessers, right when they come to this world, not later, and not more. This time we come to educate the land, to save it, not to conquer. Those are the…"

"Oh, no, heh. You are so precious, so precious you are in your attempts to not adapt. Rules? Heh, hee, heh!" Fobos or Deemos had been starting to shave the bristle of hair over his head but kept interrupting himself to steady his hand and the razor against his giggle. "There are no rules, you twit, you twat, only adaptation against an unfriendly world. Why does a Greater only make two Lessers, only passing his mind to two Homega Sapiens, upon entering this broken reality? Because the Nursery only has, only had, two functional gesta-tubes at a time, only two set up for male 'gangers' anyway. Anyway, a Greater has no patience to sit around for the recycling, for two more to be made. Rules? A Greater can't return to the Nursery? Have Lessers made copies of themselves? You immutable brother, you, heh, heh, where have you been all my life? I know, I know that some just have to tell themselves that we've all decided on some 'rules,' in order to, in order to make sense of the world we've found ourselves in, but to truly believe these stories is to be in the ultimate denial, an entirely new, new reality even scarier than…"

Fobos or Deemos put the straight razor down to scratch at his bare hairline. He was now bald and his head a patchwork of colors. "God! Gods, I'm so glad someone has come to listen to that 'scritching' sound with me. Creetch, screeeeetch!"

Antony looked to the soldier at his side, but the man did not look back. His hands covered his mouth as though he was holding something down inside his throat with all his strength. His fingers looked recently frostbit. They were as dark as the open windows in the inverted buildings lit only by the occasional flicker of the near torches.

"Go," Antony whispered, tilting his head back from the direction he thought they had come, but the man stayed, his eyelashes wet and sticking together.

"Oh, attention," Fobos or Deemos whispered before clearing his throat, "well met, brother of a doppelbrother." He gestured for Antony to sit on a nearby stack of crates. "I didn't see you there, there you go. Well met, what is the word from above? Does the war still rage? After the Virus, can there still be enough fodder left to fight on either side? Are we two all that is left of the Brotherhood?"

"I... I... am... not..." Although it had been days since Antony had eaten or drank anything, he still felt a knot in his stomach that made him feel full. But either the lack of sustenance or air was finally taking its toll. He was having difficulty focusing. At times it appeared that both Fobos *and* Deemos sat next to him, speaking to him from the same voice. He spat whatever continually moved up from his lungs. "Are... you aware of what transpires on the home front... in the Territories?"

Fobos or Deemos, or Fobos and Deemos, had brought the razor back to his head. He was clean-shaven now but continued to bring it across his scalp. "I know they are weak, weak and pathetic, and they have been surrendering to whatever hel-spawn the Army of Earth has pledged itself to."

"I mean before that. You... you haven't seen what they've done, the things they've done..."

"Who?"

"The tithingmen! In your... our absence, while we've been away at war, they've enacted laws... secured their power..."

"Who are we to judge, are we to judge them?" Fobos or Deemos pulled the blade across bone. Thin flaps of flesh hung from the back of his head like meaty hair. "We conscripted our sad sons as mayors, governors, replacing the deaf that had served the land into sinfulness. They're only doing their best... did their best... heh, hee. Are they still alive? What's the word from the surface, surface land above? Has the Virus reached its swampy fingers into Kaldera yet?"

"I..."

"Heh, we who sit here safe out in the battlefields, with solid purpose, with purpose right in front of us, easy destinies set before us like Thanksgiving dinners, plump and congealing directly in hands and laps, but… but, but, but… but those poor crippled boys we threw into positions of power, made to herd the rats back home as though they could produce anything but rancid milk… they are the real heroes those tithingmen. We can't expect them to think like we do, do we? We toss them to the pigs, expect them to eat in their wallow, and then you bitch when their breath smells like shit. Shit, you want them to do your dirty work but whine when they take some liberties… that they deserve? They deserve to take some of the cream off the top, don't they? Don't you think they… hee…"

Half his head was now exposed skull, and his cape had changed color from the slow cascade of blood over his shoulders. The remaining soldier had run off coughing and crying into some cave-in.

"I just… can't… be… the… only… one… that… hears…" He scratched his skull with the nails of all his fingers. Suddenly jumping up, he said, "Yes! Finally! Finally, another brother to drink of the blessed air beneath a god's asshole! When did you arrive, sir, well met, well met." He embraced Antony, holding him tightly to his chest. "Wait!" he said while pulling back, tracing Antony's forehead down to the crown of his nose, covering the scar with a wet finger. "You… you… I know. I know I don't know you, but you are a Prodigal aren't you? The one fighting for the Liege of Foes? Heh, hee, heh, how appropriate that we should be the last two, the last two alive, heh. How goes the war?"

"I've been down here as long as you have, brother."

Fobos or Deemos was looking at his blood-soaked hands quizzically, his lips sticking together as he spoke. "You know, you know we call ourselves brothers, heh, but all this time, heh, it's been a mistake, because we all are closer than any brothers could be. What we lost, what we sacrificed so much for to find… how we… we…" He had collapsed when reaching over to pick up a hand mirror and just rested face down in a mess of tiny bones and broken bowls. Yet Antony could hear him perfectly. "…we were all so perfectly betrayed, betrayed into a test, because it was a test, you've seen that now haven't you, that it was a test, a test to see how we would react, would live, in the face of a new beginning. We, us, I, all of us, all of I, were given something no one has ever been given… an irrefutably new beginning, new life, a chance to start completely over."

Minutes passed, and Antony picked up the mirror. Even beneath the darkness and the haze of the glass he could see his face. It was a face he had not seen for weeks, but it brought tears to his eyes he knew he could not afford to waste. He threw the mirror as hard as he could. No sound came back from the cyclopean shadows.

He took up the Davidson, trying to shield his ears before pulling the trigger at the obscure ceiling, but the gun only clicked again. It had been the last round.

"But we failed," Fobos or Deemos mumbled.

"What?"

"You know, you know you are called a 'Prodigal,' but all this time it's been a mistake, because... do you know the tale of the Parable of the Lost Father?"

Antony searched amongst the refuse but found only empty crates and piles and piles of empty bowls. He found collections of silver and goldware that appeared to have never been used.

The mumbling continued, "There was a man who had two sons. But one day he took his estate and set off for distant country and there squandered his wealth in wild living. After he had spent everything, there was a severe famine in that whole country, and he began to be in need.

"When he came to his senses he got up and went to his sons, and while he was still a long way off, one of the sons saw him and was filled with compassion for him. He ran to him, threw his arms around him, and kissed him. The son said to his brother, 'Quick! Bring the last calf and kill it. Let's have a feast and celebrate.' The brother became angry and refused to go and said, 'Look! All these years our father has wasted the estate on prostitutes and cards, and you kill the last calf for him?' And the other brother said, 'We celebrate and are glad, because this father of ours was dead and is alive again. He was lost and is found.'"

Somewhere upward and outward a section of the ground above fell. Plumes of dust and dark air lurched like great fluffy beasts across the cavern floor.

"'Prodigal' means 'wasteful,'" Antony said, wishing he had not thrown the mirror away.

"No... but it used to... it used to mean 'one who squanders health... wealth... of all sorts... but why? Why did we change the meaning? The answer to that question may be one of the most important revelations in all of this world's history!"

Antony refused to sit in the junk throne, instead settling into the softest refuse he could find, but eventually after waking to some far settling of metal against metal, he crawled to the prone form to feel the cold muscles of Fobos or Deemos.

He scratched at a tickle behind his ear. From an indeterminate direction, a distant scratching sound caused the tickle. It made his hairline itch.

It had to have been a long hour of waiting, the "critching" and "screetching" sound increasing all the while, before he could make out the shape of a figure descending from the darkness into more darkness. It shimmied down an invisible wire, dust falling with it, sometimes faster, sometimes more slowly. And it was many long minutes later until the figure had landed and walked around sudden chasms up toward Antony.

For the entire visit with Fobos or Deemos, the storm demon inside Antony had been quiet. He had kept expecting Ba'al to roar in his mind, pleading screams for Antony to unleash the nanobotic swarm upon the other Homega Sapiens, but it had been quiet. It gurgled and growled now in his mind, spitting the profanities he had so quickly become familiar with.

The figure stepped nearer, but Antony halted it with his voice. "I mean you no harm, sir, whether you're refugee or from either Army. Do with me what you will." His vision was refusing to focus again, and he just sat, looking down into hands that shook.

"Tempting." The figure said beneath a filter halfmask she unwound, along with goggles and scarf.

"Oh, goddamn it. Ivy of the Grove? Can't believe my…"

"No more. It's 'Ivy of the Nine Fingers' now." She pulled gloves off to show him. "Or 'Savior of the Tithingmen.'"

"Little late for that." The tickle had moved into Antony's throat, and only chuckling would relieve it. The demon in his body mocked his laugher.

"Are those tears of sorrow or joy?" Ivy of the Nine Fingers asked, cocking her head to the side while nearing. She handed him her canteen.

"I just realized, right now, that this is *not* Hell."

"No, Hell has some hope inherent to it. I have none to give, but I have found a way out though."

Antony's smile stretched as painfully as his laugher hurt his parched throat. It disturbed him immensely that he could not recognize the sound echoing back to him from the darkness.

LXXXVII

Meteorite, prehistoric ores, Hyperborean metals enchanted by Hyborean wizard kings?
Its origins and architecture are lost to ages a thousand times removed. But it can be said
with the utmost certainty that those trapped beneath had to evolve to be harder than even
its ancient composition to survive.

—From the oral histories of the Third World Nomads

Flames burned darkly, barely lighting twisted body and battle-field, but it was the only light under the fallen god, and the fire dripped from walls of rock and girder, and it was spat from what Janus at first thought were the corpses of volcanoes holding up the eternal night, but now could see were actually the great ruins of a city block holding up its own streets. Flickering color and heat died everywhere, smothered by the thin air and deepening shadows. No fires grew. Every soldier, of Army of Earth or Heaven, fought not only against fellow man but the settling darkness as well. Metal ribs, some man-sized, some the height of giants, jutted from precariously uneven earth, creating cold forests the armies fought against each other through. The under-gore of ages hung from the ribs like stubborn leaves surviving the winds far into winter.

Janus whispered a prayer to the green-eyed god before striking flint he suspected was too worn. The burlap tied to his torch was too thin. The dust in the shrinking air was too thick. He would have to rely on the light of whatever it was that burned in the viscous drip of the ceiling. Its smoke tickled the tip of his nose, pinched at the depths of his lungs if he breathed it too deeply. He walked up and down a collection of wooden steps and stone that only gave the ap-pearance of steps, resting with many of his soldiers, waiting to rotate back into the massive fray. In the underworld, all men, painted in the same soot and dirt they breathed, from either army, had begun to look indistinguishable over the previous days, and so both sides relied on the viridescent eyes Janus repeatedly had his battalion paint on helm and shield and breastplate. Whatever the source of their green paint, even in the bowels of the collapsed titan, they never seemed to run out. And so it was these eyes that determined friend or foe, guilty or driven.

He fell back down into the squirming masses, exchanging his weapons for those of the fallen, swirling and pushing with hatchet and dagger, striking at weak points between armor and joints. He was a legion unto himself, and he fell more of the Army of Heaven than great sections of his own soldiers even confronted. Because he could see through the dark mobs and walls of dust. Because Her great green iris lit his path for him. Because he was chosen. Because She watched and adored and protected his passage. None of the blood dripping from his eyebrows or knuckles or skirts was his own. It was the remains of the condemned. Because She had condemned them.

Before long he emerged again from the sea of war, wet and panting and coughing up whatever threatened to congeal in his throat. From a dying straggler he took up a bow and orphaned arrow and struck down a screaming assassin that had followed him up into an inverted ledge of pillars both organic and manmade. There was even less light on the height above the battlefield, but, as She certainly watched his progress, he looked as She would down upon the carnage, with supernatural insight into the deadly darkness. His green legions fought on, holding their own against superior number and armaments. With Her vision painted on their armor and cut into their skin, they knew that they too had been chosen, by Janus as he had been picked by Her. He watched over them as She did him. As long as their green symbols remained unmarred they could not be harmed.

Their commander caught his breath, looking out from unmoving shadows, across the screaming waves of men, deaf from the clang of metal on metal, dumb from throats sore from gasping at air thick as blood, to a farther darkness that grew and shrank at the whims of a new fire ignited by the sparks of axe-play. Janus watched the ebb and flow of the violent masses, the rise and fall of the flames as they ate the last of the subterranean atmosphere. To another it would appear that the Army of Heaven guarded hives of ruins staring from countless caves, and that was where he had first commanded his soldiers to strike against, but with Her eyes he now probed the dirty smog of vertical crevices to see the Horde's elite soldiers. They wore hoods over angelically feminine masks. They were a head taller than most other soldiers, and their leather and plate were relatively clean. Two even still held rifles — the first Janus had spotted in days. The elite backed into the shadows of shadows in front of a partially collapsed corridor leading out of the chamber, while the rest of the armies moved away from that side of the cavern.

And so he moved with the dance of the darkness, flickered with the dying flames, and was upon the guards before they could see him. There was little their dead bodies had that he could want. Their clothes were as moldy as his, their armor too stifling in the heavy atmosphere. They had hidden ritualistic daggers that would last only one strike in a real fight. But he took the two rifles to sling over his back. Each had one chambered round. He tried on each of their masks but found them pale comparisons to the one he had left in his troop's camp, somewhere far above ground, over the plain, in some satchel, in some tent. He felt his pack just to make sure. Sometimes he thought that maybe he had brought it with him down into the fall.

He found a scarf he wrapped around his face before heading into the cave, but an immediate coughing fit wet it beyond any use, and he tossed it aside, taking one last look back at the battlefield. An entire section of the far legion had been crushed under a very geometric piece of the cavern that had collapsed. Many of the soldiers struggled to free themselves from a quicksand that had appeared beneath them. They waded but were being struck with spears from men standing at the sudden shore.

And the Nidhogg Virus had finally found its way into the war beneath the collapsed god. Janus had heard the stories back above ground — people suddenly turning inside out, women with fingers bloating until they burst like veined balloons, children with limp bones stretching until they stood over adults before all their joints broke at once, men vomiting up their entire musculature in seconds before succumbing. The horrid stories of the Virus, its reach and immediacy, could only have been myth until one saw it. And here Janus could only stomach one quick look back before entering the deeper darkness, but he saw one soldier's face melt before the disease jumped to another, the new recipient trying desperately to pull his armor off before his chest expanded around it to suffocate blossoming organs.

Someone ran past him in the tunnel before he could react. It was too dark to determine which way the intruder had come from, which army he fought for. At the stranger's passage Janus swore he smelled fresh air for just a second. His sticky hair moved, and he pulled it from his face.

Just as he felt the tunnel narrow, and just as it began to become too steep to climb upward upright, he emerged into a room that held lantern light he had not noticed until he saw eyes of every color turn toward him. What he thought had been Her voice, beckoning him through the ruins, turned out to be the cries of the wounded. He adjusted to the green glow of burning oil and coughed to match the choking voices of the chamber. Each person appeared hurt in a different manner. Some had tied off mutilated limbs. Others held sides where their meager clothing shined wetly. Those appearing without any major wounds wheezed, prone and barely moving.

"You don't have to fear me," he said, his voice thick with phlegm and soot that brought him back into a coughing fit the room loudly returned. He loosened his mismatched breastplate, intending to continue wearing it until he realized just how shallowly he had been breathing. The reverberation it made when dropping to the metal floor sent some of the injured scurrying away beyond the lamp's reach. "I... I can heal you. She! She can heal you."

He found chalk in his side bag. It appeared white until he drew with it on a woman's forehead, where it shined like the paint on his bracer shield. When he was done, all the people still in the room had Her third eye. "See," he whispered, "all you have to do is believe in Her. Follow Her south, ahead of the glaciers, to stay warm and well. I'll be there too, to greet you. And I cannot wait." He bowed, his hands together, multiple blades and dead revolvers jingling. The last they could hear from him, as he followed a light only he could see, was the stretch of leather and the scrape of armor and a gentle, "Until then."

He heard not their continual coughs or whimpering pleas as he chose a widening plain that turned quickly into another incline. He had no idea on what it was he walked, but the strange material pulsed with a light and a warmth from fires somewhere beneath. The vegetable light lifted him through the field of carbon grasses, but the fibers still scratched at his boots, grasped at his clothing. He trudged on.

A soldier, laden with unfamiliar armor ran past him, but Janus was too slow to reach out. But he followed, unable to catch his breath enough to match the woman's speed. *Was it the wounded the Horde protected in these chambers?* he wondered. Unlikely. Was it an escape from the underworld, from the guts of the mechanical god? Or perhaps the Army of Heaven had hoarded some treasures away when the land turned upside down. He hoped he had been on the trail to liberate slaves or food but relished the idea of coming upon real spoils of war. Had the Crown of Washkington been buried along with the battalions of both armies?

A ceiling Janus could barely see collected water before it rained down in a haze. He tasted it, found it corrupted by some mechanism, spat it out into the carbon pasture, and with his pants frayed and armor scratched clear, he emerged into a hive of crisscrossing tunnels that merged and separated like the highways of man-sized ants. The rain had been replaced by steady streams of sand that ebbed and flowed according to what sounded like a parade of aurochs overhead. As soon as Janus could shake it from his hair it would stick to his eyelashes. When he shook it from his clothes it would fill his boots. And during his awkward dance someone slipped by him in the comb of tunnels. When looking to follow them, another soldier moved from behind him. Had his own soldiers made it this far into the labyrinth? Before him or after him?

But he could hear Her voice calling to him, silently echoing, leading him through the connecting corridors. He could see nothing in the now absolute darkness, not where he stepped, not even his hands that felt their way around rock and iron. Most of the tunnels were smooth, either worn over millennia or manmade, but he could feel the mark of Her eye around every turn, either formed by the natural settling of eons or the carving of knife or chisel, every one leading him through the caverns.

Up and out of the awkward climb he crawled into a humidity not experienced since his other life in the athletic stables beneath the Morbis Orbis. It was a moist heat that hit him, reminiscent of fellow gladiators preceding a day's auditions. But he was alone in the crooked chamber, except for its only other occupant. Lit by the glowing rise and fall of a great brazier, its contents tipped and scattered and rainbowed in their warmth, the massive pachyderm filled the majority of the room, and Janus could only assume that it had entered from some corridor that had since collapsed. Great and rough rubble leaned up against many of the sides of the chamber. He could not envision whether the tall room had ever been anything more than a sudden and natural opening down in the earth created when the divine machine had fallen (days? weeks ago?).

Janus walked the sparse space around the mammoth. The downed beast would sigh so deeply, so slowly, that he had to pause periodically against rock and girder to not be crushed by the immensity of the hot creature's body. It was beautiful, and Janus eventually loosened armor straps and sword belts in order to rest against its thick hair. The glow from the coals made it look even redder, while the gore thickening its hide from the numerous spear wounds appeared only as black as its tiny eyes. Its trunk had been hacked off, and it snorted through messy clots of mutilated flesh, and its exhalations slowed as Janus snuggled into masses of hair until he almost disappeared. This close he could see the designs carved into the monster's curved tusks. Letters built of figures and talons, scenes of sun and fire and trumpets, lined the ivory from base to broken tips.

Its muscles were the softening rock beneath new lava, and the crimson mammoth shuffled one last time before Janus closed his eyes. He could feel Her warmth in the humidity, Her heartbeat in the slowing thump of the great animal's blood, and it would have been difficult to determine where memory ended and dream began as the once-gladiator submerged into nostalgia and sleep. The scents were familiar, the heat not unfamiliar. His body, now many years older, was as sore as it often had been under the drumming of the stadium. He was in the athletes' pens once again, but alone. Her voice was not in his ear, but She was close. Her eyes would soon be upon him, and Her gaze would drive his sword forward. When he grounded his competitors to the sandy floor with trident or spear it was Her acceptance he sought.

~

When he woke he thought the red beast's hide had surrounded to suffocate him, but just found that the air had become even thinner yet thicker with dust. The mammoth was not cold, but no longer could Janus feel the great drum of its heart against his cheek.

With reluctance he shook the images of the dream from his head. It seemed blasphemy to wish to be rid of the visions, since She featured so prominently, but the thought of Her signaling down to him from Her gilded balcony tightened his gut and placed a lump in his throat that threatened to choke him. She was wearing his old lord Elmo's spiky headdress and weathered shield of a breastplate. Her eyes were the infected colors of Morbis Orbis' old troll ruler, and Her gaze was unrelenting. If he had not woken, Janus would have butchered every-one in and out of the stands to deserve Her approval. He wiped dry hands on the mammoth's coat until he realized they were becoming raw from the action.

For months after leaving the multitude of lives he had spent experiencing under the prolonged sleep in the City of the Seventh Day, in the infinite dream worlds of Slog Sabbaoth, he had woken daily after re-experiencing those very lives through fitful nights. Only recently had those lives faded completely from his memories, so it bothered him greatly to have suddenly had such a realistic nightmare. Was this another life he had lived in the dreamscapes of Erebus? One too willful to vanish completely from his subconsciousness? For a second it made him doubt his true memories in Below the Brook, and this was something he had not done in a long time.

Some coals still pulsed enough to show the crooked openings out of the chamber, but Janus could not see clearly for the tears in his eyes. He stood slowly, limbs stiff, unforgiving, to dress himself and wash his face in a growing pool of warm water appearing from a crack in the floor. It tasted clear enough to drink, but he knew he was taking a risk when gulping it greedily. He was immediately hungry and ate the rest of flaking rations that he could not remember finding.

After listening at each fallen exit for Her call, he circled the great creature again before finding a mass to nuzzle into. If not for Her voice, spurring him forward, he had no doubt that he would have just slept there until never waking. It would have been a fine end — drifting off to unending sleep embraced by the warmth of such a noble creature. He did not want to go forward and felt that he was leaving some part of himself behind in the chamber. But he gasped deeply at air that was not there, and he moved forward, back into darkness.

Because of a muted echo permeating the metal of surrounding passages, instead of bouncing off them, he could hear the soft sound of cheering from all directions. The revelry was not tinged by angelic song or lyrical prayer, so he assumed it to be the shouts of his own men. It was soon accompanied by the clanging of metal against metal. Blade against shield?

The darkness shifted, light appearing before dissipating, and he found himself scrambling for purchase in the sliding shadows. The ground beneath would disappear before being quickly replaced, and it sounded as if entire walls were sinking and reappearing. His hands found an alcove he pulled himself into before the chamber he was in was submerged in new metal and rock.

Something foul hung and dripped over and around him in the

chamber he crawled into, but he moved forward to the sound of a voice that could only be Her's, toward a light he was certain would turn green the closer he walked. He shed shin guards and extra belts as he moved, even dropping one of his daggers and the more misused of his two rifles. He breathed shallowly, his chest tight, and his armor and coats felt as though they had doubled in weight over the previous minutes.

The new chamber was larger than most of the tunnels, but it was still tight in room and air, for much of it was filled with rubble belying its natural shape and construction. Most of the stone filling the collapsed far side had long ago been carved into the shape of extinct creatures. Girders large and small rounded out the refuse blocking any exit.

One of Janus' soldiers was suddenly at his side. Her torch struggled in absence of oxygen, but it was strong enough to highlight a head wound that refused to heal beneath its orange infection. "They were guarding whatever's behind this recent fall, Commander," she said, coughing into the limited atmosphere and pointing to a prone figure — a stripped and unmoving warrior of the Horde that lay pushed into the only open corner of the room.

"Hold fast," Janus responded, leaning to lift a rock as large as his head. Its movement brought smaller brethren down in a small slide of dust and shiny slivers. "As long... long as you hold Her mark on your armor... you'll be safe under her watch."

The soldier smiled and looked at the green eye painted on her palm. One of her fingers was bent awkwardly in a past episode of poor healing. She began to pull at a length of iron that brought more boulders down to her boots. Janus kicked for leverage and pulled at a similar girder, but he noticed her breath despite the warmth of the chamber.

They rested frequently, their chests rising and falling as though they had been working for hours. Rock they shifted was quickly replaced, and so they climbed to the top of the mound to work against the pinnacle of the collapse. Despite their incessant coughing, the dig was loose and easy, being that the refuse was recent in its placement.

They caught little air at the bottom, hands as dirty as their faces, when the rubble shifted on its own in a wave of rolling cinder blocks and boulders. Janus tasted only dust, could see only tumbling silhouettes, could roll himself out of the way only after he would get struck by any stone. Even when his vision cleared he was waylaid even longer by a coughing fit that brought blood to his tongue.

The soldier that had helped him was nowhere to be seen in the rise and fall of a settling sea of rubble. But she was quickly replaced by another that appeared, stumbling lowly over Janus.

"We have them on a rout, Commander!" he yelled into new air that Janus only just then was realizing was flooding the low room. From his neck hung a thin chain and thick scrap of shrapnel carved with the image of Her eye. "Orders? Do we follow?"

"She watches you, man," Janus mumbled, again coughing into his red hands. "Your deeds go not... unwatched... as long as you are painted green."

The soldier saluted. But before he could turn, his face blossomed extravagantly. Geysers of fluid and cartilage shot from his ears. His limbs folded insect-like but refused to skitter. He swallowed his tongue and cheeks.

So the Nidhogg Virus continued to spread through his forces, Janus lamented, his resolve strengthened by the knowledge that it no doubt was wracking the Horde forces as well.

The chamber was now opened on its large end, but Janus would have quite a precarious climb to exit into new light. His full lungs propelled him forward however. He could smell the air for the first time in recent memory, but he did not like what the scents foretold.

A new room, dimly lit only by jagged lightning-like slivers leading into some great white void beyond another collapse, quickly surrounded him, as did deep, red shadows. The darkness appeared cast by scattered lamps that only ate any light that dared struggle to survive.

crawlch... critch... craaalch...

The sound sent Janus' skin crawling as though from encroaching worms. Even beneath the humidity and his armor, he clenched himself against the shivering of his scalp and back.

chit... chit... crawlch...

Although the movement of ceiling and floor behind him was slight, he wondered if he could have turned back. Feeling around, there was new rock suddenly from where he had come, new girders to bar the backward path, and before he could turn he lost his footing and slid down in a shower of rust and pebbles. The glove on one hand was now torn. His bare other palm was skinned to the muscle, and it stung from the air itself. He held his jaw clenched tightly against the sound, as it was directly above him then. It was the sound of turtles being smashed under boot or glass beetles being crushed in one's hand until shards ground against bone.

caaaah... cheelch... crunch, crunch, crunch...

Something moved out on the other side of the fallen walls. Their forms blocked and revealed the slivers of light and the air leaking into the cracks. So the red shadows drew back the darkness here and there across the room, pulling it like heavy drapes before a black miasma would return to hide the piles of bodies. Before their appearance was again smothered, Janus could only determine one thing. The stiff limbs, the opened rib cages, and the ever-frozen expressions all belonged to Lesser Prophets. So this, Janus realized, was where any Horde general caught beneath the fall of the gargantuan god had retreated to. They had hidden behind their suffocating forces, retreating backward and upward from divine bowels to here... and then what?

cahoop... chut... chut... chumpch...

The bloody tide of dark light shrank before quickly flooding back into the chamber, but Janus had seen him in the short moment. It had been Ammon Mars, great High Commander of the Horde forces. As all Greater Prophets, he was an immense figure, but the mound of thighs and torsos in which he was immersed made him appear even larger, even redder. There was little of his snow-white beard and mane uncaked by congealed flesh.

citch... crumpch... crumpch...

The giant's lips split and his gums bled from the splinters of bone stuck in his teeth, yet still he broke hands in his jaws. Still he picked at the piles for any leg meat unchewed, any complete ribs not snapped and sucked.

Janus took stock of the weapons still sheathed and tied to his person. He had to lighten his load while still being prepared to do battle with the High General. This was the fight he had been waiting for. This was why he had moved through his own battalion on each battlefield over the previous months, fighting at the front of his soldiers, hoping to each time come upon a worthy competitor at the summit of every battle. But he never had. But here, under god and under God's Gaze, under unlit days, weeks, warring against Horde remnant through the steaming guts of a leviathan, under the dead night of an upside down city, never certain whether he was awake or dreaming, here he found the only challenge in the entire Army of Heaven. This was the fight he had been waiting for his entire life. And She was here to applaud him. Somewhere out in the sheets of shadows of stadium and seating, beyond a silent audience, she stood from her gilded balcony to glow down her stiff green glow upon his raised arms and blades.

He knelt to retrieve the weapons he had chosen from the puddles and rubble, kissing the eyes tattooed on his worn palms. From the angle and slithering light he could see that the Nidhogg Virus had penetrated the room. Although just torn corpses, the Lesser Prophets were still affected. Their quartered figures bloated silently but violently — limbs, suddenly infected and suddenly animated into new but short lives.

It was only when Janus began to pray for victory that Ammon Mars stood, hunched in the hanging rock of the ceiling. His engorged girth created new shadows to be pulled and pushed by the red tide. His teeth, continually sucked clean, were the only pale features in the entire chamber. They were almost translucent, and Janus could see the Virus' infection working on not the great Antony himself but on the remains of those he had feasted. Blood bubbled and sharpened solidly. Flesh crackled, stretched, and inflated.

It was like a sudden thunderstorm — the Greater's steps trampling toward Janus. Countless fluids sprayed him as he leaped aside, holding his rifle near side to fire off its one round at the close immensity. He had no idea it the shot landed or where and so swung the weapon up and around. It was like striking pure an iron statue, and the gun bent before breaking. Janus immediately struck with a sword broken to the length of a dagger, following through by spinning and swinging with a backhanded hatchet. Both he left behind in the meat of his adversary. An entangling ground moved beneath his decomposing boots, and he attempted to control his fall by rolling into and with the sliding shadows. He crawled with the red darkness. He pulled bayonets from his belt before throwing them at the pursuing giant. He found a short and blunt flail to twirl from the soft refuse. He spat profanity into the wall to bounce his voice to opposite corners. He held one hand up to the phantasm stands.

High General of the Army of Heaven, Ammon Mars, shook and flailed great fists as red as volcanic rock at each end of the chamber, before his intestines flooded the floors. His stomach appeared in the air but flapped impotently, held against its will by an inflamed esophagus.

Janus was immediately upon the Greater. He climbed the hilts of the bayonets sticking from a blistering back to reach shoulders and to pummel the general with the flail. He rode the red man as though he were a bucking beast of burden until the giant collapsed in a heap amongst the remains of the Lesser Prophets. Using any blade he could find, Janus removed the general's large scalp and held it up to the bloody darkness. He was certain that green eyes flashed their approval.

Without catching his breath, he walked the uneven and moving ground. It took him longer to cross the soft refuse than it had to best his opponent, but he eventually made it to the far wall of criss-crossed bronze and fallen stone. With frequent breaks, it took him longer than expected to take down the rubble, and his unaccustomed eyes squinted at even the dim light of a clouded dusk. The cold air pained his mouth, his throat, and his lungs in its freshness, but he had returned to the surface — a place he had days ago resigned to never seeing, never feeling, again. It was as he remembered, colorless in and below the sky, but he did not even mind the bite of the atmosphere of his bare skin. For he was free at last.

He kissed what remained of the tattooed eyes on his palms, and, with his entire body steaming in the winter air, he walked the Horde camp, coughing specks of blood into his hands. The thin soldiers paid him no attention, even as he stole their rations and resupplied himself in coats and blades. They all just stared at fires they repeatedly restocked from diminishing kindle carts. Janus looked to anyone worth challenging but found only old white men and young brown boys. He climbed up a perch that had been made of girders nearly rusted through. Out across the plains, to the gray east, he could see the war still raging. He saw a hint of green in the smoke and exhaust. He would return to the war and She would return to him. He believed it down in the depths of his mute soul.

A new sun had appeared during his absence. *Wyrmwood* blossomed largely like a new bruise in the sky, fed from new fires and new blood.

LXXXVIII

Electric ebon
specter suckles the Garden.
Nectar is first sin.

—unknown

have to go back," Teca said, scanning the far western horizon for any sign of any elevation, but, as usual, she could see only smoking plains with no appearance beyond the flatness of prairie touching prairie. Occasionally, the dust of some battle would appear, or the exhaust of some dying machine exhaling its last, or the plume of some exploding Horde keg bomb, and each blossom of smoke would trick her into thinking that the remains of the Army of Earth had not left the Black Hills, or the new mountain corpse of the mechanical god, behind. But each day's trudge east told her otherwise. No one knew how far they had traveled from the collapse of the Quicken Engine, from the hills of her home — the snow-choked skies of the day and the cloud-smothered stars of the night being no navigable help — and no one could determine how far they had yet to walk. All they knew to do was to keep one day's walk ahead of the pursuing forces. And they had barely done that. "And you wouldn't even notice, would you? You'd just find some other filly to follow you into your…" The chill stilled her lips and thoughts, but only for a second. "If I die, will you forget me?"

"I would never stop until you were avenged. Your killer would die by my hand, or I would never be happy again."

"Every day I'm away…" Teca continued, naked but enjoying the presence of snowflakes as they settled on her sweat, "…every mile we walk farther from… it's the uncertainty that's actually killing me." She closed the pavilion's heavy drapery but still paused long enough for a shiver to settle, to wait for her breath to return and heart to calm before she turned back to the chimenea, to its warmth and Wulf's gaze. "It eats at me… not knowing. It could be chaos in the Needles. I just don't know… it could be mass looting. Without a High Lord, the Order could be in ruin. Or someone could have stepped in to fill the void. There're always monks with… certain ambitions… agendas." She crawled back into the cot, under the bearskin, and caressed the prominent bone of his hip with the very tips of her fingers. He had lost weight over the past week, as they all had. It seemed the constant rationing of food would never end, just as the tiring pace of their march was difficult to see beyond. She was unsure, but believed that this was the first morning the Army had rested in days.

Wulf returned her touch but sat up, and she nuzzled into the humidity of his chest.

"What if Shriven hasn't turned back to Bab'lon?" she asked herself, clicking her tongue. "What if he saw this as an opportunity to take the Order of the Creed as his own? To bring his fallen order back into the civilized parts of the country?"

Wulf moved beneath her, and she watched him take up a pair of shears as he sat up straighter, sighing deeply before holding his breath. "We can go back, love," he whispered. "Just the two of us. I'll send the Army into MANN Land where..."

She slid up and behind him on the cot, adjusting pillows and wrapping her legs around and under his arms. "Let me do it," she said. His hair was longer than she had ever seen it on him. It curled ridiculously at this length, fighting against itself. He may have technically been a northerner, but he knew not how to tame it for battle, how to wrap it under a helmet. She pulled it up into a rat king but hesitated. He was anticipating the Army of Heaven to catch up to them. He was preparing for an end to the War, one way or another. "No. They need you. When we're all safe, when they're beyond the Horde's reach, I'll go back. You can come with me, if you want. Just promise me it'll be soon."

She found his hair tougher to cut than expected. There was no longer a sharp blade in the entirety of the Army of Earth, and the scissors was no exception. Once the bulk of his mane was on the frozen ground, single and curled strands blown by hidden leaks of air into the small marquee, she went to work tidying up the hair over his neck and ears. It was still thick but no longer curly, and it was a darker blond closer to his scalp.

Done, she crawled to sit in his lap, facing him, her legs still holding firm around his waist, blushing as she settled in, skin becoming even redder. She tightened her grip until he closed his eyes. And that was when she struck.

He smiled fully, against his will, and shook his head slightly, careful of the close blades. The majority of his beard lay in clumps blowing slowly across the puddles before either of them spoke beyond laughter.

"What is the Low Coda?" he asked, still smiling as she blushed again.

"What brought that up? What is that?"

"I... heard about it... once. Do you know?"

"It... why would you ask me? It's just a rumor." But under his stare she got up, now not impervious to the coolness of the tent, and she found the soapy water that had also grown cold. She returned to him to lather his mouth and cheeks, his chin and neck, before unscrewing the single tie of the shears, bringing one of the blades to his face.

Her hand moved so slowly over his whiskers, and she never cut him, but she was obviously agitated. His eyes, so completely blue but so completely different from each other, never left her own, even though she would not meet his gaze.

"There are things best left unknown," she finally said. "Do you remember that... those things we... you and I... and Aesarean... saw under the streets of Quicken... in the sewers..."

"What?" he then stayed her hand. "Back then? Way back..."

"I know, but I'll never forget."

"I didn't know it then," Wulf said, letting her resume her slow, smooth drag of the edge up his neck, "but that being, that shiny being was a member of the Temporal Guild. Why it was..."

"No, not that. I'm talking about that ancient Greater Prophet. And Aesarean! And this... RackBreak Antony. As a paladin I was initiated into secret knowledge, old knowledge. Blind Libra made judgments that the common person is not ready for. I'm not saying I agree with it or even believe it, but just... just don't ask me to tell."

When she finished she kissed him on the smoothest areas of his cheekbones. Then his chin, then, turning the side of his face that held Yggr's Eye away from her, she nibbled his ear before whispering, "Please promise me this will all be done soon. That we'll all be safe soon, and, yes, yes I want you to come with me, come back to the Hills with me, and we can be... something... something together."

Before he could speak she had jumped from the cot to dig amongst her shoulder packs. She found pieces of her meager underarmor, re-stocked kindle in the chimenea, and continued to look through her belongings at the same time. Jumping back into the cot, silks hanging from her thin frame, she draped a long necklace over his shoulders.

"I know you manly 'midgardians' only wear rings, but I made this. It's Black Hills silver. The stone is tourmaline. It's all I could find to match your…"

He was tracing the lips of her smile with the fingers of one hand, and the pale line low on her belly with his other hand — without realizing, she thought.

"Stop it," she said, a bit too harshly for her own liking, and she stood back up to hide the old scar with her stance and new clothes she unpacked.

"I'm sorry."

"Just… just end this, please, you know you can…"

Wulf also stood to dress and to look at himself in the fog of a salvaged hand mirror. He had to crouch in some parts of the tent. The space was much smaller than his pavilion, but everyone in the Army of Earth — what was left of it — had to leave much behind in the drifts of the prairie for the pace he had set for his soldiers and refuges. They were being followed by forces twice their size. The Horde had also been wracked by the Nidhogg Virus, but its numbers seemed always to get replenished by stray forces coming from behind, where the Army of Earth daily held funerals over shallow graves for the victims of pneumonia and starvation, its ranks becoming ever smaller. It had at first always been children and elderly that the green men improvised last rites over, but the prior few days had shown that actual soldiers were not immune to the infections and worsening weather. There was no protection from wind and consumption out in the open plains.

Teca grabbed at him by his short hair, putting their foreheads together. "You know what to do…"

"I told you…"

"Just let him go!"

"It's not that easy."

"You said it yourself! The Horde out there is only following his last orders. They're trying to rescue him. Give him back to them. With… with their cities falling, there is no reason they would be out this far… to wipe us out? To kill every last one of us?"

"That is his goal."

"Bullshit!" She tried pushing him away but only managed to fall backward herself. "I don't know what you're not telling me, but you're putting yourself… or whatever you two have with each other… above the lives of all those families out there. Where're we going? We'll never make it! We'll freeze before we get there if we're not gunned down first." She pulled a dagger from her scattered bags and brought it to his throat. "Let him go!"

The light would shift in the small pavilion from time to time, constantly reminding them that it had been hastily constructed from the remains of many fallen tents. The winds moved the layers against and away from each other. It was always loud in a way Teca had yet to grow accustomed to. In the new light she could see that she had not shaved him as closely or as evenly as she had thought. And she had cut him more than once.

Before she realized it, her arm was bent at the elbow, and her dagger went one way while her wrist painfully went the other. Wulf had suddenly disappeared into her peripheral before she was lifted from below. She found herself face down on the cot again with his voice closely in her ear, and she reached back, placing her hands over his, moving them slowly and deliberately to areas that had yet to grow cold.

~

She dreamt of an event she often confused for a dream. It had happened before they had come to the Black Hills, in the weeks of warring and traveling in the opposite direction on the plains. Assassination attempts had been so common that they were tempted to host a holiday whenever a day passed without one. And this had been one of those days, so, for the first time in a week, she had slept next to him with her guard down. Yet when she woke, uneasily, she had thought it had been from his snoring, but it had been something else that took many seconds to determine. A sleet had been falling straight down against the pavilion all throughout their slumber — a wet but solid fall of flakes creating an unbroken, surrounding hum. The rhythm had permeated her dreams. She breathed according to it, so it was the barely perceptible interruption in the hum that she woke to. From this, they had caught the killer before he had snuck into the tent. He had sharpened his teeth and fingernails and covered both in a poison that would soon consume him, but his plan had been to take out the Liege of Foes first.

Now, whenever she woke to some far off sound, she would remember the incident but had difficulty telling if it had been an old nightmare, a new dream, or an actual day in the chaos that had been her life for the past half year. But this time she was waking to the familiar far confusion of exploding gunpowder. And the sound would again mean to pack up the lessening caravans and move out into increasingly unyielding drifts of what now everyone admitted was permanent snow.

Wulf stood, as she had recently, a naked silhouette in the open drapery of the tent. The chimenea's coals choked on the new breeze, their heartbeat losing all color. Surprised to find herself mostly dressed, Teca put on her mismatched boots against the frozen grass, her short coat against the flakes flittering maniacally around the tent's entrance. She had developed the curious tic of shaking her hair out to cover the burn scars above and behind her ears. She had been shaving underneath where she was growing the rest out, resigned to the fact that there were areas where her hair would never grow back.

"It's time to move on," Wulf said into the wind.

But Teca answered, "Who is it?"

"I haven't heard back in over a day, but it must be Damn Antony's men, from that direction." He talked more to himself. "If I move Janus' troops back I expose the northern family caravan... if the Horde came up from below..."

"I can pull one of my legions from the front..."

"Teca, you have to go."

"I can..."

"I mean you. *You* have to go. Go back to the Hills."

"How will that..."

"I can spare a small escort. They won't be looking for anyone heading back west. I... I think there is a dip a few miles from here, from some dried lake, with ruins of docks and cabins. You can hide there until the Horde passes. Then go home."

She touched his arm, felt the old and poorly healed scars. "Not with..."

"Why are you even here?" He did not turn but gestured to the scars, as well as others on his thigh. "See these? Before the War... before... all of this... I found what I realized were the ruins of some Libran temple... your lost Order, down in the blackest lands of Nod. I could see visions of what they found when they declared the swamp as their own. They called her Libra, at first, but came to know her as Nyctanassa, and they loved her in a way... in a way they never loved your blind angel. And she consumed their minds and body and... eventually even more. But I now think that she actually was Libra, she just had to change as they had, in order to..."

"I don't see what this..."

"Why are you here?"

"You know why! I…"

"You don't belong here, with me. Go back to your people."

"I know what you're doing, asshole, you don't have to be so cruel about it!"

They both ducked as a loud light hit closer to them than they expected. The drapes whipped shut in a warm wind, and Wulf immediately ran to gather underarmor and leather and his cloak. Yin hung from ribbons from the low pinnacle of the tent, refusing to sway in breeze or vibrations. The crimson blade, even hidden, made Teca's skin crawl by appearance alone, whether it cooed or cried somewhere in the howl of the wind. She had never been able to determine what hide had been tanned for the dark sheath or grip.

"I can go…"

"Go home!" Wulf interrupted. "There's nothing for you here. You could be doing some good with… whatever waits back at the Needles." He called at the entrance for his man-at-arms, and as the curtains and ties opened there were far more lights out in the storm of the prairie than when the tent had just closed. "Run," he told the split-lip man, "spread the word. We are to move out immediately. Within the hour!"

Wulf held his head, and Teca buckled sword and assorted other knives. Neither moved toward each other, but she eventually said, as fireworks burned nearby, "You do know why I stayed. I know…"

"You said it yourself, girl. These people need me. This is my life, however much shorter it may be. Your life lies elsewhere. Go! You're not a soldier!" he shouted, tearing Yin down and heading out into the brightening sky.

"And you're not a king!" he heard her say from behind the falling curtain.

He had no idea what time of day it was. With clouds so thick, it could have been night for all he could remember. Whether the families all around him had already heard his command or not, most of the yurts and tents were already being broken down.

"Master?" an elderly soldier with a face so pinched it appeared painful asked, "my Crimson Queen asks as to what battalion should join the engagement. What is the…"

"None," Wulf answered, quickly leaving the messenger behind. "All camps are to move forward, but send three riders to the tail legions to report back as soon as possible."

The Agent of MANN was suddenly at his side, but his size and multiple legs were making it difficult to keep up in the drifts and collapsing camps. "I will once again, Wulf, warn you away from your present course. I can give no guarantee that what's left of the Army of Earth will be welcomed in MANN states."

"We're not an army anymore. You'll turn refugees away? Even as the Horde moves in on your territory?"

There was a long silence from the metallic insectoid, but he continued to follow Wulf directly through arming legion and packing commune until they both stood outside a tall but thin yurt that still stood touched only by the accumulating snow.

Wulf found another messenger. "Tell the High Plains Drifters to collect and burn any of the faering planks that are left. They're staying to guard the rear. When the Horde is close enough, they can lob the remaining powder kegs at the fires."

The Agent of MANN interjected with, "You do realize that will be the last of the fuel for any night fires?" Wulf waited to enter the tent, just staring at the multiple opaque eyes until the Agent said, "I am an objective observer, only present to record and report." The mechanical avatar was left outside in the rising commotion.

A tent sentry closed the partially solid, partially fabric door behind Wulf. The cage inside took up most of the interior, dwarfing the shriveled prisoner, but it was not the sad sight that affected Wulf as he first entered but the smell. From the stench, one would have expected to find a drowned hound open and spilling from infected bowels, but the cage held only a man — one emaciated to unfamiliarity. He was close-shaven, and his gaunt cheeks were covered in scratches that would not heal. From refusing to eat, malnutrition had thinned his hair, discolored his sagging skin, and colored his finger and toenails.

"Let the peace ah the Choir rule in head and heart. As members ah one body you ah, and you ah called to peace. In this way you will be seen as thankful. As thankful, you will rule."

Wulf noticed immediately that the starved man did not stutter when he sang his quiet prayer. He did not choke over the stump of his tongue when he was immersed in his song.

"Every effort to live in peace with everyone is ah holy act. Without holiness you will never hear the rhythm ah the Watchers in your soul.

Your spiritual body will forever be beyond your reach."

Wulf mumbled, "Peacemakers who sow in peace reap a harvest of joy here and beyond. Live as brothers with the enemy."

The starved man woke at this, and behind the layers of lids his eyes had clouded, and it was impossible to determine what faded color they were. He seemed to gag on a throat near collapse before he went back to his prayers.

"Surprised?" Wulf said. "The Song has penetrated even into those that follow me. I hear it from time to time."

"Repay no evil for evil," the prisoner sang. "Play not insult against insult. You ah called to present blessing to evil, for in this example will you open ears to the Choir, and in this life will you rise again with deserved body, new and strong." Beside him sat a bowl of untouched broth, its odd spoon partially hidden behind it. "Whoever would love life would live lovingly. Always turn from evil and do good always. Pursue peace. Seek the hand ah the enemy as he hangs from the cliff ah evil."

The guard shivered in the corner before saying, barely louder than the prisoner, "He... he asks to be shaved daily, sir, but don't worry I have him tied, even though he couldn't harm any of his fleas. But he won't eat, sir, so I've always had to make him, force him some. Otherwise, he ain't no trouble. Just sings day and night." The guard was sweating despite the breeze that blew in beneath each corner of the fabric.

The constant draft did nothing for the stench though, and Wulf pulled his scarf up, beneath his hood and over half his face, before sighing and looking around at the interior. Every scrap of fabric and hide left was becoming increasingly as valuable as gold. Yet here he had kept Handsome Gibbet hidden away in the tent for far too long.

"If I let you out, will you call off your troops?"

Seeing the old man stretch closely was like watching the dead press against the inside of their coffins. His legs made louder sounds than the coming battles when he stood, rickety and unused to the movement. He pressed his head against the bars of the cage, and they immediately made colorful marks on his face.

"If you let me out..." he whispered, his multiple eyelids closed. The guard shuffled uncomfortably in the back of the tent as Handsome's voice rose in anger if not in volume. "Ah will make sure that every shit-eating grinner in this ah... entire camp of murderers and lying prostitutes is wiped off the face of the dirt! I won't stop ah... ah, until you are all hanging from perches made from the bones of your sh... sh, children!" The stutter had returned, creeping past his double layers of missing teeth and receded gums. He stumbled back onto his haunches, going immediately back into his song. "You know these things, so that in the Choir you will have peace. In this world you will have trouble, but take heart. As the Song overcomes the world with peace, so too should it overcome your heart with the same, so that you too can show the face of peace unto the world."

"The war is over," Wulf said.

"Oh, yeah, ah... ah, know," Handsome said, quickly and loudly back on his feet and against the bars. "The Enemy has conquered and rapes teh... the... the Territories! You broke the Library ah Panoply! All those histories lost! Puh... plague puh, punishes the Sons ah the Righteous, newives — by your word, on a holiday, no less — rose up in the Capital and beyond to cut the throats ah their husbands as they slept in righteous sleep, but Heaven still lives in muh... me, you befouling ass. Ah... hugh... have been saved. The plague does not teh... touch me. Ah am chosen. As lugh... as long as ah still breathe, Heaven lives in me, and the War will go on!"

"You live only because I had you quarantined, but no matter. If you promise to call off your armies, I will let you go, and you will never hear of me or my people again."

"Yuh... you are the Devil's foul excretion, yuh, you know that? Yeh... you come to me now... you must really be desperate!" Wulf had to lean closer in order to hear the whispers. "You lost your traitor wuh... wizard. All your fuh... forces... decimated..." He knocked away a cup of water the guard had been trying to wet his drooling mouth with. "Yuh... you're scared. You better be! You're on the verge ah extinction. Show you muh... mercy? Have you ever showed the fugh... faithful mercy? Ah wuh... watched as Ablution burned, you pious fraud! You even remember that town? Ah saw you buh... butcher an entire legion as it retreated. Speak not teh... to me ah mercy!" The blood left his face as he fell to the bottom of the bars, wheezing and with old scars appearing across his face like tiny maggots working their way into his wrinkles.

Wulf sighed as Handsome resumed his prayer, his breath slowing, his voice growing to a loud whisper. "In the peace ah the Song, ah will lie down and sleep, for the Divine Choir alone makes me dwell far from the Deaf and Blind, and it is this peace ah will gift to the land in turn." But, like a coiled snake of bones, he sprang at the cage. "Huh, have you ever huh... heard ah Mad Rocks? Uh... ah course not, you ignorant, stupid, ass fart! When Washkington and his men came to the suh... surface, lifetimes ago, they found ah commune far east ah gardeners, vegetarians, stupid ass fart pacifists. They had buh... built a grand kingdom of pyramids, aquaducts, sewers, buh... but they were lazy, stagnant. They had not expanded. So much land to grow out into, but they just wallowed in mud, eating their turnips, making love to the dirt. Washkington saw the puh... potential. It was ah shee... short war, and some coward shit-eater stabbed Washkington in the back. The commune went back to their shrinking land, and eventually they faded away. Their pyramid crumbled in time, gardens grew back into the land, and finally, ah juh... generation later, Mad Rocks and his families were forgotten. And who duh... do we remember today?" His voice whistled through weedy teeth, and Wulf adjusted his scarf over his nose. "Ah... ah will... ah have been chosen to write the history, of the now and the forever, and you will not appear anywhere ah... in it! Nuh... no one will remember your nuh... name! You and your puh... people... all you puh... pagan bullies will die horribly, puh... painfully out on these cold fields, and you will all be forgotten. No one will ever hear your story! Ah will make sure of that!"

The thought of peering into Handsome's mind brought bile to Wulf's lips, but he began to consider it as the old man pulled himself back up against the bars. Thin fingers turned white in their clenching.

"You ah all luh... lazy sluts. Why couldn't you just luh... leave us ah... alone? We of the *Ashmedai Adat El* just wanted to be left alone, in our Territories, live and worship in peace. The one ugh... eternal right ah man, the only unassailable, universally agreed upon, natural right ah the individual, that ah the right to worship in peace, you felt to become insulted by. Ugh... oh yes, you ah the victim in this world. You and your gaggle ah misfits ah so imposed upon by people's freedom you would burn the world to the ground just so everyone nuh... knows how upset you ah. Wuh... well, cry to the sky wuh... why don't you!"

Wulf closed his eyes and folded his hands. It would take some work, and it would mean spending more time in the old man's mind than he knew would be healthy, but he could think of no other solution in such a short time. The vibrations and shouts of war sounded louder with each passing minute. He steeled himself for the process, preparing to pick through despicable thoughts and perspective to erase Handsome's every memory of ever meeting Wulf. Peeking into his mind, he started searching for the encounters in Megrim and was struck with heartbreaking nostalgia for the home and friends he had found there, the nights warming in...

"Well, well, what we have here?"

Wulf collapsed on the ground. The clenching pain had appeared so suddenly that he did not have the chance to catch himself. An arm hit the floor awkwardly. His cheek scraped tent pole or hard ground. The voice — a scorpion's skitter over his psyche before the burning hot poisonous stab of its stinger into the soft meat of his brain — continued its assault.

"You forget, wretched worm, me always protect flock!"

"Ahhhrghhh!" Wulf's mind burned as coldly as the depths of some long forgotten sea trench never touched by light, with the ice of the universe's last comet as it spun and slowed irresistibly beyond the last galaxy that had turned away from expansion eons before. *"I know..."* he thought to the Angel, *"...that you are..."*

"No more tricks!"

Chem-Oshmelech's frozen words branded directly into the gray matter of his brain.

"Me free! Faithful flock no need fear wretched worm's mind rapes ever again!"

Slayd had warned him of divine intervention, but the pinching vibrations in Wulf's head kept him from being able to recall any defense the sorcerer had readied him with. "You... can't... interfere...directly... in... the... lives..."

"When wretched worm sins against faithful flock me must make presence known! Wretched worm seeks to rape mind of me favored shepherd! Oh, wretched worm think it hero of story? Wretched worm is warmonger! Wretched worm is mind raper!"

Wulf was barely aware of the sensation at the sides of his head as his own fingers dug into his temples, trying desperately to release the frigid pressure. "Because they invaded first!"

"What is word... invade? Faithful flock saves souls!"

"Enslaves them!"

"That their choice! Who you, wretched worm, to insult free will? You mortals obsessed with free will! You no respect this?"

And the presence was gone as suddenly as it had appeared, but the angel left behind pain that only slowly melted, an ice that cracked before its drool still slithered to chill the wrinkles of Wulf's brain. The pain shivered down his spine, freezing his arms and hands into twisted rigor and numbing his legs into paralysis. He could barely inhale for the cold air in his lungs. But he could feel the steaming dung of someone else's breath as his eyelids were forced open.

"Yuh... you see now, yuh... you despicable ass lick?" Handsome spat. "Ah... ah can't be touched, can ah... I?" The curved tip of a sharpened spoon wavered near, tickling the tips of Wulf's eyelashes. His face twitched, trying desperately to turn and close his eye. "Would your goat-fucking followers recognize you without this eye? Ah... I wonder. Ah... all your flags will be torn down by then." The spoon, caked with cold mold, scratched at the granite with its jagged edge, bringing new vibrations to Wulf's brain. "Ah... all your banners and books burned by then."

"This wasn't part of the deal," the guard said behind him, his eyes watering as he called the tent sentry inside. Both cringed at the sight and sound of metal against granite. "Sorry, um... sir, my liege, but he promised... I mean, I got nothing to go home to... no home to go home to, and he promised a newife and... we can't jus'... we can't just leave 'im..."

"Shut up," the sentry said, adjusting scarf over mouth and furred visor over forehead. "Let's go."

And Wulf was suddenly alone with the tithingman and the stink of the tent. The breeze beneath the canvas, skittering over snowflake and pebble frozen to unyielding dirt, did nothing to lessen the unclean and hanging atmosphere.

"Can you hear it?" The tithingman gestured backward to the cracks of explosions sounding outside over the camps. "You have nothing left to lose. Just guh... give up, guh... give in. You teh... took from me once. Now ah return the favor. The ah... only difference is ah... I became stronger. You won't survive your crucible. You don't nuh... know the love, the comfort, of nuh... never being lonely. Ah... of being chosen. Can you see it? The ah... end ah your kind's reign?" He tilted the spoon, and the meager light of the interior bent awkwardly across the slant of its curve as it slid between quivering eyelids.

Outside the prison tent, in a wind that was appearing lowly as the yurts were disassembled and tent poles taken down, the Agent of MANN was scanning the nearing fires of the western horizon. The camps all around him were disappearing respectably quickly, although he would have expected nothing less from something that had become a daily occurrence. Did what was left of the Army of Earth know how close they were veering into MANN Lands? More importantly, he wondered, did they realize how close they were to the verge of extinction? He predicted they would all be dead from old wounds, disease, or the dropping temperatures within days. But, from the looks of the encroaching searchlights, and the sounds of the nearing cannon fire, it did not appear that they would last even that long. The vocalizer on the avatar unit made a sound akin to a sigh, and he was glad that the wind had picked up to absorb the sound before the two men came out of the tent flaps.

One of them, chewing his lower lip until it appeared gangrenous, turned a shade of green at the Agent of MANN's appearance. He started to sputter excuses until the other soldier, who had been previously guarding the entrance to the tent, whispered, "Don't mind him. He can't do nothing. He don't care." They argued over the best route out of the moving camps, but quickly decided just to head around south of the closing sounds of battle.

If a mechanoidis virtual unit could appear anxious, the Agent of MANN would have. Something was wrong. He scanned the horizon in additional wavelengths but found such chaos in temperature and movement that no definitive picture could be established. Scanning the tent found only two figures in an uncompromising position, with only one having a categorized se'print. He parted the untied curtains with one pod and entered on the metal trotters of the other five.

Handsome jumped up, standing above the moaning Wulf, wiping more blood from his hands than could be absorbed by the dirty scraps of his nightshirt. The old man froze, unmoving except for the long strands of his remaining hair tickling his gaunt shoulders. He stared at the metallic monstrosity, unable to judge where the seven flat disks of eyes where looking.

"Drop it," the Agent of MANN said, his voice obviously cracking through the hidden vocalizer, but it took many quiet seconds before the tithingman rolled his fingers open to drop the eyeball on the ground. It just stuck to the congealed sand, unable to roll.

Handsome just stared at his twisted and dark reflection in the low shine of the giant insect. When he stared long enough he swore he could see colored lights from deep within the metal thorax. They swam slowly, disappearing, reappearing, intermittently changing. Those of warm colors only mutated warmly. Those of cold colors evolved only amongst the cool.

The tithingman, almost imperceptibly, stretched the hand holding the sharp spoon back toward Wulf's wet face. His opposite leg lifted, slower than a clock, to eventually settle on top of the gore-flecked eyeball.

The Agent of MANN was just a large tin statue barring the curtains to the outside world.

The eyeball popped under the pressure of Handsome's toes, and an invisible pinprick of light seared the air in the tent, connecting the tithingman to the Agent. Handsome felt no pain, only a tickling in the knuckles of his spoon hand as all the fingers were laser scalpeled away in the blink of his many eyelids. His legs gave out at the sight of his cleanly mutilated hand, but he found them kicking at the sharp floor, pushing him toward the far corner of the tent where he could remember the under-breeze blowing strongest. He held the cauterized wounds with his other hand as he crawled backward, considering only briefly to collect the scattered fingers, before burning himself on his own tiny stumps. This sent him scrambling even more quickly, and he was soon scraped and bruised after climbing under the tent into new wind and war.

Looking from Wulf to corner to tent ceiling, the Agent of MANN just scanned all the surroundings, realizing that there was nothing he would see in any wavelength that would tell him what to do next. His hexapods folded beneath him so that he could look at Wulf face to face. The man still bled from the empty socket, so after a quick ultra and altersound scan, the Agent of MANN moved even closer and initiated a lower ocelli laser.

Not long after, the avatar emerged from the tent, striking four insectoid legs into the solid ground for purchase. The two other pods held Wulf. The man's empty eye socket smoldered, but the smoke disappeared into the wind just as his screams did. As the Agent of MANN set him on the ground, wrapping him in his cloak, his metathoraxal sensors alerted him of the approaching men, but he just crouched prone as the machete struck against the back of his prothorax plates.

"It killed the Liege!" a voice was heard to say.

A pitchfork bent against one of his legs, but it shattered, and a joint twisted.

"Quick! Look what it's done!" another voice shouted, as a blunt object was brought across the avatar's triangular head.

"Before it can get up!"

"Shoot it close up!"

"It won't break!"

But it did. Carbon bindings did not crack, but they broke free. Limbs turned until the Agent of MANN was crumbled in a heap on the snow. Something solid was being wrenched between his thoracic connections, while a block of cinder was repeatedly being brought down over the main sensor array of his head.

"It's killed him! The Liege of Foes! Over here!"

The last scan package sent, far over the miles to the MANN city of Simon, before the internnae was shook from the avatar's head, was of the masses of the Army of Heaven moving slowly and deliberately closer and closer.

LXXXIX

We ironically call it Crater Hill — and retroactively and subsequentially the Battle of Crater Hill — for nothing less than literal reasons. Ancient maps show the area as one of a rolling plain topped by a small hill. But after the last battle of the Winter of the Sword there was nothing left but a hole in the ground.

—From the oral histories of the Third World Nomads

He had been talking to the young woman next to him, giving her the instructions on when to cover him and how exactly to aim the sling at so angled a target, when he noticed the smell leaking from her slightly parted lips. How long exactly had she been dead? Damn Antony could not say. The frozen air preserved any bodies to a confusing degree, but the abandoned farm had only been under siege for a couple of hours, the trenches being dug only an hour prior, so he closed her eyes knowing that he had to have been the only person to notice. He took and tied her scarf around the elbow in his coat that had been wearing away over the past week, and he pocketed her satchel of stones and bearings and the sling they were meant for. He passed the information down the line to let others know that a small parka and boots were up for grabs. Then he began repeating his instructions to a flaking and oozing elderly woman that crawled by at the bottom of the trench. She was one of the few in the Army of Earth that he had seen recently holding a rifle, and she scowled as he kept repeating his questions, the dimples in her chin joining the wrinkles at the edge of her lips.

"Do you have the ammo for that thing?" he asked again, receiving just more of the same glare. He had stopped hiding his face over the past week, figuring that what was left of the Army either would not recognize nor care anymore if a Lesser Antony fought amongst them. He often wondered if his face had become too scarred or sickly lately to be confused with a member of the Brotherhood. Did anyone care of such things anymore? He himself was having difficulty even remembering which side of the war he fought on. None of it mattered anymore. Only survival mattered. And to survive he had to take out the sniper at the top of the silo, and to do that he needed someone to cover his run.

He named the old woman "Pat," as she refused to talk to him, and Pat dug the heels of her boots into the ice of the trench as she prepared to peek over the drifts. Antony leapt up and over and ran, sometimes on two feet, sometimes on all fours, sliding to a halt behind what he thought was a pile of tractor tires. Despite the gloominess of the sky, there was still a glare from all around the ground. He had found himself snow blind over most of the afternoon. His goggles did little good, as scratched and fogged as they had gotten. And so he only now realized that what he hid behind was a pile of bodies. They were soldiers, no doubt, but from which side he could not tell. He could see only broken chainmail linking them together, as did the trails of frozen snot and blood.

The old woman had not fired, and Antony lifted his goggles to glare back toward the trenches, but snow devils had whipped up, and he could barely see along the snow drifts, so he ran for it, across the grounds and over terrain hardened by the passage of soldiers and smoothed by a wind that had not let up in days. He fell on his side behind a wooden cart half-submerged a season ago in a drift built up over the past year. This time he had heard the rifle fire from the trenches, but it was doubtful she had hit anything in the glare and snow. But it only mattered that he was closer to the silo, so he ran again, forward and diagonally between the corncribs and fallen stable, twisting and slipping over the grooves in the ice. He landed facing backward, seeing the old woman grimace as her rifle failed to fire. There was a shot, echoing oddly between the desiccated shelters, that came from the silo, and Antony skated on mismatched boots up behind the bloated carcass of an auroch. The snow that had drifted over one side of the dead animal created a shadow Antony froze in, but the wind had lessened. Outside the grounds of the farm, he could hear the sound of one or both of the Armies, marching on the dusty fields, pounding the snow ever flatter, ever harder. The plains no longer crunched under foot. It had been stomped to cold glass under the long retreat, crushed to white iron under pursuing treads.

He knew he had no chance of hitting the sniper with a slingshot. The breeze above could not be accounted for. The shine of the sky off the ground was still all-encompassing. The demon's screams in the back of his head were too distracting. But he needed to scare the sniper into retreating back into the silo if he had any hope of getting any closer. And he had to take out the sniper if there was any hope of any of the entrenched escaping the farm to return to the retreating camps. And so he spun the sling, stood, and flung the shot at the exposed area of the upper silo, rolling with his momentum to move out in the open toward a disheveled shack on the opposite side of the mainway. He heard another rifle round go off but could not determine its origin or target. He had to keep moving. The shack provided little shelter from elements or gunfire, but he did have to tear a skeletal board from its brethren and ice before moving into the barn holding the silo. Here, he quickly moved into concrete and aluminum — an indication he had entered the cylinder. Ancient furniture, broken ladders, masses of springs, and splintered pallets were stacked to a rounded but broken ceiling he could barely see. It was here that Ba'al spoke a language he could understand. The storm demon obviously wished to distract him, hoping the sniper would kill him, hoping freedom would come from Antony's death. Ba'al insulted his clan, his race, his place in the Army, his skill, but Antony no longer held any of those things in high regard. If the demon wished to disturb his confidence, he would have to work harder and find something that Antony himself had not long ago betrayed. He shook his head to no avail. The monster's words still bounced around in Lantean throughout his head.

The Lesser climbed upward on broken wood and precarious hanging shrapnel, the devil shouting obscenities all the way. The marching outside the farm was somehow louder in the silo, and so he could not forget that, even once he moved these few families and troops out of the farm trenches, he still had to lead them out of the battlefield and back on the trail of the retreat. He had to keep reminding himself that he was no longer in the middle of a war, that an offense was no longer an option. Everything was just a shadow of what it once was. The trenches they dug were not in earth but snow and permafrost. It was unlikely the plains people would ever see dirt again. The legion he led was not a group of soldiers but their families, and it was unlikely that gangrene or the persistent consumption wracking their lungs would even allow them to raise their spears against the gaining Horde. He was uncertain whether those that followed him into the farm were even fully Army of Earth. The chaos of the past week had mixed the soldiers of both armies until he sometimes wondered if he was also commanding soldiers of the Horde looking for a way out of the fighting as well.

Very slowly, and deliberately very quietly, Antony emerged up on a wobbly platform, but was immediately turned upon by the sniper. Even beneath the woolen cap and scarf, Antony could tell the sniper was a boy barely into pubescence, and his long rifle made no sound as he pulled the trigger. And Antony's revolver only clicked as his last round turned out to be a dud. He grabbed at the child before punching him in the jaw, and they both fell through breaking boards, plunging into the depths of the silo.

Hanging from torn clothing and splintered ladders crisscrossing walkways, Antony could barely see the mess of limbs the boy had become when he struck the floor. As they had struggled he had noticed that the boy's ears had been clipped and his forehead branded with the Mark of Ashmedai. Both mutilations indicated he had been a slave, although a slave with a big responsibility.

The bottom of the silo was comprised of layer upon layer of bird remains and tiny hills of snow that had found their way in through the maze leading upward. Antony pulled the boy's dark body from shadows and filth, hoping to find any winterwear of a close size to replace his torn jacket and gloves. He had split his knuckles against the sniper's teeth, but he did not bleed. Did the Nidhogg Virus leak from his wounds, he wondered, or would it only escape at his leisure?

He realized he was smiling uncontrollably again. It concerned him to no end that he had gotten used to the pain in his cheeks as the grin stretched to both extremes of his face. There were few mirrors left in the land to remind him. The boy had a scarf that would fit his face perfectly.

~

"Then why are we even here," one of RackBreak's men-at arms asked.

Snowflakes shook in the air, not from any wind but from a vibration that also made the drifts, long-settled in the ranch village, leaning against the homestead structures, shift. But the Greater Antony could tell by the sensations that it would be a small force sent against the village. The tanks would be small and few in number, with the faster moving Horde forces following the rest of the battalion east, as his own soldiers would when finished here.

"Stop trying to fortify," another of his men-at-arms answered. "We're moving out in the hour. Commander says we're meeting up with the home force." Beneath the cheers she tried to continue passing along the orders. A terrible cough weakened her voice, but still she yelled, "Says any bombardment will come at the stables' side, so, if the

Horde still cares about its own men, they won't have trenched in on the eastern end of town. That'll be how we go, then a quick jog north about a mile in."

A revolver fired closer than RackBreak would have expected, just on the other side of an ancient feedlot. "Down and out!" he shouted, massive lungs breaking through the storm and the rising commotion of his troops.

The curtain of falling flakes was parted by a black cloud descending rapidly into the wide space connecting all the ranch structures, and RackBreak's forces dove for empty doorways, behind fallen carts, and overturned barrels, as blond-ribboned arrows covered the wind-blown streets, decks, and shutters of path and building as though they had suddenly popped from the ground — a forest bed of foul winter weeds. The sharp heads glanced off his cast-iron helmet, or he easily swatted them away, but he was surprised at the sudden assault, and he stepped back, plucking arrows from hidden mail between the joints in his armor. It was not ice that crunched beneath his boot but the hand of his fallen messenger. Her neck and shoulder had been pinned to the ground by one of the pale wooden bolts. Someone had taken the time to attach tiny streamers to the arrows, each one imprinted with the sigil of Ashmedai, that of a broken seal surrounded by nine crowns carved from starry rock. The flags would have made the arrows inaccurate, but, looking around at the yellowed snow, RackBreak understood the embellishment. The field of arrows held the only color in the ranch, with the snow on the one side of all the bent trees seemingly absorbing any other hue.

Any color the hidden sky would have leaked to the ground was blocked by the great perches a year ago raised around the buildings of the village, placing the main path through the mansion and stables in perpetual shadows. Perhaps in a better season, a better day, the street would have see sunlight peek through, but with the crooked structures being so covered in the corpses of the ranch's original inhabitants, only the weather sometimes found its way around and onto the ground beneath RackBreak's boots. The earth here was broken and uneven, made of layers of inconsistently submerged and risen plates of petrified dirt and desiccated ice. When one walked this settlement, whatever its name had been, one walked the Arctic as an archeologist, with only remains that seemed so ancient but could not have been that old.

He was ignoring the shouts of his troops, staring from beneath obscuring helm up to the perches, when the Horde troops had entered from a near and drifted path. The great structures stood to a height just above the tallest of the low buildings and were made from a wood that had to have been hauled from afar, being that the plains stretched at least for a day in every direction. And the perches whistled with any wind from pores quickly bored by the elements, leaving the wood as dry as trees dead from generations of sun. But he had to keep telling himself that this scene could not have been that old — perhaps only from the Horde's last passage. The foul scrawl on the buildings, no doubt written with the hung ranchers' own bowels, spoke of betrayal. But RackBreak had seen it all too much in the prior year. A healthy crop returning after famine. A prosperous family revived after pestilence. A recently successful ranch growing despite constant winter. These were all too tempting for the Horde to pass up. Suddenly there were stories of treason concerning hermit cowboys and neutral farmsteads, and the Horde Army was suddenly fat with corn, powder monkeys and newives, and aurochs and horses to pull machines of destruction.

He did not want to, but RackBreak looked down at the Horde soldiers suddenly kneeling before him. His own troops were just then breaking from the scavenging to notice the interlopers.

One of the enemy men pulled a breather from his face, cords like plump leeches stretched before popping from his throat and nostrils as he continued, "...came to see if the rumors was true, oh great, oh Greater one."

The other two men, sporting oily shoulder armor larger than their torsos, removed goggles to pull the flannel covering their heads. Their sweat-plastered hair instantly became iced in the shadows and lilting air. One of them said, "We come to pledge and pray, Greater, great master. We hope to turn..." But two of RackBreak's men drove a spear through the mass of chainmail covering the soldier. Links stretched and burst before the blade plunged into the ice. The soldier was still squirming, mittens reaching out against the ground as his chest slid down along the shaft of the weapon. With pink scraps of lung skittering away with the snow, he could only scream silently. His companions were similarly skewered, with one of them almost breaking in half and releasing a spray of blood that quickly disappeared down the cracks in the ice before he even stopped moving.

RackBreak looked once again to the holy perches. He was amazed at the fortitude of the bodies. Some had been tied, but most were hanging from splintered notches cut into the wood. Limbs had blown away in the seasons' winds, but most of the remains had collected ice and used it to hold tightly to the sky. Mandrakes had grown impossibly from the snow directly beneath the figures, feeding from frozen strands of gore that reached all the way to the drifts.

His great boots broke the shifting plates as he trod toward what appeared to be a guesthouse. The wood and bundled weed meant to insulate the shelter had mostly disappeared beneath piling snow, and it appeared as though some of the roof had collapsed beneath the feet of heavy down collecting over it. Before entering he gestured to his closest lieutenant to start the widening gyre maneuver. It would send his outer forces around the ranches, trapping the Horde's front lines, using the growing storm to confuse their middle front, and weaken the nascent trenches before he would command his legion out into the prairie. It would be expected that they would hole up in the dead village, but he had no such plans.

Even walking the few porch steps aggravated his joints — muscles, throughout his limbs and back, pinching near the surface, burning deep inside and near the bone. One last look to the perches reminded him again of his torture beneath the camps outside Erebus — his stretching above the sleeping then exploding city — he found that no amount of cold deadened the pain, no degree of warmth numbed the very physical memories.

Inside the shelter, his men-at-arms took him to the small fire that had been built to warm its occupants. He recognized some of those gathered around the pyre as troops in the Army of Earth, for some still wore green on their faces or the bloody eyed badge of the Liege of Foes. Others warming themselves had the scarred forehead of the different marks of the Horde. But they all ate together. And what they were feasting upon, he looked away before he could determine. It was small and too familiar to even comprehend — if anything existed in the War of Heaven and Earth.

None of the group would meet his eyes. He ordered his troops to clear out all the buildings, to force any of these "strays" out onto the roads with the rest of the retreat, for the Horde was closer than he had thought, and there would be nothing left of the ranch village before long.

A cannonball landed near his feet outside the home, with the force of an exploding iceberg. His armor glowed with the streaks of melting shrapnel, and, from the looks of the broken sphere as it submerged beneath a sudden pool, he surmised that the enemy was heating its iron before launching it. Now there was color burning through the snow. Now there was warmth in the gory spray, the appearing fires.

As the hissing of the misting snow lessened, RackBreak could hear revolvers sounding throughout the paths connecting the shelters. In the clearing from stable to stable ran Horde soldiers, their voluminous pants, tucked into iron-clad boots, made their feet appear ridiculously small. One soldier, with armor obviously making up half his weight, landed on the Greater Antony's shoulders. RackBreak did not know where he had come from, nor did he care. Ligaments pinching in electrifying pain, he snatched the man from his neck and dragged him across the ice of the earth. Jagged drifts burst, as did the man's clothing. When brought up face to face, there was barely any flesh on his head to designate him as being alive. But pure white eyes twitched from a cleanly scraped skull. The Greater threw his heavy body across the square, immediately sinking to one knee from the tightening grasp of arthritic claws in his back. Rounds both leaden and wooden chimed and shattered against his armor, so he struggled to stand. The Horde soldier he had thrown stood starkly in the air across from him, impaled but crumbled and hanging from some open and obvious rafter on a far stable. Like some demented weed flower breaking to open at growing *Wyrmwood*, the man spread his crooked limbs wide and open as though he meant to fly above it all.

~

"Goddamn it, wind!" Janus could not even tell if his impeccable aim was failing him, for his arrows were becoming lost in the sudden blankets of snow that would hide the encroaching Horde, just as his own face would become lost in the sleet buffeting him from atop the overturned trailer. He wiped the mask of wet ice from his eyes, yet still had no idea if he had struck deadly into the descent of the lower prairie below. The steeps and deeps of the plains could not be told in such all-consuming yet dull brilliance of the weather. Except for the glaring purpling of *Wyrmwood*, the drifted land was the same uniform color as the sky. And, even now, as the clouds became tainted by the falling star, with the rolls of the heavens slowly becoming infected by veins of color, the wind-wracked prairie mirrored the celestial disease.

"Stab the gods!" he yelled as another shot from his long bow veered from sight. "This is no fight!" He jumped to the ground in the shelter provided by the side of the trailer. One of his soldiers neared, falling behind his group, holding a shield out toward his commander. Janus set down the bow to paint an eye, covering the shield in a viscous green with a brush of hardened bristles. "Damn the gods!" The shield ended up being flung into the storm, the paint can into the side of the trailer. Beneath the torpid layer there was paint that had not congealed yet, but before Janus could recover he began a fit of coughing that had become all too familiar since his time spent beneath the clockwork titan.

"Let me know if that helps," a familiar voice in the storm said. "We're on our own either way." Wulf appeared, holding himself up by grasping the edge of the trailer. He hid the side of his head, but not his smirk, in the many shadows of his hood, but Janus approached and reached out a hand.

Cringing, Wulf pulled his face away.

"So, it's true then," Janus said, dipping a finger in the spilled green. "The prisoner escaped. I'll catch him. He's been spotted then, in the south camp…"

"No, leave him. And your company? There is no more offensive."

"I won't just…"

"Pick your best… stay behind to cover the retreat if you must… but all others must keep moving… all… all…" Wulf caught himself from stumbling over abandoned supplies or wagon wheel rut. "We must all keep moving forward. Where's Teca?"

"Last I heard? She's evacuating the center. Have you ordered the other…" But the cloaked figure had floated back into the snowfall, leaving Janus to mark an eye in the middle of his forehead with paint that crumbled in his fingers.

"Legion! Your orders?" his nearest man-at-arms asked before ducking at the sound of something burning and whistling overhead. It was as though a cooked bird had flamed back to life and had dive-bombed the camp in a suicide run. After Janus stopped coughing, the soldier asked again, "Who'll make up the back defense?"

"Everyone," Janus croaked. "Gather the rest of the company, and send every man, mine or others, to evacuate and move anyone still lingering. Split up the units, if you must. Make sure every man, woman, and child is heading east by the minute. No exceptions."

"Any message for the reinforcements?" asked a pigeon. The child had found paint elsewhere. There was no exposed area of skin that was not an obnoxious shade of green.

"Ha! There are no reinforcements, girl."

"But, Legion, sir, have you not heard…"

"Now move, tell your Liege of Foes the west and south camps are clear and… and they will be protected."

When he was left alone in the horizontal snow, and was certain that his latest coughing fit had subsided, he urinated, spit and wet his mouth with ice, tucked his hair back into neck and collar, tightened a half-helm with broken guard on the tip of his head while tying a scarf under his chin, scavenged for the lightest gloves and thickest socks and heaviest boots and any mail that could be hung over his leather armor, and he tightened every belt and scabbard he wore before giving his long bow one last inspection. He could find no goggles or glasses in the remains of the retreating camps, but the glare on the plain was deadening as the bruising light of *Wyrmwood* grew over the land.

And he jumped. Short jumps. Mail jingling. Throwing knives jangling. He stretched to find any tightness in his armor, in his muscles, and so he stretched until it was all loose. And then he ran, grabbing his pathetic quiver. And then he stopped and kneeled, chastising himself and apologizing, and then he prayed, and he squinted through the flakes flecking his eyelashes to look up to find the curves of the coliseum and to follow those curves and those crowded seats to find the Lord's balcony to find Her approval and Her favor, but he could not see anything in the rush of white against his face. But he could hear those stands, could feel the thunder of the impatient spectators. And he could understand, for his blood was impatient too. It pressed from beneath his skin. His fingers could not keep from tightening around the bow and a drawn arrow. The ground shook. The air roared. And the Horde, clothed in smog and dyed furs and starkly branded in differing angelic sigils, darkly grew out of the very blankets of storm that parted and dissipated mere feet in front of him. Boots pounded the snow like skin drums stretched too thinly. The tread of a man-shaped tank turned even the permafrost beneath the drifts. They all sang a song, but to Janus it was just more wind smothering itself in weird updrafts.

He was too close to logically use a long bow, but he drew, pulled, and released anyway, barely aiming. One soldier, with a torso heavily armored to the point of near immobility, saw the bicep of one arm torn away. Tendons steamed and shrank from the weather, and drops of blood froze in the air before flying to cut the eyes of a nearby peer. A soldier, in, except for a great brimmed hat over an oversized gas mask, tight leather covering his entire body, swung at the air with an electrified pike before the next arrow tore through his groin up into his bladder. Brown and red urine mixed to soak his leather before marking his passage, while his companion dived to avoid the next arrow. The buckles on his winged boots caught each other, and the soldier went down with the shaft sliding beneath his kneecap. The more he struggled for cover, the more bone and cartilage was lubricated by new blood. Both ends of the arrow kept becoming lodged in the ice of the earth, and his cries for help were drowned out by his comrades' march. Someone stepped on his heel and the last thing he felt was his leg twisting and his knee popping into two pieces.

Gunfire rang out over the snow, but Janus felt the bullet graze his helm first. A tap, tap, tapping pecked against his armor, against his skull, over and over against his skull until he could hear, rather than feel, a hairline crack spread across the bone. He realized, not remembered, that he had tossed the bow and quiver, and found himself landing on top of a Horde soldier and driving two arrows into the man's face up and under his cheekbones. Eyeballs popped from the inside out to cloud over, unprotected by lids in the chilling breeze. But the ringing in Janus' scalp continued until its weight grounded him, his head too heavy to lift.

But he found himself back in the fray without remembering how he had returned to his feet. A heavily furred soldier rushed him. The hides were all dyed white, and as they whipped in the soldier's run, they parted to show layers of tubing feeding into the soldier's elephantine mask. Realizing that he had at some time drawn a hatchet, Janus dropped and rolled backward, using the enemy's momentum to bring him into and over his feet. The Horde soldier stood, trying desperately to catch hissing bowels continuously streaming from the gaps crisscrossing his belly.

Janus spun to mark the surrounding enemy troops and was immediately hit by vertigo centered in the pounding in his skull. His hand struck the air open-handedly, and throwing knives flashed out to implant themselves in thigh and shoulder. As men kneeled to work them free, Janus was upon them. One found the bones in his wrist splintering as his arm was pinned to the meaty area between his own ribs by a long dagger. The other man breathed blood and ice and choked on cartilage as Janus jerked and twisted and wrenched on his neck with a hand sickle until he found and severed the spinal cord. The man continued to whistle through many new openings as Janus searched to collect his weapons. But more soldiers were upon him, so he grabbed a nearby whip, cracking the air to keep them at bay until he had found a sword and a revolver. The gun's first round exploded in a soldier's mouth after passing through his raised hand. The broken bits of teeth and shattered jaw tore the rest of his face off while blinding him. His tongue hung down to his chestplate but he refused to stop screaming, so Janus kicked him over while launching himself at another soldier that had failed to get his rifle to fire. The sword glanced off mail, then rib, then another rib, before breaking a rib to slide up into the man's heart. With his revolver spent, Janus was able to swing the sword two-handedly, and it came stabbing down through the thigh of a man he had pounded down into a kneeling position. It pinned the man leg to heel, and to the ice beneath, but Janus wasted no time yanking the blade free in a spray of blood that flecked his lips. The enemy's electric mace glanced across Janus' helm before the blood rush fell him.

Again the pain repeated, echoed, screamed from one side of his head to the other, and again he felt himself fall, again held strongly to the ground by its weight. But again he immediately found himself in the thick of battle, swinging an unfamiliar battle axe and knowing that time had passed but not how it had passed. He left the axe embedded in the heavy helm of a soldier — a man that then staggered away, not noticeably bleeding but impossibly continuing the march with a blade that looked to be bisecting halfway into his armored head. Vomit was coloring his beard. His loose pants turned the same hue.

Janus scavenged a short sword and a long dagger from two unmoving and different soldiers he stepped over. But he got caught up in their limbs as he struck out at two more that jumped at him. He planted the dagger upward under one man's chin, and it came out splitting the face from the nose downward. Keeping the other man at bay with the sword, he struggled to wrench the dagger free, and something eventually hit Janus from behind. His head started the reverberating thunder yet again, but he managed to cut off enough fingers from one man before turning to plunge the blade up into the other man's groin and rectum before being pinned to the ground by his head again.

The thunder of the crowds woke him this time, but he knew, before opening his eyes, that he was not in the Morbis Orbis, not fighting in the sand of the coliseum but the equally gritty snow of some unfamiliar prairie. This time he knew better than to expect Her to be standing far above, looking down for Her chosen fighter.

Yet there she was. Far and above, on some hillock or massively drifted plain, watching the battles, surrounded by new men of unknown armor and tattoos. And Janus changed direction. It was appropriate that he had pulled a machete from some prone figure's meat, for he now cut his way through the Horde as though they were some leathery vegetation. He hacked until limbs gave way in splinters and liquid. He cut low at boots until men screamed at severed tendons. He chopped high until men grasped at necks that, opened, would no longer allow them to scream.

But Janus still had so far to go. The closer he neared, the deeper and untrodden the snow became. He never took his eyes off her, however. Her hair was the darkest color on the battlefield, and it streamed like ebony blood from a hood almost as dark. He could not see her eyes for the shadows, but the little of the skin bared on her face and hands was whiter than the winter had become in her absence. Her night cloak was tattered to the appearance of a flood of feathers, white armor standing in contrast to black leathers. On top her hood, disappearing into the storm, was an antlered crown with the appearance of glass.

Flames surged near, and he took his eyes off Mew for just a second to search his belts for his last throwing blade. He flung it to catch the fingers of the operator of the flamethrower, just long enough to divert the spray elsewhere and to distract the man until Janus could move in close enough to bring the machete down upon his shoulder. He embedded blade and broken scales of armor in bone and meat, tripping him to hack again and again at the same spot until the man was separate from his arm. The blood spurting from neck met the blood squirting from shoulder, and the growing pool opened up a deepening hole in the snow that the arm slid into.

Janus continued his swinging plod toward the drifted hill, but now, looking upward, he watched as someone appeared next to Mew. He was suddenly aware of the battle in ways he had not been. The echoing pain in his head had disappeared, so he could hear the crash of metal against metal, the tearing of leather, and the butcher's block sound of blades connecting with heads and limbs. He looked around at the sights of the new fighters clashing with the Horde. Men wrestled on the ground, sometimes with spears that had pinned them to ice, sometimes with enemy soldiers that gave no mercy, striking again and again to find purchase between armor plates. He heard someone call out, sounding as though he were drowning, for an angel's boon. Someone else, beneath the repeated clanking of mace again helm, called out for a beloved.

Back above the fray, a nearly naked man, that Janus felt he should remember the sight of, took the interior of Mew's hood in his many-colored hands, drawing her near. The figure was twice the size of the average man, with unavoidable muscles rippling beneath entirely tattooed flesh. He was painted permanently from toe to face, and he continued to pull Mew even closer.

Janus did not remember falling again, did not remember his head being weighted to the cold earth, but he suddenly found himself running, not remembering how he had returned to the collapsing camps. He slowed to pluck an arrow that had been stuck in his mail. The head had made it through the links, cutting and grinding against a rib. He had no time to staunch the wound with more than a scrap of fabric he tore from the ice. The evacuation looked mostly complete, but by the tents left behind he could still navigate to where he had left his tiny pavilion. It was in shambles, flipped and wind-born, with only the flaps of canvas that had been frosted to the ground still remaining. Looters ran at his approach, but he ignored them and his scattered belongings for a small chest that had been broken and turned and emptied. The traps guarding the lock, needles and flash powders bought by him from Slayd, had been set off.

He ran again, broken links of mail digging into his side, but it was not long before, following the last route of the looters, he found the Elder Mask. The old man stopped seizuring as Janus slowed to draw near. He knelt but hesitated. The mask looked different, but he could not describe in what way, as he picked it from the moaning man's face by its eye holes.

Something rolled around in Janus' bruised mouth, and he spit out a tooth. He had to get his bearings, and quickly. Reports from earlier in the day had suggested that the head force of the Horde, the mobile city of Phaeton, had been approaching from a very specific direction.

The commander camp would be heavily guarded.

There was a distracting glow as Janus placed the Elder Mask over his face, and a familiar warmth in his belly and the very tips of his limbs as he once more became The Warrior and The Assassin and such a host of other things he thought he had forgotten. The sun was dim against the falling star, but he still quickly found direction. And he found himself running yet again.

~

Sinuses caved and an eye socket cracked, but, instead of popping out, the eyeball disappeared back into the head. And even after all she had witnessed recently, Teca stilled gasped and swallowed cold air and warm bile to avoid retching any more than she already had. She shook the half a head from her oversized boot, only then realizing the gore stuck to both her heels. She barely had time to stomp her feet on the dark snow before another enemy was upon her. He wore the skull of some unknown pig-like creature over his head. It still dripped with war paint or the remains of his victims, and Teca could not tell how he could ever see out of the makeshift helm, but he ran swinging a spiked flail above his tusks.

She used hand and sword to catch herself over and over as she stumbled and backed over ice and trampled organs. The camps had periodically placed the last of their bear traps behind them as they fled over the prior days, hiding them under any loose snow the winds had not blown to the horizon. Her peripheral had alerted her to the presence of something dark under the flakes nearby, and she had lost sight of it, lost her sense of direction with the flail's spiked ball whipping past her face, its near passage drying the slush and sweat caught in her eyelashes.

A rush of air, just at a pitch higher than the storm whizzed nearby, and the soldier's mask shattered in a spray of bone and ice. Staggered, the blinded man was strangled on his own flail before Teca ran him through with her short sword. She twisted the blade before pulling it free, and it caught and scraped and dulled against multiple ribs on its way out. This close, she could hear him apologizing to someone, not her, as he choked on tears and a darkening tongue.

This isn't my fight. Why am I even here?

She heard the whizzing of the sling again but could not see Ivy for the plumes of snow kicked up by a nearby gatling gun as it struck the drifts in rapid succession. Teca dived for an upcropping, hoping she hid behind rock as well as ice. The prairie had begun to rise and fall as the march progressed over the day, signifying a hopeful end to the plains, but she had not a chance to check her maps, even if they still existed out in the moving camps.

These're just men playing at their games, as it always has been. Endless and pointless, and I'm just feeding into it.

The slingshot whizzed by again, and she thought she may have seen Ivy's distinctly pied figure duck back behind an abandoned truck door. When last Teca had seen her, she had been completely covered in patchwork leather of all colors and grains, and her face was painted with smeared colors that had streamed in the sleet and sweat dripping from her top-knotted scalp. Teca had lost track of how many people that sling had saved in the last few minutes alone.

This is not important! What's back at the Black Hills is all that's important.

She could hear the distinct sound of a jamming gun, along with the profanities of a Horde soldier, so, without looking, she rolled around her cover to run, taking care not to stumble in her loose boots and hanging swords. She had a revolver drawn and a dead round clicked away before her last good bullet fired at the gatling operator. She fired too low, but it still hit the oxman that pulled the gun's cart. The ricochet screamed off his full helmet, and he fell, seizuring throughout his bare body. Stepping over him, up onto the cart, and over the hissing barrels of the gatling gun, Teca had already thrown her revolver to unsheathe her swords. She caught the enemy's splintered dagger on her own broken blade and used her momentum to unbalance him, thrusting her short sword up into his armpit. Warmth flooded over her hand, soaking her glove and leaking down into her sleeve, sticking all the way down to her elbow. The soldier had sharpened all his front teeth into canines, and he now bit deeply into his own tongue as Teca lowered him to the ground. The *Sol Sistere* repeated itself over and over in her head. She did not even realize it.

Held in splendor, dancing finger and wing
Felled by engendering wellspring
Bring this low man from earthen Hell
String him from Heaven until his heart swells.

The enemy was upon her as soon as she dismounted from the cart. They were already wrestling with some of her soldiers, locking bayonets and machetes, and so some backed into her as others struck with spiked gauntlets and electrified bludgeons. She dropped, and her attackers accidently struck each other, so she swung upward and downward with both broken and complete blades. She swung wide with both before curling to stab with the short sword. Shrapnel or bone cut high on her cheek. Had it been an inch higher she would have lost on eye. Her attackers collapsed into each other in entangled and mutilated arms.

I don't belong here! I have to go home.

And then, appearing out of the blur of snow settling from burning cannon fire — it could have only been Wulf. He stood on the far side of a line of her own soldiers, seemingly directing them to continue the march eastward. She tripped but stood to approach, but she found one of her legs gripped by a man wearing no designation of either Army. He had no visible tattoos, wore neither the bloody tear or a brand upon his forehead. He was not even wearing any variation of the color green. But he growled like a fevered mongrel, hissed like a cornered snake, spit into the boot he had just stolen. He did not even have a foot left to put it on. Teca still watched Wulf, yet now the cloaked figure just looked up, past storm and thinning clouds, to a sky that darkened into dusk. This was the first indication of the time of day Teca had seen in hours. With *Wyrmwood* burning the heavens an unfamiliar version of violet, however, she guessed that it may have been any time of the day. Still, she now noticed what Wulf was apparently watching — the cascade of falling stars as they presented a dark rainbow over the curve of the sky. But she had to turn away. The undead hue that *Wyrmwood* was mutating the light into pained the very backs of her eyes.

She shook off the auras and kicked at the boot thief with a foot barely covered in layers of holey socks. He bit at her until she pinned his neck to the ground, taking her property back. But buckling the boot back on was all the distraction it took before Wulf disappeared. In his place were new fighters Teca did not recognize. They had hands painted blue and red, and they fought without gloves and with iron knuckles, finger knives, clawed rings, and wrist blades. These must have been the followers of the Painted God. Battlefield gossip had told her to keep an eye out for them. Their weapons were limited against the Horde soldiers, but she saw many of them retrieving the blades of fallen foes.

A green man was split down the middle beside her, his spastic limbs flicking her in the face. He had had no weapons and apparently leaped to parry a particularly nasty-looking bludgeon that had descended toward a young boy running through with a box of revolver rounds. Teca had been using her broken broadsword for deflecting, but she now plunged it where she thought her enemy's neck was unprotected. It glanced away from some hidden plate, and she lost it. Her boots slipped on a hand or got caught up on broken snow or armor, but she was still able to plunge her short sword under chest plate that ground against the blade like stone. She hit the ground rolling, and without being able to look she knew to continue to roll and crawl as the jagged bludgeon came down into the drift between her side and arm, so she rolled back over it, the plate over her chest and back protecting her as she grabbed the weapon's shaft over and around its owners hands. Using the new leverage, she pulled herself close and head-butted helm against helm. Her head rang with the sound and impact, but she did it again when something flowed out from under her attacker's eye-guard. He was on the ground, but she repeated it to the sound of cartilage crackling and metal bending. He had stopped moving, but she smashed her head again into his, sure this time that the crumbling cartilage was her own.

Her cheek bled anew as she turned her helm back and forth to pull its bent frame from her bruised face. She tweaked her nose to make sure it was not broken. Shouts of warning and darkness in her peripheral sent her diving to the ground again, just ahead of a massive foot — as large as her entire body — that broke the field beneath the ice where she had just been standing. Framed by falling stars, the giant looked down toward her with jaundiced eyes but kept trampling the earth ahead. With great, pegged morning stars that had at some point in his life replaced his hands, he crushed the young ammo boy to pulp and to the prairie, adding to the collage of haggard torsos already stuck to the spikes. From somewhere hidden, Ivy was slinging shot into the creature's bony brow.

"Don't waste the ammo," Damn Antony, who, breathless, had suddenly appeared next to Teca, said.

She swatted his hand from her shoulder. She had found a rifle under the decapitated remains of an old woman and had been trying to break the hinge to check the chamber. The inside was so gummed with rust and rot to be unpredictable and possibly dangerous, so she swung it at a Horde soldier that was only standing, only laughing at the sights all around him. Any wood in the make of the gun shattered as loudly as the man's teeth.

On the ground, on the man's back, she choked him with one of the many cords coming from beneath his leathers, but she watched as Damn Antony followed the giant's rampage, seemingly talking to himself from beneath his scarf.

"He's not a beast... just... a boy... just a tithingman... perhaps the last..."

Her own soldiers tried striking at the creature's arms, but their spears barely grazed its pimpled flesh. Yellow liquid dripped from where his hands had been replaced, where infection itched its way to his elbows, where his diaper chafed his thighs. She could not look away and barely noticed as Antony raised a hand.

The giant turned back, and Teca could then see the collar that was meant to harm both him and any attacker, and she also could not help but notice the look of sudden affection on the great boy's face as he sniffed the cold air in Antony's direction.

"Rest now," Antony whispered into the wind. "You deserve peace."

Two snowmobiles, each piled with what looked like at least four Horde soldiers — all scrambling for purchase against each other — raced crookedly by, veering through crowds of spear-wielders. Immersed in clouds of pluming smog, they turned the air to oil with their passage.

"Keep moving!" Teca yelled to the remnants of the Army of Earth. "All east!" she even shouted to the followers of the Painted God. She grabbed at a circle of soldiers that had practically dug their own trench, implanting their boots into the crust, aiming with bows and the last rounds of rifles out into the sheets of snow where fires were becoming frenzied. She dragged several of them to their feet while kicking them in the direction of the moving camps. "Don't stop!"

Both airy and settled particles danced as the giant tithingman sat on the drifts nearby. Blades had failed to break through the barnacles freckling his shoulders and back, but his voluminous chest now deflated, his neck sucked inward with a sickening sound, and the flesh over his gut revealed the shape of his bowels as the Nidhogg Virus ravaged his system. Teca searched the drifts, tearing hardened bodies free from the ice to find her broadsword. By crushing the crust of a drift, she found a jagged short sword to replace her own. She had to first break and peel the previous owner's disembodied hand from the hilt. But she kept looking back at the tithingman as his core continued to shrink and his frostbitten feet began to bloat, expanding around dark nails until they disappeared into flesh that rose like dough in an oven.

She ran past him to spur others into continuing their passage, and that was when his stretched skin could take no more.

"We'll regroup at the coming..." she started to say before the giant boy's right foot exploded. The air pushed before pulling and Teca found herself on her hands and knees. The gorge in her throat that had been threatening now was pulled up through her lips. She was surprised to find she had anything more to vomit, considering she was certain she had not eaten this day.

She barely took time to wipe her chin before she had staggered to two soldiers that had stopped to tie up the arm of an old man that had fallen, exhausted, into snow he appeared unable to pull himself out of. All three of them covered their faces to deflect chunks of spongy meat that was falling from the sky. One of them had a fresh wound on his chin from where a splinter of the tithingman's bone stood out. Teca was reminded of her cheek and she removed a glove to feel the gash, as it had opened anew and was soaking her scarves.

"You'll have to carry him," she yelled into the quickening storm around them. "But you just can't stop..." She paused at the harried glance of one of the soldiers. The girl wore dark sunglasses so her eyes could not be seen, but her silent murmurings and the sudden pale veins appearing in her dark temples said it all. Within seconds, every color of liquid had leaked from all the spaces in her face. Teca found herself habitually singing a prayer. Instead of finishing she just took up the girl's crossbow before closing her wet eyes. Before the new corpse blackened and blistered from the appearance of the Nidhogg Virus, Teca noticed the symbols of both the Lonely Forgotten Sun of God and the Liege of Foes on arms and armor.

The scream of iron and wood turned everyone's face back to the storm behind them, and from out of the darkening snow came a sight too quick and large to avoid. Teca's new crossbow exploded and the two men next to her were impaled and pinned to the ice and earth by a massive bolt of barbed cast iron. Before either of them could cry their last, the great chain of the bolt straightened and pulled them out into the smoke and steam of the Horde. Teca scrambled to stand in what was left behind — scraps of clothing, leather, and fur that still held body pieces indistinguishable from each other.

Her hands were unbroken from the attack, but her fingers were sore enough to keep her from clenching her fists, so she ran without brandished weapons, yelling to all she saw to keep up the pace, to not stop moving, to not let scenes of what followed them sap the strength from their legs, and it was only when some of the freezing fog dissipated into a bare tree line that she realized how long that she had been running — without food, without drinking anything other than her own sweat or the sprays of an enemy's blood on her face.

There was rock all around, dark boulders piled and fallen and emerging from drifts that had grown more slowly in the cluster of thick and tall trees. Rusty moss covered one side of all the stone and wood, and it had long ago stiffened under ice, beneath the broken limbs of the tall and skeletal forest. The patchwork ground was littered with icicles of all sizes where neither tree nor boulder had yet met a wind that was constantly changing directions to find its way into the grove. The people around her slowed, obviously feeling secure in the shelter from the full effects of the winter, the flame-spun arrows of the Horde, and the violent violet of crackling *Wyrmwood*.

Caught between a boulder and a precariously leaning tree, she found a young man stripped of armor or clothes. He was too dark-skinned to be from the Horde, but she found no tattoo nor jewelry indicating his allegiance. But she did find a water bladder, and she shook it to break the ice up and prompt a trickle of the best water she had ever tasted, pausing periodically to yell at anyone who staggered by to "keep moving." But by the time she finished her drink she could no longer tell if she was shouting at those following the Liege of Foes or those of the Horde. The storm had darkened under night and dark star.

A sudden crowd of soldiers pushed against each other, rock, and tree, and they were soon all around her. She was shouting at them to push forward, to not rest in the shelter of the grove, and to protect the forward caravans, but then she realized that they were not of her battalion. Some had cowboy hats and some had gasmasks. Their leather was tight and adorned with all color and size of scalps. They all wore greatly over-sized shoulder armor studded with tusks, and they were all burned with angelic marks scarring forehead or cheek. They were all clean-shaven, and no two carried the same weapon. Teca envied them for their soft skin gloves.

The Horde troops ignored her in a sudden run through the grove, but she was caught up among them none-the-less. At first the mob kept her limbs pressed against her sides, unable to grasp at her weapons, but as she was trampled beneath them her arms and blades were thrown to the side, and she clawed at the frozen ground to find anything that could be used. One of the men was upon her, the many facets of his iron chastity belt grinding into her hipbone. She could feel the soreness of instant bruising and curled her legs up under him to lock her knees beneath his dropping chin. Her arms twisted under his and between his face and hers, and she jammed an icicle into an exposed ear. There was no sound, but the little of his face she could see contorted, foam dripping from mossy teeth onto her nose, his breath condensing on the open wound of her cheek. She could feel the soldier's muscles harden under his leather, but she did not loosen her hold, only twisting her back to roll over on top of him, grinding her teeth as she pressed the ice deeper. She had to pull the shard out an inch before putting all her weight back into it again.

She smelled sizzling grease as a prod was put to her side, and for a second she could not control the turn of her hips or arms or legs. Her neck lurched, sprained and pained, and she sluggishly sat up, thrown to the uneven forest floor by the electric weapon. New soldiers moved toward her, but she surprised them by meeting them halfway with the blade of whatever hilt she found on the ground. In the confusion of limbs and leather and masses of buckles she struck closely and almost parallel to her own body. Her other hand had lost its glove, and she clawed and grasped at a neck she quickly realized belonged to one of her own men. The short sword broke off under plate or sternum, and she could only push, trying to find a way out of the mass of grappling hands and daggers.

She dropped and crawled and rolled between boots stomping for leverage, but someone grabbed at the roots of her hair and started strangling her with her own scarf. She thrust her pained neck backward and felt a nose splinter against the back of her head. Turning, she watched a wild-eyed and deeply frowning Horde soldier fall backward onto dark ground. When he planted a hand to propel himself back up, a bear trap closed on his torso and head. One side of his mouth now grinned before a sickening sucking sound separated the hemispheres of his face. She thought for a second that the sectioned body was going to stand, but it was only the weight of the trap turning the halves of the body as it fell.

Teca tried to inhale through the sour taste thickening the back of her throat, but she just wheezed and grasped at the bony branches around her to stay upright. She had found her original blades, but could only find the strength to pick up her broken broadsword. Libra's figure, long ago carved into her old mentor's hilt, shined like nothing else in the grove, in the dark star's blanketing shadow, and she held the feathery and warm metal to her forehead, feeling a presence she had not felt in a long time, and it warmed her neck down to her chest down to her belly. Her limbs suddenly found the strength that had bled away over a day of running and fighting.

The Horde soldiers had passed her by — she assumed as they were chased by her own men — but their faces, she then noticed, looked fearfully backward at a cold figure entering the grove and holding a barbed leash attached to a trotting boar. The figure wore only mold-eaten overalls that were too loose in some places while being too small in others. The goggles of a gasmask obscured his face, but a worm-eaten cranium stood out starkly from behind its cords.

Families and soldiers from the camps continued to appear and pass through the grove. Those aware of the hog-handler ran at his sight. Those preoccupied with the march were spurred on by Teca's shouts.

The hog began to shiver and retch dryly, an ingrown tusk digging up towards its brain. Quivers lined and bunched down the swine's back darkened, grew, thickened, and began to drip and curve and quiver themselves.

From behind Teca the air moved and buffeted as though some great winged creature landed, and a pale and sharp hand on her shoulder brought her and her broken blade around. It was Sera, in great drapes of the blackest and fieriest of fox furs that made her slender frame appear three times larger than it was, and she had caught the edge of the Libran's sword in her hand. And she was pregnant.

"You still pray, little knight?" the Crimson Queen asked.

"I…"

"Do not be embarrassed. Shame is for lesser beings."

Teca tried to pull her sword away, to turn back to the scattering mobs, but the pale lady held firm to the broken edge. The thinnest line of blood glittered by an absent light down her palm.

Sera continued, "'T'was not *reason* that compelled you to sing the song of your angel's glory when you were a lonely wee babe, crying for judgment against the fathers that killed your mother… the fathers you grew to love and make love to." The demon queen's face was rarely seen behind locks that flickered like fiery serpents down over her face, but Teca caught a glimpse of eyes the color of what she could only assume a doomed person would see flooding their senses as they drowned in the depths of the *Jormungandr*. Had her eyes always been that color? "So it should not be *reason* that pulls you from your prayers." The thick tendrils of hair moved again, and Teca thought she saw the slightest of scars on both her temples, as through something precious had been plucked from her long ago.

And it was in that instant that everything was revealed to Dhani Teca Libran. The face before her did not change, but she saw it for what it really was, and she became instantly blinded for the deluge of tears that salted all the way to her lips.

I have to warn Wulf.

In a flutter of tails and silk, the Crimson Queen launched into the air over Teca, bringing heat to the grove and driving a barb-handled and bladed trident down to pin the convulsing boar to the stone beneath it. Its quivers, on the verge of exploding outward, settled and shrank as did the hog's deflating flesh. It gave one last snort through a congested snout before squirming its last.

Ivy ran by Teca to flick her spinning sling at the swine's handler. His goggles exploded under a steel bearing that exited out the back of his doughy head.

Teca turned every which way, slowly, as though the sudden heat caught her up in wavering warmth suffocating her every movement. Any snow of the dark grove had evaporated. Any ice hanging from moss and branch shriveled and dripped into steaming streams that gathered around the dreamy mobs before snaking away. It was impossible to see beyond those near, since appeared new and hot a fog obscuring anything beyond the closest of broken branches and wetly shimmering boulders. The bloody bone of the trident that had impaled the boar was now just a rotten tree that looked to have once struggled to grow out of the cracks of rock and pebbled soil.

Sera stepped, ethereal and languid, back toward Teca, layers of furs parting to reveal the silk and cream beneath, the splintered and red horns emerging from her tendriled mass of hair bobbing as she tilted her face to smile.

Teca was not sure if she could move through the heat, or if she had tried, but the Crimson Queen's hand cradled the side of her face before she realized it. "We are all our fathers' daughters," she purred, "until we kill them."

And with a rush of sulfurous air, as though some beast beat the grove with flaming wings, Sera had joined the fray of soldiers fighting at the top of a wall of boulders, and Teca gathered her broken swords to do the same. But she first felt for the cut over her cheekbone. It had vanished. The pain and wound were gone.

The little forest was winter-wracked again. There was no sign of the sudden spring that Teca had seen. Ice smothered moss. Snow stuck to dead bark. Icicles stabbed toward the frozen ground.

I have to warn Wulf.

~

Her arm was beautiful, long and shining with the reflections of destruction when the light of the outside fires hit it just right. Damn Antony imagined it to be just as slender as her real arm, which he had not seen, as it was kept warm with the far side of her body beneath a drape of curly bison fur.

"I just don't understand why you follow him," Antony said, unsure as to whether he spoke loud enough over the nearing sound of cannon fire. He could not look away from her arm, imagining what it would be like to hold it in his hands. Its sophistication was far beyond what he would have imagined for this land, with smoothly sliding scales over the main joints but mostly a silver skin that moved just as flesh would. It reminded him of what he knew of the appearance of a member of the Temporal Guild — beings of organic metal he had forgotten how much he once feared. But, he knew, if she had been an agent of the time-stream regulators, that he would already be dead.

"Because you are a very binary-oriented being. You can't help it," Speaks with Skulls responded. Her voice came not from her mouth or some speaker but floated above them like evening mists in the long metal trailer, eventually settling upon him like morning frost.

"The midgardians are the enemy of your people." Antony's hands were failing to warm in the heat of the fire they had made from burning shrapnel, far into the closed back end of the trailer. The flames were their only light source, despite the light of *Wyrmwood* dripping down from the crooked ceiling.

"The tiospaye, my 'people,' does not fight for the Liege of Foes, nor does he fight for us, but we push back, pushed back, against the imposters, against those that present in the form of the natural, those claiming to be descended from both Unki, the Earth and Sky, Feather and Star, and all those under their sway." She had threads in her long braid as silver as her bionic limb, and they fell, knotted, from her war bonnet. "You ask about the men of the pale bear? Do they even exist still? Who are you to cling to old ways? Should I not be asking you a similar thing?"

He moved closer to the fire, hoping to feel the sting of heat on the exposed tips of his fingers. Pain often distracted him from the demon screaming in his mind and memories. "To understand... you would have to... to know... know something you wouldn't..."

"Grandmother, unki, was very old when she told me a story that grandmother had told her when she was very old." Speaks with Skulls moved around behind him, taking herself farther from the flames. The griffin feathers draping from her head moved from one shoulder to another. The great bony beak hiding her face peaked from behind one shoulder of Antony to the other. "First, you must know that the Family comes from a time before even the Old Ones, but when the land you call Kaldera opened and the great burning mouth of Unki spat its fiery stomach into Sky, then did the Family help the Old Ones find shelter under the hills and mountains. My grandmothers' grandmothers showed them the way into the secret caves to hide them from the falling Sky. But they closed the doors behind themselves, leaving the Family behind to die in the rising and falling land and to breathe air that burned lungs to ash."

Speaks with Skulls' war bonnet shook, as did the trailer at the outside sound of some lurching machine that tipped and gasped its last. Antony waited a second before he stopped expecting the bear traps placed at the other end of the shelter to go off. He was not familiar with how sensitive the catches were.

He had heard that a group of Natives had joined up with the Army of Earth back when it had moved out of N'Midgaard, and the Family had been fighting in the war, led by their chief, Speaks with Skulls, ever since. He had not seen any of the Native fighters, neither on the first crossing of the plains, nor on this last running retreat back toward the east, until his own men had been ambushed in the last evening. The Natives had fought valiantly, without regard to their own lives, to protect their own or the fleeing remnant of the Army, but, in the violet haze of oil fires, night, and growing *Wyrmwood*, Antony had no estimate as to how many of his soldiers remained, nor how many of Speaks with Skulls' people still fought. In the lull of the fighting, he had hidden to catch his breath inside the remains of a long trailer. The Native chief had found him shortly after. She had carried a long weapon that doubled as both rifle and spear, and he picked it up now to aim it at a mob of Horde soldiers just outside the far open end of the shelter, as she continued her story, sitting down next to him.

"But beneath an eternal night of ash and snow, and upon a land that lurched and burned and bubbled and sank, through plains of knee-deep soot and mountains that rose and fell, the tiospaye survived. We adapted, we negotiated with others left behind and others appearing from the doors to other lands that the great eruption had opened — doors to realms long closed. We traded thought with tin men, resource with trolls, prayer with curious new spirits, and we made this new angry land our own, as we adapted to such harsh climate."

Antony sighted against the men that drew nearer. Oily faces were lit by the light of the torch emanating from a flamethrower. So near the opening, their broken-toothed cackles bounced all the way back toward the campfire, but Antony could not get himself to pull the trigger. He convinced himself that it was because the sound and commotion would bring others, but deep down he knew that with each killing blow that he had delivered over the past week, he would see each previous killing, and each individual image was becoming more difficult to block out. He had been in so many wars over his multiple lives — most of which he had waged. Why was this war threatening to consume him? It should have been just another skirmish in a hundred-year-old life, but something kept telling him that this was different. It could not have been the demon gestating inside him. Its words were only of doubt and self-immolation.

And so he set the rifle aside, waiting for the inevitable breaking chime of any of the bear traps to go off. But they never did. The Horde men had moved on without checking the interior of the shelter.

Speaks with Skulls had been continuing her story, her voice an ever-whisper. With her so close to him and the fire now, he could almost see her face beneath the great bone and beak, but it was painted and as blue as the shadows. "And so we cultivated the choked land in the Old Ones' absence, as new and old spirits bred the foul out of the blood of our furred and feathered sisters, and the wind moved for the return of seasons and a view back into the star realm above. And we waited. And we changed. And then one day the ash smothering the sun and stars opened, and we rejoiced for forgotten warmth, but what was thought to be a good spirit, a wichahpi returned, was a new beginning for a new end, an end only just now appearing, one thousand moons later."

Ba'al's screams had changed their tone. What was usually cries of pain, at the touch of the microscopic automatons flowing through Antony's possessed biology, or screams of demonic epithets, had changed suddenly to a maniacal laughter giving Antony a spasm in his cheek and eyelid on one side of his face. He pulled the scarf up higher to make sure his painful smile remained hidden.

"It was a starship, and it had crashed in the northern forests of what would some day become your 'Territories,' and from this sica vessel came little green men with large black eyes, and they too wanted a place in this healing land, and they too wanted to trade, with those left behind and those of the doors to other realms, except what they wanted to trade was not of the world. Two by two they brought your phony brothers and your phony sisters, sometimes as warriors, sometimes as workers, sometimes as lovers, and they wanted to trade them for a place in this new land. But the Family would not allow such abomination, such sica, in our healing world, and they attacked the slavers and drove them back to their lame star ship, killing them all but leaving their vessel to corrode in the claiming forests. But we would not touch the thing. No, it was poisonous, *wosiliyagle*... ah, cursed. The Family would not touch it, preferring to keep it a secret of our people."

Antony could hear the distinct 'whoosh' of flame from outside, could smell the near air burn acidly, could see the cracks in the metal surrounding him glow from one end of the trailer to the other. Their own campfire twisted wickedly as though it yearned to reach out to its deadly brethren. Speaks with Skulls reached out her hands, both silver and bronze, to sculpt the flame to her story.

"But then came what you call *tanka*... men — your Greater Prophets. No, my people had been telling stories of them even from the time of the Old Ones, but now they sought out the sica ship. The secret was somehow theirs as well. So now they would one by one seek out the vessel and now they would leave the ship followed by two of your brothers, and your brothers would introduce themselves to all parts of the land, under and over and also preparing yourselves for the Old Ones' return. And they spread and they became to know the land in a way the Family never had.

"So, yes, I do know you, damned one, I do know of your many…"

The chief was thrown against Antony as the trailer was lifted into the air and turned violently in an explosion of sight and sound. And just as quickly, she was lost to him as he found himself equally twisted and turned, from one side of the metal to another, lifted and tossed and burned by old and new flames, cut by bent and exposed shrapnel. He was deafened by either cannon, vacuum rush of air, or the debris pummeling his head. Yet he could still hear the possessing demon cackling deeply as he attempted to remove himself from the settling remains of the trailer.

He still looked down the long tunnel of the shelter, but now its turned wreckage let in more light — of its own fires and the fireworks of the outside battles. It was a rainbow of colors, an oily glow at all ends of the spectrum.

His hearing slowly returned as he pulled numbly to release his arm from something heavy. There was no sight of Speaks with Skulls, but he found her bony beak mask, and her wicked-looking hatchet was imbedded in debris near his foot. He had assumed it to be ceremonial, but upon closer look the blade was too sharp to be anything other than deadly. What he thought was the beating of his heart in his ears was the thumping treads of some great tank crushing the ice of the prairie while moving past and beyond the outside of the trailer. The sound was quickly replaced by the grumblings of Ba'al, but at least Antony found that he could hear again, as soldiers armored or barely clothed appeared at the edge of the wrecked shelter. They were lit by near piles of burning bodies and by torches stuck in standards above the head of one of their kind. The light was enough to show Antony that this was a mix of fighters and civilians from many allegiances. They were all driving spears into anything that crawled or begged.

It was then that Antony noticed that his numb arm had not been trapped under a wall of the trailer, as he had thought, but caught in one of the bear traps, its mangled flesh and bent bone only now just beginning to spark twinges of pain up toward his shoulder.

But the spear-wielders then decided to probe among the refuse of the shelter.

Antony picked up the hatchet, thumbing the hidden activator and feeling the vibro-blade hum to life. He looked to the soldiers, then to his limited reach and close quarters, then to his twisted arm. Its flesh, already blue and so caught up in the teeth of the trap as to make it unrecognizable, only then began to bleed, slowly into the cooling air.

The soldiers chuckled when spotting him, and he considered revealing his face, but instead tried to adjust for uneven leverage, his elbow and knee hitting the near wreckage. He had no cover or range against their moving spears. He looked once more to their grinning faces before back to his chewed and stuck arm.

More Horde men appeared at the far end, the pale brands on their forehead shining in the falling star's glow. Ba'al was cackling maniacally.

~

RackBreak Antony pulled the Horde soldier from the woman, tearing an arm from the shoulder socket before tossing him back out into the storm, but the woman was unmoving on the ground, her face scraped from her skull, her arms and legs burnt to jelly. The Greater moved on, wincing as he jumped over the trenches, hip joints shrieking with an arthritis akin to the pain of acid. He had to pause after nearly every step, legs burning in pain. He had been fighting for nearly a day, and his younger self would have been disgusted at such weakness, but age and the torture in the outskirt suburbs of Erebus, while lately, constant reminders, had now become all-consuming. Each joint ground against another as though connected by glass dust. Every ligament and tendon felt stretched to stringy fibrous nerves.

The scent of candied sweets hit RackBreak's nostrils when the wind dipped low, and a Horde man, of toothy mask and fleshy overcoat, ran near to jump into the air toward the closest drop of a trench. He was covered in tubes of dynamite, some with lines smoldering as cleanly as the storm, some just gleaming with sweat. The Greater Antony jumped into action, wincing again through the pain of clenching muscles to pluck the mad bomber from the air. He spun twice before launching the man back into the curtains of snow where he guessed the enemy to be coming from. Between the blizzard and the smog of the Horde's engines, the explosion appeared smothered in upon itself. Still, a boot landed upright nearby before tipping and spilling out its steaming stew of quickly congealing mush.

Gunfire, muffled by smoke and suffocating clouds of down, rang out, and bullets and short arrows invisibly struck at the fleeing crowds, and RackBreak crouched over a fallen group of people that wore too little for the temperature. One of them, a woman that had shaved her head to paint it green, looked at him pleadingly, but he pushed them forward, urging them not to stop until they saw the lights of some hint at civilization. She handed him a cloverleaf that was impossibly surviving against the winter, and he scoffed at it but tucked it as deeply as he could into the folds beneath his chest plate. He could barely feel the rounds striking the back section of his armor, but the sounds of the ricochet chimed in his head and neck like church bells.

Somewhere far off, a sound that had become familiar as of late, the wobbling twang of overused springs sounded, and the rotting carcasses of all shapes and sizes splattered around and in the trenches. RackBreak's long hair and sweat was obscuring his eyes, and he tucked it into the sides of his great helmet. The bloated yet broken sow on the drift near him spewed ugly plumes of dust from too many teats and from around a tongue that looked to have grown too large for her mouth and shattered jaw. He wiped its collection from his jungle of a beard, hoping, like most of the poisons of this land, that he would remain unaffected. He punched off the head of a Horde soldier running past, jumping into the trench its body had tripped into.

There were already signs of the enemy inside. RackBreak pulled and threw to the ground a soldier that had been tearing at a man's throat with metal claws he wore over his fists. He could both feel and hear the teeth of a chainsaw as it scratched at his armor and the skin between the cast iron plates. He turned to clap his massive hands around the chainsaw wielder's owner, and helm and mask and skull crumpled inward. Splintered teeth and flecks of lips and gums sputtered out through the tiny crack left collecting the mess. An enemy locked fork and knife with a young boy another step down the gutter of the trench. The boy sank deeper into the slush, the knife pushing closer to his unarmored chest. RackBreak kicked to step on the soldier. Chain armor twisted under the Greater's turning boot, links bursting into kidney, pelvis bone exploding and tearing a bladder apart. The upper half of the man jerked like a tin-man, unable to focus on, but still trying to reach for, the lower half that was now out of reach.

RackBreak looked to spur the remnants of the Army of Earth onward, those soldiers, families, and strays that had lingered to build and defend the ditches, but none that he could see appeared able to even climb out of the trenches, much less be able to keep up with the retreat east. The boy he had just saved had feet so swollen they had split his shoes open, with flesh beneath that was as discolored as his soles. A woman nearby was working the tourniquet of her own gangrenous forearm, while a green man sewed a tiny satchel of herbs into an open sore running the length of an old man's exposed thigh. All around him, the wounded mumbled to themselves — some of the weeks' past battles, some of sunnier days RackBreak was surprised they could remember. They had a gaze that looked at not what was before them. Unfocused, their eyes were not even seeing the darkening tips of their uncovered fingers, how their nails were splitting before they picked them completely off. Once in a while, he was greeted by gums melting into pus and blood. He could only now assume the rumors of stragglers choking to death on their infections were true. He pulled down a whiffer soldier that had veered to close to the edge of the trench as the man lined up a blast from his flamethrower. The man's arms were quickly snapped backward, broken each in multiple places, and as they flopped impotently at his sides, RackBreak tore the mask from his head, the tubes from his throat, and shoved the barrel of his own thrower into his mouth. Each orifice barely had a second to glow as the triggers were squeezed before his head simultaneously melted and exploded in the only color of the trench. Bone glanced off RackBreak's helmet. Glowing gray matter sizzled in the hair of his beard.

The Greater bounded from the trenches, the bones in his pelvis shrieking, and he lowered his head like a bison to plow through a mass of Horde men, his flat and full helmet breaking armor and softening chest, his great metal boots stomping organs from rectums. He stood with aching arms outstretched and roared through beard and hair and iron face-mask through an immediate steam that plumed around him from the pile of open bodies and new gore in which he rose. From the thickening mass he pulled a double-headed battle axe with one hand, a great broad sword with the other, and he swung both at a group of men tipping a covered wagon full of the bandaged and prone. Any blade or shield that attempted to parry was broken, along with any limb holding them. Splintered steel and jagged bone stood out from the burst flesh of soldiers trying desperately to escape. RackBreak left behind a field of pale wheat dappled with dark buds dripping but reaching for the light of the falling star above.

Bullets and spear tips glanced off his cast iron chest plate, arrows the great linked chain of his skirt, swords off the bronze of any exposed skin, of which there was little. Yet still they swarmed him, keeping a distance with pikes and rifles until he pulled them in or chased them down. A man of bandoliers and trophies, with spiked vambraces, clawed gauntlets, and belts of fresh scalps, was cleaved from hairline to groin artery. RackBreak pulled the axe from the mess of a body to find brain and spine attached to the wicked blades, and when he swung it, it now hacked amongst its sailing streamers of vertebrae, nerves, and blood vessels. The broadsword in his other hand had also acquired accessories, as a disembodied and impaled hand and thigh slid down the blade to the hilt.

He opened the chest of a nearby soldier that had strayed too closely. Ribs bent outward and were as clear as the snow in the wind, but his heart glistened, pounding out the rhythm of the battle before shrinking to freeze in the open air. RackBreak cut out the legs of a soldier wearing an oversized helmet and a cape stitched from dark skin. The enemy fell upon his own curved sword, punctured bladder melting the snow beneath him into a puddle others caught their boots in. Another Horde man's helmet was detached from his body. It rolled, with a spasming jaw chewing the ice of the earth and swallowing out the stump of its neck.

Snowmobiles raced in a circle around the carnage, their clouded single eyes trying desperately to make sense of the time of day under clouded darkness and bright *Wyrmwood*. RackBreak threw the battle-axe at one, and its nose dragged the ice before it flipped forward into the air. The Greater caught the machine and swung it like a tree trunk at another. A driver and rider were compressed into shredded metal and engine. Their limbs stuck out from each others' torsos, heads screaming from each other's abdomens, as the wrecked ball of machinery continued to roll back into the storm. Intending to dislodge a chunk of ice to throw at the remaining machine, RackBreak instead lifted a jutting piece of the frozen prairie, and the driver tipped back over his bucking snowmobile, breaking his face in twain against steering column and pillar of ice. His mask and nose choked him to death, as lodged in the back of his throat as they were.

The Greater stomped one man's arm into the snowdrifts and then pulled him apart from his shoulder, tossing him to the snow. He grabbed another that advanced with electrified pike, ignoring the weapon to pull the Horde soldier apart by his legs. His head and neck were all that still held his body together. Arms, far from each other, flapped against the near drifts, making the appearance of wings in the snow.

~

Every being caught up in the fighting assumed that what settled upon their cold faces was snow, but it was in actuality ash.

Sir Teca Libran, paladin of the Order of the Creed of the Northern Librans, brought her old mentor's family sword down again and again against the Horde soldier's arm. The great-sword's broad blade had broken early in her involvement with the war, and it had only become pitted and chipped as the battles had progressed. She rarely swung it as a sword anymore. It had become a bludgeon, a dull shield to catch up an enemy's thrust while she slipped beneath to drive some other blade upward under armor and sternum. She used the heavy hilt and squared iron now to smash through plate and bone. The soldier shrieked and cried and called her the names of female dogs he had owned, but still she crushed him to the frozen ground, breaking his spear and shield, cracking any fingers or elbows that still dared to try to ward off her blows. Eventually she crawled off the top of him. He still moved from the effort of breathing beneath collapsed facemask, but he no longer cried out. One shoulder revealed long and bare bones turning the color of the snow in the wind. The other leaked long and slow strands of gore from where the forearm had previously been connected.

Teca's own arms felt disconnected. They felt as bloodless as her face as the blush left it, and she felt cold all over. It was only in these brief seconds, when she stood as still as the piles of dead coagulating all around her, that she actually noticed the storms engulfing the purple fields of slush. One storm rushed ice and wind to move the limbs floating down streams before freezing the blood rivers. The other storm raged above, with falling stars disintegrating overhead, burning the blizzard before it could fully drop. These were the aborted children of *Wyrmwood*, shattering in the atmosphere, transmogrifying ice into rain before it dissolved into the mists of gore that hung like fog. The bloody mess became a sleet of its own. Teca could no longer tell what substance sleeted upon her face. It was sometimes as cold as frozen daggers and burned sometimes as hot as the blood of reopened wounds.

The prayers came to her silent lips so quickly that she was surprised she had ever forgotten them, and with their ceasing her hands warmed and her shoulders found renewed strength. The dragging weight in her legs lifted. Her muscles felt as airy and light as when their latest fight had begun.

With a downward rush of warmth and a scatter of frozen dust that left disturbing designs in the drifts, the Crimson Queen appeared again. With multiple pitchforks and spears in each hand, Sera had stuck to the earth a group of men that had been approaching Teca from behind. They squirmed, their breath taken by the wind, their lungs — some internal, some torn and poking out their backs — filling with snow and fluid. If they still had control of their dancing limbs they were choosing to shake them at a falling sky that only darkened into complacency.

"If we can make it through the night," Sera, Queen of the absent Necrophim, yelled to any who could hear her, "we may survive yet."

Teca refused to look to her. She had seen her true face and had not looked back since. *It's nighttime?* she instead thought to herself. *How can anyone tell?* Before she could search the dark swirl the heavens had become, she was roughly thrown to the side by what she could barely tell were her own soldiers. She immediately ducked a jagged axe aimed at her head, pulling a long dagger from a solid mass of wormy ice that could have only been frozen bowels. The axe swirled overhead to come at her again, but it became caught in the armor of a different Horde soldier that ventured too closely. Teca took advantage of the pause in the fight to drive the dagger into the man's exposed armpit. The blade glanced on cartilage but poked through into his throat, where he called out some man's name before staggering and cutting gloves and fingers on the edge grinding against his pink and open larynx. He backed and whirled, but Teca kept pressing, bringing her broken sword around, intending to connect it with the dagger, but it was caught behind her.

Two men — of which army she could not tell — fought behind her, grappling over a spear as slick as they were. Cheeks had been split open. Noses sliced to the bone beneath. Her sword was stuck in the shoulder plate of one, and, before she could wrench it free, a spearhead glanced off her breastplate. She fell, unharmed, but she had dropped her weapons and lost her sense of direction. She knew she had to press with her legs, but she had lost a boot, and now the heel of one foot was cutting itself on either broken ice or someone's hot blade. So she pushed with her hands against what she assumed was cold field but turned out to be the legs of stampeding fighting all around her, and as soon as she found herself upright, caught between bare faces head-butting themselves into crumpled mush, she was tangled in spear and armored knees and tripped to the stiff prairie again.

And so she prayed again, inadvertently, suddenly remembering lyrics to an obscure part of the *Sol Sistere*.

"Beloved, my God, I can only take
refuge in the Fall you..."

A cleated boot came down upon one of her hands, and, song forgotten, she was relieved that, when her mitten was ripped away, her hand was only scratched by ice and spike. She grabbed and pushed at all around her, some pointed stick sticking up under her half-helm to tear against her ear and scalp. She found someone else's wrist in the mass of writhing and screaming fighters and drove whatever size blade it held into a face before her. But then her feet lost any purchase and she found the ground beneath disappearing, either crumbling or lifting up into the battlefield. She fell, head over feet, stuck between armored legs kicking and bleeding arms grasping at her and the loose land.

Teca found herself in a trench, but it was so clogged with the hard particles of frozen blood and the windswept drifts of melted snow and hardened dirt that she could not tell whether it was natural or hand-dug.

Encroaching *Wyrmwood* filled the space above the trench, haloed the cutting light of streaking meteors. She struggled beneath those that had fallen on top of her, only to realize that they were both dead. One man's guts had been ripped from one end to the other, and his bladder and intestines had exploded all over her chest. The other, a soldier tattooed with both red and green eyes, leaked grey matter from a missing forehead. Teca applied pressure against her own head to slow the bleeding from a scrape behind her ear, realizing that sweat cooled in what was left of her hair, her helm now missing. Before she could stand, a body landed at her feet to pin her legs to the others. A woman, blocking the strange violet light from above, came screaming down on top of her, knocking any shallow breath from Teca's tired lungs. There was then a sudden and new pressure she had to assume was yet another person falling into the trench. Near her, the crunch of snow and bones sounded as yet another person landed. Armor against armor clanged as the crowded descents continued. Teca's right arm would not move for fear of even more pain, and so she could not even roll to flinch her face away from the increasing pressures against her nose and mouth. Any air she lost in collisions from above she could not regain for the flesh and leather crushing her face. She kicked, but apparently only against herself. Something wormy pooled around her temple and into one eye. A constant scream to one side was muffled by her coat. Another scream to the other side pinched directly into her inner ear. The darkness was suddenly overwhelming as the last dark light was blocked by yet another body from above. And all she could see, but only in her mind, was the true face of Sera.

A sharp hand snaked through fighting or dead limb to grab Teca's arm, and she was quickly pulled from the squirming piles. Back out into the land and storms, she knelt beside the pregnant Crimson Queen, fighting to find air and to prevent herself from being wrapped in the flowing vines of every shade of fox fur and fiery silks.

"Someone needs to evacuate a camp that has appeared just over that tree line," Sera said. The splintered horns emerging from her serpentine mass of hair, from crown or skull, moved as she looked around, and they changed the near night shadows. "You have to keep them moving, little Libran. There are more of Ashmedai's forces appearing from the south."

But Teca did not look up, did not look beyond the puppetry of shadows that played out in the alternating melting and freezing pools of crushed organs beneath her. She could not see anywhere in the storm anyway, even as it started to sizzle from the pressure and fires from the sky. A thin rain of blood and dust and snow had appeared, and it tickled as it evaporated just above the skin of the back of her neck.

And what she thought were shadows flickering over the dead, she quickly realized were crows, and she could not help but smile — lips cracking at the rare movement — seeing that, even in the mess of a storm, the birds continued their duty as Wulf had explained it.

"Eating eyeballs to protect us," she mumbled to herself, "from seeing the forbidden through a dead man's eyes… to the holiest of blinding holies." She had been distracted over the last few days, tempted to look deeply into the occasional corpse's eyes, curious to gaze upon God on his throne, willing to drink of the madness the sight would bring. Would she continue fighting, she wondered, in insanity, or would she lurch into a drift to let the winter take her as she had seen so many do?

"How long…" she squeaked, still trying to breathe anything more than a shallow gasp, "…how… long… before we reach… how much longer…"

"Until MANN Lands? Why, my knight in lackluster armor, we have been in the outskirts of the city Simon for most of the night."

"What?" Teca then stood, the softness of the ground or the weakness in her knees helping little. The occasional abandoned shack she had crossed near over the past few hours must have, in actuality, been from the infamous refugee suburbs of Simon. She saw one of the huts now, an easy target of the Horde's flamethrowers. Either bones or jury-rigged scaffolding gleamed from inside the fire.

Suddenly aware of a crooked cramp in her shoulder, she bit her tongue and readied herself to fall again as the clamor of pike against dagger neared in a crowd of soldiers and scavengers fighting each other to avoid a new round of cannon balls appearing and driving up crowds of ice and deadly shrapnel of permafrost. She grabbed at any weapons she could find with her good arm but found herself in the grip of a suddenly appearing Ivy. The top-knotted girl massaged Teca's chest before yanking on her arm to put her dislocated shoulder back into place. The pain was immense, but it almost immediately dulled to a burning sensation as she revolved the arm around to loosen it up.

"We… we need to pull the Flash Company back… from the northern evacuations," she whispered, still finding it difficult to inhale.

Ivy stepped back, a hand hovering over her holster, her gaze fixating near Teca's ear. "Flash Company? They were wiped out days ago." She drew and fired, Teca ducked, and a man of armor went flying. He almost immediately started to get back up, and so Ivy launched herself at him with daggers splintering the purple light. Teca turned but winced at the sight of Ivy's quick blades. She scalped both helm and skin as the screaming man called for mercy. But still, Ivy spoke over the crying, "We're rallying around any stragglers in the woods. Anyone else runs the end of the plain." New specks of blood freckled her face as she dropped the soldier to point in a direction Teca would not have suspected. The girl looked taller than she remembered. She opened the cylinder of her revolver, and, with a look of obvious disappointment, holstered it to started spinning one of the slings at her belt.

"There are wounded over the next rise." The voice was familiar. It should not have been. But Teca could not deny the very specific memories the sight of the Alabaster Princess dug up. She had always disappeared into the storm when seen from afar, but here, so close and so bloody under the burning cosmos, Mew equally had become one with the gory drifts.

"The next rise," she repeated, from a dark and heavy hood hiding eyes that Teca guessed would be equally familiar and equally nostalgic. "We can protect them. Make a stand. But that will be less of a guard to the south. I'll see to it."

"We just have to last out the…" Teca's words were cut off as she was jumped by two men in armor as spiky as an anklyosaurus. She broke one of their swords with her own before bringing her blade down upon his companion's shoulder. Metal reverberated and everyone was staggered, but she recovered first to drive her weapon through a chainmail skirt into thigh meat. With both hands she jerked the sword upward and around through muscle and rectum, spraying the immediate area with flecks of gore. But she slipped on an uneven pile of torsos and legs, some frozen, some still steaming, and her other pursuer was quickly on top of her. He had no weapons but the hangnails of his fingers at her scarves and throat. His rotten emanations stung her eyes no matter how tightly she closed them. She quickly lost any breath she had scrounged.

She could feel the tip of *Tiwaz* appear at her groin as it pushed slowly through the man from his back, bursting his kidney and stomach. He squirmed off of her as Mew pulled the sword free, and he cried out the names of his children before she lopped off his head. Teca could feel the stare of his watery eyes in her peripheral as she gathered herself. She, however, could not look away from the sword in Mew's red hand. She remembered the first time she had seen its crude design, under a dawn's weak reflections of a waning *Brandr Moon*. The shadows it had captured that morning were not all that differently hued from the falling sky it now caught.

"Where's your 'painted path?'" Teca asked through a throat so sore it became a chore to breathe, much less talk, through.

"The mobile city of Phaeton moves against us. They're confronting it head on. I go to join them now."

The women cringed as they were showered in a rain of guts. Meaty ribcages, severed hands, and organs still plump with fluids of all colors fell about and over their heads. The Crimson Queen screamed like a carousing hawk as she landed between the two of them.

Scowling with pearly teeth untouched by the violet light — although with lips every bit as dark as the night — Mew turned to run, saying, "And they are not *my* 'painted men.'"

Sera handed Teca her old Libran broadsword, saying, in turn, "That meek soul has not the taste for true passion. She lives in a world she does not even believe is entirely real. Not like us, eh, noble knight?"

She could not look at the pale woman's face. It did not look the same anymore. She just felt the heft of the broken broadsword, noticing how, whenever she retrieved it, it always felt lighter than any previous time swinging it. And she swung it now at a spear that approached. Blunt blade met crooked wood, and the knight moved inward to two-handedly bring her weapon down on the helmet of the Horde soldier. She then tripped over someone crying on the ground. The left side of the person's body was frozen to the earth, exposed tendons and snow had dried and become one, but its screams and broken fingers still reached for anyone near.

The enemy blubbered through cracked lips and flooded tongue. Teca struggled on the mess of the ground, unable to understand him, but did not look away before he wrenched his caved helmet off. The sound brought bile to her throat. Along with his helmet came the back of his head, and he staggered away, the flurries cooling his skull.

Teca found herself lucky to be stuck in the continual freezing and melting of the brown slop of the battlefield, as a cacophony of shots resounded. A flaming mass of garbage roared overhead and past the drifts, scattering cinders of refuse through the bleeding sleet. Tiny geysers of gory scum erupted all around as bullets broke the drifts. Teca crawled toward a bisected shield of wood and hide to scurry beneath but could see Sera out of the corner of her eyes.

The Crimson Queen, lean but so obviously pregnant, wrapped in a whirling windstorm of furs and silks and leathers and bone jewelry and strung rubies and an emberous headdress of hair, blew a hellish cloud of nether fey out into the direction of the Horde troops. The storm parted. The plain whipped and tore apart. When the exhale ended, Sera, her jaw rehinging, looked no longer pregnant, and seven sticky dark faeries attacked the eyes and ears of any riflemen. They squirmed beneath faceguard to claw at nostrils. They flew and scampered beneath scarves to bite at lips and drink the blood of carotid arteries.

Teca had not realized that she had been praying again, with only the remembrance of Sera's true face branded into her brain. The angelic figure carved into the hilt of her sword shook off the dark light of *Wyrmwood*'s glory.

Wulf has to know, she thought to herself as quietly as she could.

~

Handsome Gibbet, frostbitten fingers trembling to untie knots as solid and bulbous as winter fungi, wiped the tears from his cheek with an elbow. There was disturbingly no one to greet him at the entrance into his great tent, no one to guard against any interlopers. He had, after time indeterminate, after his imprisonment in the Army of Earth, finally returned to his command pavilion. The canvas had faded under the glacial season, its flags apparently long since blowing away in some storm not unlike the current one. He could not remember truly what the color of the tent had been originally, but knew that the bronze violet it now appeared in the light of the falling sky was far from it. Embers lilting from a near tree lighted upon the drapery, but the biting air extinguished them before they could burn the skins. The tree had obviously been hit by a piece of the descending night. Its girth was split in twain down to the core. Smoldering veins ran its length. A massive branch had crushed a cart, along with whatever rations or ammunition its crates had held. The horse that had been bridled to the cart looked to have straggled itself in the following fear, and men of the Army of Heaven — now just strangers to Handsome — had already begun to fight over the rights to butcher the animal. As they slid knives into each others' throats, he parted heavy ropes and heavier curtains to enter what he expected would be familiar surroundings.

"Who duh fuck duh you think you are!" came a voice from beneath barely waking layers of naked flesh. But then the speaker appeared to literally choke on any more words. He coughed rather than exclaimed. He snorted deep in the back of his sinuses, desperately jerking his head to swallow but still able to, in an obvious panic, push the brown-skinned newives aside to stand — in more than one way — at attention. He quickly found a robe that was desperately too short for him before finding the words he sought.

"Suh... master? Is that you? High Former Handsome? Singular Lord Gibbet... I... uh, we all thought you were dead, master! You... your hand!"

Handsome had turned away from the mounds of pillows and limbs and fetters, stopping in front of the only area of his old pavilion that had not changed in its preceding move across the vast prairies. The scraps of clothing he had wrapped around his stumps had soaked through.

Schism still sat in his finely carved palanquin, above dais, above Handsome, above the lurid scene stinking up the tent. Everything surrounding the Lesser Prophet had been left as Handsome remembered. Schism still wore Washkington's crown, was still surrounded by the tiny reliquaries — angelic boons given to the Army of Heaven. Of the original seven, only three had been left unopened.

"Is it really you? You duh look so good. But we never stopped from your last command, High Former, we just keep…"

Handsome searched scattered briefcases and bundles, whispering loudly to the openness of the tent, "Uh, are… uh, all remaining forces directed uh, at the enemy?" Amongst a box of mixed belongings he found another small wooden box — the congratulatory gift given to him in another part of the land. He opened it so quickly and so widely that the simple hinges and weak wood broke.

"Enemy? Master Handsome, duh war is over. Yes! Yes, we're just taking a break as duh fire from duh sky… I mean, a couple of machine units… a lot of… have turned back from… you see, many of duh men are worried about their families… with all duh rumors of Territories falling back home to…"

Handsome turned to fire the pepperbox at the man, but the round struck one of the waking newives in the temple. Without bleeding, she fell on the others as they jumped, screaming in various pitches and falling over each other in an attempt to escape the ribbons tying their wrists and ankles. Some hopped, some crawled, but all of them scrambled toward the exit of the tent, around and past the man who squatted and covered his head with his hands.

"I'll drive them out, my lord!" the man yelled as the pepperbox cracked again. "I'll send all duh Army out!"

Handsome struggled with a mutilated hand to twist the barrel of the small revolver. It finally clicked into place again, and he fired toward the curtains, realizing the sergeant and his harem had disappeared into the dark morning. The entrance to the pavilion flapped its heavy doors against the sound of storm and meteorite.

"Fuh… forgive them, O' Leader on High," Handsome said, turning and balancing on one knee before Schism, "fuh… for they know not what they do." He sank even lower then to crawl toward the Boons of the Choir, to pull one of the small boxes from the alcove in the palanquin, and to flick and break the wax holding the ribbon holding the chest shut. Without tongue, he whispered, holding the box to his forehead before opening it, "MANN Lands, the city of Simon."

A wind overturned pillows, blew loose tobacco, moved the few sticky strands of hair Handsome had left, before vanishing as quickly as it had appeared.

"MANN Lands, the capital city of Joseph." He coughed as he opened another seal and box.

The third one he took his time with, as difficult as the temptation was to release the *galgalim* as quickly as possible. He set this last box down after chewing the wax from the seal with both rows of his gums. He closed both layers of his eyelids to picture the devil in his mind — not as he was certainly now, withered and one-eyed and left behind, already beaten, but as he had been the night in Handsome's bedchamber. The figure had loomed above the governor, shrouded as an incubus as he had pinned him down to bloody sheets with both hand and mind.

The old tithingman kept his eyes closed but opened the final reliquary to the roar of the sudden and quickly disappearing wind while whispering, "a man called Wulf."

~

The arrows sticking from Janus' hunched form stood out in all directions. Blood had stopped streaming down his back, but the metal heads ground against his shoulder blades, caught up in muscle and armor. He staggered through the trees in the middle of where the mobile city of Phaeton had rested, barely noticed, for most of the occupants had scattered to defend the massive camp from the followers of the Painted Path. But the occasional soldier of the Horde ran past to shovel snow onto fires that had appeared. *Wyrmwood*, in its disturbing proximity, was burning the winter away from the immediate plains. The blizzard had abated, quelled by an even stronger wind conjured by the falling star, but the air burned humidly from meteors that fell upon the battlefields with as much warning as the Horde's cannonballs, and so soldiers — too busy throwing slush at smoking tree and smoldering tent to notice the great green eyes painted on Janus' armor and mask — ran, too distracted to join the packing of the great camp or their brethren out in the bloody fields of the chase.

He stumbled past a temporary stable. It was empty. He limped near a slave pen. It was equally ramshackle and quiet. He staggered by a mound of garbage, and even through his the Elder Mask he could smell the thick stench of rotted meat and paper, the heavy crud of congealed gasoline and dusty exhaust. He pulled a knife from the back of his thigh, its wet edge revealing only more of the purple haze all air was becoming under the violent mists. His leg only hurt all the more, mirrored as its steps were by its bullet-riddled twin. Janus' body had taken a terrible toll across the battlefield and into the mobile battle-city, but he had fought like an entire legion just by himself, taking out just as many of the Horde troops. The mask had come through intact. No one would have been able to tell its pale true color at this point, however, as splatter-covered as it was. The ichors dripping from its curves pooled over the ex-gladiator's faux lips to moisten his own through the mask's mouth slit.

The garbage pile shifted and rose, and suddenly there stood a form as hunched but wider than he. From the stinking refuse came the heavy steps of an Unfeigned, one of those in the Horde that had traded organs and humanity and lifespan for a fleeting chance at physical power. The being's head resided deep within a glass bulb filled within electrical current, while the rest of its cast iron body lurked in the smog pluming from multiple exhaust pipes. It brought most of the garbage pile with it as it lurched forward.

Janus became The Assassin, disappearing into the Unfeigned's smoke to strike at it from blind spots too close for its buzzsaw to reach. He left daggers behind in the soft parts under the plates and bolts of its joints, and, when it wavered after trying to walk, Janus became The Warrior, breaking an axe on gatling gun, shattered panels, and glass. The buzzsaw had opened Janus' chest. A wide swing from a cinder-block fist had bruised a hip and ribs. But he, now covered from head to toe in the sweet soak of gasoline, walked toward what could have only been Phaeton's command pavilion. Behind him, the Unfeigned shook as it tried to move away from near flames, but it too was covered in the pool of fuel, and fires ran and arced and found the few still natural bits beneath the iron. The scream was both organic and metallic, and it brought three soldiers out from their packing.

Janus ran ahead of them, blood pooling in one of his boots, shoulder blades screaming in anguish from the blades and arrows stuck in bone and muscle. He stopped short around the corner of a portable outhouse, draped in the stench of ordure and the gory dark light of what he assumed was evening. As one Horde man ran by, he stabbed like lightning, like The Assassin, pricking tendons of the legs and feet, sticking arteries beneath arms and between legs. Janus turned to see the next two soldiers drawing near. He threw the knives at the nearest man — one wearing chains for clothing — surprising but deliberately missing him. Both daggers struck the soldier behind him, but the sound they made was edge on armor. In closed the chain-man, but his raised hatchet was too slow, too off-balance, and so Janus kneed the man in his ribs while simultaneously dislocating his arm, bringing his own ax down upon his own face. The nose guard bent inward and the man was down.

"I got gold!" the next soldier yelled. "I can get you boys... or girls... anything you..."

He too held an ax, but Janus was now The Warrior, and he smashed weapon, hand, arm, faceguard, forehead, and brain with one blow of his sword.

He could barely feel the tiny blade slide into his lower back amongst all the other punctures and slices and bullet holes wracking his body, but it made him turn to find the first soldier — now sinking into an expanding puddle of his own arterial blood — trembling and blind and trying desperately to stick him again with a rusty pocket knife. Janus' sword came down with all his might to sever the man above the shoulder. His head, without bone still connecting it, flopped against the opposite shoulder, but his hands still clenched the canvas of a nearby pavilion as it slid to the melting dirt.

For a second, back out in the main pathway of the great camp, Janus could have sworn he saw Mew in some adjoining alley. But, his eyes glancing across the smoldering effigies and stretched bodies of children hanging from makeshift perches, then saw only the encroaching carnage of the Painted Path — Maahesehaam's closing followers. The fully tattooed warriors were taking sickles to any of the Horde that had not moved yet to the battlefields.

With the Elder Mask on, he no longer saw Mew in every glimpse of the winter sun, no longer heard her voice in each rise of the wind, no longer smelled her nectarous scent whenever he breathed. Amongst all the memories in his head (in the mask), many worshipped, at the very least, her image, at the most, her grace, but focusing on The Assassin and The Warrior drove him forward, with thoughts of her being embraced by the rebel Maahesehaam only in his peripheral.

There were no guards outside the obvious command pavilion, just the scaffolding of refuse shaped into an archway. The hastily constructed ritual looked to be using rotted woods from defiled coffins. He could only hope the tiny bones woven into the arch were from birds. They dripped from a fog that could not be blown away — a mist of sticky atmosphere and lights from an unknown direction.

The handles and arrows protruding from his slumped, aching body caught against the curtains of the entrance, but he shambled through. The lights inside were dying as the glares from hidden sun and falling star fought and grew outside, but he could still see the mess of the interior. Golden trinkets were scattered. Pillows had been thrown. A young girl, dark and dead, bald and bleeding, lay strewn in one corner. Coffee percolated in the stones of a small fire in another. The drink smelled like cat urine, and its odor had permeated everything in the spacious tent. Janus had become The Assassin, and, despite the shuddering pain of each step, he had crept soundlessly in, and so Handsome Gibbet had not even noticed his presence. But Janus recognized his shrunken form at once, just as he did the familiar scene. The tithingman was standing up upon the disassembled platform, his ear to the sewn lips of Schism. He nodded, whispered in response, and nodded again. When something alerted him to Janus' presence, he fell, bone-thin limbs getting tangled amongst each other, but he quickly pulled himself to a step and aimed a shaking pepperbox at Janus.

"Nuh, not again... nuh, never..."

Janus could not understand the tiny voice, nor did he feel anything more than the impact from the round of the small revolver. He assumed himself to be beyond pain at this point. Handsome fired again, and neither of the men were sure if the round hit Janus or not. The tithingman's knuckles bulged obscenely as he tried again to turn the barrel of the gun with shaking and mutilated hands and even his mouth, quickly giving up to turn over a number of crates, never looking away from Janus.

Janus, however, was not watching him. Handsome's whisper was indiscernible, and his presence was inferior to the thing sitting up on the dais. In another life, the first time Janus had snuck into Phaeton, he had paid the figure little attention. Now he recognized it as the Horde's High Brother of the Advancing Forces — Schism of the Abysmal Well.

Handsome Gibbet ran out the back of the adjoining tent with a small chest the length of his forearm.

Janus took each step up toward Schism deliberately, taking his time to imprint every distinguishing mark of the preserved Lesser Antony in his mind. He would want to tell Mew everything. Thinking of her suddenly made him disturbingly aware of his own exhalations. He had never known it to echo around his face beneath the Elder Mask, had never felt his breath condense on its interior or his chin beneath it.

Had he noticed last time that Schism had been wearing what was most certainly Washkington's Crown? Its gilded surface had been worn mostly away. Its thorns had opened the Lesser's parchment skin in many spots over the stretched forehead. Eyelids twitched under the stitching. Lips moved from something beneath, as though Schism whispered something to him.

He took out a dagger and a hatchet. He just did not care what the Lesser had to say. Closely, he swung widely, tearing jerky flesh wide, paper skin shredding in all directions. Instantly, Janus was swarmed by a cloud of abysmal locusts. He fell backward, downward and outward from the palanquin, with the critters' tiny metal legs skittering over every inch of exposed skin, under every inch of covered limb. He twisted against their needling smiles, convulsed from the venom of their cursing stingers, but it was their tiny fiery crowns of blond hair that he feared most. He burst into flames, and the locusts cracked like popcorn over his body. Looking out beyond the wavering and scalding air, all he could see was Mew once more.

~

The first thing Mew remembered waking to was some sort of sensation in what she would in time realize must have been her feet or hands or perhaps even her entire limbs. The feeling was not pain, not yet, and it certainly was not pleasure. It was an awareness, perhaps, in burgeoning nerve endings of existence, a striving in regenerating flesh for meaning. Her other senses were a long way from life at that point, so her shallow lucidity spent an unknown amount of time (with even "time" itself being incomprehensible at this moment) swimming amongst these sensations that she later realized must have been the blooming sparks of nerves as they ignited again after cell death. But even more remarkable, as had later been recounted to her by the Painted Path, was that the twinges of primitive tactile experience must have been sparked by her mutilated form's desperate attempt toward movement. Could it be that her desire for escape and progress resided not just in her mind, that her spirit for freedom permeated down into every cell of her body? That even before she was aware of her new life her mangled hands had pulled her forward over the bottom of the canyon bed, her shattered knees and disembodied legs had pushed the rest of what remained along the ice and rock until her skull would knit itself back together, until her unraveled circulatory system could itself crawl to join back with the scattered pieces of her spinal column.

She barely remembered falling, but she remembered it as being a calm experience. Only later would she have flashes of insight into the actual hundred-foot plummet, of struggling, with the onrush of air and the tithingman's close and heavy body, to flip her assailant underneath her to cushion her from whatever frozen rock dwelled down in the shadowed reaches of the canyon. But, as muscle adhered to bone, as neuron stretched to reach neuron, and as her senses slowly reemerged through the fleshy haze, she could only recall the peace she felt in the fall, of a fulfilled calling, of all the green people across the land that would spread her word in her passing. She felt safe in the knowledge that the land would become a better place than she had known it.

The Painted Path had told her that what they had come upon in the forest barely resembled anything that had once been human. Nests of burst veins crawled together to wrap around bare winter weeds before pulling a mass of rib meat along. Bladders of fluid slithered to stick themselves to knitting muscle and splintered bone that jerked to reattach to each other. Tendons reached for joints and stuck and pulled tightly. Mew could only remember that, when her inner ears and humors had aligned enough, she could actually hear her neck bones bend to straighten and hold up her jigsaw skull.

Maahesehaam and his disciples had already followed her original trail to punish her captors. They bragged as they led her to an overlook to survey the carnage of the massacre. Her eyes, rods and cones and lenses, had still been regenerating and shifting at this point, but she could still make out a camp piled full of corpses that would have been as indistinguishable as she had been half a day earlier. Her senses were mostly emerging from resurrection, but she could still smell the slow rot of cold decay in the clinging mists.

Under the smiling reverence of the one called the Painted God, his followers, all standing above the gore-melted hill, then pledged their allegiance to vengeance and to the Lonely Forgotten Sun of God, and, despite her pleas otherwise, despite the renewed winter that killed many of them in their sleep on the deadly cold trek from Kaldera to the plains, and now nearing MANN Lands, the Painted Path waged war on the Horde, straight to the stalled mobile camps of Phaeton.

Mew stood beneath the camps' ornamentation, grotesque structures of scavenged wood and scrap metal. From the crooked perch above her hung the lanky form of a small person. He had been stuck to a hook and had the frozen engine of some small machine tied to his feet. He had to now be twice the height he had been when alive. It reminded her again of the carnage the Painted Path had left in her wake. Many of their warriors were only children, and they knew nothing other than lives of violent rebellion, constantly freeing the slaves of Below the Brook before the land had shrunk beyond capacity. With the pocket dimension gone, they had come through looking for new purpose, and they had found it when her wretched and wrecked form had appeared to them. Her resurrection had made even those that had grown used to Maahesehaam's miracles bow down in reverence. In their eyes they could never stop avenging her. Every time they beheaded a Horde soldier with one of their sickles they felt it was striking a blow against those that condemned her in the trial of the mountains. And as they ran all around her, storming tents and armories, putting the Horde men to quick and loud deaths, she could only wonder what Janus would think that she saw in all of this. Could he have guessed what she thought about all the blood shed in her name? She had searched him out in the fleeing camps of what was left of Wulf's army but to no avail. Some said that he had deserted. Some said that he was dead. Some claimed to have seen the pale face of a masked man possessed by a hundred fighters clearing the way to the Horde's commanders. Mew believed no one.

Would Janus think that she was appalled by the Painted Path's prayer through murder? Or would he believe that she reveled in such bloodshed, if he knew of her treatment by the *Ashmedai Adat El's* judges and jurors? In truth, when she looked around, at blade against blade against throat, all she now saw was the world, the ultimate expression of her ultimate truth — that of love — being exemplified in every angry eye. And that is why, since her latest resurrection, her heart had not stopped crying — in relief or sadness, she could not tell.

She wrapped her heavy cloak around herself even tighter, pulled its thick black bear hood down lower over her face. The air did not affect her. The swirl of wind was no more than the lightest of breezes to her. The sticky and low fog avoided her passage. But she could not abide by the weird day's light. Ever since entering back into the prairies of the North, she had to consistently remind herself that night was day and day was night. *Wyrmwood* pressed down against the plain, and it was dragging the horrors of Heaven down with it. And every time she let that strange vegetable light touch her skin it felt like the rape of the familiar.

But she could no longer stand outside the pavilion, waiting, doing nothing, as the wretched ran into and from the vulva of its entrance. Slave girls, generals, tithingmen, warriors and assassins came and went. Its interior had been a hive of gunshot, shouts, and whispers, and now it had become a womb of dancing and screaming light, and so she finally entered through the fleshy curtains, having no idea what she would find but knowing it would not be good.

And she was right. Janus' body crackled in flames both natural and supernatural. A line of abysmal locusts swarmed him, some skittering, some flittering, from the desiccate and collapsing shell of a figure she refused to look too closely at. The clockwork insects sparked at the viridescent light emanating from her eyes and mouth as she screamed at them. Their tiny bodies popped like embers in a new wind, and each metal shell crumbled before its lost soul was released to a new abyss.

She was at Janus' charred side in an instant. His smoldering armor and clothing had melted to a body blackened beyond recognition, but she knew the unbelieving and brown eyes watching her through the holes in the Elder Mask. They were the eyes from beneath the ring and pens of the Morbis Orbis, the eyes that would never quite touch hers when she made a late morning visit, would never completely meet her gaze as they talked into the dangerous afternoons. The heavy scent of smoldering hair burned her nostrils.

Any air he exhaled would light itself on the flames that died under

Mew's touch as she rapidly brushed away the shriveled shells of the locusts. Her knees crunched more beneath her as her hands caught a light unfamiliar under the tent and a sky emanating an unnatural hue. And she took his pain into herself.

Her hands burned.

Her arms charred.

Her limbs stung with the electric venom of a hundred spurs.

Her back was stuck with arrows.

Her thighs and sides were slashed from dagger, ax, and spear.

But she took it all in silently, biting her tongue until it bled, until he pushed her away. The strength of his blackened arms was surprising, and she rolled backward to convulse with the seizures of shock as her flesh mended. Her near instantaneous healing hurt almost as badly as the wounds she had taken upon herself.

"No..." Janus was able to croak. "No... I don't... I can't... never again..."

Mew wondered just how many lives she had left.

~

"...repeat... not head... you will be turned away! ...you hear me, Wulf?"

He could hear him, but Wulf ignored the Agent of MANN as he did all sounds around him. His voice was mostly static now, the nearer *Wyrmwood* fell. The air itself outside the sweat lodge crackled with magnetic electricity, so it was no wonder that the signal inside the insectoid helmet did the same. But despite the constant communications blathering next to his ears, Wulf found using the Agent of MANN's avatar's body as armor quite comfortable. Certain parts of its exoskeleton had been quickly dissembled and refitted to perfectly protect his legs and chest. The head, mostly gutted, now protruded from his hood. The children surrounding him, with all they had seen over the previous seasons, were not even frightened by the specter that meditated in the middle of the quickly assembled lodge. Still, many cried or whimpered from the explosions that neared. But Wulf ignored them as well to turn inward before stretching his mental senses outward. He had been focusing all his meditative energies toward the healing of his eye socket, after the remaining green women and men had packed it with oils and herb satchels, but, as the Horde neared yet again, he bedded down to direct the last of his army.

Super sensitive telekinetic waves pulsed out from his position, over the new terrain. Anyone with any utensil that could be used as a weapon walked the sludge the falling sky was melting, and many may have felt the creep along the back of their necks or the tickle of the hairs on their arms as the invisible feelers reached out. At the same time, Wulf also reached out to touch the minds of any remaining soldiers, any of his original fighters left that could lead one final push back before storm and Horde trampled the scattered retreat.

His mind searched among the crowds for the thoughts of Librans, and upon finding them he gave any foot troops slight nudges with telekinetic feeler and telepathic suggestion. The Librans walked slowly forward, those with spear and/or shield leading the charge. Nearby Horde troops took up the bait, and whether they became impaled or engaged with shield, any Libran with smaller blade or club entered the line to stab or beat the distracted. And when any other Horde soldiers came to any rescue, Wulf nudged the Librans aside so that cavalry knights could charge, raising the field's pitch by trampling or jousting through. The front line of the Horde was quickly in disarray, even though most of the horses had their necks impaled or cleaved.

But before the last mount had fallen, Wulf had already sent the mental message to a line of green archers. They had established a rhythm with pollen bombs and cloud after preceding cloud of arrows coated with a sap that prevented wounds from closing. They would keep up this rhythm until all arrows were exhausted, which would not be much longer. Wulf had waited until the wind was just right, pushing the seeds and pollens deeper into the Army of Heaven. If the fog dared dip in a different direction, he would telekinetically push it back toward the Horde. And all the while the Libran foot fighters slowly moved forward, revolving to periodically halt the Horde's forward progress and let their knights and lances through.

And then came the bear shirts. Wulf sent the midgardian berserkers around and forward. They circled on both sides of the red fields, around the main engagement, and plowed the ground and the Horde with hammer and axe. They beat the ground, themselves, and the enemy, running bare-chested, furred capes billowing over their left arms, and without regard to their own safety they ran into the men and machines of the Horde. They were torn and bullet-riddled, but never did they stop or even slow. They inhaled the allergen clouds and took the arrows of their own army unnoticed. Their eyes became as red as their chest turned the deeper they then pushed. Their assault was one long, loud, and deep charge into the enemy force. And the Army of Heaven continued to scatter, with arrows falling in the same pattern their soldiers paused to cringe beneath. And every time they stopped, every time they ducked beneath each other or truck, the Army of Earth's footmen would revolve to let knights through to reappear with a harmonic slashing and ancient swords adorned with Black Hills silver.

After a couple more revolutions, the rhythm of arrows slowed, and the bear shirts — howling like dogs, growling ursine — also slowed along the sides of the fields. They took synchronized steps, hairy boots crushing snow and skull, but with whirling hammers of stone and broken axes of iron. The enemy fought itself in between the opposite lines, crushing itself to flee only against the other row of midgardians. Into all of this, every surviving member of the Army of Earth ran. Mothers swung walking sticks they had been whittling sharp since the beginning of the war. Fathers threw spears they had been taught to drive since the peregrination out of Erebus. The elderly moved as close as they could before firing off the last of the Army's wet rounds. Children ran in the slop to collect shields to drag to the back of the lines.

And then Wulf whispered into the minds of the masses. He pulled them back to pause, to catch breath, to reload meager rations of ammunition and arrows, to realign breaking lines, to adjust the leverage of the uneven ground to the people's advantage. As the lines regrouped and resupplied, the bear shirts continued their thrum against the ground. As the sky vibrated from falling star, the softening ground did the same under midgardian boot. At the rear of the Horde forces, enemy reinforcements found themselves trampled by the retreat of their running forbearers. And Wulf could sense those reinforcements, could feel the minds of a multitude of new companies of enemy coming up from the southern prairie. A league away, under hide hut, sweat, and the unknown metal of alien armor, he knew of the growing threat.

"…sssstt… hear me? Wulf… do it…" the interior of the helmet sizzled in his ear.

And he did then actually stop to listen, to the Agent of MANN speaking from the near city, to the murmurs and cries of the children sharing tiny lodge, to the fear creeping coldly down into his stomach.

He stood to crouch, again surprised at how light his new armor was, how the new space in his skull improved his equilibrium, but also how the Eye of Yggr compensated for an expected loss of peripheral. He drew up to his full height outside the lodge and scanned the roll of the hillocks leading out from the thin lines of trees framing the base camp. His electronic voice said to a near soldier, "Move anyone remaining as deep into the forest as you can. Find the city on the other side."

"...repeat!" the Agent of MANN broadcasted to him. "Bring them, Wulf... fsssk... bring them all. I'll let... in. I'll let you in! Ssssst... care. I will let... fsssst... ksssst."

Wulf turned, releasing the clasps of his heavy cloak before wrapping it around the dirty children that were emerging behind him. They stared out at him from the hot interior, but all he could see was the multitude of dark, wet eyes. They were the biggest he had ever seen.

"Run, as fast as you can, but run together, always together, hold together, but run as fast as you can."

Wulf strode away from them, out into the strangely earthy yet celestial evening, feeling the humid freeze that characterized the unnatural winter that could only come from a war-torn plain being crushed under a collapsing heavens. His bizarre armor shielded him from most of it, but the grit from exploding meteorites and the icy shrapnel of blood-soaked mists stung his arms. He stopped at the beginning of the rolling ground, amongst abandoned wagons and stretchers. A group of women, too exposed in only the lightest of hides and worn mittens, had cannibalized yurts to build fencing between the few trees available. They had spears to set up in the uneven ground as shallow pitfalls. There was only one rifle to share amongst the group.

"We're almost ready," one of them said to him. Her doeskin skirt was so torn, her furred moccasins so short, that her calves were easily open to the corrupt breeze. She had once been a newife, he could tell, for it appeared that the *noli me tangere* tattoo on her ankle had been burned away. The wound was still healing, if it ever entirely would. "We just have to..."

The ground moved up toward them as though some great worm writhed beneath it. In fact, Wulf would have suspected that the Beast of the Core had come, that his long ago fevered summons had come to fruition, had not the quake come with the sound of enemy cannon and gunpowder.

He righted himself, shifting the grain of snowdrifts from his back. Nearby trees either split or fell, yellow interiors now showing before being tainted by the bruise of the sky. Wulf removed himself from the refuse of fallen branches and piles of boards from whatever wagon's remains had exploded. The clang of metal and tread, armor and rifle, grew like an inconsistent song to a manic pitch. There was movement all around as the Horde flowed over him like a sea of rusty chains and rotted rubber. And he waded into this dark moisture, hungry Yin flashing out before him, refusing to reflect the ugly light of the atmosphere for it own wine color, whining immediately from its foul leather sheath for subsistence.

"Alright, girl!" Wulf shouted from his mandibled speaker. "Let's see just how insatiable you are!"

The blade moved faster than any Horde soldier could follow, augmented by Wulf's years of training under *SHE'* serpentine eyes and his telekinesis to give each slice extra speed and strength, for he struck with both his hand and his mind.

A soldier with shoulder armor both spiked and hairy lost his head, his facemask already giving him the expression of wide incredulity. Another man was cut from groin to goiter, and the spray of blood hid a body trying desperately to steady itself without a center. On came the Horde, with a new batch of soldiers completely covered in full-environmental armor. Great plates covered their arms and barrel chests. Their heads appeared tiny in small rounded helmets protected by great shoulder pauldrons. From a distance they would have looked squat, but up close they were taller than Wulf. Yet Yin sliced through each man as though he were wearing no armor at all. The possessed blade passed through iron and steel as easily as it did muscle and bone. He swung it without resistance. And she drank up both blood and soul with each murder.

Wulf dropped low to avoid the swing of short pikes, and below the whizzing axe blades he cut the legs out from under all that neared. Some would struggle to move, limbless in their heavy armor, before their spirits were torn from their warm flesh to be gobbled up by the eldritch blade. He leaped above the low stab of spears and electric tridents, only to descend upon heads with Yin piercing helmet, skull, spine, bladder, and artery. Any blood the vampiric sword did not immediately drink would be flung wide with the next swing, falling like the obscene rain storming down from *Wyrmwood*.

He dived into the thickest of Horde squads, where their long pikes and flamecasters would be inhibited, and they struck their comrades trying to pin him down. Any that were able to avoid the claws and spiked knuckles of each other fell by his quick and close jabs to their kidneys. Any who ran would be pulled back by his mental suggestions, both telekinetic and empathic, and he would separate the organs and the souls from their bodies with one sweeping circular swing.

Next to him, one of Wulf's own fighters took a mace to the face, her jaw tearing off to be thrown to the piles of gory excrement soaking the melted fields. She probed but never touched the gaping hole in her face and neck before joining her friends on the top of one of these dark mounds. Wulf reached the side of a Libran too late, as the knight's lungs were punctured by an inward-bent chestplate. A bucket of blood geysered from his blue lips, drenching his assailant before Wulf severed the Horde soldier's torso from his waist. He turned to a scream from behind as a midgardian was impaled on the horns of a charging snow-mobile. Its driver and rider both quickly lost their heads to Yin, never getting the chance to scream in return.

He leaped over a crowd of hardhats in duster jackets down to their sharp boots. They held no weapons except for gauntlets that ended, instead of fingers, in wicked meat hooks. The leather of their heavy sleeves was soaked in blood so thickly that the hooks were connected to the ground by thin veins streaming behind their march. The open coats revealed segmented tubing and belts tangled around their pelvises that led to hip-held battery packs. Wulf could not feel their hooks against his telekinetic or MANN exoskeleton. The enemy, however, could feel the rush of his crimson sword through their spines, but only for a second. One man staggered before falling upon his own messy ropes of intestines and cords, asking for help from above. Many of them fell with their hooks looped in the ribcages of their fellow soldiers, as Wulf darted around and around them, behind and over and under them.

He kicked low, smashing greaves and shins, and was always ahead of any spear or halberd, always behind any enemy before they realized it. Any Horde soldier was more likely to strike a companion that him, and they often did when swinging at the liquid shadow.

He could see what no one else did on the battlefield. Yggr's Eye revealed each man's soul as Yin tore it from body. Their spirits, all rainbows of cloudy ectoplasmic expression, stretched like distressed cotton, in rigored and silent howls, before being sucked into the blade's supernatural edge. Wulf was determined to find an end to her hunger, but he feared it was without limit, as she binged on both soul and blood. The gory streams on her unknown metal turned to rivulets that shrank to droplets that disappeared into the very blade itself. Yet still she cried, puerilly and infernally, forever more.

Flaming cannonballs, cooking away the fog into spiraling, horizontal tornados, burned the air of those escaping all carnage. Wulf pushed with his mind against any on these lights as they appeared, and the crackling metal would careen off its course to destroy some other target.

A great mace came down within an inch of his leg. Wulf rolled to the side. It was as unevenly yet demonically spiked as the full armor of the being wielding it. Somewhere beneath the mass of sharp scales and razored segments strode a soldier Yin could not reach. Impossibly, she could not break the wards placed on the armor, could not pierce the enchantments strengthening the man's equally spiked shield. Again and again he struck, to no avail, as the soldier's great mace would swing, impaling other Horde soldiers Wulf would leap behind. He struck at any points in the charmed armor he thought openings, but only dark sparks would result. He tried slicing away at the numerous sigils of Asmodeus, but nothing worked. He slid beneath the brute to stab at what he hoped were soft points, and in doing so he noticed, through Yggr's Eye, a slight discoloration in the gauntlet holding the great shield. It was a replacement piece, not a part of the original suit. Still rolling, he swiped fingers from hand with a close strike, before plunging his sword into the same hand and completely down the length inside of the armored arm. Yin had drunk up deeply of heart's blood before the man's soul even appeared just to disappear just as greedily.

The mists moved above as a tin trailer's turning rectangular form appeared from above. With grimace and grinding teeth, Wulf pushed against it, telekinetically slowing it revolution before tossing it sideways. It would have landed atop him. Instead, its twisting bulk smashed nearby, and its contents scrambled and screamed from new openings in the metal.

"Goddamn, do I hate Gregors." He flew at the scarecrow creatures before they could swarm the nearest refugees. Rotten clothing, moldy straw, and assorted blunt teeth flew about in a storm of elderly limbs and heads. Yin whined her displeasure at the rancid souls linked to the brainless effigies. The creatures ran in too many directions for Wulf to follow.

"...ssssss... be last... imaging report... ssst... can... something fast, very, very fast..." Between the electricity in the air and the guttural barking of the Horde at all sides, Wulf could not hear the Agent of MANN trying to get his attention. He dove deep into his mind to find the peace of "the way," the calm the *SHE*' had shown him all those decades ago. In this peaceful flow of opposites he found the strength to push outward with his mind, feeling in all directions with invisible tendrils, sensing the minds in all directions for fear, anger, and vigilance. And he struck. Yin bit through the top of a bald soldier's head, from angelic branding to thigh's artery. He cut through another's heavily armored neck to lop a head off that, for less than a second, blotted out the flaming star above. Wulf cut off arms to let men wander for the second before their eternal spirit was sucked into his blade. He cut off their feet to use their bodies to push off against as an alternative to a prairie littered with lungs and livers, leaping over and about to kick off Horde heads. As Yin ate, Wulf struck out with his mind and hand, smashing chestplate and rib and heart with telekinetic palm strikes. He kicked low with mind and foot, shattering spiked greaves and fibulas, leaving only messes of shrapnel and bone splinters below knees, and leaving the victims behind to plead for mercy against storm and sky. His mind pushed against treaded trucks, topped by gaseous flamethrowers, throwing them into the deeper pools of bloody slush. Telekinesis pulled the enemy from their individual fights, bringing them within Yin's thirsty reach.

Often he would find himself fighting alongside other remnants from the Army of Earth. They swung broken weapons or stabbed with common utensils or whittled spears from the bare woodlands. Some were cut down before he could help them, others disappeared into the struggling crowds only to reappear later with even more wounds. Still, they all fought on.

A group of wild men rushed him. They were all barely armored with the lightest of leathers but branded heavily with what looked like all the pink shapes of the entire Divine Choir on their white and rosy skin. Every feature that could be pierced, was, with angelic arms reaching out from every ornament. Wulf leaped between their charges, and each man cut his brethren trying to stab him. Those that were left were sliced from shoulder to hip, some sliding in half cleanly without blood left to bleed. He spun and ducked around and under them, over and behind them, leaving few near tendons untouched, few arteries unopened.

"Wulf! Can you hear me? Something fast... kssk... way!"

One of his own soldiers landed nearby, flung from a nearby man-sized slingshot. The man had been quartered beforehand but landed almost back in his original shape. Wulf flicked his wrist and telekinetically pushed the sling into the air and into some distant trees. The controller of the sling, he pulled at with his mind, and the man was instantaneously impaled and hollow from Yin's touch.

"It's coming here, to Simon, but... tsssst... kssssss... another one just as fast..."

Wulf paused, alone on an island of chunks of ice, earth, and machinery. His voice command broke the seals of his helmet, and beneath the hiss of the armor's atmospheric release, he listened to the Agent of MANN's frantic last warning. "Something... ssss... coming straight... your location! ...immense speed..." He dropped the insectoidal head to the gore of the ground. The fuzzy communications had given him a headache. He had felt that the helmet hampered his peripheral, dulled his mental senses, and interfered with the Eye of Yggr. Despite the stomach-churning stench of the fields, and the humid pressure of the crushing mists, it was a relief to taste real air.

But there was something wrong with the atmosphere. It fought against itself in whirling gusts. It ignited, sometimes close to the warped earth, sometimes high above in electric clouds seeded with grit from exploding meteorites. *Wyrmwood* grew and grew closer, and the battlefields sometimes seemed to rise, drawn to the falling star, while other times the drifts of dirt and quartered bodies, the melted remains of man and frost, spread, repulsed by the sky. This celestial and chthonic struggle gave the appearance of a deep sleeping land that snored through its traumatic dreams. While beneath the clamor of the fighting — under the sounds of stalling machines and jagged shields against broken faces — Wulf could now hear a rising groan akin to the sound of some great instrument. He heard everything around him as a piece of that sound. The jamming of a gatling gun, the whines of barely living invalids, the scream of a pike scraping platemail — all rang out together as the voice of one trumpet. And as he felt outward with his mind, both caressing the land with psionic waves and tendrils and searching amongst the fevered brains of the fighting, he noticed something alien far beyond hillock and rise. He sensed something nearing the close prairie, traveling at an impossible speed, made of some superorganic substance — neither the consistency of the material or immaterial — and bearing down toward the very spot he stood. And as soon as he opened his eyes he could see it, as fast as it flew. He pushed at it with more effort than he ever had any object ever with his mind, but it did not slow until he pushed even harder. Wulf believed that he had never reached the upper limits of his telekinesis, but knew he could push no harder than he was pushing now against the angelic "wheel within wheels." He was certain no one else on the bloody fields saw the translucent being until it plowed bodies over with the rest of the carnage, was certain no one else was hearing the infernal trumpets until they burst ear drums with its passage. But, with Yggr's Eye, he could see the celestial rims and spokes turning faster than light within each other — all covered in eyes — could feel the form as he slowed it with his mind. It only partially spun in this reality, and so, as it neared ever closer, Wulf felt as though, as he gathered all his strength, mental and physical, to push back against it, he was touching against another world — one of only flesh and crystals and an obscene hybrid of both.

He sank into the grotesque muck of guts the ground had become, trying to gather any leverage from earth and mind, with the "wheel within wheels" too tearing into the battlefield to push forward, ice and bodies — fresh and otherwise — being flung behind its revolution for a mile or more. Both Armies, buffeted by supernatural pressures, were now aware of the spinning anomaly, and most ran from the plains never to be seen again. The being they saw would fill their short days with nightmares they could not differentiate from the waking hours. Still it creeped closer. Still Wulf strained, blood vessels in his temples bursting, his granite eye bleeding. He could feel the pressure as though the being spun right in front of him, and in response his nose bent sideways, his cheekbones cracked and outspread fingers broke. The air filling his lungs was sucked out as though he pushed in a vacuum, and he breathed only the blood leaking from capillaries. But with one final exertion he pushed again, and something popped in the back of his brain, followed by what felt like a stream of something cold dripping down from the interior of his skull to his spine.

The *galgalim*, the wheel within wheels, hit Wulf, and the sound of his inner ears bursting, a multitude of bones breaking, and organs liquefying, deafened him to all that came next. In the mere seconds he bounced across the land he woke up several times, only to see the world spinning on all sides. When he came to rest in a pile of bodies and ice, a throne of snow and bone, on the far side of a battlefield he thought he knew, Yggr's Eye refused to close, showing him the continuation of the fighting he thought diminished by his presence. Obscure men wrestled nearby with knives sharpened out of shrapnel, shields fastened out of refuse. Woman tricked armored men into falling upon spears sharpened out of bone. Flamecasters scorched any horse or straggler that could not remove themselves from the bloody mess the plains had become. Any functioning rifle or dry round that could be found was used against its holder to block out the disgusting trumpet blare of the horizons. Packs of all color of dogs, senses overloaded, plunged sticky muzzles into the immense meat gardens. The mists at this angle even more reflected the scum of the drifts, the organic violet of the sky, and the scene was darkening so quickly that Wulf could not make out the birds of the sky. They circled and dived and he could only assume that they were crows by their size and shape.

But the wheel within wheels approached again. He still was uncertain as to if anyone else could see it, but everyone and everything seemed eternally distracted. It had shifted to another (its true?) form, and Wulf could not know whether any others saw it as he did through his enchanted eye. It had slowed its four-dimensional spinning until it stood and walked upright like a man, in a similar, although bone-thin, shape. It stepped as though the movement was unfamiliar. Without exception, it was completely covered in eyes.

With his spine broken at some height, he could feel no pain, but, as far as he could tell, he could not move himself in any way. Positioned as he was, however he was, he could only watch events fold around him. There was the slightest rise and fall in his view, telling him that his body was at least attempting to breathe.

The being neared, looking, watching, glancing, studying, and staring in every possible direction but striding still straight for Wulf. The uneven corpse-piles of the ground did not slow it, but it eventually did stagger as it stood two of its staccato paces away. Yin still stuck diagonally through its belly like an unwanted erection from when the being had struck Wulf. It tried again to pull the weapon from its womb, grasping both handle and blade, puncturing the eyes covering its hands. Finally, the sword moved and was dropped to a pool of gore it greedily drank from. The being took one more, obviously painful, step toward Wulf, swatting a crow from the back of its neck. But another appeared, landing and pecking at its narrow waist, with another landing on a shoulder to appraise its banquet. These were knocked or scared away but not before a flock of the dark birds descended upon what served as the wheel within wheels' head. It fell backward, swinging arms full of eyes before all its limbs were covered by the cacophony of wings and "caws" and "carghs" of the crows. The consuming cloud was so thick he could not even tell when the being had stopped moving.

But still, all he could do was watch, without pain, without movement, and when a partially eaten limb peeked out from the mound of fighting crows, with one eye not wholly pecked away yet, Wulf could not resist but look into it. If he was going to die out on this flooded plain, on a hill of skulls and entrails, under a bruised sky, all broken and twisted, let it be in madness, so he stared into the dead eye to look at the forbidden throne room of God.

Untold seconds turned to nondescript minutes as the murder of crows picked the being's form entirely clean. The night darkened even more, so, as far as Wulf could tell, there was nothing left of the wheel within wheels. He could not look in any other direction so could not tell if the moon was rising or if it was just more bones bleaching in the wind next to his head. Bubbles rose, appeared, and burst in front of him. He assumed he was barely breathing through a puddle of blood that had probably drained from him. Yin, wherever she rested, was more than likely drinking her fill. Would the sword then feast upon his soul as well? He wondered.

Oddly enough, he found that some of his hearing was returning, or perhaps he was just starting to be able to decipher the smothered grunts and creaks of his surroundings through the vibrations in his broken skull. He could have sworn he heard the sound of a beast sniffing near.

"Well... well... well... well... it sure's a stink I never thought I'd smell again. I almost missed it, eh, Emla? Not easy to smell anything out here, but I's always the Pack's best sniffer. One've the reasons I'd…"

A face came into view. It was filthy, but not like everyone else's out in the battlefields. This one was stained by dirt and time, not blood. The beard, probably once black, was mostly gray. The head appeared shiny and bare expect for a long hood and cowl made from the head and hide of an equally frosted black wolf.

"But it ain't just the man I sniffed, eh Emla?" the old man continued. "I sniffed that there hunk'a pure Bifrost granite in his cracked head. You sniff it? That reek of black magik? 'Course you don't, you stuffed up, bitch. That there's Woden's Glare. The Egg of Madness. Muninn's Gizzard…"

In and out of his shrinking sightline, Wulf saw the dirty Garm's companion. She was just as filthy, just as emaciated, but much more pregnant. The wolf skin covering her head was a dulled gray, black at every tip.

"You probably don't remember me, you dumb mumblecrust, but the nose of Flowstone Skoll…"

Wulf did not recognize the man exactly, but he certainly knew the dead eyes of the wolf that stared down from the top of his head. It was easier now, with the distance of time, to think back to that night than it had been for many years. It was a nightmare night but an important one. For Wulf had seen his first Garm that night, had met Aesarean, but he had also found the Eye of Yggr in that barn and had met Teca shortly after. That night he had crouched beneath the terrible howl of the man that, two decades later, again stood above him.

"Shame you won't live to see it all, rakefire, but few'll. Be grateful you lasted this long. Your daddy'd be proud, I guess. Back off, bitch!" he growled at his companion before turning back to Wulf. "Watch this now!"

He blocked Wulf's line of sight with a palm so callused it appeared like the granite of their homelands. It was knotted and hardened like the driftwood that would sometimes appear on the shore of the *Jormungandr*. The hand changed. Bulbous knuckles buckled and broke before sprouting thick patches of graying black fur that joined together to cover a sudden great paw. When Wulf could see again, he could only stare at the great hunched werewolf drooling and panting over him. A missing patch of fur in the middle of its barrel chest revealed a pale and old scar — the result of Meri's attack on that night so long ago. Wulf could not help but think of blood-speckled sunflowers.

"See? See me?" The words were rough coming from the great canine muzzle, through missing and dulled wolven teeth. This was a beast inexperienced in human speech. "So... so... so... so... much blood in air... makes ever night... *Brandr Moon*! Aaaaahhh woooo! Gah... craaach... aahhh!"

The beast coughed up something Wulf was glad he could not make out. And then the claws moved in again, mangy fur obscuring his vision. He could not feel what was being done to him, but the scene jerked from side to side, telling him his body was being defiled in some manner. A speck of what must have been blood blurred his view for a second before rolling away. When the Garm that Skoll had become was finished, he stood back upright on his small hind legs to sniff and lap a too pink tongue at the large flap of skin that had been cut from Wulf's chest and left arm. The Garm's eyes were paradoxically pale in the dead light of the evening as they squinted at the tattooed flesh. "This... map..." the creature's furry jaws twisted to try to say, "... reward me back to... pack."

Skoll's companion, Emla, asked, "What about the Eye, sweets? It's here for the..."

"Cursed, bitch!" Tongue sticking, curved teeth catching on each other, the creature's jaws chewed each word before drooling them out. "Must'b given away... before... true power... no... knowledge!"

Emla began her change then, in full sight of Wulf's new perspective, under a moon he could not see. Fur of dirty snow sprouted unevenly before spreading to each other, even before her back cracked and limbs bloated. Her hollow face exploded outward into a mass of black teeth and blacker gums. Her legs broke backward before she stood to her new full height. All of her mangy flesh twisted around her bulbous belly, and she screamed so loudly even Wulf could hear her. The sound quickly turned canine but at the same high pitch. Limbs thin for a Garm, gut dragging the purple drifts, she lumbered near, sniffing him up and down, before the both of them lurched to run on all fours toward a tilted grove that darkened and deepened as the night neared.

Wulf could see nothing for a long time. Living shadows sluggishly fell over and around. A line of arrows appeared as though they had sprouted from the macabre garden. Each were featured from a bird he did not recognize. Long after the two Garm had left, dogs reappeared on the battlefield. He had not realized that they had scattered early in the battles, but was not surprised to see them reappear to pick up and avoid the scent of the werewolves. At the farthest peripheral of Wulf's sight, someone struggled to regain their boots from the sludge with each step while stabbing at any complete body. Some of the remains fought back to no avail. Others just continued to intermittently freeze and melt without reaction. A crow landed on Wulf's broken face, tapped its beak against granite, flew off almost as suddenly. The pressure of the falling sky had become so great that even Wulf could feel it — not physically but against a brain that he had assumed had mostly leaked out through any cracks in his head.

His view changed as a vibration from behind jostled him face down into the dead muck, but he was immediately pulled from the mire and embraced, wrapped in the Crimson Queen's arms and silks and furs and otherwise. She wiped the guts from his cheeks, picked them from his hair, and went about cutting a tiny and quickly bleeding slit in her exposed breast to press his mutilated lips against. Not all his bones knit. Most of his organs were still bruised. Absent skin was quickly covered over with tight scars. But by the time he was done suckling he could at least sleep peacefully in Sera's arms as she waited for Ashmedai's descent to complete.

And it did. On some far battlefield, over the collapsed hills, through overturned woodlands and thrown plains, where the snow had begun to collect again in drifts so deep the blood would not immediately soak upward, the falling star of *Wyrmwood* collided with Earth. The countryside shifted for miles around. Miles beyond that the quakes were felt. The blare of a shattering trumpet was heard even further. Armies that were not flattened or buried were scattered to the electric wind. The prairie cracked open at ground zero, and after years of descent from the abysmal cosmos, the holy immensity of the chimerubimic Architect, the archangel prince *Ashmedai Deva*, now ascended and began his cataclysmic crawl to the surface.

XC

When the Man was to death resigned
he left Woman and Girls behind

(for you had other new loves to
find and remember
remember and find)

He found Perdition
not all-together unkind

He did not mind the unfamiliar fields
the golden wheat of lying yields.
There was no heat. Nothing was dying.
Yet he rested in ash at nightfall,
in hut's bare bones,
but not at all alone.

For before eternal sleep he woke
to the whisper of whiskers

A whistling kiss, remembered bliss
the rumble of humbled heart…

…remembered wish

…a decent descent into endless night.
—from the Love Song of Smeagol Gibbons

M y first memories are of peeking into my… father's… quarters. I hesitate to call him that — my 'father.' It gives him too much credit. It imbues him with a title that should be prestigious, and I certainly do not mean to gift him with any honors… or anything other than complete and utter oblivion. Calling him 'father' presents him with a reward he has always searched for and never achieved — a purpose, a meaning, some sort of inspired providence that has always eluded him.

"My 'mother' I appreciate barely any better. The so-called 'morning star.' Or is she too my father? The father of my own destiny. It was she or he that first seduced my father. First by giving him yet another illusion of free will by offering choices she knew he would accept or ignore. Then by appearing to him in multitudes. His own harem pulled from the fetishistic dreams of a violent pubescence, all of the 'women' plucked from her substance like ribs and filled with her essence. All my father's harem was of her and of him. An intemporal orgy more akin to divine masturbation... as if that is any sort of rare event. But it served its purpose. His purpose. Her purpose. And I was born. Yes, I cannot fault my mother, for she was what she was without excuse. She, the limbless Venus, cursed by God to go upon her belly and eat the dirt beneath mankind's foot. But she was allowed to strike at his heel, and so she had. And I was born.

"I was left under the 'tutelage' of the only remaining archangel, what you call Asmodeus. And what he taught me was nothing but grave grief. I was made into a plaything. Nothing more. My only refuge being the stolen peeks into my father's chambers. He was majestic, that man, and he was my everything — my everything being 'hope.' Hope for a future in which he would save me from my servitude to the Prince Ashmedai Deva, the demon clothed in the gown and wings of an angel.

"Timeless days after days I spent under the unspeakable cruelties of Ashmedai. At times his foul trickery would involve actually teaching me from his forbidden libraries, attempting to give me hope that he could later crush beneath his multiple heads or wormy belly. But I learned, not only from his spellbooks, but from his hate. I learned not to trust in hope. Or so I thought. For still I believed that one day my father would break from his carnal prison and free me from Ashmedai's wet embrace.

"But the day came when he left, my father, without word or promise. He left and fled to this world, without me. Left me behind in a hell then devoid of hope."

"But you escaped," Ivy said, hanging on the Crimson Queen's every word.

"Eventually, Ashmedai, satisfied that he had coaxed every last ounce of innocence out of a little child, also left me behind. With the gods fleeing this land, he came here, leaving what he believed to be a suitably corrupted replacement to rule in his absence. And that is when I became known as the Crimson Queen," Sera said.

"But you escaped," Ivy said.

"I found hope again. I was no longer a child, and, with what I had learned through all the immeasurable seconds of my life, I watched this world through rooms covered in scrying glass, through spells clairvoyant and omniscient, and I found something else to believe in."

Wulf walked away. He had heard the story before and looked

around to what remained of the immediate area during the occasional tremor of the already uneven ground. Dogs and crows scuttled everywhere to peruse the hills of dead. Most of the scavengers were finding themselves stuck in the bloody muck as the cooling night refroze the prairies and woodlands. A hound whimpered nearby, its snout congealing to whatever corpse it sniffed or chewed. A crow flapped its wings wildly on a far branch, caught up in the frosted mess a hung bundle of intestines had become.

Each step hurt for Wulf. He had scavenged rags from the dead and refuse to tie around his face, to cover his open eye socket, to bind an elbow and knee that still felt as though they were coming apart. His musculature had mostly mended. His bones lost their breaks. But he walked sore, with each limb feeling nearly undone with even the slightest vibration. While somewhere back in his brain, or maybe somewhere deep in something more incorporeal, he felt permanently broken, forever leaking. The thing Sera described as a *galgalim* — a lesser manifestation of angelic tribiology — the wheel within wheels that had struck him with the force of the Divine Chariot, had made Wulf push his abilities further than they had ever been pushed. His brain may have scarred over, but it was over tissue that would never spark again. He could still pull things toward him, as he did then, with new ice and snow coming into his hands to wipe away the blood from his chin. He could still reach out to others' minds, as he did to any stragglers that remained, urging them to continue quickly through the sparse woodlands, the following plain, to what remained of the MANN city of Simon. But he could no longer "push" at things telekinetically. When he tried, to force items away or create a mental armor around himself, he expected that spot deep in his cranium to squeal with postpartum pain, but he did not even have that luxury — some sort of pinch to remind him what he had lost. It was just as though he never had the ability to begin with.

The night cooled after the earthquakes, and he was thankful for the temperature on his aching body. Aching muscles welcomed the numbness. With the amount of celestial dust and chthonic eruption from Asmodeus' bombardment, Wulf feared the color the atmosphere would be at sunrise. He was afraid it would be familiar to only a few.

"But," Sera whispered to Ivy, back on the battlefield, looking out across the miles of purple hills and fallen trees, "I'm afraid to admit that Ashmedai taught me only too well. The hate he engendered within me, the pain he nurtured in that little girl, will always overcome any optimism and enlightenment I may have found since. You see, in this sense, he too was my father. And an unforgiving vengeance will be his legacy. And I will tear the stars from the heavens for my revenge. I will chain and unchain ghosts and turn Hell inside out to right wrongs. I will unleash the fire of the atom to end all existence if it means the end to those that spurn me!"

Far off across those mutilated miles, to where what was once called *Wyrmwood* had fallen, the antediluvian archangel stirred from the pit it had created in its collapse. Some that still wandered far out in the plains, that had not died yet from exposure or infection, that had not been crushed or tossed from the quake, neared out of truly morbid curiosity. If they were able to traverse the upheaval and the sudden heat, the rictus and palsies shocking their features at the sight of the Divine Prince would wrack their last few living minutes. But their forbidden glances revealed a voluminous crown of satin and golden ores held aloft by a mass of eels posing as the angel's mane. The celestial being's heads each were as large as villages, and indeed was each filled with crowds of inhabitants — lustful sinners copulating like lice while biting at their own and others' infesting pubic mites. The main face of Ashmedai, a mockery of a 175 year-old man, stared upward with eyes so black that no light could escape their pull. The monster's other heads — horned mule, weeping ewe, and tusked and furred serpent — grasped at the sides of the crater for purchase, while atrophied bat wings fluttered impotently. Its body, lengthening into lion and lizard-like features, scrambled for purchase and threatened to tear the entirety of the land apart from below. The archangel had one arm. Its elbow and wrist and fingers each bent backward in their own directions, but it held a scepter befitting its station. Obviously noxious poisons dripped from the pores of its backward hand down onto glass gems. The celestial being appeared unable to remove its own girth from the earth.

And so great chains crawled — giant links the length and thickness of twisted elder trees. Forged from the spirits of the irresolute, the chains had the appearance of old iron but sang with the wails of the venially sinful as they turned and straightened. On one end the iron was secured into the deformed horns growing from the bone of Ashmedai's neck, pierced through the azure nipples of his shrunken teats and seven tumorous scrotums. At the other end of each length of gargantuan chain was a headless mass of unbaptized infants. Fourteen in all, these flesh golems scurried up the interior of the plain to the surface, their patchwork bodies, like melted conglomerations of baby dolls, each impaled by the final large links of each length, pulled and pulled until the behemoth angel began to appear over the horizon.

Still the trumpeting roar of the smoldering atmosphere howled.

The bulbous crown of Ashmedai Deva, Grand Maestro of the Divine Choir, once Prince Duke of the Order of the Wandering Fly, Supreme Kingangel of the Chayot Ha Kodesh of the Mountains of Heaven, began to rise from the pit. And the earth quaked.

Still the air bellowed as a trumpet. But this time it wavered, the wail dropping before rising again in anguish. If anyone had still been alive or sane out on the plain they would have now been able to locate the source of the horn, for the locomotive burst from burning mist, shaking and propelling its iron body through drifts and fog as ghostly as itself. The train screamed from whistle and flaming smokestack. Its piercing eye, the luminescent color of death's shroud, glared ahead of itself, brightening the collapsing night. On top of the *Loco*, steering the infernal machine with chains wrapped around and from limbs and through windows, was Harlowe FelDougan, with smoking rags of vests and jackets fluttering like flames behind him. The train bucked and kicked beneath him but could not pull away from the zombie Harlow's reining, and its mystical iron hide continued its homicidal momentum over and into the pit.

Ashmedai's molten blood erupted. His seven mouths squealed and brayed and screamed. The land would be forever poisoned for leagues with toothy winter toads that oozed from hot pockets from the very spot.

The pistoleer crawled and stood from the spot he had jumped to, but he ran as the prairie shook to close upon itself, silencing the eternal siren scream of the *Loco* and the bellowing song of Ashmedai.

Wulf steadied himself, miles to the east, against the aftershocks that continued to shift the plains and thickening groves of foliage. Branches fell nearby, sending ripples through the gelatinous pools that refused to completely freeze in the weird darkness of the fallen night sky. A Horde soldier, legless, struggling to keep his head above the mush, still covered in the heaviest of plate mail, trying desperately to pull himself up onto an island of bones, cried for help. Wulf ignored his and many of the nearby pleas of the enemy fallen. With Yin he was probing the appearing *Goblin Revenant*. They were dark but ethereal, grouped so closely that he could not at times tell them apart. They had been talking to him in their squeaky and ghostly voices — a bitter breeze only he could hear, only Yggr's Eye could see — but he had not been listening until that moment.

"*...you knew the price, o' last of lieges, o' tallest of lords...*"

His hand instinctively went to his chest, chuckling to himself with heavy face and hands. Why was it, he wondered, that people always felt that their very souls resided in their chest, in their hearts. What was it about the heart that inspired the nations to such musings and poetry. It was just bloody meat, a muscle-bound bellows one so easily forgot about for days, weeks, months at a time. He looked as far as he could in the night to the rotting fruit strewn to the shaking horizon, at all the exposed ribs and impaled torsos. When was the last time any of these people had thought about their hearts? Were they at least able to be reminded by its last rhythms before it stopped in their chests?

"*We, yer last servants in life and death,*" the Goblin Revenant continued, "*did as you pleased, and now we've come for our reward, what was once yers and is now ours. A deal with spirits is binding. A deal with goblins is a deal.*"

Yin's touch barely swirled the swampy mist of their forms.

"*Your pretty, pretty sword loves ta drink, yes she does, but we have no blood, your paleness, and so she cannot eat our tiny little spirits. Now... we have come fer what is now ours. We ask not fer permission but out of respect fer yer past love, of mob and hob, we wish fer last words.*"

Wulf looked to the west, imagining the fall of Kaldera's capitals. Would the Necrophim he unleashed upon the world quit at the subjugation of the Territories? No. They had died and now lived for war. Once they trampled the last of the Horde they would turn on one another, fighting until the glaciers overtook them, each general freezing in their final swings of axe or fist like a statuesque monument to be found by some future civilization under a red sun.

He looked to the east, toward where whatever ruin lay that had been the city of Simon. The last transmission from the Agent of MANN had been ominous. If another of what Sera had called the *galgalim*, the wheel within wheels, had also come for the city, he was not sure what he was sending the last of his people off to. Just a distraction?

Wulf looked to the south to imagine what he *should* have been sending them off to. There were rumors that the far southern desert and jungles were still warm. But he knew it would only be a matter of time before the far south too would freeze, if what his northern ancestors had prophesized would come to fruition.

He slid the flat edge of Yin along his palm. It had to be the only clean blade within leagues of where he was standing. She was voraciously clean, insatiably clean. But would she drink his own blood, his own soul, if he asked it? Had she become as fond of him as he had of her? She cooed like an infant with a belly full of warm milk, but he knew she was still hungry.

The North. The North. He looked to the North, to the memories of his people and family. Everything the Church had warned the land about was coming true. Everything the Garm had dreamt was coming to be. But everyone was fleeing the North, whatever remained of it. He squinted north, trying to imagine what the lands around Bifrost now looked like, under numerous divine winters of snow.

But instead he saw Teca. And his throat seized, thinking inwardly about how the superstitious linked their souls with their breath. Was it how all cultures believed in some sort of initial, primordial "breath of life" bestowed before consciousness? Was that why "existence before essence" was so treasured, or was it the other way around? He sucked at suddenly absent air, and saw Teca trudging through the freezing swamp of floating ribcages and scalps, avoiding the grasping claws of any drowning Horde soldiers.

"It's time, o' Goblin Liege, o' grand traitor, fer yer payment, fer the soul price you owe us."

He readied his vampiric sword over his wrist, and for the second time in one night Wulf thought back to that single *Brandr Moon* in the sunflower fields. He had been so young, but she had been even younger, and he was now so regretful at how dismissive he had been of her. Before that Goblin Winter had been through she would have surprised him by facing down aliens and rakish ruffians. And now she had done nothing less than survive the War of Heaven and Earth. What else would she overcome in his absence? Wulf had potentially doomed the planet by decades-ago summoning the great Beast of the Core, yet his only regret, out on the waning night of the last battle for the countryside, was that he would not see what came next.

But the *Goblin Revenant* was gone. Before Wulf could turn the edge of his sword, the ghosts had disappeared into murky earth, and he ran in the sluggish drifts, feeling as though more than just the collapsed battlefield slowed him down. He ran to the figure of Teca, seeing, with Yggr's Eye, spectral goblins appear up from the ground behind her. A squirming mass of tiny hands fought amongst each other to be the first to snatch at her soul, but they all found it, and they pulled it from her falling body. Out of habit Wulf tried to push at her with his mind, and, when his telekinesis failed him in this, he pulled, and she was dragged through the air into his hands. Onto his sword. Yin drank eagerly her blood and, much to the squealing dismay of the ghosts, her soul. For less than a second, Teca's reaching spirit was caught between goblin hands and sword's maw, but Yin won the struggle, purring again as Wulf pulled her from the body.

"Noooo!!!!!" The *Revenant* was in a tantrum. They stomped ethereal feet, spat otherworldy epithets. *"Her soul was ours! You were ta pay the price. We hadda deal!"*

Wulf sank into the bloody mire, holding Teca's body close. It had grown cold more quickly than he could have ever imagined. Her cheek against his held little warmth, but he pressed his lips against it anyway. For some reason, he could not help but think of a different morning of the Goblin Winter. He and Teca had woken early, their bodies insufficient to stave off the night's chill, and they had climbed above the line of trees to catch the sunrise, but the light could just not penetrate the cloud cover.

"There's freedom in faith, you know," she had said sheepishly, holding her broken wrist to her heart. "Just think of letting yourself over to... love. I can't explain how..."

"The Church of Bifrost," he had interrupted, although always regretted, "preaches that 'come a terrible day, Death shall have no dominion, and we shall all throw off the shrouds of the grave to walk again.' Do I have faith that the priests tell the truth? Or faith that I will, as I don't now, wish to live again? Isn't one life lonely enough?"

But no, his memory was not serving him. It was out on the wind-dried prairie that they had greeted the sun together. They had headed out early together, the cold dust stinging their eyes awake, and they sat within his cloak together, looking to a far field where a platinum priestess prayed to herself.

Teca had asked him what he would do if he, "could live forever?" And he remembered how cold her fingertips had been that morning, and how he had ignored her question, as he had so many others. He remembered how she never talked to, and rarely about, the priestess that had accompanied them on their "quest" across the plains and into the Black Hills. Even that morning she had tried to steal his attention away from her.

"How is it you survive out here all alone? You're amazing," he had said of the squire.

"I wasn't always…"

"What would I do if I was immortal? There would be no 'I' that I would understand, actually. I cannot recognize the person I would be, cannot relate to…"

He did not remember the rest of his answer. Instead, as he now folded her arms over each other and kept her face above the mire and pulled her even closer, he remembered a night in a town (had it been Quicken?) where someone had played a squeezebox, and, in the absence of Meri, Shay had asked Teca to dance to the rousing music. She had danced closely, sticking her tongue out at Wulf whenever they circled near. At the time he could not understand the gesture, but he had laughed uncontrollably every time. But now he grimaced, as the fallen sky warped under new darkness and the dead light of an uncertain dawn. He felt for the necklace she had given him, but there were scars and scabs where it should have been.

"Her soul was not mine to give," he thought he had thought to himself.

But the *Goblin Revenant* answered, *"Yes, you fool! Yes, it was! You tricked us! Tricked us outta our reward!"* The ghosts tore and rent at themselves and each other until they sank back into the earth. He was never to see them again.

...because what you crave is a time, a place
in which forgotten a sin
can be, when and where you can see his face
—scrawled on the walls of the King of All's lower halls

ithout the Prince there was no love for the rule. Without the Queen there was no infatuation with the monarchy. There was left only a punishing father that had extended his reach beyond the millions of children that had no more patience for the decades of abuse. They had always been ungrateful flies, buzzing in his eyes and ears, but now they spread their maggots around a kingdom not even dead yet.

Some of Easarean's generals had taken to suppressing the insurrections on their own, not waiting for a break in the King's melancholy. Easarean did not care. A year after the death of the Prince, he was alone in castle and conscience. He had brooded on his amethyst throne, silent and unmoving, day after week after month, until the Queen of Quartz had left him. She had left his side, his people, and his kingdom. All of it had also been hers, in many ways even more so than his, but she had one morning looked to the sun and was never seen again. It was only then that Easarean realized he had never seen her look to the sky before, so grounded by the land and its creatures, the earth and its living and unliving denizens she was. And so he was alone, and so the people revolted, tired of war under dark sky. They had always felt special under his rule — a new, always growing, race mightier than anything they encountered, but when all else was conquered — man and nature, beast and ideal — they had nothing else to subvert but themselves, nowhere else to look but inward. And what they found they did not like.

But the wars they supported, the assimilation and genocide they approved, the horrors they rationalized, could not be so easily put behind them. Any penance would be impossible. It was much easier to blame the King. If they could see themselves as being exploited or even duped, then revolution was the only answer, and they could go on fighting. And fighting was the ultimate busywork. No longer were they alone in their thoughts. An uprising gave no time for introspection. Easarean, once the King of All, was now the Scapegoat Monarch.

But the fighting, scattered, was still far from his capital. Even with his quiet indecision his generals had kept his closest lands free from uprising, and so his castle and, especially the subterranean levels, was quiet except for his large steps across the massive bulge of earth in the Queen's cellar. It smelled as she had, of damp precious stone and frigid mineral. He lit the cellar with portable lamps but carried a primitive torch, looking for any sign of her presence, but the dirt had obviously not been disturbed since he had last seen her. There were no recently dug bed sites or glyphs shaped from agates. Her geode bed coffin lie broken, massive but shattered and dusty, still with guts shimmering in the unnatural glow. Easarean was unsure if there had ever been light in this section of the catacombs. The Queen certainly had never needed it. The blind worms and beetles crunching beneath his boots did not need it.

The Scapegoat Monarch's arms and back flexed, rippling as he lifted a large chunk of the geode to launch it at the wall. It broke again, while the pace in his heat and the shocking echo was a relief after a season of inactivity and silence in the castle.

He knew the Queen had napped below to feel the coolness of the soil, to be near the dirt's caress and the touch of its inhabitants, but Easarean knew she had another reason for hibernating beneath the castle. He knew she found the closeness of the dungeons comforting, the moans of its dwellers soothing, and he had no doubt she shared in their shivering dreams at such proximity. Similarly, the King had come to the subterranean levels for more than one reason.

Despite the odds of finding anything new, he had surveyed the Queen's bed cellars, but now moved on to the dungeons. They were equally cold and damp and had mostly been long forgotten by his castle's guards and almost by the King himself. Before the Prince had been born, Easarean would visit one part of the dungeon each year as though in anniversary. To others it would have appeared as a note of sentimentality in a ruler that was anything but sentimental. The section had been dug deliberately apart from the main rows of decay-smelling cells, built before even the castle itself.

Easarean unlocked the wall with the key from around his neck and was immediately assailed by a stench older but wetter than the one wafting between the rest of the dungeon. When was the last time anyone had attended to the First Prisoner, he wondered. Easarean had not looked for his council in a prince's age, had actually forgotten about his yearly visits, but here the Norn Fox crawled through his chains, subsisting on whatever vermin found its way into the worn stone chamber. Easarean gave him a fistful more, tossing a clump of centipedes, millipedes, and featherpedes from the cellar onto the frozen floor.

The Norn Fox was blind but could follow the skittering before him with a mole's hearing, could smell the insects with a bat's sense, arthritic joints screaming as he fell toward his food. Entangled, he could only reach with a desiccated tongue to eat only those that climbed his face.

Easarean lifted him to his atrophied feet with one hand, pulling chains from him with the other. Water trickled in some shadow the torch's light could not break.

"Has it been a year... already?" the Norn Fox said in a voice surprising Easarean with its strength. He had to assume that the shrunken man kept conversation with himself or spiders. It was the only way to explain the fact he still had any voice at all.

"How is it you see so much of other worlds, fool, but nothing of your own? It has been many years. You are an old man now. I have beaten you in yet another manner."

"Has your beloved left you yet? Has your little prince expired? In all the multiverse I watch, in all the realities I dream, your lives may be vastly different, but there are certain universal truths, certain events that ring true in each universe, that you apparently can't escape."

Easarean threw the weightless man against the smooth rock of the circular room. It was not long before blood, thick and slow, dripped from an ear.

"Why didn't you warn me?" the King asked, not waiting for an answer before striking the Norn Fox. The man's paper-thin skin split from temple to temple and bled even before he landed against the opposite side of the cell.

Easarean, of course, knew why the traitorous savant had not warned him. Among all the enemies the King of All had made on this planet, the Norn Fox was the oldest. It was the Queen of Quartz, the Cousin, and the cloaked one — the Norn Fox — that had walked the plains into the Black Hills all those years ago. Never fearing the Cousin, it was the mysterious Norn Fox that had kept Easarean from moving sooner, keeping him from taking his place at the Queen's side. Looking down on the decrepit, broken man now before him, he wondered why he had waited so long.

"Yet... yet here you need me again. Here I am in chains. Here I lie... but here you crawl... back to me again. My sidesight gave you your kingdom, no? What more could you need from me?"

There was not much resistance left in the Norn Fox's skull, but still Easarean beat him about it. The soft mess left spoke incoherently. Easarean did not listen anyway.

"You've given me nothing but treachery, fool!" the King interrupted. "But you can still redeem yourself. Make your last act one of worth. Have your stinking soul contribute something to a world you've denied before it sinks to whatever frozen bog your bow-legged ancestors saw as Heaven." He kept the torch near the man's face, hoping to burn away the stink of the chamber. The Scapegoat Monarch lowered his voice, returning it to an even tone. Yelling had aggravated his throat after months of silence. "I have seen things across this land that have opened even my eyes to the endless potentials of science and magik. I have seen men sprout from gardens and children regrow heads. I have seen messiahs killed and reborn and killed again. I know it is possible to break Death's sway." He quickly gave in to the emotion though, not stopping his voice from growing again into a shout. He needed to shout, for it was the only thing holding the tears in. "How? How can the Prince be resurrected? How can I bring back my Antony?" His voice cracked, and he knew it was futile, and he sobbed in spite of himself.

The Norn Fox wobbled precariously on white legs thin as sticks and began smearing blood across walls still hiding the hints of messages long years past. Easarean tried to make out the old writing, remembering few of the poems. The dreams the Norn Fox received from alternate worlds had warned and driven the King of All for the first few years of his reign, but they had still all led to this. Had the Norn Fox known? Could Easarean trust another prophecy from the man's blood?

The sideseer fell when finished. Stepping past the man's blood, Easarean's rapid breaths drowning out the Norn Fox's shallow ones, he read the backwards and sideways scrawl as it gleamed by torchlight.

He stared at the words until both the torch and the Norn Fox were extinguished. Whether he could not decipher the words' meaning, whether he did not want to, or whether he did not trust them, even he could not admit.

The King of All turned away in the darkness, stepping over key and body and out through the chamber to never look back.

XCII

Broke Screams
fill ears
sweet as stolen mead.
Breath congeals on beards.
Ice pools under enemy fears and exploded feet.

Relish chorus of battle

Song simmers, darkening within.
In frenzied circles hammer is swung
arms pump
strengthened from winter of winds
finding release in season of swords
with blood boiling sledge is brought down.
Bones burst through puckered face
waiting for Chooser of the Slain.

  —Excerpt from the Song of Gnos

The scattered population spoke only in whispers of shock, hushed voices speaking in an odd accent of the *wheels within the wheel* that rolled — faster than light they said — across the plains, uprooting forests before plowing through their village. It arrived with no mercy but tore into the land beneath their homes. MANN's man-tanks were no match for it. They were flung into the air as easily as the markets and suburbs. And the ground was thrown just as easily. The land shifted and fell and exploded, and before anyone could react, MANN's underground city of Simon was laid bare to the surface world for the first time.

And now, like a dying volcano, its guts exposed to air and snow, it hissed like an ancient salamandr preborn and cancerous and dissolving onto black steam and white smoke. The fresh mists ate at the predawn color slithering closer from the gory horizon. They absorbed it and reflected it outward, so that every direction would have to experience its impossible purple. But the people were warm for the first time in memory. The humid fogs and multitude of energies emanating from the cracks in the ground warmed hands and noses, and they could concentrate on something other than mere survival. They took the chance to gather all they had, which was not much, taking census of children and scraps of seeds and other freeze-dried foods. They pulled any fabric from their collapsed huts to repurpose. The scavengers that had lived in Simon Town, above the underground city of Simon, ignored the newcomers that lingered and asked too many questions. The now homeless knew that the War had been drawing near for some time, feeling, even before the sudden assault of the spinning *galgalim*, the quakes while seeing the smoke of the west. But the warmth that had always emanated from below had been too inviting to leave.

"We're at your service, sir!"

"When do we head out?"

"I can have us packed up by dawn, before dawn, if you wish, Commander."

RackBreak Antony stomped his great boots, shook the gory ice from his armor, his all-encompassing beard and mane, satisfied to be back on what he thought was solid ground. The artificial earth vibrated, however, beneath his large feet.

The crowd following him paused, shocked at the unstable plain, but not for too long.

"When do we head out?"

"I can have a hundred men at your side in an hour!"

"I'll fetch the maps. I know of rations. When'll it warm... ?"

He trod on over the uneven girders and false ground of what remained of the refugee suburbs of Simon. How much of the ramshackle civilian villages had collapsed into the open earth when the *galgalim* had attacked the underground city of MANN, RackBreak could not tell, but he was determined to save any that had survived.

"I tell you again," he murmured to anyone that could hear him, "I go alone, to the dark South, to ready the paths for you. The only path left. To the great and horrible South."

"But we fight with you, Lord!"

"I am in your debt!"

"Where you go, I go, Commander."

People peered silently from falling streets, near widening sinkholes and broken hovels filling with a new snow beginning to light in the night. RackBreak peered over the edge of one of the huge openings. It was all metal and plastic beneath, lit by dimming fluorescents and virgin fires not yet corrupted by the color the fallen sky had created. The burning of indecipherable materials smothered his gaze and lungs.

Where had the Lesser and Wulf dropped to? And why? All that mattered now was the path. The path south. Nothing else mattered.

"You do not know the responsibility I grant you!" RackBreak bellowed, and people scattered like rats from a burning shack. His back hurt from the exertion of yelling in ways it had not, even in the heat of battle. His inflamed knees buckled, but he walked from the openings into the prairie, from the refugee cities, from those he had commanded, from all those that had followed. "These people need your help. You and they are the future. Ensure there is one by collecting them, tending to them, and leading them south. I will prepare it for you!"

RackBreak turned away from the steaming carnage to find the crowd around him reappearing before dispersing at his glare, but their questions become even louder. So he turned again, this time to the lines of trees disappearing into the winter beyond any shantytown still standing. If the southern deserts and jungles of this world were as infested as those of his, then what waited any refugees of the cold would be far worse than death by glacier. It would be a long walk, and each day that passed had him finding new pains in his arthritic joints. But once the survivors of the War of Heaven and Earth decided on who would lead them, they would inevitably head south, hopefully ahead of the final winter, and they would have to decide soon. He had no more confidence in the sun. And so, he too could not wait any longer.

The Greater Antony disappeared into the drifts building at the edge of the warmth emanating from the acrid fissures. No one followed him this time.

~

"In the end, we underestimated just how much they considered themselves victims," Damn Antony said, walking the intermittent light. New snowflakes fell slowly with the dust and dirt through the spires of dark and pale illumination streaming like waterfalls from the surface world. He had to keep one eye on his guide and one on the creaking upper levels, while carefully stepping from exposed girder to any seemingly stable platform.

"Careful," the Agent of MANN warned, "some of the exposed cryoptic cables may still be active. And avoid stepping through any of the pools." He had introduced himself as John Juan Aristo and as though the two should recognize him, before laughing and revealing that he was the man that had accompanied the Army of Earth in the form of the avatar. Damn Antony could see it then, could imagine the inflections in the man's voice through the digitization of the metal insectoid that had observed the Army.

John Juan led them under sparking panels that hung from some unseen upper floors. Everything they navigated around burned or steamed, precariously leaning or hanging from tortured metals or unknown materials. Each floor was open to deeper recesses, and the surface ground opened above to the dying night. The Agent of MANN seemed to be collecting whatever he could of value. Antony could not tell what any of the artifacts he bundled even were. Juan finally responded.

"Yeah, in a short amount of time they went from conquering to seeing themselves as oppressed. We had obviously been watching them from afar and became quickly concerned when their evangelism started showing signs of supposed martyrdom. Any criticism of their faith was quickly seen as sedition... against the state no less. Any 'alternative' lifestyle — your Alabaster Princess, for example — offering up a different world view went from shunned to criminally blasphemous in such a culturally short amount of time that we very quickly started to consider countermeasures."

Juan looked and gestured to Wulf. The man had scavenged a cloak of many dark colors and now hid deep within it. He had not spoken since their descent into what remained of the underground city, but he now gestured and a crumbled door tore itself from a burning wall. The three men entered a massive laboratory, hidden from the destruction outside, lit by slowly dying white light. There was only one color in the tall room and it was almost immediately corrupted by the foul night now metastasizing inward.

Wulf carried the body of Teca in his arms.

The Agent of MANN opened panels to peruse monitors as Antony asked, "Are these... are these what I think they are?" The Lesser appeared weaker as the minutes continued. The length that was left of his missing arm, tied at many points above the elbow, had begun to bleed again — if it had ever even stopped. He could not move without holding himself steady on wall or Wulf. It appeared to be a strain just to look up at the great glass cylinder that lined one wall.

"I have always enjoyed the company of polytheists," Juan said as he focused on an array of holographic readings. "They enjoy life as though they had an almost genetic understanding of mortality — and perhaps they do. After millennia of the same old cycle repeating itself ad nauseam, perhaps our very DNA has recorded and adapted to and expects the past in the future."

"These... these are angels..." Antony, being steadied by Wulf, said more than asked. Each great round fluid-filled chamber held a fleshy chrysalis. Some had parted. Some had almost been completely eaten away. But emerging from all of them were the blind pupae of androgynous chimera. An oozing crack in one of the seven cylinders revealed that the laboratory had not been entirely undamaged. A shedding of cables poured through a split in the metal behind the instruments.

Juan tweaked hard light images, and an external humming that Antony had not noticed before started to dull. The pure light of the chamber disappeared, to be replaced by a crimson glow more akin to the night up and outside. "So, yeah," he said, "polytheists are always destined to go the way of Denisovans or Neanderthals, making way for true survivors. In a society of many gods, yeah, there may be a grace period of peace, but inevitably people will gravitate toward specific traits and specific personifications, creating tribes with patron gods, and it is, of course, not enough to just enjoy one's deity while letting one's neighbor enjoy theirs. No, how would you know if you have chosen the right one? Your neighbors' prosperity cannot be attributed to a truer god if you and yours has conquered theirs, can it? And so one is left — one unified culture under one god."

Antony could not tell if the giant fetal eruciforms could sense his presence. Their tiny wings refused to beat, their multitude of eyes refused to blink. They responded not in the least when silver umbilici detached and probes and sensors slackened. "What are you doing?"

"The city is losing all energy. I'm diverting what's left to integral systems. Simon has always been geothermically powered. The *galgalim's* attack must have severed the main connections to the grid, and, I'm sure, the quakes aren't helping. Oh, what am I doing to *them?* Yeah, you see, we weren't about to just let things take their natural course, and, as you can see, we would have been justified. The Horde was too quickly a threat. They would have never left MANN alone. Eventually, you see, after defeating your Army, they would have devolved into squabbling among themselves. 'Which angel is godlier?' 'My angel is more righteous!' And so on. They would have literally killed each other extolling the virtues of their patron gods. One would have emerged victorious, and, by virtue, the 'right' one, but, well, look around you, we didn't have time for that. So we had planned to speed the process along by, at the very least, introducing more options, or, by the very most, distracting the Horde until we could undermine them in some other way. But, well, we too underestimated their desperation for validation."

Antony approached him, leaning more to one side than he realized. "Did you… did MANN create the Divine Choir?"

"What a silly question. Hold still." Juan pressed flickering lines of lights before closing a panel. From the gross shadows transformed a low piece of the wall that folded up to Antony's height. Before the Lesser could respond, he had been injected, strapped, and pulled into the automaton's instrumentation. "We'll see if there is still enough power left in the systems to fix up your arm."

Before leading Wulf out of the chamber, the Agent of MANN took one last look up at the deflating masses of cells. "They are too immature to survive on their own, and there is not enough resources to devote to their growth. A pity. A considerable amount of Grail was used in their design. 'The best lied schemes of mousey men…' well, you know…"

Wulf followed him out into the expanse of the falling city, and they were greeted by an upper floor sucking the air out of the layers as it fell in front of and beneath them. The sounds it made below as it settled were of metal, fire, and turning earth. The platform on which they were going to walk had disappeared into the darkness. Everything on their new path was sharp or hot, and they could not trust any step without feeling around for it first.

He adjusted the unmoving form in his cloak and arms before stopping to peer into what once would have been a fortified room. Its own lights were dying as well, and the smoke from numerous sources had been collecting near its ceiling. The amount of scents in the darkness confused each breath. Juan doubled back a minute later when he realized that he had not been followed.

"We don't have much time. Hopefully, your friend's arm… I just need to quickly…" He stopped as he found Wulf looking at an incomplete doorframe standing on an alien pedestal in the middle of the hazy room. The unfamiliar materials of the object's molding had been dirtied by the cracks in the room's ceiling.

"Oh, yeah, the Moon Room," Juan said, wiping a line through the dust with a finger. It's an old design. Took an immense amount of energy to power, and, after we lost contact with its destination, or need for its use, it just, kind of, went into storage, or was cannibalized for the frame's precious ores."

The top of the frame was mostly missing. It would have almost been the length of Yin. The multitude of cords stretched from the base unit around in piles creating a nest for the Moon Room frame. The meager lights of the chamber disappeared, and the men left, returning to a precarious path that led Juan into a gallery in which he filled up another bundle full with what looked like preserved rations. He paused only long enough to place his hands on Wulf's shoulders, but he could not see into the depths of his hood. The sparks cascading outside the gallery's door did not even reflect off the Eye of Yggr.

"Thank you, friend, for coming for me. If I hadn't, well, you know, I might have just stayed down here to… you know…"

Wulf finally responded as Juan went back to packing. His voice cracked like the glowing wires hanging from the ceiling. "Are there any others…"

"They've chosen. We lost connection with the city of Joseph." Here the Agent of MANN turned away, suddenly a shrunken man, suddenly at a loss for words. When he turned back it was with swollen eyes and blushing cheeks. "I'm certain that the same thing that hit us, and you, this *galgalim*, this thing my archives described as an angelic boon, some sort of lesser celestial being, like a 'pet' of the higher orders of the enemy, another one hit Joseph." He stepped out of the room into the deadly catwalks and falling fires of the main pit. "You know, the history of cultural faith is not linear, not a dead end at all. It evolves but is circular. Once a society, through war and oppression, decides on one all-encompassing god, forgetting all others, they very quickly start to regress back to a polytheistic culture. We're hard-wired for discontent. Stress is as essential as food or sex. How can I prove that my worth is above others — in the eyes of fellowship or deity — when everyone follows the same faith? And so rifts are created, differing sects, and pedantry becomes occupation for the insecure. So many schisms and breaks that one religion becomes many, and add to this all that mankind finds to replace religion — holding coin, king, or sport as high as the divine — and we have polytheism again. Start the process anew. But, again, we were too late."

Flaming ground drifted from above in a hypnotic display. Exposed wires began to spark less. The grand creaking of the surrounding city, however, began to grow, and Juan had to shout to bring his voice above the shifting segments of Simon.

"This may be all that is left of MANN. My… friends… they've chosen… to remain as avatars. Somewhere in this mess, if they still live, they are relaxed into sensory chairs, as I was, but their minds are traveling out there, in some freezing plain or wilderness, in their other bodies. And that is their choice." He shifted his bundles over his back. They were as tall as he was. "But, again, you came for me. Thank you."

Back down through the carnage, but echoed amongst the melting walls and crashing floors, came Antony's scream.

"You may regret it," Wulf said, holding the body in his arms even more closely.

XCIII

...you can see his face,
the face of a child lost, it can still be
held, before it had been felled,
in a world close to your own, you will see

—scrawled on the walls of the King of All's lower halls

The newly ordained Scapegoat Monarch had more than one kind of dungeon. The catacombs beneath the capital's castle may have been the most legendary, and the swamp-sunk torture cities of the South may have been the most intimidating, but there were others rumored or unknown. It was even whispered amongst the people that their King warmed his northern retreat with the vapors of an imprisoned dragon. But knowledge of the most secretive prison and its one inhabitant would shock even the most jaded person of the land. The guards would run. The generals would mutiny. Even the Queen had not known whom Easarean had hidden away so closely. Why he had kept him, even Easarean could not say. He had never visited him, as he had with the Norn Fox. He had never had him tortured, as he had so many other conquered foes. He was not a trophy to be admired, as locked away as he was. Could it be that Easarean had always suspected that the day would come when he would need the advice of what was once the ruler of the largest nation in the country? No matter the reason, he was now satisfied that he had kept him. Once forgotten, the Norn Fox's final prophecy had reminded the Scapegoat Monarch of whom kept right under his nose.

Easarean had just received word that the latest insurrection had been put down with, as he had commanded, a disproportionate amount of force. Since meeting with the Norn Fox he had taken a more active role in the quelling of the uprisings. They were now short-lived and shrinking. The words of his prognosticator had been encouraging, as they always had been, and he now believed there was a chance to bring Antony back from the shroud of death. He did not know how, but he did know who had the answer.

Easarean's leisure office was purposefully different from his other offices. Where as the private war rooms scattered throughout the Kingdom of All were always windowless with long tables, no seating, and filled with maps reminding him of different conquering endeavors, this office was at the top of his castle, looking out through numerous wide windows past the castle's walls into his crimson capital city. Dust had settled over the cherry woods of the furniture and the thickly set desk, but the bloody light from outside still warmed the room in likely color. Easarean wiped a hand through what had settled on the trophy arching sharply next to the thick leather he sat in. The dragon's tooth had not yellowed or dulled. Perhaps it never would.

He stretched back in his chair. It was so much more comfortable than his rocky throne, but he rarely felt that he deserved the comfort of his office lately. He tugged at the delicate tie hanging from the taxidermied basilisk's neck until the creature leaned forward enough for Easarean to see himself in its glasses. The King picked at food crusted in his beard. He was close enough to see the trophy's empty sockets, its eyeballs years ago used in some arcane ritual by the Queen.

There were maps here too, but these were framed around paintings and photographs of the more beautiful areas of the continent — places he visited with Antony when the Prince had been a small boy. Few of the scenes still existed, but his memories of bottomless canyons, gigantic roaring waterfalls, and cyclopean redwood forests were as strong as ever.

He pulled the safe from beneath the desk to begin working the combination. There was much technology in this land, more of a variety now than ever in its history, yet Easarean chose to keep the simple, locked combination-safe for his purposes. In fact, there was only simple technology in his castle office, candled sconces being the height of progress in the room. The piece of silicon he took from the safe, however, was an all-together different manner. It was the reason he kept the office, as ridiculous as he knew the gesture was. If the prisoner wanted to escape, he would have done so over a decade ago.

Easarean removed three components from his robe, sighing and placing them on the desk in the order he planned to use them. He twisted a thumb-sized cube from his robe, connecting it to one of the numerous stray wires fraying from the circuit board. He then swapped out a tiny fuse among the many over a charred corner of the board. Unwinding a thin cord, he connected a thin copper strip to a button-sized receiver/speaker. He expected the prisoner to speak immediately, but after waiting several silent staring minutes, he started the conversation.

"I know you can hear me."

"A dire dilemma, indeed, if the conquering king comes calling the deposed dynast," Automaton the Perverted responded. His voice was slight and tinny, not what Easarean expected from memory but more than he expected from the tiny speaker. He kept his fingers wavering over the battery in anticipation of any treachery. The Pervert continued, "I did not profile you as a sentimental sort, but have you come to reminisce with this ancient adversary? I suddenly sense the passage of past into present. Do you wish to share sweet anecdotes of authority, or make amends on clearing conscience? Is the awesome King of All killed? Has illness or age assassinated my fearless foe in a way I never could?"

"No," Easarean paused. He thought back as quickly as he could. The Pervert had been conquered, every last vestige of his robotic legions ground into glass, with the tyrant himself placed in the small safe years before the King of All's christening. Yet the intelligence knew Easarean's title. How could the artificial intelligence know anything of the time after he had been shut off? The King knew that he needed to hurry. "It is true. I ask a boon. In the final stages of our war, with my army destroying or cutting you off from the last of your resources, you defiled yourself and nature by reanimating corpses with foul techno-tendrils. Abominations! You lost any right you had to this country with those gross hybrids — neither man nor machine. But these dead men lived again, walking and talking. They lived again!"

"So it is the secret of soul survival you seek? Disappointing. I had hoped for more constructive conversation. You'll be beleaguered to know the necromatons were no more alive than you acknowledge me to be."

"But…"

"A stabilizing structure animating mortified meat. Resurrection was the ruse, but I underestimated your uncaring convictions."

"I… my son…" Once again the King's voice wavered and shook like his hands. He never felt less in control then when speaking of the Prince.

"Mine is not the mind to recommend resurrection. I am a savage of science, not the immeasurable imaginings of magic. My advice? Advance your inquiry in ways unthought. Unwrap your understanding from preconceived patterns."

"What… do you want?"

"Ask not how to save Prince Antony from death," the Pervert said in a new, deeper voice, "ask how to save him from dying."

"How, damn you, how did you know?" Easarean let the wires fall from his fingers and instead readied a shaking fist, preparing to smash all that was left of the great race and nation of Automaton the Perverted.

"Simplicity, simpleton." The voice had reverted to its pale imitation. "As soon as you had connected the power source, I sent out an audio virus at a pitch too high for your inferior flesh and cartilage receptors. The virus infected the nearest human in your castle implanted with technology obviously assimilated from the GAU — impressive bio-upgrades even by my standards. This linked my core intellessence with the primitive quaputers of your capital and, now, your country. The infotecture of your entire nation has been infected, including the neurostructure of any person with any sort of cognithetic enhancement. I am once again looking through a million eyes, processing in a million homes. I can see that you have been very busy during my years of imprisonment, but not as busy as I have been during the past standard minute."

Easarean smashed the circuit board. The cracked desk groaned beneath his hands before it crashed to the floor of the office. He had not heard any indication of explosions, but he could see a power plant smoking through one window, while unusual flashes of light lit the streets out another. People were shouting out in the city while gunfire sounded from within the walls of the castle. Yet the King just sat back, reminded again how much more comfortable the leather at his back was compared to the throne.

He pondered the Pervert's words as the gunfire grew closer. Perhaps his sorrow had blinded him, narrowed his focus. Perhaps he *had* been looking at it from the wrong angle. He was being reactive and it was unbecoming of his title and, more so, his blood. Resurrection was a fool's game.

He stroked the massive tooth next to the remains of his desk, remembering its capture. He would be proactive. He would change his focus. If he could not bring Antony back from death, he would prevent Antony from dying.

By the time his royal guard breached the office, hearing and speaking the buzzing newly in their minds, the King was gone. The castle reputedly was filled with secret passages, fake walls and tunnels leading outward that only the King knew, and he would be long gone by the time any of the guard would find them.

XCIV

One last time o'horrid hammer-thrower
do I come to hear the whisper of your
thunder, to light my lips upon the fire
of lightning, and although this soldier tires,
although my swords and words dull with effort,
King Foeman vanished from this cold desert.

For this one merchant of trifles and Horde,
from throwing shares to the wind for a sword,
became a blood god, dispensing quick peace
on battlefield without fear war would cease.

Yet now not only do bent blade and bolt
lament absence of bloodied eye, but revolt
do the Dead and living without purpose.
For with Foeman gone the rot usurps us!
   —An Elegy for King Foeman

Ivy told the story of when she first came to consciousness.

"It took years to piece together the thoughts, but now they flow as one memory so well that it's difficult to believe there ever was a time I didn't know them. I don't know who originally set the Nursery's systems to create me or if it was even an intentional act. Did Shiloh Antony order the womb tubes to create a female Homega Sapiens as part of what were going to be his last acts? Or had I already been created, by some unknown agent or intelligence, and I was overlooked in his use of the ship's biotechnology?

"That is the first thing I remember — watching him from an unlit section of the Nursery as he experimented with the controls. He would order the ship to its usual programs. Supposedly you Lessers have an unwritten rule — that each Greater creates two Lessers, putting his 'essence' into both. But here was a Lesser Antony creating more Lessers, putting his mind into one of them. And it continued. I only later saw the suicides when I peeked from the ship. And it was the violence that sent me into a state of shock. Luckily! Or I would not have left and escaped the fires that eventually consumed the Nursery.

"The original Lesser — Shiloh Antony — put his mind into an empty Homega Sapiens. The original then went out and killed himself.

The new Lesser, I watched, would find the body, take its possessions, and, every single time, after hours of obvious thought and internal suffering, repeat the process. I don't know how long this continued. It was difficult but fascinating to watch. Not knowing any better, I believed this simple act to be *all* of life. I looked at this circle of death and rebirth to be all of existence. But I, at some time, realized that I was removed from it, that I was not a part of it, that I was only observing, and this was very troubling to me. Why was I *outside* of the natural order? At some point in this cycle of suicide, one of the versions of Shiloh Antony must have too had a crisis of focus, because while my mind was fragmenting and deciding on its limits of perception, the Nursery was set ablaze, and the next thing I now remember is waking in that patch of ivy that gave me my first name, being stared at by others that were not a part of nature, including Shiloh Antony. I spent the journeys and the seasons that followed watching him, looking for any indication or acknowledgement of his escape from that natural order. It took me years, I think, to realize that any Antony, Lesser or Greater, is incapable of shame. Regret? Yes. But not shame."

Damn Antony heard none of her words. Ba'alphegor the storm demon, eternal enemy to a people he once considered his own, screamed out in the most horrible of pain in his very soul. Its wails permeated Antony's every cell, as the possessing entity cried out at the touch of iron. The artificial virus coursing, held dormant in Antony's body, was already burning the demon, but the touch of the Lesser's new cybernetic arm was a new source of constant pain as well. It had become almost impossible for Antony to focus on anything else as long as the being screamed. But he would not let Ba'al free. Without the creature to ironically sustain him against the Nidhogg Virus he would succumb to its genetic targeting. And the demon would be free to continue its eternal vengeance against his former clan. But neither reason was why he held the demon in its iron and flesh prison. He enjoyed Ba'al's pain.

Antony had found a place away from the refugees of war, hidden from the remnants of the Army of Earth and also the shantytown survivors that had lived above the city of Simon. He sat in an overturned shack, still close enough to look out over the crowds of people massing around the warmth of the collapsed earth but not close enough to be seen by them. But Ivy of the Nine Fingers had found him anyway. He hid behind Speaks with Skulls' skeletal bird mask — all that he could find of her body. Within it, he tasted the warm air of his face. But Ivy had recognized him somehow.

"This is all that is left of Shiloh Antony," she said, holding up the cloth mask, its one starry eye fading. "It's torn, thinning, and as far as I know it is all that remains of the Shiloh legacy as well. I took it when he finally died, but it never fit me well. I have a feeling it will fit you just right." She laid it over Antony's head, with its sides covering his own and the face draping over his beak. Its star now overwhelmed on his forehead.

"How did you escape the Virus?" he asked. "It spread everywhere in the fighting. Your blood should..."

"I adapted." She sprang up and out of the timbers.

"I don't think that's possible."

"And that's why you haven't. Now hurry, he's speaking soon."

But Antony only sat back against the ramshackle chair he had made. For a second the demon had stopped screaming, perhaps as interested in the answer as he was. But now the entity just wailed at iron's touch again. Antony, however, felt great, wishing the pain relief from the Agent of MANN's medicine would last forever.

From the crooked church building to the far edges of the gaping and steaming crater of Simon, people were gathering, pillaging, hoarding, and packing. How many, he wondered, had not been exposed to the Nidhogg Virus? Who among them shared even just a splinter of his bloodline? How many were secure that the biotechnological disease had moved on far away across the horizon? None, he knew, suspected that it could be lying in wait so near, sometimes very near. He was bothered to find himself smiling again, and even more bothered to find that he still could not stop. His cheeks, even under the influence of painkillers hurt him tremendously. His facial muscles were so exhausted that the pain tired even the rest of his body. When would he ever find sleep?

Soon, if the sun would ever rise on this horrid night, he would have to find himself some wine. He looked for the morning even now but could not tell if any healthy light was finding its way through the dead horizon. The only comfortable light came up through the cracks in the close land, some leading up through the uneven boneyard to the dilapidated church on a hill overlooking myriad refugees.

In that church, beneath sagging steeple and the numerous trees that long ago lived and died tilting on and into the roof, sat Wulf, cradling Teca's body in his arms and lap. Someone had cleared refuse and floor planks to build a bonfire in the middle of a room probably once defined by orderly rows of benches — some of which, if surviving years of pillaging and repurposing, may have been burning before him. Windows that perhaps had once held stained glass had long ago been boarded up, but a color Wulf was increasingly unnerved by leaked through, along with a nearing morning of the same violent violence that drifted in from the openings made by the ancient trees that had once grown into the ceiling. Surrounding him on all sides were the laughable spoils of war — unique armors, pikes, and standards of angels he did not recognize, chests locked and broken holding hopefully anything that could be salvaged for a journey south, anything that could be layered with hides and worn wool, or sharpened and used against the horrors that waited. He could see the shine of precious metals, the glint of gems, from manhandled crates, but none of it meant anything in this post-war world. Most valuable was the rare dry ounce of gunpowder or wares that could be melted. Even more rare was the unspoiled piece of fruit, the slice of jerky that had not been petrified in the drifts. Wulf's stomach growled at the thought and at Sera's taloned touch.

"You would be king," she cooed, caressing his bare chest painfully before enfolding him in her furs and silks and limbs and more.

"I am a traitor, as you have described it, to people and land."

"I have said no such thing."

"What am I then? Truly? A bastard boy of a soon to be forgotten nation of upstarted barbarians?"

One would have thought Sera cold, with lips and eyes azure as the coming glaciers, skin as icy pale as the plains before the war. But her flesh burned against him, as hot as the ash of the unknown relics that flamed up in the bonfire. "A product of generations of structured, hidden breeding. Your presence was foretold and then prescribed in blasphemous and growling whispers in the sewers of Bifrost."

"I would have been better off not knowing."

"No, it is important to realize how your ancestors have attempted to manipulate you in order to rise above them. Once their machinations have been exposed, you are free to choose your own path."

"So I am what? An assassin without a contract? A failed coward killer lost in a land that has never felt like home? How do I know I am not still some tool of the *SHE*'?"

"Those paper dragons have no more lease on you. I made sure of that."

But Wulf knew that Sera's intervention had come too late. The Garm elders had contracted the *SHE'* to train him in the use of his abilities, and then he had unwittingly used them in their service on that feverish prairie decades ago. What use was this knowledge now?

"But I am still always a tool of death," he said more to himself than to her. "The Horde used the fear of me as a justification for expansion. And look at how many have…"

"They would have found another scapegoat. Their fear and their faith were interchangeable, otherwise they would have grown stagnant. And those who died would have done so either way. Now, at least, you have a following that can be saved from the Final Winter. That is where your identity should now live."

His hand went to that cool feeling in the back of his scalp, the sensation that had appeared since the breaking of his telekinesis. That part of his brain had not healed. He could still *pull* with his mind but not *push*. It was like finding oneself suddenly without a limb. He then felt his chest and left arm, where Flowstone Skoll had flayed him, and where so much flesh had scarred over. Movement on that side was stiff under the new skin, and he knew it always would be.

"But the Garm now know where the entrance into the earth is, the path to their chained god. Is that who I am? Some fallen hero on a collision course with redemption, to prevent Ragnarok?"

"They still have no way to break his bonds, love, no unimaginable blade to sever unbreakable fetters."

"So I am…"

"The man who would be king. Your masses await."

He immediately shivered upon standing from her embrace. And Teca's body gave off no warmth. The fire in the middle of the church held no pleasure for him, and he walked around it to the front doors, suddenly overcome by the memories of images carved in every church door in his hometown. The doors in front of him now were uncovered, just some recent replacements, but the churches in Bifrost were often a source of pride for the parishes, always designed with the scenes of the end of the world.

Harbingers will prepare the land for the Winter of Winds and the Winter of the Sword. The serpent Nidhogg will poison the unfaithful. Vengeful dead will walk. Finally, in the Season of the Beast, the great Wolf of the Core will become unleashed to swallow the sun. The hidden giant Surt will throw fire down from the sky, over the land, consuming anything and everything. Only two will survive the destruction to repopulate Earth.

Wulf clumsily tightened the thin scarf he had wrapped around his head to cover his missing eye, finding his cloak among the spoils. It was so darkly crimson it appeared like a shadow amongst the other clothes. Sera, behind him, stretched her arms and otherwise and walked to the largest branch hanging down into the chamber. She bit her lip, and it bled.

He looked amongst the rest of the clutter — piles of crooked shields and brain-stained helms, flags and banners to be restitched into underwear, crates to be repurposed into carts, meager grains to be soaked and cooked in melted snow. In one corner were stacked chests most prized to the Horde — forbidden wands, broken family swords, relics from the Kalderan Knights. The big chest holding Washkington's Crown stood out in one of the few beams of morning spreading from the collapsed roof.

The Crimson Queen dipped her horned head, long and thick ringlets of bloody hair hanging over her face and bare chest, and she kissed the branch of the long dead tree. With a shudder of limbs, as from some unseen, unfelt, unheard breeze, garlands of red leaves sprouted, grew, and hung like castle drapery. The air of the church was suddenly crisp and the freshest Wulf remembered breathing. For the first time in weeks he smelled something other than infection, opened guts, or the sweetness of death. With a twitch of his full hands, sheathed Yin flew out from the darkness and into his busy embrace.

"Once and future Wulf," Sera called before he stepped outside, "if you could go back, to any other time and place, what would you do differently?"

He looked out past the graveyards and watched the masses gathering around the rises and yards and glowing, open grounds. A mist noticeably grew from below before the promise of dawn and a horizontal hue he could not help but shiver at. Why did he fear a color so much? Where had he seen it before? And why could he not exactly describe it? He searched the crowds for anyone he knew.

And Mew, down amongst the open earth and fallen shacks,

crouched under crooked beams before returning to her full height under one of those huts. Children immediately ran from Maahesehaam's side to touch her gowns. She wore only ivory drapery that hung, hiding her arms, and culminated, after spreading thickly, in strands dirtied by the charcoal accumulating on the surface of the cracked plain like moss. Her boots, as pearly white as the masses of ribbons that hid her hair tightly to her head, appeared impervious to the bubbling mud of the hut. Her snowy hand did then appear, but only for a second as she removed her filigreed cat's eye medallion, handing it to one of the children that had been admiring it. Mew's eyes were the only other source of green in the dilapidated structure. She peeked backwards to check on the commotion building near the graveyard hill.

Maahesehaam's golden eyes, however, never left the woman whose bed he kneeled at. The Painted God fed her from a bowl of foggy broth. "You deserve every bit of the heat escaping from the undercity, good mother," he said. "MANN enslaved you and yours' attentions for far too long. See how much they hoarded? Feeding you just enough warmth to keep you from straying, from looking elsewhere? While they fed on your hope, that someday you would be let inside, into the grand establishment of their 'society.'"

Mew was about to ask who the woman was, but she knew Maahesehaam did not know. It was enough *that* she "was." That she existed. And that was all the tattooed man needed to know to give her value. All people were equal in his eyes, all deserving of salvation. It was the indigent, he had told her, the oppressed, that had an easier time finding it. They were not distracted by the pleasures of wealth. They saw more clearly without temptations. She had disagreed with him, finding the downtrodden of this land to be distracted by hope — hope that they too would one day, without exception, become gold-bearers, the very oppressors that had held them down. He had conceded, agreeing that it was not enough to help man become comfortable with his lot in life but to help him see the evil of the oppressor.

"He will speak soon," Mew said, as some of the dirty but no longer cold children ran back to the painted man's side. They made up stories about the scenes tattooed on his neck and shoulders, gasping as the images appeared to change when he shrugged.

"I have no interest in the words of a warlord who wishes to become king."

"Some have called you the same, if I remember, back home."

"That was never your home." He still did not look away from the old woman he tended to. "I remember the rumors, before I became liberator, of how you had come from another world, as a babe, left behind by a green-eyed god."

"I was not alone."

He stood then to his full imposing self, and the children fell, wide-eyed, claiming the stories tattooed on his flesh were evolving on their own. "It is the future you see," he told them, chuckling. "The images change as our choices change. There is no such thing as destiny, my little lords. Never let anyone tell you otherwise about fate. It is not written by anyone but you, no matter who you are."

Mew neared in the ugly predawn light, under broken rafter and torn canvas, to look at the muscular tapestry once again. She had once thought she saw the image of herself, but she could not find it now. Instead, on his dark arm she found the representation of a cat bleeding all color into fang and pyramid.

"I know him," Mew said at last, "he has no ambitions. This whole 'Liege of Foes' façade was out of necessity."

"Was it necessary to sunder the entire countryside in his own personal war? To drag the population along with him?"

"Says the man who uprooted Below the Brook in rebellion. The man who avenged me with bloodshed." She placed her head on his shoulder.

"You'll see. Before the sun rises, your Wulf will have a crown on his head, and the land will have just another despot taking advantage of tragedy."

Mew stepped back, silently under fallen structure and out into the morbid light. "Is that what your tattoos tell you?"

"It is what history dictates. My tattoos tell me that you are the only one who can prevent it, the one that can get closest to him."

Maahesehaam said more, but she could not hear him as she strolled the new paths between hissing fissures and shifted graveyards, using the church obscured by mists as an endpoint.

A raven, of the deepest violet in the coming morning, had been soaring in the weird and loud updrafts of the open earth, but he now folded, dropped, and settled on Wulf's shoulder, digging his talons into cloak and skin.

Wulf winced. "I haven't missed that."

"What about my sage advice?" Coyote cawed.

"Why did you do it? All those years ago? I was only a child."

"This again?"

"But I know more now. Did you? Whom were you working for?"

"Yes, you were a child, and your life was in greater danger the longer you stayed in that court! You needed to be scuttled away for a while."

"They tortured me!"

"The *SHE'* educated you, beyond most schools out in this land, certainly beyond anything you would have been taught in N'Midgaard. And they trained you. Your potential..."

"In order to unleash the end of the world!"

"Yes, well, we'll have to do something about that, I guess. But the Garm only have the way, not the means."

"Wulf!" Mew said above the growing crowds, pushing through them as she talked. She was quickly followed by many green followers and surrounded by sickle-bearing believers of the Painted Path. She dismissed all of them, but the tattooed men of Maahesehaam lurked near, keeping other groups of wanderers from approaching the hill of the church. She stepped around the hastily built platform settled at the bottom of the hill to near Wulf.

"You have to tell them," Wulf told her as he stopped to examine the stage that had been built out of the worst of the leftover supplies from the retreat, "all of them, to start heading south. There is nothing more for us here." He stifled a shudder as Coyote pinched his shoulder. Where had he seen that extra-normal color before? The East colored. The strange purple should not have been possible in reality, in this world.

"Wulf, they've been running for... how long? I don't even know. And the people that lived here... their whole world has just been destroyed. We've all lost... so much. Just let them rest."

Coyote balanced from foot to foot. "We'll lose even more after these fogs settle. The heat from the city below is exhausting itself, and the winter — the Final Winter — will be upon us soon."

"You once told me," Wulf sighed, "to take care of their bodies, their lives, here and now, and you would take care of their souls."

"An odd distinction," Coyote cawed.

"Yes," Mew said, looking out over ancient grave stones that had appeared from the sudden thaw. They were lit from beneath by the interior burning earth, but now too on their eastern sides. The spectacle made it look as though the worn rocks were on fire by some color of flame she had never seen before, an entire hue she was certain that had actually never even existed before this odd dawn. "I now know that those are the same thing. We both have their salvation in mind. But I have failed. For the man who believes in eternal life is unrecognizable to his kin. Earthly concerns are unknown to him. And this evolves one to a psychological state beyond mortal understanding. His demeanor transcends the understanding of the common populace. But all these people that have gathered, I recognize them. I know their words. They are known to me, so I have failed." She appeared to be reading the impossible marks on gravestones that had worn down to almost nothing even before the winters of goblin, wind, and war had blown snow over the land. "But what is your plan here? What are your intentions for these people?"

"Everyone wants to be king," the raven said, "except the intelligent. I can't think of a better way to paint a big target on your head right now."

"What is salvation?" Wulf asked.

"Freedom," Coyote answered, "freedom in every single manner and form, from chains you cannot even realize, conceive that you are bound by."

"Freedom," Mew answered, "from this horrible world, into the embrace of Mother, where the drudgery and violence of this life cannot distract us from the all-encompassing ultimate reality of the peace of the *gentle constants*."

She had never more reminded him of her mother than she did right then — the rise of her chin, the way the golden embers in her eyes had disappeared, leaving only the primordial green that had consumed his every thought for those long-ago months. With Yggr's Eye, the only eye he had left, he tried to look past the impossible color of the sunrise, realizing he was gazing in the wrong direction, stared back into the memory of the battlefield. As he had been broken and dying, unable to look away, he had stared into one of the dead eyes of the *galgalim*.

"I saw... something... out there."

"It doesn't matter," interrupted Coyote, "it changes nothing."

Wulf continued, "Like the thing that destroyed this city... one attacked me, and as it lay dying... no... dead, I looked into its eyes, past its eyes, through its eyes, its dead eyes..."

"Yes," Mew relented.

"I could see through to God's Throne Room, just as the old tales tell."

"Yes."

"It was empty. The Throne was empty." Wulf remembered just then where he had seen the worrisome color of the burgeoning dawn before. It was blushing Mew's alabaster cheeks into bruises, just as it had the Crimson Queen's when he first woke to meet her. He had opened his eyes on that sulfurous beach to find that same netherworldy morn blossoming on her face. She said he had been calling out of nightmares for "Sera," and so he had called her by that name ever since. "We are alone."

"Yes," Coyote squawked.

"No," Mew said, now smiling. "Look out there. Those are your people now. They have no saviors now except what they choose. But that must be the key in this... this..."

"Dying land," Coyote said, turning on his shoulder to face away from the dawn.

"...new world. But that is why I ask, Wulf. Who will you be in this new world? Now that you've saved their lives, they adore you. Look at them. What you decide now is part of a great responsibility. It is not to be taken lightly. Take care not to become what you've sacrificed so much to destroy."

He stepped forward, adjusting the body he carried, and the crowds started turning from the horizon. Some began cheering. Mew stepped into his gory shadow, her hand appearing from beneath darkening gowns. She held the wrapped hilt of the short sword tighter than she ever had, and its blade was another sharp line alongside all the long lines of her fabrics. It was similarly bloodied by the necrochromatic heavens.

"Who's your friend?" Nine-fingered Ivy suddenly asked. She had at some time sneaked behind Wulf and gone into the church to retrieve the chest containing Washkington's Crown. Her little muscles tightened and stretched outside of her furred vest as she pulled the chest past him.

"John Juan Aristo," the Agent of MANN, who had also just

appeared from the far side of the graveyards, announced. "You wouldn't recognize me, Ivy, not by how I look now, but I definitely have a lot of questions for you."

"No thanks," she said, "I'm pretty busy."

Wulf watched her drag the chest out onto the platform. She looked different to him every day — even more so since the fall of the Quicken Machine, even more so under the light of the dead dawn. "No advice," he asked, "before you run off again?"

"Sure, never trust a hastily built stage," she replied before disappearing into the crowds, quickly reappearing and heading out into the torn fields and fallen forests.

The crowds started cheering again. It was a rolling call that someone would begin on one end, and it would last from one side of the churchyard to the other. Wulf saw midgardians out in the masses. Heavily furred shoulders shook. Blue jay feathered caps turned. He watched as what could have possibly been the last of the Northern Order gathered, the remnants of their plate armor glinting off an untold number of scratches. A few dwarves lingered. The multitude of scorched refugees from the near infernos joined the crowds. Even those that, within the last few days, worked to cut or burn angelic sigils off their foreheads went unnoticed in the gathering. Mew's green people moved between all of them, rationing tea and new herbs they had grown just in the past few hours.

Wulf looked to the dark faces of the masses — none of them clean, none of them unscarred — and he recognized them. They held the same look he had been seeing for years now, not only fighting at his side but against him. After all this, had nothing changed?

"Your mother trusted me," he said to Mew as she moved closer behind him.

"No. She found you predictable. That's not the same thing."

"I'm not ready." He turned and pushed *Tiwaz* aside with the very tips of his fingers, but its quick touch brought back a wave of nostalgia for a time when he could just walk the plains and forests of a countryside not far from where he was standing now — just him and *Tiwaz* and his phlegmy horse Slippy — a time when odd jobs and exorcisms kept him on a casual move. He was beholden to none back then. Or so he thought. He now knew that he was part of some insidious plan, but it did not matter. Without the knowledge of manipulations was he not happier? Was there no turning back? No.

He walked the remains of ice as hardened as steel, stones as worn as river rocks, and a path from the time of the Old Ones. The simple stage creaked but was surprisingly level, set into cool mud and hot sod. He pulled his hood low on the side of his missing eye, his cloak close against a cool breeze that had appeared with the sudden sun. It had been so long since he had seen the light unclouded. But it too was soaked in the unnatural violet, and he thought for a second that any ground the light grew to touch quivered like a shiver after a remembered nightmare. He set Teca and Yin on the ground, uncertain as to why he had brought her with, and waited a few breaths before he stood back up. Those faces, those familiar faces looked back to him. He looked specifically for one face, knowing he would not see her although knowing exactly what she would have said if she had been there that day. And he knew exactly what he would have said in response. The conversation played out in his mind as though it was a memory, and perhaps it had been.

"Many years ago," Wulf started, and the entirety of the gathering moved closer together and began nearing the stage, "I crossed fields and forests not far from here." Her voice was still in his head, and he suddenly could not speak, could only see her sleepy eyes and suppressed smile lying down against his chest, could only feel her slight warmth against his neck. And then all he could see was her sallow complexion as he had carried her across the murky battlefield. He had then wrapped her arms over his shoulders, fooling himself into thinking that he could feel her holding on by her own strength. He wished to go back to holding her again but spoke first.

"I was ill, feverish, as many were back then, and I dreamed, as many did, the nightmares induced by Plaag. But the difference is that, in my delirium, I reached out... reached out to the very center of the world... for anyone... anything... that could hear me. What I did not realize, however, was that I was only answering a call."

The crowds mingled, occasionally looking amongst each other, moving even closer to ensure they could hear.

"I let loose the Call of the Beast, and its followers answered, and they are on the move, and they worship Death." He remembered some oft-forgotten lesson from one of the few times he had been unable to sneak out of church as a child. The Beast of the Core will defy description. Whole civilizations have evolved into inbred, cannibalistic tribes in the bacteria of its teeth. The creation and collapse of the universe is reflected in the void of its eyes. Who had taught him that? No one had taught him that. Had he said that out loud?

Someone had started cheering over his words, and, as Wulf continued, his voice was quickly drowned out as hoots and howls spread.

"I want you to know that... I need you to know that... this final winter is my..."

The cheering had become rhythmic, and it did not lesson as he crouched to open the chest beside him. Inside was sand, a shocking contrast to the earth he had been trudging through for years now. He could only guess that it, along with the crown, had been transported from the far eastern beaches, where a population had worshipped mollusks and bewigged, ivory-toothed, old, white men. He stuck a hand into the golden sand, and the cold shocked him, but not enough to numb the prick of a finger as he started to pull the crown out. The tiny jewel of blood stood out against his pale hand but was quickly subsumed by the similar light of Heaven. He dug again, this time careful to avoid the petrified thorns. He held the crown and stood. The gold had apparently long ago worn away from the sharpest parts. His finger had gone numb. He could only feel an uncomfortable tingle when he tried to move it.

"If the world opens, splits, yawns wide to reveal the Beast of the Core, and if the Bastard God swallows the sun, and we are plunged into eternal night, you need to know that..."

The crowd stomped the softening grounds. Mud, some steaming, some frozen, speckled boot and skirt. Flags were raised. Songs were improvised loudly. "Liege of Kings!" was becoming the chant.

The numbness had spread up Wulf's arm. He could feel nothing yet it paradoxically tickled painfully. The sensation crossed his chest, cooling his heart, paralyzing his lungs. When it reached his unmoving lips, spreading over his head, he watched the crowds as they appeared to vibrate out of his range of sight. He could not focus on his surroundings, no matter how hard he tried. Everything vibrated into obscurity and against each other. Objects that vibrated a world away touched each other and others until the sensation reached across the land to vibrate against him.

The near masses went suddenly silent and still as they, in unison, turned back to the stage to watch Wulf just… disappear. His clothes fell to a heap without him. Coyote pecked and scratched quizzically at the empty cloak. Yin started to stir nearby on the stage. She hungered again.

And then those same masses turned to the boneyards scattered around the church, and to the battlefields behind them, beyond the thin forest. Wherever the unpleasant dawn touched, the dead rose as though from a rotting garden. Ancient bones fought their way upward and outward, through melting graves and ice, moving aside shrunken gravestones. Mutilated figures shuffled, breaking themselves from frost and each other, from the piles stretching back out into the plains. Recent funeral pyres fell as charred remains emerged, some staggering, some crawling, some just screaming from ashen lungs, through unhinged jaws. Everywhere the violent violet dawn laid its hands, the bruised touch spreading as the sun rose, dead struggled and stood.

Splintered bone burst through soft flesh. Splintered armor stretched from ice-burnt skin. Plates sang as they scraped against spines. Corroded clothing squeaked as it hung from bare frames. Beards sloughed off shedding skulls. Joints lost their ligaments. Guts fell in unraveling heaps before fleshless toes. But the vengeful dead all moved forward. Born again in the resurrection dawn, some reached, some pulled, some rolled, some crawled, some skittered, some shambled, and some ran. But they were all envious of the warmth and the breath of the living, and they all moved toward the crowds.

Across the land — from the eastern segments of what remained of MANN's Land, to the war-torn cities of the Kalderan Territories, to the far western desert and sea — wherever the dawn — filtered by the dust and smog of the war of Heaven and Earth, and the blood and fire of Ashmedai's descent, ascent, and demise — fell — dead, both long buried or recently murdered, rose to exact unrighteous hunger on the living.

~

He vibrated beyond sensation, but the feeling was slowing. The numbness turned to an aching tingle in his brain and limbs. The crowds all around had disappeared into an all-encompassing quiver that lost all differentiation before losing all light. But the darkness now formed into something new. Wulf could see and feel his hands, could now make out cold corners barely recognizable as substance in a room without light or shadows. He still thought his senses deprived, but realized that he was floating. On one side of him also floated Washkington's Crown, on the other he could read the letters 'S' and 'E' and 'R' and 'T' stenciled onto the metallic gray of the wall.

"Who Is It That Disturbs My Slumber? Tell Me Your Name, Son Of Man."

God's voice was as Wulf expected — as cold as the walls in the room, as digitally distant as a choir of children's bells.

Already aloft, living tendrils of aluminum and plastic lifted Wulf farther and around toward a window filling one side of the room. The planet Earth revolved before him. So much of it had already turned white. A silver pin, alive with fiber optics, grew from one of the feelers before it stuck into the back of his head, somewhere where his spine met his skull.

God searched and searched, and Wulf once more had to relive his life in mere seconds. But there was one area He could not immediately probe. He knocked and knocked against the lobotomized brainweezle in Wulf's head, but it would not open. He banged against the hidden cache, but it would not reveal its contents. Here, the man's entire existence was laid bare, but God was not satisfied. He was being denied. So Wulf let him in.

XCV

...in a world close to your own you will see
choices were made, then and now, the son still
lives past Time's terrible sieves
you will have to pass before he was killed

—scrawled on the walls of the King of All's lower halls

Easarean was unused to this much discomfort in his later years. This made the slush melting in his boots all the more bothersome. His years of opulence made the sulfurous rain stinging his eyes that much more annoying, the muddy snow sucking at every step twice as encumbering. Yet he still found the journey pleasing to a king that had grown used to heavily armed escorts and travels surrounded by the steel of a tank. On this quest he could turn his head without vision obscured by a mass of troops or a line of crawlers. He could make a decision, change a direction or his mind without having to send it down through the ranks. With his kingdom under the control of the Pervert's unified hive mind, Easarean's thoughts were once again his own. It was, in fact, liberating.

There was actually a good chance he was the only man in the country with a mind of his own. As he snuck out through wall and capital and border and nation he had seen few people not under the Pervert's control, and even those few had been submitting themselves to the neuroplants that would link their minds to the collective. The temptation of unity was too great in an uncertain world, Easarean guessed.

His escape from the cities to Lake of the Truthful Head had been mostly unhindered, and he could only assume it was by design. The Pervert's eyes were everywhere, and so if he looked the other way it was only because he wanted Easarean to live in a world that reminded him every day of what he had so quickly lost. It certainly would be the Pervert's style.

But Easarean still knew better than to just walk right into the front door of his northernmost retreat. He took a wide berth around the low-lying hills the resort sat on, coming up behind to the secret entrance leading into the lowest of the above ground levels. The halls were silent except for the patter of the greasy rain on streaked windows. The resort was massive, but he could tell by dust and disrepair that he was the only one in the resort in months. It looked to have been neglected long before he was overthrown. It was true it had been years since he had vacationed here, with or without Antony, and the moist heat had turned the interior into a hot bed of mold creeping into the corners of the darkly stained wood. Easarean knew exactly where the heat was coming from. It was why he was here.

Not trusting the conveniences of the resort, he took the stairway down to the cellars below. The rooms were still heavily stocked for vacations he would never take and guests the Queen would never entertain. He surprised himself by not breaking into one of the great barrels of wine, momentarily considering taking a cask with him in his descent, but he needed his wits about him when dealing with a dragon. They were a tricky lot.

Down and down he went, through stairwell after stairwell built only to bring him to his final prisoner — an enemy neither he nor even his son could kill but only imprison. And it was Antony that had suggested using the beast's heat to warm the northern resort to encourage his mother to vacation with them. Back then the snow had actually stuck to the ground, sometimes even stranding them for weeks, and the Queen felt cut off from the soil of the land and eventually stopped coming with them. The imprisonment of Phlegethon had changed all that, warming the surrounding countryside, but the Queen had then avoided the resort for other reasons — seeing the earth spoiled and corrupted by the creature's breath.

Easarean strode into the massive chamber, wrapping a scarf across his face to protect from the choking exhalation. The air flickered all around him, periodically flaming near the loud filters working overtime. The machines were on the verge of overloading.

The dragon squatted before him, wings clipped and limbs spread, tangled in chains of quartz, thin wires and thick conductors entwining around and through scaly flesh. Segmented tubes thicker than Easarean's arms threaded around each other and into Phlegethon's unhinged jaw, spreading his maw wide and continuing down into his gullet. The black beast looked a part of the glossy stone of the wall, and did not even twitch — could not even twitch — as Easarean entered, but one yellow eye rolled to follow the man's steps.

"Greetings, monster." His voice cracked. Easarean felt small in the chamber among the massive machinery, the giant tangles of chains and cords, and the great fire dragon himself. The creature was toothless and declawed, neutered and spellbound, yet Easarean still feared him. Just the sight of the giant lizard kept him cool in the sweltering chamber.

"It is humbling, I'm certain," Easarean continued, "to be seen by your conqueror in this state, but I can tell you that all kings fall. Your shame will only make you stronger, trust my words. All rules fall, but what makes you a true king is when you rise again. And I am here to let you know you can rise again, if only you heed my words." Easarean moved, pacing across the slick stone, pretending to examine rattling machinery he could not understand. He could feel the yellow eye not only following him, but picking through his brain. His bravado was wasted on the dragon. He could not lie to a creature that knew what he was thinking before even he himself did. And so he just went straight to the point.

"Unfettered, you have power over time. Free from enchantment and chain and enchanted chain, you divert time like a rancher diverts the simplest of streams. You mold histories like a potter does clay. The future is a painting in which only you hold the inks, brushing into it only events and peoples you choose. Is this true?"

There was no response — no lip quiver, no docked tail twitch — just the yellow eye Easarean could not escape. He moved to the other side of the monster and the chamber, his nonchalant poise breaking as the other eye took up the task of staring past his steps and into his soul. In the distant past, the parapsyte, and more recently the Queen, would have shielded his mind from such intrusions, but he was alone now. If his bargain worked, however, he would never be alone again.

"You, dragon, are the mightiest of the great tempomagi. Eons break under your great gaze. The future is no more a mystery to you than the past. The past is no less inevitable to you than the future. Yet you still ended up here, warming my bath, tempering my sauna. Such is my might." At this Easarean thought he detected a wincing around the yellow eye. "But my might also comes through my mercy and my ability to recognize a fellow king. Your time, great Phlegethon, has come again, and this time you will not spend it wasting under some crumbling mountain, napping over a rusting hoard. This time rule over smoldering cities and the cooking populations you deserve." There were lessons from the Academy, techniques taught to shield one's mind from invasion, and he girded his thoughts now as he learned then, so long ago.

"I offer you this," he yelled over the stuttering filters, both he and the machines coughing from the inhalation of the burning air. "I offer you your freedom, and I offer you all of the Kingdom... all the Kingdom of All, and in return you use your mastery of time to send this king back before the death of his Prince... send this... father... back before the death of his son."

But still no response, still just the great yellow eye, blinding in contrast to the shadows of ebony scales. Easarean had no idea if the dragon still crept through his mind, for could he surely not do it without being noticed?

"But this king is no fool. For your freedom, for the opportunity to scald the continent from sea to boiling sea, I will have your word. A dragon's word is legendary, chiseled in adamantine, spellbinding. I will have your word that you will send me back before Antony was killed. Do I have it?"

Despite the rocking echoes of failing ventilation, Easarean's choking breaths and manic heart, it was as though the chamber were silent as he waited for a response.

Yes

Later, he would tell himself he collapsed from the steaming atmosphere in the dungeon instead of, in truth, fainting at the hellish voice.

"Brevity is a virtue in love and war"
—Hyper Khan's "The War of Art"

In all the worlds Damn Antony had visited, all the lives he had lived, he had never seen such a color. It was an affront to nature, but it also spat in the face of any supernatural elements he had ever witnessed as well. He could not imagine any person not taking offense at the light creeping over the morning. The sun was filtered through the bloody mists rising from the near countryside, the celestial and burning dust from the falling sky, and the still-lingering plume of earth that had erupted when Ashmedai attempted to make his presence known. It all corrupted the dawn, and the dawn woke the dead. Resurrection was everywhere. Dead citizens of Simon and its ramshackle aboveground suburbs crawled from the ground. Ancient bones fought to free themselves from frozen graves in the churchyard, and the near battlefields squirmed to life as piles of bodies pulled apart in an effort to be the first to feast upon the warmth of the screaming living. Antony could even see victims of the Nidhogg Virus struggling to stand and follow the scattering crowds. For rare minutes, the demon in his body and mind was quiet. With all the death the entity had been responsible for over the ages, all the carnage its vengeance had wrought, Ba'alphegor was even too stunned to laugh.

Nearby, but out of sight of Antony, Mew burst into the cabin she had hidden Janus in. He had been nearly unresponsive since she had found him in the Horde camp. His only action had been repeatedly to push her away, and so she had some of her green people sequester him to one of the numerous abandoned shacks of the suburbs. They were to tend to him as best they could. As Mew suddenly appeared in the leaning cabin, bleeding from the bites and scratches of the hungry dead crowds, she found Janus wrapped and near comatose, as she had left him, but with what looked like the clothed statues of his green caretakers. Elusive scales flickered and moved in the darkness with the grotesque light peeking in through the wood of the walls, and, without seeing it fully, she could hear the basilisk finishing his speech to the unconscious man.

"...myself. You may call me Mister Kasssk, and I am what you may call a collector... a collector of the rare and unique. Some years ago I made a deal to acquire…"

Mew brandished *Tiwaz* in both her bleeding hands, but the basilisk, with a defunct chicken wing, doffed mirrored sunglasses from his beak. His abominable gaze turned her to stone — the finest of alabasters.

"Well then, it seems I have little time," Mister Kasssk continued. He fluttered up to the bed with his tiny briefcase, opening it, revealing the flowery light from within. "I have the rights to the heir of Aesarean, whom you have claimed to be." Janus shrank beneath his gauze, stretched and twisted beneath wrappings. Within seconds he had disappeared into the briefcase. The basilisk said, "Pleasant doing business with you," before he climbed in himself. The cabin was then empty except for statues.

"Help me help you, you dumb bastard." Out from the shacks and the steaming camps, past the hungry scramble of the resurrected of the grounds and yards, Ivy of the Nine Fingers pulled the Zombie Pistoleer out from under the cooling carcass of a great lizard beast she could not help but find familiar. It was larger but reminded her of the thing that had attacked her companions on the top of the Tower of Gog all those seasons ago. Its head was riddled with bullets with an accuracy that could have only been Harlowe's. Even freed from beneath the girth of the coldblooded creature, the gunslinger was caught up in his chains and thorny vines. His clothes were as shredded as his gray skin. The odd sunrise had just appeared, and it oozed over his balding head. At the weird dawn's touch, the coffin blossoms opened on his hand, opposite wrist, and forearm. Tiny leaves snaked.

"How many rounds you have left?" Ivy asked, checking her own bandolier.

"Not enough," he answered, watching the cold battlefields come back to life. The world was so quiet without the horrid scream of the *Loco* tainting it. He was so excited — anxious even — to begin getting used to that silence. He looked to the gross heavens and the corruption of color they had become. He could only describe them as, "A nighttime rainbow tied ta its black bed."

"What?"

"Nothin'"

Femurs cracked and spines snapped as the recently killed tore themselves from the frost. Some lost heads and hands when standing from the gore of others. Some still carried blades and poles as broken as their bodies. All crawled or staggered toward the only warmth they could find.

The pistoleers exchanged revolvers and bullets, checking both before reloading and spinning cylinders. "Hey, Harlowe," Ivy said, holstering and readying her hands at her sides.

"Yep?"

"Good to have you back."

"Yep."

The lizard beast stirred nearby. Congealed strands of brain hung from its crocodilian head as it shrugged off ice and earth and skin.

Harlowe and Ivy looked at each other before they both smiled and ran off, to the south, with the vengeful dead at their heels.

Across that prairie of war and the plain of growing resurrection, to fields that had not just yet received the glory of the dawn, held a hidden little hamlet still receiving the snow of night. Drifts blew against the eastern sides of the houses, soon to be warmed by a violent violet. Inside one of the small buildings sat Handsome Gibbet. Now toothless, he whispered past two layers of gums into the dim room. The sleepers he talked to gave off a heat that was an instant and welcome relief from the storm-wracked night he had spent tracking them toward the quiet town.

"Ever muh... make a muh... man drink gasoline? You get him to drink so muh... much, and before he gags or spits up you tell him ah dirty story about his muh... mommy. Then, when he laughs, you stick a hot muh... match in his muh... mouth. It's called ah 'dragon's joke.'"

The men in the human mound finally stirred. Many of them had been sniffing the air even before Handsome had sat down. The scent of something near was obviously giving them nightmares. Flowstone Skoll rose from the furs to approach the tithingman. Handsome was tiny, starved, and he looked every bit his little stature in layers of coats and blankets. Only his prune of a head stuck out.

"Ever buh... boil ah man alive? Ah got ah buh... bronze... buh... bull as ah reward for throwing down ah uprising once. Buh... back in the South. Long time ago."

Skoll neared and sniffed. "You think you can get in good with us, eh, muck-spout? With your brave tales? Yeah, you're a real hero, man." The windows and doors of the house had been lost to war or time and appeared to have been recently replaced by stretched skin — much of which was still in the shape of a person. If one looked out into the snow, the flayed remnants were slowly being covered by the snowfall. One window's flaps blew open from the wind, and, for a second, the ugly sunrise gleamed in the sewn eyes of Skoll's wolfen headdress. "What's your name, gobermouch?"

Handsome's eyes, glossy beneath all their lids, did not look at anything in the room. "We had ah barbeque tuh... to celebrate some wedding, and ah wanted tuh... to put the leader ah the uprising inside the bull, put it over the firepit, but he didn't fit, so ah found his son or nephew or something. The moans sounded like ah cow in heat. You got tuh... to cut their feet up first, so they have something tuh... to boil in. We didn't eat him, ah course. Ah'm not ah savage. No offense."

Laughter came from the waking mound, and Busy Emla, her furs and skin shining with sweat, approached. "Sweets! He thinks we did this!" But she scurried backward at Skoll's growling, bulbously pregnant belly pulling her down to the floor.

"This?" Skoll asked, pointing a black fingernail at the windows and door. "This, numb nuts, is your own people's doing. They wanted the wells in this here town, and what good're they now? Your people fight for water as it freezes! For glass and shiny stones! For oil for trucks that won't turn in the blizzard! None of it matters! This's the coming of the *Fimbulvetr!* Don't you..."

"Yes," Handsome squeaked.

"What's that? Speak up, yeasty."

"Ah nuh... know. Just please tell me your stories ain't just myths."

"Miss?" Skoll asked.

"Miss who?" Emla barked.

Mad Hati was suddenly filling the space of the room, smelling and smiling at something near. When dawn peeked through the skin of the window, his mane, beard, and furry headdress looked to be lit by the fires of Hell. All the Garm were awake now, and, as curious as their noses had made them, all except Hati had slunk back into the corners.

"Woof! He said 'myths,' my sad heathens!" Hati slammed the axe-head of *Manhood* into the floor, missing Handsome by an earthworm's length. The tattooed map on his chest and right arm were gangrene green, but it matched up perfectly with the shriveling hide he wore over his left shoulder. It was a complete map to the South and beyond. "Our course, of course, is of divine offering, you coarse little ewe litter.

Drink from the vine and die, dink."

Handsome had too few fingers left to hold onto the little wooden box he presented, and it broke on the floor, spilling its humble contents in front of Hati.

"Puh... please, just puh... promise me one thing."

The great red Garm gingerly picked up the *Shear* by its elongated finger ring. Its counterintuitive blade rocked in the breeze.

"Promise me that the one you call Wulf will suffer. Huh... hurt... huh... him before..."

"Arrooooooo! Death is salvation from life, my good man," Hati growled. He gently bit the edge of the *Shear* to test its worth, cracking a tooth in the action. "And you have just made us the world's greatest saviors."

But you will not listen, you will not hear,
for Warrior to the core
you are, and losing to pride you fear,
but the Warrior's own will still is not free.
Life, in all its prescribed strife,
binds and blinds you as much as you have me,
but again I give you this boon, this clue.
To the past look for whom few
seek — find Antony and he will find you!

—scrawled on the walls of the King of All's lower halls

asarean's was a life of betrayal. Looking back, all he could see was a mass of traitors building the architecture of his life around him. If he had a fault, it was that he had given all of them his trust. But he knew he had no faults. He was built on a grander scale than all who had come before him. He had been built for a grander world — a reality worthy of his bold tastes and massive appetites.

Perhaps this was that world. Perhaps his life full of traitors had only been meant to lead him to a reality large enough to fulfill his lusts.

From the day of his birth he had been betrayed. He thought back to the Academy and its propaganda. His training mates and those that came before him had never known life outside the Clan, had never known the wonders of the universe. They had never experienced beyond the phalanx, life unstructured or the love of a child. They knew only what the Clan told them, burning out their short lives in wars where they gained nothing but the promise, and only the promise, of prestige. Easarean still remembered the epics of the heroes he had so admired. He had surpassed them of his own accord, the Empire be damned. He had fought for himself, not some vague ideal that would have only led to death on some god-forsaken colony for some weakly justified cause. Of all that betrayed him he hated his dead clan the most. They sent him on the path of trusting too much. They taught him to rigidly follow orders, a version of history and an idea of a future based on faith. They molded him in a way that made it difficult to see the world through a critical lens, and it led him to trust others when he had no reason to, except for faith. Faith may have been a good trait, necessary even, for a soldier, but it crippled him when he entered the real world, leaving him to rely on hollow promises while trusting others without reason.

He had trusted the Shining One, the angel, and its empty promises. He had trusted the parapsyte and the basilisk and then the beautiful priestess, the Queen of Quartz, the most of all. Caught in the well of depression after Antony's death he had trusted the Norn Fox and Automaton the Perverted. They had all betrayed him, taken advantage of his faith in them. And now, as he looked out at the brave new world he found himself in, he realized that one more had betrayed him. He had trusted in the honor of the dragon, but now knew that Phlegethon had gotten his ultimate revenge.

He was certain that the creature's twisted sense of honor had been fulfilled, for he had in fact sent him back in time — of that there was no doubt — but, after years of walking across a bizarrely askew landscape, Easarean knew that this was not his reality.

In this world, this world's Easarean had not followed the same path. He had not become the King of All nor united the land under his banner. This world had banished its own Automaton centuries ago in evolutionary wars, worshipped unfamiliar gods such as the avenging B'stet, fecund *MGGT*, and an angelic choir. Here, strange knights scoured the land in search of darkness to light in the name of Blind Libra. Here, MANN spied in the absence of the GAU. Here, an Alabaster Priestess had risen instead of a Queen of Quartz.

Was there room in this world for Easarean? Or — as he found over the years of exploring this reality — was there room in this world for *another* Easarean? As he walked the land, spreading the gospel of *A World Broken*, he heard rumors of others like him, others that, along with him, became known as the Prophets Greater. Over time he surmised that they too had lived lives similar to his own. They had all been kings of their own realities, warriors betrayed over and over again, leading to the death of the one constant in all of their worlds — the Prince Antony. They had all been as desperate as he, making bargains with demons and dragons, being sent back in time, but never ending up back in their own world. They were all strangers to this reality, preaching the way things should have been, should be and could still be. In this world they took their son's name, in memoriam, for they knew he would never be again — not in this dimension.

Some had come before Easarean, creating the myths already

ingrained in the countryside. Some had come after him, still coming to terms, as he had to, of a mutant reality divergent of their own.

But no matter when they came, they all grew tired. The Prophets Greater were older than their age for all they had seen and done, and they could not bear to live it again. This world was wrong, and they had not the resolve to make it right, to live through it all again, to make the bargains and face the betrayals it took to build the Kingdom of All again. Antony would live in this reality in name only.

But before retiring to the life of a soldier, warlord, or hermit, each Greater Antony would predictably do one last thing in their quest to make the world right. In each of their own realities they had destroyed the Nursery before it had become a continuing threat to their nations, but here it still existed, as hidden in forest and earth as they remembered it. With the Nursery each Greater Antony made two Lessers to carry the word of *A World Broken*. Two Homega Sapiens for each Greater Prophet to save the land from itself.

Easarean, of course, was no different. If there was irony in using the Nursery, he did not see it as he copied his mind into the ship's systems, transferring them then into two fresh bodies grown from the standard blank templates. These bodies were smaller, inferior to his own, but they stood amongst the weak of this land in speed, strength, and endurance. They would not fall prey to the disease or famine rearing its head, and could easily lead the lower men in coming wars.

Besides, he mused, as he sent them on their way, *they have what is most important. The mind of the King! The essence of the Warrior!*

Two for every one. And these men became known through the generations and their words as the Prophets Lesser. With new bodies, they were not tired and could sing the stories of a better world — a world without robot or werewolf or the uncertainty of the differing cultures and men of the country. These Lesser Antonys also integrated themselves into the generations of legends, spreading even farther than the Greaters in the culture of the land — their minds, at one time indistinguishable, eventually evolving as the world affected them as much as they affected the world.

Easarean watched as eventually the Prophets Lesser unified their common cause under the Divine Choir. Here was a force that could claim the country, combine the nations under one creed, and make the land a sight Prince Antony would have been proud of. Through the

Divine Choir the people would know peace. And no one would ever have to be hurt again.

Easarean, now known as Silent Antony the Greater, watched all of it slowly unfold over the years. He saw the other Greater Antonys retreat into petty power grabs or seclusion. He observed the eventual corruption of the Prophets Lesser by both the Horde and their own bodies. He was old now, older than he should ever have been, and he wished he would have died long before seeing his twisted legacy. But as he closed his eyes, as Libran Knights burst into his humble chambers with beaming swords to fulfill their *Low Coda*, as they struck and stabbed, Easarean did realize one thing — that the Shining One actually had fulfilled his promise. In the end, Easarean had not been betrayed by *everyone* in his life. He may die, but his children had become heroes of the land, and they would make it greater, even greater than he ever could. The Shining One had fulfilled his bargain. The King of All's children would be great. His legacy would reign forever.

GOBLIN WINTER
of puppet kings and telling sins

the Fimbulvetr Books

book one
WIND OF CHAINS

book two
LIE BY THE SWORD

book three
SEASON OF THE BEAST

Daniel Scott Westby was born in Minnesota in 1975. He teaches ethical rhetoric and literature, and he lives with his family in Colorado. Inspired by romantic poetry and progressive rock, Herman Melville and Philip K. Dick, Lie by the Sword *follows* Wind of Chains *and is the penultimate book of the* Fimbulvetr Trilogy, *concerning the rise and fall of the future.*